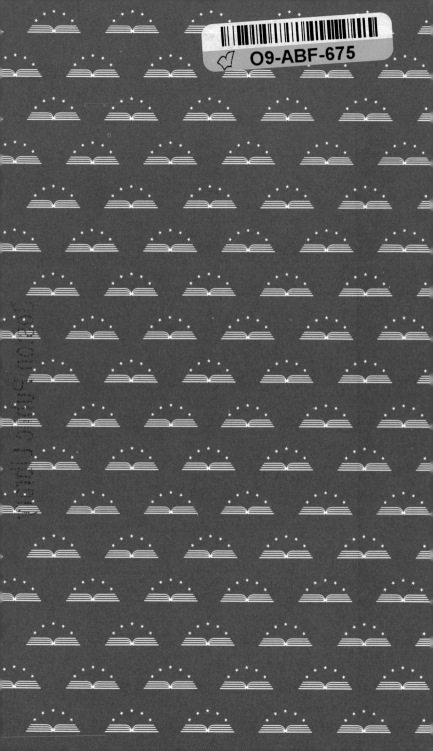

THEODORE DREISER

THEODORE DREISER

SISTER CARRIE
JENNIE GERHARDT
TWELVE MEN

THE LIBRARY OF AMERICA

First Printing
Library of America—36

Manufactured in the United States of America

RICHARD LEHAN
WROTE THE NOTES AND SELECTED
THE TEXTS FOR THIS VOLUME

Grateful acknowledgement is made to the National Endowment for the Humanities, the Ford Foundation, and the Andrew W. Mellon Foundation for their generous financial support of this series.

Contents

SISTER CARRIE

TO MY FRIEND
ARTHUR HENRY
WHOSE STEADFAST IDEALS AND SERENE
DEVOTION TO TRUTH AND BEAUTY
HAVE SERVED TO LIGHTEN THE METHOD
AND STRENGTHEN THE PURPOSE OF
THIS VOLUME.

Chapter I

The Magnet Attracting: A Waif Amid Forces

WHEN Caroline Meeber boarded the afternoon train for Chicago, her total outfit consisted of a small trunk, a cheap imitation alligator-skin satchel, a small lunch in a paper box, and a yellow leather snap purse, containing her ticket, a scrap of paper with her sister's address in Van Buren Street, and four dollars in money. It was in August, 1889. She was eighteen years of age, bright, timid, and full of the illusions of ignorance and youth. Whatever touch of regret at parting characterised her thoughts, it was certainly not for advantages now being given up. A gush of tears at her mother's farewell kiss, a touch in her throat when the cars clacked by the flour mill where her father worked by the day, a pathetic sigh as the familiar green environs of the village passed in review, and the threads which bound her so lightly to girlhood and home were irretrievably broken.

To be sure there was always the next station, where one might descend and return. There was the great city, bound more closely by these very trains which came up daily. Columbia City was not so very far away, even once she was in Chicago. What, pray, is a few hours—a few hundred miles? She looked at the little slip bearing her sister's address and wondered. She gazed at the green landscape, now passing in swift review, until her swifter thoughts replaced its impression with vague conjectures of what Chicago might be.

When a girl leaves her home at eighteen, she does one of two things. Either she falls into saving hands and becomes better, or she rapidly assumes the cosmopolitan standard of virtue and becomes worse. Of an intermediate balance, under the circumstances, there is no possibility. The city has its cunning wiles, no less than the infinitely smaller and more human tempter. There are large forces which allure with all the soulfulness of expression possible in the most cultured human. The gleam of a thousand lights is often as effective as the persuasive light in a wooing and fascinating eye. Half the undoing of the unsophisticated and natural mind is accomplished by forces wholly superhuman. A blare of sound, a roar of life, a vast array of human hives, appeal to the astonished senses in equivocal terms. Without a counsellor at hand to whisper cautious interpretations, what falsehoods may not these things breathe into the unguarded ear! Unrecognised for what they are, their beauty, like music, too often relaxes, then weakens, then perverts the simpler human perceptions.

Caroline, or Sister Carrie, as she had been half affectionately termed by the family, was possessed of a mind rudimentary in its power of observation and analysis. Self-interest with her was high, but not strong. It was, nevertheless, her guiding characteristic. Warm with the fancies of youth, pretty with the insipid prettiness of the formative period, possessed of a figure promising eventual shapeliness and an eye alight with certain native intelligence, she was a fair example of the middle American class—two generations removed from the emigrant. Books were beyond her interest—knowledge a sealed book. In the intuitive graces she was still crude. She could scarcely toss her head gracefully. Her hands were almost ineffectual. The feet, though small, were set flatly. And yet she was interested in her charms, quick to understand the keener pleasures of life, ambitious to gain in material things. A half-equipped little knight she was, venturing to reconnoitre the mysterious city and dreaming wild dreams of some vague, far-off supremacy, which should make it prey and subject—the proper penitent, grovelling at a woman's slipper.

"That," said a voice in her ear, "is one of the prettiest little resorts in Wisconsin."

"Is it?" she answered nervously.

The train was just pulling out of Waukesha. For some time she had been conscious of a man behind. She felt him observing her mass of hair. He had been fidgetting, and with natural intuition she felt a certain interest growing in that quarter. Her maidenly reserve, and a certain sense of what was conventional under the circumstances, called her to forestall and deny this familiarity, but the daring and magnetism of the individual, born of past experiences and triumphs, prevailed. She answered.

He leaned forward to put his elbows upon the back of her seat and proceeded to make himself volubly agreeable.

"Yes, that is a great resort for Chicago people. The hotels are swell. You are not familiar with this part of the country, are you?"

"Oh, yes, I am," answered Carrie. "That is, I live at Columbia City. I have never been through here, though."

"And so this is your first visit to Chicago," he observed.

All the time she was conscious of certain features out of the side of her eye. Flush, colourful cheeks, a light moustache, a grey fedora hat. She now turned and looked upon him in full, the instincts of self-protection and coquetry mingling confusedly in her brain.

"I didn't say that," she said.

"Oh," he answered, in a very pleasing way and with an assumed air of mistake, "I thought you did."

Here was a type of the travelling canvasser for a manufacturing house—a class which at that time was first being dubbed by the slang of the day "drummers." He came within the meaning of a still newer term, which had sprung into general use among Americans in 1880, and which concisely expressed the thought of one whose dress or manners are calculated to elicit the admiration of susceptible young women—a "masher." His suit was of a striped and crossed pattern of brown wool, new at that time, but since become familiar as a business suit. The low crotch of the vest revealed a stiff shirt bosom of white and pink stripes. From his coat sleeves protruded a pair of linen cuffs of the same pattern, fastened with large, gold plate buttons, set with the common yellow agates known as "cat's-eyes." His fingers bore several rings—one, the ever-enduring heavy seal—and from his vest dangled a neat gold watch chain, from which was suspended the secret insignia of the Order of Elks. The whole suit was rather tight-fitting, and was finished off with heavy-soled tan shoes, highly polished, and the grey fedora hat. He was, for the order of intellect represented, attractive, and whatever he had to recommend him, you may be sure was not lost upon Carrie, in this, her first glance.

Lest this order of individual should permanently pass, let me put down some of the most striking characteristics of his most successful manner and method. Good clothes, of course, were the first essential, the things without which he was nothing. A strong physical nature, actuated by a keen desire for the feminine, was the next. A mind free of any consideration of the problems or forces of the world and actuated not by greed, but an insatiable love of variable pleasure. His method was always simple. Its principal element was daring, backed, of course, by an intense desire and admiration for the sex. Let him meet with a young woman twice and he would straighten her necktie for her and perhaps address her by her first name. In the great department stores he was at his ease. If he caught the attention of some young woman while waiting for the cash boy to come back with his change, he would find out her name, her favourite flower, where a note would reach her, and perhaps pursue the delicate task of friendship until it proved unpromising, when it would be relinquished. He would do very well with more pretentious women, though the burden of expense was a slight deterrent. Upon entering a parlour car, for instance, he would select a chair next to the most promising bit of femininity and soon enquire if she cared to have the shade lowered. Before the train cleared the yards he would have the porter bring her a footstool. At the next lull in his conversational progress he would find her something to read, and from then on, by dint of compliment gently insinuated, personal narrative, exaggeration and service, he would win her tolerance, and, mayhap, regard.

A woman should some day write the complete philosophy of clothes. No matter how young, it is one of the things she wholly comprehends. There is an indescribably faint line in the matter of man's apparel which somehow divides for her those who are worth glancing at and those who are not. Once an individual has passed this faint line on the way downward he will get no glance from her. There is another line at which the dress of a man will cause her to study her own. This line the individual at her elbow now marked for Carrie. She became conscious of an inequality. Her own plain blue dress, with its black cotton tape trimmings, now seemed to her shabby. She felt the worn state of her shoes.

"Let's see," he went on, "I know quite a number of people in your town. Morgenroth the clothier and Gibson the dry goods man."

"Oh, do you?" she interrupted, aroused by memories of longings their show windows had cost her.

At last he had a clew to her interest, and followed it deftly. In a few minutes he had come about into her seat. He talked of sales of clothing, his travels, Chicago, and the amusements of that city.

"If you are going there, you will enjoy it immensely. Have you relatives?"

"I am going to visit my sister," she explained.

"You want to see Lincoln Park," he said, "and Michigan Boulevard. They are putting up great buildings there. It's a second New York—great. So much to see—theatres, crowds, fine houses—oh, you'll like that."

There was a little ache in her fancy of all he described. Her insignificance in the presence of so much magnificence faintly affected her. She realised that hers was not to be a round of pleasure, and yet there was something promising in all the material prospect he set forth. There was something satisfactory in the attention of this individual with his good clothes. She could not help smiling as he told her of some popular actress of whom she reminded him. She was not silly, and yet attention of this sort had its weight.

"You will be in Chicago some little time, won't you?" he observed at one turn of the now easy conversation.

"I don't know," said Carrie vaguely—a flash vision of the possibility of her not securing employment rising in her mind.

"Several weeks, anyhow," he said, looking steadily into her eyes.

There was much more passing now than the mere words indicated. He recognised the indescribable thing that made up for fascination and beauty in her. She realised that she was of interest to him from the one standpoint which a woman both delights in and fears. Her manner was simple, though for the very reason that she had not yet learned the many little affectations with which women conceal their true feelings. Some things she did appeared bold. A clever companion—had she ever had one—would have warned her never to look a man in the eyes so steadily.

"Why do you ask?" she said.

"Well, I'm going to be there several weeks. I'm going to study stock at our place and get new samples. I might show you 'round."

"I don't know whether you can or not. I mean I don't know whether I can. I shall be living with my sister, and——"

"Well, if she minds, we'll fix that." He took out his pencil and a little pocket note-book as if it were all settled. "What is your address there?"

She fumbled her purse which contained the address slip.

He reached down in his hip pocket and took out a fat purse. It was filled with slips of paper, some mileage books, a roll of greenbacks. It impressed her deeply. Such a purse had never been carried by any one attentive to her. Indeed, an experienced traveller, a brisk man of the world, had never come within such close range before. The purse, the shiny tan shoes, the smart new suit, and the *air* with which he did things, built up for her a dim world of fortune, of which he was the centre. It disposed her pleasantly toward all he might do.

He took out a neat business card, on which was engraved Bartlett, Caryoe & Company, and down in the lefthand corner, Chas. H. Drouet.

"That's me," he said, putting the card in her hand and touching his name. "It's pronounced Drew-eh. Our family was French, on my father's side."

She looked at it while he put up his purse. Then he got out a letter from a bunch in his coat pocket. "This is the house I travel for," he went on, pointing to a picture on it, "corner of State and Lake." There was pride in his voice. He felt that it was something to be connected with such a place, and he made her feel that way.

"What is your address?" he began again, fixing his pencil to write.

She looked at his hand.

"Carrie Meeber," she said slowly. "Three hundred and fifty-four West Van Buren Street, care S. C. Hanson."

He wrote it carefully down and got out the purse again. "You'll be at home if I come around Monday night?" he said.

"I think so," she answered.

How true it is that words are but the vague shadows of the

volumes we mean. Little audible links, they are, chaining together great inaudible feelings and purposes. Here were these
two, bandying little phrases, drawing purses, looking at cards,
and both unconscious of how inarticulate all their real feelings
were. Neither was wise enough to be sure of the working of
the mind of the other. He could not tell how his luring succeeded. She could not realise that she was drifting, until he
secured her address. Now she felt that she had yielded something—he, that he had gained a victory. Already they felt that
they were somehow associated. Already he took control in
directing the conversation. His words were easy. Her manner
was relaxed.

They were nearing Chicago. Signs were everywhere numerous. Trains flashed by them. Across wide stretches of flat,
open prairie they could see lines of telegraph poles stalking
across the fields toward the great city. Far away were indications of suburban towns, some big smoke-stacks towering
high in the air.

Frequently there were two-story frame houses standing out
in the open fields, without fence or trees, lone outposts of the
approaching army of homes.

To the child, the genius with imagination, or the wholly
untravelled, the approach to a great city for the first time is a
wonderful thing. Particularly if it be evening—that mystic period between the glare and gloom of the world when life is
changing from one sphere or condition to another. Ah, the
promise of the night. What does it not hold for the weary!
What old illusion of hope is not here forever repeated! Says
the soul of the toiler to itself, "I shall soon be free. I shall be
in the ways and the hosts of the merry. The streets, the lamps,
the lighted chamber set for dining, are for me. The theatre,
the halls, the parties, the ways of rest and the paths of song—
these are mine in the night." Though all humanity be still
enclosed in the shops, the thrill runs abroad. It is in the air.
The dullest feel something which they may not always express
or describe. It is the lifting of the burden of toil.

Sister Carrie gazed out of the window. Her companion,
affected by her wonder, so contagious are all things, felt anew
some interest in the city and pointed out its marvels.

"This is Northwest Chicago," said Drouet. "This is the

Chicago River," and he pointed to a little muddy creek, crowded with the huge masted wanderers from far-off waters nosing the black-posted banks. With a puff, a clang, and a clatter of rails it was gone. "Chicago is getting to be a great town," he went on. "It's a wonder. You'll find lots to see here."

She did not hear this very well. Her heart was troubled by a kind of terror. The fact that she was alone, away from home, rushing into a great sea of life and endeavour, began to tell. She could not help but feel a little choked for breath— a little sick as her heart beat so fast. She half closed her eyes and tried to think it was nothing, that Columbia City was only a little way off.

"Chicago! Chicago!" called the brakeman, slamming open the door. They were rushing into a more crowded yard, alive with the clatter and clang of life. She began to gather up her poor little grip and closed her hand firmly upon her purse. Drouet arose, kicked his legs to straighten his trousers, and seized his clean yellow grip.

"I suppose your people will be here to meet you?" he said. "Let me carry your grip."

"Oh, no," she said. "I'd rather you wouldn't. I'd rather you wouldn't be with me when I meet my sister."

"All right," he said in all kindness. "I'll be near, though, in case she isn't here, and take you out there safely."

"You're so kind," said Carrie, feeling the goodness of such attention in her strange situation.

"Chicago!" called the brakeman, drawing the word out long. They were under a great shadowy train shed, where the lamps were already beginning to shine out, with passenger cars all about and the train moving at a snail's pace. The people in the car were all up and crowding about the door.

"Well, here we are," said Drouet, leading the way to the door. "Good-bye, till I see you Monday."

"Good-bye," she answered, taking his proffered hand.

"Remember, I'll be looking till you find your sister."

She smiled into his eyes.

They filed out, and he affected to take no notice of her. A lean-faced, rather commonplace woman recognised Carrie on the platform and hurried forward.

"Why, Sister Carrie!" she began, and there was a perfunctory embrace of welcome.

Carrie realised the change of affectional atmosphere at once. Amid all the maze, uproar, and novelty she felt cold reality taking her by the hand. No world of light and merriment. No round of amusement. Her sister carried with her most of the grimness of shift and toil.

"Why, how are all the folks at home?" she began; "how is father, and mother?"

Carrie answered, but was looking away. Down the aisle, toward the gate leading into the waiting-room and the street, stood Drouet. He was looking back. When he saw that she saw him and was safe with her sister he turned to go, sending back the shadow of a smile. Only Carrie saw it. She felt something lost to her when he moved away. When he disappeared she felt his absence thoroughly. With her sister she was much alone, a lone figure in a tossing, thoughtless sea.

Chapter II

What Poverty Threatened: Of Granite and Brass

MINNIE'S FLAT, as the one-floor resident apartments were then being called, was in a part of West Van Buren Street inhabited by families of labourers and clerks, men who had come, and were still coming, with the rush of population pouring in at the rate of 50,000 a year. It was on the third floor, the front windows looking down into the street, where, at night, the lights of grocery stores were shining and children were playing. To Carrie, the sound of the little bells upon the horse-cars, as they tinkled in and out of hearing, was as pleasing as it was novel. She gazed into the lighted street when Minnie brought her into the front room, and wondered at the sounds, the movement, the murmur of the vast city which stretched for miles and miles in every direction.

Mrs. Hanson, after the first greetings were over, gave Carrie the baby and proceeded to get supper. Her husband asked a few questions and sat down to read the evening paper. He was a silent man, American born, of a Swede father, and now employed as a cleaner of refrigerator cars at the stock-yards. To him the presence or absence of his wife's sister was a matter of indifference. Her personal appearance did not affect him one way or the other. His one observation to the point was concerning the chances of work in Chicago.

"It's a big place," he said. "You can get in somewhere in a few days. Everybody does."

It had been tacitly understood beforehand that she was to get work and pay her board. He was of a clean, saving disposition, and had already paid a number of monthly instalments on two lots far out on the West Side. His ambition was some day to build a house on them.

In the interval which marked the preparation of the meal Carrie found time to study the flat. She had some slight gift of observation and that sense, so rich in every woman— intuition.

She felt the drag of a lean and narrow life. The walls of the rooms were discordantly papered. The floors were covered with matting and the hall laid with a thin rag carpet. One could see that the furniture was of that poor, hurriedly patched together quality sold by the instalment houses.

She sat with Minnie, in the kitchen, holding the baby until it began to cry. Then she walked and sang to it, until Hanson, disturbed in his reading, came and took it. A pleasant side to his nature came out here. He was patient. One could see that he was very much wrapped up in his offspring.

"Now, now," he said, walking. "There, there," and there was a certain Swedish accent noticeable in his voice.

"You'll want to see the city first, won't you?" said Minnie, when they were eating. "Well, we'll go out Sunday and see Lincoln Park."

Carrie noticed that Hanson had said nothing to this. He seemed to be thinking of something else.

"Well," she said, "I think I'll look around to-morrow. I've got Friday and Saturday, and it won't be any trouble. Which way is the business part?"

Minnie began to explain, but her husband took this part of the conversation to himself.

"It's that way," he said, pointing east. "That's east." Then he went off into the longest speech he had yet indulged in, concerning the lay of Chicago. "You'd better look in those big manufacturing houses along Franklin Street and just the other side of the river," he concluded. "Lots of girls work there. You could get home easy, too. It isn't very far."

Carrie nodded and asked her sister about the neighbourhood. The latter talked in a subdued tone, telling the little she knew about it, while Hanson concerned himself with the baby. Finally he jumped up and handed the child to his wife.

"I've got to get up early in the morning, so I'll go to bed," and off he went, disappearing into the dark little bedroom off the hall, for the night.

"He works way down at the stock-yards," explained Minnie, "so he's got to get up at half-past five."

"What time do you get up to get breakfast?" asked Carrie.

"At about twenty minutes of five."

Together they finished the labour of the day, Carrie washing the dishes while Minnie undressed the baby and put it to bed. Minnie's manner was one of trained industry, and Carrie could see that it was a steady round of toil with her.

She began to see that her relations with Drouet would have to be abandoned. He could not come here. She read from the manner of Hanson, in the subdued air of Minnie, and, indeed, the whole atmosphere of the flat, a settled opposition to anything save a conservative round of toil. If Hanson sat every evening in the front room and read his paper, if he went to bed at nine, and Minnie a little later, what would they expect of her? She saw that she would first need to get work and establish herself on a paying basis before she could think of having company of any sort. Her little flirtation with Drouet seemed now an extraordinary thing.

"No," she said to herself, "he can't come here."

She asked Minnie for ink and paper, which were upon the mantel in the dining-room, and when the latter had gone to bed at ten, got out Drouet's card and wrote him.

"I cannot have you call on me here. You will have to wait until you hear from me again. My sister's place is so small."

She troubled herself over what else to put in the letter. She wanted to make some reference to their relations upon the train, but was too timid. She concluded by thanking him for his kindness in a crude way, then puzzled over the formality of signing her name, and finally decided upon the severe, winding up with a "Very truly," which she subsequently changed to "Sincerely." She sealed and addressed the letter, and going in the front room, the alcove of which contained her bed, drew the one small rocking-chair up to the open window, and sat looking out upon the night and streets in silent wonder. Finally, wearied by her own reflections, she began to grow dull in her chair, and feeling the need of sleep, arranged her clothing for the night and went to bed.

When she awoke at eight the next morning, Hanson had gone. Her sister was busy in the dining-room, which was also the sitting-room, sewing. She worked, after dressing, to arrange a little breakfast for herself, and then advised with Minnie as to which way to look. The latter had changed considerably since Carrie had seen her. She was now a thin, though rugged, woman of twenty-seven, with ideas of life coloured by her husband's, and fast hardening into narrower conceptions of pleasure and duty than had ever been hers in a thoroughly circumscribed youth. She had invited Carrie, not because she longed for her presence, but because the latter was dissatisfied at home, and could probably get work and pay her board here. She was pleased to see her in a way, but reflected her husband's point of view in the matter of work. Anything was good enough so long as it paid—say, five dollars a week to begin with. A shop girl was the destiny prefigured for the newcomer. She would get in one of the great shops and do well enough until—well, until something happened. Neither of them knew exactly what. They did not figure on promotion. They did not exactly count on marriage. Things would go on, though, in a dim kind of way until the better thing would eventuate, and Carrie would be rewarded for coming and toiling in the city. It was under such auspicious circumstances that she started out this morning to look for work.

Before following her in her round of seeking, let us look at the sphere in which her future was to lie. In 1889 Chicago had the peculiar qualifications of growth which made such adventuresome pilgrimages even on the part of young girls plausible. Its many and growing commercial opportunities gave it widespread fame, which made of it a giant magnet, drawing to itself, from all quarters, the hopeful and the hopeless— those who had their fortune yet to make and those whose fortunes and affairs had reached a disastrous climax elsewhere. It was a city of over 500,000, with the ambition, the daring, the activity of a metropolis of a million. Its streets and houses were already scattered over an area of seventy-five square miles. Its population was not so much thriving upon established commerce as upon the industries which prepared for the arrival of others. The sound of the hammer engaged upon the erection of new structures was everywhere heard. Great industries were moving in. The huge railroad corporations which had long before recognised the prospects of the place had seized upon vast tracts of land for transfer and shipping purposes. Street-car lines had been extended far out into the open country in anticipation of rapid growth. The city had laid miles and miles of streets and sewers through regions where, perhaps, one solitary house stood out alone—a pioneer of the populous ways to be. There were regions open to the sweeping winds and rain, which were yet lighted throughout the night with long, blinking lines of gas-lamps, fluttering in the wind. Narrow board walks extended out, passing here a house, and there a store, at far intervals, eventually ending on the open prairie.

In the central portion was the vast wholesale and shopping district, to which the uninformed seeker for work usually drifted. It was a characteristic of Chicago then, and one not generally shared by other cities, that individual firms of any pretension occupied individual buildings. The presence of ample ground made this possible. It gave an imposing appearance to most of the wholesale houses, whose offices were upon the ground floor and in plain view of the street. The large plates of window glass, now so common, were then rapidly coming into use, and gave to the ground floor offices a distinguished and prosperous look. The casual wanderer could see as he passed a polished array of office fixtures, much frosted glass, clerks hard at work, and genteel business men in "nobby" suits and clean linen lounging about or sitting in groups. Polished brass or nickel signs at the square stone entrances announced the firm and the nature of the business in rather neat and reserved terms. The entire metropolitan centre possessed a high and mighty air calculated to overawe and abash the common applicant, and to make the gulf between poverty and success seem both wide and deep.

Into this important commercial region the timid Carrie went. She walked east along Van Buren Street through a region of lessening importance, until it deteriorated into a mass of shanties and coal-yards, and finally verged upon the river. She walked bravely forward, led by an honest desire to find employment and delayed at every step by the interest of the unfolding scene, and a sense of helplessness amid so much evidence of power and force which she did not understand. These vast buildings, what were they? These strange energies and huge interests, for what purposes were they there? She could have understood the meaning of a little stone-cutter's yard at Columbia City, carving little pieces of marble for individual use, but when the yards of some huge stone corporation came into view, filled with spur tracks and flat cars, transpierced by docks from the river and traversed overhead by immense trundling cranes of wood and steel, it lost all significance in her little world.

It was so with the vast railroad yards, with the crowded array of vessels she saw at the river, and the huge factories over the way, lining the water's edge. Through the open windows she could see the figures of men and women in working aprons, moving busily about. The great streets were wall-lined mysteries to her; the vast offices, strange mazes which concerned far-off individuals of importance. She could only think of people connected with them as counting money, dressing magnificently, and riding in carriages. What they dealt in, how they laboured, to what end it all came, she had only the vaguest conception. It was all wonderful, all vast, all far removed, and she sank in spirit inwardly and fluttered feebly at the heart as she thought of entering any one of these mighty concerns and asking for something to do—something that she could do—anything.

Chapter III

ONCE ACROSS the river and into the wholesale district, she glanced about her for some likely door at which to apply. As she contemplated the wide windows and imposing signs, she became conscious of being gazed upon and understood for what she was—a wage-seeker. She had never done this thing before, and lacked courage. To avoid a certain indefinable shame she felt at being caught spying about for a position, she quickened her steps and assumed an air of indifference supposedly common to one upon an errand. In this way she passed many manufacturing and wholesale houses without once glancing in. At last, after several blocks of walking, she felt that this would not do, and began to look about again, though without relaxing her pace. A little way on she saw a great door which, for some reason, attracted her attention. It was ornamented by a small brass sign, and seemed to be the entrance to a vast hive of six or seven floors. "Perhaps," she thought, "they may want some one," and crossed over to enter. When she came within a score of feet of the desired goal, she saw through the window a young man in a grey checked suit. That he had anything to do with the concern, she could not tell, but because he happened to be looking in her direction her weakening heart misgave her and she hurried by, too overcome with shame to enter. Over the way stood a great six-story structure, labelled Storm and King, which she viewed with rising hope. It was a wholesale dry goods concern and employed women. She could see them moving about now and then upon the upper floors. This place she decided to enter, no matter what. She crossed over and walked directly toward the entrance. As she did so, two men came out and paused in the door. A telegraph messenger in blue dashed past her and up the few steps that led to the entrance and disappeared. Several pedestrians out of the hurrying throng which filled the sidewalks passed about her as she paused, hesitating. She looked helplessly around, and then, seeing herself observed, retreated. It was too difficult a task. She could not go past them.

So severe a defeat told sadly upon her nerves. Her feet carried her mechanically forward, every foot of her progress being a satisfactory portion of a flight which she gladly made. Block after block passed by. Upon street-lamps at the various corners she read names such as Madison, Monroe, La Salle, Clark, Dearborn, State, and still she went, her feet beginning to tire upon the broad stone flagging. She was pleased in part that the streets were bright and clean. The morning sun, shining down with steadily increasing warmth, made the shady side of the streets pleasantly cool. She looked at the blue sky overhead with more realisation of its charm than had ever come to her before.

Her cowardice began to trouble her in a way. She turned back, resolving to hunt up Storm and King and enter. On the way she encountered a great wholesale shoe company, through the broad plate windows of which she saw an enclosed executive department, hidden by frosted glass. Without this enclosure, but just within the street entrance, sat a grey-haired gentleman at a small table, with a large open ledger before him. She walked by this institution several times hesitating, but, finding herself unobserved, faltered past the screen door and stood humbly waiting.

"Well, young lady," observed the old gentleman, looking at her somewhat kindly, " what is it you wish?"

"I am, that is, do you—I mean, do you need any help?" she stammered.

"Not just at present," he answered smiling. "Not just at present. Come in some time next week. Occasionally we need some one."

She received the answer in silence and backed awkwardly out. The pleasant nature of her reception rather astonished her. She had expected that it would be more difficult, that something cold and harsh would be said—she knew not what. That she had not been put to shame and made to feel her unfortunate position, seemed remarkable.

Somewhat encouraged, she ventured into another large structure. It was a clothing company, and more people were in evidence—well-dressed men of forty and more, surrounded by brass railings.

An office boy approached her.

"Who is it you wish to see?" he asked.

"I want to see the manager," she said.

He ran away and spoke to one of a group of three men who were conferring together. One of these came towards her.

"Well?" he said coldly. The greeting drove all courage from her at once.

"Do you need any help?" she stammered.

"No," he replied abruptly, and turned upon his heel.

She went foolishly out, the office boy deferentially swinging the door for her, and gladly sank into the obscuring crowd. It was a severe setback to her recently pleased mental state.

Now she walked quite aimlessly for a time, turning here and there, seeing one great company after another, but finding no courage to prosecute her single inquiry. High noon came, and with it hunger. She hunted out an unassuming restaurant and entered, but was disturbed to find that the prices were exorbitant for the size of her purse. A bowl of soup was all that she could afford, and, with this quickly eaten, she went out again. It restored her strength somewhat and made her moderately bold to pursue the search.

In walking a few blocks to fix upon some probable place, she again encountered the firm of Storm and King, and this time managed to get in. Some gentlemen were conferring close at hand, but took no notice of her. She was left standing, gazing nervously upon the floor. When the limit of her distress had been nearly reached, she was beckoned to by a man at one of the many desks within the near-by railing.

"Who is it you wish to see?" he inquired.

"Why, any one, if you please," she answered. "I am looking for something to do."

"Oh, you want to see Mr. McManus," he returned. "Sit down," and he pointed to a chair against the neighbouring wall. He went on leisurely writing, until after a time a short, stout gentleman came in from the street.

"Mr. McManus," called the man at the desk, "this young woman wants to see you."

The short gentleman turned about towards Carrie, and she arose and came forward.

"What can I do for you, miss?" he inquired, surveying her curiously.

"I want to know if I can get a position," she inquired.

"As what?" he asked.

"Not as anything in particular," she faltered.

"Have you ever had any experience in the wholesale dry goods business?" he questioned.

"No, sir," she replied.

"Are you a stenographer or typewriter?"

"No, sir."

"Well, we haven't anything here," he said. "We employ only experienced help."

She began to step backward toward the door, when something about her plaintive face attracted him.

"Have you ever worked at anything before?" he inquired.

"No, sir," she said.

"Well, now, it's hardly possible that you would get anything to do in a wholesale house of this kind. Have you tried the department stores?"

She acknowledged that she had not.

"Well, if I were you," he said, looking at her rather genially, "I would try the department stores. They often need young women as clerks."

"Thank you," she said, her whole nature relieved by this spark of friendly interest.

"Yes," he said, as she moved toward the door, "you try the department stores," and off he went.

At that time the department store was in its earliest form of successful operation, and there were not many. The first three in the United States, established about 1884, were in Chicago. Carrie was familiar with the names of several through the advertisements in the "Daily News," and now proceeded to seek them. The words of Mr. McManus had somehow managed to restore her courage, which had fallen low, and she dared to hope that this new line would offer her something. Some time she spent in wandering up and down, thinking to encounter the buildings by chance, so readily is the mind, bent upon prosecuting a hard but needful errand, eased by that self-deception which the semblance of search, without the reality, gives. At last she inquired of a police officer, and was directed to proceed "two blocks up," where she would find "The Fair."

The nature of these vast retail combinations, should they ever permanently disappear, will form an interesting chapter in the commercial history of our nation. Such a flowering out of a modest trade principle the world had never witnessed up to that time. They were along the line of the most effective retail organisation, with hundreds of stores coördinated into one and laid out upon the most imposing and economic basis. They were handsome, bustling, successful affairs, with a host of clerks and a swarm of patrons. Carrie passed along the busy aisles, much affected by the remarkable displays of trinkets, dress goods, stationery, and jewelry. Each separate counter was a show place of dazzling interest and attraction. She could not help feeling the claim of each trinket and valuable upon her personally, and yet she did not stop. There was nothing there which she could not have used—nothing which she did not long to own. The dainty slippers and stockings, the delicately frilled skirts and petticoats, the laces, ribbons, hair-combs, purses, all touched her with individual desire, and she felt keenly the fact that not any of these things were in the range of her purchase. She was a work-seeker, an outcast without employment, one whom the average employee could tell at a glance was poor and in need of a situation.

It must not be thought that any one could have mistaken her for a nervous, sensitive, high-strung nature, cast unduly upon a cold, calculating, and unpoetic world. Such certainly she was not. But women are peculiarly sensitive to their adornment.

Not only did Carrie feel the drag of desire for all which was new and pleasing in apparel for women, but she noticed too, with a touch at the heart, the fine ladies who elbowed and ignored her, brushing past in utter disregard of her presence, themselves eagerly enlisted in the materials which the store contained. Carrie was not familiar with the appearance of her more fortunate sisters of the city. Neither had she before known the nature and appearance of the shop girls with whom she now compared poorly. They were pretty in the main, some even handsome, with an air of independence and indifference which added, in the case of the more favoured, a certain piquancy. Their clothes were neat, in many instances fine, and wherever she encountered the eye of one it was only to recognise in it a keen analysis of her own position—her individual shortcomings of dress and that shadow of *manner* which she thought must hang about her and make clear to all who and what she was. A flame of envy lighted in her heart. She realised in a dim way how much the city held—wealth, fashion, ease—every adornment for women, and she longed for dress and beauty with a whole heart.

On the second floor were the managerial offices, to which, after some inquiry, she was now directed. There she found other girls ahead of her, applicants like herself, but with more of that self-satisfied and independent air which experience of the city lends; girls who scrutinised her in a painful manner. After a wait of perhaps three-quarters of an hour, she was called in turn.

"Now," said a sharp, quick-mannered Jew, who was sitting at a roll-top desk near the window, "have you ever worked in any other store?"

"No, sir," said Carrie.

"Oh, you haven't," he said, eyeing her keenly.

"No, sir," she replied.

"Well, we prefer young women just now with some experience. I guess we can't use you."

Carrie stood waiting a moment, hardly certain whether the interview had terminated.

"Don't wait!" he exclaimed. "Remember we are very busy here."

Carrie began to move quickly to the door.

"Hold on," he said, calling her back. "Give me your name and address. We want girls occasionally."

When she had gotten safely into the street, she could scarcely restrain the tears. It was not so much the particular rebuff which she had just experienced, but the whole abashing trend of the day. She was tired and nervous. She abandoned the thought of appealing to the other department stores and now wandered on, feeling a certain safety and relief in mingling with the crowd.

In her indifferent wandering she turned into Jackson Street, not far from the river, and was keeping her way along the south side of that imposing thoroughfare, when a piece of wrapping paper, written on with marking ink and tacked up on the door, attracted her attention. It read, "Girls wanted—wrappers & stitchers." She hesitated a moment, then entered.

The firm of Speigelheim & Co., makers of boys' caps, occupied one floor of the building, fifty feet in width and some eighty feet in depth. It was a place rather dingily lighted, the darkest portions having incandescent lights, filled with machines and work benches. At the latter laboured quite a company of girls and some men. The former were drabby-looking creatures, stained in face with oil and dust, clad in thin, shapeless, cotton dresses and shod with more or less worn shoes. Many of them had their sleeves rolled up, revealing bare arms, and in some cases, owing to the heat, their dresses were open at the neck. They were a fair type of nearly the lowest order of shop-girls—careless, slouchy, and more or less pale from confinement. They were not timid, however; were rich in curiosity, and strong in daring and slang.

Carrie looked about her, very much disturbed and quite sure that she did not want to work here. Aside from making her uncomfortable by sidelong glances, no one paid her the least attention. She waited until the whole department was aware of her presence. Then some word was sent around, and a foreman, in an apron and shirt sleeves, the latter rolled up to his shoulders, approached.

"Do you want to see me?" he asked.

"Do you need any help?" said Carrie, already learning directness of address.

"Do you know how to stitch caps?" he returned.

"No, sir," she replied.

"Have you ever had any experience at this kind of work?" he inquired.

She answered that she had not.

"Well," said the foreman, scratching his ear meditatively, " we do need a stitcher. We like experienced help, though. We've hardly got time to break people in." He paused and looked away out of the window. "We might, though, put you at finishing," he concluded reflectively.

"How much do you pay a week?" ventured Carrie, emboldened by a certain softness in the man's manner and his simplicity of address.

"Three and a half," he answered.

"Oh," she was about to exclaim, but checked herself and allowed her thoughts to die without expression.

"We're not exactly in need of anybody," he went on vaguely, looking her over as one would a package. "You can come on Monday morning, though," he added, "and I'll put you to work."

"Thank you," said Carrie weakly.

"If you come, bring an apron," he added.

He walked away and left her standing by the elevator, never so much as inquiring her name.

While the appearance of the shop and the announcement of the price paid per week operated very much as a blow to Carrie's fancy, the fact that work of any kind was offered after so rude a round of experience was gratifying. She could not begin to believe that she would take the place, modest as her aspirations were. She had been used to better than that. Her mere experience and the free out-of-door life of the country caused her nature to revolt at such confinement. Dirt had never been her share. Her sister's flat was clean. This place was grimy and low, the girls were careless and hardened. They must be bad-minded and hearted, she imagined. Still, a place had been offered her. Surely Chicago was not so bad if she could find one place in one day. She might find another and better later.

Her subsequent experiences were not of a reassuring nature, however. From all the more pleasing or imposing places she was turned away abruptly with the most chilling formality. In others where she applied only the experienced were required. She met with painful rebuffs, the most trying of which had been in a manufacturing cloak house, where she had gone to the fourth floor to inquire.

"No, no," said the foreman, a rough, heavily built individual, who looked after a miserably lighted workshop, " we don't want any one. Don't come here."

With the wane of the afternoon went her hopes, her courage, and her strength. She had been astonishingly persistent.

So earnest an effort was well deserving of a better reward. On every hand, to her fatigued senses, the great business portion grew larger, harder, more stolid in its indifference. It seemed as if it was all closed to her, that the struggle was too fierce for her to hope to do anything at all. Men and women hurried by in long, shifting lines. She felt the flow of the tide of effort and interest—felt her own helplessness without quite realising the wisp on the tide that she was. She cast about vainly for some possible place to apply, but found no door which she had the courage to enter. It would be the same thing all over. The old humiliation of her plea, rewarded by curt denial. Sick at heart and in body, she turned to the west, the direction of Minnie's flat, which she had now fixed in mind, and began that wearisome, baffled retreat which the seeker for employment at nightfall too often makes. In passing through Fifth Avenue, south towards Van Buren Street, where she intended to take a car, she passed the door of a large wholesale shoe house, through the plate-glass window of which she could see a middle-aged gentleman sitting at a small desk. One of those forlorn impulses which often grow out of a fixed sense of defeat, the last sprouting of a baffled and uprooted growth of ideas, seized upon her. She walked deliberately through the door and up to the gentleman, who looked at her weary face with partially awakened interest.

"What is it?" he said.

"Can you give me something to do?" said Carrie.

"Now, I really don't know," he said kindly. "What kind of work is it you want—you're not a typewriter, are you?"

"Oh, no," answered Carrie.

"Well, we only employ book-keepers and typewriters here. You might go around to the side and inquire upstairs. They did want some help upstairs a few days ago. Ask for Mr. Brown."

She hastened around to the side entrance and was taken up by the elevator to the fourth floor.

"Call Mr. Brown, Willie," said the elevator man to a boy near by.

Willie went off and presently returned with the information that Mr. Brown said she should sit down and that he would be around in a little while.

It was a portion of the stock room which gave no idea of the general character of the place, and Carrie could form no opinion of the nature of the work.

"So you want something to do," said Mr. Brown, after he inquired concerning the nature of her errand. "Have you ever been employed in a shoe factory before?"

"No, sir," said Carrie.

"What is your name?" he inquired, and being informed, "Well, I don't know as I have anything for you. Would you work for four and a half a week?"

Carrie was too worn by defeat not to feel that it was considerable. She had not expected that he would offer her less than six. She acquiesced, however, and he took her name and address.

"Well," he said, finally, "you report here at eight o'clock Monday morning. I think I can find something for you to do."

He left her revived by the possibilities, sure that she had found something at last. Instantly the blood crept warmly over her body. Her nervous tension relaxed. She walked out into the busy street and discovered a new atmosphere. Behold, the throng was moving with a lightsome step. She noticed that men and women were smiling. Scraps of conversation and notes of laughter floated to her. The air was light. People were already pouring out of the buildings, their labour ended for the day. She noticed that they were pleased, and thoughts of her sister's home and the meal that would be awaiting her quickened her steps. She hurried on, tired perhaps, but no longer weary of foot. What would not Minnie say! Ah, the long winter in Chicago—the lights, the crowd, the amusement! This was a great, pleasing metropolis after all. Her new firm was a goodly institution. Its windows were of huge plate glass. She could probably do well there. Thoughts of Drouet returned—of the things he had told her. She now felt that life was better, that it was livelier, sprightlier. She boarded a car in the best of spirits, feeling her blood still flowing pleasantly. She would live in Chicago, her mind kept saying to itself. She would have a better time than she had ever had before—she would be happy.

Chapter IV

THE SPENDINGS OF FANCY: FACTS ANSWER WITH SNEERS

FOR THE NEXT two days Carrie indulged in the most high-flown speculations.

Her fancy plunged recklessly into privileges and amusements which would have been much more becoming had she been cradled a child of fortune. With ready will and quick mental selection she scattered her meagre four-fifty per week with a swift and graceful hand. Indeed, as she sat in her rocking-chair these several evenings before going to bed and looked out upon the pleasantly lighted street, this money cleared for its prospective possessor the way to every joy and every bauble which the heart of woman may desire. "I will have a fine time," she thought.

Her sister Minnie knew nothing of these rather wild cerebrations, though they exhausted the markets of delight. She was too busy scrubbing the kitchen wood-work and calculating the purchasing power of eighty cents for Sunday's dinner. When Carrie had returned home, flushed with her first success and ready, for all her weariness, to discuss the now interesting events which led up to her achievement, the former had merely smiled approvingly and inquired whether she would have to spend any of it for car fare. This consideration had not entered in before, and it did not now for long affect the glow of Carrie's enthusiasm. Disposed as she then was to calculate upon that vague basis which allows the subtraction of one sum from another without any perceptible diminution, she was happy.

When Hanson came home at seven o'clock, he was inclined to be a little crusty—his usual demeanour before supper. This never showed so much in anything he said as in a certain solemnity of countenance and the silent manner in which he slopped about. He had a pair of yellow carpet slippers which he enjoyed wearing, and these he would immediately substitute for his solid pair of shoes. This, and washing his face with the aid of common washing soap until it glowed a shiny red, constituted his only preparation for his evening meal. He would then get his evening paper and read in silence.

For a young man, this was rather a morbid turn of character, and so affected Carrie. Indeed, it affected the entire atmosphere of the flat, as such things are inclined to do, and gave to his wife's mind its subdued and tactful turn, anxious to avoid taciturn replies. Under the influence of Carrie's announcement he brightened up somewhat.

"You didn't lose any time, did you?" he remarked, smiling a little.

"No," returned Carrie with a touch of pride.

He asked her one or two more questions and then turned to play with the baby, leaving the subject until it was brought up again by Minnie at the table.

Carrie, however, was not to be reduced to the common level of observation which prevailed in the flat.

"It seems to be such a large company," she said, at one place. "Great big plate-glass windows and lots of clerks. The man I saw said they hired ever so many people."

"It's not very hard to get work now," put in Hanson, "if you look right."

Minnie, under the warming influence of Carrie's good spirits and her husband's somewhat conversational mood, began to tell Carrie of some of the well-known things to see— things the enjoyment of which cost nothing.

"You'd like to see Michigan Avenue. There are such fine houses. It is such a fine street."

"Where is 'H. R. Jacob's'?" interrupted Carrie, mentioning one of the theatres devoted to melodrama which went by that name at the time.

"Oh, it's not very far from here," answered Minnie. "It's in Halstead Street, right up here."

"How I'd like to go there. I crossed Halstead Street to-day, didn't I?"

At this there was a slight halt in the natural reply. Thoughts are a strangely permeating factor. At her suggestion of going to the theatre, the unspoken shade of disapproval to the doing of those things which involved the expenditure of money—shades of feeling which arose in the mind of Hanson and then in Minnie—slightly affected the atmosphere of the table. Minnie answered "yes," but Carrie could feel that going to the theatre was poorly advocated here. The subject was put off for a little while until Hanson, through with his meal, took his paper and went into the front room.

When they were alone, the two sisters began a somewhat freer conversation, Carrie interrupting it to hum a little, as they worked at the dishes.

"I should like to walk up and see Halstead Street, if it isn't too far," said Carrie, after a time. "Why don't we go to the theatre to-night?"

"Oh, I don't think Sven would want to go to-night," returned Minnie. "He has to get up so early."

"He wouldn't mind—he'd enjoy it," said Carrie.

"No, he doesn't go very often," returned Minnie.

"Well, I'd like to go," rejoined Carrie. "Let's you and me go."

Minnie pondered a while, not upon whether she could or would go—for that point was already negatively settled with her—but upon some means of diverting the thoughts of her sister to some other topic.

"We'll go some other time," she said at last, finding no ready means of escape.

Carrie sensed the root of the opposition at once.

"I have some money," she said. "You go with me."

Minnie shook her head.

"He could go along," said Carrie.

"No," returned Minnie softly, and rattling the dishes to drown the conversation. "He wouldn't."

It had been several years since Minnie had seen Carrie, and in that time the latter's character had developed a few shades. Naturally timid in all things that related to her own advancement, and especially so when without power or resource, her craving for pleasure was so strong that it was the one stay of her nature. She would speak for that when silent on all else.

"Ask him," she pleaded softly.

Minnie was thinking of the resource which Carrie's board would add. It would pay the rent and would make the subject of expenditure a little less difficult to talk about with her husband. But if Carrie was going to think of running around in the beginning there would be a hitch somewhere. Unless

Carrie submitted to a solemn round of industry and saw the need of hard work without longing for play, how was her coming to the city to profit them? These thoughts were not those of a cold, hard nature at all. They were the serious reflections of a mind which invariably adjusted itself, without much complaining, to such surroundings as its industry could make for it.

At last she yielded enough to ask Hanson. It was a half-hearted procedure without a shade of desire on her part.

"Carrie wants us to go to the theatre," she said, looking in upon her husband. Hanson looked up from his paper, and they exchanged a mild look, which said as plainly as anything: "This isn't what we expected."

"I don't care to go," he returned. "What does she want to see?"

"H. R. Jacob's," said Minnie.

He looked down at his paper and shook his head negatively.

When Carrie saw how they looked upon her proposition, she gained a still clearer feeling of their way of life. It weighed on her, but took no definite form of opposition.

"I think I'll go down and stand at the foot of the stairs," she said, after a time.

Minnie made no objection to this, and Carrie put on her hat and went below.

"Where has Carrie gone?" asked Hanson, coming back into the dining-room when he heard the door close.

"She said she was going down to the foot of the stairs," answered Minnie. "I guess she just wants to look out a while."

"She oughtn't to be thinking about spending her money on theatres already, do you think?" he said.

"She just feels a little curious, I guess," ventured Minnie. "Everything is so new."

"I don't know," said Hanson, and went over to the baby, his forehead slightly wrinkled.

He was thinking of a full career of vanity and wastefulness which a young girl might indulge in, and wondering how Carrie could contemplate such a course when she had so little, as yet, with which to do.

On Saturday Carrie went out by herself—first toward the river, which interested her, and then back along Jackson Street, which was then lined by the pretty houses and fine lawns which subsequently caused it to be made into a boulevard. She was struck with the evidences of wealth, although there was, perhaps, not a person on the street worth more than a hundred thousand dollars. She was glad to be out of the flat, because already she felt that it was a narrow, humdrum place, and that interest and joy lay elsewhere. Her thoughts now were of a more liberal character, and she punctuated them with speculations as to the whereabouts of Drouet. She was not sure but that he might call anyhow Monday night, and, while she felt a little disturbed at the possibility, there was, nevertheless, just the shade of a wish that he would.

On Monday she arose early and prepared to go to work. She dressed herself in a worn shirt-waist of dotted blue percale, a skirt of light-brown serge rather faded, and a small straw hat which she had worn all summer at Columbia City. Her shoes were old, and her necktie was in that crumpled, flattened state which time and much wearing impart. She made a very average looking shop-girl with the exception of her features. These were slightly more even than common, and gave her a sweet, reserved, and pleasing appearance.

It is no easy thing to get up early in the morning when one is used to sleeping until seven and eight, as Carrie had been at home. She gained some inkling of the character of Hanson's life when, half asleep, she looked out into the diningroom at six o'clock and saw him silently finishing his breakfast. By the time she was dressed he was gone, and she, Minnie, and the baby ate together, the latter being just old enough to sit in a high chair and disturb the dishes with a spoon. Her spirits were greatly subdued now when the fact of entering upon strange and untried duties confronted her. Only the ashes of all her fine fancies were remaining—ashes still concealing, nevertheless, a few red embers of hope. So subdued was she by her weakening nerves, that she ate quite in silence, going over imaginary conceptions of the character of the shoe company, the nature of the work, her employer's attitude. She was vaguely feeling that she would come in contact with the great owners, that her work would be where grave, stylishly dressed men occasionally look on.

"Well, good luck," said Minnie, when she was ready to go. They had agreed it was best to walk, that morning at least, to see if she could do it every day—sixty cents a week for car fare being quite an item under the circumstances.

"I'll tell you how it goes to-night," said Carrie.

Once in the sunlit street, with labourers tramping by in either direction, the horse-cars passing crowded to the rails with the small clerks and floor help in the great wholesale houses, and men and women generally coming out of doors and passing about the neighbourhood, Carrie felt slightly re-assured. In the sunshine of the morning, beneath the wide, blue heavens, with a fresh wind astir, what fears, except the most desperate, can find a harbourage? In the night, or the gloomy chambers of the day, fears and misgivings wax strong, but out in the sunlight there is, for a time, cessation even of the terror of death.

Carrie went straight forward until she crossed the river, and then turned into Fifth Avenue. The thoroughfare, in this part, was like a walled cañon of brown stone and dark red brick. The big windows looked shiny and clean. Trucks were rumbling in increasing numbers; men and women, girls and boys were moving onward in all directions. She met girls of her own age, who looked at her as if with contempt for her dif-fidence. She wondered at the magnitude of this life and at the importance of knowing much in order to do anything in it at all. Dread at her own inefficiency crept upon her. She would not know how, she would not be quick enough. Had not all the other places refused her because she did not know some-thing or other? She would be scolded, abused, ignominiously discharged.

It was with weak knees and a slight catch in her breathing that she came up to the great shoe company at Adams and Fifth Avenue and entered the elevator. When she stepped out on the fourth floor there was no one at hand, only great aisles of boxes piled to the ceiling. She stood, very much fright-ened, awaiting some one.

Presently Mr. Brown came up. He did not seem to recog-nise her.

"What is it you want?" he inquired.

Carrie's heart sank.

"You said I should come this morning to see about work——"

"Oh," he interrupted. "Um—yes. What is your name?"

"Carrie Meeber."

"Yes," said he. "You come with me."

He led the way through dark, box-lined aisles which had the smell of new shoes, until they came to an iron door which opened into the factory proper. There was a large, low-ceiled room, with clacking, rattling machines at which men in white shirt sleeves and blue gingham aprons were working. She followed him diffidently through the clattering automatons, keeping her eyes straight before her, and flushing slightly. They crossed to a far corner and took an elevator to the sixth floor. Out of the array of machines and benches, Mr. Brown signalled a foreman.

"This is the girl," he said, and turning to Carrie, "You go with him." He then returned, and Carrie followed her new superior to a little desk in a corner, which he used as a kind of official centre.

"You've never worked at anything like this before, have you?" he questioned, rather sternly.

"No, sir," she answered.

He seemed rather annoyed at having to bother with such help, but put down her name and then led her across to where a line of girls occupied stools in front of clacking machines. On the shoulder of one of the girls who was punching eye-holes in one piece of the upper, by the aid of the machine, he put his hand.

"You," he said, "show this girl how to do what you're doing. When you get through, come to me."

The girl so addressed rose promptly and gave Carrie her place.

"It isn't hard to do," she said, bending over. "You just take this so, fasten it with this clamp, and start the machine."

She suited action to word, fastened the piece of leather, which was eventually to form the right half of the upper of a man's shoe, by little adjustable clamps, and pushed a small steel rod at the side of the machine. The latter jumped to the task of punching, with sharp, snapping clicks, cutting circular bits of leather out of the side of the upper, leaving the holes which were to hold the laces. After observing a few times, the girl let her work at it alone. Seeing that it was fairly well done, she went away.

The pieces of leather came from the girl at the machine to her right, and were passed on to the girl at her left. Carrie saw at once that an average speed was necessary or the work would pile up on her and all those below would be delayed. She had no time to look about, and bent anxiously to her task. The girls at her left and right realised her predicament and feelings, and, in a way, tried to aid her, as much as they dared, by working slower.

At this task she laboured incessantly for some time, finding relief from her own nervous fears and imaginings in the humdrum, mechanical movement of the machine. She felt, as the minutes passed, that the room was not very light. It had a thick odour of fresh leather, but that did not worry her. She felt the eyes of the other help upon her, and troubled lest she was not working fast enough.

Once, when she was fumbling at the little clamp, having made a slight error in setting in the leather, a great hand appeared before her eyes and fastened the clamp for her. It was the foreman. Her heart thumped so that she could scarcely see to go on.

"Start your machine," he said, "start your machine. Don't keep the line waiting."

This recovered her sufficiently and she went excitedly on, hardly breathing until the shadow moved away from behind her. Then she heaved a great breath.

As the morning wore on the room became hotter. She felt the need of a breath of fresh air and a drink of water, but did not venture to stir. The stool she sat on was without a back or foot-rest, and she began to feel uncomfortable. She found, after a time, that her back was beginning to ache. She twisted and turned from one position to another slightly different, but it did not ease her for long. She was beginning to weary.

"Stand up, why don't you?" said the girl at her right, without any form of introduction. "They won't care."

Carrie looked at her gratefully. "I guess I will," she said.

She stood up from her stool and worked that way for a while, but it was a more difficult position. Her neck and shoulders ached in bending over.

The spirit of the place impressed itself on her in a rough way. She did not venture to look around, but above the clack of the machine she could hear an occasional remark. She could also note a thing or two out of the side of her eye.

"Did you see Harry last night?" said the girl at her left, addressing her neighbour.

"No."

"You ought to have seen the tie he had on. Gee, but he was a mark."

"S-s-t," said the other girl, bending over her work. The first, silenced, instantly assumed a solemn face. The foreman passed slowly along, eyeing each worker distinctly. The moment he was gone, the conversation was resumed again.

"Say," began the girl at her left, " what jeh think he said?"

"I don't know."

"He said he saw us with Eddie Harris at Martin's last night."

"No!" They both giggled.

A youth with tan-coloured hair, that needed clipping very badly, came shuffling along between the machines, bearing a basket of leather findings under his left arm, and pressed against his stomach. When near Carrie, he stretched out his right hand and gripped one girl under the arm.

"Aw, let me go," she exclaimed angrily. "Duffer."

He only grinned broadly in return.

"Rubber!" he called back as she looked after him. There was nothing of the gallant in him.

Carrie at last could scarcely sit still. Her legs began to tire and she wanted to get up and stretch. Would noon never come? It seemed as if she had worked an entire day. She was not hungry at all, but weak, and her eyes were tired, straining at the one point where the eye-punch came down. The girl at the right noticed her squirmings and felt sorry for her. She was concentrating herself too thoroughly—what she did really required less mental and physical strain. There was nothing to be done, however. The halves of the uppers came piling steadily down. Her hands began to ache at the wrists and then in the fingers, and towards the last she seemed one mass of dull, complaining muscles, fixed in an eternal position and performing a single mechanical movement which became more and more distasteful, until at last it was absolutely nauseating. When she was wondering whether the strain would ever cease, a dull-sounding bell clanged somewhere down an elevator shaft, and the end came. In an instant there was a buzz of action and conversation. All the girls instantly left their stools and hurried away in an adjoining room, men passed through, coming from some department which opened on the right. The whirling wheels began to sing in a steadily modifying key, until at last they died away in a low buzz. There was an audible stillness, in which the common voice sounded strange.

Carrie got up and sought her lunch box. She was stiff, a little dizzy, and very thirsty. On the way to the small space portioned off by wood, where all the wraps and lunches were kept, she encountered the foreman, who stared at her hard.

"Well," he said, "did you get along all right?"

"I think so," she replied, very respectfully.

"Um," he replied, for want of something better, and walked on.

Under better material conditions, this kind of work would not have been so bad, but the new socialism which involves pleasant working conditions for employees had not then taken hold upon manufacturing companies.

The place smelled of the oil of the machines and the new leather—a combination which, added to the stale odours of the building, was not pleasant even in cold weather. The floor, though regularly swept every evening, presented a littered surface. Not the slightest provision had been made for the comfort of the employees, the idea being that something was gained by giving them as little and making the work as hard and unremunerative as possible. What we know of footrests, swivel-back chairs, dining-rooms for the girls, clean aprons and curling irons supplied free, and a decent cloak room, were unthought of. The washrooms were disagreeable, crude, if not foul places, and the whole atmosphere was sordid.

Carrie looked about her, after she had drunk a tinful of

water from a bucket in one corner, for a place to sit and eat. The other girls had ranged themselves about the windows or the work-benches of those of the men who had gone out. She saw no place which did not hold a couple or a group of girls, and being too timid to think of intruding herself, she sought out her machine and, seated upon her stool, opened her lunch on her lap. There she sat listening to the chatter and comment about her. It was, for the most part, silly and graced by the current slang. Several of the men in the room exchanged compliments with the girls at long range.

"Say, Kitty," called one to a girl who was doing a waltz step in a few feet of space near one of the windows, "are you going to the ball with me?"

"Look out, Kitty," called another, "you'll jar your back hair."

"Go on, Rubber," was her only comment.

As Carrie listened to this and much more of similar familiar badinage among the men and girls, she instinctively withdrew into herself. She was not used to this type, and felt that there was something hard and low about it all. She feared that the young boys about would address such remarks to her—boys who, beside Drouet, seemed uncouth and ridiculous. She made the average feminine distinction between clothes, putting worth, goodness, and distinction in a dress suit, and leaving all the unlovely qualities and those beneath notice in overalls and jumper.

She was glad when the short half hour was over and the wheels began to whirr again. Though wearied, she would be inconspicuous. This illusion ended when another young man passed along the aisle and poked her indifferently in the ribs with his thumb. She turned about, indignation leaping to her eyes, but he had gone on and only once turned to grin. She found it difficult to conquer an inclination to cry.

The girl next her noticed her state of mind. "Don't you mind," she said. "He's too fresh."

Carrie said nothing, but bent over her work. She felt as though she could hardly endure such a life. Her idea of work had been so entirely different. All during the long afternoon she thought of the city outside and its imposing show, crowds, and fine buildings. Columbia City and the better side of her home life came back. By three o'clock she was sure it must be six, and by four it seemed as if they had forgotten to note the hour and were letting all work overtime. The foreman became a true ogre, prowling constantly about, keeping her tied down to her miserable task. What she heard of the conversation about her only made her feel sure that she did not want to make friends with any of these. When six o'clock came she hurried eagerly away, her arms aching and her limbs stiff from sitting in one position.

As she passed out along the hall after getting her hat, a young machine hand, attracted by her looks, made bold to jest with her.

"Say, Maggie," he called, "if you wait, I'll walk with you."

It was thrown so straight in her direction that she knew who was meant, but never turned to look.

In the crowded elevator, another dusty, toil-stained youth tried to make an impression on her by leering in her face.

One young man, waiting on the walk outside for the appearance of another, grinned at her as she passed.

"Ain't going my way, are you?" he called jocosely.

Carrie turned her face to the west with a subdued heart. As she turned the corner, she saw through the great shiny window the small desk at which she had applied. There were the crowds, hurrying with the same buzz and energy-yielding enthusiasm. She felt a slight relief, but it was only at her escape. She felt ashamed in the face of better dressed girls who went by. She felt as though she should be better served, and her heart revolted.

Chapter V

A Glittering Night Flower: The Use of a Name

Drouet did not call that evening. After receiving the letter, he had laid aside all thought of Carrie for the time being and was floating around having what he considered a gay time. On this particular evening he dined at "Rector's," a restaurant of some local fame, which occupied a basement at Clark and Monroe Streets. Thereafter he visited the resort of Fitzgerald and Moy's in Adams Street, opposite the imposing Federal Building. There he leaned over the splendid bar and swallowed a glass of plain whiskey and purchased a couple of cigars, one of which he lighted. This to him represented in part high life—a fair sample of what the whole must be.

Drouet was not a drinker in excess. He was not a moneyed man. He only craved the best, as his mind conceived it, and such doings seemed to him a part of the best. Rector's, with its polished marble walls and floor, its profusion of lights, its show of china and silverware, and, above all, its reputation as a resort for actors and professional men, seemed to him the proper place for a successful man to go. He loved fine clothes, good eating, and particularly the company and acquaintance-ship of successful men. When dining, it was a source of keen satisfaction to him to know that Joseph Jefferson was wont to come to this same place, or that Henry E. Dixie, a well-known performer of the day, was then only a few tables off. At Rector's he could always obtain this satisfaction, for there one could encounter politicians, brokers, actors, some rich young "rounders" of the town, all eating and drinking amid a buzz of popular commonplace conversation.

"That's So-and-so over there," was a common remark of these gentlemen among themselves, particularly among those who had not yet reached, but hoped to do so, the dazzling height which money to dine here lavishly represented.

"You don't say so," would be the reply.

"Why, yes, didn't you know that? Why, he's manager of the Grand Opera House."

When these things would fall upon Drouet's ears, he would straighten himself a little more stiffly and eat with solid comfort. If he had any vanity, this augmented it, and if he had any ambition, this stirred it. He would be able to flash a roll of greenbacks too some day. As it was, he could eat where *they* did.

His preference for Fitzgerald and Moy's Adams Street place was another yard off the same cloth. This was really a gorgeous saloon from a Chicago standpoint. Like Rector's, it was also ornamented with a blaze of incandescent lights, held in handsome chandeliers. The floors were of brightly coloured tiles, the walls a composition of rich, dark, polished wood, which reflected the light, and coloured stucco-work, which gave the place a very sumptuous appearance. The long bar was a blaze of lights, polished wood-work, coloured and cut glassware, and many fancy bottles. It was a truly swell saloon, with rich screens, fancy wines, and a line of bar goods unsurpassed in the country.

At Rector's, Drouet had met Mr. G. W. Hurstwood, manager of Fitzgerald and Moy's. He had been pointed out as a very successful and well-known man about town. Hurstwood looked the part, for, besides being slightly under forty, he had a good, stout constitution, an active manner, and a solid, substantial air, which was composed in part of his fine clothes, his clean linen, his jewels, and, above all, his own sense of his importance. Drouet immediately conceived a notion of him as being some one worth knowing, and was glad not only to meet him, but to visit the Adams Street bar thereafter whenever he wanted a drink or a cigar.

Hurstwood was an interesting character after his kind. He was shrewd and clever in many little things, and capable of creating a good impression. His managerial position was fairly important—a kind of stewardship which was imposing, but lacked financial control. He had risen by perseverance and industry, through long years of service, from the position of barkeeper in a commonplace saloon to his present altitude. He had a little office in the place, set off in polished cherry and grill-work, where he kept, in a roll-top desk, the rather simple accounts of the place—supplies ordered and needed. The chief executive and financial functions devolved upon the owners—Messrs. Fitzgerald and Moy—and upon a cashier who looked after the money taken in.

For the most part he lounged about, dressed in excellent tailored suits of imported goods, a solitaire ring, a fine blue diamond in his tie, a striking vest of some new pattern, and a watch-chain of solid gold, which held a charm of rich design, and a watch of the latest make and engraving. He knew by name, and could greet personally with a "Well, old fellow," hundreds of actors, merchants, politicians, and the general run of successful characters about town, and it was part of his success to do so. He had a finely graduated scale of informality and friendship, which improved from the "How do you do?" addressed to the fifteen-dollar-a-week clerks and office attachés, who, by long frequenting of the place, became aware of his position, to the "Why, old man, how are you?" which he addressed to those noted or rich individuals who knew him and were inclined to be friendly. There was a class, however, too rich, too famous, or too successful, with whom he could not attempt any familiarity of address, and with these he was professionally tactful, assuming a grave and dignified attitude, paying them the deference which would win their good feeling without in the least compromising his own bearing and opinions. There were, in the last place, a few good followers, neither rich nor poor, famous, nor yet remarkably successful, with whom he was friendly on the score of good-fellowship. These were the kind of men with whom he would converse longest and most seriously. He loved to go out and have a good time once in a while—to go to the races, the theatres, the sporting entertainments at some of the clubs. He kept a horse and neat trap, had his wife and two children, who were well established in a neat house on the North Side near Lincoln Park, and was altogether a very acceptable individual of our great American upper class—the first grade below the luxuriously rich.

Hurstwood liked Drouet. The latter's genial nature and dressy appearance pleased him. He knew that Drouet was only a travelling salesman—and not one of many years at that—but the firm of Bartlett, Caryoe & Company was a large and prosperous house, and Drouet stood well. Hurstwood knew Caryoe quite well, having drunk a glass now and then with him, in company with several others, when the conversation was general. Drouet had what was a help in his business, a moderate sense of humour, and could tell a good story when the occasion required. He could talk races with Hurstwood, tell interesting incidents concerning himself and his experiences with women, and report the state of trade in the cities which he visited, and so managed to make himself almost invariably agreeable. To-night he was particularly so, since his report to the company had been favourably commented upon, his new samples had been satisfactorily selected, and his trip marked out for the next six weeks.

"Why, hello, Charlie, old man," said Hurstwood, as Drouet came in that evening about eight o'clock. "How goes it?" The room was crowded.

Drouet shook hands, beaming good nature, and they strolled towards the bar.

"Oh, all right."

"I haven't seen you in six weeks. When did you get in?"

"Friday," said Drouet. "Had a fine trip."

"Glad of it," said Hurstwood, his black eyes lit with a warmth which half displaced the cold make-believe that usually dwelt in them. "What are you going to take?" he added, as the barkeeper, in snowy jacket and tie, leaned toward them from behind the bar.

"Old Pepper," said Drouet.

"A little of the same for me," put in Hurstwood.

"How long are you in town this time?" inquired Hurstwood.

"Only until Wednesday. I'm going up to St. Paul."

"George Evans was in here Saturday and said he saw you in Milwaukee last week."

"Yes, I saw George," returned Drouet. "Great old boy, isn't he? We had quite a time there together."

The barkeeper was setting out the glasses and bottle before them, and they now poured out the draught as they talked, Drouet filling his to within a third of full, as was considered proper, and Hurstwood taking the barest suggestion of whiskey and modifying it with seltzer.

"What's become of Caryoe?" remarked Hurstwood. "I haven't seen him around here in two weeks."

"Laid up, they say," exclaimed Drouet. "Say, he's a gouty old boy!"

"Made a lot of money in his time, though, hasn't he?"

"Yes, wads of it," returned Drouet. "He won't live much longer. Barely comes down to the office now."

"Just one boy, hasn't he?" asked Hurstwood.

"Yes, and a swift-pacer," laughed Drouet.

"I guess he can't hurt the business very much, though, with the other members all there."

"No, he can't injure that any, I guess."

Hurstwood was standing, his coat open, his thumbs in his pockets, the light on his jewels and rings relieving them with agreeable distinctness. He was the picture of fastidious comfort.

To one not inclined to drink, and gifted with a more serious turn of mind, such a bubbling, chattering, glittering chamber must ever seem an anomaly, a strange commentary on nature and life. Here come the moths, in endless procession, to bask in the light of the flame. Such conversation as one may hear would not warrant a commendation of the scene upon intellectual grounds. It seems plain that schemers would choose more sequestered quarters to arrange their plans, that politicians would not gather here in company to discuss anything save formalities, where the sharp-eared may hear, and it would scarcely be justified on the score of thirst, for the majority of those who frequent these more gorgeous places have no craving for liquor. Nevertheless, the fact that here men gather, here chatter, here love to pass and rub elbows, must be explained upon some grounds. It must be that a strange bundle of passions and vague desires give rise to such a curious social institution or it would not be.

Drouet, for one, was lured as much by his longing for pleasure as by his desire to shine among his betters. The many friends he met here dropped in because they craved, without, perhaps, consciously analysing it, the company, the glow, the atmosphere which they found. One might take it, after all, as an augur of the better social order, for the things which they satisfied here, though sensory, were not evil. No evil could come out of the contemplation of an expensively decorated chamber. The worst effect of such a thing would be, perhaps, to stir up in the material-minded an ambition to arrange their lives upon a similarly splendid basis. In the last analysis, that would scarcely be called the fault of the decorations, but rather of the innate trend of the mind. That such a scene might stir the less expensively dressed to emulate the more expensively dressed could scarcely be laid at the door of anything save the false ambition of the minds of those so affected. Remove the element so thoroughly and solely complained of—liquor—and there would not be one to gainsay the qualities of beauty and enthusiasm which would remain. The pleased eye with which our modern restaurants of fashion are looked upon is proof of this assertion.

Yet, here is the fact of the lighted chamber, the dressy, greedy company, the small, self-interested palaver, the disorganized, aimless, wandering mental action which it represents—the love of light and show and finery which, to one outside, under the serene light of the eternal stars, must seem a strange and shiny thing. Under the stars and sweeping night winds, what a lamp-flower it must bloom; a strange, glittering night-flower, odour-yielding, insect-drawing, insect-infested rose of pleasure.

"See that fellow coming in there?" said Hurstwood, glancing at a gentleman just entering, arrayed in a high hat and Prince Albert coat, his fat cheeks puffed and red as with good eating.

"No, where?" said Drouet.

"There," said Hurstwood, indicating the direction by a cast of his eye, "the man with the silk hat."

"Oh, yes," said Drouet, now affecting not to see. "Who is he?"

"That's Jules Wallace, the spiritualist."

Drouet followed him with his eyes, much interested.

"Doesn't look much like a man who sees spirits, does he?" said Drouet.

"Oh, I don't know," returned Hurstwood. "He's got the money, all right," and a little twinkle passed over his eyes.

"I don't go much on those things, do you?" asked Drouet.

"Well, you never can tell," said Hurstwood. "There may be something to it. I wouldn't bother about it myself, though. By the way," he added, "are you going anywhere to-night?"

" 'The Hole in the Ground,' " said Drouet, mentioning the popular farce of the time.

"Well, you'd better be going. It's half after eight already," and he drew out his watch.

The crowd was already thinning out considerably—some bound for the theatres, some to their clubs, and some to that most fascinating of all the pleasures—for the type of man there represented, at least—the ladies.

"Yes, I will," said Drouet.

"Come around after the show. I have something I want to show you," said Hurstwood.

"Sure," said Drouet, elated.

"You haven't anything on hand for the night, have you?" added Hurstwood.

"Not a thing."

"Well, come round, then."

"I struck a little peach coming in on the train Friday," remarked Drouet, by way of parting. "By George, that's so, I must go and call on her before I go away."

"Oh, never mind her," Hurstwood remarked.

"Say, she was a little dandy, I tell you," went on Drouet confidentially, and trying to impress his friend.

"Twelve o'clock," said Hurstwood.

"That's right," said Drouet, going out.

Thus was Carrie's name bandied about in the most frivolous and gay of places, and that also when the little toiler was bemoaning her narrow lot, which was almost inseparable from the early stages of this, her unfolding fate.

Chapter VI

At the flat that evening Carrie felt a new phase of its atmosphere. The fact that it was unchanged, while her feelings were different, increased her knowledge of its character. Minnie, after the good spirits Carrie manifested at first, expected a fair report. Hanson supposed that Carrie would be satisfied.

"Well," he said, as he came in from the hall in his working clothes, and looked at Carrie through the dining-room door, "how did you make out?"

"Oh," said Carrie, "it's pretty hard. I don't like it."

There was an air about her which showed plainer than any words that she was both weary and disappointed.

"What sort of work is it?" he asked, lingering a moment as he turned upon his heel to go into the bathroom.

"Running a machine," answered Carrie.

It was very evident that it did not concern him much, save from the side of the flat's success. He was irritated a shade because it could not have come about in the throw of fortune for Carrie to be pleased.

Minnie worked with less elation than she had just before Carrie arrived. The sizzle of the meat frying did not sound quite so pleasing now that Carrie had reported her discontent. To Carrie, the one relief of the whole day would have been a jolly home, a sympathetic reception, a bright supper table, and some one to say: "Oh, well, stand it a little while. You will get something better," but now this was ashes. She began to see that they looked upon her complaint as unwarranted, and that she was supposed to work on and say nothing. She knew that she was to pay four dollars for her board and room, and now she felt that it would be an exceedingly gloomy round, living with these people.

Minnie was no companion for her sister—she was too old. Her thoughts were staid and solemnly adapted to a condition. If Hanson had any pleasant thoughts or happy feelings he concealed them. He seemed to do all his mental operations

47

without the aid of physical expression. He was as still as a deserted chamber. Carrie, on the other hand, had the blood of youth and some imagination. Her day of love and the mysteries of courtship were still ahead. She could think of things she would like to do, of clothes she would like to wear, and of places she would like to visit. These were the things upon which her mind ran, and it was like meeting with opposition at every turn to find no one here to call forth or respond to her feelings.

She had forgotten, in considering and explaining the result of her day, that Drouet might come. Now, when she saw how unreceptive these two people were, she hoped he would not. She did not know exactly what she would do or how she would explain to Drouet, if he came. After supper she changed her clothes. When she was trimly dressed she was rather a sweet little being, with large eyes and a sad mouth. Her face expressed the mingled expectancy, dissatisfaction, and depression she felt. She wandered about after the dishes were put away, talked a little with Minnie, and then decided to go down and stand in the door at the foot of the stairs. If Drouet came, she could meet him there. Her face took on the semblance of a look of happiness as she put on her hat to go below.

"Carrie doesn't seem to like her place very well," said Minnie to her husband when the latter came out, paper in hand, to sit in the dining-room a few minutes.

"She ought to keep it for a time, anyhow," said Hanson. "Has she gone downstairs?"

"Yes," said Minnie.

"I'd tell her to keep it if I were you. She might be here weeks without getting another one."

Minnie said she would, and Hanson read his paper.

"If I were you," he said a little later, "I wouldn't let her stand in the door down there. It don't look good."

"I'll tell her," said Minnie.

The life of the streets continued for a long time to interest Carrie. She never wearied of wondering where the people in the cars were going or what their enjoyments were. Her imagination trod a very narrow round, always winding up at points which concerned money, looks, clothes, or enjoyment. She would have a far-off thought of Columbia City now and then, or an irritating rush of feeling concerning her experiences of the present day, but, on the whole, the little world about her enlisted her whole attention.

The first floor of the building, of which Hanson's flat was the third, was occupied by a bakery, and to this, while she was standing there, Hanson came down to buy a loaf of bread. She was not aware of his presence until he was quite near her.

"I'm after bread," was all he said as he passed.

The contagion of thought here demonstrated itself. While Hanson really came for bread, the thought dwelt with him that now he would see what Carrie was doing. No sooner did he draw near her with that in mind than she felt it. Of course, she had no understanding of what put it into her head, but, nevertheless, it aroused in her the first shade of real antipathy to him. She knew now that she did not like him. He was suspicious.

A thought will colour a world for us. The flow of Carrie's meditations had been disturbed, and Hanson had not long gone upstairs before she followed. She had realised with the lapse of the quarter hours that Drouet was not coming, and somehow she felt a little resentful, a little as if she had been forsaken—was not good enough. She went upstairs, where everything was silent. Minnie was sewing by a lamp at the table. Hanson had already turned in for the night. In her weariness and disappointment Carrie did no more than announce that she was going to bed.

"Yes, you'd better," returned Minnie. "You've got to get up early, you know."

The morning was no better. Hanson was just going out the door as Carrie came from her room. Minnie tried to talk with her during breakfast, but there was not much of interest which they could mutually discuss. As on the previous morning, Carrie walked down town, for she began to realise now that her four-fifty would not even allow her car fare after she paid her board. This seemed a miserable arrangement. But the morning light swept away the first misgivings of the day, as morning light is ever wont to do.

At the shoe factory she put in a long day, scarcely so wearisome as the preceding, but considerably less novel. The head foreman, on his round, stopped by her machine.

"Where did you come from?" he inquired.

"Mr. Brown hired me," she replied.

"Oh, he did, eh!" and then, "See that you keep things going."

The machine girls impressed her even less favourably. They seemed satisfied with their lot, and were in a sense "common." Carrie had more imagination than they. She was not used to slang. Her instinct in the matter of dress was naturally better. She disliked to listen to the girl next to her, who was rather hardened by experience.

"I'm going to quit this," she heard her remark to her neighbour. "What with the stipend and being up late, it's too much for me health."

They were free with the fellows, young and old, about the place, and exchanged banter in rude phrases, which at first shocked her. She saw that she was taken to be of the same sort and addressed accordingly.

"Hello," remarked one of the stout-wristed sole-workers to her at noon. "You're a daisy." He really expected to hear the common "Aw! go chase yourself!" in return, and was sufficiently abashed, by Carrie's silently moving away, to retreat, awkwardly grinning.

That night at the flat she was even more lonely—the dull situation was becoming harder to endure. She could see that the Hansons seldom or never had any company. Standing at the street door looking out, she ventured to walk out a little way. Her easy gait and idle manner attracted attention of an offensive but common sort. She was slightly taken back at the overtures of a well-dressed man of thirty, who in passing looked at her, reduced his pace, turned back, and said:

"Out for a little stroll, are you, this evening?"

Carrie looked at him in amazement, and then summoned sufficient thought to reply: "Why, I don't know you," backing away as she did so.

"Oh, that don't matter," said the other affably.

She bandied no more words with him, but hurried away, reaching her own door quite out of breath. There was something in the man's look which frightened her.

During the remainder of the week it was very much the

same. One or two nights she found herself too tired to walk home, and expended car fare. She was not very strong, and sitting all day affected her back. She went to bed one night before Hanson.

Transplantation is not always successful in the matter of flowers or maidens. It requires sometimes a richer soil, a better atmosphere to continue even a natural growth. It would have been better if her acclimatization had been more gradual—less rigid. She would have done better if she had not secured a position so quickly, and had seen more of the city which she constantly troubled to know about.

On the first morning it rained she found that she had no umbrella. Minnie loaned her one of hers, which was worn and faded. There was the kind of vanity in Carrie that troubled at this. She went to one of the great department stores and bought herself one, using a dollar and a quarter of her small store to pay for it.

"What did you do that for, Carrie?" asked Minnie, when she saw it.

"Oh, I need one," said Carrie.

"You foolish girl."

Carrie resented this, though she did not reply. She was not going to be a common shop-girl, she thought; they need not think it, either.

On the first Saturday night Carrie paid her board, four dollars. Minnie had a quaver of conscience as she took it, but did not know how to explain to Hanson if she took less. That worthy gave up just four dollars less toward the household expenses with a smile of satisfaction. He contemplated increasing his Building and Loan payments. As for Carrie, she studied over the problem of finding clothes and amusement on fifty cents a week. She brooded over this until she was in a state of mental rebellion.

"I'm going up the street for a walk," she said after supper.

"Not alone, are you?" asked Hanson.

"Yes," returned Carrie.

"I wouldn't," said Minnie.

"I want to see *something*," said Carrie, and by the tone she put into the last word they realised for the first time she was not pleased with them.

"What's the matter with her?" asked Hanson, when she went into the front room to get her hat.

"I don't know," said Minnie.

"Well, she ought to know better than to want to go out alone."

Carrie did not go very far, after all. She returned and stood in the door. The next day they went out to Garfield Park, but it did not please her. She did not look well enough. In the shop next day she heard the highly coloured reports which girls give of their trivial amusements. They had been happy. On several days it rained and she used up car fare. One night she got thoroughly soaked, going to catch the car at Van Buren Street. All that evening she sat alone in the front room looking out upon the street, where the lights were reflected on the wet pavements, thinking. She had imagination enough to be moody.

On Saturday she paid another four dollars and pocketed her fifty cents in despair. The speaking acquaintanceship which she formed with some of the girls at the shop discovered to her the fact that they had more of their earnings to use for themselves than she did. They had young men of the kind whom she, since her experience with Drouet, felt above, who took them about. She came to thoroughly dislike the light-headed young fellows of the shop. Not one of them had a show of refinement. She saw only their work-day side.

There came a day when the first premonitory blast of winter swept over the city. It scudded the fleecy clouds in the heavens, trailed long, thin streamers of smoke from the tall stacks, and raced about the streets and corners in sharp and sudden puffs. Carrie now felt the problem of winter clothes. What was she to do? She had no winter jacket, no hat, no shoes. It was difficult to speak to Minnie about this, but at last she summoned the courage.

"I don't know what I'm going to do about clothes," she said one evening when they were together. "I need a hat."

Minnie looked serious.

"Why don't you keep part of your money and buy yourself one?" she suggested, worried over the situation which the withholding of Carrie's money would create.

"I'd like to for a week or so, if you don't mind," ventured Carrie.

"Could you pay two dollars?" asked Minnie.

Carrie readily acquiesced, glad to escape the trying situation, and liberal now that she saw a way out. She was elated and began figuring at once. She needed a hat first of all. How Minnie explained to Hanson she never knew. He said nothing at all, but there were thoughts in the air which left disagreeable impressions.

The new arrangement might have worked if sickness had not intervened. It blew up cold after a rain one afternoon when Carrie was still without a jacket. She came out of the warm shop at six and shivered as the wind struck her. In the morning she was sneezing, and going down town made it worse. That day her bones ached and she felt light-headed. Towards evening she felt very ill, and when she reached home was not hungry. Minnie noticed her drooping actions and asked her about herself.

"I don't know," said Carrie. "I feel real bad."

She hung about the stove, suffered a chattering chill, and went to bed sick. The next morning she was thoroughly feverish.

Minnie was truly distressed at this, but maintained a kindly demeanour. Hanson said perhaps she had better go back home for a while. When she got up after three days, it was taken for granted that her position was lost. The winter was near at hand, she had no clothes, and now she was out of work.

"I don't know," said Carrie; "I'll go down Monday and see if I can't get something."

If anything, her efforts were more poorly rewarded on this trial than the last. Her clothes were nothing suitable for fall wearing. Her last money she had spent for a hat. For three days she wandered about, utterly dispirited. The attitude of the flat was fast becoming unbearable. She hated to think of going back there each evening. Hanson was so cold. She knew it could not last much longer. Shortly she would have to give up and go home.

On the fourth day she was down town all day, having borrowed ten cents for lunch from Minnie. She had applied in the cheapest kind of places without success. She even answered for a waitress in a small restaurant where she saw a card in the window, but they wanted an experienced girl. She moved through the thick throng of strangers, utterly subdued in spirit. Suddenly a hand pulled her arm and turned her about.

"Well, well!" said a voice. In the first glance she beheld Drouet. He was not only rosy-cheeked, but radiant. He was the essence of sunshine and good-humour. "Why, how are you, Carrie?" he said. "You're a daisy. Where have you been?"

Carrie smiled under his irresistible flood of geniality.

"I've been out home," she said.

"Well," he said, "I saw you across the street there. I thought it was you. I was just coming out to your place. How are you, anyhow?"

"I'm all right," said Carrie, smiling.

Drouet looked her over and saw something different.

"Well," he said, "I want to talk to you. You're not going anywhere in particular, are you?"

"Not just now," said Carrie.

"Let's go up here and have something to eat. George! but I'm glad to see you again."

She felt so relieved in his radiant presence, so much looked after and cared for, that she assented gladly, though with the slightest air of holding back.

"Well," he said, as he took her arm—and there was an exuberance of good-fellowship in the word which fairly warmed the cockles of her heart.

They went through Monroe Street to the old Windsor dining-room, which was then a large, comfortable place, with an excellent cuisine and substantial service. Drouet selected a table close by the window, where the busy rout of the street could be seen. He loved the changing panorama of the street—to see and be seen as he dined.

"Now," he said, getting Carrie and himself comfortably settled, " what will you have?"

Carrie looked over the large bill of fare which the waiter handed her without really considering it. She was very hungry, and the things she saw there awakened her desires, but the high prices held her attention. "Half broiled spring chicken—seventy-five. Sirloin steak with mushrooms—one twenty-five." She had dimly heard of these things, but it seemed strange to be called to order from the list.

"I'll fix this," exclaimed Drouet. "Sst! waiter."

That officer of the board, a full-chested, round-faced negro, approached, and inclined his ear.

"Sirloin with mushrooms," said Drouet. "Stuffed to-matoes."

"Yassah," assented the negro, nodding his head.

"Hashed brown potatoes."

"Yassah."

"Asparagus."

"Yassah."

"And a pot of coffee."

Drouet turned to Carrie. "I haven't had a thing since break-fast. Just got in from Rock Island. I was going off to dine when I saw you."

Carrie smiled and smiled.

"What have you been doing?" he went on. "Tell me all about yourself. How is your sister?"

"She's well," returned Carrie, answering the last query.

He looked at her hard.

"Say," he said, "you haven't been sick, have you?"

Carrie nodded.

"Well, now, that's a blooming shame, isn't it? You don't look very well. I thought you looked a little pale. What have you been doing?"

"Working," said Carrie.

"You don't say so! At what?"

She told him.

"Rhodes, Morgenthau and Scott—why, I know that house. Over there on Fifth Avenue, isn't it? They're a close-fisted concern. What made you go there?"

"I couldn't get anything else," said Carrie frankly.

"Well, that's an outrage," said Drouet. "You oughtn't to be working for those people. Have the factory right back of the store, don't they?"

"Yes," said Carrie.

"That isn't a good house," said Drouet. "You don't want to work at anything like that, anyhow."

He chattered on at a great rate, asking questions, explaining things about himself, telling her what a good restaurant it was, until the waiter returned with an immense tray, bearing the hot savoury dishes which had been ordered. Drouet fairly shone in the matter of serving. He appeared to great advantage behind the white napery and silver platters of the table and displaying his arms with a knife and fork. As he cut the meat his rings almost spoke. His new suit creaked as he stretched to reach the plates, break the bread, and pour the coffee. He helped Carrie to a rousing plateful and contributed the warmth of his spirit to her body until she was a new girl. He was a splendid fellow in the true popular understanding of the term, and captivated Carrie completely.

That little soldier of fortune took her good turn in an easy way. She felt a little out of place, but the great room soothed her and the view of the well-dressed throng outside seemed a splendid thing. Ah, what was it not to have money! What a thing it was to be able to come in here and dine! Drouet must be fortunate. He rode on trains, dressed in such nice clothes, was so strong, and ate in these fine places. He seemed quite a figure of a man, and she wondered at his friendship and regard for her.

"So you lost your place because you got sick, eh?" he said. "What are you going to do now?"

"Look around," she said, a thought of the need that hung outside this fine restaurant like a hungry dog at her heels passing into her eyes.

"Oh, no," said Drouet, "that won't do. How long have you been looking?"

"Four days," she answered.

"Think of that!" he said, addressing some problematical individual. "You oughtn't to be doing anything like that. These girls," and he waved an inclusion of all shop and factory girls, "don't get anything. Why, you can't live on it, can you?"

He was a brotherly sort of creature in his demeanour. When he had scouted the idea of that kind of toil, he took another tack. Carrie was really very pretty. Even then, in her commonplace garb, her figure was evidently not bad, and her eyes were large and gentle. Drouet looked at her and his thoughts reached home. She felt his admiration. It was

powerfully backed by his liberality and good-humour. She felt
that she liked him—that she could continue to like him ever
so much. There was something even richer than that, running
as a hidden strain, in her mind. Every little while her eyes
would meet his, and by that means the interchanging current
of feeling would be fully connected.

"Why don't you stay down town and go to the theatre with
me?" he said, hitching his chair closer. The table was not very
wide.

"Oh, I can't," she said.

"What are you going to do to-night?"

"Nothing," she answered, a little drearily.

"You don't like out there where you are, do you?"

"Oh, I don't know."

"What are you going to do if you don't get work?"

"Go back home, I guess."

There was the least quaver in her voice as she said this.
Somehow, the influence he was exerting was powerful. They
came to an understanding of each other without words—he
of her situation, she of the fact that he realised it.

"No," he said, "you can't make it!" genuine sympathy filling his mind for the time. "Let me help you. You take some
of my money."

"Oh, no!" she said, leaning back.

"What are you going to do?" he said.

She sat meditating, merely shaking her head.

He looked at her quite tenderly for his kind. There were
some loose bills in his vest pocket—greenbacks. They were
soft and noiseless, and he got his fingers about them and
crumpled them up in his hand.

"Come on," he said, "I'll see you through all right. Get
yourself some clothes."

It was the first reference he had made to that subject, and
now she realised how bad off she was. In his crude way he
had struck the key-note. Her lips trembled a little.

She had her hand out on the table before her. They were
quite alone in their corner, and he put his larger, warmer
hand over it.

"Aw, come, Carrie," he said, " what can you do alone? Let
me help you."

He pressed her hand gently and she tried to withdraw it. At this he held it fast, and she no longer protested. Then he slipped the greenbacks he had into her palm, and when she began to protest, he whispered:

"I'll loan it to you—that's all right. I'll loan it to you."

He made her take it. She felt bound to him by a strange tie of affection now. They went out, and he walked with her far out south toward Polk Street, talking.

"You don't want to live with those people?" he said in one place, abstractedly. Carrie heard it, but it made only a slight impression.

"Come down and meet me to-morrow," he said, "and we'll go to the matinée. Will you?"

Carrie protested a while, but acquiesced.

"You're not doing anything. Get yourself a nice pair of shoes and a jacket."

She scarcely gave a thought to the complication which would trouble her when he was gone. In his presence, she was of his own hopeful, easy-way-out mood.

"Don't you bother about those people out there," he said at parting. "I'll help you."

Carrie left him, feeling as though a great arm had slipped out before her to draw off trouble. The money she had accepted was two soft, green, handsome ten-dollar bills.

Chapter VII

THE LURE OF THE MATERIAL: BEAUTY SPEAKS FOR ITSELF

THE TRUE meaning of money yet remains to be popularly explained and comprehended. When each individual realises for himself that this thing primarily stands for and should only be accepted as a moral due—that it should be paid out as honestly stored energy, and not as a usurped privilege—many of our social, religious, and political troubles will have permanently passed. As for Carrie, her understanding of the moral significance of money was the popular understanding, nothing more. The old definition: "Money: something everybody else has and I must get," would have expressed her understanding of it thoroughly. Some of it she now held in her hand—two soft, green ten-dollar bills—and she felt that she was immensely better off for the having of them. It was something that was power in itself. One of her order of mind would have been content to be cast away upon a desert island with a bundle of money, and only the long strain of starvation would have taught her that in some cases it could have no value. Even then she would have had no conception of the relative value of the thing; her one thought would, undoubtedly, have concerned the pity of having so much power and the inability to use it.

The poor girl thrilled as she walked away from Drouet. She felt ashamed in part because she had been weak enough to take it, but her need was so dire, she was still glad. Now she would have a nice new jacket! Now she would buy a nice pair of pretty button shoes. She would get stockings, too, and a skirt, and, and—until already, as in the matter of her prospective salary, she had got beyond, in her desires, twice the purchasing power of her bills.

She conceived a true estimate of Drouet. To her, and indeed to all the world, he was a nice, good-hearted man. There was nothing evil in the fellow. He gave her the money out of a good heart—out of a realisation of her want. He would not have given the same amount to a poor young man, but we must not forget that a poor young man could not, in the nature of things, have appealed to him like a poor young girl. Femininity affected his feelings. He was the creature of an inborn desire. Yet no beggar could have caught his eye and said, "My God, mister, I'm starving," but he would gladly have handed out what was considered the proper portion to give beggars and thought no more about it. There would have been no speculation, no philosophising. He had no mental process in him worthy the dignity of either of those terms. In his good clothes and fine health, he was a merry, unthinking moth of the lamp. Deprived of his position, and struck by a few of the involved and baffling forces which sometimes play upon man, he would have been as helpless as Carrie—as helpless, as non-understanding, as pitiable, if you will, as she.

Now, in regard to his pursuit of women, he meant them no harm, because he did not conceive of the relation which he hoped to hold with them as being harmful. He loved to make advances to women, to have them succumb to his charms, not because he was a cold-blooded, dark, scheming villain, but because his inborn desire urged him to that as a chief delight. He was vain, he was boastful, he was as deluded by fine clothes as any silly-headed girl. A truly deep-dyed villain could have hornswaggled him as readily as he could have flattered a pretty shop-girl. His fine success as a salesman lay in his geniality and the thoroughly reputable standing of his house. He bobbed about among men, a veritable bundle of enthusiasm—no power worthy the name of intellect, no thoughts worthy the adjective noble, no feelings long continued in one strain. A Madame Sappho would have called him a pig; a Shakespeare would have said "my merry child;" old, drinking Caryoe thought him a clever, successful business man. In short, he was as good as his intellect conceived.

The best proof that there was something open and commendable about the man was the fact that Carrie took the money. No deep, sinister soul with ulterior motives could have given her fifteen cents under the guise of friendship. The unintellectual are not so helpless. Nature has taught the beasts of the field to fly when some unheralded danger threatens. She has put into the small, unwise head of the chipmunk the untutored fear of poisons. "He keepeth His creatures whole," was not written of beasts alone. Carrie was unwise, and, therefore, like the sheep in its unwisdom, strong in feeling. The instinct of self-protection, strong in all such natures, was roused but feebly, if at all, by the overtures of Drouet.

When Carrie had gone, he felicitated himself upon her good opinion. By George, it was a shame young girls had to be knocked around like that. Cold weather coming on and no clothes. Tough. He would go around to Fitzgerald and Moy's and get a cigar. It made him feel light of foot as he thought about her.

Carrie reached home in high good spirits, which she could scarcely conceal. The possession of the money involved a number of points which perplexed her seriously. How should she buy any clothes when Minnie knew that she had no money? She had no sooner entered the flat than this point was settled for her. It could not be done. She could think of no way of explaining.

"How did you come out?" asked Minnie, referring to the day.

Carrie had none of the small deception which could feel one thing and say something directly opposed. She would prevaricate, but it would be in the line of her feelings at least. So instead of complaining when she felt so good, she said:

"I have the promise of something."

"Where?"

"At the Boston Store."

"Is it sure promised?" questioned Minnie.

"Well, I'm to find out to-morrow," returned Carrie, disliking to draw out a lie any longer than was necessary.

Minnie felt the atmosphere of good feeling which Carrie brought with her. She felt now was the time to express to Carrie the state of Hanson's feeling about her entire Chicago venture.

"If you shouldn't get it—" she paused, troubled for an easy way.

"If I don't get something pretty soon, I think I'll go home."

Minnie saw her chance.

"Sven thinks it might be best for the winter, anyhow."

The situation flashed on Carrie at once. They were un-

willing to keep her any longer, out of work. She did not
blame Minnie, she did not blame Hanson very much. Now,
as she sat there digesting the remark, she was glad she had
Drouet's money.

"Yes," she said after a few moments, "I thought of doing
that."

She did not explain that the thought, however, had aroused
all the antagonism of her nature. Columbia City, what was
there for her? She knew its dull, little round by heart. Here
was the great, mysterious city which was still a magnet for
her. What she had seen only suggested its possibilities. Now
to turn back on it and live the little old life out there—she
almost exclaimed against the thought.

She had reached home early and went in the front room
to think. What could she do? She could not buy new shoes
and wear them here. She would need to save part of the
twenty to pay her fare home. She did not want to borrow of
Minnie for that. And yet, how could she explain where she
even got that money? If she could only get enough to let her
out easy.

She went over the tangle again and again. Here, in the
morning, Drouet would expect to see her in a new jacket, and
that couldn't be. The Hansons expected her to go home, and
she wanted to get away, and yet she did not want to go
home. In the light of the way they would look on her getting
money without work, the taking of it now seemed dreadful.
She began to be ashamed. The whole situation depressed her.
It was all so clear when she was with Drouet. Now it was all
so tangled, so hopeless—much worse than it was before, because she had the semblance of aid in her hand which she
could not use.

Her spirits sank so that at supper Minnie felt that she must
have had another hard day. Carrie finally decided that she
would give the money back. It was wrong to take it. She
would go down in the morning and hunt for work. At noon
she would meet Drouet as agreed and tell him. At this decision her heart sank, until she was the old Carrie of distress.

Curiously, she could not hold the money in her hand without feeling some relief. Even after all her depressing conclusions, she could sweep away all thought about the matter and

then the twenty dollars seemed a wonderful and delightful thing. Ah, money, money, money! What a thing it was to have. How plenty of it would clear away all these troubles.

In the morning she got up and started out a little early. Her decision to hunt for work was moderately strong, but the money in her pocket, after all her troubling over it, made the work question the least shade less terrible. She walked into the wholesale district, but as the thought of applying came with each passing concern, her heart shrank. What a coward she was, she thought to herself. Yet she had applied so often. It would be the same old story. She walked on and on, and finally did go into one place, with the old result. She came out feeling that luck was against her. It was no use.

Without much thinking, she reached Dearborn Street. Here was the great Fair store with its multitude of delivery wagons about, its long window display, its crowd of shoppers. It readily changed her thoughts, she who was so weary of them. It was here that she had intended to come and get her new things. Now for relief from distress, she thought she would go in and see. She would look at the jackets.

There is nothing in this world more delightful than that middle state in which we mentally balance at times, possessed of the means, lured by desire, and yet deterred by conscience or want of decision. When Carrie began wandering around the store amid the fine displays she was in this mood. Her original experience in this same place had given her a high opinion of its merits. Now she paused at each individual bit of finery, where before she had hurried on. Her woman's heart was warm with desire for them. How would she look in this, how charming that would make her! She came upon the corset counter and paused in rich reverie as she noted the dainty concoctions of colour and lace there displayed. If she would only make up her mind, she could have one of those now. She lingered in the jewelry department. She saw the earrings, the bracelets, the pins, the chains. What would she not have given if she could have had them all! She would look fine too, if only she had some of these things.

The jackets were the greatest attraction. When she entered the store, she already had her heart fixed upon the peculiar little tan jacket with large mother-of-pearl buttons which was all the rage that fall. Still she delighted to convince herself that there was nothing she would like better. She went about among the glass cases and racks where these things were displayed, and satisfied herself that the one she thought of was the proper one. All the time she wavered in mind, now persuading herself that she could buy it right away if she chose, now recalling to herself the actual condition. At last the noon hour was dangerously near, and she had done nothing. She must go now and return the money.

Drouet was on the corner when she came up.

"Hello," he said, "where is the jacket and"—looking down—"the shoes?"

Carrie had thought to lead up to her decision in some intelligent way, but this swept the whole fore-schemed situation by the board.

"I came to tell you that—that I can't take the money."

"Oh, that's it, is it?" he returned. "Well, you come on with me. Let's go over here to Partridge's."

Carrie walked with him. Behold, the whole fabric of doubt and impossibility had slipped from her mind. She could not get at the points that were so serious, the things she was going to make plain to him.

"Have you had lunch yet? Of course you haven't. Let's go in here," and Drouet turned into one of the very nicely furnished restaurants off State Street, in Monroe.

"I mustn't take the money," said Carrie, after they were settled in a cosey corner, and Drouet had ordered the lunch. "I can't wear those things out there. They—they wouldn't know where I got them."

"What do you want to do," he smiled, "go without them?"

"I think I'll go home," she said, wearily.

"Oh, come," he said, "you've been thinking it over too long. I'll tell you what you do. You say you can't wear them out there. Why don't you rent a furnished room and leave them in that for a week?"

Carrie shook her head. Like all women, she was there to object and be convinced. It was for him to brush the doubts away and clear the path if he could.

"Why are you going home?" he asked.

"Oh, I can't get anything here."

"They won't keep you?" he remarked, intuitively.

"They can't," said Carrie.

"I'll tell you what you do," he said. "You come with me. I'll take care of you."

Carrie heard this passively. The peculiar state which she was in made it sound like the welcome breath of an open door. Drouet seemed of her own spirit and pleasing. He was clean, handsome, well-dressed, and sympathetic. His voice was the voice of a friend.

"What can you do back at Columbia City?" he went on, rousing by the words in Carrie's mind a picture of the dull world she had left. "There isn't anything down there. Chicago's the place. You can get a nice room here and some clothes, and then you can do something."

Carrie looked out through the window into the busy street. There it was, the admirable, great city, so fine when you are not poor. An elegant coach, with a prancing pair of bays, passed by, carrying in its upholstered depths a young lady.

"What will you have if you go back?" asked Drouet. There was no subtle undercurrent to the question. He imagined that she would have nothing at all of the things he thought worth while.

Carrie sat still, looking out. She was wondering what she could do. They would be expecting her to go home this week.

Drouet turned to the subject of the clothes she was going to buy.

"Why not get yourself a nice little jacket? You've got to have it. I'll loan you the money. You needn't worry about taking it. You can get yourself a nice room by yourself. I won't hurt you."

Carrie saw the drift, but could not express her thoughts. She felt more than ever the helplessness of her case.

"If I could only get something to do," she said.

"Maybe you can," went on Drouet, "if you stay here. You can't if you go away. They won't let you stay out there. Now, why not let me get you a nice room? I won't bother you— you needn't be afraid. Then, when you get fixed up, maybe you could get something."

He looked at her pretty face and it vivified his mental resources. She was a sweet little mortal to him—there was no doubt of that. She seemed to have some power back of her actions. She was not like the common run of store-girls. She wasn't silly.

In reality, Carrie had more imagination than he—more taste. It was a finer mental strain in her that made possible her depression and loneliness. Her poor clothes were neat, and she held her head unconsciously in a dainty way.

"Do you think I could get something?" she asked.

"Sure," he said, reaching over and filling her cup with tea. "I'll help you."

She looked at him, and he laughed reassuringly.

"Now I'll tell you what we'll do. We'll go over here to Partridge's and you pick out what you want. Then we'll look around for a room for you. You can leave the things there. Then we'll go to the show to-night."

Carrie shook her head.

"Well, you can go out to the flat then, that's all right. You don't need to stay in the room. Just take it and leave your things there."

She hung in doubt about this until the dinner was over.

"Let's go over and look at the jackets," he said.

Together they went. In the store they found that shine and rustle of new things which immediately laid hold of Carrie's heart. Under the influence of a good dinner and Drouet's radiating presence, the scheme proposed seemed feasible. She looked about and picked a jacket like the one which she had admired at The Fair. When she got it in her hand it seemed so much nicer. The saleswoman helped her on with it, and, by accident, it fitted perfectly. Drouet's face lightened as he saw the improvement. She looked quite smart.

"That's the thing," he said.

Carrie turned before the glass. She could not help feeling pleased as she looked at herself. A warm glow crept into her cheeks.

"That's the thing," said Drouet. "Now pay for it."

"It's nine dollars," said Carrie.

"That's all right—take it," said Drouet.

She reached in her purse and took out one of the bills. The woman asked if she would wear the coat and went off. In a few minutes she was back and the purchase was closed.

From Partridge's they went to a shoe store, where Carrie was fitted for shoes. Drouet stood by, and when he saw how nice they looked, said, "Wear them." Carrie shook her head, however. She was thinking of returning to the flat. He bought her a purse for one thing, and a pair of gloves for another, and let her buy the stockings.

"To-morrow," he said, "you come down here and buy yourself a skirt."

In all of Carrie's actions there was a touch of misgiving. The deeper she sank into the entanglement, the more she imagined that the thing hung upon the few remaining things she had not done. Since she had not done these, there was a way out.

Drouet knew a place in Wabash Avenue where there were rooms. He showed Carrie the outside of these, and said: "Now, you're my sister." He carried the arrangement off with an easy hand when it came to the selection, looking around, criticising, opining. "Her trunk will be here in a day or so," he observed to the landlady, who was very pleased.

When they were alone, Drouet did not change in the least. He talked in the same general way as if they were out in the street. Carrie left her things.

"Now," said Drouet, " why don't you move to-night?"

"Oh, I can't," said Carrie.

"Why not?"

"I don't want to leave them so."

He took that up as they walked along the avenue. It was a warm afternoon. The sun had come out and the wind had died down. As he talked with Carrie, he secured an accurate detail of the atmosphere of the flat.

"Come out of it," he said, "they won't care. I'll help you get along."

She listened until her misgivings vanished. He would show her about a little and then help her get something. He really imagined that he would. He would be out on the road and she could be working.

"Now, I'll tell you what you do," he said, "you go out there and get whatever you want and come away."

She thought a long time about this. Finally she agreed. He would come out as far as Peoria Street and wait for her. She was to meet him at half-past eight. At half-past five she reached home, and at six her determination was hardened.

"So you didn't get it?" said Minnie, referring to Carrie's story of the Boston Store.

Carrie looked at her out of the corner of her eye. "No," she answered.

"I don't think you'd better try any more this fall," said Minnie.

Carrie said nothing.

When Hanson came home he wore the same inscrutable demeanour. He washed in silence and went off to read his paper. At dinner Carrie felt a little nervous. The strain of her own plans was considerable, and the feeling that she was not welcome here was strong.

"Didn't find anything, eh?" said Hanson.

"No."

He turned to his eating again, the thought that it was a burden to have her here dwelling in his mind. She would have to go home, that was all. Once she was away, there would be no more coming back in the spring.

Carrie was afraid of what she was going to do, but she was relieved to know that this condition was ending. They would not care. Hanson particularly would be glad when she went. He would not care what became of her.

After dinner she went into the bathroom, where they could not disturb her, and wrote a little note.

"Good-bye, Minnie," it read. "I'm not going home. I'm going to stay in Chicago a little while and look for work. Don't worry. I'll be all right."

In the front room Hanson was reading his paper. As usual, she helped Minnie clear away the dishes and straighten up. Then she said:

"I guess I'll stand down at the door a little while." She could scarcely prevent her voice from trembling.

Minnie remembered Hanson's remonstrance.

"Sven doesn't think it looks good to stand down there," she said.

"Doesn't he?" said Carrie. "I won't do it any more after this."

She put on her hat and fidgeted around the table in the

little bedroom, wondering where to slip the note. Finally she put it under Minnie's hair-brush.

When she had closed the hall-door, she paused a moment and wondered what they would think. Some thought of the queerness of her deed affected her. She went slowly down the stairs. She looked back up the lighted step, and then affected to stroll up the street. When she reached the corner she quickened her pace.

As she was hurrying away, Hanson came back to his wife.

"Is Carrie down at the door again?" he asked.

"Yes," said Minnie; "she said she wasn't going to do it any more."

He went over to the baby where it was playing on the floor and began to poke his finger at it.

Drouet was on the corner waiting, in good spirits.

"Hello, Carrie," he said, as a sprightly figure of a girl drew near him. "Got here safe, did you? Well, we'll take a car."

Chapter VIII

Intimations by Winter: An Ambassador Summoned

AMONG THE FORCES which sweep and play throughout the universe, untutored man is but a wisp in the wind. Our civilisation is still in a middle stage, scarcely beast, in that it is no longer wholly guided by instinct; scarcely human, in that it is not yet wholly guided by reason. On the tiger no responsibility rests. We see him aligned by nature with the forces of life—he is born into their keeping and without thought he is protected. We see man far removed from the lairs of the jungles, his innate instincts dulled by too near an approach to free-will, his free-will not sufficiently developed to replace his instincts and afford him perfect guidance. He is becoming too wise to hearken always to instincts and desires; he is still too weak to always prevail against them. As a beast, the forces of life aligned him with them; as a man, he has not yet wholly learned to align himself with the forces. In this intermediate stage he wavers—neither drawn in harmony with nature by his instincts nor yet wisely putting himself into harmony by his own free-will. He is even as a wisp in the wind, moved by every breath of passion, acting now by his will and now by his instincts, erring with one, only to retrieve by the other, falling by one, only to rise by the other—a creature of incalculable variability. We have the consolation of knowing that evolution is ever in action, that the ideal is a light that cannot fail. He will not forever balance thus between good and evil. When this jangle of free-will and instinct shall have been adjusted, when perfect understanding has given the former the power to replace the latter entirely, man will no longer vary. The needle of understanding will yet point steadfast and unwavering to the distant pole of truth.

In Carrie—as in how many of our worldlings do they not?—instinct and reason, desire and understanding, were at war for the mastery. She followed whither her craving led. She was as yet more drawn than she drew.

When Minnie found the note next morning, after a night of mingled wonder and anxiety, which was not exactly touched by yearning, sorrow, or love, she exclaimed: "Well, what do you think of that?"

"What?" said Hanson.

"Sister Carrie has gone to live somewhere else."

Hanson jumped out of bed with more celerity than he usually displayed and looked at the note. The only indication of his thoughts came in the form of a little clicking sound made by his tongue; the sound some people make when they wish to urge on a horse.

"Where do you suppose she's gone to?" said Minnie, thoroughly aroused.

"I don't know," a touch of cynicism lighting his eye. "Now she has gone and done it."

Minnie moved her head in a puzzled way.

"Oh, oh," she said, "she doesn't know what she has done."

"Well," said Hanson, after a while, sticking his hands out before him, "what can you do?"

Minnie's womanly nature was higher than this. She figured the possibilities in such cases.

"Oh," she said at last, "poor Sister Carrie!"

At the time of this particular conversation, which occurred at 5 A.M., that little soldier of fortune was sleeping a rather troubled sleep in her new room, alone.

Carrie's new state was remarkable in that she saw possibilities in it. She was no sensualist, longing to drowse sleepily in the lap of luxury. She turned about, troubled by her daring, glad of her release, wondering whether she would get something to do, wondering what Drouet would do. That worthy had his future fixed for him beyond a peradventure. He could not help what he was going to do. He could not see clearly enough to wish to do differently. He was drawn by his innate desire to act the old pursuing part. He would need to delight himself with Carrie as surely as he would need to eat his heavy breakfast. He might suffer the least rudimentary twinge of conscience in whatever he did, and in just so far he was evil and sinning. But whatever twinges of conscience he might have would be rudimentary, you may be sure.

The next day he called upon Carrie, and she saw him in her chamber. He was the same jolly, enlivening soul.

"Aw," he said, "what are you looking so blue about? Come on out to breakfast. You want to get your other clothes to-day."

Carrie looked at him with the hue of shifting thought in her large eyes.

"I wish I could get something to do," she said.

"You'll get that all right," said Drouet. "What's the use worrying right now? Get yourself fixed up. See the city. I won't hurt you."

"I know you won't," she remarked, half truthfully.

"Got on the new shoes, haven't you? Stick 'em out. George, they look fine. Put on your jacket."

Carrie obeyed.

"Say, that fits like a T, don't it?" he remarked, feeling the set of it at the waist and eyeing it from a few paces with real pleasure. "What you need now is a new skirt. Let's go to breakfast."

Carrie put on her hat.

"Where are the gloves?" he inquired.

"Here," she said, taking them out of the bureau drawer.

"Now, come on," he said.

Thus the first hour of misgiving was swept away.

It went this way on every occasion. Drouet did not leave her much alone. She had time for some lone wanderings, but mostly he filled her hours with sight-seeing. At Carson, Pirie's he bought her a nice skirt and shirt waist. With his money she purchased the little necessaries of toilet, until at last she looked quite another maiden. The mirror convinced her of a few things which she had long believed. She was pretty, yes, indeed! How nice her hat set, and weren't her eyes pretty. She caught her little red lip with her teeth and felt her first thrill of power. Drouet was so good.

They went to see "The Mikado" one evening, an opera which was hilariously popular at that time. Before going, they made off for the Windsor dining-room, which was in Dearborn Street, a considerable distance from Carrie's room. It was blowing up cold, and out of her window Carrie could see the western sky, still pink with the fading light, but steely blue at the top where it met the darkness. A long, thin cloud of pink hung in midair, shaped like some island in a far-off sea. Somehow the swaying of some dead branches of trees across the way brought back the picture with which she was familiar when she looked from their front window in December days at home.

She paused and wrung her little hands.

"What's the matter?" said Drouet.

"Oh, I don't know," she said, her lip trembling.

He sensed something, and slipped his arm over her shoulder, patting her arm.

"Come on," he said gently, "you're all right."

She turned to slip on her jacket.

"Better wear that boa about your throat to-night."

They walked north on Wabash to Adams Street and then west. The lights in the stores were already shining out in gushes of golden hue. The arc lights were sputtering overhead, and high up were the lighted windows of the tall office buildings. The chill wind whipped in and out in gusty breaths. Homeward bound, the six o'clock throng bumped and jostled. Light overcoats were turned up about the ears, hats were pulled down. Little shop-girls went fluttering by in pairs and fours, chattering, laughing. It was a spectacle of warm-blooded humanity.

Suddenly a pair of eyes met Carrie's in recognition. They were looking out from a group of poorly dressed girls. Their clothes were faded and loose-hanging, their jackets old, their general make-up shabby.

Carrie recognised the glance and the girl. She was one of those who worked at the machines in the shoe factory. The latter looked, not quite sure, and then turned her head and looked. Carrie felt as if some great tide had rolled between them. The old dress and the old machine came back. She actually started. Drouet didn't notice until Carrie bumped into a pedestrian.

"You must be thinking," he said.

They dined and went to the theatre. That spectacle pleased Carrie immensely. The colour and grace of it caught her eye. She had vain imaginings about place and power, about far-off lands and magnificent people. When it was over, the clatter of coaches and the throng of fine ladies made her stare.

"Wait a minute," said Drouet, holding her back in the

showy foyer where ladies and gentlemen were moving in a social crush, skirts rustling, lace-covered heads nodding, white teeth showing through parted lips. "Let's see."

"Sixty-seven," the coach-caller was saying, his voice lifted in a sort of euphonious cry. "Sixty-seven."

"Isn't it fine?" said Carrie.

"Great," said Drouet. He was as much affected by this show of finery and gayety as she. He pressed her arm warmly. Once she looked up, her even teeth glistening through her smiling lips, her eyes alight. As they were moving out he whispered down to her, "You look lovely!" They were right where the coach-caller was swinging open a coach-door and ushering in two ladies.

"You stick to me and we'll have a coach," laughed Drouet.

Carrie scarcely heard, her head was so full of the swirl of life.

They stopped in at a restaurant for a little after-theatre lunch. Just a shade of a thought of the hour entered Carrie's head, but there was no household law to govern her now. If any habits ever had time to fix upon her, they would have operated here. Habits are peculiar things. They will drive the really non-religious mind out of bed to say prayers that are only a custom and not a devotion. The victim of habit, when he has neglected the thing which it was his custom to do, feels a little scratching in the brain, a little irritating something which comes of being out of the rut, and imagines it to be the prick of conscience, the still, small voice that is urging him ever to righteousness. If the digression is unusual enough, the drag of habit will be heavy enough to cause the unreasoning victim to return and perform the perfunctory thing. "Now, bless me," says such a mind, "I have done my duty," when, as a matter of fact, it has merely done its old, unbreakable trick once again.

Carrie had no excellent home principles fixed upon her. If she had, she would have been more consciously distressed. Now the lunch went off with considerable warmth. Under the influence of the varied occurrences, the fine, invisible passion which was emanating from Drouet, the food, the still unusual luxury, she relaxed and heard with open ears. She was again the victim of the city's hypnotic influence.

"Well," said Drouet at last, " we had better be going."

They had been dawdling over the dishes, and their eyes had frequently met. Carrie could not help but feel the vibration of force which followed, which, indeed, was his gaze. He had a way of touching her hand in explanation, as if to impress a fact upon her. He touched it now as he spoke of going.

They arose and went out into the street. The downtown section was now bare, save for a few whistling strollers, a few *owl* cars, a few open resorts whose windows were still bright. Out Wabash Avenue they strolled, Drouet still pouring forth his volume of small information. He had Carrie's arm in his, and held it closely as he explained. Once in a while, after some witticism, he would look down, and his eyes would meet hers. At last they came to the steps, and Carrie stood up on the first one, her head now coming even with his own. He took her hand and held it genially. He looked steadily at her as she glanced about, warmly musing.

At about that hour, Minnie was soundly sleeping, after a long evening of troubled thought. She had her elbow in an awkward position under her side. The muscles so held irritated a few nerves, and now a vague scene floated in on the drowsy mind. She fancied she and Carrie were somewhere beside an old coal-mine. She could see the tall runway and the heap of earth and coal cast out. There was a deep pit, into which they were looking; they could see the curious wet stones far down where the wall disappeared in vague shadows. An old basket, used for descending, was hanging there, fastened by a worn rope.

"Let's get in," said Carrie.

"Oh, no," said Minnie.

"Yes, come on," said Carrie.

She began to pull the basket over, and now, in spite of all protest, she had swung over and was going down.

"Carrie," she called, "Carrie, come back;" but Carrie was far down now and the shadow had swallowed her completely.

She moved her arm.

Now the mystic scenery merged queerly and the place was by waters she had never seen. They were upon some board or ground or something that reached far out, and at the end of this was Carrie. They looked about, and now the thing was sinking, and Minnie heard the low sip of the encroaching water.

"Come on, Carrie," she called, but Carrie was reaching farther out. She seemed to recede, and now it was difficult to call to her.

"Carrie," she called, "Carrie," but her own voice sounded far away, and the strange waters were blurring everything. She came away suffering as though she had lost something. She was more inexpressibly sad than she had ever been in life.

It was this way through many shifts of the tired brain, those curious phantoms of the spirit slipping in, blurring strange scenes, one with the other. The last one made her cry out, for Carrie was slipping away somewhere over a rock, and her fingers had let loose and she had seen her falling.

"Minnie! What's the matter? Here, wake up," said Hanson, disturbed, and shaking her by the shoulder.

"Wha—what's the matter?" said Minnie, drowsily.

"Wake up," he said, "and turn over. You're talking in your sleep."

A week or so later Drouet strolled into Fitzgerald and Moy's, spruce in dress and manner.

"Hello, Charley," said Hurstwood, looking out from his office door.

Drouet strolled over and looked in upon the manager at his desk.

"When do you go out on the road again?" he inquired.

"Pretty soon," said Drouet.

"Haven't seen much of you this trip," said Hurstwood.

"Well, I've been busy," said Drouet.

They talked some few minutes on general topics.

"Say," said Drouet, as if struck by a sudden idea, "I want you to come out some evening."

"Out where?" inquired Hurstwood.

"Out to my house, of course," said Drouet, smiling.

Hurstwood looked up quizzically, the least suggestion of a smile hovering about his lips. He studied the face of Drouet in his wise way, and then with the demeanour of a gentleman, said: "Certainly; glad to."

"We'll have a nice game of euchre."

"May I bring a nice little bottle of Sec?" asked Hurstwood.

"Certainly," said Drouet. "I'll introduce you."

Chapter IX

Convention's Own Tinder-box:
The Eye That Is Green

HURSTWOOD'S RESIDENCE on the North Side, near Lincoln Park, was a brick building of a very popular type then, a three-story affair with the first floor sunk a very little below the level of the street. It had a large bay window bulging out from the second floor, and was graced in front by a small grassy plot, twenty-five feet wide and ten feet deep. There was also a small rear yard, walled in by the fences of the neighbours and holding a stable where he kept his horse and trap.

The ten rooms of the house were occupied by himself, his wife Julia, and his son and daughter, George, Jr., and Jessica. There were besides these a maid-servant, represented from time to time by girls of various extraction, for Mrs. Hurstwood was not always easy to please.

"George, I let Mary go yesterday," was not an unfrequent salutation at the dinner table.

"All right," was his only reply. He had long since wearied of discussing the rancorous subject.

A lovely home atmosphere is one of the flowers of the world, than which there is nothing more tender, nothing more delicate, nothing more calculated to make strong and just the natures cradled and nourished within it. Those who have never experienced such a beneficent influence will not understand wherefore the tear springs glistening to the eyelids at some strange breath in lovely music. The mystic chords which bind and thrill the heart of the nation, they will never know.

Hurstwood's residence could scarcely be said to be infused with this home spirit. It lacked that toleration and regard without which the home is nothing. There was fine furniture, arranged as soothingly as the artistic perception of the occupants warranted. There were soft rugs, rich, upholstered chairs and divans, a grand piano, a marble carving of some unknown Venus by some unknown artist, and a number of small bronzes gathered from heaven knows where, but generally sold by the large furniture houses along with everything else which goes to make the "perfectly appointed house."

In the dining-room stood a sideboard laden with glistening decanters and other utilities and ornaments in glass, the arrangement of which could not be questioned. Here was something Hurstwood knew about. He had studied the subject for years in his business. He took no little satisfaction in telling each Mary, shortly after she arrived, something of what the art of the thing required. He was not garrulous by any means. On the contrary, there was a fine reserve in his manner toward the entire domestic economy of his life which was all that is comprehended by the popular term, gentlemanly. He would not argue, he would not talk freely. In his manner was something of the dogmatist. What he could not correct, he would ignore. There was a tendency in him to walk away from the impossible thing.

There was a time when he had been considerably enamoured of his Jessica, especially when he was younger and more confined in his success. Now, however, in her seventeenth year, Jessica had developed a certain amount of reserve and independence which was not inviting to the richest form of parental devotion. She was in the high school, and had notions of life which were decidedly those of a patrician. She liked nice clothes and urged for them constantly. Thoughts of love and elegant individual establishments were running in her head. She met girls at the high school whose parents were truly rich and whose fathers had standing locally as partners or owners of solid businesses. These girls gave themselves the airs befitting the thriving domestic establishments from whence they issued. They were the only ones of the school about whom Jessica concerned herself.

Young Hurstwood, Jr., was in his twentieth year, and was already connected in a promising capacity with a large real estate firm. He contributed nothing for the domestic expenses of the family, but was thought to be saving his money to invest in real estate. He had some ability, considerable vanity, and a love of pleasure that had not, as yet, infringed upon his duties, whatever they were. He came in and went out, pursuing his own plans and fancies, addressing a few words to his mother occasionally, relating some little incident to his father, but for the most part confining himself to those generalities with which most conversation concerns itself. He was not laying bare his desires for any one to see. He did not find any one in the house who particularly cared to see.

Mrs. Hurstwood was the type of the woman who has ever endeavoured to shine and has been more or less chagrined at the evidences of superior capability in this direction elsewhere. Her knowledge of life extended to that little conventional round of society of which she was not—but longed to be—a member. She was not without realisation already that this thing was impossible, so far as she was concerned. For her daughter, she hoped better things. Through Jessica she might rise a little. Through George, Jr.'s, possible success she might draw to herself the privilege of pointing proudly. Even Hurstwood was doing well enough, and she was anxious that his small real estate adventures should prosper. His property holdings, as yet, were rather small, but his income was pleasing and his position with Fitzgerald and Moy was fixed. Both those gentlemen were on pleasant and rather informal terms with him.

The atmosphere which such personalities would create must be apparent to all. It worked out in a thousand little conversations, all of which were of the same calibre.

"I'm going up to Fox Lake to-morrow," announced George, Jr., at the dinner table one Friday evening.

"What's going on up there?" queried Mrs. Hurstwood.

"Eddie Fahrway's got a new steam launch, and he wants me to come up and see how it works."

"How much did it cost him?" asked his mother.

"Oh, over two thousand dollars. He says it's a dandy."

"Old Fahrway must be making money," put in Hurstwood.

"He is, I guess. Jack told me they were shipping Vega-cura to Australia now—said they sent a whole box to Cape Town last week."

"Just think of that!" said Mrs. Hurstwood, "and only four years ago they had that basement in Madison Street."

"Jack told me they were going to put up a six-story building next spring in Robey Street."

"Just think of that!" said Jessica.

On this particular occasion Hurstwood wished to leave early.

"I guess I'll be going down town," he remarked, rising.

"Are we going to McVicker's Monday?" questioned Mrs. Hurstwood, without rising.

"Yes," he said indifferently.

They went on dining, while he went upstairs for his hat and coat. Presently the door clicked.

"I guess papa's gone," said Jessica.

The latter's school news was of a particular stripe.

"They're going to give a performance in the Lyceum, upstairs," she reported one day, "and I'm going to be in it."

"Are you?" said her mother.

"Yes, and I'll have to have a new dress. Some of the nicest girls in the school are going to be in it. Miss Palmer is going to take the part of Portia."

"Is she?" said Mrs. Hurstwood.

"They've got that Martha Griswold in it again. She thinks she can act."

"Her family doesn't amount to anything, does it?" said Mrs. Hurstwood sympathetically. "They haven't anything, have they?"

"No," returned Jessica, "they're poor as church mice."

She distinguished very carefully between the young boys of the school, many of whom were attracted by her beauty.

"What do you think?" she remarked to her mother one evening; "that Herbert Crane tried to make friends with me."

"Who is he, my dear?" inquired Mrs. Hurstwood.

"Oh, no one," said Jessica, pursing her pretty lips. "He's just a student there. He hasn't anything."

The other half of this picture came when young Blyford, son of Blyford, the soap manufacturer, walked home with her. Mrs. Hurstwood was on the third floor, sitting in a rocking-chair reading, and happened to look out at the time.

"Who was that with you, Jessica?" she inquired, as Jessica came upstairs.

"It's Mr. Blyford, mamma," she replied.

"Is it?" said Mrs. Hurstwood.

"Yes, and he wants me to stroll over into the park with him," explained Jessica, a little flushed with running up the stairs.

"All right, my dear," said Mrs. Hurstwood. "Don't be gone long."

As the two went down the street, she glanced interestedly out of the window. It was a most satisfactory spectacle indeed, most satisfactory.

In this atmosphere Hurstwood had moved for a number of years, not thinking deeply concerning it. His was not the order of nature to trouble for something better, unless the better was immediately and sharply contrasted. As it was, he received and gave, irritated sometimes by the little displays of selfish indifference, pleased at times by some show of finery which supposedly made for dignity and social distinction. The life of the resort which he managed was his life. There he spent most of his time. When he went home evenings the house looked nice. With rare exceptions the meals were acceptable, being the kind that an ordinary servant can arrange. In part, he was interested in the talk of his son and daughter, who always looked well. The vanity of Mrs. Hurstwood caused her to keep her person rather showily arrayed, but to Hurstwood this was much better than plainness. There was no love lost between them. There was no great feeling of dissatisfaction. Her opinion on any subject was not startling. They did not talk enough together to come to the argument of any one point. In the accepted and popular phrase, she had her ideas and he had his. Once in a while he would meet a woman whose youth, sprightliness, and humour would make his wife seem rather deficient by contrast, but the temporary dissatisfaction which such an encounter might arouse would be counterbalanced by his social position and a certain matter of policy. He could not complicate his home life, because it might affect his relations with his employers. They wanted no scandals. A man, to hold his position, must have a dignified manner, a clean record, a respectable home anchorage. Therefore he was circumspect in all he did, and whenever he appeared in the public ways in the afternoon, or on Sunday, it was with his wife, and sometimes his children. He would visit the local resorts, or those near by in Wisconsin, and spend a few stiff, polished days strolling about conventional places doing conventional things. He knew the need of it.

When some one of the many middle-class individuals whom he knew, who had money, would get into trouble, he would shake his head. It didn't do to talk about those things. If it came up for discussion among such friends as with him passed for close, he would deprecate the folly of the thing. "It was all right to do it—all men do those things—but why wasn't he careful? A man can't be too careful." He lost sympathy for the man that made a mistake and was found out.

On this account he still devoted some time to showing his wife about—time which would have been wearisome indeed if it had not been for the people he would meet and the little enjoyments which did not depend upon her presence or absence. He watched her with considerable curiosity at times, for she was still attractive in a way and men looked at her. She was affable, vain, subject to flattery, and this combination, he knew quite well, might produce a tragedy in a woman of her home position. Owing to his order of mind, his confidence in the sex was not great. His wife never possessed the virtues which would win the confidence and admiration of a man of his nature. As long as she loved him vigorously he could see how confidence could be, but when that was no longer the binding chain—well, something might happen.

During the last year or two the expenses of the family seemed a large thing. Jessica wanted fine clothes, and Mrs. Hurstwood, not to be outshone by her daughter, also frequently enlivened her apparel. Hurstwood had said nothing in the past, but one day he murmured.

"Jessica must have a new dress this month," said Mrs. Hurstwood one morning.

Hurstwood was arraying himself in one of his perfection vests before the glass at the time.

"I thought she just bought one," he said.

"That was just something for evening wear," returned his wife complacently.

"It seems to me," returned Hurstwood, "that she's spending a good deal for dresses of late."

"Well, she's going out more," concluded his wife, but the tone of his voice impressed her as containing something she had not heard there before.

He was not a man who travelled much, but when he did, he had been accustomed to take her along. On one occasion recently a local aldermanic junket had been arranged to visit Philadelphia—a junket that was to last ten days. Hurstwood had been invited.

"Nobody knows us down there," said one, a gentleman whose face was a slight improvement over gross ignorance and sensuality. He always wore a silk hat of most imposing proportions. "We can have a good time." His left eye moved with just the semblance of a wink. "You want to come along, George."

The next day Hurstwood announced his intention to his wife.

"I'm going away, Julia," he said, "for a few days."

"Where?" she asked, looking up.

"To Philadelphia, on business."

She looked at him consciously, expecting something else.

"I'll have to leave you behind this time."

"All right," she replied, but he could see that she was thinking that it was a curious thing. Before he went she asked him a few more questions, and that irritated him. He began to feel that she was a disagreeable attachment.

On this trip he enjoyed himself thoroughly, and when it was over he was sorry to get back. He was not willingly a prevaricator, and hated thoroughly to make explanations concerning it. The whole incident was glossed over with general remarks, but Mrs. Hurstwood gave the subject considerable thought. She drove out more, dressed better, and attended theatres freely to make up for it.

Such an atmosphere could hardly come under the category of home life. It ran along by force of habit, by force of conventional opinion. With the lapse of time it must necessarily become dryer and dryer—must eventually be tinder, easily lighted and destroyed.

Chapter X

THE COUNSEL OF WINTER:
FORTUNE'S AMBASSADOR CALLS

IN THE LIGHT of the world's attitude toward woman and her duties, the nature of Carrie's mental state deserves consideration. Actions such as hers are measured by an arbitrary scale. Society possesses a conventional standard whereby it judges all things. All men should be good, all women virtuous. Wherefore, villain, hast thou failed?

For all the liberal analysis of Spencer and our modern naturalistic philosophers, we have but an infantile perception of morals. There is more in the subject than mere conformity to a law of evolution. It is yet deeper than conformity to things of earth alone. It is more involved than we, as yet, perceive. Answer, first, why the heart thrills; explain wherefore some plaintive note goes wandering about the world, undying; make clear the rose's subtle alchemy evolving its ruddy lamp in light and rain. In the essence of these facts lie the first principles of morals.

"Oh," thought Drouet, "how delicious is my conquest."

"Ah," thought Carrie, with mournful misgivings, "what is it I have lost?"

Before this world-old proposition we stand, serious, interested, confused; endeavouring to evolve the true theory of morals—the true answer to what is right.

In the view of a certain stratum of society, Carrie was comfortably established—in the eyes of the starveling, beaten by every wind and gusty sheet of rain, she was safe in a halcyon harbour. Drouet had taken three rooms, furnished, in Ogden Place, facing Union Park, on the West Side. That was a little, green-carpeted breathing spot, than which, to-day, there is nothing more beautiful in Chicago. It afforded a vista pleasant to contemplate. The best room looked out upon the lawn of the park, now sear and brown, where a little lake lay sheltered. Over the bare limbs of the trees, which now swayed in the wintry wind, rose the steeple of the Union Park Congregational Church, and far off the towers of several others.

The rooms were comfortably enough furnished. There was

a good Brussels carpet on the floor, rich in dull red and lemon shades, and representing large jardinières filled with gorgeous, impossible flowers. There was a large pier-glass mirror between the two windows. A large, soft, green, plush-covered couch occupied one corner, and several rocking-chairs were set about. Some pictures, several rugs, a few small pieces of bric-à-brac, and the tale of contents is told.

In the bedroom, off the front room, was Carrie's trunk, bought by Drouet, and in the wardrobe built into the wall quite an array of clothing—more than she had ever possessed before, and of very becoming designs. There was a third room for possible use as a kitchen, where Drouet had Carrie establish a little portable gas stove for the preparation of small lunches, oysters, Welsh rarebits, and the like, of which he was exceedingly fond; and, lastly, a bath. The whole place was cosey, in that it was lighted by gas and heated by furnace registers, possessing also a small grate, set with an asbestos back, a method of cheerful warming which was then first coming into use. By her industry and natural love of order, which now developed, the place maintained an air pleasing in the extreme.

Here, then, was Carrie, established in a pleasant fashion, free of certain difficulties which most ominously confronted her, laden with many new ones which were of a mental order, and altogether so turned about in all of her earthly relationships that she might well have been a new and different individual. She looked into her glass and saw a prettier Carrie than she had seen before; she looked into her mind, a mirror prepared of her own and the world's opinions, and saw a worse. Between these two images she wavered, hesitating which to believe.

"My, but you're a little beauty," Drouet was wont to exclaim to her.

She would look at him with large, pleased eyes.

"You know it, don't you?" he would continue.

"Oh, I don't know," she would reply, feeling delight in the fact that one should think so, hesitating to believe, though she really did, that she was vain enough to think so much of herself.

Her conscience, however, was not a Drouet, interested to

praise. There she heard a different voice, with which she argued, pleaded, excused. It was no just and sapient counsellor, in its last analysis. It was only an average little conscience, a thing which represented the world, her past environment, habit, convention, in a confused way. With it, the voice of the people was truly the voice of God.

"Oh, thou failure!" said the voice.

"Why?" she questioned.

"Look at those about," came the whispered answer. "Look at those who are good. How would they scorn to do what you have done. Look at the good girls; how will they draw away from such as you when they know you have been weak. You had not tried before you failed."

It was when Carrie was alone, looking out across the park, that she would be listening to this. It would come infrequently—when something else did not interfere, when the pleasant side was not too apparent, when Drouet was not there. It was somewhat clear in utterance at first, but never wholly convincing. There was always an answer, always the December days threatened. She was alone; she was desireful; she was fearful of the whistling wind. The voice of want made answer for her.

Once the bright days of summer pass by, a city takes on that sombre garb of grey, wrapt in which it goes about its labours during the long winter. Its endless buildings look grey, its sky and its streets assume a sombre hue; the scattered, leafless trees and wind-blown dust and paper but add to the general solemnity of colour. There seems to be something in the chill breezes which scurry through the long, narrow thoroughfares productive of rueful thoughts. Not poets alone, nor artists, nor that superior order of mind which arrogates to itself all refinement, feel this, but dogs and all men. These feel as much as the poet, though they have not the same power of expression. The sparrow upon the wire, the cat in the doorway, the dray horse tugging his weary load, feel the long, keen breaths of winter. It strikes to the heart of all life, animate and inanimate. If it were not for the artificial fires of merriment, the rush of profit-seeking trade, and pleasure-selling amusements; if the various merchants failed to make the customary display within and without their establishments; if our streets were not strung with signs of gorgeous hues and thronged with hurrying purchasers, we would quickly discover how firmly the chill hand of winter lays upon the heart; how dispiriting are the days during which the sun withholds a portion of our allowance of light and warmth. We are more dependent upon these things than is often thought. We are insects produced by heat, and pass without it.

In the drag of such a grey day the secret voice would reassert itself, feebly and more feebly.

Such mental conflict was not always uppermost. Carrie was not by any means a gloomy soul. More, she had not the mind to get firm hold upon a definite truth. When she could not find her way out of the labyrinth of ill-logic which thought upon the subject created, she would turn away entirely.

Drouet, all the time, was conducting himself in a model way for one of his sort. He took her about a great deal, spent money upon her, and when he travelled he took her with him. There were times when she would be alone for two or three days, while he made the shorter circuits of his business, but, as a rule, she saw a great deal of him.

"Say, Carrie," he said one morning, shortly after they had so established themselves, "I've invited my friend Hurstwood to come out some day and spend the evening with us."

"Who is he?" asked Carrie, doubtfully.

"Oh, he's a nice man. He's manager of Fitzgerald and Moy's."

"What's that?" said Carrie.

"The finest resort in town. It's a way-up, swell place."

Carrie puzzled a moment. She was wondering what Drouet had told him, what her attitude would be.

"That's all right," said Drouet, feeling her thought. "He doesn't know anything. You're Mrs. Drouet now."

There was something about this which struck Carrie as slightly inconsiderate. She could see that Drouet did not have the keenest sensibilities.

"Why don't we get married?" she inquired, thinking of the voluble promises he had made.

"Well, we will," he said, "just as soon as I get this little deal of mine closed up."

He was referring to some property which he said he had, and which required so much attention, adjustment, and what not, that somehow or other it interfered with his free moral, personal actions.

"Just as soon as I get back from my Denver trip in January we'll do it."

Carrie accepted this as a basis for hope—it was a sort of salve to her conscience, a pleasant way out. Under the circumstances, things would be righted. Her actions would be justified.

She really was not enamoured of Drouet. She was more clever than he. In a dim way, she was beginning to see where he lacked. If it had not been for this, if she had not been able to measure and judge him in a way, she would have been worse off than she was. She would have adored him. She would have been utterly wretched in her fear of not gaining his affection, of losing his interest, of being swept away and left without an anchorage. As it was, she wavered a little, slightly anxious, at first, to gain him completely, but later feeling at ease in waiting. She was not exactly sure what she thought of him—what she wanted to do.

When Hurstwood called, she met a man who was more clever than Drouet in a hundred ways. He paid that peculiar deference to women which every member of the sex appreciates. He was not overawed, he was not overbold. His great charm was attentiveness. Schooled in winning those birds of fine feather among his own sex, the merchants and professionals who visited his resort, he could use even greater tact when endeavouring to prove agreeable to some one who charmed him. In a pretty woman of any refinement of feeling whatsoever he found his greatest incentive. He was mild, placid, assured, giving the impression that he wished to be of service only—to do something which would make the lady more pleased.

Drouet had ability in this line himself when the game was worth the candle, but he was too much the egotist to reach the polish which Hurstwood possessed. He was too buoyant, too full of ruddy life, too assured. He succeeded with many who were not quite schooled in the art of love. He failed dismally where the woman was slightly experienced and possessed innate refinement. In the case of Carrie he found a woman who was all of the latter, but none of the former. He was lucky in the fact that opportunity tumbled into his lap, as it were. A few years later, with a little more experience, the slightest tide of success, and he had not been able to approach Carrie at all.

"You ought to have a piano here, Drouet," said Hurstwood, smiling at Carrie, on the evening in question, "so that your wife could play."

Drouet had not thought of that.

"So we ought," he observed readily.

"Oh, I don't play," ventured Carrie.

"It isn't very difficult," returned Hurstwood. "You could do very well in a few weeks."

He was in the best form for entertaining this evening. His clothes were particularly new and rich in appearance. The coat lapels stood out with that medium stiffness which excellent cloth possesses. The vest was of a rich Scotch plaid, set with a double row of round mother-of-pearl buttons. His cravat was a shiny combination of silken threads, not loud, not inconspicuous. What he wore did not strike the eye so forcibly as that which Drouet had on, but Carrie could see the elegance of the material. Hurstwood's shoes were of soft, black calf, polished only to a dull shine. Drouet wore patent leather, but Carrie could not help feeling that there was a distinction in favour of the soft leather, where all else was so rich. She noticed these things almost unconsciously. They were things which would naturally flow from the situation. She was used to Drouet's appearance.

"Suppose we have a little game of euchre?" suggested Hurstwood, after a light round of conversation. He was rather dexterous in avoiding everything that would suggest that he knew anything of Carrie's past. He kept away from personalities altogether, and confined himself to those things which did not concern individuals at all. By his manner, he put Carrie at her ease, and by his deference and pleasantries he amused her. He pretended to be seriously interested in all she said.

"I don't know how to play," said Carrie.

"Charlie, you are neglecting a part of your duty," he observed to Drouet most affably. "Between us, though," he went on, " we can show you."

By his tact he made Drouet feel that he admired his choice. There was something in his manner that showed that he was pleased to be there. Drouet felt really closer to him than ever before. It gave him more respect for Carrie. Her appearance came into a new light, under Hurstwood's appreciation. The situation livened considerably.

"Now, let me see," said Hurstwood, looking over Carrie's shoulder very deferentially. "What have you?" He studied for a moment. "That's rather good," he said.

"You're lucky. Now, I'll show you how to trounce your husband. You take my advice."

"Here," said Drouet, "if you two are going to scheme together, I won't stand a ghost of a show. Hurstwood's a regular sharp."

"No, it's your wife. She brings me luck. Why shouldn't she win?"

Carrie looked gratefully at Hurstwood, and smiled at Drouet. The former took the air of a mere friend. He was simply there to enjoy himself. Anything that Carrie did was pleasing to him, nothing more.

"There," he said, holding back one of his own good cards, and giving Carrie a chance to take a trick. "I count that clever playing for a beginner."

The latter laughed gleefully as she saw the hand coming her way. It was as if she were invincible when Hurstwood helped her.

He did not look at her often. When he did, it was with a mild light in his eye. Not a shade was there of anything save geniality and kindness. He took back the shifty, clever gleam, and replaced it with one of innocence. Carrie could not guess but that it was pleasure with him in the immediate thing. She felt that he considered she was doing a great deal.

"It's unfair to let such playing go without earning something," he said after a time, slipping his finger into the little coin pocket of his coat. "Let's play for dimes."

"All right," said Drouet, fishing for bills.

Hurstwood was quicker. His fingers were full of new ten-cent pieces. "Here we are," he said, supplying each one with a little stack.

"Oh, this is gambling," smiled Carrie. "It's bad."

"No," said Drouet, "only fun. If you never play for more than that, you will go to Heaven."

"Don't you moralise," said Hurstwood to Carrie gently, "until you see what becomes of the money."

Drouet smiled.

"If your husband gets them, he'll tell you how bad it is."

Drouet laughed loud.

There was such an ingratiating tone about Hurstwood's voice, the insinuation was so perceptible that even Carrie got the humour of it.

"When do you leave?" said Hurstwood to Drouet.

"On Wednesday," he replied.

"It's rather hard to have your husband running about like that, isn't it?" said Hurstwood, addressing Carrie.

"She's going along with me this time," said Drouet.

"You must both go with me to the theatre before you go."

"Certainly," said Drouet. "Eh, Carrie?"

"I'd like it ever so much," she replied.

Hurstwood did his best to see that Carrie won the money. He rejoiced in her success, kept counting her winnings, and finally gathered and put them in her extended hand. They spread a little lunch, at which he served the wine, and afterwards he used fine tact in going.

"Now," he said, addressing first Carrie and then Drouet with his eyes, "you must be ready at 7.30. I'll come and get you."

They went with him to the door and there was his cab waiting, its red lamps gleaming cheerfully in the shadow.

"Now," he observed to Drouet, with a tone of good-fellowship, "when you leave your wife alone, you must let me show her around a little. It will break up her loneliness."

"Sure," said Drouet, quite pleased at the attention shown.

"You're so kind," observed Carrie.

"Not at all," said Hurstwood, "I would want your husband to do as much for me."

He smiled and went lightly away. Carrie was thoroughly impressed. She had never come in contact with such grace. As for Drouet, he was equally pleased.

"There's a nice man," he remarked to Carrie, as they returned to their cosey chamber. "A good friend of mine, too."

"He seems to be," said Carrie.

Chapter XI

THE PERSUASION OF FASHION:
FEELING GUARDS O'ER ITS OWN

CARRIE WAS an apt student of fortune's ways—of fortune's superficialities. Seeing a thing, she would immediately set to inquiring how she would look, properly related to it. Be it known that this is not fine feeling, it is not wisdom. The greatest minds are not so afflicted; and, on the contrary, the lowest order of mind is not so disturbed. Fine clothes to her were a vast persuasion; they spoke tenderly and Jesuitically for themselves. When she came within earshot of their pleading, desire in her bent a willing ear. The voice of the so-called inanimate! Who shall translate for us the language of the stones?

"My dear," said the lace collar she secured from Partridge's, "I fit you beautifully; don't give me up."

"Ah, such little feet," said the leather of the soft new shoes; "how effectively I cover them. What a pity they should ever want my aid."

Once these things were in her hand, on her person, she might dream of giving them up; the method by which they came might intrude itself so forcibly that she would ache to be rid of the thought of it, but she would not give them up. "Put on the old clothes—that torn pair of shoes," was called to her by her conscience in vain. She could possibly have conquered the fear of hunger and gone back; the thought of hard work and a narrow round of suffering would, under the last pressure of conscience, have yielded, but spoil her appearance?—be old-clothed and poor-appearing?—never!

Drouet heightened her opinion on this and allied subjects in such a manner as to weaken her power of resisting their influence. It is so easy to do this when the thing opined is in the line of what we desire. In his hearty way, he insisted upon her good looks. He looked at her admiringly, and she took it at its full value. Under the circumstances, she did not need to carry herself as pretty women do. She picked that knowledge up fast enough for herself. Drouet had a habit, characteristic of his kind, of looking after stylishly dressed or pretty women on the street and remarking upon them. He had just enough of the feminine love of dress to be a good judge—not of intellect, but of clothes. He saw how they set their little feet, how they carried their chins, with what grace and sinuosity they swung their bodies. A dainty, self-conscious swaying of the hips by a woman was to him as alluring as the glint of rare wine to a toper. He would turn and follow the disappearing vision with his eyes. He would thrill as a child with the unhindered passion that was in him. He loved the thing that women love in themselves, grace. At this, their own shrine, he knelt with them, an ardent devotee.

"Did you see that woman who went by just now?" he said to Carrie on the first day they took a walk together. "Fine stepper, wasn't she?"

Carrie looked, and observed the grace commended.

"Yes, she is," she returned, cheerfully, a little suggestion of possible defect in herself awakening in her mind. If that was so fine, she must look at it more closely. Instinctively, she felt a desire to imitate it. Surely she could do that too.

When one of her mind sees many things emphasized and reëmphasized and admired, she gathers the logic of it and applies accordingly. Drouet was not shrewd enough to see that this was not tactful. He could not see that it would be better to make her feel that she was competing with herself, not others better than herself. He would not have done it with an older, wiser woman, but in Carrie he saw only the novice. Less clever than she, he was naturally unable to comprehend her sensibility. He went on educating and wounding her, a thing rather foolish in one whose admiration for his pupil and victim was apt to grow.

Carrie took the instructions affably. She saw what Drouet liked; in a vague way she saw where he was weak. It lessens a woman's opinion of a man when she learns that his admiration is so pointedly and generously distributed. She sees but one object of supreme compliment in this world, and that is herself. If a man is to succeed with many women, he must be all in all to each.

In her own apartments Carrie saw things which were lessons in the same school.

In the same house with her lived an official of one of the theatres, Mr. Frank A. Hale, manager of the Standard, and his wife, a pleasing-looking brunette of thirty-five. They were people of a sort very common in America to-day, who live respectably from hand to mouth. Hale received a salary of forty-five dollars a week. His wife, quite attractive, affected the feeling of youth, and objected to that sort of home life which means the care of a house and the raising of a family. Like Drouet and Carrie, they also occupied three rooms on the floor above.

Not long after she arrived Mrs. Hale established social relations with her, and together they went about. For a long time this was her only companionship, and the gossip of the manager's wife formed the medium through which she saw the world. Such trivialities, such praises of wealth, such conventional expression of morals as sifted through this passive creature's mind, fell upon Carrie and for the while confused her.

On the other hand, her own feelings were a corrective influence. The constant drag to something better was not to be denied. By those things which address the heart was she steadily recalled. In the apartments across the hall were a young girl and her mother. They were from Evansville, Indiana, the wife and daughter of a railroad treasurer. The daughter was here to study music, the mother to keep her company.

Carrie did not make their acquaintance, but she saw the daughter coming in and going out. A few times she had seen her at the piano in the parlour, and not infrequently had heard her play. This young woman was particularly dressy for her station, and wore a jewelled ring or two which flashed upon her white fingers as she played.

Now Carrie was affected by music. Her nervous composition responded to certain strains, much as certain strings of a harp vibrate when a corresponding key of a piano is struck. She was delicately moulded in sentiment, and answered with vague ruminations to certain wistful chords. They awoke longings for those things which she did not have. They

caused her to cling closer to things she possessed. One short
song the young lady played in a most soulful and tender
mood. Carrie heard it through the open door from the parlour below. It was at that hour between afternoon and night
when, for the idle, the wanderer, things are apt to take on a
wistful aspect. The mind wanders forth on far journeys and
returns with sheaves of withered and departed joys. Carrie sat
at her window looking out. Drouet had been away since ten
in the morning. She had amused herself with a walk, a book
by Bertha M. Clay which Drouet had left there, though she
did not wholly enjoy the latter, and by changing her dress for
the evening. Now she sat looking out across the park as wistful and depressed as the nature which craves variety and life
can be under such circumstances. As she contemplated her
new state, the strain from the parlour below stole upward.
With it her thoughts became coloured and enmeshed. She
reverted to the things which were best and saddest within the
small limit of her experience. She became for the moment a
repentant.

While she was in this mood Drouet came in, bringing with
him an entirely different atmosphere. It was dusk and Carrie
had neglected to light the lamp. The fire in the grate, too,
had burned low.

"Where are you, Cad?" he said, using a pet name he had
given her.

"Here," she answered.

There was something delicate and lonely in her voice, but
he could not hear it. He had not the poetry in him that would
seek a woman out under such circumstances and console her
for the tragedy of life. Instead, he struck a match and lighted
the gas.

"Hello," he exclaimed, "you've been crying."

Her eyes were still wet with a few vague tears.

"Pshaw," he said, "you don't want to do that."

He took her hand, feeling in his good-natured egotism that
it was probably lack of his presence which had made her
lonely.

"Come on, now," he went on; "it's all right. Let's waltz a
little to that music."

He could not have introduced a more incongruous proposition. It made clear to Carrie that he could not sympathise with her. She could not have framed thoughts which would have expressed his defect or made clear the difference between them, but she felt it. It was his first great mistake.

What Drouet said about the girl's grace, as she tripped out evenings accompanied by her mother, caused Carrie to perceive the nature and value of those little modish ways which women adopt when they would presume to be something. She looked in the mirror and pursed up her lips, accompanying it with a little toss of the head, as she had seen the railroad treasurer's daughter do. She caught up her skirts with an easy swing, for had not Drouet remarked that in her and several others, and Carrie was naturally imitative. She began to get the hang of those little things which the pretty woman who has vanity invariably adopts. In short, her knowledge of grace doubled, and with it her appearance changed. She became a girl of considerable taste.

Drouet noticed this. He saw the new bow in her hair and the new way of arranging her locks which she affected one morning.

"You look fine that way, Cad," he said.

"Do I?" she replied, sweetly. It made her try for other effects that selfsame day.

She used her feet less heavily, a thing that was brought about by her attempting to imitate the treasurer's daughter's graceful carriage. How much influence the presence of that young woman in the same house had upon her it would be difficult to say. But, because of all these things, when Hurstwood called he had found a young woman who was much more than the Carrie to whom Drouet had first spoken. The primary defects of dress and manner had passed. She was pretty, graceful, rich in the timidity born of uncertainty, and with a something childlike in her large eyes which captured the fancy of this starched and conventional poser among men. It was the ancient attraction of the fresh for the stale. If there was a touch of appreciation left in him for the bloom and unsophistication which is the charm of youth, it rekindled now. He looked into her pretty face and felt the subtle waves of young life radiating therefrom. In that large clear eye he could see nothing that his *blasé* nature could understand as guile. The little vanity, if he could have perceived it there, would have touched him as a pleasant thing.

"I wonder," he said, as he rode away in his cab, "how Drouet came to win her."

He gave her credit for feelings superior to Drouet at the first glance.

The cab plopped along between the far-receding lines of gas lamps on either hand. He folded his gloved hands and saw only the lighted chamber and Carrie's face. He was pondering over the delight of youthful beauty.

"I'll have a bouquet for her," he thought. "Drouet won't mind."

He never for a moment concealed the fact of her attraction for himself. He troubled himself not at all about Drouet's priority. He was merely floating those gossamer threads of thought which, like the spider's, he hoped would lay hold somewhere. He did not know, he could not guess, what the result would be.

A few weeks later Drouet, in his peregrinations, encountered one of his well-dressed lady acquaintances in Chicago on his return from a short trip to Omaha. He had intended to hurry out to Ogden Place and surprise Carrie, but now he fell into an interesting conversation and soon modified his original intention.

"Let's go to dinner," he said, little recking any chance meeting which might trouble his way.

"Certainly," said his companion.

They visited one of the better restaurants for a social chat. It was five in the afternoon when they met; it was seven-thirty before the last bone was picked.

Drouet was just finishing a little incident he was relating, and his face was expanding into a smile, when Hurstwood's eye caught his own. The latter had come in with several friends, and, seeing Drouet and some woman, not Carrie, drew his own conclusion.

"Ah, the rascal," he thought, and then, with a touch of righteous sympathy, "that's pretty hard on the little girl."

Drouet jumped from one easy thought to another as he caught Hurstwood's eye. He felt but very little misgiving, until he saw that Hurstwood was cautiously pretending not to see. Then some of the latter's impression forced itself upon him. He thought of Carrie and their last meeting. By George, he would have to explain this to Hurstwood. Such a chance half-hour with an old friend must not have anything more attached to it than it really warranted.

For the first time he was troubled. Here was a moral complication of which he could not possibly get the ends. Hurstwood would laugh at him for being a fickle boy. He would laugh with Hurstwood. Carrie would never hear, his present companion at table would never know, and yet he could not help feeling that he was getting the worst of it—there was some faint stigma attached, and he was not guilty. He broke up the dinner by becoming dull, and saw his companion on her car. Then he went home.

"He hasn't talked to me about any of these later flames," thought Hurstwood to himself. "He thinks I think he cares for the girl out there."

"He ought not to think I'm knocking around, since I have just introduced him out there," thought Drouet.

"I saw you," Hurstwood said, genially, the next time Drouet drifted in to his polished resort, from which he could not stay away. He raised his forefinger indicatively, as parents do to children.

"An old acquaintance of mine that I ran into just as I was coming up from the station," explained Drouet. "She used to be quite a beauty."

"Still attracts a little, eh?" returned the other, affecting to jest.

"Oh, no," said Drouet, "just couldn't escape her this time."

"How long are you here?" asked Hurstwood.

"Only a few days."

"You must bring the girl down and take dinner with me," he said. "I'm afraid you keep her cooped up out there. I'll get a box for Joe Jefferson."

"Not me," answered the drummer. "Sure I'll come."

This pleased Hurstwood immensely. He gave Drouet no credit for any feelings toward Carrie whatever. He envied him, and now, as he looked at the well-dressed, jolly salesman, whom he so much liked, the gleam of the rival glowed in his eye. He began to "size up" Drouet from the standpoints of wit and fascination. He began to look to see where he was weak. There was no disputing that, whatever he might think of him as a good fellow, he felt a certain amount of contempt for him as a lover. He could hoodwink him all right. Why, if he would just let Carrie see one such little incident as that of Thursday, it would settle the matter. He ran on in thought, almost exulting, the while he laughed and chatted, and Drouet felt nothing. He had no power of analysing the glance and the atmosphere of a man like Hurstwood. He stood and smiled and accepted the invitation while his friend examined him with the eye of a hawk.

The object of this peculiarly involved comedy was not thinking of either. She was busy adjusting her thoughts and feelings to newer conditions, and was not in danger of suffering disturbing pangs from either quarter.

One evening Drouet found her dressing herself before the glass.

"Cad," said he, catching her, "I believe you're getting vain."

"Nothing of the kind," she returned, smiling.

"Well, you're mighty pretty," he went on, slipping his arm around her. "Put on that navy-blue dress of yours and I'll take you to the show."

"Oh, I've promised Mrs. Hale to go with her to the Exposition to-night," she returned, apologetically.

"You did, eh?" he said, studying the situation abstractedly. "I wouldn't care to go to that myself."

"Well, I don't know," answered Carrie, puzzling, but not offering to break her promise in his favour.

Just then a knock came at their door and the maid-servant handed a letter in.

"He says there's an answer expected," she explained.

"It's from Hurstwood," said Drouet, noting the superscription as he tore it open.

"You are to come down and see Joe Jefferson with me to-night," it ran in part. "It's my turn, as we agreed the other day. All other bets are off."

"Well, what do you say to this?" asked Drouet, innocently, while Carrie's mind bubbled with favourable replies.

"You had better decide, Charlie," she said, reservedly.

"I guess we had better go, if you can break that engagement upstairs," said Drouet.

"Oh, I can," returned Carrie without thinking.

Drouet selected writing paper while Carrie went to change her dress. She hardly explained to herself why this latest invitation appealed to her most.

"Shall I wear my hair as I did yesterday?" she asked, as she came out with several articles of apparel pending.

"Sure," he returned, pleasantly.

She was relieved to see that he felt nothing. She did not credit her willingness to go to any fascination Hurstwood held for her. It seemed that the combination of Hurstwood, Drouet, and herself was more agreeable than anything else that had been suggested. She arrayed herself most carefully and they started off, extending excuses upstairs.

"I say," said Hurstwood, as they came up the theatre lobby, " we are exceedingly charming this evening."

Carrie fluttered under his approving glance.

"Now, then," he said, leading the way up the foyer into the theatre.

If ever there was dressiness it was here. It was the personification of the old term spick and span.

"Did you ever see Jefferson?" he questioned, as he leaned toward Carrie in the box.

"I never did," she returned.

"He's delightful, delightful," he went on, giving the commonplace rendition of approval which such men know. He sent Drouet after a programme, and then discoursed to Carrie concerning Jefferson as he had heard of him. The former was pleased beyond expression, and was really hypnotised by the environment, the trappings of the box, the elegance of her companion. Several times their eyes accidentally met, and then there poured into hers such a flood of feeling as she had never before experienced. She could not for the moment explain it, for in the next glance or the next move of the hand there was seeming indifference, mingled only with the kindest attention.

Drouet shared in the conversation, but he was almost dull in comparison. Hurstwood entertained them both, and now it was driven into Carrie's mind that here was the superior man. She instinctively felt that he was stronger and higher, and yet withal so simple. By the end of the third act she was sure that Drouet was only a kindly soul, but otherwise defective. He sank every moment in her estimation by the strong comparison.

"I have had such a nice time," said Carrie, when it was all over and they were coming out.

"Yes, indeed," added Drouet, who was not in the least aware that a battle had been fought and his defences weakened. He was like the Emperor of China, who sat glorying in himself, unaware that his fairest provinces were being wrested from him.

"Well, you have saved me a dreary evening," returned Hurstwood. "Good-night."

He took Carrie's little hand, and a current of feeling swept from one to the other.

"I'm so tired," said Carrie, leaning back in the car when Drouet began to talk.

"Well, you rest a little while I smoke," he said, rising, and then he foolishly went to the forward platform of the car and left the game as it stood.

Chapter XII

Of the Lamps of the Mansions:
The Ambassador's Plea

M RS. HURSTWOOD was not aware of any of her husband's moral defections, though she might readily have suspected his tendencies, which she well understood. She was a woman upon whose action under provocation you could never count. Hurstwood, for one, had not the slightest idea of what she would do under certain circumstances. He had never seen her thoroughly aroused. In fact, she was not a woman who would fly into a passion. She had too little faith in mankind not to know that they were erring. She was too calculating to jeopardise any advantage she might gain in the way of information by fruitless clamour. Her wrath would never wreak itself in one fell blow. She would wait and brood, studying the details and adding to them until her power might be commensurate with her desire for revenge. At the same time, she would not delay to inflict any injury, big or little, which would wound the object of her revenge and still leave him uncertain as to the source of the evil. She was a cold, self-centred woman, with many a thought of her own which never found expression, not even by so much as the glint of an eye.

Hurstwood felt some of this in her nature, though he did not actually perceive it. He dwelt with her in peace and some satisfaction. He did not fear her in the least—there was no cause for it. She still took a faint pride in him, which was augmented by her desire to have her social integrity maintained. She was secretly somewhat pleased by the fact that much of her husband's property was in her name, a precaution which Hurstwood had taken when his home interests were somewhat more alluring than at present. His wife had not the slightest reason to feel that anything would ever go amiss with their household, and yet the shadows which run before gave her a thought of the good of it now and then. She was in a position to become refractory with considerable advantage, and Hurstwood conducted himself circumspectly because he felt that he could not be sure of anything once she became dissatisfied.

It so happened that on the night when Hurstwood, Carrie, and Drouet were in the box at McVickar's, George, Jr., was in the sixth row of the parquet with the daughter of H. B. Carmichael, the third partner of a wholesale dry-goods house of that city. Hurstwood did not see his son, for he sat, as was his wont, as far back as possible, leaving himself just partially visible, when he bent forward, to those within the first six rows in question. It was his wont to sit this way in every theatre—to make his personality as inconspicuous as possible where it would be no advantage to him to have it otherwise.

He never moved but what, if there was any danger of his conduct being misconstrued or ill-reported, he looked carefully about him and counted the cost of every inch of conspicuity.

The next morning at breakfast his son said:

"I saw you, Governor, last night."

"Were you at McVickar's?" said Hurstwood, with the best grace in the world.

"Yes," said young George.

"Who with?"

"Miss Carmichael."

Mrs. Hurstwood directed an inquiring glance at her husband, but could not judge from his appearance whether it was any more than a casual look into the theatre which was referred to.

"How was the play?" she inquired.

"Very good," returned Hurstwood, "only it's the same old thing, 'Rip Van Winkle.' "

"Whom did you go with?" queried his wife, with assumed indifference.

"Charlie Drouet and his wife. They are friends of Moy's, visiting here."

Owing to the peculiar nature of his position, such a disclosure as this would ordinarily create no difficulty. His wife took it for granted that his situation called for certain social movements in which she might not be included. But of late he had pleaded office duty on several occasions when his wife asked for his company to any evening entertainment. He had done so in regard to the very evening in question only the morning before.

"I thought you were going to be busy," she remarked, very carefully.

"So I was," he exclaimed. "I couldn't help the interruption, but I made up for it afterward by working until two."

This settled the discussion for the time being, but there was a residue of opinion which was not satisfactory. There was no time at which the claims of his wife could have been more unsatisfactorily pushed. For years he had been steadily modifying his matrimonial devotion, and found her company dull. Now that a new light shone upon the horizon, this older luminary paled in the west. He was satisfied to turn his face away entirely, and any call to look back was irksome.

She, on the contrary, was not at all inclined to accept anything less than a complete fulfilment of the letter of their relationship, though the spirit might be wanting.

"We are coming down town this afternoon," she remarked, a few days later. "I want you to come over to Kinsley's and meet Mr. Phillips and his wife. They're stopping at the Tremont, and we're going to show them around a little."

After the occurrence of Wednesday, he could not refuse, though the Phillips were about as uninteresting as vanity and ignorance could make them. He agreed, but it was with short grace. He was angry when he left the house.

"I'll put a stop to this," he thought. "I'm not going to be bothered fooling around with visitors when I have work to do."

Not long after this Mrs. Hurstwood came with a similar proposition, only it was to a matinée this time.

"My dear," he returned, "I haven't time. I'm too busy."

"You find time to go with other people, though," she replied, with considerable irritation.

"Nothing of the kind," he answered. "I can't avoid business relations, and that's all there is to it."

"Well, never mind," she exclaimed. Her lips tightened. The feeling of mutual antagonism was increased.

On the other hand, his interest in Drouet's little shop-girl grew in an almost evenly balanced proportion. That young lady, under the stress of her situation and the tutelage of her new friend, changed effectively. She had the aptitude of the struggler who seeks emancipation. The glow of a more showy life was not lost upon her. She did not grow in knowledge so much as she awakened in the matter of desire. Mrs. Hale's extended harangues upon the subjects of wealth and position taught her to distinguish between degrees of wealth.

Mrs. Hale loved to drive in the afternoon in the sun when it was fine, and to satisfy her soul with a sight of those mansions and lawns which she could not afford. On the North Side had been erected a number of elegant mansions along what is now known as the North Shore Drive. The present lake wall of stone and granitoid was not then in place, but the road had been well laid out, the intermediate spaces of lawn were lovely to look upon, and the houses were thoroughly new and imposing. When the winter season had passed and the first fine days of the early spring appeared, Mrs. Hale secured a buggy for an afternoon and invited Carrie. They rode first through Lincoln Park and on far out towards Evanston, turning back at four and arriving at the north end of the Shore Drive at about five o'clock. At this time of year the days are still comparatively short, and the shadows of the evening were beginning to settle down upon the great city. Lamps were beginning to burn with that mellow radiance which seems almost watery and translucent to the eye. There was a softness in the air which speaks with an infinite delicacy of feeling to the flesh as well as to the soul. Carrie felt that it was a lovely day. She was ripened by it in spirit for many suggestions. As they drove along the smooth pavement an occasional carriage passed. She saw one stop and the footman dismount, opening the door for a gentleman who seemed to be leisurely returning from some afternoon pleasure. Across the broad lawns, now first freshening into green, she saw lamps faintly glowing upon rich interiors. Now it was but a chair, now a table, now an ornate corner, which met her eye, but it appealed to her as almost nothing else could. Such childish fancies as she had had of fairy palaces and kingly quarters now came back. She imagined that across these richly carved entrance-ways, where the globed and crystalled lamps shone upon panelled doors set with stained and designed panes of glass, was neither care nor unsatisfied desire. She was perfectly certain that here was happiness. If she could but stroll up yon broad walk, cross that rich entrance-way, which to her was of the beauty of a jewel, and sweep in grace and luxury to possession and command— oh! how quickly would sadness flee; how, in an instant, would the heartache end. She gazed and gazed, wondering, delighting, longing, and all the while the siren voice of the unrestful was whispering in her ear.

"If we could have such a home as that," said Mrs. Hale sadly, "how delightful it would be."

"And yet they do say," said Carrie, "that no one is ever happy."

She had heard so much of the canting philosophy of the grapeless fox.

"I notice," said Mrs. Hale, "that they all try mighty hard, though, to take their misery in a mansion."

When she came to her own rooms, Carrie saw their comparative insignificance. She was not so dull but that she could perceive they were but three small rooms in a moderately well-furnished boarding-house. She was not contrasting it now with what she had had, but what she had so recently seen. The glow of the palatial doors was still in her eye, the roll of cushioned carriages still in her ears. What, after all, was Drouet? What was she? At her window, she thought it over, rocking to and fro, and gazing out across the lamp-lit park toward the lamp-lit houses on Warren and Ashland avenues. She was too wrought up to care to go down to eat, too pensive to do aught but rock and sing. Some old tunes crept to her lips, and, as she sang them, her heart sank. She longed and longed and longed. It was now for the old cottage room in Columbia City, now the mansion upon the Shore Drive, now the fine dress of some lady, now the elegance of some scene. She was sad beyond measure, and yet uncertain, wishing, fancying. Finally, it seemed as if all her state was one of loneliness and forsakenness, and she could scarce refrain from trembling at the lip. She hummed and hummed as the moments went by, sitting in the shadow by the window, and was therein as happy, though she did not perceive it, as she ever would be.

While Carrie was still in this frame of mind, the house-servant brought up the intelligence that Mr. Hurstwood was in the parlour asking to see Mr. and Mrs. Drouet.

"I guess he doesn't know that Charlie is out of town," thought Carrie.

She had seen comparatively little of the manager during the winter, but had been kept constantly in mind of him by one thing and another, principally by the strong impression he had made. She was quite disturbed for the moment as to her appearance, but soon satisfied herself by the aid of the mirror, and went below.

Hurstwood was in his best form, as usual. He hadn't heard that Drouet was out of town. He was but slightly affected by the intelligence, and devoted himself to the more general topics which would interest Carrie. It was surprising—the ease with which he conducted a conversation. He was like every man who has had the advantage of practice and knows he has sympathy. He knew that Carrie listened to him pleasurably, and, without the least effort, he fell into a train of observation which absorbed her fancy. He drew up his chair and modulated his voice to such a degree that what he said seemed wholly confidential. He confined himself almost exclusively to his observation of men and pleasures. He had been here and there, he had seen this and that. Somehow he made Carrie wish to see similar things, and all the while kept her aware of himself. She could not shut out the consciousness of his individuality and presence for a moment. He would raise his eyes slowly in smiling emphasis of something, and she was fixed by their magnetism. He would draw out, with the easiest grace, her approval. Once he touched her hand for emphasis and she only smiled. He seemed to radiate an atmosphere which suffused her being. He was never dull for a minute, and seemed to make her clever. At least, she brightened under his influence until all her best side was exhibited. She felt that she was more clever with him than with others. At least, he seemed to find so much in her to applaud. There was not the slightest touch of patronage. Drouet was full of it.

There had been something so personal, so subtle, in each meeting between them, both when Drouet was present and when he was absent, that Carrie could not speak of it without feeling a sense of difficulty. She was no talker. She could never arrange her thoughts in fluent order. It was always a matter of feeling with her, strong and deep. Each time there had been no sentence of importance which she could relate, and as for the glances and sensations, what woman would reveal them? Such things had never been between her and Drouet. As a matter of fact, they could never be. She had been dominated by distress and the enthusiastic forces of relief which Drouet represented at an opportune moment when she yielded to him. Now she was persuaded by secret current feelings which Drouet had never understood. Hurstwood's glance was as effective as the spoken words of a lover, and more. They called for no immediate decision, and could not be answered.

People in general attach too much importance to words. They are under the illusion that talking effects great results. As a matter of fact, words are, as a rule, the shallowest portion of all the argument. They but dimly represent the great surging feelings and desires which lie behind. When the distraction of the tongue is removed, the heart listens.

In this conversation she heard, instead of his words, the voices of the things which he represented. How suave was the counsel of his appearance! How feelingly did his superior state speak for itself! The growing desire he felt for her lay upon her spirit as a gentle hand. She did not need to tremble at all, because it was invisible; she did not need to worry over what other people would say—what she herself would say— because it had no tangibility. She was being pleaded with, persuaded, led into denying old rights and assuming new ones, and yet there were no words to prove it. Such conversation as was indulged in held the same relationship to the actual mental enactments of the twain that the low music of the orchestra does to the dramatic incident which it is used to cover.

"Have you ever seen the houses along the Lake Shore on the North Side?" asked Hurstwood.

"Why, I was just over there this afternoon—Mrs. Hale and I. Aren't they beautiful?"

"They're very fine," he answered.

"Oh, me," said Carrie, pensively. "I wish I could live in such a place."

"You're not happy," said Hurstwood, slowly, after a slight pause.

He had raised his eyes solemnly and was looking into her own. He assumed that he had struck a deep chord. Now was a slight chance to say a word in his own behalf. He leaned over quietly and continued his steady gaze. He felt the critical character of the period. She endeavoured to stir, but it was useless. The whole strength of a man's nature was working. He had good cause to urge him on. He looked and looked, and the longer the situation lasted the more difficult it became. The little shop-girl was getting into deep water. She was letting her few supports float away from her.

"Oh," she said at last, "you mustn't look at me like that."

"I can't help it," he answered.

She relaxed a little and let the situation endure, giving him strength.

"You are not satisfied with life, are you?"

"No," she answered, weakly.

He saw he was the master of the situation—he felt it. He reached over and touched her hand.

"You mustn't," she exclaimed, jumping up.

"I didn't intend to," he answered, easily.

She did not run away, as she might have done. She did not terminate the interview, but he drifted off into a pleasant field of thought with the readiest grace. Not long after he rose to go, and she felt that he was in power.

"You mustn't feel bad," he said, kindly; "things will straighten out in the course of time."

She made no answer, because she could think of nothing to say.

"We are good friends, aren't we?" he said, extending his hand.

"Yes," she answered.

"Not a word, then, until I see you again."

He retained a hold on her hand.

"I can't promise," she said, doubtfully.

"You must be more generous than that," he said, in such a simple way that she was touched.

"Let's not talk about it any more," she returned.

"All right," he said, brightening.

He went down the steps and into his cab. Carrie closed the door and ascended into her room. She undid her broad lace collar before the mirror and unfastened her pretty alligator belt which she had recently bought.

"I'm getting terrible," she said, honestly affected by a feeling of trouble and shame. "I don't seem to do anything right."

She unloosed her hair after a time, and let it hang in loose brown waves. Her mind was going over the events of the evening.

"I don't know," she murmured at last, " what I can do."

"Well," said Hurstwood as he rode away, "she likes me all right; that I know."

The aroused manager whistled merrily for a good four miles to his office an old melody that he had not recalled for fifteen years.

Chapter XIII

His Credentials Accepted: A Babel of Tongues

It was not quite two days after the scene between Carrie and Hurstwood in the Ogden Place parlour before he again put in his appearance. He had been thinking almost uninterruptedly of her. Her leniency had, in a way, inflamed his regard. He felt that he must succeed with her, and that speedily.

The reason for his interest, not to say fascination, was deeper than mere desire. It was a flowering out of feelings which had been withering in dry and almost barren soil for many years. It is probable that Carrie represented a better order of woman than had ever attracted him before. He had had no love affair since that which culminated in his marriage, and since then time and the world had taught him how raw and erroneous was his original judgment. Whenever he thought of it, he told himself that, if he had it to do over again, he would never marry such a woman. At the same time, his experience with women in general had lessened his respect for the sex. He maintained a cynical attitude, well grounded on numerous experiences. Such women as he had known were of nearly one type, selfish, ignorant, flashy. The wives of his friends were not inspiring to look upon. His own wife had developed a cold, commonplace nature which to him was anything but pleasing. What he knew of that underworld where grovel the beast-men of society (and he knew a great deal) had hardened his nature. He looked upon most women with suspicion—a single eye to the utility of beauty and dress. He followed them with a keen, suggestive glance. At the same time, he was not so dull but that a good woman commanded his respect. Personally, he did not attempt to analyse the marvel of a saintly woman. He would take off his hat, and would silence the light-tongued and the vicious in her presence—much as the Irish keeper of a Bowery hall will humble himself before a Sister of Mercy, and pay toll to charity with a willing and reverent hand. But he would not think much upon the question of why he did so.

A man in his situation who comes, after a long round of worthless or hardening experiences, upon a young, unsophisticated, innocent soul, is apt either to hold aloof, out of a sense of his own remoteness, or to draw near and become fascinated and elated by his discovery. It is only by a roundabout process that such men ever do draw near such a girl. They have no method, no understanding of how to ingratiate themselves in youthful favour, save when they find virtue in the toils. If, unfortunately, the fly has got caught in the net, the spider can come forth and talk business upon its own terms. So when maidenhood has wandered into the moil of the city, when it is brought within the circle of the "rounder" and the roué, even though it be at the outermost rim, they can come forth and use their alluring arts.

Hurstwood had gone, at Drouet's invitation, to meet a new baggage of fine clothes and pretty features. He entered, expecting to indulge in an evening of lightsome frolic, and then lose track of the newcomer forever. Instead he found a woman whose youth and beauty attracted him. In the mild light of Carrie's eye was nothing of the calculation of the mistress. In the diffident manner was nothing of the art of the courtesan. He saw at once that a mistake had been made, that some difficult conditions had pushed this troubled creature into his presence, and his interest was enlisted. Here sympathy sprang to the rescue, but it was not unmixed with selfishness. He wanted to win Carrie because he thought her fate mingled with his was better than if it were united with Drouet's. He envied the drummer his conquest as he had never envied any man in all the course of his experience.

Carrie was certainly better than this man, as she was superior, mentally, to Drouet. She came fresh from the air of the village, the light of the country still in her eye. Here was neither guile nor rapacity. There were slight inherited traits of both in her, but they were rudimentary. She was too full of wonder and desire to be greedy. She still looked about her upon the great maze of the city without understanding. Hurstwood felt the bloom and the youth. He picked her as he would the fresh fruit of a tree. He felt as fresh in her presence as one who is taken out of the flash of summer to the first cool breath of spring.

Carrie, left alone since the scene in question, and having no one with whom to counsel, had at first wandered from one strange mental conclusion to another, until at last, tired out, she gave it up. She owed something to Drouet, she thought. It did not seem more than yesterday that he had aided her when she was worried and distressed. She had the kindliest feelings for him in every way. She gave him credit for his good looks, his generous feelings, and even, in fact, failed to recollect his egotism when he was absent; but she could not feel any binding influence keeping her for him as against all others. In fact, such a thought had never had any grounding, even in Drouet's desires.

The truth is, that this goodly drummer carried the doom of all enduring relationships in his own lightsome manner and unstable fancy. He went merrily on, assured that he was alluring all, that affection followed tenderly in his wake, that things would endure unchangingly for his pleasure. When he missed some old face, or found some door finally shut to him, it did not grieve him deeply. He was too young, too successful. He would remain thus young in spirit until he was dead.

As for Hurstwood, he was alive with thoughts and feelings concerning Carrie. He had no definite plans regarding her, but he was determined to make her confess an affection for him. He thought he saw in her drooping eye, her unstable glance, her wavering manner, the symptoms of a budding passion. He wanted to stand near her and make her lay her hand in his—he wanted to find out what her next step would be—what the next sign of feeling for him would be. Such anxiety and enthusiasm had not affected him for years. He was a youth again in feeling—a cavalier in action.

In his position opportunity for taking his evenings out was excellent. He was a most faithful worker in general, and a man who commanded the confidence of his employers in so far as the distribution of his time was concerned. He could take such hours off as he chose, for it was well known that he fulfilled his managerial duties successfully, whatever time he might take. His grace, tact, and ornate appearance gave the place an air which was most essential, while at the same time his long experience made him a most excellent judge of its stock necessities. Bartenders and assistants might come and go, singly or in groups, but, so long as he was present, the host of old-time customers would barely notice the change. He gave the place the atmosphere to which they were used. Consequently, he arranged his hours very much to suit himself, taking now an afternoon, now an evening, but invariably returning between eleven and twelve to witness the last hour or two of the day's business and look after the closing details.

"You see that things are safe and all the employees are out when you go home, George," Moy had once remarked to him, and he never once, in all the period of his long service, neglected to do this. Neither of the owners had for years been in the resort after five in the afternoon, and yet their manager as faithfully fulfilled this request as if they had been there regularly to observe.

On this Friday afternoon, scarcely two days after his previous visit, he made up his mind to see Carrie. He could not stay away longer.

"Evans," he said, addressing the head barkeeper, "if any one calls, I will be back between four and five."

He hurried to Madison Street and boarded a horse-car, which carried him to Ogden Place in half an hour.

Carrie had thought of going for a walk, and had put on a light grey woollen dress with a jaunty double-breasted jacket. She had out her hat and gloves, and was fastening a white lace tie about her throat when the housemaid brought up the information that Mr. Hurstwood wished to see her.

She started slightly at the announcement, but told the girl to say that she would come down in a moment, and proceeded to hasten her dressing.

Carrie could not have told herself at this moment whether she was glad or sorry that the impressive manager was awaiting her presence. She was slightly flurried and tingling in the cheeks, but it was more nervousness than either fear or favour. She did not try to conjecture what the drift of the conversation would be. She only felt that she must be careful, and that Hurstwood had an indefinable fascination for her. Then she gave her tie its last touch with her fingers and went below.

The deep-feeling manager was himself a little strained in

the nerves by the thorough consciousness of his mission. He felt that he must make a strong play on this occasion, but now that the hour was come, and he heard Carrie's feet upon the stair, his nerve failed him. He sank a little in determination, for he was not so sure, after all, what her opinion might be.

When she entered the room, however, her appearance gave him courage. She looked simple and charming enough to strengthen the daring of any lover. Her apparent nervousness dispelled his own.

"How are you?" he said, easily. "I could not resist the temptation to come out this afternoon, it was so pleasant."

"Yes," said Carrie, halting before him, "I was just preparing to go for a walk myself."

"Oh, were you?" he said. "Supposing, then, you get your hat and we both go?"

They crossed the park and went west along Washington Boulevard, beautiful with its broad macadamised road, and large frame houses set back from the sidewalks. It was a street where many of the more prosperous residents of the West Side lived, and Hurstwood could not help feeling nervous over the publicity of it. They had gone but a few blocks when a livery stable sign in one of the side streets solved the difficulty for him. He would take her to drive along the new Boulevard.

The Boulevard at that time was little more than a country road. The part he intended showing her was much farther out on this same West Side, where there was scarcely a house. It connected Douglas Park with Washington or South Park, and was nothing more than a neatly *made* road, running due south for some five miles over an open, grassy prairie, and then due east over the same kind of prairie for the same distance. There was not a house to be encountered anywhere along the larger part of the route, and any conversation would be pleasantly free of interruption.

At the stable he picked a gentle horse, and they were soon out of range of either public observation or hearing.

"Can you drive?" he said, after a time.

"I never tried," said Carrie.

He put the reins in her hand, and folded his arms.

"You see there's nothing to it much," he said, smilingly.

"Not when you have a gentle horse," said Carrie.

"You can handle a horse as well as any one, after a little practice," he added, encouragingly.

He had been looking for some time for a break in the conversation when he could give it a serious turn. Once or twice he had held his peace, hoping that in silence her thoughts would take the colour of his own, but she had lightly continued the subject. Presently, however, his silence controlled the situation. The drift of his thoughts began to tell. He gazed fixedly at nothing in particular, as if he were thinking of something which concerned her not at all. His thoughts, however, spoke for themselves. She was very much aware that a climax was pending.

"Do you know," he said, "I have spent the happiest evenings in years since I have known you?"

"Have you?" she said, with assumed airiness, but still excited by the conviction which the tone of his voice carried.

"I was going to tell you the other evening," he added, "but somehow the opportunity slipped away."

Carrie was listening without attempting to reply. She could think of nothing worth while to say. Despite all the ideas concerning right which had troubled her vaguely since she had last seen him, she was now influenced again strongly in his favour.

"I came out here to-day," he went on, solemnly, "to tell you just how I feel—to see if you wouldn't listen to me."

Hurstwood was something of a romanticist after his kind. He was capable of strong feelings—often poetic ones—and under a stress of desire, such as the present, he waxed eloquent. That is, his feelings and his voice were coloured with that seeming repression and pathos which is the essence of eloquence.

"You know," he said, putting his hand on her arm, and keeping a strange silence while he formulated words, "that I love you?"

Carrie did not stir at the words. She was bound up completely in the man's atmosphere. He would have church-like silence in order to express his feelings, and she kept it. She did not move her eyes from the flat, open scene before her.

Hurstwood waited for a few moments, and then repeated the words.

"You must not say that," she said, weakly.

Her words were not convincing at all. They were the result of a feeble thought that something ought to be said. He paid no attention to them whatever.

"Carrie," he said, using her first name with sympathetic familiarity, "I want you to love me. You don't know how much I need some one to waste a little affection on me. I am practically alone. There is nothing in my life that is pleasant or delightful. It's all work and worry with people who are nothing to me."

As he said this, Hurstwood really imagined that his state was pitiful. He had the ability to get off at a distance and view himself objectively—of seeing what he wanted to see in the things which made up his existence. Now, as he spoke, his voice trembled with that peculiar vibration which is the result of tensity. It went ringing home to his companion's heart.

"Why, I should think," she said, turning upon him large eyes which were full of sympathy and feeling, "that you would be very happy. You know so much of the world."

"That is it," he said, his voice dropping to a soft minor, "I know too much of the world."

It was an important thing to her to hear one so well-positioned and powerful speaking in this manner. She could not help feeling the strangeness of her situation. How was it that, in so little a while, the narrow life of the country had fallen from her as a garment, and the city, with all its mystery, taken its place? Here was this greatest mystery, the man of money and affairs sitting beside her, appealing to her. Behold, he had ease and comfort, his strength was great, his position high, his clothing rich, and yet he was appealing to her. She could formulate no thought which would be just and right. She troubled herself no more upon the matter. She only basked in the warmth of his feeling, which was as a grateful blaze to one who is cold. Hurstwood glowed with his own intensity, and the heat of his passion was already melting the wax of his companion's scruples.

"You think," he said, "I am happy; that I ought not to

complain? If you were to meet all day with people who care absolutely nothing about you, if you went day after day to a place where there was nothing but show and indifference, if there was not one person in all those you knew to whom you could appeal for sympathy or talk to with pleasure, perhaps you would be unhappy too."

He was striking a chord now which found sympathetic response in her own situation. She knew what it was to meet with people who were indifferent, to walk alone amid so many who cared absolutely nothing about you. Had not she? Was not she at this very moment quite alone? Who was there among all whom she knew to whom she could appeal for sympathy? Not one. She was left to herself to brood and wonder.

"I could be content," went on Hurstwood, "if I had you to love me. If I had you to go to; you for a companion. As it is, I simply move about from place to place without any satisfaction. Time hangs heavily on my hands. Before you came I did nothing but idle and drift into anything that offered itself. Since you came—well, I've had you to think about."

The old illusion that here was some one who needed her aid began to grow in Carrie's mind. She truly pitied this sad, lonely figure. To think that all his fine state should be so barren for want of her; that he needed to make such an appeal when she herself was lonely and without anchor. Surely, this was too bad.

"I am not very bad," he said, apologetically, as if he owed it to her to explain on this score. "You think, probably, that I roam around, and get into all sorts of evil? I have been rather reckless, but I could easily come out of that. I need you to draw me back, if my life ever amounts to anything."

Carrie looked at him with the tenderness which virtue ever feels in its hope of reclaiming vice. How could such a man need reclaiming? His errors, what were they, that she could correct? Small they must be, where all was so fine. At worst, they were gilded affairs, and with what leniency are gilded errors viewed.

He put himself in such a lonely light that she was deeply moved.

"Is it that way?" she mused.

He slipped his arm about her waist, and she could not find the heart to draw away. With this free hand he seized upon her fingers. A breath of soft spring wind went bounding over the road, rolling some brown twigs of the previous autumn before it. The horse paced leisurely on, unguided.

"Tell me," he said, softly, "that you love me."

Her eyes fell consciously.

"Own to it, dear," he said, feelingly; "you do, don't you?"

She made no answer, but he felt his victory.

"Tell me," he said, richly, drawing her so close that their lips were near together. He pressed her hand warmly, and then released it to touch her cheek.

"You do?" he said, pressing his lips to her own.

For answer, her lips replied.

"Now," he said, joyously, his fine eyes ablaze, "you're my own girl, aren't you?"

By way of further conclusion, her head lay softly upon his shoulder.

Chapter XIV

CARRIE in her rooms that evening was in a fine glow, physically and mentally. She was deeply rejoicing in her affection for Hurstwood and his love, and looked forward with fine fancy to their next meeting Sunday night. They had agreed, without any feeling of enforced secrecy, that she should come down town and meet him, though, after all, the need of it was the cause.

Mrs. Hale, from her upper window, saw her come in.

"Um," she thought to herself, "she goes riding with another man when her husband is out of the city. He had better keep an eye on her."

The truth is that Mrs. Hale was not the only one who had a thought on this score. The house-maid who had welcomed Hurstwood had her opinion also. She had no particular regard for Carrie, whom she took to be cold and disagreeable. At the same time, she had a fancy for the merry and easy-mannered Drouet, who threw her a pleasant remark now and then, and in other ways extended her the evidence of that regard which he had for all members of the sex. Hurstwood was more reserved and critical in his manner. He did not appeal to this bodiced functionary in the same pleasant way. She wondered that he came so frequently, that Mrs. Drouet should go out with him this afternoon when Mr. Drouet was absent. She gave vent to her opinions in the kitchen where the cook was. As a result, a hum of gossip was set going which moved about the house in that secret manner common to gossip.

Carrie, now that she had yielded sufficiently to Hurstwood to express her affection, no longer troubled about her attitude towards him. Temporarily she gave little thought to Drouet, thinking only of the dignity and grace of her lover and of his consuming affection for her. On the first evening, she did little but go over the details of the afternoon. It was the first time her sympathies had ever been thoroughly aroused, and they threw a new light on her character. She had some power of initiative, latent before, which now began to exert itself. She looked more practically upon her state and began to see glimmerings of a way out. Hurstwood seemed a drag in the direction of honour. Her feelings were exceedingly creditable, in that they constructed out of these recent developments something which conquered freedom from dishonour. She had no idea what Hurstwood's next word would be. She only took his affection to be a fine thing, and appended better, more generous results accordingly.

As yet, Hurstwood had only a thought of pleasure without responsibility. He did not feel that he was doing anything to complicate his life. His position was secure, his home-life, if not satisfactory, was at least undisturbed, his personal liberty rather untrammelled. Carrie's love represented only so much added pleasure. He would enjoy this new gift over and above his ordinary allowance of pleasure. He would be happy with her and his own affairs would go on as they had, undisturbed.

On Sunday evening Carrie dined with him at a place he had selected in East Adams Street, and thereafter they took a cab to what was then a pleasant evening resort out on Cottage Grove Avenue near 39th Street. In the process of his declaration he soon realised that Carrie took his love upon a higher basis than he had anticipated. She kept him at a distance in a rather earnest way, and submitted only to those tender tokens of affection which better become the inexperienced lover. Hurstwood saw that she was not to be possessed for the asking, and deferred pressing his suit too warmly.

Since he feigned to believe in her married state he found that he had to carry out the part. His triumph, he saw, was still at a little distance. How far he could not guess.

They were returning to Ogden Place in the cab, when he asked:

"When will I see you again?"

"I don't know," she answered, wondering herself.

"Why not come down to The Fair," he suggested, "next Tuesday?"

She shook her head.

"Not so soon," she answered.

"I'll tell you what I'll do," he added. "I'll write you, care of this West Side Post-office. Could you call next Tuesday?"

Carrie assented.

The cab stopped one door out of the way according to his call.

"Good-night," he whispered, as the cab rolled away.

Unfortunately for the smooth progression of this affair, Drouet returned. Hurstwood was sitting in his imposing little office the next afternoon when he saw Drouet enter.

"Why, hello, Charles," he called affably; "back again?"

"Yes," smiled Drouet, approaching and looking in at the door.

Hurstwood arose.

"Well," he said, looking the drummer over, "rosy as ever, eh?"

They began talking of the people they knew and things that had happened.

"Been home yet?" finally asked Hurstwood.

"No, I am going, though," said Drouet.

"I remembered the little girl out there," said Hurstwood, "and called once. Thought you wouldn't want her left quite alone."

"Right you are," agreed Drouet. "How is she?"

"Very well," said Hurstwood. "Rather anxious about you, though. You'd better go out now and cheer her up."

"I will," said Drouet, smilingly.

"Like to have you both come down and go to the show with me Wednesday," concluded Hurstwood at parting.

"Thanks, old man," said his friend, "I'll see what the girl says and let you know."

They separated in the most cordial manner.

"There's a nice fellow," Drouet thought to himself as he turned the corner towards Madison.

"Drouet is a good fellow," Hurstwood thought to himself as he went back into his office, "but he's no man for Carrie."

The thought of the latter turned his mind into a most pleasant vein, and he wondered how he would get ahead of the drummer.

When Drouet entered Carrie's presence, he caught her in his arms as usual, but she responded to his kiss with a tremour of opposition.

"Well," he said, "I had a great trip."

"Did you? How did you come out with that La Crosse man you were telling me about?"

"Oh, fine; sold him a complete line. There was another fellow there, representing Burnstein, a regular hook-nosed sheeny, but he wasn't in it. I made him look like nothing at all."

As he undid his collar and unfastened his studs, preparatory to washing his face and changing his clothes, he dilated upon his trip. Carrie could not help listening with amusement to his animated descriptions.

"I tell you," he said, "I surprised the people at the office. I've sold more goods this last quarter than any other man of our house on the road. I sold three thousand dollars' worth in La Crosse."

He plunged his face in a basin of water, and puffed and blew as he rubbed his neck and ears with his hands, while Carrie gazed upon him with mingled thoughts of recollection and present judgment. He was still wiping his face, when he continued:

"I'm going to strike for a raise in June. They can afford to pay it, as much business as I turn in. I'll get it too, don't you forget."

"I hope you do," said Carrie.

"And then if that little real estate deal I've got on goes through, we'll get married," he said with a great show of earnestness, the while he took his place before the mirror and began brushing his hair.

"I don't believe you ever intend to marry me, Charlie," Carrie said ruefully. The recent protestations of Hurstwood had given her courage to say this.

"Oh, yes I do—course I do—what put that into your head?"

He had stopped his trifling before the mirror now and crossed over to her. For the first time Carrie felt as if she must move away from him.

"But you've been saying that so long," she said, looking with her pretty face upturned into his.

"Well, and I mean it too, but it takes money to live as I want to. Now, when I get this increase, I can come pretty near fixing things all right, and I'll do it. Now, don't you worry, girlie."

He patted her reassuringly upon the shoulder, but Carrie felt how really futile had been her hopes. She could clearly see that this easy-going soul intended no move in her behalf. He was simply letting things drift because he preferred the free round of his present state to any legal trammellings.

In contrast, Hurstwood appeared strong and sincere. He had no easy manner of putting her off. He sympathised with her and showed her what her true value was. He needed her, while Drouet did not care.

"Oh, no," she said remorsefully, her tone reflecting some of her own success and more of her helplessness, "you never will."

"Well, you wait a little while and see," he concluded. "I'll marry you all right."

Carrie looked at him and felt justified. She was looking for something which would calm her conscience, and here it was, a light, airy disregard of her claims upon his justice. He had faithfully promised to marry her, and this was the way he fulfilled his promise.

"Say," he said, after he had, as he thought, pleasantly disposed of the marriage question, "I saw Hurstwood to-day, and he wants us to go to the theatre with him."

Carrie started at the name, but recovered quickly enough to avoid notice.

"When?" she asked, with assumed indifference.

"Wednesday. We'll go, won't we?"

"If you think so," she answered, her manner being so enforcedly reserved as to almost excite suspicion. Drouet noticed something, but he thought it was due to her feelings concerning their talk about marriage.

"He called once, he said."

"Yes," said Carrie, "he was out here Sunday evening."

"Was he?" said Drouet. "I thought from what he said that he had called a week or so ago."

"So he did," answered Carrie, who was wholly unaware of what conversation her lovers might have held. She was all at sea mentally, and fearful of some entanglement which might ensue from what she would answer.

"Oh, then he called twice?" said Drouet, the first shade of misunderstanding showing in his face.

"Yes," said Carrie innocently, feeling now that Hurstwood must have mentioned but one call.

Drouet imagined that he must have misunderstood his friend. He did not attach particular importance to the information, after all.

"What did he have to say?" he queried, with slightly increased curiosity.

"He said he came because he thought I might be lonely. You hadn't been in there so long he wondered what had become of you."

"George is a fine fellow," said Drouet, rather gratified by his conception of the manager's interest. "Come on and we'll go out to dinner."

When Hurstwood saw that Drouet was back he wrote at once to Carrie, saying:

"I told him I called on you, dearest, when he was away. I did not say how often, but he probably thought once. Let me know of anything you may have said. Answer by special messenger when you get this, and, darling, I must see you. Let me know if you can't meet me at Jackson and Throop Streets Wednesday afternoon at two o'clock. I want to speak with you before we meet at the theatre."

Carrie received this Tuesday morning when she called at the West Side branch of the post-office, and answered at once.

"I said you called twice," she wrote. "He didn't seem to mind. I will try and be at Throop Street if nothing interferes. I seem to be getting very bad. It's wrong to act as I do, I know."

Hurstwood, when he met her as agreed, reassured her on this score.

"You mustn't worry, sweetheart," he said. "Just as soon as he goes on the road again we will arrange something. We'll fix it so that you won't have to deceive any one."

Carrie imagined that he would marry her at once, though he had not directly said so, and her spirits rose. She proposed to make the best of the situation until Drouet left again.

"Don't show any more interest in me than you ever have," Hurstwood counselled concerning the evening at the theatre.

"You mustn't look at me steadily then," she answered, mindful of the power of his eyes.

"I won't," he said, squeezing her hand at parting and giving the glance she had just cautioned against.

"There," she said playfully, pointing a finger at him.

"The show hasn't begun yet," he returned.

He watched her walk from him with tender solicitation. Such youth and prettiness reacted upon him more subtly than wine.

At the theatre things passed as they had in Hurstwood's favour. If he had been pleasing to Carrie before, how much more so was he now. His grace was more permeating because it found a readier medium. Carrie watched his every movement with pleasure. She almost forgot poor Drouet, who babbled on as if he were the host.

Hurstwood was too clever to give the slightest indication of a change. He paid, if anything, more attention to his old friend than usual, and yet in no way held him up to that subtle ridicule which a lover in favour may so secretly practise before the mistress of his heart. If anything, he felt the injustice of the game as it stood, and was not cheap enough to add to it the slightest mental taunt.

Only the play produced an ironical situation, and this was due to Drouet alone.

The scene was one in "The Covenant," in which the wife listened to the seductive voice of a lover in the absence of her husband.

"Served him right," said Drouet afterward, even in view of her keen expiation of her error. "I haven't any pity for a man who would be such a chump as that."

"Well, you never can tell," returned Hurstwood gently. "He probably thought he was right."

"Well, a man ought to be more attentive than that to his wife if he wants to keep her."

They had come out of the lobby and made their way through the showy crush about the entrance way.

"Say, mister," said a voice at Hurstwood's side, "would you mind giving me the price of a bed?"

Hurstwood was interestedly remarking to Carrie.

"Honest to God, mister, I'm without a place to sleep."

The plea was that of a gaunt-faced man of about thirty, who looked the picture of privation and wretchedness. Drouet was the first to see. He handed over a dime with an upwelling feeling of pity in his heart. Hurstwood scarcely noticed the incident. Carrie quickly forgot.

Chapter XV

THE IRK OF THE OLD TIES: THE MAGIC OF YOUTH

THE COMPLETE ignoring by Hurstwood of his own home came with the growth of his affection for Carrie. His actions, in all that related to his family, were of the most perfunctory kind. He sat at breakfast with his wife and children, absorbed in his own fancies, which reached far without the realm of their interests. He read his paper, which was heightened in interest by the shallowness of the themes discussed by his son and daughter. Between himself and his wife ran a river of indifference.

Now that Carrie had come, he was in a fair way to be blissful again. There was delight in going down town evenings. When he walked forth in the short days, the street lamps had a merry twinkle. He began to experience the almost forgotten feeling which hastens the lover's feet. When he looked at his fine clothes, he saw them with her eyes—and her eyes were young.

When in the flush of such feelings he heard his wife's voice, when the insistent demands of matrimony recalled him from dreams to a stale practice, how it grated. He then knew that this was a chain which bound his feet.

"George," said Mrs. Hurstwood, in that tone of voice which had long since come to be associated in his mind with demands, "we want you to get us a season ticket to the races."

"Do you want to go to all of them?" he said with a rising inflection.

"Yes," she answered.

The races in question were soon to open at Washington Park, on the South Side, and were considered quite society affairs among those who did not affect religious rectitude and conservatism. Mrs. Hurstwood had never asked for a whole season ticket before, but this year certain considerations decided her to get a box. For one thing, one of her neighbours, a certain Mr. and Mrs. Ramsey, who were possessors of money, made out of the coal business, had done so. In the next place, her favourite physician, Dr. Beale, a gentleman inclined to horses and betting, had talked with her concerning his intention to enter a two-year-old in the Derby. In the third place, she wished to exhibit Jessica, who was gaining in maturity and beauty, and whom she hoped to marry to a man of means. Her own desire to be about in such things and parade among her acquaintances and the common throng was as much an incentive as anything.

Hurstwood thought over the proposition a few moments without answering. They were in the sitting-room on the second floor, waiting for supper. It was the evening of his engagement with Carrie and Drouet to see "The Covenant," which had brought him home to make some alterations in his dress.

"You're sure separate tickets wouldn't do as well?" he asked, hesitating to say anything more rugged.

"No," she replied impatiently.

"Well," he said, taking offence at her manner, "you needn't get mad about it. I'm just asking you."

"I'm not mad," she snapped. "I'm merely asking you for a season ticket."

"And I'm telling you," he returned, fixing a clear, steady eye on her, "that it's no easy thing to get. I'm not sure whether the manager will give it to me."

He had been thinking all the time of his "pull" with the race-track magnates.

"We can buy it then," she exclaimed sharply.

"You talk easy," he said. "A season family ticket costs one hundred and fifty dollars."

"I'll not argue with you," she replied with determination. "I want the ticket and that's all there is to it."

She had risen, and now walked angrily out of the room.

"Well, you get it then," he said grimly, though in a modified tone of voice.

As usual, the table was one short that evening.

The next morning he had cooled down considerably, and later the ticket was duly secured, though it did not heal matters. He did not mind giving his family a fair share of all that he earned, but he did not like to be forced to provide against his will.

"Did you know, mother," said Jessica another day, "the Spencers are getting ready to go away?"

"No. Where, I wonder?"

"Europe," said Jessica. "I met Georgine yesterday and she told me. She just put on more airs about it."

"Did she say when?"

"Monday, I think. They'll get a notice in the papers again—they always do."

"Never mind," said Mrs. Hurstwood consolingly, "we'll go one of these days."

Hurstwood moved his eyes over the paper slowly, but said nothing.

"'We sail for Liverpool from New York,'" Jessica exclaimed, mocking her acquaintance. "'Expect to spend most of the "summah" in France,'—vain thing. As if it was anything to go to Europe."

"It must be if you envy her so much," put in Hurstwood.

It grated upon him to see the feeling his daughter displayed.

"Don't worry over them, my dear," said Mrs. Hurstwood.

"Did George get off?" asked Jessica of her mother another day, thus revealing something that Hurstwood had heard nothing about.

"Where has he gone?" he asked, looking up. He had never before been kept in ignorance concerning departures.

"He was going to Wheaton," said Jessica, not noticing the slight put upon her father.

"What's out there?" he asked, secretly irritated and chagrined to think that he should be made to pump for information in this manner.

"A tennis match," said Jessica.

"He didn't say anything to me," Hurstwood concluded, finding it difficult to refrain from a bitter tone.

"I guess he must have forgotten," exclaimed his wife blandly.

In the past he had always commanded a certain amount of respect, which was a compound of appreciation and awe. The familiarity which in part still existed between himself and his daughter he had courted. As it was, it did not go beyond the light assumption of words. The *tone* was always modest.

Whatever had been, however, had lacked affection, and now he saw that he was losing track of their doings. His knowledge was no longer intimate. He sometimes saw them at table, and sometimes did not. He heard of their doings occasionally, more often not. Some days he found that he was all at sea as to what they were talking about—things they had arranged to do or that they had done in his absence. More affecting was the feeling that there were little things going on of which he no longer heard. Jessica was beginning to feel that her affairs were her own. George, Jr., flourished about as if he were a man entirely and must needs have private matters. All this Hurstwood could see, and it left a trace of feeling, for he was used to being considered—in his official position, at least—and felt that his importance should not begin to wane here. To darken it all, he saw the same indifference and independence growing in his wife, while he looked on and paid the bills.

He consoled himself with the thought, however, that, after all, he was not without affection. Things might go as they would at his house, but he had Carrie outside of it. With his mind's eye he looked into her comfortable room in Ogden Place, where he had spent several such delightful evenings, and thought how charming it would be when Drouet was disposed of entirely and she was waiting evenings in cosey little quarters for him. That no cause would come up whereby Drouet would be led to inform Carrie concerning his married state, he felt hopeful. Things were going so smoothly that he believed they would not change. Shortly now he would persuade Carrie and all would be satisfactory.

The day after their theatre visit he began writing her regularly—a letter every morning, and begging her to do as much for him. He was not literary by any means, but experience of the world and his growing affection gave him somewhat of a style. This he exercised at his office desk with perfect deliberation. He purchased a box of delicately coloured and scented writing paper in monogram, which he kept locked in one of the drawers. His friends now wondered at the cleric and very official-looking nature of his position. The five bartenders viewed with respect the duties which could call a man to do so much desk-work and penmanship.

Hurstwood surprised himself with his fluency. By the natural law which governs all effort, what he wrote reacted upon him. He began to feel those subtleties which he could find words to express. With every expression came increased conception. Those inmost breathings which there found words took hold upon him. He thought Carrie worthy of all the affection he could there express.

Carrie was indeed worth loving if ever youth and grace are to command that token of acknowledgment from life in their bloom. Experience had not yet taken away that freshness of the spirit which is the charm of the body. Her soft eyes contained in their liquid lustre no suggestion of the knowledge of disappointment. She had been troubled in a way by doubt and longing, but these had made no deeper impression than could be traced in a certain open wistfulness of glance and speech. The mouth had the expression at times, in talking and in repose, of one who might be upon the verge of tears. It was not that grief was thus ever present. The pronunciation of certain syllables gave to her lips this peculiarity of formation—a formation as suggestive and moving as pathos itself.

There was nothing bold in her manner. Life had not taught her domination—superciliousness of grace, which is the lordly power of some women. Her longing for consideration was not sufficiently powerful to move her to demand it. Even now she lacked self-assurance, but there was that in what she had already experienced which left her a little less than timid. She wanted pleasure, she wanted position, and yet she was confused as to what these things might be. Every hour the kaleidoscope of human affairs threw a new lustre upon something, and therewith it became for her the desired—the all. Another shift of the box, and some other had become the beautiful, the perfect.

On her spiritual side, also, she was rich in feeling, as such a nature well might be. Sorrow in her was aroused by many a spectacle—an uncritical upwelling of grief for the weak and the helpless. She was constantly pained by the sight of the white-faced, ragged men who slopped desperately by her in a sort of wretched mental stupor. The poorly clad girls who went blowing by her window evenings, hurrying home from some of the shops of the West Side, she pitied from the depths of her heart. She would stand and bite her lips as they passed, shaking her little head and wondering. They had so little, she thought. It was so sad to be ragged and poor. The hang of faded clothes pained her eyes.

"And they have to work so hard!" was her only comment.

On the street sometimes she would see men working—Irishmen with picks, coal-heavers with great loads to shovel, Americans busy about some work which was a mere matter of strength—and they touched her fancy. Toil, now that she was free of it, seemed even a more desolate thing than when she was part of it. She saw it through a mist of fancy—a pale, sombre half-light, which was the essence of poetic feeling. Her old father, in his flour-dusted miller's suit, sometimes returned to her in memory, revived by a face in a window. A shoemaker pegging at his last, a blastman seen through a narrow window in some basement where iron was being melted, a bench-worker seen high aloft in some window, his coat off, his sleeves rolled up; these took her back in fancy to the details of the mill. She felt, though she seldom expressed them, sad thoughts upon this score. Her sympathies were ever with that under-world of toil from which she had so recently sprung, and which she best understood.

Though Hurstwood did not know it, he was dealing with one whose feelings were as tender and as delicate as this. He did not know, but it was this in her, after all, which attracted him. He never attempted to analyse the nature of his affection. It was sufficient that there was tenderness in her eye, weakness in her manner, good-nature and hope in her thoughts. He drew near this lily, which had sucked its waxen beauty and perfume from below a depth of waters which he had never penetrated, and out of ooze and mould which he could not understand. He drew near because it was waxen and fresh. It lightened his feelings for him. It made the morning worth while.

In a material way, she was considerably improved. Her awkwardness had all but passed, leaving, if anything, a quaint residue which was as pleasing as perfect grace. Her little shoes now fitted her smartly and had high heels. She had learned much about laces and those little neck-pieces which add so much to a woman's appearance. Her form had filled out until it was admirably plump and well-rounded.

Hurstwood wrote her one morning, asking her to meet him in Jefferson Park, Monroe Street. He did not consider it policy to call any more, even when Drouet was at home.

The next afternoon he was in the pretty little park by one, and had found a rustic bench beneath the green leaves of a lilac bush which bordered one of the paths. It was at that season of the year when the fulness of spring had not yet worn quite away. At a little pond near by some cleanly dressed children were sailing white canvas boats. In the shade of a green pagoda a bebuttoned officer of the law was resting, his arms folded, his club at rest in his belt. An old gardener was upon the lawn, with a pair of pruning shears, looking after some bushes. High overhead was the clear blue sky of the new summer, and in the thickness of the shiny green leaves of the trees hopped and twittered the busy sparrows.

Hurstwood had come out of his own home that morning feeling much of the same old annoyance. At his store he had idled, there being no need to write. He had come away to this place with the lightness of heart which characterises those who put weariness behind. Now, in the shade of this cool, green bush, he looked about him with the fancy of the lover. He heard the carts go lumbering by upon the neighbouring streets, but they were far off, and only buzzed upon his ear. The hum of the surrounding city was faint, the clang of an occasional bell was as music. He looked and dreamed a new dream of pleasure which concerned his present fixed condition not at all. He got back in fancy to the old Hurstwood, who was neither married nor fixed in a solid position for life. He remembered the light spirit in which he once looked after the girls—how he had danced, escorted them home, hung over their gates. He almost wished he was back there again— here in this pleasant scene he felt as if he were wholly free.

At two Carrie came tripping along the walk toward him, rosy and clean. She had just recently donned a sailor hat for the season with a band of pretty white-dotted blue silk. Her skirt was of a rich blue material, and her shirt waist matched it, with a thin stripe of blue upon a snow-white ground— stripes that were as fine as hairs. Her brown shoes peeped occasionally from beneath her skirt. She carried her gloves in her hand.

Hurstwood looked up at her with delight.

"You came, dearest," he said eagerly, standing to meet her and taking her hand.

"Of course," she said, smiling; "did you think I wouldn't?"

"I didn't know," he replied.

He looked at her forehead, which was moist from her brisk walk. Then he took out one of his own soft, scented silk handkerchiefs and touched her face here and there.

"Now," he said affectionately, "you're all right."

They were happy in being near one another—in looking into each other's eyes. Finally, when the long flush of delight had subsided, he said:

"When is Charlie going away again?"

"I don't know," she answered. "He says he has some things to do for the house here now."

Hurstwood grew serious, and he lapsed into quiet thought. He looked up after a time to say:

"Come away and leave him."

He turned his eyes to the boys with the boats, as if the request were of little importance.

"Where would we go?" she asked in much the same manner, rolling her gloves, and looking into a neighbouring tree.

"Where do you want to go?" he enquired.

There was something in the tone in which he said this which made her feel as if she must record her feelings against any local habitation.

"We can't stay in Chicago," she replied.

He had no thought that this was in her mind—that any removal would be suggested.

"Why not?" he asked softly.

"Oh, because," she said, "I wouldn't want to."

He listened to this with but dull perception of what it meant. It had no serious ring to it. The question was not up for immediate decision.

"I would have to give up my position," he said.

The tone he used made it seem as if the matter deserved only slight consideration. Carrie thought a little, the while enjoying the pretty scene.

"I wouldn't like to live in Chicago and him here," she said, thinking of Drouet.

"It's a big town, dearest," Hurstwood answered. "It would be as good as moving to another part of the country to move to the South Side."

He had fixed upon that region as an objective point.

"Anyhow," said Carrie, "I shouldn't want to get married as long as he is here. I wouldn't want to run away."

The suggestion of marriage struck Hurstwood forcibly. He saw clearly that this was her idea—he felt that it was not to be gotten over easily. Bigamy lightened the horizon of his shadowy thoughts for a moment. He wondered for the life of him how it would all come out. He could not see that he was making any progress save in her regard. When he looked at her now, he thought her beautiful. What a thing it was to have her love him, even if it be entangling! She increased in value in his eyes because of her objection. She was something to struggle for, and that was everything. How different from the women who yielded willingly! He swept the thought of them from his mind.

"And you don't know when he'll go away?" asked Hurstwood, quietly.

She shook her head.

He sighed.

"You're a determined little miss, aren't you?" he said, after a few moments, looking up into her eyes.

She felt a wave of feeling sweep over her at this. It was pride at what seemed his admiration—affection for the man who could feel this concerning her.

"No," she said coyly, "but what can I do?"

Again he folded his hands and looked away over the lawn into the street.

"I wish," he said pathetically, "you would come to me. I don't like to be away from you this way. What good is there in waiting? You're not any happier, are you?"

"Happier!" she exclaimed softly, "you know better than that."

"Here we are then," he went on in the same tone, " wasting our days. If you are not happy, do you think I am? I sit and write to you the biggest part of the time. I'll tell you what,

Carrie," he exclaimed, throwing sudden force of expression into his voice and fixing her with his eyes, "I can't live without you, and that's all there is to it. Now," he concluded, showing the palm of one of his white hands in a sort of at-an-end, helpless expression, "what shall I do?"

This shifting of the burden to her appealed to Carrie. The semblance of the load without the weight touched the woman's heart.

"Can't you wait a little while yet?" she said tenderly. "I'll try and find out when he's going."

"What good will it do?" he asked, holding the same strain of feeling.

"Well, perhaps we can arrange to go somewhere."

She really did not see anything clearer than before, but she was getting into that frame of mind where, out of sympathy, a woman yields.

Hurstwood did not understand. He was wondering how she was to be persuaded—what appeal would move her to forsake Drouet. He began to wonder how far her affection for him would carry her. He was thinking of some question which would make her tell.

Finally he hit upon one of those problematical propositions which often disguise our own desires while leading us to an understanding of the difficulties which others make for us, and so discover for us a way. It had not the slightest connection with anything intended on his part, and was spoken at random before he had given it a moment's serious thought.

"Carrie," he said, looking into her face and assuming a serious look which he did not feel, "suppose I were to come to you next week, or this week for that matter—to-night say— and tell you I had to go away—that I couldn't stay another minute and wasn't coming back any more—would you come with me?"

His sweetheart viewed him with the most affectionate glance, her answer ready before the words were out of his mouth.

"Yes," she said.

"You wouldn't stop to argue or arrange?"

"Not if you couldn't wait."

He smiled when he saw that she took him seriously, and

he thought what a chance it would afford for a possible junket of a week or two. He had a notion to tell her that he was joking and so brush away her sweet seriousness, but the effect of it was too delightful. He let it stand.

"Suppose we didn't have time to get married here?" he added, an afterthought striking him.

"If we got married as soon as we got to the other end of the journey it would be all right."

"I meant that," he said.

"Yes."

The morning seemed peculiarly bright to him now. He wondered whatever could have put such a thought into his head. Impossible as it was, he could not help smiling at its cleverness. It showed how she loved him. There was no doubt in his mind now, and he would find a way to win her.

"Well," he said, jokingly, "I'll come and get you one of these evenings," and then he laughed.

"I wouldn't stay with you, though, if you didn't marry me," Carrie added reflectively.

"I don't want you to," he said tenderly, taking her hand.

She was extremely happy now that she understood. She loved him the more for thinking that he would rescue her so. As for him, the marriage clause did not dwell in his mind. He was thinking that with such affection there could be no bar to his eventual happiness.

"Let's stroll about," he said gayly, rising and surveying all the lovely park.

"All right," said Carrie.

They passed the young Irishman, who looked after them with envious eyes.

" 'Tis a foine couple," he observed to himself. "They must be rich."

Chapter XVI

A Witless Aladdin: The Gate to the World

In the course of his present stay in Chicago, Drouet paid some slight attention to the secret order to which he belonged. During his last trip he had received a new light on its importance.

"I tell you," said another drummer to him, "it's a great thing. Look at Hazenstab. He isn't so deuced clever. Of course he's got a good house behind him, but that won't do alone. I tell you it's his degree. He's a way-up Mason, and that goes a long way. He's got a secret sign that stands for something."

Drouet resolved then and there that he would take more interest in such matters. So when he got back to Chicago he repaired to his local lodge headquarters.

"I say, Drouet," said Mr. Harry Quincel, an individual who was very prominent in this local branch of the Elks, "you're the man that can help us out."

It was after the business meeting and things were going socially with a hum. Drouet was bobbing around chatting and joking with a score of individuals whom he knew.

"What are you up to?" he inquired genially, turning a smiling face upon his secret brother.

"We're trying to get up some theatricals for two weeks from to-day, and we want to know if you don't know some young lady who could take a part—it's an easy part."

"Sure," said Drouet, "what is it?" He did not trouble to remember that he knew no one to whom he could appeal on this score. His innate good-nature, however, dictated a favourable reply.

"Well, now, I'll tell you what we are trying to do," went on Mr. Quincel. "We are trying to get a new set of furniture for the lodge. There isn't enough money in the treasury at the present time, and we thought we would raise it by a little entertainment."

"Sure," interrupted Drouet, "that's a good idea."

"Several of the boys around here have got talent. There's

Harry Burbeck, he does a fine black-face turn. Mac Lewis is all right at heavy dramatics. Did you ever hear him recite 'Over the Hills'?"

"Never did."

"Well, I tell you, he does it fine."

"And you want me to get some woman to take a part?" questioned Drouet, anxious to terminate the subject and get on to something else. "What are you going to play?"

" 'Under the Gaslight,' " said Mr. Quincel, mentioning Augustin Daly's famous production, which had worn from a great public success down to an amateur theatrical favourite, with many of the troublesome accessories cut out and the *dramatis personæ* reduced to the smallest possible number.

Drouet had seen this play some time in the past.

"That's it," he said; "that's a fine play. It will go all right. You ought to make a lot of money out of that."

"We think we'll do very well," Mr. Quincel replied. "Don't you forget now," he concluded, Drouet showing signs of restlessness; "some young woman to take the part of Laura."

"Sure, I'll attend to it."

He moved away, forgetting almost all about it the moment Mr. Quincel had ceased talking. He had not even thought to ask the time or place.

Drouet was reminded of his promise a day or two later by the receipt of a letter announcing that the first rehearsal was set for the following Friday evening, and urging him to kindly forward the young lady's address at once, in order that the part might be delivered to her.

"Now, who the deuce do I know?" asked the drummer reflectively, scratching his rosy ear. "I don't know any one that knows anything about amateur theatricals."

He went over in memory the names of a number of women he knew, and finally fixed on one, largely because of the convenient location of her home on the West Side, and promised himself that as he came out that evening he would see her. When, however, he started west on the car he forgot, and was only reminded of his delinquency by an item in the "Evening News"—a small three-line affair under the head of Secret Society Notes—which stated the Custer

Lodge of the Order of Elks would give a theatrical performance in Avery Hall on the 16th, when "Under the Gaslight" would be produced.

"George!" exclaimed Drouet, "I forgot that."

"What?" inquired Carrie.

They were at their little table in the room which might have been used for a kitchen, where Carrie occasionally served a meal. To-night the fancy had caught her, and the little table was spread with a pleasing repast.

"Why, my lodge entertainment. They're going to give a play, and they wanted me to get them some young lady to take a part."

"What is it they're going to play?"

" 'Under the Gaslight.' "

"When?"

"On the 16th."

"Well, why don't you?" asked Carrie.

"I don't know any one," he replied.

Suddenly he looked up.

"Say," he said, "how would you like to take the part?"

"Me?" said Carrie. "I can't act."

"How do you know?" questioned Drouet reflectively.

"Because," answered Carrie, "I never did."

Nevertheless, she was pleased to think he would ask. Her eyes brightened, for if there was anything that enlisted her sympathies it was the art of the stage.

True to his nature, Drouet clung to this idea as an easy way out.

"That's nothing. You can act all you have to down there."

"No, I can't," said Carrie weakly, very much drawn toward the proposition and yet fearful.

"Yes, you can. Now, why don't you do it? They need some one, and it will be lots of fun for you."

"Oh, no, it won't," said Carrie seriously.

"You'd like that. I know you would. I've seen you dancing around here and giving imitations and that's why I asked you. You're clever enough, all right."

"No, I'm not," said Carrie shyly.

"Now, I'll tell you what you do. You go down and see about it. It'll be fun for you. The rest of the company isn't going to be any good. They haven't any experience. What do they know about theatricals?"

He frowned as he thought of their ignorance.

"Hand me the coffee," he added.

"I don't believe I could act, Charlie," Carrie went on pettishly. "You don't think I could, do you?"

"Sure. Out o' sight. I bet you make a hit. Now you want to go, I know you do. I knew it when I came home. That's why I asked you."

"What is the play, did you say?"

" 'Under the Gaslight.' "

"What part would they want me to take?"

"Oh, one of the heroines—I don't know."

"What sort of a play is it?"

"Well," said Drouet, whose memory for such things was not the best, "it's about a girl who gets kidnapped by a couple of crooks—a man and a woman that live in the slums. She had some money or something and they wanted to get it. I don't know now how it did go exactly."

"Don't you know what part I would have to take?"

"No, I don't, to tell the truth." He thought a moment. "Yes, I do, too. Laura, that's the thing—you're to be Laura."

"And you can't remember what the part is like?"

"To save me, Cad, I can't," he answered. "I ought to, too; I've seen the play enough. There's a girl in it that was stolen when she was an infant—was picked off the street or something—and she's the one that's hounded by the two old criminals I was telling you about." He stopped with a mouthful of pie poised on a fork before his face. "She comes very near getting drowned—no, that's not it. I'll tell you what I'll do," he concluded hopelessly, "I'll get you the book. I can't remember now for the life of me."

"Well, I don't know," said Carrie, when he had concluded, her interest and desire to shine dramatically struggling with her timidity for the mastery. "I might go if you thought I'd do all right."

"Of course, you'll do," said Drouet, who, in his efforts to enthuse Carrie, had interested himself. "Do you think I'd come home here and urge you to do something that I didn't think you would make a success of? You can act all right. It'll be good for you."

"When must I go?" said Carrie, reflectively.

"The first rehearsal is Friday night. I'll get the part for you to-night."

"All right," said Carrie resignedly, "I'll do it, but if I make a failure now it's your fault."

"You won't fail," assured Drouet. "Just act as you do around here. Be natural. You're all right. I've often thought you'd make a corking good actress."

"Did you really?" asked Carrie.

"That's right," said the drummer.

He little knew as he went out of the door that night what a secret flame he had kindled in the bosom of the girl he left behind. Carrie was possessed of that sympathetic, impressionable nature which, ever in the most developed form, has been the glory of the drama. She was created with that passivity of soul which is always the mirror of the active world. She possessed an innate taste for imitation and no small ability. Even without practice, she could sometimes restore dramatic situations she had witnessed by re-creating, before her mirror, the expressions of the various faces taking part in the scene. She loved to modulate her voice after the conventional manner of the distressed heroine, and repeat such pathetic fragments as appealed most to her sympathies. Of late, seeing the airy grace of the *ingenue* in several well-constructed plays, she had been moved to secretly imitate it, and many were the little movements and expressions of the body in which she indulged from time to time in the privacy of her chamber. On several occasions, when Drouet had caught her admiring herself, as he imagined, in the mirror, she was doing nothing more than recalling some little grace of the mouth or the eyes which she had witnessed in another. Under his airy accusation she mistook this for vanity and accepted the blame with a faint sense of error, though, as a matter of fact, it was nothing more than the first subtle outcroppings of an artistic nature, endeavouring to re-create the perfect likeness of some phase of beauty which appealed to her. In such feeble tendencies, be it known, such outworking of desire to reproduce life, lies the basis of all dramatic art.

Now, when Carrie heard Drouet's laudatory opinion of her dramatic ability, her body tingled with satisfaction. Like the flame which welds the loosened particles into a solid mass, his words united those floating wisps of feeling which she had felt, but never believed, concerning her possible ability, and made them into a gaudy shred of hope. Like all human beings, she had a touch of vanity. She felt that she could do things if she only had a chance. How often had she looked at the well-dressed actresses on the stage and wondered how she would look, how delightful she would feel if only she were in their place. The glamour, the tense situation, the fine clothes, the applause, these had lured her until she felt that she, too, could act—that she, too, could compel acknowledgment of power. Now she was told that she really could—that little things she had done about the house had made even him feel her power. It was a delightful sensation while it lasted.

When Drouet was gone, she sat down in her rocking-chair by the window to think about it. As usual, imagination exaggerated the possibilities for her. It was as if he had put fifty cents in her hand and she had exercised the thoughts of a thousand dollars. She saw herself in a score of pathetic situations in which she assumed a tremulous voice and suffering manner. Her mind delighted itself with scenes of luxury and refinement, situations in which she was the cynosure of all eyes, the arbiter of all fates. As she rocked to and fro she felt the tensity of woe in abandonment, the magnificence of wrath after deception, the languour of sorrow after defeat. Thoughts of all the charming women she had seen in plays— every fancy, every illusion which she had concerning the stage—now came back as a returning tide after the ebb. She built up feelings and a determination which the occasion did not warrant.

Drouet dropped in at the lodge when he went down town, and swashed around with a great *air*, as Quincel met him.

"Where is that young lady you were going to get for us?" asked the latter.

"I've got her," said Drouet.

"Have you?" said Quincel, rather surprised by his promptness; "that's good. What's her address?" and he pulled out his note-book in order to be able to send her part to her.

"You want to send her her part?" asked the drummer.

"Yes."

"Well, I'll take it. I'm going right by her house in the morning."

"What did you say her address was? We only want it in case we have any information to send her."

"Twenty-nine Ogden Place."

"And her name?"

"Carrie Madenda," said the drummer, firing at random. The lodge members knew him to be single.

"That sounds like somebody that can act, doesn't it?" said Quincel.

"Yes, it does."

He took the part home to Carrie and handed it to her with the manner of one who does a favour.

"He says that's the best part. Do you think you can do it?"

"I don't know until I look it over. You know I'm afraid, now that I've said I would."

"Oh, go on. What have you got to be afraid of? It's a cheap company. The rest of them aren't as good as you are."

"Well, I'll see," said Carrie, pleased to have the part, for all her misgivings.

He sidled around, dressing and fidgeting before he arranged to make his next remark.

"They were getting ready to print the programmes," he said, "and I gave them the name of Carrie Madenda. Was that all right?"

"Yes, I guess so," said his companion, looking up at him. She was thinking it was slightly strange.

"If you didn't make a hit, you know," he went on.

"Oh, yes," she answered, rather pleased now with his caution. It was clever for Drouet.

"I didn't want to introduce you as my wife, because you'd feel worse then if you didn't *go*. They all know me so well. But you'll *go* all right. Anyhow, you'll probably never meet any of them again."

"Oh, I don't care," said Carrie desperately. She was determined now to have a try at the fascinating game.

Drouet breathed a sigh of relief. He had been afraid that

he was about to precipitate another conversation upon the marriage question.

The part of Laura, as Carrie found out when she began to examine it, was one of suffering and tears. As delineated by Mr. Daly, it was true to the most sacred traditions of melodrama as he found it when he began his career. The sorrowful demeanour, the tremolo music, the long, explanatory, cumulative addresses, all were there.

"Poor fellow," read Carrie, consulting the text and drawing her voice out pathetically. "Martin, be sure and give him a glass of wine before he goes."

She was surprised at the briefness of the entire part, not knowing that she must be on the stage while others were talking, and not only be there, but also keep herself in harmony with the dramatic movement of the scenes.

"I think I can do that, though," she concluded.

When Drouet came the next night, she was very much satisfied with her day's study.

"Well, how goes it, Caddie?" he said.

"All right," she laughed. "I think I have it memorised nearly."

"That's good," he said. "Let's hear some of it."

"Oh, I don't know whether I can get up and say it off here," she said bashfully.

"Well, I don't know why you shouldn't. It'll be easier here than it will there."

"I don't know about that," she answered.

Eventually she took off the ball-room episode with considerable feeling, forgetting, as she got deeper in the scene, all about Drouet, and letting herself rise to a fine state of feeling.

"Good," said Drouet; "fine; out o' sight! You're all right, Caddie, I tell you."

He was really moved by her excellent representation and the general appearance of the pathetic little figure as it swayed and finally fainted to the floor. He had bounded up to catch her, and now held her laughing in his arms.

"Ain't you afraid you'll hurt yourself?" he asked.

"Not a bit."

"Well, you're a wonder. Say, I never knew you could do anything like that."

"I never did, either," said Carrie merrily, her face flushed with delight.

"Well, you can bet that you're all right," said Drouet. "You can take my word for that. You won't fail."

Chapter XVII

A Glimpse Through the Gateway:
Hope Lightens the Eye

THE, TO CARRIE, very important theatrical performance was to take place at the Avery on conditions which were to make it more noteworthy than was at first anticipated. The little dramatic student had written to Hurstwood the very morning her part was brought her that she was going to take part in a play.

"I really am," she wrote, feeling that he might take it as a jest; "I have my part now, honest, truly."

Hurstwood smiled in an indulgent way as he read this.

"I wonder what it is going to be? I must see that."

He answered at once, making a pleasant reference to her ability. "I haven't the slightest doubt you will make a success. You must come to the park to-morrow morning and tell me all about it."

Carrie gladly complied, and revealed all the details of the undertaking as she understood it.

"Well," he said, "that's fine. I'm glad to hear it. Of course, you will do well, you're so clever."

He had truly never seen so much spirit in the girl before. Her tendency to discover a touch of sadness had for the nonce disappeared. As she spoke her eyes were bright, her cheeks red. She radiated much of the pleasure which her undertakings gave her. For all her misgivings—and they were as plentiful as the moments of the day—she was still happy. She could not repress her delight in doing this little thing which, to an ordinary observer, had no importance at all.

Hurstwood was charmed by the development of the fact that the girl had capabilities. There is nothing so inspiring in life as the sight of a legitimate ambition, no matter how incipient. It gives colour, force, and beauty to the possessor.

Carrie was now lightened by a touch of this divine afflatus. She drew to herself commendation from her two admirers which she had not earned. Their affection for her naturally heightened their perception of what she was trying to do and their approval of what she did. Her inexperience conserved her own exuberant fancy, which ran riot with every straw of opportunity, making of it a golden divining rod whereby the treasure of life was to be discovered.

"Let's see," said Hurstwood, "I ought to know some of the boys in the lodge. I'm an Elk myself."

"Oh, you mustn't let him know I told you."

"That's so," said the manager.

"I'd like for you to be there, if you want to come, but I don't see how you can unless he asks you."

"I'll be there," said Hurstwood affectionately. "I can fix it so he won't know you told me. You leave it to me."

This interest of the manager was a large thing in itself for the performance, for his standing among the Elks was something worth talking about. Already he was thinking of a box with some friends, and flowers for Carrie. He would make it a dress-suit affair and give the little girl a chance.

Within a day or two, Drouet dropped into the Adams Street resort, and he was at once spied by Hurstwood. It was at five in the afternoon and the place was crowded with merchants, actors, managers, politicians, a goodly company of rotund, rosy figures, silk-hatted, starchy-bosomed, beringed and bescarfpinned to the queen's taste. John L. Sullivan, the pugilist, was at one end of the glittering bar, surrounded by a company of loudly dressed sports, who were holding a most animated conversation. Drouet came across the floor with a festive stride, a new pair of tan shoes squeaking audibly at his progress.

"Well, sir," said Hurstwood, "I was wondering what had become of you. I thought you had gone out of town again."

Drouet laughed.

"If you don't report more regularly we'll have to cut you off the list."

"Couldn't help it," said the drummer, "I've been busy."

They strolled over toward the bar amid the noisy, shifting company of notables. The dressy manager was shaken by the hand three times in as many minutes.

"I hear your lodge is going to give a performance," observed Hurstwood, in the most offhand manner.

"Yes, who told you?"

"No one," said Hurstwood. "They just sent me a couple of tickets, which I can have for two dollars. Is it going to be any good?"

"I don't know," replied the drummer. "They've been trying to get me to get some woman to take a part."

"I wasn't intending to go," said the manager easily. "I'll subscribe, of course. How are things over there?"

"All right. They're going to fit things up out of the proceeds."

"Well," said the manager, "I hope they make a success of it. Have another?"

He did not intend to say any more. Now, if he should appear on the scene with a few friends, he could say that he had been urged to come along. Drouet had a desire to wipe out the possibility of confusion.

"I think the girl is going to take a part in it," he said abruptly, after thinking it over.

"You don't say so! How did that happen?"

"Well, they were short and wanted me to find them some one. I told Carrie, and she seems to want to try."

"Good for her," said the manager. "It'll be a real nice affair. Do her good, too. Has she ever had any experience?"

"Not a bit."

"Oh, well, it isn't anything very serious."

"She's clever, though," said Drouet, casting off any imputation against Carrie's ability. "She picks up her part quick enough."

"You don't say so!" said the manager.

"Yes, sir; she surprised me the other night. By George, if she didn't."

"We must give her a nice little send-off," said the manager. "I'll look after the flowers."

Drouet smiled at his good-nature.

"After the show you must come with me and we'll have a little supper."

"I think she'll do all right," said Drouet.

"I want to see her. She's got to do all right. We'll make her," and the manager gave one of his quick, steely half-smiles, which was a compound of good-nature and shrewdness.

Carrie, meanwhile, attended the first rehearsal. At this performance Mr. Quincel presided, aided by Mr. Millice, a young man who had some qualifications of past experience, which were not exactly understood by any one. He was so experienced and so business-like, however, that he came very near being rude—failing to remember, as he did, that the individuals he was trying to instruct were volunteer players and not salaried underlings.

"Now, Miss Madenda," he said, addressing Carrie, who stood in one part uncertain as to what move to make, "you don't want to stand like that. Put expression in your face. Remember, you are troubled over the intrusion of the stranger. Walk so," and he struck out across the Avery stage in a most drooping manner.

Carrie did not exactly fancy the suggestion, but the novelty of the situation, the presence of strangers, all more or less nervous, and the desire to do anything rather than make a failure, made her timid. She walked in imitation of her mentor as requested, inwardly feeling that there was something strangely lacking.

"Now, Mrs. Morgan," said the director to one young married woman who was to take the part of Pearl, "you sit here. Now, Mr. Bamberger, you stand here, so. Now, what is it you say?"

"Explain," said Mr. Bamberger feebly. He had the part of Ray, Laura's lover, the society individual who was to waver in his thoughts of marrying her, upon finding that she was a waif and a nobody by birth.

"How is that—what does your text say?"

"Explain," repeated Mr. Bamberger, looking intently at his part.

"Yes, but it also says," the director remarked, "that you are to look shocked. Now, say it again, and see if you can't look shocked."

"Explain!" demanded Mr. Bamberger vigorously.

"No, no, that won't do! Say it this way—*explain*."

"Explain," said Mr. Bamberger, giving a modified imitation.

"That's better. Now go on."

"One night," resumed Mrs. Morgan, whose lines came

next, "father and mother were going to the opera. When they were crossing Broadway, the usual crowd of children accosted them for alms——"

"Hold on," said the director, rushing forward, his arm extended. "Put more feeling into what you are saying."

Mrs. Morgan looked at him as if she feared a personal assault. Her eye lightened with resentment.

"Remember, Mrs. Morgan," he added, ignoring the gleam, but modifying his manner, "that you're detailing a pathetic story. You are now supposed to be telling something that is a grief to you. It requires feeling, repression, thus: 'The usual crowd of children accosted them for alms.' "

"All right," said Mrs. Morgan.

"Now, go on."

"As mother felt in her pocket for some change, her fingers touched a cold and trembling hand which had clutched her purse."

"Very good," interrupted the director, nodding his head significantly.

"A pickpocket! Well!" exclaimed Mr. Bamberger, speaking the lines that here fell to him.

"No, no, Mr. Bamberger," said the director, approaching, "not that way. 'A pickpocket—well?' so. That's the idea."

"Don't you think," said Carrie weakly, noticing that it had not been proved yet whether the members of the company knew their lines, let alone the details of expression, "that it would be better if we just went through our lines once to see if we know them? We might pick up some points."

"A very good idea, Miss Madenda," said Mr. Quincel, who sat at the side of the stage, looking serenely on and volunteering opinions which the director did not heed.

"All right," said the latter, somewhat abashed, "it might be well to do it." Then brightening, with a show of authority, "Suppose we run right through, putting in as much expression as we can."

"Good," said Mr. Quincel.

"This hand," resumed Mrs. Morgan, glancing up at Mr. Bamberger and down at her book, as the lines proceeded, "my mother grasped in her own, and so tight that a small, feeble voice uttered an exclamation of pain. Mother looked down, and there beside her was a little ragged girl."

"Very good," observed the director, now hopelessly idle.

"The thief!" exclaimed Mr. Bamberger.

"Louder," put in the director, finding it almost impossible to keep his hands off.

"The thief!" roared poor Bamberger.

"Yes, but a thief hardly six years old, with a face like an angel's. 'Stop,' said my mother. 'What are you doing?'

" 'Trying to steal,' said the child.

" 'Don't you know that it is wicked to do so?' asked my father.

" 'No,' said the girl, 'but it is dreadful to be hungry.'

" 'Who told you to steal?' asked my mother.

" 'She—there,' said the child, pointing to a squalid woman in a doorway opposite, who fled suddenly down the street. 'That is old Judas,' said the girl."

Mrs. Morgan read this rather flatly, and the director was in despair. He fidgeted around, and then went over to Mr. Quincel.

"What do you think of them?" he asked.

"Oh, I guess we'll be able to whip them into shape," said the latter, with an air of strength under difficulties.

"I don't know," said the director. "That fellow Bamberger strikes me as being a pretty poor shift for a lover."

"He's all we've got," said Quincel, rolling up his eyes. "Harrison went back on me at the last minute. Who else can we get?"

"I don't know," said the director. "I'm afraid he'll never pick up."

At this moment Bamberger was exclaiming, "Pearl, you are joking with me."

"Look at that now," said the director, whispering behind his hand. "My Lord! what can you do with a man who drawls out a sentence like that?"

"Do the best you can," said Quincel consolingly.

The rendition ran on in this wise until it came to where Carrie, as Laura, comes into the room to explain to Ray, who, after hearing Pearl's statement about her birth, had written the letter repudiating her, which, however, he did not deliver. Bamberger was just concluding the words of Ray, "I must go before she returns. Her step! Too late," and was cramming the letter in his pocket, when she began sweetly with:

"Ray!"

"Miss—Miss Courtland," Bamberger faltered weakly.

Carrie looked at him a moment and forgot all about the company present. She began to feel the part, and summoned an indifferent smile to her lips, turning as the lines directed and going to a window, as if he were not present. She did it with a grace which was fascinating to look upon.

"Who is that woman?" asked the director, watching Carrie in her little scene with Bamberger.

"Miss Madenda," said Quincel.

"I know her name," said the director, "but what does she do?"

"I don't know," said Quincel. "She's a friend of one of our members."

"Well, she's got more gumption than any one I've seen here so far—seems to take an interest in what she's doing."

"Pretty, too, isn't she?" said Quincel.

The director strolled away without answering.

In the second scene, where she was supposed to face the company in the ball-room, she did even better, winning the smile of the director, who volunteered, because of her fascination for him, to come over and speak with her.

"Were you ever on the stage?" he asked insinuatingly.

"No," said Carrie.

"You do so well, I thought you might have had some experience."

Carrie only smiled consciously.

He walked away to listen to Bamberger, who was feebly spouting some ardent line.

Mrs. Morgan saw the drift of things and gleamed at Carrie with envious and snapping black eyes.

"She's some cheap professional," she gave herself the satisfaction of thinking, and scorned and hated her accordingly.

The rehearsal ended for one day, and Carrie went home feeling that she had acquitted herself satisfactorily. The words of the director were ringing in her ears, and she longed for an opportunity to tell Hurstwood. She wanted him to know just how well she was doing. Drouet, too, was an object for her confidences. She could hardly wait until he should ask her, and yet she did not have the vanity to bring it up. The drummer, however, had another line of thought to-night, and her little experience did not appeal to him as important. He let the conversation drop, save for what she chose to recite without solicitation, and Carrie was not good at that. He took it for granted that she was doing very well and he was relieved of further worry. Consequently he threw Carrie into repression, which was irritating. She felt his indifference keenly and longed to see Hurstwood. It was as if he were now the only friend she had on earth. The next morning Drouet was interested again, but the damage had been done.

She got a pretty letter from the manager, saying that by the time she got it he would be waiting for her in the park. When she came, he shone upon her as the morning sun.

"Well, my dear," he asked, "how did you come out?"

"Well enough," she said, still somewhat reduced after Drouet.

"Now, tell me just what you did. Was it pleasant?"

Carrie related the incidents of the rehearsal, warming up as she proceeded.

"Well, that's delightful," said Hurstwood. "I'm so glad. I must get over there to see you. When is the next rehearsal?"

"Tuesday," said Carrie, "but they don't allow visitors."

"I imagine I could get in," said Hurstwood significantly.

She was completely restored and delighted by his consideration, but she made him promise not to come around.

"Now, you must do your best to please me," he said encouragingly. "Just remember that I want you to succeed. We will make the performance worth while. You do that now."

"I'll try," said Carrie, brimming with affection and enthusiasm.

"That's the girl," said Hurstwood fondly. "Now, remember," shaking an affectionate finger at her, "your best."

"I will," she answered, looking back.

The whole earth was brimming sunshine that morning. She tripped along, the clear sky pouring liquid blue into her soul.

Oh, blessed are the children of endeavour in this, that they try and are hopeful. And blessed also are they who, knowing, smile and approve.

Chapter XVIII

BY THE EVENING of the 16th the subtle hand of Hurstwood had made itself apparent. He had given the word among his friends—and they were many and influential—that here was something which they ought to attend, and, as a consequence, the sale of tickets by Mr. Quincel, acting for the lodge, had been large. Small four-line notes had appeared in all of the daily newspapers. These he had arranged for by the aid of one of his newspaper friends on the "Times," Mr. Harry McGarren, the managing editor.

"Say, Harry," Hurstwood said to him one evening, as the latter stood at the bar drinking before wending his belated way homeward, "you can help the boys out, I guess."

"What is it?" said McGarren, pleased to be consulted by the opulent manager.

"The Custer Lodge is getting up a little entertainment for their own good, and they'd like a little newspaper notice. You know what I mean—a squib or two saying that it's going to take place."

"Certainly," said McGarren, "I can fix that for you, George."

At the same time Hurstwood kept himself wholly in the background. The members of Custer Lodge could scarcely understand why their little affair was taking so well. Mr. Harry Quincel was looked upon as quite a star for this sort of work.

By the time the 16th had arrived Hurstwood's friends had rallied like Romans to a senator's call. A well-dressed, good-natured, flatteringly-inclined audience was assured from the moment he thought of assisting Carrie.

That little student had mastered her part to her own satisfaction, much as she trembled for her fate when she should once face the gathered throng, behind the glare of the footlights. She tried to console herself with the thought that a score of other persons, men and women, were equally tremulous concerning the outcome of their efforts, but she could not disassociate the general danger from her own individual liability. She feared that she would forget her lines, that she might be unable to master the feeling which she now felt concerning her own movements in the play. At times she wished that she had never gone into the affair; at others, she trembled lest she should be paralysed with fear and stand white and gasping, not knowing what to say and spoiling the entire performance.

In the matter of the company, Mr. Bamberger had disappeared. That hopeless example had fallen under the lance of the director's criticism. Mrs. Morgan was still present, but envious and determined, if for nothing more than spite, to do as well as Carrie at least. A loafing professional had been called in to assume the rôle of Ray, and, while he was a poor stick of his kind, he was not troubled by any of those qualms which attack the spirit of those who have never faced an audience. He swashed about (cautioned though he was to maintain silence concerning his past theatrical relationships) in such a self-confident manner that he was like to convince every one of his identity by mere matter of circumstantial evidence.

"It is so easy," he said to Mrs. Morgan, in the usual affected stage voice. "An audience would be the last thing to trouble me. It's the spirit of the part, you know, that is difficult."

Carrie disliked his appearance, but she was too much the actress not to swallow his qualities with complaisance, seeing that she must suffer his fictitious love for the evening.

At six she was ready to go. Theatrical paraphernalia had been provided over and above her care. She had practised her make-up in the morning, had rehearsed and arranged her material for the evening by one o'clock, and had gone home to have a final look at her part, waiting for the evening to come.

On this occasion the lodge sent a carriage. Drouet rode with her as far as the door, and then went about the neighbouring stores, looking for some good cigars. The little actress marched nervously into her dressing-room and began that painfully anticipated matter of make-up which was to transform her, a simple maiden, to Laura, The Belle of Society.

The flare of the gas-jets, the open trunks, suggestive of

travel and display, the scattered contents of the make-up box—rouge, pearl powder, whiting, burnt cork, India ink, pencils for the eyelids, wigs, scissors, looking-glasses, drapery—in short, all the nameless paraphernalia of disguise, have a remarkable atmosphere of their own. Since her arrival in the city many things had influenced her, but always in a far-removed manner. This new atmosphere was more friendly. It was wholly unlike the great brilliant mansions which waved her coldly away, permitting her only awe and distant wonder. This took her by the hand kindly, as one who says, "My dear, come in." It opened for her as if for its own. She had wondered at the greatness of the names upon the bill-boards, the marvel of the long notices in the papers, the beauty of the dresses upon the stage, the atmosphere of carriages, flowers, refinement. Here was no illusion. Here was an open door to see all of that. She had come upon it as one who stumbles upon a secret passage, and, behold, she was in the chamber of diamonds and delight!

As she dressed with a flutter, in her little stage room, hearing the voices outside, seeing Mr. Quincel hurrying here and there, noting Mrs. Morgan and Mrs. Hoagland at their nervous work of preparation, seeing all the twenty members of the cast moving about and worrying over what the result would be, she could not help thinking what a delight this would be if it would endure; how perfect a state, if she could only do well now, and then some time get a place as a real actress. The thought had taken a mighty hold upon her. It hummed in her ears as the melody of an old song.

Outside in the little lobby another scene was being enacted. Without the interest of Hurstwood, the little hall would probably have been comfortably filled, for the members of the lodge were moderately interested in its welfare. Hurstwood's word, however, had gone the rounds. It was to be a full-dress affair. The four boxes had been taken. Dr. Norman McNeill Hale and his wife were to occupy one. This was quite a card. C. R. Walker, dry-goods merchant and possessor of at least two hundred thousand dollars, had taken another; a well-known coal merchant had been induced to take the third, and Hurstwood and his friends the fourth. Among the latter was Drouet. The people who were now pouring here were not celebrities, nor even local notabilities, in a general sense. They were the lights of a certain circle—the circle of small fortunes and secret order distinctions. These gentlemen Elks knew the standing of one another. They had regard for the ability which could amass a small fortune, own a nice home, keep a barouche or carriage, perhaps, wear fine clothes, and maintain a good mercantile position. Naturally, Hurstwood, who was a little above the order of mind which accepted this standard as perfect, who had shrewdness and much assumption of dignity, who held an imposing and authoritative position, and commanded friendship by intuitive tact in handling people, was quite a figure. He was more generally known than most others in the same circle, and was looked upon as some one whose reserve covered a mine of influence and solid financial prosperity.

To-night he was in his element. He came with several friends directly from Rector's in a carriage. In the lobby he met Drouet, who was just returning from a trip for more cigars. All five now joined in an animated conversation concerning the company present and the general drift of lodge affairs.

"Who's here?" said Hurstwood, passing into the theatre proper, where the lights were turned up and a company of gentlemen were laughing and talking in the open space back of the seats.

"Why, how do you do, Mr. Hurstwood?" came from the first individual recognised.

"Glad to see you," said the latter, grasping his hand lightly. "Looks quite an affair, doesn't it?"

"Yes, indeed," said the manager.

"Custer seems to have the backing of its members," observed the friend.

"So it should," said the knowing manager. "I'm glad to see it."

"Well, George," said another rotund citizen, whose avoirdupois made necessary an almost alarming display of starched shirt bosom, "how goes it with you?"

"Excellent," said the manager.

"What brings you over here? You're not a member of Custer."

"Good-nature," returned the manager. "Like to see the boys, you know."

"Wife here?"

"She couldn't come to-night. She's not well."

"Sorry to hear it—nothing serious, I hope."

"No, just feeling a little ill."

"I remember Mrs. Hurstwood when she was travelling once with you over to St. Joe—" and here the newcomer launched off in a trivial recollection, which was terminated by the arrival of more friends.

"Why, George, how are you?" said another genial West Side politician and lodge member. "My, but I'm glad to see you again; how are things, anyhow?"

"Very well; I see you got that nomination for alderman."

"Yes, we whipped them out over there without much trouble."

"What do you suppose Hennessy will do now?"

"Oh, he'll go back to his brick business. He has a brick-yard, you know."

"I didn't know that," said the manager. "Felt pretty sore, I suppose, over his defeat."

"Perhaps," said the other, winking shrewdly.

Some of the more favoured of his friends whom he had invited began to roll up in carriages now. They came shuffling in with a great show of finery and much evident feeling of content and importance.

"Here we are," said Hurstwood, turning to one from a group with whom he was talking.

"That's right," returned the newcomer, a gentleman of about forty-five.

"And say," he whispered, jovially, pulling Hurstwood over by the shoulder so that he might whisper in his ear, "if this isn't a good show, I'll punch your head."

"You ought to pay for seeing your old friends. Bother the show!"

To another who inquired, "Is it something really good?" the manager replied:

"I don't know. I don't suppose so." Then, lifting his hand graciously, "For the lodge."

"Lots of boys out, eh?"

"Yes, look up Shanahan. He was just asking for you a moment ago."

It was thus that the little theatre resounded to a babble of successful voices, the creak of fine clothes, the commonplace of good-nature, and all largely because of this man's bidding. Look at him any time within the half hour before the curtain was up, he was a member of an eminent group—a rounded company of five or more whose stout figures, large white bosoms, and shining pins bespoke the character of their success. The gentlemen who brought their wives called him out to shake hands. Seats clicked, ushers bowed while he looked blandly on. He was evidently a light among them, reflecting in his personality the ambitions of those who greeted him. He was acknowledged, fawned upon, in a way lionised. Through it all one could see the standing of the man. It was greatness in a way, small as it was.

Chapter XIX

An Hour in Elfland: A Clamour Half Heard

At last the curtain was ready to go up. All the details of the make-up had been completed, and the company settled down as the leader of the small, hired orchestra tapped significantly upon his music rack with his baton and began the soft curtain-raising strain. Hurstwood ceased talking, and went with Drouet and his friend Sagar Morrison around to the box.

"Now, we'll see how the little girl does," he said to Drouet, in a tone which no one else could hear.

On the stage, six of the characters had already appeared in the opening parlour scene. Drouet and Hurstwood saw at a glance that Carrie was not among them, and went on talking in a whisper. Mrs. Morgan, Mrs. Hoagland, and the actor who had taken Bamberger's part were representing the principal rôles in this scene. The professional, whose name was Patton, had little to recommend him outside of his assurance, but this at the present moment was most palpably needed. Mrs. Morgan, as Pearl, was stiff with fright. Mrs. Hoagland was husky in the throat. The whole company was so weak-kneed that the lines were merely spoken, and nothing more. It took all the hope and uncritical good-nature of the audience to keep from manifesting pity by that unrest which is the agony of failure.

Hurstwood was perfectly indifferent. He took it for granted that it would be worthless. All he cared for was to have it endurable enough to allow for pretension and congratulation afterward.

After the first rush of fright, however, the players got over the danger of collapse. They rambled weakly forward, losing nearly all the expression which was intended, and making the thing dull in the extreme, when Carrie came in.

One glance at her, and both Hurstwood and Drouet saw plainly that she also was weak-kneed. She came faintly across the stage, saying:

"And you, sir; we have been looking for you since eight

o'clock," but with so little colour and in such a feeble voice that it was positively painful.

"She's frightened," whispered Drouet to Hurstwood.

The manager made no answer.

She had a line presently which was supposed to be funny.

"Well, that's as much as to say that I'm a sort of life pill."

It came out so flat, however, that it was a deathly thing. Drouet fidgeted. Hurstwood moved his toe the least bit.

There was another place in which Laura was to rise and, with a sense of impending disaster, say, sadly:

"I wish you hadn't said that, Pearl. You know the old proverb, 'Call a maid by a married name.'"

The lack of feeling in the thing was ridiculous. Carrie did not get it at all. She seemed to be talking in her sleep. It looked as if she were certain to be a wretched failure. She was more hopeless than Mrs. Morgan, who had recovered somewhat, and was now saying her lines clearly at least. Drouet looked away from the stage at the audience. The latter held out silently, hoping for a general change, of course. Hurstwood fixed his eye on Carrie, as if to hypnotise her into doing better. He was pouring determination of his own in her direction. He felt sorry for her.

In a few more minutes it fell to her to read the letter sent in by the strange villain. The audience had been slightly diverted by a conversation between the professional actor and a character called Snorky, impersonated by a short little American, who really developed some humour as a half-crazed, one-armed soldier, turned messenger for a living. He bawled his lines out with such defiance that, while they really did not partake of the humour intended, they were funny. Now he was off, however, and it was back to pathos, with Carrie as the chief figure. She did not recover. She wandered through the whole scene between herself and the intruding villain, straining the patience of the audience, and finally exiting, much to their relief.

"She's too nervous," said Drouet, feeling in the mildness of the remark that he was lying for once.

"Better go back and say a word to her."

Drouet was glad to do anything for relief. He fairly hustled around to the side entrance, and was let in by the friendly doorkeeper. Carrie was standing in the wings, weakly waiting her next cue, all the snap and nerve gone out of her.

"Say, Cad," he said, looking at her, "you mustn't be nervous. Wake up. Those guys out there don't amount to anything. What are you afraid of?"

"I don't know," said Carrie. "I just don't seem to be able to do it."

She was grateful for the drummer's presence, though. She had found the company so nervous that her own strength had gone.

"Come on," said Drouet. "Brace up. What are you afraid of? Go on out there now, and do the trick. What do you care?"

Carrie revived a little under the drummer's electrical, nervous condition.

"Did I do so very bad?"

"Not a bit. All you need is a little more ginger. Do it as you showed me. Get that toss of your head you had the other night."

Carrie remembered her triumph in the room. She tried to think she could do it.

"What's next?" he said, looking at her part, which she had been studying.

"Why, the scene between Ray and me when I refuse him."

"Well, now you do that lively," said the drummer. "Put in snap, that's the thing. Act as if you didn't care."

"Your turn next, Miss Madenda," said the prompter.

"Oh, dear," said Carrie.

"Well, you're a chump for being afraid," said Drouet. "Come on now, brace up. I'll watch you from right here."

"Will you?" said Carrie.

"Yes, now go on. Don't be afraid."

The prompter signalled her.

She started out, weak as ever, but suddenly her nerve partially returned. She thought of Drouet looking.

"Ray," she said, gently, using a tone of voice much more calm than when she had last appeared. It was the scene which had pleased the director at the rehearsal.

"She's easier," thought Hurstwood to himself.

She did not do the part as she had at rehearsal, but she was better. The audience was at least not irritated. The improvement of the work of the entire company took away direct observation from her. They were making very fair progress, and now it looked as if the play would be passable, in the less trying parts at least.

Carrie came off warm and nervous.

"Well," she said, looking at him, " was it any better?"

"Well, I should say so. That's the way. Put life into it. You did that about a thousand per cent. better than you did the other scene. Now go on and fire up. You can do it. Knock 'em."

"Was it really better?"

"Better, I should say so. What comes next?"

"That ballroom scene."

"Well, you can do that all right," he said.

"I don't know," answered Carrie.

"Why, woman," he exclaimed, "you did it for me! Now you go out there and do it. It'll be fun for you. Just do as you did in the room. If you'll reel it off that way, I'll bet you make a hit. Now, what'll you bet? You do it."

The drummer usually allowed his ardent good-nature to get the better of his speech. He really did think that Carrie had acted this particular scene very well, and he wanted her to repeat it in public. His enthusiasm was due to the mere spirit of the occasion.

When the time came, he buoyed Carrie up most effectually. He began to make her feel as if she had done very well. The old melancholy of desire began to come back as he talked at her, and by the time the situation rolled around she was running high in feeling.

"I think I can do this."

"Sure you can. Now you go ahead and see."

On the stage, Mrs. Van Dam was making her cruel insinuation against Laura.

Carrie listened, and caught the infection of something— she did not know what. Her nostrils sniffed thinly.

"It means," the professional actor began, speaking as Ray, "that society is a terrible avenger of insult. Have you ever heard of the Siberian wolves? When one of the pack falls through weakness, the others devour him. It is not an elegant comparison, but there is something wolfish in society. Laura has mocked it with a pretence, and society, which is made up of pretence, will bitterly resent the mockery."

At the sound of her stage name Carrie started. She began to feel the bitterness of the situation. The feelings of the outcast descended upon her. She hung at the wing's edge, wrapt in her own mounting thoughts. She hardly heard anything more, save her own rumbling blood.

"Come, girls," said Mrs. Van Dam, solemnly, "let us look after our things. They are no longer safe when such an accomplished thief enters."

"Cue," said the prompter, close to her side, but she did not hear. Already she was moving forward with a steady grace, born of inspiration. She dawned upon the audience, handsome and proud, shifting, with the necessity of the situation, to a cold, white, helpless object, as the social pack moved away from her scornfully.

Hurstwood blinked his eyes and caught the infection. The radiating waves of feeling and sincerity were already breaking against the farthest walls of the chamber. The magic of passion, which will yet dissolve the world, was here at work.

There was a drawing, too, of attention, a riveting of feeling, heretofore wandering.

"Ray! Ray! Why do you not come back to her?" was the cry of Pearl.

Every eye was fixed on Carrie, still proud and scornful. They moved as she moved. Their eyes were with her eyes.

Mrs. Morgan, as Pearl, approached her.

"Let us go home," she said.

"No," answered Carrie, her voice assuming for the first time a penetrating quality which it had never known. "Stay with him!"

She pointed an almost accusing hand toward her lover. Then, with a pathos which struck home because of its utter simplicity, "He shall not suffer long."

Hurstwood realised that he was seeing something extraordinarily good. It was heightened for him by the applause of the audience as the curtain descended and the fact that it was Carrie. He thought now that she was beautiful. She had done something which was above his sphere. He felt a keen delight in realising that she was his.

"Fine," he said, and then, seized by a sudden impulse, arose and went about to the stage door.

When he came in upon Carrie she was still with Drouet. His feelings for her were most exuberant. He was almost swept away by the strength and feeling she exhibited. His desire was to pour forth his praise with the unbounded feelings of a lover, but here was Drouet, whose affection was also rapidly reviving. The latter was more fascinated, if anything, than Hurstwood. At least, in the nature of things, it took a more ruddy form.

"Well, well," said Drouet, "you did out of sight. That was simply great. I knew you could do it. Oh, but you're a little daisy!"

Carrie's eyes flamed with the light of achievement.

"Did I do all right?"

"Did you? Well, I guess. Didn't you hear the applause?"

There was some faint sound of clapping yet.

"I thought I got it something like—I felt it."

Just then Hurstwood came in. Instinctively he felt the change in Drouet. He saw that the drummer was near to Carrie, and jealousy leaped alight in his bosom. In a flash of thought, he reproached himself for having sent him back. Also, he hated him as an intruder. He could scarcely pull himself down to the level where he would have to congratulate Carrie as a friend. Nevertheless, the man mastered himself, and it was a triumph. He almost jerked the old subtle light to his eyes.

"I thought," he said, looking at Carrie, "I would come around and tell you how well you did, Mrs. Drouet. It was delightful."

Carrie took the cue, and replied:

"Oh, thank you."

"I was just telling her," put in Drouet, now delighted with his possession, "that I thought she did fine."

"Indeed you did," said Hurstwood, turning upon Carrie eyes in which she read more than the words.

Carrie laughed luxuriantly.

"If you do as well in the rest of the play, you will make us all think you are a born actress."

Carrie smiled again. She felt the acuteness of Hurstwood's

position, and wished deeply that she could be alone with him, but she did not understand the change in Drouet. Hurstwood found that he could not talk, repressed as he was, and grudging Drouet every moment of his presence, he bowed himself out with the elegance of a Faust. Outside he set his teeth with envy.

"Damn it!" he said, "is he always going to be in the way?" He was moody when he got back to the box, and could not talk for thinking of his wretched situation.

As the curtain for the next act arose, Drouet came back. He was very much enlivened in temper and inclined to whisper, but Hurstwood pretended interest. He fixed his eyes on the stage, although Carrie was not there, a short bit of melodramatic comedy preceding her entrance. He did not see what was going on, however. He was thinking his own thoughts, and they were wretched.

The progress of the play did not improve matters for him. Carrie, from now on, was easily the centre of interest. The audience, which had been inclined to feel that nothing could be good after the first gloomy impression, now went to the other extreme and saw power where it was not. The general feeling reacted on Carrie. She presented her part with some felicity, though nothing like the intensity which had aroused the feeling at the end of the long first act.

Both Hurstwood and Drouet viewed her pretty figure with rising feelings. The fact that such ability should reveal itself in her, that they should see it set forth under such effective circumstances, framed almost in massy gold and shone upon by the appropriate lights of sentiment and personality, heightened her charm for them. She was more than the old Carrie to Drouet. He longed to be at home with her until he could tell her. He awaited impatiently the end, when they should go home alone.

Hurstwood, on the contrary, saw in the strength of her new attractiveness his miserable predicament. He could have cursed the man beside him. By the Lord, he could not even applaud feelingly as he would. For once he must simulate when it left a taste in his mouth.

It was in the last act that Carrie's fascination for her lovers assumed its most effective character.

Hurstwood listened to its progress, wondering when Carrie would come on. He had not long to wait. The author had used the artifice of sending all the merry company for a drive, and now Carrie came in alone. It was the first time that Hurstwood had had a chance to see her facing the audience quite alone, for nowhere else had she been without a foil of some sort. He suddenly felt, as she entered, that her old strength—the power that had grasped him at the end of the first act—had come back. She seemed to be gaining feeling, now that the play was drawing to a close and the opportunity for great action was passing.

"Poor Pearl," she said, speaking with natural pathos. "It is a sad thing to want for happiness, but it is a terrible thing to see another groping about blindly for it, when it is almost within the grasp."

She was gazing now sadly out upon the open sea, her arm resting listlessly upon the polished door-post.

Hurstwood began to feel a deep sympathy for her and for himself. He could almost feel that she was talking to him. He was, by a combination of feelings and entanglements, almost deluded by that quality of voice and manner which, like a pathetic strain of music, seems ever a personal and intimate thing. Pathos has this quality, that it seems ever addressed to one alone.

"And yet, she can be very happy with him," went on the little actress. "Her sunny temper, her joyous face will brighten any home."

She turned slowly toward the audience without seeing. There was so much simplicity in her movements that she seemed wholly alone. Then she found a seat by a table, and turned over some books, devoting a thought to them.

"With no longings for what I may not have," she breathed in conclusion—and it was almost a sigh—"my existence hidden from all save two in the wide world, and making my joy out of the joy of that innocent girl who will soon be his wife."

Hurstwood was sorry when a character, known as Peach Blossom, interrupted her. He stirred irritably, for he wished her to go on. He was charmed by the pale face, the lissome figure, draped in pearl grey, with a coiled string of pearls at the throat. Carrie had the air of one who was weary and in need of protection, and, under the fascinating make-believe of the moment, he rose in feeling until he was ready in spirit to go to her and ease her out of her misery by adding to his own delight.

In a moment Carrie was alone again, and was saying, with animation:

"I must return to the city, no matter what dangers may lurk here. I must go, secretly if I can; openly, if I must."

There was a sound of horses' hoofs outside, and then Ray's voice saying:

"No, I shall not ride again. Put him up."

He entered, and then began a scene which had as much to do with the creation of the tragedy of affection in Hurstwood as anything in his peculiar and involved career. For Carrie had resolved to make something of this scene, and, now that the cue had come, it began to take a feeling hold upon her. Both Hurstwood and Drouet noted the rising sentiment as she proceeded.

"I thought you had gone with Pearl," she said to her lover.

"I did go part of the way, but I left the party a mile down the road."

"You and Pearl had no disagreement?"

"No—yes; that is, we always have. Our social barometers always stand at 'cloudy' and 'overcast.' "

"And whose fault is that?" she said, easily.

"Not mine," he answered, pettishly. "I know I do all I can—I say all I can—but she——"

This was rather awkwardly put by Patton, but Carrie redeemed it with a grace which was inspiring.

"But she is your wife," she said, fixing her whole attention upon the stilled actor, and softening the quality of her voice until it was again low and musical. "Ray, my friend, courtship is the text from which the whole sermon of married life takes its theme. Do not let yours be discontented and unhappy."

She put her two little hands together and pressed them appealingly.

Hurstwood gazed with slightly parted lips. Drouet was fidgeting with satisfaction.

"To be my wife, yes," went on the actor in a manner which

was weak by comparison, but which could not now spoil the tender atmosphere which Carrie had created and maintained. She did not seem to feel that he was wretched. She would have done nearly as well with a block of wood. The accessories she needed were within her own imagination. The acting of others could not affect them.

"And you repent already?" she said, slowly.

"I lost you," he said, seizing her little hand, "and I was at the mercy of any flirt who chose to give me an inviting look. It was your fault—you know it was—why did you leave me?"

Carrie turned slowly away, and seemed to be mastering some impulse in silence. Then she turned back.

"Ray," she said, "the greatest happiness I have ever felt has been the thought that all your affection was forever bestowed upon a virtuous woman, your equal in family, fortune, and accomplishments. What a revelation do you make to me now! What is it makes you continually war with your happiness?"

The last question was asked so simply that it came to the audience and the lover as a personal thing.

At last it came to the part where the lover exclaimed, "Be to me as you used to be."

Carrie answered, with affecting sweetness, "I cannot be that to you, but I can speak in the spirit of the Laura who is dead to you forever."

"Be it as you will," said Patton.

Hurstwood leaned forward. The whole audience was silent and intent.

"Let the woman you look upon be wise or vain," said Carrie, her eyes bent sadly upon the lover, who had sunk into a seat, "beautiful or homely, rich or poor, she has but one thing she can really give or refuse—her heart."

Drouet felt a scratch in his throat.

"Her beauty, her wit, her accomplishments, she may sell to you; but her love is the treasure without money and without price."

The manager suffered this as a personal appeal. It came to him as if they were alone, and he could hardly restrain the tears for sorrow over the hopeless, pathetic, and yet dainty and appealing woman whom he loved. Drouet also was beside himself. He was resolving that he would be to Carrie

what he had never been before. He would marry her, by
George! She was worth it.

"She asks only in return," said Carrie, scarcely hearing the
small, scheduled reply of her lover, and putting herself even
more in harmony with the plaintive melody now issuing from
the orchestra, "that when you look upon her your eyes shall
speak devotion; that when you address her your voice shall
be gentle, loving, and kind; that you shall not despise her
because she cannot understand all at once your vigorous
thoughts and ambitious designs; for, when misfortune and
evil have defeated your greatest purposes, her love remains to
console you. You look to the trees," she continued, while
Hurstwood restrained his feelings only by the grimmest
repression, "for strength and grandeur; do not despise the
flowers because their fragrance is all they have to give. Remember," she concluded, tenderly, "love is all a woman has
to give," and she laid a strange, sweet accent on the all, "but
it is the only thing which God permits us to carry beyond the
grave."

The two men were in the most harrowed state of affection.
They scarcely heard the few remaining words with which the
scene concluded. They only saw their idol, moving about
with appealing grace, continuing a power which to them was
a revelation.

Hurstwood resolved a thousand things, Drouet as well.
They joined equally in the burst of applause which called Carrie out. Drouet pounded his hands until they ached. Then he
jumped up again and started out. As he went, Carrie came
out, and, seeing an immense basket of flowers being hurried
down the aisle toward her, she waited. They were Hurstwood's. She looked toward the manager's box for a moment,
caught his eye, and smiled. He could have leaped out of the
box to enfold her. He forgot the need of circumspectness
which his married state enforced. He almost forgot that he
had with him in the box those who knew him. By the Lord,
he would have that lovely girl if it took his all. He would act
at once. This should be the end of Drouet, and don't you
forget it. He would not wait another day. The drummer
should not have her.

He was so excited that he could not stay in the box. He

went into the lobby, and then into the street, thinking. Drouet did not return. In a few minutes the last act was over, and he was crazy to have Carrie alone. He cursed the luck that could keep him smiling, bowing, shamming, when he wanted to tell her that he loved her, when he wanted to whisper to her alone. He groaned as he saw that his hopes were futile. He must even take her to supper, shamming. He finally went about and asked how she was getting along. The actors were all dressing, talking, hurrying about. Drouet was palavering himself with the looseness of excitement and passion. The manager mastered himself only by a great effort.

"We are going to supper, of course," he said, with a voice that was a mockery of his heart.

"Oh, yes," said Carrie, smiling.

The little actress was in fine feather. She was realising now what it was to be petted. For once she was the admired, the sought-for. The independence of success now made its first faint showing. With the tables turned, she was looking down, rather than up, to her lover. She did not fully realise that this was so, but there was something in condescension coming from her which was infinitely sweet. When she was ready they climbed into the waiting coach and drove down town; once, only, did she find an opportunity to express her feeling, and that was when the manager preceded Drouet in the coach and sat beside her. Before Drouet was fully in she had squeezed Hurstwood's hand in a gentle, impulsive manner. The manager was beside himself with affection. He could have sold his soul to be with her alone. "Ah," he thought, "the agony of it."

Drouet hung on, thinking he was all in all. The dinner was spoiled by his enthusiasm. Hurstwood went home feeling as if he should die if he did not find affectionate relief. He whispered "to-morrow" passionately to Carrie, and she understood. He walked away from the drummer and his prize at parting feeling as if he could slay him and not regret. Carrie also felt the misery of it.

"Good-night," he said, simulating an easy friendliness.

"Good-night," said the little actress, tenderly.

"The fool!" he said, now hating Drouet. "The idiot! I'll do him yet, and that quick! We'll see to-morrow."

"Well, if you aren't a wonder," Drouet was saying, complacently, squeezing Carrie's arm. "You are the dandiest little girl on earth."

Chapter XX

THE LURE OF THE SPIRIT: THE FLESH IN PURSUIT

PASSION IN a man of Hurstwood's nature takes a vigorous form. It is no musing, dreamy thing. There is none of the tendency to sing outside of my lady's window—to languish and repine in the face of difficulties. In the night he was long getting to sleep because of too much thinking, and in the morning he was early awake, seizing with alacrity upon the same dear subject and pursuing it with vigour. He was out of sorts physically, as well as disordered mentally, for did he not delight in a new manner in his Carrie, and was not Drouet in the way? Never was man more harassed than he by the thoughts of his love being held by the elated, flush-mannered drummer. He would have given anything, it seemed to him, to have the complication ended—to have Carrie acquiesce to an arrangement which would dispose of Drouet effectually and forever.

What to do. He dressed thinking. He moved about in the same chamber with his wife, unmindful of her presence.

At breakfast he found himself without an appetite. The meat to which he helped himself remained on his plate untouched. His coffee grew cold, while he scanned the paper indifferently. Here and there he read a little thing, but remembered nothing. Jessica had not yet come down. His wife sat at one end of the table revolving thoughts of her own in silence. A new servant had been recently installed and had forgot the napkins. On this account the silence was irritably broken by a reproof.

"I've told you about this before, Maggie," said Mrs. Hurstwood. "I'm not going to tell you again."

Hurstwood took a glance at his wife. She was frowning. Just now her manner irritated him excessively. Her next remark was addressed to him.

"Have you made up your mind, George, when you will take your vacation?"

It was customary for them to discuss the regular summer outing at this season of the year.

"Not yet," he said, "I'm very busy just now."

"Well, you'll want to make up your mind pretty soon, won't you, if we're going?" she returned.

"I guess we have a few days yet," he said.

"Hmff," she returned. "Don't wait until the season's over." She stirred in aggravation as she said this.

"There you go again," he observed. "One would think I never did anything, the way you begin."

"Well, I want to know about it," she reiterated.

"You've got a few days yet," he insisted. "You'll not want to start before the races are over."

He was irritated to think that this should come up when he wished to have his thoughts for other purposes.

"Well, we may. Jessica doesn't want to stay until the end of the races."

"What did you want with a season ticket, then?"

"Uh!" she said, using the sound as an exclamation of disgust, "I'll not argue with you," and therewith arose to leave the table.

"Say," he said, rising, putting a note of determination in his voice which caused her to delay her departure, " what's the matter with you of late? Can't I talk with you any more?"

"Certainly, you can *talk* with me," she replied, laying emphasis on the word.

"Well, you wouldn't think so by the way you act. Now, you want to know when I'll be ready—not for a month yet. Maybe not then."

"We'll go without you."

"You will, eh?" he sneered.

"Yes, we will."

He was astonished at the woman's determination, but it only irritated him the more.

"Well, we'll see about that. It seems to me you're trying to run things with a pretty high hand of late. You talk as though you settled my affairs for me. Well, you don't. You don't regulate anything that's connected with me. If you want to go, go, but you won't hurry me by any such talk as that."

He was thoroughly aroused now. His dark eyes snapped, and he crunched his paper as he laid it down. Mrs. Hurstwood said nothing more. He was just finishing when she turned on her heel and went out into the hall and upstairs. He paused for a moment, as if hesitating, then sat down and drank a little coffee, and thereafter arose and went for his hat and gloves upon the main floor.

His wife had really not anticipated a row of this character. She had come down to the breakfast table feeling a little out of sorts with herself and revolving a scheme which she had in her mind. Jessica had called her attention to the fact that the races were not what they were supposed to be. The social opportunities were not what they had thought they would be this year. The beautiful girl found going every day a dull thing. There was an earlier exodus this year of people who were anybody to the watering places and Europe. In her own circle of acquaintances several young men in whom she was interested had gone to Waukesha. She began to feel that she would like to go too, and her mother agreed with her.

Accordingly, Mrs. Hurstwood decided to broach the subject. She was thinking this over when she came down to the table, but for some reason the atmosphere was wrong. She was not sure, after it was all over, just how the trouble had begun. She was determined now, however, that her husband was a brute, and that, under no circumstances, would she let this go by unsettled. She would have more lady-like treatment or she would know why.

For his part, the manager was loaded with the care of this new argument until he reached his office and started from there to meet Carrie. Then the other complications of love, desire, and opposition possessed him. His thoughts fled on before him upon eagles' wings. He could hardly wait until he should meet Carrie face to face. What was the night, after all, without her—what the day? She must and should be his.

For her part, Carrie had experienced a world of fancy and feeling since she had left him, the night before. She had listened to Drouet's enthusiastic maunderings with much regard for that part which concerned herself, with very little for that which affected his own gain. She kept him at such lengths as she could, because her thoughts were with her own triumph. She felt Hurstwood's passion as a delightful background to her own achievement, and she wondered what he would have to say. She was sorry for him, too, with that peculiar sorrow which finds something complimentary to itself in the misery of another. She was now experiencing the first shades of feeling of that subtle change which removes one out of the ranks of the suppliants into the lines of the dispensers of charity. She was, all in all, exceedingly happy.

On the morrow, however, there was nothing in the papers concerning the event, and, in view of the flow of common, everyday things about, it now lost a shade of the glow of the previous evening. Drouet himself was not talking so much *of* as *for* her. He felt instinctively that, for some reason or other, he needed reconstruction in her regard.

"I think," he said, as he spruced around their chambers the next morning, preparatory to going down town, "that I'll straighten out that little deal of mine this month and then we'll get married. I was talking with Mosher about that yesterday."

"No, you won't," said Carrie, who was coming to feel a certain faint power to jest with the drummer.

"Yes, I will," he exclaimed, more feelingly than usual, adding, with the tone of one who pleads, "Don't you believe what I've told you?"

Carrie laughed a little.

"Of course I do," she answered.

Drouet's assurance now misgave him. Shallow as was his mental observation, there was that in the things which had happened which made his little power of analysis useless. Carrie was still with him, but not helpless and pleading. There was a lilt in her voice which was new. She did not study him with eyes expressive of dependence. The drummer was feeling the shadow of something which was coming. It coloured his feelings and made him develop those little attentions and say those little words which were mere forefendations against danger.

Shortly afterward he departed, and Carrie prepared for her meeting with Hurstwood. She hurried at her toilet, which was soon made, and hastened down the stairs. At the corner she passed Drouet, but they did not see each other.

The drummer had forgotten some bills which he wished to

turn into his house. He hastened up the stairs and burst into the room, but found only the chambermaid, who was cleaning up.

"Hello," he exclaimed, half to himself, "has Carrie gone?"

"Your wife? Yes, she went out just a few minutes ago."

"That's strange," thought Drouet. "She didn't say a word to me. I wonder where she went?"

He hastened about, rummaging in his valise for what he wanted, and finally pocketing it. Then he turned his attention to his fair neighbour, who was good-looking and kindly disposed towards him.

"What are you up to?" he said, smiling.

"Just cleaning," she replied, stopping and winding a dusting towel about her hand.

"Tired of it?"

"Not so very."

"Let me show you something," he said, affably, coming over and taking out of his pocket a little lithographed card which had been issued by a wholesale tobacco company. On this was printed a picture of a pretty girl, holding a striped parasol, the colours of which could be changed by means of a revolving disk in the back, which showed red, yellow, green, and blue through little interstices made in the ground occupied by the umbrella top.

"Isn't that clever?" he said, handing it to her and showing her how it worked. "You never saw anything like that before."

"Isn't it nice?" she answered.

"You can have it if you want it," he remarked.

"That's a pretty ring you have," he said, touching a commonplace setting which adorned the hand holding the card he had given her.

"Do you think so?"

"That's right," he answered, making use of a pretence at examination to secure her finger. "That's fine."

The ice being thus broken, he launched into further observation, pretending to forget that her fingers were still retained by his. She soon withdrew them, however, and retreated a few feet to rest against the window-sill.

"I didn't see you for a long time," she said, coquettishly,

repulsing one of his exuberant approaches. "You must have been away."

"I was," said Drouet.

"Do you travel far?"

"Pretty far—yes."

"Do you like it?"

"Oh, not very well. You get tired of it after a while."

"I wish I could travel," said the girl, gazing idly out of the window.

"What has become of your friend, Mr. Hurstwood?" she suddenly asked, bethinking herself of the manager, who, from her own observation, seemed to contain promising material.

"He's here in town. What makes you ask about him?"

"Oh, nothing, only he hasn't been here since you got back."

"How did you come to know him?"

"Didn't I take up his name a dozen times in the last month?"

"Get out," said the drummer, lightly. "He hasn't called more than half a dozen times since we've been here."

"He hasn't, eh?" said the girl, smiling. "That's all you know about it."

Drouet took on a slightly more serious tone. He was uncertain as to whether she was joking or not.

"Tease," he said, " what makes you smile that way?"

"Oh, nothing."

"Have you seen him recently?"

"Not since you came back," she laughed.

"Before?"

"Certainly."

"How often?"

"Why, nearly every day."

She was a mischievous newsmonger, and was keenly wondering what the effect of her words would be.

"Who did he come to see?" asked the drummer, incredulously.

"Mrs. Drouet."

He looked rather foolish at this answer, and then attempted to correct himself so as not to appear a dupe.

"Well," he said, " what of it?"

"Nothing," replied the girl, her head cocked coquettishly on one side.

"He's an old friend," he went on, getting deeper into the mire.

He would have gone on further with his little flirtation, but the taste for it was temporarily removed. He was quite relieved when the girl's name was called from below.

"I've got to go," she said, moving away from him airily.

"I'll see you later," he said, with a pretence of disturbance at being interrupted.

When she was gone, he gave freer play to his feelings. His face, never easily controlled by him, expressed all the perplexity and disturbance which he felt. Could it be that Carrie had received so many visits and yet said nothing about them? Was Hurstwood lying? What did the chambermaid mean by it, anyway? He had thought there was something odd about Carrie's manner at the time. Why did she look so disturbed when he had asked her how many times Hurstwood had called? By George! he remembered now. There was something strange about the whole thing.

He sat down in a rocking-chair to think the better, drawing up one leg on his knee and frowning mightily. His mind ran on at a great rate.

And yet Carrie hadn't acted out of the ordinary. It couldn't be, by George, that she was deceiving him. She hadn't acted that way. Why, even last night she had been as friendly toward him as could be, and Hurstwood too. Look how they acted! He could hardly believe they would try to deceive him.

His thoughts burst into words.

"She did act sort of funny at times. Here she had dressed and gone out this morning and never said a word."

He scratched his head and prepared to go down town. He was still frowning. As he came into the hall he encountered the girl, who was now looking after another chamber. She had on a white dusting cap, beneath which her chubby face shone good-naturedly. Drouet almost forgot his worry in the fact that she was smiling on him. His put his hand familiarly on her shoulder, as if only to greet her in passing.

"Got over being mad?" she said, still mischievously inclined.

"I'm not mad," he answered.

"I thought you were," she said, smiling.

"Quit your fooling about that," he said, in an offhand way. "Were you serious?"

"Certainly," she answered. Then, with an air of one who did not intentionally mean to create trouble, "He came lots of times. I thought you knew."

The game of deception was up with Drouet. He did not try to simulate indifference further.

"Did he spend the evenings here?" he asked.

"Sometimes. Sometimes they went out."

"In the evening?"

"Yes. You mustn't look so mad, though."

"I'm not," he said. "Did any one else see him?"

"Of course," said the girl, as if, after all, it were nothing in particular.

"How long ago was this?"

"Just before you came back."

The drummer pinched his lip nervously.

"Don't say anything, will you?" he asked, giving the girl's arm a gentle squeeze.

"Certainly not," she returned. "I wouldn't worry over it."

"All right," he said, passing on, seriously brooding for once, and yet not wholly unconscious of the fact that he was making a most excellent impression upon the chambermaid.

"I'll see her about that," he said to himself, passionately, feeling that he had been unduly wronged. "I'll find out, b'George, whether she'll act that way or not."

Chapter XXI

THE LURE OF THE SPIRIT: THE FLESH IN PURSUIT

WHEN CARRIE came Hurstwood had been waiting many minutes. His blood was warm; his nerves wrought up. He was anxious to see the woman who had stirred him so profoundly the night before.

"Here you are," he said, repressedly, feeling a spring in his limbs and an elation which was tragic in itself.

"Yes," said Carrie.

They walked on as if bound for some objective point, while Hurstwood drank in the radiance of her presence. The rustle of her pretty skirt was like music to him.

"Are you satisfied?" he asked, thinking of how well she did the night before.

"Are you?"

He tightened his fingers as he saw the smile she gave him.

"It was wonderful."

Carrie laughed ecstatically.

"That was one of the best things I've seen in a long time," he added.

He was dwelling on her attractiveness as he had felt it the evening before, and mingling it with the feeling her presence inspired now.

Carrie was dwelling in the atmosphere which this man created for her. Already she was enlivened and suffused with a glow. She felt his drawing toward her in every sound of his voice.

"Those were such nice flowers you sent me," she said, after a moment or two. "They were beautiful."

"Glad you liked them," he answered, simply.

He was thinking all the time that the subject of his desire was being delayed. He was anxious to turn the talk to his own feelings. All was ripe for it. His Carrie was beside him. He wanted to plunge in and expostulate with her, and yet he found himself fishing for words and feeling for a way.

"You got home all right," he said, gloomily, of a sudden, his tone modifying itself to one of self-commiseration.

"Yes," said Carrie, easily.

He looked at her steadily for a moment, slowing his pace and fixing her with his eye.

She felt the flood of feeling.

"How about me?" he asked.

This confused Carrie considerably, for she realised the floodgates were open. She didn't know exactly what to answer.

"I don't know," she answered.

He took his lower lip between his teeth for a moment, and then let it go. He stopped by the walk side and kicked the grass with his toe. He searched her face with a tender, appealing glance.

"Won't you come away from him?" he asked, intensely.

"I don't know," returned Carrie, still illogically drifting and finding nothing at which to catch.

As a matter of fact, she was in a most hopeless quandary. Here was a man whom she thoroughly liked, who exercised an influence over her, sufficient almost to delude her into the belief that she was possessed of a lively passion for him. She was still the victim of his keen eyes, his suave manners, his fine clothes. She looked and saw before her a man who was most gracious and sympathetic, who leaned toward her with a feeling that was a delight to observe. She could not resist the glow of his temperament, the light of his eye. She could hardly keep from feeling what he felt.

And yet she was not without thoughts which were disturbing. What did he know? What had Drouet told him? Was she a wife in his eyes, or what? Would he marry her? Even while he talked, and she softened, and her eyes were lighted with a tender glow, she was asking herself if Drouet had told him they were not married. There was never anything at all convincing about what Drouet said.

And yet she was not grieved at Hurstwood's love. No strain of bitterness was in it for her, whatever he knew. He was evidently sincere. His passion was real and warm. There was power in what he said. What should she do? She went on thinking this, answering vaguely, languishing affectionately, and altogether drifting, until she was on a borderless sea of speculation.

"Why don't you come away?" he said, tenderly. "I will arrange for you whatever—"

"Oh, don't," said Carrie.

"Don't what?" he asked. "What do you mean?"

There was a look of confusion and pain in her face. She was wondering why that miserable thought must be brought in. She was struck as by a blade with the miserable provision which was outside the pale of marriage.

He himself realised that it was a wretched thing to have dragged in. He wanted to weigh the effects of it, and yet he could not see. He went beating on, flushed by her presence, clearly awakened, intensely enlisted in his plan.

"Won't you come?" he said, beginning over and with a more reverent feeling. "You know I can't do without you—you know it—it can't go on this way—can it?"

"I know," said Carrie.

"I wouldn't ask if I—I wouldn't argue with you if I could help it. Look at me, Carrie. Put yourself in my place. You don't want to stay away from me, do you?"

She shook her head as if in deep thought.

"Then why not settle the whole thing, once and for all?"

"I don't know," said Carrie.

"Don't know! Ah, Carrie, what makes you say that? Don't torment me. Be serious."

"I am," said Carrie, softly.

"You can't be, dearest, and say that. Not when you know how I love you. Look at last night."

His manner as he said this was the most quiet imaginable. His face and body retained utter composure. Only his eyes moved, and they flashed a subtle, dissolving fire. In them the whole intensity of the man's nature was distilling itself.

Carrie made no answer.

"How can you act this way, dearest?" he inquired, after a time. "You love me, don't you?"

He turned on her such a storm of feeling that she was overwhelmed. For the moment all doubts were cleared away.

"Yes," she answered, frankly and tenderly.

"Well, then you'll come, won't you—come to-night?"

Carrie shook her head in spite of her distress.

"I can't wait any longer," urged Hurstwood. "If that is too soon, come Saturday."

"When will we be married?" she asked, diffidently, forgetting in her difficult situation that she had hoped he took her to be Drouet's wife.

The manager started, hit as he was by a problem which was more difficult than hers. He gave no sign of the thoughts that flashed like messages to his mind.

"Any time you say," he said, with ease, refusing to discolour his present delight with this miserable problem.

"Saturday?" asked Carrie.

He nodded his head.

"Well, if you will marry me then," she said, "I'll go."

The manager looked at his lovely prize, so beautiful, so winsome, so difficult to be won, and made strange resolutions. His passion had gotten to that stage now where it was no longer coloured with reason. He did not trouble over little barriers of this sort in the face of so much loveliness. He would accept the situation with all its difficulties; he would not try to answer the objections which cold truth thrust upon him. He would promise anything, everything, and trust to fortune to disentangle him. He would make a try for Paradise, whatever might be the result. He would be happy, by the Lord, if it cost all honesty of statement, all abandonment of truth.

Carrie looked at him tenderly. She could have laid her head upon his shoulder, so delightful did it all seem.

"Well," she said, "I'll try and get ready then."

Hurstwood looked into her pretty face, crossed with little shadows of wonder and misgiving, and thought he had never seen anything more lovely.

"I'll see you again to-morrow," he said, joyously, "and we'll talk over the plans."

He walked on with her, elated beyond words, so delightful had been the result. He impressed a long story of joy and affection upon her, though there was but here and there a word. After a half-hour he began to realise that the meeting must come to an end, so exacting is the world.

"To-morrow," he said at parting, a gayety of manner adding wonderfully to his brave demeanour.

"Yes," said Carrie, tripping elatedly away.

There had been so much enthusiasm engendered that she was believing herself deeply in love. She sighed as she thought of her handsome adorer. Yes, she would get ready by Saturday. She would go, and they would be happy.

Chapter XXII

THE BLAZE OF THE TINDER:
FLESH WARS WITH THE FLESH

THE MISFORTUNE of the Hurstwood household was due to the fact that jealousy, having been born of love, did not perish with it. Mrs. Hurstwood retained this in such form that subsequent influences could transform it into hate. Hurstwood was still worthy, in a physical sense, of the affection his wife had once bestowed upon him, but in a social sense he fell short. With his regard died his power to be attentive to her, and this, to a woman, is much greater than outright crime toward another. Our self-love dictates our appreciation of the good or evil in another. In Mrs. Hurstwood it discoloured the very hue of her husband's indifferent nature. She saw design in deeds and phrases which sprung only from a faded appreciation of her presence.

As a consequence, she was resentful and suspicious. The jealousy that prompted her to observe every falling away from the little amenities of the married relation on his part served to give her notice of the airy grace with which he still took the world. She could see from the scrupulous care which he exercised in the matter of his personal appearance that his interest in life had abated not a jot. Every motion, every glance had something in it of the pleasure he felt in Carrie, of the zest this new pursuit of pleasure lent to his days. Mrs. Hurstwood felt something, sniffing change, as animals do danger, afar off.

This feeling was strengthened by actions of a direct and more potent nature on the part of Hurstwood. We have seen with what irritation he shirked those little duties which no longer contained any amusement or satisfaction for him, and the open snarls with which, more recently, he resented her irritating goads. These little rows were really precipitated by an atmosphere which was surcharged with dissension. That it would shower, with a sky so full of blackening thunderclouds, would scarcely be thought worthy of comment. Thus, after leaving the breakfast table this morning, raging inwardly at his blank declaration of indifference at her plans, Mrs. Hurstwood encountered Jessica in her dressing-room, very leisurely arranging her hair. Hurstwood had already left the house.

"I wish you wouldn't be so late coming down to breakfast," she said, addressing Jessica, while making for her crochet basket. "Now here the things are quite cold, and you haven't eaten."

Her natural composure was sadly ruffled, and Jessica was doomed to feel the fag end of the storm.

"I'm not hungry," she answered.

"Then why don't you say so, and let the girl put away the things, instead of keeping her waiting all morning?"

"She doesn't mind," answered Jessica, coolly.

"Well, I do, if she doesn't," returned the mother, "and, anyhow, I don't like you to talk that way to me. You're too young to put on such an air with your mother."

"Oh, mamma, don't row," answered Jessica. "What's the matter this morning, anyway?"

"Nothing's the matter, and I'm not rowing. You mustn't think because I indulge you in some things that you can keep everybody waiting. I won't have it."

"I'm not keeping anybody waiting," returned Jessica, sharply, stirred out of a cynical indifference to a sharp defence. "I said I wasn't hungry. I don't want any breakfast."

"Mind how you address me, missy. I'll not have it. Hear me now; I'll not have it!"

Jessica heard this last while walking out of the room, with a toss of her head and a flick of her pretty skirts indicative of the independence and indifference she felt. She did not propose to be quarrelled with.

Such little arguments were all too frequent, the result of a growth of natures which were largely independent and selfish. George, Jr., manifested even greater touchiness and exaggeration in the matter of his individual rights, and attempted to make all feel that he was a man with a man's privileges—an assumption which, of all things, is most groundless and pointless in a youth of nineteen.

Hurstwood was a man of authority and some fine feeling,

and it irritated him excessively to find himself surrounded more and more by a world upon which he had no hold, and of which he had a lessening understanding.

Now, when such little things, such as the proposed earlier start to Waukesha, came up, they made clear to him his position. He was being made to follow, was not leading. When, in addition, a sharp temper was manifested, and to the process of shouldering him out of his authority was added a rousing intellectual kick, such as a sneer or a cynical laugh, he was unable to keep his temper. He flew into hardly repressed passion, and wished himself clear of the whole household. It seemed a most irritating drag upon all his desires and opportunities.

For all this, he still retained the semblance of leadership and control, even though his wife was straining to revolt. Her display of temper and open assertion of opposition were based upon nothing more than the feeling that she could do it. She had no special evidence wherewith to justify herself— the knowledge of something which would give her both authority and excuse. The latter was all that was lacking, however, to give a solid foundation to what, in a way, seemed groundless discontent. The clear proof of one overt deed was the cold breath needed to convert the lowering clouds of suspicion into a rain of wrath.

An inkling of untoward deeds on the part of Hurstwood had come. Doctor Beale, the handsome resident physician of the neighbourhood, met Mrs. Hurstwood at her own doorstep some days after Hurstwood and Carrie had taken the drive west on Washington Boulevard. Dr. Beale, coming east on the same drive, had recognised Hurstwood, but not before he was quite past him. He was not so sure of Carrie—did not know whether it was Hurstwood's wife or daughter.

"You don't speak to your friends when you meet them out driving, do you?" he said, jocosely, to Mrs. Hurstwood.

"If I see them, I do. Where was I?"

"On Washington Boulevard," he answered, expecting her eye to light with immediate remembrance.

She shook her head.

"Yes, out near Hoyne Avenue. You were with your husband."

"I guess you're mistaken," she answered. Then, remembering her husband's part in the affair, she immediately fell a prey to a host of young suspicions, of which, however, she gave no sign.

"I know I saw your husband," he went on. "I wasn't so sure about you. Perhaps it was your daughter."

"Perhaps it was," said Mrs. Hurstwood, knowing full well that such was not the case, as Jessica had been her companion for weeks. She had recovered herself sufficiently to wish to know more of the details.

"Was it in the afternoon?" she asked, artfully, assuming an air of acquaintanceship with the matter.

"Yes, about two or three."

"It must have been Jessica," said Mrs. Hurstwood, not wishing to seem to attach any importance to the incident.

The physician had a thought or two of his own, but dismissed the matter as worthy of no further discussion on his part at least.

Mrs. Hurstwood gave this bit of information considerable thought during the next few hours, and even days. She took it for granted that the doctor had really seen her husband, and that he had been riding, most likely, with some other woman, after announcing himself as *busy* to her. As a consequence, she recalled, with rising feeling, how often he had refused to go to places with her, to share in little visits, or, indeed, take part in any of the social amenities which furnished the diversion of her existence. He had been seen at the theatre with people whom he called Moy's friends; now he was seen driving, and, most likely, would have an excuse for that. Perhaps there were others of whom she did not hear, or why should he be so busy, so indifferent, of late? In the last six weeks he had become strangely irritable—strangely satisfied to pick up and go out, whether things were right or wrong in the house. Why?

She recalled, with more subtle emotions, that he did not look at her now with any of the old light of satisfaction or approval in his eye. Evidently, along with other things, he was taking her to be getting old and uninteresting. He saw her wrinkles, perhaps. She was fading, while he was still preening himself in his elegance and youth. He was still an interested factor in the merry-makings of the world, while she—but she did not pursue the thought. She only found the whole situation bitter, and hated him for it thoroughly.

Nothing came of this incident at the time, for the truth is it did not seem conclusive enough to warrant any discussion. Only the atmosphere of distrust and ill-feeling was strengthened, precipitating every now and then little sprinklings of irritable conversation, enlivened by flashes of wrath. The matter of the Waukesha outing was merely a continuation of other things of the same nature.

The day after Carrie's appearance on the Avery stage, Mrs. Hurstwood visited the races with Jessica and a youth of her acquaintance, Mr. Bart Taylor, the son of the owner of a local house-furnishing establishment. They had driven out early, and, as it chanced, encountered several friends of Hurstwood, all Elks, and two of whom had attended the performance the evening before. A thousand chances the subject of the performance had never been brought up had Jessica not been so engaged by the attentions of her young companion, who usurped as much time as possible. This left Mrs. Hurstwood in the mood to extend the perfunctory greetings of some who knew her into short conversations, and the short conversations of friends into long ones. It was from one who meant but to greet her perfunctorily that this interesting intelligence came.

"I see," said this individual, who wore sporting clothes of the most attractive pattern, and had a field-glass strung over his shoulder, "that you did not get over to our little entertainment last evening."

"No?" said Mrs. Hurstwood, inquiringly, and wondering why he should be using the tone he did in noting the fact that she had not been to something she knew nothing about. It was on her lips to say, "What was it?" when he added, "I saw your husband."

Her wonder was at once replaced by the more subtle quality of suspicion.

"Yes," she said, cautiously, "was it pleasant? He did not tell me much about it."

"Very. Really one of the best private theatricals I ever attended. There was one actress who surprised us all."

"Indeed," said Mrs. Hurstwood.

"It's too bad you couldn't have been there, really. I was sorry to hear you weren't feeling well."

Feeling well! Mrs. Hurstwood could have echoed the words after him open-mouthed. As it was, she extricated herself from her mingled impulse to deny and question, and said, almost raspingly:

"Yes, it is too bad."

"Looks like there will be quite a crowd here to-day, doesn't it?" the acquaintance observed, drifting off upon another topic.

The manager's wife would have questioned farther, but she saw no opportunity. She was for the moment wholly at sea, anxious to think for herself, and wondering what new deception was this which caused him to give out that she was ill when she was not. Another case of her company not wanted, and excuses being made. She resolved to find out more.

"Were you at the performance last evening?" she asked of the next of Hurstwood's friends who greeted her, as she sat in her box.

"Yes. You didn't get around."

"No," she answered, "I was not feeling very well."

"So your husband told me," he answered. "Well, it was really very enjoyable. Turned out much better than I expected."

"Were there many there?"

"The house was full. It was quite an Elk night. I saw quite a number of your friends—Mrs. Harrison, Mrs. Barnes, Mrs. Collins."

"Quite a social gathering."

"Indeed it was. My wife enjoyed it very much."

Mrs. Hurstwood bit her lip.

"So," she thought, "that's the way he does. Tells my friends I am sick and cannot come."

She wondered what could induce him to go alone. There was something back of this. She rummaged her brain for a reason.

By evening, when Hurstwood reached home, she had brooded herself into a state of sullen desire for explanation and revenge. She wanted to know what this peculiar action

of his imported. She was certain there was more behind it all
than what she had heard, and evil curiosity mingled well with
distrust and the remnants of her wrath of the morning. She,
impending disaster itself, walked about with gathered shadow
at the eyes and the rudimentary muscles of savagery fixing the
hard lines of her mouth.

On the other hand, as we may well believe, the manager
came home in the sunniest mood. His conversation and
agreement with Carrie had raised his spirits until he was in
the frame of mind of one who sings joyously. He was proud
of himself, proud of his success, proud of Carrie. He could
have been genial to all the world, and he bore no grudge
against his wife. He meant to be pleasant, to forget her presence, to live in the atmosphere of youth and pleasure which
had been restored to him.

So now, the house, to his mind, had a most pleasing and
comfortable appearance. In the hall he found an evening paper, laid there by the maid and forgotten by Mrs. Hurstwood.
In the dining-room the table was clean laid with linen and
napery and shiny with glasses and decorated china. Through
an open door he saw into the kitchen, where the fire was
crackling in the stove and the evening meal already well under
way. Out in the small back yard was George, Jr., frolicking
with a young dog he had recently purchased, and in the parlour Jessica was playing at the piano, the sounds of a merry
waltz filling every nook and corner of the comfortable home.
Every one, like himself, seemed to have regained his good
spirits, to be in sympathy with youth and beauty, to be inclined to joy and merry-making. He felt as if he could say a
good word all around himself, and took a most genial glance
at the spread table and polished sideboard before going upstairs to read his paper in the comfortable arm-chair of the
sitting-room which looked through the open windows into
the street. When he entered there, however, he found his wife
brushing her hair and musing to herself the while.

He came lightly in, thinking to smooth over any feeling
that might still exist by a kindly word and a ready promise,
but Mrs. Hurstwood said nothing. He seated himself in the
large chair, stirred lightly in making himself comfortable,
opened his paper, and began to read. In a few moments he was

smiling merrily over a very comical account of a baseball game which had taken place between the Chicago and Detroit teams.

The while he was doing this Mrs. Hurstwood was observing him casually through the medium of the mirror which was before her. She noticed his pleasant and contented manner, his airy grace and smiling humour, and it merely aggravated her the more. She wondered how he could think to carry himself so in her presence after the cynicism, indifference, and neglect he had heretofore manifested and would continue to manifest so long as she would endure it. She thought how she should like to tell him—what stress and emphasis she would lend her assertions, how she should drive over this whole affair until satisfaction should be rendered her. Indeed, the shining sword of her wrath was but weakly suspended by a thread of thought.

In the meanwhile Hurstwood encountered a humorous item concerning a stranger who had arrived in the city and became entangled with a bunco-steerer. It amused him immensely, and at last he stirred and chuckled to himself. He wished that he might enlist his wife's attention and read it to her.

"Ha, ha," he exclaimed softly, as if to himself, "that's funny."

Mrs. Hurstwood kept on arranging her hair, not so much as deigning a glance.

He stirred again and went on to another subject. At last he felt as if his good-humour must find some outlet. Julia was probably still out of humour over that affair of this morning, but that could easily be straightened. As a matter of fact, she was in the wrong, but he didn't care. She could go to Waukesha right away if she wanted to. The sooner the better. He would tell her that as soon as he got a chance, and the whole thing would blow over.

"Did you notice," he said, at last, breaking forth concerning another item which he had found, "that they have entered suit to compel the Illinois Central to get off the lake front, Julia?" he asked.

She could scarcely force herself to answer, but managed to say "No," sharply.

Hurstwood pricked up his ears. There was a note in her voice which vibrated keenly.

"It would be a good thing if they did," he went on, half to himself, half to her, though he felt that something was amiss in that quarter. He withdrew his attention to his paper very circumspectly, listening mentally for the little sounds which should show him what was on foot.

As a matter of fact, no man as clever as Hurstwood—as observant and sensitive to atmospheres of many sorts, particularly upon his own plane of thought—would have made the mistake which he did in regard to his wife, wrought up as she was, had he not been occupied mentally with a very different train of thought. Had not the influence of Carrie's regard for him, the elation which her promise aroused in him, lasted over, he would not have seen the house in so pleasant a mood. It was not extraordinarily bright and merry this evening. He was merely very much mistaken, and would have been much more fitted to cope with it had he come home in his normal state.

After he had studied his paper a few moments longer, he felt that he ought to modify matters in some way or other. Evidently his wife was not going to patch up peace at a word. So he said:

"Where did George get the dog he has there in the yard?"

"I don't know," she snapped.

He put his paper down on his knees and gazed idly out of the window. He did not propose to lose his temper, but merely to be persistent and agreeable, and by a few questions bring around a mild understanding of some sort.

"Why do you feel so bad about that affair of this morning?" he said, at last. "We needn't quarrel about that. You know you can go to Waukesha if you want to."

"So you can stay here and trifle around with some one else?" she exclaimed, turning to him a determined countenance upon which was drawn a sharp and wrathful sneer.

He stopped as if slapped in the face. In an instant his persuasive, conciliatory manner fled. He was on the defensive at a wink and puzzled for a word to reply.

"What do you mean?" he said at last, straightening himself and gazing at the cold, determined figure before him, who paid no attention, but went on arranging herself before the mirror.

"You know what I mean," she said, finally, as if there were a world of information which she held in reserve—which she did not need to tell.

"Well, I don't," he said, stubbornly, yet nervous and alert for what should come next. The finality of the woman's manner took away his feeling of superiority in battle.

She made no answer.

"Hmph!" he murmured, with a movement of his head to one side. It was the weakest thing he had ever done. It was totally unassured.

Mrs. Hurstwood noticed the lack of colour in it. She turned upon him, animal-like, able to strike an effectual second blow.

"I want the Waukesha money to-morrow morning," she said.

He looked at her in amazement. Never before had he seen such a cold, steely determination in her eye—such a cruel look of indifference. She seemed a thorough master of her mood—thoroughly confident and determined to wrest all control from him. He felt that all his resources could not defend him. He must attack.

"What do you mean?" he said, jumping up. "*You* want! I'd like to know what's got into you to-night."

"Nothing's *got* into me," she said, flaming. "I want that money. You can do your swaggering afterwards."

"Swaggering, eh! What! You'll get nothing from me. What do you mean by your insinuations, anyhow?"

"Where were you last night?" she answered. The words were hot as they came. "Who were you driving with on Washington Boulevard? Who were you with at the theatre when George saw you? Do you think I'm a fool to be duped by you? Do you think I'll sit at home here and take your 'too busys' and 'can't come,' while you parade around and make out that I'm unable to come? I want you to know that lordly airs have come to an end so far as I am concerned. You can't dictate to me nor my children. I'm through with you entirely."

"It's a lie," he said, driven to a corner and knowing no other excuse.

"Lie, eh!" she said, fiercely, but with returning reserve; "you may call it a lie if you want to, but I know."

"It's a lie, I tell you," he said, in a low, sharp voice. "You've been searching around for some cheap accusation for months, and now you think you have it. You think you'll spring something and get the upper hand. Well, I tell you, you can't. As long as I'm in this house I'm master of it, and you or any one else won't dictate to me—do you hear?"

He crept toward her with a light in his eye that was ominous. Something in the woman's cool, cynical, upper-handish manner, as if she were already master, caused him to feel for the moment as if he could strangle her.

She gazed at him—a pythoness in humour.

"I'm not dictating to you," she returned; "I'm telling you what I want."

The answer was so cool, so rich in bravado, that somehow it took the wind out of his sails. He could not attack her, he could not ask her for proofs. Somehow he felt evidence, law, the remembrance of all his property which she held in her name, to be shining in her glance. He was like a vessel, powerful and dangerous, but rolling and floundering without sail.

"And I'm telling you," he said in the end, slightly recovering himself, " what you'll not get."

"We'll see about it," she said. "I'll find out what my rights are. Perhaps you'll talk to a lawyer, if you won't to me."

It was a magnificent play, and had its effect. Hurstwood fell back beaten. He knew now that he had more than mere bluff to contend with. He felt that he was face to face with a dull proposition. What to say he hardly knew. All the merriment had gone out of the day. He was disturbed, wretched, resentful. What should he do?

"Do as you please," he said, at last. "I'll have nothing more to do with you," and out he strode.

Chapter XXIII

A Spirit in Travail: One Rung Put Behind

WHEN CARRIE reached her own room she had already fallen a prey to those doubts and misgivings which are ever the result of a lack of decision. She could not persuade herself as to the advisability of her promise, or that now, having given her word, she ought to keep it. She went over the whole ground in Hurstwood's absence, and discovered little objections that had not occurred to her in the warmth of the manager's argument. She saw where she had put herself in a peculiar light, namely, that of agreeing to marry when she was already supposedly married. She remembered a few things Drouet had done, and now that it came to walking away from him without a word, she felt as if she were doing wrong. Now, she was comfortably situated, and to one who is more or less afraid of the world, this is an urgent matter, and one which puts up strange, uncanny arguments. "You do not know what will come. There are miserable things outside. People go a-begging. Women are wretched. You never can tell what will happen. Remember the time you were hungry. Stick to what you have."

Curiously, for all her leaning towards Hurstwood, he had not taken a firm hold on her understanding. She was listening, smiling, approving, and yet not finally agreeing. This was due to a lack of power on his part, a lack of that majesty of passion that sweeps the mind from its seat, fuses and melts all arguments and theories into a tangled mass, and destroys for the time being the reasoning power. This majesty of passion is possessed by nearly every man once in his life, but it is usually an attribute of youth and conduces to the first successful mating.

Hurstwood, being an older man, could scarcely be said to retain the fire of youth, though he did possess a passion warm and unreasoning. It was strong enough to induce the leaning toward him which, on Carrie's part, we have seen. She might have been said to be imagining herself in love, when she was not. Women frequently do this. It flows from the fact that in each exists a bias toward affection, a craving for the pleasure of being loved. The longing to be shielded, bettered, sympathised with, is one of the attributes of the sex. This, coupled with sentiment and a natural tendency to emotion, often makes refusing difficult. It persuades them that they are in love.

Once at home, she changed her clothes and straightened the rooms for herself. In the matter of the arrangement of the furniture she never took the house-maid's opinion. That young woman invariably put one of the rocking-chairs in the corner, and Carrie as regularly moved it out. To-day she hardly noticed that it was in the wrong place, so absorbed was she in her own thoughts. She worked about the room until Drouet put in appearance at five o'clock. The drummer was flushed and excited and full of determination to know all about her relations with Hurstwood. Nevertheless, after going over the subject in his mind the livelong day, he was rather weary of it and wished it over with. He did not foresee serious consequences of any sort, and yet he rather hesitated to begin. Carrie was sitting by the window when he came in, rocking and looking out.

"Well," she said innocently, weary of her own mental discussion and wondering at his haste and ill-concealed excitement, "what makes you hurry so?"

Drouet hesitated, now that he was in her presence, uncertain as to what course to pursue. He was no diplomat. He could neither read nor see.

"When did you get home?" he asked foolishly.

"Oh, an hour or so ago. What makes you ask that?"

"You weren't here," he said, "when I came back this morning, and I thought you had gone out."

"So I did," said Carrie simply. "I went for a walk."

Drouet looked at her wonderingly. For all his lack of dignity in such matters he did not know how to begin. He stared at her in the most flagrant manner until at last she said:

"What makes you stare at me so? What's the matter?"

"Nothing," he answered. "I was just thinking."

"Just thinking what?" she returned smilingly, puzzled by his attitude.

"Oh, nothing—nothing much."

"Well, then, what makes you look so?"

Drouet was standing by the dresser, gazing at her in a comic manner. He had laid off his hat and gloves and was now fidgeting with the little toilet pieces which were nearest him. He hesitated to believe that the pretty woman before him was involved in anything so unsatisfactory to himself. He was very much inclined to feel that it was all right, after all. Yet the knowledge imparted to him by the chambermaid was rankling in his mind. He wanted to plunge in with a straight remark of some sort, but he knew not what.

"Where did you go this morning?" he finally asked weakly.

"Why, I went for a walk," said Carrie.

"Sure you did?" he asked.

"Yes, what makes you ask?"

She was beginning to see now that he knew something. Instantly she drew herself into a more reserved position. Her cheeks blanched slightly.

"I thought maybe you didn't," he said, beating about the bush in the most useless manner.

Carrie gazed at him, and as she did so her ebbing courage halted. She saw that he himself was hesitating, and with a woman's intuition realised that there was no occasion for great alarm.

"What makes you talk like that?" she asked, wrinkling her pretty forehead. "You act so funny to-night."

"I feel funny," he answered.

They looked at one another for a moment, and then Drouet plunged desperately into his subject.

"What's this about you and Hurstwood?" he asked.

"Me and Hurstwood—what do you mean?"

"Didn't he come here a dozen times while I was away?"

"A dozen times," repeated Carrie, guiltily. "No, but what do you mean?"

"Somebody said that you went out riding with him and that he came here every night."

"No such thing," answered Carrie. "It isn't true. Who told you that?"

She was flushing scarlet to the roots of her hair, but Drouet did not catch the full hue of her face, owing to the modified

light of the room. He was regaining much confidence as
Carrie defended herself with denials.

"Well, some one," he said. "You're sure you didn't?"

"Certainly," said Carrie. "You know how often he came."

Drouet paused for a moment and thought.

"I know what you told me," he said finally.

He moved nervously about, while Carrie looked at him
confusedly.

"Well, I know that I didn't tell you any such thing as that,"
said Carrie, recovering herself.

"If I were you," went on Drouet, ignoring her last remark,
"I wouldn't have anything to do with him. He's a married
man, you know."

"Who—who is?" said Carrie, stumbling at the word.

"Why, Hurstwood," said Drouet, noting the effect and
feeling that he was delivering a telling blow.

"Hurstwood!" exclaimed Carrie, rising. Her face had
changed several shades since this announcement was made.
She looked within and without herself in a half-dazed
way.

"Who told you this?" she asked, forgetting that her interest
was out of order and exceedingly incriminating.

"Why, I know it. I've always known it," said Drouet.

Carrie was feeling about for a right thought. She was
making a most miserable showing, and yet feelings were gen-
erating within her which were anything but crumbling
cowardice.

"I thought I told you," he added.

"No, you didn't," she contradicted, suddenly recovering
her voice. "You didn't do anything of the kind."

Drouet listened to her in astonishment. This was something new.

"I thought I did," he said.

Carrie looked around her very solemnly, and then went
over to the window.

"You oughn't to have had anything to do with him," said
Drouet in an injured tone, "after all I've done for you."

"You," said Carrie, "you! What have you done for me?"

Her little brain had been surging with contradictory feelings—shame at exposure, shame at Hurstwood's perfidy,

anger at Drouet's deception, the mockery he had made of her. Now one clear idea came into her head. He was at fault. There was no doubt about it. Why did he bring Hurstwood out—Hurstwood, a married man, and never say a word to her? Never mind now about Hurstwood's perfidy—why had he done this? Why hadn't he warned her? There he stood now, guilty of this miserable breach of confidence and talking about what he had done for her!

"Well, I like that," exclaimed Drouet, little realising the fire his remark had generated. "I think I've done a good deal."

"You have, eh?" she answered. "You've deceived me—that's what you've done. You've brought your old friends out here under false pretences. You've made me out to be— Oh," and with this her voice broke and she pressed her two little hands together tragically.

"I don't see what that's got to do with it," said the drummer quaintly.

"No," she answered, recovering herself and shutting her teeth. "No, of course you don't see. There isn't anything you see. You couldn't have told me in the first place, could you? You had to make me out wrong until it was too late. Now you come sneaking around with your information and your talk about what you have done."

Drouet had never suspected this side of Carrie's nature. She was alive with feeling, her eyes snapping, her lips quivering, her whole body sensible of the injury she felt, and partaking of her wrath.

"Who's sneaking?" he asked, mildly conscious of error on his part, but certain that he was wronged.

"You are," stamped Carrie. "You're a horrid, conceited coward, that's what you are. If you had any sense of manhood in you, you wouldn't have thought of doing any such thing."

The drummer stared.

"I'm not a coward," he said. "What do you mean by going with other men, anyway?"

"Other men!" exclaimed Carrie. "Other men—you know better than that. I did go with Mr. Hurstwood, but whose fault was it? Didn't you bring him here? You told him yourself that he should come out here and take me out. Now, after it's all over, you come and tell me that I oughtn't to go with him and that he's a married man."

She paused at the sound of the last two words and wrung her hands. The knowledge of Hurstwood's perfidy wounded her like a knife.

"Oh," she sobbed, repressing herself wonderfully and keeping her eyes dry. "Oh, oh!"

"Well, I didn't think you'd be running around with him when I was away," insisted Drouet.

"Didn't think!" said Carrie, now angered to the core by the man's peculiar attitude. "Of course not. You thought only of what would be to your satisfaction. You thought you'd make a toy of me—a plaything. Well, I'll show you that you won't. I'll have nothing more to do with you at all. You can take your old things and keep them," and unfastening a little pin he had given her, she flung it vigorously upon the floor and began to move about as if to gather up the things which belonged to her.

By this Drouet was not only irritated but fascinated the more. He looked at her in amazement, and finally said:

"I don't see where your wrath comes in. I've got the right of this thing. You oughtn't to have done anything that wasn't right after all I did for you."

"What have you done for me?" asked Carrie blazing, her head thrown back and her lips parted.

"I think I've done a good deal," said the drummer, looking around. "I've given you all the clothes you wanted, haven't I? I've taken you everywhere you wanted to go. You've had as much as I've had, and more too."

Carrie was not ungrateful, whatever else might be said of her. In so far as her mind could construe, she acknowledged benefits received. She hardly knew how to answer this, and yet her wrath was not placated. She felt that the drummer had injured her irreparably.

"Did I ask you to?" she returned.

"Well, I did it," said Drouet, "and you took it."

"You talk as though I had persuaded you," answered Carrie. "You stand there and throw up what you've done. I don't want your old things. I'll not have them. You take them to-night and do what you please with them. I'll not stay here another minute."

"That's nice!" he answered, becoming angered now at the sense of his own approaching loss. "Use everything and abuse me and then walk off. That's just like a woman. I take you when you haven't got anything, and then when some one else comes along, why I'm no good. I always thought it'd come out that way."

He felt really hurt as he thought of his treatment, and looked as if he saw no way of obtaining justice.

"It's not so," said Carrie, "and I'm not going with any-body else. You have been as miserable and inconsiderate as you can be. I hate you, I tell you, and I wouldn't live with you another minute. You're a big, insulting"—here she hes-itated and used no word at all—"or you wouldn't talk that way."

She had secured her hat and jacket and slipped the latter on over her little evening dress. Some wisps of wavy hair had loosened from the bands at the side of her head and were straggling over her hot, red cheeks. She was angry, mortified, grief-stricken. Her large eyes were full of the anguish of tears, but her lids were not yet wet. She was distracted and uncer-tain, deciding and doing things without an aim or conclusion, and she had not the slightest conception of how the whole difficulty would end.

"Well, that's a fine finish," said Drouet. "Pack up and pull out, eh? You take the cake. I bet you were knocking around with Hurstwood or you wouldn't act like that. I don't want the old rooms. You needn't pull out for me. You can have them for all I care, but b'George, you haven't done me right."

"I'll not live with you," said Carrie. "I don't want to live with you. You've done nothing but brag around ever since you've been here."

"Aw, I haven't anything of the kind," he answered.

Carrie walked over to the door.

"Where are you going?" he said, stepping over and heading her off.

"Let me out," she said.

"Where are you going?" he repeated.

He was, above all, sympathetic, and the sight of Carrie

wandering out, he knew not where, affected him, despite his grievance.

Carrie merely pulled at the door.

The strain of the situation was too much for her, however. She made one more vain effort and then burst into tears.

"Now, be reasonable, Cad," said Drouet gently. "What do you want to rush out for this way? You haven't any place to go. Why not stay here now and be quiet? I'll not bother you. I don't want to stay here any longer."

Carrie had gone sobbing from the door to the window. She was so overcome she could not speak.

"Be reasonable now," he said. "I don't want to hold you. You can go if you want to, but why don't you think it over? Lord knows, I don't want to stop you."

He received no answer. Carrie was quieting, however, under the influence of his plea.

"You stay here now, and I'll go," he added at last.

Carrie listened to this with mingled feelings. Her mind was shaken loose from the little mooring of logic that it had. She was stirred by this thought, angered by that—her own injustice, Hurstwood's, Drouet's, their respective qualities of kindness and favour, the threat of the world outside, in which she had failed once before, the impossibility of this state inside, where the chambers were no longer justly hers, the effect of the argument upon her nerves, all combined to make her a mass of jangling fibres—an anchorless, storm-beaten little craft which could do absolutely nothing but drift.

"Say," said Drouet, coming over to her after a few moments, with a new idea, and putting his hand upon her.

"Don't!" said Carrie, drawing away, but not removing her handkerchief from her eyes.

"Never mind about this quarrel now. Let it go. You stay here until the month's out, anyhow, and then you can tell better what you want to do. Eh?"

Carrie made no answer.

"You'd better do that," he said. "There's no use your packing up now. You can't go anywhere."

Still he got nothing for his words.

"If you'll do that, we'll call it off for the present and I'll get out."

Carrie lowered her handkerchief slightly and looked out of the window.

"Will you do that?" he asked.

Still no answer.

"Will you?" he repeated.

She only looked vaguely into the street.

"Aw! come on," he said, "tell me. Will you?"

"I don't know," said Carrie softly, forced to answer.

"Promise me you'll do that," he said, "and we'll quit talking about it. It'll be the best thing for you."

Carrie heard him, but she could not bring herself to answer reasonably. She felt that the man was gentle, and that his interest in her had not abated, and it made her suffer a pang of regret. She was in a most helpless plight.

As for Drouet, his attitude had been that of the jealous lover. Now his feelings were a mixture of anger at deception, sorrow at losing Carrie, misery at being defeated. He wanted his rights in some way or other, and yet his rights included the retaining of Carrie, the making her feel her error.

"Will you?" he urged.

"Well, I'll see," said Carrie.

This left the matter as open as before, but it was something. It looked as if the quarrel would blow over, if they could only get some way of talking to one another. Carrie was ashamed, and Drouet aggrieved. He pretended to take up the task of packing some things in a valise.

Now, as Carrie watched him out of the corner of her eye, certain sound thoughts came into her head. He had erred, true, but what had she done? He was kindly and good-natured for all his egotism. Throughout this argument he had said nothing very harsh. On the other hand, there was Hurstwood—a greater deceiver than he. He had pretended all this affection, all this passion, and he was lying to her all the while. Oh, the perfidy of men! And she had loved him. There could be nothing more in that quarter. She would see Hurstwood no more. She would write him and let him know what she thought. Thereupon what would she do? Here were these rooms. Here was Drouet, pleading for her to remain. Evidently things could go on here somewhat as before, if all were arranged. It would be better than the street, without a place to lay her head.

All this she thought of as Drouet rummaged the drawers for collars and laboured long and painstakingly at finding a shirt-stud. He was in no hurry to rush this matter. He felt an attraction to Carrie which would not down. He could not think that the thing would end by his walking out of the room. There must be some way round, some way to make her own up that he was right and she was wrong—to patch up a peace and shut out Hurstwood for ever. Mercy, how he turned at the man's shameless duplicity.

"Do you think," he said, after a few moments' silence, "that you'll try and get on the stage?"

He was wondering what she was intending.

"I don't know what I'll do yet," said Carrie.

"If you do, maybe I can help you. I've got a lot of friends in that line."

She made no answer to this.

"Don't go and try to knock around now without any money. Let me help you," he said. "It's no easy thing to go on your own hook here."

Carrie only rocked back and forth in her chair.

"I don't want you to go up against a hard game that way."

He bestirred himself about some other details and Carrie rocked on.

"Why don't you tell me all about this thing," he said, after a time, "and let's call it off? You don't really care for Hurstwood, do you?"

"Why do you want to start on that again?" said Carrie. "You were to blame."

"No, I wasn't," he answered.

"Yes, you were, too," said Carrie. "You shouldn't have ever told me such a story as that."

"But you didn't have much to do with him, did you?" went on Drouet, anxious for his own peace of mind to get some direct denial from her.

"I won't talk about it," said Carrie, pained at the quizzical turn the peace arrangement had taken.

"What's the use of acting like that now, Cad?" insisted the

drummer, stopping in his work and putting up a hand expressively. "You might let me know where I stand, at least."

"I won't," said Carrie, feeling no refuge but in anger. "Whatever has happened is your own fault."

"Then you do care for him?" said Drouet, stopping completely and experiencing a rush of feeling.

"Oh, stop!" said Carrie.

"Well, I'll not be made a fool of," exclaimed Drouet. "You may trifle around with him if you want to, but you can't lead me. You can tell me or not, just as you want to, but I won't fool any longer!"

He shoved the last few remaining things he had laid out into his valise and snapped it with a vengeance. Then he grabbed his coat, which he had laid off to work, picked up his gloves, and started out.

"You can go to the deuce as far as I am concerned," he said, as he reached the door. "I'm no sucker," and with that he opened it with a jerk and closed it equally vigorously.

Carrie listened at her window view, more astonished than anything else at this sudden rise of passion in the drummer. She could hardly believe her senses—so good-natured and tractable had he invariably been. It was not for her to see the wellspring of human passion. A real flame of love is a subtle thing. It burns as a will-o'-the-wisp, dancing onward to fairylands of delight. It roars as a furnace. Too often jealousy is the quality upon which it feeds.

Chapter XXIV

ASHES OF TINDER: A FACE AT THE WINDOW

THAT NIGHT Hurstwood remained down town entirely, going to the Palmer House for a bed after his work was through. He was in a fevered state of mind, owing to the blight his wife's action threatened to cast upon his entire future. While he was not sure how much significance might be attached to the threat she had made, he was sure that her attitude, if long continued, would cause him no end of trouble. She was determined, and had worsted him in a very important contest. How would it be from now on? He walked the floor of his little office, and later that of his room, putting one thing and another together to no avail.

Mrs. Hurstwood, on the contrary, had decided not to lose her advantage by inaction. Now that she had practically cowed him, she would follow up her work with demands, the acknowledgment of which would make her word *law* in the future. He would have to pay her the money which she would now regularly demand or there would be trouble. It did not matter what he did. She really did not care whether he came home any more or not. The household would move along much more pleasantly without him, and she could do as she wished without consulting any one. Now she proposed to consult a lawyer and hire a detective. She would find out at once just what advantages she could gain.

Hurstwood walked the floor, mentally arranging the chief points of his situation. "She has that property in her name," he kept saying to himself. "What a fool trick that was. Curse it! What a fool move that was."

He also thought of his managerial position. "If she raises a row now I'll lose this thing. They won't have me around if my name gets in the papers. My friends, too!" He grew more angry as he thought of the talk any action on her part would create. How would the papers talk about it? Every man he knew would be wondering. He would have to explain and deny and make a general mark of himself. Then Moy would come and confer with him and there would be the devil to pay.

Many little wrinkles gathered between his eyes as he contemplated this, and his brow moistened. He saw no solution of anything—not a loophole left.

Through all this thoughts of Carrie flashed upon him, and the approaching affair of Saturday. Tangled as all his matters were, he did not worry over that. It was the one pleasing thing in this whole rout of trouble. He could arrange that satisfactorily, for Carrie would be glad to wait, if necessary. He would see how things turned out to-morrow, and then he would talk to her. They were going to meet as usual. He saw only her pretty face and neat figure and wondered why life was not arranged so that such joy as he found with her could be steadily maintained. How much more pleasant it would be. Then he would take up his wife's threat again, and the wrinkles and moisture would return.

In the morning he came over from the hotel and opened his mail, but there was nothing in it outside the ordinary run. For some reason he felt as if something might come that way, and was relieved when all the envelopes had been scanned and nothing suspicious noticed. He began to feel the appetite that had been wanting before he had reached the office, and decided before going out to the park to meet Carrie to drop in at the Grand Pacific and have a pot of coffee and some rolls. While the danger had not lessened, it had not as yet materialised, and with him no news was good news. If he could only get plenty of time to think, perhaps something would turn up. Surely, surely, this thing would not drift along to catastrophe and he not find a way out.

His spirits fell, however, when, upon reaching the park, he waited and waited and Carrie did not come. He held his favourite post for an hour or more, then arose and began to walk about restlessly. Could something have happened out there to keep her away? Could she have been reached by his wife? Surely not. So little did he consider Drouet that it never once occurred to him to worry about his finding out. He grew restless as he ruminated, and then decided that perhaps it was nothing. She had not been able to get away this morning. That was why no letter notifying him had come. He would get one to-day. It would probably be on his desk when he got back. He would look for it at once.

After a time he gave up waiting and drearily headed for the Madison car. To add to his distress, the bright blue sky became overcast with little fleecy clouds which shut out the sun. The wind veered to the east, and by the time he reached his office it was threatening to drizzle all afternoon.

He went in and examined his letters, but there was nothing from Carrie. Fortunately, there was nothing from his wife either. He thanked his stars that he did not have to confront that proposition just now when he needed to think so much. He walked the floor again, pretending to be in an ordinary mood, but secretly troubled beyond the expression of words.

At one-thirty he went to Rector's for lunch, and when he returned a messenger was waiting for him. He looked at the little chap with a feeling of doubt.

"I'm to bring an answer," said the boy.

Hurstwood recognised his wife's writing. He tore it open and read without a show of feeling. It began in the most formal manner and was sharply and coldly worded throughout.

"I want you to send the money I asked for at once. I need it to carry out my plans. You can stay away if you want to. It doesn't matter in the least. But I must have some money. So don't delay, but send it by the boy."

When he had finished it, he stood holding it in his hands. The audacity of the thing took his breath. It roused his ire also—the deepest element of revolt in him. His first impulse was to write but four words in reply—"Go to the devil!"—but he compromised by telling the boy that there would be no reply. Then he sat down in his chair and gazed without seeing, contemplating the result of his work. What would she do about that? The confounded wretch! Was she going to try to bulldoze him into submission? He would go up there and have it out with her, that's what he would do. She was carrying things with too high a hand. These were his first thoughts.

Later, however, his old discretion asserted itself. Something had to be done. A climax was near and she would not sit idle. He knew her well enough to know that when she had decided upon a plan she would follow it up. Possibly matters would go into a lawyer's hands at once.

"Damn her!" he said softly, with his teeth firmly set, "I'll make it hot for her if she causes me trouble. I'll make her change her tone if I have to use force to do it!"

He arose from his chair and went and looked out into the street. The long drizzle had begun. Pedestrians had turned up collars, and trousers at the bottom. Hands were hidden in the pockets of the umbrellaless; umbrellas were up. The street looked like a sea of round black cloth roofs, twisting, bobbing, moving. Trucks and vans were rattling in a noisy line and everywhere men were shielding themselves as best they could. He scarcely noticed the picture. He was forever confronting his wife, demanding of her to change her attitude toward him before he worked her bodily harm.

At four o'clock another note came, which simply said that if the money was not forthcoming that evening the matter would be laid before Fitzgerald and Moy on the morrow, and other steps would be taken to get it.

Hurstwood almost exclaimed out loud at the insistency of this thing. Yes, he would send her the money. He'd take it to her—he would go up there and have a talk with her, and that at once.

He put on his hat and looked around for his umbrella. He would have some arrangement of this thing.

He called a cab and was driven through the dreary rain to the North Side. On the way his temper cooled as he thought of the details of the case. What did she know? What had she done? Maybe she'd got hold of Carrie, who knows—or—or Drouet. Perhaps she really had evidence, and was prepared to fell him as a man does another from secret ambush. She was shrewd. Why should she taunt him this way unless she had good grounds?

He began to wish that he had compromised in some way or other—that he had sent the money. Perhaps he could do it up here. He would go in and see, anyhow. He would have no row.

By the time he reached his own street he was keenly alive to the difficulties of his situation and wished over and over that some solution would offer itself, that he could see his way out. He alighted and went up the steps to the front door, but it was with a nervous palpitation of the heart. He pulled out his key and tried to insert it, but another key was on the inside. He shook at the knob, but the door was locked. Then he rang the bell. No answer. He rang again—this time harder. Still no answer. He jangled it fiercely several times in succession, but without avail. Then he went below.

There was a door which opened under the steps into the kitchen, protected by an iron grating, intended as a safeguard against burglars. When he reached this he noticed that it also was bolted and that the kitchen windows were down. What could it mean? He rang the bell and then waited. Finally, seeing that no one was coming, he turned and went back to his cab.

"I guess they've gone out," he said apologetically to the individual who was hiding his red face in a loose tarpaulin rain-coat.

"I saw a young girl up in that winder," returned the cabby.

Hurstwood looked, but there was no face there now. He climbed moodily into the cab, relieved and distressed.

So this was the game, was it? Shut him out and make him pay. Well, by the Lord, that did beat all!

Chapter XXV

ASHES OF TINDER: THE LOOSING OF STAYS

WHEN HURSTWOOD got back to his office again he was in a greater quandary than ever. Lord, Lord, he thought, what had he got into? How could things have taken such a violent turn, and so quickly? He could hardly realise how it had all come about. It seemed a monstrous, unnatural, unwarranted condition which had suddenly descended upon him without his let or hindrance.

Meanwhile he gave a thought now and then to Carrie. What could be the trouble in that quarter? No letter had come, no word of any kind, and yet here it was late in the evening and she had agreed to meet him that morning. To-morrow they were to have met and gone off—where? He saw that in the excitement of recent events he had not formulated a plan upon that score. He was desperately in love, and would have taken great chances to win her under ordinary circumstances, but now—now what? Supposing she had found out something? Supposing she, too, wrote him and told him that she knew all—that she would have nothing more to do with him? It would be just like this to happen as things were going now. Meanwhile he had not sent the money.

He strolled up and down the polished floor of the resort, his hands in his pockets, his brow wrinkled, his mouth set. He was getting some vague comfort out of a good cigar, but it was no panacea for the ill which affected him. Every once in a while he would clinch his fingers and tap his foot—signs of the stirring mental process he was undergoing. His whole nature was vigorously and powerfully shaken up, and he was finding what limits the mind has to endurance. He drank more brandy and soda than he had any evening in months. He was altogether a fine example of great mental perturbation.

For all his study nothing came of the evening except this— he sent the money. It was with great opposition, after two or three hours of the most urgent mental affirmation and denial, that at last he got an envelope, placed in it the requested amount, and slowly sealed it up.

Then he called Harry, the boy of all work around the place.

"You take this to this address," he said, handing him the envelope, "and give it to Mrs. Hurstwood."

"Yes, sir," said the boy.

"If she isn't there bring it back."

"Yes, sir."

"You've seen my wife?" he asked as a precautionary measure as the boy turned to go.

"Oh, yes, sir. I know her."

"All right, now. Hurry right back."

"Any answer?"

"I guess not."

The boy hastened away and the manager fell to his musings. Now he had done it. There was no use speculating over that. He was beaten for to-night and he might just as well make the best of it. But, oh, the wretchedness of being forced this way! He could see her meeting the boy at the door and smiling sardonically. She would take the envelope and know that she had triumphed. If he only had that letter back he wouldn't send it. He breathed heavily and wiped the moisture from his face.

For relief, he arose and joined in conversation with a few friends who were drinking. He tried to get the interest of things about him, but it was not to be. All the time his thoughts would run out to his home and see the scene being therein enacted. All the time he was wondering what she would say when the boy handed her the envelope.

In about an hour and three-quarters the boy returned. He had evidently delivered the package, for, as he came up, he made no sign of taking anything out of his pocket.

"Well?" said Hurstwood.

"I gave it to her."

"My wife?"

"Yes, sir."

"Any answer?"

"She said it was high time."

Hurstwood scowled fiercely.

There was no more to be done upon that score that night.

He went on brooding over his situation until midnight, when he repaired again to the Palmer House. He wondered what the morning would bring forth, and slept anything but soundly upon it.

Next day he went again to the office and opened his mail, suspicious and hopeful of its contents. No word from Carrie. Nothing from his wife, which was pleasant.

The fact that he had sent the money and that she had received it worked to the ease of his mind, for, as the thought that he had done it receded, his chagrin at it grew less and his hope of peace more. He fancied, as he sat at his desk, that nothing would be done for a week or two. Meanwhile, he would have time to think.

This process of *thinking* began by a reversion to Carrie and the arrangement by which he was to get her away from Drouet. How about that now? His pain at her failure to meet or write him rapidly increased as he devoted himself to this subject. He decided to write her care of the West Side Post-office and ask for an explanation, as well as to have her meet him. The thought that this letter would probably not reach her until Monday chafed him exceedingly. He must get some speedier method—but how?

He thought upon it for a half-hour, not contemplating a messenger or a cab direct to the house, owing to the exposure of it, but finding that time was slipping away to no purpose, he wrote the letter and then began to think again.

The hours slipped by, and with them the possibility of the union he had contemplated. He had thought to be joyously aiding Carrie by now in the task of joining her interests to his, and here it was afternoon and nothing done. Three o'clock came, four, five, six, and no letter. The helpless manager paced the floor and grimly endured the gloom of defeat. He saw a busy Saturday ushered out, the Sabbath in, and nothing done. All day, the bar being closed, he brooded alone, shut out from home, from the excitement of his resort, from Carrie, and without the ability to alter his condition one iota. It was the worst Sunday he had spent in his life.

In Monday's second mail he encountered a very legal-looking letter, which held his interest for some time. It bore the imprint of the law offices of McGregor, James and Hay, and with a very formal "Dear Sir," and "We beg to state," went on to inform him briefly that they had been retained by Mrs. Julia Hurstwood to adjust certain matters which related to her sustenance and property rights, and would he kindly call and see them about the matter at once.

He read it through carefully several times, and then merely shook his head. It seemed as if his family troubles were just beginning.

"Well!" he said after a time, quite audibly, "I don't know."

Then he folded it up and put it in his pocket.

To add to his misery there was no word from Carrie. He was quite certain now that she knew he was married and was angered at his perfidy. His loss seemed all the more bitter now that he needed her most. He thought he would go out and insist on seeing her if she did not send him word of some sort soon. He was really affected most miserably of all by this desertion. He had loved her earnestly enough, but now that the possibility of losing her stared him in the face she seemed much more attractive. He really pined for a word, and looked out upon her with his mind's eye in the most wistful manner. He did not propose to lose her, whatever she might think. Come what might, he would adjust this matter, and soon. He would go to her and tell her all his family complications. He would explain to her just where he stood and how much he needed her. Surely she couldn't go back on him now? It wasn't possible. He would plead until her anger would melt—until she would forgive him.

Suddenly he thought: "Supposing she isn't out there—suppose she has gone?"

He was forced to take his feet. It was too much to think of and sit still.

Nevertheless, his rousing availed him nothing.

On Tuesday it was the same way. He did manage to bring himself into the mood to go out to Carrie, but when he got in Ogden Place he thought he saw a man watching him and went away. He did not go within a block of the house.

One of the galling incidents of this visit was that he came back on a Randolph Street car, and without noticing arrived almost opposite the building of the concern with which his son was connected. This sent a pang through his heart. He had called on his boy there several times. Now the lad had not sent him a word. His absence did not seem to be noticed by either of his children. Well, well, fortune plays a man queer tricks. He got back to his office and joined in a conversation with friends. It was as if idle chatter deadened the sense of misery.

That night he dined at Rector's and returned at once to his office. In the bustle and show of the latter was his only relief. He troubled over many little details and talked perfunctorily to everybody. He stayed at his desk long after all others had gone, and only quitted it when the night watchman on his round pulled at the front door to see if it was safely locked.

On Wednesday he received another polite note from McGregor, James and Hay. It read:

> "*Dear Sir:* We beg to inform you that we are instructed to wait until to-morrow (Thursday) at one o'clock, before filing suit against you, on behalf of Mrs. Julia Hurstwood, for divorce and alimony. If we do not hear from you before that time we shall consider that you do not wish to compromise the matter in any way and act accordingly.
>
> "Very truly yours, etc."

"Compromise!" exclaimed Hurstwood bitterly. "Compromise!"

Again he shook his head.

So here it was spread out clear before him, and now he knew what to expect. If he didn't go and see them they would sue him promptly. If he did, he would be offered terms that would make his blood boil. He folded the letter and put it with the other one. Then he put on his hat and went for a turn about the block.

Chapter XXVI

The Ambassador Fallen: A Search for the Gate

C ARRIE, LEFT ALONE by Drouet, listened to his retreating steps, scarcely realising what had happened. She knew that he had stormed out. It was some moments before she questioned whether he would return, not now exactly, but ever. She looked around her upon the rooms, out of which the evening light was dying, and wondered why she did not feel quite the same towards them. She went over to the dresser and struck a match, lighting the gas. Then she went back to the rocker to think.

It was some time before she could collect her thoughts, but when she did, this truth began to take on importance. She was quite alone. Suppose Drouet did not come back? Suppose she should never hear anything more of him? This fine arrangement of chambers would not last long. She would have to quit them.

To her credit, be it said, she never once counted on Hurstwood. She could only approach that subject with a pang of sorrow and regret. For a truth, she was rather shocked and frightened by this evidence of human depravity. He would have tricked her without turning an eyelash. She would have been led into a newer and worse situation. And yet she could not keep out the pictures of his looks and manners. Only this one deed seemed strange and miserable. It contrasted sharply with all she felt and knew concerning the man.

But she was alone. That was the greater thought just at present. How about that? Would she go out to work again? Would she begin to look around in the business district? The stage! Oh, yes. Drouet had spoken about that. Was there any hope there? She moved to and fro, in deep and varied thoughts, while the minutes slipped away and night fell completely. She had had nothing to eat, and yet there she sat, thinking it over.

She remembered that she was hungry and went to the little cupboard in the rear room where were the remains of one of their breakfasts. She looked at these things with certain misgivings. The contemplation of food had more significance than usual.

While she was eating she began to wonder how much money she had. It struck her as exceedingly important, and without ado she went to look for her purse. It was on the dresser, and in it were seven dollars in bills and some change. She quailed as she thought of the insignificance of the amount and rejoiced because the rent was paid until the end of the month. She began also to think what she would have done if she had gone out into the street when she first started. By the side of that situation, as she looked at it now, the present seemed agreeable. She had a little time at least, and then, perhaps, everything would come out all right, after all.

Drouet had gone, but what of it? He did not seem seriously angry. He only acted as if he were huffy. He would come back—of course he would. There was his cane in the corner. Here was one of his collars. He had left his light overcoat in the wardrobe. She looked about and tried to assure herself with the sight of a dozen such details, but, alas, the secondary thought arrived. Supposing he did come back. Then what?

Here was another proposition nearly, if not quite, as disturbing. She would have to talk with and explain to him. He would want her to admit that he was right. It would be impossible for her to live with him.

On Friday Carrie remembered her appointment with Hurstwood, and the passing of the hour when she should, by all right of promise, have been in his company served to keep the calamity which had befallen her exceedingly fresh and clear. In her nervousness and stress of mind she felt it necessary to act, and consequently put on a brown street dress, and at eleven o'clock started to visit the business portion once again. She must look for work.

The rain, which threatened at twelve and began at one, served equally well to cause her to retrace her steps and remain within doors as it did to reduce Hurstwood's spirits and give him a wretched day.

The morrow was Saturday, a half-holiday in many business quarters, and besides it was a balmy, radiant day, with the trees and grass shining exceedingly green after the rain of the

night before. When she went out the sparrows were twittering merrily in joyous choruses. She could not help feeling, as
she looked across the lovely park, that life was a joyous thing
for those who did not need to worry, and she wished over
and over that something might interfere now to preserve for
her the comfortable state which she had occupied. She did
not want Drouet or his money when she thought of it, nor
anything more to do with Hurstwood, but only the content
and ease of mind she had experienced, for, after all, she had
been happy—happier, at least, than she was now when confronted by the necessity of making her way alone.

When she arrived in the business part it was quite eleven
o'clock, and the business had little longer to run. She did not
realise this at first, being affected by some of the old distress
which was a result of her earlier adventure into this strenuous
and exacting quarter. She wandered about, assuring herself
that she was making up her mind to look for something, and
at the same time feeling that perhaps it was not necessary to
be in such haste about it. The thing was difficult to encounter, and she had a few days. Besides, she was not sure that
she was really face to face again with the bitter problem of
self-sustenance. Anyhow, there was one change for the better.
She knew that she had improved in appearance. Her manner
had vastly changed. Her clothes were becoming, and men—
well-dressed men, some of the kind who before had gazed at
her indifferently from behind their polished railings and imposing office partitions—now gazed into her face with a soft
light in their eyes. In a way, she felt the power and satisfaction of the thing, but it did not wholly reassure her. She
looked for nothing save what might come legitimately and
without the appearance of special favour. She wanted something, but no man should buy her by false protestations or
favour. She proposed to earn her living honestly.

"This store closes at one on Saturdays," was a pleasing and
satisfactory legend to see upon doors which she felt she ought
to enter and inquire for work. It gave her an excuse, and after
encountering quite a number of them, and noting that the
clock registered 12.15, she decided that it would be no use to
seek further to-day, so she got on a car and went to Lincoln
Park. There was always something to see there—the flowers,

the animals, the lake—and she flattered herself that on Monday she would be up betimes and searching. Besides, many things might happen between now and Monday.

Sunday passed with equal doubts, worries, assurances, and heaven knows what vagaries of mind and spirit. Every half-hour in the day the thought would come to her most sharply, like the tail of a swishing whip, that action—immediate action—was imperative. At other times she would look about her and assure herself that things were not so bad—that certainly she would come out safe and sound. At such times she would think of Drouet's advice about going on the stage, and saw some chance for herself in that quarter. She decided to take up that opportunity on the morrow.

Accordingly, she arose early Monday morning and dressed herself carefully. She did not know just how such applications were made, but she took it to be a matter which related more directly to the theatre buildings. All you had to do was to inquire of some one about the theatre for the manager and ask for a position. If there was anything, you might get it, or, at least, he could tell you how.

She had had no experience with this class of individuals whatsoever, and did not know the salacity and humour of the theatrical tribe. She only knew of the position which Mr. Hale occupied, but, of all things, she did not wish to encounter that personage, on account of her intimacy with his wife.

There was, however, at this time, one theatre, the Chicago Opera House, which was considerably in the public eye, and its manager, David A. Henderson, had a fair local reputation. Carrie had seen one or two elaborate performances there and had heard of several others. She knew nothing of Henderson nor of the methods of applying, but she instinctively felt that this would be a likely place, and accordingly strolled about in that neighbourhood. She came bravely enough to the showy entrance way, with the polished and begilded lobby, set with framed pictures out of the current attraction, leading up to the quiet box-office, but she could get no further. A noted comic opera comedian was holding forth that week, and the air of distinction and prosperity overawed her. She could not imagine that there would be anything in such a lofty sphere for her. She almost trembled at the audacity which might have carried her on to a terrible rebuff. She could find heart only to look at the pictures which were showy and then walk out. It seemed to her as if she had made a splendid escape and that it would be foolhardy to think of applying in that quarter again.

This little experience settled her hunting for one day. She looked around elsewhere, but it was from the outside. She got the location of several playhouses fixed in her mind—notably the Grand Opera House and McVickar's, both of which were leading in attractions—and then came away. Her spirits were materially reduced, owing to the newly restored sense of magnitude of the great interests and the insignificance of her claims upon society, such as she understood them to be.

That night she was visited by Mrs. Hale, whose chatter and protracted stay made it impossible to dwell upon her predicament or the fortune of the day. Before retiring, however, she sat down to think, and gave herself up to the most gloomy forebodings. Drouet had not put in an appearance. She had had no word from any quarter, she had spent a dollar of her precious sum in procuring food and paying car fare. It was evident that she would not endure long. Besides, she had discovered no resource.

In this situation her thoughts went out to her sister in Van Buren Street, whom she had not seen since the night of her flight, and to her home at Columbia City, which seemed now a part of something that could not be again. She looked for no refuge in that direction. Nothing but sorrow was brought her by thoughts of Hurstwood, which would return. That he could have chosen to dupe her in so ready a manner seemed a cruel thing.

Tuesday came, and with it appropriate indecision and speculation. She was in no mood, after her failure of the day before, to hasten forth upon her work-seeking errand, and yet she rebuked herself for what she considered her weakness the day before. Accordingly she started out to revisit the Chicago Opera House, but possessed scarcely enough courage to approach.

She did manage to inquire at the box-office, however.

"Manager of the company or the house?" asked the smartly

dressed individual who took care of the tickets. He was favourably impressed by Carrie's looks.

"I don't know," said Carrie, taken back by the question.

"You couldn't see the manager of the house to-day, anyhow," volunteered the young man. "He's out of town."

He noted her puzzled look, and then added: "What is it
you wish to see about?"

"I want to see about getting a position," she answered.

"You'd better see the manager of the company," he returned, "but he isn't here now."

"When will he be in?" asked Carrie, somewhat relieved by
this information.

"Well, you might find him in between eleven and twelve.
He's here after two o'clock."

Carrie thanked him and walked briskly out, while the
young man gazed after her through one of the side windows
of his gilded coop.

"Good-looking," he said to himself, and proceeded to visions of condescensions on her part which were exceedingly
flattering to himself.

One of the principal comedy companies of the day was
playing an engagement at the Grand Opera House. Here Carrie asked to see the manager of the company. She little knew
the trivial authority of this individual, or that had there been
a vacancy an actor would have been sent on from New York
to fill it.

"His office is upstairs," said a man in the box-office.

Several persons were in the manager's office, two lounging
near a window, another talking to an individual sitting at a
roll-top desk—the manager. Carrie glanced nervously about,
and began to fear that she should have to make her appeal
before the assembled company, two of whom—the occupants
of the window—were already observing her carefully.

"I can't do it," the manager was saying; "it's a rule of Mr.
Frohman's never to allow visitors back of the stage. No, no!"

Carrie timidly waited, standing. There were chairs, but no
one motioned her to be seated. The individual to whom the
manager had been talking went away quite crestfallen. That
luminary gazed earnestly at some papers before him, as if they
were of the greatest concern.

"Did you see that in the 'Herald' this morning about Nat Goodwin, Harris?"

"No," said the person addressed. "What was it?"

"Made quite a curtain address at Hooley's last night. Better look it up."

Harris reached over to a table and began to look for the "Herald."

"What is it?" said the manager to Carrie, apparently noticing her for the first time. He thought he was going to be held up for free tickets.

Carrie summoned up all her courage, which was little at best. She realised that she was a novice, and felt as if a rebuff were certain. Of this she was so sure that she only wished now to pretend she had called for advice.

"Can you tell me how to go about getting on the stage?"

It was the best way after all to have gone about the matter. She was interesting, in a manner, to the occupant of the chair, and the simplicity of her request and attitude took his fancy. He smiled, as did the others in the room, who, however, made some slight effort to conceal their humour.

"I don't know," he answered, looking her brazenly over. "Have you ever had any experience upon the stage?"

"A little," answered Carrie. "I have taken part in amateur performances."

She thought she had to make some sort of showing in order to retain his interest.

"Never studied for the stage?" he said, putting on an air intended as much to impress his friends with his discretion as Carrie.

"No, sir."

"Well, I don't know," he answered, tipping lazily back in his chair while she stood before him. "What makes you want to get on the stage?"

She felt abashed at the man's daring, but could only smile in answer to his engaging smirk, and say:

"I need to make a living."

"Oh," he answered, rather taken by her trim appearance, and feeling as if he might scrape up an acquaintance with her. "That's a good reason, isn't it? Well, Chicago is not a good place for what you want to do. You ought to be in New York.

There's more chance there. You could hardly expect to get started out here."

Carrie smiled genially, grateful that he should condescend to advise her even so much. He noticed the smile, and put a slightly different construction on it. He thought he saw an easy chance for a little flirtation.

"Sit down," he said, pulling a chair forward from the side of his desk and dropping his voice so that the two men in the room should not hear. Those two gave each other the suggestion of a wink.

"Well, I'll be going, Barney," said one, breaking away and so addressing the manager. "See you this afternoon."

"All right," said the manager.

The remaining individual took up a paper as if to read.

"Did you have any idea what sort of part you would like to get?" asked the manager softly.

"Oh, no," said Carrie. "I would take anything to begin with."

"I see," he said. "Do you live here in the city?"

"Yes, sir."

The manager smiled most blandly.

"Have you ever tried to get in as a chorus girl?" he asked, assuming a more confidential air.

Carrie began to feel that there was something exuberant and unnatural in his manner.

"No," she said.

"That's the way most girls begin," he went on, " who go on the stage. It's a good way to get experience."

He was turning on her a glance of the companionable and persuasive manner.

"I didn't know that," said Carrie.

"It's a difficult thing," he went on, "but there's always a chance, you know." Then, as if he suddenly remembered, he pulled out his watch and consulted it. "I've an appointment at two," he said, "and I've got to go to lunch now. Would you care to come and dine with me? We can talk it over there."

"Oh, no," said Carrie, the whole motive of the man flashing on her at once. "I have an engagement myself."

"That's too bad," he said, realising that he had been a little beforehand in his offer and that Carrie was about to go away. "Come in later. I may know of something."

"Thank you," she answered, with some trepidation, and went out.

"She was good-looking, wasn't she?" said the manager's companion, who had not caught all the details of the game he had played.

"Yes, in a way," said the other, sore to think the game had been lost. "She'd never make an actress, though. Just another chorus girl—that's all."

This little experience nearly destroyed her ambition to call upon the manager at the Chicago Opera House, but she decided to do so after a time. He was of a more sedate turn of mind. He said at once that there was no opening of any sort, and seemed to consider her search foolish.

"Chicago is no place to get a start," he said. "You ought to be in New York."

Still she persisted, and went to McVickar's, where she could not find any one. "The Old Homestead" was running there, but the person to whom she was referred was not to be found.

These little expeditions took up her time until quite four o'clock, when she was weary enough to go home. She felt as if she ought to continue and inquire elsewhere, but the results so far were too dispiriting. She took the car and arrived at Ogden Place in three-quarters of an hour, but decided to ride on to the West Side branch of the Post-office, where she was accustomed to receive Hurstwood's letters. There was one there now, written Saturday, which she tore open and read with mingled feelings. There was so much warmth in it and such tense complaint at her having failed to meet him, and her subsequent silence, that she rather pitied the man. That he loved her was evident enough. That he had wished and dared to do so, married as he was, was the evil. She felt as if the thing deserved an answer, and consequently decided that she would write and let him know that she knew of his married state and was justly incensed at his deception. She would tell him that it was all over between them.

At her room, the wording of this missive occupied her

for some time, for she fell to the task at once. It was most difficult.

"You do not need to have me explain why I did not meet you," she wrote in part. "How could you deceive me so? You cannot expect me to have anything more to do with you. I wouldn't under any circumstances. Oh, how could you act so?" she added in a burst of feeling. "You have caused me more misery than you can think. I hope you will get over your infatuation for me. We must not meet any more. Good-bye."

She took the letter the next morning, and at the corner dropped it reluctantly into the letter-box, still uncertain as to whether she should do so or not. Then she took the car and went down town.

This was the dull season with the department stores, but she was listened to with more consideration than was usually accorded to young women applicants, owing to her neat and attractive appearance. She was asked the same old questions with which she was already familiar.

"What can you do? Have you ever worked in a retail store before? Are you experienced?"

At The Fair, See and Company's, and all the great stores it was much the same. It was the dull season, she might come in a little later, possibly they would like to have her.

When she arrived at the house at the end of the day, weary and disheartened, she discovered that Drouet had been there. His umbrella and light overcoat were gone. She thought she missed other things, but could not be sure. Everything had not been taken.

So his going was crystallising into staying. What was she to do now? Evidently she would be facing the world in the same old way within a day or two. Her clothes would get poor. She put her two hands together in her customary expressive way and pressed her fingers. Large tears gathered in her eyes and broke hot across her cheeks. She was alone, very much alone.

Drouet really had called, but it was with a very different mind from that which Carrie had imagined. He expected to find her, to justify his return by claiming that he came to get the remaining portion of his wardrobe, and before he got away again to patch up a peace.

Accordingly, when he arrived, he was disappointed to find Carrie out. He trifled about, hoping that she was somewhere in the neighbourhood and would soon return. He constantly listened, expecting to hear her foot on the stair.

When he did so, it was his intention to make believe that he had just come in and was disturbed at being caught. Then he would explain his need of his clothes and find out how things stood.

Wait as he did, however, Carrie did not come. From pottering around among the drawers, in momentary expectation of her arrival, he changed to looking out of the window, and from that to resting himself in the rocking-chair. Still no Carrie. He began to grow restless and lit a cigar. After that he walked the floor. Then he looked out of the window and saw clouds gathering. He remembered an appointment at three. He began to think that it would be useless to wait, and got hold of his umbrella and light coat, intending to take these things, any way. It would scare her, he hoped. To-morrow he would come back for the others. He would find out how things stood.

As he started to go he felt truly sorry that he had missed her. There was a little picture of her on the wall, showing her arrayed in the little jacket he had first bought her—her face a little more wistful than he had seen it lately. He was really touched by it, and looked into the eyes of it with a rather rare feeling for him.

"You didn't do me right, Cad," he said, as if he were addressing her in the flesh.

Then he went to the door, took a good look around, and went out.

Chapter XXVII

WHEN WATERS ENGULF US WE REACH FOR A STAR

IT WAS WHEN he returned from his disturbed stroll about the streets, after receiving the decisive note from McGregor, James and Hay, that Hurstwood found the letter Carrie had written him that morning. He thrilled intensely as he noted the handwriting, and rapidly tore it open.

"Then," he thought, "she loves me or she would not have written to me at all."

He was slightly depressed at the tenor of the note for the first few minutes, but soon recovered. "She wouldn't write at all if she didn't care for me."

This was his one resource against the depression which held him. He could extract little from the wording of the letter, but the spirit he thought he knew.

There was really something exceedingly human—if not pathetic—in his being thus relieved by a clearly worded reproof. He who had for so long remained satisfied with himself now looked outside of himself for comfort—and to such a source. The mystic cords of affection! How they bind us all.

The colour came to his cheeks. For the moment he forgot the letter from McGregor, James and Hay. If he could only have Carrie, perhaps he could get out of the whole entanglement—perhaps it would not matter. He wouldn't care what his wife did with herself if only he might not lose Carrie. He stood up and walked about, dreaming his delightful dream of a life continued with this lovely possessor of his heart.

It was not long, however, before the old worry was back for consideration, and with it what weariness! He thought of the morrow and the suit. He had done nothing, and here was the afternoon slipping away. It was now a quarter of four. At five the attorneys would have gone home. He still had the morrow until noon. Even as he thought, the last fifteen minutes passed away and it was five. Then he abandoned the thought of seeing them any more that day and turned to Carrie.

It is to be observed that the man did not justify himself to himself. He was not troubling about that. His whole thought was the possibility of persuading Carrie. Nothing was wrong in that. He loved her dearly. Their mutual happiness depended upon it. Would that Drouet were only away!

While he was thinking thus elatedly, he remembered that he wanted some clean linen in the morning.

This he purchased, together with a half-dozen ties, and went to the Palmer House. As he entered he thought he saw Drouet ascending the stairs with a key. Surely not Drouet! Then he thought, perhaps they had changed their abode temporarily. He went straight up to the desk.

"Is Mr. Drouet stopping here?" he asked of the clerk.

"I think he is," said the latter, consulting his private registry list. "Yes."

"Is that so?" exclaimed Hurstwood, otherwise concealing his astonishment. "Alone?" he added.

"Yes," said the clerk.

Hurstwood turned away and set his lips so as best to express and conceal his feelings.

"How's that?" he thought. "They've had a row."

He hastened to his room with rising spirits and changed his linen. As he did so, he made up his mind that if Carrie was alone, or if she had gone to another place, it behooved him to find out. He decided to call at once.

"I know what I'll do," he thought. "I'll go to the door and ask if Mr. Drouet is at home. That will bring out whether he is there or not and where Carrie is."

He was almost moved to some muscular display as he thought of it. He decided to go immediately after supper.

On coming down from his room at six, he looked carefully about to see if Drouet was present and then went out to lunch. He could scarcely eat, however, he was so anxious to be about his errand. Before starting he thought it well to discover where Drouet would be, and returned to his hotel.

"Has Mr. Drouet gone out?" he asked of the clerk.

"No," answered the latter, "he's in his room. Do you wish to send up a card?"

"No, I'll call around later," answered Hurstwood, and strolled out.

He took a Madison car and went direct to Ogden Place, this time walking boldly up to the door. The chambermaid answered his knock.

"Is Mr. Drouet in?" said Hurstwood blandly.

"He is out of the city," said the girl, who had heard Carrie tell this to Mrs. Hale.

"Is Mrs. Drouet in?"

"No, she has gone to the theatre."

"Is that so?" said Hurstwood, considerably taken back; then, as if burdened with something important, "You don't know to which theatre?"

The girl really had no idea where she had gone, but not liking Hurstwood, and wishing to cause him trouble, answered: "Yes, Hooley's."

"Thank you," returned the manager, and, tipping his hat slightly, went away.

"I'll look in at Hooley's," thought he, but as a matter of fact he did not. Before he had reached the central portion of the city he thought the whole matter over and decided it would be useless. As much as he longed to see Carrie, he knew she would be with some one and did not wish to intrude with his plea there. A little later he might do so—in the morning. Only in the morning he had the lawyer question before him.

This little pilgrimage threw quite a wet blanket upon his rising spirits. He was soon down again to his old worry, and reached the resort anxious to find relief. Quite a company of gentlemen were making the place lively with their conversation. A group of Cook County politicians were conferring about a round cherry-wood table in the rear portion of the room. Several young merry-makers were chattering at the bar before making a belated visit to the theatre. A shabbily-genteel individual, with a red nose and an old high hat, was sipping a quiet glass of ale alone at one end of the bar. Hurstwood nodded to the politicians and went into his office.

About ten o'clock a friend of his, Mr. Frank L. Taintor, a local sport and racing man, dropped in, and seeing Hurstwood alone in his office came to the door.

"Hello, George!" he exclaimed.

"How are you, Frank?" said Hurstwood, somewhat relieved

by the sight of him. "Sit down," and he motioned him to one of the chairs in the little room.

"What's the matter, George?" asked Taintor. "You look a little glum. Haven't lost at the track, have you?"

"I'm not feeling very well to-night. I had a slight cold the other day."

"Take whiskey, George," said Taintor. "You ought to know that."

Hurstwood smiled.

While they were still conferring there, several other of Hurstwood's friends entered, and not long after eleven, the theatres being out, some actors began to drop in—among them some notabilities.

Then began one of those pointless social conversations so common in American resorts where the would-be *gilded* attempt to rub off gilt from those who have it in abundance. If Hurstwood had one leaning, it was toward notabilities. He considered that, if anywhere, he belonged among them. He was too proud to toady, too keen not to strictly observe the plane he occupied when there were those present who did not appreciate him, but, in situations like the present, where he could shine as a gentleman and be received without equivocation as a friend and equal among men of known ability, he was most delighted. It was on such occasions, if ever, that he would "take something." When the social flavour was strong enough he would even unbend to the extent of drinking glass for glass with his associates, punctiliously observing his turn to pay as if he were an outsider like the others. If he ever approached intoxication—or rather that ruddy warmth and comfortableness which precedes the more sloven state—it was when individuals such as these were gathered about him, when he was one of a circle of chatting celebrities. To-night, disturbed as was his state, he was rather relieved to find company, and now that notabilities were gathered, he laid aside his troubles for the nonce, and joined in right heartily.

It was not long before the imbibing began to tell. Stories began to crop up—those ever-enduring, droll stories which form the major portion of the conversation among American men under such circumstances.

Twelve o'clock arrived, the hour for closing, and with it the company took leave. Hurstwood shook hands with them most cordially. He was very roseate physically. He had arrived at that state where his mind, though clear, was, nevertheless, warm in its fancies. He felt as if his troubles were not very serious. Going into his office, he began to turn over certain accounts, awaiting the departure of the bartenders and the cashier, who soon left.

It was the manager's duty, as well as his custom, after all were gone to see that everything was safely closed up for the night. As a rule, no money except the cash taken in after banking hours was kept about the place, and that was locked in the safe by the cashier, who, with the owners, was joint keeper of the secret combination, but, nevertheless, Hurstwood nightly took the precaution to try the cash drawers and the safe in order to see that they were tightly closed. Then he would lock his own little office and set the proper light burning near the safe, after which he would take his departure.

Never in his experience had he found anything out of order, but to-night, after shutting down his desk, he came out and tried the safe. His way was to give a sharp pull. This time the door responded. He was slightly surprised at that, and looking in found the money cases as left for the day, apparently unprotected. His first thought was, of course, to inspect the drawers and shut the door.

"I'll speak to Mayhew about this to-morrow," he thought.

The latter had certainly imagined upon going out a half-hour before that he had turned the knob on the door so as to spring the lock. He had never failed to do so before. But to-night Mayhew had other thoughts. He had been revolving the problem of a business of his own.

"I'll look in here," thought the manager, pulling out the money drawers. He did not know why he wished to look in there. It was quite a superfluous action, which another time might not have happened at all.

As he did so, a layer of bills, in parcels of a thousand, such as banks issue, caught his eye. He could not tell how much they represented, but paused to view them. Then he pulled out the second of the cash drawers. In that were the receipts of the day.

"I didn't know Fitzgerald and Moy ever left any money this way," his mind said to itself. "They must have forgotten it."

He looked at the other drawer and paused again.

"Count them," said a voice in his ear.

He put his hand into the first of the boxes and lifted the stack, letting the separate parcels fall. They were bills of fifty and one hundred dollars done in packages of a thousand. He thought he counted ten such.

"Why don't I shut the safe?" his mind said to itself, lingering. "What makes me pause here?"

For answer there came the strangest words:

"Did you ever have ten thousand dollars in ready money?"

Lo, the manager remembered that he had never had so much. All his property had been slowly accumulated, and now his wife owned that. He was worth more than forty thousand, all told—but she would get that.

He puzzled as he thought of these things, then pushed in the drawers and closed the door, pausing with his hand upon the knob, which might so easily lock it all beyond temptation. Still he paused. Finally he went to the windows and pulled down the curtains. Then he tried the door, which he had previously locked. What was this thing, making him suspicious? Why did he wish to move about so quietly. He came back to the end of the counter as if to rest his arm and think. Then he went and unlocked his little office door and turned on the light. He also opened his desk, sitting down before it, only to think strange thoughts.

"The safe is open," said a voice. "There is just the least little crack in it. The lock has not been sprung."

The manager floundered among a jumble of thoughts. Now all the entanglement of the day came back. Also the thought that here was a solution. That money would do it. If he had that and Carrie. He rose up and stood stock-still, looking at the floor.

"What about it?" his mind asked, and for answer he put his hand slowly up and scratched his head.

The manager was no fool to be led blindly away by such an errant proposition as this, but his situation was peculiar. Wine was in his veins. It had crept up into his head and given him a warm view of the situation. It also coloured the possibilities of ten thousand for him. He could see great opportunities with that. He could get Carrie. Oh, yes, he could! He could get rid of his wife. That letter, too, was waiting discussion to-morrow morning. He would not need to answer that. He went back to the safe and put his hand on the knob. Then he pulled the door open and took the drawer with the money quite out.

With it once out and before him, it seemed a foolish thing to think about leaving it. Certainly it would. Why, he could live quietly with Carrie for years.

Lord! what was that? For the first time he was tense, as if a stern hand had been laid upon his shoulder. He looked fearfully around. Not a soul was present. Not a sound. Some one was shuffling by on the sidewalk. He took the box and the money and put it back in the safe. Then he partly closed the door again.

To those who have never wavered in conscience, the predicament of the individual whose mind is less strongly constituted and who trembles in the balance between duty and desire is scarcely appreciable, unless graphically portrayed. Those who have never heard that solemn voice of the ghostly clock which ticks with awful distinctness, "thou shalt," "thou shalt not," "thou shalt," "thou shalt not," are in no position to judge. Not alone in sensitive, highly organised natures is such a mental conflict possible. The dullest specimen of humanity, when drawn by desire toward evil, is recalled by a sense of right, which is proportionate in power and strength to his evil tendency. We must remember that it may not be a knowledge of right, for no knowledge of right is predicated of the animal's instinctive recoil at evil. Men are still led by instinct before they are regulated by knowledge. It is instinct which recalls the criminal—it is instinct (where highly organised reasoning is absent) which gives the criminal his feeling of danger, his fear of wrong.

At every first adventure, then, into some untried evil, the mind wavers. The clock of thought ticks out its wish and its denial. To those who have never experienced such a mental dilemma, the following will appeal on the simple ground of revelation.

When Hurstwood put the money back, his nature again

resumed its ease and daring. No one had observed him. He was quite alone. No one could tell what he wished to do. He could work this thing out for himself.

The imbibation of the evening had not yet worn off. Moist as was his brow, tremble as did his hand once after the nameless fright, he was still flushed with the fumes of liquor. He scarcely noticed that the time was passing. He went over his situation once again, his eye always seeing the money in a lump, his mind always seeing what it would do. He strolled into his little room, then to the door, then to the safe again. He put his hand on the knob and opened it. There was the money! Surely no harm could come from looking at it!

He took out the drawer again and lifted the bills. They were so smooth, so compact, so portable. How little they made, after all. He decided he would take them. Yes, he would. He would put them in his pocket. Then he looked at that and saw they would not go there. His hand satchel! To be sure, his hand satchel. They would go in that—all of it would. No one would think anything of it either. He went into the little office and took it from the shelf in the corner. Now he set it upon the desk and went out toward the safe. For some reason he did not want to fill it out in the big room.

First he brought the bills and then the loose receipts of the day. He would take it all. He put the empty drawers back and pushed the iron door almost to, then stood beside it meditating.

The wavering of a mind under such circumstances is an almost inexplicable thing, and yet it is absolutely true. Hurstwood could not bring himself to act definitely. He wanted to think about it—to ponder over it, to decide whether it were best. He was drawn by such a keen desire for Carrie, driven by such a state of turmoil in his own affairs that he thought constantly it would be best, and yet he wavered. He did not know what evil might result from it to him—how soon he might come to grief. The true ethics of the situation never once occurred to him, and never would have, under any circumstances.

After he had all the money in the hand bag, a revulsion of feeling seized him. He would not do it—no! Think of what a scandal it would make. The police! They would be after him. He would have to fly, and where? Oh, the terror of being a fugitive from justice! He took out the two boxes and put all the money back. In his excitement he forgot what he was doing, and put the sums in the wrong boxes. As he pushed the door to, he thought he remembered doing it wrong and opened the door again. There were the two boxes mixed.

He took them out and straightened the matter, but now the terror had gone. Why be afraid?

While the money was in his hand the lock clicked. It had sprung! Did he do it? He grabbed at the knob and pulled vigorously. It had closed. Heavens! he was in for it now, sure enough.

The moment he realised that the safe was locked for a surety, the sweat burst out upon his brow and he trembled violently. He looked about him and decided instantly. There was no delaying now.

"Supposing I do lay it on the top," he said, "and go away, they'll know who took it. I'm the last to close up. Besides, other things will happen."

At once he became the man of action.

"I must get out of this," he thought.

He hurried into his little room, took down his light overcoat and hat, locked his desk, and grabbed the satchel. Then he turned out all but one light and opened the door. He tried to put on his old assured air, but it was almost gone. He was repenting rapidly.

"I wish I hadn't done that," he said. "That was a mistake."

He walked steadily down the street, greeting a night watchman whom he knew who was trying doors. He must get out of the city, and that quickly.

"I wonder how the trains run?" he thought.

Instantly he pulled out his watch and looked. It was nearly half-past one.

At the first drug store he stopped, seeing a long-distance telephone booth inside. It was a famous drug store, and contained one of the first private telephone booths ever erected.

"I want to use your 'phone a minute," he said to the night clerk.

The latter nodded.

"Give me 1643," he called to Central, after looking up the Michigan Central depot number. Soon he got the ticket agent.

"How do the trains leave here for Detroit?" he asked.

The man explained the hours.

"No more to-night?"

"Nothing with a sleeper. Yes, there is, too," he added. "There is a mail train out of here at three o'clock."

"All right," said Hurstwood. "What time does that get to Detroit?"

He was thinking if he could only get there and cross the river into Canada, he could take his time about getting to Montreal. He was relieved to learn that it would reach there by noon.

"Mayhew won't open the safe till nine," he thought. "They can't get on my track before noon."

Then he thought of Carrie. With what speed must he get her, if he got her at all. She would have to come along. He jumped into the nearest cab standing by.

"To Ogden Place," he said sharply. "I'll give you a dollar more if you make good time."

The cabby beat his horse into a sort of imitation gallop, which was fairly fast, however. On the way Hurstwood thought what to do. Reaching the number, he hurried up the steps and did not spare the bell in waking the servant.

"Is Mrs. Drouet in?" he asked.

"Yes," said the astonished girl.

"Tell her to dress and come to the door at once. Her husband is in the hospital, injured, and wants to see her."

The servant girl hurried upstairs, convinced by the man's strained and emphatic manner.

"What!" said Carrie, lighting the gas and searching for her clothes.

"Mr. Drouet is hurt and in the hospital. He wants to see you. The cab's downstairs."

Carrie dressed very rapidly, and soon appeared below, forgetting everything save the necessities.

"Drouet is hurt," said Hurstwood quickly. "He wants to see you. Come quickly."

Carrie was so bewildered that she swallowed the whole story.

"Get in," said Hurstwood, helping her and jumping after.

The cabby began to turn the horse around.

"Michigan Central depot," he said, standing up and speaking so low that Carrie could not hear, "as fast as you can go."

Chapter XXVIII

A Pilgrim, an Outlaw: The Spirit Detained

THE CAB had not travelled a short block before Carrie, settling herself and thoroughly waking in the night atmosphere, asked:

"What's the matter with him? Is he hurt badly?"

"It isn't anything very serious," Hurstwood said solemnly. He was very much disturbed over his own situation, and now that he had Carrie with him, he only wanted to get safely out of reach of the law. Therefore he was in no mood for anything save such words as would further his plans distinctly.

Carrie did not forget that there was something to be settled between her and Hurstwood, but the thought was ignored in her agitation. The one thing was to finish this strange pilgrimage.

"Where is he?"

"Way out on the South Side," said Hurstwood. "We'll have to take the train. It's the quickest way."

Carrie said nothing, and the horse gambolled on. The weirdness of the city by night held her attention. She looked at the long receding rows of lamps and studied the dark, silent houses.

"How did he hurt himself?" she asked—meaning what was the nature of his injuries. Hurstwood understood. He hated to lie any more than necessary, and yet he wanted no protests until he was out of danger.

"I don't know exactly," he said. "They just called me up to go and get you and bring you out. They said there wasn't any need for alarm, but that I shouldn't fail to bring you."

The man's serious manner convinced Carrie, and she became silent, wondering.

Hurstwood examined his watch and urged the man to hurry. For one in so delicate a position he was exceedingly cool. He could only think of how needful it was to make the train and get quietly away. Carrie seemed quite tractable, and he congratulated himself.

In due time they reached the depot, and after helping her out he handed the man a five-dollar bill and hurried on.

"You wait here," he said to Carrie, when they reached the waiting-room, " while I get the tickets."

"Have I much time to catch that train for Detroit?" he asked of the agent.

"Four minutes," said the latter.

He paid for two tickets as circumspectly as possible.

"Is it far?" said Carrie, as he hurried back.

"Not very," he said. "We must get right in."

He pushed her before him at the gate, stood between her and the ticket man while the latter punched their tickets, so that she could not see, and then hurried after.

There was a long line of express and passenger cars and one or two common day coaches. As the train had only recently been made up and few passengers were expected, there were only one or two brakemen waiting. They entered the rear day coach and sat down. Almost immediately, "All aboard," resounded faintly from the outside, and the train started.

Carrie began to think it was a little bit curious—this going to a depot—but said nothing. The whole incident was so out of the natural that she did not attach too much weight to anything she imagined.

"How have you been?" asked Hurstwood gently, for he now breathed easier.

"Very well," said Carrie, who was so disturbed that she could not bring a proper attitude to bear in the matter. She was still nervous to reach Drouet and see what could be the matter. Hurstwood contemplated her and felt this. He was not disturbed that it should be so. He did not trouble because she was moved sympathetically in the matter. It was one of the qualities in her which pleased him exceedingly. He was only thinking how he should explain. Even this was not the most serious thing in his mind, however. His own deed and present flight were the great shadows which weighed upon him.

"What a fool I was to do that," he said over and over. "What a mistake!"

In his sober senses, he could scarcely realise that the thing had been done. He could not begin to feel that he was a fugitive from justice. He had often read of such things, and had thought they must be terrible, but now that the thing was upon him, he only sat and looked into the past. The future was a thing which concerned the Canadian line. He wanted to reach that. As for the rest, he surveyed his actions for the evening, and counted them parts of a great mistake.

"Still," he said, " what could I have done?"

Then he would decide to make the best of it, and would begin to do so by starting the whole inquiry over again. It was a fruitless, harassing round, and left him in a queer mood to deal with the proposition he had in the presence of Carrie.

The train clacked through the yards along the lake front, and ran rather slowly to Twenty-fourth Street. Brakes and signals were visible without. The engine gave short calls with its whistle, and frequently the bell rang. Several brakemen came through, bearing lanterns. They were locking the vestibules and putting the cars in order for a long run.

Presently it began to gain speed, and Carrie saw the silent streets flashing by in rapid succession. The engine also began its whistle-calls of four parts, with which it signalled danger to important crossings.

"It is very far?" asked Carrie.

"Not so very," said Hurstwood. He could hardly repress a smile at her simplicity. He wanted to explain and conciliate her, but he also wanted to be well out of Chicago.

In the lapse of another half-hour it became apparent to Carrie that it was quite a run to wherever he was taking her, anyhow.

"Is it in Chicago?" she asked nervously. They were now far beyond the city limits, and the train was scudding across the Indiana line at a great rate.

"No," he said, "not where we are going."

There was something in the way he said this which aroused her in an instant.

Her pretty brow began to contract.

"We are going to see Charlie, aren't we?" she asked.

He felt that the time was up. An explanation might as well come now as later. Therefore, he shook his head in the most gentle negative.

"What?" said Carrie. She was nonplussed at the possibility of the errand being different from what she had thought.

He only looked at her in the most kindly and mollifying way.

"Well, where are you taking me, then?" she asked, her voice showing the quality of fright.

"I'll tell you, Carrie, if you'll be quiet. I want you to come along with me to another city."

"Oh," said Carrie, her voice rising into a weak cry. "Let me off. I don't want to go with you."

She was quite appalled at the man's audacity. This was something which had never for a moment entered her head. Her one thought now was to get off and away. If only the flying train could be stopped, the terrible trick would be amended.

She arose and tried to push out into the aisle—anywhere. She knew she had to do something. Hurstwood laid a gentle hand on her.

"Sit still, Carrie," he said. "Sit still. It won't do you any good to get up here. Listen to me and I'll tell you what I'll do. Wait a moment."

She was pushing at his knees, but he only pulled her back. No one saw this little altercation, for very few persons were in the car, and they were attempting to doze.

"I won't," said Carrie, who was, nevertheless, complying against her will. "Let me go," she said. "How dare you?" and large tears began to gather in her eyes.

Hurstwood was now fully aroused to the immediate difficulty, and ceased to think of his own situation. He must do something with this girl, or she would cause him trouble. He tried the art of persuasion with all his powers aroused.

"Look here now, Carrie," he said, "you mustn't act this way. I didn't mean to hurt your feelings. I don't want to do anything to make you feel bad."

"Oh," sobbed Carrie, "oh, oh—oo—o!"

"There, there," he said, "you mustn't cry. Won't you listen to me? Listen to me a minute, and I'll tell you why I came to do this thing. I couldn't help it. I assure you I couldn't. Won't you listen?"

Her sobs disturbed him so that he was quite sure she did not hear a word he said.

"Won't you listen?" he asked.

"No, I won't," said Carrie, flashing up. "I want you to take me out of this, or I'll tell the conductor. I won't go with you. It's a shame," and again sobs of fright cut off her desire for expression.

Hurstwood listened with some astonishment. He felt that she had just cause for feeling as she did, and yet he wished that he could straighten this thing out quickly. Shortly the conductor would come through for the tickets. He wanted no noise, no trouble of any kind. Before everything he must make her quiet.

"You couldn't get out until the train stops again," said Hurstwood. "It won't be very long until we reach another station. You can get out then if you want to. I won't stop you. All I want you to do is to listen a moment. You'll let me tell you, won't you?"

Carrie seemed not to listen. She only turned her head toward the window, where outside all was black. The train was speeding with steady grace across the fields and through patches of wood. The long whistles came with sad, musical effect as the lonely woodland crossings were approached.

Now the conductor entered the car and took up the one or two fares that had been added at Chicago. He approached Hurstwood, who handed out the tickets. Poised as she was to act, Carrie made no move. She did not look about.

When the conductor had gone again Hurstwood felt relieved.

"You're angry at me because I deceived you," he said. "I didn't mean to, Carrie. As I live I didn't. I couldn't help it. I couldn't stay away from you after the first time I saw you."

He was ignoring the last deception as something that might go by the board. He wanted to convince her that his wife could no longer be a factor in their relationship. The money he had stolen he tried to shut out of his mind.

"Don't talk to me," said Carrie, "I hate you. I want you to go away from me. I am going to get out at the very next station."

She was in a tremble of excitement and opposition as she spoke.

"All right," he said, "but you'll hear me out, won't you?

After all you have said about loving me, you might hear me. I don't want to do you any harm. I'll give you the money to go back with when you go. I merely want to tell you, Carrie. You can't stop me from loving you, whatever you may think."

He looked at her tenderly, but received no reply.

"You think I have deceived you badly, but I haven't. I didn't do it willingly. I'm through with my wife. She hasn't any claims on me. I'll never see her any more. That's why I'm here to-night. That's why I came and got you."

"You said Charlie was hurt," said Carrie, savagely. "You deceived me. You've been deceiving me all the time, and now you want to force me to run away with you."

She was so excited that she got up and tried to get by him again. He let her, and she took another seat. Then he followed.

"Don't run away from me, Carrie," he said gently. "Let me explain. If you will only hear me out you will see where I stand. I tell you my wife is nothing to me. She hasn't been anything for years or I wouldn't have ever come near you. I'm going to get a divorce just as soon as I can. I'll never see her again. I'm done with all that. You're the only person I want. If I can have you I won't ever think of another woman again."

Carrie heard all this in a very ruffled state. It sounded sincere enough, however, despite all he had done. There was a tenseness in Hurstwood's voice and manner which could but have some effect. She did not want anything to do with him. He was married, he had deceived her once, and now again, and she thought him terrible. Still there is something in such daring and power which is fascinating to a woman, especially if she can be made to feel that it is all prompted by love of her.

The progress of the train was having a great deal to do with the solution of this difficult situation. The speeding wheels and disappearing country put Chicago farther and farther behind. Carrie could feel that she was being borne a long distance off—that the engine was making an almost through run to some distant city. She felt at times as if she could cry out and make such a row that some one would come to her aid; at other times it seemed an almost useless thing—so far was she from any aid, no matter what she did. All the while Hurstwood was endeavouring to formulate his plea in such a way that it would strike home and bring her into sympathy with him.

"I was simply put where I didn't know what else to do."

Carrie deigned no suggestion of hearing this.

"When I saw you wouldn't come unless I could marry you, I decided to put everything else behind me and get you to come away with me. I'm going off now to another city. I want to go to Montreal for a while, and then anywhere you want to. We'll go and live in New York, if you say."

"I'll not have anything to do with you," said Carrie. "I want to get off this train. Where are we going?"

"To Detroit," said Hurstwood.

"Oh!" said Carrie, in a burst of anguish. So distant and definite a point seemed to increase the difficulty.

"Won't you come along with me?" he said, as if there was great danger that she would not. "You won't need to do anything but travel with me. I'll not trouble you in any way. You can see Montreal and New York, and then if you don't want to stay you can go back. It will be better than trying to go back to-night."

The first gleam of fairness shone in this proposition for Carrie. It seemed a plausible thing to do, much as she feared his opposition if she tried to carry it out. Montreal and New York! Even now she was speeding toward those great, strange lands, and could see them if she liked. She thought, but made no sign.

Hurstwood thought he saw a shade of compliance in this. He redoubled his ardour.

"Think," he said, "what I've given up. I can't go back to Chicago any more. I've got to stay away and live alone now, if you don't come with me. You won't go back on me entirely, will you, Carrie?"

"I don't want you to talk to me," she answered forcibly.

Hurstwood kept silent for a while.

Carrie felt the train to be slowing down. It was the moment to act if she was to act at all. She stirred uneasily.

"Don't think of going, Carrie," he said. "If you ever cared for me at all, come along and let's start right. I'll do whatever you say. I'll marry you, or I'll let you go back. Give yourself time to think it over. I wouldn't have wanted you to come if I hadn't loved you. I tell you, Carrie, before God, I can't live without you. I won't!"

There was the tensity of fierceness in the man's plea which appealed deeply to her sympathies. It was a dissolving fire which was actuating him now. He was loving her too intensely to think of giving her up in this, his hour of distress. He clutched her hand nervously and pressed it with all the force of an appeal.

The train was now all but stopped. It was running by some cars on a side track. Everything outside was dark and dreary. A few sprinkles on the window began to indicate that it was raining. Carrie hung in a quandary, balancing between decision and helplessness. Now the train stopped, and she was listening to his plea. The engine backed a few feet and all was still.

She wavered, totally unable to make a move. Minute after minute slipped by and still she hesitated, he pleading.

"Will you let me come back if I want to?" she asked, as if she now had the upper hand and her companion was utterly subdued.

"Of course," he answered, "you know I will."

Carrie only listened as one who has granted a temporary amnesty. She began to feel as if the matter were in her hands entirely.

The train was again in rapid motion. Hurstwood changed the subject.

"Aren't you very tired?" he said.

"No," she answered.

"Won't you let me get you a berth in the sleeper?"

She shook her head, though for all her distress and his trickery she was beginning to notice what she had always felt—his thoughtfulness.

"Oh, yes," he said, "you will feel so much better."

She shook her head.

"Let me fix my coat for you, anyway," and he arose and arranged his light coat in a comfortable position to receive her head.

"There," he said tenderly, "now see if you can't rest a

little." He could have kissed her for her compliance. He took his seat beside her and thought a moment.

"I believe we're in for a heavy rain," he said.

"So it looks," said Carrie, whose nerves were quieting under the sound of the rain drops, driven by a gusty wind, as the train swept on frantically through the shadow to a newer world.

The fact that he had in a measure mollified Carrie was a source of satisfaction to Hurstwood, but it furnished only the most temporary relief. Now that her opposition was out of the way, he had all of his time to devote to the consideration of his own error.

His condition was bitter in the extreme, for he did not want the miserable sum he had stolen. He did not want to be a thief. That sum or any other could never compensate for the state which he had thus foolishly doffed. It could not give him back his host of friends, his name, his house and family, nor Carrie, as he had meant to have her. He was shut out from Chicago—from his easy, comfortable state. He had robbed himself of his dignity, his merry meetings, his pleasant evenings. And for what? The more he thought of it the more unbearable it became. He began to think that he would try and restore himself to his old state. He would return the miserable thievings of the night and explain. Perhaps Moy would understand. Perhaps they would forgive him and let him come back.

By noontime the train rolled into Detroit and he began to feel exceedingly nervous. The police must be on his track by now. They had probably notified all the police of the big cities, and detectives would be watching for him. He remembered instances in which defaulters had been captured. Consequently, he breathed heavily and paled somewhat. His hands felt as if they must have something to do. He simulated interest in several scenes without which he did not feel. He repeatedly beat his foot upon the floor.

Carrie noticed his agitation, but said nothing. She had no idea what it meant or that it was important.

He wondered now why he had not asked whether this train went on through to Montreal or some Canadian point. Perhaps he could have saved time. He jumped up and sought the conductor.

"Does any part of this train go to Montreal?" he asked.

"Yes, the next sleeper back does."

He would have asked more, but it did not seem wise, so he decided to inquire at the depot.

The train rolled into the yards, clanging and puffing.

"I think we had better go right on through to Montreal," he said to Carrie. "I'll see what the connections are when we get off."

He was exceedingly nervous, but did his best to put on a calm exterior. Carrie only looked at him with large, troubled eyes. She was drifting mentally, unable to say to herself what to do.

The train stopped and Hurstwood led the way out. He looked warily around him, pretending to look after Carrie. Seeing nothing that indicated studied observation, he made his way to the ticket office.

"The next train for Montreal leaves when?" he asked.

"In twenty minutes," said the man.

He bought two tickets and Pullman berths. Then he hastened back to Carrie.

"We go right out again," he said, scarcely noticing that Carrie looked tired and weary.

"I wish I was out of all this," she exclaimed gloomily.

"You'll feel better when we reach Montreal," he said.

"I haven't an earthly thing with me," said Carrie; "not even a handkerchief."

"You can buy all you want as soon as you get there, dearest," he explained. "You can call in a dressmaker."

Now the crier called the train ready and they got on. Hurstwood breathed a sigh of relief as it started. There was a short run to the river, and there they were ferried over. They had barely pulled the train off the ferry-boat when he settled back with a sigh.

"It won't be so very long now," he said, remembering her in his relief. "We get there the first thing in the morning."

Carrie scarcely deigned to reply.

"I'll see if there is a dining-car," he added. "I'm hungry."

Chapter XXIX

To the untravelled, territory other than their own familiar heath is invariably fascinating. Next to love, it is the one thing which solaces and delights. Things new are too important to be neglected, and mind, which is a mere reflection of sensory impressions, succumbs to the flood of objects. Thus lovers are forgotten, sorrows laid aside, death hidden from view. There is a world of accumulated feeling back of the trite dramatic expression—"I am going away."

As Carrie looked out upon the flying scenery she almost forgot that she had been tricked into this long journey against her will and that she was without the necessary apparel for travelling. She quite forgot Hurstwood's presence at times, and looked away to homely farmhouses and cosey cottages in villages with wondering eyes. It was an interesting world to her. Her life had just begun. She did not feel herself defeated at all. Neither was she blasted in hope. The great city held much. Possibly she would come out of bondage into freedom—who knows? Perhaps she would be happy. These thoughts raised her above the level of erring. She was saved in that she was hopeful.

The following morning the train pulled safely into Montreal and they stepped down, Hurstwood glad to be out of danger, Carrie wondering at the novel atmosphere of the northern city. Long before, Hurstwood had been here, and now he remembered the name of the hotel at which he had stopped. As they came out of the main entrance of the depot he heard it called anew by a busman.

"We'll go right up and get rooms," he said.

At the clerk's office Hurstwood swung the register about while the clerk came forward. He was thinking what name he would put down. With the latter before him he found no time for hesitation. A name he had seen out of the car window came swiftly to him. It was pleasing enough. With an easy hand he wrote, "G. W. Murdock and wife." It was the largest concession to necessity he felt like making. His initials he could not spare.

When they were shown their room Carrie saw at once that he had secured her a lovely chamber.

"You have a bath there," said he. "Now you can clean up when you get ready."

Carrie went over and looked out the window, while Hurstwood looked at himself in the glass. He felt dusty and unclean. He had no trunk, no change of linen, not even a hairbrush.

"I'll ring for soap and towels," he said, "and send you up a hair-brush. Then you can bathe and get ready for breakfast. I'll go for a shave and come back and get you, and then we'll go out and look for some clothes for you."

He smiled good-naturedly as he said this.

"All right," said Carrie.

She sat down in one of the rocking-chairs, while Hurstwood waited for the boy, who soon knocked.

"Soap, towels, and a pitcher of ice-water."

"Yes, sir."

"I'll go now," he said to Carrie, coming toward her and holding out his hands, but she did not move to take them.

"You're not mad at me, are you?" he asked softly.

"Oh, no!" she answered, rather indifferently.

"Don't you care for me at all?"

She made no answer, but looked steadily toward the window.

"Don't you think you could love me a little?" he pleaded, taking one of her hands, which she endeavoured to draw away. "You once said you did."

"What made you deceive me so?" asked Carrie.

"I couldn't help it," he said, "I wanted you too much."

"You didn't have any right to want me," she answered, striking cleanly home.

"Oh, well, Carrie," he answered, "here I am. It's too late now. Won't you try and care for me a little?"

He looked rather worsted in thought as he stood before her.

She shook her head negatively.

"Let me start all over again. Be my wife from to-day on."

Carrie rose up as if to step away, he holding her hand. Now he slipped his arm about her and she struggled, but in vain. He held her quite close. Instantly there flamed up in his body the all-compelling desire. His affection took an ardent form.

"Let me go," said Carrie, who was folded close to him.

"Won't you love me?" he said. "Won't you be mine from now on?"

Carrie had never been ill-disposed toward him. Only a moment before she had been listening with some complacency, remembering her old affection for him. He was so handsome, so daring!

Now, however, this feeling had changed to one of opposition, which rose feebly. It mastered her for a moment, and then, held close as she was, began to wane. Something else in her spoke. This man, to whose bosom she was being pressed, was strong; he was passionate, he loved her, and she was alone. If she did not turn to him—accept of his love—where else might she go? Her resistance half dissolved in the flood of his strong feeling.

She found him lifting her head and looking into her eyes. What magnetism there was she could never know. His many sins, however, were for the moment all forgotten.

He pressed her closer and kissed her, and she felt that further opposition was useless.

"Will you marry me?" she asked, forgetting *how*.

"This very day," he said, with all delight.

Now the hall-boy pounded on the door and he released his hold upon her regretfully.

"You get ready now, will you," he said, "at once?"

"Yes," she answered.

"I'll be back in three-quarters of an hour."

Carrie, flushed and excited, moved away as he admitted the boy.

Below stairs, he halted in the lobby to look for a barber shop. For the moment, he was in fine feather. His recent victory over Carrie seemed to atone for much he had endured during the last few days. Life seemed worth fighting for. This eastward flight from all things customary and attached seemed as if it might have happiness in store. The storm showed a rainbow at the end of which might be a pot of gold.

He was about to cross to a little red-and-white striped bar which was fastened up beside a door when a voice greeted him familiarly. Instantly his heart sank.

"Why, hello, George, old man!" said the voice. "What are you doing down here?"

Hurstwood was already confronted, and recognised his friend Kenny, the stock-broker.

"Just attending to a little private matter," he answered, his mind working like a key-board of a telephone station. This man evidently did not know—he had not read the papers.

"Well, it seems strange to see you way up here," said Mr. Kenny genially. "Stopping here?"

"Yes," said Hurstwood uneasily, thinking of his hand-writing on the register.

"Going to be in town long?"

"No, only a day or so."

"Is that so? Had your breakfast?"

"Yes," said Hurstwood, lying blandly. "I'm just going for a shave."

"Won't you come have a drink?"

"Not until afterwards," said the ex-manager. "I'll see you later. Are you stopping here?"

"Yes," said Mr. Kenny, and then, turning the word again, added: "How are things out in Chicago?"

"About the same as usual," said Hurstwood, smiling genially.

"Wife with you?"

"No."

"Well, I must see more of you to-day. I'm just going in here for breakfast. Come in when you're through."

"I will," said Hurstwood, moving away. The whole conversation was a trial to him. It seemed to add complications with every word. This man called up a thousand memories. He represented everything he had left. Chicago, his wife, the elegant resort—all these were in his greeting and inquiries. And here he was in this same hotel expecting to confer with him, unquestionably waiting to have a good time with him. All at once the Chicago papers would arrive. The local papers would have accounts in them this very day. He forgot his triumph with Carrie in the possibility of soon being known for what he was, in this man's eyes, a safe-breaker. He could have groaned as he went into the barber shop. He decided to escape and seek a more secluded hotel.

Accordingly, when he came out he was glad to see the lobby clear, and hastened toward the stairs. He would get Carrie and go out by the ladies' entrance. They would have breakfast in some more inconspicuous place.

Across the lobby, however, another individual was surveying him. He was of a commonplace Irish type, small of stature, cheaply dressed, and with a head that seemed a smaller edition of some huge ward politician's. This individual had been evidently talking with the clerk, but now he surveyed the ex-manager keenly.

Hurstwood felt the long-range examination and recognised the type. Instinctively he felt that the man was a detective— that he was being watched. He hurried across, pretending not to notice, but in his mind was a world of thoughts. What would happen now? What could these people do? He began to trouble concerning the extradition laws. He did not understand them absolutely. Perhaps he could be arrested. Oh, if Carrie should find out! Montreal was too warm for him. He began to long to be out of it.

Carrie had bathed and was waiting when he arrived. She looked refreshed—more delightful than ever, but reserved. Since he had gone she had resumed somewhat of her cold attitude towards him. Love was not blazing in her heart. He felt it, and his troubles seemed increased. He could not take her in his arms; he did not even try. Something about her forbade it. In part his opinion was the result of his own experiences and reflections below stairs.

"You're ready, are you?" he said kindly.

"Yes," she answered.

"We'll go out for breakfast. This place down here doesn't appeal to me very much."

"All right," said Carrie.

They went out, and at the corner the commonplace Irish individual was standing, eyeing him. Hurstwood could scarcely refrain from showing that he knew of this chap's presence. The insolence in the fellow's eye was galling. Still they passed, and he explained to Carrie concerning the city. Another restaurant was not long in showing itself, and here they entered.

"What a queer town this is," said Carrie, who marvelled at it solely because it was not like Chicago.

"It isn't as lively as Chicago," said Hurstwood. "Don't you like it?"

"No," said Carrie, whose feelings were already localised in the great Western city.

"Well, it isn't as interesting," said Hurstwood.

"What's here?" asked Carrie, wondering at his choosing to visit this town.

"Nothing much," returned Hurstwood. "It's quite a resort. There's some pretty scenery about here."

Carrie listened, but with a feeling of unrest. There was much about her situation which destroyed the possibility of appreciation.

"We won't stay here long," said Hurstwood, who was now really glad to note her dissatisfaction. "You pick out your clothes as soon as breakfast is over and we'll run down to New York soon. You'll like that. It's a lot more like a city than any place outside Chicago."

He was really planning to slip out and away. He would see what these detectives would do—what move his employers at Chicago would make—then he would slip away—down to New York, where it was easy to hide. He knew enough about that city to know that its mysteries and possibilities of mystification were infinite.

The more he thought, however, the more wretched his situation became. He saw that getting here did not exactly clear up the ground. The firm would probably employ detectives to watch him—Pinkerton men or agents of Mooney and Boland. They might arrest him the moment he tried to leave Canada. So he might be compelled to remain here months, and in what a state!

Back at the hotel Hurstwood was anxious and yet fearful to see the morning papers. He wanted to know how far the news of his criminal deed had spread. So he told Carrie he would be up in a few moments, and went to secure and scan the dailies. No familiar or suspicious faces were about, and yet he did not like reading in the lobby, so he sought the main parlour on the floor above and, seated by a window there, looked them over. Very little was given to his crime, but it was there, several "sticks" in all, among all the riffraff of telegraphed murders, accidents, marriages, and other news. He wished, half sadly, that he could undo it all. Every moment of his time in this far-off abode of safety but added to his feeling that he had made a great mistake. There could have been an easier way out if he had only known.

He left the papers before going to the room, thinking thus to keep them out of the hands of Carrie.

"Well, how are you feeling?" he asked of her. She was engaged in looking out of the window.

"Oh, all right," she answered.

He came over, and was about to begin a conversation with her, when a knock came at their door.

"Maybe it's one of my parcels," said Carrie.

Hurstwood opened the door, outside of which stood the individual whom he had so thoroughly suspected.

"You're Mr. Hurstwood, are you?" said the latter, with a volume of affected shrewdness and assurance.

"Yes," said Hurstwood calmly. He knew the type so thoroughly that some of his old familiar indifference to it returned. Such men as these were of the lowest stratum welcomed at the resort. He stepped out and closed the door.

"Well, you know what I am here for, don't you?" said the man confidentially.

"I can guess," said Hurstwood softly.

"Well, do you intend to try and keep the money?"

"That's my affair," said Hurstwood grimly.

"You can't do it, you know," said the detective, eyeing him coolly.

"Look here, my man," said Hurstwood authoritatively, "you don't understand anything about this case, and I can't explain to you. Whatever I intend to do I'll do without advice from the outside. You'll have to excuse me."

"Well, now, there's no use of your talking that way," said the man, "when you're in the hands of the police. We can make a lot of trouble for you if we want to. You're not registered right in this house, you haven't got your wife with you, and the newspapers don't know you're here yet. You might as well be reasonable."

"What do you want to know?" asked Hurstwood.

"Whether you're going to send back that money or not."

Hurstwood paused and studied the floor.

"There's no use explaining to you about this," he said at last. "There's no use of your asking me. I'm no fool, you know. I know just what you can do and what you can't. You can create a lot of trouble if you want to. I know that all right, but it won't help you to get the money. Now, I've made up my mind what to do. I've already written Fitzgerald and Moy, so there's nothing I can say. You wait until you hear more from them."

All the time he had been talking he had been moving away from the door, down the corridor, out of the hearing of Carrie. They were now near the end where the corridor opened into the large general parlour.

"You won't give it up?" said the man.

The words irritated Hurstwood greatly. Hot blood poured into his brain. Many thoughts formulated themselves. He was no thief. He didn't want the money. If he could only explain to Fitzgerald and Moy, maybe it would be all right again.

"See here," he said, "there's no use my talking about this at all. I respect your power all right, but I'll have to deal with the people who know."

"Well, you can't get out of Canada with it," said the man.

"I don't want to get out," said Hurstwood. "When I get ready there'll be nothing to stop me for."

He turned back, and the detective watched him closely. It seemed an intolerable thing. Still he went on and into the room.

"Who was it?" asked Carrie.

"A friend of mine from Chicago."

The whole of this conversation was such a shock that, coming as it did after all the other worry of the past week, it sufficed to induce a deep gloom and moral revulsion in Hurstwood. What hurt him most was the fact that he was being pursued as a thief. He began to see the nature of that social injustice which sees but one side—often but a single point in a long tragedy. All the newspapers noted but one thing, his taking the money. How and wherefore were but indifferently dealt with. All the complications which led up to it were unknown. He was accused without being understood.

Sitting in his room with Carrie the same day, he decided to send the money back. He would write Fitzgerald and Moy, explain all, and then send it by express. Maybe they would forgive him. Perhaps they would ask him back. He would make good the false statement he had made about writing them. Then he would leave this peculiar town.

For an hour he thought over this plausible statement of the tangle. He wanted to tell them about his wife, but couldn't. He finally narrowed it down to an assertion that he was light-headed from entertaining friends, had found the safe open, and having gone so far as to take the money out, had accidentally closed it. This act he regretted very much. He was sorry he had put them to so much trouble. He would undo what he could by sending the money back—the major portion of it. The remainder he would pay up as soon as he could. Was there any possibility of his being restored? This he only hinted at.

The troubled state of the man's mind may be judged by the very construction of this letter. For the nonce he forgot what a painful thing it would be to resume his old place, even if it were given him. He forgot that he had severed himself from the past as by a sword, and that if he did manage to in some way reunite himself with it, the jagged line of separation and reunion would always show. He was always forgetting something—his wife, Carrie, his need of money, present situation, or something—and so did not reason clearly. Nevertheless, he sent the letter, waiting a reply before sending the money.

Meanwhile, he accepted his present situation with Carrie, getting what joy out of it he could.

Out came the sun by noon, and poured a golden flood through their open windows. Sparrows were twittering. There were laughter and song in the air. Hurstwood could not keep his eyes from Carrie. She seemed the one ray of sunshine in all his trouble. Oh, if she would only love him wholly—only throw her arms around him in the blissful spirit in which he had seen her in the little park in Chicago—

how happy he would be! It would repay him; it would show him that he had not lost all. He would not care.

"Carrie," he said, getting up once and coming over to her, "are you going to stay with me from now on?"

She looked at him quizzically, but melted with sympathy as the value of the look upon his face forced itself upon her. It was love now, keen and strong—love enhanced by difficulty and worry. She could not help smiling.

"Let me be everything to you from now on," he said. "Don't make me worry any more. I'll be true to you. We'll go to New York and get a nice flat. I'll go into business again, and we'll be happy. Won't you be mine?"

Carrie listened quite solemnly. There was no great passion in her, but the drift of things and this man's proximity created a semblance of affection. She felt rather sorry for him—a sorrow born of what had only recently been a great admiration. True love she had never felt for him. She would have known as much if she could have analysed her feelings, but this thing which she now felt aroused by his great feeling broke down the barriers between them.

"You'll stay with me, won't you?" he asked.

"Yes," she said, nodding her head.

He gathered her to himself, imprinting kisses upon her lips and cheeks.

"You must marry me, though," she said.

"I'll get a license to-day," he answered.

"How?" she asked.

"Under a new name," he answered. "I'll take a new name and live a new life. From now on I'm Murdock."

"Oh, don't take that name," said Carrie.

"Why not?" he said.

"I don't like it."

"Well, what shall I take?" he asked.

"Oh, anything, only don't take that."

He thought a while, still keeping his arms about her, and then said:

"How would Wheeler do?"

"That's all right," said Carrie.

"Well, then, Wheeler," he said. "I'll get the license this afternoon."

They were married by a Baptist minister, the first divine they found convenient.

At last the Chicago firm answered. It was by Mr. Moy's dictation. He was astonished that Hurstwood had done this; very sorry that it had come about as it had. If the money were returned, they would not trouble to prosecute him, as they really bore him no ill-will. As for his returning, or their restoring him to his former position, they had not quite decided what the effect of it would be. They would think it over and correspond with him later, possibly, after a little time, and so on.

The sum and substance of it was that there was no hope, and they wanted the money with the least trouble possible. Hurstwood read his doom. He decided to pay $9,500 to the agent whom they said they would send, keeping $1,300 for his own use. He telegraphed his acquiescence, explained to the representative who called at the hotel the same day, took a certificate of payment, and told Carrie to pack her trunk. He was slightly depressed over this newest move at the time he began to make it, but eventually restored himself. He feared that even yet he might be seized and taken back, so he tried to conceal his movements, but it was scarcely possible. He ordered Carrie's trunk sent to the depot, where he had it sent by express to New York. No one seemed to be observing him, but he left at night. He was greatly agitated lest at the first station across the border or at the depot in New York there should be waiting for him an officer of the law.

Carrie, ignorant of his theft and his fears, enjoyed the entry into the latter city in the morning. The round green hills sentinelling the broad, expansive bosom of the Hudson held her attention by their beauty as the train followed the line of the stream. She had heard of the Hudson River, the great city of New York, and now she looked out, filling her mind with the wonder of it.

As the train turned east at Spuyten Duyvil and followed the east bank of the Harlem River, Hurstwood nervously called her attention to the fact that they were on the edge of the city. After her experience with Chicago, she expected long lines of cars—a great highway of tracks—and noted the difference. The sight of a few boats in the Harlem and more in the East River tickled her young heart. It was the first sign of the great sea. Next came a plain street with five-story brick flats, and then the train plunged into the tunnel.

"Grand Central Station!" called the trainman, as, after a few minutes of darkness and smoke, daylight reappeared. Hurstwood arose and gathered up his small grip. He was screwed up to the highest tension. With Carrie he waited at the door and then dismounted. No one approached him, but he glanced furtively to and fro as he made for the street entrance. So excited was he that he forgot all about Carrie, who fell behind, wondering at his self-absorption. As he passed through the depot proper the strain reached its climax and began to wane. All at once he was on the sidewalk, and none but cabmen hailed him. He heaved a great breath and turned, remembering Carrie.

"I thought you were going to run off and leave me," she said.

"I was trying to remember which car takes us to the Gilsey," he answered.

Carrie hardly heard him, so interested was she in the busy scene.

"How large is New York?" she asked.

"Oh, a million or more," said Hurstwood.

He looked around and hailed a cab, but he did so in a changed way.

For the first time in years the thought that he must count these little expenses flashed through his mind. It was a disagreeable thing.

He decided he would lose no time living in hotels but would rent a flat. Accordingly he told Carrie, and she agreed.

"We'll look to-day, if you want to," she said.

Suddenly he thought of his experience in Montreal. At the more important hotels he would be certain to meet Chicagoans whom he knew. He stood up and spoke to the driver.

"Take me to the Belford," he said, knowing it to be less frequented by those whom he knew. Then he sat down.

"Where is the residence part?" asked Carrie, who did not take the tall five-story walls on either hand to be the abodes of families.

"Everywhere," said Hurstwood, who knew the city fairly well. "There are no lawns in New York. All these are houses."

"Well, then, I don't like it," said Carrie, who was coming to have a few opinions of her own.

Chapter XXX

WHATEVER A MAN like Hurstwood could be in Chicago, it is very evident that he would be but an inconspicuous drop in an ocean like New York. In Chicago, whose population still ranged about 500,000, millionaires were not numerous. The rich had not become so conspicuously rich as to drown all moderate incomes in obscurity. The attention of the inhabitants was not so distracted by local celebrities in the dramatic, artistic, social, and religious fields as to shut the well-positioned man from view. In Chicago the two roads to distinction were politics and trade. In New York the roads were any one of a half-hundred, and each had been diligently pursued by hundreds, so that celebrities were numerous. The sea was already full of whales. A common fish must needs disappear wholly from view—remain unseen. In other words, Hurstwood was nothing.

There is a more subtle result of such a situation as this, which, though not always taken into account, produces the tragedies of the world. The great create an atmosphere which reacts badly upon the small. This atmosphere is easily and quickly felt. Walk among the magnificent residences, the splendid equipages, the gilded shops, restaurants, resorts of all kinds; scent the flowers, the silks, the wines; drink of the laughter springing from the soul of luxurious content, of the glances which gleam like light from defiant spears; feel the quality of the smiles which cut like glistening swords and of strides born of place, and you shall know of what is the atmosphere of the high and mighty. Little use to argue that of such is not the kingdom of greatness, but so long as the world is attracted by this and the human heart views this as the one desirable realm which it must attain, so long, to that heart, will this remain the realm of greatness. So long, also, will the atmosphere of this realm work its desperate results in the soul of man. It is like a chemical reagent. One day of it, like one drop of the other, will so affect and discolour the views, the aims, the desire of the mind, that it will thereafter

remain forever dyed. A day of it to the untried mind is like
opium to the untried body. A craving is set up which, if gratified, shall eternally result in dreams and death. Aye! dreams
unfulfilled—gnawing, luring, idle phantoms which beckon
and lead, beckon and lead, until death and dissolution dissolve their power and restore us blind to nature's heart.

A man of Hurstwood's age and temperament is not subject
to the illusions and burning desires of youth, but neither has
he the strength of hope which gushes as a fountain in the
heart of youth. Such an atmosphere could not incite in him
the cravings of a boy of eighteen, but in so far as they were
excited, the lack of hope made them proportionately bitter.
He could not fail to notice the signs of affluence and luxury
on every hand. He had been to New York before and knew
the resources of its folly. In part it was an awesome place to
him, for here gathered all that he most respected on this
earth—wealth, place, and fame. The majority of the celebrities with whom he had tipped glasses in his day as manager
hailed from this self-centred and populous spot. The most inviting stories of pleasure and luxury had been told of places
and individuals here. He knew it to be true that unconsciously he was brushing elbows with fortune the livelong
day; that a hundred or five hundred thousand gave no one
the privilege of living more than comfortably in so wealthy a
place. Fashion and pomp required more ample sums, so that
the poor man was nowhere. All this he realised, now quite
sharply, as he faced the city, cut off from his friends, de-
spoiled of his modest fortune, and even his name, and forced
to begin the battle for place and comfort all over again. He
was not old, but he was not so dull but that he could feel he
soon would be. Of a sudden, then, this show of fine clothes,
place, and power took on peculiar significance. It was emphasised by contrast with his own distressing state.

And it was distressing. He soon found that freedom from
fear of arrest was not the *sine qua non* of his existence. That
danger dissolved, the next necessity became the grievous
thing. The paltry sum of thirteen hundred and some odd dollars set against the need of rent, clothing, food, and pleasure
for years to come was a spectacle little calculated to induce
peace of mind in one who had been accustomed to spend five

times that sum in the course of a year. He thought upon the subject rather actively the first few days he was in New York, and decided that he must act quickly. As a consequence, he consulted the business opportunities advertised in the morning papers and began investigations on his own account.

That was not before he had become settled, however. Carrie and he went looking for a flat, as arranged, and found one in Seventy-eighth Street near Amsterdam Avenue. It was a five-story building, and their flat was on the third floor. Owing to the fact that the street was not yet built up solidly, it was possible to see east to the green tops of the trees in Central Park and west to the broad waters of the Hudson, a glimpse of which was to be had out of the west windows. For the privilege of six rooms and a bath, running in a straight line, they were compelled to pay thirty-five dollars a month—an average, and yet exorbitant, rent for a home at the time. Carrie noticed the difference between the size of the rooms here and in Chicago and mentioned it.

"You'll not find anything better, dear," said Hurstwood, "unless you go into one of the old-fashioned houses, and then you won't have any of these conveniences."

Carrie picked out the new abode because of its newness and bright wood-work. It was one of the very new ones supplied with steam heat, which was a great advantage. The stationary range, hot and cold water, dumb-waiter, speaking tubes, and call-bell for the janitor pleased her very much. She had enough of the instincts of a housewife to take great satisfaction in these things.

Hurstwood made arrangement with one of the instalment houses whereby they furnished the flat complete and accepted fifty dollars down and ten dollars a month. He then had a little plate, bearing the name G. W. Wheeler, made, which he placed on his letter-box in the hall. It sounded exceedingly odd to Carrie to be called Mrs. Wheeler by the janitor, but in time she became used to it and looked upon the name as her own.

These house details settled, Hurstwood visited some of the advertised opportunities to purchase an interest in some flourishing down-town bar. After the palatial resort in Adams Street, he could not stomach the commonplace saloons which he found advertised. He lost a number of days looking up these and finding them disagreeable. He did, however, gain considerable knowledge by talking, for he discovered the influence of Tammany Hall and the value of standing in with the police. The most profitable and flourishing places he found to be those which conducted anything but a legitimate business, such as that controlled by Fitzgerald and Moy. Elegant back rooms and private drinking booths on the second floor were usually adjuncts of very profitable places. He saw by portly keepers, whose shirt fronts shone with large diamonds, and whose clothes were properly cut, that the liquor business here, as elsewhere, yielded the same golden profit.

At last he found an individual who had a resort in Warren Street, which seemed an excellent venture. It was fairly well-appearing and susceptible of improvement. The owner claimed the business to be excellent, and it certainly looked so.

"We deal with a very good class of people," he told Hurstwood. "Merchants, salesmen, and professionals. It's a well-dressed class. No bums. We don't allow 'em in the place."

Hurstwood listened to the cash-register ring, and watched the trade for a while.

"It's profitable enough for two, is it?" he asked.

"You can see for yourself if you're any judge of the liquor trade," said the owner. "This is only one of the two places I have. The other is down in Nassau Street. I can't tend to them both alone. If I had some one who knew the business thoroughly I wouldn't mind sharing with him in this one and letting him manage it."

"I've had experience enough," said Hurstwood blandly, but he felt a little diffident about referring to Fitzgerald and Moy.

"Well, you can suit yourself, Mr. Wheeler," said the proprietor.

He only offered a third interest in the stock, fixtures, and good-will, and this in return for a thousand dollars and managerial ability on the part of the one who should come in. There was no property involved, because the owner of the saloon merely rented from an estate.

The offer was genuine enough, but it was a question with Hurstwood whether a third interest in that locality could be made to yield one hundred and fifty dollars a month, which he figured he must have in order to meet the ordinary family expenses and be comfortable. It was not the time, however, after many failures to find what he wanted, to hesitate. It looked as though a third would pay a hundred a month now. By judicious management and improvement, it might be made to pay more. Accordingly he agreed to enter into partnership, and made over his thousand dollars, preparing to enter the next day.

His first inclination was to be elated, and he confided to Carrie that he thought he had made an excellent arrangement. Time, however, introduced food for reflection. He found his partner to be very disagreeable. Frequently he was the worse for liquor, which made him surly. This was the last thing which Hurstwood was used to in business. Besides, the business varied. It was nothing like the class of patronage which he had enjoyed in Chicago. He found that it would take a long time to make friends. These people hurried in and out without seeking the pleasures of friendship. It was no gathering or lounging place. Whole days and weeks passed without one such hearty greeting as he had been wont to enjoy every day in Chicago.

For another thing, Hurstwood missed the celebrities— those well-dressed, *élite* individuals who lend grace to the average bars and bring news from far-off and exclusive circles. He did not see one such in a month. Evenings, when still at his post, he would occasionally read in the evening papers incidents concerning celebrities whom he knew—whom he had drunk a glass with many a time. They would visit a bar like Fitzgerald and Moy's in Chicago, or the Hoffman House, uptown, but he knew that he would never see them down here.

Again, the business did not pay as well as he thought. It increased a little, but he found he would have to watch his household expenses, which was humiliating.

In the very beginning it was a delight to go home late at night, as he did, and find Carrie. He managed to run up and take dinner with her between six and seven, and to remain home until nine o'clock in the morning, but the novelty of this waned after a time, and he began to feel the drag of his duties.

The first month had scarcely passed before Carrie said in a very natural way: "I think I'll go down this week and buy a dress."

"What kind?" said Hurstwood.

"Oh, something for street wear."

"All right," he answered, smiling, although he noted mentally that it would be more agreeable to his finances if she didn't. Nothing was said about it the next day, but the following morning he asked:

"Have you done anything about your dress?"

"Not yet," said Carrie.

He paused a few moments, as if in thought, and then said: "Would you mind putting it off a few days?"

"No," replied Carrie, who did not catch the drift of his remarks. She had never thought of him in connection with money troubles before. "Why?"

"Well, I'll tell you," said Hurstwood. "This investment of mine is taking a lot of money just now. I expect to get it all back shortly, but just at present I am running close."

"Oh!" answered Carrie. "Why, certainly, dear. Why didn't you tell me before?"

"It wasn't necessary," said Hurstwood.

For all her acquiescence, there was something about the way Hurstwood spoke which reminded Carrie of Drouet and his little deal which he was always about to put through. It was only the thought of a second, but it was a beginning. It was something new in her thinking of Hurstwood.

Other things followed from time to time, little things of the same sort, which in their cumulative effect were eventually equal to a full revelation. Carrie was not dull by any means. Two persons cannot long dwell together without coming to an understanding of one another. The mental difficulties of an individual reveal themselves whether he voluntarily confesses them or not. Trouble gets in the air and contributes gloom, which speaks for itself. Hurstwood dressed as nicely as usual, but they were the same clothes he had in Canada. Carrie noticed that he did not install a large wardrobe, though his own was anything but large. She noticed, also, that he did not suggest many amusements, said nothing about the food, seemed concerned about his business. This was not the easy Hurstwood of Chicago—not the liberal, opulent Hurstwood she had known. The change was too obvious to escape detection.

In time she began to feel that a change had come about, and that she was not in his confidence. He was evidently secretive and kept his own counsel. She found herself asking him questions about little things. This is a disagreeable state to a woman. Great love makes it seem reasonable, sometimes plausible, but never satisfactory. Where great love is not, a more definite and less satisfactory conclusion is reached.

As for Hurstwood, he was making a great fight against the difficulties of a changed condition. He was too shrewd not to realise the tremendous mistake he had made, and appreciate that he had done well in getting where he was, and yet he could not help contrasting his present state with his former, hour after hour, and day after day.

Besides, he had the disagreeable fear of meeting old-time friends, ever since one such encounter which he made shortly after his arrival in the city. It was in Broadway that he saw a man approaching him whom he knew. There was no time for simulating non-recognition. The exchange of glances had been too sharp, the knowledge of each other too apparent. So the friend, a buyer for one of the Chicago wholesale houses, felt, perforce, the necessity of stopping.

"How are you?" he said, extending his hand with an evident mixture of feeling and a lack of plausible interest.

"Very well," said Hurstwood, equally embarrassed. "How is it with you?"

"All right; I'm down here doing a little buying. Are you located here now?"

"Yes," said Hurstwood, "I have a place down in Warren Street."

"Is that so?" said the friend. "Glad to hear it. I'll come down and see you."

"Do," said Hurstwood.

"So long," said the other, smiling affably and going on.

"He never asked for my number," thought Hurstwood; "he wouldn't think of coming." He wiped his forehead, which had grown damp, and hoped sincerely he would meet no one else.

These things told upon his good-nature, such as it was. His one hope was that things would change for the better in a money way. He had Carrie. His furniture was being paid for. He was maintaining his position. As for Carrie, the amusements he could give her would have to do for the present. He could probably keep up his pretensions sufficiently long without exposure to make good, and then all would be well. He failed therein to take account of the frailties of human nature—the difficulties of matrimonial life. Carrie was young. With him and with her varying mental states were common. At any moment the extremes of feeling might be anti-polarised at the dinner table. This often happens in the best regulated families. Little things brought out on such occasions need great love to obliterate them afterward. Where that is not, both parties count two and two and make a problem after a while.

Chapter XXXI

A PET OF GOOD FORTUNE: BROADWAY FLAUNTS ITS JOYS

THE EFFECT of the city and his own situation on Hurstwood was paralleled in the case of Carrie, who accepted the things which fortune provided with the most genial good-nature. New York, despite her first expression of disapproval, soon interested her exceedingly. Its clear atmosphere, more populous thoroughfares, and peculiar indifference struck her forcibly. She had never seen such a little flat as hers, and yet it soon enlisted her affection. The new furniture made an excellent showing, the sideboard which Hurstwood himself arranged gleamed brightly. The furniture for each room was appropriate, and in the so-called parlour, or front room, was installed a piano, because Carrie said she would like to learn to play. She kept a servant and developed rapidly in household tactics and information. For the first time in her life she felt settled, and somewhat justified in the eyes of society as she conceived of it. Her thoughts were merry and innocent enough. For a long while she concerned herself over the arrangement of New York flats, and wondered at ten families living in one building and all remaining strange and indifferent to each other. She also marvelled at the whistles of the hundreds of vessels in the harbour—the long, low cries of the Sound steamers and ferry-boats when fog was on. The mere fact that these things spoke from the sea made them wonderful. She looked much at what she could see of the Hudson from her west windows and of the great city building up rapidly on either hand. It was much to ponder over, and sufficed to entertain her for more than a year without becoming stale.

For another thing, Hurstwood was exceedingly interesting in his affection for her. Troubled as he was, he never exposed his difficulties to her. He carried himself with the same self-important air, took his new state with easy familiarity, and rejoiced in Carrie's proclivities and successes. Each evening he arrived promptly to dinner, and found the little dining-room a most inviting spectacle. In a way, the smallness of the room added to its luxury. It looked full and replete. The white-covered table was arrayed with pretty dishes and lighted with a four-armed candelabra, each light of which was topped with a red shade. Between Carrie and the girl the steaks and chops came out all right, and canned goods did the rest for a while. Carrie studied the art of making biscuit, and soon reached the stage where she could show a plate of light, palatable morsels for her labour.

In this manner the second, third, and fourth months passed. Winter came, and with it a feeling that indoors was best, so that the attending of theatres was not much talked of. Hurstwood made great efforts to meet all expenditures without a show of feeling one way or the other. He pretended that he was reinvesting his money in strengthening the business for greater ends in the future. He contented himself with a very moderate allowance of personal apparel, and rarely suggested anything for Carrie. Thus the first winter passed.

In the second year, the business which Hurstwood managed did increase somewhat. He got out of it regularly the $150 per month which he had anticipated. Unfortunately, by this time Carrie had reached certain conclusions, and he had scraped up a few acquaintances.

Being of a passive and receptive rather than an active and aggressive nature, Carrie accepted the situation. Her state seemed satisfactory enough. Once in a while they would go to a theatre together, occasionally in season to the beaches and different points about the city, but they picked up no acquaintances. Hurstwood naturally abandoned his show of fine manners with her and modified his attitude to one of easy familiarity. There were no misunderstandings, no apparent differences of opinion. In fact, without money or visiting friends, he led a life which could neither arouse jealousy nor comment. Carrie rather sympathised with his efforts and thought nothing upon her lack of entertainment such as she had enjoyed in Chicago. New York as a corporate entity and her flat temporarily seemed sufficient.

However, as Hurstwood's business increased, he, as stated, began to pick up acquaintances. He also began to allow himself more clothes. He convinced himself that his home life was very precious to him, but allowed that he could occasionally stay away from dinner. The first time he did this he sent a message saying that he would be detained. Carrie ate alone, and wished that it might not happen again. The second time, also, he sent word, but at the last moment. The third time he forgot entirely and explained afterwards. These events were months apart, each.

"Where were you, George?" asked Carrie, after the first absence.

"Tied up at the office," he said genially. "There were some accounts I had to straighten."

"I'm sorry you couldn't get home," she said kindly. "I was fixing to have such a nice dinner."

The second time he gave a similar excuse, but the third time the feeling about it in Carrie's mind was a little bit out of the ordinary.

"I couldn't get home," he said, when he came in later in the evening, "I was so busy."

"Couldn't you have sent me word?" asked Carrie.

"I meant to," he said, "but you know I forgot it until it was too late to do any good."

"And I had such a good dinner!" said Carrie.

Now, it so happened that from his observations of Carrie he began to imagine that she was of the thoroughly domestic type of mind. He really thought, after a year, that her chief expression in life was finding its natural channel in household duties. Notwithstanding the fact that he had observed her act in Chicago, and that during the past year he had only seen her limited in her relations to her flat and him by conditions which he made, and that she had not gained any friends or associates, he drew this peculiar conclusion. With it came a feeling of satisfaction in having a wife who could thus be content, and this satisfaction worked its natural result. That is, since he imagined he saw her satisfied, he felt called upon to give only that which contributed to such satisfaction. He supplied the furniture, the decorations, the food, and the necessary clothing. Thoughts of entertaining her, leading her out into the shine and show of life, grew less and less. He felt attracted to the outer world, but did not think she would care to go along. Once he went to the theatre alone. Another time he joined a couple of his new friends at an evening game of poker. Since his money-feathers were beginning to grow again he felt like sprucing about. All this, however, in a much less imposing way than had been his wont in Chicago. He avoided the gay places where he would be apt to meet those who had known him.

Now, Carrie began to feel this in various sensory ways. She was not the kind to be seriously disturbed by his actions. Not loving him greatly, she could not be jealous in a disturbing way. In fact, she was not jealous at all. Hurstwood was pleased with her placid manner, when he should have duly considered it. When he did not come home it did not seem anything like a terrible thing to her. She gave him credit for having the usual allurements of men—people to talk to, places to stop, friends to consult with. She was perfectly willing that he should enjoy himself in his way, but she did not care to be neglected herself. Her state still seemed fairly reasonable, however. All she did observe was that Hurstwood was somewhat different.

Some time in the second year of their residence in Seventy-eighth Street the flat across the hall from Carrie became vacant, and into it moved a very handsome young woman and her husband, with both of whom Carrie afterwards became acquainted. This was brought about solely by the arrangement of the flats, which were united in one place, as it were, by the dumb-waiter. This useful elevator, by which fuel, groceries, and the like were sent up from the basement, and garbage and waste sent down, was used by both residents of one floor; that is, a small door opened into it from each flat.

If the occupants of both flats answered to the whistle of the janitor at the same time, they would stand face to face when they opened the dumb-waiter doors. One morning, when Carrie went to remove her paper, the newcomer, a handsome brunette of perhaps twenty-three years of age, was there for a like purpose. She was in a night-robe and dressing-gown, with her hair very much tousled, but she looked so pretty and good-natured that Carrie instantly conceived a liking for her. The newcomer did no more than smile shamefacedly, but it was sufficient. Carrie felt that she would like to know her, and a similar feeling stirred in the mind of the other, who admired Carrie's innocent face.

"That's a real pretty woman who has moved in next door," said Carrie to Hurstwood at the breakfast table.

"Who are they?" asked Hurstwood.

"I don't know," said Carrie. "The name on the bell is Vance. Some one over there plays beautifully. I guess it must be she."

"Well, you never can tell what sort of people you're living next to in this town, can you?" said Hurstwood, expressing the customary New York opinion about neighbours.

"Just think," said Carrie, "I have been in this house with nine other families for over a year and I don't know a soul. These people have been here over a month and I haven't seen any one before this morning."

"It's just as well," said Hurstwood. "You never know who you're going to get in with. Some of these people are pretty bad company."

"I expect so," said Carrie, agreeably.

The conversation turned to other things, and Carrie thought no more upon the subject until a day or two later, when, going out to market, she encountered Mrs. Vance coming in. The latter recognised her and nodded, for which Carrie returned a smile. This settled the probability of acquaintanceship. If there had been no faint recognition on this occasion, there would have been no future association.

Carrie saw no more of Mrs. Vance for several weeks, but she heard her play through the thin walls which divided the front rooms of the flats, and was pleased by the merry selection of pieces and the brilliance of their rendition. She could play only moderately herself, and such variety as Mrs. Vance exercised bordered, for Carrie, upon the verge of great art. Everything she had seen and heard thus far—the merest scraps and shadows—indicated that these people were, in a measure, refined and in comfortable circumstances. So Carrie was ready for any extension of the friendship which might follow.

One day Carrie's bell rang and the servant, who was in the kitchen, pressed the button which caused the front door of the general entrance on the ground floor to be electrically unlatched. When Carrie waited at her own door on the third floor to see who it might be coming up to call on her, Mrs. Vance appeared.

"I hope you'll excuse me," she said. "I went out a while ago and forgot my outside key, so I thought I'd ring your bell."

This was a common trick of other residents of the building, whenever they had forgotten their outside keys. They did not apologise for it, however.

"Certainly," said Carrie. "I'm glad you did. I do the same thing sometimes."

"Isn't it just delightful weather?" said Mrs. Vance, pausing for a moment.

Thus, after a few more preliminaries, this visiting acquaintance was well launched, and in the young Mrs. Vance Carrie found an agreeable companion.

On several occasions Carrie visited her and was visited. Both flats were good to look upon, though that of the Vances tended somewhat more to the luxurious.

"I want you to come over this evening and meet my husband," said Mrs. Vance, not long after their intimacy began. "He wants to meet you. You play cards, don't you?"

"A little," said Carrie.

"Well, we'll have a game of cards. If your husband comes home bring him over."

"He's not coming to dinner to-night," said Carrie.

"Well, when he does come we'll call him in."

Carrie acquiesced, and that evening met the portly Vance, an individual a few years younger than Hurstwood, and who owed his seemingly comfortable matrimonial state much more to his money than to his good looks. He thought well of Carrie upon the first glance and laid himself out to be genial, teaching her a new game of cards and talking to her about New York and its pleasures. Mrs. Vance played some upon the piano, and at last Hurstwood came.

"I am very glad to meet you," he said to Mrs. Vance when Carrie introduced him, showing much of the old grace which had captivated Carrie.

"Did you think your wife had run away?" said Mr. Vance, extending his hand upon introduction.

"I didn't know but what she might have found a better husband," said Hurstwood.

He now turned his attention to Mrs. Vance, and in a flash Carrie saw again what she for some time had sub-consciously missed in Hurstwood—the adroitness and flattery of which he was capable. She also saw that she was not well dressed—not nearly as well dressed—as Mrs. Vance. These were not vague ideas any longer. Her situation was cleared up for her. She felt that her life was becoming stale, and therein she felt cause for gloom. The old helpful, urging melancholy was restored. The desirous Carrie was whispered to concerning her possibilities.

There were no immediate results to this awakening, for Carrie had little power of initiative; but, nevertheless, she seemed ever capable of getting herself into the tide of change where she would be easily borne along. Hurstwood noticed nothing. He had been unconscious of the marked contrasts which Carrie had observed. He did not even detect the shade of melancholy which settled in her eyes. Worst of all, she now began to feel the loneliness of the flat and seek the company of Mrs. Vance, who liked her exceedingly.

"Let's go to the matinée this afternoon," said Mrs. Vance, who had stepped across into Carrie's flat one morning, still arrayed in a soft pink dressing-gown, which she had donned upon rising. Hurstwood and Vance had gone their separate ways nearly an hour before.

"All right," said Carrie, noticing the air of the petted and well-groomed woman in Mrs. Vance's general appearance. She looked as though she was dearly loved and her every wish gratified. "What shall we see?"

"Oh, I do want to see Nat Goodwin," said Mrs. Vance. "I do think he is the jolliest actor. The papers say this is such a good play."

"What time will we have to start?" asked Carrie.

"Let's go at one and walk down Broadway from Thirty-fourth Street," said Mrs. Vance. "It's such an interesting walk. He's at the Madison Square."

"I'll be glad to go," said Carrie. "How much will we have to pay for seats?"

"Not more than a dollar," said Mrs. Vance.

The latter departed, and at one o'clock reappeared, stunningly arrayed in a dark-blue walking dress, with a nobby hat to match. Carrie had gotten herself up charmingly enough, but this woman pained her by contrast. She seemed to have so many dainty little things which Carrie had not. There were trinkets of gold, an elegant green leather purse set with her initials, a fancy handkerchief, exceedingly rich in design, and the like. Carrie felt that she needed more and better clothes to compare with this woman, and that any one looking at the two would pick Mrs. Vance for her raiment alone. It was a trying, though rather unjust thought, for Carrie had now developed an equally pleasing figure, and had grown in comeliness until she was a thoroughly attractive type of her colour of beauty. There was some difference in the clothing of the two, both of quality and age, but this difference was not especially noticeable. It served, however, to augment Carrie's dissatisfaction with her state.

The walk down Broadway, then as now, was one of the remarkable features of the city. There gathered, before the matinée and afterwards, not only all the pretty women who love a showy parade, but the men who love to gaze upon and admire them. It was a very imposing procession of pretty faces and fine clothes. Women appeared in their very best hats, shoes, and gloves, and walked arm in arm on their way to the fine shops or theatres strung along from Fourteenth to Thirty-fourth streets. Equally the men paraded with the very latest they could afford. A tailor might have secured hints on suit measurements, a shoemaker on proper lasts and colours, a hatter on hats. It was literally true that if a lover of fine clothes secured a new suit, it was sure to have its first airing on Broadway. So true and well understood was this fact, that several years later a popular song, detailing this and other facts concerning the afternoon parade on matinée days, and entitled "What Right Has He on Broadway?" was published, and had quite a vogue about the music-halls of the city.

In all her stay in the city, Carrie had never heard of this showy parade; had never even been on Broadway when it was taking place. On the other hand, it was a familiar thing to Mrs. Vance, who not only knew of it as an entity, but had often been in it, going purposely to see and be seen, to create a stir with her beauty and dispel any tendency to fall short in dressiness by contrasting herself with the beauty and fashion of the town.

Carrie stepped along easily enough after they got out of the car at Thirty-fourth Street, but soon fixed her eyes upon the lovely company which swarmed by and with them as they proceeded. She noticed suddenly that Mrs. Vance's manner had rather stiffened under the gaze of handsome men and elegantly dressed ladies, whose glances were not modified by any rules of propriety. To stare seemed the proper and natural thing. Carrie found herself stared at and ogled. Men in flaw-less top-coats, high hats, and silver-headed walking sticks el-bowed near and looked too often into conscious eyes. Ladies rustled by in dresses of stiff cloth, shedding affected smiles and perfume. Carrie noticed among them the sprinkling of goodness and the heavy percentage of vice. The rouged and powdered cheeks and lips, the scented hair, the large, misty, and languorous eye, were common enough. With a start she awoke to find that she was in fashion's crowd, on parade in a show place—and such a show place! Jewellers' windows gleamed along the path with remarkable frequency. Florist shops, furriers, haberdashers, confectioners—all followed in rapid succession. The street was full of coaches. Pompous doormen in immense coats, shiny brass belts and buttons, waited in front of expensive salesrooms. Coachmen in tan boots, white tights, and blue jackets waited obsequiously for the mistresses of carriages who were shopping inside. The whole street bore the flavour of riches and show, and Carrie felt that she was not of it. She could not, for the life of her, assume the attitude and smartness of Mrs. Vance, who, in her beauty, was all assurance. She could only imagine that it must be evident to many that she was the less handsomely dressed of the two. It cut her to the quick, and she resolved that she would not come here again until she looked better. At the same time she longed to feel the delight of parading here as an equal. Ah, then she would be happy!

Chapter XXXII

The Feast of Belshazzar: A Seer to Translate

S UCH FEELINGS as were generated in Carrie by this walk put her in an exceedingly receptive mood for the pathos which followed in the play. The actor whom they had gone to see had achieved his popularity by presenting a mellow type of comedy, in which sufficient sorrow was introduced to lend contrast and relief to humour. For Carrie, as we well know, the stage had a great attraction. She had never forgotten her one histrionic achievement in Chicago. It dwelt in her mind and occupied her consciousness during many long afternoons in which her rocking-chair and her latest novel contributed the only pleasures of her state. Never could she witness a play without having her own ability vividly brought to consciousness. Some scenes made her long to be a part of them—to give expression to the feelings which she, in the place of the character represented, would feel. Almost invariably she would carry the vivid imaginations away with her and brood over them the next day alone. She lived as much in these things as in the realities which made up her daily life.

It was not often that she came to the play stirred to her heart's core by actualities. To-day a low song of longing had been set singing in her heart by the finery, the merriment, the beauty she had seen. Oh, these women who had passed her by, hundreds and hundreds strong, who were they? Whence came the rich, elegant dresses, the astonishingly coloured buttons, the knick-knacks of silver and gold? Where were these lovely creatures housed? Amid what elegancies of carved furniture, decorated walls, elaborate tapestries did they move? Where were their rich apartments, loaded with all that money could provide? In what stables champed these sleek, nervous horses and rested the gorgeous carriages? Where lounged the richly groomed footmen? Oh, the mansions, the lights, the perfume, the loaded boudoirs and tables! New York must be filled with such bowers, or the beautiful, insolent, supercilious creatures could not be. Some hot-houses held them. It ached her to know that she was not one of them—that, alas, she had dreamed a dream and it had not come true. She wondered at her own solitude these two years past—her indifference to the fact that she had never achieved what she had expected.

The play was one of those drawing-room concoctions in which charmingly overdressed ladies and gentlemen suffer the pangs of love and jealousy amid gilded surroundings. Such bon-mots are ever enticing to those who have all their days longed for such material surroundings and have never had them gratified. They have the charm of showing suffering under ideal conditions. Who would not grieve upon a gilded chair? Who would not suffer amid perfumed tapestries, cushioned furniture, and liveried servants? Grief under such circumstances becomes an enticing thing. Carrie longed to be of it. She wanted to take her sufferings, whatever they were, in such a world, or failing that, at least to simulate them under such charming conditions upon the stage. So affected was her mind by what she had seen, that the play now seemed an extraordinarily beautiful thing. She was soon lost in the world it represented, and wished that she might never return. Between the acts she studied the galaxy of matinée attendants in front rows and boxes, and conceived a new idea of the possibilities of New York. She was sure she had not seen it all— that the city was one whirl of pleasure and delight.

Going out, the same Broadway taught her a sharper lesson. The scene she had witnessed coming down was now augmented and at its height. Such a crush of finery and folly she had never seen. It clinched her convictions concerning her state. She had not lived, could not lay claim to having lived, until something of this had come into her own life. Women were spending money like water; she could see that in every elegant shop she passed. Flowers, candy, jewelry, seemed the principal things in which the elegant dames were interested. And she—she had scarcely enough pin money to indulge in such outings as this a few times a month.

That night the pretty little flat seemed a commonplace thing. It was not what the rest of the world was enjoying. She saw the servant working at dinner with an indifferent eye. In her mind were running scenes of the play. Particularly she remembered one beautiful actress—the sweetheart who had

been wooed and won. The grace of this woman had won
Carrie's heart. Her dresses had been all that art could suggest,
her sufferings had been so real. The anguish which she had
portrayed Carrie could feel. It was done as she was sure she
could do it. There were places in which she could even do
better. Hence she repeated the lines to herself. Oh, if she
could only have such a part, how broad would be her life!
She, too, could act appealingly.

When Hurstwood came, Carrie was moody. She was sitting, rocking and thinking, and did not care to have her enticing imaginations broken in upon; so she said little or
nothing.

"What's the matter, Carrie?" said Hurstwood after a time,
noticing her quiet, almost moody state.

"Nothing," said Carrie. "I don't feel very well to-night."

"Not sick, are you?" he asked, approaching very close.

"Oh, no," she said, almost pettishly, "I just don't feel very
good."

"That's too bad," he said, stepping away and adjusting his
vest after his slight bending over. "I was thinking we might
go to a show to-night."

"I don't want to go," said Carrie, annoyed that her fine
visions should have thus been broken into and driven out of
her mind. "I've been to the matinée this afternoon."

"Oh, you have?" said Hurstwood. "What was it?"

" 'A Gold Mine.' "

"How was it?"

"Pretty good," said Carrie.

"And you don't want to go again to-night?"

"I don't think I do," she said.

Nevertheless, wakened out of her melancholia and called to
the dinner table, she changed her mind. A little food in the
stomach does wonders. She went again, and in so doing temporarily recovered her equanimity. The great awakening blow
had, however, been delivered. As often as she might recover
from these discontented thoughts now, they would occur
again. Time and repetition—ah, the wonder of it! The dropping water and the solid stone—how utterly it yields at last!

Not long after this matinée experience—perhaps a
month—Mrs. Vance invited Carrie to an evening at the

theatre with them. She heard Carrie say that Hurstwood was not coming home to dinner.

"Why don't you come with us? Don't get dinner for yourself. We're going down to Sherry's for dinner and then over to the Lyceum. Come along with us."

"I think I will," answered Carrie.

She began to dress at three o'clock for her departure at half-past five for the noted dining-room which was then crowding Delmonico's for position in society. In this dressing Carrie showed the influence of her association with the dashing Mrs. Vance. She had constantly had her attention called by the latter to novelties in everything which pertains to a woman's apparel.

"Are you going to get such and such a hat?" or, "Have you seen the new gloves with the oval pearl buttons?" were but sample phrases out of a large selection.

"The next time you get a pair of shoes, dearie," said Mrs. Vance, "get button, with thick soles and patent-leather tips. They're all the rage this fall."

"I will," said Carrie.

"Oh, dear, have you seen the new shirtwaists at Altman's? They have some of the loveliest patterns. I saw one there that I know would look stunning on you. I said so when I saw it."

Carrie listened to these things with considerable interest, for they were suggested with more of friendliness than is usually common between pretty women. Mrs. Vance liked Carrie's stable good-nature so well that she really took pleasure in suggesting to her the latest things.

"Why don't you get yourself one of those nice serge skirts they're selling at Lord & Taylor's?" she said one day. "They're the circular style, and they're going to be worn from now on. A dark blue one would look so nice on you."

Carrie listened with eager ears. These things never came up between her and Hurstwood. Nevertheless, she began to suggest one thing and another, which Hurstwood agreed to without any expression of opinion. He noticed the new tendency on Carrie's part, and finally, hearing much of Mrs. Vance and her delightful ways, suspected whence the change came. He was not inclined to offer the slightest objection so soon, but he felt that Carrie's wants were expanding. This did not appeal to him exactly, but he cared for her in his own way, and so the thing stood. Still, there was something in the details of the transactions which caused Carrie to feel that her requests were not a delight to him. He did not enthuse over the purchases. This led her to believe that neglect was creeping in, and so another small wedge was entered.

Nevertheless, one of the results of Mrs. Vance's suggestions was the fact that on this occasion Carrie was dressed somewhat to her own satisfaction. She had on her best, but there was comfort in the thought that if she must confine herself to a *best*, it was neat and fitting. She looked the well-groomed woman of twenty-one, and Mrs. Vance praised her, which brought colour to her plump cheeks and a noticeable brightness into her large eyes. It was threatening rain, and Mr. Vance, at his wife's request, had called a coach.

"Your husband isn't coming?" suggested Mr. Vance, as he met Carrie in his little parlour.

"No; he said he wouldn't be home for dinner."

"Better leave a little note for him, telling him where we are. He might turn up."

"I will," said Carrie, who had not thought of it before.

"Tell him we'll be at Sherry's until eight o'clock. He knows, though, I guess."

Carrie crossed the hall with rustling skirts, and scrawled the note, gloves on. When she returned a newcomer was in the Vance flat.

"Mrs. Wheeler, let me introduce Mr. Ames, a cousin of mine," said Mrs. Vance. "He's going along with us, aren't you, Bob?"

"I'm very glad to meet you," said Ames, bowing politely to Carrie.

The latter caught in a glance the dimensions of a very stalwart figure. She also noticed that he was smooth-shaven, good looking, and young, but nothing more.

"Mr. Ames is just down in New York for a few days," put in Vance, "and we're trying to show him around a little."

"Oh, are you?" said Carrie, taking another glance at the newcomer.

"Yes; I am just on here from Indianapolis for a week or

so," said young Ames, seating himself on the edge of a chair to wait while Mrs. Vance completed the last touches of her toilet.

"I guess you find New York quite a thing to see, don't you?" said Carrie, venturing something to avoid a possible deadly silence.

"It is rather large to get around in a week," answered Ames, pleasantly.

He was an exceedingly genial soul, this young man, and wholly free of affectation. It seemed to Carrie he was as yet only overcoming the last traces of the bashfulness of youth. He did not seem apt at conversation, but he had the merit of being well dressed and wholly courageous. Carrie felt as if it were not going to be hard to talk to him.

"Well, I guess we're ready now. The coach is outside."

"Come on, people," said Mrs. Vance, coming in smiling. "Bob, you'll have to look after Mrs. Wheeler."

"I'll try to," said Bob smiling, and edging closer to Carrie. "You won't need much watching, will you?" he volunteered, in a sort of ingratiating and help-me-out kind of way.

"Not very, I hope," said Carrie.

They descended the stairs, Mrs. Vance offering suggestions, and climbed into the open coach.

"All right," said Vance, slamming the coach door, and the conveyance rolled away.

"What is it we're going to see?" asked Ames.

"Sothern," said Vance, "in 'Lord Chumley.' "

"Oh, he is so good!" said Mrs. Vance. "He's just the funniest man."

"I notice the papers praise it," said Ames.

"I haven't any doubt," put in Vance, "but we'll all enjoy it very much."

Ames had taken a seat beside Carrie, and accordingly he felt it his bounden duty to pay her some attention. He was interested to find her so young a wife, and so pretty, though it was only a respectful interest. There was nothing of the dashing lady's man about him. He had respect for the married state, and thought only of some pretty marriageable girls in Indianapolis.

"Are you a born New Yorker?" asked Ames of Carrie.

"Oh, no; I've only been here for two years."

"Oh, well, you've had time to see a great deal of it, anyhow."

"I don't seem to have," answered Carrie. "It's about as strange to me as when I first came here."

"You're not from the West, are you?"

"Yes. I'm from Wisconsin," she answered.

"Well, it does seem as if most people in this town haven't been here so very long. I hear of lots of Indiana people in my line who are here."

"What is your line?" asked Carrie.

"I'm connected with an electrical company," said the youth.

Carrie followed up this desultory conversation with occasional interruptions from the Vances. Several times it became general and partially humorous, and in that manner the restaurant was reached.

Carrie had noticed the appearance of gayety and pleasure-seeking in the streets which they were following. Coaches were numerous, pedestrians many, and in Fifty-ninth Street the street cars were crowded. At Fifty-ninth Street and Fifth Avenue a blaze of lights from several new hotels which bordered the Plaza Square gave a suggestion of sumptuous hotel life. Fifth Avenue, the home of the wealthy, was noticeably crowded with carriages, and gentlemen in evening dress. At Sherry's an imposing doorman opened the coach door and helped them out. Young Ames held Carrie's elbow as he helped her up the steps. They entered the lobby already swarming with patrons, and then, after divesting themselves of their wraps, went into a sumptuous dining-room.

In all Carrie's experience she had never seen anything like this. In the whole time she had been in New York Hurstwood's modified state had not permitted his bringing her to such a place. There was an almost indescribable atmosphere about it which convinced the newcomer that this was the proper thing. Here was the place where the matter of expense limited the patrons to the moneyed or pleasure-loving class. Carrie had read of it often in the "Morning" and "Evening World." She had seen notices of dances, parties, balls, and suppers at Sherry's. The Misses So-and-so would give a party on Wednesday evening at Sherry's. Young Mr. So-and-so would entertain a party of friends at a private luncheon on the sixteenth, at Sherry's. The common run of conventional, perfunctory notices of the doings of society, which she could scarcely refrain from scanning each day, had given her a distinct idea of the gorgeousness and luxury of this wonderful temple of gastronomy. Now, at last, she was really in it. She had come up the imposing steps, guarded by the large and portly doorman. She had seen the lobby, guarded by another large and portly gentleman, and been waited upon by uniformed youths who took care of canes, overcoats, and the like. Here was the splendid dining-chamber, all decorated and aglow, where the wealthy ate. Ah, how fortunate was Mrs. Vance; young, beautiful, and well off—at least, sufficiently so to come here in a coach. What a wonderful thing it was to be rich.

Vance led the way through lanes of shining tables, at which were seated parties of two, three, four, five, or six. The air of assurance and dignity about it all was exceedingly noticeable to the novitiate. Incandescent lights, the reflection of their glow in polished glasses, and the shine of gilt upon the walls, combined into one tone of light which it requires minutes of complacent observation to separate and take particular note of. The white shirt fronts of the gentlemen, the bright costumes of the ladies, diamonds, jewels, fine feathers—all were exceedingly noticeable.

Carrie walked with an air equal to that of Mrs. Vance, and accepted the seat which the head waiter provided for her. She was keenly aware of all the little things that were done—the little genuflections and attentions of the waiters and head waiter which Americans pay for. The air with which the latter pulled out each chair, and the wave of the hand with which he motioned them to be seated, were worth several dollars in themselves.

Once seated, there began that exhibition of showy, wasteful, and unwholesome gastronomy as practised by wealthy Americans, which is the wonder and astonishment of true culture and dignity the world over. The large bill of fare held an array of dishes sufficient to feed an army, sidelined with prices which made reasonable expenditure a ridiculous impossibility —an order of soup at fifty cents or a dollar, with a dozen kinds to choose from; oysters in forty styles and at sixty cents the half-dozen; entrées, fish, and meats at prices which would house one over night in an average hotel. One dollar fifty and two dollars seemed to be the most common figures upon this most tastefully printed bill of fare.

Carrie noticed this, and in scanning it the price of spring chicken carried her back to that other bill of fare and far different occasion when, for the first time, she sat with Drouet in a good restaurant in Chicago. It was only momentary—a sad note as out of an old song—and then it was gone. But in that flash was seen the other Carrie—poor, hungry, drifting at her wits' ends, and all Chicago a cold and closed world, from which she only wandered because she could not find work.

On the walls were designs in colour, square spots of robin's-egg blue, set in ornate frames of gilt, whose corners were elaborate mouldings of fruit and flowers, with fat cupids hovering in angelic comfort. On the ceilings were coloured traceries with more gilt, leading to a centre where spread a cluster of lights—incandescent globes mingled with glittering prisms and stucco tendrils of gilt. The floor was of a reddish hue, waxed and polished, and in every direction were mirrors—tall, brilliant, bevel-edged mirrors—reflecting and re-reflecting forms, faces, and candelabra a score and a hundred times.

The tables were not so remarkable in themselves, and yet the imprint of Sherry upon the napery, the name of Tiffany upon the silverware, the name of Haviland upon the china, and over all the glow of the small, red-shaded candelabra and the reflected tints of the walls on garments and faces, made them seem remarkable. Each waiter added an air of exclusiveness and elegance by the manner in which he bowed, scraped, touched, and trifled with things. The exclusively personal attention which he devoted to each one, standing half bent, ear to one side, elbows akimbo, saying: "Soup—green turtle, yes. One portion, yes. Oysters—certainly—half-dozen—yes. Asparagus. Olives—yes."

It would be the same with each one, only Vance essayed to order for all, inviting counsel and suggestions. Carrie studied the company with open eyes. So this was high life in New

York. It was so that the rich spent their days and evenings. Her poor little mind could not rise above applying each scene to all society. Every fine lady must be in the crowd on Broadway in the afternoon, in the theatre at the matinée, in the coaches and dining-halls at night. It must be glow and shine everywhere, with coaches waiting, and footmen attending, and she was out of it all. In two long years she had never even been in such a place as this.

Vance was in his element here, as Hurstwood would have been in former days. He ordered freely of soup, oysters, roast meats, and side dishes, and had several bottles of wine brought, which were set down beside the table in a wicker basket.

Ames was looking away rather abstractedly at the crowd and showed an interesting profile to Carrie. His forehead was high, his nose rather large and strong, his chin moderately pleasing. He had a good, wide, well-shaped mouth, and his dark-brown hair was parted slightly on one side. He seemed to have the least touch of boyishness to Carrie, and yet he was a man full grown.

"Do you know," he said, turning back to Carrie, after his reflection, "I sometimes think it is a shame for people to spend so much money this way."

Carrie looked at him a moment with the faintest touch of surprise at his seriousness. He seemed to be thinking about something over which she had never pondered.

"Do you?" she answered, interestedly.

"Yes," he said, "they pay so much more than these things are worth. They put on so much show."

"I don't know why people shouldn't spend when they have it," said Mrs. Vance.

"It doesn't do any harm," said Vance, who was still studying the bill of fare, though he had ordered.

Ames was looking away again, and Carrie was again looking at his forehead. To her he seemed to be thinking about strange things. As he studied the crowd his eye was mild.

"Look at that woman's dress over there," he said, again turning to Carrie, and nodding in a direction.

"Where?" said Carrie, following his eyes.

"Over there in the corner—way over. Do you see that brooch?"

"Isn't it large?" said Carrie.

"One of the largest clusters of jewels I have ever seen," said Ames.

"It is, isn't it?" said Carrie. She felt as if she would like to be agreeable to this young man, and also there came with it, or perhaps preceded it, the slightest shade of a feeling that he was better educated than she was—that his mind was better. He seemed to look it, and the saving grace in Carrie was that she could understand that people could be wiser. She had seen a number of people in her life who reminded her of what she had vaguely come to think of as scholars. This strong young man beside her, with his clear, natural look, seemed to get a hold of things which she did not quite understand, but approved of. It was fine to be so, as a man, she thought.

The conversation changed to a book that was having its vogue at the time—"Moulding a Maiden," by Albert Ross. Mrs. Vance had read it. Vance had seen it discussed in some of the papers.

"A man can make quite a strike writing a book," said Vance. "I notice this fellow Ross is very much talked about." He was looking at Carrie as he spoke.

"I hadn't heard of him," said Carrie, honestly.

"Oh, I have," said Mrs. Vance. "He's written lots of things. This last story is pretty good."

"He doesn't amount to much," said Ames.

Carrie turned her eyes toward him as to an oracle.

"His stuff is nearly as bad as 'Dora Thorne,'" concluded Ames.

Carrie felt this as a personal reproof. She read "Dora Thorne," or had a great deal in the past. It seemed only fair to her, but she supposed that people thought it very fine. Now this clear-eyed, fine-headed youth, who looked something like a student to her, made fun of it. It was poor to him, not worth reading. She looked down, and for the first time felt the pain of not understanding.

Yet there was nothing sarcastic or supercilious in the way Ames spoke. He had very little of that in him. Carrie felt that it was just kindly thought of a high order—the right thing to think, and wondered what else was right, according to him. He seemed to notice that she listened and rather sympathised with him, and from now on he talked mostly to her.

As the waiter bowed and scraped about, felt the dishes to see if they were hot enough, brought spoons and forks, and did all those little attentive things calculated to impress the luxury of the situation upon the diner, Ames also leaned slightly to one side and told her of Indianapolis in an intelligent way. He really had a very bright mind, which was finding its chief development in electrical knowledge. His sympathies for other forms of information, however, and for types of people, were quick and warm. The red glow on his head gave it a sandy tinge and put a bright glint in his eye. Carrie noticed all these things as he leaned toward her and felt exceedingly young. This man was far ahead of her. He seemed wiser than Hurstwood, saner and brighter than Drouet. He seemed innocent and clean, and she thought that he was exceedingly pleasant. She noticed, also, that his interest in her was a far-off one. She was not in his life, nor any of the things that touched his life, and yet now, as he spoke of these things, they appealed to her.

"I shouldn't care to be rich," he told her, as the dinner proceeded and the supply of food warmed up his sympathies; "not rich enough to spend my money this way."

"Oh, wouldn't you?" said Carrie, the, to her, new attitude forcing itself distinctly upon her for the first time.

"No," he said. "What good would it do? A man doesn't need this sort of thing to be happy."

Carrie thought of this doubtfully; but, coming from him, it had weight with her.

"He probably could be happy," she thought to herself, "all alone. He's so strong."

Mr. and Mrs. Vance kept up a running fire of interruptions, and these impressive things by Ames came at odd moments. They were sufficient, however, for the atmosphere that went with this youth impressed itself upon Carrie without words. There was something in him, or the world he moved in, which appealed to her. He reminded her of scenes she had seen on the stage—the sorrows and sacrifices that always went with she knew not what. He had taken away some of the bitterness of the contrast between this life and her life, and all by a certain calm indifference which concerned only him.

As they went out, he took her arm and helped her into the coach, and then they were off again, and so to the show.

During the acts Carrie found herself listening to him very attentively. He mentioned things in the play which she most approved of—things which swayed her deeply.

"Don't you think it rather fine to be an actor?" she asked once.

"Yes, I do," he said, "to be a good one. I think the theatre a great thing."

Just this little approval set Carrie's heart bounding. Ah, if she could only be an actress—a good one! This man was wise—he knew—and he approved of it. If she were a fine actress, such men as he would approve of her. She felt that he was good to speak as he had, although it did not concern her at all. She did not know why she felt this way.

At the close of the show it suddenly developed that he was not going back with them.

"Oh, aren't you?" said Carrie, with an unwarrantable feeling.

"Oh, no," he said; "I'm stopping right around here in Thirty-third Street."

Carrie could not say anything else, but somehow this development shocked her. She had been regretting the wane of a pleasant evening, but she had thought there was a half-hour more. Oh, the half-hours, the minutes of the world; what miseries and griefs are crowded into them!

She said good-bye with feigned indifference. What matter could it make? Still, the coach seemed lorn.

When she went into her own flat she had this to think about. She did not know whether she would ever see this man any more. What difference could it make—what difference could it make?

Hurstwood had returned, and was already in bed. His clothes were scattered loosely about. Carrie came to the door and saw him, then retreated. She did not want to go in yet a while. She wanted to think. It was disagreeable to her.

Back in the dining-room she sat in her chair and rocked.

Her little hands were folded tightly as she thought. Through a fog of longing and conflicting desires she was beginning to see. Oh, ye legions of hope and pity—of sorrow and pain! She was rocking, and beginning to see.

Chapter XXXIII

Without the Walled City: The Slope of the Years

THE IMMEDIATE result of this was nothing. Results from such things are usually long in growing. Morning brings a change of feeling. The existent condition invariably pleads for itself. It is only at odd moments that we get glimpses of the misery of things. The heart understands when it is confronted with contrasts. Take them away and the ache subsides.

Carrie went on, leading much this same life for six months thereafter or more. She did not see Ames any more. He called once upon the Vances, but she only heard about it through the young wife. Then he went West, and there was a gradual subsidence of whatever personal attraction had existed. The mental effect of the thing had not gone, however, and never would entirely. She had an ideal to contrast men by—particularly men close to her.

During all this time—a period rapidly approaching three years—Hurstwood had been moving along in an even path. There was no apparent slope downward, and distinctly none upward, so far as the casual observer might have seen. But psychologically there was a change, which was marked enough to suggest the future very distinctly indeed. This was in the mere matter of the halt his career had received when he departed from Chicago. A man's fortune or material progress is very much the same as his bodily growth. Either he is growing stronger, healthier, wiser, as the youth approaching manhood, or he is growing weaker, older, less incisive mentally, as the man approaching old age. There are no other states. Frequently there is a period between the cessation of youthful accretion and the setting in, in the case of the middle-aged man, of the tendency toward decay when the two processes are almost perfectly balanced and there is little doing in either direction. Given time enough, however, the balance becomes a sagging to the grave side. Slowly at first, then with a modest momentum, and at last the graveward process is in the full swing. So it is frequently with man's fortune. If its process of accretion is never halted, if the balancing stage is never reached, there will be no toppling. Rich men are, frequently, in these days, saved from this dissolution of their fortune by their ability to hire younger brains. These younger brains look upon the interests of the fortune as their own, and so steady and direct its progress. If each individual were left absolutely to the care of his own interests, and were given time enough in which to grow exceedingly old, his fortune would pass as his strength and will. He and his would be utterly dissolved and scattered unto the four winds of the heavens.

But now see wherein the parallel changes. A fortune, like a man, is an organism which draws to itself other minds and other strength than that inherent in the founder. Beside the young minds drawn to it by salaries, it becomes allied with young forces, which make for its existence even when the strength and wisdom of the founder are fading. It may be conserved by the growth of a community or of a state. It may be involved in providing something for which there is a growing demand. This removes it at once beyond the special care of the founder. It needs not so much foresight now as direction. The man wanes, the need continues or grows, and the fortune, fallen into whose hands it may, continues. Hence, some men never recognise the turning in the tide of their abilities. It is only in chance cases, where a fortune or a state of success is wrested from them, that the lack of ability to do as they did formerly becomes apparent. Hurstwood, set down under new conditions, was in a position to see that he was no longer young. If he did not, it was due wholly to the fact that his state was so well balanced that an absolute change for the worse did not show.

Not trained to reason or introspect himself, he could not analyse the change that was taking place in his mind, and hence his body, but he felt the depression of it. Constant comparison between his old state and his new showed a balance for the worse, which produced a constant state of gloom or, at least, depression. Now, it has been shown experimentally that a constantly subdued frame of mind produces certain poisons in the blood, called katastates, just as virtuous feelings of pleasure and delight produce helpful chemicals called anastates. The poisons generated by remorse inveigh against the system, and eventually produce marked physical deterioration. To these Hurstwood was subject.

In the course of time it told upon his temper. His eye no longer possessed that buoyant, searching shrewdness which had characterised it in Adams Street. His step was not as sharp and firm. He was given to thinking, thinking, thinking. The new friends he made were not celebrities. They were of a cheaper, a slightly more sensual and cruder, grade. He could not possibly take the pleasure in this company that he had in that of those fine frequenters of the Chicago resort. He was left to brood.

Slowly, exceedingly slowly, his desire to greet, conciliate, and make at home these people who visited the Warren Street place passed from him. More and more slowly the significance of the realm he had left began to be clear. It did not seem so wonderful to be in it when he was in it. It had seemed very easy for any one to get up there and have ample raiment and money to spend, but now that he was out of it, how far off it became. He began to see as one sees a city with a wall about it. Men were posted at the gates. You could not get in. Those inside did not care to come out to see who you were. They were so merry inside there that all those outside were forgotten, and he was on the outside.

Each day he could read in the evening papers of the doings within this walled city. In the notices of passengers for Europe he read the names of eminent frequenters of his old resort. In the theatrical column appeared, from time to time, announcements of the latest successes of men he had known. He knew that they were at their old gayeties. Pullmans were hauling them to and fro about the land, papers were greeting them with interesting mentions, the elegant lobbies of hotels and the glow of polished dining-rooms were keeping them close within the walled city. Men whom he had known, men whom he had tipped glasses with—rich men, and he was forgotten! Who was Mr. Wheeler? What was the Warren Street resort? Bah!

If one thinks that such thoughts do not come to so common a type of mind—that such feelings require a higher mental development—I would urge for their consideration the fact that it is the higher mental development that does away with such thoughts. It is the higher mental development which induces philosophy and that fortitude which refuses to dwell upon such things—refuses to be made to suffer by their consideration. The common type of mind is exceedingly keen on all matters which relate to its physical welfare—exceedingly keen. It is the unintellectual miser who sweats blood at the loss of a hundred dollars. It is the Epictetus who smiles when the last vestige of physical welfare is removed.

The time came, in the third year, when this thinking began to produce results in the Warren Street place. The tide of patronage dropped a little below what it had been at its best since he had been there. This irritated and worried him.

There came a night when he confessed to Carrie that the business was not doing as well this month as it had the month before. This was in lieu of certain suggestions she had made concerning little things she wanted to buy. She had not failed to notice that he did not seem to consult her about buying clothes for himself. For the first time, it struck her as a ruse, or that he said it so that she would not think of asking for things. Her reply was mild enough, but her thoughts were rebellious. He was not looking after her at all. She was depending for her enjoyment upon the Vances.

And now the latter announced that they were going away. It was approaching spring, and they were going North.

"Oh, yes," said Mrs. Vance to Carrie, " we think we might as well give up the flat and store our things. We'll be gone for the summer, and it would be a useless expense. I think we'll settle a little farther down town when we come back."

Carrie heard this with genuine sorrow. She had enjoyed Mrs. Vance's companionship so much. There was no one else in the house whom she knew. Again she would be all alone.

Hurstwood's gloom over the slight decrease in profits and the departure of the Vances came together. So Carrie had loneliness and this mood of her husband to enjoy at the same time. It was a grievous thing. She became restless and dissatisfied, not exactly, as she thought, with Hurstwood, but with life. What was it? A very dull round indeed. What did she have? Nothing but this narrow, little flat. The Vances could travel, they could do the things worth doing, and here she was. For what was she made, anyhow? More thought followed, and then tears—tears seemed justified, and the only relief in the world.

For another period this state continued, the twain leading a rather monotonous life, and then there was a slight change for the worse. One evening, Hurstwood, after thinking about a way to modify Carrie's desire for clothes and the general strain upon his ability to provide, said:

"I don't think I'll ever be able to do much with Shaughnessy."

"What's the matter?" said Carrie.

"Oh, he's a slow, greedy 'mick'! He won't agree to anything to improve the place, and it won't ever pay without it."

"Can't you make him?" said Carrie.

"No; I've tried. The only thing I can see, if I want to improve, is to get hold of a place of my own."

"Why don't you?" said Carrie.

"Well, all I have is tied up in there just now. If I had a chance to save a while I think I could open a place that would give us plenty of money."

"Can't we save?" said Carrie.

"We might try it," he suggested. "I've been thinking that if we'd take a smaller flat down town and live economically for a year, I would have enough, with what I have invested, to open a good place. Then we could arrange to live as you want to."

"It would suit me all right," said Carrie, who, nevertheless, felt badly to think it had come to this. Talk of a smaller flat sounded like poverty.

"There are lots of nice little flats down around Sixth Avenue, below Fourteenth Street. We might get one down there."

"I'll look at them if you say so," said Carrie.

"I think I could break away from this fellow inside of a year," said Hurstwood. "Nothing will ever come of this arrangement as it's going on now."

"I'll look around," said Carrie, observing that the proposed change seemed to be a serious thing with him.

The upshot of this was that the change was eventually effected; not without great gloom on the part of Carrie. It really affected her more seriously than anything that had yet happened. She began to look upon Hurstwood wholly as a man, and not as a lover or husband. She felt thoroughly bound to him as a wife, and that her lot was cast with his, whatever it might be; but she began to see that he was gloomy and taciturn, not a young, strong, and buoyant man. He looked a little bit old to her about the eyes and mouth now, and there were other things which placed him in his true rank, so far as her estimation was concerned. She began to feel that she had made a mistake. Incidentally, she also began to recall the fact that he had practically forced her to flee with him.

The new flat was located in Thirteenth Street, a half block west of Sixth Avenue, and contained only four rooms. The new neighbourhood did not appeal to Carrie as much. There were no trees here, no west view of the river. The street was solidly built up. There were twelve families here, respectable enough, but nothing like the Vances. Richer people required more space.

Being left alone in this little place, Carrie did without a girl. She made it charming enough, but could not make it delight her. Hurstwood was not inwardly pleased to think that they should have to modify their state, but he argued that he could do nothing. He must put the best face on it, and let it go at that.

He tried to show Carrie that there was no cause for financial alarm, but only congratulation over the chance he would have at the end of the year by taking her rather more frequently to the theatre and by providing a liberal table. This was for the time only. He was getting in the frame of mind where he wanted principally to be alone and to be allowed to think. The disease of brooding was beginning to claim him as a victim. Only the newspapers and his own thoughts were worth while. The delight of love had again slipped away. It was a case of live, now, making the best you can out of a very commonplace station in life.

The road downward has but few landings and level places. The very state of his mind, superinduced by his condition, caused the breach to widen between him and his partner. At last that individual began to wish that Hurstwood was out of it. It so happened, however, that a real estate deal on the part of the owner of the land arranged things even more effectually than ill-will could have schemed.

"Did you see that?" said Shaughnessy one morning to Hurstwood, pointing to the real estate column in a copy of the "Herald," which he held.

"No, what is it?" said Hurstwood, looking down the items of news.

"The man who owns this ground has sold it."

"You don't say so?" said Hurstwood.

He looked, and there was the notice. Mr. August Viele had yesterday registered the transfer of the lot, 25 × 75 feet, at the corner of Warren and Hudson streets, to J. F. Slawson for the sum of $57,000.

"Our lease expires when?" asked Hurstwood, thinking. "Next February, isn't it?"

"That's right," said Shaughnessy.

"It doesn't say what the new man's going to do with it," remarked Hurstwood, looking back to the paper.

"We'll hear, I guess, soon enough," said Shaughnessy.

Sure enough, it did develop. Mr. Slawson owned the property adjoining, and was going to put up a modern office building. The present one was to be torn down. It would take probably a year and a half to complete the other one.

All these things developed by degrees, and Hurstwood began to ponder over what would become of the saloon. One day he spoke about it to his partner.

"Do you think it would be worth while to open up somewhere else in the neighbourhood?"

"What would be the use?" said Shaughnessy. "We couldn't get another corner around here."

"It wouldn't pay anywhere else, do you think?"

"I wouldn't try it," said the other.

The approaching change now took on a most serious aspect to Hurstwood. Dissolution meant the loss of his thousand dollars, and he could not save another thousand in the time. He understood that Shaughnessy was merely tired of the arrangement, and would probably lease the new corner, when completed, alone. He began to worry about the necessity of a new connection and to see impending serious financial straits unless something turned up. This left him in no mood to enjoy his flat or Carrie, and consequently the depression invaded that quarter.

Meanwhile, he took such time as he could to look about, but opportunities were not numerous. More, he had not the same impressive personality which he had when he first came to New York. Bad thoughts had put a shade into his eyes which did not impress others favourably. Neither had he thirteen hundred dollars in hand to talk with. About a month later, finding that he had not made any progress, Shaughnessy reported definitely that Slawson would not extend the lease.

"I guess this thing's got to come to an end," he said, affecting an air of concern.

"Well, if it has, it has," answered Hurstwood, grimly. He would not give the other a key to his opinions, whatever they were. He should not have the satisfaction.

A day or two later he saw that he must say something to Carrie.

"You know," he said, "I think I'm going to get the worst of my deal down there."

"How is that?" asked Carrie in astonishment.

"Well, the man who owns the ground has sold it, and the new owner won't re-lease it to us. The business may come to an end."

"Can't you start somewhere else?"

"There doesn't seem to be any place. Shaughnessy doesn't want to."

"Do you lose what you put in?"

"Yes," said Hurstwood, whose face was a study.

"Oh, isn't that too bad?" said Carrie.

"It's a trick," said Hurstwood. "That's all. They'll start another place there all right."

Carrie looked at him, and gathered from his whole demeanour what it meant. It was serious, very serious.

"Do you think you can get something else?" she ventured, timidly.

Hurstwood thought a while. It was all up with the bluff about money and investment. She could see now that he was "broke."

"I don't know," he said solemnly; "I can try."

Chapter XXXIV

THE GRIND OF THE MILLSTONES: A SAMPLE OF CHAFF

CARRIE PONDERED over this situation as consistently as Hurstwood, once she got the facts adjusted in her mind. It took several days for her to fully realise that the approach of the dissolution of her husband's business meant commonplace struggle and privation. Her mind went back to her early venture in Chicago, the Hansons and their flat, and her heart revolted. That was terrible! Everything about poverty was terrible. She wished she knew a way out. Her recent experiences with the Vances had wholly unfitted her to view her own state with complacence. The glamour of the high life of the city had, in the few experiences afforded her by the former, seized her completely. She had been taught how to dress and where to go without having ample means to do either. Now, these things—ever-present realities as they were—filled her eyes and mind. The more circumscribed became her state, the more entrancing seemed this other. And now poverty threatened to seize her entirely and to remove this other world far upward like a heaven to which any Lazarus might extend, appealingly, his hands.

So, too, the ideal brought into her life by Ames remained. He had gone, but here was his word that riches were not everything; that there was a great deal more in the world than she knew; that the stage was good, and the literature she read poor. He was a strong man and clean—how much stronger and better than Hurstwood and Drouet she only half formulated to herself, but the difference was painful. It was something to which she voluntarily closed her eyes.

During the last three months of the Warren Street connection, Hurstwood took parts of days off and hunted, tracking the business advertisements. It was a more or less depressing business, wholly because of the thought that he must soon get something or he would begin to live on the few hundred dollars he was saving, and then he would have nothing to invest—he would have to hire out as a clerk.

Everything he discovered in his line advertised as an

opportunity, was either too expensive or too wretched for him. Besides, winter was coming, the papers were announcing hardships, and there was a general feeling of hard times in the air, or, at least, he thought so. In his worry, other people's worries became apparent. No item about a firm failing, a family starving, or a man dying upon the streets, supposedly of starvation, but arrested his eye as he scanned the morning papers. Once the "World" came out with a flaring announcement about "80,000 people out of employment in New York this winter," which struck as a knife at his heart.

"Eighty thousand!" he thought. "What an awful thing that is."

This was new reasoning for Hurstwood. In the old days the world had seemed to be getting along well enough. He had been wont to see similar things in the "Daily News," in Chicago, but they did not hold his attention. Now, these things were like grey clouds hovering along the horizon of a clear day. They threatened to cover and obscure his life with chilly greyness. He tried to shake them off, to forget and brace up. Sometimes he said to himself, mentally:

"What's the use worrying? I'm not out yet. I've got six weeks more. Even if worst comes to worst, I've got enough to live on for six months."

Curiously, as he troubled over his future, his thoughts occasionally reverted to his wife and family. He had avoided such thoughts for the first three years as much as possible. He hated her, and he could get along without her. Let her go. He would do well enough. Now, however, when he was not doing well enough, he began to wonder what she was doing, how his children were getting along. He could see them living as nicely as ever, occupying the comfortable house and using his property.

"By George! it's a shame they should have it all," he vaguely thought to himself on several occasions. "I didn't do anything."

As he looked back now and analysed the situation which led up to his taking the money, he began mildly to justify himself. What had he done—what in the world—that should bar him out this way and heap such difficulties upon him? It seemed only yesterday to him since he was comfortable and well-to-do. But now it was all wrested from him.

"She didn't deserve what she got out of me, that is sure. I didn't do so much, if everybody could just know."

There was no thought that the facts ought to be advertised. It was only a mental justification he was seeking from himself—something that would enable him to bear his state as a righteous man.

One afternoon, five weeks before the Warren Street place closed up, he left the saloon to visit three or four places he saw advertised in the "Herald." One was down in Gold Street, and he visited that, but did not enter. It was such a cheap looking place he felt that he could not abide it. Another was on the Bowery, which he knew contained many showy resorts. It was near Grand Street, and turned out to be very handsomely fitted up. He talked around about investments for fully three-quarters of an hour with the proprietor, who maintained that his health was poor, and that was the reason he wished a partner.

"Well, now, just how much money would it take to buy a half interest here?" said Hurstwood, who saw seven hundred dollars as his limit.

"Three thousand," said the man.

Hurstwood's jaw fell.

"Cash?" he said.

"Cash."

He tried to put on an air of deliberation, as one who might really buy; but his eyes showed gloom. He wound up by saying he would think it over, and came away. The man he had been talking to sensed his condition in a vague way.

"I don't think he wants to buy," he said to himself. "He doesn't talk right."

The afternoon was as grey as lead and cold. It was blowing up a disagreeable winter wind. He visited a place far up on the east side, near Sixty-ninth Street, and it was five o'clock, and growing dim, when he reached there. A portly German kept this place.

"How about this ad. of yours?" asked Hurstwood, who rather objected to the looks of the place.

"Oh, dat iss all over," said the German. "I vill not sell now."

"Oh, is that so?"

"Yes; dere is nothing to dat. It iss all over."

"Very well," said Hurstwood, turning around.

The German paid no more attention to him, and it made him angry.

"The crazy ass!" he said to himself. "What does he want to advertise for?"

Wholly depressed, he started for Thirteenth Street. The flat had only a light in the kitchen, where Carrie was working. He struck a match and, lighting the gas, sat down in the dining-room without even greeting her. She came to the door and looked in.

"It's you, is it?" she said, and went back.

"Yes," he said, without even looking up from the evening paper he had bought.

Carrie saw things were wrong with him. He was not so handsome when gloomy. The lines at the sides of the eyes were deepened. Naturally dark of skin, gloom made him look slightly sinister. He was quite a disagreeable figure.

Carrie set the table and brought in the meal.

"Dinner's ready," she said, passing him for something.

He did not answer, reading on.

She came in and sat down at her place, feeling exceedingly wretched.

"Won't you eat now?" she asked.

He folded his paper and drew near, silence holding for a time, except for the "Pass me's."

"It's been gloomy to-day, hasn't it?" ventured Carrie, after a time.

"Yes," he said.

He only picked at his food.

"Are you still sure to close up?" said Carrie, venturing to take up the subject which they had discussed often enough.

"Of course we are," he said, with the slightest modification of sharpness.

This retort angered Carrie. She had had a dreary day of it herself.

"You needn't talk like that," she said.

"Oh!" he exclaimed, pushing back from the table, as if to say more, but letting it go at that. Then he picked up his paper. Carrie left her seat, containing herself with difficulty. He saw she was hurt.

"Don't go 'way," he said, as she started back into the kitchen. "Eat your dinner."

She passed, not answering.

He looked at the paper a few moments, and then rose up and put on his coat.

"I'm going down town, Carrie," he said, coming out. "I'm out of sorts to-night."

She did not answer.

"Don't be angry," he said. "It will be all right to-morrow."

He looked at her, but she paid no attention to him, working at her dishes.

"Good-bye!" he said finally, and went out.

This was the first strong result of the situation between them, but with the nearing of the last day of the business the gloom became almost a permanent thing. Hurstwood could not conceal his feelings about the matter. Carrie could not help wondering where she was drifting. It got so that they talked even less than usual, and yet it was not Hurstwood who felt any objection to Carrie. It was Carrie who shied away from him. This he noticed. It aroused an objection to her becoming indifferent to him. He made the possibility of friendly intercourse almost a giant task, and then noticed with discontent that Carrie added to it by her manner and made it more impossible.

At last the final day came. When it actually arrived, Hurstwood, who had got his mind into such a state where a thunder-clap and raging storm would have seemed highly appropriate, was rather relieved to find that it was a plain, ordinary day. The sun shone, the temperature was pleasant. He felt, as he came to the breakfast table, that it wasn't so terrible, after all.

"Well," he said to Carrie, "to-day's my last day on earth."

Carrie smiled in answer to his humour.

Hurstwood glanced over his paper rather gayly. He seemed to have lost a load.

"I'll go down for a little while," he said after breakfast, "and then I'll look around. To-morrow I'll spend the whole day looking about. I think I can get something, now this thing's off my hands."

He went out smiling and visited the place. Shaughnessy was there. They had made all arrangements to share according to their interests. When, however, he had been there several hours, gone out three more, and returned, his elation had departed. As much as he had objected to the place, now that it was no longer to exist, he felt sorry. He wished that things were different.

Shaughnessy was coolly business-like.

"Well," he said at five o'clock, " we might as well count the change and divide."

They did so. The fixtures had already been sold and the sum divided.

"Good-night," said Hurstwood at the final moment, in a last effort to be genial.

"So long," said Shaughnessy, scarcely deigning a notice.

Thus the Warren Street arrangement was permanently concluded.

Carrie had prepared a good dinner at the flat, but after his ride up, Hurstwood was in a solemn and reflective mood.

"Well?" said Carrie, inquisitively.

"I'm out of that," he answered, taking off his coat.

As she looked at him, she wondered what his financial state was now. They ate and talked a little.

"Will you have enough to buy in anywhere else?" asked Carrie.

"No," he said. "I'll have to get something else and save up."

"It would be nice if you could get some place," said Carrie, prompted by anxiety and hope.

"I guess I will," he said reflectively.

For some days thereafter he put on his overcoat regularly in the morning and sallied forth. On these ventures he first consoled himself with the thought that with the seven hundred dollars he had he could still make some advantageous arrangement. He thought about going to some brewery, which, as he knew, frequently controlled saloons which they leased, and get them to help him. Then he remembered

that he would have to pay out several hundred any way for
fixtures and that he would have nothing left for his monthly
expenses. It was costing him nearly eighty dollars a month to
live.

"No," he said, in his sanest moments, "I can't do it. I'll get
something else and save up."

This getting-something proposition complicated itself the
moment he began to think of what it was he wanted to do.
Manage a place? Where should he get such a position? The
papers contained no requests for managers. Such positions,
he knew well enough, were either secured by long years of
service or were bought with a half or third interest. Into a
place important enough to need such a manager he had not
money enough to buy.

Nevertheless, he started out. His clothes were very good
and his appearance still excellent, but it involved the trouble
of deluding. People, looking at him, imagined instantly that a
man of his age, stout and well dressed, must be well off. He
appeared a comfortable owner of something, a man from
whom the common run of mortals could well expect gratu-
ities. Being now forty-three years of age, and comfortably
built, walking was not easy. He had not been used to exercise
for many years. His legs tired, his shoulders ached, and his
feet pained him at the close of the day, even when he took
street cars in almost every direction. The mere getting up and
down, if long continued, produced this result.

The fact that people took him to be better off than he was,
he well understood. It was so painfully clear to him that it
retarded his search. Not that he wished to be less well-appearing, but that he was ashamed to belie his appearance by
incongruous appeals. So he hesitated, wondering what to do.

He thought of the hotels, but instantly he remembered that
he had had no experience as a clerk, and, what was more important, no acquaintances or friends in that line to whom he
could go. He did know some hotel owners in several cities,
including New York, but they knew of his dealings with Fitzgerald and Moy. He could not apply to them. He thought of
other lines suggested by large buildings or businesses which
he knew of—wholesale groceries, hardware, insurance concerns, and the like—but he had had no experience.

How to go about getting anything was a bitter thought. Would he have to go personally and ask; wait outside an office door, and, then, distinguished and affluent looking, announce that he was looking for something to do? He strained painfully at the thought. No, he could not do that.

He really strolled about, thinking, and then, the weather being cold, stepped into a hotel. He knew hotels well enough to know that any decent looking individual was welcome to a chair in the lobby. This was in the Broadway Central, which was then one of the most important hotels in the city. Taking a chair here was a painful thing to him. To think he should come to this! He had heard loungers about hotels called chair-warmers. He had called them that himself in his day. But here he was, despite the possibility of meeting some one who knew him, shielding himself from cold and the weariness of the streets in a hotel lobby.

"I can't do this way," he said to himself. "There's no use of my starting out mornings without first thinking up some place to go. I'll think of some places and then look them up."

It occurred to him that the positions of bartenders were sometimes open, but he put this out of his mind. Bartender—he, the ex-manager!

It grew awfully dull sitting in the hotel lobby, and so at four he went home. He tried to put on a business air as he went in, but it was a feeble imitation. The rocking-chair in the dining-room was comfortable. He sank into it gladly, with several papers he had bought, and began to read.

As she was going through the room to begin preparing dinner, Carrie said:

"The man was here for the rent to-day."

"Oh, was he?" said Hurstwood.

The least wrinkle crept into his brow as he remembered that this was February 2d, the time the man always called. He fished down in his pocket for his purse, getting the first taste of paying out when nothing is coming in. He looked at the fat, green roll as a sick man looks at the one possible saving cure. Then he counted off twenty-eight dollars.

"Here you are," he said to Carrie, when she came through again.

He buried himself in his papers and read. Oh, the rest of

it—the relief from walking and thinking! What Lethean waters were these floods of telegraphed intelligence! He forgot his troubles, in part. Here was a young, handsome woman, if you might believe the newspaper drawing, suing a rich, fat, candy-making husband in Brooklyn for divorce. Here was another item detailing the wrecking of a vessel in ice and snow off Prince's Bay on Staten Island. A long, bright column told of the doings in the theatrical world—the plays produced, the actors appearing, the managers making announcements. Fannie Davenport was just opening at the Fifth Avenue. Daly was producing "King Lear." He read of the early departure for the season of a party composed of the Vanderbilts and their friends for Florida. An interesting shooting affray was on in the mountains of Kentucky. So he read, read, read, rocking in the warm room near the radiator and waiting for dinner to be served.

Chapter XXXV

THE PASSING OF EFFORT: THE VISAGE OF CARE

THE NEXT MORNING he looked over the papers and waded through a long list of advertisements, making a few notes. Then he turned to the male-help-wanted column, but with disagreeable feelings. The day was before him—a long day in which to discover something—and this was how he must begin to discover. He scanned the long column, which mostly concerned bakers, bushelmen, cooks, compositors, drivers, and the like, finding two things only which arrested his eye. One was a cashier wanted in a wholesale furniture house, and the other a salesman for a whiskey house. He had never thought of the latter. At once he decided to look that up.

The firm in question was Alsbery & Co., whiskey brokers.

He was admitted almost at once to the manager on his appearance.

"Good-morning, sir," said the latter, thinking at first that he was encountering one of his out-of-town customers.

"Good-morning," said Hurstwood. "You advertised, I believe, for a salesman?"

"Oh," said the man, showing plainly the enlightenment which had come to him. "Yes. Yes, I did."

"I thought I'd drop in," said Hurstwood, with dignity. "I've had some experience in that line myself."

"Oh, have you?" said the man. "What experience have you had?"

"Well, I've managed several liquor houses in my time. Recently I owned a third-interest in a saloon at Warren and Hudson streets."

"I see," said the man.

Hurstwood ceased, waiting for some suggestion.

"We did want a salesman," said the man. "I don't know as it's anything you'd care to take hold of, though."

"I see," said Hurstwood. "Well, I'm in no position to choose, just at present. If it were open, I should be glad to get it."

The man did not take kindly at all to his "No position to choose." He wanted some one who wasn't thinking of a choice or something better. Especially not an old man. He wanted some one young, active, and glad to work actively for a moderate sum. Hurstwood did not please him at all. He had more of an air than his employers.

"Well," he said in answer, "we'd be glad to consider your application. We shan't decide for a few days yet. Suppose you send us your references."

"I will," said Hurstwood.

He nodded good-morning and came away. At the corner he looked at the furniture company's address, and saw that it was in West Twenty-third Street. Accordingly, he went up there. The place was not large enough, however. It looked moderate, the men in it idle and small salaried. He walked by, glancing in, and then decided not to go in there.

"They want a girl, probably, at ten a week," he said.

At one o'clock he thought of eating, and went to a restaurant in Madison Square. There he pondered over places which he might look up. He was tired. It was blowing up grey again. Across the way, through Madison Square Park, stood the great hotels, looking down upon a busy scene. He decided to go over to the lobby of one and sit a while. It was warm in there and bright. He had seen no one he knew at the Broadway Central. In all likelihood he would encounter no one here. Finding a seat on one of the red plush divans close to the great windows which look out on Broadway's busy rout, he sat musing. His state did not seem so bad in here. Sitting still and looking out, he could take some slight consolation in the few hundred dollars he had in his purse. He could forget, in a measure, the weariness of the street and his tiresome searches. Still, it was only escape from a severe to a less severe state. He was still gloomy and disheartened. There, minutes seemed to go very slowly. An hour was a long, long time in passing. It was filled for him with observations and mental comments concerning the actual guests of the hotel, who passed in and out, and those more prosperous pedestrians whose good fortune showed in their clothes and spirits as they passed along Broadway, outside. It was nearly the first time since he had arrived in the city that his leisure afforded him ample opportunity to contemplate this spectacle. Now, being, perforce, idle himself, he wondered at the activity of others. How gay were the youths he saw, how pretty the women. Such fine clothes they all wore. They were so intent upon getting somewhere. He saw coquettish glances cast by magnificent girls. Ah, the money it required to train with such—how well he knew! How long it had been since he had had the opportunity to do so!

The clock outside registered four. It was a little early, but he thought he would go back to the flat.

This going back to the flat was coupled with the thought that Carrie would think he was sitting around too much if he came home early. He hoped he wouldn't have to, but the day hung heavily on his hands. Over there he was on his own ground. He could sit in his rocking-chair and read. This busy, distracting, suggestive scene was shut out. He could read his papers. Accordingly, he went home. Carrie was reading, quite alone. It was rather dark in the flat, shut in as it was.

"You'll hurt your eyes," he said when he saw her.

After taking off his coat, he felt it incumbent upon him to make some little report of his day.

"I've been talking with a wholesale liquor company," he said. "I may go out on the road."

"Wouldn't that be nice!" said Carrie.

"It wouldn't be such a bad thing," he answered.

Always from the man at the corner now he bought two papers—the "Evening World" and "Evening Sun." So now he merely picked his papers up, as he came by, without stopping.

He drew up his chair near the radiator and lighted the gas. Then it was as the evening before. His difficulties vanished in the items he so well loved to read.

The next day was even worse than the one before, because now he could not think of where to go. Nothing he saw in the papers he studied—till ten o'clock—appealed to him. He felt that he ought to go out, and yet he sickened at the thought. Where to, where to?

"You mustn't forget to leave me my money for this week," said Carrie, quietly.

They had an arrangement by which he placed twelve dollars

a week in her hands, out of which to pay current expenses. He heaved a little sigh as she said this, and drew out his purse. Again he felt the dread of the thing. Here he was taking off, taking off, and nothing coming in.

"Lord!" he said, in his own thoughts, "this can't go on."

To Carrie he said nothing whatsoever. She could feel that her request disturbed him. To pay her would soon become a distressing thing.

"Yet, what have I got to do with it?" she thought. "Oh, why should I be made to worry?"

Hurstwood went out and made for Broadway. He wanted to think up some place. Before long, though, he reached the Grand Hotel at Thirty-first Street. He knew of its comfortable lobby. He was cold after his twenty blocks' walk.

"I'll go in their barber shop and get a shave," he thought.

Thus he justified himself in sitting down in here after his tonsorial treatment.

Again, time hanging heavily on his hands, he went home early, and this continued for several days, each day the need to hunt paining him, and each day disgust, depression, shamefacedness driving him into lobby idleness.

At last three days came in which a storm prevailed, and he did not go out at all. The snow began to fall late one afternoon. It was a regular flurry of large, soft, white flakes. In the morning it was still coming down with a high wind, and the papers announced a blizzard. From out the front windows one could see a deep, soft bedding.

"I guess I'll not try to go out to-day," he said to Carrie at breakfast. "It's going to be awful bad, so the papers say."

"The man hasn't brought my coal, either," said Carrie, who ordered by the bushel.

"I'll go over and see about it," said Hurstwood. This was the first time he had ever suggested doing an errand, but, somehow, the wish to sit about the house prompted it as a sort of compensation for the privilege.

All day and all night it snowed, and the city began to suffer from a general blockade of traffic. Great attention was given to the details of the storm by the newspapers, which played up the distress of the poor in large type.

Hurstwood sat and read by his radiator in the corner. He

did not try to think about his need of work. This storm being so terrific, and tying up all things, robbed him of the need. He made himself wholly comfortable and toasted his feet.

Carrie observed his ease with some misgiving. For all the fury of the storm she doubted his comfort. He took his situation too philosophically.

Hurstwood, however, read on and on. He did not pay much attention to Carrie. She fulfilled her household duties and said little to disturb him.

The next day it was still snowing, and the next, bitter cold. Hurstwood took the alarm of the paper and sat still. Now he volunteered to do a few other little things. One was to go to the butcher, another to the grocery. He really thought nothing of these little services in connection with their true significance. He felt as if he were not wholly useless—indeed, in such a stress of weather, quite worth while about the house.

On the fourth day, however, it cleared, and he read that the storm was over. Now, however, he idled, thinking how sloppy the streets would be.

It was noon before he finally abandoned his papers and got under way. Owing to the slightly warmer temperature the streets were bad. He went across Fourteenth Street on the car and got a transfer south on Broadway. One little advertisement he had, relating to a saloon down in Pearl Street. When he reached the Broadway Central, however, he changed his mind.

"What's the use?" he thought, looking out upon the slop and snow. "I couldn't buy into it. It's a thousand to one nothing comes of it. I guess I'll get off," and off he got. In the lobby he took a seat and waited again, wondering what he could do.

While he was idly pondering, satisfied to be inside, a well-dressed man passed up the lobby, stopped, looked sharply, as if not sure of his memory, and then approached. Hurstwood recognised Cargill, the owner of the large stables in Chicago of the same name, whom he had last seen at Avery Hall, the night Carrie appeared there. The remembrance of how this individual brought up his wife to shake hands on that occasion was also on the instant clear.

Hurstwood was greatly abashed. His eyes expressed the difficulty he felt.

"Why, it's Hurstwood!" said Cargill, remembering now, and sorry that he had not recognised him quickly enough in the beginning to have avoided this meeting.

"Yes," said Hurstwood. "How are you?"

"Very well," said Cargill, troubled for something to talk about. "Stopping here?"

"No," said Hurstwood, "just keeping an appointment."

"I knew you had left Chicago. I was wondering what had become of you."

"Oh, I'm here now," answered Hurstwood, anxious to get away.

"Doing well, I suppose?"

"Excellent."

"Glad to hear it."

They looked at one another, rather embarrassed.

"Well, I have an engagement with a friend upstairs. I'll leave you. So long."

Hurstwood nodded his head.

"Damn it all," he murmured, turning toward the door. "I knew that would happen."

He walked several blocks up the street. His watch only registered 1.30. He tried to think of some place to go or something to do. The day was so bad he wanted only to be inside. Finally his feet began to feel wet and cold, and he boarded a car. This took him to Fifty-ninth Street, which was as good as anywhere else. Landed here, he turned to walk back along Seventh Avenue, but the slush was too much. The misery of lounging about with nowhere to go became intolerable. He felt as if he were catching cold.

Stopping at a corner, he waited for a car south bound. This was no day to be out; he would go home.

Carrie was surprised to see him at a quarter of three.

"It's a miserable day out," was all he said. Then he took off his coat and changed his shoes.

That night he felt a cold coming on and took quinine. He was feverish until morning, and sat about the next day while Carrie waited on him. He was a helpless creature in sickness, not very handsome in a dull-coloured bath gown and his hair uncombed. He looked haggard about the eyes and quite old. Carrie noticed this, and it did not appeal to her. She wanted to be good-natured and sympathetic, but something about the man held her aloof.

Toward evening he looked so badly in the weak light that she suggested he go to bed.

"You'd better sleep alone," she said, "you'll feel better. I'll open your bed for you now."

"All right," he said.

As she did all these things, she was in a most despondent state.

"What a life! What a life!" was her one thought.

Once during the day, when he sat near the radiator, hunched up and reading, she passed through, and seeing him, wrinkled her brows. In the front room, where it was not so warm, she sat by the window and cried. This was the life cut out for her, was it? To live cooped up in a small flat with some one who was out of work, idle, and indifferent to her. She was merely a servant to him now, nothing more.

This crying made her eyes red, and when, in preparing his bed, she lighted the gas, and, having prepared it, called him in, he noticed the fact.

"What's the matter with you?" he asked, looking into her face. His voice was hoarse and his unkempt head only added to its grewsome quality.

"Nothing," said Carrie, weakly.

"You've been crying," he said.

"I haven't, either," she answered.

It was not for love of him, that he knew.

"You needn't cry," he said, getting into bed. "Things will come out all right."

In a day or two he was up again, but rough weather holding, he stayed in. The Italian newsdealer now delivered the morning papers, and these he read assiduously. A few times after that he ventured out, but meeting another of his old-time friends, he began to feel uneasy sitting about hotel corridors.

Every day he came home early, and at last made no pretence of going anywhere. Winter was no time to look for anything.

Naturally, being about the house, he noticed the way Carrie did things. She was far from perfect in household methods and economy, and her little deviations on this score first caught his eye. Not, however, before her regular demand for her allowance became a grievous thing. Sitting around as he did, the weeks seemed to pass very quickly. Every Tuesday Carrie asked for her money.

"Do you think we live as cheaply as we might?" he asked one Tuesday morning.

"I do the best I can," said Carrie.

Nothing was added to this at the moment, but the next day he said:

"Do you ever go to the Gansevoort Market over here?"

"I didn't know there was such a market," said Carrie.

"They say you can get things lots cheaper there."

Carrie was very indifferent to the suggestion. These were things which she did not like at all.

"How much do you pay for a pound of meat?" he asked one day.

"Oh, there are different prices," said Carrie. "Sirloin steak is twenty-two cents."

"That's steep, isn't it?" he answered.

So he asked about other things, until finally, with the passing days, it seemed to become a mania with him. He learned the prices and remembered them.

His errand-running capacity also improved. It began in a small way, of course. Carrie, going to get her hat one morning, was stopped by him.

"Where are you going, Carrie?" he asked.

"Over to the baker's," she answered.

"I'd just as leave go for you," he said.

She acquiesced, and he went. Each afternoon he would go to the corner for the papers.

"Is there anything you want?" he would say.

By degrees she began to use him. Doing this, however, she lost the weekly payment of twelve dollars.

"You want to pay me to-day," she said one Tuesday, about this time.

"How much?" he asked.

She understood well enough what it meant.

"Well, about five dollars," she answered. "I owe the coal man."

The same day he said:

"I think this Italian up here on the corner sells coal at twenty-five cents a bushel. I'll trade with him."

Carrie heard this with indifference.

"All right," she said.

Then it came to be:

"George, I must have some coal to-day," or, "You must get some meat of some kind for dinner."

He would find out what she needed and order.

Accompanying this plan came skimpiness.

"I only got a half-pound of steak," he said, coming in one afternoon with his papers. "We never seem to eat very much."

These miserable details ate the heart out of Carrie. They blackened her days and grieved her soul. Oh, how this man had changed! All day and all day, here he sat, reading his papers. The world seemed to have no attraction. Once in a while he would go out, in fine weather, it might be four or five hours, between eleven and four. She could do nothing but view him with gnawing contempt.

It was apathy with Hurstwood, resulting from his inability to see his way out. Each month drew from his small store. Now, he had only five hundred dollars left, and this he hugged, half feeling as if he could stave off absolute necessity for an indefinite period. Sitting around the house, he decided to wear some old clothes he had. This came first with the bad days. Only once he apologised in the very beginning:

"It's so bad to-day, I'll just wear these around."

Eventually these became the permanent thing.

Also, he had been wont to pay fifteen cents for a shave, and a tip of ten cents. In his first distress, he cut down the tip to five, then to nothing. Later, he tried a ten-cent barber shop, and, finding that the shave was satisfactory, patronised regularly. Later still, he put off shaving to every other day, then to every third, and so on, until once a week became the rule. On Saturday he was a sight to see.

Of course, as his own self-respect vanished, it perished for him in Carrie. She could not understand what had gotten into the man. He had some money, he had a decent suit remaining, he was not bad looking when dressed up. She did not forget her own difficult struggle in Chicago, but she did not forget either that she had never ceased trying. He never tried. He did not even consult the ads. in the papers any more.

Finally, a distinct impression escaped from her.

"What makes you put so much butter on the steak?" he asked her one evening, standing around in the kitchen.

"To make it good, of course," she answered.

"Butter is awful dear these days," he suggested.

"You wouldn't mind it if you were working," she answered.

He shut up after this, and went in to his paper, but the retort rankled in his mind. It was the first cutting remark that had come from her.

That same evening, Carrie, after reading, went off to the front room to bed. This was unusual. When Hurstwood decided to go, he retired, as usual, without a light. It was then that he discovered Carrie's absence.

"That's funny," he said; "maybe she's sitting up."

He gave the matter no more thought, but slept. In the morning she was not beside him. Strange to say, this passed without comment.

Night approaching, and a slightly more conversational feeling prevailing, Carrie said:

"I think I'll sleep alone to-night. I have a headache."

"All right," said Hurstwood.

The third night she went to her front bed without apologies.

This was a grim blow to Hurstwood, but he never mentioned it.

"All right," he said to himself, with an irrepressible frown, "let her sleep alone."

Chapter XXXVI

A Grim Retrogression: The Phantom of Chance

THE VANCES, who had been back in the city ever since Christmas, had not forgotten Carrie; but they, or rather Mrs. Vance, had never called on her, for the very simple reason that Carrie had never sent her address. True to her nature, she corresponded with Mrs. Vance as long as she still lived in Seventy-eighth Street, but when she was compelled to move into Thirteenth, her fear that the latter would take it as an indication of reduced circumstances caused her to study some way of avoiding the necessity of giving her address. Not finding any convenient method, she sorrowfully resigned the privilege of writing to her friend entirely. The latter wondered at this strange silence, thought Carrie must have left the city, and in the end gave her up as lost. So she was thoroughly surprised to encounter her in Fourteenth Street, where she had gone shopping. Carrie was there for the same purpose.

"Why, Mrs. Wheeler," said Mrs. Vance, looking Carrie over in a glance, "where have you been? Why haven't you been to see me? I've been wondering all this time what had become of you. Really, I——"

"I'm so glad to see you," said Carrie, pleased and yet nonplussed. Of all times, this was the worst to encounter Mrs. Vance. "Why, I'm living down town here. I've been intending to come and see you. Where are you living now?"

"In Fifty-eighth Street," said Mrs. Vance, "just off Seventh Avenue—218. Why don't you come and see me?"

"I will," said Carrie. "Really, I've been wanting to come. I know I ought to. It's a shame. But you know——"

"What's your number?" said Mrs. Vance.

"Thirteenth Street," said Carrie, reluctantly. "112 West."

"Oh," said Mrs. Vance, "that's right near here, isn't it?"

"Yes," said Carrie. "You must come down and see me some time."

"Well, you're a fine one," said Mrs. Vance, laughing, the while noting that Carrie's appearance had modified somewhat. "The address, too," she added to herself. "They must be hard up."

Still she liked Carrie well enough to take her in tow.

"Come with me in here a minute," she exclaimed, turning into a store.

When Carrie returned home, there was Hurstwood, reading as usual. He seemed to take his condition with the utmost nonchalance. His beard was at least four days old.

"Oh," thought Carrie, "if she were to come here and see him?"

She shook her head in absolute misery. It looked as if her situation was becoming unbearable.

Driven to desperation, she asked at dinner:

"Did you ever hear any more from that wholesale house?"

"No," he said. "They don't want an inexperienced man."

Carrie dropped the subject, feeling unable to say more.

"I met Mrs. Vance this afternoon," she said, after a time.

"Did, eh?" he answered.

"They're back in New York now," Carrie went on. "She did look so nice."

"Well, she can afford it as long as he puts up for it," returned Hurstwood. "He's got a soft job."

Hurstwood was looking into the paper. He could not see the look of infinite weariness and discontent Carrie gave him.

"She said she thought she'd call here some day."

"She's been long getting round to it, hasn't she?" said Hurstwood, with a kind of sarcasm.

The woman didn't appeal to him from her spending side.

"Oh, I don't know," said Carrie, angered by the man's attitude. "Perhaps I didn't want her to come."

"She's too gay," said Hurstwood, significantly. "No one can keep up with her pace unless they've got a lot of money."

"Mr. Vance doesn't seem to find it very hard."

"He may not now," answered Hurstwood, doggedly, well understanding the inference; "but his life isn't done yet. You can't tell what'll happen. He may get down like anybody else."

There was something quite knavish in the man's attitude. His eye seemed to be cocked with a twinkle upon the fortunate, expecting their defeat. His own state seemed a thing apart—not considered.

This thing was the remains of his old-time cocksureness and independence. Sitting in his flat, and reading of the doings of other people, sometimes this independent, undefeated mood came upon him. Forgetting the weariness of the streets and the degradation of search, he would sometimes prick up his ears. It was as if he said:

"I can do something. I'm not down yet. There's a lot of things coming to me if I want to go after them."

It was in this mood that he would occasionally dress up, go for a shave, and, putting on his gloves, sally forth quite actively. Not with any definite aim. It was more a barometric condition. He felt just right for being outside and doing something.

On such occasions, his money went also. He knew of several poker rooms down town. A few acquaintances he had in down-town resorts and about the City Hall. It was a change to see them and exchange a few friendly commonplaces.

He had once been accustomed to hold a pretty fair hand at poker. Many a friendly game had netted him a hundred dollars or more at the time when that sum was merely sauce to the dish of the game—not the all in all. Now, he thought of playing.

"I might win a couple of hundred. I'm not out of practice."

It is but fair to say that this thought had occurred to him several times before he acted upon it.

The poker room which he first invaded was over a saloon in West Street, near one of the ferries. He had been there before. Several games were going. These he watched for a time and noticed that the pots were quite large for the ante involved.

"Deal me a hand," he said at the beginning of a new shuffle. He pulled up a chair and studied his cards. Those playing made that quiet study of him which is so unapparent, and yet invariably so searching.

Poor fortune was with him at first. He received a mixed collection without progression or pairs. The pot was opened.

"I pass," he said.

On the strength of this, he was content to lose his ante. The deals did fairly by him in the long run, causing him to come away with a few dollars to the good.

The next afternoon he was back again, seeking amusement and profit. This time he followed up three of a kind to his doom. There was a better hand across the table, held by a pugnacious Irish youth, who was a political hanger-on of the Tammany district in which they were located. Hurstwood was surprised at the persistence of this individual, whose bets came with a *sang-froid* which, if a bluff, was excellent art. Hurstwood began to doubt, but kept, or thought to keep, at least, the cool demeanour with which, in olden times, he deceived those psychic students of the gaming table, who seem to read thoughts and moods, rather than exterior evidences, however subtle. He could not down the cowardly thought that this man had something better and would stay to the end, drawing his last dollar into the pot, should he choose to go so far. Still, he hoped to win much—his hand was excellent. Why not raise it five more?

"I raise you three," said the youth.

"Make it five," said Hurstwood, pushing out his chips.

"Come again," said the youth, pushing out a small pile of reds.

"Let me have some more chips," said Hurstwood to the keeper in charge, taking out a bill.

A cynical grin lit up the face of his youthful opponent. When the chips were laid out, Hurstwood met the raise.

"Five again," said the youth.

Hurstwood's brow was wet. He was deep in now—very deep for him. Sixty dollars of his good money was up. He was ordinarily no coward, but the thought of losing so much weakened him. Finally he gave way. He would not trust to this fine hand any longer.

"I call," he said.

"A full house!" said the youth, spreading out his cards.

Hurstwood's hand dropped.

"I thought I had you," he said, weakly.

The youth raked in his chips, and Hurstwood came away, not without first stopping to count his remaining cash on the stair.

"Three hundred and forty dollars," he said.

With this loss and ordinary expenses, so much had already gone.

Back in the flat, he decided he would play no more.

Remembering Mrs. Vance's promise to call, Carrie made one other mild protest. It was concerning Hurstwood's appearance. This very day, coming home, he changed his clothes to the old togs he sat around in.

"What makes you always put on those old clothes?" asked Carrie.

"What's the use wearing my good ones around here?" he asked.

"Well, I should think you'd feel better." Then she added: "Some one might call."

"Who?" he said.

"Well, Mrs. Vance," said Carrie.

"She needn't see me," he answered, sullenly.

This lack of pride and interest made Carrie almost hate him.

"Oh," she thought, "there he sits. 'She needn't see me.' I should think he would be ashamed of himself."

The real bitterness of this thing was added when Mrs. Vance did call. It was on one of her shopping rounds. Making her way up the commonplace hall, she knocked at Carrie's door. To her subsequent and agonising distress, Carrie was out. Hurstwood opened the door, half-thinking that the knock was Carrie's. For once, he was taken honestly aback. The lost voice of youth and pride spoke in him.

"Why," he said, actually stammering, "how do you do?"

"How do you do?" said Mrs. Vance, who could scarcely believe her eyes. His great confusion she instantly perceived. He did not know whether to invite her in or not.

"Is your wife at home?" she inquired.

"No," he said, "Carrie's out; but won't you step in? She'll be back shortly."

"No-o," said Mrs. Vance, realising the change of it all. "I'm really very much in a hurry. I thought I'd just run up and look in, but I couldn't stay. Just tell your wife she must come and see me."

"I will," said Hurstwood, standing back, and feeling intense relief at her going. He was so ashamed that he folded his hands weakly, as he sat in the chair afterwards, and thought.

Carrie, coming in from another direction, thought she saw Mrs. Vance going away. She strained her eyes, but she could not make sure.

"Was anybody here just now?" she asked of Hurstwood.

"Yes," he said guiltily; "Mrs. Vance."

"Did she see you?" she asked, expressing her full despair.

This cut Hurstwood like a whip, and made him sullen.

"If she had eyes, she did. I opened the door."

"Oh," said Carrie, closing one hand tightly out of sheer nervousness. "What did she have to say?"

"Nothing," he answered. "She couldn't stay."

"And you looking like that!" said Carrie, throwing aside a long reserve.

"What of it?" he said, angering. "I didn't know she was coming, did I?"

"You knew she might," said Carrie. "I told you she said she was coming. I've asked you a dozen times to wear your other clothes. Oh, I think this is just terrible."

"Oh, let up," he answered. "What difference does it make? You couldn't associate with her, anyway. They've got too much money."

"Who said I wanted to?" said Carrie, fiercely.

"Well, you act like it, rowing around over my looks. You'd think I'd committed——"

Carrie interrupted:

"It's true," she said. "I couldn't if I wanted to, but whose fault is it? You're very free to sit and talk about who I could associate with. Why don't you get out and look for work?"

This was a thunderbolt in camp.

"What's it to you?" he said, rising, almost fiercely. "I pay the rent, don't I? I furnish the——"

"Yes, you pay the rent," said Carrie. "You talk as if there was nothing else in the world but a flat to sit around in. You haven't done a thing for three months except sit around and interfere here. I'd like to know what you married me for?"

"I didn't marry you," he said, in a snarling tone.

"I'd like to know what you did, then, in Montreal?" she answered.

"Well, I didn't marry you," he answered. "You can get that out of your head. You talk as though you didn't know."

Carrie looked at him a moment, her eyes distending. She had believed it was all legal and binding enough.

"What did you lie to me for, then?" she asked, fiercely. "What did you force me to run away with you for?"

Her voice became almost a sob.

"Force!" he said, with curled lip. "A lot of forcing I did."

"Oh!" said Carrie, breaking under the strain, and turning. "Oh, oh!" and she hurried into the front room.

Hurstwood was now hot and waked up. It was a great shaking up for him, both mental and moral. He wiped his brow as he looked around, and then went for his clothes and dressed. Not a sound came from Carrie; she ceased sobbing when she heard him dressing. She thought, at first, with the faintest alarm, of being left without money—not of losing him, though he might be going away permanently. She heard him open the top of the wardrobe and take out his hat. Then the dining-room door closed, and she knew he had gone.

After a few moments of silence, she stood up, dry-eyed, and looked out the window. Hurstwood was just strolling up the street, from the flat, toward Sixth Avenue.

The latter made progress along Thirteenth and across Fourteenth Street to Union Square.

"Look for work!" he said to himself. "Look for work! She tells me to get out and look for work."

He tried to shield himself from his own mental accusation, which told him that she was right.

"What a cursed thing that Mrs. Vance's call was, anyhow," he thought. "Stood right there, and looked me over. I know what she was thinking."

He remembered the few times he had seen her in Seventy-eighth Street. She was always a swell-looker, and he had tried to put on the air of being worthy of such as she, in front of her. Now, to think she had caught him looking this way. He wrinkled his forehead in his distress.

"The devil!" he said a dozen times in an hour.

It was a quarter after four when he left the house. Carrie was in tears. There would be no dinner that night.

"What the deuce," he said, swaggering mentally to hide his own shame from himself. "I'm not so bad. I'm not down yet."

He looked around the square, and seeing the several large

hotels, decided to go to one for dinner. He would get his papers and make himself comfortable there.

He ascended into the fine parlour of the Morton House, then one of the best New York hotels, and, finding a cushioned seat, read. It did not trouble him much that his decreasing sum of money did not allow of such extravagance. Like the morphine fiend, he was becoming addicted to his ease. Anything to relieve his mental distress, to satisfy his craving for comfort. He must do it. No thoughts for the morrow— he could not stand to think of it any more than he could of any other calamity. Like the certainty of death, he tried to shut the certainty of soon being without a dollar completely out of his mind, and he came very near doing it.

Well-dressed guests moving to and fro over the thick carpets carried him back to the old days. A young lady, a guest of the house, playing a piano in an alcove pleased him. He sat there reading.

His dinner cost him $1.50. By eight o'clock he was through, and then, seeing guests leaving and the crowd of pleasure-seekers thickening outside, wondered where he should go. Not home. Carrie would be up. No, he would not go back there this evening. He would stay out and knock around as a man who was independent—not broke—well might. He bought a cigar, and went outside on the corner where other individuals were lounging—brokers, racing people, thespians—his own flesh and blood. As he stood there, he thought of the old evenings in Chicago, and how he used to dispose of them. Many's the game he had had. This took him to poker.

"I didn't do that thing right the other day," he thought, referring to his loss of sixty dollars. "I shouldn't have weakened. I could have bluffed that fellow down. I wasn't in form, that's what ailed me."

Then he studied the possibilities of the game as it had been played, and began to figure how he might have won, in several instances, by bluffing a little harder.

"I'm old enough to play poker and do something with it. I'll try my hand to-night."

Visions of a big stake floated before him. Supposing he did win a couple of hundred, wouldn't he be in it? Lots of sports he knew made their living at this game, and a good living, too.

"They always had as much as I had," he thought.

So off he went to a poker room in the neighbourhood, feeling much as he had in the old days. In this period of self-forgetfulness, aroused first by the shock of argument and perfected by a dinner in the hotel, with cocktails and cigars, he was as nearly like the old Hurstwood as he would ever be again. It was not the old Hurstwood—only a man arguing with a divided conscience and lured by a phantom.

This poker room was much like the other one, only it was a back room in a better drinking resort. Hurstwood watched a while, and then, seeing an interesting game, joined in. As before, it went easy for a while, he winning a few times and cheering up, losing a few pots and growing more interested and determined on that account. At last the fascinating game took a strong hold on him. He enjoyed its risks and ventured, on a trifling hand, to bluff the company and secure a fair stake. To his self-satisfaction intense and strong, he did it.

In the height of this feeling he began to think his luck was with him. No one else had done so well. Now came another moderate hand, and again he tried to open the jack-pot on it. There were others there who were almost reading his heart, so close was their observation.

"I have three of a kind," said one of the players to himself. "I'll just stay with that fellow to the finish."

The result was that bidding began.

"I raise you ten."

"Good."

"Ten more."

"Good."

"Ten again."

"Right you are."

It got to where Hurstwood had seventy-five dollars up. The other man really became serious. Perhaps this individual (Hurstwood) really did have a stiff hand.

"I call," he said.

Hurstwood showed his hand. He was done. The bitter fact that he had lost seventy-five dollars made him desperate.

"Let's have another pot," he said, grimly.

"All right," said the man.

Some of the other players quit, but observant loungers took their places. Time passed, and it came to twelve o'clock. Hurstwood held on, neither winning nor losing much. Then he grew weary, and on a last hand lost twenty more. He was sick at heart.

At a quarter after one in the morning he came out of the place. The chill, bare streets seemed a mockery of his state. He walked slowly west, little thinking of his row with Carrie. He ascended the stairs and went into his room as if there had been no trouble. It was his loss that occupied his mind. Sitting down on the bedside he counted his money. There was now but a hundred and ninety dollars and some change. He put it up and began to undress.

"I wonder what's getting into me, anyhow?" he said.

In the morning Carrie scarcely spoke, and he felt as if he must go out again. He had treated her badly, but he could not afford to make up. Now desperation seized him, and for a day or two, going out thus, he lived like a gentleman—or what he conceived to be a gentleman—which took money. For his escapades he was soon poorer in mind and body, to say nothing of his purse, which had lost thirty by the process. Then he came down to cold, bitter sense again.

"The rent man comes to-day," said Carrie, greeting him thus indifferently three mornings later.

"He does?"

"Yes; this is the second," answered Carrie.

Hurstwood frowned. Then in despair he got out his purse. "It seems an awful lot to pay for rent," he said.

He was nearing his last hundred dollars.

Chapter XXXVII

THE SPIRIT AWAKENS: NEW SEARCH FOR THE GATE

IT WOULD be useless to explain how in due time the last fifty dollars was in sight. The seven hundred, by his process of handling, had only carried them into June. Before the final hundred mark was reached he began to indicate that a calamity was approaching.

"I don't know," he said one day, taking a trivial expenditure for meat as a text, "it seems to take an awful lot for us to live."

"It doesn't seem to me," said Carrie, "that we spend very much."

"My money is nearly gone," he said, "and I hardly know where it's gone to."

"All that seven hundred dollars?" asked Carrie.

"All but a hundred."

He looked so disconsolate that it scared her. She began to see that she herself had been drifting. She had felt it all the time.

"Well, George," she exclaimed, " why don't you get out and look for something? You could find something."

"I have looked," he said. "You can't make people give you a place."

She gazed weakly at him and said: "Well, what do you think you will do? A hundred dollars won't last long."

"I don't know," he said. "I can't do any more than look."

Carrie became frightened over this announcement. She thought desperately upon the subject. Frequently she had considered the stage as a door through which she might enter that gilded state which she had so much craved. Now, as in Chicago, it came as a last resource in distress. Something must be done if he did not get work soon. Perhaps she would have to go out and battle again alone.

She began to wonder how one would go about getting a place. Her experience in Chicago proved that she had not tried the right way. There must be people who would listen to and try you—men who would give you an opportunity.

They were talking at the breakfast table, a morning or two later, when she brought up the dramatic subject by saying that she saw that Sarah Bernhardt was coming to this country. Hurstwood had seen it, too.

"How do people get on the stage, George?" she finally asked, innocently.

"I don't know," he said. "There must be dramatic agents."

Carrie was sipping coffee, and did not look up.

"Regular people who get you a place?"

"Yes, I think so," he answered.

Suddenly the air with which she asked attracted his attention.

"You're not still thinking about being an actress, are you?" he asked.

"No," she answered, "I was just wondering."

Without being clear, there was something in the thought which he objected to. He did not believe any more, after three years of observation, that Carrie would ever do anything great in that line. She seemed too simple, too yielding. His idea of the art was that it involved something more pompous. If she tried to get on the stage she would fall into the hands of some cheap manager and become like the rest of them. He had a good idea of what he meant by *them*. Carrie was pretty. She would get along all right, but where would he be?

"I'd get that idea out of my head, if I were you. It's a lot more difficult than you think."

Carrie felt this to contain, in some way, an aspersion upon her ability.

"You said I did real well in Chicago," she rejoined.

"You did," he answered, seeing that he was arousing opposition, "but Chicago isn't New York, by a big jump."

Carrie did not answer this at all. It hurt her.

"The stage," he went on, "is all right if you can be one of the big guns, but there's nothing to the rest of it. It takes a long while to get up."

"Oh, I don't know," said Carrie, slightly aroused.

In a flash, he thought he foresaw the result of this thing. Now, when the worst of his situation was approaching, she would get on the stage in some cheap way and forsake him.

Strangely, he had not conceived well of her mental ability. That was because he did not understand the nature of emotional greatness. He had never learned that a person might be emotionally—instead of intellectually—great. Avery Hall was too far away for him to look back and sharply remember. He had lived with this woman too long.

"Well, I do," he answered. "If I were you I wouldn't think of it. It's not much of a profession for a woman."

"It's better than going hungry," said Carrie. "If you don't want me to do that, why don't you get work yourself?"

There was no answer ready for this. He had got used to the suggestion.

"Oh, let up," he answered.

The result of this was that she secretly resolved to try. It didn't matter about him. She was not going to be dragged into poverty and something worse to suit him. She could act. She could get something and then work up. What would he say then? She pictured herself already appearing in some fine performance on Broadway; of going every evening to her dressing-room and making up. Then she would come out at eleven o'clock and see the carriages ranged about, waiting for the people. It did not matter whether she was the star or not. If she were only once in, getting a decent salary, wearing the kind of clothes she liked, having the money to do with, going here and there as she pleased, how delightful it would all be. Her mind ran over this picture all the day long. Hurstwood's dreary state made its beauty become more and more vivid.

Curiously this idea soon took hold of Hurstwood. His vanishing sum suggested that he would need sustenance. Why could not Carrie assist him a little until he could get something?

He came in one day with something of this idea in his mind.

"I met John B. Drake to-day," he said. "He's going to open a hotel here in the fall. He says that he can make a place for me then."

"Who is he?" asked Carrie.

"He's the man that runs the Grand Pacific in Chicago."

"Oh," said Carrie.

"I'd get about fourteen hundred a year out of that."

"That would be good, wouldn't it?" she said, sympathetically.

"If I can only get over this summer," he added, "I think I'll be all right. I'm hearing from some of my friends again."

Carrie swallowed this story in all its pristine beauty. She sincerely wished he could get through the summer. He looked so hopeless.

"How much money have you left?"

"Only fifty dollars."

"Oh, mercy," she exclaimed, "what will we do? It's only twenty days until the rent will be due again."

Hurstwood rested his head on his hands and looked blankly at the floor.

"Maybe you could get something in the stage line?" he blandly suggested.

"Maybe I could," said Carrie, glad that some one approved of the idea.

"I'll lay my hand to whatever I can get," he said, now that he saw her brighten up. "I can get something."

She cleaned up the things one morning after he had gone, dressed as neatly as her wardrobe permitted, and set out for Broadway. She did not know that thoroughfare very well. To her it was a wonderful conglomeration of everything great and mighty. The theatres were there—these agencies must be somewhere about.

She decided to stop in at the Madison Square Theatre and ask how to find the theatrical agents. This seemed the sensible way. Accordingly, when she reached that theatre she applied to the clerk at the box office.

"Eh?" he said, looking out. "Dramatic agents? I don't know. You'll find them in the 'Clipper,' though. They all advertise in that."

"Is that a paper?" said Carrie.

"Yes," said the clerk, marvelling at such ignorance of a common fact. "You can get it at the news-stands," he added politely, seeing how pretty the inquirer was.

Carrie proceeded to get the "Clipper," and tried to find the agents by looking over it as she stood beside the stand. This could not be done so easily. Thirteenth Street was a number of blocks off, but she went back, carrying the precious paper and regretting the waste of time.

Hurstwood was already there, sitting in his place.

"Where were you?" he asked.

"I've been trying to find some dramatic agents."

He felt a little diffident about asking concerning her success. The paper she began to scan attracted his attention.

"What have you got there?" he asked.

"The 'Clipper.' The man said I'd find their addresses in here."

"Have you been all the way over to Broadway to find that out? I could have told you."

"Why didn't you?" she asked, without looking up.

"You never asked me," he returned.

She went hunting aimlessly through the crowded columns. Her mind was distracted by this man's indifference. The difficulty of the situation she was facing was only added to by all he did. Self-commiseration brewed in her heart. Tears trembled along her eyelids but did not fall. Hurstwood noticed something.

"Let me look."

To recover herself she went into the front room while he searched. Presently she returned. He had a pencil, and was writing upon an envelope.

"Here 're three," he said.

Carrie took it and found that one was Mrs. Bermudez, another Marcus Jenks, a third Percy Weil. She paused only a moment, and then moved toward the door.

"I might as well go right away," she said, without looking back.

Hurstwood saw her depart with some faint stirrings of shame, which were the expression of a manhood rapidly becoming stultified. He sat a while, and then it became too much. He got up and put on his hat.

"I guess I'll go out," he said to himself, and went, strolling nowhere in particular, but feeling somehow that he must go.

Carrie's first call was upon Mrs. Bermudez, whose address was quite the nearest. It was an old-fashioned residence turned into offices. Mrs. Bermudez's offices consisted of what formerly had been a back chamber and a hall bedroom, marked "Private."

As Carrie entered she noticed several persons lounging about—men, who said nothing and did nothing.

While she was waiting to be noticed, the door of the hall bedroom opened and from it issued two very mannish-looking women, very tightly dressed, and wearing white collars and cuffs. After them came a portly lady of about forty-five, light-haired, sharp-eyed, and evidently good-natured. At least she was smiling.

"Now, don't forget about that," said one of the mannish women.

"I won't," said the portly woman. "Let's see," she added, " where are you the first week in February?"

"Pittsburg," said the woman.

"I'll write you there."

"All right," said the other, and the two passed out.

Instantly the portly lady's face became exceedingly sober and shrewd. She turned about and fixed on Carrie a very searching eye.

"Well," she said, "young woman, what can I do for you?"

"Are you Mrs. Bermudez?"

"Yes."

"Well," said Carrie, hesitating how to begin, "do you get places for persons upon the stage?"

"Yes."

"Could you get me one?"

"Have you ever had any experience?"

"A very little," said Carrie.

"Whom did you play with?"

"Oh, with no one," said Carrie. "It was just a show gotten——"

"Oh, I see," said the woman, interrupting her. "No, I don't know of anything now."

Carrie's countenance fell.

"You want to get some New York experience," concluded the affable Mrs. Bermudez. "We'll take your name, though."

Carrie stood looking while the lady retired to her office.

"What is your address?" inquired a young lady behind the counter, taking up the curtailed conversation.

"Mrs. George Wheeler," said Carrie, moving over to where she was writing. The woman wrote her address in full and then allowed her to depart at her leisure.

She encountered a very similar experience in the office of Mr. Jenks, only he varied it by saying at the close: "If you could play at some local house, or had a programme with your name on it, I might do something."

In the third place the individual asked:

"What sort of work do you want to do?"

"What do you mean?" said Carrie.

"Well, do you want to get in a comedy or on the vaudeville stage or in the chorus?"

"Oh, I'd like to get a part in a play," said Carrie.

"Well," said the man, "it'll cost you something to do that."

"How much?" said Carrie, who, ridiculous as it may seem, had not thought of this before.

"Well, that's for you to say," he answered shrewdly.

Carrie looked at him curiously. She hardly knew how to continue the inquiry.

"Could you get me a part if I paid?"

"If we didn't you'd get your money back."

"Oh," she said.

The agent saw he was dealing with an inexperienced soul, and continued accordingly.

"You'd want to deposit fifty dollars, any way. No agent would trouble about you for less than that."

Carrie saw a light.

"Thank you," she said. "I'll think about it."

She started to go, and then bethought herself.

"How soon would I get a place?" she asked.

"Well, that's hard to say," said the man. "You might get one in a week, or it might be a month. You'd get the first thing that we thought you could do."

"I see," said Carrie, and then, half-smiling to be agreeable, she walked out.

The agent studied a moment, and then said to himself:

"It's funny how anxious these women are to get on the stage."

Carrie found ample food for reflection in the fifty-dollar proposition. "Maybe they'd take my money and not give me anything," she thought. She had some jewelry—a diamond ring and pin and several other pieces. She could get fifty dollars for those if she went to a pawnbroker.

Hurstwood was home before her. He had not thought she would be so long seeking.

"Well?" he said, not venturing to ask what news.

"I didn't find out anything to-day," said Carrie, taking off her gloves. "They all want money to get you a place."

"How much?" asked Hurstwood.

"Fifty dollars."

"They don't want anything, do they?"

"Oh, they're like everybody else. You can't tell whether they'd ever get you anything after you did pay them."

"Well, I wouldn't put up fifty on that basis," said Hurstwood, as if he were deciding, money in hand.

"I don't know," said Carrie. "I think I'll try some of the managers."

Hurstwood heard this, dead to the horror of it. He rocked a little to and fro, and chewed at his finger. It seemed all very natural in such extreme states. He would do better later on.

Chapter XXXVIII

IN ELF LAND DISPORTING: THE GRIM WORLD WITHOUT

WHEN CARRIE renewed her search, as she did the next day, going to the Casino, she found that in the opera chorus, as in other fields, employment is difficult to secure. Girls who can stand in a line and look pretty are as numerous as labourers who can swing a pick. She found there was no discrimination between one and the other of applicants, save as regards a conventional standard of prettiness and form. Their own opinion or knowledge of their ability went for nothing.

"Where shall I find Mr. Gray?" she asked of a sulky door-man at the stage entrance of the Casino.

"You can't see him now; he's busy."

"Do you know when I can see him?"

"Got an appointment with him?"

"No."

"Well, you'll have to call at his office."

"Oh, dear!" exclaimed Carrie. "Where is his office?"

He gave her the number.

She knew there was no need of calling there now. He would not be in. Nothing remained but to employ the inter-mediate hours in search.

The dismal story of ventures in other places is quickly told. Mr. Daly saw no one save by appointment. Carrie waited an hour in a dingy office, quite in spite of obstacles, to learn this fact of the placid, indifferent Mr. Dorney.

"You will have to write and ask him to see you."

So she went away.

At the Empire Theatre she found a hive of peculiarly listless and indifferent individuals. Everything ornately upholstered, everything carefully finished, everything remarkably reserved.

At the Lyceum she entered one of those secluded, under-stairway closets, berugged and bepanneled, which causes one to feel the greatness of all positions of authority. Here was reserve itself done into a box-office clerk, a doorman, and an assistant, glorying in their fine positions.

"Ah, be very humble now—very humble indeed. Tell us what it is you require. Tell it quickly, nervously, and without a vestige of self-respect. If no trouble to us in any way, we may see what we can do."

This was the atmosphere of the Lyceum—the attitude, for that matter, of every managerial office in the city. These little proprietors of businesses are lords indeed on their own ground.

Carrie came away wearily, somewhat more abashed for her pains.

Hurstwood heard the details of the weary and unavailing search that evening.

"I didn't get to see any one," said Carrie. "I just walked, and walked, and waited around."

Hurstwood only looked at her.

"I suppose you have to have some friends before you can get in," she added, disconsolately.

Hurstwood saw the difficulty of this thing, and yet it did not seem so terrible. Carrie was tired and dispirited, but now she could rest. Viewing the world from his rocking-chair, its bitterness did not seem to approach so rapidly. To-morrow was another day.

To-morrow came, and the next, and the next.

Carrie saw the manager at the Casino once.

"Come around," he said, "the first of next week. I may make some changes then."

He was a large and corpulent individual, surfeited with good clothes and good eating, who judged women as another would horseflesh. Carrie was pretty and graceful. She might be put in even if she did not have any experience. One of the proprietors had suggested that the chorus was a little weak on looks.

The first of next week was some days off yet. The first of the month was drawing near. Carrie began to worry as she had never worried before.

"Do you really look for anything when you go out?" she asked Hurstwood one morning as a climax to some painful thoughts of her own.

"Of course I do," he said pettishly, troubling only a little over the disgrace of the insinuation.

"I'd take anything," she said, "for the present. It will soon be the first of the month again."

She looked the picture of despair.

Hurstwood quit reading his paper and changed his clothes.

"He would look for something," he thought. "He would go and see if some brewery couldn't get him in somewhere. Yes, he would take a position as bartender, if he could get it."

It was the same sort of pilgrimage he had made before. One or two slight rebuffs, and the bravado disappeared.

"No use," he thought. "I might as well go on back home."

Now that his money was so low, he began to observe his clothes and feel that even his best ones were beginning to look commonplace. This was a bitter thought.

Carrie came in after he did.

"I went to see some of the variety managers," she said, aimlessly. "You have to have an act. They don't want anybody that hasn't."

"I saw some of the brewery people to-day," said Hurstwood. "One man told me he'd try to make a place for me in two or three weeks."

In the face of so much distress on Carrie's part, he had to make some showing, and it was thus he did so. It was lassitude's apology to energy.

Monday Carrie went again to the Casino.

"Did I tell you to come around to-day?" said the manager, looking her over as she stood before him.

"You said the first of the week," said Carrie, greatly abashed.

"Ever had any experience?" he asked again, almost severely.

Carrie owned to ignorance.

He looked her over again as he stirred among some papers. He was secretly pleased with this pretty, disturbed-looking young woman. "Come around to the theatre to-morrow morning."

Carrie's heart bounded to her throat.

"I will," she said with difficulty. She could see he wanted her, and turned to go.

"Would he really put her to work? Oh, blessed fortune, could it be?"

Already the hard rumble of the city through the open windows became pleasant.

A sharp voice answered her mental interrogation, driving away all immediate fears on that score.

"Be sure you're there promptly," the manager said roughly. "You'll be dropped if you're not."

Carrie hastened away. She did not quarrel now with Hurstwood's idleness. She had a place—she had a place! This sang in her ears.

In her delight she was almost anxious to tell Hurstwood. But, as she walked homeward, and her survey of the facts of the case became larger, she began to think of the anomaly of her finding work in several weeks and his lounging in idleness for a number of months.

"Why don't he get something?" she openly said to herself. "If I can he surely ought to. It wasn't very hard for me."

She forgot her youth and her beauty. The handicap of age she did not, in her enthusiasm, perceive.

Thus, ever, the voice of success.

Still, she could not keep her secret. She tried to be calm and indifferent, but it was a palpable sham.

"Well?" he said, seeing her relieved face.

"I have a place."

"You have?" he said, breathing a better breath.

"Yes."

"What sort of a place is it?" he asked, feeling in his veins as if now he might get something good also.

"In the chorus," she answered.

"Is it the Casino show you told me about?"

"Yes," she answered. "I begin rehearsing to-morrow."

There was more explanation volunteered by Carrie, because she was happy. At last Hurstwood said:

"Do you know how much you'll get?"

"No, I didn't want to ask," said Carrie. "I guess they pay twelve or fourteen dollars a week."

"About that, I guess," said Hurstwood.

There was a good dinner in the flat that evening, owing to the mere lifting of the terrible strain. Hurstwood went out for a shave, and returned with a fair-sized sirloin steak.

"Now, to-morrow," he thought, "I'll look around myself," and with renewed hope he lifted his eyes from the ground.

On the morrow Carrie reported promptly and was given a place in the line. She saw a large, empty, shadowy play-house, still redolent of the perfumes and blazonry of the night, and notable for its rich, oriental appearance. The wonder of it awed and delighted her. Blessed be its wondrous reality. How hard she would try to be worthy of it. It was above the common mass, above idleness, above want, above insignificance. People came to it in finery and carriages to see. It was ever a centre of light and mirth. And here she was of it. Oh, if she could only remain, how happy would be her days!

"What is your name?" said the manager, who was conducting the drill.

"Madenda," she replied, instantly mindful of the name Drouet had selected in Chicago. "Carrie Madenda."

"Well, now, Miss Madenda," he said, very affably, as Carrie thought, "you go over there."

Then he called to a young woman who was already of the company:

"Miss Clark, you pair with Miss Madenda."

This young lady stepped forward, so that Carrie saw where to go, and the rehearsal began.

Carrie soon found that while this drilling had some slight resemblance to the rehearsals as conducted at Avery Hall, the attitude of the manager was much more pronounced. She had marvelled at the insistence and superior airs of Mr. Millice, but the individual conducting here had the same insistence, coupled with almost brutal roughness. As the drilling proceeded, he seemed to wax exceedingly wroth over trifles, and to increase his lung power in proportion. It was very evident that he had a great contempt for any assumption of dignity or innocence on the part of these young women.

"Clark," he would call—meaning, of course, Miss Clark—" why don't you catch step there?"

"By fours, right! Right, I said, right! For heaven's sake, get on to yourself! Right!" and in saying this he would lift the last sounds into a vehement roar.

"Maitland! Maitland!" he called once.

A nervous, comely-dressed little girl stepped out. Carrie

trembled for her out of the fulness of her own sympathies and fear.

"Yes, sir," said Miss Maitland.

"Is there anything the matter with your ears?"

"No, sir."

"Do you know what 'column left' means?"

"Yes, sir."

"Well, what are you stumbling around the right for? Want to break up the line?"

"I was just——"

"Never mind what you were just. Keep your ears open."

Carrie pitied, and trembled for her turn.

Yet another suffered the pain of personal rebuke.

"Hold on a minute," cried the manager, throwing up his hands, as if in despair. His demeanour was fierce.

"Elvers," he shouted, " what have you got in your mouth?"

"Nothing," said Miss Elvers, while some smiled and stood nervously by.

"Well, are you talking?"

"No, sir."

"Well, keep your mouth still then. Now, all together again."

At last Carrie's turn came. It was because of her extreme anxiety to do all that was required that brought on the trouble.

She heard some one called.

"Mason," said the voice. "Miss Mason."

She looked around to see who it could be. A girl behind shoved her a little, but she did not understand.

"You, you!" said the manager. "Can't you hear?"

"Oh," said Carrie, collapsing, and blushing fiercely.

"Isn't your name Mason?" asked the manager.

"No, sir," said Carrie, "it's Madenda."

"Well, what's the matter with your feet? Can't you dance?"

"Yes, sir," said Carrie, who had long since learned this art.

"Why don't you do it then? Don't go shuffling along as if you were dead. I've got to have people with life in them."

Carrie's cheek burned with a crimson heat. Her lips trembled a little.

"Yes, sir," she said.

It was this constant urging, coupled with irascibility and energy, for three long hours. Carrie came away worn enough in body, but too excited in mind to notice it. She meant to go home and practise her evolutions as prescribed. She would not err in any way, if she could help it.

When she reached the flat Hurstwood was not there. For a wonder he was out looking for work, as she supposed. She took only a mouthful to eat and then practised on, sustained by visions of freedom from financial distress—"The sound of glory ringing in her ears."

When Hurstwood returned he was not so elated as when he went away, and now she was obliged to drop practice and get dinner. Here was an early irritation. She would have her work and this. Was she going to act and keep house?

"I'll not do it," she said, "after I get started. He can take his meals out."

Each day thereafter brought its cares. She found it was not such a wonderful thing to be in the chorus, and she also learned that her salary would be twelve dollars a week. After a few days she had her first sight of those high and mighties —the leading ladies and gentlemen. She saw that they were privileged and deferred to. She was nothing—absolutely nothing at all.

At home was Hurstwood, daily giving her cause for thought. He seemed to get nothing to do, and yet he made bold to inquire how she was getting along. The regularity with which he did this smacked of some one who was waiting to live upon her labour. Now that she had a visible means of support, this irritated her. He seemed to be depending upon her little twelve dollars.

"How are you getting along?" he would blandly inquire.

"Oh, all right," she would reply.

"Find it easy?"

"It will be all right when I get used to it."

His paper would then engross his thoughts.

"I got some lard," he would add, as an afterthought. "I thought maybe you might want to make some biscuit."

The calm suggestion of the man astonished her a little, especially in the light of recent developments. Her dawning independence gave her more courage to observe, and she felt as if she wanted to say things. Still she could not talk to him as she had to Drouet. There was something in the man's manner of which she had always stood in awe. He seemed to have some invisible strength in reserve.

One day, after her first week's rehearsal, what she expected came openly to the surface.

"We'll have to be rather saving," he said, laying down some meat he had purchased. "You won't get any money for a week or so yet."

"No," said Carrie, who was stirring a pan at the stove.

"I've only got the rent and thirteen dollars more," he added.

"That's it," she said to herself. "I'm to use my money now."

Instantly she remembered that she had hoped to buy a few things for herself. She needed clothes. Her hat was not nice.

"What will twelve dollars do towards keeping up this flat?" she thought. "I can't do it. Why doesn't he get something to do?"

The important night of the first real performance came. She did not suggest to Hurstwood that he come and see. He did not think of going. It would only be money wasted. She had such a small part.

The advertisements were already in the papers; the posters upon the bill-boards. The leading lady and many members were cited. Carrie was nothing.

As in Chicago, she was seized with stage fright as the very first entrance of the ballet approached, but later she recovered. The apparent and painful insignificance of the part took fear away from her. She felt that she was so obscure it did not matter. Fortunately, she did not have to wear tights. A group of twelve were assigned pretty golden-hued skirts which came only to a line about an inch above the knee. Carrie happened to be one of the twelve.

In standing about the stage, marching, and occasionally lifting up her voice in the general chorus, she had a chance to observe the audience and to see the inauguration of a great hit. There was plenty of applause, but she could not help noting how poorly some of the women of alleged ability did.

"I could do better than that," Carrie ventured to herself, in several instances. To do her justice, she was right.

After it was over she dressed quickly, and as the manager had scolded some others and passed her, she imagined she must have proved satisfactory. She wanted to get out quickly, because she knew but few, and the stars were gossiping. Outside were carriages and some correct youths in attractive clothing, waiting. Carrie saw that she was scanned closely. The flutter of an eyelash would have brought her a companion. That she did not give.

One experienced youth volunteered, anyhow.

"Not going home alone, are you?" he said.

Carrie merely hastened her steps and took the Sixth Avenue car. Her head was so full of the wonder of it that she had time for nothing else.

"Did you hear any more from the brewery?" she asked at the end of the week, hoping by the question to stir him on to action.

"No," he answered, "they're not quite ready yet. I think something will come of that, though."

She said nothing more then, objecting to giving up her own money, and yet feeling that such would have to be the case. Hurstwood felt the crisis, and artfully decided to appeal to Carrie. He had long since realised how good-natured she was, how much she would stand. There was some little shame in him at the thought of doing so, but he justified himself with the thought that he really would get something. Rent day gave him his opportunity.

"Well," he said, as he counted it out, "that's about the last of my money. I'll have to get something pretty soon."

Carrie looked at him askance, half-suspicious of an appeal.

"If I could only hold out a little longer I think I could get something. Drake is sure to open a hotel here in September."

"Is he?" said Carrie, thinking of the short month that still remained until that time.

"Would you mind helping me out until then?" he said appealingly. "I think I'll be all right after that time."

"No," said Carrie, feeling sadly handicapped by fate.

"We can get along if we economise. I'll pay you back all right."

"Oh, I'll help you," said Carrie, feeling quite hard-hearted at thus forcing him to humbly appeal, and yet her desire for the benefit of her earnings wrung a faint protest from her.

"Why don't you take anything, George, temporarily?" she said. "What difference does it make? Maybe, after a while, you'll get something better."

"I will take anything," he said, relieved, and wincing under reproof. "I'd just as leave dig on the streets. Nobody knows me here."

"Oh, you needn't do that," said Carrie, hurt by the pity of it. "But there must be other things."

"I'll get something!" he said, assuming determination.

Then he went back to his paper.

Chapter XXXIX

OF LIGHTS AND OF SHADOWS: THE PARTING OF WORLDS

WHAT HURSTWOOD got as the result of this determination was more self-assurance that each particular day was not the day. At the same time, Carrie passed through thirty days of mental distress.

Her need of clothes—to say nothing of her desire for ornaments—grew rapidly as the fact developed that for all her work she was not to have them. The sympathy she felt for Hurstwood, at the time he asked her to tide him over, vanished with these newer urgings of decency. He was not always renewing his request, but this love of good appearance was. It insisted, and Carrie wished to satisfy it, wished more and more that Hurstwood was not in the way.

Hurstwood reasoned, when he neared the last ten dollars, that he had better keep a little pocket change and not become wholly dependent for car-fare, shaves, and the like; so when this sum was still in his hand he announced himself as penniless.

"I'm clear out," he said to Carrie one afternoon. "I paid for some coal this morning, and that took all but ten or fifteen cents."

"I've got some money there in my purse."

Hurstwood went to get it, starting for a can of tomatoes. Carrie scarcely noticed that this was the beginning of the new order. He took out fifteen cents and bought the can with it. Thereafter it was dribs and drabs of this sort, until one morning Carrie suddenly remembered that she would not be back until close to dinner time.

"We're all out of flour," she said; "you'd better get some this afternoon. We haven't any meat, either. How would it do if we had liver and bacon?"

"Suits me," said Hurstwood.

"Better get a half or three-quarters of a pound of that."

"Half 'll be enough," volunteered Hurstwood.

She opened her purse and laid down a half dollar. He pretended not to notice it.

Hurstwood bought the flour—which all grocers sold in 3½-pound packages—for thirteen cents and paid fifteen cents for a half-pound of liver and bacon. He left the packages, together with the balance of thirty-two cents, upon the kitchen table, where Carrie found it. It did not escape her that the change was accurate. There was something sad in realising that, after all, all that he wanted of her was something to eat. She felt as if hard thoughts were unjust. Maybe he would get something yet. He had no vices.

That very evening, however, on going into the theatre, one of the chorus girls passed her all newly arrayed in a pretty mottled tweed suit, which took Carrie's eye. The young woman wore a fine bunch of violets and seemed in high spirits. She smiled at Carrie good-naturedly as she passed, showing pretty, even teeth, and Carrie smiled back.

"She can afford to dress well," thought Carrie, "and so could I, if I could only keep my money. I haven't a decent tie of any kind to wear."

She put out her foot and looked at her shoe reflectively.

"I'll get a pair of shoes Saturday, anyhow; I don't care what happens."

One of the sweetest and most sympathetic little chorus girls in the company made friends with her because in Carrie she found nothing to frighten her away. She was a gay little Manon, unwitting of society's fierce conception of morality, but, nevertheless, good to her neighbour and charitable. Little license was allowed the chorus in the matter of conversation, but, nevertheless, some was indulged in.

"It's warm to-night, isn't it?" said this girl, arrayed in pink fleshings and an imitation golden helmet. She also carried a shining shield.

"Yes; it is," said Carrie, pleased that some one should talk to her.

"I'm almost roasting," said the girl.

Carrie looked into her pretty face, with its large blue eyes, and saw little beads of moisture.

"There's more marching in this opera than ever I did before," added the girl.

"Have you been in others?" asked Carrie, surprised at her experience.

"Lots of them," said the girl; "haven't you?"

"This is my first experience."

"Oh, is it? I thought I saw you the time they ran 'The Queen's Mate' here."

"No," said Carrie, shaking her head; "not me."

This conversation was interrupted by the blare of the orchestra and the sputtering of the calcium lights in the wings as the line was called to form for a new entrance. No further opportunity for conversation occurred, but the next evening, when they were getting ready for the stage, this girl appeared anew at her side.

"They say this show is going on the road next month."

"Is it?" said Carrie.

"Yes; do you think you'll go?"

"I don't know; I guess so, if they'll take me."

"Oh, they'll take you. I wouldn't go. They won't give you any more, and it will cost you everything you make to live. I never leave New York. There are too many shows going on here."

"Can you always get in another show?"

"I always have. There's one going on up at the Broadway this month. I'm going to try and get in that if this one really goes."

Carrie heard this with aroused intelligence. Evidently it wasn't so very difficult to get on. Maybe she also could get a place if this show went away.

"Do they all pay about the same?" she asked.

"Yes. Sometimes you get a little more. This show doesn't pay very much."

"I get twelve," said Carrie.

"Do you?" said the girl. "They pay me fifteen, and you do more work than I do. I wouldn't stand it if I were you. They're just giving you less because they think you don't know. You ought to be making fifteen."

"Well, I'm not," said Carrie.

"Well, you'll get more at the next place if you want it," went on the girl, who admired Carrie very much. "You do fine, and the manager knows it."

To say the truth, Carrie did unconsciously move about with an air pleasing and somewhat distinctive. It was due wholly to her natural manner and total lack of self-consciousness.

"Do you suppose I could get more up at the Broadway?"

"Of course you can," answered the girl. "You come with me when I go. I'll do the talking."

Carrie heard this, flushing with thankfulness. She liked this little gaslight soldier. She seemed so experienced and self-reliant in her tinsel helmet and military accoutrements.

"My future must be assured if I can always get work this way," thought Carrie.

Still, in the morning, when her household duties would infringe upon her and Hurstwood sat there, a perfect load to contemplate, her fate seemed dismal and unrelieved. It did not take so very much to feed them under Hurstwood's close-measured buying, and there would possibly be enough for rent, but it left nothing else. Carrie bought the shoes and some other things, which complicated the rent problem very seriously. Suddenly, a week from the fatal day, Carrie realised that they were going to run short.

"I don't believe," she exclaimed, looking into her purse at breakfast, "that I'll have enough to pay the rent."

"How much have you?" inquired Hurstwood.

"Well, I've got twenty-two dollars, but there's everything to be paid for this week yet, and if I use all I get Saturday to pay this, there won't be any left for next week. Do you think your hotel man will open his hotel this month?"

"I think so," returned Hurstwood. "He said he would."

After a while, Hurstwood said:

"Don't worry about it. Maybe the grocer will wait. He can do that. We've traded there long enough to make him trust us for a week or two."

"Do you think he will?" she asked.

"I think so."

On this account, Hurstwood, this very day, looked grocer Oeslogge clearly in the eye as he ordered a pound of coffee, and said:

"Do you mind carrying my account until the end of every week?"

"No, no, Mr. Wheeler," said Mr. Oeslogge. "Dat iss all right."

Hurstwood, still tactful in distress, added nothing to this. It seemed an easy thing. He looked out of the door, and then gathered up his coffee when ready and came away. The game of a desperate man had begun.

Rent was paid, and now came the grocer. Hurstwood managed by paying out of his own ten and collecting from Carrie at the end of the week. Then he delayed a day next time settling with the grocer, and so soon had his ten back, with Oeslogge getting his pay on this Thursday or Friday for last Saturday's bill.

This entanglement made Carrie anxious for a change of some sort. Hurstwood did not seem to realise that she had a right to anything. He schemed to make what she earned cover all expenses, but seemed not to trouble over adding anything himself.

"He talks about worrying," thought Carrie. "If he worried enough he couldn't sit there and wait for me. He'd get something to do. No man could go seven months without finding something if he tried."

The sight of him always around in his untidy clothes and gloomy appearance drove Carrie to seek relief in other places. Twice a week there were matinées, and then Hurstwood ate a cold snack, which he prepared himself. Two other days there were rehearsals beginning at ten in the morning and lasting usually until one. Now, to this Carrie added a few visits to one or two chorus girls, including the blue-eyed soldier of the golden helmet. She did it because it was pleasant and a relief from dulness of the home over which her husband brooded.

The blue-eyed soldier's name was Osborne—Lola Osborne. Her room was in Nineteenth Street near Fourth Avenue, a block now given up wholly to office buildings. Here she had a comfortable back room, looking over a collection of back yards in which grew a number of shade trees pleasant to see.

"Isn't your home in New York?" she asked of Lola one day.

"Yes; but I can't get along with my people. They always want me to do what they want. Do you live here?"

"Yes," said Carrie.

"With your family?"

Carrie was ashamed to say that she was married. She had talked so much about getting more salary and confessed to so much anxiety about her future, that now, when the direct question of fact was waiting, she could not tell this girl.

"With some relatives," she answered.

Miss Osborne took it for granted that, like herself, Carrie's time was her own. She invariably asked her to stay, proposing little outings and other things of that sort until Carrie began neglecting her dinner hours. Hurstwood noticed it, but felt in no position to quarrel with her. Several times she came so late as scarcely to have an hour in which to patch up a meal and start for the theatre.

"Do you rehearse in the afternoons?" Hurstwood once asked, concealing almost completely the cynical protest and regret which prompted it.

"No; I was looking around for another place," said Carrie.

As a matter of fact she was, but only in such a way as furnished the least straw of an excuse. Miss Osborne and she had gone to the office of the manager who was to produce the new opera at the Broadway and returned straight to the former's room, where they had been since three o'clock.

Carrie felt this question to be an infringement on her liberty. She did not take into account how much liberty she was securing. Only the latest step, the newest freedom, must not be questioned.

Hurstwood saw it all clearly enough. He was shrewd after his kind, and yet there was enough decency in the man to stop him from making any effectual protest. In his almost inexplicable apathy he was content to droop supinely while Carrie drifted out of his life, just as he was willing supinely to see opportunity pass beyond his control. He could not help clinging and protesting in a mild, irritating, and ineffectual way, however—a way that simply widened the breach by slow degrees.

A further enlargement of this chasm between them came when the manager, looking between the wings upon the brightly lighted stage where the chorus was going through some of its glittering evolutions, said to the master of the ballet:

"Who is that fourth girl there on the right—the one coming round at the end now?"

"Oh," said the ballet-master, "that's Miss Madenda."

"She's good looking. Why don't you let her head that line?"

"I will," said the man.

"Just do that. She'll look better there than the woman you've got."

"All right. I will do that," said the master.

The next evening Carrie was called out, much as if for an error.

"You lead your company to-night," said the master.

"Yes, sir," said Carrie.

"Put snap into it," he added. "We must have snap."

"Yes, sir," replied Carrie.

Astonished at this change, she thought that the heretofore leader must be ill; but when she saw her in the line, with a distinct expression of something unfavourable in her eye, she began to think that perhaps it was merit.

She had a chic way of tossing her head to one side, and holding her arms as if for action—not listlessly. In front of the line this showed up even more effectually.

"That girl knows how to carry herself," said the manager, another evening. He began to think that he should like to talk with her. If he hadn't made it a rule to have nothing to do with the members of the chorus, he would have approached her most unbendingly.

"Put that girl at the head of the white column," he suggested to the man in charge of the ballet.

This white column consisted of some twenty girls, all in snow-white flannel trimmed with silver and blue. Its leader was most stunningly arrayed in the same colours, elaborated, however, with epaulets and a belt of silver, with a short sword dangling at one side. Carrie was fitted for this costume, and a few days later appeared, proud of her new laurels. She was especially gratified to find that her salary was now eighteen instead of twelve.

Hurstwood heard nothing about this.

"I'll not give him the rest of my money," said Carrie. "I do enough. I am going to get me something to wear."

As a matter of fact, during this second month she had been buying for herself as recklessly as she dared, regardless of the consequences. There were impending more complications rent day, and more extension of the credit system in the neighbourhood. Now, however, she proposed to do better by herself.

Her first move was to buy a shirt waist, and in studying these she found how little her money would buy—how much, if she could only use all. She forgot that if she were alone she would have to pay for a room and board, and imagined that every cent of her eighteen could be spent for clothes and things that she liked.

At last she picked upon something, which not only used up all her surplus above twelve, but invaded that sum. She knew she was going too far, but her feminine love of finery prevailed. The next day Hurstwood said:

"We owe the grocer five dollars and forty cents this week."

"Do we?" said Carrie, frowning a little.

She looked in her purse to leave it.

"I've only got eight dollars and twenty cents altogether."

"We owe the milkman sixty cents," added Hurstwood.

"Yes, and there's the coal man," said Carrie.

Hurstwood said nothing. He had seen the new things she was buying; the way she was neglecting household duties; the readiness with which she was slipping out afternoons and staying. He felt that something was going to happen. All at once she spoke:

"I don't know," she said; "I can't do it all. I don't earn enough."

This was a direct challenge. Hurstwood had to take it up. He tried to be calm.

"I don't want you to do it all," he said. "I only want a little help until I can get something to do."

"Oh, yes," answered Carrie. "That's always the way. It takes more than I can earn to pay for things. I don't see what I'm going to do."

"Well, I've tried to get something," he exclaimed. "What do you want me to do?"

"You couldn't have tried so very hard," said Carrie. "I got something."

"Well, I did," he said, angered almost to harsh words. "You needn't throw up your success to me. All I asked was a little help until I could get something. I'm not down yet. I'll come up all right."

He tried to speak steadily, but his voice trembled a little.

Carrie's anger melted on the instant. She felt ashamed.

"Well," she said, "here's the money," and emptied it out on the table. "I haven't got quite enough to pay it all. If they can wait until Saturday, though, I'll have some more."

"You keep it," said Hurstwood, sadly. "I only want enough to pay the grocer."

She put it back, and proceeded to get dinner early and in good time. Her little bravado made her feel as if she ought to make amends.

In a little while their old thoughts returned to both.

"She's making more than she says," thought Hurstwood. "She says she's making twelve, but that wouldn't buy all those things. I don't care. Let her keep her money. I'll get something again one of these days. Then she can go to the deuce."

He only said this in his anger, but it prefigured a possible course of action and attitude well enough.

"I don't care," thought Carrie. "He ought to be told to get out and do something. It isn't right that I should support him."

In these days Carrie was introduced to several youths, friends of Miss Osborne, who were of the kind most aptly described as gay and festive. They called once to get Miss Osborne for an afternoon drive. Carrie was with her at the time.

"Come and go along," said Lola.

"No, I can't," said Carrie.

"Oh, yes, come and go. What have you got to do?"

"I have to be home by five," said Carrie.

"What for?"

"Oh, dinner."

"They'll take us to dinner," said Lola.

"Oh, no," said Carrie. "I won't go. I can't."

"Oh, do come. They're awful nice boys. We'll get you back in time. We're only going for a drive in Central Park."

Carrie thought a while, and at last yielded.

"Now, I must be back by half-past four," she said.

The information went in one ear of Lola and out the other.

After Drouet and Hurstwood, there was the least touch of cynicism in her attitude toward young men—especially of the gay and frivolous sort. She felt a little older than they. Some of their pretty compliments seemed silly. Still, she was young in heart and body and youth appealed to her.

"Oh, we'll be right back, Miss Madenda," said one of the chaps, bowing. "You wouldn't think we'd keep you over time, now, would you?"

"Well, I don't know," said Carrie, smiling.

They were off for a drive—she, looking about and noticing fine clothing, the young men voicing those silly pleasantries and weak quips which pass for humour in coy circles. Carrie saw the great park parade of carriages, beginning at the Fifty-ninth Street entrance and winding past the Museum of Art to the exit at One Hundred and Tenth Street and Seventh Avenue. Her eye was once more taken by the show of wealth—the elaborate costumes, elegant harnesses, spirited horses, and, above all, the beauty. Once more the plague of poverty galled her, but now she forgot in a measure her own troubles so far as to forget Hurstwood. He waited until four, five, and even six. It was getting dark when he got up out of his chair.

"I guess she isn't coming home," he said, grimly.

"That's the way," he thought. "She's getting a start now. I'm out of it."

Carrie had really discovered her neglect, but only at a quarter after five, and the open carriage was now far up Seventh Avenue, near the Harlem River.

"What time is it?" she inquired. "I must be getting back."

"A quarter after five," said her companion, consulting an elegant, open-faced watch.

"Oh, dear me!" exclaimed Carrie. Then she settled back with a sigh. "There's no use crying over spilt milk," she said. "It's too late."

"Of course it is," said the youth, who saw visions of a fine dinner now, and such invigorating talk as would result in a reunion after the show. He was greatly taken with Carrie. "We'll drive down to Delmonico's now and have something there, won't we, Orrin?"

"To be sure," replied Orrin, gaily.

Carrie thought of Hurstwood. Never before had she neglected dinner without an excuse.

They drove back, and at 6.15 sat down to dine. It was the

Sherry incident over again, the remembrance of which came painfully back to Carrie. She remembered Mrs. Vance, who had never called again after Hurstwood's reception, and Ames.

At this figure her mind halted. It was a strong, clean vision. He liked better books than she read, better people than she associated with. His ideals burned in her heart.

"It's fine to be a good actress," came distinctly back.

What sort of an actress was she?

"What are you thinking about, Miss Madenda?" inquired her merry companion. "Come, now, let's see if I can guess."

"Oh, no," said Carrie. "Don't try."

She shook it off and ate. She forgot, in part, and was merry. When it came to the after-theatre proposition, however, she shook her head.

"No," she said, "I can't. I have a previous engagement."

"Oh, now, Miss Madenda," pleaded the youth.

"No," said Carrie, "I can't. You've been so kind, but you'll have to excuse me."

The youth looked exceedingly crestfallen.

"Cheer up, old man," whispered his companion. "We'll go around, anyhow. She may change her mind."

Chapter XL

A Public Dissension: A Final Appeal

THERE WAS no after-theatre lark, however, so far as Carrie was concerned. She made her way homeward, thinking about her absence. Hurstwood was asleep, but roused up to look as she passed through to her own bed.

"Is that you?" he said.

"Yes," she answered.

The next morning at breakfast she felt like apologising.

"I couldn't get home last evening," she said.

"Ah, Carrie," he answered, "what's the use saying that? I don't care. You needn't tell me that, though."

"I couldn't," said Carrie, her colour rising. Then, seeing that he looked as if he said "I know," she exclaimed: "Oh, all right. I don't care."

From now on, her indifference to the flat was even greater. There seemed no common ground on which they could talk to one another. She let herself be asked for expenses. It became so with him that he hated to do it. He preferred standing off the butcher and baker. He ran up a grocery bill of sixteen dollars with Oeslogge, laying in a supply of staple articles, so that they would not have to buy any of those things for some time to come. Then he changed his grocery. It was the same with the butcher and several others. Carrie never heard anything of this directly from him. He asked for such as he could expect, drifting farther and farther into a situation which could have but one ending.

In this fashion, September went by.

"Isn't Mr. Drake going to open his hotel?" Carrie asked several times.

"Yes. He won't do it before October, though, now."

Carrie became disgusted. "Such a man," she said to herself frequently. More and more she visited. She put most of her spare money in clothes, which, after all, was not an astonishing amount. At last the opera she was with announced its departure within four weeks. "Last two weeks of the Great

Comic Opera success—The ——," etc., was upon all bill-boards and in the newspapers, before she acted.

"I'm not going out on the road," said Miss Osborne.

Carrie went with her to apply to another manager.

"Ever had any experience?" was one of his questions.

"I'm with the company at the Casino now."

"Oh, you are?" he said.

The end of this was another engagement at twenty per week.

Carrie was delighted. She began to feel that she had a place in the world. People recognised ability.

So changed was her state that the home atmosphere became intolerable. It was all poverty and trouble there, or seemed to be, because it was a load to bear. It became a place to keep away from. Still she slept there, and did a fair amount of work, keeping it in order. It was a sitting place for Hurst-wood. He sat and rocked, rocked and read, enveloped in the gloom of his own fate. October went by, and November. It was the dead of winter almost before he knew it, and there he sat.

Carrie was doing better, that he knew. Her clothes were im-proved now, even fine. He saw her coming and going, some-times picturing to himself her rise. Little eating had thinned him somewhat. He had no appetite. His clothes, too, were a poor man's clothes. Talk about getting something had become even too threadbare and ridiculous for him. So he folded his hands and waited—for what, he could not anticipate.

At last, however, troubles became too thick. The hounding of creditors, the indifference of Carrie, the silence of the flat, and presence of winter, all joined to produce a climax. It was effected by the arrival of Oeslogge, personally, when Carrie was there.

"I call about my bill," said Mr. Oeslogge.

Carrie was only faintly surprised.

"How much is it?" she asked.

"Sixteen dollars," he replied.

"Oh, that much?" said Carrie. "Is this right?" she asked, turning to Hurstwood.

"Yes," he said.

"Well, I never heard anything about it."

She looked as if she thought he had been contracting some needless expense.

"Well, we had it all right," he answered. Then he went to the door. "I can't pay you anything on that to-day," he said, mildly.

"Well, when can you?" said the grocer.

"Not before Saturday, anyhow," said Hurstwood.

"Huh!" returned the grocer. "This is fine. I must have that. I need the money."

Carrie was standing farther back in the room, hearing it all. She was greatly distressed. It was so bad and commonplace. Hurstwood was annoyed also.

"Well," he said, "there's no use talking about it now. If you'll come in Saturday, I'll pay you something on it."

The grocery man went away.

"How are we going to pay it?" asked Carrie, astonished by the bill. "I can't do it."

"Well, you don't have to," he said. "He can't get what he can't get. He'll have to wait."

"I don't see how we ran up such a bill as that," said Carrie.

"Well, we ate it," said Hurstwood.

"It's funny," she replied, still doubting.

"What's the use of your standing there and talking like that, now?" he asked. "Do you think I've had it alone? You talk as if I'd taken something."

"Well, it's too much, anyhow," said Carrie. "I oughtn't to be made to pay for it. I've got more than I can pay for now."

"All right," replied Hurstwood, sitting down in silence. He was sick of the grind of this thing.

Carrie went out, and there he sat, determining to do something.

There had been appearing in the papers about this time rumours and notices of an approaching strike on the trolley lines in Brooklyn. There was general dissatisfaction as to the hours of labour required and the wages paid. As usual—and for some inexplicable reason—the men chose the winter for the forcing of the hand of their employers and the settlement of their difficulties.

Hurstwood had been reading of this thing, and wondering

concerning the huge tie-up which would follow. A day or two before this trouble with Carrie, it came. On a cold afternoon, when everything was grey and it threatened to snow, the papers announced that the men had been called out on all the lines.

Being so utterly idle, and his mind filled with the numerous predictions which had been made concerning the scarcity of labour this winter and the panicky state of the financial market, Hurstwood read this with interest. He noted the claims of the striking motormen and conductors, who said that they had been wont to receive two dollars a day in times past, but that for a year or more "trippers" had been introduced, which cut down their chance of livelihood one-half, and increased their hours of servitude from ten to twelve, and even fourteen. These "trippers" were men put on during the busy and *rush* hours, to take a car out for one trip. The compensation paid for such a trip was only twenty-five cents. When the rush or busy hours were over, they were laid off. Worst of all, no man might know when he was going to get a car. He must come to the barns in the morning and wait around in fair and foul weather until such time as he was needed. Two trips were an average reward for so much waiting—a little over three hours' work for fifty cents. The work of waiting was not counted.

The men complained that this system was extending, and that the time was not far off when but a few out of 7,000 employees would have regular two-dollar-a-day work at all. They demanded that the system be abolished, and that ten hours be considered a day's work, barring unavoidable delays, with $2.25 pay. They demanded immediate acceptance of these terms, which the various trolley companies refused.

Hurstwood at first sympathised with the demands of these men—indeed, it is a question whether he did not always sympathise with them to the end, belie him as his actions might. Reading nearly all the news, he was attracted first by the scare-heads with which the trouble was noted in the "World." He read it fully—the names of the seven companies involved, the number of men.

"They're foolish to strike in this sort of weather," he thought to himself. "Let 'em win if they can, though."

The next day there was even a larger notice of it. "Brooklynites Walk," said the "World." "Knights of Labour Tie up the Trolley Lines Across the Bridge." "About Seven Thousand Men Out."

Hurstwood read this, formulating to himself his own idea of what would be the outcome. He was a great believer in the strength of corporations.

"They can't win," he said, concerning the men. "They haven't any money. The police will protect the companies. They've got to. The public has to have its cars."

He didn't sympathise with the corporations, but strength was with them. So was property and public utility.

"Those fellows can't win," he thought.

Among other things, he noticed a circular issued by one of the companies, which read:

> "ATLANTIC AVENUE RAILROAD.
> "SPECIAL NOTICE.
>
> "The motormen and conductors and other employees of this company having abruptly left its service, an opportunity is now given to all loyal men who have struck against their will to be reinstated, providing they will make their applications by twelve o'clock noon on Wednesday, January 16th. Such men will be given employment (with guaranteed protection) in the order in which such applications are received, and runs and positions assigned them accordingly. Otherwise, they will be considered discharged, and every vacancy will be filled by a new man as soon as his services can be secured.
> "(Signed)
> "BENJAMIN NORTON,
> "*President.*"

He also noted among the want ads. one which read:

> "WANTED.—50 skilled motormen, accustomed to Westinghouse system, to run U. S. mail cars only, in the City of Brooklyn; protection guaranteed."

He noted particularly in each the "protection guaranteed." It signified to him the unassailable power of the companies.

"They've got the militia on their side," he thought. "There isn't anything those men can do."

While this was still in his mind, the incident with Oeslogge and Carrie occurred. There had been a good deal to irritate him, but this seemed much the worst. Never before had she accused him of stealing—or very near that. She doubted the naturalness of so large a bill. And he had worked so hard to make expenses seem light. He had been "doing" butcher and baker in order not to call on her. He had eaten very little— almost nothing.

"Damn it all!" he said. "I can get something. I'm not down yet."

He thought that he really must do something now. It was too cheap to sit around after such an insinuation as this. Why, after a little, he would be standing anything.

He got up and looked out the window into the chilly street. It came gradually into his mind, as he stood there, to go to Brooklyn.

"Why not?" his mind said. "Any one can get work over there. You'll get two a day."

"How about accidents?" said a voice. "You might get hurt."

"Oh, there won't be much of that," he answered. "They've called out the police. Any one who wants to run a car will be protected all right."

"You don't know how to run a car," rejoined the voice.

"I won't apply as a motorman," he answered. "I can ring up fares all right."

"They'll want motormen mostly."

"They'll take anybody; that I know."

For several hours he argued pro and con with this mental counsellor, feeling no need to act at once in a matter so sure of profit.

In the morning he put on his best clothes, which were poor enough, and began stirring about, putting some bread and meat into a page of a newspaper. Carrie watched him, interested in this new move.

"Where are you going?" she asked.

"Over to Brooklyn," he answered. Then, seeing her still inquisitive, he added: "I think I can get on over there."

"On the trolley lines?" said Carrie, astonished.

"Yes," he rejoined.

"Aren't you afraid?" she asked.

"What of?" he answered. "The police are protecting them."

"The paper said four men were hurt yesterday."

"Yes," he returned; "but you can't go by what the papers say. They'll run the cars all right."

He looked rather determined now, in a desolate sort of way, and Carrie felt very sorry. Something of the old Hurstwood was here—the least shadow of what was once shrewd and pleasant strength. Outside, it was cloudy and blowing a few flakes of snow.

"What a day to go over there," thought Carrie.

Now he left before she did, which was a remarkable thing, and tramped eastward to Fourteenth Street and Sixth Avenue, where he took the car. He had read that scores of applicants were applying at the office of the Brooklyn City Railroad building and were being received. He made his way there by horse-car and ferry—a dark, silent man—to the offices in question. It was a long way, for no cars were running, and the day was cold; but he trudged along grimly. Once in Brooklyn, he could clearly see and feel that a strike was on. People showed it in their manner. Along the routes of certain tracks not a car was running. About certain corners and nearby saloons small groups of men were lounging. Several spring wagons passed him, equipped with plain wooden chairs, and labelled "Flatbush" or "Prospect Park. Fare, Ten Cents." He noticed cold and even gloomy faces. Labour was having its little war.

When he came near the office in question, he saw a few men standing about, and some policemen. On the far corners were other men—whom he took to be strikers—watching. All the houses were small and wooden, the streets poorly paved. After New York, Brooklyn looked actually poor and hard-up.

He made his way into the heart of the small group, eyed by policemen and the men already there. One of the officers addressed him.

"What are you looking for?"

"I want to see if I can get a place."

"The offices are up those steps," said the bluecoat. His face was a very neutral thing to contemplate. In his heart of hearts, he sympathised with the strikers and hated this "scab." In his heart of hearts, also, he felt the dignity and use of the police force, which commanded order. Of its true social significance, he never once dreamed. His was not the mind for that. The two feelings blended in him—neutralised one another and him. He would have fought for this man as determinedly as for himself, and yet only so far as commanded. Strip him of his uniform, and he would have soon picked his side.

Hurstwood ascended a dusty flight of steps and entered a small, dust-coloured office, in which were a railing, a long desk, and several clerks.

"Well, sir?" said a middle-aged man, looking up at him from the long desk.

"Do you want to hire any men?" inquired Hurstwood.

"What are you—a motorman?"

"No; I'm not anything," said Hurstwood.

He was not at all abashed by his position. He knew these people needed men. If one didn't take him, another would. This man could take him or leave him, just as he chose.

"Well, we prefer experienced men, of course," said the man. He paused, while Hurstwood smiled indifferently. Then he added: "Still, I guess you can learn. What is your name?"

"Wheeler," said Hurstwood.

The man wrote an order on a small card. "Take that to our barns," he said, "and give it to the foreman. He'll show you what to do."

Hurstwood went down and out. He walked straight away in the direction indicated, while the policemen looked after.

"There's another wants to try it," said Officer Kiely to Officer Macey.

"I have my mind he'll get his fill," returned the latter, quietly.

They had been in strikes before.

Chapter XLI

THE STRIKE

THE BARN at which Hurstwood applied was exceedingly short-handed, and was being operated practically by three men as directors. There were a lot of green hands around—queer, hungry-looking men, who looked as if want had driven them to desperate means. They tried to be lively and willing, but there was an air of hang-dog diffidence about the place.

Hurstwood went back through the barns and out into a large, enclosed lot, where were a series of tracks and loops. A half-dozen cars were there, manned by instructors, each with a pupil at the lever. More pupils were waiting at one of the rear doors of the barn.

In silence Hurstwood viewed this scene, and waited. His companions took his eye for a while, though they did not interest him much more than the cars. They were an uncomfortable-looking gang, however. One or two were very thin and lean. Several were quite stout. Several others were raw-boned and sallow, as if they had been beaten upon by all sorts of rough weather.

"Did you see by the paper they are going to call out the militia?" Hurstwood heard one of them remark.

"Oh, they'll do that," returned the other. "They always do."

"Think we're liable to have much trouble?" said another, whom Hurstwood did not see.

"Not very."

"That Scotchman that went out on the last car," put in a voice, "told me that they hit him in the ear with a cinder."

A small, nervous laugh accompanied this.

"One of those fellows on the Fifth Avenue line must have had a hell of a time, according to the papers," drawled another. "They broke his car windows and pulled him off into the street 'fore the police could stop 'em."

"Yes; but there are more police around to-day," was added by another.

Hurstwood hearkened without much mental comment. These talkers seemed scared to him. Their gabbling was feverish—things said to quiet their own minds. He looked out into the yard and waited.

Two of the men got around quite near him, but behind his back. They were rather social, and he listened to what they said.

"Are you a railroad man?" said one.

"Me? No. I've always worked in a paper factory."

"I had a job in Newark until last October," returned the other, with reciprocal feeling.

There were some words which passed too low to hear. Then the conversation became strong again.

"I don't blame these fellers for striking," said one. "They've got the right of it, all right, but I had to get something to do."

"Same here," said the other. "If I had any job in Newark I wouldn't be over here takin' chances like these."

"It's hell these days, ain't it?" said the man. "A poor man ain't nowhere. You could starve, by God, right in the streets, and there ain't most no one would help you."

"Right you are," said the other. "The job I had I lost 'cause they shut down. They run all summer and lay up a big stock, and then shut down."

Hurstwood paid some little attention to this. Somehow, he felt a little superior to these two—a little better off. To him these were ignorant and commonplace, poor sheep in a driver's hand.

"Poor devils," he thought, speaking out of the thoughts and feelings of a bygone period of success.

"Next," said one of the instructors.

"You're next," said a neighbour, touching him.

He went out and climbed on the platform. The instructor took it for granted that no preliminaries were needed.

"You see this handle," he said, reaching up to an electric cut-off, which was fastened to the roof. "This throws the current off or on. If you want to reverse the car you turn it over here. If you want to send it forward, you put it over here. If you want to cut off the power, you keep it in the middle."

Hurstwood smiled at the simple information.

"Now, this handle here regulates your speed. To here," he said, pointing with his finger, "gives you about four miles an hour. This is eight. When it's full on, you make about fourteen miles an hour."

Hurstwood watched him calmly. He had seen motormen work before. He knew just about how they did it, and was sure he could do as well, with a very little practice.

The instructor explained a few more details, and then said: "Now, we'll back her up."

Hurstwood stood placidly by, while the car rolled back into the yard.

"One thing you want to be careful about, and that is to start easy. Give one degree time to act before you start another. The one fault of most men is that they always want to throw her wide open. That's bad. It's dangerous, too. Wears out the motor. You don't want to do that."

"I see," said Hurstwood.

He waited and waited, while the man talked on.

"Now you take it," he said, finally.

The ex-manager laid hand to the lever and pushed it gently, as he thought. It worked much easier than he imagined, however, with the result that the car jerked quickly forward, throwing him back against the door. He straightened up sheepishly, while the instructor stopped the car with the brake.

"You want to be careful about that," was all he said.

Hurstwood found, however, that handling a brake and regulating speed were not so instantly mastered as he had imagined. Once or twice he would have ploughed through the rear fence if it had not been for the hand and word of his companion. The latter was rather patient with him, but he never smiled.

"You've got to get the knack of working both arms at once," he said. "It takes a little practice."

One o'clock came while he was still on the car practising, and he began to feel hungry. The day set in snowing, and he was cold. He grew weary of running to and fro on the short track.

They ran the car to the end and both got off. Hurstwood went into the barn and sought a car step, pulling out his paper-wrapped lunch from his pocket. There was no water and the bread was dry, but he enjoyed it. There was no ceremony about dining. He swallowed and looked about, contemplating the dull, homely labour of the thing. It was disagreeable—miserably disagreeable—in all its phases. Not because it was bitter, but because it was hard. It would be hard to any one, he thought.

After eating, he stood about as before, waiting until his turn came.

The intention was to give him an afternoon of practice, but the greater part of the time was spent in waiting about.

At last evening came, and with it hunger and a debate with himself as to how he should spend the night. It was half-past five. He must soon eat. If he tried to go home, it would take him two hours and a half of cold walking and riding. Besides, he had orders to report at seven the next morning, and going home would necessitate his rising at an unholy and disagreeable hour. He had only something like a dollar and fifteen cents of Carrie's money, with which he had intended to pay the two weeks' coal bill before the present idea struck him.

"They must have some place around here," he thought. "Where does that fellow from Newark stay?"

Finally he decided to ask. There was a young fellow standing near one of the doors in the cold, waiting a last turn. He was a mere boy in years—twenty-one about—but with a body lank and long, because of privation. A little good living would have made this youth plump and swaggering.

"How do they arrange this, if a man hasn't any money?" inquired Hurstwood, discreetly.

The fellow turned a keen, watchful face on the inquirer.

"You mean eat?" he replied.

"Yes, and sleep. I can't go back to New York to-night."

"The foreman 'll fix that if you ask him, I guess. He did me."

"That so?"

"Yes. I just told him I didn't have anything. Gee, I couldn't go home. I live way over in Hoboken."

Hurstwood only cleared his throat by way of acknowledgment.

"They've got a place upstairs here, I understand. I don't know what sort of a thing it is. Purty tough, I guess. He gave me a meal ticket this noon. I know that wasn't much."

Hurstwood smiled grimly, and the boy laughed.

"It ain't no fun, is it?" he inquired, wishing vainly for a cheery reply.

"Not much," answered Hurstwood.

"I'd tackle him now," volunteered the youth. "He may go 'way."

Hurstwood did so.

"Isn't there some place I can stay around here to-night?" he inquired. "If I have to go back to New York, I'm afraid I won't——"

"There're some cots upstairs," interrupted the man, "if you want one of them."

"That'll do," he assented.

He meant to ask for a meal ticket, but the seemingly proper moment never came, and he decided to pay himself that night.

"I'll ask him in the morning."

He ate in a cheap restaurant in the vicinity, and, being cold and lonely, went straight off to seek the loft in question. The company was not attempting to run cars after nightfall. It was so advised by the police.

The room seemed to have been a lounging place for night workers. There were some nine cots in the place, two or three wooden chairs, a soap box, and a small, round-bellied stove, in which a fire was blazing. Early as he was, another man was there before him. The latter was sitting beside the stove warming his hands.

Hurstwood approached and held out his own toward the fire. He was sick of the bareness and privation of all things connected with his venture, but was steeling himself to hold out. He fancied he could for a while.

"Cold, isn't it?" said the early guest.

"Rather."

A long silence.

"Not much of a place to sleep in, is it?" said the man.

"Better than nothing," replied Hurstwood.

Another silence.

"I believe I'll turn in," said the man.

Rising, he went to one of the cots and stretched himself, removing only his shoes, and pulling the one blanket and dirty old comforter over him in a sort of bundle. The sight disgusted Hurstwood, but he did not dwell on it, choosing to gaze into the stove and think of something else. Presently he decided to retire, and picked a cot, also removing his shoes.

While he was doing so, the youth who had advised him to come here entered, and, seeing Hurstwood, tried to be genial.

"Better'n nothin'," he observed, looking around.

Hurstwood did not take this to himself. He thought it to be an expression of individual satisfaction, and so did not answer. The youth imagined he was out of sorts, and set to whistling softly. Seeing another man asleep, he quit that and lapsed into silence.

Hurstwood made the best of a bad lot by keeping on his clothes and pushing away the dirty covering from his head, but at last he dozed in sheer weariness. The covering became more and more comfortable, its character was forgotten, and he pulled it about his neck and slept.

In the morning he was aroused out of a pleasant dream by several men stirring about in the cold, cheerless room. He had been back in Chicago in fancy, in his own comfortable home. Jessica had been arranging to go somewhere, and he had been talking with her about it. This was so clear in his mind, that he was startled now by the contrast of this room. He raised his head, and the cold, bitter reality jarred him into wakefulness.

"Guess I'd better get up," he said.

There was no water on this floor. He put on his shoes in the cold and stood up, shaking himself in his stiffness. His clothes felt disagreeable, his hair bad.

"Hell!" he muttered, as he put on his hat.

Downstairs things were stirring again.

He found a hydrant, with a trough which had once been used for horses, but there was no towel here, and his handkerchief was soiled from yesterday. He contented himself with wetting his eyes with the ice-cold water. Then he sought the foreman, who was already on the ground.

"Had your breakfast yet?" inquired that worthy.

"No," said Hurstwood.

"Better get it, then; your car won't be ready for a little while."

Hurstwood hesitated.

"Could you let me have a meal ticket?" he asked, with an effort.

"Here you are," said the man, handing him one.

He breakfasted as poorly as the night before on some fried steak and bad coffee. Then he went back.

"Here," said the foreman, motioning him, when he came in. "You take this car out in a few minutes."

Hurstwood climbed up on the platform in the gloomy barn and waited for a signal. He was nervous, and yet the thing was a relief. Anything was better than the barn.

On this the fourth day of the strike, the situation had taken a turn for the worse. The strikers, following the counsel of their leaders and the newspapers, had struggled peaceably enough. There had been no great violence done. Cars had been stopped, it is true, and the men argued with. Some crews had been won over and led away, some windows broken, some jeering and yelling done; but in no more than five or six instances had men been seriously injured. These by crowds whose acts the leaders disclaimed.

Idleness, however, and the sight of the company, backed by the police, triumphing, angered the men. They saw that each day more cars were going on, each day more declarations were being made by the company officials that the effective opposition of the strikers was broken. This put desperate thoughts in the minds of the men. Peaceful methods meant, they saw, that the companies would soon run all their cars and those who had complained would be forgotten. There was nothing so helpful to the companies as peaceful methods.

All at once they blazed forth, and for a week there was storm and stress. Cars were assailed, men attacked, policemen struggled with, tracks torn up, and shots fired, until at last street fights and mob movements became frequent, and the city was invested with militia.

Hurstwood knew nothing of the change of temper.

"Run your car out," called the foreman, waving a vigorous hand at him. A green conductor jumped up behind and rang the bell twice as a signal to start. Hurstwood turned the lever and ran the car out through the door into the street in front of the barn. Here two brawny policemen got up beside him on the platform—one on either hand.

At the sound of a gong near the barn door, two bells were given by the conductor and Hurstwood opened his lever.

The two policemen looked about them calmly.

" 'Tis cold, all right, this morning," said the one on the left, who possessed a rich brogue.

"I had enough of it yesterday," said the other. "I wouldn't want a steady job of this."

"Nor I."

Neither paid the slightest attention to Hurstwood, who stood facing the cold wind, which was chilling him completely, and thinking of his orders.

"Keep a steady gait," the foreman had said. "Don't stop for any one who doesn't look like a real passenger. Whatever you do, don't stop for a crowd."

The two officers kept silent for a few moments.

"The last man must have gone through all right," said the officer on the left. "I don't see his car anywhere."

"Who's on there?" asked the second officer, referring, of course, to its complement of policemen.

"Schaeffer and Ryan."

There was another silence, in which the car ran smoothly along. There were not so many houses along this part of the way. Hurstwood did not see many people either. The situation was not wholly disagreeable to him. If he were not so cold, he thought he would do well enough.

He was brought out of this feeling by the sudden appearance of a curve ahead, which he had not expected. He shut off the current and did an energetic turn at the brake, but not in time to avoid an unnaturally quick turn. It shook him up and made him feel like making some apologetic remarks, but he refrained.

"You want to look out for them things," said the officer on the left, condescendingly.

"That's right," agreed Hurstwood, shamefacedly.

"There's lots of them on this line," said the officer on the right.

Around the corner a more populated way appeared. One or two pedestrians were in view ahead. A boy coming out of a gate with a tin milk bucket gave Hurstwood his first objectionable greeting.

"Scab!" he yelled. "Scab!"

Hurstwood heard it, but tried to make no comment, even to himself. He knew he would get that, and much more of the same sort, probably.

At a corner farther up a man stood by the track and signalled the car to stop.

"Never mind him," said one of the officers. "He's up to some game."

Hurstwood obeyed. At the corner he saw the wisdom of it. No sooner did the man perceive the intention to ignore him, than he shook his fist.

"Ah, you bloody coward!" he yelled.

Some half dozen men, standing on the corner, flung taunts and jeers after the speeding car.

Hurstwood winced the least bit. The real thing was slightly worse than the thoughts of it had been.

Now came in sight, three or four blocks farther on, a heap of something on the track.

"They've been at work, here, all right," said one of the policemen.

"We'll have an argument, maybe," said the other.

Hurstwood ran the car close and stopped. He had not done so wholly, however, before a crowd gathered about. It was composed of ex-motormen and conductors in part, with a sprinkling of friends and sympathisers.

"Come off the car, pardner," said one of the men in a voice meant to be conciliatory. "You don't want to take the bread out of another man's mouth, do you?"

Hurstwood held to his brake and lever, pale and very uncertain what to do.

"Stand back," yelled one of the officers, leaning over the platform railing. "Clear out of this, now. Give the man a chance to do his work."

"Listen, pardner," said the leader, ignoring the policeman

and addressing Hurstwood. "We're all working men, like yourself. If you were a regular motorman, and had been treated as we've been, you wouldn't want any one to come in and take your place, would you? You wouldn't want any one to do you out of your chance to get your rights, would you?"

"Shut her off! shut her off!" urged the other of the policemen, roughly. "Get out of this, now," and he jumped the railing and landed before the crowd and began shoving. Instantly the other officer was down beside him.

"Stand back, now," they yelled. "Get out of this. What the hell do you mean? Out, now."

It was like a small swarm of bees.

"Don't shove me," said one of the strikers, determinedly. "I'm not doing anything."

"Get out of this!" cried the officer, swinging his club. "I'll give ye a bat on the sconce. Back, now."

"What the hell!" cried another of the strikers, pushing the other way, adding at the same time some lusty oaths.

Crack came an officer's club on his forehead. He blinked his eyes blindly a few times, wabbled on his legs, threw up his hands, and staggered back. In return, a swift fist landed on the officer's neck.

Infuriated by this, the latter plunged left and right, laying about madly with his club. He was ably assisted by his brother of the blue, who poured ponderous oaths upon the troubled waters. No severe damage was done, owing to the agility of the strikers in keeping out of reach. They stood about the sidewalk now and jeered.

"Where is the conductor?" yelled one of the officers, getting his eye on that individual, who had come nervously forward to stand by Hurstwood. The latter had stood gazing upon the scene with more astonishment than fear.

"Why don't you come down here and get these stones off the track?" inquired the officer. "What you standing there for? Do you want to stay here all day? Get down."

Hurstwood breathed heavily in excitement and jumped down with the nervous conductor as if he had been called.

"Hurry up, now," said the other policeman.

Cold as it was, these officers were hot and mad. Hurstwood

worked with the conductor, lifting stone after stone and warming himself by the work.

"Ah, you scab, you!" yelled the crowd. "You coward! Steal a man's job, will you? Rob the poor, will you, you thief? We'll get you yet, now. Wait."

Not all of this was delivered by one man. It came from here and there, incorporated with much more of the same sort and curses.

"Work, you blackguards," yelled a voice. "Do the dirty work. You're the suckers that keep the poor people down!"

"May God starve ye yet," yelled an old Irish woman, who now threw open a nearby window and stuck out her head.

"Yes, and you," she added, catching the eye of one of the policemen. "You bloody, murtherin' thafe! Crack my son over the head, will you, you hard-hearted, murtherin' divil? Ah, ye——"

But the officer turned a deaf ear.

"Go to the devil, you old hag," he half muttered as he stared round upon the scattered company.

Now the stones were off, and Hurstwood took his place again amid a continued chorus of epithets. Both officers got up beside him and the conductor rang the bell, when, bang! bang! through window and door came rocks and stones. One narrowly grazed Hurstwood's head. Another shattered the window behind.

"Throw open your lever," yelled one of the officers, grabbing at the handle himself.

Hurstwood complied and the car shot away, followed by a rattle of stones and a rain of curses.

"That —————— hit me in the neck," said one of the officers. "I gave him a good crack for it, though."

"I think I must have left spots on some of them," said the other.

"I know that big guy that called us a ——————," said the first. "I'll get him yet for that."

"I thought we were in for it sure, once there," said the second.

Hurstwood, warmed and excited, gazed steadily ahead. It was an astonishing experience for him. He had read of these things, but the reality seemed something altogether new. He was no coward in spirit. The fact that he had suffered this much now rather operated to arouse a stolid determination to stick it out. He did not recur in thought to New York or the flat. This one trip seemed a consuming thing.

They now ran into the business heart of Brooklyn uninterrupted. People gazed at the broken windows of the car and at Hurstwood in his plain clothes. Voices called "scab" now and then, as well as other epithets, but no crowd attacked the car. At the down-town end of the line, one of the officers went to call up his station and report the trouble.

"There's a gang out there," he said, "laying for us yet. Better send some one over there and clean them out."

The car ran back more quietly—hooted, watched, flung at, but not attacked. Hurstwood breathed freely when he saw the barns.

"Well," he observed to himself, "I came out of that all right."

The car was turned in and he was allowed to loaf a while, but later he was again called. This time a new team of officers was aboard. Slightly more confident, he sped the car along the commonplace streets and felt somewhat less fearful. On one side, however, he suffered intensely. The day was raw, with a sprinkling of snow and a gusty wind, made all the more intolerable by the speed of the car. His clothing was not intended for this sort of work. He shivered, stamped his feet, and beat his arms as he had seen other motormen do in the past, but said nothing. The novelty and danger of the situation modified in a way his disgust and distress at being compelled to be here, but not enough to prevent him from feeling grim and sour. This was a dog's life, he thought. It was a tough thing to have to come to.

The one thought that strengthened him was the insult offered by Carrie. He was not down so low as to take all that, he thought. He could do something—this, even—for a while. It would get better. He would save a little.

A boy threw a clod of mud while he was thus reflecting and hit him upon the arm. It hurt sharply and angered him more than he had been any time since morning.

"The little cur!" he muttered.

"Hurt you?" asked one of the policemen.

"No," he answered.

At one of the corners, where the car slowed up because of a turn, an ex-motorman, standing on the sidewalk, called to him:

"Won't you come out, pardner, and be a man? Remember we're fighting for decent day's wages, that's all. We've got families to support." The man seemed most peaceably inclined.

Hurstwood pretended not to see him. He kept his eyes straight on before and opened the lever wide. The voice had something appealing in it.

All morning this went on and long into the afternoon. He made three such trips. The dinner he had was no stay for such work and the cold was telling on him. At each end of the line he stopped to thaw out, but he could have groaned at the anguish of it. One of the barnmen, out of pity, loaned him a heavy cap and a pair of sheepskin gloves, and for once he was extremely thankful.

On the second trip of the afternoon he ran into a crowd about half way along the line, that had blocked the car's progress with an old telegraph pole.

"Get that thing off the track," shouted the two policemen.

"Yah, yah, yah!" yelled the crowd. "Get it off yourself."

The two policemen got down and Hurstwood started to follow.

"You stay there," one called. "Some one will run away with your car."

Amid the babel of voices, Hurstwood heard one close beside him.

"Come down, pardner, and be a man. Don't fight the poor. Leave that to the corporations."

He saw the same fellow who had called to him from the corner. Now, as before, he pretended not to hear him.

"Come down," the man repeated gently. "You don't want to fight poor men. Don't fight at all." It was a most philosophic and jesuitical motorman.

A third policeman joined the other two from somewhere and some one ran to telephone for more officers. Hurstwood gazed about, determined but fearful.

A man grabbed him by the coat.

"Come off of that," he exclaimed, jerking at him and trying to pull him over the railing.

"Let go," said Hurstwood, savagely.

"I'll show you—you scab!" cried a young Irishman, jumping up on the car and aiming a blow at Hurstwood. The latter ducked and caught it on the shoulder instead of the jaw.

"Away from here," shouted an officer, hastening to the rescue, and adding, of course, the usual oaths.

Hurstwood recovered himself, pale and trembling. It was becoming serious with him now. People were looking up and jeering at him. One girl was making faces.

He began to waver in his resolution, when a patrol wagon rolled up and more officers dismounted. Now the track was quickly cleared and the release effected.

"Let her go now, quick," said the officer, and again he was off.

The end came with a real mob, which met the car on its return trip a mile or two from the barns. It was an exceedingly poor-looking neighbourhood. He wanted to run fast through it, but again the track was blocked. He saw men carrying something out to it when he was yet a half-dozen blocks away.

"There they are again!" exclaimed one policeman.

"I'll give them something this time," said the second officer, whose patience was becoming worn. Hurstwood suffered a qualm of body as the car rolled up. As before, the crowd began hooting, but now, rather than come near, they threw things. One or two windows were smashed and Hurstwood dodged a stone.

Both policemen ran out toward the crowd, but the latter replied by running toward the car. A woman—a mere girl in appearance—was among these, bearing a rough stick. She was exceedingly wrathful and struck at Hurstwood, who dodged. Thereupon, her companions, duly encouraged, jumped on the car and pulled Hurstwood over. He had hardly time to speak or shout before he fell.

"Let go of me," he said, falling on his side.

"Ah, you sucker," he heard some one say. Kicks and blows rained on him. He seemed to be suffocating. Then two men seemed to be dragging him off and he wrestled for freedom.

"Let up," said a voice, "you're all right. Stand up."

He was let loose and recovered himself. Now he recognised two officers. He felt as if he would faint from exhaustion. Something was wet on his chin. He put up his hand and felt, then looked. It was red.

"They cut me," he said, foolishly, fishing for his handkerchief.

"Now, now," said one of the officers. "It's only a scratch."

His senses became cleared now and he looked around. He was standing in a little store, where they left him for the moment. Outside, he could see, as he stood wiping his chin, the car and the excited crowd. A patrol wagon was there, and another.

He walked over and looked out. It was an ambulance, backing in.

He saw some energetic charging by the police and arrests being made.

"Come on, now, if you want to take your car," said an officer, opening the door and looking in.

He walked out, feeling rather uncertain of himself. He was very cold and frightened.

"Where's the conductor?" he asked.

"Oh, he's not here now," said the policeman.

Hurstwood went toward the car and stepped nervously on. As he did so there was a pistol shot. Something stung his shoulder.

"Who fired that?" he heard an officer exclaim. "By God! who did that?" Both left him, running toward a certain building. He paused a moment and then got down.

"George!" exclaimed Hurstwood, weakly, "this is too much for me."

He walked nervously to the corner and hurried down a side street.

"Whew!" he said, drawing in his breath.

A half block away, a small girl gazed at him.

"You'd better sneak," she called.

He walked homeward in a blinding snowstorm, reaching the ferry by dusk. The cabins were filled with comfortable souls, who studied him curiously. His head was still in such a whirl that he felt confused. All the wonder of the twinkling lights of the river in a white storm passed for nothing. He trudged doggedly on until he reached the flat. There he entered and found the room warm. Carrie was gone. A couple of evening papers were lying on the table where she left them. He lit the gas and sat down. Then he got up and stripped to examine his shoulder. It was a mere scratch. He washed his hands and face, still in a brown study, apparently, and combed his hair. Then he looked for something to eat, and finally, his hunger gone, sat down in his comfortable rocking-chair. It was a wonderful relief.

He put his hand to his chin, forgetting, for the moment, the papers.

"Well," he said, after a time, his nature recovering itself, "that's a pretty tough game over there."

Then he turned and saw the papers. With half a sigh he picked up the "World."

"Strike Spreading in Brooklyn," he read. "Rioting Breaks Out in all Parts of the City."

He adjusted his paper very comfortably and continued. It was the one thing he read with absorbing interest.

Chapter XLII

A Touch of Spring: The Empty Shell

THOSE WHO LOOK upon Hurstwood's Brooklyn venture as an error of judgment will none the less realise the negative influence on him of the fact that he had tried and failed. Carrie got a wrong idea of it. He said so little that she imagined he had encountered nothing worse than the ordinary roughness—quitting so soon in the face of this seemed trifling. He did not want to work.

She was now one of a group of oriental beauties who, in the second act of the comic opera, were paraded by the vizier before the new potentate as the treasures of his harem. There was no word assigned to any of them, but on the evening when Hurstwood was housing himself in the loft of the street-car barn, the leading comedian and star, feeling exceedingly facetious, said in a profound voice, which created a ripple of laughter:

"Well, who are you?"

It merely happened to be Carrie who was courtesying before him. It might as well have been any of the others, so far as he was concerned. He expected no answer and a dull one would have been reproved. But Carrie, whose experience and belief in herself gave her daring, courtesied sweetly again and answered:

"I am yours truly."

It was a trivial thing to say, and yet something in the way she did it caught the audience, which laughed heartily at the mock-fierce potentate towering before the young woman. The comedian also liked it, hearing the laughter.

"I thought your name was Smith," he returned, endeavouring to get the last laugh.

Carrie almost trembled for her daring after she had said this. All members of the company had been warned that to interpolate lines or "business" meant a fine or worse. She did not know what to think.

As she was standing in her proper position in the wings, awaiting another entry, the great comedian made his exit past her and paused in recognition.

"You can just leave that in hereafter," he remarked, seeing how intelligent she appeared. "Don't add any more, though."

"Thank you," said Carrie, humbly. When he went on she found herself trembling violently.

"Well, you're in luck," remarked another member of the chorus. "There isn't another one of us has got a line."

There was no gainsaying the value of this. Everybody in the company realised that she had got a start. Carrie hugged herself when next evening the lines got the same applause. She went home rejoicing, knowing that soon something must come of it. It was Hurstwood who, by his presence, caused her merry thoughts to flee and replaced them with sharp longings for an end of distress.

The next day she asked him about his venture.

"They're not trying to run any cars except with police. They don't want anybody just now—not before next week."

Next week came, but Carrie saw no change. Hurstwood seemed more apathetic than ever. He saw her off mornings to rehearsals and the like with the utmost calm. He read and read. Several times he found himself staring at an item, but thinking of something else. The first of these lapses that he sharply noticed concerned a hilarious party he had once attended at a driving club, of which he had been a member. He sat, gazing downward, and gradually thought he heard the old voices and the clink of glasses.

"You're a dandy, Hurstwood," his friend Walker said. He was standing again well dressed, smiling, good-natured, the recipient of encores for a good story.

All at once he looked up. The room was so still it seemed ghostlike. He heard the clock ticking audibly and half suspected that he had been dozing. The paper was so straight in his hands, however, and the items he had been reading so directly before him, that he rid himself of the doze idea. Still, it seemed peculiar. When it occurred a second time, however, it did not seem quite so strange.

Butcher and grocery man, baker and coal man—not the group with whom he was then dealing, but those who had trusted him to the limit—called. He met them all blandly, becoming deft in excuse. At last he became bold, pretended to be out, or waved them off.

"They can't get blood out of a turnip," he said. "If I had it I'd pay them."

Carrie's little soldier friend, Miss Osborne, seeing her succeeding, had become a sort of satellite. Little Osborne could never of herself amount to anything. She seemed to realise it in a sort of pussy-like way and instinctively concluded to cling with her soft little claws to Carrie.

"Oh, you'll get up," she kept telling Carrie with admiration. "You're so good."

Timid as Carrie was, she was strong in capability. The reliance of others made her feel as if she must, and when she must she dared. Experience of the world and of necessity was in her favour. No longer the lightest word of a man made her head dizzy. She had learned that men could change and fail. Flattery in its most palpable form had lost its force with her. It required superiority—kindly superiority—to move her—the superiority of a genius like Ames.

"I don't like the actors in our company," she told Lola one day. "They're all so stuck on themselves."

"Don't you think Mr. Barclay's pretty nice?" inquired Lola, who had received a condescending smile or two from that quarter.

"Oh, he's nice enough," answered Carrie; "but he isn't sincere. He assumes such an air."

Lola felt for her first hold upon Carrie in the following manner:

"Are you paying room-rent where you are?"

"Certainly," answered Carrie. "Why?"

"I know where I could get the loveliest room and bath, cheap. It's too big for me, but it would be just right for two, and the rent is only six dollars a week for both."

"Where?" said Carrie.

"In Seventeenth Street."

"Well, I don't know as I'd care to change," said Carrie, who was already turning over the three-dollar rate in her mind. She was thinking if she had only herself to support this would leave her seventeen for herself.

Nothing came of this until after the Brooklyn adventure of Hurstwood's and her success with the speaking part. Then she began to feel as if she must be free. She thought of leaving Hurstwood and thus making him act for himself, but he had developed such peculiar traits she feared he might resist any effort to throw him off. He might hunt her out at the show and hound her in that way. She did not wholly believe that he would, but he might. This, she knew, would be an embarrassing thing if he made himself conspicuous in any way. It troubled her greatly.

Things were precipitated by the offer of a better part. One of the actresses playing the part of a modest sweetheart gave notice of leaving and Carrie was selected.

"How much are you going to get?" asked Miss Osborne, on hearing the good news.

"I didn't ask him," said Carrie.

"Well, find out. Goodness, you'll never get anything if you don't ask. Tell them you must have forty dollars, anyhow."

"Oh, no," said Carrie.

"Certainly!" exclaimed Lola. "Ask 'em, anyway."

Carrie succumbed to this prompting, waiting, however, until the manager gave her notice of what clothing she must have to fit the part.

"How much do I get?" she inquired.

"Thirty-five dollars," he replied.

Carrie was too much astonished and delighted to think of mentioning forty. She was nearly beside herself, and almost hugged Lola, who clung to her at the news.

"It isn't as much as you ought to get," said the latter, "especially when you've got to buy clothes."

Carrie remembered this with a start. Where to get the money? She had none laid up for such an emergency. Rent day was drawing near.

"I'll not do it," she said, remembering her necessity. "I don't use the flat. I'm not going to give up my money this time. I'll move."

Fitting into this came another appeal from Miss Osborne, more urgent than ever.

"Come live with me, won't you?" she pleaded. "We can have the loveliest room. It won't cost you hardly anything that way."

"I'd like to," said Carrie, frankly.

"Oh, do," said Lola. "We'll have such a good time."

Carrie thought a while.

"I believe I will," she said, and then added: "I'll have to see first, though."

With the idea thus grounded, rent day approaching, and clothes calling for instant purchase, she soon found excuse in Hurstwood's lassitude. He said less and drooped more than ever.

As rent day approached, an idea grew in him. It was fostered by the demands of creditors and the impossibility of holding up many more. Twenty-eight dollars was too much for rent. "It's hard on her," he thought. "We could get a cheaper place."

Stirred with this idea, he spoke at the breakfast table.

"Don't you think we pay too much rent here?" he asked.

"Indeed I do," said Carrie, not catching his drift.

"I should think we could get a smaller place," he suggested. "We don't need four rooms."

Her countenance, had he been scrutinising her, would have exhibited the disturbance she felt at this evidence of his determination to stay by her. He saw nothing remarkable in asking her to come down lower.

"Oh, I don't know," she answered, growing wary.

"There must be places around here where we could get a couple of rooms, which would do just as well."

Her heart revolted. "Never!" she thought. Who would furnish the money to move? To think of being in two rooms with him! She resolved to spend her money for clothes quickly, before something terrible happened. That very day she did it. Having done so, there was but one other thing to do.

"Lola," she said, visiting her friend, "I think I'll come."

"Oh, jolly!" cried the latter.

"Can we get it right away?" she asked, meaning the room.

"Certainly," cried Lola.

They went to look at it. Carrie had saved ten dollars from her expenditures—enough for this and her board beside. Her enlarged salary would not begin for ten days yet—would not reach her for seventeen. She paid half of the six dollars with her friend.

"Now, I've just enough to get on to the end of the week," she confided.

"Oh, I've got some," said Lola. "I've got twenty-five dollars, if you need it."

"No," said Carrie. "I guess I'll get along."

They decided to move Friday, which was two days away. Now that the thing was settled, Carrie's heart misgave her. She felt very much like a criminal in the matter. Each day looking at Hurstwood, she had realised that, along with the disagreeableness of his attitude, there was something pathetic.

She looked at him the same evening she had made up her mind to go, and now he seemed not so shiftless and worthless, but run down and beaten upon by chance. His eyes were not keen, his face marked, his hands flabby. She thought his hair had a touch of grey. All unconscious of his doom, he rocked and read his paper, while she glanced at him.

Knowing that the end was so near, she became rather solicitous.

"Will you go over and get some canned peaches?" she asked Hurstwood, laying down a two-dollar bill.

"Certainly," he said, looking in wonder at the money.

"See if you can get some nice asparagus," she added. "I'll cook it for dinner."

Hurstwood rose and took the money, slipping on his overcoat and getting his hat. Carrie noticed that both of these articles of apparel were old and poor looking in appearance. It was plain enough before, but now it came home with peculiar force. Perhaps he couldn't help it, after all. He had done well in Chicago. She remembered his fine appearance the days he had met her in the park. Then he was so sprightly, so clean. Had it been all his fault?

He came back and laid the change down with the food.

"You'd better keep it," she observed. "We'll need other things."

"No," he said, with a sort of pride; "you keep it."

"Oh, go on and keep it," she replied, rather unnerved. "There'll be other things."

He wondered at this, not knowing the pathetic figure he

had become in her eyes. She restrained herself with difficulty
from showing a quaver in her voice.

To say truly, this would have been Carrie's attitude in any
case. She had looked back at times upon her parting from
Drouet and had regretted that she had served him so badly.
She hoped she would never meet him again, but she was
ashamed of her conduct. Not that she had any choice in the
final separation. She had gone willingly to seek him, with
sympathy in her heart, when Hurstwood had reported him
ill. There was something cruel somewhere, and not being able
to track it mentally to its logical lair, she concluded with feeling that he would never understand what Hurstwood had
done and would see hard-hearted decision in her deed; hence
her shame. Not that she cared for him. She did not want to
make any one who had been good to her feel badly.

She did not realise what she was doing by allowing these
feelings to possess her. Hurstwood, noticing the kindness,
conceived better of her. "Carrie's good-natured, anyhow," he
thought.

Going to Miss Osborne's that afternoon, she found that
little lady packing and singing.

"Why don't you come over with me to-day?" she asked.

"Oh, I can't," said Carrie. "I'll be there Friday. Would you
mind lending me the twenty-five dollars you spoke of?"

"Why, no," said Lola, going for her purse.

"I want to get some other things," said Carrie.

"Oh, that's all right," answered the little girl, good-
naturedly, glad to be of service.

It had been days since Hurstwood had done more than go
to the grocery or to the news-stand. Now the weariness of
indoors was upon him—had been for two days—but chill,
grey weather had held him back. Friday broke fair and warm.
It was one of those lovely harbingers of spring, given as a
sign in dreary winter that earth is not forsaken of warmth and
beauty. The blue heaven, holding its one golden orb, poured
down a crystal wash of warm light. It was plain, from the
voice of the sparrows, that all was halcyon outside. Carrie
raised the front windows, and felt the south wind blowing.

"It's lovely out to-day," she remarked.

"Is it?" said Hurstwood.

After breakfast, he immediately got his other clothes. "Will you be back for lunch?" asked Carrie, nervously. "No," he said.

He went out into the streets and tramped north, along Seventh Avenue, idly fixing upon the Harlem River as an objective point. He had seen some ships up there, the time he had called upon the brewers. He wondered how the territory thereabouts was growing.

Passing Fifty-ninth Street, he took the west side of Central Park, which he followed to Seventy-eighth Street. Then he remembered the neighbourhood and turned over to look at the mass of buildings erected. It was very much improved. The great open spaces were filling up. Coming back, he kept to the Park until 110th Street, and then turned into Seventh Avenue again, reaching the pretty river by one o'clock.

There it ran winding before his gaze, shining brightly in the clear light, between the undulating banks on the right and the tall, tree-covered heights on the left. The spring-like atmosphere woke him to a sense of its loveliness, and for a few moments he stood looking at it, folding his hands behind his back. Then he turned and followed it toward the east side, idly seeking the ships he had seen. It was four o'clock before the waning day, with its suggestion of a cooler evening, caused him to return. He was hungry and would enjoy eating in the warm room.

When he reached the flat by half-past five, it was still dark. He knew that Carrie was not there, not only because there was no light showing through the transom, but because the evening papers were stuck between the outside knob and the door. He opened with his key and went in. Everything was still dark. Lighting the gas, he sat down, preparing to wait a little while. Even if Carrie did come now, dinner would be late. He read until six, then got up to fix something for himself.

As he did so, he noticed that the room seemed a little queer. What was it? He looked around, as if he missed something, and then saw an envelope near where he had been sitting. It spoke for itself, almost without further action on his part.

Reaching over, he took it, a sort of chill settling upon him even while he reached. The crackle of the envelope in his hands was loud. Green paper money lay soft within the note.

"Dear George," he read, crunching the money in one hand. "I'm going away. I'm not coming back any more. It's no use trying to keep up the flat; I can't do it. I wouldn't mind helping you, if I could, but I can't support us both, and pay the rent. I need what little I make to pay for my clothes. I'm leaving twenty dollars. It's all I have just now. You can do whatever you like with the furniture. I won't want it.—CARRIE."

He dropped the note and looked quietly round. Now he knew what he missed. It was the little ornamental clock, which was hers. It had gone from the mantel-piece. He went into the front room, his bedroom, the parlour, lighting the gas as he went. From the chiffonier had gone the knick-knacks of silver and plate. From the table-top, the lace coverings. He opened the wardrobe—no clothes of hers. He opened the drawers—nothing of hers. Her trunk was gone from its accustomed place. Back in his own room hung his old clothes, just as he had left them. Nothing else was gone.

He stepped into the parlour and stood for a few moments looking vacantly at the floor. The silence grew oppressive. The little flat seemed wonderfully deserted. He wholly forgot that he was hungry, that it was only dinner-time. It seemed later in the night.

Suddenly, he found that the money was still in his hands. There were twenty dollars in all, as she had said. Now he walked back, leaving the lights ablaze, and feeling as if the flat were empty.

"I'll get out of this," he said to himself.

Then the sheer loneliness of his situation rushed upon him in full.

"Left me!" he muttered, and repeated, "left me!"

The place that had been so comfortable, where he had spent so many days of warmth, was now a memory. Something colder and chillier confronted him. He sank down in his chair, resting his chin in his hand—mere sensation, without thought, holding him.

Then something like a bereaved affection and self-pity swept over him.

"She needn't have gone away," he said. "I'd have got something."

He sat a long while without rocking, and added quite clearly, out loud:

"I tried, didn't I?"

At midnight he was still rocking, staring at the floor.

Chapter XLIII

THE WORLD TURNS FLATTERER: AN EYE IN THE DARK

INSTALLED in her comfortable room, Carrie wondered how Hurstwood had taken her departure. She arranged a few things hastily and then left for the theatre, half expecting to encounter him at the door. Not finding him, her dread lifted, and she felt more kindly toward him. She quite forgot him until about to come out, after the show, when the chance of his being there frightened her. As day after day passed and she heard nothing at all, the thought of being bothered by him passed. In a little while she was, except for occasional thoughts, wholly free of the gloom with which her life had been weighed in the flat.

It is curious to note how quickly a profession absorbs one. Carrie became wise in theatrical lore, hearing the gossip of little Lola. She learned what the theatrical papers were, which ones published items about actresses and the like. She began to read the newspaper notices, not only of the opera in which she had so small a part, but of others. Gradually the desire for notice took hold of her. She longed to be renowned like others, and read with avidity all the complimentary or critical comments made concerning others high in her profession. The showy world in which her interest lay completely absorbed her.

It was about this time that the newspapers and magazines were beginning to pay that illustrative attention to the beauties of the stage which has since become fervid. The newspapers, and particularly the Sunday newspapers, indulged in large decorative theatrical pages, in which the faces and forms of well-known theatrical celebrities appeared, enclosed with artistic scrolls. The magazines also—or at least one or two of the newer ones—published occasional portraits of pretty stars, and now and again photos of scenes from various plays. Carrie watched these with growing interest. When would a scene from her opera appear? When would some paper think her photo worth while?

The Sunday before taking her new part she scanned the

theatrical pages for some little notice. It would have accorded
with her expectations if nothing had been said, but there in
the squibs, tailing off several more substantial items, was a
wee notice. Carrie read it with a tingling body:

> "The part of Katisha, the country maid, in 'The Wives
> of Abdul' at the Broadway, heretofore played by Inez
> Carew, will be hereafter filled by Carrie Madenda, one of
> the cleverest members of the chorus."

Carrie hugged herself with delight. Oh, wasn't it just fine!
At last! The first, the long-hoped for, the delightful notice!
And they called her clever. She could hardly restrain herself
from laughing loudly. Had Lola seen it?

"They've got a notice here of the part I'm going to play
to-morrow night," said Carrie to her friend.

"Oh, jolly! Have they?" cried Lola, running to her. "That's
all right," she said, looking. "You'll get more now, if you do
well. I had my picture in the 'World' once."

"Did you?" asked Carrie.

"Did I? Well, I should say," returned the little girl. "They
had a frame around it."

Carrie laughed.

"They've never published my picture."

"But they will," said Lola. "You'll see. You do better than
most that get theirs in now."

Carrie felt deeply grateful for this. She almost loved Lola
for the sympathy and praise she extended. It was so helpful
to her—so almost necessary.

Fulfilling her part capably brought another notice in the
papers that she was doing her work acceptably. This pleased
her immensely. She began to think the world was taking note
of her.

The first week she got her thirty-five dollars, it seemed an
enormous sum. Paying only three dollars for room rent
seemed ridiculous. After giving Lola her twenty-five, she still
had seven dollars left. With four left over from previous earnings, she had eleven. Five of this went to pay the regular installment on the clothes she had to buy. The next week she
was even in greater feather. Now, only three dollars need be

paid for room rent and five on her clothes. The rest she had for food and her own whims.

"You'd better save a little for summer," cautioned Lola. "We'll probably close in May."

"I intend to," said Carrie.

The regular entrance of thirty-five dollars a week to one who has endured scant allowances for several years is a demoralising thing. Carrie found her purse bursting with good green bills of comfortable denominations. Having no one dependent upon her, she began to buy pretty clothes and pleasing trinkets, to eat well, and to ornament her room. Friends were not long in gathering about. She met a few young men who belonged to Lola's staff. The members of the opera company made her acquaintance without the formality of introduction. One of these discovered a fancy for her. On several occasions he strolled home with her.

"Let's stop in and have a rarebit," he suggested one midnight.

"Very well," said Carrie.

In the rosy restaurant, filled with the merry lovers of late hours, she found herself criticising this man. He was too stilted, too self-opinionated. He did not talk of anything that lifted her above the common run of clothes and material success. When it was all over, he smiled most graciously.

"Got to go straight home, have you?" he said.

"Yes," she answered, with an air of quiet understanding.

"She's not so inexperienced as she looks," he thought, and thereafter his respect and ardour were increased.

She could not help sharing in Lola's love for a good time. There were days when they went carriage riding, nights when after the show they dined, afternoons when they strolled along Broadway, tastefully dressed. She was getting in the metropolitan whirl of pleasure.

At last her picture appeared in one of the weeklies. She had not known of it, and it took her breath. "Miss Carrie Madenda," it was labelled. "One of the favourites of 'The Wives of Abdul' company." At Lola's advice she had had some pictures taken by Sarony. They had got one there. She thought of going down and buying a few copies of the paper, but remembered that there was no one she knew well enough to send them to. Only Lola, apparently, in all the world was interested.

The metropolis is a cold place socially, and Carrie soon found that a little money brought her nothing. The world of wealth and distinction was quite as far away as ever. She could feel that there was no warm, sympathetic friendship back of the easy merriment with which many approached her. All seemed to be seeking their own amusement, regardless of the possible sad consequence to others. So much for the lessons of Hurstwood and Drouet.

In April she learned that the opera would probably last until the middle or the end of May, according to the size of the audiences. Next season it would go on the road. She wondered if she would be with it. As usual, Miss Osborne, owing to her moderate salary, was for securing a home engagement.

"They're putting on a summer play at the Casino," she announced, after figuratively putting her ear to the ground. "Let's try and get in that."

"I'm willing," said Carrie.

They tried in time and were apprised of the proper date to apply again. That was May 16th. Meanwhile their own show closed May 5th.

"Those that want to go with the show next season," said the manager, " will have to sign this week."

"Don't you sign," advised Lola. "I wouldn't go."

"I know," said Carrie, "but maybe I can't get anything else."

"Well, I won't," said the little girl, who had a resource in her admirers. "I went once and I didn't have anything at the end of the season."

Carrie thought this over. She had never been on the road.

"We can get along," added Lola. "I always have."

Carrie did not sign.

The manager who was putting on the summer skit at the Casino had never heard of Carrie, but the several notices she had received, her published picture, and the programme bearing her name had some little weight with him. He gave her a silent part at thirty dollars a week.

"Didn't I tell you?" said Lola. "It doesn't do you any good to go away from New York. They forget all about you if you do."

Now, because Carrie was pretty, the gentlemen who made up the advance illustrations of shows about to appear for the Sunday papers selected Carrie's photo along with others to illustrate the announcement. Because she was very pretty, they gave it excellent space and drew scrolls about it. Carrie was delighted. Still, the management did not seem to have seen anything of it. At least, no more attention was paid to her than before. At the same time there seemed very little in her part. It consisted of standing around in all sorts of scenes, a silent little Quakeress. The author of the skit had fancied that a great deal could be made of such a part, given to the right actress, but now, since it had been doled out to Carrie, he would as leave have had it cut out.

"Don't kick, old man," remarked the manager. "If it don't go the first week we will cut it out."

Carrie had no warning of this halcyon intention. She practised her part ruefully, feeling that she was effectually shelved. At the dress rehearsal she was disconsolate.

"That isn't so bad," said the author, the manager noting the curious effect which Carrie's blues had upon the part. "Tell her to frown a little more when Sparks dances."

Carrie did not know it, but there was the least show of wrinkles between her eyes and her mouth was puckered quaintly.

"Frown a little more, Miss Madenda," said the stage manager.

Carrie instantly brightened up, thinking he had meant it as a rebuke.

"No; frown," he said. "Frown as you did before."

Carrie looked at him in astonishment.

"I mean it," he said. "Frown hard when Mr. Sparks dances. I want to see how it looks."

It was easy enough to do. Carrie scowled. The effect was something so quaint and droll it caught even the manager.

"That *is* good," he said. "If she'll do that all through, I think it will take."

Going over to Carrie, he said:

"Suppose you try frowning all through. Do it hard. Look mad. It'll make the part really funny."

On the opening night it looked to Carrie as if there were nothing to her part, after all. The happy, sweltering audience did not seem to see her in the first act. She frowned and frowned, but to no effect. Eyes were riveted upon the more elaborate efforts of the stars.

In the second act, the crowd, wearied by a dull conversation, roved with its eyes about the stage and sighted her. There she was, grey-suited, sweet-faced, demure, but scowling. At first the general idea was that she was temporarily irritated, that the look was genuine and not fun at all. As she went on frowning, looking now at one principal and now at the other, the audience began to smile. The portly gentlemen in the front rows began to feel that she was a delicious little morsel. It was the kind of frown they would have loved to force away with kisses. All the gentlemen yearned toward her. She was capital.

At last, the chief comedian, singing in the centre of the stage, noticed a giggle where it was not expected. Then another and another. When the place came for loud applause it was only moderate. What could be the trouble? He realised that something was up.

All at once, after an exit, he caught sight of Carrie. She was frowning alone on the stage and the audience was giggling and laughing.

"By George, I won't stand that!" thought the thespian. "I'm not going to have my work cut up by some one else. Either she quits that when I do my turn or I quit."

"Why, that's all right," said the manager, when the kick came. "That's what she's supposed to do. You needn't pay any attention to that."

"But she ruins my work."

"No, she don't," returned the former, soothingly. "It's only a little fun on the side."

"It is, eh?" exclaimed the big comedian. "She killed my hand all right. I'm not going to stand that."

"Well, wait until after the show. Wait until to-morrow. We'll see what we can do."

The next act, however, settled what was to be done. Carrie

was the chief feature of the play. The audience, the more it studied her, the more it indicated its delight. Every other feature paled beside the quaint, teasing, delightful atmosphere which Carrie contributed while on the stage. Manager and company realised she had made a hit.

The critics of the daily papers completed her triumph. There were long notices in praise of the quality of the burlesque, touched with recurrent references to Carrie. The contagious mirth of the thing was repeatedly emphasised.

"Miss Madenda presents one of the most delightful bits of character work ever seen on the Casino stage," observed the sage critic of the "Sun." "It is a bit of quiet, unassuming drollery which warms like good wine. Evidently the part was not intended to take precedence, as Miss Madenda is not often on the stage, but the audience, with the characteristic perversity of such bodies, selected for itself. The little Quakeress was marked for a favourite the moment she appeared, and thereafter easily held attention and applause. The vagaries of fortune are indeed curious."

The critic of the "Evening World," seeking as usual to establish a catch phrase which should "go" with the town, wound up by advising: "If you wish to be merry, see Carrie frown."

The result was miraculous so far as Carrie's fortune was concerned. Even during the morning she received a congratulatory message from the manager.

"You seem to have taken the town by storm," he wrote. "This is delightful. I am as glad for your sake as for my own."

The author also sent word.

That evening when she entered the theatre the manager had a most pleasant greeting for her.

"Mr. Stevens," he said, referring to the author, "is preparing a little song, which he would like you to sing next week."

"Oh, I can't sing," returned Carrie.

"It isn't anything difficult. 'It's something that is very simple,' he says, 'and would suit you exactly.'"

"Of course, I wouldn't mind trying," said Carrie, archly.

"Would you mind coming to the box-office a few moments before you dress?" observed the manager, in addition. "There's a little matter I want to speak to you about."

"Certainly," replied Carrie.

In that latter place the manager produced a paper.

"Now, of course," he said, "we want to be fair with you in the matter of salary. Your contract here only calls for thirty dollars a week for the next three months. How would it do to make it, say, one hundred and fifty a week and extend it for twelve months?"

"Oh, very well," said Carrie, scarcely believing her ears.

"Supposing, then, you just sign this."

Carrie looked and beheld a new contract made out like the other one, with the exception of the new figures of salary and time. With a hand trembling from excitement she affixed her name.

"One hundred and fifty a week!" she murmured, when she was again alone. She found, after all—as what millionaire has not?—that there was no realising, in consciousness, the meaning of large sums. It was only a shimmering, glittering phrase in which lay a world of possibilities.

Down in a third-rate Bleecker Street hotel, the brooding Hurstwood read the dramatic item covering Carrie's success, without at first realising who was meant. Then suddenly it came to him and he read the whole thing over again.

"That's her, all right, I guess," he said.

Then he looked about upon a dingy, moth-eaten hotel lobby.

"I guess she's struck it," he thought, a picture of the old shiny, plush-covered world coming back, with its lights, its ornaments, its carriages, and flowers. Ah, she was in the walled city now! Its splendid gates had opened, admitting her from a cold, dreary outside. She seemed a creature afar off— like every other celebrity he had known.

"Well, let her have it," he said. "I won't bother her."

It was the grim resolution of a bent, bedraggled, but unbroken pride.

Chapter XLIV

And This Is Not Elf Land: What Gold Will Not Buy

WHEN CARRIE got back on the stage, she found that over night her dressing-room had been changed.

"You are to use this room, Miss Madenda," said one of the stage lackeys.

No longer any need of climbing several flights of steps to a small coop shared with another. Instead, a comparatively large and commodious chamber with conveniences not enjoyed by the small fry overhead. She breathed deeply and with delight. Her sensations were more physical than mental. In fact, she was scarcely thinking at all. Heart and body were having their say.

Gradually the deference and congratulation gave her a mental appreciation of her state. She was no longer ordered, but requested, and that politely. The other members of the cast looked at her enviously as she came out arrayed in her simple habit, which she wore all through the play. All those who had supposedly been her equals and superiors now smiled the smile of sociability, as much as to say: "How friendly we have always been." Only the star comedian whose part had been so deeply injured stalked by himself. Figuratively, he could not kiss the hand that smote him.

Doing her simple part, Carrie gradually realised the meaning of the applause which was for her, and it was sweet. She felt mildly guilty of something—perhaps unworthiness. When her associates addressed her in the wings she only smiled weakly. The pride and daring of place were not for her. It never once crossed her mind to be reserved or haughty—to be other than she had been. After the performances she rode to her room with Lola, in a carriage provided.

Then came a week in which the first fruits of success were offered to her lips—bowl after bowl. It did not matter that her splendid salary had not begun. The world seemed satisfied with the promise. She began to get letters and cards. A Mr. Withers—whom she did not know from Adam—having learned by some hook or crook where she resided, bowed himself politely in.

"You will excuse me for intruding," he said; "but have you been thinking of changing your apartments?"

"I hadn't thought of it," returned Carrie.

"Well, I am connected with the Wellington—the new hotel on Broadway. You have probably seen notices of it in the papers."

Carrie recognised the name as standing for one of the newest and most imposing hostelries. She had heard it spoken of as having a splendid restaurant.

"Just so," went on Mr. Withers, accepting her acknowledgment of familiarity. "We have some very elegant rooms at present which we would like to have you look at, if you have not made up your mind where you intend to reside for the summer. Our apartments are perfect in every detail—hot and cold water, private baths, special hall service for every floor, elevators, and all that. You know what our restaurant is."

Carrie looked at him quietly. She was wondering whether he took her to be a millionaire.

"What are your rates?" she inquired.

"Well, now, that is what I came to talk with you privately about. Our regular rates are anywhere from three to fifty dollars a day."

"Mercy!" interrupted Carrie. "I couldn't pay any such rate as that."

"I know how you feel about it," exclaimed Mr. Withers, halting. "But just let me explain. I said those are our regular rates. Like every other hotel we make special ones, however. Possibly you have not thought about it, but your name is worth something to us."

"Oh!" ejaculated Carrie, seeing at a glance.

"Of course. Every hotel depends upon the repute of its patrons. A well-known actress like yourself," and he bowed politely, while Carrie flushed, "draws attention to the hotel, and—although you may not believe it—patrons."

"Oh, yes," returned Carrie, vacantly, trying to arrange this curious proposition in her mind.

"Now," continued Mr. Withers, swaying his derby hat softly and beating one of his polished shoes upon the floor,

"I want to arrange, if possible, to have you come and stop at the Wellington. You need not trouble about terms. In fact, we need hardly discuss them. Anything will do for the summer—a mere figure—anything that you think you could afford to pay."

Carrie was about to interrupt, but he gave her no chance.

"You can come to-day or to-morrow—the earlier the better—and we will give you your choice of nice, light, outside rooms—the very best we have."

"You're very kind," said Carrie, touched by the agent's extreme affability. "I should like to come very much. I would want to pay what is right, however. I shouldn't want to——"

"You need not trouble about that at all," interrupted Mr. Withers. "We can arrange that to your entire satisfaction at any time. If three dollars a day is satisfactory to you, it will be so to us. All you have to do is to pay that sum to the clerk at the end of the week or month, just as you wish, and he will give you a receipt for what the rooms would cost if charged for at our regular rates."

The speaker paused.

"Suppose you come and look at the rooms," he added.

"I'd be glad to," said Carrie, "but I have a rehearsal this morning."

"I did not mean at once," he returned. "Any time will do. Would this afternoon be inconvenient?"

"Not at all," said Carrie.

Suddenly she remembered Lola, who was out at the time.

"I have a room-mate," she added, " who will have to go wherever I do. I forgot about that."

"Oh, very well," said Mr. Withers, blandly. "It is for you to say whom you want with you. As I say, all that can be arranged to suit yourself."

He bowed and backed toward the door.

"At four, then, we may expect you?"

"Yes," said Carrie.

"I will be there to show you," and so Mr. Withers withdrew.

After rehearsal Carrie informed Lola.

"Did they really?" exclaimed the latter, thinking of the

Wellington as a group of managers. "Isn't that fine? Oh, jolly! It's so swell. That's where we dined that night we went with those two Cushing boys. Don't you know?"

"I remember," said Carrie.

"Oh, it's as fine as it can be."

"We'd better be going up there," observed Carrie, later in the afternoon.

The rooms which Mr. Withers displayed to Carrie and Lola were three and bath—a suite on the parlour floor. They were done in chocolate and dark red, with rugs and hangings to match. Three windows looked down into busy Broadway on the east, three into a side street which crossed there. There were two lovely bedrooms, set with brass and white enamel beds, white, ribbon-trimmed chairs and chiffoniers to match. In the third room, or parlour, was a piano, a heavy piano lamp, with a shade of gorgeous pattern, a library table, several huge easy rockers, some dado book shelves, and a gilt curio case, filled with oddities. Pictures were upon the walls, soft Turkish pillows upon the divan, footstools of brown plush upon the floor. Such accommodations would ordinarily cost a hundred dollars a week.

"Oh, lovely!" exclaimed Lola, walking about.

"It is comfortable," said Carrie, who was lifting a lace curtain and looking down into crowded Broadway.

The bath was a handsome affair, done in white enamel, with a large, blue-bordered stone tub and nickel trimmings. It was bright and commodious, with a bevelled mirror set in the wall at one end and incandescent lights arranged in three places.

"Do you find these satisfactory?" observed Mr. Withers.

"Oh, very," answered Carrie.

"Well, then, any time you find it convenient to move in, they are ready. The boy will bring you the keys at the door."

Carrie noted the elegantly carpeted and decorated hall, the marbled lobby, and showy waiting-room. It was such a place as she had often dreamed of occupying.

"I guess we'd better move right away, don't you think so?" she observed to Lola, thinking of the commonplace chamber in Seventeenth Street.

"Oh, by all means," said the latter.

The next day her trunks left for the new abode.

Dressing, after the matinée on Wednesday, a knock came at her dressing-room door.

Carrie looked at the card handed by the boy and suffered a shock of surprise.

"Tell her I'll be right out," she said softly. Then, looking at the card, added: "Mrs. Vance."

"Why, you little sinner," the latter exclaimed, as she saw Carrie coming toward her across the now vacant stage. "How in the world did this happen?"

Carrie laughed merrily. There was no trace of embarrassment in her friend's manner. You would have thought that the long separation had come about accidentally.

"I don't know," returned Carrie, warming, in spite of her first troubled feelings, toward this handsome, good-natured young matron.

"Well, you know, I saw your picture in the Sunday paper, but your name threw me off. I thought it must be you or somebody that looked just like you, and I said: 'Well, now, I will go right down there and see.' I was never more surprised in my life. How are you, anyway?"

"Oh, very well," returned Carrie. "How have you been?"

"Fine. But aren't you a success! Dear, oh! All the papers talking about you. I should think you would be just too proud to breathe. I was almost afraid to come back here this afternoon."

"Oh, nonsense," said Carrie, blushing. "You know I'd be glad to see you."

"Well, anyhow, here you are. Can't you come up and take dinner with me now? Where are you stopping?"

"At the Wellington," said Carrie, who permitted herself a touch of pride in the acknowledgment.

"Oh, are you?" exclaimed the other, upon whom the name was not without its proper effect.

Tactfully, Mrs. Vance avoided the subject of Hurstwood, of whom she could not help thinking. No doubt Carrie had left him. That much she surmised.

"Oh, I don't think I can," said Carrie, "to-night. I have so little time. I must be back here by 7.30. Won't you come and dine with me?"

"I'd be delighted, but I can't to-night," said Mrs. Vance, studying Carrie's fine appearance. The latter's good fortune made her seem more than ever worthy and delightful in the other's eyes. "I promised faithfully to be home at six." Glancing at the small gold watch pinned to her bosom, she added: "I must be going, too. Tell me when you're coming up, if at all."

"Why, any time you like," said Carrie.

"Well, to-morrow then. I'm living at the Chelsea now."

"Moved again?" exclaimed Carrie, laughing.

"Yes. You know I can't stay six months in one place. I just have to move. Remember now—half-past five."

"I won't forget," said Carrie, casting a glance at her as she went away. Then it came to her that she was as good as this woman now—perhaps better. Something in the other's solicitude and interest made her feel as if she were the one to condescend.

Now, as on each preceding day, letters were handed her by the doorman at the Casino. This was a feature which had rapidly developed since Monday. What they contained she well knew. *Mash notes* were old affairs in their mildest form. She remembered having received her first one far back in Columbia City. Since then, as a chorus girl, she had received others—gentlemen who prayed for an engagement. They were common sport between her and Lola, who received some also. They both frequently made light of them.

Now, however, they came thick and fast. Gentlemen with fortunes did not hesitate to note, as an addition to their own amiable collection of virtues, that they had their horses and carriages. Thus one:

"I have a million in my own right. I could give you every luxury. There isn't anything you could ask for that you couldn't have. I say this, not because I want to speak of my money, but because I love you and wish to gratify your every desire. It is love that prompts me to write. Will you not give me one half-hour in which to plead my cause?"

Such of these letters as came while Carrie was still in the Seventeenth Street place were read with more interest—though never delight—than those which arrived after she was installed in her luxurious quarters at the Wellington. Even there her vanity—or that self-appreciation which, in its more rabid form, is called vanity—was not sufficiently cloyed to make these things wearisome. Adulation, being new in any form, pleased her. Only she was sufficiently wise to distinguish between her old condition and her new one. She had not had fame or money before. Now they had come. She had not had adulation and affectionate propositions before. Now they had come. Wherefore? She smiled to think that men should suddenly find her so much more attractive. In the least way it incited her to coolness and indifference.

"Do look here," she remarked to Lola. "See what this man says: 'If you will only deign to grant me one half-hour,' " she repeated, with an imitation of languor. "The idea. Aren't men silly?"

"He must have lots of money, the way he talks," observed Lola.

"That's what they all say," said Carrie, innocently.

"Why don't you see him," suggested Lola, "and hear what he has to say?"

"Indeed I won't," said Carrie. "I know what he'd say. I don't want to meet anybody that way."

Lola looked at her with big, merry eyes.

"He couldn't hurt you," she returned. "You might have some fun with him."

Carrie shook her head.

"You're awfully queer," returned the little, blue-eyed soldier.

Thus crowded fortune. For this whole week, though her large salary had not yet arrived, it was as if the world understood and trusted her. Without money—or the requisite sum, at least—she enjoyed the luxuries which money could buy. For her the doors of fine places seemed to open quite without the asking. These palatial chambers, how marvellously they came to her. The elegant apartments of Mrs. Vance in the Chelsea—these were hers. Men sent flowers, love notes, offers of fortune. And still her dreams ran riot. The one hundred and fifty! the one hundred and fifty! What a door to an Aladdin's cave it seemed to be. Each day, her head almost turned by developments, her fancies of what her fortune must be, with ample money, grew and multiplied. She conceived of delights which were not—saw lights of joy that never were on land or sea. Then, at last, after a world of anticipation, came her first installment of one hundred and fifty dollars.

It was paid to her in greenbacks—three twenties, six tens, and six fives. Thus collected it made a very convenient roll. It was accompanied by a smile and a salutation from the cashier who paid it.

"Ah, yes," said the latter, when she applied; "Miss Madenda—one hundred and fifty dollars. Quite a success the show seems to have made."

"Yes, indeed," returned Carrie.

Right after came one of the insignificant members of the company, and she heard the changed tone of address.

"How much?" said the same cashier, sharply. One, such as she had only recently been, was waiting for her modest salary. It took her back to the few weeks in which she had collected—or rather had received—almost with the air of a domestic, four-fifty per week from a lordly foreman in a shoe factory—a man who, in distributing the envelopes, had the manner of a prince doling out favours to a servile group of petitioners. She knew that out in Chicago this very day the same factory chamber was full of poor homely-clad girls working in long lines of clattering machines; that at noon they would eat a miserable lunch in a half-hour; that Saturday they would gather, as they had when she was one of them, and accept the small pay for work a hundred times harder than she was now doing. Oh, it was so easy now! The world was so rosy and bright. She felt so thrilled that she must needs walk back to the hotel to think, wondering what she should do.

It does not take money long to make plain its impotence, providing the desires are in the realm of affection. With her one hundred and fifty in hand, Carrie could think of nothing particularly to do. In itself, as a tangible, apparent thing which she could touch and look upon, it was a diverting thing for a few days, but this soon passed. Her hotel bill did not require its use. Her clothes had for some time been wholly satisfactory. Another day or two and she would receive another hundred and fifty. It began to appear as if this were not so startlingly necessary to maintain her present state. If she wanted to do anything better or move higher she must have more—a great deal more.

Now a critic called to get up one of those tinsel interviews which shine with clever observations, show up the wit of critics, display the folly of celebrities, and divert the public. He liked Carrie, and said so, publicly—adding, however, that she was merely pretty, good-natured, and lucky. This cut like a knife. The "Herald," getting up an entertainment for the benefit of its free ice fund, did her the honour to beg her to appear along with celebrities for nothing. She was visited by a young author, who had a play which he thought she could produce. Alas, she could not judge. It hurt her to think it. Then she found she must put her money in the bank for safety, and so moving, finally reached the place where it struck her that the door to life's perfect enjoyment was not open.

Gradually she began to think it was because it was summer. Nothing was going on much save such entertainments as the one in which she was star. Fifth Avenue was boarded up where the rich had deserted their mansions. Madison Avenue was little better. Broadway was full of loafing thespians in search of next season engagements. The whole city was quiet and her nights were taken up with her work. Hence the feeling that there was little to do.

"I don't know," she said to Lola one day, sitting at one of the windows which looked down into Broadway, "I get lonely; don't you?"

"No," said Lola, "not very often. You won't go anywhere. That's what's the matter with you."

"Where can I go?"

"Why, there're lots of places," returned Lola, who was thinking of her own lightsome tourneys with the gay youths. "You won't go with anybody."

"I don't want to go with these people who write to me. I know what kind they are."

"You oughtn't to be lonely," said Lola, thinking of Carrie's success. "There're lots would give their ears to be in your shoes."

Carrie looked out again at the passing crowd.

"I don't know," she said.

Unconsciously her idle hands were beginning to weary.

Chapter XLV

CURIOUS SHIFTS OF THE POOR

THE GLOOMY Hurstwood, sitting in his cheap hotel, where he had taken refuge with seventy dollars—the price of his furniture—between him and nothing, saw a hot summer out and a cool fall in, reading. He was not wholly indifferent to the fact that his money was slipping away. As fifty cents after fifty cents were paid out for a day's lodging he became uneasy, and finally took a cheaper room—thirty-five cents a day—to make his money last longer. Frequently he saw notices of Carrie. Her picture was in the "World" once or twice, and an old "Herald" he found in a chair informed him that she had recently appeared with some others at a benefit for something or other. He read these things with mingled feelings. Each one seemed to put her farther and farther away into a realm which became more imposing as it receded from him. On the bill-boards, too, he saw a pretty poster, showing her as the Quaker Maid, demure and dainty. More than once he stopped and looked at these, gazing at the pretty face in a sullen sort of way. His clothes were shabby, and he presented a marked contrast to all that she now seemed to be.

Somehow, so long as he knew she was at the Casino, though he had never any intention of going near her, there was a sub-conscious comfort for him—he was not quite alone. The show seemed such a fixture that, after a month or two, he began to take it for granted that it was still running. In September it went on the road and he did not notice it. When all but twenty dollars of his money was gone, he moved to a fifteen-cent lodging-house in the Bowery, where there was a bare lounging-room filled with tables and benches as well as some chairs. Here his preference was to close his eyes and dream of other days, a habit which grew upon him. It was not sleep at first, but a mental hearkening back to scenes and incidents in his Chicago life. As the present became darker, the past grew brighter, and all that concerned it stood in relief.

He was unconscious of just how much this habit had hold

of him until one day he found his lips repeating an old answer he had made to one of his friends. They were in Fitzgerald and Moy's. It was as if he stood in the door of his elegant little office, comfortably dressed, talking to Sagar Morrison about the value of South Chicago real estate in which the latter was about to invest.

"How would you like to come in on that with me?" he heard Morrison say.

"Not me," he answered, just as he had years before. "I have my hands full now."

The movement of his lips aroused him. He wondered whether he had really spoken. The next time he noticed anything of the sort he really did talk.

"Why don't you jump, you bloody fool?" he was saying. "Jump!"

It was a funny English story he was telling to a company of actors. Even as his voice recalled him, he was smiling. A crusty old codger, sitting near by, seemed disturbed; at least, he stared in a most pointed way. Hurstwood straightened up. The humour of the memory fled in an instant and he felt ashamed. For relief, he left his chair and strolled out into the streets.

One day, looking down the ad. columns of the "Evening World," he saw where a new play was at the Casino. Instantly, he came to a mental halt. Carrie had gone! He remembered seeing a poster of her only yesterday, but no doubt it was one left uncovered by the new signs. Curiously, this fact shook him up. He had almost to admit that somehow he was depending upon her being in the city. Now she was gone. He wondered how this important fact had skipped him. Goodness knows when she would be back now. Impelled by a nervous fear, he rose and went into the dingy hall, where he counted his remaining money, unseen. There were but ten dollars in all.

He wondered how all these other lodging-house people around him got along. They didn't seem to do anything. Perhaps they begged—unquestionably they did. Many was the dime he had given to such as they in his day. He had seen other men asking for money on the streets. Maybe he could get some that way. There was horror in this thought.

Sitting in the lodging-house room, he came to his last fifty cents. He had saved and counted until his health was affected. His stoutness had gone. With it, even the semblance of a fit in his clothes. Now he decided he must do something, and, walking about, saw another day go by, bringing him down to his last twenty cents—not enough to eat for the morrow.

Summoning all his courage, he crossed to Broadway and up to the Broadway Central hotel. Within a block he halted, undecided. A big, heavy-faced porter was standing at one of the side entrances, looking out. Hurstwood purposed to appeal to him. Walking straight up, he was upon him before he could turn away.

"My friend," he said, recognising even in his plight the man's inferiority, "is there anything about this hotel that I could get to do?"

The porter stared at him the while he continued to talk.

"I'm out of work and out of money and I've got to get something—it doesn't matter what. I don't care to talk about what I've been, but if you'd tell me how to get something to do, I'd be much obliged to you. It wouldn't matter if it only lasted a few days just now. I've got to have something."

The porter still gazed, trying to look indifferent. Then, seeing that Hurstwood was about to go on, he said:

"I've nothing to do with it. You'll have to ask inside."

Curiously, this stirred Hurstwood to further effort.

"I thought you might tell me."

The fellow shook his head irritably.

Inside went the ex-manager and straight to an office off the clerk's desk. One of the managers of the hotel happened to be there. Hurstwood looked him straight in the eye.

"Could you give me something to do for a few days?" he said. "I'm in a position where I have to get something at once."

The comfortable manager looked at him, as much as to say: "Well, I should judge so."

"I came here," explained Hurstwood, nervously, "because I've been a manager myself in my day. I've had bad luck in a way, but I'm not here to tell you that. I want something to do, if only for a week."

The man imagined he saw a feverish gleam in the appli-cant's eye.

"What hotel did you manage?" he inquired.

"It wasn't a hotel," said Hurstwood. "I was manager of Fitzgerald and Moy's place in Chicago for fifteen years."

"Is that so?" said the hotel man. "How did you come to get out of that?"

The figure of Hurstwood was rather surprising in contrast to the fact.

"Well, by foolishness of my own. It isn't anything to talk about now. You could find out if you wanted to. I'm 'broke' now and, if you will believe me, I haven't eaten anything to-day."

The hotel man was slightly interested in this story. He could hardly tell what to do with such a figure, and yet Hurstwood's earnestness made him wish to do something.

"Call Olsen," he said, turning to the clerk.

In reply to a bell and a disappearing hall-boy, Olsen, the head porter, appeared.

"Olsen," said the manager, "is there anything downstairs you could find for this man to do? I'd like to give him some-thing."

"I don't know, sir," said Olsen. "We have about all the help we need. I think I could find something, sir, though, if you like."

"Do. Take him to the kitchen and tell Wilson to give him something to eat."

"All right, sir," said Olsen.

Hurstwood followed. Out of the manager's sight, the head porter's manner changed.

"I don't know what the devil there is to do," he observed.

Hurstwood said nothing. To him the big trunk hustler was a subject for private contempt.

"You're to give this man something to eat," he observed to the cook.

The latter looked Hurstwood over, and seeing something keen and intellectual in his eyes, said:

"Well, sit down over there."

Thus was Hurstwood installed in the Broadway Central, but not for long. He was in no shape or mood to do the scrub work that exists about the foundation of every hotel. Nothing better offering, he was set to aid the fireman, to work about the basement, to do anything and everything that might offer. Porters, cooks, firemen, clerks—all were over him. Moreover his appearance did not please these individuals—his temper was too lonely—and they made it disagreeable for him.

With the stolidity and indifference of despair, however, he endured it all, sleeping in an attic at the roof of the house, eating what the cook gave him, accepting a few dollars a week, which he tried to save. His constitution was in no shape to endure.

One day the following February he was sent on an errand to a large coal company's office. It had been snowing and thawing and the streets were sloppy. He soaked his shoes in his progress and came back feeling dull and weary. All the next day he felt unusually depressed and sat about as much as possible, to the irritation of those who admired energy in others.

In the afternoon some boxes were to be moved to make room for new culinary supplies. He was ordered to handle a truck. Encountering a big box, he could not lift it.

"What's the matter there?" said the head porter. "Can't you handle it?"

He was straining hard to lift it, but now he quit.

"No," he said, weakly.

The man looked at him and saw that he was deathly pale.

"Not sick, are you?" he asked.

"I think I am," returned Hurstwood.

"Well, you'd better go sit down, then."

This he did, but soon grew rapidly worse. It seemed all he could do to crawl to his room, where he remained for a day.

"That man Wheeler's sick," reported one of the lackeys to the night clerk.

"What's the matter with him?"

"I don't know. He's got a high fever."

The hotel physician looked at him.

"Better send him to Bellevue," he recommended. "He's got pneumonia."

Accordingly, he was carted away.

In three weeks the worst was over, but it was nearly the first of May before his strength permitted him to be turned out. Then he was discharged.

No more weakly looking object ever strolled out into the spring sunshine than the once hale, lusty manager. All his corpulency had fled. His face was thin and pale, his hands white, his body flabby. Clothes and all, he weighed but one hundred and thirty-five pounds. Some old garments had been given him—a cheap brown coat and misfit pair of trousers. Also some change and advice. He was told to apply to the charities.

Again he resorted to the Bowery lodging-house, brooding over where to look. From this it was but a step to beggary.

"What can a man do?" he said. "I can't starve."

His first application was in sunny Second Avenue. A well-dressed man came leisurely strolling toward him out of Stuyvesant Park. Hurstwood nerved himself and sidled near.

"Would you mind giving me ten cents?" he said, directly. "I'm in a position where I must ask some one."

The man scarcely looked at him, but fished in his vest pocket and took out a dime.

"There you are," he said.

"Much obliged," said Hurstwood, softly, but the other paid no more attention to him.

Satisfied with his success and yet ashamed of his situation, he decided that he would only ask for twenty-five cents more, since that would be sufficient. He strolled about sizing up people, but it was long before just the right face and situation arrived. When he asked, he was refused. Shocked by this result, he took an hour to recover and then asked again. This time a nickel was given him. By the most watchful effort he did get twenty cents more, but it was painful.

The next day he resorted to the same effort, experiencing a variety of rebuffs and one or two generous receptions. At last it crossed his mind that there was a science of faces, and that a man could pick the liberal countenance if he tried.

It was no pleasure to him, however, this stopping of passers-by. He saw one man taken up for it and now troubled lest he should be arrested. Nevertheless, he went on, vaguely anticipating that indefinite something which is always better.

It was with a sense of satisfaction, then, that he saw announced one morning the return of the Casino Company, "with Miss Carrie Madenda." He had thought of her often enough in days past. How successful she was—how much money she must have! Even now, however, it took a severe run of ill-luck to decide him to appeal to her. He was truly hungry before he said:

"I'll ask her. She won't refuse me a few dollars."

Accordingly, he headed for the Casino one afternoon, passing it several times in an effort to locate the stage entrance. Then he sat in Bryant Park, a block away, waiting. "She can't refuse to help me a little," he kept saying to himself.

Beginning with half-past six, he hovered like a shadow about the Thirty-ninth Street entrance, pretending always to be a hurrying pedestrian and yet fearful lest he should miss his object. He was slightly nervous, too, now that the eventful hour had arrived; but being weak and hungry, his ability to suffer was modified. At last he saw that the actors were beginning to arrive, and his nervous tension increased, until it seemed as if he could not stand much more.

Once he thought he saw Carrie coming and moved forward, only to see that he was mistaken.

"She can't be long, now," he said to himself, half fearing to encounter her and equally depressed at the thought that she might have gone in by another way. His stomach was so empty that it ached.

Individual after individual passed him, nearly all well dressed, almost all indifferent. He saw coaches rolling by, gentlemen passing with ladies—the evening's merriment was beginning in this region of theatres and hotels.

Suddenly a coach rolled up and the driver jumped down to open the door. Before Hurstwood could act, two ladies flounced across the broad walk and disappeared in the stage door. He thought he saw Carrie, but it was so unexpected, so elegant and far away, he could hardly tell. He waited a while longer, growing feverish with want, and then seeing that the stage door no longer opened, and that a merry audience was arriving, he concluded it must have been Carrie and turned away.

"Lord," he said, hastening out of the street into which the more fortunate were pouring, "I've got to get something."

At that hour, when Broadway is wont to assume its most interesting aspect, a peculiar individual invariably took his stand at the corner of Twenty-sixth Street and Broadway—a spot which is also intersected by Fifth Avenue. This was the hour when the theatres were just beginning to receive their patrons. Fire signs announcing the night's amusements blazed on every hand. Cabs and carriages, their lamps gleaming like yellow eyes, pattered by. Couples and parties of three and four freely mingled in the common crowd, which poured by in a thick stream, laughing and jesting. On Fifth Avenue were loungers—a few wealthy strollers, a gentleman in evening dress with his lady on his arm, some clubmen passing from one smoking-room to another. Across the way the great hotels showed a hundred gleaming windows, their cafés and billiard-rooms filled with a comfortable, well-dressed, and pleasure-loving throng. All about was the night, pulsating with the thoughts of pleasure and exhilaration—the curious enthusiasm of a great city bent upon finding joy in a thousand different ways.

This unique individual was no less than an ex-soldier turned religionist, who, having suffered the whips and privations of our peculiar social system, had concluded that his duty to the God which he conceived lay in aiding his fellow-man. The form of aid which he chose to administer was entirely original with himself. It consisted of securing a bed for all such homeless wayfarers as should apply to him at this particular spot, though he had scarcely the wherewithal to provide a comfortable habitation for himself.

Taking his place amid this lightsome atmosphere, he would stand, his stocky figure cloaked in a great cape overcoat, his head protected by a broad slouch hat, awaiting the applicants who had in various ways learned the nature of his charity. For a while he would stand alone, gazing like any idler upon an ever-fascinating scene. On the evening in question, a policeman passing saluted him as "captain," in a friendly way. An urchin who had frequently seen him before, stopped to gaze.

All others took him for nothing out of the ordinary, save in the matter of dress, and conceived of him as a stranger whistling and idling for his own amusement.

As the first half-hour waned, certain characters appeared. Here and there in the passing crowds one might see, now and then, a loiterer edging interestedly near. A slouchy figure crossed the opposite corner and glanced furtively in his direction. Another came down Fifth Avenue to the corner of Twenty-sixth Street, took a general survey, and hobbled off again. Two or three noticeable Bowery types edged along the Fifth Avenue side of Madison Square, but did not venture over. The soldier, in his cape overcoat, walked a short line of ten feet at his corner, to and fro, indifferently whistling.

As nine o'clock approached, some of the hubbub of the earlier hour passed. The atmosphere of the hotels was not so youthful. The air, too, was colder. On every hand curious figures were moving—watchers and peepers, without an imaginary circle, which they seemed afraid to enter—a dozen in all. Presently, with the arrival of a keener sense of cold, one figure came forward. It crossed Broadway from out the shadow of Twenty-sixth Street, and, in a halting, circuitous way, arrived close to the waiting figure. There was something shamefaced or diffident about the movement, as if the intention were to conceal any idea of stopping until the very last moment. Then suddenly, close to the soldier, came the halt.

The captain looked in recognition, but there was no especial greeting. The newcomer nodded slightly and murmured something like one who waits for gifts. The other simply motioned toward the edge of the walk.

"Stand over there," he said.

By this the spell was broken. Even while the soldier resumed his short, solemn walk, other figures shuffled forward. They did not so much as greet the leader, but joined the one, sniffling and hitching and scraping their feet.

"Cold, ain't it?"

"I'm glad winter's over."

"Looks as though it might rain."

The motley company had increased to ten. One or two knew each other and conversed. Others stood off a few feet, not wishing to be in the crowd and yet not counted out. They were peevish, crusty, silent, eying nothing in particular and moving their feet.

There would have been talking soon, but the soldier gave them no chance. Counting sufficient to begin, he came forward.

"Beds, eh, all of you?"

There was a general shuffle and murmur of approval.

"Well, line up here. I'll see what I can do. I haven't a cent myself."

They fell into a sort of broken, ragged line. One might see, now, some of the chief characteristics by contrast. There was a wooden leg in the line. Hats were all drooping, a group that would ill become a second-hand Hester Street basement collection. Trousers were all warped and frayed at the bottom and coats worn and faded. In the glare of the store lights, some of the faces looked dry and chalky; others were red with blotches and puffed in the cheeks and under the eyes; one or two were rawboned and reminded one of railroad hands. A few spectators came near, drawn by the seemingly conferring group, then more and more, and quickly there was a pushing, gaping crowd. Some one in the line began to talk.

"Silence!" exclaimed the captain. "Now, then, gentlemen, these men are without beds. They have to have some place to sleep to-night. They can't lie out in the streets. I need twelve cents to put one of them to bed. Who will give it to me?"

No reply.

"Well, we'll have to wait here, boys, until some one does. Twelve cents isn't so very much for one man."

"Here's fifteen," exclaimed a young man, peering forward with strained eyes. "It's all I can afford."

"All right. Now I have fifteen. Step out of the line," and seizing one by the shoulder, the captain marched him off a little way and stood him up alone.

Coming back, he resumed his place and began again.

"I have three cents left. These men must be put to bed somehow. There are"—counting—"one, two, three, four, five, six, seven, eight, nine, ten, eleven, twelve men. Nine cents more will put the next man to bed; give him a good, comfortable bed for the night. I go right along and look after that myself. Who will give me nine cents?"

One of the watchers, this time a middle-aged man, handed him a five-cent piece.

"Now, I have eight cents. Four more will give this man a bed. Come, gentlemen. We are going very slow this evening. You all have good beds. How about these?"

"Here you are," remarked a bystander, putting a coin into his hand.

"That," said the captain, looking at the coin, "pays for two beds for two men and gives me five on the next one. Who will give me seven cents more?"

"I will," said a voice.

Coming down Sixth Avenue this evening, Hurstwood chanced to cross east through Twenty-sixth Street toward Third Avenue. He was wholly disconsolate in spirit, hungry to what he deemed an almost mortal extent, weary, and defeated. How should he get at Carrie now? It would be eleven before the show was over. If she came in a coach, she would go away in one. He would need to interrupt under most trying circumstances. Worst of all, he was hungry and weary, and at best a whole day must intervene, for he had not heart to try again to-night. He had no food and no bed.

When he neared Broadway, he noticed the captain's gathering of wanderers, but thinking it to be the result of a street preacher or some patent medicine fakir, was about to pass on. However, in crossing the street toward Madison Square Park, he noticed the line of men whose beds were already secured, stretching out from the main body of the crowd. In the glare of the neighbouring electric light he recognised a type of his own kind—the figures whom he saw about the streets and in the lodging-houses, drifting in mind and body like himself. He wondered what it could be and turned back.

There was the captain curtly pleading as before. He heard with astonishment and a sense of relief the oft-repeated words: "These men must have a bed." Before him was the line of unfortunates whose beds were yet to be had, and seeing a newcomer quietly edge up and take a position at the end of the line, he decided to do likewise. What use to contend? He was weary to-night. It was a simple way out of one difficulty, at least. To-morrow, maybe, he would do better.

Back of him, where some of those were whose beds were

safe, a relaxed air was apparent. The strain of uncertainty being removed, he heard them talking with moderate freedom and some leaning toward sociability. Politics, religion, the state of the government, some newspaper sensations, and the more notorious facts the world over, found mouthpieces and auditors there. Cracked and husky voices pronounced forcibly upon odd matters. Vague and rambling observations were made in reply.

There were squints, and leers, and some dull, ox-like stares from those who were too dull or too weary to converse.

Standing tells. Hurstwood became more weary waiting. He thought he should drop soon and shifted restlessly from one foot to the other. At last his turn came. The man ahead had been paid for and gone to the blessed line of success. He was now first, and already the captain was talking for him.

"Twelve cents, gentlemen—twelve cents puts this man to bed. He wouldn't stand here in the cold if he had any place to go."

Hurstwood swallowed something that rose to his throat. Hunger and weakness had made a coward of him.

"Here you are," said a stranger, handing money to the captain.

Now the latter put a kindly hand on the ex-manager's shoulder.

"Line up over there," he said.

Once there, Hurstwood breathed easier. He felt as if the world were not quite so bad with such a good man in it. Others seemed to feel like himself about this.

"Captain's a great feller, ain't he?" said the man ahead—a little, woe-begone, helpless-looking sort of individual, who looked as though he had ever been the sport and care of fortune.

"Yes," said Hurstwood, indifferently.

"Huh! there's a lot back there yet," said a man farther up, leaning out and looking back at the applicants for whom the captain was pleading.

"Yes. Must be over a hundred to-night," said another.

"Look at the guy in the cab," observed a third.

A cab had stopped. Some gentleman in evening dress reached out a bill to the captain, who took it with simple

thanks and turned away to his line. There was a general cran-
ing of necks as the jewel in the white shirt front sparkled and
the cab moved off. Even the crowd gaped in awe.

"That fixes up nine men for the night," said the captain,
counting out as many of the line near him. "Line up over
there. Now, then, there are only seven. I need twelve cents."

Money came slowly. In the course of time the crowd
thinned out to a meagre handful. Fifth Avenue, save for an
occasional cab or foot passenger, was bare. Broadway was
thinly peopled with pedestrians. Only now and then a
stranger passing noticed the small group, handed out a coin,
and went away, unheeding.

The captain remained stolid and determined. He talked on,
very slowly, uttering the fewest words and with a certain assurance, as though he could not fail.

"Come; I can't stay out here all night. These men are getting tired and cold. Some one give me four cents."

There came a time when he said nothing at all. Money was
handed him, and for each twelve cents he singled out a man
and put him in the other line. Then he walked up and down
as before, looking at the ground.

The theatres let out. Fire signs disappeared. A clock struck
eleven. Another half-hour and he was down to the last two
men.

"Come, now," he exclaimed to several curious observers;
"eighteen cents will fix us all up for the night. Eighteen cents.
I have six. Somebody give me the money. Remember, I have
to go over to Brooklyn yet to-night. Before that I have to
take these men down and put them to bed. Eighteen cents."

No one responded. He walked to and fro, looking down
for several minutes, occasionally saying softly: "Eighteen
cents." It seemed as if this paltry sum would delay the desired
culmination longer than all the rest had. Hurstwood, buoyed
up slightly by the long line of which he was a part, refrained
with an effort from groaning, he was so weak.

At last a lady in opera cape and rustling skirts came down
Fifth Avenue, accompanied by her escort. Hurstwood gazed
wearily, reminded by her both of Carrie in her new world
and of the time when he had escorted his own wife in like
manner.

While he was gazing, she turned and, looking at the remarkable company, sent her escort over. He came, holding a bill in his fingers, all elegant and graceful.

"Here you are," he said.

"Thanks," said the captain, turning to the two remaining applicants. "Now we have some for to-morrow night," he added.

Therewith he lined up the last two and proceeded to the head, counting as he went.

"One hundred and thirty-seven," he announced. "Now, boys, line up. Right dress there. We won't be much longer about this. Steady, now."

He placed himself at the head and called out "Forward." Hurstwood moved with the line. Across Fifth Avenue, through Madison Square by the winding paths, east on Twenty-third Street, and down Third Avenue wound the long, serpentine company. Midnight pedestrians and loiterers stopped and stared as the company passed. Chatting policemen, at various corners, stared indifferently or nodded to the leader, whom they had seen before. On Third Avenue they marched, a seemingly weary way, to Eighth Street, where there was a lodging-house, closed, apparently, for the night. They were expected, however.

Outside in the gloom they stood, while the leader parleyed within. Then doors swung open and they were invited in with a "Steady, now."

Some one was at the head showing rooms, so that there was no delay for keys. Toiling up the creaky stairs, Hurstwood looked back and saw the captain, watching; the last one of the line being included in his broad solicitude. Then he gathered his cloak about him and strolled out into the night.

"I can't stand much of this," said Hurstwood, whose legs ached him painfully, as he sat down upon the miserable bunk in the small, lightless chamber allotted to him. "I've got to eat, or I'll die."

Chapter XLVI

STIRRING TROUBLED WATERS

PLAYING IN New York one evening on this her return, Carrie was putting the finishing touches to her toilet before leaving for the night, when a commotion near the stage door caught her ear. It included a familiar voice.

"Never mind, now. I want to see Miss Madenda."

"You'll have to send in your card."

"Oh, come off! Here."

A half-dollar was passed over, and now a knock came at her dressing-room door.

Carrie opened it.

"Well, well!" said Drouet. "I do swear! Why, how are you? I knew that was you the moment I saw you."

Carrie fell back a pace, expecting a most embarrassing conversation.

"Aren't you going to shake hands with me? Well, you're a dandy! That's all right, shake hands."

Carrie put out her hand, smiling, if for nothing more than the man's exuberant good-nature. Though older, he was but slightly changed. The same fine clothes, the same stocky body, the same rosy countenance.

"That fellow at the door there didn't want to let me in, until I paid him. I knew it was you, all right. Say, you've got a great show. You do your part fine. I knew you would. I just happened to be passing to-night and thought I'd drop in for a few minutes. I saw your name on the programme, but I didn't remember it until you came on the stage. Then it struck me all at once. Say, you could have knocked me down with a feather. That's the same name you used out there in Chicago, isn't it?"

"Yes," answered Carrie, mildly, overwhelmed by the man's assurance.

"I knew it was, the moment I saw you. Well, how have you been, anyhow?"

"Oh, very well," said Carrie, lingering in her dressing-room. She was rather dazed by the assault. "How have you been?"

"Me? Oh, fine. I'm here now."

"Is that so?" said Carrie.

"Yes. I've been here for six months. I've got charge of a branch here."

"How nice!"

"Well, when did you go on the stage, anyhow?" inquired Drouet.

"About three years ago," said Carrie.

"You don't say so! Well, sir, this is the first I've heard of it. I knew you would, though. I always said you could act— didn't I?"

Carrie smiled.

"Yes, you did," she said.

"Well, you do look great," he said. "I never saw anybody improve so. You're taller, aren't you?"

"Me? Oh, a little, maybe."

He gazed at her dress, then at her hair, where a becoming hat was set jauntily, then into her eyes, which she took all occasion to avert. Evidently he expected to restore their old friendship at once and without modification.

"Well," he said, seeing her gather up her purse, handkerchief, and the like, preparatory to departing, "I want you to come out to dinner with me; won't you? I've got a friend out here."

"Oh, I can't," said Carrie. "Not to-night. I have an early engagement to-morrow."

"Aw, let the engagement go. Come on. I can get rid of him. I want to have a good talk with you."

"No, no," said Carrie; "I can't. You mustn't ask me any more. I don't care for a late dinner."

"Well, come on and have a talk, then, anyhow."

"Not to-night," she said, shaking her head. "We'll have a talk some other time."

As a result of this, she noticed a shade of thought pass over his face, as if he were beginning to realise that things were changed. Good-nature dictated something better than this for one who had always liked her.

"You come around to the hotel to-morrow," she said, as sort of penance for error. "You can take dinner with me."

"All right," said Drouet, brightening. "Where are you stopping?"

"At the Waldorf," she answered, mentioning the fashionable hostelry then but newly erected.

"What time?"

"Well, come at three," said Carrie, pleasantly.

The next day Drouet called, but it was with no especial delight that Carrie remembered her appointment. However, seeing him, handsome as ever, after his kind, and most genially disposed, her doubts as to whether the dinner would be disagreeable were swept away. He talked as volubly as ever.

"They put on a lot of lugs here, don't they?" was his first remark.

"Yes; they do," said Carrie.

Genial egotist that he was, he went at once into a detailed account of his own career.

"I'm going to have a business of my own pretty soon," he observed in one place. "I can get backing for two hundred thousand dollars."

Carrie listened most good-naturedly.

"Say," he said, suddenly; "where is Hurstwood now?"

Carrie flushed a little.

"He's here in New York, I guess," she said. "I haven't seen him for some time."

Drouet mused for a moment. He had not been sure until now that the ex-manager was not an influential figure in the background. He imagined not; but this assurance relieved him. It must be that Carrie had got rid of him—as well she ought, he thought.

"A man always makes a mistake when he does anything like that," he observed.

"Like what?" said Carrie, unwitting of what was coming.

"Oh, you know," and Drouet waved her intelligence, as it were, with his hand.

"No, I don't," she answered. "What do you mean?"

"Why that affair in Chicago—the time he left."

"I don't know what you are talking about," said Carrie. Could it be he would refer so rudely to Hurstwood's flight with her?

"Oho!" said Drouet, incredulously. "You knew he took ten thousand dollars with him when he left, didn't you?"

"What!" said Carrie. "You don't mean to say he stole money, do you?"

"Why," said Drouet, puzzled at her tone, "you knew that, didn't you?"

"Why, no," said Carrie. "Of course I didn't."

"Well, that's funny," said Drouet. "He did, you know. It was in all the papers."

"How much did you say he took?" said Carrie.

"Ten thousand dollars. I heard he sent most of it back afterwards, though."

Carrie looked vacantly at the richly carpeted floor. A new light was shining upon all the years since her enforced flight. She remembered now a hundred things that indicated as much. She also imagined that he took it on her account. Instead of hatred springing up there was a kind of sorrow generated. Poor fellow! What a thing to have had hanging over his head all the time.

At dinner Drouet, warmed up by eating and drinking and softened in mood, fancied he was winning Carrie to her old-time good-natured regard for him. He began to imagine it would not be so difficult to enter into her life again, high as she was. Ah, what a prize! he thought. How beautiful, how elegant, how famous! In her theatrical and Waldorf setting, Carrie was to him the all-desirable.

"Do you remember how nervous you were that night at the Avery?" he asked.

Carrie smiled to think of it.

"I never saw anybody do better than you did then, Cad," he added ruefully, as he leaned an elbow on the table; "I thought you and I were going to get along fine those days."

"You mustn't talk that way," said Carrie, bringing in the least touch of coldness.

"Won't you let me tell you——"

"No," she answered, rising. "Besides, it's time I was getting ready for the theatre. I'll have to leave you. Come, now."

"Oh, stay a minute," pleaded Drouet. "You've got plenty of time."

"No," said Carrie, gently.

Reluctantly Drouet gave up the bright table and followed. He saw her to the elevator and, standing there, said:

"When do I see you again?"

"Oh, some time, possibly," said Carrie. "I'll be here all summer. Good-night!"

The elevator door was open.

"Good-night!" said Drouet, as she rustled in.

Then he strolled sadly down the hall, all his old longing revived, because she was now so far off. The merry frou-frou of the place spoke all of her. He thought himself hardly dealt with. Carrie, however, had other thoughts.

That night it was that she passed Hurstwood, waiting at the Casino, without observing him.

The next night, walking to the theatre, she encountered him face to face. He was waiting, more gaunt than ever, determined to see her, if he had to send in word. At first she did not recognise the shabby, baggy figure. He frightened her, edging so close, a seemingly hungry stranger.

"Carrie," he half whispered, "can I have a few words with you?"

She turned and recognised him on the instant. If there ever had lurked any feeling in her heart against him, it deserted her now. Still, she remembered what Drouet said about his having stolen the money.

"Why, George," she said; "what's the matter with you?"

"I've been sick," he answered. "I've just got out of the hospital. For God's sake, let me have a little money, will you?"

"Of course," said Carrie, her lip trembling in a strong effort to maintain her composure. "But what's the matter with you, anyhow?"

She was opening her purse, and now pulled out all the bills in it—a five and two twos.

"I've been sick, I told you," he said, peevishly, almost resenting her excessive pity. It came hard to him to receive it from such a source.

"Here," she said. "It's all I have with me."

"All right," he answered, softly. "I'll give it back to you some day."

Carrie looked at him, while pedestrians stared at her. She felt the strain of publicity. So did Hurstwood.

"Why don't you tell me what's the matter with you?" she asked, hardly knowing what to do. "Where are you living?"

"Oh, I've got a room down in the Bowery," he answered. "There's no use trying to tell you here. I'm all right now."

He seemed in a way to resent her kindly inquiries—so much better had fate dealt with her.

"Better go on in," he said. "I'm much obliged, but I won't bother you any more."

She tried to answer, but he turned away and shuffled off toward the east.

For days this apparition was a drag on her soul before it began to wear partially away. Drouet called again, but now he was not even seen by her. His attentions seemed out of place.

"I'm out," was her reply to the boy.

So peculiar, indeed, was her lonely, self-withdrawing temper, that she was becoming an interesting figure in the public eye—she was so quiet and reserved.

Not long after the management decided to transfer the show to London. A second summer season did not seem to promise well here.

"How would you like to try subduing London?" asked her manager, one afternoon.

"It might be just the other way," said Carrie.

"I think we'll go in June," he answered.

In the hurry of departure, Hurstwood was forgotten. Both he and Drouet were left to discover that she was gone. The latter called once, and exclaimed at the news. Then he stood in the lobby, chewing the ends of his moustache. At last he reached a conclusion—the old days had gone for good.

"She isn't so much," he said; but in his heart of hearts he did not believe this.

Hurstwood shifted by curious means through a long summer and fall. A small job as janitor of a dance hall helped him for a month. Begging, sometimes going hungry, sometimes sleeping in the park, carried him over more days. Resorting to those peculiar charities, several of which, in the press of hungry search, he accidentally stumbled upon, did the rest. Toward the dead of winter, Carrie came back, appearing on Broadway in a new play; but he was not aware of it. For weeks he wandered about the city, begging, while the fire sign, announcing her engagement, blazed nightly upon the crowded street of amusements. Drouet saw it, but did not venture in.

About this time Ames returned to New York. He had made a little success in the West, and now opened a laboratory in Wooster Street. Of course, he encountered Carrie through Mrs. Vance; but there was nothing responsive between them. He thought she was still united to Hurstwood, until otherwise informed. Not knowing the facts then, he did not profess to understand, and refrained from comment.

With Mrs. Vance, he saw the new play, and expressed himself accordingly.

"She ought not to be in comedy," he said. "I think she could do better than that."

One afternoon they met at the Vances' accidentally, and began a very friendly conversation. She could hardly tell why the one-time keen interest in him was no longer with her. Unquestionably, it was because at that time he had represented something which she did not have; but this she did not understand. Success had given her the momentary feeling that she was now blessed with much of which he would approve. As a matter of fact, her little newspaper fame was nothing at all to him. He thought she could have done better, by far.

"You didn't go into comedy-drama, after all?" he said, remembering her interest in that form of art.

"No," she answered; "I haven't, so far."

He looked at her in such a peculiar way that she realised she had failed. It moved her to add: "I want to, though."

"I should think you would," he said. "You have the sort of disposition that would do well in comedy-drama."

It surprised her that he should speak of disposition. Was she, then, so clearly in his mind?

"Why?" she asked.

"Well," he said, "I should judge you were rather sympathetic in your nature."

Carrie smiled and coloured slightly. He was so innocently frank with her that she drew nearer in friendship. The old call of the ideal was sounding.

"I don't know," she answered, pleased, nevertheless, beyond all concealment.

"I saw your play," he remarked. "It's very good."

"I'm glad you liked it."

"Very good, indeed," he said, "for a comedy."

This is all that was said at the time, owing to an interruption, but later they met again. He was sitting in a corner after dinner, staring at the floor, when Carrie came up with another of the guests. Hard work had given his face the look of one who is weary. It was not for Carrie to know the thing in it which appealed to her.

"All alone?" she said.

"I was listening to the music."

"I'll be back in a moment," said her companion, who saw nothing in the inventor.

Now he looked up in her face, for she was standing a moment, while he sat.

"Isn't that a pathetic strain?" he inquired, listening.

"Oh, very," she returned, also catching it, now that her attention was called.

"Sit down," he added, offering her the chair beside him.

They listened a few moments in silence, touched by the same feeling, only hers reached her through the heart. Music still charmed her as in the old days.

"I don't know what it is about music," she started to say, moved by the inexplicable longings which surged within her; "but it always makes me feel as if I wanted something—I——"

"Yes," he replied; "I know how you feel."

Suddenly he turned to considering the peculiarity of her disposition, expressing her feelings so frankly.

"You ought not to be melancholy," he said.

He thought a while, and then went off into a seemingly alien observation which, however, accorded with their feelings.

"The world is full of desirable situations, but, unfortunately, we can occupy but one at a time. It doesn't do us any good to wring our hands over the far-off things."

The music ceased and he arose, taking a standing position before her, as if to rest himself.

"Why don't you get into some good, strong comedy-drama?" he said. He was looking directly at her now, studying her face. Her large, sympathetic eyes and pain-touched mouth appealed to him as proofs of his judgment.

"Perhaps I shall," she returned.

"That's your field," he added.

"Do you think so?"

"Yes," he said; "I do. I don't suppose you're aware of it, but there is something about your eyes and mouth which fits you for that sort of work."

Carrie thrilled to be taken so seriously. For the moment, loneliness deserted her. Here was praise which was keen and analytical.

"It's in your eyes and mouth," he went on abstractedly. "I remember thinking, the first time I saw you, that there was something peculiar about your mouth. I thought you were about to cry."

"How odd," said Carrie, warm with delight. This was what her heart craved.

"Then I noticed that that was your natural look, and to-night I saw it again. There's a shadow about your eyes, too, which gives your face much this same character. It's in the depth of them, I think."

Carrie looked straight into his face, wholly aroused.

"You probably are not aware of it," he added.

She looked away, pleased that he should speak thus, longing to be equal to this feeling written upon her countenance. It unlocked the door to a new desire.

She had cause to ponder over this until they met again— several weeks or more. It showed her she was drifting away from the old ideal which had filled her in the dressing-rooms of the Avery stage and thereafter, for a long time. Why had she lost it?

"I know why you should be a success," he said, another time, "if you had a more dramatic part. I've studied it out——"

"What is it?" said Carrie.

"Well," he said, as one pleased with a puzzle, "the expression in your face is one that comes out in different things. You get the same thing in a pathetic song, or any picture which moves you deeply. It's a thing the world likes to see, because it's a natural expression of its longing."

Carrie gazed without exactly getting the import of what he meant.

"The world is always struggling to express itself," he went on. "Most people are not capable of voicing their feelings. They depend upon others. That is what genius is for. One man expresses their desires for them in music; another one in poetry; another one in a play. Sometimes nature does it in a face—it makes the face representative of all desire. That's what has happened in your case."

He looked at her with so much of the import of the thing in his eyes that she caught it. At least, she got the idea that her look was something which represented the world's longing. She took it to heart as a creditable thing, until he added:

"That puts a burden of duty on you. It so happens that you have this thing. It is no credit to you—that is, I mean, you might not have had it. You paid nothing to get it. But now that you have it, you must do something with it."

"What?" asked Carrie.

"I should say, turn to the dramatic field. You have so much sympathy and such a melodious voice. Make them valuable to others. It will make your powers endure."

Carrie did not understand this last. All the rest showed her that her comedy success was little or nothing.

"What do you mean?" she asked.

"Why, just this. You have this quality in your eyes and mouth and in your nature. You can lose it, you know. If you turn away from it and live to satisfy yourself alone, it will go fast enough. The look will leave your eyes. Your mouth will change. Your power to act will disappear. You may think they won't, but they will. Nature takes care of that."

He was so interested in forwarding all good causes that he sometimes became enthusiastic, giving vent to these preachments. Something in Carrie appealed to him. He wanted to stir her up.

"I know," she said, absently, feeling slightly guilty of neglect.

"If I were you," he said, "I'd change."

The effect of this was like roiling helpless waters. Carrie troubled over it in her rocking-chair for days.

"I don't believe I'll stay in comedy so very much longer," she eventually remarked to Lola.

"Oh, why not?" said the latter.

"I think," she said, "I can do better in a serious play."

"What put that idea in your head?"

"Oh, nothing," she answered; "I've always thought so."

Still, she did nothing—grieving. It was a long way to this better thing—or seemed so—and comfort was about her; hence the inactivity and longing.

Chapter XLVII

THE WAY OF THE BEATEN: A HARP IN THE WIND

IN THE CITY, at that time, there were a number of charities similar in nature to that of the captain's, which Hurstwood now patronised in a like unfortunate way. One was a convent mission-house of the Sisters of Mercy in Fifteenth Street—a row of red brick family dwellings, before the door of which hung a plain wooden contribution box, on which was painted the statement that every noon a meal was given free to all those who might apply and ask for aid. This simple announcement was modest in the extreme, covering, as it did, a charity so broad. Institutions and charities are so large and so numerous in New York that such things as this are not often noticed by the more comfortably situated. But to one whose mind is upon the matter, they grow exceedingly under inspection. Unless one were looking up this matter in particular, he could have stood at Sixth Avenue and Fifteenth Street for days around the noon hour and never have noticed that out of the vast crowd that surged along that busy thoroughfare there turned out, every few seconds, some weather-beaten, heavy-footed specimen of humanity, gaunt in countenance and dilapidated in the matter of clothes. The fact is none the less true, however, and the colder the day the more apparent it became. Space and a lack of culinary room in the mission-house, compelled an arrangement which permitted of only twenty-five or thirty eating at one time, so that a line had to be formed outside and an orderly entrance effected. This caused a daily spectacle which, however, had become so common by repetition during a number of years that now nothing was thought of it. The men waited patiently, like cattle, in the coldest weather—waited for several hours before they could be admitted. No questions were asked and no service rendered. They ate and went away again, some of them returning regularly day after day the winter through.

A big, motherly looking woman invariably stood guard at the door during the entire operation and counted the admissible number. The men moved up in solemn order. There was no haste and no eagerness displayed. It was almost a dumb procession. In the bitterest weather this line was to be found here. Under an icy wind there was a prodigious slapping of hands and a dancing of feet. Fingers and the features of the face looked as if severely nipped by the cold. A study of these men in broad light proved them to be nearly all of a type. They belonged to the class that sit on the park benches during the endurable days and sleep upon them during the summer nights. They frequent the Bowery and those down-at-the-heels East Side streets where poor clothes and shrunken features are not singled out as curious. They are the men who are in the lodging-house sitting-rooms during bleak and bitter weather and who swarm about the cheaper shelters which only open at six in a number of the lower East Side streets. Miserable food, ill-timed and greedily eaten, had played havoc with bone and muscle. They were all pale, flabby, sunken-eyed, hollow-chested, with eyes that glinted and shone and lips that were a sickly red by contrast. Their hair was but half attended to, their ears anæmic in hue, and their shoes broken in leather and run down at heel and toe. They were of the class which simply floats and drifts, every wave of people washing up one, as breakers do driftwood upon a stormy shore.

For nearly a quarter of a century, in another section of the city, Fleischmann, the baker, had given a loaf of bread to any one who would come for it to the side door of his restaurant at the corner of Broadway and Tenth Street, at midnight. Every night during twenty years about three hundred men had formed in line and at the appointed time marched past the doorway, picked their loaf from a great box placed just outside, and vanished again into the night. From the beginning to the present time there had been little change in the character or number of these men. There were two or three figures that had grown familiar to those who had seen this little procession pass year after year. Two of them had missed scarcely a night in fifteen years. There were about forty, more or less, regular callers. The remainder of the line was formed of strangers. In times of panic and unusual hardships there were seldom more than three hundred. In times of prosperity, when little is heard of the unemployed, there were seldom less. The same number, winter and summer, in storm or calm, in good times and bad, held this melancholy midnight rendezvous at Fleischmann's bread box.

At both of these two charities, during the severe winter which was now on, Hurstwood was a frequent visitor. On one occasion it was peculiarly cold, and finding no comfort in begging about the streets, he waited until noon before seeking this free offering to the poor. Already, at eleven o'clock of this morning, several such as he had shambled forward out of Sixth Avenue, their thin clothes flapping and fluttering in the wind. They leaned against the iron railing which protects the walls of the Ninth Regiment Armory, which fronts upon that section of Fifteenth Street, having come early in order to be first in. Having an hour to wait, they at first lingered at a respectful distance; but others coming up, they moved closer in order to protect their right of precedence. To this collection Hurstwood came up from the west out of Seventh Avenue and stopped close to the door, nearer than all the others. Those who had been waiting before him, but farther away, now drew near, and by a certain stolidity of demeanour, no words being spoken, indicated that they were first.

Seeing the opposition to his action, he looked sullenly along the line, then moved out, taking his place at the foot. When order had been restored, the animal feeling of opposition relaxed.

"Must be pretty near noon," ventured one.

"It is," said another. "I've been waiting nearly an hour."

"Gee, but it's cold!"

They peered eagerly at the door, where all must enter. A grocery man drove up and carried in several baskets of eatables. This started some words upon grocery men and the cost of food in general.

"I see meat's gone up," said one.

"If there wuz war, it would help this country a lot."

The line was growing rapidly. Already there were fifty or more, and those at the head, by their demeanour, evidently congratulated themselves upon not having so long to wait as those at the foot. There was much jerking of heads, and looking down the line.

"It don't matter how near you get to the front, so long as you're in the first twenty-five," commented one of the first twenty-five. "You all go in together."

"Humph!" ejaculated Hurstwood, who had been so sturdily displaced.

"This here Single Tax is the thing," said another. "There ain't going to be no order till it comes."

For the most part there was silence; gaunt men shuffling, glancing, and beating their arms.

At last the door opened and the motherly-looking sister appeared. She only looked an order. Slowly the line moved up and, one by one, passed in, until twenty-five were counted. Then she interposed a stout arm, and the line halted, with six men on the steps. Of these the ex-manager was one. Waiting thus, some talked, some ejaculated concerning the misery of it; some brooded, as did Hurstwood. At last he was admitted, and, having eaten, came away, almost angered because of his pains in getting it.

At eleven o'clock of another evening, perhaps two weeks later, he was at the midnight offering of a loaf—waiting patiently. It had been an unfortunate day with him, but now he took his fate with a touch of philosophy. If he could secure no supper, or was hungry late in the evening, here was a place he could come. A few minutes before twelve, a great box of bread was pushed out, and exactly on the hour a portly, round-faced German took position by it, calling "Ready." The whole line at once moved forward, each taking his loaf in turn and going his separate way. On this occasion, the ex-manager ate his as he went, plodding the dark streets in silence to his bed.

By January he had about concluded that the game was up with him. Life had always seemed a precious thing, but now constant want and weakened vitality had made the charms of earth rather dull and inconspicuous. Several times, when fortune pressed most harshly, he thought he would end his troubles; but with a change of weather, or the arrival of a quarter or a dime, his mood would change, and he would wait. Each day he would find some old paper lying about and look into it, to see if there was any trace of Carrie, but all summer and fall he had looked in vain. Then he noticed that his eyes were beginning to hurt him, and this ailment rapidly increased until, in the dark chambers of the lodgings he frequented, he did not attempt to read. Bad and irregular eating was weakening every function of his body. The one recourse left him was to doze when a place offered and he could get the money to occupy it.

He was beginning to find, in his wretched clothing and meagre state of body, that people took him for a chronic type of bum and beggar. Police hustled him along, restaurant and lodging-house keepers turned him out promptly the moment he had his due; pedestrians waved him off. He found it more and more difficult to get anything from anybody.

At last he admitted to himself that the game was up. It was after a long series of appeals to pedestrians, in which he had been refused and refused—every one hastening from contact.

"Give me a little something, will you, mister?" he said to the last one. "For God's sake, do; I'm starving."

"Aw, get out," said the man, who happened to be a common type himself. "You're no good. I'll give you nawthin'."

Hurstwood put his hands, red from cold, down in his pockets. Tears came into his eyes.

"That's right," he said; "I'm no good now. I was all right. I had money. I'm going to quit this," and, with death in his heart, he started down toward the Bowery. People had turned on the gas before and died; why shouldn't he? He remembered a lodging-house where there were little, close rooms, with gas-jets in them, almost pre-arranged, he thought, for what he wanted to do, which rented for fifteen cents. Then he remembered that he had no fifteen cents.

On the way he met a comfortable-looking gentleman, coming, clean-shaven, out of a fine barber shop.

"Would you mind giving me a little something?" he asked this man boldly.

The gentleman looked him over and fished for a dime. Nothing but quarters were in his pocket.

"Here," he said, handing him one, to be rid of him. "Be off, now."

Hurstwood moved on, wondering. The sight of the large, bright coin pleased him a little. He remembered that he was hungry and that he could get a bed for ten cents. With this, the idea of death passed, for the time being, out of his mind. It was only when he could get nothing but insults that death seemed worth while.

One day, in the middle of the winter, the sharpest spell of the season set in. It broke grey and cold in the first day, and on the second snowed. Poor luck pursuing him, he had secured but ten cents by nightfall, and this he had spent for food. At evening he found himself at the Boulevard and Sixty-seventh Street, where he finally turned his face Bowery-ward. Especially fatigued because of the wandering propensity which had seized him in the morning, he now half dragged his wet feet, shuffling the soles upon the sidewalk. An old, thin coat was turned up about his red ears—his cracked derby hat was pulled down until it turned them outward. His hands were in his pockets.

"I'll just go down Broadway," he said to himself.

When he reached Forty-second Street, the fire signs were already blazing brightly. Crowds were hastening to dine. Through bright windows, at every corner, might be seen gay companies in luxuriant restaurants. There were coaches and crowded cable cars.

In his weary and hungry state, he should never have come here. The contrast was too sharp. Even he was recalled keenly to better things.

"What's the use?" he thought. "It's all up with me. I'll quit this."

People turned to look after him, so uncouth was his shambling figure. Several officers followed him with their eyes, to see that he did not beg of anybody.

Once he paused in an aimless, incoherent sort of way and looked through the windows of an imposing restaurant, before which blazed a fire sign, and through the large, plate windows of which could be seen the red and gold decorations, the palms, the white napery, and shining glassware, and, above all, the comfortable crowd. Weak as his mind had become, his hunger was sharp enough to show the importance of this. He stopped stock still, his frayed trousers soaking in the slush, and peered foolishly in.

"Eat," he mumbled. "That's right, eat. Nobody else wants any."

Then his voice dropped even lower, and his mind half lost the fancy it had.

"It's mighty cold," he said. "Awful cold."

At Broadway and Thirty-ninth Street was blazing, in incandescent fire, Carrie's name. "Carrie Madenda," it read, "and the Casino Company." All the wet, snowy sidewalk was bright with this radiated fire. It was so bright that it attracted Hurstwood's gaze. He looked up, and then at a large, gilt-framed poster-board, on which was a fine lithograph of Carrie, life-size.

Hurstwood gazed at it a moment, snuffling and hunching one shoulder, as if something were scratching him. He was so run down, however, that his mind was not exactly clear.

"That's you," he said at last, addressing her. "Wasn't good enough for you, was I? Huh!"

He lingered, trying to think logically. This was no longer possible with him.

"She's got it," he said, incoherently, thinking of money. "Let her give me some."

He started around to the side door. Then he forgot what he was going for and paused, pushing his hands deeper to warm the wrists. Suddenly it returned. The stage door! That was it.

He approached that entrance and went in.

"Well?" said the attendant, staring at him. Seeing him pause, he went over and shoved him. "Get out of here," he said.

"I want to see Miss Madenda," he said.

"You do, eh?" the other said, almost tickled at the spectacle. "Get out of here," and he shoved him again. Hurstwood had no strength to resist.

"I want to see Miss Madenda," he tried to explain, even as he was being hustled away. "I'm all right. I——"

The man gave him a last push and closed the door. As he did so, Hurstwood slipped and fell in the snow. It hurt him, and some vague sense of shame returned. He began to cry and swear foolishly.

"God damned dog!" he said. "Damned old cur," wiping the slush from his worthless coat. "I—I hired such people as you once."

Now a fierce feeling against Carrie welled up—just one fierce, angry thought before the whole thing slipped out of his mind.

"She owes me something to eat," he said. "She owes it to me."

Hopelessly he turned back into Broadway again and slopped onward and away, begging, crying, losing track of his thoughts, one after another, as a mind decayed and disjointed is wont to do.

It was truly a wintry evening, a few days later, when his one distinct mental decision was reached. Already, at four o'clock, the sombre hue of night was thickening the air. A heavy snow was falling—a fine picking, whipping snow, borne forward by a swift wind in long, thin lines. The streets were bedded with it—six inches of cold, soft carpet, churned to a dirty brown by the crush of teams and the feet of men. Along Broadway men picked their way in ulsters and umbrellas. Along the Bowery, men slouched through it with collars and hats pulled over their ears. In the former thoroughfare business men and travellers were making for comfortable hotels. In the latter, crowds on cold errands shifted past dingy stores, in the deep recesses of which lights were already gleaming. There were early lights in the cable cars, whose usual clatter was reduced by the mantle about the wheels. The whole city was muffled by this fast-thickening mantle.

In her comfortable chambers at the Waldorf, Carrie was reading at this time "Père Goriot," which Ames had recommended to her. It was so strong, and Ames's mere recommendation had so aroused her interest, that she caught nearly the full sympathetic significance of it. For the first time, it was being borne in upon her how silly and worthless had been her earlier reading, as a whole. Becoming wearied, however, she yawned and came to the window, looking out upon the old winding procession of carriages rolling up Fifth Avenue.

"Isn't it bad?" she observed to Lola.

"Terrible!" said that little lady, joining her. "I hope it snows enough to go sleigh riding."

"Oh, dear," said Carrie, with whom the sufferings of Father Goriot were still keen. "That's all you think of. Aren't you sorry for the people who haven't anything to-night?"

"Of course I am," said Lola; "but what can I do? I haven't anything."

Carrie smiled.

"You wouldn't care, if you had," she returned.

"I would, too," said Lola. "But people never gave me anything when I was hard up."

"Isn't it just awful?" said Carrie, studying the winter's storm.

"Look at that man over there," laughed Lola, who had caught sight of some one falling down. "How sheepish men look when they fall, don't they?"

"We'll have to take a coach to-night," answered Carrie, absently.

In the lobby of the Imperial, Mr. Charles Drouet was just arriving, shaking the snow from a very handsome ulster. Bad weather had driven him home early and stirred his desire for those pleasures which shut out the snow and gloom of life. A good dinner, the company of a young woman, and an evening at the theatre were the chief things for him.

"Why, hello, Harry!" he said, addressing a lounger in one of the comfortable lobby chairs. "How are you?"

"Oh, about six and six," said the other.

"Rotten weather, isn't it?"

"Well, I should say," said the other. "I've been just sitting here thinking where I'd go to-night."

"Come along with me," said Drouet. "I can introduce you to something dead swell."

"Who is it?" said the other.

"Oh, a couple of girls over here in Fortieth Street. We could have a dandy time. I was just looking for you."

"Supposing we get 'em and take 'em out to dinner?"

"Sure," said Drouet. "Wait'll I go upstairs and change my clothes."

"Well, I'll be in the barber shop," said the other. "I want to get a shave."

"All right," said Drouet, creaking off in his good shoes toward the elevator. The old butterfly was as light on the wing as ever.

*   *   *

On an incoming vestibuled Pullman, speeding at forty miles and hour through the snow of the evening, were three others, all related.

"First call for dinner in the dining-car," a Pullman servitor was announcing, as he hastened through the aisle in snow-white apron and jacket.

"I don't believe I want to play any more," said the youngest, a black-haired beauty, turned supercilious by fortune, as she pushed a euchre hand away from her.

"Shall we go into dinner?" inquired her husband, who was all that fine raiment can make.

"Oh, not yet," she answered. "I don't want to play any more, though."

"Jessica," said her mother, who was also a study in what good clothing can do for age, "push that pin down in your tie—it's coming up."

Jessica obeyed, incidentally touching at her lovely hair and looking at a little jewel-faced watch. Her husband studied her, for beauty, even cold, is fascinating from one point of view.

"Well, we won't have much more of this weather," he said. "It only takes two weeks to get to Rome."

Mrs. Hurstwood nestled comfortably in her corner and smiled. It was so nice to be the mother-in-law of a rich young man—one whose financial state had borne her personal inspection.

"Do you suppose the boat will sail promptly?" asked Jessica, "if it keeps up like this?"

"Oh, yes," answered her husband. "This won't make any difference."

Passing down the aisle came a very fair-haired banker's son, also of Chicago, who had long eyed this supercilious beauty. Even now he did not hesitate to glance at her, and she was conscious of it. With a specially conjured show of indifference, she turned her pretty face wholly away. It was not wifely modesty at all. By so much was her pride satisfied.

At this moment Hurstwood stood before a dirty four-story building in a side street quite near the Bowery, whose one-time coat of buff had been changed by soot and rain. He mingled with a crowd of men—a crowd which had been, and was still, gathering by degrees.

It began with the approach of two or three, who hung about the closed wooden doors and beat their feet to keep them warm. They had on faded derby hats with dents in them. Their misfit coats were heavy with melted snow and turned up at the collars. Their trousers were mere bags, frayed at the bottom and wobbling over big, soppy shoes, torn at the sides and worn almost to shreds. They made no effort to go in, but shifted ruefully about, digging their hands deep in their pockets and leering at the crowd and the increasing lamps. With the minutes, increased the number. There were old men with grizzled beards and sunken eyes, men who were comparatively young but shrunken by diseases, men who were middle-aged. None were fat. There was a face in the thick of the collection which was as white as drained veal. There was another red as brick. Some came with thin, rounded shoulders, others with wooden legs, still others with frames so lean that clothes only flapped about them. There were great ears, swollen noses, thick lips, and, above all, red, blood-shot eyes. Not a normal, healthy face in the whole mass; not a straight figure; not a straightforward, steady glance.

In the drive of the wind and sleet they pushed in on one another. There were wrists, unprotected by coat or pocket, which were red with cold. There were ears, half covered by every conceivable semblance of a hat, which still looked stiff and bitten. In the snow they shifted, now one foot, now another, almost rocking in unison.

With the growth of the crowd about the door came a murmur. It was not conversation, but a running comment directed at any one in general. It contained oaths and slang phrases.

"By damn, I wish they'd hurry up."

"Look at the copper watchin'."

"Maybe it ain't winter, nuther!"

"I wisht I was in Sing Sing."

Now a sharper lash of wind cut down and they huddled closer. It was an edging, shifting, pushing throng. There was no anger, no pleading, no threatening words. It was all sullen endurance, unlightened by either wit or good fellowship.

A carriage went jingling by with some reclining figure in it. One of the men nearest the door saw it.

"Look at the bloke ridin'."

"He ain't so cold."

"Eh, eh, eh!" yelled another, the carriage having long since passed out of hearing.

Little by little the night crept on. Along the walk a crowd turned out on its way home. Men and shop-girls went by with quick steps. The cross-town cars began to be crowded. The gas lamps were blazing, and every window bloomed ruddy with a steady flame. Still the crowd hung about the door, unwavering.

"Ain't they ever goin' to open up?" queried a hoarse voice, suggestively.

This seemed to renew the general interest in the closed door, and many gazed in that direction. They looked at it as dumb brutes look, as dogs paw and whine and study the knob. They shifted and blinked and muttered, now a curse, now a comment. Still they waited and still the snow whirled and cut them with biting flakes. On the old hats and peaked shoulders it was piling. It gathered in little heaps and curves and no one brushed it off. In the centre of the crowd the warmth and steam melted it, and water trickled off hat rims and down noses, which the owners could not reach to scratch. On the outer rim the piles remained unmelted. Hurstwood, who could not get in the centre, stood with head lowered to the weather and bent his form.

A light appeared through the transom overhead. It sent a thrill of possibility through the watchers. There was a murmur of recognition. At last the bars grated inside and the crowd pricked up its ears. Footsteps shuffled within and it murmured again. Some one called: "Slow up there, now," and then the door opened. It was push and jam for a minute, with grim, beast silence to prove its quality, and then it melted inward, like logs floating, and disappeared. There were wet hats and wet shoulders, a cold, shrunken, disgruntled mass, pouring in between bleak walls. It was just six o'clock and there was supper in every hurrying pedestrian's face. And yet no supper was provided here—nothing but beds.

Hurstwood laid down his fifteen cents and crept off with weary steps to his allotted room. It was a dingy affair—wooden, dusty, hard. A small gas-jet furnished sufficient light for so rueful a corner.

"Hm!" he said, clearing his throat and locking the door.

Now he began leisurely to take off his clothes, but stopped first with his coat, and tucked it along the crack under the door. His vest he arranged in the same place. His old wet, cracked hat he laid softly upon the table. Then he pulled off his shoes and lay down.

It seemed as if he thought a while, for now he arose and turned the gas out, standing calmly in the blackness, hidden from view. After a few moments, in which he reviewed nothing, but merely hesitated, he turned the gas on again, but applied no match. Even then he stood there, hidden wholly in that kindness which is night, while the uprising fumes filled the room. When the odour reached his nostrils, he quit his attitude and fumbled for the bed.

"What's the use?" he said, weakly, as he stretched himself to rest.

And now Carrie had attained that which in the beginning seemed life's object, or, at least, such fraction of it as human beings ever attain of their original desires. She could look about on her gowns and carriage, her furniture and bank account. Friends there were, as the world takes it—those who would bow and smile in acknowledgment of her success. For these she had once craved. Applause there was, and publicity—once far off, essential things, but now grown trivial and indifferent. Beauty also—her type of loveliness—and yet she was lonely. In her rocking-chair she sat, when not otherwise engaged—singing and dreaming.

Thus in life there is ever the intellectual and the emotional nature—the mind that reasons, and the mind that feels. Of one come the men of action—generals and statesmen; of the other, the poets and dreamers—artists all.

As harps in the wind, the latter respond to every breath of fancy, voicing in their moods all the ebb and flow of the ideal.

Man has not yet comprehended the dreamer any more than he has the ideal. For him the laws and morals of the world are unduly severe. Ever hearkening to the sound of beauty, straining for the flash of its distant wings, he watches to follow, wearying his feet in travelling. So watched Carrie, so followed, rocking and singing.

And it must be remembered that reason had little part in this. Chicago dawning, she saw the city offering more of loveliness than she had ever known, and instinctively, by force of her moods alone, clung to it. In fine raiment and elegant surroundings, men seemed to be contented. Hence, she drew near these things. Chicago, New York; Drouet, Hurstwood; the world of fashion and the world of stage—these were but incidents. Not them, but that which they represented, she longed for. Time proved the representation false.

Oh, the tangle of human life! How dimly as yet we see. Here was Carrie, in the beginning poor, unsophisticated, emotional; responding with desire to everything most lovely in life, yet finding herself turned as by a wall. Laws to say: "Be allured, if you will, by everything lovely, but draw not nigh unless by righteousness." Convention to say: "You shall not better your situation save by honest labour." If honest labour be unremunerative and difficult to endure; if it be the long, long road which never reaches beauty, but wearies the feet and the heart; if the drag to follow beauty be such that one abandons the admired way, taking rather the despised path leading to her dreams quickly, who shall cast the first stone? Not evil, but longing for that which is better, more often directs the steps of the erring. Not evil, but goodness more often allures the feeling mind unused to reason.

Amid the tinsel and shine of her state walked Carrie, unhappy. As when Drouet took her, she had thought: "Now am I lifted into that which is best"; as when Hurstwood seemingly offered her the better way: "Now am I happy." But since the world goes its way past all who will not partake of its folly, she now found herself alone. Her purse was open to him whose need was greatest. In her walks on Broadway, she no longer thought of the elegance of the creatures who passed her. Had they more of that peace and beauty which glimmered afar off, then were they to be envied.

Drouet abandoned his claim and was seen no more. Of Hurstwood's death she was not even aware. A slow, black boat setting out from the pier at Twenty-seventh Street upon its weekly errand bore, with many others, his nameless body to the Potter's Field.

Thus passed all that was of interest concerning these twain in their relation to her. Their influence upon her life is explicable alone by the nature of her longings. Time was when both represented for her all that was most potent in earthly success. They were the personal representatives of a state most blessed to attain—the titled ambassadors of comfort and peace, aglow with their credentials. It is but natural that when the world which they represented no longer allured her, its ambassadors should be discredited. Even had Hurstwood returned in his original beauty and glory, he could not now have allured her. She had learned that in his world, as in her own present state, was not happiness.

Sitting alone, she was now an illustration of the devious ways by which one who feels, rather than reasons, may be led in the pursuit of beauty. Though often disillusioned, she was still waiting for that halcyon day when she should be led forth among dreams become real. Ames had pointed out a farther step, but on and on beyond that, if accomplished, would lie others for her. It was forever to be the pursuit of that radiance of delight which tints the distant hilltops of the world.

Oh, Carrie, Carrie! Oh, blind strivings of the human heart! Onward, onward, it saith, and where beauty leads, there it follows. Whether it be the tinkle of a lone sheep bell o'er some quiet landscape, or the glimmer of beauty in sylvan places, or the show of soul in some passing eye, the heart knows and makes answer, following. It is when the feet weary and hope seems vain that the heartaches and the longings arise. Know, then, that for you is neither surfeit nor content. In your rocking-chair, by your window dreaming, shall you long, alone. In your rocking-chair, by your window, shall you dream such happiness as you may never feel.

THE END

JENNIE GERHARDT

Chapter I

ONE MORNING, in the fall of 1880, a middle-aged woman, accompanied by a young girl of eighteen, presented herself at the clerk's desk of the principal hotel in Columbus, Ohio, and made inquiry as to whether there was anything about the place that she could do. She was of a helpless, fleshy build, with a frank, open countenance and an innocent, diffident manner. Her eyes were large and patient, and in them dwelt such a shadow of distress as only those who have looked sympathetically into the countenances of the distraught and helpless poor know anything about. Any one could see where the daughter behind her got the timidity and shamefacedness which now caused her to stand back and look indifferently away. She was a product of the fancy, the feeling, the innate affection of the untutored but poetic mind of her mother combined with the gravity and poise which were characteristic of her father. Poverty was driving them. Together they presented so appealing a picture of honest necessity that even the clerk was affected.

"What is it you would like to do?" he said.

"Maybe you have some cleaning or scrubbing," she replied, timidly. "I could wash the floors."

The daughter, hearing the statement, turned uneasily, not because it irritated her to work, but because she hated people to guess at the poverty that made it necessary. The clerk, manlike, was affected by the evidence of beauty in distress. The innocent helplessness of the daughter made their lot seem hard indeed.

"Wait a moment," he said; and, stepping into a back office, he called the head housekeeper.

There was work to be done. The main staircase and parlor hall were unswept because of the absence of the regular scrubwoman.

"Is that her daughter with her?" asked the housekeeper, who could see them from where she was standing.

"Yes, I believe so."

"She might come this afternoon if she wants to. The girl helps her, I suppose?"

"You go see the housekeeper," said the clerk, pleasantly, as he came back to the desk. "Right through there"—pointing to a near-by door. "She'll arrange with you about it."

A succession of misfortunes, of which this little scene might have been called the tragic culmination, had taken place in the life and family of William Gerhardt, a glass-blower by trade. Having suffered the reverses so common in the lower walks of life, this man was forced to see his wife, his six children, and himself dependent for the necessaries of life upon whatever windfall of fortune the morning of each recurring day might bring. He himself was sick in bed. His oldest boy, Sebastian, or "Bass," as his associates transformed it, worked as an apprentice to a local freight-car builder, but received only four dollars a week. Genevieve, the oldest of the girls, was past eighteen, but had not as yet been trained to any special work. The other children, George, aged fourteen; Martha, twelve; William ten, and Veronica, eight, were too young to do anything, and only made the problem of existence the more complicated. Their one mainstay was the home, which, barring a six-hundred-dollar mortgage, the father owned. He had borrowed this money at a time when, having saved enough to buy the house, he desired to add three rooms and a porch, and so make it large enough for them to live in. A few years were still to run on the mortgage, but times had been so bad that he had been forced to use up not only the little he had saved to pay off the principal, but the annual interest also. Gerhardt was helpless, and the consciousness of his precarious situation—the doctor's bill, the interest due upon the mortgage, together with the sums owed butcher and baker, who, through knowing him to be absolutely honest, had trusted him until they could trust no longer—all these perplexities weighed upon his mind and racked him so nervously as to delay his recovery.

Mrs. Gerhardt was no weakling. For a time she took in washing, what little she could get, devoting the intermediate hours to dressing the children, cooking, seeing that they got off to school, mending their clothes, waiting on her husband, and occasionally weeping. Not infrequently she went personally to some new grocer, each time farther and farther away, and, starting an account with a little cash, would receive credit until other grocers warned the philanthropist of his folly. Corn was cheap. Sometimes she would make a kettle of lye hominy, and this would last, with scarcely anything else, for an entire week. Corn-meal also, when made into mush, was better than nothing, and this, with a little milk, made almost a feast. Potatoes fried was the nearest they ever came to luxurious food, and coffee was an infrequent treat. Coal was got by picking it up in buckets and baskets along the maze of tracks in the nearby railroad yard. Wood, by similar journeys to surrounding lumber-yards. Thus they lived from day to day, each hour hoping that the father would get well and that the glass-works would soon start up. But as the winter approached Gerhardt began to feel desperate.

"I must get out of this now pretty soon," was the sturdy German's regular comment, and his anxiety found but weak expression in the modest quality of his voice.

To add to all this trouble little Veronica took the measles, and, for a few days, it was thought that she would die. The mother neglected everything else to hover over her and pray for the best. Doctor Ellwanger came every day, out of purely human sympathy, and gravely examined the child. The Lutheran minister, Pastor Wundt, called to offer the consolation of the Church. Both of these men brought an atmosphere of grim ecclesiasticism into the house. They were the black-garbed, sanctimonious emissaries of superior forces. Mrs. Gerhardt felt as if she were going to lose her child, and watched sorrowfully by the cot-side. After three days the worst was over, but there was no bread in the house. Sebastian's wages had been spent for medicine. Only coal was free for the picking, and several times the children had been scared from the railroad yards. Mrs. Gerhardt thought of all the places to which she might apply, and despairingly hit upon the hotel. Now, by a miracle, she had her chance.

"How much do you charge?" the housekeeper asked her.

Mrs. Gerhardt had not thought this would be left to her, but need emboldened her.

"Would a dollar a day be too much?"

"No," said the housekeeper; "there is only about three days' work to do every week. If you would come every afternoon you could do it."

"Very well," said the applicant. "Shall we start to-day?"

"Yes; if you'll come with me now I'll show you where the cleaning things are."

The hotel, into which they were thus summarily introduced, was a rather remarkable specimen for the time and place. Columbus, being the State capital, and having a population of fifty thousand and a fair passenger traffic, was a good field for the hotel business, and the opportunity had been improved; so at least the Columbus people proudly thought. The structure, five stories in height, and of imposing proportions, stood at one corner of the central public square, where were the Capitol building and principal stores. The lobby was large and had been recently redecorated. Both floor and wainscot were of white marble, kept shiny by frequent polishing. There was an imposing staircase with hand-rails of walnut and toe-strips of brass. An inviting corner was devoted to a news and cigar-stand. Where the staircase curved upward the clerk's desk and offices had been located, all done in hardwood and ornamented by novel gas-fixtures. One could see through a door at one end of the lobby to the barber-shop, with its chairs and array of shaving-mugs. Outside were usually two or three buses, arriving or departing, in accordance with the movement of the trains.

To this caravanserai came the best of the political and social patronage of the State. Several Governors had made it their permanent abiding place during their terms of office. The two United States Senators, whenever business called them to Columbus, invariably maintained parlor chambers at the hotel. One of them, Senator Brander, was looked upon by the proprietor as more or less of a permanent guest, because he was not only a resident of the city, but an otherwise homeless bachelor. Other and more transient guests included Congressmen, State legislators and lobbyists, merchants, professional men, and, after them, the whole raft of indescribables who, coming and going, make up the glow and stir of this kaleidoscopic world.

Mother and daughter, suddenly flung into this realm of superior brightness, felt immeasurably overawed. They went about too timid to touch anything for fear of giving offense. The great red-carpeted hallway, which they were set to sweep, had for them all the magnificence of a palace; they kept their eyes down and spoke in their lowest tones. When it came to scrubbing the steps and polishing the brass-work of the splendid stairs both needed to steel themselves, the mother against her timidity, the daughter against the shame at so public an exposure. Wide beneath lay the imposing lobby, and men, lounging, smoking, passing constantly in and out, could see them both.

"Isn't it fine?" whispered Genevieve, and started nervously at the sound of her own voice.

"Yes," returned her mother, who, upon her knees, was wringing out her cloth with earnest but clumsy hands.

"It must cost a good deal to live here, don't you think?"

"Yes," said her mother. "Don't forget to rub into these little corners. Look here what you've left."

Jennie, mortified by this correction, fell earnestly to her task, and polished vigorously, without again daring to lift her eyes.

With painstaking diligence they worked downward until about five o'clock; it was dark outside, and all the lobby was brightly lighted. Now they were very near the bottom of the stairway.

Through the big swinging doors there entered from the chilly world without a tall, distinguished, middle-aged gentleman, whose silk hat and loose military cape-coat marked him at once, among the crowd of general idlers, as some one of importance. His face was of a dark and solemn cast, but broad and sympathetic in its lines, and his bright eyes were heavily shaded with thick, bushy, black eyebrows. Passing to the desk he picked up the key that had already been laid out for him, and coming to the staircase, started up.

The middle-aged woman, scrubbing at his feet, he acknowledged not only by walking around her, but by graciously waving his hand, as much as to say, "Don't move for me."

The daughter, however, caught his eye by standing up, her troubled glance showing that she feared she was in his way.

He bowed and smiled pleasantly.

"You shouldn't have troubled yourself," he said.

Jennie only smiled.

When he had reached the upper landing an impulsive sidewise glance assured him, more clearly than before, of her uncommonly prepossessing appearance. He noted the high, white forehead, with its smoothly parted and plaited hair. The eyes he saw were blue and the complexion fair. He had even time to admire the mouth and the full cheeks—above all, the well-rounded, graceful form, full of youth, health, and that hopeful expectancy which to the middle-aged is so suggestive of all that is worth begging of Providence. Without another look he went dignifiedly upon his way, but the impression of her charming personality went with him. This was the Hon. George Sylvester Brander, junior Senator.

"Wasn't that a fine-looking man who went up just now?" observed Jennie a few moments later.

"Yes, he was," said her mother.

"He had a gold-headed cane."

"You mustn't stare at people when they pass," cautioned her mother, wisely. "It isn't nice."

"I didn't stare at him," returned Jennie, innocently. "He bowed to me."

"Well, don't you pay any attention to anybody," said her mother. "They may not like it."

Jennie fell to her task in silence, but the glamor of the great world was having its effect upon her senses. She could not help giving ear to the sounds, the brightness, the buzz of conversation and laughter surrounding her. In one section of the parlor floor was the dining-room, and from the clink of dishes one could tell that supper was being prepared. In another was the parlor proper, and there some one came to play on the piano. That feeling of rest and relaxation which comes before the evening meal pervaded the place. It touched the heart of the innocent working-girl with hope, for hers were the years, and poverty could not as yet fill her young mind with cares. She rubbed diligently always, and sometimes forgot the troubled mother at her side, whose kindly eyes were becoming invested with crows' feet, and whose lips half repeated the hundred cares of the day. She could only think that all of this was very fascinating, and wish that a portion of it might come to her.

At half-past five the housekeeper, remembering them, came and told them that they might go. The fully finished stairway was relinquished by both with a sigh of relief, and, after putting their implements away, they hastened homeward, the mother, at least, pleased to think that at last she had something to do.

As they passed several fine houses Jennie was again touched by that half-defined emotion which the unwonted novelty of the hotel life had engendered in her consciousness.

"Isn't it fine to be rich?" she said.

"Yes," answered her mother, who was thinking of the suffering Veronica.

"Did you see what a big dining-room they had there?"

"Yes."

They went on past the low cottages and among the dead leaves of the year.

"I wish we were rich," murmured Jennie, half to herself.

"I don't know just what to do," confided her mother with a long-drawn sigh. "I don't believe there's a thing to eat in the house."

"Let's stop and see Mr. Bauman again," exclaimed Jennie, her natural sympathies restored by the hopeless note in her mother's voice.

"Do you think he would trust us any more?"

"Let's tell him where we're working. I will."

"Well," said her mother, wearily.

Into the small, dimly lighted grocery store, which was two blocks from their house, they ventured nervously. Mrs. Gerhardt was about to begin, but Jennie spoke first.

"Will you let us have some bread to-night, and a little bacon? We're working now at the Columbus House, and we'll be sure to pay you Saturday."

"Yes," added Mrs. Gerhardt, "I have something to do."

Bauman, who had long supplied them before illness and trouble began, knew that they told the truth.

"How long have you been working there?" he asked.

"Just this afternoon."

"You know, Mrs. Gerhardt," he said, "how it is with me. I don't want to refuse you. Mr. Gerhardt is good for it, but I am poor, too. Times are hard," he explained further, "I have my family to keep."

"Yes, I know," said Mrs. Gerhardt, weakly.

Her old shoddy shawl hid her rough hands, red from the day's work, but they were working nervously. Jennie stood by in strained silence.

"Well," concluded Mr. Bauman, "I guess it's all right this time. Do what you can for me Saturday."

He wrapped up the bread and bacon, and, handing Jennie the parcel, he added, with a touch of cynicism:

"When you get money again I guess you'll go and trade somewhere else."

"No," returned Mrs. Gerhardt; "you know better than that." But she was too nervous to parley long.

They went out into the shadowy street, and on past the low cottages to their own home.

"I wonder," said the mother, wearily, when they neared the door, "if they've got any coal?"

"Don't worry," said Jennie. "If they haven't I'll go."

"A man run us away," was almost the first greeting that the perturbed George offered when the mother made her inquiry about the coal. "I got a little, though," he added. "I threw it off a car."

Mrs. Gerhardt only smiled, but Jennie laughed.

"How is Veronica?" she inquired.

"She seems to be sleeping," said the father. "I gave her medicine again at five."

While the scanty meal was being prepared the mother went to the sick child's bedside, taking up another long night's vigil quite as a matter of course.

While the supper was being eaten Sebastian offered a suggestion, and his larger experience in social and commercial matters made his proposition worth considering. Though only a car-builder's apprentice, without any education except such as pertained to Lutheran doctrine, to which he objected very strongly, he was imbued with American color and energy. His transformed name of Bass suited him exactly. Tall, athletic, and well-featured for his age, he was a typical stripling of the town. Already he had formulated a philosophy of life. To succeed one must do something—one must associate, or at least seem to associate, with those who were foremost in the world of appearances.

For this reason the young boy loved to hang about the

Columbus House. It seemed to him that this hotel was the center and circumference of all that was worth while in the social sense. He would go down-town evenings, when he first secured money enough to buy a decent suit of clothes, and stand around the hotel entrance with his friends, kicking his heels, smoking a two-for-five-cent cigar, preening himself on his stylish appearance, and looking after the girls. Others were there with him—town dandies and nobodies, young men who came there to get shaved or to drink a glass of whisky. And all of these he admired and sought to emulate. Clothes were the main touchstone. If men wore nice clothes and had rings and pins, whatever they did seemed appropriate. He wanted to be like them and to act like them, and so his experience of the more pointless forms of life rapidly broadened.

"Why don't you get some of those hotel fellows to give you their laundry?" he asked of Jennie after she had related the afternoon's experiences. "It would be better than scrubbing the stairs."

"How do you get it?" she replied.

"Why, ask the clerk, of course."

This plan struck Jennie as very much worth while.

"Don't you ever speak to me if you meet me around there," he cautioned her a little later, privately. "Don't you let on that you know me."

"Why?" she asked, innocently.

"Well, you know why," he answered, having indicated before that when they looked so poor he did not want to be disgraced by having to own them as relatives. "Just you go on by. Do you hear?"

"All right," she returned, meekly, for although this youth was not much over a year her senior, his superior will dominated.

The next day on their way to the hotel she spoke of it to her mother.

"Bass said we might get some of the laundry of the men at the hotel to do."

Mrs. Gerhardt, whose mind had been straining all night at the problem of adding something to the three dollars which her six afternoons would bring her, approved of the idea.

"So we might," she said. "I'll ask that clerk."

When they reached the hotel, however, no immediate opportunity presented itself. They worked on until late in the afternoon. Then, as fortune would have it, the housekeeper sent them in to scrub up the floor behind the clerk's desk. That important individual felt very kindly toward mother and daughter. He liked the former's sweetly troubled countenance and the latter's pretty face. So he listened graciously when Mrs. Gerhardt ventured meekly to put the question which she had been revolving in her mind all the afternoon.

"Is there any gentleman here," she said, "who would give me his washing to do? I'd be so very much obliged for it."

The clerk looked at her, and again recognized that absolute want was written all over her anxious face.

"Let's see," he answered, thinking of Senator Brander and Marshall Hopkins. Both were charitable men, who would be more than glad to aid a poor woman. "You go up and see Senator Brander," he continued. "He's in twenty-two. Here," he added, writing out the number, "you go up and tell him I sent you."

Mrs. Gerhardt took the card with a tremor of gratefulness. Her eyes looked the words she could not say.

"That's all right," said the clerk, observing her emotion. "You go right up. You'll find him in his room now."

With the greatest diffidence Mrs. Gerhardt knocked at number twenty-two. Jennie stood silently at her side.

After a moment the door was opened, and in the full radiance of the bright room stood the Senator. Attired in a handsome smoking-coat, he looked younger than at their first meeting.

"Well, madam," he said, recognizing the couple, and particularly the daughter, "what can I do for you?"

Very much abashed, the mother hesitated in her reply.

"We would like to know if you have any washing you could let us have to do?"

"Washing?" he repeated after her, in a voice which had a peculiarly resonant quality. "Washing? Come right in. Let me see."

He stepped aside with much grace, waved them in and closed the door. "Let me see," he repeated, opening and closing drawer after drawer of the massive black-walnut bureau. Jennie studied the room with interest. Such an array of nicknacks and pretty things on mantel and dressing-case she had never seen before. The Senator's easy chair, with a green-shaded lamp beside it, the rich heavy carpet and the fine rugs upon the floor—what comfort, what luxury!

"Sit down; take those two chairs there," said the Senator, graciously, disappearing into a closet.

Still overawed, mother and daughter thought it more polite to decline, but now the Senator had completed his researches and he reiterated his invitation. Very uncomfortably they yielded and took chairs.

"Is this your daughter?" he continued, with a smile at Jennie.

"Yes, sir," said the mother; "she's my oldest girl."

"Is your husband alive?"

"What is his name?"

"Where does he live?"

To all of these questions Mrs. Gerhardt very humbly answered.

"How many children have you?" he went on.

"Six," said Mrs. Gerhardt.

"Well," he returned, "that's quite a family. You've certainly done your duty to the nation."

"Yes, sir," returned Mrs. Gerhardt, who was touched by his genial and interesting manner.

"And you say this is your oldest daughter?"

"Yes, sir."

"What does your husband do?"

"He's a glass-blower. But he's sick now."

During the colloquy Jennie's large blue eyes were wide with interest. Whenever he looked at her she turned upon him such a frank, unsophisticated gaze, and smiled in such a vague, sweet way, that he could not keep his eyes off of her for more than a minute of the time.

"Well," he continued, sympathetically, "that is too bad! I have some washing here—not very much—but you are welcome to it. Next week there may be more."

He went about now, stuffing articles of apparel into a blue cotton bag with a pretty design on the side.

"Do you want these any certain day?" questioned Mrs. Gerhardt.

"No," he said, reflectively; "any day next week will do."

She thanked him with a simple phrase, and started to go.

"Let me see," he said, stepping ahead of them and opening the door, "you may bring them back Monday."

"Yes, sir," said Mrs. Gerhardt. "Thank you."

They went out and the Senator returned to his reading, but it was with a peculiarly disturbed mind.

"Too bad," he said, closing his volume. "There's something very pathetic about those people." Jennie's spirit of wonder and appreciation was abroad in the room.

Mrs. Gerhardt and Jennie made their way anew through the shadowy streets. They felt immeasurably encouraged by this fortunate venture.

"Didn't he have a fine room?" whispered Jennie.

"Yes," answered the mother; "he's a great man."

"He's a senator, isn't he?" continued the daughter.

"Yes."

"It must be nice to be famous," said the girl, softly.

Chapter II

THE SPIRIT of Jennie—who shall express it? This daughter of poverty, who was now to fetch and carry the laundry of this distinguished citizen of Columbus, was a creature of a mellowness of temperament which words can but vaguely suggest. There are natures born to the inheritance of flesh that come without understanding, and that go again without seeming to have wondered why. Life, so long as they endure it, is a true wonderland, a thing of infinite beauty, which could they but wander into it wonderingly, would be heaven enough. Opening their eyes, they see a conformable and perfect world. Trees, flowers, the world of sound and the world of color. These are the valued inheritance of their state. If no one said to them "Mine," they would wander radiantly forth, singing the song which all the earth may some day hope to hear. It is the song of goodness.

Caged in the world of the material, however, such a nature is almost invariably an anomaly. That other world of flesh into which has been woven pride and greed looks askance at the idealist, the dreamer. If one says it is sweet to look at the clouds, the answer is a warning against idleness. If one seeks to give ear to the winds, it shall be well with his soul, but they will seize upon his possessions. If all the world of the so-called inanimate delay one, calling with tenderness in sounds that seem to be too perfect to be less than understanding, it shall be ill with the body. The hands of the actual are forever reaching toward such as these—forever seizing greedily upon them. It is of such that the bond servants are made.

In the world of the actual, Jennie was such a spirit. From her earliest youth goodness and mercy had molded her every impulse. Did Sebastian fall and injure himself, it was she who struggled with straining anxiety, carried him safely to his mother. Did George complain that he was hungry, she gave him all of her bread. Many were the hours in which she had rocked her younger brothers and sisters to sleep, singing whole-heartedly betimes and dreaming far dreams. Since her earliest walking period she had been as the right hand of her mother. What scrubbing, baking, errand-running, and nursing

there had been to do she did. No one had ever heard her
rudely complain, though she often thought of the hardness of
her lot. She knew that there were other girls whose lives were
infinitely freer and fuller, but, it never occurred to her to be
meanly envious; her heart might be lonely, but her lips continued to sing. When the days were fair she looked out of her
kitchen window and longed to go where the meadows were.
Nature's fine curves and shadows touched her as a song itself.
There were times when she had gone with George and the
others, leading them away to where a patch of hickory-trees
flourished, because there were open fields, with shade for
comfort and a brook of living water. No artist in the formulating of conceptions, her soul still responded to these things,
and every sound and every sigh were welcome to her because
of their beauty.

When the soft, low call of the wood-doves, those spirits of
the summer, came out of the distance, she would incline her
head and listen, the whole spiritual quality of it dropping like
silver bubbles into her own great heart.

Where the sunlight was warm and the shadows flecked
with its splendid radiance she delighted to wonder at the pattern of it, to walk where it was most golden, and follow with
instinctive appreciation the holy corridors of the trees.

Color was not lost upon her. That wonderful radiance
which fills the western sky at evening touched and unbur-
dened her heart.

"I wonder," she said once with girlish simplicity, "how it
would feel to float away off there among those clouds."

She had discovered a natural swing of a wild grape-vine,
and was sitting in it with Martha and George.

"Oh, wouldn't it be nice if you had a boat up there," said
George.

She was looking with uplifted face at a far-off cloud, a red
island in a sea of silver.

"Just supposing," she said, "people could live on an island
like that."

Her soul was already up there, and its elysian paths knew
the lightness of her feet.

"There goes a bee," said George, noting a bumbler wing-
ing by.

"Yes," she said, dreamily, "it's going home."

"Does everything have a home?" asked Martha.

"Nearly everything," she answered.

"Do the birds go home?" questioned George.

"Yes," she said, deeply feeling the poetry of it herself, "the birds go home."

"Do the bees go home?" urged Martha.

"Yes, the bees go home."

"Do the dogs go home?" said George, who saw one traveling lonesomely along the nearby road.

"Why, of course," she said, "you know that dogs go home."

"Do the gnats?" he persisted, seeing one of those curious spirals of minute insects turning energetically in the waning light.

"Yes," she said, half believing her remark. "Listen!"

"Oho," exclaimed George, incredulously, "I wonder what kind of houses they live in."

"Listen!" she gently persisted, putting out her hand to still him.

It was that halcyon hour when the Angelus falls like a benediction upon the waning day. Far off the notes were sounding gently, and nature, now that she listened, seemed to have paused also. A scarlet-breasted robin was hopping in short spaces upon the grass before her. A humming bee hummed, a cow-bell tinkled, while some suspicious cracklings told of a secretly reconnoitering squirrel. Keeping her pretty hand weighed in the air, she listened until the long, soft notes spread and faded and her heart could hold no more. Then she arose.

"Oh," she said, clenching her fingers in an agony of poetic feeling. There were crystal tears overflowing in her eyes. The wondrous sea of feeling in her had stormed its banks. Of such was the spirit of Jennie.

Chapter III

THE JUNIOR Senator, George Sylvester Brander, was a man of peculiar mold. In him there were joined, to a remarkable degree, the wisdom of the opportunist and the sympathetic nature of the true representative of the people. Born a native of southern Ohio, he had been raised and educated there, if one might except the two years in which he had studied law at Columbia University. He knew common and criminal law, perhaps, as well as any citizen of his State, but he had never practised with that assiduity which makes for pre-eminent success at the bar. He had made money, and had had splendid opportunities to make a great deal more if he had been willing to stultify his conscience, but that he had never been able to do. And yet his integrity had not been at all times proof against the claims of friendship. Only in the last presidential election he had thrown his support to a man for Governor who, he well knew, had no claim which a strictly honorable conscience could have recognized.

In the same way, he had been guilty of some very questionable, and one or two actually unsavory, appointments. Whenever his conscience pricked him too keenly he would endeavor to hearten himself with his pet phrase, "All in a lifetime." Thinking over things quite alone in his easy-chair, he would sometimes rise up with these words on his lips, and smile sheepishly as he did so. Conscience was not by any means dead in him. His sympathies, if anything, were keener than ever.

This man, three times Congressman from the district of which Columbus was a part, and twice United States Senator, had never married. In his youth he had had a serious love affair, but there was nothing discreditable to him in the fact that it came to nothing. The lady found it inconvenient to wait for him. He was too long in earning a competence upon which they might subsist.

Tall, straight-shouldered, neither lean nor stout, he was to-day an imposing figure. Having received his hard knocks and endured his losses, there was that about him which touched and awakened the sympathies of the imaginative. People

thought him naturally agreeable, and his senatorial peers
looked upon him as not any too heavy mentally, but personally a fine man.

His presence in Columbus at this particular time was due
to the fact that his political fences needed careful repairing.
The general election had weakened his party in the State Legislature. There were enough votes to re-elect him, but it
would require the most careful political manipulation to hold
them together. Other men were ambitious. There were a half-
dozen available candidates, any one of whom would have rejoiced to step into his shoes. He realized the exigencies of the
occasion. They could not well beat him, he thought; but even
if this should happen, surely the President could be induced
to give him a ministry abroad.

Yes, he might be called a successful man, but for all that
Senator Brander felt that he had missed something. He had
wanted to do so many things. Here he was, fifty-two years of
age, clean, honorable, highly distinguished, as the world takes
it, but single. He could not help looking about him now and
then and speculating upon the fact that he had no one to care
for him. His chamber seemed strangely hollow at times—his
own personality exceedingly disagreeable.

"Fifty!" he often thought to himself. "Alone—absolutely
alone."

Sitting in his chamber that Saturday afternoon, a rap at his
door aroused him. He had been speculating upon the futility
of his political energy in the light of the impermanence of life
and fame.

"What a great fight we make to sustain ourselves!" he
thought. "How little difference it will make to me a few years
hence!"

He arose, and opening wide his door, perceived Jennie. She
had come, as she had suggested to her mother, at this time,
instead of on Monday, in order to give a more favorable
impression of promptness.

"Come right in," said the Senator; and, as on the first occasion, he graciously made way for her.

Jennie passed in, momentarily expecting some compliment
upon the promptitude with which the washing had been
done. The Senator never noticed it at all.

"Well, my young lady," he said when she had put the bundle down, "how do you find yourself this evening?"

"Very well," replied Jennie. "We thought we'd better bring your clothes to-day instead of Monday."

"Oh, that would not have made any difference," replied Brander lightly. "Just leave them on the chair."

Jennie, without considering the fact that she had been offered no payment for the service rendered, was about to retire, had not the Senator detained her.

"How is your mother?" he asked pleasantly.

"She's very well," said Jennie simply.

"And your little sister? Is she any better?"

"The doctor thinks so," she replied.

"Sit down," he continued graciously. "I want to talk to you."

Moving to a nearby chair, the young girl seated herself.

"Hem!" he went on, clearing his throat lightly. "What seems to be the matter with her?"

"She has the measles," returned Jennie. "We thought once that she was going to die."

Brander studied her face as she said this, and he thought he saw something exceedingly pathetic there. The girl's poor clothes and her wondering admiration for his exalted station in life affected him. It made him feel almost ashamed of the comfort and luxury that surrounded him. How high up he was in the world, indeed!

"I am glad she is better now," he said kindly. "How old is your father?"

"Fifty-seven."

"And is he any better?"

"Oh yes, sir; he's around now, although he can't go out just yet."

"I believe your mother said he was a glass-blower by trade?"

"Yes, sir."

Brander well knew the depressed local conditions in this branch of manufacture. It had been part of the political issue in the last campaign. They must be in a bad way truly.

"Do all of the children go to school?" he inquired.

"Why yes, sir," returned Jennie, stammering. She was too

shamefaced to own that one of the children had been obliged to leave school for the lack of shoes. The utterance of the falsehood troubled her.

He reflected awhile; then realizing that he had no good excuse for further detaining her, he arose and came over to her. From his pocket he took a thin layer of bills, and removing one, handed it to her.

"You take that," he said, "and tell your mother that I said she should use it for whatever she wants."

Jennie accepted the money with mingled feelings; it did not occur to her to look and see how much it was. The great man was so near her, the wonderful chamber in which he dwelt so impressive, that she scarcely realized what she was doing.

"Thank you," she said. "Is there any day you want your washing called for?" she added.

"Oh yes," he answered; "Monday—Monday evenings."

She went away, and in a half reverie he closed the door behind her. The interest that he felt in these people was unusual. Poverty and beauty certainly made up an affecting combination. He sat down in his chair and gave himself over to the pleasant speculations which her coming had aroused. Why should he not help them?

"I'll find out where they live," he finally resolved.

In the days that followed Jennie regularly came for the clothes. Senator Brander found himself more and more interested in her, and in time he managed to remove from her mind that timidity and fear which had made her feel uncomfortable in his presence. One thing which helped toward this was his calling her by her first name. This began with her third visit, and thereafter he used it with almost unconscious frequency.

It could scarcely be said that he did this in a fatherly spirit, for he had little of that attitude toward any one. He felt exceedingly young as he talked to this girl, and he often wondered whether it were not possible for her to perceive and appreciate him on his youthful side.

As for Jennie, she was immensely taken with the comfort and luxury surrounding this man, and subconsciously with the man himself, the most attractive she had ever known. Everything he had was fine, everything he did was gentle, distinguished, and considerate. From some far source, perhaps some old German ancestors, she had inherited an understanding and appreciation of all this. Life ought to be lived as he lived it; the privilege of being generous particularly appealed to her.

Part of her attitude was due to that of her mother, in whose mind sympathy was always a more potent factor than reason. For instance, when she brought to her the ten dollars Mrs. Gerhardt was transported with joy.

"Oh," said Jennie, "I didn't know until I got outside that it was so much. He said I should give it to you."

Mrs. Gerhardt took it, and holding it loosely in her folded hands, saw distinctly before her the tall Senator with his fine manners.

"What a fine man he is!" she said. "He has a good heart."

Frequently throughout the evening and the next day Mrs. Gerhardt commented upon this wonderful treasure-trove, repeating again and again how good he must be or how large must be his heart. When it came to washing his clothes she almost rubbed them to pieces, feeling that whatever she did she could scarcely do enough. Gerhardt was not to know. He had such stern views about accepting money without earning it that even in their distress, she would have experienced some difficulty in getting him to take it. Consequently she said nothing, but used it to buy bread and meat, and going as it did such a little way, the sudden windfall was never noticed.

Jennie, from now on, reflected this attitude toward the Senator, and, feeling so grateful toward him, she began to talk more freely. They came to be on such good terms that he gave her a little leather picture-case from his dresser which he had observed her admiring. Every time she came he found excuse to detain her, and soon discovered that, for all her soft girlishness, there lay deep-seated in her a conscious deprecation of poverty and a shame of having to own any need. He honestly admired her for this, and, seeing that her clothes were poor and her shoes worn, he began to wonder how he could help her without offending.

Not infrequently he thought to follow her some evening, and see for himself what the condition of the family might be. He was a United States Senator, however. The neighbor-

hood they lived in must be very poor. He stopped to consider, and for the time the counsels of prudence prevailed.
Consequently the contemplated visit was put off.

Early in December Senator Brander returned to Washington for three weeks, and both Mrs. Gerhardt and Jennie were
surprised to learn one day that he had gone. Never had he
given them less than two dollars a week for his washing, and
several times it had been five. He had not realized, perhaps,
what a breach his absence would make in their finances. But
there was nothing to do about it; they managed to pinch
along. Gerhardt, now better, searched for work at the various
mills, and finding nothing, procured a saw-buck and saw, and
going from door to door, sought for the privilege of sawing
wood. There was not a great deal of this to do, but he managed, by the most earnest labor to earn two, and sometimes
three, dollars a week. This added to what his wife earned and
what Sebastian gave was enough to keep bread in their
mouths, but scarcely more.

It was at the opening of the joyous Christmas-time that the
bitterness of their poverty affected them most. The Germans
love to make a great display at Christmas. It is the one season
of the year when the fullness of their large family affection
manifests itself. Warm in the appreciation of the joys of childhood, they love to see the little ones enjoy their toys and
games. Father Gerhardt at his saw-buck during the weeks before Christmas thought of this very often. What would little
Veronica not deserve after her long illness! How he would
have liked to give each of the children a stout pair of shoes,
the boys a warm cap, the girls a pretty hood. Toys and games
and candy they always had had before. He hated to think of
the snow-covered Christmas morning and no table richly
piled with what their young hearts would most desire.

As for Mrs. Gerhardt, one could better imagine than describe her feelings. She felt so keenly about it that she could
hardly bring herself to speak of the dreaded hour to her husband. She had managed to lay aside three dollars in the hope
of getting enough to buy a ton of coal, and so put an end to
poor George's daily pilgrimage to the coal yard, but now as
the Christmas week drew near she decided to use it for gifts.
Father Gerhardt was also secreting two dollars without the

knowledge of his wife, thinking that on Christmas Eve he could produce it at a critical moment, and so relieve her maternal anxiety.

When the actual time arrived, however, there was very little to be said for the comfort that they got out of the occasion. The whole city was rife with Christmas atmosphere. Grocery stores and meat markets were strung with holly. The toy shops and candy stores were radiant with fine displays of everything that a self-respecting Santa Claus should have about him. Both parents and children observed it all—the former with serious thoughts of need and anxiety, the latter with wild fancy and only partially suppressed longings.

Frequently had Gerhardt said in their presence:

"Kriss Kringle is very poor this year. He hasn't so very much to give."

But no child, however poverty-stricken, could be made to believe this. Every time after so saying he looked into their eyes, but in spite of the warning, expectation flamed in them undiminished.

Christmas coming on Tuesday, the Monday before there was no school. Before going to the hotel Mrs. Gerhardt had cautioned George that he must bring enough coal from the yards to last over Christmas day. The latter went at once with his two younger sisters, but there being a dearth of good picking, it took them a long time to fill their baskets, and by night they had gathered only a scanty supply.

"Did you go for the coal?" asked Mrs. Gerhardt the first thing when she returned from the hotel that evening.

"Yes," said George.

"Did you get enough for to-morrow?"

"Yes," he replied, "I guess so."

"Well, now, I'll go and look," she replied. Taking the lamp, they went out into the woodshed where the coal was deposited.

"Oh, my!" she exclaimed when she saw it; "why, that isn't near enough. You must go right off and get some more."

"Oh," said George, pouting his lips, "I don't want to go. Let Bass go."

Bass, who had returned promptly at a quarter past six, was

already busy in the back bedroom washing and dressing pre-paratory to going down-town.

"No," said Mrs. Gerhardt. "Bass has worked hard all day. You must go."

"I don't want to," pouted George.

"All right," said Mrs. Gerhardt, "maybe to-morrow you'll be without a fire, and then what?"

They went back to the house, but George's conscience was too troubled to allow him to consider the case as closed.

"Bass, you come, too," he called to his elder brother when he was inside.

"Go where?" said Bass.

"To get some coal."

"No," said the former, "I guess not. What do you take me for?"

"Well, then, I'll not," said George, with an obstinate jerk of his head.

"Why didn't you get it up this afternoon?" questioned his brother sharply; "you've had all day to do it."

"Aw, I did try," said George. "We couldn't find enough. I can't get any when there ain't any, can I?"

"I guess you didn't try very hard," said the dandy.

"What's the matter now?" asked Jennie, who, coming in after having stopped at the grocer's for her mother, saw George with a solemn pout on his face.

"Oh, Bass won't go with me to get any coal!"

"Didn't you get any this afternoon?"

"Yes," said George, "but ma says I didn't get enough."

"I'll go with you," said his sister. "Bass, will you come along?"

"No," said the young man, indifferently, "I won't." He was adjusting his necktie and felt irritated.

"There ain't any," said George, "unless we get it off the cars. There wasn't any cars where I was."

"There are, too," exclaimed Bass.

"There ain't," said George.

"Oh, don't quarrel," said Jennie. "Get the baskets and let's go right now before it gets too late."

The other children, who had a fondness for their big sis-ter, got out the implements of supply—Veronica a basket,

Martha and William buckets, and George, a big clothes-basket, which he and Jennie were to fill and carry between them. Bass, moved by his sister's willingness and the little regard he still maintained for her, now made a suggestion.

"I'll tell you what you do, Jen," he said. "You go over there with the kids to Eighth Street and wait around those cars. I'll be along in a minute. When I come by don't any of you pretend to know me. Just you say, 'Mister, won't you please throw us some coal down?' and then I'll get up on the cars and pitch off enough to fill the baskets. D'ye understand?"

"All right," said Jennie, very much pleased.

Out into the snowy night they went, and made their way to the railroad tracks. At the intersection of the street and the broad railroad yard were many heavily laden cars of bituminous coal newly backed in. All of the children gathered within the shadow of one. While they were standing there, waiting the arrival of their brother, the Washington Special arrived, a long, fine train with several of the new style drawing-room cars, the big plate-glass windows shining and the passengers looking out from the depths of their comfortable chairs. The children instinctively drew back as it thundered past.

"Oh, wasn't it long?" said George.

"Wouldn't I like to be a brakeman, though," sighed William.

Jennie, alone, kept silent, but to her particularly the suggestion of travel and comfort had appealed. How beautiful life must be for the rich!

Sebastian now appeared in the distance, a mannish spring in his stride, and with every evidence that he took himself seriously. He was of that peculiar stubbornness and determination that had the children failed to carry out his plan of procedure he would have gone deliberately by and refused to help them at all.

Martha, however, took the situation as it needed to be taken, and piped out childishly, "Mister, won't you please throw us down some coal?"

Sebastian stopped abruptly, and looking sharply at them as though he were really a stranger, exclaimed, "Why, certainly," and proceeded to climb up on the car, from whence he cast down with remarkable celerity more than enough chunks to fill their baskets. Then as though not caring to linger any longer amid such plebeian company, he hastened across the network of tracks and was lost to view.

On their way home they encountered another gentleman, this time a real one, with high hat and distinguished cape coat, whom Jennie immediately recognized. This was the honorable Senator himself, newly returned from Washington, and anticipating a very unprofitable Christmas. He had arrived upon the express which had enlisted the attention of the children, and was carrying his light grip for the pleasure of it to the hotel. As he passed he thought that he recognized Jennie.

"Is that you, Jennie?" he said, and paused to be more certain.

The latter, who had discovered him even more quickly than he had her, exclaimed, "Oh, there is Mr. Brander!" Then, dropping her end of the basket, with a caution to the children to take it right home, she hurried away in the opposite direction.

The Senator followed, vainly calling three or four times "Jennie! Jennie!" Losing hope of overtaking her, and suddenly recognizing, and thereupon respecting, her simple, girlish shame, he stopped, and turning back, decided to follow the children. Again he felt that same sensation which he seemed always to get from this girl—the far cry between her estate and his. It was something to be a Senator to-night, here where these children were picking coal. What could the joyous holiday of the morrow hold for them? He tramped along sympathetically, an honest lightness coming into his step, and soon he saw them enter the gateway of the low cottage. Crossing the street, he stood in the weak shade of the snowladen trees. The light was burning with a yellow glow in a rear window. All about was the white snow. In the woodshed he could hear the voices of the children, and once he thought he detected the form of Mrs. Gerhardt. After a time another form came shadow-like through the side gate. He knew who it was. It touched him to the quick, and he bit his lip sharply to suppress any further show of emotion. Then he turned vigorously on his heel and walked away.

The chief grocery of the city was conducted by one

Manning, a stanch adherent of Brander, and one who felt honored by the Senator's acquaintance. To him at his busy desk came the Senator this same night.

"Manning," he said, "could I get you to undertake a little work for me this evening?"

"Why, certainly, Senator, certainly," said the grocery-man. "When did you get back? Glad to see you. Certainly."

"I want you to get everything together that would make a nice Christmas for a family of eight—father and mother and six children—Christmas tree, groceries, toys—you know what I mean."

"Certainly, certainly, Senator."

"Never mind the cost now. Send plenty of everything. I'll give you the address," and he picked up a note-book to write it.

"Why, I'll be delighted, Senator," went on Mr. Manning, rather affected himself. "I'll be delighted. You always were generous."

"Here you are, Manning," said the Senator, grimly, from the mere necessity of preserving his senatorial dignity. "Send everything at once, and the bill to me."

"I'll be delighted," was all the astonished and approving grocery-man could say.

The Senator passed out, but remembering the old people, visited a clothier and shoe man, and, finding that he could only guess at what sizes might be required, ordered the several articles with the privilege of exchange. When his labors were over, he returned to his room.

"Carrying coal," he thought, over and over. "Really, it was very thoughtless in me. I mustn't forget them any more."

Chapter IV

THE DESIRE to flee which Jennie experienced upon seeing the Senator again was attributable to what she considered the disgrace of her position. She was ashamed to think that he, who thought so well of her, should discover her doing so common a thing. Girl-like, she was inclined to imagine that his interest in her depended upon something else than her mere personality.

When she reached home Mrs. Gerhardt had heard of her flight from the other children.

"What was the matter with you, anyhow?" asked George, when she came in.

"Oh, nothing," she answered, but immediately turned to her mother and said, "Mr. Brander came by and saw us."

"Oh, did he?" softly exclaimed her mother. "He's back then. What made you run, though, you foolish girl?"

"Well, I didn't want him to see me."

"Well, maybe he didn't know you, anyhow," she said, with a certain sympathy for her daughter's predicament.

"Oh yes, he did, too," whispered Jennie. "He called after me three or four times."

Mrs. Gerhardt shook her head.

"What is it?" said Gerhardt, who had been hearing the conversation from the adjoining room, and now came out.

"Oh, nothing," said the mother, who hated to explain the significance which the Senator's personality had come to have in their lives. "A man frightened them when they were bringing the coal."

The arrival of the Christmas presents later in the evening threw the household into an uproar of excitement. Neither Gerhardt nor the mother could believe their eyes when a grocery wagon halted in front of their cottage and a lusty clerk began to carry in the gifts. After failing to persuade the clerk that he had made a mistake, the large assortment of good things was looked over with very human glee.

"Just you never mind," was the clerk's authoritative words. "I know what I'm about. Gerhardt, isn't it? Well, you're the people."

Mrs. Gerhardt moved about, rubbing her hands in her excitement, and giving vent to an occasional "Well, isn't that nice now!"

Gerhardt himself was melted at the thought of the generosity of the unknown benefactor, and was inclined to lay it all to the goodness of a great local mill owner, who knew him and wished him well. Mrs. Gerhardt tearfully suspected the source, but said nothing. Jennie knew, by instinct, the author of it all.

The afternoon of the day after Christmas Brander encountered the mother in the hotel, Jennie having been left at home to look after the house.

"How do you do, Mrs. Gerhardt," he exclaimed genially extending his hand. "How did you enjoy your Christmas?"

Poor Mrs. Gerhardt took it nervously; her eyes filled rapidly with tears.

"There, there," he said, patting her on the shoulder. "Don't cry. You mustn't forget to get my laundry to-day."

"Oh no, sir," she returned, and would have said more had he not walked away.

From this on, Gerhardt heard continually of the fine Senator at the hotel, how pleasant he was, and how much he paid for his washing. With the simplicity of a German workingman, he was easily persuaded that Mr. Brander must be a very great and a very good man.

Jennie, whose feelings needed no encouragement in this direction, was more than ever prejudiced in his favor.

There was developing in her that perfection of womanhood, the full mold of form, which could not help but attract any man. Already she was well built, and tall for a girl. Had she been dressed in the trailing skirts of a woman of fashion she would have made a fitting companion for a man the height of the Senator. Her eyes were wondrously clear and bright, her skin fair, and her teeth white and even. She was clever, too, in a sensible way, and by no means deficient in observation. All that she lacked was training and the assurance of which the knowledge of utter dependency despoils one. But the carrying of washing and the compulsion to acknowledge almost anything as a favor put her at a disadvantage.

Nowadays when she came to the hotel upon her semi-weekly errand Senator Brander took her presence with easy grace, and to this she responded. He often gave her little presents for herself, or for her brothers and sisters, and he talked to her so unaffectedly that finally the overawing sense of the great difference between them was brushed away, and she looked upon him more as a generous friend than as a distinguished Senator. He asked her once how she would like to go to a seminary, thinking all the while how attractive she would be when she came out. Finally, one evening, he called her to his side.

"Come over here, Jennie," he said, "and stand by me."

She came, and, moved by a sudden impulse, he took her hand.

"Well, Jennie," he said, studying her face in a quizzical, interrogative way, "what do you think of me, anyhow?"

"Oh," she answered, looking consciously away, "I don't know. What makes you ask me that?"

"Oh yes, you do," he returned. "You have some opinion of me. Tell me now, what is it?"

"No, I haven't," she said, innocently.

"Oh yes, you have," he went on, pleasantly, interested by her transparent evasiveness. "You must think something of me. Now, what is it?"

"Do you mean do I like you?" she asked, frankly, looking down at the big mop of black hair well streaked with gray which hung about his forehead, and gave an almost lionine cast to his fine face.

"Well, yes," he said, with a sense of disappointment. She was barren of the art of the coquette.

"Why, of course I like you," she replied, prettily.

"Haven't you ever thought anything else about me?" he went on.

"I think you're very kind," she went on, even more bashfully; she realized now that he was still holding her hand.

"Is that all?" he asked.

"Well," she said, with fluttering eyelids, "isn't that enough?"

He looked at her, and the playful, companionable directness of her answering gaze thrilled him through and through.

He studied her face in silence while she turned and twisted, feeling, but scarcely understanding, the deep import of his scrutiny.

"Well," he said at last, "I think you're a fine girl. Don't you think I'm a pretty nice man?"

"Yes," said Jennie, promptly.

He leaned back in his chair and laughed at the unconscious drollery of her reply. She looked at him curiously, and smiled.

"What made you laugh?" she inquired.

"Oh, your answer," he returned. "I really ought not to laugh, though. You don't appreciate me in the least. I don't believe you like me at all."

"But I do, though," she replied, earnestly. "I think you're so good." Her eyes showed very plainly that she felt what she was saying.

"Well," he said, drawing her gently down to him; then, at the same instant, he pressed his lips to her cheek.

"Oh!" she cried, straightening up, at once startled and frightened.

It was a new note in their relationship. The senatorial quality vanished in an instant. She recognized in him something that she had not felt before. He seemed younger, too. She was a woman to him, and he was playing the part of a lover. She hesitated, but not knowing just what to do, did nothing at all.

"Well," he said, "did I frighten you?"

She looked at him, but moved by her underlying respect for this great man, she said, with a smile, "Yes, you did."

"I did it because I like you so much."

She meditated upon this a moment, and then said, "I think I'd better be going."

"Now then," he pleaded, "are you going to run away because of that?"

"No," she said, moved by a curious feeling of ingratitude; "but I ought to be going. They'll be wondering where I am."

"You're sure you're not angry about it?"

"No," she replied, and with more of a womanly air than she had ever shown before. It was a novel experience to be in so authoritative a position. It was so remarkable that it was somewhat confusing to both of them.

"You're my girl, anyhow," the Senator said, rising. "I'm going to take care of you in the future."

Jennie heard this, and it pleased her. He was so well fitted, she thought, to do wondrous things; he was nothing less than a veritable magician. She looked about her, and the thought of coming into such a life and such an atmosphere was heavenly. Not that she fully understood his meaning, however. He meant to be good and generous, and to give her fine things. Naturally she was happy. She took up the package that she had come for, not seeing or feeling the incongruity of her position, while he felt it as a direct reproof.

"She ought not to carry that," he thought. A great wave of sympathy swept over him. He took her cheeks between his hands, this time in a superior and more generous way. "Never mind, little girl," he said. "You won't have to do this always. I'll see what I can do."

The outcome of this was simply a more sympathetic relationship between them. He did not hesitate to ask her to sit beside him on the arm of his chair the next time she came, and to question her intimately about the family's condition and her own desires. Several times he noticed that she was evading his questions, particularly in regard to what her father was doing. She was ashamed to own that he was sawing wood. Fearing lest something more serious was impending, he decided to go out some day and see for himself.

This he did when a convenient morning presented itself and his other duties did not press upon him. It was three days before the great fight in the Legislature began which ended in his defeat. Nothing could be done in these few remaining days. So he took his cane and strolled forth, coming to the cottage in the course of a half hour, and knocked boldly at the door.

Mrs. Gerhardt opened it.

"Good-morning," he said, cheerily; then, seeing her hesitate, he added, "May I come in?"

The good mother, who was all but overcome by his astonishing presence, wiped her hands furtively upon her much-mended apron, and, seeing that he waited for a reply, said:

"Oh yes. Come right in."

She hurried forward, forgetting to close the door, and, offering him a chair, asked him to be seated.

Brander, feeling sorry that he was the occasion of so much confusion, said: "Don't trouble yourself, Mrs. Gerhardt. I was passing and thought I'd come in. How is your husband?"

"He's well, thank you," returned the mother. "He's out working to-day."

"Then he has found employment?"

"Yes, sir," said Mrs. Gerhardt, who hesitated, like Jennie, to say what it was.

"The children are all well now, and in school, I hope?"

"Yes," replied Mrs. Gerhardt. She had now unfastened her apron, and was nervously turning it in her lap.

"That's good, and where is Jennie?"

The latter, who had been ironing, had abandoned the board and had concealed herself in the bedroom, where she was busy tidying herself in the fear that her mother would not have the forethought to say that she was out, and so let her have a chance for escape.

"She's here," returned the mother. "I'll call her."

"What did you tell him I was here for?" said Jennie, weakly.

"What could I do?" asked the mother.

Together they hesitated while the Senator surveyed the room. He felt sorry to think that such deserving people must suffer so; he intended, in a vague way, to ameliorate their condition if possible.

"Good-morning," the Senator said to Jennie, when finally she came hesitatingly into the room. "How do you do to-day?"

Jennie came forward, extending her hand and blushing. She found herself so much disturbed by this visit that she could hardly find tongue to answer his questions.

"I thought," he said, "I'd come out and find where you live. This is a quite comfortable house. How many rooms have you?"

"Five," said Jennie. "You'll have to excuse the looks this morning. We've been ironing, and it's all upset."

"I know," said Brander, gently. "Don't you think I understand, Jennie? You mustn't feel nervous about me."

She noticed the comforting, personal tone he always used with her when she was at his room, and it helped to subdue her flustered senses.

"You musn't think it anything if I come here occasionally. I intend to come. I want to meet your father."

"Oh," said Jennie, "he's out to-day."

While they were talking, however, the honest woodcutter was coming in at the gate with his buck and saw. Brander saw him, and at once recognized him by a slight resemblance to his daughter.

"There he is now, I believe," he said.

"Oh, is he?" said Jennie, looking out.

Gerhardt, who was given to speculation these days, passed by the window without looking up. He put his wooden buck down, and, hanging his saw on a nail on the side of the house, came in.

"Mother," he called, in German, and, then not seeing her, he came to the door of the front room and looked in.

Brander arose and extended his hand. The knotted and weather-beaten German came forward, and took it with a very questioning expression of countenance.

"This is my father, Mr. Brander," said Jennie, all her diffidence dissolved by sympathy. "This is the gentleman from the hotel, papa, Mr. Brander."

"What's the name?" said the German, turning his head.

"Brander," said the Senator.

"Oh yes," he said, with a considerable German accent. "Since I had the fever I don't hear good. My wife, she spoke to me of you."

"Yes," said the Senator, "I thought I'd come out and make your acquaintance. You have quite a family."

"Yes," said the father, who was conscious of his very poor garments and anxious to get away. "I have six children—all young. She's the oldest girl."

Mrs. Gerhardt now came back, and Gerhardt, seeing his chance, said hurriedly:

"Well, if you'll excuse me, I'll go. I broke my saw, and so I had to stop work."

"Certainly," said Brander, graciously, realizing now why Jennie had never wanted to explain. He half wished that she were courageous enough not to conceal anything.

"Well, Mrs. Gerhardt," he said, when the mother was stiffly seated, "I want to tell you that you mustn't look on me as a stranger. Hereafter I want you to keep me informed of how things are going with you. Jennie won't always do it."

Jennie smiled quietly. Mrs. Gerhardt only rubbed her hands.

"Yes," she answered, humbly grateful.

They talked for a few minutes, and then the Senator rose.

"Tell your husband," he said, "to come and see me next Monday at my office in the hotel. I want to do something for him."

"Thank you," faltered Mrs. Gerhardt.

"I'll not stay any longer now," he added. "Don't forget to have him come."

"Oh, he'll come," she returned.

Adjusting a glove on one hand, he extended the other to Jennie.

"Here is your finest treasure, Mrs. Gerhardt," he said. "I think I'll take her."

"Well, I don't know," said her mother, "whether I could spare her or not."

"Well," said the Senator, going toward the door, and giving Mrs. Gerhardt his hand, "good-morning."

He nodded and walked out, while a half-dozen neighbors, who had observed his entrance, peeked from behind curtains and drawn blinds at the astonishing sight.

"Who can that be, anyhow?" was the general query.

"See what he gave me," said the innocent mother to her daughter the moment he had closed the door.

It was a ten-dollar bill. He had placed it softly in her hand as he said good-by.

Chapter V

HAVING BEEN led by circumstances into an attitude of obligation toward the Senator, it was not unnatural that Jennie should become imbued with a most generous spirit of appreciation for everything he had done and now continued to do. The Senator gave her father a letter to a local mill owner, who saw that he received something to do. It was not much, to be sure, a mere job as night-watchman, but it helped, and old Gerhardt's gratitude was extravagant. Never was there such a great, such a good man!

Nor was Mrs. Gerhardt overlooked. Once Brander sent her a dress, and at another time a shawl. All these benefactions were made in a spirit of mingled charity and self-gratification, but to Mrs. Gerhardt they glowed with but one motive. Senator Brander was good-hearted.

As for Jennie, he drew nearer to her in every possible way, so that at last she came to see him in a light which would require considerable analysis to make clear. This fresh, young soul, however, had too much innocence and buoyancy to consider for a moment the world's point of view. Since that one notable and halcyon visit upon which he had robbed her of her original shyness, and implanted a tender kiss upon her cheek, they had lived in a different atmosphere. Jennie was his companion now, and as he more and more unbended, and even joyously flung aside the habiliments of his dignity, her perception of him grew clearer. They laughed and chatted in a natural way, and he keenly enjoyed this new entrance into the radiant world of youthful happiness.

One thing that disturbed him, however, was the occasional thought, which he could not repress, that he was not doing right. Other people must soon discover that he was not confining himself strictly to conventional relations with this washer-woman's daughter. He suspected that the housekeeper was not without knowledge that Jennie almost invariably lingered from a quarter to three-quarters of an hour whenever she came for or returned his laundry. He knew that it might come to the ears of the hotel clerks, and so, in a general way, get about town and work serious injury, but the reflection did not cause him to modify his conduct. Sometimes he consoled himself with the thought that he was not doing her any actual harm, and at other times he would argue that he could not put this one delightful tenderness out of his life. Did he not wish honestly to do her much good?

He thought of these things occasionally, and decided that he could not stop. The self-approval which such a resolution might bring him was hardly worth the inevitable pain of the abnegation. He had not so very many more years to live. Why die unsatisfied?

One evening he put his arm around her and strained her to his breast. Another time he drew her to his knee, and told her of his life at Washington. Always now he had a caress and a kiss for her, but it was still in a tentative, uncertain way. He did not want to reach for her soul too deeply.

Jennie enjoyed it all innocently. Elements of fancy and novelty entered into her life. She was an unsophisticated creature, emotional, totally inexperienced in the matter of the affections, and yet mature enough mentally to enjoy the attentions of this great man who had thus bowed from his high position to make friends with her.

One evening she pushed his hair back from his forehead as she stood by his chair, and, finding nothing else to do, took out his watch. The great man thrilled as he looked at her pretty innocence.

"Would you like to have a watch, too?" he asked.

"Yes, indeed, I would," said Jennie, with a deep breath.

The next day he stopped as he was passing a jewelry store and bought one. It was gold, and had pretty ornamented hands.

"Jennie," he said, when she came the next time, "I want to show you something. See what time it is by my watch."

Jennie drew out the watch from his waistcoat pocket and started in surprise.

"This isn't your watch!" she exclaimed, her face full of innocent wonder.

"No," he said, delighted with his little deception. "It's yours."

"Mine!" exclaimed Jennie. "Mine! Oh, isn't it lovely!"

"Do you think so?" he said.

Her delight touched and pleased him immensely. Her face shone with light and her eyes fairly danced.

"That's yours," he said. "See that you wear it now, and don't lose it."

"You're so good!" she exclaimed.

"No," he said, but he held her at arm's length by the waist, to make up his mind what his reward should be. Slowly he drew her toward him until, when very close, she put her arms about his neck, and laid her cheek in gratitude against his own. This was the quintessence of pleasure for him. He felt as he had been longing to feel for years.

The progress of his idyl suffered a check when the great senatorial fight came on in the Legislature. Attacked by a combination of rivals, Brander was given the fight of his life. To his amazement he discovered that a great railroad corporation, which had always been friendly, was secretly throwing its strength in behalf of an already too powerful candidate. Shocked by this defection, he was thrown alternately into the deepest gloom and into paroxysms of wrath. These slings of fortune, however lightly he pretended to receive them, never failed to lacerate him. It had been long since he had suffered a defeat—too long.

During this period Jennie received her earliest lesson in the vagaries of men. For two weeks she did not even see him, and one evening, after an extremely comfortless conference with his leader, he met her with the most chilling formality. When she knocked at his door he only troubled to open it a foot, exclaiming almost harshly: "I can't bother about the clothes to-night. Come to-morrow."

Jennie retreated, shocked and surprised by this reception. She did not know what to think of it. He was restored on the instant to his far-off, mighty throne, and left to rule in peace. Why should he not withdraw the light of his countenance if it pleased him. But why—

A day or two later he repented mildly, but had no time to readjust matters. His washing was taken and delivered with considerable formality, and he went on toiling forgetfully, until at last he was miserably defeated by two votes. Astounded by this result, he lapsed into gloomy dejection of soul. What was he to do now?

Into this atmosphere came Jennie, bringing with her the lightness and comfort of her own hopeful disposition. Nagged to desperation by his thoughts, Brander first talked to her to amuse himself; but soon his distress imperceptibly took flight; he found himself actually smiling.

"Ah, Jennie," he said, speaking to her as he might have done to a child, "youth is on your side. You possess the most valuable thing in life."

"Do I?"

"Yes, but you don't realize it. You never will until it is too late."

"I love that girl," he thought to himself that night. "I wish I could have her with me always."

But fortune had another fling for him to endure. It got about the hotel that Jennie was, to use the mildest expression, conducting herself strangely. A girl who carries washing must expect criticism if anything not befitting her station is observed in her apparel. Jennie was seen wearing the gold watch. Her mother was informed by the housekeeper of the state of things.

"I thought I'd speak to you about it," she said. "People are talking. You'd better not let your daughter go to his room for the laundry."

Mrs. Gerhardt was too astonished and hurt for utterance. Jennie had told her nothing, but even now she did not believe there was anything to tell. The watch had been both approved of and admired by her. She had not thought that it was endangering her daughter's reputation.

Going home she worried almost incessantly, and talked with Jennie about it. The latter did not admit the implication that things had gone too far. In fact, she did not look at it in that light. She did not own, it is true, what really had happened while she was visiting the Senator.

"It's so terrible that people should begin to talk!" said her mother. "Did you really stay so long in the room?"

"I don't know," returned Jennie, compelled by her conscience to admit at least part of the truth. "Perhaps I did."

"He has never said anything out of the way to you, has he?"

"No," answered her daughter, who did not attach any suspicion of evil to what had passed between them.

If the mother had only gone a little bit further she might have learned more, but she was only too glad, for her own peace of mind, to hush the matter up. People were slandering a good man, that she knew. Jennie had been the least bit indiscreet. People were always so ready to talk. How could the poor girl, amid such unfortunate circumstances, do otherwise than she did. It made her cry to think of it.

The result of it all was that she decided to get the washing herself.

She came to his door the next Monday after this decision. Brander, who was expecting Jennie, was both surprised and disappointed.

"Why," he said to her, " what has become of Jennie?"

Having hoped that he would not notice, or, at least, not comment upon the change, Mrs. Gerhardt did not know what to say. She looked up at him weakly in her innocent, motherly way, and said, "She couldn't come to-night."

"Not ill, is she?" he inquired.

"No."

"I'm glad to hear that," he said resignedly. "How have you been?"

Mrs. Gerhardt answered his kindly inquiries and departed. After she had gone he got to thinking the matter over, and wondered what could have happened. It seemed rather odd that he should be wondering over it.

On Saturday, however, when she returned the clothes he felt that there must be something wrong.

"What's the matter, Mrs. Gerhardt?" he inquired. "Has anything happened to your daughter?"

"No, sir," she returned, too troubled to wish to deceive him.

"Isn't she coming for the laundry any more?"

"I—I—" ventured the mother, stammering in her perturbation; "she—they have been talking about her," she at last forced herself to say.

"Who has been talking?" he asked gravely.

"The people here in the hotel."

"Who, what people?" he interrupted, a touch of annoyance showing in his voice.

"The housekeeper."

"The housekeeper, eh!" he exclaimed. "What has she got to say?"

The mother related to him her experience.

"And she told you that, did she?" he remarked in wrath. "She ventures to trouble herself about my affairs, does she? I wonder people can't mind their own business without interfering with mine. Your daughter, Mrs. Gerhardt, is perfectly safe with me. I have no intention of doing her an injury. It's a shame," he added indignantly, "that a girl can't come to my room in this hotel without having her motive questioned. I'll look into this matter."

"I hope you don't think that I have anything to do with it," said the mother apologetically. "I know you like Jennie and wouldn't injure her. You've done so much for her and all of us, Mr. Brander, I feel ashamed to keep her away."

"That's all right, Mrs. Gerhardt," he said quietly. "You did perfectly right. I don't blame you in the least. It is the lying accusation passed about in this hotel that I object to. We'll see about that."

Mrs. Gerhardt stood there, pale with excitement. She was afraid she had deeply offended this man who had done so much for them. If she could only say something, she thought, that would clear this matter up and make him feel that she was no tattler. Scandal was distressing to her.

"I thought I was doing everything for the best," she said at last.

"So you were," he replied. "I like Jennie very much. I have always enjoyed her coming here. It is my intention to do well by her, but perhaps it will be better to keep her away, at least for the present."

Again that evening the Senator sat in his easy-chair and brooded over this new development. Jennie was really much more precious to him than he had thought. Now that he had no hope of seeing her there any more, he began to realize how much these little visits of hers had meant. He thought the matter over very carefully, realized instantly that there was nothing to be done so far as the hotel gossip was concerned, and concluded that he had really placed the girl in a very unsatisfactory position.

"Perhaps I had better end this little affair," he thought. "It isn't a wise thing to pursue."

On the strength of this conclusion he went to Washington and finished his term. Then he returned to Columbus to await the friendly recognition from the President which was to send him upon some ministry abroad. Jennie had not been forgotten in the least. The longer he stayed away the more eager he was to get back. When he was again permanently settled in his old quarters he took up his cane one morning and strolled out in the direction of the cottage. Arriving there, he made up his mind to go in, and knocking at the door, he was greeted by Mrs. Gerhardt and her daughter with astonished and diffident smiles. He explained vaguely that he had been away, and mentioned his laundry as if that were the object of his visit. Then, when chance gave him a few moments with Jennie alone, he plunged in boldly.

"How would you like to take a drive with me to-morrow evening?" he asked.

"I'd like it," said Jennie, to whom the proposition was a glorious novelty.

He smiled and patted her cheek, foolishly happy to see her again. Every day seemed to add to her beauty. Graced with her clean white apron, her shapely head crowned by the glory of her simply plaited hair, she was a pleasing sight for any man to look upon.

He waited until Mrs. Gerhardt returned, and then, having accomplished the purpose of his visit, he arose.

"I'm going to take your daughter out riding to-morrow evening," he explained. "I want to talk to her about her future."

"Won't that be nice?" said the mother. She saw nothing incongruous in the proposal. They parted with smiles and much handshaking.

"That man has the best heart," commented Mrs. Gerhardt. "Doesn't he always speak so nicely of you? He may help you to an education. You ought to be proud."

"I am," said Jennie frankly.

"I don't know whether we had better tell your father or not," concluded Mrs. Gerhardt. "He doesn't like for you to be out evenings."

Finally they decided not to tell him. He might not understand.

Jennie was ready when he called. He could see by the weak-flamed, unpretentious parlor-lamp that she was dressed for him, and that the occasion had called out the best she had. A pale lavender gingham, starched and ironed, until it was a model of laundering, set off her pretty figure to perfection. There were little lace-edged cuffs and a rather high collar attached to it. She had no gloves, nor any jewelry, nor yet a jacket good enough to wear, but her hair was done up in such a dainty way that it set off her well-shaped head better than any hat, and the few ringlets that could escape crowned her as with a halo. When Brander suggested that she should wear a jacket she hesitated a moment; then she went in and borrowed her mother's cape, a plain gray woolen one. Brander realized now that she had no jacket, and suffered keenly to think that she had contemplated going without one.

"She would have endured the raw night air," he thought, "and said nothing of it."

He looked at her and shook his head reflectively. Then they started, and he quickly forgot everything but the great fact that she was at his side. She talked with freedom and with a gentle girlish enthusiasm that he found irresistibly charming.

"Why, Jennie," he said, when she had called upon him to notice how soft the trees looked, where, outlined dimly against the new rising moon, they were touched with its yellow light, "you're a great one. I believe you would write poetry if you were schooled a little."

"Do you suppose I could?" she asked innocently.

"Do I suppose, little girl?" he said, taking her hand. "Do I suppose? Why, I know. You're the dearest little day-dreamer in the world. Of course you could write poetry. You live it. You are poetry, my dear. Don't you worry about writing any."

This eulogy touched her as nothing else possibly could have done. He was always saying such nice things. No one ever seemed to like or to appreciate her half as much as he did. And how good he was! Everybody said that. Her own father.

They rode still farther, until suddenly remembering, he

said: "I wonder what time it is. Perhaps we had better be turning back. Have you your watch?"

Jennie started, for this watch had been the one thing of which she had hoped he would not speak. Ever since he had returned it had been on her mind.

In his absence the family finances had become so strained that she had been compelled to pawn it. Martha had got to that place in the matter of apparel where she could no longer go to school unless something new were provided for her. And so, after much discussion, it was decided that the watch must go.

Bass took it, and after much argument with the local pawn broker, he had been able to bring home ten dollars. Mrs. Gerhardt expended the money upon her children, and heaved a sigh of relief. Martha looked very much better. Naturally, Jennie was glad.

Now, however, when the Senator spoke of it, her hour of retribution seemed at hand. She actually trembled, and he noticed her discomfiture.

"Why, Jennie," he said gently, " what made you start like that?"

"Nothing," she answered.

"Haven't you your watch?"

She paused, for it seemed impossible to tell a deliberate falsehood. There was a strained silence; then she said, with a voice that had too much of a sob in it for him not to suspect the truth, "No, sir." He persisted, and she confessed everything.

"Well," he said, "dearest, don't feel badly about it. There never was such another girl. I'll get your watch for you. Hereafter when you need anything I want you to come to me. Do you hear? I want you to promise me that. If I'm not here, I want you to write me. I'll always be in touch with you from now on. You will have my address. Just let me know, and I'll help you. Do you understand?"

"Yes," said Jennie.

"You'll promise to do that now, will you?"

"Yes," she replied.

For a moment neither of them spoke.

"Jennie," he said at last, the spring-like quality of the night moving him to a burst of feeling, "I've about decided that I can't do without you. Do you think you could make up your mind to live with me from now on?"

Jennie looked away, not clearly understanding his words as he meant them.

"I don't know," she said vaguely.

"Well, you think about it," he said pleasantly. "I'm serious. Would you be willing to marry me, and let me put you away in a seminary for a few years?"

"Go away to school?"

"Yes, after you marry me."

"I guess so," she replied. Her mother came into her mind. Maybe she could help the family.

He looked around at her, and tried to make out the expression on her face. It was not dark. The moon was now above the trees in the east, and already the vast host of stars were paling before it.

"Don't you care for me at all, Jennie?" he asked.

"Yes!"

"You never come for my laundry any more, though," he returned pathetically. It touched her to hear him say this.

"I didn't do that," she answered. "I couldn't help it; Mother thought it was best."

"So it was," he assented. "Don't feel badly. I was only joking with you. You'd be glad to come if you could, wouldn't you?"

"Yes, I would," she answered frankly.

He took her hand and pressed it so feelingly that all his kindly words seemed doubly emphasized to her. Reaching up impulsively, she put her arms about him. "You're so good to me," she said with the loving tone of a daughter.

"You're my girl, Jennie," he said with deep feeling. "I'd do anything in the world for you."

Chapter VI

THE FATHER of this unfortunate family, William Gerhardt, was a man of considerable interest on his personal side. Born in the kingdom of Saxony, he had had character enough to oppose the army conscription iniquity, and to flee, in his eighteenth year, to Paris. From there he had set forth for America, the land of promise.

Arrived in this country, he had made his way, by slow stages, from New York to Philadelphia, and thence westward, working for a time in the various glass factories in Pennsylvania. In one romantic village of this new world he had found his heart's ideal. With her, a simple American girl of German extraction, he had removed to Youngstown, and thence to Columbus, each time following a glass manufacturer by the name of Hammond, whose business prospered and waned by turns.

Gerhardt was an honest man, and he liked to think that others appreciated his integrity. "William," his employer used to say to him, "I want you because I can trust you," and this, to him, was more than silver and gold.

This honesty, like his religious convictions, was wholly due to inheritance. He had never reasoned about it. Father and grandfather before him were sturdy German artisans, who had never cheated anybody out of a dollar, and this honesty of intention came into his veins undiminished.

His Lutheran proclivities had been strengthened by years of church-going and the religious observances of home life. In his father's cottage the influence of the Lutheran minister had been all-powerful; he had inherited the feeling that the Lutheran Church was a perfect institution, and that its teachings were of all-importance when it came to the issue of the future life. His wife, nominally of the Mennonite faith, was quite willing to accept her husband's creed. And so his household became a God-fearing one; wherever they went their first public step was to ally themselves with the local Lutheran church, and the minister was always a welcome guest in the Gerhardt home.

Pastor Wundt, the shepherd of the Columbus church, was

a sincere and ardent Christian, but his bigotry and hard-and-fast orthodoxy made him intolerant. He considered that the members of his flock were jeopardizing their eternal salvation if they danced, played cards, or went to theaters, and he did not hesitate to declare vociferously that hell was yawning for those who disobeyed his injunctions. Drinking, even temperately, was a sin. Smoking—well, he smoked himself. Right conduct in marriage, however, and innocence before that state were absolute essentials of Christian living. Let no one talk of salvation, he had said, for a daughter who had failed to keep her chastity unstained, or for the parents who, by negligence, had permitted her to fall. Hell was yawning for all such. You must walk the straight and narrow way if you would escape eternal punishment, and a just God was angry with sinners every day.

Gerhardt and his wife, and also Jennie, accepted the doctrines of their Church as expounded by Mr. Wundt without reserve. With Jennie, however, the assent was little more than nominal. Religion had as yet no striking hold upon her. It was a pleasant thing to know that there was a heaven, a fearsome one to realize that there was a hell. Young girls and boys ought to be good and obey their parents. Otherwise the whole religious problem was badly jumbled in her mind.

Gerhardt was convinced that everything spoken from the pulpit of his church was literally true. Death and the future life were realities to him.

Now that the years were slipping away and the problem of the world was becoming more and more inexplicable, he clung with pathetic anxiety to the doctrines which contained a solution. Oh, if he could only be so honest and upright that the Lord might have no excuse for ruling him out. He trembled not only for himself, but for his wife and children. Would he not some day be held responsible for them? Would not his own laxity and lack of system in inculcating the laws of eternal life to them end in his and their damnation? He pictured to himself the torments of hell, and wondered how it would be with him and his in the final hour.

Naturally, such a deep religious feeling made him stern with his children. He was prone to scan with a narrow eye the pleasures and foibles of youthful desire. Jennie was never to have a lover if her father had any voice in the matter. Any flirtation with the youths she might meet upon the streets of Columbus could have no continuation in her home. Gerhardt forgot that he was once young himself, and looked only to the welfare of her spirit. So the Senator was a novel factor in her life.

When he first began to be a part of their family affairs the conventional standards of Father Gerhardt proved untrustworthy. He had no means of judging such a character. This was no ordinary person coquetting with his pretty daughter. The manner in which the Senator entered the family life was so original and so plausible that he became an active part before any one thought anything about it. Gerhardt himself was deceived, and, expecting nothing but honor and profit to flow to the family from such a source, accepted the interest and the service, and plodded peacefully on. His wife did not tell him of the many presents which had come before and since the wonderful Christmas.

But one morning as Gerhardt was coming home from his night work a neighbor named Otto Weaver accosted him.

"Gerhardt," he said, "I want to speak a word with you. As a friend of yours, I want to tell you what I hear. The neighbors, you know, they talk now about the man who comes to see your daughter."

"My daughter?" said Gerhardt, more puzzled and pained by this abrupt attack than mere words could indicate. "Whom do you mean? I don't know of any one who comes to see my daughter."

"No?" inquired Weaver, nearly as much astonished as the recipient of his confidences. "The middle-aged man, with gray hair. He carries a cane sometimes. You don't know him?"

Gerhardt racked his memory with a puzzled face.

"They say he was a senator once," went on Weaver, doubtful of what he had got into; "I don't know."

"Ah," returned Gerhardt, measurably relieved. "Senator Brander. Yes. He has come sometimes—so. Well, what of it?"

"It is nothing," returned the neighbor, "only they talk. He is no longer a young man, you know. Your daughter, she goes out with him now a few times. These people, they see that, and now they talk about her. I thought you might want to know."

Gerhardt was shocked to the depths of his being by these terrible words. People must have a reason for saying such things. Jennie and her mother were seriously at fault. Still he did not hesitate to defend his daughter.

"He is a friend of the family," he said confusedly. "People should not talk until they know. My daughter has done nothing."

"That is so. It is nothing," continued Weaver. "People talk before they have any grounds. You and I are old friends. I thought you might want to know."

Gerhardt stood there motionless another minute or so, his jaw fallen and a strange helplessness upon him. The world was such a grim thing to have antagonistic to you. Its opinions and good favor were so essential. How hard he had tried to live up to its rules! Why should it not be satisfied and let him alone?

"I am glad you told me," he murmured as he started homeward. "I will see about it. Good-by."

Gerhardt took the first opportunity to question his wife.

"What is this about Senator Brander coming out to call on Jennie?" he asked in German. "The neighbors are talking about it."

"Why, nothing," answered Mrs. Gerhardt, in the same language. She was decidedly taken aback at his question. "He did call two or three times."

"You didn't tell me that," he returned, a sense of her frailty in tolerating and shielding such weakness in one of their children irritating him.

"No," she replied, absolutely nonplussed. "He has only been here two or three times."

"Two or three times!" exclaimed Gerhardt, the German tendency to talk loud coming upon him. "Two or three times! The whole neighborhood talks about it. What is this, then?"

"He only called two or three times," Mrs. Gerhardt repeated weakly.

"Weaver comes to me on the street," continued Gerhardt, "and tells me that my neighbors are talking of the man my daughter is going with. I didn't know anything about it.

There I stood. I didn't know what to say. What kind of a way is that? What must the man think of me?"

"There is nothing the matter," declared the mother, using an effective German idiom. "Jennie has gone walking with him once or twice. He has called here at the house. What is there now in that for the people to talk about? Can't the girl have any pleasure at all?"

"But he is an old man," returned Gerhardt, voicing the words of Weaver. "He is a public citizen. What should he want to call on a girl like Jennie for?"

"I don't know," said Mrs. Gerhardt, defensively. "He comes here to the house. I don't know anything but good about the man. Can I tell him not to come?"

Gerhardt paused at this. All that he knew of the Senator was excellent. What was there now that was so terrible about it?

"The neighbors are so ready to talk. They haven't got anything else to talk about now, so they talk about Jennie. You know whether she is a good girl or not. Why should they say such things?" and tears came into the soft little mother's eyes.

"That is all right," grumbled Gerhardt, "but he ought not to want to come around and take a girl of her age out walking. It looks bad, even if he don't mean any harm."

At this moment Jennie came in. She had heard the talking in the front bedroom, where she slept with one of the children, but had not suspected its import. Now her mother turned her back and bent over the table where she was making biscuit, in order that her daughter might not see her red eyes.

"What's the matter?" she inquired, vaguely troubled by the tense stillness in the attitude of both her parents.

"Nothing," said Gerhardt firmly.

Mrs. Gerhardt made no sign, but her very immobility told something. Jennie went over to her and quickly discovered that she had been weeping.

"What's the matter?" she repeated wonderingly, gazing at her father.

Gerhardt only stood there, his daughter's innocence dominating his terror of evil.

"What's the matter?" she urged softly of her mother.

"Oh, it's the neighbors," returned the mother brokenly. "They're always ready to talk about something they don't know anything about."

"Is it me again?" inquired Jennie, her face flushing faintly.

"You see," observed Gerhardt, apparently addressing the world in general, "she knows. Now, why didn't you tell me that he was coming here? The neighbors talk, and I hear nothing about it until to-day. What kind of a way is that, anyhow?"

"Oh," exclaimed Jennie, out of the purest sympathy for her mother, "what difference does it make?"

"What difference?" cried Gerhardt, still talking in German, although Jennie answered in English. "Is it no difference that men stop me on the street and speak of it? You should be ashamed of yourself to say that. I always thought well of this man, but now, since you don't tell me about him, and the neighbors talk, I don't know what to think. Must I get my knowledge of what is going on in my own home from my neighbors?"

Mother and daughter paused. Jennie had already begun to think that their error was serious.

"I didn't keep anything from you because it was evil," she said. "Why, he only took me out riding once."

"Yes, but you didn't tell me that," answered her father.

"You know you don't like for me to go out after dark," replied Jennie. "That's why I didn't. There wasn't anything else to hide about it."

"He shouldn't want you to go out after dark with him," observed Gerhardt, always mindful of the world outside. "What can he want with you. Why does he come here? He is too old, anyhow. I don't think you ought to have anything to do with him—such a young girl as you are."

"He doesn't want to do anything except help me," murmured Jennie. "He wants to marry me."

"Marry you? Ha! Why doesn't he tell me that!" exclaimed Gerhardt. "I shall look into this. I won't have him running around with my daughter, and the neighbors talking. Besides, he is too old. I shall tell him that. He ought to know better than to put a girl where she gets talked about. It is better he should stay away altogether."

This threat of Gerhardt's, that he would tell Brander to stay away, seemed simply terrible to Jennie and to her mother. What good could come of any such attitude? Why must they be degraded before him? Of course Brander did call again, while Gerhardt was away at work, and they trembled lest the father should hear of it. A few days later the Senator came and took Jennie for a long walk. Neither she nor her mother said anything to Gerhardt. But he was not to be put off the scent for long.

"Has Jennie been out again with that man?" he inquired of Mrs. Gerhardt the next evening.

"He was here last night," returned the mother, evasively.

"Did she tell him he shouldn't come any more?"

"I don't know. I don't think so."

"Well, now, I will see for myself once whether this thing will be stopped or not," said the determined father. "I shall talk with him. Wait till he comes again."

In accordance with this, he took occasion to come up from his factory on three different evenings, each time carefully surveying the house, in order to discover whether any visitor was being entertained. On the fourth evening Brander came, and inquiring for Jennie, who was exceedingly nervous, he took her out for a walk. She was afraid of her father, lest some unseemly things should happen, but did not know exactly what to do.

Gerhardt, who was on his way to the house at the time, observed her departure. That was enough for him. Walking deliberately in upon his wife, he said:

"Where is Jennie?"

"She is out somewhere," said her mother.

"Yes, I know where," said Gerhardt. "I saw her. Now wait till she comes home. I will tell him."

He sat down calmly, reading a German paper and keeping an eye upon his wife, until, at last, the gate clicked, and the front door opened. Then he got up.

"Where have you been?" he exclaimed in German.

Brander, who had not suspected that any trouble of this character was pending, felt irritated and uncomfortable. Jennie was covered with confusion. Her mother was suffering an agony of torment in the kitchen.

"Why, I have been out for a walk," she answered con-fusedly.

"Didn't I tell you not to go out any more after dark?" said Gerhardt, utterly ignoring Brander.

Jennie colored furiously, unable to speak a word.

"What is the trouble?" inquired Brander gravely. "Why should you talk to her like that?"

"She should not go out after dark," returned the father rudely. "I have told her two or three times now. I don't think you ought to come here any more, either."

"And why?" asked the Senator, pausing to consider and choose his words. "Isn't this rather peculiar? What has your daughter done?"

"What has she done!" exclaimed Gerhardt, his excitement growing under the strain he was enduring, and speaking al-most unaccented English in consequence. "She is running around the streets at night when she oughtn't to be. I don't want my daughter taken out after dark by a man of your age. What do you want with her anyway? She is only a child yet."

"Want!" said the Senator, straining to regain his ruffled dignity. "I want to talk with her, of course. She is old enough to be interesting to me. I want to marry her if she will have me."

"I want you to go out of here and stay out of here," re-turned the father, losing all sense of logic, and descending to the ordinary level of parental compulsion. "I don't want you to come around my house any more. I have enough trouble without my daughter being taken out and given a bad name."

"I tell you frankly," said the Senator, drawing himself up to his full height, "that you will have to make clear your meaning. I have done nothing that I am ashamed of. Your daughter has not come to any harm through me. Now, I want to know what you mean by conducting yourself in this manner."

"I mean," said Gerhardt, excitedly repeating himself, "I mean, I mean that the whole neighborhood talks about how you come around here, and have buggy-rides and walks with my daughter when I am not here—that's what I mean. I mean that you are no man of honorable intentions, or you would not come taking up with a little girl who is only old enough to be your daughter. People tell me well enough what you are. Just you go and leave my daughter alone."

"People!" said the Senator. "Well, I care nothing for your people. I love your daughter, and I am here to see her because I do love her. It is my intention to marry her, and if your neighbors have anything to say to that, let them say it. There is no reason why you should conduct yourself in this manner before you know what my intentions are."

Unnerved by this unexpected and terrible altercation, Jennie had backed away to the door leading out into the dining-room, and her mother, seeing her, came forward.

"Oh," said the latter, breathing excitedly, "he came home when you were away. What shall we do?" They clung together, as women do, and wept silently. The dispute continued.

"Marry, eh," exclaimed the father. "Is that it?"

"Yes," said the Senator, "marry, that is exactly it. Your daughter is eighteen years of age and can decide for herself. You have insulted me and outraged your daughter's feelings. Now, I wish you to know that it cannot stop here. If you have any cause to say anything against me outside of mere hearsay I wish you to say it."

The Senator stood before him, a very citadel of righteousness. He was neither loud-voiced nor angry-mannered, but there was a tightness about his lips which bespoke the man of force and determination.

"I don't want to talk to you any more," returned Gerhardt, who was checked but not overawed. "My daughter is my daughter. I am the one who will say whether she shall go out at night, or whether she shall marry you, either. I know what you politicians are. When I first met you I thought you were a fine man, but now, since I see the way you conduct yourself with my daughter, I don't want anything more to do with you. Just you go and stay away from here. That's all I ask of you."

"I am sorry, Mrs. Gerhardt," said Brander, turning deliberately away from the angry father, "to have had such an argument in your home. I had no idea that your husband was opposed to my visits. However, I will leave the matter as it stands for the present. You must not take all this as badly as it seems."

Gerhardt looked on in astonishment at his coolness.

"I will go now," he said, again addressing Gerhardt, "but you mustn't think that I am leaving this matter for good. You have made a serious mistake this evening. I hope you will realize that. I bid you good-night." He bowed slightly and went out.

Gerhardt closed the door firmly. "Now," he said, turning to his daughter and wife, " we will see whether we are rid of him or not. I will show you how to go after night upon the streets when everybody is talking already."

In so far as words were concerned, the argument ceased, but looks and feeling ran strong and deep, and for days thereafter scarcely a word was spoken in the little cottage. Gerhardt began to brood over the fact that he had accepted his place the Senator and decided to give it up. He made it known that no more of the Senator's washing was to be done in their house, and if he had not been sure that Mrs. Gerhardt's hotel work was due to her own efforts in finding it he would have stopped that. No good would come out of it, anyway. If she had never gone to the hotel all this talk would never have come upon them.

As for the Senator, he went away decidedly ruffled by this crude occurrence. Neighborhood slanders are bad enough on their own plane, but for a man of his standing to descend and become involved in one struck him now as being a little bit unworthy. He did not know what to do about the situation, and while he was trying to come to some decision several days went by. Then he was called to Washington, and he went away without having seen Jennie again.

In the mean time the Gerhardt family struggled along as before. They were poor, indeed, but Gerhardt was willing to face poverty if only it could be endured with honor. The grocery bills were of the same size, however. The children's clothing was steadily wearing out. Economy had to be practised, and payments stopped on old bills that Gerhardt was trying to adjust.

Then came a day when the annual interest on the mortgage was due, and yet another when two different grocery-men met Gerhardt on the street and asked about their little bills. He did not hesitate to explain just what the situation was, and to tell them with convincing honesty that he would try hard and do the best he could. But his spirit was unstrung by his misfortunes. He prayed for the favor of Heaven while at his labor, and did not hesitate to use the daylight hours that he should have had for sleeping to go about—either looking for a more remunerative position or to obtain such little jobs as he could now and then pick up. One of them was that of cutting grass.

Mrs. Gerhardt protested that he was killing himself, but he explained his procedure by pointing to their necessity.

"When people stop me on the street and ask me for money I have no time to sleep."

It was a distressing situation for all of them.

To cap it all, Sebastian got in jail. It was that old coal-stealing ruse of his practised once too often. He got up on a car one evening while Jennie and the children waited for him, and a railroad detective arrested him. There had been a good deal of coal stealing during the past two years, but so long as it was confined to moderate quantities the railroad took no notice. When, however, customers of shippers complained that cars from the Pennsylvania fields lost thousands of pounds in transit to Cleveland, Cincinnati, Chicago, and other points, detectives were set to work. Gerhardt's children were not the only ones who preyed upon the railroad in this way. Other families in Columbus—many of them—were constantly doing the same thing, but Sebastian happened to be seized upon as the Columbus example.

"You come off that car now," said the detective, suddenly appearing out of the shadow. Jennie and the other children dropped their baskets and buckets and fled for their lives. Sebastian's first impulse was to jump and run, but when he tried it the detective grabbed him by the coat.

"Hold on here," he exclaimed. "I want you."

"Aw, let go," said Sebastian savagely, for he was no weakling. There was nerve and determination in him, as well as a keen sense of his awkward predicament.

"Let go, I tell you," he reiterated, and giving a jerk, he almost upset his captor.

"Come here now," said the detective, pulling him viciously in an effort to establish his authority.

Sebastian came, but it was with a blow which staggered his adversary.

There was more struggling, and then a passing railroad hand came to the detective's assistance. Together they hurried him toward the depot, and there discovering the local officer, turned him over. It was with a torn coat, scarred hands and face, and a black eye that Sebastian was locked up for the night.

When the children came home they could not say what had happened to their brother, but as nine o'clock struck, and then ten and eleven, and Sebastian did not return, Mrs. Gerhardt was beside herself. He had stayed out many a night as late as twelve and one, but his mother had a foreboding of something terrible to-night. When half-past one arrived, and no Sebastian, she began to cry.

"Some one ought to go up and tell your father," she said. "He may be in jail."

Jennie volunteered, but George, who was soundly sleeping, was awakened to go along with her.

"What!" said Gerhardt, astonished to see his two children.

"Bass hasn't come yet," said Jennie, and then told the story of the evening's adventure in explanation.

Gerhardt left his work at once, walking back with his two children to a point where he could turn off to go to the jail. He guessed what had happened, and his heart was troubled.

"Is that so, now!" he repeated nervously, rubbing his clumsy hands across his wet forehead.

Arrived at the station-house, the sergeant in charge told him curtly that Bass was under arrest.

"Sebastian Gerhardt?" he said, looking over his blotter; "yes, here he is. Stealing coal and resisting an officer. Is he your boy?"

"Oh, my!" said Gerhardt, *"Ach Gott!"* He actually wrung his hands in distress.

"Want to see him?" asked the Sergeant.

"Yes, yes," said the father.

"Take him back, Fred," said the other to the old watchman in charge, "and let him see the boy."

When Gerhardt stood in the back room, and Sebastian was brought out all marked and tousled, he broke down and began to cry. No word could cross his lips because of his emotion.

"Don't cry, pop," said Sebastian bravely. "I couldn't help it. It's all right. I'll be out in the morning."

Gerhardt only shook with his grief.

"Don't cry," continued Sebastian, doing his very best to restrain his own tears. "I'll be all right. What's the use of crying?"

"I know, I know," said the gray-headed parent brokenly, "but I can't help it. It is my fault that I should let you do that."

"No, no, it isn't," said Sebastian. "You couldn't help it. Does mother know anything about it?"

"Yes, she knows," he returned. "Jennie and George just came up where I was and told me. I didn't know anything about it until just now," and he began to cry again.

"Well, don't you feel badly," went on Bass, the finest part of his nature coming to the surface. "I'll be all right. Just you go back to work now, and don't worry. I'll be all right."

"How did you hurt your eye?" asked the father, looking at him with red eyes.

"Oh, I had a little wrestling match with the man who nabbed me," said the boy, smiling bravely. "I thought I could get away."

"You shouldn't do that, Sebastian," said the father. "It may go harder with you on that account. When does your case come up?"

"In the morning, they told me," said Bass. "Nine o'clock."

Gerhardt stayed with his son for some time, and discussed the question of bail, fine, and the dire possibility of a jail sentence without arriving at any definite conclusion. Finally he was persuaded by Bass to go away, but the departure was the occasion for another outburst of feeling; he was led away shaking and broken with emotion.

"It's pretty tough," said Bass to himself as he was led back to his cell. He was thinking solely of his father. "I wonder what ma will think."

The thought of this touched him tenderly. "I wish I'd knocked the dub over the first crack," he said. "What a fool I was not to get away."

Chapter VII

GERHARDT WAS in despair; he did not know any one to whom he could appeal between the hours of two and nine o'clock in the morning. He went back to talk with his wife, and then to his post of duty. What was to be done? He could think of only one friend who was able, or possibly willing to do anything. This was the glass manufacturer, Hammond; but he was not in the city. Gerhardt did not know this, however.

When nine o'clock came, he went alone to the court, for it was thought advisable that the others should stay away. Mrs. Gerhardt was to hear immediately what happened. He would come right back.

When Sebastian was lined up inside the dock he had to wait a long time, for there were several prisoners ahead of him. Finally his name was called, and the boy was pushed forward to the bar. "Stealing coal, Your Honor, and resisting arrest," explained the officer who had arrested him.

The magistrate looked at Sebastian closely; he was unfavorably impressed by the lad's scratched and wounded face.

"Well, young man," he said, "what have you to say for yourself? How did you get your black eye?"

Sebastian looked at the judge, but did not answer.

"I arrested him," said the detective. "He was on one of the company's cars. He tried to break away from me, and when I held him he assaulted me. This man here was a witness," he added, turning to the railroad hand who had helped him.

"Is that where he struck you?" asked the Court, observing the detective's swollen jaw.

"Yes, sir," he returned, glad of an opportunity to be further revenged.

"If you please," put in Gerhardt, leaning forward, "he is my boy. He was sent to get the coal. He—"

"We don't mind what they pick up around the yard," interrupted the detective, "but he was throwing it off the cars to half a dozen others."

"Can't you earn enough to keep from taking coal off the

coal cars?" asked the Court; but before either father or son had time to answer he added, "What is your business?"

"Car builder," said Sebastian.

"And what do you do?" he questioned, addressing Gerhardt.

"I am watchman at Miller's furniture factory."

"Um," said the court, feeling that Sebastian's attitude remained sullen and contentious. "Well, this young man might be let off on the coal-stealing charge, but he seems to be somewhat too free with his fists. Columbus is altogether too rich in that sort of thing. Ten dollars."

"If you please," began Gerhardt, but the court officer was already pushing him away.

"I don't want to hear any more about it," said the judge. "He's stubborn, anyhow. What's the next case?"

Gerhardt made his way over to his boy, abashed and yet very glad it was no worse. Somehow, he thought, he could raise the money. Sebastian looked at him solicitously as he came forward.

"It's all right," said Bass soothingly. "He didn't give me half a chance to say anything."

"I'm only glad it wasn't more," said Gerhardt nervously. "We will try and get the money."

Going home to his wife, Gerhardt informed the troubled household of the result. Mrs. Gerhardt stood white and yet relieved, for ten dollars seemed something that might be had. Jennie heard the whole story with open mouth and wide eyes. It was a terrible blow to her. Poor Bass! He was always so lively and good-natured. It seemed awful that he should be in jail.

Gerhardt went hurriedly to Hammond's fine residence, but he was not in the city. He thought then of a lawyer by the name of Jenkins, whom he knew in a casual way, but Jenkins was not at his office. There were several grocers and coal merchants whom he knew well enough, but he owed them money. Pastor Wundt might let him have it, but the agony such a disclosure to that worthy would entail held him back. He did call on one or two acquaintances, but these, surprised at the unusual and peculiar request, excused themselves. At four o'clock he returned home, weary and exhausted.

"I don't know what to do," he said despairingly. "If I could only think."

Jennie thought of Brander, but the situation had not accentuated her desperation to the point where she could brave her father's opposition and his terrible insult to the Senator, so keenly remembered, to go and ask. Her watch had been pawned a second time, and she had no other means of obtaining money.

The family council lasted until half-past ten, but still there was nothing decided. Mrs. Gerhardt persistently and monotonously turned one hand over in the other and stared at the floor. Gerhardt ran his hand through his reddish brown hair distractedly. "It's no use," he said at last. "I can't think of anything."

"Go to bed, Jennie," said her mother solicitously; "get the others to go. There's no use their sitting up. I may think of something. You go to bed."

Jennie went to her room, but the very thought of repose was insupportable. She had read in the paper, shortly after her father's quarrel with the Senator, that the latter had departed for Washington. There had been no notice of his return. Still he might be in the city. She stood before a short, narrow mirror that surmounted a shabby bureau, thinking. Her sister Veronica, with whom she slept, was already composing herself to dreams. Finally a grim resolution fixed itself in her consciousness. She would go and see Senator Brander. If *he* were in town he would help Bass. Why shouldn't she — he loved her. He had asked over and over to marry her. Why should she not go and ask him for help?

She hesitated a little while, then hearing Veronica breathing regularly, she put on her hat and jacket, and noiselessly opened the door into the sitting-room to see if any one were stirring.

There was no sound save that of Gerhardt rocking nervously to and fro in the kitchen. There was no light save that of her own small room-lamp and a gleam from under the kitchen door. She turned and blew the former out—then slipped quietly to the front door, opened it and stepped out into the night.

A waning moon was shining, and a hushed sense of

growing life filled the air, for it was nearing spring again. As Jennie hurried along the shadowy streets—the arc light had not yet been invented—she had a sinking sense of fear; what was this rash thing she was about to do? How would the Senator receive her? What would he think? She stood stock-still, wavering and doubtful; then the recollection of Bass in his night cell came over her again, and she hurried on.

The character of the Capitol Hotel was such that it was not difficult for a woman to find ingress through the ladies' entrance to the various floors of the hotel at any hour of the night. The hotel, not unlike many others of the time, was in no sense loosely conducted, but its method of supervision in places was lax. Any person could enter, and, by applying at a rear entrance to the lobby, gain the attention of the clerk. Otherwise not much notice was taken of those who came and went.

When she came to the door it was dark save for a low light burning in the entry-way. The distance to the Senator's room was only a short way along the hall of the second floor. She hurried up the steps, nervous and pale, but giving no other outward sign of the storm that was surging within her. When she came to his familiar door she paused; she feared that she might not find him in his room; she trembled again to think that he might be there. A light shone through the transom, and, summoning all her courage, she knocked. A man coughed and bestirred himself.

His surprise as he opened the door knew no bounds. "Why, Jennie!" he exclaimed. "How delightful! I was thinking of you. Come in—come in."

He welcomed her with an eager embrace.

"I was coming out to see you, believe me, I was. I was thinking all along how I could straighten this matter out. And now you come. But what's the trouble?"

He held her at arm's length and studied her distressed face. The fresh beauty of her seemed to him like cut lilies wet with dew.

He felt a great surge of tenderness.

"I have something to ask you," she at last brought herself to say. "My brother is in jail. We need ten dollars to get him out, and I didn't know where else to go."

"My poor child!" he said, chafing her hands. "Where else should you go? Haven't I told you always to come to me? Don't you know, Jennie, I would do anything in the world for you?"

"Yes," she gasped.

"Well, then, don't worry about that any more. But won't fate ever cease striking at you, poor child? How did your brother come to get in jail?"

"They caught him throwing coal down from the cars," she replied.

"Ah!" he replied, his sympathies touched and awakened. Here was this boy arrested and fined for what fate was practically driving him to do. Here was this girl pleading with him at night, in his room, for what to her was a great necessity—ten dollars; to him, a mere nothing. "I will arrange about your brother," he said quickly. "Don't worry. I can get him out in half an hour. You sit here now and be comfortable until I return."

He waved her to his easy-chair beside a large lamp, and hurried out of the room.

Brander knew the sheriff who had personal supervision of the county jail. He knew the judge who had administered the fine. It was but a five minutes' task to write a note to the judge asking him to revoke the fine, for the sake of the boy's character, and send it by a messenger to his home. Another ten minutes' task to go personally to the jail and ask his friend, the sheriff, to release the boy then and there.

"Here is the money," he said. "If the fine is revoked you can return it to me. Let him go now."

The sheriff was only too glad to comply. He hastened below to personally supervise the task, and Bass, a very much astonished boy, was set free. No explanations were vouchsafed him.

"That's all right now," said the turnkey. "You're at liberty. Run along home and don't let them catch you at anything like that again."

Bass went his way wondering, and the ex-Senator returned to his hotel trying to decide just how this delicate situation should be handled. Obviously Jennie had not told her father of her mission. She had come as a last resource. She was now waiting for him in his room.

There are crises in all men's lives when they waver between the strict fulfilment of justice and duty and the great possibilities for personal happiness which another line of conduct seems to assure. And the dividing line is not always marked and clear. He knew that the issue of taking her, even as his wife, was made difficult by the senseless opposition of her father. The opinion of the world brought up still another complication. Supposing he should take her openly, what would the world say? She was a significant type emotionally, that he knew. There was something there—artistically, temperamentally, which was far and beyond the keenest suspicion of the herd. He did not know himself quite what it was, but he felt a largeness of feeling not altogether squared with intellect, or perhaps better yet, experience, which was worthy of any man's desire. "This remarkable girl," he thought, seeing her clearly in his mind's eye.

Meditating as to what he should do, he returned to his hotel, and the room. As he entered he was struck anew with her beauty, and with the irresistible appeal of her personality. In the glow of the shaded lamp she seemed a figure of marvelous potentiality.

"Well," he said, endeavoring to appear calm, "I have looked after your brother. He is out."

She rose.

"Oh," she exclaimed, clasping her hands and stretching her arms out toward him. There were tears of gratefulness in her eyes.

He saw them and stepped close to her. "Jennie, for heaven's sake don't cry," he entreated. "You angel! You sister of mercy! To think you should have to add tears to your other sacrifices."

He drew her to him, and then all the caution of years deserted him. There was a sense both of need and of fulfilment in his mood. At last, in spite of other losses, fate had brought him what he most desired—love, a woman whom he could love. He took her in his arms, and kissed her again and again.

The English Jefferies has told us that it requires a hundred and fifty years to make a perfect maiden. "From all enchanted things of earth and air, this preciousness has been drawn. From the south wind that breathed a century and a half over the green wheat; from the perfume of the growing grasses waving over heavy-laden clover and laughing veronica, hiding the green finches, baffling the bee; from rose-lined hedge, woodbine, and cornflower, azure blue, where yellowing wheat stalks crowd up under the shadow of green firs. All the devious brooklets' sweetness where the iris stays the sunlight; all the wild woods hold of beauty; all the broad hills of thyme and freedom—thrice a hundred years repeated.

"A hundred years of cowslips, bluebells, violets; purple spring and golden autumn; sunshine, shower, and dewy mornings; the night immortal; all the rhythm of time unrolling. A chronicle unwritten and past all power of writing; who shall preserve a record of the petals that fell from the roses a century ago? The swallows to the house-tops three hundred times—think of that! Thence she sprang, and the world yearns toward her beauty as to flowers that are past. The loveliness of seventeen is centuries old. That is why passion is almost sad."

If you have understood and appreciated the beauty of hare-bells three hundred times repeated; if the quality of the roses, of the music, of the ruddy mornings and evenings of the world has ever touched your heart; if all beauty were passing, and you were given these things to hold in your arms before the world slipped away, would you give them up?

Chapter VIII

THE SIGNIFICANCE of the material and spiritual changes which sometimes overtake us are not very clear at the time. A sense of shock, a sense of danger, and then apparently we subside to old ways, but the change has come. Never again, here or elsewhere, will we be the same. Jennie pondering after the subtle emotional turn which her evening's sympathetic expedition had taken, was lost in a vague confusion of emotions. She had no definite realization of what social and physical changes this new relationship to the Senator might entail. She was not conscious as yet of that shock which the possibility of maternity, even under the most favorable conditions, must bring to the average woman. Her present attitude was one of surprise, wonder, uncertainty; and at the same time she experienced a genuine feeling of quiet happiness. Brander was a good man; now he was closer to her than ever. He loved her. Because of this new relationship a change in her social condition was to inevitably follow. Life was to be radically different from now on—was different at this moment. Brander assured her over and over of his enduring affection.

"I tell you, Jennie," he repeated, as she was leaving, "I don't want you to worry. This emotion of mine got the best of me, but I'll marry you. I've been carried off my feet, but I'll make it up to you. Go home and say nothing at all. Caution your brother, if it isn't too late. Keep your own counsel, and I will marry you and take you away. I can't do it right now. I don't want to do it here. But I'm going to Washington, and I'll send for you. And here"—he reached for his purse and took from it a hundred dollars, practically all he had with him, "take that. I'll send you more to-morrow. You're my girl now—remember that. You belong to me."

He embraced her tenderly.

She went out into the night, thinking. No doubt he would do as he said. She dwelt, in imagination, upon the possibilities of a new and fascinating existence. Of course he would marry her. Think of it! She would go to Washington—that far-off place. And her father and mother—they would not need to work so hard any more. And Bass, and Martha—she fairly glowed as she recounted to herself the many ways in which she could help them all.

A block away she waited for Brander, who accompanied her to her own gate, and waited while she made a cautious reconnaissance. She slipped up the steps and tried the door. It was open. She paused a moment to indicate to her lover that she was safe, and entered. All was silent within. She slipped to her own room and heard Veronica breathing. She went quietly to where Bass slept with George. He was in bed, stretched out as if asleep. When she entered he asked, "Is that you, Jennie?"

"Yes."

"Where have you been?"

"Listen," she whispered. "Have you seen papa and mamma?"

"Yes."

"Did they know I had gone out?"

"Ma did. She told me not to ask after you. Where have you been?"

"I went to see Senator Brander for you."

"Oh, that was it. They didn't say why they let me out."

"Don't tell any one," she pleaded. "I don't want any one to know. You know how papa feels about him."

"All right," he replied. But he was curious as to what the ex-Senator thought, what he had done, and how she had appealed to him. She explained briefly; then she heard her mother come to the door.

"Jennie," she whispered.

Jennie went out.

"Oh, why did you go?" she asked.

"I couldn't help it, ma," she replied. "I thought I must do something."

"Why did you stay so long?"

"He wanted to talk to me," she answered evasively.

Her mother looked at her nervously, wanly.

"I have been so afraid, oh, so afraid. Your father went to your room, but I said you were asleep. He locked the front door, but I opened it again. When Bass came in he wanted to call you, but I persuaded him to wait until morning."

Again she looked wistfully at her daughter.

"I'm all right, mamma," said Jennie encouragingly. "I'll tell you all about it to-morrow. Go to bed. How does he think Bass got out?"

"He doesn't know. He thought maybe they just let him go because he couldn't pay the fine."

Jennie laid her hand lovingly on her mother's shoulder.

"Go to bed," she said.

She was already years older in thought and act. She felt as though she must help her mother now as well as herself.

The days which followed were ones of dreamy uncertainty to Jennie. She went over in her mind these dramatic events time and time and time and again. It was not such a difficult matter to tell her mother that the Senator had talked again of marriage, that he proposed to come and get her after his next trip to Washington, that he had given her a hundred dollars and intended to give her more, but of that other matter—the one all-important thing, she could not bring herself to speak. It was too sacred. The balance of the money that he had promised her arrived by messenger the following day, four hundred dollars in bills, with the admonition that she should put it in a local bank. The ex-Senator explained that he was already on his way to Washington, but that he would come back or send for her. "Keep a stout heart," he wrote. "There are better days in store for you."

Brander was gone, and Jennie's fate was really in the balance. But her mind still retained all of the heart-innocence, and unsophistication of her youth; a certain gentle wistfulness was the only outward change in her demeanor. He would surely send for her. There was the mirage of a distant country and wondrous scenes looming up in her mind. She had a little fortune in the bank, more than she had ever dreamed of, with which to help her mother. There were natural, girlish anticipations of good still holding over, which made her less apprehensive than she could otherwise possibly have been. All nature, life, possibility was in the balance. It might turn good, or ill, but with so inexperienced a soul it would not be entirely evil until it was so.

How a mind under such uncertain circumstances could retain so comparatively placid a vein is one of those marvels which find their explanation in the inherent trustfulness of the spirit of youth. It is not often that the minds of men retain the perceptions of their younger days. The marvel is not that one should thus retain, but that any should ever lose them. Go the world over, and after you have put away the wonder and tenderness of youth what is there left? The few sprigs of green that sometimes invade the barrenness of your material- ism, the few glimpses of summer which flash past the eye of the wintry soul, the half hours off during the long tedium of burrowing, these reveal to the hardened earth-seeker the uni- verse which the youthful mind has with it always. No fear and no favor; the open fields and the light upon the hills; morning, noon, night; stars, the bird-calls, the water's purl— these are the natural inheritance of the mind of the child. Men call it poetic, those who are hardened fanciful. In the days of their youth it was natural, but the receptiveness of youth has departed, and they cannot see.

How this worked out in her personal actions was to be seen only in a slightly accentuated wistfulness, a touch of which was in every task. Sometimes she would wonder that no letter came, but at the same time she would recall the fact that he had specified a few weeks, and hence the six that ac- tually elapsed did not seem so long.

In the meanwhile the distinguished ex-Senator had gone light-heartedly to his conference with the President, he had joined in a pleasant round of social calls, and he was about to pay a short country visit to some friends in Maryland, when he was seized with a slight attack of fever, which confined him to his room for a few days. He felt a little irritated that he should be laid up just at this time, but never suspected that there was anything serious in his indisposition. Then the doctor discovered that he was suffering from a virulent form of typhoid, the ravages of which took away his senses for a time and left him very weak. He was thought to be conva- lescing, however, when just six weeks after he had last parted with Jennie, he was seized with a sudden attack of heart fail- ure and never regained consciousness. Jennie remained bliss- fully ignorant of his illness and did not even see the heavy- typed headlines of the announcement of his death until Bass came home that evening.

"Look here, Jennie," he said excitedly, "Brander's dead!"

He held up the newspaper, on the first column of which was printed in heavy block type:

DEATH OF EX-SENATOR BRANDER

Sudden Passing of Ohio's Distinguished Son.
Succumbs to Heart Failure at the Arlington, in
Washington.

Recent attack of typhoid, from which he was thought
to be recovering, proves fatal. Notable phases
of a remarkable career.

Jennie looked at it in blank amazement. "Dead?" she exclaimed.

"There it is in the paper," returned Bass, his tone being that of one who is imparting a very interesting piece of news. "He died at ten o'clock this morning."

Chapter IX

JENNIE TOOK the paper with but ill-concealed trembling and went into the adjoining room. There she stood by the front window and looked at it again, a sickening sensation of dread holding her as though in a trance.

"He is dead," was all that her mind could formulate for the time, and as she stood there the voice of Bass recounting the fact to Gerhardt in the adjoining room sounded in her ears. "Yes, he is dead," she heard him say; and once again she tried to get some conception of what it meant to her. But her mind seemed a blank.

A moment later Mrs. Gerhardt joined her. She had heard Bass's announcement and had seen Jennie leave the room, but her trouble with Gerhardt over the Senator had caused her to be careful of any display of emotion. No conception of the real state of affairs ever having crossed her mind, she was only interested in seeing how Jennie would take this sudden annihilation of her hopes.

"Isn't it too bad?" she said, with real sorrow. "To think that he should have to die just when he was going to do so much for you—for us all."

She paused, expecting some word of agreement, but Jennie remained unwontedly dumb.

"I wouldn't feel badly," continued Mrs. Gerhardt. "It can't be helped. He meant to do a good deal, but you mustn't think of that now. It's all over, and it can't be helped, you know."

She paused again, and still Jennie remained motionless and mute. Mrs. Gerhardt, seeing how useless her words were, concluded that Jennie wished to be alone, and she went away.

Still Jennie stood there, and now, as the real significance of the news began to formulate itself into consecutive thought, she began to realize the wretchedness of her position, its helplessness. She went into her bedroom and sat down upon the side of the bed, from which position she saw a very pale, distraught face staring at her from out of the small mirror. She looked at it uncertainly; could that really be her own countenance? "I'll have to go away," she thought, and began, with the courage of despair, to wonder what refuge would be open to her.

In the mean time the evening meal was announced, and, to maintain appearances, she went out and joined the family; the naturalness of her part was very difficult to sustain. Gerhardt observed her subdued condition without guessing the depth of emotion which it covered. Bass was too much interested in his own affairs to pay particular attention to anybody.

During the days that followed Jennie pondered over the difficulties of her position and wondered what she should do. Money she had, it was true; but no friends, no experience, no place to go. She had always lived with her family. She began to feel unaccountable sinkings of spirit, nameless and formless fears seemed to surround and haunt her. Once when she arose in the morning she felt an uncontrollable desire to cry, and frequently thereafter this feeling would seize upon her at the most inopportune times. Mrs. Gerhardt began to note her moods, and one afternoon she resolved to question her daughter.

"Now you must tell me what's the matter with you," she said quietly. "Jennie, you must tell your mother everything."

Jennie, to whom confession had seemed impossible, under the sympathetic persistence of her mother broke down at last and made the fatal confession. Mrs. Gerhardt stood there, too dumb with misery to give vent to a word.

"Oh!" she said at last, a great wave of self-accusation sweeping over her, "it is all my fault. I might have known. But we'll do what we can." She broke down and sobbed aloud.

After a time she went back to the washing she had to do, and stood over her tub rubbing and crying. The tears ran down her cheeks and dropped into the suds. Once in a while she stopped and tried to dry her eyes with her apron, but they soon filled again.

Now that the first shock had passed, there came the vivid consciousness of ever-present danger. What would Gerhardt do if he learned the truth? He had often said that if ever one of his daughters should act like some of those he knew he would turn her out of doors. "She should not stay under my roof!" he had exclaimed.

"I'm so afraid of your father," Mrs. Gerhardt often said to Jennie in this intermediate period. "I don't know what he'll say."

"Perhaps I'd better go away," suggested her daughter.

"No," she said; "he needn't know just yet. Wait awhile." But in her heart of hearts she knew that the evil day could not be long postponed.

One day, when her own suspense had reached such a pitch that it could no longer be endured, Mrs. Gerhardt sent Jennie away with the children, hoping to be able to tell her husband before they returned. All the morning she fidgeted about, dreading the opportune moment and letting him retire to his slumber without speaking. When afternoon came she did not go out to work, because she could not leave with her painful duty unfulfilled. Gerhardt arose at four, and still she hesitated, knowing full well that Jennie would soon return and that the specially prepared occasion would then be lost. It is almost certain that she would not have had the courage to say anything if he himself had not brought up the subject of Jennie's appearance.

"She doesn't look well," he said. "There seems to be something the matter with her."

"Oh," began Mrs. Gerhardt, visibly struggling with her fears, and moved to make an end of it at any cost, "Jennie is in trouble. I don't know what to do. She—"

Gerhardt, who had unscrewed a door-lock and was trying to mend it, looked up sharply from his work.

"What do you mean?" he asked.

Mrs. Gerhardt had her apron in her hands at the time, her nervous tendency to roll it coming upon her. She tried to summon sufficient courage to explain, but fear mastered her completely; she lifted the apron to her eyes and began to cry.

Gerhardt looked at her and rose. He was a man with the Calvin type of face, rather spare, with skin sallow and discolored as the result of age and work in the wind and rain. When he was surprised or angry sparks of light glittered in his eyes. He frequently pushed his hair back when he was troubled, and almost invariably walked the floor; just now he looked alert and dangerous.

"What is that you say?" he inquired in German, his voice

straining to a hard note. "In trouble—has some one—" He paused and flung his hand upward. "Why don't you speak?" he demanded.

"I never thought," went on Mrs. Gerhardt, frightened, and yet following her own train of thought, "that anything like that would happen to her. She was such a good girl. Oh!" she concluded, "to think he should ruin Jennie."

"By thunder!" shouted Gerhardt, giving way to a fury of feeling, "I thought so! Brander! Ha! Your fine man! That comes of letting her go running around at nights, buggy-riding, walking the streets. I thought so. God in heaven!—"

He broke from his dramatic attitude and struck out in a fierce stride across the narrow chamber, turning like a caged animal.

"Ruined!" he exclaimed. "Ruined! Ha! So he has ruined her, has he?"

Suddenly he stopped like an image jerked by a string. He was directly in front of Mrs. Gerhardt, who had retired to the table at the side of the wall, and was standing there pale with fear.

"He is dead now!" he shouted, as if this fact had now first occurred to him. "He is dead!"

He put both hands to his temples, as if he feared his brain would give way, and stood looking at her, the mocking irony of the situation seeming to burn in his brain like fire.

"Dead!" he repeated, and Mrs. Gerhardt, fearing for the reason of the man, shrank still farther away, her wits taken up rather with the tragedy of the figure he presented than with the actual substance of his woe.

"He intended to marry her," she pleaded nervously. "He would have married her if he had not died."

"Would have!" shouted Gerhardt, coming out of his trance at the sound of her voice. "Would have! That's a fine thing to talk about now. Would have! The hound! May his soul burn in hell—the dog! Ah, God, I hope—I hope— If I were not a Christian—" He clenched his hands, the awfulness of his passion shaking him like a leaf.

Mrs. Gerhardt burst into tears, and her husband turned away, his own feelings far too intense for him to have any sympathy with her. He walked to and fro, his heavy step shaking the kitchen floor. After a time he came back, a new phase of the dread calamity having offered itself to his mind.

"When did this happen?" he demanded.

"I don't know," returned Mrs. Gerhardt, too terror-stricken to tell the truth. "I only found it out the other day."

"You lie!" he exclaimed in his excitement. "You were always shielding her. It is your fault that she is where she is. If you had let me have my way there would have been no cause for our trouble to-night.

"A fine ending," he went on to himself. "A fine ending. My boy gets into jail; my daughter walks the streets and gets herself talked about; the neighbors come to me with open remarks about my children; and now this scoundrel ruins her. By the God in heaven, I don't know what has got into my children!

"I don't know how it is," he went on, unconsciously commiserating himself. "I try, I try! Every night I pray that the Lord will let me do right, but it is no use. I might work and work. My hands—look at them—are rough with work. All my life I have tried to be an honest man. Now—now—" His voice broke, and it seemed for a moment as if he would give way to tears. Suddenly he turned on his wife, the major passion of anger possessing him.

"You are the cause of this," he exclaimed. "You are the sole cause. If you had done as I told you to do this would not have happened. No, you wouldn't do that. She must go out! out!! out!!! She has become a street-walker, that's what she has become. She has set herself right to go to hell. Let her go. I wash my hands of the whole thing. This is enough for me."

He made as if to go off to his little bedroom, but he had no sooner reached the door than he came back.

"She shall get out!" he said electrically. "She shall not stay under my roof! To-night! At once! I will not let her enter my door again. I will show her whether she will disgrace me or not!"

"You mustn't turn her out on the streets to-night," pleaded Mrs. Gerhardt. "She has no place to go."

"To-night!" he repeated. "This very minute! Let her find a home. She did not want this one. Let her get out now. We will see how the world treats her." He walked out of the room, inflexible resolution fixed upon his rugged features.

At half-past five, when Mrs. Gerhardt was tearfully going about the duty of getting supper, Jennie returned. Her mother started when she heard the door open, for now she knew the storm would burst afresh. Her father met her on the threshold.

"Get out of my sight!" he said savagely. "You shall not stay another hour in my house. I don't want to see you any more. Get out!"

Jennie stood before him, pale, trembling a little, and silent. The children she had brought home with her crowded about in frightened amazement. Veronica and Martha, who loved her dearly, began to cry.

"What's the matter?" George asked, his mouth open in wonder.

"She shall get out," reiterated Gerhardt. "I don't want her under my roof. If she wants to be a street-walker, let her be one, but she shall not stay here. Pack your things," he added, staring at her.

Jennie had no word to say, but the children cried loudly.

"Be still," said Gerhardt. "Go into the kitchen."

He drove them all out and followed stubbornly himself.

Jennie went quietly to her room. She gathered up her few little belongings and began, with tears, to put them into a valise her mother brought her. The little girlish trinkets that she had accumulated from time to time she did not take. She saw them, but thought of her younger sisters, and let them stay. Martha and Veronica would have assisted her, but their father forbade them to go.

At six o'clock Bass came in, and seeing the nervous assembly in the kitchen, inquired what the trouble was.

Gerhardt looked at him grimly, but did not answer.

"What's the trouble?" insisted Bass. "What are you all sitting around for?"

"He is driving Jennie away," whispered Mrs. Gerhardt tearfully.

"What for?" asked Bass, opening his eyes in astonishment.

"I shall tell you what for," broke in Gerhardt, still speaking in German. "Because she's a street-walker, that's what for.

She goes and gets herself ruined by a man thirty years older than she is, a man old enough to be her father. Let her get out of this. She shall not stay here another minute."

Bass looked about him, and the children opened their eyes. All felt clearly that something terrible had happened, even the little ones. None but Bass understood.

"What do you want to send her out to-night for?" he inquired. "This is no time to send a girl out on the streets. Can't she stay here until morning?"

"No," said Gerhardt.

"He oughtn't to do that," put in the mother.

"She goes now," said Gerhardt. "Let that be an end of it."

"Where is she going to go?" insisted Bass.

"I don't know," Mrs. Gerhardt interpolated weakly.

Bass looked around, but did nothing until Mrs. Gerhardt motioned him toward the front door when her husband was not looking.

"Go in! Go in!" was the import of her gesture.

Bass went in, and then Mrs. Gerhardt dared to leave her work and follow. The children stayed awhile, but, one by one, even they slipped away, leaving Gerhardt alone. When he thought that time enough had elapsed he arose.

In the interval Jennie had been hastily coached by her mother.

Jennie should go to a private boarding-house somewhere, and send back her address. Bass should not accompany her, but she should wait a little way up the street, and he would follow. When her father was away the mother might get to see her, or Jennie could come home. All else must be postponed until they could meet again.

While the discussion was still going on, Gerhardt came in.

"Is she going?" he asked harshly.

"Yes," answered Mrs. Gerhardt, with her first and only note of defiance.

Bass said, "What's the hurry?" But Gerhardt frowned too mightily for him to venture on any further remonstrance.

Jennie entered, wearing her one good dress and carrying her valise. There was fear in her eyes, for she was passing through a fiery ordeal, but she had become a woman. The strength of love was with her, the support of patience and the ruling sweetness of sacrifice. Silently she kissed her mother, while tears fell fast. Then she turned, and the door closed upon her as she went forth to a new life.

Chapter X

THE WORLD into which Jennie was thus unduly thrust forth was that in which virtue has always vainly struggled since time immemorial; for virtue is the wishing well and the doing well unto others. Virtue is that quality of generosity which offers itself willingly for another's service, and, being this, it is held by society to be nearly worthless. Sell yourself cheaply and you shall be used lightly and trampled under foot. Hold yourself dearly, however unworthily, and you will be respected. Society, in the mass, lacks woefully in the matter of discrimination. Its one criterion is the opinion of others. Its one test that of self-preservation. Has he preserved his fortune? Has she preserved her purity? Only in rare instances and with rare individuals does there seem to be any guiding light from within.

Jennie had not sought to hold herself dear. Innate feeling in her made for self-sacrifice. She could not be readily corrupted by the world's selfish lessons on how to preserve oneself from the evil to come.

It is in such supreme moments that growth is greatest. It comes as with a vast surge, this feeling of strength and sufficiency. We may still tremble, the fear of doing wretchedly may linger, but we grow. Flashes of inspiration come to guide the soul. In nature there is no outside. When we are cast from a group or a condition we have still the companionship of all that is. Nature is not ungenerous. Its winds and stars are fellows with you. Let the soul be but gentle and receptive, and this vast truth will come home—not in set phrases, perhaps, but as a feeling, a comfort, which, after all, is the last essence of knowledge. In the universe peace is wisdom.

Jennie had hardly turned from the door when she was overtaken by Bass. "Give me your grip," he said; and then seeing that she was dumb with unutterable feeling, he added, "I think I know where I can get you a room."

He led the way to the southern part of the city, where they were not known, and up to the door of an old lady whose parlor clock had been recently purchased from the instalment firm by whom he was now employed. She was not well off, he knew, and had a room to rent.

"Is that room of yours still vacant?" he asked.

"Yes," she said, looking at Jennie.

"I wish you'd let my sister have it. We're moving away, and she can't go yet."

The old lady expressed her willingness, and Jennie was soon temporarily installed.

"Don't worry now," said Bass, who felt rather sorry for her. "This'll blow over. Ma said I should tell you not to worry. Come up to-morrow when he's gone."

Jennie said she would, and, after giving her further oral encouragement, he arranged with the old lady about board, and took his leave.

"It's all right now," he said encouragingly as he went out. "You'll come out all right. Don't worry. I've got to go back, but I'll come around in the morning."

He went away, and the bitter stress of it blew lightly over his head, for he was thinking that Jennie had made a mistake. This was shown by the manner in which he had asked her questions as they had walked together, and that in the face of her sad and doubtful mood.

"What'd you want to do that for?" and "Didn't you ever think what you were doing?" he persisted.

"Please don't ask me to-night," Jennie had said, which put an end to the sharpest form of his queries. She had no excuse to offer and no complaint to make. If any blame attached, very likely it was hers. His own misfortune and the family's and her sacrifice were alike forgotten.

Left alone in her strange abode, Jennie gave way to her saddened feelings. The shock and shame of being banished from her home overcame her, and she wept. Although of a naturally long-suffering and uncomplaining disposition, the catastrophic wind-up of all her hopes was too much for her. What was this element in life that could seize and overwhelm one as does a great wind? Why this sudden intrusion of death to shatter all that had seemed most promising in life?

As she thought over the past, a very clear recollection of the details of her long relationship with Brander came back to her, and for all her suffering she could only feel a loving affection for him. After all, he had not deliberately willed her any harm. His kindness, his generosity—these things had been real. He had been essentially a good man, and she was sorry—more for his sake than for her own—that his end had been so untimely.

These cogitations, while not at all reassuring, at least served to pass the night away, and the next morning Bass stopped on his way to work to say that Mrs. Gerhardt wished her to come home that same evening. Gerhardt would not be present, and they could talk it over. She spent the day lonesomely enough, but when night fell her spirits brightened, and at a quarter of eight she set out.

There was not much of comforting news to tell her. Gerhardt was still in a direfully angry and outraged mood. He had already decided to throw up his place on the following Saturday and go to Youngstown. Any place was better than Columbus after this; he could never expect to hold up his head here again. Its memories were odious. He would go away now, and if he succeeded in finding work the family should follow, a decision which meant the abandoning of the little home. He was not going to try to meet the mortgage on the house—he could not hope to.

At the end of the week Gerhardt took his leave, Jennie returned home, and for a time at least there was a restoration of the old order, a condition which, of course, could not endure.

Bass saw it. Jennie's trouble and its possible consequences weighed upon him disagreeably. Columbus was no place to stay. Youngstown was no place to go. If they should all move away to some larger city it would be much better.

He pondered over the situation, and hearing that a manufacturing boom was on in Cleveland, he thought it might be wise to try his luck there. If he succeeded, the others might follow. If Gerhardt still worked on in Youngstown, as he was now doing, and the family came to Cleveland, it would save Jennie from being turned out in the streets.

Bass waited a little while before making up his mind, but finally announced his purpose.

"I believe I'll go up to Cleveland," he said to his mother one evening as she was getting supper.

"Why?" she asked, looking up uncertainly. She was rather afraid that Bass would desert her.

"I think I can get work there," he returned. "We oughtn't to stay in this darned old town."

"Don't swear," she returned reprovingly.

"Oh, I know," he said, "but it's enough to make any one swear. We've never had anything but rotten luck here. I'm going to go, and maybe if I get anything we can all move. We'd be better off if we'd get some place where people don't know us. We can't be anything here."

Mrs. Gerhardt listened with a strong hope for a betterment of their miserable life creeping into her heart. If Bass would only do this. If he would go and get work, and come to her rescue, as a strong bright young son might, what a thing it would be! They were in the rapids of a life which was moving toward a dreadful calamity. If only something would happen.

"Do you think you could get something to do?" she asked interestedly.

"I ought to," he said. "I've never looked for a place yet that I didn't get it. Other fellows have gone up there and done all right. Look at the Millers."

He shoved his hands into his pockets and looked out the window.

"Do you think you could get along until I try my hand up there?" he asked.

"I guess we could," she replied. "Papa's at work now and we have some money that, that—" she hesitated to name the source, so ashamed was she of their predicament.

"Yes, I know," said Bass, grimly.

"We won't have to pay any rent here before fall and then we'll have to give it up anyhow," she added.

She was referring to the mortgage on the house, which fell due the next September and which unquestionably could not be met. "If we could move away from here before then, I guess we could get along."

"I'll do it," said Bass determinedly. "I'll go."

Accordingly, he threw up his place at the end of the month, and the day after he left for Cleveland.

Chapter XI

THE INCIDENTS of the days that followed, relating as they did peculiarly to Jennie, were of an order which the morality of our day has agreed to taboo.

Certain processes of the all-mother, the great artificing wisdom of the power that works and weaves in silence and in darkness, when viewed in the light of the established opinion of some of the little individuals created by it, are considered very vile. We turn our faces away from the creation of life as if that were the last thing that man should dare to interest himself in, openly.

It is curious that a feeling of this sort should spring up in a world whose very essence is generative, the vast process dual, and where wind, water, soil, and light alike minister to the fruition of that which is all that we are. Although the whole earth, not we alone, is moved by passions hymeneal, and everything terrestrial has come into being by the one common road, yet there is that ridiculous tendency to close the eyes and turn away the head as if there were something unclean in nature itself. "Conceived in iniquity and born in sin," is the unnatural interpretation put upon the process by the extreme religionist, and the world, by its silence, gives assent to a judgment so marvelously warped.

Surely there is something radically wrong in this attitude. The teachings of philosophy and the deductions of biology should find more practical application in the daily reasoning of man. No process is vile, no condition is unnatural. The accidental variation from a given social practice does not necessarily entail sin. No poor little earthling, caught in the enormous grip of chance, and so swerved from the established customs of men, could possibly be guilty of that depth of vileness which the attitude of the world would seem to predicate so inevitably.

Jennie was now to witness the unjust interpretation of that wonder of nature, which, but for Brander's death, might have been consecrated and hallowed as one of the ideal functions of life. Although herself unable to distinguish the separateness of this from every other normal process of life, yet was she made to feel, by the actions of all about her, that degradation was her portion and sin the foundation as well as the condition of her state. Almost, not quite, it was sought to extinguish the affection, the consideration, the care which, afterward, the world would demand of her, for her child. Almost, not quite, was the budding and essential love looked upon as evil. Although her punishment was neither the gibbet nor the jail of a few hundred years before, yet the ignorance and immobility of the human beings about her made it impossible for them to see anything in her present condition but a vile and premeditated infraction of the social code, the punishment of which was ostracism. All she could do now was to shun the scornful gaze of men, and to bear in silence the great change that was coming upon her. Strangely enough, she felt no useless remorse, no vain regrets. Her heart was pure, and she was conscious that it was filled with peace. Sorrow there was, it is true, but only a mellow phase of it, a vague uncertainty and wonder, which would sometimes cause her eyes to fill with tears.

You have heard the wood-dove calling in the lone stillness of the summertime; you have found the unheeded brooklet singing and babbling where no ear comes to hear. Under dead leaves and snow-banks the delicate arbutus unfolds its simple blossom, answering some heavenly call for color. So, too, this other flower of womanhood.

Jennie was left alone, but, like the wood-dove, she was a voice of sweetness in the summer-time. Going about her household duties, she was content to wait, without a murmur, the fulfilment of that process for which, after all, she was but the sacrificial implement. When her duties were lightest she was content to sit in quiet meditation, the marvel of life holding her as in a trance. When she was hardest pressed to aid her mother, she would sometimes find herself quietly singing, the pleasure of work lifting her out of herself. Always she was content to face the future with a serene and unfaltering courage. It is not so with all women. Nature is unkind in permitting the minor type to bear a child at all. The larger natures in their maturity welcome motherhood, see in it the immense possibilities of racial fulfilment, and find joy and satisfaction in being the hand-maiden of so immense a purpose.

Jennie, a child in years, was potentially a woman physically and mentally, but not yet come into rounded conclusions as to life and her place in it. The great situation which had forced her into this anomalous position was from one point of view a tribute to her individual capacity. It proved her courage, the largeness of her sympathy, her willingness to sacrifice for what she considered a worthy cause. That it resulted in an unexpected consequence, which placed upon her a larger and more complicated burden, was due to the fact that her sense of self-protection had not been commensurate with her emotions. There were times when the prospective coming of the child gave her a sense of fear and confusion, because she did not know but that the child might eventually reproach her; but there was always that saving sense of eternal justice in life which would not permit her to be utterly crushed. To her way of thinking, people were not intentionally cruel. Vague thoughts of sympathy and divine goodness permeated her soul. Life at worst or best was beautiful—had always been so.

These thoughts did not come to her all at once, but through the months during which she watched and waited. It was a wonderful thing to be a mother, even under these untoward conditions. She felt that she would love this child, would be a good mother to it if life permitted. That was the problem—what would life permit?

There were many things to be done—clothes to be made; certain provisions of hygiene and diet to be observed. One of her fears was that Gerhardt might unexpectedly return, but he did not. The old family doctor who had nursed the various members of the Gerhardt family through their multitudinous ailments—Doctor Ellwanger—was taken into consultation, and he gave sound and practical advice. Despite his Lutheran upbringing, the practice of medicine in a large and kindly way had led him to the conclusion that there are more things in heaven and earth than are dreamed of in our philosophies and in our small neighborhood relationships. "So it is," he observed to Mrs. Gerhardt when she confided to him nervously what the trouble was. "Well, you mustn't worry. These things happen in more places than you think. If you knew as much about life as I do, and about your neighbors, you would not cry. Your girl will be all right. She is very healthy. She can go away somewhere afterward, and people will never know. Why should you worry about what your neighbors think. It is not so uncommon as you imagine."

Mrs. Gerhardt marveled. He was such a wise man. It gave her a little courage. As for Jennie, she listened to his advice with interest and without fear. She wanted things not so much for herself as for her child, and she was anxious to do whatever she was told. The doctor was curious to know who the father was; when informed he lifted his eyes. "Indeed," he commented. "That ought to be a bright baby."

There came the final hour when the child was ushered into the world. It was Doctor Ellwanger who presided, assisted by the mother, who, having brought forth six herself, knew exactly what to do. There was no difficulty, and at the first cry of the new-born infant there awakened in Jennie a tremendous yearning toward it. This was *her* child! It was weak and feeble—a little girl, and it needed her care. She took it to her breast, when it had been bathed and swaddled, with a tremendous sense of satisfaction and joy. This was her child, her little girl. She wanted to live to be able to work for it, and rejoiced, even in her weakness, that she was so strong. Doctor Ellwanger predicted a quick recovery. He thought two weeks would be the outside limit of her need to stay in bed. As a matter of fact, in ten days she was up and about, as vigorous and healthy as ever. She had been born with strength and with that nurturing quality which makes the ideal mother.

The great crisis had passed, and now life went on much as before. The children, outside of Bass, were too young to understand fully, and had been deceived by the story that Jennie was married to Senator Brander, who had died. They did not know that a child was coming until it was there. The neighbors were feared by Mrs. Gerhardt, for they were ever watchful and really knew all. Jennie would never have braved this local atmosphere except for the advice of Bass, who, having secured a place in Cleveland some time before, had written that he thought when she was well enough it would be advisable for the whole family to seek a new start in Cleveland. Things were flourishing there. Once away they would never hear of their present neighbors and Jennie could find something to do. So she stayed at home.

Chapter XII

BASS WAS no sooner in Cleveland than the marvel of that growing city was sufficient to completely restore his equanimity of soul and to stir up new illusions as to the possibility of rehabilitation for himself and his family. "If only they could come here," he thought. "If only they could all get work and do right." Here was no evidence of any of their recent troubles, no acquaintances who could suggest by their mere presence the troubles of the past. All was business, all activity. The very turning of the corner seemed to rid one of old times and crimes. It was as if a new world existed in every block.

He soon found a place in a cigar store, and, after working a few weeks, he began to write home the cheering ideas he had in mind. Jennie ought to come as soon as she was able, and then, if she found something to do, the others might follow. There was plenty of work for girls of her age. She could live in the same house with him temporarily; or maybe they could take one of the fifteen-dollar-a-month cottages that were for rent. There were big general furnishing houses, where one could buy everything needful for a small house on very easy monthly terms. His mother could come and keep house for them. They would be in a clean, new atmosphere, unknown and untalked about. They could start life all over again; they could be decent, honorable, prosperous.

Filled with this hope and the glamor which new scenes and new environment invariably throw over the unsophisticated mind, he wrote a final letter, in which he suggested that Jennie should come at once. This was when the baby was six months old. There were theaters here, he said, and beautiful streets. Vessels from the lakes came into the heart of the city. It was a wonderful city, and growing very fast. It was thus that the new life appealed to him.

The effect which all this had upon Mrs. Gerhardt, Jennie, and the rest of the family was phenomenal. Mrs. Gerhardt, long weighed upon by the misery which Jennie's error had entailed, was for taking measures for carrying out this plan at once. So buoyant was her natural temperament that she was completely carried away by the glory of Cleveland, and already saw fulfilled therein not only her own desires for a nice home, but the prosperous advancement of her children. "Of course they could get work," she said. Bass was right. She had always wanted Gerhardt to go to some large city, but he would not. Now it was necessary, and they would go and become better off than they ever had been.

And Gerhardt did take this view of the situation. In answer to his wife's letter he wrote that it was not advisable for him to leave his place, but if Bass saw a way for them, it might be a good thing to go. He was the more ready to acquiesce in the plan for the simple reason that he was half distracted with the worry of supporting the family and of paying the debts already outstanding. Every week he laid by five dollars out of his salary, which he sent in the form of a postal order to Mrs. Gerhardt. Three dollars he paid for board, and fifty cents he kept for spending money, church dues, a little tobacco and occasionally a glass of beer. Every week he put a dollar and a half in a little iron bank against a rainy day. His room was a bare corner in the topmost loft of the mill. To this he would ascend after sitting alone on the doorstep of the mill in this lonely, forsaken neighborhood, until nine o'clock of an evening; and here, amid the odor of machinery wafted up from the floor below, by the light of a single tallow candle, he would conclude his solitary day, reading his German paper, folding his hands and thinking, kneeling by an open window in the shadow of the night to say his prayers, and silently stretching himself to rest. Long were the days, dreary the prospect. Still he lifted his hands in utmost faith to God, praying that his sins might be forgiven and that he might be vouchsafed a few more years of comfort and of happy family life.

So the momentous question was finally decided. There was the greatest longing and impatience among the children, and Mrs. Gerhardt shared their emotions in a suppressed way. Jennie was to go first, as Bass had suggested; later on they would all follow.

When the hour came for Jennie's departure there was great excitement in the household.

"How long you going to be 'fore you send for us?" was Martha's inquiry, several times repeated.

"Tell Bass to hurry up," said the eager George.

"I want to go to Cleveland, I want to go to Cleveland," Veronica was caught singing to herself.

"Listen to her," exclaimed George, sarcastically.

"Aw, you hush up," was her displeased rejoinder.

When the final hour came, however, it required all of Jennie's strength to go through with the farewells. Though everything was being done in order to bring them together again under better conditions, she could not help feeling depressed. Her little one, now six months old, was being left behind. The great world was to her one undiscovered bourne. It frightened her.

"You mustn't worry, Ma," she found courage enough to say. "I'll be all right. I'll write you just as soon as I get there. It won't be so very long."

But when it came to bending over her baby for the last time her courage went out like a blown lamp. Stooping over the cradle in which the little one was resting, she looked into its face with passionate, motherly yearning.

"Is it going to be a good little girl?" she cooed.

Then she caught it up into her arms, and hugging it closely to her neck and bosom, she buried her face against its little body. Mrs. Gerhardt saw that she was trembling.

"Come now," she said, coaxingly, "you mustn't carry on so. She will be all right with me. I'll take care of her. If you're going to act this way, you'd better not try to go at all."

Jennie lifted her head, her blue eyes wet with tears, and handed the little one to her mother.

"I can't help it," she said, half crying, half smiling.

Quickly she kissed her mother and the children; then she hurried out.

As she went down the street with George she looked back and bravely waved her hand. Mrs. Gerhardt responded, noticing how much more like a woman she looked. It had been necessary to invest some of her money in new clothes to wear on the train. She had selected a neat, ready-made suit of brown, which fitted her nicely. She wore the skirt of this with a white shirt-waist, and a sailor hat with a white veil wound around it in such fashion that it could be easily drawn over her face. As she went farther and farther away Mrs. Gerhardt followed her lovingly with her glance; and when she disappeared from view she said tenderly, through her own tears:

"I'm glad she looked so nice, anyhow."

Chapter XIII

BASS MET JENNIE at the depot in Cleveland and talked hopefully of the prospects. "The first thing is to get work," he began, while the jingling sounds and the changing odors which the city thrust upon her were confusing and almost benumbing her senses. "Get something to do. It doesn't matter what, so long as you get something. If you don't get more than three or four dollars a week, it will pay the rent. Then, with what George can earn, when he comes, and what Pop sends, we can get along all right. It'll be better than being down in that hole," he concluded.

"Yes," said Jennie, vaguely, her mind so hypnotized by the new display of life about her that she could not bring it forcibly to bear upon the topic under discussion. "I know what you mean. I'll get something."

She was much older now, in understanding if not in years. The ordeal through which she had so recently passed had aroused in her a clearer conception of the responsibilities of life. Her mother was always in her mind, her mother and the children. In particular Martha and Veronica must have a better opportunity to do for themselves than she had had. They should be dressed better; they ought to be kept longer in school; they must have more companionship, more opportunity to broaden their lives.

Cleveland, like every other growing city at this time, was crowded with those who were seeking employment. New enterprises were constantly springing up, but those who were seeking to fulfil the duties they provided were invariably in excess of the demand. A stranger coming to the city might walk into a small position of almost any kind on the very day he arrived; and he might as readily wander in search of employment for weeks and even months. Bass suggested the shops and department stores as a first field in which to inquire. The factories and other avenues of employment were to be her second choice.

"Don't pass a place, though," he had cautioned her, "if you think there's any chance of getting anything to do. Go right in."

"What must I say?" asked Jennie, nervously.

"Tell them you want work. You don't care what you do to begin with."

In compliance with this advice, Jennie set out the very first day, and was rewarded by some very chilly experiences. Wherever she went, no one seemed to want any help. She applied at the stores, the factories, the little shops that lined the outlying thoroughfares, but was always met by a rebuff. As a last resource she turned to housework, although she had hoped to avoid that; and, studying the want columns, she selected four which seemed more promising than the others. To these she decided to apply. One had already been filled when she arrived, but the lady who came to the door was so taken by her appearance that she invited her in and questioned her as to her ability.

"I wish you had come a little earlier," she said. "I like you better than I do the girl I have taken. Leave me your address, anyhow."

Jennie went away, smiling at her reception. She was not quite so youthful looking as she had been before her recent trouble, but the thinner cheeks and the slightly deeper eyes added to the pensiveness and delicacy of her countenance. She was a model of neatness. Her clothes, all newly cleaned and ironed before leaving home, gave her a fresh and inviting appearance. There was growth coming to her in the matter of height, but already in appearance and intelligence she looked to be a young woman of twenty. Best of all, she was of that naturally sunny disposition, which, in spite of toil and privation, kept her always cheerful. Any one in need of a servant-girl or house companion would have been delighted to have had her.

The second place at which she applied was a large residence in Euclid Avenue; it seemed far too imposing for anything she might have to offer in the way of services, but having come so far she decided to make the attempt. The servant who met her at the door directed her to wait a few moments, and finally ushered her into the boudoir of the mistress of the house on the second floor. The latter, a Mrs. Bracebridge, a prepossessing brunette of the conventionally fashionable type, had a keen eye for feminine values and was impressed rather favorably with Jennie. She talked with her a little while, and finally decided to try her in the general capacity of maid.

"I will give you four dollars a week, and you can sleep here if you wish," said Mrs. Bracebridge.

Jennie explained that she was living with her brother, and would soon have her family with her.

"Oh, very well," replied her mistress. "Do as you like about that. Only I expect you to be here promptly."

She wished her to remain for the day and to begin her duties at once, and Jennie agreed. Mrs. Bracebridge provided her a dainty cap and apron, and then spent some little time in instructing her in her duties. Her principal work would be to wait on her mistress, to brush her hair and to help her dress. She was also to answer the bell, wait on the table if need be, and do any other errand which her mistress might indicate. Mrs. Bracebridge seemed a little hard and formal to her prospective servant, but for all that Jennie admired the dash and go and the obvious executive capacity of her employer.

At eight o'clock that evening Jennie was dismissed for the day. She wondered if she could be of any use in such a household, and marveled that she had got along as well as she had. Her mistress had set her to cleaning her jewelry and boudoir ornaments as an opening task, and though she had worked steadily and diligently, she had not finished by the time she left. She hurried away to her brother's apartment, delighted to be able to report that she had found a situation. Now her mother could come to Cleveland. Now she could have her baby with her. Now they could really begin that new life which was to be so much better and finer and sweeter than anything they had ever had before.

At Bass's suggestion Jennie wrote her mother to come at once, and a week or so later a suitable house was found and rented. Mrs. Gerhardt, with the aid of the children, packed up the simple belongings of the family, including a single vanload of furniture, and at the end of a fortnight they were on their way to the new home.

Mrs. Gerhardt always had had a keen desire for a really comfortable home. Solid furniture, upholstered and trimmed, a thick, soft carpet of some warm, pleasing color, plenty of chairs, settees, pictures, a lounge, and a piano—she had wanted these nice things all her life, but her circumstances had never been good enough for her hopes to be realized. Still she did not despair. Some day, maybe, before she died these things would be added to her, and she would be happy. Perhaps her chance was coming now.

Arrived at Cleveland, this feeling of optimism was encouraged by the sight of Jennie's cheerful face. Bass assured her that they would get along all right. He took them out to the house, and George was shown the way to go back to the depot and have the freight looked after. Mrs. Gerhardt had still fifty dollars left out of the money which Senator Brander had sent to Jennie, and with this a way of getting a little extra furniture on the instalment plan was provided. Bass had already paid the first month's rent, and Jennie had spent her evenings for the last few days in washing the windows and floors of this new house and in getting it into a state of perfect cleanliness. Now, when the first night fell, they had two new mattresses and comfortables spread upon a clean floor; a new lamp, purchased from one of the nearby stores, a single box, borrowed by Jennie from a grocery store, for cleaning purposes, upon which Mrs. Gerhardt could sit, and some sausages and bread to stay them until morning. They talked and planned for the future until nine o'clock came, when all but Jennie and her mother retired. These two talked on, the burden of responsibilities resting on the daughter. Mrs. Gerhardt had come to feel in a way dependent upon her.

In the course of a week the entire cottage was in order, with a half-dozen pieces of new furniture, a new carpet, and some necessary kitchen utensils. The most disturbing thing was the need of a new cooking-stove, the cost of which added greatly to the bill. The younger children were entered at the public school, but it was decided that George must find some employment. Both Jennie and her mother felt the injustice of this keenly, but knew no way of preventing the sacrifice.

"We will let him go to school next year if we can," said Jennie.

Auspiciously as the new life seemed to have begun, the closeness with which their expenses were matching their income was an ever-present menace. Bass, originally very

generous in his propositions, soon announced that he felt
four dollars a week for his room and board to be a sufficient
contribution from himself. Jennie gave everything she earned,
and protested that she did not stand in need of anything, so
long as the baby was properly taken care of. George secured
a place as an overgrown cash-boy, and brought in two dollars
and fifty cents a week, all of which, at first, he gladly contributed. Later on he was allowed the fifty cents for himself as
being meet and just. Gerhardt, from his lonely post of labor,
contributed five dollars by mail, always arguing that a little
money ought to be saved in order that his honest debts back
in Columbus might be paid. Out of this total income of
fifteen dollars a week all of these individuals had to be fed
and clothed, the rent paid, coal purchased, and the regular
monthly instalment of three dollars paid on the outstanding
furniture bill of fifty dollars.

How it was done, those comfortable individuals, who
frequently discuss the social aspects of poverty, might well
trouble to inform themselves. Rent, coal, and light alone
consumed the goodly sum of twenty dollars a month; food,
another unfortunately necessary item, used up twenty-five
more; clothes, instalments, dues, occasional items of medicine
and the like, were met out of the remaining eleven dollars—
how, the ardent imagination of the comfortable reader can
guess. It was done, however, and for a time the hopeful members considered that they were doing fairly well.

During this period the little family presented a picture of
honorable and patient toil, which was interesting to contemplate. Every day Mrs. Gerhardt, who worked like a servant
and who received absolutely no compensation either in
clothes, amusements, or anything else, arose in the morning
while the others slept, and built the fire. Then she took up
the task of getting the breakfast. Often as she moved about
noiselessly in her thin, worn slippers, cushioned with pieces
of newspaper to make them fit, she looked in on Jennie, Bass,
and George, wrapped in their heavy slumbers, and with that
divine sympathy which is born in heaven she wished that they
did not need to rise so early or to work so hard. Sometimes
she would pause before touching her beloved Jennie, gaze at
her white face, so calm in sleep, and lament that life had not

dealt more kindly with her. Then she would lay her hand gently upon her shoulder and whisper, "Jennie, Jennie," until the weary sleeper would wake.

When they arose breakfast was always ready. When they returned at night supper was waiting. Each of the children received a due share of Mrs. Gerhardt's attention. The little baby was closely looked after by her. She protested that she needed neither clothes nor shoes so long as one of the children would run errands for her.

Jennie, of all the children, fully understood her mother; she alone strove, with the fullness of a perfect affection, to ease her burden.

"Ma, you let me do this."

"Now, ma, I'll 'tend to that."

"You go sit down, ma."

These were the every-day expressions of the enduring affection that existed between them. Always there was perfect understanding between Jennie and her mother, and as the days passed this naturally widened and deepened. Jennie could not bear to think of her as being always confined to the house. Daily she thought as she worked of that humble home where her mother was watching and waiting. How she longed to give her those comforts which she had always craved!

Chapter XIV

THE DAYS spent in the employ of the Bracebridge household were of a broadening character. This great house
was a school to Jennie, not only in the matter of dress and
manners, but as formulating a theory of existence. Mrs.
Bracebridge and her husband were the last word in the
matter of self-sufficiency, taste in the matter of appointments,
care in the matter of dress, good form in the matter of
reception, entertainment, and the various usages of social life.
Now and then, apropos of nothing save her own mood,
Mrs. Bracebridge would indicate her philosophy of life in an
epigram.

"Life is a battle, my dear. If you gain anything you will
have to fight for it."

"In my judgment it is silly not to take advantage of any aid
which will help you to be what you want to be." (This while
applying a faint suggestion of rouge.)

"Most people are born silly. They are exactly what they are
capable of being. I despise lack of taste; it is the worst crime."

Most of these worldly-wise counsels were not given directly
to Jennie. She overheard them, but to her quiet and reflective
mind they had their import. Like seeds fallen upon good
ground, they took root and grew. She began to get a faint
perception of hierarchies and powers. They were not for her,
perhaps, but they were in the world, and if fortune were kind
one might better one's state. She worked on, wondering,
however, just how better fortune might come to her. Who
would have her to wife knowing her history? How could she
ever explain the existence of her child?

Her child, her child, the one transcendent, gripping theme
of joy and fear. If she could only do something for it—sometime, somehow!

For the first winter things went smoothly enough. By the
closest economy the children were clothed and kept in school,
the rent paid, and the instalments met. Once it looked as
though there might be some difficulty about the continuance
of the home life, and that was when Gerhardt wrote that he
would be home for Christmas. The mill was to close down

for a short period at that time. He was naturally anxious to see what the new life of his family at Cleveland was like.

Mrs. Gerhardt would have welcomed his return with unalloyed pleasure had it not been for the fear she entertained of his creating a scene. Jennie talked it over with her mother, and Mrs. Gerhardt in turn spoke of it to Bass, whose advice was to brave it out.

"Don't worry," he said; "he won't do anything about it. I'll talk to him if he says anything."

The scene did occur, but it was not so unpleasant as Mrs. Gerhardt had feared. Gerhardt came home during the afternoon, while Bass, Jennie, and George were at work. Two of the younger children went to the train to meet him. When he entered Mrs. Gerhardt greeted him affectionately, but she trembled for the discovery which was sure to come. Her suspense was not for long. Gerhardt opened the front bedroom door only a few minutes after he arrived. On the white counterpane of the bed was a pretty child, sleeping. He could not but know on the instant whose it was, but he pretended ignorance.

"Whose child is that?" he questioned.

"It's Jennie's," said Mrs. Gerhardt, weakly.

"When did that come here?"

"Not so very long ago," answered the mother, nervously.

"I guess she is here, too," he declared, contemptuously, refusing to pronounce her name, a fact which he had already anticipated.

"She's working in a family," returned his wife in a pleading tone. "She's doing so well now. She had no place to go. Let her alone."

Gerhardt had received a light since he had been away. Certain inexplicable thoughts and feelings had come to him in his religious meditations. In his prayers he had admitted to the All-seeing that he might have done differently by his daughter. Yet he could not make up his mind how to treat her for the future. She had committed a great sin; it was impossible to get away from that.

When Jennie came home that night a meeting was unavoidable. Gerhardt saw her coming, and pretended to be deeply engaged in a newspaper. Mrs. Gerhardt, who had begged him not to ignore Jennie entirely, trembled for fear he would say or do something which would hurt her feelings.

"She is coming now," she said, crossing to the door of the front room, where he was sitting; but Gerhardt refused to look up. "Speak to her, anyhow," was her last appeal before the door opened; but he made no reply.

When Jennie came in her mother whispered, "He is in the front room."

Jennie paled, put her thumb to her lip and stood irresolute, not knowing how to meet the situation.

"Has he seen?"

Jennie paused as she realized from her mother's face and nod that Gerhardt knew of the child's existence.

"Go ahead," said Mrs. Gerhardt; "it's all right. He won't say anything."

Jennie finally went to the door, and, seeing her father, his brow wrinkled as if in serious but not unkindly thought, she hesitated, but made her way forward.

"Papa," she said, unable to formulate a definite sentence.

Gerhardt looked up, his grayish-brown eyes a study under their heavy sandy lashes. At the sight of his daughter he weakened internally; but with the self-adjusted armor of resolve about him he showed no sign of pleasure at seeing her. All the forces of his conventional understanding of morality and his naturally sympathetic and fatherly disposition were battling within him, but, as in so many cases where the average mind is concerned, convention was temporarily the victor.

"Yes," he said.

"Won't you forgive me, Papa?"

"I do," he returned grimly.

She hesitated a moment, and then stepped forward, for what purpose he well understood.

"There," he said, pushing her gently away, as her lips barely touched his grizzled cheek.

It had been a frigid meeting.

When Jennie went out into the kitchen after this very trying ordeal she lifted her eyes to her waiting mother and tried to make it seem as though all had been well, but her emotional disposition got the better of her.

"Did he make up to you?" her mother was about to ask;

but the words were only half out of her mouth before her daughter sank down into one of the chairs close to the kitchen table and, laying her head on her arm, burst forth into soft, convulsive, inaudible sobs.

"Now, now," said Mrs. Gerhardt. "There now, don't cry. What did he say?"

It was some time before Jennie recovered herself sufficiently to answer. Her mother tried to treat the situation lightly.

"I wouldn't feel bad," she said. "He'll get over it. It's his way."

Chapter XV

THE RETURN of Gerhardt brought forward the child question in all its bearings. He could not help considering it from the standpoint of a grandparent, particularly since it was a human being possessed of a soul. He wondered if it had been baptized. Then he inquired.

"No, not yet," said his wife, who had not forgotten this duty, but had been uncertain whether the little one would be welcome in the faith.

"No, of course not," sneered Gerhardt, whose opinion of his wife's religious devotion was not any too great. "Such carelessness! Such irreligion! That is a fine thing."

He thought it over a few moments, and felt that this evil should be corrected at once.

"It should be baptized," he said. "Why don't she take it and have it baptized?"

Mrs. Gerhardt reminded him that some one would have to stand godfather to the child, and there was no way to have the ceremony performed without confessing the fact that it was without a legitimate father.

Gerhardt listened to this, and it quieted him for a few moments, but his religion was something which he could not see put in the background by any such difficulty. How would the Lord look upon quibbling like this? It was not Christian, and it was his duty to attend to the matter. It must be taken, forthwith, to the church, Jennie, himself, and his wife accompanying it as sponsors; or, if he did not choose to condescend thus far to his daughter, he must see that it was baptized when she was not present. He brooded over this difficulty, and finally decided that the ceremony should take place on one of these week-days between Christmas and New Year's, when Jennie would be at her work. This proposal he broached to his wife, and, receiving her approval, he made his next announcement. "It has no name," he said.

Jennie and her mother had talked over this very matter, and Jennie had expressed a preference for Vesta. Now her mother made bold to suggest it as her own choice.

"How would Vesta do?"

Gerhardt heard this with indifference. Secretly he had settled the question in his own mind. He had a name in store,
left over from the halcyon period of his youth, and never op-
portunely available in the case of his own children—Wilhelmina. Of course he had no idea of unbending in the least
toward his small granddaughter. He merely liked the name,
and the child ought to be grateful to get it. With a far-off,
gingerly air he brought forward this first offering upon the
altar of natural affection, for offering it was, after all.

"That is nice," he said, forgetting his indifference. "But
how would Wilhelmina do?"

Mrs. Gerhardt did not dare cross him when he was thus
unconsciously weakening. Her woman's tact came to the
rescue.

"We might give her both names," she compromised.

"It makes no difference to me," he replied, drawing back
into the shell of opposition from which he had been inadvertently drawn. "Just so she is baptized."

Jennie heard of this with pleasure, for she was anxious that
the child should have every advantage, religious or otherwise,
that it was possible to obtain. She took great pains to starch
and iron the clothes it was to wear on the appointed day.

Gerhardt sought out the minister of the nearest Lutheran
church, a round-headed, thick-set theologian of the most formal type, to whom he stated his errand.

"Your grandchild?" inquired the minister.

"Yes," said Gerhardt, "her father is not here."

"So," replied the minister, looking at him curiously.

Gerhardt was not to be disturbed in his purpose. He explained that he and his wife would bring her. The minister,
realizing the probable difficulty, did not question him further.

"The church cannot refuse to baptize her so long as you,
as grandparent, are willing to stand sponsor for her," he said.

Gerhardt came away, hurt by the shadow of disgrace in
which he felt himself involved, but satisfied that he had done
his duty. Now he would take the child and have it baptized,
and when that was over his present responsibility would
cease.

When it came to the hour of the baptism, however, he
found that another influence was working to guide him into

greater interest and responsibility. The stern religion with which he was enraptured, its insistence upon a higher law, was there, and he heard again the precepts which had helped to bind him to his own children.

"Is it your intention to educate this child in the knowledge and love of the gospel?" asked the black-gowned minister, as they stood before him in the silent little church whither they had brought the infant; he was reading from the form provided for such occasions. Gerhardt answered "Yes," and Mrs. Gerhardt added her affirmative.

"Do you engage to use all necessary care and diligence, by prayerful instruction, admonition, example, and discipline that this child may renounce and avoid everything that is evil and that she may keep God's will and commandments as declared in His sacred word?"

A thought flashed through Gerhardt's mind as the words were uttered of how it had fared with his own children. They, too, had been thus sponsored. They too, had heard his solemn pledge to care for their spiritual welfare. He was silent.

"We do," prompted the minister.

"We do," repeated Gerhardt and his wife weakly.

"Do you now dedicate this child by the rite of baptism unto the Lord, who brought it?"

"We do."

"And, finally, if you can conscientiously declare before God that the faith to which you have assented is your faith, and that the solemn promises you have made are the serious resolutions of your heart, please to announce the same in the presence of God, by saying 'Yes.'"

"Yes," they replied.

"I baptize thee, Wilhelmina Vesta," concluded the minister, stretching out his hand over her, "in the name of the Father and of the Son and of the Holy Ghost. Let us pray."

Gerhardt bent his gray head and followed with humble reverence the beautiful invocation which followed:

"Almighty and everlasting God! we adore Thee as the great Parent of the children of men, as the Father of our spirits and the Former of our bodies. We praise Thee for giving existence to this infant and for preserving her until this day. We bless Thee that she is called to virtue and glory, that she has now been dedicated to Thee, and brought within the pale of the Christian Church. We thank Thee that by the Gospel of the Son she is furnished with everything necessary to her spiritual happiness; that it supplies light for her mind and comfort for her heart, encouragement and power to discharge her duty, and the precious hope of mercy and immortality to sustain and make her faithful. And we beseech Thee, O most merciful God, that this child may be enlightened and sanctified from her early years by the Holy Spirit, and be everlastingly saved by Thy mercy. Direct and bless Thy servants who are intrusted with the care of her in the momentous work of her education. Inspire them with just conception of the absolute necessity of religious instruction and principles. Forbid that they should ever forget that this offspring belongs to Thee, and that, if through their criminal neglect or bad example Thy reasonable creature be lost, Thou wilt requite it at their hands. Give them a deep sense of the divinity of her nature, of the worth of her soul, of the dangers to which she will be exposed, of the honor and felicity to which she is capable of ascending with Thy blessing, and of the ruin in this world and the misery in the world to come which springs from wicked passion and conduct. Give them grace to check the first risings of forbidden inclinations in her breast, to be her defense against the temptations incident to childhood and youth, and, as she grows up, to enlarge her understanding and to lead her to an acquaintance with Thee and with Jesus Christ, whom Thou hast sent. Give them grace to cultivate in her heart a supreme reverence and love for Thee, a grateful attachment to the Gospel of Thy Son, her Saviour, a due regard for all its ordinances and institutions, a temper of kindness and good-will to all mankind, and an invincible love of sincerity and truth. Help them to watch continually over her with tender solicitude, to be studious, that by their conversation and deportment her heart may not be corrupted, and at all times to set before her such an example that she may safely tread in their footsteps. If it please Thee to prolong her days on earth, grant that she may prove an honor and a comfort to her parents and friends, be useful in the world, and find in Thy Providence an unfailing defense and support. Whether she live, let her live to Thee; or whether she die, let her die to Thee. And, at the great day of account, may she and her parents meet each other with rapture and rejoice together in Thy redeeming love, through Jesus Christ, forever and ever, Amen."

As this solemn admonition was read a feeling of obligation descended upon the grandfather of this little outcast; a feeling that he was bound to give the tiny creature lying on his wife's arm the care and attention which God in His sacrament had commanded. He bowed his head in utmost reverence, and when the service was concluded and they left the silent church he was without words to express his feelings. Religion was a consuming thing with him. God was a person, a dominant reality. Religion was not a thing of mere words or of interesting ideas to be listened to on Sunday, but a strong, vital expression of the Divine Will handed down from a time when men were in personal contact with God. Its fulfilment was a matter of joy and salvation with him, the one consolation of a creature sent to wander in a vale whose explanation was not here but in heaven. Slowly Gerhardt walked on, and as he brooded on the words and the duties which the sacrament involved the shade of lingering disgust that had possessed him when he had taken the child to church disappeared and a feeling of natural affection took its place. However much the daughter had sinned, the infant was not to blame. It was a helpless, puling, tender thing, demanding his sympathy and his love. Gerhardt felt his heart go out to the little child, and yet he could not yield his position all in a moment.

"That is a nice man," he said of the minister to his wife as they walked along, rapidly softening in his conception of his duty.

"Yes, he was," agreed Mrs. Gerhardt timidly.

"It's a good-sized little church," he continued.

"Yes."

Gerhardt looked around him, at the street, the houses, the show of brisk life on this sunshiny, winter's day, and then finally at the child that his wife was carrying.

"She must be heavy," he said, in his characteristic German. "Let me take her."

Mrs. Gerhardt, who was rather weary, did not refuse.

"There!" he said, as he looked at her and then fixed her

comfortably upon his shoulder. "Let us hope she proves worthy of all that has been done to-day."

Mrs. Gerhardt listened, and the meaning in his voice interpreted itself plainly enough. The presence of the child in the house might be the cause of recurring spells of depression and unkind words, but there would be another and greater influence restraining him. There would always be her soul to consider. He would never again be utterly unconscious of her soul.

Chapter XVI

URING THE remainder of Gerhardt's stay he was shy in Jennie's presence and endeavored to act as though he were unconscious of her existence. When the time came for parting he even went away without bidding her good-by, telling his wife she might do that for him; but after he was actually on his way back to Youngstown he regretted the omission. "I might have bade her good-by," he thought to himself as the train rumbled heavily along. But it was too late.

For the time being the affairs of the Gerhardt family drifted. Jennie continued her work with Mrs. Bracebridge. Sebastian fixed himself firmly in his clerkship in the cigar store. George was promoted to the noble sum of three dollars, and then three-fifty. It was a narrow, humdrum life the family led. Coal, groceries, shoes, and clothing were the uppermost topics of their conversation; every one felt the stress and strain of trying to make ends meet.

That which worried Jennie most, and there were many things which weighed upon her sensitive soul, was the outcome of her own life—not so much for herself as for her baby and the family. She could not really see where she fitted in. "Who would have me?" she asked herself over and over. "How was she to dispose of Vesta in the event of a new love affair?" Such a contingency was quite possible. She was young, good-looking, and men were inclined to flirt with her, or rather to attempt it. The Bracebridges entertained many masculine guests, and some of them had made unpleasant overtures to her.

"My dear, you're a very pretty girl," said one old rake of fifty-odd when she knocked at his door one morning to give him a message from his hostess.

"I beg your pardon," she said, confusedly, and colored.

"Indeed, you're quite sweet. And you needn't beg my pardon. I'd like to talk to you some time."

He attempted to chuck her under the chin, but Jennie hurried away. She would have reported the matter to her mistress but a nervous shame deterred her. "Why would men always be doing this?" she thought. Could it be because there was something innately bad about her, an inward corruption that attracted its like?

It is a curious characteristic of the non-defensive disposition that it is like a honey-jar to flies. Nothing is brought to it and much is taken away. Around a soft, yielding, unselfish disposition men swarm naturally. They sense this generosity, this non-protective attitude from afar. A girl like Jennie is like a comfortable fire to the average masculine mind; they gravitate to it, seek its sympathy, yearn to possess it. Hence she was annoyed by many unwelcome attentions.

One day there arrived from Cincinnati a certain Lester Kane, the son of a wholesale carriage builder of great trade distinction in that city and elsewhere throughout the country, who was wont to visit this house frequently in a social way. He was a friend of Mrs. Bracebridge more than of her husband, for the former had been raised in Cincinnati and as a girl had visited at his father's house. She knew his mother, his brother and sisters and to all intents and purposes socially had always been considered one of the family.

"Lester's coming to-morrow, Henry," Jennie heard Mrs. Bracebridge tell her husband. "I had a wire from him this noon. He's such a scamp. I'm going to give him the big east front room up-stairs. Be sociable and pay him some attention. His father was so good to me."

"I know it," said her husband calmly. "I like Lester. He's the biggest one in that family. But he's too indifferent. He doesn't care enough."

"I know; but he's so nice. I do think he's one of the nicest men I ever knew."

"I'll be decent to him. Don't I always do pretty well by your people?"

"Yes, pretty well."

"Oh, I don't know about that," he replied, dryly.

When this notable person arrived Jennie was prepared to see some one of more than ordinary importance, and she was not disappointed. There came into the reception-hall to greet her mistress a man of perhaps thirty-six years of age, above the medium in height, clear-eyed, firm-jawed, athletic, direct, and vigorous. He had a deep, resonant voice that carried clearly everywhere; people somehow used to stop and listen whether they knew him or not. He was simple and abrupt in his speech.

"Oh, there you are," he began. "I'm glad to see you again. How's Mr. Bracebridge? How's Fannie?"

He asked his questions forcefully, whole-heartedly, and his hostess answered with an equal warmth. "I'm glad to see you, Lester," she said. "George will take your things up-stairs. Come up into my room. It's more comfy. How are grandpa and Louise?"

He followed her up the stairs, and Jennie, who had been standing at the head of the stairs listening, felt the magnetic charm of his personality. It seemed, why she could hardly say, that a real personage had arrived. The house was cheerier. The attitude of her mistress was much more complaisant. Everybody seemed to feel that something must be done for this man.

Jennie went about her work, but the impression persisted; his name ran in her mind. Lester Kane. And he was from Cincinnati. She looked at him now and then on the sly, and felt, for the first time in her life, an interest in a man on his own account. He was so big, so handsome, so forceful. She wondered what his business was. At the same time she felt a little dread of him. Once she caught him looking at her with a steady, incisive stare. She quailed inwardly, and took the first opportunity to get out of his presence. Another time he tried to address a few remarks to her, but she pretended that her duties called her away. She knew that often his eyes were on her when her back was turned, and it made her nervous. She wanted to run away from him, although there was no very definite reason why she should do so.

As a matter of fact, this man, so superior to Jennie in wealth, education, and social position, felt an instinctive interest in her unusual personality. Like the others, he was attracted by the peculiar softness of her disposition and her pre-eminent femininity. There was that about her which suggested the luxury of love. He felt as if somehow she could be reached—why, he could not have said. She did not bear any outward marks of her previous experience. There were no evidences of coquetry about her, but still he "felt that he might." He was inclined to make the venture on his first visit, but business called him away; he left after four days and was absent from Cleveland for three weeks. Jennie thought he was gone for good, and she experienced a queer sense of relief as well as of regret. Then, suddenly, he returned. He came apparently unexpectedly, explaining to Mrs. Bracebridge that business interests again demanded his presence in Cleveland. As he spoke he looked at Jennie sharply, and she felt as if somehow his presence might also concern her a little.

On this second visit she had various opportunities of seeing him, at breakfast, where she sometimes served, at dinner, when she could see the guests at the table from the parlor or sitting-room, and at odd times when he came to Mrs. Bracebridge's boudoir to talk things over. They were very friendly.

"Why don't you settle down, Lester, and get married?" Jennie heard her say to him the second day he was there. "You know it's time."

"I know," he replied, "but I'm in no mood for that. I want to browse around a little while yet."

"Yes, I know about your browsing. You ought to be ashamed of yourself. Your father is really worried."

He chuckled amusedly. "Father doesn't worry much about me. He has got all he can attend to to look after the business."

Jennie looked at him curiously. She scarcely understood what she was thinking, but this man drew her. If she had realized in what way she would have fled his presence then and there.

Now he was more insistent in his observation of her—addressed an occasional remark to her—engaged her in brief, magnetic conversations. She could not help answering him— he was pleasing to her. Once he came across her in the hall on the second floor searching in a locker for some linen. They were all alone, Mrs. Bracebridge having gone out to do some morning shopping and the other servants being below stairs. On this occasion he made short work of the business. He approached her in a commanding, unhesitating, and thoroughly determined way.

"I want to talk to you," he said. "Where do you live?"

"I—I—" she stammered, and blanched perceptibly. "I live out on Lorrie Street."

"What number?" he questioned, as though she were compelled to tell him.

She quailed and shook inwardly. "Thirteen fourteen," she replied mechanically.

He looked into her big, soft-blue eyes with his dark, vigorous brown ones. A flash that was hypnotic, significant, insistent passed between them.

"You belong to me," he said. "I've been looking for you. When can I see you?"

"Oh, you mustn't," she said, her fingers going nervously to her lips. "I can't see you—I—I—"

"Oh, I mustn't, mustn't I? Look here"—he took her arm and drew her slightly closer—"you and I might as well understand each other right now. I like you. Do you like me? Say?"

She looked at him, her eyes wide, filled with wonder, with fear, with a growing terror.

"I don't know," she gasped, her lips dry.

"Do you?" He fixed her grimly, firmly with his eyes.

"I don't know."

"Look at me," he said.

"Yes," she replied.

He pulled her to him quickly. "I'll talk to you later," he said, and put his lips masterfully to hers.

She was horrified, stunned, like a bird in the grasp of a cat; but through it all something tremendously vital and insistent was speaking to her. He released her with a short laugh. "We won't do any more of this here, but, remember, you belong to me," he said, as he turned and walked nonchalantly down the hall. Jennie, in sheer panic, ran to her mistress's room and locked the door behind her.

Chapter XVII

The shock of this sudden encounter was so great to Jennie that she was hours in recovering herself. At first she did not understand clearly just what had happened. Out of clear sky, as it were, this astonishing thing had taken place. She had yielded herself to another man. Why? Why? she asked herself, and yet within her own consciousness there was an answer. Though she could not explain her own emotions, she belonged to him temperamentally and he belonged to her.

There is a fate in love and a fate in fight. This strong, intellectual bear of a man, son of a wealthy manufacturer, stationed, so far as material conditions were concerned, in a world immensely superior to that in which Jennie moved, was, nevertheless, instinctively, magnetically, and chemically drawn to this poor serving-maid. She was his natural affinity, though he did not know it—the one woman who answered somehow the biggest need of his nature. Lester Kane had known all sorts of women, rich and poor, the highly bred maidens of his own class, the daughters of the proletariat, but he had never yet found one who seemed to combine for him the traits of an ideal woman—sympathy, kindliness of judgment, youth, and beauty. Yet this ideal remained fixedly seated in the back of his brain—when the right woman appeared he intended to take her. He had the notion that, for purposes of marriage, he ought perhaps to find this woman on his own plane. For purposes of temporary happiness he might take her from anywhere, leaving marriage, of course, out of the question. He had no idea of making anything like a serious proposal to a servant-girl. But Jennie was different. He had never seen a servant quite like her. And she was lady-like and lovely without appearing to know it. Why, this girl was a rare flower. Why shouldn't he try to seize her? Let us be just to Lester Kane; let us try to understand him and his position. Not every mind is to be estimated by the weight of a single folly; not every personality is to be judged by the drag of a single passion. We live in an age in which the impact of materialized forces is well-nigh irresistible; the spiritual nature is overwhelmed by the shock. The tremendous and

complicated development of our material civilization, the
multiplicity, and variety of our social forms, the depth, subtlety, and sophistry of our imaginative impressions, gathered,
remultiplied, and disseminated by such agencies as the railroad, the express and the post-office, the telephone, the telegraph, the newspaper, and, in short, the whole machinery of
social intercourse—these elements of existence combine to
produce what may be termed a kaleidoscopic glitter, a dazzling and confusing phantasmagoria of life that wearies and
stultifies the mental and moral nature. It induces a sort of
intellectual fatigue through which we see the ranks of the victims of insomnia, melancholia, and insanity constantly recruited. Our modern brain-pan does not seem capable as yet
of receiving, sorting, and storing the vast army of facts and
impressions which present themselves daily. The white light
of publicity is too white. We are weighed upon by too many
things. It is as if the wisdom of the infinite were struggling
to beat itself into finite and cup-big minds.

Lester Kane was the natural product of these untoward
conditions. His was a naturally observing mind, Rabelaisian
in its strength and tendencies, but confused by the multiplicity of things, the vastness of the panorama of life, the glitter
of its details, the unsubstantial nature of its forms, the uncertainty of their justification. Born a Catholic, he was no longer
a believer in the divine inspiration of Catholicism; raised a
member of the social elect, he had ceased to accept the fetish
that birth and station presuppose any innate superiority;
brought up as the heir to a comfortable fortune and expected
to marry in his own sphere, he was by no means sure that he
wanted marriage on any terms. Of course the conjugal state
was an institution. It was established. Yes, certainly. But what
of it? The whole nation believed in it. True, but other nations
believed in polygamy. There were other questions that bothered him—such questions as the belief in a single deity or
ruler of the universe, and whether a republican, monarchial,
or aristocratic form of government were best. In short, the
whole body of things material, social, and spiritual had come
under the knife of his mental surgery and been left but half
dissected. Life was not proved to him. Not a single idea of
his, unless it were the need of being honest, was finally

settled. In all other things he wavered, questioned, procrastinated, leaving to time and to the powers back of the universe the solution of the problems that vexed him. Yes, Lester Kane was the natural product of a combination of elements—religious, commercial, social—modified by that pervading atmosphere of liberty in our national life which is productive of almost uncounted freedom of thought and action. Thirty-six years of age, and apparently a man of vigorous, aggressive, and sound personality, he was, nevertheless, an essentially animal-man, pleasantly veneered by education and environment. Like the hundreds of thousands of Irishmen who in his father's day had worked on the railroad tracks, dug in the mines, picked and shoveled in the ditches, and carried up bricks and mortar on the endless structures of a new land, he was strong, hairy, axiomatic, and witty.

"Do you want me to come back here next year?" he had asked of Brother Ambrose, when, in his seventeenth year, that ecclesiastical member was about to chastise him for some school-boy misdemeanor.

The other stared at him in astonishment. "Your father will have to look after that," he replied.

"Well, my father won't look after it," Lester returned. "If you touch me with that whip I'll take things into my own hands. I'm not committing any punishable offenses, and I'm not going to be knocked around any more."

Words, unfortunately, did not avail in this case, but a good, vigorous Irish-American wrestle did, in which the whip was broken and the discipline of the school so far impaired that he was compelled to take his clothes and leave. After that he looked his father in the eye and told him that he was not going to school any more.

"I'm perfectly willing to jump in and work," he explained. "There's nothing in a classical education for me. Let me go into the office, and I guess I'll pick up enough to carry me through."

Old Archibald Kane, keen, single-minded, of unsullied commercial honor, admired his son's determination, and did not attempt to coerce him.

"Come down to the office," he said; "perhaps there is something you can do."

Entering upon a business life at the age of eighteen, Lester had worked faithfully, rising in his father's estimation, until now he had come to be, in a way, his personal representative. Whenever there was a contract to be entered upon, an important move to be decided, or a representative of the manufactory to be sent anywhere to consummate a deal, Lester was the agent selected. His father trusted him implicitly, and so diplomatic and earnest was he in the fulfilment of his duties that this trust had never been impaired.

"Business is business," was a favorite axiom with him, and the very tone in which he pronounced the words was a reflex of his character and personality.

There were molten forces in him, flames which burst forth now and then in spite of the fact that he was sure that he had them under control. One of these impulses was a taste for liquor, of which he was perfectly sure he had the upper hand. He drank but very little, he thought, and only, in a social way, among friends; never to excess. Another weakness lay in his sensual nature; but here again he believed that he was the master. If he chose to have irregular relations with women, he was capable of deciding where the danger point lay. If men were only guided by a sense of the brevity inherent in all such relationships there would not be so many troublesome consequences growing out of them. Finally, he flattered himself that he had a grasp upon a right method of living, a method which was nothing more than a quiet acceptance of social conditions as they were, tempered by a little personal judgment as to the right and wrong of individual conduct. Not to fuss and fume, not to cry out about anything, not to be mawkishly sentimental; to be vigorous and sustain your personality intact—such was his theory of life, and he was satisfied that it was a good one.

As to Jennie, his original object in approaching her had been purely selfish. But now that he had asserted his masculine prerogatives, and she had yielded, at least in part, he began to realize that she was no common girl, no toy of the passing hour.

There is a time in some men's lives when they unconsciously begin to view feminine youth and beauty not so much in relation to the ideal of happiness, but rather with regard to the social conventions by which they are environed.

"Must it be?" they ask themselves, in speculating concerning the possibility of taking a maiden to wife, "that I shall be compelled to swallow the whole social code, make a covenant with society, sign a pledge of abstinence, and give to another a life interest in all my affairs, when I know too well that I am but taking to my arms a variable creature like myself, whose wishes are apt to become insistent and burdensome in proportion to the decrease of her beauty and interest?" These are the men, who, unwilling to risk the manifold contingencies of an authorized connection, are led to consider the advantages of a less-binding union, a temporary companionship. They seek to seize the happiness of life without paying the cost of their indulgence. Later on, they think, the more definite and conventional relationship may be established without reproach or the necessity of radical readjustment.

Lester Kane was past the youthful love period, and he knew it. The innocence and unsophistication of younger ideals had gone. He wanted the comfort of feminine companionship, but he was more and more disinclined to give up his personal liberty in order to obtain it. He would not wear the social shackles if it were possible to satisfy the needs of his heart and nature and still remain free and unfettered. Of course he must find the right woman, and in Jennie he believed that he had discovered her. She appealed to him on every side; he had never known anybody quite like her. Marriage was not only impossible but unnecessary. He had only to say "Come" and she must obey; it was her destiny.

Lester thought the matter over calmly, dispassionately. He strolled out to the shabby street where she lived; he looked at the humble roof that sheltered her. Her poverty, her narrow and straitened environment touched his heart. Ought he not to treat her generously, fairly, honorably? Then the remembrance of her marvelous beauty swept over him and changed his mood. No, he must possess her if he could—to-day, quickly, as soon as possible. It was in that frame of mind that he returned to Mrs. Bracebridge's home from his visit to Lorrie Street.

Chapter XVIII

JENNIE WAS now going through the agony of one who has a varied and complicated problem to confront. Her baby, her father, her brothers, and sisters all rose up to confront her. What was this thing that she was doing? Was she allowing herself to slip into another wretched, unsanctified relationship? How was she to explain to her family about this man? He would not marry her, that was sure, if he knew all about her. He would not marry her, anyhow, a man of his station and position. Yet here she was parleying with him. What ought she to do? She pondered over the problem until evening, deciding first that it was best to run away, but remembering painfully that she had told him where she lived. Then she resolved that she would summon up her courage and refuse him—tell him she couldn't, wouldn't have anything to do with him. This last solution of the difficulty seemed simple enough—in his absence. And she would find work where he could not follow her up so easily. It all seemed simple enough as she put on her things in the evening to go home.

Her aggressive lover, however, was not without his own conclusion in this matter. Since leaving Jennie he had thought concisely and to the point. He came to the decision that he must act at once. She might tell her family, she might tell Mrs. Bracebridge, she might leave the city. He wanted to know more of the conditions which surrounded her, and there was only one way to do that—talk to her. He must persuade her to come and live with him. She would, he thought. She admitted that she liked him. That soft, yielding note in her character which had originally attracted him seemed to presage that he could win her without much difficulty, if he wished to try. He decided to do so, anyhow, for truly he desired her greatly.

At half-past five he returned to the Bracebridge home to see if she were still there. At six he had an opportunity to say to her, unobserved, "I am going to walk home with you. Wait for me at the next corner, will you?"

"Yes," she said, a sense of compulsion to do his bidding

seizing her. She explained to herself afterward that she ought to talk to him, that she must tell him finally of her decision not to see him again, and this was as good an opportunity as any. At half-past six he left the house on a pretext—a forgotten engagement—and a little after seven he was waiting for her in a closed carriage near the appointed spot. He was calm, absolutely satisfied as to the result, and curiously elated beneath a sturdy, shock-proof exterior. It was as if he breathed some fragrant perfume, soft, grateful, entrancing.

A few minutes after eight he saw Jennie coming along. The flare of the gas-lamp was not strong, but it gave sufficient light for his eyes to make her out. A wave of sympathy passed over him, for there was a great appeal in her personality. He stepped out as she neared the corner and confronted her. "Come," he said, "and get in this carriage with me. I'll take you home."

"No," she replied. "I don't think I ought to."

"Come with me. I'll take you home. It's a better way to talk."

Once more that sense of dominance on his part, that power of compulsion. She yielded, feeling all the time that she should not; he called out to the cabman, "Anywhere for a little while." When she was seated beside him he began at once.

"Listen to me, Jennie, I want you. Tell me something about yourself."

"I have to talk to you," she replied, trying to stick to her original line of defense.

"About what?" he inquired, seeking to fathom her expression in the half light.

"I can't go on this way," she murmured nervously. "I can't act this way. You don't know how it all is. I shouldn't have done what I did this morning. I mustn't see you any more. Really I mustn't."

"You didn't do what you did this morning," he remarked, paradoxically, seizing on that one particular expression. "I did that. And as for seeing me any more, I'm going to see you." He seized her hand. "You don't know me, but I like you. I'm crazy about you, that's all. You belong to me. Now listen. I'm going to have you. Are you going to come to me?"

"No, no, no!" she replied in an agonized voice. "I can't do anything like that, Mr. Kane. Please listen to me. It can't be. You don't know. Oh, you don't know. I can't do what you want. I don't want to. I couldn't, even if I wanted to. You don't know how things are. But I don't want to do anything wrong. I mustn't. I can't. I won't. Oh, no! no!! no!!! Please let me go home."

He listened to this troubled, feverish outburst with sympathy, with even a little pity.

"What do you mean by you can't?" he asked, curiously.

"Oh, I can't tell you," she replied. "Please don't ask me. You oughtn't to know. But I mustn't see you any more. It won't do any good."

"But you like me," he retorted.

"Oh yes, yes, I do. I can't help that. But you mustn't come near me any more. Please don't."

He turned his proposition over in his mind with the solemnity of a judge. He knew that this girl liked him—loved him really, brief as their contact had been. And he was drawn to her, perhaps not irrevocably, but with exceeding strength. What prevented her from yielding, especially since she wanted to? He was curious.

"See here, Jennie," he replied. "I hear what you say. I don't know what you mean by 'can't' if you want to. You say you like me. Why can't you come to me? You're my sort. We will get along beautifully together. You're suited to me temperamentally. I'd like to have you with me. What makes you say you can't come?"

"I can't," she replied. "I can't. I don't want to. I oughtn't. Oh, please don't ask me any more. You don't know. I can't tell you why." She was thinking of her baby.

The man had a keen sense of justice and fair play. Above all things he wanted to be decent in his treatment of people. In this case he intended to be tender and considerate, and yet he must win her. He turned this over in his mind.

"Listen to me," he said finally, still holding her hand. "I may not want you to do anything immediately. I want you to think it over. But you belong to me. You say you care for me. You admitted that this morning. I know you do. Now why should you stand out against me? I like you, and I can do a lot of things for you. Why not let us be good friends now? Then we can talk the rest of this over later."

"But I mustn't do anything wrong," she insisted. "I don't want to. Please don't come near me any more. I can't do what you want."

"Now, look here," he said. "You don't mean that. Why did you say you liked me? Have you changed your mind? Look at me." (She had lowered her eyes.) "Look at me! You haven't, have you?"

"Oh no, no, no," she half sobbed, swept by some force beyond her control.

"Well, then, why stand out against me? I love you, I tell you—I'm crazy about you. That's why I came back this time. It was to see you!"

"Was it?" asked Jennie, surprised.

"Yes, it was. And I would have come again and again if necessary. I tell you I'm crazy about you. I've got to have you. Now tell me you'll come with me."

"No, no, no," she pleaded. "I can't. I must work. I want to work. I don't want to do anything wrong. Please don't ask me. You mustn't. You must let me go. Really you must. I can't do what you want."

"Tell me, Jennie," he said, changing the subject. "What does your father do?"

"He's a glass-blower."

"Here in Cleveland?"

"No, he works in Youngstown."

"Is your mother alive?"

"Yes, sir."

"You live with her?"

"Yes, sir."

He smiled at the "sir." "Don't say 'sir' to me, sweet!" he pleaded in his gruff way. "And don't insist on the *Mr.* Kane. I'm not 'mister' to you any more. You belong to me, little girl, me." And he pulled her close to him.

"Please don't, Mr. Kane," she pleaded. "Oh, please don't. I can't! I can't! You mustn't."

But he sealed her lips with his own.

"Listen to me, Jennie," he repeated, using his favorite expression. "I tell you you belong to me. I like you better every moment. I haven't had a chance to know you. I'm not going to give you up. You've got to come to me eventually. And I'm not going to have you working as a lady's maid. You can't stay in that place except for a little while. I'm going to take you somewhere else. And I'm going to leave you some money, do you hear? You have to take it."

At the word money she quailed and withdrew her hand.

"No, no, no!" she repeated. "No, I won't take it."

"Yes, you will. Give it to your mother. I'm not trying to buy you. I know what you think. But I'm not. I want to help you. I want to help your family. I know where you live. I saw the place to-day. How many are there of you?"

"Six," she answered faintly.

"The families of the poor," he thought.

"Well, you take this from me," he insisted, drawing a purse from his coat. "And I'll see you very soon again. There's no escape, sweet."

"No, no," she protested. "I won't. I don't need it. No, you mustn't ask me."

He insisted further, but she was firm, and finally he put the money away.

"One thing is sure, Jennie, you're not going to escape me," he said soberly. "You'll have to come to me eventually. Don't you know you will? Your own attitude shows that. I'm not going to leave you alone."

"Oh, if you knew the trouble you're causing me."

"I'm not causing you any real trouble, am I?" he asked. "Surely not."

"Yes. I can never do what you want."

"You will! You will!" he exclaimed eagerly, the bare thought of this prize escaping him heightening his passion. "You'll come to me." And he drew her close in spite of all her protests.

"There," he said when, after the struggle, that mystic some-thing between them spoke again, and she relaxed. Tears were in her eyes, but he did not see them. "Don't you see how it is? You like me too."

"I can't," she repeated, with a sob.

Her evident distress touched him. "You're not crying, little girl, are you?" he asked.

She made no answer.

"I'm sorry," he went on. "I'll not say anything more to-night. We're almost at your home. I'm leaving to-morrow, but I'll see you again. Yes, I will, sweet. I can't give you up now. I'll do anything in reason to make it easy for you, but I can't, do you hear?"

She shook her head.

"Here's where you get out," he said, as the carriage drew up near the corner. He could see the evening lamp gleaming behind the Gerhardt cottage curtains.

"Good-by," he said as she stepped out.

"Good-by," she murmured.

"Remember," he said, "this is just the beginning."

"Oh no, no!" she pleaded.

He looked after her as she walked away.

"The beauty!" he exclaimed.

Jennie stepped into the house weary, discouraged, ashamed. What had she done? There was no denying that she had compromised herself irretrievably. He would come back.

He would come back. And he had offered her money. That was the worst of all.

Chapter XIX

THE INCONCLUSIVE nature of this interview, exciting as it was, did not leave any doubt in either Lester Kane's or Jennie's mind; certainly this was not the end of the affair. Kane knew that he was deeply fascinated. This girl was lovely. She was sweeter than he had had any idea of. Her hesitancy, her repeated protests, her gentle "no, no, no" moved him as music might. Depend upon it, this girl was for him, and he would get her. She was too sweet to let go. What did he care about what his family or the world might think?

It was curious that Kane held the well-founded idea that in time Jennie would yield to him physically, as she had already done spiritually. Just why he could not say. Something about her—a warm womanhood, a guileless expression of countenance—intimated a sympathy toward sex relationship which had nothing to do with hard, brutal immorality. She was the kind of a woman who was made for a man—one man. All her attitude toward sex was bound up with love, tenderness, service. When the one man arrived she would love him and she would go to him. That was Jennie as Lester understood her. He felt it. She would yield to him because he was the one man.

On Jennie's part there was a great sense of complication and of possible disaster. If he followed her of course he would learn all. She had not told him about Brander, because she was still under the vague illusion that, in the end, she might escape. When she left him she knew that he would come back. She knew, in spite of herself that she wanted him to do so. Yet she felt that she must not yield, she must go on leading her straitened, humdrum life. This was her punishment for having made a mistake. She had made her bed, and she must lie on it.

The Kane family mansion at Cincinnati to which Lester returned after leaving Jennie was an imposing establishment, which contrasted strangely with the Gerhardt home. It was a great, rambling, two-story affair, done after the manner of the French châteaux, but in red brick and brownstone. It was set down, among flowers and trees, in an almost park-like inclosure, and its very stones spoke of a splendid dignity and of a refined luxury. Old Archibald Kane, the father, had amassed a tremendous fortune, not by grabbing and browbeating and unfair methods, but by seeing a big need and filling it. Early in life he had realized that America was a growing country. There was going to be a big demand for vehicles—wagons, carriages, drays—and he knew that some one would have to supply them. Having founded a small wagon industry, he had built it up into a great business; he made good wagons, and he sold them at a good profit. It was his theory that most men were honest; he believed that at bottom they wanted honest things, and if you gave them these they would buy of you, and come back and buy again and again, until you were an influential and rich man. He believed in the measure "heaped full and running over." All through his life and now in his old age he enjoyed the respect and approval of every one who knew him. "Archibald Kane," you would hear his competitors say, "Ah, there is a fine man. Shrewd, but honest. He's a big man."

This man was the father of two sons and three daughters, all healthy, all good-looking, all blessed with exceptional minds, but none of them so generous and forceful as their long-living and big-hearted sire. Robert, the eldest, a man forty years of age, was his father's right-hand man in financial matters, having a certain hard incisiveness which fitted him for the somewhat sordid details of business life. He was of medium height, of a rather spare build, with a high forehead, slightly inclined to baldness, bright, liquid-blue eyes, an eagle nose, and thin, firm, even lips. He was a man of few words, rather slow to action and of deep thought. He sat close to his father as vice-president of the big company which occupied two whole blocks in an outlying section of the city. He was a strong man—a coming man, as his father well knew.

Lester, the second boy, was his father's favorite. He was not by any means the financier that Robert was, but he had a larger vision of the subtleties that underlie life. He was softer, more human, more good-natured about everything. And, strangely enough, old Archibald admired and trusted him. He knew he had the bigger vision. Perhaps he turned to Robert when it was a question of some intricate financial problem, but Lester was the most loved as a son.

Then there was Amy, thirty-two years of age, married, handsome, the mother of one child—a boy; Imogene, twenty-eight, also married, but as yet without children, and Louise, twenty-five, single, the best-looking of the girls, but also the coldest and most critical. She was the most eager of all for social distinction, the most vigorous of all in her love of family prestige, the most desirous that the Kane family should outshine every other. She was proud to think that the family was so well placed socially, and carried herself with an air and a hauteur which was sometimes amusing, sometimes irritating to Lester! He liked her—in a way she was his favorite sister—but he thought she might take herself with a little less seriousness and not do the family standing any harm.

Mrs. Kane, the mother, was a quiet, refined woman, sixty years of age, who, having come up from comparative poverty with her husband, cared but little for social life. But she loved her children and her husband, and was naïvely proud of their position and attainments. It was enough for her to shine only in their reflected glory. A good woman, a good wife, and a good mother.

Lester arrived at Cincinnati early in the evening, and drove at once to his home. An old Irish servitor met him at the door.

"Ah, Mr. Lester," he began, joyously, "sure I'm glad to see you back. I'll take your coat. Yes, yes, it's been fine weather we're having. Yes, yes, the family's all well. Sure your sister Amy is just after leavin' the house with the boy. Your mother's up-stairs in her room. Yes, yes."

Lester smiled cheerily and went up to his mother's room. In this, which was done in white and gold and overlooked the garden to the south and east, sat Mrs. Kane, a subdued, graceful, quiet woman, with smoothly laid gray hair. She looked up when the door opened, laid down the volume that she had been reading, and rose to greet him.

"There you are, Mother," he said, putting his arms around her and kissing her. "How are you?"

"Oh, I'm just about the same, Lester. How have you been?"

"Fine. I was up with the Bracebridges for a few days again. I had to stop off in Cleveland to see Parsons. They all asked after you."

"How is Minnie?"

"Just the same. She doesn't change any that I can see. She's just as interested in entertaining as she ever was."

"She's a bright girl," remarked his mother, recalling Mrs. Bracebridge as a girl in Cincinnati. "I always liked her. She's so sensible."

"She hasn't lost any of that, I can tell you," replied Lester significantly. Mrs. Kane smiled and went on to speak of various family happenings. Imogene's husband was leaving for St. Louis on some errand. Robert's wife was sick with a cold. Old Zwingle, the yard watchman at the factory, who had been with Mr. Kane for over forty years, had died. Her husband was going to the funeral. Lester listened dutifully, albeit a trifle absently.

Lester, as he walked down the hall, encountered Louise. "Smart" was the word for her. She was dressed in a beaded black silk dress, fitting close to her form, with a burst of rubies at her throat which contrasted effectively with her dark complexion and black hair. Her eyes were black and piercing.

"Oh, there you are, Lester," she exclaimed. "When did you get in? Be careful how you kiss me. I'm going out, and I'm all fixed, even to the powder on my nose. Oh, you bear!" Lester had gripped her firmly and kissed her soundly. She pushed him away with her strong hands.

"I didn't brush much of it off," he said. "You can always dust more on with that puff of yours." He passed on to his own room to dress for dinner. Dressing for dinner was a custom that had been adopted by the Kane family in the last few years. Guests had become so common that in a way it was a necessity, and Louise, in particular, made a point of it. To-night Robert was coming, and a Mr. and Mrs. Burnett, old friends of his father and mother, and so, of course, the meal would be a formal one. Lester knew that his father was around somewhere, but he did not trouble to look him up now. He was thinking of his last two days in Cleveland and wondering when he would see Jennie again.

Chapter XX

As LESTER CAME down-stairs after making his toilet he found his father in the library reading.

"Hello, Lester," he said, looking up from his paper over the top of his glasses and extending his hand. "Where do you come from?"

"Cleveland," replied his son, shaking hands heartily, and smiling.

"Robert tells me you've been to New York."

"Yes, I was there."

"How did you find my old friend Arnold?"

"Just about the same," returned Lester. "He doesn't look any older."

"I suppose not," said Archibald Kane genially, as if the report were a compliment to his own hardy condition. "He's been a temperate man. A fine old gentleman."

He led the way back to the sitting-room where they chatted over business and home news until the chime of the clock in the hall warned the guests up-stairs that dinner had been served.

Lester sat down in great comfort amid the splendors of the great Louis Quinze dining-room. He liked this homey home atmosphere—his mother and father and his sisters—the old family friends. So he smiled and was exceedingly genial.

Louise announced that the Leverings were going to give a dance on Tuesday, and inquired whether he intended to go.

"You know I don't dance," he returned dryly. "Why should I go?"

"Don't dance? Won't dance, you mean. You're getting too lazy to move. If Robert is willing to dance occasionally I think you might."

"Robert's got it on me in lightness," Lester replied, airily.

"And politeness," retorted Louise.

"Be that as it may," said Lester.

"Don't try to stir up a fight, Louise," observed Robert, sagely.

After dinner they adjourned to the library, and Robert talked with his brother a little on business. There were some contracts coming up for revision. He wanted to see what suggestions Lester had to make. Louise was going to a party, and the carriage was now announced. "So you are not coming?" she asked, a trifle complainingly.

"Too tired," said Lester lightly. "Make my excuses to Mrs. Knowles."

"Letty Pace asked about you the other night," Louise called back from the door.

"Kind," replied Lester. "I'm greatly obliged."

"She's a nice girl, Lester," put in his father, who was standing near the open fire. "I only wish you would marry her and settle down. You'd have a good wife in her."

"She's charming," testified Mrs. Kane.

"What is this?" asked Lester jocularly—"a conspiracy? You know I'm not strong on the matrimonial business."

"And I well know it," replied his mother semi-seriously. "I wish you were."

Lester changed the subject. He really could not stand for this sort of thing any more, he told himself. And as he thought his mind wandered back to Jennie and her peculiar "Oh no, no!" There was some one that appealed to him. That was a type of womanhood worth while. Not sophisticated, not self-seeking, not watched over and set like a man-trap in the path of men, but a sweet little girl—sweet as a flower, who was without anybody, apparently, to watch over her. That night in his room he composed a letter, which he dated a week later, because he did not want to appear too urgent and because he could not again leave Cincinnati for at least two weeks.

"MY DEAR JENNIE,—Although it has been a week, and I have said nothing, I have not forgotten you—believe me. Was the impression I gave of myself very bad? I will make it better from now on, for I love you, little girl—I really do. There is a flower on my table which reminds me of you very much—white, delicate, beautiful. Your personality, lingering with me, is just that. You are the essence of everything beautiful to me. It is in your power to strew flowers in my path if you will.

"But what I want to say here is that I shall be in Cleveland

on the 18th, and I shall expect to see you. I arrive Thursday
night, and I want you to meet me in the ladies' parlor of the
Dornton at noon Friday. Will you? You can lunch with me.

"You see, I respect your suggestion that I should not call.
(I will not—on condition.) These separations are dangerous
to good friendship. Write me that you will. I throw myself
on your generosity. But I can't take 'no' for an answer, not
now.

"With a world of affection.

"LESTER KANE."

He sealed the letter and addressed it. "She's a remarkable
girl in her way," he thought. "She really is."

Chapter XXI

THE ARRIVAL of this letter, coming after a week of silence and after she had had a chance to think, moved Jennie deeply. What did she want to do? What ought she to do? How did she truly feel about this man? Did she sincerely wish to answer his letter? If she did so, what should she say? Heretofore all her movements, even the one in which she had sought to sacrifice herself for the sake of Bass in Columbus, had not seemed to involve any one but herself. Now, there seemed to be others to consider—her family, above all, her child. The little Vesta was now eighteen months of age; she was an interesting child; her large, blue eyes and light hair giving promise of a comeliness which would closely approximate that of her mother, while her mental traits indicated a clear and intelligent mind. Mrs. Gerhardt had become very fond of her. Gerhardt had unbended so gradually that his interest was not even yet clearly discernible, but he had a distinct feeling of kindliness toward her. And this readjustment of her father's attitude had aroused in Jennie an ardent desire to so conduct herself that no pain should ever come to him again. Any new folly on her part would not only be base ingratitude to her father, but would tend to injure the prospects of her little one. Her life was a failure, she fancied, but Vesta's was a thing apart; she must do nothing to spoil it. She wondered whether it would not be better to write Lester and explain everything. She had told him that she did not wish to do wrong. Suppose she went on to inform him that she had a child, and beg him to leave her in peace. Would he obey her? She doubted it. Did she really want him to take her at her word?

The need of making this confession was a painful thing to Jennie. It caused her to hesitate, to start a letter in which she tried to explain, and then to tear it up. Finally, fate intervened in the sudden home-coming of her father, who had been seriously injured by an accident at the glass-works in Youngstown where he worked.

It was on a Wednesday afternoon, in the latter part of August, when a letter came from Gerhardt. But instead of the customary fatherly communication, written in German and inclosing the regular weekly remittance of five dollars, there was only a brief note, written by another hand, and explaining that the day before Gerhardt had received a severe burn on both hands, due to the accidental overturning of a dipper of molten glass. The letter added that he would be home the next morning.

"What do you think of that?" exclaimed William, his mouth wide open.

"Poor papa!" said Veronica, tears welling up in her eyes.

Mrs. Gerhardt sat down, clasped her hands in her lap, and stared at the floor. "Now, what to do?" she nervously exclaimed. The possibility that Gerhardt was disabled for life opened long vistas of difficulties which she had not the courage to contemplate.

Bass came home at half-past six and Jennie at eight. The former heard the news with an astonished face.

"Gee! that's tough, isn't it?" he exclaimed. "Did the letter say how bad he was hurt?"

"No," replied Mrs. Gerhardt.

"Well, I wouldn't worry about it," said Bass easily. "It won't do any good. We'll get along somehow. I wouldn't worry like that if I were you."

The truth was, he wouldn't, because his nature was wholly different. Life did not rest heavily upon his shoulders. His brain was not large enough to grasp the significance and weigh the results of things.

"I know," said Mrs. Gerhardt, endeavoring to recover herself. "I can't help it, though. To think that just when we were getting along fairly well this new calamity should be added. It seems sometimes as if we were under a curse. We have so much bad luck."

When Jennie came her mother turned to her instinctively; here was her one stay.

"What's the matter, ma?" asked Jennie as she opened the door and observed her mother's face. "What have you been crying about?"

Mrs. Gerhardt looked at her, and then turned half away.

"Pa's had his hands burned," put in Bass solemnly. "He'll be home to-morrow."

Jennie turned and stared at him. "His hands burned!" she exclaimed.

"Yes," said Bass.

"How did it happen?"

"A pot of glass was turned over."

Jennie looked at her mother, and her eyes dimmed with tears. Instinctively she ran to her and put her arms around her.

"Now, don't you cry, ma," she said, barely able to control herself. "Don't you worry. I know how you feel, but we'll get along. Don't cry now." Then her own lips lost their evenness, and she struggled long before she could pluck up courage to contemplate this new disaster. And now without volition upon her part there leaped into her consciousness a new and subtly persistent thought. What about Lester's offer of assistance now? What about his declaration of love? Somehow it came back to her—his affection, his personality, his desire to help her, his sympathy, so like that which Brander had shown when Bass was in jail. Was she doomed to a second sacrifice? Did it really make any difference? Wasn't her life a failure already? She thought this over as she looked at her mother sitting there so silent, haggard, and distraught. "What a pity," she thought, "that her mother must always suffer! Wasn't it a shame that she could never have any real happiness?"

"I wouldn't feel so badly," she said, after a time. "Maybe pa isn't burned so badly as we think. Did the letter say he'd be home in the morning?"

"Yes," said Mrs. Gerhardt, recovering herself.

They talked more quietly from now on, and gradually, as the details were exhausted, a kind of dumb peace settled down upon the household.

"One of us ought to go to the train to meet him in the morning," said Jennie to Bass. "I will. I guess Mrs. Bracebridge won't mind."

"No," said Bass gloomily, "you mustn't. I can go."

He was sour at this new fling of fate, and he looked his feelings; he stalked off gloomily to his room and shut himself in. Jennie and her mother saw the others off to bed, and then sat out in the kitchen talking.

"I don't see what's to become of us now," said Mrs.

Gerhardt at last, completely overcome by the financial complications which this new calamity had brought about. She looked so weak and helpless that Jennie could hardly contain herself.

"Don't worry, mamma dear," she said, softly, a peculiar resolve coming into her heart. The world was wide. There was comfort and ease in it scattered by others with a lavish hand. Surely, surely misfortune could not press so sharply but that they could live!

She sat down with her mother, the difficulties of the future seeming to approach with audible and ghastly steps.

"What do you suppose will become of us now?" repeated her mother, who saw how her fanciful conception of this Cleveland home had crumbled before her eyes.

"Why," said Jennie, who saw clearly and knew what could be done, "it will be all right. I wouldn't worry about it. Something will happen. We'll get something."

She realized, as she sat there, that fate had shifted the burden of the situation to her. She must sacrifice herself; there was no other way.

Bass met his father at the railway station in the morning. He looked very pale, and seemed to have suffered a great deal. His cheeks were slightly sunken and his bony profile appeared rather gaunt. His hands were heavily bandaged, and altogether he presented such a picture of distress that many stopped to look at him on the way home from the station.

"By chops," he said to Bass, "that was a burn I got. I thought once I couldn't stand the pain any longer. Such pain I had! Such pain! By chops! I will never forget it."

He related just how the accident had occurred, and said that he did not know whether he would ever be able to use his hands again. The thumb on his right hand and the first two fingers on the left had been burned to the bone. The latter had been amputated at the first joint—the thumb he might save, but his hands would be in danger of being stiff.

"By chops!" he added, "just at the time when I needed the money most. Too bad! Too bad!"

When they reached the house, and Mrs. Gerhardt opened the door, the old mill-worker, conscious of her voiceless sympathy, began to cry. Mrs. Gerhardt sobbed also. Even Bass lost control of himself for a moment or two, but quickly recovered. The other children wept, until Bass called a halt on all of them.

"Don't cry now," he said cheeringly. "What's the use of crying? It isn't so bad as all that. You'll be all right again. We can get along."

Bass's words had a soothing effect, temporarily, and, now that her husband was home, Mrs. Gerhardt recovered her composure. Though his hands were bandaged, the mere fact that he could walk and was not otherwise injured was some consolation. He might recover the use of his hands and be able to undertake light work again. Anyway, they would hope for the best.

When Jennie came home that night she wanted to run to her father and lay the treasury of her services and affection at his feet, but she trembled lest he might be as cold to her as formerly.

Gerhardt, too, was troubled. Never had he completely recovered from the shame which his daughter had brought upon him. Although he wanted to be kindly, his feelings were so tangled that he hardly knew what to say or do.

"Papa," said Jennie, approaching him timidly.

Gerhardt looked confused and tried to say something natural, but it was unavailing. The thought of his helplessness, the knowledge of her sorrow and of his own responsiveness to her affection—it was all too much for him; he broke down again and cried helplessly.

"Forgive me, papa," she pleaded, "I'm so sorry. Oh, I'm so sorry."

He did not attempt to look at her, but in the swirl of feeling that their meeting created he thought that he could forgive, and he did.

"I have prayed," he said brokenly. "It is all right."

When he recovered himself he felt ashamed of his emotion, but a new relationship of sympathy and of understanding had been established. From that time, although there was always a great reserve between them, Gerhardt tried not to ignore her completely, and she endeavored to show him the simple affection of a daughter, just as in the old days.

But while the household was again at peace, there were

other cares and burdens to be faced. How were they to get along now with five dollars taken from the weekly budget, and with the cost of Gerhardt's presence added? Bass might have contributed more of his weekly earnings, but he did not feel called upon to do it. And so the small sum of nine dollars weekly must meet as best it could the current expenses of rent, food, and coal, to say nothing of incidentals, which now began to press very heavily. Gerhardt had to go to a doctor to have his hands dressed daily. George needed a new pair of shoes. Either more money must come from some source or the family must beg for credit and suffer the old tortures of want. The situation crystallized the half-formed resolve in Jennie's mind.

Lester's letter had been left unanswered. The day was drawing near. Should she write? He would help them. Had he not tried to force money on her? She finally decided that it was her duty to avail herself of this proffered assistance. She sat down and wrote him a brief note. She would meet him as he had requested, but he would please not come to the house. She mailed the letter, and then waited, with mingled feelings of trepidation and thrilling expectancy, the arrival of the fateful day.

Chapter XXII

THE FATAL FRIDAY came, and Jennie stood face to face with this new and overwhelming complication in her modest scheme of existence. There was really no alternative, she thought. Her own life was a failure. Why go on fighting? If she could make her family happy, if she could give Vesta a good education, if she could conceal the true nature of this older story and keep Vesta in the background—perhaps, perhaps—well, rich men had married poor girls before this, and Lester was very kind, he certainly liked her. At seven o'clock she went to Mrs. Bracebridge's; at noon she excused herself on the pretext of some work for her mother and left the house for the hotel.

Lester, leaving Cincinnati a few days earlier than he expected, had failed to receive her reply; he arrived at Cleveland feeling sadly out of tune with the world. He had a lingering hope that a letter from Jennie might be awaiting him at the hotel, but there was no word from her. He was a man not easily wrought up, but to-night he felt depressed, and so went gloomily up to his room and changed his linen. After supper he proceeded to drown his dissatisfaction in a game of billiards with some friends, from whom he did not part until he had taken very much more than his usual amount of alcoholic stimulant. The next morning he arose with a vague idea of abandoning the whole affair, but as the hours elapsed and the time of his appointment drew near he decided that it might not be unwise to give her one last chance. She might come. Accordingly, when it still lacked a quarter of an hour of the time, he went down into the parlor. Great was his delight when he beheld her sitting in a chair and waiting—the outcome of her acquiescence. He walked briskly up, a satisfied, gratified smile on his face.

"So you did come after all," he said, gazing at her with the look of one who has lost and recovered a prize. "What do you mean by not writing me? I thought from the way you neglected me that you had made up your mind not to come at all."

"I did write," she replied.

"Where?"

"To the address you gave me. I wrote three days ago."

"That explains it. It came too late. You should have written me before. How have you been?"

"Oh, all right," she replied.

"You don't look it!" he said. "You look worried. What's the trouble, Jennie? Nothing gone wrong out at your house, has there?"

It was a fortuitous question. He hardly knew why he had asked it. Yet it opened the door to what she wanted to say.

"My father's sick," she replied.

"What's happened to him?"

"He burned his hands at the glass-works. We've been terribly worried. It looks as though he would not be able to use them any more."

She paused, looking the distress she felt, and he saw plainly that she was facing a crisis.

"That's too bad," he said. "That certainly is. When did this happen?"

"Oh, almost three weeks ago now."

"It certainly is bad. Come in to lunch, though. I want to talk with you. I've been wanting to get a better understanding of your family affairs ever since I left." He led the way into the dining-room and selected a secluded table. He tried to divert her mind by asking her to order the luncheon, but she was too worried and too shy to do so and he had to make out the menu by himself. Then he turned to her with a cheering air. "Now, Jennie," he said, "I want you to tell me all about your family. I got a little something of it last time, but I want to get it straight. Your father, you said, was a glass-blower by trade. Now he can't work any more at that, that's obvious."

"Yes," she said.

"How many other children are there?"

"Six."

"Are you the oldest?"

"No, my brother Sebastian is. He's twenty-two."

"And what does he do?"

"He's a clerk in a cigar store."

"Do you know how much he makes?"

"I think it's twelve dollars," she replied thoughtfully.

"And the other children?"

"Martha and Veronica don't do anything yet. They're too young. My brother George works at Wilson's. He's a cash-boy. He gets three dollars and a half."

"And how much do you make?"

"I make four."

He stopped, figuring up mentally just what they had to live on. "How much rent do you pay?" he continued.

"Twelve dollars."

"How old is your mother?"

"She's nearly fifty now."

He turned a fork in his hands back and forth; he was think-ing earnestly.

"To tell you the honest truth, I fancied it was something like that, Jennie," he said. "I've been thinking about you a lot. Now, I know. There's only one answer to your problem, and it isn't such a bad one, if you'll only believe me." He paused for an inquiry, but she made none. Her mind was running on her own difficulties.

"Don't you want to know?" he inquired.

"Yes," she answered mechanically.

"It's me," he replied. "You have to let me help you. I wanted to last time. Now you have to; do you hear?"

"I thought I wouldn't," she said simply.

"I knew what you thought," he replied. "That's all over now. I'm going to 'tend to that family of yours. And I'll do it right now while I think of it."

He drew out his purse and extracted several ten and twenty-dollar bills—two hundred and fifty dollars in all. "I want you to take this," he said. "It's just the beginning. I will see that your family is provided for from now on. Here, give me your hand."

"Oh no," she said. "Not so much. Don't give me all that."

"Yes," he replied. "Don't argue. Here. Give me your hand."

She put it out in answer to the summons of his eyes, and he shut her fingers on the money, pressing them gently at the same time. "I want you to have it, sweet. I love you, little girl. I'm not going to see you suffer, nor any one belonging to you."

Her eyes looked a dumb thankfulness, and she bit her lips.

"I don't know how to thank you," she said.

"You don't need to," he replied. "The thanks are all the other way—believe me."

He paused and looked at her, the beauty of her face holding him. She looked at the table, wondering what would come next.

"How would you like to leave what you're doing and stay at home?" he asked. "That would give you your freedom day times."

"I couldn't do that," she replied. "Papa wouldn't allow it. He knows I ought to work."

"That's true enough," he said. "But there's so little in what you're doing. Good heavens! Four dollars a week! I would be glad to give you fifty times that sum if I thought there was any way in which you could use it." He idly thrummed the cloth with his fingers.

"I couldn't," she said. "I hardly know how to use this. They'll suspect. I'll have to tell mamma."

From the way she said it he judged there must be some bond of sympathy between her and her mother which would permit of a confidence such as this. He was by no means a hard man, and the thought touched him. But he would not relinquish his purpose.

"There's only one thing to be done, as far as I can see," he went on very gently. "You're not suited for the kind of work you're doing. You're too refined. I object to it. Give it up and come with me down to New York; I'll take good care of you. I love you and want you. As far as your family is concerned, you won't have to worry about them any more. You can take a nice home for them and furnish it in any style you please. Wouldn't you like that?"

He paused, and Jennie's thoughts reverted quickly to her mother, her dear mother. All her life long Mrs. Gerhardt had been talking of this very thing—a nice home. If they could just have a larger house, with good furniture and a yard filled with trees, how happy she would be. In such a home she would be free of the care of rent, the discomfort of poor furniture, the wretchedness of poverty; she would be so happy. She hesitated there while his keen eye followed her in spirit, and he saw what a power he had set in motion. It had been a happy inspiration—the suggestion of a decent home for the family. He waited a few minutes longer, and then said:

"Well, wouldn't you better let me do that?"

"It would be very nice," she said, "but it can't be done now. I couldn't leave home. Papa would want to know all about where I was going. I wouldn't know what to say."

"Why couldn't you pretend that you are going down to New York with Mrs. Bracebridge?" he suggested. "There couldn't be any objection to that, could there?"

"Not if they didn't find out," she said, her eyes opening in amazement. "But if they should!"

"They won't," he replied calmly. "They're not watching Mrs. Bracebridge's affairs. Plenty of mistresses take their maids on long trips. Why not simply tell them you're invited to go—have to go—and then go?"

"Do you think I could?" she inquired.

"Certainly," he replied. "What is there peculiar about that?"

She thought it over, and the plan did seem feasible. Then she looked at this man and realized that relationship with him meant possible motherhood for her again. The tragedy of giving birth to a child—ah, she could not go through that a second time, at least under the same conditions. She could not bring herself to tell him about Vesta, but she must voice this insurmountable objection.

"I—" she said, formulating the first word of her sentence, and then stopping.

"Yes," he said. "I—what?"

"I—" She paused again.

He loved her shy ways, her sweet, hesitating lips.

"What is it, Jennie?" he asked helpfully. "You're so delicious. Can't you tell me?"

Her hand was on the table. He reached over and laid his strong brown one on top of it.

"I couldn't have a baby," she said, finally, and looked down.

He gazed at her, and the charm of her frankness, her innate decency under conditions so anomalous, her simple unaffected recognition of the primal facts of life lifted her to a plane in his esteem which she had not occupied until that moment.

"You're a great girl, Jennie," he said. "You're wonderful. But don't worry about that. It can be arranged. You don't need to have a child unless you want to, and I don't want you to."

He saw the question written in her wondering, shamed face.

"It's so," he said. "You believe me, don't you? You think I know, don't you?"

"Yes," she faltered.

"Well, I do. But anyway, I wouldn't let any trouble come to you. I'll take you away. Besides, I don't want any children. There wouldn't be any satisfaction in that proposition for me at this time. I'd rather wait. But there won't be—don't worry."

"Yes," she said faintly. Not for worlds could she have met his eyes.

"Look here, Jennie," he said, after a time. "You care for me, don't you? You don't think I'd sit here and plead with you if I didn't care for you? I'm crazy about you, and that's the literal truth. You're like wine to me. I want you to come with me. I want you to do it quickly. I know how difficult this family business is, but you can arrange it. Come with me down to New York. We'll work out something later. I'll meet your family. We'll pretend a courtship, anything you like—only come now."

"You don't mean right away, do you?" she asked, startled.

"Yes, to-morrow if possible. Monday sure. You can arrange it. Why, if Mrs. Bracebridge asked you you'd go fast enough, and no one would think anything about it. Isn't that so?"

"Yes," she admitted slowly.

"Well, then, why not now?"

"It's always so much harder to work out a falsehood," she replied thoughtfully.

"I know it, but you can come. Won't you?"

"Won't you wait a little while?" she pleaded. "It's so very sudden. I'm afraid."

"Not a day, sweet, that I can help. Can't you see how I feel? Look in my eyes. Will you?"

"Yes," she replied sorrowfully, and yet with a strange thrill of affection. "I will."

Chapter XXIII

THE BUSINESS of arranging for this sudden departure was really not so difficult as it first appeared. Jennie proposed to tell her mother the whole truth, and there was nothing to say to her father except that she was going with Mrs. Bracebridge at the latter's request. He might question her, but he really could not doubt. Before going home that afternoon she accompanied Lester to a department store, where she was fitted out with a trunk, a suit-case, and a traveling suit and hat. Lester was very proud of his prize. "When we get to New York I am going to get you some real things," he told her. "I am going to show you what you can be made to look like." He had all the purchased articles packed in the trunk and sent to his hotel. Then he arranged to have Jennie come there and dress Monday for the trip which began in the afternoon.

When she came home Mrs. Gerhardt, who was in the kitchen, received her with her usual affectionate greeting. "Have you been working very hard?" she asked. "You look tired."

"No," she said, "I'm not tired. It isn't that. I just don't feel good."

"What's the trouble?"

"Oh, I have to tell you something, mamma. It's so hard." She paused, looking inquiringly at her mother, and then away.

"Why, what is it?" asked her mother nervously. So many things had happened in the past that she was always on the alert for some new calamity. "You haven't lost your place, have you?"

"No," replied Jennie, with an effort to maintain her mental poise, "but I'm going to leave it."

"No!" exclaimed her mother. "Why?"

"I'm going to New York."

Her mother's eyes opened widely. "Why, when did you decide to do that?" she inquired.

"To-day."

"You don't mean it!"

"Yes, I do, mamma. Listen. I've got something I want to tell you. You know how poor we are. There isn't any way we can make things come out right. I have found some one who wants to help us. He says he loves me, and he wants me to go to New York with him Monday. I've decided to go."

"Oh, Jennie!" exclaimed her mother. "Surely not! You wouldn't do anything like that after all that's happened. Think of your father."

"I've thought it all out," went on Jennie, firmly. "It's really for the best. He's a good man. I know he is. He has lots of money. He wants me to go with him, and I'd better go. He will take a new house for us when we come back and help us to get along. No one will ever have me as a wife—you know that. It might as well be this way. He loves me. And I love him. Why shouldn't I go?"

"Does he know about Vesta?" asked her mother cautiously.

"No," said Jennie guiltily. "I thought I'd better not tell him about her. She oughtn't to be brought into it if I can help it."

"I'm afraid you're storing up trouble for yourself, Jennie," said her mother. "Don't you think he is sure to find it out some time?"

"I thought maybe that she could be kept here," suggested Jennie, "until she's old enough to go to school. Then maybe I could send her somewhere."

"She might," assented her mother; "but don't you think it would be better to tell him now? He won't think any the worse of you."

"It isn't that. It's her," said Jennie passionately. "I don't want her to be brought into it."

Her mother shook her head. "Where did you meet him?" she inquired.

"At Mrs. Bracebridge's."

"How long ago?"

"Oh, it's been almost two months now."

"And you never said anything about him," protested Mrs. Gerhardt reproachfully.

"I didn't know that he cared for me this way," said Jennie defensively.

"Why didn't you wait and let him come out here first?"

asked her mother. "It will make things so much easier. You can't go and not have your father find out."

"I thought I'd say I was going with Mrs. Bracebridge. Papa can't object to my going with her."

"No," agreed her mother thoughtfully.

The two looked at each other in silence. Mrs. Gerhardt, with her imaginative nature, endeavored to formulate some picture of this new and wonderful personality that had come into Jennie's life. He was wealthy; he wanted to take Jennie; he wanted to give them a good home. What a story!

"And he gave me this," put in Jennie, who, with some instinctive psychic faculty, had been following her mother's mood. She opened her dress at the neck, and took out the two hundred and fifty dollars; she placed the money in her mother's hands.

The latter stared at it wide-eyed. Here was the relief for all her woes—food, clothes, rent, coal—all done up in one small package of green and yellow bills. If there were plenty of money in the house Gerhardt need not worry about his burned hands; George and Martha and Veronica could be clothed in comfort and made happy. Jennie could dress better; there would be a future education for Vesta.

"Do you think he might ever want to marry you?" asked her mother finally.

"I don't know," replied Jennie, "he might. I know he loves me."

"Well," said her mother after a long pause, "if you're going to tell your father you'd better do it right away. He'll think it's strange as it is."

Jennie realized that she had won. Her mother had acquiesced from sheer force of circumstances. She was sorry, but somehow it seemed to be for the best. "I'll help you out with it," her mother had concluded, with a little sigh.

The difficulty of telling this lie was very great for Mrs. Gerhardt, but she went through the falsehood with a seeming nonchalance which allayed Gerhardt's suspicions. The children were also told, and when, after the general discussion, Jennie repeated the falsehood to her father it seemed natural enough.

"How long do you think you'll be gone?" he inquired.

"About two or three weeks," she replied.

"That's a nice trip," he said. "I came through New York in 1844. It was a small place then compared to what it is now."

Secretly he was pleased that Jennie should have this fine chance. Her employer must like her.

When Monday came Jennie bade her parents good-by and left early, going straight to the Dornton, where Lester awaited her.

"So you came," he said gaily, greeting her as she entered the ladies' parlor.

"Yes," she said simply.

"You are my niece," he went on. "I have engaged a room for you near mine. I'll call for the key, and you go dress. When you're ready I'll have the trunk sent to the depot. The train leaves at one o'clock."

She went to her room and dressed, while he fidgeted about, read, smoked, and finally knocked at her door.

She replied by opening to him, fully clad.

"You look charming," he said with a smile.

She looked down, for she was nervous and distraught. The whole process of planning, lying, nerving herself to carry out her part had been hard on her. She looked tired and worried.

"Not grieving, are you?" he asked, seeing how things stood.

"No-o," she replied.

"Come now, sweet. You mustn't feel this way. It's coming out all right." He took her in his arms and kissed her, and they strolled down the hall. He was astonished to see how well she looked in even these simple clothes—the best she had ever had.

They reached the depot after a short carriage ride. The accommodations had been arranged for before hand, and Kane had allowed just enough time to make the train. When they settled themselves in a Pullman state-room it was with a keen sense of satisfaction on his part. Life looked rosy. Jennie was beside him. He had succeeded in what he had started out to do. So might it always be.

As the train rolled out of the depot and the long reaches of the fields succeeded Jennie studied them wistfully. There were the forests, leafless and bare; the wide, brown fields, wet with the rains of winter; the low farm-houses sitting amid flat stretches of prairie, their low roofs making them look as if they were hugging the ground. The train roared past little hamlets, with cottages of white and yellow and drab, their roofs blackened by frost and rain. Jennie noted one in particular which seemed to recall the old neighborhood where they used to live at Columbus; she put her handkerchief to her eyes and began silently to cry.

"I hope you're not crying, are you, Jennie?" said Lester, looking up suddenly from the letter he had been reading. "Come, come," he went on as he saw a faint tremor shaking her. "This won't do. You have to do better than this. You'll never get along if you act that way."

She made no reply, and the depth of her silent grief filled him with strange sympathies.

"Don't cry," he continued soothingly; "everything will be all right. I told you that. You needn't worry about anything."

Jennie made a great effort to recover herself, and began to dry her eyes.

"You don't want to give way like that," he continued. "It doesn't do you any good. I know how you feel about leaving home, but tears won't help it any. It isn't as if you were going away for good, you know. Besides, you'll be going back shortly. You care for me, don't you, sweet? I'm something?"

"Yes," she said, and managed to smile back at him.

Lester returned to his correspondence and Jennie fell to thinking of Vesta. It troubled her to realize that she was keeping this secret from one who was already very dear to her. She knew that she ought to tell Lester about the child, but she shrank from the painful necessity. Perhaps later on she might find the courage to do it.

"I'll have to tell him something," she thought with a sudden upwelling of feeling as regarded the seriousness of this duty. "If I don't do it soon and I should go and live with him and he should find it out he would never forgive me. He might turn me out, and then where would I go? I have no home now. What would I do with Vesta?"

She turned to contemplate him, a premonitory wave of terror sweeping over her, but she only saw that imposing and comfort-loving soul quietly reading his letters, his smoothly shaved red cheek and comfortable head and body looking anything but militant or like an avenging Nemesis. She was just withdrawing her gaze when he looked up.

"Well, have you washed all your sins away?" he inquired merrily.

She smiled faintly at the allusion. The touch of fact in it made it slightly piquant.

"I expect so," she replied.

He turned to some other topic, while she looked out of the window, the realization that one impulse to tell him had proved unavailing dwelling in her mind. "I'll have to do it shortly," she thought, and consoled herself with the idea that she would surely find courage before long.

Their arrival in New York the next day raised the important question in Lester's mind as to where he should stop. New York was a very large place, and he was not in much danger of encountering people who would know him, but he thought it just as well not to take chances. Accordingly he had the cabman drive them to one of the more exclusive apartment hotels, where he engaged a suite of rooms; and they settled themselves for a stay of two or three weeks.

This atmosphere into which Jennie was now plunged was so wonderful, so illuminating, that she could scarcely believe this was the same world that she had inhabited before. Kane was no lover of vulgar display. The appointments with which he surrounded himself were always simple and elegant. He knew at a glance what Jennie needed, and bought for her with discrimination and care. And Jennie, a woman, took a keen pleasure in the handsome gowns and pretty fripperies that he lavished upon her. Could this be really Jennie Gerhardt, the washerwoman's daughter, she asked herself, as she gazed in her mirror at the figure of a girl clad in blue velvet, with yellow French lace at her throat and upon her arms? Could these be her feet, clad in soft shapely shoes at ten dollars a pair, these her hands adorned with flashing jewels? What wonderful good fortune she was enjoying! And Lester had promised that her mother would share in it. Tears sprang to her eyes at the thought. The dear mother, how she loved her!

It was Lester's pleasure in these days to see what he could

do to make her look like some one truly worthy of him. He exercised his most careful judgment, and the result surprised even himself. People turned in the halls, in the dining-rooms, and on the street to gaze at Jennie.

"A stunning woman that man has with him," was a frequent comment.

Despite her altered state Jennie did not lose her judgment of life or her sense of perspective or proportion. She felt as though life were tentatively loaning her something which would be taken away after a time. There was no petty vanity in her bosom. Lester realized this as he watched her. "You're a big woman, in your way," he said. "You'll amount to something. Life hasn't given you much of a deal up to now."

He wondered how he could justify this new relationship to his family, should they chance to hear about it. If he should decide to take a home in Chicago or St. Louis (there was such a thought running in his mind) could he maintain it secretly? Did he want to? He was half persuaded that he really, truly loved her.

As the time drew near for their return he began to counsel her as to her future course of action. "You ought to find some way of introducing me, as an acquaintance, to your father," he said. "It will ease matters up. I think I'll call. Then if you tell him you're going to marry me he'll think nothing of it." Jennie thought of Vesta, and trembled inwardly. But perhaps her father could be induced to remain silent.

Lester had made the wise suggestion that she should retain the clothes she had worn in Cleveland in order that she might wear them home when she reached there. "There won't be any trouble about this other stuff," he said. "I'll have it cared for until we make some other arrangement." It was all very simple and easy; he was a master strategist.

Jennie had written her mother almost daily since she had been East. She had inclosed little separate notes to be read by Mrs. Gerhardt only. In one she explained Lester's desire to call, and urged her mother to prepare the way by telling her father that she had met some one who liked her. She spoke of the difficulty concerning Vesta, and her mother at once began to plan a campaign to have Gerhardt hold his peace. There must be no hitch now. Jennie must be given an opportunity to better herself. When she returned there was great rejoicing. Of course she could not go back to her work, but Mrs. Gerhardt explained that Mrs. Bracebridge had given Jennie a few weeks' vacation in order that she might look for something better, something at which she could make more money.

Chapter XXIV

THE PROBLEM of the Gerhardt family and its relationship to himself comparatively settled, Kane betook himself to Cincinnati and to his business duties. He was heartily interested in the immense plant, which occupied two whole blocks in the outskirts of the city, and its conduct and development was as much a problem and a pleasure to him as to either his father or his brother. He liked to feel that he was a vital part of this great and growing industry. When he saw freight cars going by on the railroads labelled "The Kane Manufacturing Company—Cincinnati" or chanced to notice displays of the company's products in the windows of carriage sales companies in the different cities he was conscious of a warm glow of satisfaction. It was something to be a factor in an institution so stable, so distinguished, so honestly worth while. This was all very well, but now Kane was entering upon a new phase of his personal existence—in a word, there was Jennie. He was conscious as he rode toward his home city that he was entering on a relationship which might involve disagreeable consequences. He was a little afraid of his father's attitude; above all, there was his brother Robert.

Robert was cold and conventional in character; an excellent business man; irreproachable in both his public and in his private life. Never overstepping the strict boundaries of legal righteousness, he was neither warm-hearted nor generous—in fact, he would turn any trick which could be speciously, or at best necessitously, recommended to his conscience. How he reasoned Lester did not know—he could not follow the ramifications of a logic which could combine hard business tactics with moral rigidity, but somehow his brother managed to do it. "He's got a Scotch Presbyterian conscience mixed with an Asiatic perception of the main chance," Lester once told somebody, and he had the situation accurately measured. Nevertheless he could not rout his brother from his positions nor defy him, for he had the public conscience with him. He was in line with convention practically, and perhaps sophisticatedly.

The two brothers were outwardly friendly; inwardly they were far apart. Robert liked Lester well enough personally, but he did not trust his financial judgment, and, temperamentally, they did not agree as to how life and its affairs should be conducted. Lester had a secret contempt for his brother's chill, persistent chase of the almighty dollar. Robert was sure that Lester's easy-going ways were reprehensible, and bound to create trouble sooner or later. In the business they did not quarrel much—there was not so much chance with the old gentleman still in charge—but there were certain minor differences constantly cropping up which showed which way the wind blew. Lester was for building up trade through friendly relationship, concessions, personal contact, and favors. Robert was for pulling everything tight, cutting down the cost of production, and offering such financial inducements as would throttle competition.

The old manufacturer always did his best to pour oil on these troubled waters, but he foresaw an eventual clash. One or the other would have to get out or perhaps both. "If only you two boys could agree!" he used to say.

Another thing which disturbed Lester was his father's attitude on the subject of marriage—Lester's marriage, to be specific. Archibald Kane never ceased to insist on the fact that Lester ought to get married, and that he was making a big mistake in putting it off. All the other children, save Louise, were safely married. Why not his favorite son? It was doing him injury morally, socially, commercially, that he was sure of.

"The world expects it of a man in your position," his father had argued from time to time. "It makes for social solidity and prestige. You ought to pick out a good woman and raise a family. Where will you be when you get to my time of life if you haven't any children, any home?"

"Well, if the right woman came along," said Lester, "I suppose I'd marry her. But she hasn't come along. What do you want me to do? Take anybody?"

"No, not anybody, of course, but there are lots of good women. You can surely find some one if you try. There's that Pace girl. What about her? You used to like her. I wouldn't drift on this way, Lester; it can't come to any good."

His son would only smile. "There, father, let it go now. I'll come around some time, no doubt. I've got to be thirsty when I'm led to water."

The old gentleman gave over, time and again, but it was a sore point with him. He wanted his son to settle down and be a real man of affairs.

The fact that such a situation as this might militate against any permanent arrangement with Jennie was obvious even to Lester at this time. He thought out his course of action carefully. Of course he would not give Jennie up, whatever the possible consequences. But he must be cautious; he must take no unnecessary risks. Could he bring her to Cincinnati? What a scandal if it were ever found out! Could he install her in a nice home somewhere near the city? The family would probably eventually suspect something. Could he take her along on his numerous business journeys? This first one to New York had been successful. Would it always be so? He turned the question over in his mind. The very difficulty gave it zest. Perhaps St. Louis, or Pittsburg, or Chicago would be best after all. He went to these places frequently, and particularly to Chicago. He decided finally that it should be Chicago if he could arrange it. He could always make excuses to run up there, and it was only a night's ride. Yes, Chicago was best. The very size and activity of the city made concealment easy. After two weeks' stay at Cincinnati Lester wrote Jennie that he was coming to Cleveland soon, and she answered that she thought it would be all right for him to call and see her. Her father had been told about him. She had felt it unwise to stay about the house, and so had secured a position in a store at four dollars a week. He smiled as he thought of her working, and yet the decency and energy of it appealed to him. "She's all right," he said. "She's the best I've come across yet."

He ran up to Cleveland the following Saturday, and, calling at her place of business, he made an appointment to see her that evening. He was anxious that his introduction, as her beau, should be gotten over with as quickly as possible. When he did call the shabbiness of the house and the manifest poverty of the family rather disgusted him, but somehow Jennie seemed as sweet to him as ever. Gerhardt came in the front-room, after he had been there a few minutes, and shook hands with him, as did also Mrs. Gerhardt, but Lester paid little attention to them. The old German appeared to him to be merely commonplace—the sort of man who was hired by hundreds in common capacities in his father's factory. After some desultory conversation Lester suggested to Jennie that they should go for a drive. Jennie put on her hat, and together they departed. As a matter of fact, they went to an apartment which he had hired for the storage of her clothes. When she returned at eight in the evening the family considered it nothing amiss.

Chapter XXV

A month later Jennie was able to announce that Lester intended to marry her. His visits had of course paved the way for this, and it seemed natural enough. Only Gerhardt seemed a little doubtful. He did not know just how this might be. Perhaps it was all right. Lester seemed a fine enough man in all conscience, and really, after Brander, why not? If a United States Senator could fall in love with Jennie, why not a business man? There was just one thing—the child. "Has she told him about Vesta?" he asked his wife.

"No," said Mrs. Gerhardt, "not yet."

"Not yet, not yet. Always something underhanded. Do you think he wants her if he knows? That's what comes of such conduct in the first place. Now she has to slip around like a thief. The child cannot even have an honest name."

Gerhardt went back to his newspaper reading and brooding. His life seemed a complete failure to him and he was only waiting to get well enough to hunt up another job as watchman. He wanted to get out of this mess of deception and dishonesty.

A week or two later Jennie confided to her mother that Lester had written her to join him in Chicago. He was not feeling well, and could not come to Cleveland. The two women explained to Gerhardt that Jennie was going away to be married to Mr. Kane. Gerhardt flared up at this, and his suspicions were again aroused. But he could do nothing but grumble over the situation; it would lead to no good end, of that he was sure.

When the day came for Jennie's departure she had to go without saying farewell to her father. He was out looking for work until late in the afternoon, and before he had returned she had been obliged to leave for the station. "I will write a note to him when I get there," she said. She kissed her baby over and over. "Lester will take a better house for us soon," she went on hopefully. "He wants us to move." The night train bore her to Chicago; the old life had ended and the new one had begun.

The curious fact should be recorded here that, although

Lester's generosity had relieved the stress upon the family finances, the children and Gerhardt were actually none the wiser. It was easy for Mrs. Gerhardt to deceive her husband as to the purchase of necessities and she had not as yet indulged in any of the fancies which an enlarged purse permitted. Fear deterred her. But, after Jennie had been in Chicago for a few days, she wrote to her mother saying that Lester wanted them to take a new home. This letter was shown to Gerhardt, who had been merely biding her return to make a scene. He frowned, but somehow it seemed an evidence of regularity. If he had not married her why should he want to help them? Perhaps Jennie was well married after all. Perhaps she really had been lifted to a high station in life, and was now able to help the family. Gerhardt almost concluded to forgive her everything once and for all.

The end of it was that a new house was decided upon, and Jennie returned to Cleveland to help her mother move. Together they searched the streets for a nice, quiet neighborhood, and finally found one. A house of nine rooms, with a yard, which rented for thirty dollars, was secured and suitably furnished. There were comfortable fittings for the dining-room and sitting-room, a handsome parlor set and bedroom sets complete for each room. The kitchen was supplied with every convenience, and there was even a bath-room, a luxury the Gerhardts had never enjoyed before. Altogether the house was attractive, though plain, and Jennie was happy to know that her family could be comfortable in it.

When the time came for the actual moving Mrs. Gerhardt was fairly beside herself with joy, for was not this the realization of her dreams? All through the long years of her life she had been waiting, and now it had come. A new house, new furniture, plenty of room—things finer than she had ever even imagined—think of it! Her eyes shone as she looked at the new beds and tables and bureaus and whatnots. "Dear, dear, isn't this nice!" she exclaimed. "Isn't it beautiful!" Jennie smiled and tried to pretend satisfaction without emotion, but there were tears in her eyes. She was so glad for her mother's sake. She could have kissed Lester's feet for his goodness to her family.

The day the furniture was moved in Mrs. Gerhardt, Martha,

and Veronica were on hand to clean and arrange things. At the sight of the large rooms and pretty yard, bare enough in winter, but giving promise of a delightful greenness in spring, and the array of new furniture standing about in excelsior, the whole family fell into a fever of delight. Such beauty, such spaciousness! George rubbed his feet over the new carpets and Bass examined the quality of the furniture critically. "Swell," was his comment. Mrs. Gerhardt roved to and fro like a person in a dream. She could not believe that these bright bedrooms, this beautiful parlor, this handsome dining-room were actually hers.

Gerhardt came last of all. Although he tried hard not to show it, he, too, could scarcely refrain from enthusiastic comment. The sight of an opal-globed chandelier over the dining-room table was the finishing touch.

"Gas, yet!" he said.

He looked grimly around, under his shaggy eyebrows, at the new carpets under his feet, the long oak extension table covered with a white cloth and set with new dishes, at the pictures on the walls, the bright, clean kitchen. He shook his head. "By chops, it's fine!" he said. "It's very nice. Yes, it's very nice. We want to be careful now not to break anything. It's so easy to scratch things up, and then it's all over."

Yes, even Gerhardt was satisfied.

Chapter XXVI

It would be useless to chronicle the events of the three years that followed—events and experiences by which the family grew from an abject condition of want to a state of comparative self-reliance, based, of course, on the obvious prosperity of Jennie and the generosity (through her) of her distant husband. Lester was seen now and then, a significant figure, visiting Cleveland, and sometimes coming out to the house where he occupied with Jennie the two best rooms of the second floor. There were hurried trips on her part—in answer to telegraph messages—to Chicago, to St. Louis, to New York. One of his favorite pastimes was to engage quarters at the great resorts—Hot Springs, Mt. Clemens, Saratoga—and for a period of a week or two at a stretch enjoy the luxury of living with Jennie as his wife. There were other times when he would pass through Cleveland only for the privilege of seeing her for a day. All the time he was aware that he was throwing on her the real burden of a rather difficult situation, but he did not see how he could remedy it at this time. He was not sure as yet that he really wanted to. They were getting along fairly well.

The attitude of the Gerhardt family toward this condition of affairs was peculiar. At first, in spite of the irregularity of it, it seemed natural enough. Jennie said she was married. No one had seen her marriage certificate, but she said so, and she seemed to carry herself with the air of one who holds that relationship. Still, she never went to Cincinnati, where his family lived, and none of his relatives ever came near her. Then, too, his attitude, in spite of the money which had first blinded them, was peculiar. He really did not carry himself like a married man. He was so indifferent. There were weeks in which she appeared to receive only perfunctory notes. There were times when she would only go away for a few days to meet him. Then there were the long periods in which she absented herself—the only worthwhile testimony toward a real relationship, and that, in a way, unnatural.

Bass, who had grown to be a young man of twenty-five, with some business judgment and a desire to get out in the world, was suspicious. He had come to have a pretty keen knowledge of life, and intuitively he felt that things were not right. George, nineteen, who had gained a slight foothold in a wall-paper factory and was looking forward to a career in that field, was also restless. He felt that something was wrong. Martha, seventeen, was still in school, as were William and Veronica. Each was offered an opportunity to study indefinitely; but there was unrest with life. They knew about Jennie's child. The neighbors were obviously drawing conclusions for themselves. They had few friends. Gerhardt himself finally concluded that there was something wrong, but he had let himself into this situation, and was not in much of a position now to raise an argument. He wanted to ask her at times—proposed to make her do better if he could—but the worst had already been done. It depended on the man now, he knew that.

Things were gradually nearing a state where a general upheaval would have taken place had not life stepped in with one of its fortuitous solutions. Mrs. Gerhardt's health failed. Although stout and formerly of a fairly active disposition, she had of late years become decidedly sedentary in her habits and grown weak, which, coupled with a mind naturally given to worry, and weighed upon as it had been by a number of serious and disturbing ills, seemed now to culminate in a slow but very certain case of systemic poisoning. She became decidedly sluggish in her motions, wearied more quickly at the few tasks left for her to do, and finally complained to Jennie that it was very hard for her to climb stairs. "I'm not feeling well," she said. "I think I'm going to be sick."

Jennie now took alarm and proposed to take her to some near-by watering-place, but Mrs. Gerhardt wouldn't go. "I don't think it would do any good," she said. She sat about or went driving with her daughter, but the fading autumn scenery depressed her. "I don't like to get sick in the fall," she said. "The leaves coming down make me think I am never going to get well."

"Oh, ma, how you talk!" said Jennie; but she felt frightened, nevertheless.

How much the average home depends upon the mother was seen when it was feared the end was near. Bass, who had thought of getting married and getting out of this atmosphere, abandoned the idea temporarily. Gerhardt, shocked and greatly depressed, hung about like one expectant of and greatly awed by the possibility of disaster. Jennie, too inexperienced in death to feel that she could possibly lose her mother, felt as if somehow her living depended on her. Hoping in spite of all opposing circumstances, she hung about, a white figure of patience, waiting and serving.

The end came one morning after a month of illness and several days of unconsciousness, during which silence reigned in the house and all the family went about on tip-toe. Mrs. Gerhardt passed away with her dying gaze fastened on Jennie's face for the last few minutes of consciousness that life vouchsafed her. Jennie stared into her eyes with a yearning horror. "Oh, mamma! mamma!" she cried. "Oh no, no!"

Gerhardt came running in from the yard, and, throwing himself down by the bedside, wrung his bony hands in anguish. "I should have gone first!" he cried. "I should have gone first!"

The death of Mrs. Gerhardt hastened the final breaking up of the family. Bass was bent on getting married at once, having had a girl in town for some time. Martha, whose views of life had broadened and hardened, was anxious to get out also. She felt that a sort of stigma attached to the home—to herself, in fact, so long as she remained there. Martha looked to the public schools as a source of income; she was going to be a teacher. Gerhardt alone scarcely knew which way to turn. He was again at work as a night watchman. Jennie found him crying one day alone in the kitchen, and immediately burst into tears herself. "Now, papa!" she pleaded, "it isn't as bad as that. You will always have a home—you know that—as long as I have anything. You can come with me."

"No, no," he protested. He really did not want to go with her. "It isn't that," he continued. "My whole life comes to nothing."

It was some little time before Bass, George and Martha finally left, but, one by one, they got out, leaving Jennie, her father, Veronica, and William, and one other—Jennie's child. Of course Lester knew nothing of Vesta's parentage, and curiously enough he had never seen the little girl. During the short periods in which he deigned to visit the house—two or three days at most—Mrs. Gerhardt took good care that Vesta was kept in the background. There was a play-room on the top floor, and also a bedroom there, and concealment was easy. Lester rarely left his rooms, he even had his meals served to him in what might have been called the living-room of the suite. He was not at all inquisitive or anxious to meet any one of the other members of the family. He was perfectly willing to shake hands with them or to exchange a few perfunctory words, but perfunctory words only. It was generally understood that the child must not appear, and so it did not.

There is an inexplicable sympathy between old age and childhood, an affinity which is as lovely as it is pathetic. During that first year in Lorrie Street, when no one was looking, Gerhardt often carried Vesta about on his shoulders and pinched her soft, red cheeks. When she got old enough to walk he it was who, with a towel fastened securely under her arms, led her patiently around the room until she was able to take a few steps of her own accord. When she actually reached the point where she could walk he was the one who coaxed her to the effort, shyly, grimly, but always lovingly. By some strange leading of fate this stigma on his family's honor, this blotch on conventional morality, had twined its helpless baby fingers about the tendons of his heart. He loved this little outcast ardently, hopefully. She was the one bright ray in a narrow, gloomy life, and Gerhardt early took upon himself the responsibility of her education in religious matters. Was it not he who had insisted that the infant should be baptized?

"Say 'Our Father,' " he used to demand of the lisping infant when he had her alone with him.

"Ow Fowvaw," was her vowel-like interpretation of his words.

" 'Who art in heaven.' "

" 'Ooh ah in aven,' " repeated the child.

"Why do you teach her so early?" pleaded Mrs. Gerhardt, overhearing the little one's struggles with stubborn consonants and vowels.

"Because I want she should learn the Christian faith," returned Gerhardt determinedly. "She ought to know her prayers. If she don't begin now she never will know them."

Mrs. Gerhardt smiled. Many of her husband's religious idiosyncrasies were amusing to her. At the same time she liked to see this sympathetic interest he was taking in the child's upbringing. If he were only not so hard, so narrow at times. He made himself a torment to himself and to every one else.

On the earliest bright morning of returning spring he was wont to take her for her first little journeys in the world. "Come, now," he would say, " we will go for a little walk."

"Walk," chirped Vesta.

"Yes, walk," echoed Gerhardt.

Mrs. Gerhardt would fasten on one of her little hoods, for in these days Jennie kept Vesta's wardrobe beautifully replete. Taking her by the hand, Gerhardt would issue forth, satisfied to drag first one foot and then the other in order to accommodate his gait to her toddling steps.

One beautiful May day, when Vesta was four years old, they started on one of their walks. Everywhere nature was budding and bourgeoning; the birds twittering their arrival from the south; the insects making the best of their brief span of life. Sparrows chirped in the road; robins strutted upon the grass; bluebirds built in the eaves of the cottages. Gerhardt took a keen delight in pointing out the wonders of nature to Vesta, and she was quick to respond. Every new sight and sound interested her.

"Ooh!—ooh!" exclaimed Vesta, catching sight of a low, flashing touch of red as a robin lighted upon a twig nearby. Her hand was up, and her eyes were wide open.

"Yes," said Gerhardt, as happy as if he himself had but newly discovered this marvelous creature. "Robin. Bird. Robin. Say robin."

"Wobin," said Vesta.

"Yes, robin," he answered. "It is going to look for a worm now. We will see if we cannot find its nest. I think I saw a nest in one of these trees."

He plodded peacefully on, seeking to rediscover an old abandoned nest that he had observed on a former walk. "Here it is," he said at last, coming to a small and leafless tree, in which a winter-beaten remnant of a home was still clinging. "Here, come now, see," and he lifted the baby up at arm's length.

"See," said Gerhardt, indicating the wisp of dead grasses with his free hand, "nest. That is a bird's nest. See!"

"Ooh!" repeated Vesta, imitating his pointing finger with one of her own. "Ness—ooh!"

"Yes," said Gerhardt, putting her down again. "That was a *wren's* nest. They have all gone now. They will not come any more."

Still further they plodded, he unfolding the simple facts of life, she wondering with the wide wonder of a child. When they had gone a block or two he turned slowly about as if the end of the world had been reached.

"We must be going back!" he said.

And so she had come to her fifth year, growing in sweetness, intelligence, and vivacity. Gerhardt was fascinated by the questions she asked, the puzzles she pronounced. "Such a girl!" he would exclaim to his wife. "What is it she doesn't want to know? 'Where is God? What does He do? Where does He keep His feet?' she asks me. I gotta laugh sometimes." From rising in the morning, to dress her to laying her down at night after she had said her prayers, she came to be the chief solace and comfort of his days. Without Vesta, Gerhardt would have found his life hard indeed to bear.

Chapter XXVII

FOR THREE YEARS now Lester had been happy in the companionship of Jennie. Irregular as the connection might be in the eyes of the church and of society, it had brought him peace and comfort, and he was perfectly satisfied with the outcome of the experiment. His interest in the social affairs of Cincinnati was now practically *nil*, and he had consistently refused to consider any matrimonial proposition which had himself as the object. He looked on his father's business organization as offering a real chance for himself if he could get control of it; but he saw no way of doing so. Robert's interests were always in the way, and, if anything, the two brothers were farther apart than ever in their ideas and aims. Lester had thought once or twice of entering some other line of business or of allying himself with another carriage company, but he did not feel that he could conscientiously do this. Lester had his salary—fifteen thousand a year as secretary and treasurer of the company (his brother was vice-president)—and about five thousand from some outside investments. He had not been so lucky or so shrewd in speculation as Robert had been; aside from the principal which yielded his five thousand, he had nothing. Robert, on the other hand, was unquestionably worth between three and four hundred thousand dollars, in addition to his future interest in the business, which both brothers shrewdly suspected would be divided somewhat in their favor. Robert and Lester would get a fourth each, they thought; their sisters a sixth. It seemed natural that Kane senior should take this view, seeing that the brothers were actually in control and doing the work. Still, there was no certainty. The old gentleman might do anything or nothing. The probabilities were that he would be very fair and liberal. At the same time, Robert was obviously beating Lester in the game of life. What did Lester intend to do about it?

There comes a time in every thinking man's life when he pauses and "takes stock" of his condition; when he asks himself how it fares with his individuality as a whole, mental, moral, physical, material. This time comes after the first heed-

less flights of youth have passed, when the initiative and more
powerful efforts have been made, and he begins to feel the
uncertainty of results and final values which attaches itself to
everything. There is a deadening thought of uselessness which
creeps into many men's minds—the thought which has been
best expressed by the Preacher in Ecclesiastes.

Yet Lester strove to be philosophical. "What difference
does it make," he used to say to himself, "whether I live at
the White House, or here at home, or at the Grand Pacific?"
But in the very question was the implication that there were
achievements in life which he had failed to realize in his own
career. The White House represented the rise and success of
a great public character. His home and the Grand Pacific were
what had come to him without effort.

He decided for the time being—it was about the period of
the death of Jennie's mother—that he would make some effort to rehabilitate himself. He would cut out idling—these
numerous trips with Jennie had cost him considerable time.
He would make some outside investments. If his brother
could find avenues of financial profit, so could he. He would
endeavor to assert his authority—he would try to make himself of more importance in the business, rather than let Robert gradually absorb everything. Should he forsake Jennie?—
that thought also came to him. She had no claim on him. She
could make no protest. Somehow he did not see how it could
be done. It seemed cruel, useless; above all (though he disliked to admit it) it would be uncomfortable for himself. He
liked her—loved her, perhaps, in a selfish way. He didn't see
how he could desert her very well.

Just at this time he had a really serious difference with
Robert. His brother wanted to sever relations with an old and
well established paint company in New York, which had manufactured paints especially for the house, and invest in a new
concern in Chicago, which was growing and had a promising
future. Lester, knowing the members of the Eastern firm,
their reliability, their long and friendly relations with the
house, was in opposition. His father at first seemed to agree
with Lester. But Robert argued out the question in his cold,
logical way, his blue eyes fixed uncompromisingly upon his
brother's face. "We can't go on forever," he said, "standing

by old friends, just because father here has dealt with them, or you like them. We must have a change. The business must be stiffened up; we're going to have more and stronger competition."

"It's just as father feels about it," said Lester at last. "I have no deep feeling in the matter. It won't hurt me one way or the other. You say the house is going to profit eventually. I've stated the arguments on the other side."

"I'm inclined to think Robert is right," said Archibald Kane calmly. "Most of the things he has suggested so far have worked out."

Lester colored. "Well, we won't have any more discussion about it then," he said. He rose and strolled out of the office.

The shock of this defeat, coming at a time when he was considering pulling himself together, depressed Lester considerably. It wasn't much but it was a straw, and his father's remark about his brother's business acumen was even more irritating. He was beginning to wonder whether his father would discriminate in any way in the distribution of the property. Had he heard anything about his entanglement with Jennie? Had he resented the long vacations he had taken from business? It did not appear to Lester that he could be justly chargeable with either incapacity or indifference, so far as the company was concerned. He had done his work well. He was still the investigator of propositions put up to the house, the student of contracts, the trusted adviser of his father and mother—but he was being worsted. Where would it end? He thought about this, but could reach no conclusion.

Later in this same year Robert came forward with a plan for reorganization in the executive department of the business. He proposed that they should build an immense exhibition and storage warehouse on Michigan Avenue in Chicago, and transfer a portion of their completed stock there. Chicago was more central than Cincinnati. Buyers from the West and country merchants could be more easily reached and dealt with there. It would be a big advertisement for the house, a magnificent evidence of its standing and prosperity. Kane senior and Lester immediately approved of this. Both saw its advantages. Robert suggested that Lester should undertake the construction of the new buildings. It would probably be advisable for him to reside in Chicago a part of the time.

The idea appealed to Lester, even though it took him away from Cincinnati, largely if not entirely. It was dignified and not unrepresentative of his standing in the company. He could live in Chicago and he could have Jennie with him. The scheme he had for taking an apartment could now be arranged without difficulty. He voted yes. Robert smiled. "I'm sure we'll get good results from this all around," he said.

As construction work was soon to begin, Lester decided to move to Chicago immediately. He sent word for Jennie to meet him, and together they selected an apartment on the North Side, a very comfortable suite of rooms on a side street near the lake, and he had it fitted up to suit his taste. He figured that living in Chicago he could pose as a bachelor. He would never need to invite his friends to his rooms. There were his offices, where he could always be found, his clubs and the hotels. To his way of thinking the arrangement was practically ideal.

Of course Jennie's departure from Cleveland brought the affairs of the Gerhardt family to a climax. Probably the home would be broken up, but Gerhardt himself took the matter philosophically. He was an old man, and it did not matter much where he lived. Bass, Martha, and George were already taking care of themselves. Veronica and William were still in school, but some provision could be made for boarding them with a neighbor. The one real concern of Jennie and Gerhardt was Vesta. It was Gerhardt's natural thought that Jennie must take the child with her. What else should a mother do?

"Have you told him yet?" he asked her, when the day of her contemplated departure had been set.

"No; but I'm going to soon," she assured him.

"Always soon," he said.

He shook his head. His throat swelled.

"It's too bad," he went on. "It's a great sin. God will punish you, I'm afraid. The child needs some one. I'm getting old—otherwise I would keep her. There is no one here all day now to look after her right, as she should be." Again he shook his head.

"I know," said Jennie weakly. "I'm going to fix it now. I'm going to have her live with me soon. I won't neglect her—you know that."

"But the child's name," he insisted. "She should have a name. Soon in another year she goes to school. People will want to know who she is. It can't go on forever like this."

Jennie understood well enough that it couldn't. She was crazy about her baby. The heaviest cross she had to bear was the constant separations and the silence she was obliged to maintain about Vesta's very existence. It did seem unfair to the child, and yet Jennie did not see clearly how she could have acted otherwise. Vesta had good clothes, everything she needed. She was at least comfortable. Jennie hoped to give her a good education. If only she had told the truth to Lester in the first place. Now it was almost too late, and yet she felt that she had acted for the best. Finally she decided to find some good woman or family in Chicago who would take charge of Vesta for a consideration. In a Swedish colony to the west of La Salle Avenue she came across an old lady who seemed to embody all the virtues she required—cleanliness, simplicity, honesty. She was a widow, doing work by the day, but she was glad to make an arrangement by which she should give her whole time to Vesta. The latter was to go to kindergarten when a suitable one should be found. She was to have toys and kindly attention, and Mrs. Olsen was to inform Jennie of any change in the child's health. Jennie proposed to call every day, and she thought that sometimes, when Lester was out of town, Vesta might be brought to the apartment. She had had her with her at Cleveland, and he had never found out anything.

The arrangements completed, Jennie returned at the first opportunity to Cleveland to take Vesta away. Gerhardt, who had been brooding over his approaching loss, appeared most solicitous about her future. "She should grow up to be a fine girl," he said. "You should give her a good education—she is so smart." He spoke of the advisability of sending her to a Lutheran school and church, but Jennie was not so sure of that. Time and association with Lester had led her to think that perhaps the public school was better than any private institution. She had no particular objection to the church, but she no longer depended upon its teachings as a guide in the affairs of life. Why should she?

The next day it was necessary for Jennie to return to Chicago. Vesta, excited and eager, was made ready for the journey. Gerhardt had been wandering about, restless as a lost spirit, while the process of dressing was going on; now that the hour had actually struck he was doing his best to control his feelings. He could see that the five-year-old child had no conception of what it meant to him. She was happy and self-interested, chattering about the ride and the train.

"Be a good little girl," he said, lifting her up and kissing her. "See that you study your catechism and say your prayers. And you won't forget the grandpa—what?—" He tried to go on, but his voice failed him.

Jennie, whose heart ached for her father, choked back her emotion. "There," she said, "if I'd thought you were going to act like that—" She stopped.

"Go," said Gerhardt, manfully, "go. It is best this way." And he stood solemnly by as they went out of the door. Then he turned back to his favorite haunt, the kitchen, and stood there staring at the floor. One by one they were leaving him—Mrs. Gerhardt, Bass, Martha, Jennie, Vesta. He clasped his hands together, after his old-time fashion, and shook his head again and again. "So it is! So it is!" he repeated. "They all leave me. All my life goes to pieces."

Chapter XXVIII

DURING the three years in which Jennie and Lester had been associated there had grown up between them a strong feeling of mutual sympathy and understanding. Lester truly loved her in his own way. It was a strong, self-satisfying, determined kind of way, based solidly on a big natural foundation, but rising to a plane of genuine spiritual affinity. The yielding sweetness of her character both attracted and held him. She was true, and good, and womanly to the very center of her being; he had learned to trust her, to depend upon her, and the feeling had but deepened with the passing of the years.

On her part Jennie had sincerely, deeply, truly learned to love this man. At first when he had swept her off her feet, overawed her soul, and used her necessity as a chain wherewith to bind her to him, she was a little doubtful, a little afraid of him, although she had always liked him. Now, however, by living with him, by knowing him better, by watching his moods, she had come to love him. He was so big, so vocal, so handsome. His point of view and opinions of anything and everything were so positive. His pet motto, "Hew to the line, let the chips fall where they may," had clung in her brain as something immensely characteristic. Apparently he was not afraid of anything—God, man, or devil. He used to look at her, holding her chin between the thumb and fingers of his big brown hand, and say: "You're sweet, all right, but you need courage and defiance. You haven't enough of those things." And her eyes would meet his in dumb appeal. "Never mind," he would add, "you have other things." And then he would kiss her.

One of the most appealing things to Lester was the simple way in which she tried to avoid exposure of her various social and educational shortcomings. She could not write very well, and once he found a list of words he had used written out on a piece of paper with the meanings opposite. He smiled, but he liked her better for it. Another time in the Southern hotel in St. Louis he watched her pretending a loss of appetite because she thought that her lack of table manners was being observed by nearby diners. She could not always be sure of the right forks and knives, and the strange-looking dishes bothered her; how did one eat asparagus and artichokes?

"Why don't you eat something?" he asked good-naturedly. "You're hungry, aren't you?"

"Not very."

"You must be. Listen, Jennie. I know what it is. You mustn't feel that way. Your manners are all right. I wouldn't bring you here if they weren't. Your instincts are all right. Don't be uneasy. I'd tell you quick enough when there was anything wrong." His brown eyes held a friendly gleam.

She smiled gratefully. "I do feel a little nervous at times," she admitted.

"Don't," he repeated. "You're all right. Don't worry. I'll show you." And he did.

By degrees Jennie grew into an understanding of the usages and customs of comfortable existence. All that the Gerhardt family had ever had were the bare necessities of life. Now she was surrounded with whatever she wanted—trunks, clothes, toilet articles, the whole varied equipment of comfort—and while she liked it all, it did not upset her sense of proportion and her sense of the fitness of things. There was no element of vanity in her, only a sense of joy in privilege and opportunity. She was grateful to Lester for all that he had done and was doing for her. If only she could hold him—always!

The details of getting Vesta established once adjusted, Jennie settled down into the routine of home life. Lester, busy about his multitudinous affairs, was in and out. He had a suite of rooms reserved for himself at the Grand Pacific, which was then the exclusive hotel of Chicago, and this was his ostensible residence. His luncheon and evening appointments were kept at the Union Club. An early patron of the telephone, he had one installed in the apartment, so that he could reach Jennie quickly and at any time. He was home two or three nights a week, sometimes oftener. He insisted at first on Jennie having a girl of general housework, but acquiesced in the more sensible arrangement which she suggested later of letting some one come in to do the cleaning. She liked to work around her own home. Her natural industry and love of order prompted this feeling.

Lester liked his breakfast promptly at eight in the morning. He wanted dinner served nicely at seven. Silverware, cut glass, imported china—all the little luxuries of life appealed to him. He kept his trunks and wardrobe at the apartment.

During the first few months everything went smoothly. He was in the habit of taking Jennie to the theater now and then, and if he chanced to run across an acquaintance he always introduced her as Miss Gerhardt. When he registered her as his wife it was usually under an assumed name; where there was no danger of detection he did not mind using his own signature. Thus far there had been no difficulty or unpleasantness of any kind.

The trouble with this situation was that it was criss-crossed with the danger and consequent worry which the deception in regard to Vesta had entailed, as well as with Jennie's natural anxiety about her father and the disorganized home. Jennie feared, as Veronica hinted, that she and William would go to live with Martha, who was installed in a boarding-house in Cleveland, and that Gerhardt would be left alone. He was such a pathetic figure to her, with his injured hands and his one ability—that of being a watchman—that she was hurt to think of his being left alone. Would he come to her? She knew that he would not—feeling as he did at present. Would Lester have him—she was not sure of that. If he came Vesta would have to be accounted for. So she worried.

The situation in regard to Vesta was really complicated. Owing to the feeling that she was doing her daughter a great injustice, Jennie was particularly sensitive in regard to her, anxious to do a thousand things to make up for the one great duty that she could not perform. She daily paid a visit to the home of Mrs. Olsen, always taking with her toys, candy, or whatever came into her mind as being likely to interest and please the child. She liked to sit with Vesta and tell her stories of fairy and giant, which kept the little girl wide-eyed. At last she went so far as to bring her to the apartment, when Lester was away visiting his parents, and she soon found it possible, during his several absences, to do this regularly. After that, as time went on and she began to know his habits, she became more bold—although bold is scarcely the word to use in connection with Jennie. She became venturesome much as a mouse might; she would risk Vesta's presence on the assurance of even short absences—two or three days. She even got into the habit of keeping a few of Vesta's toys at the apartment, so that she could have something to play with when she came.

During these several visits from her child Jennie could not but realize the lovely thing life would be were she only an honored wife and a happy mother. Vesta was a most observant little girl. She could by her innocent childish questions give a hundred turns to the dagger of self-reproach which was already planted deeply in Jennie's heart.

"Can I come to live with you?" was one of her simplest and most frequently repeated questions. Jennie would reply that mamma could not have her just yet, but that very soon now, just as soon as she possibly could, Vesta should come to stay always.

"Don't you know just when?" Vesta would ask.

"No, dearest, not just when. Very soon now. You won't mind waiting a little while. Don't you like Mrs. Olsen?"

"Yes," replied Vesta; "but then she ain't got any nice things now. She's just got old things." And Jennie, stricken to the heart, would take Vesta to the toy shop, and load her down with a new assortment of playthings.

Of course Lester was not in the least suspicious. His observations of things relating to the home were rather casual. He went about his work and his pleasures believing Jennie to be the soul of sincerity and good-natured service, and it never occurred to him that there was anything underhanded in her actions. Once he did come home sick in the afternoon and found her absent—an absence which endured from two o'clock to five. He was a little irritated and grumbled on her return, but his annoyance was as nothing to her astonishment and fright when she found him there. She blanched at the thought of his suspecting something, and explained as best she could. She had gone to see her washerwoman. She was slow about her marketing. She didn't dream he was there. She was sorry, too, that her absence had lost her an opportunity to serve him. It showed her what a mess she was likely to make of it all.

It happened that about three weeks after the above occurrence Lester had occasion to return to Cincinnati for a week, and during this time Jennie again brought Vesta to the flat; for four days there was the happiest goings on between the mother and child.

Nothing would have come of this little reunion had it not been for an oversight on Jennie's part, the far-reaching effects of which she could only afterward regret. This was the leaving of a little toy lamb under the large leather divan in the front room, where Lester was wont to lie and smoke. A little bell held by a thread of blue ribbon was fastened about its neck, and this tinkled feebly whenever it was shaken. Vesta, with the unaccountable freakishness of children had deliberately dropped it behind the divan, an action which Jennie did not notice at the time. When she gathered up the various playthings after Vesta's departure she overlooked it entirely, and there it rested, its innocent eyes still staring upon the sunlit regions of toyland, when Lester returned.

That same evening, when he was lying on the divan, quietly enjoying his cigar and his newspaper, he chanced to drop the former, fully lighted. Wishing to recover it before it should do any damage, he leaned over and looked under the divan. The cigar was not in sight, so he rose and pulled the lounge out, a move which revealed to him the little lamb still standing where Vesta had dropped it. He picked it up, turning it over and over, and wondering how it had come there.

A lamb! It must belong to some neighbor's child in whom Jennie had taken an interest, he thought. He would have to go and tease her about this.

Accordingly he held the toy jovially before him, and, coming out into the dining-room, where Jennie was working at the sideboard, he exclaimed in a mock solemn voice, "Where did this come from?"

Jennie, who was totally unconscious of the existence of this evidence of her duplicity, turned, and was instantly possessed with the idea that he had suspected all and was about to visit his just wrath upon her. Instantly the blood flamed in her cheeks and as quickly left them.

"Why, why!" she stuttered, "it's a little toy I bought."

"I see it is," he returned genially, her guilty tremor not escaping his observation, but having at the same time no explicable significance to him. "It's frisking around a mighty lone sheepfold."

He touched the little bell at its throat, while Jennie stood there, unable to speak. It tinkled feebly, and then he looked at her again. His manner was so humorous that she could tell he suspected nothing. However, it was almost impossible for her to recover her self-possession.

"What's ailing you?" he asked.

"Nothing," she replied.

"You look as though a lamb was a terrible shock to you."

"I forgot to take it out from there, that was all," she went on blindly.

"It looks as though it has been played with enough," he added more seriously, and then seeing that the discussion was evidently painful to her, he dropped it. The lamb had not furnished him the amusement that he had expected.

Lester went back into the front room, stretched himself out and thought it over. Why was she nervous? What was there about a toy to make her grow pale? Surely there was no harm in her harboring some youngster of the neighborhood when she was alone—having it come in and play. Why should she be so nervous? He thought it over, but could come to no conclusion.

Nothing more was said about the incident of the toy lamb. Time might have wholly effaced the impression from Lester's memory had nothing else intervened to arouse his suspicions; but a mishap of any kind seems invariably to be linked with others which follow close upon its heels.

One evening when Lester happened to be lingering about the flat later than usual the door bell rang, and, Jennie being busy in the kitchen, Lester went himself to open the door. He was greeted by a middle-aged lady, who frowned very nervously upon him, and inquired in broken Swedish accents for Jennie.

"Wait a moment," said Lester; and stepping to the rear door he called her.

Jennie came, and seeing who the visitor was, she stepped nervously out in the hall and closed the door after her. The action instantly struck Lester as suspicious. He frowned and determined to inquire thoroughly into the matter. A moment later Jennie reappeared. Her face was white and her fingers seemed to be nervously seeking something to seize upon.

"What's the trouble?" he inquired, the irritation he had felt the moment before giving his voice a touch of gruffness.

"I've got to go out for a little while," she at last managed to reply.

"Very well," he assented unwillingly. "But you can tell me what's the trouble with you, can't you? Where do you have to go?"

"I—I," began Jennie, stammering. "I—have—"

"Yes," he said grimly.

"I have to go on an errand," she stumbled on. "I—I can't wait. I'll tell you when I come back, Lester. Please don't ask me now."

She looked vainly at him, her troubled countenance still marked by preoccupation and anxiety to get away, and Lester, who had never seen this look of intense responsibility in her before, was moved and irritated by it.

"That's all right," he said, "but what's the use of all this secrecy? Why can't you come out and tell what's the matter with you? What's the use of this whispering behind doors? Where do you have to go?"

He paused, checked by his own harshness, and Jennie, who was intensely wrought up by the information she had received, as well as the unwonted verbal castigation she was now enduring, rose to an emotional state never reached by her before.

"I will, Lester, I will," she exclaimed. "Only not now. I haven't time. I'll tell you everything when I come back. Please don't stop me now."

She hurried to the adjoining chamber to get her wraps, and Lester, who had even yet no clear conception of what it all meant, followed her stubbornly to the door.

"See here," he exclaimed in his vigorous, brutal way, "you're not acting right. What's the matter with you? I want to know."

He stood in the doorway, his whole frame exhibiting the pugnacity and settled determination of a man who is bound to be obeyed. Jennie, troubled and driven to bay, turned at last.

"It's my child, Lester," she exclaimed. "It's dying. I haven't time to talk. Oh, please don't stop me. I'll tell you everything when I come back."

"Your child!" he exclaimed. "What the hell are you talking about?"

"I couldn't help it," she returned. "I was afraid— I should have told you long ago. I meant to only—only— Oh, let me go now, and I'll tell you all when I come back!"

He stared at her in amazement; then he stepped aside, unwilling to force her any further for the present. "Well, go ahead," he said quietly. "Don't you want some one to go along with you?"

"No," she replied. "Mrs. Olsen is right here. I'll go with her."

She hurried forth, white-faced, and he stood there, pondering. Could this be the woman he had thought he knew? Why, she had been deceiving him for years. Jennie! The white-faced! The simple!

He choked a little as he muttered:

"Well, I'll be damned!"

Chapter XXIX

THE REASON why Jennie had been called was nothing more than one of those infantile seizures the coming and result of which no man can predict two hours beforehand. Vesta had been seriously taken with membranous croup only a few hours before, and the development since had been so rapid that the poor old Swedish mother was half frightened to death herself, and hastily despatched a neighbor to say that Vesta was very ill and Mrs. Kane was to come at once. This message, delivered as it was in a very nervous manner by one whose only object was to bring her, had induced the soul-racking fear of death in Jennie and caused her to brave the discovery of Lester in the manner described. Jennie hurried on anxiously, her one thought being to reach her child before the arm of death could interfere and snatch it from her, her mind weighed upon by a legion of fears. What if it should already be too late when she got there; what if Vesta already should be no more. Instinctively she quickened her pace and as the street lamps came and receded in the gloom she forgot all the sting of Lester's words, all fear that he might turn her out and leave her alone in a great city with a little child to care for, and remembered only the fact that her Vesta was very ill, possibly dying, and that she was the direct cause of the child's absence from her; that perhaps but for the want of her care and attention Vesta might be well to-night.

"If I can only get there," she kept saying to herself; and then, with that frantic unreason which is the chief characteristic of the instinct-driven mother: "I might have known that God would punish me for my unnatural conduct. I might have known—I might have known."

When she reached the gate she fairly sped up the little walk and into the house, where Vesta was lying pale, quiet, and weak, but considerably better. Several Swedish neighbors and a middle-aged physician were in attendance, all of whom looked at her curiously as she dropped beside the child's bed and spoke to her.

Jennie's mind had been made up. She had sinned, and sinned grievously, against her daughter, but now she would make amends so far as possible. Lester was very dear to her, but she would no longer attempt to deceive him in anything, even if he left her—she felt an agonized stab, a pain at the thought—she must still do the one right thing. Vesta must not be an outcast any longer. Her mother must give her a home. Where Jennie was, there must Vesta be.

Sitting by the bedside in this humble Swedish cottage, Jennie realized the fruitlessness of her deception, the trouble and pain it had created in her home, the months of suffering it had given her with Lester, the agony it had heaped upon her this night—and to what end? The truth had been discovered anyhow. She sat there and meditated, not knowing what next was to happen, while Vesta quieted down, and then went soundly to sleep.

Lester, after recovering from the first heavy import of this discovery, asked himself some perfectly natural questions. "Who was the father of the child? How old was it? How did it chance to be in Chicago, and who was taking care of it?" He could ask, but he could not answer; he knew absolutely nothing.

Curiously, now, as he thought, his first meeting with Jennie at Mrs. Bracebridge's came back to him. What was it about her then that had attracted him? What made him think, after a few hours' observation, that he could seduce her to do his will? What was it—moral looseness, or weakness, or what? There must have been art in the sorry affair, the practised art of the cheat, and, in deceiving such a confiding nature as his, she had done even more than practise deception—she had been ungrateful.

Now the quality of ingratitude was a very objectionable thing to Lester—the last and most offensive trait of a debased nature, and to be able to discover a trace of it in Jennie was very disturbing. It is true that she had not exhibited it in any other way before—quite to the contrary—but nevertheless he saw strong evidences of it now, and it made him very bitter in his feeling toward her. How could she be guilty of any such conduct toward him? Had he not picked her up out of nothing, so to speak, and befriended her?

He moved from his chair in this silent room and began to pace slowly to and fro, the weightiness of this subject exercising to the full his power of decision. She was guilty of a misdeed which he felt able to condemn. The original concealment was evil; the continued deception more. Lastly, there was the thought that her love after all had been divided, part for him, part for the child, a discovery which no man in his position could contemplate with serenity. He moved irritably as he thought of it, shoved his hands in his pockets and walked to and fro across the floor.

That a man of Lester's temperament should consider himself wronged by Jennie merely because she had concealed a child whose existence was due to conduct no more irregular than was involved later in the yielding of herself to him was an example of those inexplicable perversions of judgment to which the human mind, in its capacity of keeper of the honor of others, seems permanently committed. Lester, aside from his own personal conduct (for men seldom judge with that in the balance), had faith in the ideal that a woman should reveal herself completely to the one man with whom she is in love; and the fact that she had not done so was a grief to him. He had asked her once tentatively about her past. She begged him not to press her. That was the time she should have spoken of any child. Now—he shook his head.

His first impulse, after he had thought the thing over, was to walk out and leave her. At the same time he was curious to hear the end of this business. He did put on his hat and coat, however, and went out, stopping at the first convenient saloon to get a drink. He took a car and went down to the club, strolling about the different rooms and chatting with several people whom he encountered. He was restless and irritated; and finally, after three hours of meditation, he took a cab and returned to his apartment.

The distraught Jennie, sitting by her sleeping child, was at last made to realize, by its peaceful breathing that all danger was over. There was nothing more that she could do for Vesta, and now the claims of the home that she had deserted began to reassert themselves, the promise to Lester and the need of being loyal to her duties unto the very end. Lester might possibly be waiting for her. It was just probable that he wished to hear the remainder of her story before breaking with her entirely. Although anguished and frightened by the

certainty, as she deemed it, of his forsaking her, she nevertheless felt that it was no more than she deserved—a just punishment for all her misdoings.

When Jennie arrived at the flat it was after eleven, and the
hall light was already out. She first tried the door, and then
inserted her key. No one stirred, however, and, opening the
door, she entered in the expectation of seeing Lester sternly
confronting her. He was not there, however. The burning gas
had merely been an oversight on his part. She glanced quickly
about, but seeing only the empty room, she came instantly to
the other conclusion, that he had forsaken her—and so stood
there, a meditative, helpless figure.

"Gone!" she thought.

At this moment his footsteps sounded on the stairs. He
came in with his derby hat pulled low over his broad forehead, close to his sandy eyebrows, and with his overcoat but-
toned up closely about his neck. He took off the coat without
looking at Jennie and hung it on the rack. Then he deliberately took off his hat and hung that up also. When he was
through he turned to where she was watching him with wide
eyes.

"I want to know about this thing now from beginning to
end," he began. "Whose child is that?"

Jennie wavered a moment, as one who might be going to
take a leap in the dark, then opened her lips mechanically and
confessed:

"It's Senator Brander's."

"Senator Brander!" echoed Lester, the familiar name of the
dead but still famous statesman ringing with shocking and unexpected force in his ears. "How did you come to know him?"

"We used to do his washing for him," she rejoined simply
—"my mother and I."

Lester paused, the baldness of the statements issuing from
her sobering even his rancorous mood. "Senator Brander's
child," he thought to himself. So that great representative of
the interests of the common people was the undoer of her—
a self-confessed washerwoman's daughter. A fine tragedy of
low life all this was.

"How long ago was this?" he demanded, his face the picture of a darkling mood.

"It's been nearly six years now," she returned.

He calculated the time that had elapsed since he had known her, and then continued:

"How old is the child?"

"She's a little over five."

Lester moved a little. The need for serious thought made his tone more peremptory but less bitter.

"Where have you been keeping her all this time?"

"She was at home until you went to Cincinnati last spring. I went down and brought her then."

"Was she there the times I came to Cleveland?"

"Yes," said Jennie; "but I didn't let her come out anywhere where you could see her."

"I thought you said you told your people that you were married," he exclaimed, wondering how this relationship of the child to the family could have been adjusted.

"I did," she replied, "but I didn't want to tell you about her. They thought all the time I intended to."

"Well, why didn't you?"

"Because I was afraid."

"Afraid of what?"

"I didn't know what was going to become of me when I went with you, Lester. I didn't want to do her any harm if I could help it. I was ashamed, afterward; when you said you didn't like children I was afraid."

"Afraid I'd leave you?"

"Yes."

He stopped, the simplicity of her answers removing a part of the suspicion of artful duplicity which had originally weighed upon him. After all, there was not so much of that in it as mere wretchedness of circumstance and cowardice of morals. What a family she must have! What queer non-moral natures they must have to have brooked any such a combination of affairs!

"Didn't you know that you'd be found out in the long run?" he at last demanded. "Surely you might have seen that you couldn't raise her that way. Why didn't you tell me in the first place? I wouldn't have thought anything of it then."

"I know," she said. "I wanted to protect her."

"Where is she now?" he asked.

Jennie explained.

She stood there, the contradictory aspect of these questions and of his attitude puzzling even herself. She did try to explain them after a time, but all Lester could gain was that she had blundered along without any artifice at all—a condition that was so manifest that, had he been in any other position than that he was, he might have pitied her. As it was, the revelation concerning Brander was hanging over him, and he finally returned to that.

"You say your mother used to do washing for him. How did you come to get in with him?"

Jennie, who until now had borne his questions with unmoving pain, winced at this. He was now encroaching upon the period that was by far the most distressing memory of her life. What he had just asked seemed to be a demand upon her to make everything clear.

"I was so young, Lester," she pleaded. "I was only eighteen. I didn't know. I used to go to the hotel where he was stopping and get his laundry, and at the end of the week I'd take it to him again."

She paused, and as he took a chair, looking as if he expected to hear the whole story, she continued: "We were so poor. He used to give me money to give to my mother. I didn't know."

She paused again, totally unable to go on, and he, seeing that it would be impossible for her to explain without prompting, took up his questioning again—eliciting by degrees the whole pitiful story. Brander had intended to marry her. He had written to her, but before he could come to her he died.

The confession was complete. It was followed by a period of five minutes, in which Lester said nothing at all; he put his arm on the mantel and stared at the wall, while Jennie waited, not knowing what would follow—not wishing to make a single plea. The clock ticked audibly. Lester's face betrayed no sign of either thought or feeling. He was now quite calm, quite sober, wondering what he should do. Jennie was before him as the criminal at the bar. He, the righteous, the moral, the pure of heart, was in the judgment seat. Now to sentence her—to make up his mind what course of action he should pursue.

It was a disagreeable tangle, to be sure, something that a man of his position and wealth really ought not to have anything to do with. This child, the actuality of it, put an almost unbearable face upon the whole matter—and yet he was not quite prepared to speak. He turned after a time, the silvery tinkle of the French clock on the mantel striking three and causing him to become aware of Jennie, pale, uncertain, still standing as she had stood all this while.

"Better go to bed," he said at last, and fell again to pondering this difficult problem.

But Jennie continued to stand there wide-eyed, expectant, ready to hear at any moment his decision as to her fate. She waited in vain, however. After a long time of musing he turned and went to the clothes-rack near the door.

"Better go to bed," he said, indifferently. "I'm going out."

She turned instinctively, feeling that even in this crisis there was some little service that she might render, but he did not see her. He went out, vouchsafing no further speech.

She looked after him, and as his footsteps sounded on the stair she felt as if she were doomed and hearing her own death-knell. What had she done? What would he do now? She stood there a dissonance of despair, and when the lower door clicked moved her hand out of the agony of her suppressed hopelessness.

"Gone!" she thought. "Gone!"

In the light of a late dawn she was still sitting there pondering, her state far too urgent for idle tears.

Chapter XXX

THE SULLEN, philosophic Lester was not so determined upon his future course of action as he appeared to be. Stern as was his mood, he did not see, after all, exactly what grounds he had for complaint. And yet the child's existence complicated matters considerably. He did not like to see the evidence of Jennie's previous misdeeds walking about in the shape of a human being; but, as a matter of fact, he admitted to himself that long ago he might have forced Jennie's story out of her if he had gone about it in earnest. She would not have lied, he knew that. At the very outset he might have demanded the history of her past. He had not done so; well, now it was too late. The one thing it did fix in his mind was that it would be useless to ever think of marrying her. It couldn't be done, not by a man in his position. The best solution of the problem was to make reasonable provision for Jennie and then leave her. He went to his hotel with his mind made up, but he did not actually say to himself that he would do it at once.

It is an easy thing for a man to theorize in a situation of this kind, quite another to act. Our comforts, appetites and passions grow with usage, and Jennie was not only a comfort, but an appetite, with him. Almost four years of constant association had taught him so much about her and himself that he was not prepared to let go easily or quickly. It was too much of a wrench. He could think of it bustling about the work of a great organization during the daytime, but when night came it was a different matter. He could be lonely, too, he discovered much to his surprise, and it disturbed him.

One of the things that interested him in this situation was Jennie's early theory that the intermingling of Vesta with him and her in this new relationship would injure the child. Just how did she come by that feeling, he wanted to know? His place in the world was better than hers, yet it dawned on him after a time that there might have been something in her point of view. She did not know who he was or what he would do with her. He might leave her shortly. Being uncertain, she wished to protect her baby. That wasn't so bad.

Then again, he was curious to know what the child was like. The daughter of a man like Senator Brander might be somewhat of an infant. He was a brilliant man and Jennie was a charming woman. He thought of this, and, while it irritated him, it aroused his curiosity. He ought to go back and see the child—he was really entitled to a view of it—but he hesitated because of his own attitude in the beginning. It seemed to him that he really ought to quit, and here he was parleying with himself.

The truth was that he couldn't. These years of living with Jennie had made him curiously dependent upon her. Who had ever been so close to him before? His mother loved him, but her attitude toward him had not so much to do with real love as with ambition. His father—well, his father was a man, like himself. All of his sisters were distinctly wrapped up in their own affairs; Robert and he were temperamentally uncongenial. With Jennie he had really been happy, he had truly lived. She was necessary to him; the longer he stayed away from her the more he wanted her. He finally decided to have a straight-out talk with her, to arrive at some sort of understanding. She ought to get the child and take care of it. She must understand that he might eventually want to quit. She ought to be made to feel that a definite change had taken place, though no immediate break might occur. That same evening he went out to the apartment. Jennie heard him enter, and her heart began to flutter. Then she took her courage in both hands, and went to meet him.

"There's just one thing to be done about this as far as I can see," began Lester, with characteristic directness. "Get the child and bring her here where you can take care of her. There's no use leaving her in the hands of strangers."

"I will, Lester," said Jennie submissively. "I always wanted to."

"Very well, then, you'd better do it at once." He took an evening newspaper out of his pocket and strolled toward one of the front windows; then he turned to her. "You and I might as well understand each other, Jennie," he went on. "I can see how this thing came about. It was a piece of foolishness on my part not to have asked you before, and made you tell me. It was silly for you to conceal it, even if you didn't want the child's life mixed with mine. You might have known that it couldn't be done. That's neither here nor there, though, now. The thing that I want to point out is that one can't live and hold a relationship such as ours without confidence. You and I had that, I thought. I don't see my way clear to ever hold more than a tentative relationship with you on this basis. The thing is too tangled. There's too much cause for scandal."

"I know," said Jennie.

"Now, I don't propose to do anything hasty. For my part I don't see why things can't go on about as they are—certainly for the present—but I want you to look the facts in the face."

Jennie sighed. "I know, Lester," she said, "I know."

He went to the window and stared out. There were some trees in the yard, where the darkness was settling. He wondered how this would really come out, for he liked a home atmosphere. Should he leave the apartment and go to his club?

"You'd better get the dinner," he suggested, after a time, turning toward her irritably; but he did not feel so distant as he looked. It was a shame that life could not be more decently organized. He strolled back to his lounge, and Jennie went about her duties. She was thinking of Vesta, of her ungrateful attitude toward Lester, of his final decision never to marry her. So that was how one dream had been wrecked by folly.

She spread the table, lighted the pretty silver candles, made his favorite biscuit, put a small leg of lamb in the oven to roast, and washed some lettuce-leaves for a salad. She had been a diligent student of a cook-book for some time, and she had learned a good deal from her mother. All the time she was wondering how the situation would work out. He would leave her eventually—no doubt of that. He would go away and marry some one else.

"Oh, well," she thought finally, "he is not going to leave me right away—that is something. And I can bring Vesta here." She sighed as she carried the things to the table. If life would only give her Lester and Vesta together—but that hope was over.

Chapter XXXI

THERE WAS peace and quiet for some time after this storm. Jennie went the next day and brought Vesta away with her. The joy of the reunion between mother and child made up for many other worries. "Now I can do by her as I ought," she thought; and three or four times during the day she found herself humming a little song.

Lester came only occasionally at first. He was trying to make himself believe that he ought to do something toward reforming his life—toward bringing about that eventual separation which he had suggested. He did not like the idea of a child being in this apartment—particularly that particular child. He fought his way through a period of calculated neglect, and then began to return to the apartment more regularly. In spite of all its drawbacks, it was a place of quiet, peace, and very notable personal comfort.

During the first days of Lester's return it was difficult for Jennie to adjust matters so as to keep the playful, nervous, almost uncontrollable child from annoying the staid, emphatic, commercial-minded man. Jennie gave Vesta a severe talking to the first night Lester telephoned that he was coming, telling her that he was a very bad-tempered man who didn't like children, and that she mustn't go near him. "You mustn't talk," she said. "You mustn't ask questions. Let mamma ask you what you want. And don't reach, ever."

Vesta agreed solemnly, but her childish mind hardly grasped the full significance of the warning.

Lester came at seven. Jennie, who had taken great pains to array Vesta as attractively as possible, had gone into her bedroom to give her own toilet a last touch. Vesta was supposedly in the kitchen. As a matter of fact, she had followed her mother to the door of the sitting-room, where now she could be plainly seen. Lester hung up his hat and coat, then, turning, he caught his first glimpse. The child looked very sweet—he admitted that at a glance. She was arrayed in a blue-dotted, white flannel dress, with a soft roll collar and cuffs, and the costume was completed by white stockings and shoes. Her corn-colored ringlets hung gaily about her face. Blue eyes, rosy lips, rosy cheeks completed the picture. Lester stared, almost inclined to say something, but restrained himself. Vesta shyly retreated.

When Jennie came out he commented on the fact that Vesta had arrived. "Rather sweet-looking child," he said. "Do you have much trouble in making her mind?"

"Not much," she returned.

Jennie went on to the dining-room, and Lester overheard a scrap of their conversation.

"Who are he?" asked Vesta.

"Sh! That's your Uncle Lester. Didn't I tell you you mustn't talk?"

"Are he your uncle?"

"No, dear. Don't talk now. Run into the kitchen."

"Are he only my uncle?"

"Yes. Now run along."

"All right."

In spite of himself Lester had to smile.

What might have followed if the child had been homely, misshapen, peevish, or all three, can scarcely be conjectured. Had Jennie been less tactful, even in the beginning, he might have obtained a disagreeable impression. As it was, the natural beauty of the child, combined with the mother's gentle diplomacy in keeping her in the background, served to give him that fleeting glimpse of innocence and youth which is always pleasant. The thought struck him that Jennie had been the mother of a child all these years; she had been separated from it for months at a time; she had never even hinted at its existence, and yet her affection for Vesta was obviously great. "It's queer," he said. "She's a peculiar woman."

One morning Lester was sitting in the parlor reading his paper when he thought he heard something stir. He turned, and was surprised to see a large blue eye fixed upon him through the crack of a neighboring door—the effect was most disconcerting. It was not like the ordinary eye, which, under such embarrassing circumstances, would have been immediately withdrawn; it kept its position with deliberate boldness. He turned his paper solemnly and looked again.

There was the eye. He turned it again. Still was the eye present. He crossed his legs and looked again. Now the eye was gone.

This little episode, unimportant in itself, was yet informed with the saving grace of comedy, a thing to which Lester was especially responsive. Although not in the least inclined to relax his attitude of aloofness, he found his mind, in the minutest degree, tickled by the mysterious appearance; the corners of his mouth were animated by a desire to turn up. He did not give way to the feeling, and stuck by his paper, but the incident remained very clearly in his mind. The young wayfarer had made her first really important impression upon him.

Not long after this Lester was sitting one morning at breakfast, calmly eating his chop and conning his newspaper, when he was aroused by another visitation—this time not quite so simple. Jennie had given Vesta her breakfast, and set her to amuse herself alone until Lester should leave the house. Jennie was seated at the table, pouring out the coffee, when Vesta suddenly appeared, very business-like in manner, and marched through the room. Lester looked up, and Jennie colored and arose.

"What is it, Vesta?" she inquired, following her.

By this time, however, Vesta had reached the kitchen, secured a little broom, and returned, a droll determination lighting her face.

"I want my little broom," she exclaimed and marched sedately past, at which manifestation of spirit Lester again twitched internally, this time allowing the slightest suggestion of a smile to play across his mouth.

The final effect of this intercourse was gradually to break down the feeling of distaste Lester had for the child, and to establish in its place a sort of tolerant recognition of her possibilities as a human being.

The developments of the next six months were of a kind to further relax the strain of opposition which still existed in Lester's mind. Although not at all resigned to the somewhat tainted atmosphere in which he was living, he yet found himself so comfortable that he could not persuade himself to give it up. It was too much like a bed of down. Jennie was too worshipful. The condition of unquestioned liberty, so far as all his old social relationships were concerned, coupled with the privilege of quiet, simplicity, and affection in the home was too inviting. He lingered on, and began to feel that perhaps it would be just as well to let matters rest as they were.

During this period his friendly relations with the little Vesta insensibly strengthened. He discovered that there was a real flavor of humor about Vesta's doings, and so came to watch for its development. She was forever doing something interesting, and although Jennie watched over her with a care that was in itself a revelation to him, nevertheless Vesta managed to elude every effort to suppress her and came straight home with her remarks. Once, for example, she was sawing away at a small piece of meat upon her large plate with her big knife, when Lester remarked to Jennie that it might be advisable to get her a little breakfast set.

"She can hardly handle these knives."

"Yes," said Vesta instantly. "I need a little knife. My hand is just so very little."

She held it up. Jennie, who never could tell what was to follow, reached over and put it down, while Lester with difficulty restrained a desire to laugh.

Another morning, not long after, she was watching Jennie put the lumps of sugar in Lester's cup, when she broke in with, "I want two lumps in mine, mamma."

"No, dearest," replied Jennie, "you don't need any in yours. You have milk to drink."

"Uncle Lester has two," she protested.

"Yes," returned Jennie; "but you're only a little girl. Besides you mustn't say anything like that at the table. It isn't nice."

"Uncle Lester eats too much sugar," was her immediate rejoinder, at which that fine gourmet smiled broadly.

"I don't know about that," he put in, for the first time deigning to answer her directly. "That sounds like the fox and grapes to me." Vesta smiled back at him, and now that the ice was broken she chattered on unrestrainedly. One thing led to another, and at last Lester felt as though, in a way, the little girl belonged to him; he was willing even that she should share in such opportunities as his position and wealth might make possible—provided, of course, that he stayed with

Jennie, and that they worked out some arrangement which would not put him hopelessly out of touch with the world which was back of him, and which he had to keep constantly in mind.

Chapter XXXII

THE FOLLOWING spring the show-rooms and warehouse were completed, and Lester removed his office to the new building. Heretofore, he had been transacting all his business affairs at the Grand Pacific and the club. From now on he felt himself to be firmly established in Chicago—as if that was to be his future home. A large number of details were thrown upon him—the control of a considerable office force, and the handling of various important transactions. It took away from him the need of traveling, that duty going to Amy's husband, under the direction of Robert. The latter was doing his best to push his personal interests, not only through the influence he was bringing to bear upon his sisters, but through his reorganization of the factory. Several men whom Lester was personally fond of were in danger of elimination. But Lester did not hear of this, and Kane senior was inclined to give Robert a free hand. Age was telling on him. He was glad to see some one with a strong policy come up and take charge. Lester did not seem to mind. Apparently he and Robert were on better terms than ever before.

Matters might have gone on smoothly enough were it not for the fact that Lester's private life with Jennie was not a matter which could be permanently kept under cover. At times he was seen driving with her by people who knew him in a social and commercial way. He was for brazening it out on the ground that he was a single man, and at liberty to associate with anybody he pleased. Jennie might be any young woman of good family in whom he was interested. He did not propose to introduce her to anybody if he could help it, and he always made it a point to be a fast traveler in driving, in order that others might not attempt to detain and talk to him. At the theater, as has been said, she was simply "Miss Gerhardt."

The trouble was that many of his friends were also keen observers of life. They had no quarrel to pick with Lester's conduct. Only he had been seen in other cities, in times past, with this same woman. She must be some one whom he was maintaining irregularly. Well, what of it? Wealth and youthful spirits must have their fling. Rumors came to Robert, who, however, kept his own counsel. If Lester wanted to do this sort of thing, well and good. But there must come a time when there would be a show-down.

This came about in one form about a year and a half after Lester and Jennie had been living in the north side apartment. It so happened that, during a stretch of inclement weather in the fall, Lester was seized with a mild form of grip. When he felt the first symptoms he thought that his indisposition would be a matter of short duration, and tried to overcome it by taking a hot bath and a liberal dose of quinine. But the infection was stronger than he counted on; by morning he was flat on his back, with a severe fever and a splitting headache.

His long period of association with Jennie had made him incautious. Policy would have dictated that he should betake himself to his hotel and endure his sickness alone. As a matter of fact, he was very glad to be in the house with her. He had to call up the office to say that he was indisposed and would not be down for a day or so; then he yielded himself comfortably to her patient ministrations.

Jennie, of course, was delighted to have Lester with her, sick or well. She persuaded him to see a doctor and have him prescribe. She brought him potions of hot lemonade, and bathed his face and hands in cold water over and over. Later, when he was recovering, she made him appetizing cups of beef-tea or gruel.

It was during this illness that the first real contretemps occurred. Lester's sister Louise, who had been visiting friends in St. Paul, and who had written him that she might stop off to see him on her way, decided upon an earlier return than she had originally planned. While Lester was sick at his apartment she arrived in Chicago. Calling up the office, and finding that he was not there and would not be down for several days, she asked where he could be reached.

"I think he is at his rooms in the Grand Pacific," said an incautious secretary. "He's not feeling well." Louise, a little disturbed, telephoned to the Grand Pacific, and was told that Mr. Kane had not been there for several days—did not, as a matter of fact, occupy his rooms more than one or two days a week. Piqued by this, she telephoned his club.

It so happened that at the club there was a telephone boy who had called up the apartment a number of times for Lester himself. He had not been cautioned not to give its number—as a matter of fact, it had never been asked for by any one else. When Louise stated that she was Lester's sister, and was anxious to find him, the boy replied, "I think he lives at 19 Schiller Place."

"Whose address is that you're giving?" inquired a passing clerk.

"Mr. Kane's."

"Well, don't be giving out addresses. Don't you know that yet?"

The boy apologized, but Louise had hung up the receiver and was gone.

About an hour later, curious as to this third residence of her brother, Louise arrived at Schiller Place. Ascending the steps—it was a two-apartment house—she saw the name of Kane on the door leading to the second floor. Ringing the bell, she was opened to by Jennie, who was surprised to see so fashionably attired a young woman.

"This is Mr. Kane's apartment, I believe," began Louise, condescendingly, as she looked in at the open door behind Jennie. She was a little surprised to meet a young woman, but her suspicions were as yet only vaguely aroused.

"Yes," replied Jennie.

"He's sick, I believe. I'm his sister. May I come in?"

Jennie, had she had time to collect her thoughts, would have tried to make some excuse, but Louise, with the audacity of her birth and station, swept past before Jennie could say a word. Once inside Louise looked about her inquiringly. She found herself in the sitting-room, which gave into the bed-room where Lester was lying. Vesta happened to be playing in one corner of the room, and stood up to eye the new-comer. The open bedroom showed Lester quite plainly lying in bed, a window to the left of him, his eyes closed.

"Oh, there you are, old fellow!" exclaimed Louise. "What's ailing you?" she hurried on.

Lester, who at the sound of her voice had opened his eyes, realized in an instant how things were. He pulled himself up on one elbow, but words failed him.

"Why, hello, Louise," he finally forced himself to say. "Where did you come from?"

"St. Paul. I came back sooner than I thought," she answered lamely, a sense of something wrong irritating her. "I had a hard time finding you, too. Who's your—" she was about to say "pretty housekeeper," but turned to find Jennie dazedly gathering up certain articles in the adjoining room and looking dreadfully distraught.

Lester cleared his throat hopelessly.

His sister swept the place with an observing eye. It took in the home atmosphere, which was both pleasing and suggestive. There was a dress of Jennie's lying across a chair, in a familiar way, which caused Miss Kane to draw herself up warily. She looked at her brother, who had a rather curious expression in his eyes—he seemed slightly nonplussed, but cool and defiant.

"You shouldn't have come out here," said Lester finally, before Louise could give vent to the rising question in her mind.

"Why shouldn't I?" she exclaimed, angered at the brazen confession. "You're my brother, aren't you? Why should you have any place that I couldn't come. Well, I like that—and from you to me."

"Listen, Louise," went on Lester, drawing himself up further on one elbow. "You know as much about life as I do. There is no need of our getting into an argument. I didn't know you were coming, or I would have made other arrangements."

"Other arrangements, indeed," she sneered. "I should think as much. The idea!"

She was greatly irritated to think that she had fallen into this trap; it was really disgraceful of Lester.

"I wouldn't be so haughty about it," he declared, his color rising. "I'm not apologizing to you for my conduct. I'm saying I would have made other arrangements, which is a very different thing from begging your pardon. If you don't want to be civil, you needn't."

"Why, Lester Kane!" she exclaimed, her cheeks flaming. "I thought better of you, honestly I did. I should think you would be ashamed of yourself living here in open—" she paused without using the word—"and our friends scattered all over the city. It's terrible! I thought you had more sense of decency and consideration."

"Decency nothing," he flared. "I tell you I'm not apologizing to you. If you don't like this you know what you can do."

"Oh!" she exclaimed. "This from my own brother! And for the sake of that creature! Whose child is that?" she demanded, savagely and yet curiously.

"Never mind, it's not mine. If it were it wouldn't make any difference. I wish you wouldn't busy yourself about my affairs."

Jennie, who had been moving about the dining-room beyond the sitting-room, heard the cutting references to herself. She winced with pain.

"Don't flatter yourself. I won't any more," retorted Louise. "I should think, though, that you, of all men, would be above anything like this—and that with a woman so obviously beneath you. Why, I thought she was—" she was again going to add "your housekeeper," but she was interrupted by Lester, who was angry to the point of brutality.

"Never mind what you thought she was," he growled. "She's better than some who do the so-called superior thinking. I know what you think. It's neither here nor there, I tell you. I'm doing this, and I don't care what you think. I have to take the blame. Don't bother about me."

"Well, I won't, I assure you," she flung back. "It's quite plain that your family means nothing to you. But if you had any sense of decency, Lester Kane, you would never let your sister be trapped into coming into a place like this. I'm disgusted, that's all, and so will the others be when they hear of it."

She turned on her heel and walked scornfully out, a withering look being reserved for Jennie, who had unfortunately stepped near the door of the dining-room. Vesta had disappeared. Jennie came in a little while later and closed the door. She knew of nothing to say. Lester, his thick hair pushed back from his vigorous face, leaned back moodily on his pillow. "What a devilish trick of fortune," he thought. Now she would go home and tell it to the family. His father would know, and his mother. Robert, Imogene, Amy—all would hear. He would have no explanation to make—she had seen. He stared at the wall meditatively.

Meanwhile Jennie, moving about her duties, also found food for reflection. So this was her real position in another woman's eyes. Now she could see what the world thought. This family was as aloof from her as if it lived on another planet. To his sisters and brothers, his father and mother, she was a bad woman, a creature far beneath him socially, far beneath him mentally and morally, a creature of the streets. And she had hoped somehow to rehabilitate herself in the eyes of the world. It cut her as nothing before had ever done. The thought tore a great, gaping wound in her sensibilities. She was really low and vile in her—Louise's—eyes, in the world's eyes, basically so in Lester's eyes. How could it be otherwise? She went about numb and still, but the ache of defeat and disgrace was under it all. Oh, if she could only see some way to make herself right with the world, to live honorably, to be decent. How could that possibly be brought about? It ought to be—she knew that. But how?

Chapter XXXIII

OUTRAGED in her family pride, Louise lost no time in returning to Cincinnati, where she told the story of her discovery, embellished with many details. According to her, she was met at the door by a "silly-looking, white-faced woman," who did not even offer to invite her in when she announced her name, but stood there "looking just as guilty as a person possibly could." Lester also had acted shamefully, having outbrazened the matter to her face. When she had demanded to know whose the child was he had refused to tell her. "It isn't mine," was all he would say.

"Oh dear, oh dear!" exclaimed Mrs. Kane, who was the first to hear the story. "My son, my Lester! How could he have done it!"

"And such a creature!" exclaimed Louise emphatically, as though the words needed to be reiterated to give them any shadow of reality.

"I went there solely because I thought I could help him," continued Louise. "I thought when they said he was indisposed that he might be seriously ill. How should I have known?"

"Poor Lester!" exclaimed her mother. "To think he would come to anything like that!"

Mrs. Kane turned the difficult problem over in her mind and, having no previous experiences whereby to measure it, telephoned for old Archibald, who came out from the factory and sat through the discussion with a solemn countenance. So Lester was living openly with a woman of whom they had never heard. He would probably be as defiant and indifferent as his nature was strong. The standpoint of parental authority was impossible. Lester was a centralized authority in himself, and if any overtures for a change of conduct were to be made, they would have to be very diplomatically executed.

Archibald Kane returned to the manufactory sore and disgusted, but determined that something ought to be done. He held a consultation with Robert, who confessed that he had heard disturbing rumors from time to time, but had not wanted to say anything. Mrs. Kane suggested that Robert might go to Chicago and have a talk with Lester.

"He ought to see that this thing, if continued, is going to do him irreparable damage," said Mr. Kane. "He cannot hope to carry it off successfully. Nobody can. He ought to marry her or he ought to quit. I want you to tell him that for me."

"All well and good," said Robert, "but who's going to convince him? I'm sure I don't want the job."

"I hope to," said old Archibald, "eventually; but you'd better go up and try, anyhow. It can't do any harm. He might come to his senses."

"I don't believe it," replied Robert. "He's a strong man. You see how much good talk does down here. Still, I'll go if it will relieve your feelings any. Mother wants it."

"Yes, yes," said his father distractedly, "better go."

Accordingly Robert went. Without allowing himself to anticipate any particular measure of success in this venture, he rode pleasantly into Chicago confident in the reflection that he had all the powers of morality and justice on his side.

Upon Robert's arrival, the third morning after Louise's interview, he called up the warerooms, but Lester was not there. He then telephoned to the house, and tactfully made an appointment. Lester was still indisposed, but he preferred to come down to the office, and he did. He met Robert in his cheerful, nonchalant way, and together they talked business for a time. Then followed a pregnant silence.

"Well, I suppose you know what brought me up here," began Robert tentatively.

"I think I could make a guess at it," Lester replied.

"They were all very much worried over the fact that you were sick—mother particularly. You're not in any danger of having a relapse, are you?"

"I think not."

"Louise said there was some sort of a peculiar *ménage* she ran into up here. You're not married, are you?"

"No."

"The young woman Louise saw is just—" Robert waved his hand expressively.

Lester nodded.

"I don't want to be inquisitive, Lester. I didn't come up for that. I'm simply here because the family felt that I ought to come. Mother was so very much distressed that I couldn't do less than see you for her sake—" he paused, and Lester, touched by the fairness and respect of his attitude, felt that mere courtesy at least made some explanation due.

"I don't know that anything I can say will help matters much," he replied thoughtfully. "There's really nothing to be said. I have the woman and the family has its objections. The chief difficulty about the thing seems to be the bad luck in being found out."

He stopped, and Robert turned over the substance of this worldly reasoning in his mind. Lester was very calm about it. He seemed, as usual, to be most convincingly sane.

"You're not contemplating marrying her, are you?" queried Robert hesitatingly.

"I hadn't come to that," answered Lester coolly.

They looked at each other quietly for a moment, and then Robert turned his glance to the distant scene of the city.

"It's useless to ask whether you are seriously in love with her, I suppose," ventured Robert.

"I don't know whether I'd be able to discuss that divine afflatus with you or not," returned Lester, with a touch of grim humor. "I have never experienced the sensation myself. All I know is that the lady is very pleasing to me."

"Well, it's all a question of your own well-being and the family's, Lester," went on Robert, after another pause. "Morality doesn't seem to figure in it anyway—at least you and I can't discuss that together. Your feelings on that score naturally relate to you alone. But the matter of your own personal welfare seems to me to be substantial enough ground to base a plea on. The family's feelings and pride are also fairly important. Father's the kind of a man who sets more store by the honor of his family than most men. You know that as well as I do, of course."

"I know how father feels about it," returned Lester. "The whole business is as clear to me as it is to any of you, though off-hand I don't see just what's to be done about it. These matters aren't always of a day's growth, and they can't be settled in a day. The girl's here. To a certain extent I'm responsible that she is here. While I'm not willing to go into details, there's always more in these affairs than appears on the court calendar."

"Of course I don't know what your relations with her have been," returned Robert, "and I'm not curious to know, but it does look like a bit of injustice all around, don't you think—unless you intend to marry her?" This last was put forth as a feeler.

"I might be willing to agree to that, too," was Lester's baffling reply, "if anything were to be gained by it. The point is, the woman is here, and the family is in possession of the fact. Now if there is anything to be done I have to do it. There isn't anybody else who can act for me in this matter."

Lester lapsed into a silence, and Robert rose and paced the floor, coming back after a time to say: "You say you haven't any idea of marrying her—or rather you haven't come to it. I wouldn't, Lester. It seems to me you would be making the mistake of your life, from every point of view. I don't want to orate, but a man of your position has so much to lose; you can't afford to do it. Aside from family considerations, you have too much at stake. You'd be simply throwing your life away—"

He paused, with his right hand held out before him, as was customary when he was deeply in earnest, and Lester felt the candor and simplicity of this appeal. Robert was not criticizing him now. He was making an appeal to him, and this was somewhat different.

The appeal passed without comment, however, and then Robert began on a new tack, this time picturing old Archibald's fondness for Lester and the hope he had always entertained that he would marry some well-to-do Cincinnati girl, Catholic, if agreeable to him, but at least worthy of his station. And Mrs. Kane felt the same way; surely Lester must realize that.

"I know just how all of them feel about it," Lester interrupted at last, "but I don't see that anything's to be done right now."

"You mean that you don't think it would be policy for you to give her up just at present?"

"I mean that she's been exceptionally good to me, and that

I'm morally under obligations to do the best I can by her. What that may be, I can't tell."

"To live with her?" inquired Robert coolly.

"Certainly not to turn her out bag and baggage if she has been accustomed to live with me," replied Lester. Robert sat down again, as if he considered his recent appeal futile.

"Can't family reasons persuade you to make some amicable arrangements with her and let her go?"

"Not without due consideration of the matter; no."

"You don't think you could hold out some hope that the thing will end quickly—something that would give me a reasonable excuse for softening down the pain of it to the family?"

"I would be perfectly willing to do anything which would take away the edge of this thing for the family, but the truth's the truth, and I can't see any room for equivocation between you and me. As I've said before, these relationships are in-volved with things which make it impossible to discuss them—unfair to me, unfair to the woman. No one can see how they are to be handled, except the people that are in them, and even they can't always see. I'd be a damned dog to stand up here and give you my word to do anything except the best I can."

Lester stopped, and now Robert rose and paced the floor again, only to come back after a time and say, "You don't think there's anything to be done just at present?"

"Not at present."

"Very well, then, I expect I might as well be going. I don't know that there's anything else we can talk about."

"Won't you stay and take lunch with me? I think I might manage to get down to the hotel if you'll stay."

"No, thank you," answered Robert. "I believe I can make that one o'clock train for Cincinnati. I'll try, anyhow."

They stood before each other now, Lester pale and rather flaccid, Robert clear, wax-like, well-knit, and shrewd, and one could see the difference time had already made. Robert was the clean, decisive man, Lester the man of doubts. Robert was the spirit of business energy and integrity embodied, Lester the spirit of commercial self-sufficiency, looking at life with an uncertain eye. Together they made a striking picture, which was none the less powerful for the thoughts that were now running through their minds.

"Well," said the older brother, after a time, "I don't suppose there is anything more I can say. I had hoped to make you feel just as we do about this thing, but of course you are your own best judge of this. If you don't see it now, nothing I could say would make you. It strikes me as a very bad move on your part though."

Lester listened. He said nothing, but his face expressed an unchanged purpose.

Robert turned for his hat, and they walked to the office door together.

"I'll put the best face I can on it," said Robert, and walked out.

Chapter XXXIV

IN THIS WORLD of ours the activities of animal life seem to be limited to a plane or circle, as if that were an inherent necessity to the creatures of a planet which is perforce compelled to swing about the sun. A fish, for instance, may not pass out of the circle of the seas without courting annihilation; a bird may not enter the domain of the fishes without paying for it dearly. From the parasites of the flowers to the monsters of the jungle and the deep we see clearly the circumscribed nature of their movements—the emphatic manner in which life has limited them to a sphere; and we are content to note the ludicrous and invariably fatal results which attend any effort on their part to depart from their environment.

In the case of man, however, the operation of this theory of limitations has not as yet been so clearly observed. The laws governing our social life are not so clearly understood as to permit of a clear generalization. Still, the opinions, pleas, and judgments of society serve as boundaries which are none the less real for being intangible. When men or women err—that is, pass out from the sphere in which they are accustomed to move—it is not as if the bird had intruded itself into the water, or the wild animal into the haunts of man. Annihilation is not the immediate result. People may do no more than elevate their eyebrows in astonishment, laugh sarcastically, lift up their hands in protest. And yet so well defined is the sphere of social activity that he who departs from it is doomed. Born and bred in this environment, the individual is practically unfitted for any other state. He is like a bird accustomed to a certain density of atmosphere, and which cannot live comfortably at either higher or lower level.

Lester sat down in his easy-chair by the window after his brother had gone and gazed ruminatively out over the flourishing city. Yonder was spread out before him life with its concomitant phases of energy, hope, prosperity, and pleasure, and here he was suddenly struck by a wind of misfortune and blown aside for the time being—his prospects and purposes dissipated. Could he continue as cheerily in the paths he had

hitherto pursued? Would not his relations with Jennie be necessarily affected by this sudden tide of opposition? Was not
his own home now a thing of the past so far as his old easygoing relationship was concerned? All the atmosphere of unstained affection would be gone out of it now. That hearty
look of approval which used to dwell in his father's eye—
would it be there any longer? Robert, his relations with the
manufactory, everything that was a part of his old life, had
been affected by this sudden intrusion of Louise.

"It's unfortunate," was all that he thought to himself, and
therewith turned from what he considered senseless brooding to the consideration of what, if anything, was to be
done.

"I'm thinking I'd take a run up to Mt. Clemens to-morrow,
or Thursday anyhow, if I feel strong enough," he said to
Jennie after he had returned. "I'm not feeling as well as I
might. A few days will do me good." He wanted to get off
by himself and think. Jennie packed his bag for him at the
given time, and he departed, but he was in a sullen, meditative mood.

During the week that followed he had ample time to think
it all over, the result of his cogitations being that there was
no need of making a decisive move at present. A few weeks
more, one way or the other, could not make any practical
difference. Neither Robert nor any other member of the family was at all likely to seek another conference with him. His
business relations would necessarily go on as usual, since they
were coupled with the welfare of the manufactory; certainly
no attempt to coerce him would be attempted. But the consciousness that he was at hopeless variance with his family
weighed upon him. "Bad business," he meditated—"bad
business." But he did not change.

For the period of a whole year this unsatisfactory state of
affairs continued. Lester did not go home for six months;
then an important business conference demanding his presence, he appeared and carried it off quite as though nothing
important had happened. His mother kissed him affectionately, if a little sadly; his father gave him his customary greeting, a hearty handshake; Robert, Louise, Amy, Imogene,
concertedly, though without any verbal understanding,

agreed to ignore the one real issue. But the feeling of estrangement was there, and it persisted. Hereafter his visits to Cincinnati were as few and far between as he could possibly make them.

Chapter XXXV

I N THE MEANTIME Jennie had been going through a moral crisis of her own. For the first time in her life, aside from the family attitude, which had afflicted her greatly, she realized what the world thought of her. She was bad—she knew that. She had yielded on two occasions to the force of circumstances which might have been fought out differently. If only she had had more courage! If she did not always have this haunting sense of fear! If she could only make up her mind to do the right thing! Lester would never marry her. Why should he? She loved him, but she could leave him, and it would be better for him. Probably her father would live with her if she went back to Cleveland. He would honor her for at last taking a decent stand. Yet the thought of leaving Lester was a terrible one to her—he had been so good. As for her father, she was not sure whether he would receive her or not.

After the tragic visit of Louise she began to think of saving a little money, laying it aside as best she could from her allowance. Lester was generous and she had been able to send home regularly fifteen dollars a week to maintain the family— as much as they had lived on before, without any help from the outside. She spent twenty dollars to maintain the table, for Lester required the best of everything—fruits, meats, desserts, liquors, and what not. The rent was fifty-five dollars, with clothes and extras a varying sum. Lester gave her fifty dollars a week, but somehow it had all gone. She thought how she might economize but this seemed wrong. Better go without taking anything, if she were going, was the thought that came to her. It was the only decent thing to do.

She thought over this week after week, after the advent of Louise, trying to nerve herself to the point where she could speak or act. Lester was consistently generous and kind, but she felt at times that he himself might wish it. He was thoughtful, abstracted. Since the scene with Louise it seemed to her that he had been a little different. If she could only say to him that she was not satisfied with the way she was living, and then leave. But he himself had plainly indicated after his discovery of Vesta that her feelings on that score could not matter so very much to him, since he thought the presence of the child would definitely interfere with his ever marrying her. It was her presence he wanted on another basis. And he was so forceful, she could not argue with him very well. She decided if she went it would be best to write a letter and tell him why. Then maybe when he knew how she felt he would forgive her and think nothing more about it.

The condition of the Gerhardt family was not improving. Since Jennie had left Martha had married. After several years of teaching in the public schools of Cleveland she had met a young architect, and they were united after a short engagement. Martha had been always a little ashamed of her family, and now, when this new life dawned, she was anxious to keep the connection as slight as possible. She barely notified the members of the family of the approaching marriage—Jennie not at all—and to the actual ceremony she invited only Bass and George. Gerhardt, Veronica, and William resented the slight. Gerhardt ventured upon no comment. He had had too many rebuffs. But Veronica was angry. She hoped that life would give her an opportunity to pay her sister off. William, of course, did not mind particularly. He was interested in the possibilities of becoming an electrical engineer, a career which one of his school-teachers had pointed out to him as being attractive and promising.

Jennie heard of Martha's marriage after it was all over, a note from Veronica giving her the main details. She was glad from one point of view, but realized that her brothers and sisters were drifting away from her.

A little while after Martha's marriage Veronica and William went to reside with George, a break which was brought about by the attitude of Gerhardt himself. Ever since his wife's death and the departure of the other children he had been subject to moods of profound gloom, from which he was not easily aroused. Life, it seemed, was drawing to a close for him, although he was only sixty-five years of age. The earthly ambitions he had once cherished were gone forever. He saw Sebastian, Martha, and George out in the world practically ignoring him, contributing nothing at all to a home which should never have taken a dollar from Jennie. Veronica and William were restless. They objected to leaving school and

going to work, apparently preferring to live on money which
Gerhardt had long since concluded was not being come by
honestly. He was now pretty well satisfied as to the true relations of Jennie and Lester. At first he had believed them to
be married, but the way Lester had neglected Jennie for long
periods, the humbleness with which she ran at his beck and
call, her fear of telling him about Vesta—somehow it all
pointed to the same thing. She had not been married at
home. Gerhardt had never had sight of her marriage certificate. Since she was away she might have been married, but he
did not believe it.

The real trouble was that Gerhardt had grown intensely
morose and crotchety, and it was becoming impossible for
young people to live with him. Veronica and William felt it.
They resented the way in which he took charge of the expenditures after Martha left. He accused them of spending too
much on clothes and amusements, he insisted that a smaller
house should be taken, and he regularly sequestered a part of
the money which Jennie sent, for what purpose they could
hardly guess. As a matter of fact, Gerhardt was saving as
much as possible in order to repay Jennie eventually. He
thought it was sinful to go on in this way, and this was his
one method, outside of his meager earnings, to redeem himself. If his other children had acted rightly by him he felt that
he would not now be left in his old age the recipient of charity from one, who, despite her other good qualities, was certainly not leading a righteous life. So they quarreled.

It ended one winter month when George agreed to receive
his complaining brother and sister on condition that they
should get something to do. Gerhardt was nonplussed for a
moment, but invited them to take the furniture and go their
way. His generosity shamed them for the moment; they even
tentatively invited him to come and live with them, but this
he would not do. He would ask the foreman of the mill he
watched for the privilege of sleeping in some out-of-the-way
garret. He was always liked and trusted. And this would save
him a little money.

So in a fit of pique he did this, and there was seen the
spectacle of an old man watching through a dreary season of
nights, in a lonely trafficless neighborhood while the city

pursued its gaiety elsewhere. He had a wee small corner in the topmost loft of a warehouse away from the tear and grind of the factory proper. Here Gerhardt slept by day. In the afternoon he would take a little walk, strolling toward the business center, or out along the banks of the Cuyahoga, or the lake. As a rule his hands were below his back, his brow bent in meditation. He would even talk to himself a little—an occasional "By chops!" or "So it is" being indicative of his dreary mood. At dusk he would return, taking his stand at the lonely gate which was his post of duty. His meals he secured at a nearby workingmen's boarding-house, such as he felt he must have.

The nature of the old German's reflections at this time were of a peculiarly subtle and somber character. What was this thing—life? What did it all come to after the struggle, and the worry, and the grieving? Where does it all go to? People die; you hear nothing more from them. His wife, now, she had gone. Where had her spirit taken its flight?

Yet he continued to hold some strongly dogmatic convictions. He believed there was a hell, and that people who sinned would go there. How about Mrs. Gerhardt? How about Jennie? He believed that both had sinned woefully. He believed that the just would be rewarded in heaven. But who were the just? Mrs. Gerhardt had not had a bad heart. Jennie was the soul of generosity. Take his son Sebastian. Sebastian was a good boy, but he was cold, and certainly indifferent to his father. Take Martha—she was ambitious, but obviously selfish. Somehow the children, outside of Jennie, seemed self-centered. Bass walked off when he got married, and did nothing more for anybody. Martha insisted that she needed all she made to live on. George had contributed for a little while, but had finally refused to help out. Veronica and William had been content to live on Jennie's money so long as he would allow it, and yet they knew it was not right. His very existence, was it not a commentary on the selfishness of his children? And he was getting so old. He shook his head. Mystery of mysteries. Life was truly strange, and dark, and uncertain. Still he did not want to go and live with any of his children. Actually they were not worthy of him—none but Jennie, and she was not good. So he grieved.

This woeful condition of affairs was not made known to Jennie for some time. She had been sending her letters to Martha, but, on her leaving, Jennie had been writing directly to Gerhardt. After Veronica's departure Gerhardt wrote to Jennie saying that there was no need of sending any more money. Veronica and William were going to live with George. He himself had a good place in a factory, and would live there a little while. He returned her a moderate sum that he had saved—one hundred and fifteen dollars—with the word that he would not need it.

Jennie did not understand, but as the others did not write, she was not sure but what it might be all right—her father was so determined. But by degrees, however, a sense of what it really must mean overtook her—a sense of something wrong, and she worried, hesitating between leaving Lester and going to see about her father, whether she left him or not. Would he come with her? Not here certainly. If she were married, yes, possibly. If she were alone—probably. Yet if she did not get some work which paid well they would have a difficult time. It was the same old problem. What could she do? Nevertheless, she decided to act. If she could get five or six dollars a week they could live. This hundred and fifteen dollars which Gerhardt had saved would tide them over the worst difficulties perhaps.

Chapter XXXVI

THE TROUBLE with Jennie's plan was that it did not definitely take into consideration Lester's attitude. He did care for her in an elemental way, but he was hedged about by the ideas of the conventional world in which he had been reared. To say that he loved her well enough to take her for better or worse—to legalize her anomalous position and to face the world bravely with the fact that he had chosen a wife who suited him—was perhaps going a little too far, but he did really care for her, and he was not in a mood, at this particular time, to contemplate parting with her for good.

Lester was getting along to that time of life when his ideas of womanhood were fixed and not subject to change. Thus far, on his own plane and within the circle of his own associates, he had met no one who appealed to him as did Jennie. She was gentle, intelligent, gracious, a handmaiden to his every need; and he had taught her the little customs of polite society, until she was as agreeable a companion as he cared to have. He was comfortable, he was satisfied—why seek further?

But Jennie's restlessness increased day by day. She tried writing out her views, and started a half dozen letters before she finally worded one which seemed, partially at least, to express her feelings. It was a long letter for her, and it ran as follows:

"Lester dear,—When you get this I won't be here, and I want you not to think harshly of me until you have read it all. I am taking Vesta and leaving, and I think it is really better that I should. Lester, I ought to do it. You know when you met me we were very poor, and my condition was such that I didn't think any good man would ever want me. When you came along and told me you loved me I was hardly able to think just what I ought to do. You made me love you, Lester, in spite of myself.

"You know I told you that I oughtn't to do anything wrong any more and that I wasn't good, but somehow when you were near me I couldn't think just right, and I didn't see just how I was to get away from you. Papa was sick at home that time, and there was hardly anything in the house to eat. We were all doing so poorly. My brother George didn't have good shoes, and mamma was so worried. I have often thought, Lester, if mamma had not been compelled to worry so much she might be alive to-day. I thought if you liked me and I really liked you—I love you, Lester—maybe it wouldn't make so much difference about me. You know you told me right away you would like to help my family, and I felt that maybe that would be the right thing to do. We were so terribly poor.

"Lester, dear, I am ashamed to leave you this way; it seems so mean, but if you knew how I have been feeling these days you would forgive me. Oh, I love you, Lester, I do, I do. But for months past—ever since your sister came—I felt that I was doing wrong, and that I oughtn't to go on doing it, for I know how terribly wrong it is. It was wrong for me ever to have anything to do with Senator Brander, but I was such a girl then—I hardly knew what I was doing. It was wrong of me not to tell you about Vesta when I first met you, though I thought I was doing right when I did it. It was terribly wrong of me to keep her here all that time concealed, Lester, but I was afraid of you then—afraid of what you would say and do. When your sister Louise came it all came over me somehow, clearly, and I have never been able to think right about it since. It can't be right, Lester, but I don't blame you. I blame myself.

"I don't ask you to marry me, Lester. I know how you feel about me and how you feel about your family, and I don't think it would be right. They would never want you to do it, and it isn't right that I should ask you. At the same time I know I oughtn't to go on living this way. Vesta is getting along where she understands everything. She thinks you are her really truly uncle. I have thought of it all so much. I have thought a number of times that I would try to talk to you about it, but you frighten me when you get serious, and I don't seem to be able to say what I want to. So I thought if I could just write you this and then go you would understand. You do, Lester, don't you? You won't be angry with me? I know it's for the best for you and for me. I ought to do it. Please forgive me, Lester, please; and don't think of me

any more. I will get along. But I love you—oh yes, I do—
and I will never be grateful enough for all you have done for
me. I wish you all the luck that can come to you. Please forgive me, Lester. I love you, yes, I do. I love you.

"JENNIE.

"P. S. I expect to go to Cleveland with papa. He needs
me. He is all alone. But don't come for me, Lester. It's best
that you shouldn't."

She put this in an envelope, sealed it, and, having hidden
it in her bosom, for the time being, awaited the hour when
she could conveniently take her departure.

It was several days before she could bring herself to the
actual execution of the plan, but one afternoon, Lester, having telephoned that he would not be home for a day or two,
she packed some necessary garments for herself and Vesta in
several trunks, and sent for an expressman. She thought of
telegraphing her father that she was coming; but, seeing he
had no home, she thought it would be just as well to go and
find him. George and Veronica had not taken all the furniture. The major portion of it was in storage—so Gerhardt
had written. She might take that and furnish a little home or
flat. She was ready for the end, waiting for the expressman,
when the door opened and in walked Lester.

For some unforeseen reason he had changed his mind. He
was not in the least psychic or intuitional, but on this occasion his feelings had served him a peculiar turn. He had
thought of going for a day's duck-shooting with some friends
in the Kankakee Marshes south of Chicago, but had finally
changed his mind; he even decided to go out to the house
early. What prompted this he could not have said.

As he neared the house he felt a little peculiar about coming home so early; then at the sight of the two trunks standing in the middle of the room he stood dumfounded. What
did it mean—Jennie dressed and ready to depart? And Vesta
in a similar condition? He stared in amazement, his brown
eyes keen in inquiry.

"Where are you going?" he asked.

"Why—why—" she began, falling back. "I was going
away."

"Where to?"

"I thought I would go to Cleveland," she replied.

"What for?"

"Why—why—I meant to tell you, Lester, that I didn't think I ought to stay here any longer this way. I didn't think it was right. I thought I'd tell you, but I couldn't. I wrote you a letter."

"A letter," he exclaimed. "What the deuce are you talking about? Where is the letter?"

"There," she said, mechanically pointing to a small center-table where the letter lay conspicuous on a large book.

"And you were really going to leave me, Jennie, with just a letter?" said Lester, his voice hardening a little as he spoke. "I swear to heaven you are beyond me. What's the point?" He tore open the envelope and looked at the beginning. "Better send Vesta from the room," he suggested.

She obeyed. Then she came back and stood there pale and wide-eyed, looking at the wall, at the trunks, and at him. Lester read the letter thoughtfully. He shifted his position once or twice, then dropped the paper on the floor.

"Well, I'll tell you, Jennie," he said finally, looking at her curiously and wondering just what he was going to say. Here again was his chance to end this relationship if he wished. He couldn't feel that he did wish it, seeing how peacefully things were running. They had gone so far together it seemed ridiculous to quit now. He truly loved her—there was no doubt of that. Still he did not want to marry her—could not very well. She knew that. Her letter said as much. "You have this thing wrong," he went on slowly. "I don't know what comes over you at times, but you don't view the situation right. I've told you before that I can't marry you—not now, anyhow. There are too many big things involved in this, which you don't know anything about. I love you, you know that. But my family has to be taken into consideration, and the business. You can't see the difficulties raised on these scores, but I can. Now I don't want you to leave me. I care too much about you. I can't prevent you, of course. You can go if you want to. But I don't think you ought to want to. You don't really, do you? Sit down a minute."

Jennie, who had been counting on getting away without

being seen, was now thoroughly nonplussed. To have him begin a quiet argument—a plea as it were. It hurt her. He, Lester, pleading with her, and she loved him so.

She went over to him, and he took her hand.

"Now, listen," he said. "There's really nothing to be gained by your leaving me at present. Where did you say you were going?"

"To Cleveland," she replied.

"Well, how did you expect to get along?"

"I thought I'd take papa, if he'd come with me—he's alone now—and get something to do, maybe."

"Well, what can you do, Jennie, different from what you ever have done? You wouldn't expect to be a lady's maid again, would you? Or clerk in a store?"

"I thought I might get some place as a housekeeper," she suggested. She had been counting up her possibilities, and this was the most promising idea that had occurred to her.

"No, no," he grumbled, shaking his head. "There's nothing to that. There's nothing in this whole move of yours except a notion. Why, you won't be any better off morally than you are right now. You can't undo the past. It doesn't make any difference, anyhow. I can't marry you now. I might in the future, but I can't tell anything about that, and I don't want to promise anything. You're not going to leave me though with my consent, and if you were going I wouldn't have you dropping back into any such thing as you're contemplating. I'll make some provision for you. You don't really want to leave me, do you, Jennie?"

Against Lester's strong personality and vigorous protest Jennie's own conclusions and decisions went to pieces. Just the pressure of his hand was enough to upset her. Now she began to cry.

"Don't cry, Jennie," he said. "This thing may work out better than you think. Let it rest for a while. Take off your things. You're not going to leave me any more, are you?"

"No-o-o!" she sobbed.

He took her in his lap. "Let things rest as they are," he went on. "It's a curious world. Things can't be adjusted in a minute. They may work out. I'm putting up with some things myself that I ordinarily wouldn't stand for."

He finally saw her restored to comparative calmness, smiling sadly through her tears.

"Now you put those things away," he said genially, pointing to the trunks. "Besides, I want you to promise me one thing."

"What's that?" asked Jennie.

"No more concealment of anything, do you hear? No more thinking things out for yourself, and acting without my knowing anything about it. If you have anything on your mind, I want you to come out with it. I'm not going to eat you! Talk to me about whatever is troubling you. I'll help you solve it, or, if I can't, at least there won't be any concealment between us."

"I know, Lester," she said earnestly, looking him straight in the eyes. "I promise I'll never conceal anything any more—truly I won't. I've been afraid, but I won't be now. You can trust me."

"That sounds like what you ought to be," he replied. "I know you will." And he let her go.

A few days later, and in consequence of this agreement, the future of Gerhardt came up for discussion. Jennie had been worrying about him for several days; now it occurred to her that this was something to talk over with Lester. Accordingly, she explained one night at dinner what had happened in Cleveland. "I know he is very unhappy there all alone," she said, "and I hate to think of it. I was going to get him if I went back to Cleveland. Now I don't know what to do about it."

"Why don't you send him some money?" he inquired.

"He won't take any more money from me, Lester," she explained. "He thinks I'm not good—not acting right. He doesn't believe I'm married."

"He has pretty good reason, hasn't he?" said Lester calmly.

"I hate to think of him sleeping in a factory. He's so old and lonely."

"What's the matter with the rest of the family in Cleveland? Won't they do anything for him? Where's your brother Bass?"

"I think maybe they don't want him, he's so cross," she said simply.

"I hardly know what to suggest in that case," smiled Lester. "The old gentleman oughtn't to be so fussy."

"I know," she said, "but he's old now, and he has had so much trouble."

Lester ruminated for a while, toying with his fork. "I'll tell you what I've been thinking, Jennie," he said finally. "There's no use living this way any longer, if we're going to stick it out. I've been thinking that we might take a house out in Hyde Park. It's something of a run from the office, but I'm not much for this apartment life. You and Vesta would be better off for a yard. In that case you might bring your father on to live with us. He couldn't do any harm pottering about; indeed, he might help keep things straight."

"Oh, that would just suit papa, if he'd come," she replied. "He loves to fix things, and he'd cut the grass and look after the furnace. But he won't come unless he's sure I'm married."

"I don't know how that could be arranged unless you could show the old gentleman a marriage certificate. He seems to want something that can't be produced very well. A steady job he'd have running the furnace of a country house," he added meditatively.

Jennie did not notice the grimness of the jest. She was too busy thinking what a tangle she had made of her life. Gerhardt would not come now, even if they had a lovely home to share with him. And yet he ought to be with Vesta again. She would make him happy.

She remained lost in a sad abstraction, until Lester, following the drift of her thoughts, said: "I don't see how it can be arranged. Marriage certificate blanks aren't easily procurable. It's bad business—a criminal offense to forge one, I believe. I wouldn't want to be mixed up in that sort of thing."

"Oh, I don't want you to do anything like that, Lester. I'm just sorry papa is so stubborn. When he gets a notion you can't change him."

"Suppose we wait until we get settled after moving," he suggested. "Then you can go to Cleveland and talk to him personally. You might be able to persuade him." He liked her attitude toward her father. It was so decent that he rather wished he could help her carry out her scheme. While not very interesting, Gerhardt was not objectionable to Lester, and if the old man wanted to do the odd jobs around a big place, why not?

Chapter XXXVII

THE PLAN for a residence in Hyde Park was not long in taking shape. After several weeks had passed, and things had quieted down again, Lester invited Jennie to go with him to South Hyde Park to look for a house. On the first trip they found something which seemed to suit admirably—an old-time home of eleven large rooms, set in a lawn fully two hundred feet square and shaded by trees which had been planted when the city was young. It was ornate, homelike, peaceful. Jennie was fascinated by the sense of space and country, although depressed by the reflection that she was not entering her new home under the right auspices. She had vaguely hoped that in planning to go away she was bringing about a condition under which Lester might have come after her and married her. Now all that was over. She had promised to stay, and she would have to make the best of it. She suggested that they would never know what to do with so much room, but he waved that aside. "We will very likely have people in now and then," he said. "We can furnish it up anyhow, and see how it looks." He had the agent make out a five-year lease, with an option for renewal, and set at once the forces to work to put the establishment in order.

The house was painted and decorated, the lawn put in order, and everything done to give the place a trim and satisfactory appearance. There was a large, comfortable library and sitting-room, a big dining-room, a handsome reception-hall, a parlor, a large kitchen, serving-room, and in fact, all the ground-floor essentials of a comfortable home. On the second floor were bedrooms, baths, and the maid's room. It was all very comfortable and harmonious, and Jennie took an immense pride and pleasure in getting things in order.

Immediately after moving in, Jennie, with Lester's permission, wrote to her father asking him to come to her. She did not say that she was married, but left it to be inferred. She descanted on the beauty of the neighborhood, the size of the yard, and the manifold conveniences of the establishment. "It is so very nice," she added, "you would like it, papa. Vesta is here and goes to school every day. Won't you come and stay

676

with us? It's so much better than living in a factory. And I would like to have you so."

Gerhardt read this letter with a solemn countenance. Was it really true? Would they be taking a larger house if they were not permanently united? After all these years and all this lying? Could he have been mistaken? Well, it was high time— but should he go? He had lived alone this long time now— should he go to Chicago and live with Jennie? Her appeal did touch him, but somehow he decided against it. That would be too generous an acknowledgment of the fact that there had been fault on his side as well as on hers.

Jennie was disappointed at Gerhardt's refusal. She talked it over with Lester, and decided that she would go on to Cleveland and see him. Accordingly, she made the trip, hunted up the factory, a great rumbling furniture concern in one of the poorest sections of the city, and inquired at the office for her father. The clerk directed her to a distant warehouse, and Gerhardt was informed that a lady wished to see him. He crawled out of his humble cot and came down, curious as to who it could be. When Jennie saw him in his dusty, baggy clothes, his hair gray, his eye brows shaggy, coming out of the dark door, a keen sense of the pathetic moved her again. "Poor papa!" she thought. He came toward her, his inquisitorial eye softened a little by his consciousness of the affection that had inspired her visit. "What are you come for?" he asked cautiously.

"I want you to come home with me, papa," she pleaded yearningly. "I don't want you to stay here any more. I can't think of you living alone any longer."

"So," he said, nonplussed, "that brings you?"

"Yes," she replied; "Won't you? Don't stay here."

"I have a good bed," he explained by way of apology for his state.

"I know," she replied, "but we have a good home now and Vesta is there. Won't you come? Lester wants you to."

"Tell me one thing," he demanded. "Are you married?"

"Yes," she replied, lying hopelessly. "I have been married a long time. You can ask Lester when you come." She could scarcely look him in the face, but she managed somehow, and he believed her.

"Well," he said, "it is time."

"Won't you come, papa?" she pleaded.

He threw out his hands after his characteristic manner. The urgency of her appeal touched him to the quick. "Yes, I come," he said, and turned; but she saw by his shoulders what was happening. He was crying.

"Now, papa?" she pleaded.

For answer he walked back into the dark warehouse to get his things.

Chapter XXXVIII

GERHARDT, HAVING become an inmate of the Hyde Park home, at once bestirred himself about the labors which he felt instinctively concerned him. He took charge of the furnace and the yard, outraged at the thought that good money should be paid to any outsider when he had nothing to do. The trees, he declared to Jennie, were in a dreadful condition. If Lester would get him a pruning knife and a saw he would attend to them in the spring. In Germany they knew how to care for such things, but these Americans were so shiftless. Then he wanted tools and nails, and in time all the closets and shelves were put in order. He found a Lutheran Church almost two miles away, and declared that it was better than the one in Cleveland. The pastor, of course, was a heaven-sent son of divinity. And nothing would do but that Vesta must go to church with him regularly.

Jennie and Lester settled down into the new order of living with some misgivings; certain difficulties were sure to arise. On the North Side it had been easy for Jennie to shun neighbors and say nothing. Now they were occupying a house of some pretensions; their immediate neighbors would feel it their duty to call, and Jennie would have to play the part of an experienced hostess. She and Lester had talked this situation over. It might as well be understood here, he said, that they were husband and wife. Vesta was to be introduced as Jennie's daughter by her first marriage, her husband, a Mr. Stover (her mother's maiden name), having died immediately after the child's birth. Lester, of course, was the stepfather. This particular neighborhood was so far from the fashionable heart of Chicago that Lester did not expect to run into many of his friends. He explained to Jennie the ordinary formalities of social intercourse, so that when the first visitor called Jennie might be prepared to receive her. Within a fortnight this first visitor arrived in the person of Mrs. Jacob Stendahl, a woman of considerable importance in this particular section. She lived five doors from Jennie—the houses of the neighborhood were all set in spacious lawns—and drove up in her carriage, on her return from her shopping, one afternoon.

"Is Mrs. Kane in?" she asked of Jeannette, the new maid.

"I think so, mam," answered the girl. "Won't you let me have your card?"

The card was given and taken to Jennie, who looked at it curiously.

When Jennie came into the parlor Mrs. Stendahl, a tall, dark, inquisitive-looking woman, greeted her most cordially.

"I thought I would take the liberty of intruding on you," she said most winningly. "I am one of your neighbors. I live on the other side of the street, some few doors up. Perhaps you have seen the house—the one with the white stone gate-posts."

"Oh, yes indeed," replied Jennie. "I know it well. Mr. Kane and I were admiring it the first day we came out here."

"I know of your husband, of course, by reputation. My husband is connected with the Wilkes Frog and Switch Company."

Jennie bowed her head. She knew that the latter concern must be something important and profitable from the way in which Mrs. Stendahl spoke of it.

"We have lived here quite a number of years, and I know how you must feel coming as a total stranger to a new section of the city. I hope you will find time to come in and see me some afternoon. I shall be most pleased. My regular reception day is Thursday."

"Indeed I shall," answered Jennie, a little nervously, for the ordeal was a trying one. "I appreciate your goodness in call-ing. Mr. Kane is very busy as a rule, but when he is at home I am sure he would be most pleased to meet you and your husband."

"You must both come over some evening," replied Mrs. Stendahl. "We lead a very quiet life. My husband is not much for social gatherings. But we enjoy our neighborhood friends."

Jennie smiled her assurances of good-will. She accompanied Mrs. Stendahl to the door, and shook hands with her. "I'm so glad to find you so charming," observed Mrs. Stendahl frankly.

"Oh, thank you," said Jennie flushing a little. "I'm sure I don't deserve so much praise."

"Well, now I will expect you some afternoon. Good-by," and she waved a gracious farewell.

"That wasn't so bad," thought Jennie as she watched Mrs. Stendahl drive away. "She is very nice, I think. I'll tell Lester about her."

Among the other callers were a Mr. and Mrs. Carmichael Burke, a Mrs. Hanson Field, and a Mrs. Timothy Ballinger— all of whom left cards, or stayed to chat a few minutes. Jennie found herself taken quite seriously as a woman of importance, and she did her best to support the dignity of her position. And, indeed, she did exceptionally well. She was most hospitable and gracious. She had a kindly smile and a manner wholly natural; she succeeded in making a most favorable impression. She explained to her guests that she had been living on the North Side until recently, that *her husband*, Mr. Kane, had long wanted to have a home in Hyde Park, that her father and daughter were living here, and that Lester was the child's stepfather. She said she hoped to repay all these nice attentions and to be a good neighbor.

Lester heard about these calls in the evening, for he did not care to meet these people. Jennie came to enjoy it in a mild way. She liked making new friends, and she was hoping that something definite could be worked out here which would make Lester look upon her as a good wife and an ideal companion. Perhaps, some day, he might really want to marry her.

First impressions are not always permanent, as Jennie was soon to discover. The neighborhood had accepted her perhaps a little too hastily, and now rumors began to fly about. A Mrs. Sommerville, calling on Mrs. Craig, one of Jennie's near neighbors, intimated that she knew who Lester was— "oh, yes, indeed. You know, my dear," she went on, "his reputation is just a little—" she raised her eyebrows and her hand at the same time.

"You don't say!" commented her friend curiously. "He looks like such a staid, conservative person."

"Oh, no doubt, in a way, he is," went on Mrs. Sommerville. "His family is of the very best. There was some young woman he went with—so my husband tells me. I don't know whether this is the one or not, but she was introduced as a

Miss Gorwood, or some such name as that, when they were living together as husband and wife on the North Side."

"Tst! Tst! Tst!" clicked Mrs. Craig with her tongue at this astonishing news. "You don't tell me! Come to think of it, it must be the same woman. Her father's name is Gerhardt."

"Gerhardt!" exclaimed Mrs. Sommerville. "Yes, that's the name. It seems to me that there was some earlier scandal in connection with her—at least there was a child. Whether he married her afterward or not, I don't know. Anyhow, I understand his family will not have anything to do with her."

"How very interesting!" exclaimed Mrs. Craig. "And to think he should have married her afterward, if he really did. I'm sure you can't tell with whom you're coming in contact these days, can you?"

"It's so true. Life does get badly mixed at times. She appears to be a charming woman."

"Delightful!" exclaimed Mrs. Craig. "Quite naïve. I was really taken with her."

"Well, it may be," went on her guest, "that this isn't the same woman after all. I may be mistaken."

"Oh, I hardly think so. Gerhardt! She told me they had been living on the North Side."

"Then I'm sure it's the same person. How curious that you should speak of her!"

"It is, indeed," went on Mrs. Craig, who was speculating as to what her attitude toward Jennie should be in the future.

Other rumors came from other sources. There were people who had seen Jennie and Lester out driving on the North Side, who had been introduced to her as Miss Gerhardt, who knew what the Kane family thought. Of course her present position, the handsome house, the wealth of Lester, the beauty of Vesta—all these things helped to soften the situation. She was apparently too circumspect, too much the good wife and mother, too really nice to be angry with; but she had a past, and that had to be taken into consideration.

An opening bolt of the coming storm fell upon Jennie one day when Vesta, returning from school, suddenly asked: "Mamma, who was my papa?"

"His name was Stover, dear," replied her mother, struck at once by the thought that there might have been some

criticism—that some one must have been saying something.
"Why do you ask?"

"Where was I born?" continued Vesta, ignoring the last inquiry, and interested in clearing up her own identity.

"In Columbus, Ohio, pet. Why?"

"Anita Ballinger said I didn't have any papa, and that you
weren't ever married when you had me. She said I wasn't a
really, truly girl at all—just a nobody. She made me so mad
I slapped her."

Jennie's face grew rigid. She sat staring straight before her.
Mrs. Ballinger had called, and Jennie had thought her peculiarly gracious and helpful in her offer of assistance, and now
her little daughter had said this to Vesta. Where did the child
hear it?

"You mustn't pay any attention to her, dearie," said Jennie
at last. "She doesn't know. Your papa was Mr. Stover, and
you were born in Columbus. You mustn't fight other little
girls. Of course they say nasty things when they fight—sometimes things they don't really mean. Just let her alone and
don't go near her any more. Then she won't say anything to
you."

It was a lame explanation, but it satisfied Vesta for the time
being. "I'll slap her if she tries to slap me," she persisted.

"You mustn't go near her, pet, do you hear? Then she can't
try to slap you," returned her mother. "Just go about your
studies, and don't mind her. She can't quarrel with you if you
don't let her."

Vesta went away leaving Jennie brooding over her words.
The neighbors were talking. Her history was becoming common gossip. How had they found out.

It is one thing to nurse a single thrust, another to have the
wound opened from time to time by additional stabs. One
day Jennie, having gone to call on Mrs. Hanson Field, who
was her immediate neighbor, met a Mrs. Williston Baker,
who was there taking tea. Mrs. Baker knew of the Kanes, of
Jennie's history on the North Side, and of the attitude of the
Kane family. She was a thin, vigorous, intellectual woman,
somewhat on the order of Mrs. Bracebridge, and very careful
of her social connections. She had always considered Mrs.
Field a woman of the same rigid circumspectness of attitude,

and when she found Jennie calling there she was outwardly calm but inwardly irritated. "This is Mrs. Kane, Mrs. Baker," said Mrs. Field, introducing her guests with a smiling countenance. Mrs. Baker looked at Jennie ominously.

"Mrs. Lester Kane?" she inquired.

"Yes," replied Mrs. Field.

"Indeed," she went on freezingly. "I've heard a great deal about Mrs.—" accenting the word—"Mrs. Lester Kane."

She turned to Mrs. Field, ignoring Jennie completely, and started an intimate conversation in which Jennie could have no possible share. Jennie stood helplessly by, unable to formulate a thought which would be suitable to so trying a situation. Mrs. Baker soon announced her departure, although she had intended to stay longer. "I can't remain another minute," she said; "I promised Mrs. Neil that I would stop in to see her to-day. I'm sure I've bored you enough already as it is."

She walked to the door, not troubling to look at Jennie until she was nearly out of the room. Then she looked in her direction, and gave her a frigid nod.

"We meet such curious people now and again," she observed finally to her hostess as she swept away.

Mrs. Field did not feel able to defend Jennie, for she herself was in no notable social position, and was endeavoring, like every other middle-class woman of means, to get along. She did not care to offend Mrs. Williston Baker, who was socially so much more important than Jennie. She came back to where Jennie was sitting, smiling apologetically, but she was a little bit flustered. Jennie was out of countenance, of course. Presently she excused herself and went home. She had been cut deeply by the slight offered her, and she felt that Mrs. Field realized that she had made a mistake in ever taking her up. There would be no additional exchange of visits there— that she knew. The old hopeless feeling came over her that her life was a failure. It couldn't be made right, or, if it could, it wouldn't be. Lester was not inclined to marry her and put her right.

Time went on and matters remained very much as they were. To look at this large house, with its smooth lawn and well grown trees, its vines clambering about the pillars of the veranda and interlacing themselves into a transparent veil of green; to see Gerhardt pottering about the yard, Vesta coming home from school, Lester leaving in the morning in his smart trap—one would have said that here is peace and plenty, no shadow of unhappiness hangs over this charming home.

And as a matter of fact existence with Lester and Jennie did run smoothly. It is true that the neighbors did not call any more, or only a very few of them, and there was no social life to speak of; but the deprivation was hardly noticed; there was so much in the home life to please and interest. Vesta was learning to play the piano, and to play quite well. She had a good ear for music. Jennie was a charming figure in blue, lavender, and olive-green house-gowns as she went about her affairs, sewing, dusting, getting Vesta off to school, and seeing that things generally were put to rights. Gerhardt busied himself about his multitudinous duties, for he was not satisfied unless he had his hands into all the domestic economies of the household. One of his self-imposed tasks was to go about the house after Lester, or the servants, turning out the gas-jets or electric-light bulbs which might accidentally have been left burning. That was a sinful extravagance.

Again, Lester's expensive clothes, which he carelessly threw aside after a few months' use, were a source of woe to the thrifty old German. Moreover, he grieved over splendid shoes discarded because of a few wrinkles in the leather or a slightly run down heel or sole. Gerhardt was for having them repaired, but Lester answered the old man's querulous inquiry as to what was wrong " with them shoes" by saying that they weren't comfortable any more.

"Such extravagance!" Gerhardt complained to Jennie. "Such waste! No good can come of anything like that. It will mean want one of these days."

"He can't help it, papa," Jennie excused. "That's the way he was raised."

"Ha! A fine way to be raised. These Americans, they know nothing of economy. They ought to live in Germany awhile. Then they would know what a dollar can do."

Lester heard something of this through Jennie, but he only smiled. Gerhardt was amusing to him.

Another grievance was Lester's extravagant use of matches. He had the habit of striking a match, holding it while he talked, instead of lighting his cigar, and then throwing it away. Sometimes he would begin to light a cigar two or three minutes before he would actually do so, tossing aside match after match. There was a place out in one corner of the veranda where he liked to sit of a spring or summer evening, smoking and throwing away half-burned matches. Jennie would sit with him, and a vast number of matches would be lit and flung out on the lawn. At one time, while engaged in cutting the grass, Gerhardt found, to his horror, not a handful, but literally boxes of half-burned match-sticks lying unconsumed and decaying under the fallen blades. He was discouraged, to say the least. He gathered up this damning evidence in a newspaper and carried it back into the sitting-room where Jennie was sewing.

"See here, what I find!" he demanded. "Just look at that! That man, he has no more sense of economy than a—than a—" the right term failed him. "He sits and smokes, and this is the way he uses matches. Five cents a box they cost—five cents. How can a man hope to do well and carry on like that, I like to know. Look at them."

Jennie looked. She shook her head. "Lester is extravagant," she said.

Gerhardt carried them to the basement. At least they should be burned in the furnace. He would have used them as lighters for his own pipe, sticking them in the fire to catch a blaze, only old newspapers were better, and he had stacks of these—another evidence of his lord and master's wretched, spendthrift disposition. It was a sad world to work in. Almost everything was against him. Still he fought as valiantly as he could against waste and shameless extravagance. His own economies were rigid. He would wear the same suit of black—cut down from one of Lester's expensive investments of years before—every Sunday for a couple of years. Lester's shoes, by a little stretch of the imagination, could be made to seem to fit, and these he wore. His old ties also—the black ones—they were fine. If he could have cut down Lester's shirts he would have done so; he did make over the underwear, with the friendly aid of the cook's needle. Lester's socks, of course, were just right. There was never any expense for Gerhardt's clothing.

The remaining stock of Lester's discarded clothing—shoes, shirts, collars, suits, ties, and what not—he would store away for weeks and months, and then, in a sad and gloomy frame of mind, he would call in a tailor, or an old-shoe man, or a ragman, and dispose of the lot at the best price he could. He learned that all second-hand clothes men were sharks; that there was no use in putting the least faith in the protests of any rag dealer or old-shoe man. They all lied. They all claimed to be very poor, when as a matter of fact they were actually rolling in wealth. Gerhardt had investigated these stories; he had followed them up; he had seen what they were doing with the things he sold them.

"Scoundrels!" he declared. "They offer me ten cents for a pair of shoes, and then I see them hanging out in front of their places marked two dollars. Such robbery! My God! They could afford to give me a dollar."

Jennie smiled. It was only to her that he complained, for he could expect no sympathy from Lester. So far as his own meager store of money was concerned, he gave the most of it to his beloved church, where he was considered to be a model of propriety, honesty, faith—in fact, the embodiment of all the virtues.

And so, for all the ill winds that were beginning to blow socially, Jennie was now leading the dream years of her existence. Lester, in spite of the doubts which assailed him at times as to the wisdom of his career, was invariably kind and considerate, and he seemed to enjoy his home life.

"Everything all right?" she would ask when he came in of an evening.

"Sure!" he would answer, and pinch her chin or cheek.

She would follow him in while Jeannette, always alert, would take his coat and hat. In the winter-time they would sit in the library before the big grate-fire. In the spring, summer, or fall Lester preferred to walk out on the porch, one corner of which commanded a sweeping view of the lawn and the distant street, and light his before-dinner cigar. Jennie would sit on the side of his chair and stroke his head. "Your hair is not getting the least bit thin, Lester; aren't you glad?"

she would say; or, "Oh, see how your brow is wrinkled now. You mustn't do that. You didn't change your tie, mister, this morning. Why didn't you? I laid one out for you."

"Oh, I forgot," he would answer, or he would cause the wrinkles to disappear, or laughingly predict that he would soon be getting bald if he wasn't so now.

In the drawing-room or library, before Vesta and Gerhardt, she was not less loving, though a little more circumspect. She loved odd puzzles like pigs in clover, the spider's hole, baby billiards, and the like. Lester shared in these simple amusements. He would work by the hour, if necessary, to make a difficult puzzle come right. Jennie was clever at solving these mechanical problems. Sometimes she would have to show him the right method, and then she would be immensely pleased with herself. At other times she would stand behind him watching, her chin on his shoulder, her arms about his neck. He seemed not to mind—indeed, he was happy in the wealth of affection she bestowed. Her cleverness, her gentleness, her tact created an atmosphere which was immensely pleasing; above all her youth and beauty appealed to him. It made him feel young, and if there was one thing Lester objected to, it was the thought of drying up into an aimless old age. "I want to keep young, or die young," was one of his pet remarks; and Jennie came to understand. She was glad that she was so much younger now for his sake.

Another pleasant feature of the home life was Lester's steadily increasing affection for Vesta. The child would sit at the big table in the library in the evening conning her books, while Jennie would sew, and Gerhardt would read his interminable list of German Lutheran papers. It grieved the old man that Vesta should not be allowed to go to a German Lutheran parochial school, but Lester would listen to nothing of the sort. "We'll not have any thick-headed German training in this," he said to Jennie, when she suggested that Gerhardt had complained. "The public schools are good enough for any child. You tell him to let her alone."

There were really some delightful hours among the four. Lester liked to take the little seven-year-old school-girl between his knees and tease her. He liked to invert the so-called facts of life, to propound its paradoxes, and watch how the child's budding mind took them. "What's water?" he would ask; and being informed that it was "what we drink," he would stare and say, "That's so, but what is it? Don't they teach you any better than that?"

"Well, it is what we drink, isn't it?" persisted Vesta.

"The fact that we drink it doesn't explain what it is," he would retort. "You ask your teacher what water is"; and then he would leave her with this irritating problem troubling her young soul.

Food, china, her dress, anything was apt to be brought back to its chemical constituents, and he would leave her to struggle with these dark suggestions of something else back of the superficial appearance of things until she was actually in awe of him. She had a way of showing him how nice she looked before she started to school in the morning, a habit that arose because of his constant criticism of her appearance. He wanted her to look smart, he insisted on a big bow of blue ribbon for her hair, he demanded that her shoes be changed from low quarter to high boots with the changing character of the seasons, and that her clothing be carried out on a color scheme suited to her complexion and disposition.

"That child's light and gay by disposition. Don't put anything somber on her," he once remarked.

Jennie had come to realize that he must be consulted in this, and would say, "Run to your papa and show him how you look."

Vesta would come and turn briskly around before him, saying, "See."

"Yes. You're all right. Go on"; and on she would go.

He grew so proud of her that on Sundays and some week-days when they drove he would always have her in between them. He insisted that Jennie send her to dancing-school, and Gerhardt was beside himself with rage and grief. "Such irreligion!" he complained to Jennie. "Such devil's fol-de-rol. Now she goes to dance. What for? To make a no-good out of her—a creature to be ashamed of?"

"Oh no, papa," replied Jennie. "It isn't as bad as that. This is an awful nice school. Lester says she has to go."

"Lester, Lester; that man! A fine lot he knows about what is good for a child. A card-player, a whisky-drinker!"

"Now, hush, papa; I won't have you talk like that," Jennie would reply warmly. "He's a good man, and you know it."

"Yes, yes, a good man. In some things, maybe. Not in this. No."

He went away groaning. When Lester was near he said nothing, and Vesta could wind him around her finger.

"Oh you," she would say, pulling at his arm or rubbing his grizzled cheek. There was no more fight in Gerhardt when Vesta did this. He lost control of himself—something welled up and choked his throat. "Yes, I know how you do," he would exclaim.

Vesta would tweak his ear.

"Stop now!" he would say. "That is enough."

It was noticeable, however, that she did not have to stop unless she herself willed it. Gerhardt adored the child, and she could do anything with him; he was always her devoted servitor.

Chapter XXXIX

DURING THIS PERIOD the dissatisfaction of the Kane family with Lester's irregular habit of life grew steadily stronger. That it could not help but become an open scandal, in the course of time, was sufficiently obvious to them. Rumors were already going about. People seemed to understand in a wise way, though nothing was ever said directly. Kane senior could scarcely imagine what possessed his son to fly in the face of conventions in this manner. If the woman had been some one of distinction—some sorceress of the stage, or of the world of art, or letters, his action would have been explicable if not commendable, but with this creature of very ordinary capabilities, as Louise had described her, this putty-faced nobody—he could not possibly understand it.

Lester was his son, his favorite son; it was too bad that he had not settled down in the ordinary way. Look at the women in Cincinnati who knew him and liked him. Take Letty Pace, for instance. Why in the name of common sense had he not married her? She was good looking, sympathetic, talented. The old man grieved bitterly, and then, by degrees, he began to harden. It seemed a shame that Lester should treat him so. It wasn't natural, or justifiable, or decent. Archibald Kane brooded over it until he felt that some change ought to be enforced, but just what it should be he could not say. Lester was his own boss, and he would resent any criticism of his actions. Apparently, nothing could be done.

Certain changes helped along an approaching denouement. Louise married not many months after her very disturbing visit to Chicago, and then the home property was fairly empty except for visiting grandchildren. Lester did not attend the wedding, though he was invited. For another thing, Mrs. Kane died, making a readjustment of the family will necessary. Lester came home on this occasion, grieved to think he had lately seen so little of his mother—that he had caused her so much pain—but he had no explanation to make. His father thought at the time of talking to him, but put it off because of his obvious gloom. He went back to Chicago, and there were more months of silence.

After Mrs. Kane's death and Louise's marriage, the father went to live with Robert, for his three grandchildren afforded him his greatest pleasure in his old age. The business, except for the final adjustment which would come after his death, was in Robert's hands. The latter was consistently agreeable to his sisters and their husbands and to his father, in view of the eventual control he hoped to obtain. He was not a sycophant in any sense of the word, but a shrewd, cold business man, far shrewder than his brother gave him credit for. He was already richer than any two of the other children put together, but he chose to keep his counsel and to pretend modesty of fortune. He realized the danger of envy, and preferred a Spartan form of existence, putting all the emphasis on inconspicuous but very ready and very hard cash. While Lester was drifting Robert was working—working all the time.

Robert's scheme for eliminating his brother from participation in the control of the business was really not very essential, for his father, after long brooding over the details of the Chicago situation, had come to the definite conclusion that any large share of his property ought not to go to Lester. Obviously, Lester was not so strong a man as he had thought him to be. Of the two brothers, Lester might be the bigger intellectually or sympathetically—artistically and socially there was no comparison—but Robert got commercial results in a silent, effective way. If Lester was not going to pull himself together at this stage of the game, when would he? Better leave his property to those who would take care of it. Archibald Kane thought seriously of having his lawyer revise his will in such a way that, unless Lester should reform, he would be cut off with only a nominal income. But he decided to give Lester one more chance—to make a plea, in fact, that he should abandon his false way of living, and put himself on a sound basis before the world. It wasn't too late. He really had a great future. Would he deliberately choose to throw it away? Old Archibald wrote Lester that he would like to have a talk with him at his convenience, and within the lapse of thirty-six hours Lester was in Cincinnati.

"I thought I'd have one more talk with you, Lester, on a subject that's rather difficult for me to bring up," began the elder Kane. "You know what I'm referring to?"

"Yes, I know," replied Lester, calmly.

"I used to think, when I was much younger that my son's matrimonial ventures would never concern me, but I changed my views on that score when I got a little farther along. I began to see through my business connections how much the right sort of a marriage helps a man, and then I got rather anxious that my boys should marry well. I used to worry about you, Lester, and I'm worrying yet. This recent connection you've made has caused me no end of trouble. It worried your mother up to the very last. It was her one great sorrow. Don't you think you have gone far enough with it? The scandal has reached down here. What it is in Chicago I don't know, but it can't be a secret. That can't help the house in business there. It certainly can't help you. The whole thing has gone on so long that you have injured your prospects all around, and yet you continue. Why do you?"

"I suppose because I love her," Lester replied.

"You can't be serious in that," said his father. "If you had loved her, you'd have married her in the first place. Surely you wouldn't take a woman and live with her as you have with this woman for years, disgracing her and yourself, and still claim that you love her. You may have a passion for her, but it isn't love."

"How do you know I haven't married her?" inquired Lester coolly. He wanted to see how his father would take to that idea.

"You're not serious!" The old gentleman propped himself up on his arms and looked at him.

"No, I'm not," replied Lester, "but I might be. I might marry her."

"Impossible!" exclaimed his father vigorously. "I can't believe it. I can't believe a man of your intelligence would do a thing like that, Lester. Where is your judgment? Why, you've lived in open adultery with her for years, and now you talk of marrying her. Why, in heaven's name, if you were going to do anything like that, didn't you do it in the first place? Disgrace your parents, break your mother's heart, injure the business, become a public scandal, and then marry the cause of it? I don't believe it."

Old Archibald got up.

"Don't get excited, father," said Lester quickly. "We won't get anywhere that way. I say I might marry her. She's not a bad woman, and I wish you wouldn't talk about her as you do. You've never seen her. You know nothing about her."

"I know enough," insisted old Archibald, determinedly. "I know that no good woman would act as she has done. Why, man, she's after your money. What else could she want? It's as plain as the nose on your face."

"Father," said Lester, his voice lowering ominously, " why do you talk like that? You never saw the woman. You wouldn't know her from Adam's off ox. Louise comes down here and gives an excited report, and you people swallow it whole. She isn't as bad as you think she is, and I wouldn't use the language you're using about her if I were you. You're doing a good woman an injustice, and you won't, for some reason, be fair."

"Fair! Fair!" interrupted Archibald. "Talk about being fair. Is it fair to me, to your family, to your dead mother to take a woman of the streets and live with her? Is it—"

"Stop now, father," exclaimed Lester, putting up his hand. "I warn you. I won't listen to talk like that. You're talking about the woman that I'm living with—that I may marry. I love you, but I won't have you saying things that aren't so. She isn't a woman of the streets. You know, as well as you know anything, that I wouldn't take up with a woman of that kind. We'll have to discuss this in a calmer mood, or I won't stay here. I'm sorry. I'm awfully sorry. But I won't listen to any such language as that."

Old Archibald quieted himself. In spite of his opposition, he respected his son's point of view. He sat back in his chair and stared at the floor. "How was he to handle this thing?" he asked himself.

"Are you living in the same place?" he finally inquired.

"No, we've moved out to Hyde Park. I've taken a house out there."

"I hear there's a child. Is that yours?"

"No."

"Have you any children of your own?"

"No."

"Well, that's a God's blessing."

Lester merely scratched his chin.

"And you insist you will marry her?" Archibald went on.

"I didn't say that," replied his son. "I said I might."

"Might! Might!" exclaimed his father, his anger bubbling again. "What a tragedy! You with your prospects! Your outlook! How do you suppose I can seriously contemplate entrusting any share of my fortune to a man who has so little regard for what the world considers as right and proper? Why, Lester, this carriage business, your family, your personal reputation appear to be as nothing at all to you. I can't understand what has happened to your pride. It seems like some wild, impossible fancy."

"It's pretty hard to explain, father, and I can't do it very well. I simply know that I'm in this affair, and that I'm bound to see it through. It may come out all right. I may not marry her—I may. I'm not prepared now to say what I'll do. You'll have to wait. I'll do the best I can."

Old Archibald merely shook his head disapprovingly.

"You've made a bad mess of this, Lester," he said finally. "Surely you have. But I suppose you are determined to go your way. Nothing that I have said appears to move you."

"Not now, father. I'm sorry."

"Well, I warn you, then, that, unless you show some consideration for the dignity of your family and the honor of your position it will make a difference in my will. I can't go on countenancing this thing, and not be a party to it morally and every other way. I won't do it. You can leave her, or you can marry her. You certainly ought to do one or the other. If you leave her, everything will be all right. You can make any provision for her you like. I have no objection to that. I'll gladly pay whatever you agree to. You will share with the rest of the children, just as I had planned. If you marry her it will make a difference. Now do as you please. But don't blame me. I love you. I'm your father. I'm doing what I think is my bounden duty. Now you think that over and let me know."

Lester sighed. He saw how hopeless this argument was. He felt that his father probably meant what he said, but how could he leave Jennie, and justify himself to himself? Would his father really cut him off? Surely not. The old gentleman loved him even now—he could see it. Lester felt troubled and distressed; this attempt at coercion irritated him. The idea—he, Lester Kane, being made to do such a thing—to throw Jennie down. He stared at the floor.

Old Archibald saw that he had let fly a telling bullet.

"Well," said Lester finally, "there's no use of our discussing it any further now—that's certain, isn't it? I can't say what I'll do. I'll have to take time and think. I can't decide this offhand."

The two looked at each other. Lester was sorry for the world's attitude and for his father's keen feeling about the affair. Kane senior was sorry for his son, but he was determined to see the thing through. He wasn't sure whether he had converted Lester or not, but he was hopeful. Maybe he would come around yet.

"Good-by, father," said Lester, holding out his hand. "I think I'll try and make that two-ten train. There isn't anything else you wanted to see me about?"

"No."

The old man sat there after Lester had gone, thinking deeply. What a twisted career! What an end to great possibilities! What a foolhardy persistence in evil and error! He shook his head. Robert was wiser. He was the one to control a business. He was cool and conservative. If Lester were only like that. He thought and thought. It was a long time before he stirred. And still, in the bottom of his heart, his erring son continued to appeal to him.

Chapter XL

LESTER RETURNED to Chicago. He realized that he had offended his father seriously, how seriously he could not say. In all his personal relations with old Archibald he had never seen him so worked up. But even now Lester did not feel that the breach was irreparable; he hardly realized that it was necessary for him to act decisively if he hoped to retain his father's affection and confidence. As for the world at large, what did it matter how much people talked or what they said. He was big enough to stand alone. But was he? People turn so quickly from weakness or the shadow of it. To get away from failure—even the mere suspicion of it—that seems to be a subconscious feeling with the average man and woman; we all avoid non-success as though we fear that it may prove contagious. Lester was soon to feel the force of this prejudice.

One day Lester happened to run across Berry Dodge, the millionaire head of Dodge, Holbrook & Kingsbury, a firm that stood in the dry-goods world, where the Kane Company stood in the carriage world. Dodge had been one of Lester's best friends. He knew him as intimately as he knew Henry Bracebridge, of Cleveland, and George Knowles, of Cincinnati. He visited at his handsome home on the North Shore Drive, and they met constantly in a business and social way. But since Lester had moved out to Hyde Park, the old intimacy had lapsed. Now they came face to face on Michigan Avenue near the Kane building.

"Why, Lester, I'm glad to see you again," said Dodge. He extended a formal hand, and seemed just a little cool. "I hear you've gone and married since I saw you."

"No, nothing like that," replied Lester, easily, with the air of one who prefers to be understood in the way of the world sense.

"Why so secret about it, if you have?" asked Dodge, attempting to smile, but with a wry twist to the corners of his mouth. He was trying to be nice, and to go through a difficult situation gracefully. "We fellows usually make a fuss about that sort of thing. You ought to let your friends know."

"Well," said Lester, feeling the edge of the social blade that was being driven into him, "I thought I'd do it in a new way. I'm not much for excitement in that direction, anyhow."

"It is a matter of taste, isn't it?" said Dodge a little absently. "You're living in the city, of course?"

"In Hyde Park."

"That's a pleasant territory. How are things otherwise?" And he deftly changed the subject before waving him a perfunctory farewell.

Lester missed at once the inquiries which a man like Dodge would have made if he had really believed that he was married. Under ordinary circumstances his friend would have wanted to know a great deal about the new Mrs. Kane. There would have been all those little familiar touches common to people living on the same social plane. Dodge would have asked Lester to bring his wife over to see them, would have definitely promised to call. Nothing of the sort happened, and Lester noticed the significant omission.

It was the same with the Burnham Moores, the Henry Aldriches, and a score of other people whom he knew equally well. Apparently they all thought that he had married and settled down. They were interested to know where he was living, and they were rather disposed to joke him about being so very secretive on the subject, but they were not willing to discuss the supposed Mrs. Kane. He was beginning to see that this move of his was going to tell against him notably.

One of the worst stabs—it was the cruelest because, in a way, it was the most unintentional—he received from an old acquaintance, Will Whitney, at the Union Club. Lester was dining there one evening, and Whitney met him in the main reading-room as he was crossing from the cloak-room to the cigar-stand. The latter was a typical society figure, tall, lean, smoothfaced, immaculately garbed, a little cynical, and tonight a little the worse for liquor. "Hi, Lester!" he called out, " what's this talk about a *ménage* of yours out in Hyde Park? Say, you're going some. How are you going to explain all this to your wife when you get married?"

"I don't have to explain it," replied Lester irritably. "Why should you be so interested in my affairs? You're not living in a stone house, are you?"

"Say, ha! ha! that's pretty good now, isn't it? You didn't marry that little beauty you used to travel around with on the North Side, did you? Eh, now! Ha, ha! Well, I swear. You married! You didn't, now, did you?"

"Cut it out, Whitney," said Lester roughly. "You're talking wild."

"Pardon, Lester," said the other aimlessly, but sobering. "I beg your pardon. Remember, I'm just a little warm. Eight whisky-sours straight in the other room there. Pardon. I'll talk to you some time when I'm all right. See, Lester? Eh! Ha! ha! I'm a little loose, that's right. Well, so long! Ha! ha!"

Lester could not get over that cacaphonous "ha! ha!" It cut him, even though it came from a drunken man's mouth. "That little beauty you used to travel with on the North Side. You didn't marry her, did you?" He quoted Whitney's impertinences resentfully. George! But this was getting a little rough! He had never endured anything like this before—he, Lester Kane. It set him thinking. Certainly he was paying dearly for trying to do the kind thing by Jennie.

Chapter XLI

B UT WORSE WAS to follow. The American public likes gossip about well-known people, and the Kanes were wealthy and socially prominent. The report was that Lester, one of its principal heirs, had married a servant girl. He, an heir to millions! Could it be possible? What a piquant morsel for the newspapers! Very soon the paragraphs began to appear. A small society paper, called the *South Side Budget*, referred to him anonymously as "the son of a famous and wealthy carriage manufacturer of Cincinnati," and outlined briefly what it knew of the story. "Of Mrs. ——" it went on, sagely, "not so much is known, except that she once worked in a well-known Cleveland society family as a maid and was, before that, a working-girl in Columbus, Ohio. After such a picturesque love-affair in high society, who shall say that romance is dead?"

Lester saw this item. He did not take the paper, but some kind soul took good care to see that a copy was marked and mailed to him. It irritated him greatly, for he suspected at once that it was a scheme to blackmail him. But he did not know exactly what to do about it. He preferred, of course, that such comments should cease, but he also thought that if he made any effort to have them stopped he might make matters worse. So he did nothing. Naturally, the paragraph in the *Budget* attracted the attention of other newspapers. It sounded like a good story, and one Sunday editor, more enterprising than the others, conceived the notion of having this romance written up. A full-page Sunday story with a scarehead such as "Sacrifices Millions for His Servant Girl Love," pictures of Lester, Jennie, the house at Hyde Park, the Kane manufactory at Cincinnati, the warehouse on Michigan Avenue—certainly, such a display would make a sensation. The Kane Company was not an advertiser in any daily or Sunday paper. The newspaper owed him nothing. If Lester had been forewarned he might have put a stop to the whole business by putting an advertisement in the paper or appealing to the publisher. He did not know, however, and so was without power to prevent the publication. The editor made a thorough job of the business. Local newspaper men in Cincinnati, Cleveland, and Columbus were instructed to report by wire whether anything of Jennie's history was known in their city. The Bracebridge family in Cleveland was asked whether Jennie had ever worked there. A garbled history of the Gerhardts was obtained from Columbus. Jennie's residence on the North Side, for several years prior to her supposed marriage, was discovered and so the whole story was nicely pieced together. It was not the idea of the newspaper editor to be cruel or critical, but rather complimentary. All the bitter things, such as the probable illegitimacy of Vesta, the suspected immorality of Lester and Jennie in residing together as man and wife, the real grounds of the well-known objections of his family to the match, were ignored. The idea was to frame up a Romeo and Juliet story in which Lester should appear as an ardent, self-sacrificing lover, and Jennie as a poor and lovely working-girl, lifted to great financial and social heights by the devotion of her millionaire lover. An exceptional newspaper artist was engaged to make scenes depicting the various steps of the romance and the whole thing was handled in the most approved yellow-journal style. There was a picture of Lester obtained from his Cincinnati photographer for a consideration; Jennie had been surreptitiously "snapped" by a staff artist while she was out walking.

And so, apparently out of a clear sky, the story appeared—highly complimentary, running over with sugary phrases, but with all the dark, sad facts looming up in the background. Jennie did not see it at first. Lester came across the page accidentally, and tore it out. He was stunned and chagrined beyond words. "To think the damned newspaper would do that to a private citizen who was quietly minding his own business!" he thought. He went out of the house, the better to conceal his deep inward mortification. He avoided the more populous parts of the town, particularly the down-town section, and rode far out on Cottage Grove Avenue to the open prairie. He wondered, as the trolley-car rumbled along, what his friends were thinking—Dodge, and Burnham Moore, and Henry Aldrich, and the others. This was a smash, indeed. The best he could do was to put a brave face on it and say nothing, or else wave it off with an indifferent motion of the hand. One thing was sure—he would prevent further comment. He returned to the house calmer, his self-poise restored, but he was eager for Monday to come in order that he might get in touch with his lawyer, Mr. Watson. But when he did see Mr. Watson it was soon agreed between the two men that it would be foolish to take any legal action. It was the part of wisdom to let the matter drop. "But I won't stand for anything more," concluded Lester.

"I'll attend to that," said the lawyer, consolingly.

Lester got up. "It's amazing—this damned country of ours!" he exclaimed. "A man with a little money hasn't any more privacy than a public monument."

"A man with a little money," said Mr. Watson, "is just like a cat with a bell around its neck. Every rat knows exactly where it is and what it is doing."

"That's an apt simile," assented Lester, bitterly.

Jennie knew nothing of this newspaper story for several days. Lester felt that he could not talk it over, and Gerhardt never read the wicked Sunday newspapers. Finally, one of Jennie's neighborhood friends, less tactful than the others, called her attention to the fact of its appearance by announcing that she had seen it. Jennie did not understand at first. "A story about me?" she exclaimed.

"You and Mr. Kane, yes," replied her guest. "Your love romance."

Jennie colored swiftly. "Why, I hadn't seen it," she said. "Are you sure it was about us?"

"Why, of course," laughed Mrs. Stendahl. "How could I be mistaken? I have the paper over at the house. I'll send Marie over with it when I get back. You look very sweet in your picture."

Jennie winced.

"I wish you would," she said, weakly.

She was wondering where they had secured her picture, what the article said. Above all, she was dismayed to think of its effect upon Lester. Had he seen the article? Why had he not spoken to her about it?

The neighbor's daughter brought over the paper, and Jennie's heart stood still as she glanced at the title-page. There it all was—uncompromising and direct. How dreadfully conspicuous the headline—"This Millionaire Fell in Love With This Lady's Maid," which ran between a picture of Lester on the left and Jennie on the right. There was an additional caption which explained how Lester, son of the famous carriage family of Cincinnati, had sacrificed great social opportunity and distinction to marry his heart's desire. Below were scattered a number of other pictures—Lester addressing Jennie in the mansion of Mrs. Bracebridge, Lester standing with her before an imposing and conventional-looking parson, Lester driving with her in a handsome victoria, Jennie standing beside the window of an imposing mansion (the fact that it was a mansion being indicated by most sumptuous-looking hangings) and gazing out on a very modest working-man's cottage pictured in the distance. Jennie felt as though she must die for very shame. She did not so much mind what it meant to her, but Lester, Lester, how must he feel? And his family? Now they would have another club with which to strike him and her. She tried to keep calm about it, to exert emotional control, but again the tears would rise, only this time they were tears of opposition to defeat. She did not want to be hounded this way. She wanted to be let alone. She was trying to do right now. Why couldn't the world help her, instead of seeking to push her down?

Chapter XLII

THE FACT that Lester had seen this page was made perfectly clear to Jennie that evening, for he brought it home himself, having concluded, after mature deliberation, that he ought to. He had told her once that there was to be no concealment between them, and this thing, coming so brutally to disturb their peace, was nevertheless a case in point. He had decided to tell her not to think anything of it—that it did not make much difference, though to him it made all the difference in the world. The effect of this chill history could never be undone. The wise—and they included all his social world and many who were not of it—could see just how he had been living. The article which accompanied the pictures told how he had followed Jennie from Cleveland to Chicago, how she had been coy and distant and that he had to court her a long time to win her consent. This was to explain their living together on the North Side. Lester realized that this was an asinine attempt to sugar-coat the true story and it made him angry. Still he preferred to have it that way rather than in some more brutal vein. He took the paper out of his pocket when he arrived at the house, spreading it on the library table. Jennie, who was close by, watched him, for she knew what was coming.

"Here's something that will interest you, Jennie," he said dryly, pointing to the array of text and pictures.

"I've already seen it, Lester," she said wearily. "Mrs. Stendahl showed it to me this afternoon. I was wondering whether you had."

"Rather high-flown description of my attitude, isn't it? I didn't know I was such an ardent Romeo."

"I'm awfully sorry, Lester," said Jennie, reading behind the dry face of humor the serious import of this affair to him. She had long since learned that Lester did not express his real feeling, his big ills in words. He was inclined to jest and make light of the inevitable, the inexorable. This light comment merely meant "this matter cannot be helped, so we will make the best of it."

"Oh, don't feel badly about it," he went on. "It isn't anything which can be adjusted now. They probably meant well enough. We just happen to be in the limelight."

"I understand," said Jennie, coming over to him. "I'm sorry, though, anyway." Dinner was announced a moment later and the incident was closed.

But Lester could not dismiss the thought that matters were getting in a bad way. His father had pointed it out to him rather plainly at the last interview, and now this newspaper notoriety had capped the climax. He might as well abandon his pretension to intimacy with his old world. It would have none of him, or at least the more conservative part of it would not. There were a few bachelors, a few gay married men, some sophisticated women, single and married, who saw through it all and liked him just the same, but they did not make society. He was virtually an outcast, and nothing could save him but to reform his ways; in other words, he must give up Jennie once and for all.

But he did not want to do this. The thought was painful to him—objectionable in every way. Jennie was growing in mental acumen. She was beginning to see things quite as clearly as he did. She was not a cheap, ambitious, climbing creature. She was a big woman and a good one. It would be a shame to throw her down, and besides she was good-looking. He was forty-six and she was twenty-nine; and she looked twenty-four or five. It is an exceptional thing to find beauty, youth, compatibility, intelligence, your own point of view—softened and charmingly emotionalized—in another. He had made his bed, as his father had said. He had better lie on it.

It was only a little while after this disagreeable newspaper incident that Lester had word that his father was quite ill and failing; it might be necessary for him to go to Cincinnati at any moment. Pressure of work was holding him pretty close when the news came that his father was dead. Lester, of course, was greatly shocked and grieved, and he returned to Cincinnati in a retrospective and sorrowful mood. His father had been a great character to him—a fine and interesting old gentleman entirely aside from his relationship to him as his son. He remembered him now dandling him upon his knee as a child, telling him stories of his early life in Ireland, and of his subsequent commercial struggle when he was a little older, impressing the maxims of his business career and his commercial wisdom on him as he grew to manhood. Old Archibald had been radically honest. It was to him that Lester owed his instincts for plain speech and direct statement of fact. "Never lie," was Archibald's constant, reiterated statement. "Never try to make a thing look different from what it is to you. It's the breath of life—truth—it's the basis of real worth, while commercial success—it will make a notable character of any one who will stick to it." Lester believed this. He admired his father intensely for his rigid insistence on truth, and now that he was really gone he felt sorry. He wished he might have been spared to be reconciled to him. He half fancied that old Archibald would have liked Jennie if he had known her. He did not imagine that he would ever have had the opportunity to straighten things out, although he still felt that Archibald would have liked her.

When he reached Cincinnati it was snowing, a windy, blustery snow. The flakes were coming down thick and fast. The traffic of the city had a muffled sound. When he stepped down from the train he was met by Amy, who was glad to see him in spite of all their past differences. Of all the girls she was the most tolerant. Lester put his arms about her, and kissed her.

"It seems like old times to see you, Amy," he said, "your coming to meet me this way. How's the family? I suppose they're all here. Well, poor father, his time had to come. Still, he lived to see everything that he wanted to see. I guess he was pretty well satisfied with the outcome of his efforts."

"Yes," replied Amy, "and since mother died he was very lonely."

They rode up to the house in kindly good feeling, chatting of old times and places. All the members of the immediate family, and the various relatives, were gathered in the old family mansion. Lester exchanged the customary condolences with the others, realizing all the while that his father had lived long enough. He had had a successful life, and had fallen like a ripe apple from the tree. Lester looked at him where he lay in the great parlor, in his black coffin, and a feeling of the old-time affection swept over him. He smiled at the clean-cut, determined, conscientious face.

"The old gentleman was a big man all the way through," he said to Robert, who was present. "We won't find a better figure of a man soon."

"We will not," said his brother, solemnly.

After the funeral it was decided to read the will at once. Louise's husband was anxious to return to Buffalo; Lester was compelled to be in Chicago. A conference of the various members of the family was called for the second day after the funeral, to be held at the offices of Messrs. Knight, Keatley & O'Brien, counselors of the late manufacturer.

As Lester rode to the meeting he had the feeling that his father had not acted in any way prejudicial to his interests. It had not been so very long since they had had their last conversation; he had been taking his time to think about things, and his father had given him time. He always felt that he had stood well with the old gentleman, except for his alliance with Jennie. His business judgment had been valuable to the company. Why should there be any discrimination against him? He really did not think it possible.

When they reached the offices of the law firm, Mr. O'Brien, a short, fussy, albeit comfortable-looking little person, greeted all the members of the family and the various heirs and assigns with a hearty handshake. He had been personal counsel to Archibald Kane for twenty years. He knew his whims and idiosyncrasies, and considered himself very much in the light of a father confessor. He liked all the children, Lester especially.

"Now I believe we are all here," he said, finally, extracting a pair of large horn reading-glasses from his coat pocket and looking sagely about. "Very well. We might as well proceed to business. I will just read the will without any preliminary remarks."

He turned to his desk, picked up a paper lying upon it, cleared his throat, and began.

It was a peculiar document, in some respects, for it began with all the minor bequests; first, small sums to old employes, servants, and friends. It then took up a few institutional bequests, and finally came to the immediate family, beginning with the girls. Imogene, as a faithful and loving daughter was left a sixth of the stock of the carriage company and a fourth of the remaining properties of the deceased, which roughly aggregated (the estate—not her share) about eight hundred thousand dollars. Amy and Louise were provided for in exactly the same proportion. The grandchildren were given certain little bonuses for good conduct, when they should come of age. Then it took up the cases of Robert and Lester.

"Owing to certain complications which have arisen in the affairs of my son Lester," it began, "I deem it my duty to make certain conditions which shall govern the distribution of the remainder of my property, to wit: One-fourth of the stock of the Kane Manufacturing Company and one-fourth of the remainder of my various properties, real, personal, moneys, stocks and bonds, to go to my beloved son Robert, in recognition of the faithful performance of his duty, and one-fourth of the stock of the Kane Manufacturing Company and the remaining fourth of my various properties, real, personal, moneys, stocks and bonds, to be held in trust by him for the benefit of his brother Lester, until such time as such conditions as may hereinafter be set forth shall have been complied with. And it is my wish and desire that my children shall concur in his direction of the Kane Manufacturing Company, and of such other interests as are entrusted to him, until such time as he shall voluntarily relinquish such control, or shall indicate another arrangement which shall be better."

Lester swore under his breath. His cheeks changed color, but he did not move. He was not inclined to make a show. It appeared that he was not even mentioned separately.

The conditions "hereinafter set forth" dealt very fully with his case, however, though they were not read aloud to the family at the time, Mr. O'Brien stating that this was in accordance with their father's wish. Lester learned immediately afterward that he was to have ten thousand a year for three years, during which time he had the choice of doing either one of two things: First, he was to leave Jennie, if he had not already married her, and so bring his life into moral conformity with the wishes of his father. In this event Lester's share of the estate was to be immediately turned over to him. Secondly, he might elect to marry Jennie, if he had not already done so, in which case the ten thousand a year, specifically set aside to him for three years, was to be continued for life— but for his life only. Jennie was not to have anything of it after his death. The ten thousand in question represented the annual interest on two hundred shares of L. S. and M. S. stock which were also to be held in trust until his decision had been reached and their final disposition effected. If Lester refused to marry Jennie, or to leave her, he was to have nothing at all after the three years were up. At Lester's death the stock on which his interest was drawn was to be divided pro rata among the surviving members of the family. If any heir or assign contested the will, his or her share was thereby forfeited entirely.

It was astonishing to Lester to see how thoroughly his father had taken his case into consideration. He half suspected, on reading these conditions, that his brother Robert had had something to do with the framing of them, but of course he could not be sure. Robert had not given any direct evidence of enmity.

"Who drew this will?" he demanded of O'Brien, a little later.

"Well, we all had a hand in it," replied O'Brien, a little shamefacedly. "It was a very difficult document to draw up. You know, Mr. Kane, there was no budging your father. He was adamant. He has come very near defeating his own wishes in some of these clauses. Of course, you know, we had nothing to do with its spirit. That was between you and him. I hated very much to have to do it."

"Oh, I understand all that!" said Lester. "Don't let that worry you."

Mr. O'Brien was very grateful.

During the reading of the will Lester had sat as stolid as an ox.

He got up after a time, as did the others, assuming an air of nonchalance. Robert, Amy, Louise and Imogene all felt shocked, but not exactly, not unqualifiedly regretful. Certainly Lester had acted very badly. He had given his father great provocation.

"I think the old gentleman has been a little rough in this," said Robert, who had been sitting next him. "I certainly did not expect him to go as far as that. So far as I am concerned some other arrangement would have been satisfactory."

Lester smiled grimly. "It doesn't matter," he said.

Imogene, Amy, and Louise were anxious to be consolatory, but they did not know what to say. Lester had brought it all on himself. "I don't think papa acted quite right, Lester," ventured Amy, but Lester waved her away almost gruffly.

"I can stand it," he said.

He figured out, as he stood there, what his income would be in case he refused to comply with his father's wishes. Two hundred shares of L. S. and M. S., in open market, were worth a little over one thousand each. They yielded from five to six per cent., sometimes more, sometimes less. At this rate he would have ten thousand a year, not more.

The family gathering broke up, each going his way, and Lester returned to his sister's house. He wanted to get out of the city quickly, gave business as an excuse to avoid lunching with any one, and caught the earliest train back to Chicago. As he rode he meditated.

So this was how much his father really cared for him! Could it really be so? He, Lester Kane, ten thousand a year, for only three years, and then longer only on condition that he married Jennie! "Ten thousand a year," he thought, "and that for three years! Good Lord! Any smart clerk can earn that. To think he should have done that to me!"

Chapter XLIII

THIS ATTEMPT at coercion was the one thing which would definitely set Lester in opposition to his family, at least for the time being. He had realized clearly enough of late that he had made a big mistake; first in not having married Jennie, thus avoiding scandal; and in the second place in not having accepted her proposition at the time when she wanted to leave him. There were no two ways about it, he had made a mess of this business. He could not afford to lose his fortune entirely. He did not have enough money of his own. Jennie was unhappy, he could see that. Why shouldn't she be? He was unhappy. Did he want to accept the shabby ten thousand a year, even if he were willing to marry her? Finally, did he want to lose Jennie, to have her go out of his life once and for all? He could not make up his mind; the problem was too complicated.

When Lester returned to his home, after the funeral, Jennie saw at once that something was amiss with him, something beyond a son's natural grief for his father's death was weighing upon his spirits. What was it, she wondered. She tried to draw near to him sympathetically, but his wounded spirit could not be healed so easily. When hurt in his pride he was savage and sullen—he could have struck any man who irritated him. She watched him interestedly, wishing to do something for him, but he would not give her his confidence. He grieved, and she could only grieve with him.

Days passed, and now the financial situation which had been created by his father's death came up for careful consideration. The factory management had to be reorganized. Robert would have to be made president, as his father wished. Lester's own relationship to the business would have to come up for adjudication. Unless he changed his mind about Jennie, he was not a stockholder. As a matter of fact, he was not anything. To continue to be secretary and treasurer, it was necessary that he should own at least one share of the company's stock. Would Robert give him any? Would Amy, Louise, or Imogene? Would they sell him any? Would the other members of the family care to do anything which would infringe on Robert's prerogatives under the will? They were all rather unfriendly to Lester at present, and he realized that he was facing a ticklish situation. The solution was—to get rid of Jennie. If he did that he would not need to be begging for stock. If he didn't, he was flying in the face of his father's last will and testament. He turned the matter over in his mind slowly and deliberately. He could quite see how things were coming out. He must abandon either Jennie or his prospects in life. What a dilemma!

Despite Robert's assertion, that so far as he was concerned another arrangement would have been satisfactory, he was really very well pleased with the situation; his dreams were slowly nearing completion. Robert had long had his plans perfected, not only for a thorough reorganization of the company proper, but for an extension of the business in the direction of a combination of carriage companies. If he could get two or three of the larger organizations in the East and West to join with him, selling costs could be reduced, overproduction would be avoided, and the general expenses could be materially scaled down. Through a New York representative, he had been picking up stock in outside carriage companies for some time and he was almost ready to act. In the first place he would have himself elected president of the Kane Company, and since Lester was no longer a factor, he could select Amy's husband as vice-president, and possibly some one other than Lester as secretary and treasurer. Under the conditions of the will, the stock and other properties set aside temporarily for Lester, in the hope that he would come to his senses, were to be managed and voted by Robert. His father had meant, obviously, that he, Robert, should help him coerce his brother. He did not want to appear mean, but this was such an easy way. It gave him a righteous duty to perform. Lester must come to his senses or he must let Robert run the business to suit himself.

Lester, attending to his branch duties in Chicago, foresaw the drift of things. He realized now that he was permanently out of the company, a branch manager at his brother's sufferance, and the thought irritated him greatly. Nothing had been said by Robert to indicate that such a change had taken place—things went on very much as before—but Robert's suggestions were now obviously law. Lester was really his brother's employe at so much a year. It sickened his soul.

There came a time, after a few weeks, when he felt as if he could not stand this any longer. Hitherto he had been a free and independent agent. The approaching annual stock-holder's meeting which hitherto had been a one-man affair and a formality, his father doing all the voting, would be now a combination of voters, his brother presiding, his sisters very likely represented by their husbands, and he not there at all. It was going to be a great come-down, but as Robert had not said anything about offering to give or sell him any stock which would entitle him to sit as a director or hold any offi-cial position in the company, he decided to write and resign. That would bring matters to a crisis. It would show his brother that he felt no desire to be under obligations to him in any way or to retain anything which was not his—and gladly so—by right of ability and the desire of those with whom he was associated. If he wanted to move back into the company by deserting Jennie he would come in a very differ-ent capacity from that of branch manager. He dictated a simple, straightforward business letter, saying:

"DEAR ROBERT,—I know the time is drawing near when the company must be reorganized under your direction. Not having any stock, I am not entitled to sit as a director, or to hold the joint position of secretary and treasurer. I want you to accept this letter as formal notice of my resignation from both positions, and I want to have your directors consider what disposition should be made of this position and my ser-vices. I am not anxious to retain the branch-managership as a branch-managership merely; at the same time I do not want to do anything which will embarrass you in your plans for the future. You see by this that I am not ready to accept the prop-osition laid down in father's will—at least, not at present. I would like a definite understanding of how you feel in this matter. Will you write and let me know?

"Yours,

"LESTER."

Robert, sitting in his office at Cincinnati, considered this letter gravely. It was like his brother to come down to "brass tacks." If Lester were only as cautious as he was straight-forward and direct, what a man he would be! But there was no guile in the man—no subtlety. He would never do a snaky thing—and Robert knew, in his own soul, that to suc-ceed greatly one must. "You have to be ruthless at times— you have to be subtle," Robert would say to himself. "Why not face the facts to yourself when you are playing for big stakes?" He would, for one, and he did.

Robert felt that although Lester was a tremendously decent fellow and his brother, he wasn't pliable enough to suit his needs. He was too outspoken, too inclined to take issue. If Lester yielded to his father's wishes, and took possession of his share of the estate, he would become, necessarily, an active partner in the affairs of the company. Lester would be a bar-rier in Robert's path. Did Robert want this? Decidedly he did not. He much preferred that Lester should hold fast to Jennie, for the present at least, and so be quietly shelved by his own act.

After long consideration, Robert dictated a politic letter. He hadn't made up his mind yet just what he wanted to do. He did not know what his sisters' husbands would like. A consultation would have to be held. For his part, he would be very glad to have Lester remain as secretary and treasurer, if it could be arranged. Perhaps it would be better to let the matter rest for the present.

Lester cursed. What did Robert mean by beating around the bush? He knew well enough how it could be arranged. One share of stock would be enough for Lester to qualify. Robert was afraid of him—that was the basic fact. Well, he would not retain any branch-managership, depend on that. He would resign at once. Lester accordingly wrote back, say-ing that he had considered all sides, and had decided to look after some interests of his own, for the time being. If Robert could arrange it, he would like to have some one come on to Chicago and take over the branch agency. Thirty days would be time enough. In a few days came a regretful reply, saying that Robert was awfully sorry, but that if Lester was deter-mined he did not want to interfere with any plans he might have in view. Imogene's husband, Jefferson Midgely, had long thought he would like to reside in Chicago. He could undertake the work for the time being.

Lester smiled. Evidently Robert was making the best of a very subtle situation. Robert knew that he, Lester, could sue and tie things up, and also that he would be very loath to do so. The newspapers would get hold of the whole story. This matter of his relationship to Jennie was in the air, anyhow. He could best solve the problem by leaving her. So it all came back to that.

Chapter XLIV

For a man of Lester's years—he was now forty-six—to be tossed out in the world without a definite connection, even though he did have a present income (including this new ten thousand) of fifteen thousand a year, was a disturbing and discouraging thing. He realized now that, unless he made some very fortunate and profitable arrangements in the near future, his career was virtually at an end. Of course he could marry Jennie. That would give him the ten thousand for the rest of his life, but it would also end his chance of getting his legitimate share of the Kane estate. Again, he might sell out the seventy-five thousand dollars' worth of moderate interest-bearing stocks, which now yielded him about five thousand, and try a practical investment of some kind—say a rival carriage company. But did he want to jump in, at this stage of the game, and begin a running fight on his father's old organization? Moreover, it would be a hard row to hoe. There was the keenest rivalry for business as it was, with the Kane Company very much in the lead. Lester's only available capital was his seventy-five thousand dollars. Did he want to begin in a picayune, obscure way? It took money to get a foothold in the carriage business as things were now.

The trouble with Lester was that, while blessed with a fine imagination and considerable insight, he lacked the ruthless, narrow-minded insistence on his individual superiority which is a necessary element in almost every great business success. To be a forceful figure in the business world means, as a rule, that you must be an individual of one idea, and that idea the God-given one that life has destined you for a tremendous future in the particular field you have chosen. It means that one thing, a cake of soap, a new can-opener, a safety razor, or speed-accelerator, must seize on your imagination with tremendous force, burn as a raging flame, and make itself the be-all and end-all of your existence. As a rule, a man needs poverty to help him to this enthusiasm, and youth. The thing he has discovered, and with which he is going to busy himself, must be the door to a thousand opportunities and a thousand joys. Happiness must be beyond or the fire will not burn as brightly as it might—the urge will not be great enough to make a great success.

Lester did not possess this indispensable quality of enthusiasm. Life had already shown him the greater part of its so-called joys. He saw through the illusions that are so often and so noisily labeled pleasure. Money, of course, was essential, and he had already had money—enough to keep him comfortably. Did he want to risk it? He looked about him thoughtfully. Perhaps he did. Certainly he could not comfortably contemplate the thought of sitting by and watching other people work for the rest of his days.

In the end he decided that he would bestir himself and look into things. He was, as he said to himself, in no hurry; he was not going to make a mistake. He would first give the trade, the people who were identified with the manufacture and sale of carriages, time to realize that he was out of the Kane Company, for the time being, anyhow, and open to other connections. So he announced that he was leaving the Kane Company and going to Europe, ostensibly for a rest. He had never been abroad, and Jennie, too, would enjoy it. Vesta could be left at home with Gerhardt and a maid, and he and Jennie would travel around a bit, seeing what Europe had to show. He wanted to visit Venice and Baden-Baden, and the great watering-places that had been recommended to him. Cairo and Luxor and the Parthenon had always appealed to his imagination. After he had had his outing he could come back and seriously gather up the threads of his intentions.

The spring after his father died, he put his plan into execution. He had wound up the work of the warerooms and with a pleasant deliberation had studied out a tour. He made Jennie his confidante, and now, having gathered together their traveling comforts they took a steamer from New York to Liverpool. After a few weeks in the British Isles they went to Egypt. From there they came back, through Greece and Italy, into Austria and Switzerland, and then later, through France and Paris, to Germany and Berlin. Lester was diverted by the novelty of the experience and yet he had an uncomfortable feeling that he was wasting his time. Great business enterprises were not built by travelers, and he was not looking for health.

Jennie, on the other hand, was transported by what she saw, and enjoyed the new life to the full. Before Luxor and Karnak—places which Jennie had never dreamed existed—she learned of an older civilization, powerful, complex, complete. Millions of people had lived and died here, believing in other gods, other forms of government, other conditions of existence. For the first time in her life Jennie gained a clear idea of how vast the world is. Now from this point of view—of decayed Greece, of fallen Rome, of forgotten Egypt, she saw how pointless are our minor difficulties, our minor beliefs. Her father's Lutheranism—it did not seem so significant any more; and the social economy of Columbus, Ohio—rather pointless, perhaps. Her mother had worried so of what people—her neighbors—thought, but here were dead worlds of people, some bad, some good. Lester explained that their differences in standards of morals were due sometimes to climate, sometimes to religious beliefs, and sometimes to the rise of peculiar personalities like Mohammed. Lester liked to point out how small conventions bulked in this, the larger world, and vaguely she began to see. Admitting that she had been bad—locally it was important, perhaps, but in the sum of civilization, in the sum of big forces, what did it all amount to? They would be dead after a little while, she and Lester and all these people. Did anything matter except goodness—goodness of heart? What else was there that was real?

Chapter XLV

IT WAS WHILE traveling abroad that Lester came across, first at the Carlton in London and later at Shepheards in Cairo, the one girl, before Jennie, whom it might have been said he truly admired—Letty Pace. He had not seen her for a long time, and she had been Mrs. Malcolm Gerald for nearly four years, and a charming widow for nearly two years more. Malcolm Gerald had been a wealthy man, having amassed a fortune in banking and stock-brokering in Cincinnati, and he had left Mrs. Malcolm Gerald very well off. She was the mother of one child, a little girl, who was safely in charge of a nurse and maid at all times, and she was invariably the picturesque center of a group of admirers recruited from every capital of the civilized world. Letty Gerald was a talented woman, beautiful, graceful, artistic, a writer of verse, an omnivorous reader, a student of art, and a sincere and ardent admirer of Lester Kane.

In her day she had truly loved him, for she had been a wise observer of men and affairs, and Lester had always appealed to her as a real man. He was so sane, she thought, so calm. He was always intolerant of sham, and she liked him for it. He was inclined to wave aside the petty little frivolities of common society conversation, and to talk of simple and homely things. Many and many a time, in years past, they had deserted a dance to sit out on a balcony somewhere, and talk while Lester smoked. He had argued philosophy with her, discussed books, described political and social conditions in other cities—in a word, he had treated her like a sensible human being, and she had hoped and hoped and hoped that he would propose to her. More than once she had looked at his big, solid head with its short growth of hardy brown hair, and wished that she could stroke it. It was a hard blow to her when he finally moved away to Chicago; at that time she knew nothing of Jennie, but she felt instinctively that her chance of winning him was gone.

Then Malcolm Gerald, always an ardent admirer, proposed for something like the sixty-fifth time, and she took him. She did not love him, but she was getting along, and she had to marry some one. He was forty-four when he married her, and he lived only four years—just long enough to realize that he had married a charming, tolerant, broad-minded woman. Then he died of pneumonia and Mrs. Gerald was a rich widow, sympathetic, attractive, delightful in her knowledge of the world, and with nothing to do except to live and to spend her money.

She was not inclined to do either indifferently. She had long since had her ideal of a man established by Lester. These whipper-snappers of counts, earls, lords, barons, whom she met in one social world and another (for her friendship and connections had broadened notably with the years), did not interest her a particle. She was terribly weary of the superficial veneer of the titled fortune-hunter whom she met abroad. A good judge of character, a student of men and manners, a natural reasoner along sociologic and psychologic lines, she saw through them and through the civilization which they represented. "I could have been happy in a cottage with a man I once knew out in Cincinnati," she told one of her titled women friends who had been an American before her marriage. "He was the biggest, cleanest, sanest fellow. If he had proposed to me I would have married him if I had had to work for a living myself."

"Was he so poor?" asked her friend.

"Indeed he wasn't. He was comfortably rich, but that did not make any difference to me. It was the man I wanted."

"It would have made a difference in the long run," said the other.

"You misjudge me," replied Mrs. Gerald. "I waited for him for a number of years, and I know."

Lester had always retained pleasant impressions and kindly memories of Letty Pace, or Mrs. Gerald, as she was now. He had been fond of her in a way, very fond. Why hadn't he married her? He had asked himself that question time and again. She would have made him an ideal wife, his father would have been pleased, everybody would have been delighted. Instead he had drifted and drifted, and then he had met Jennie; and somehow, after that, he did not want her any more. Now after six years of separation he met her again. He knew she was married. She was vaguely aware he had had some sort of an affair—she had heard that he had subsequently married the woman and was living on the South Side. She did not know of the loss of his fortune. She ran across him first in the Carlton one June evening. The windows were open, and the flowers were blooming everywhere, odorous with that sense of new life in the air which runs through the world when spring comes back. For the moment she was a little beside herself. Something choked in her throat; but she collected herself and extended a graceful arm and hand.

"Why, Lester Kane," she exclaimed. "How *do* you do! I am so glad. And this is Mrs. Kane? Charmed, I'm sure. It seems truly like a breath of spring to see you again. I hope you'll excuse me, Mrs. Kane, but I'm delighted to see your husband. I'm ashamed to say how many years it is, Lester, since I saw you last! I feel quite old when I think of it. Why, Lester, think; it's been all of six or seven years! And I've been married and had a child, and poor Mr. Gerald has died, and oh, dear, I don't know what all hasn't happened to me."

"You don't look it," commented Lester, smiling. He was pleased to see her again, for they had been good friends. She liked him still—that was evident, and he truly liked her.

Jennie smiled. She was glad to see this old friend of Lester's. This woman, trailing a magnificent yellow lace train over pale, mother-of-pearl satin, her round, smooth arms bare to the shoulder, her corsage cut low and a dark red rose blowing at her waist, seemed to her the ideal of what a woman should be. She liked looking at lovely women quite as much as Lester; she enjoyed calling his attention to them, and teasing him, in the mildest way, about their charms. "Wouldn't you like to run and talk to her, Lester, instead of to me?" she would ask when some particularly striking or beautiful woman chanced to attract her attention. Lester would examine her choice critically, for he had come to know that her judge of feminine charms was excellent. "Oh, I'm pretty well off where I am," he would retort, looking into her eyes; or, jestingly, "I'm not as young as I used to be, or I'd get in tow of that."

"Run on," was her comment. "I'll wait for you."

"What would you do if I really should?"

"Why, Lester, I wouldn't do anything. You'd come back to me, maybe."

"Wouldn't you care?"

"You know I'd care. But if you felt that you wanted to, I wouldn't try to stop you. I wouldn't expect to be all in all to one man, unless he wanted me to be."

"Where do you get those ideas, Jennie?" he asked her once, curious to test the breadth of her philosophy.

"Oh, I don't know, why?"

"They're so broad, so good-natured, so charitable. They're not common, that's sure."

"Why, I don't think we ought to be selfish, Lester. I don't know why. Some women think differently, I know, but a man and a woman ought to want to live together, or they ought not to—don't you think? It doesn't make so much difference if a man goes off for a little while—just so long as he doesn't stay—if he wants to come back at all."

Lester smiled, but he respected her for the sweetness of her point of view—he had to.

To-night, when she saw this woman so eager to talk to Lester, she realized at once that they must have a great deal in common to talk over; whereupon she did a characteristic thing. "Won't you excuse me for a little while?" she asked, smiling. "I left some things uncared for in our rooms. I'll be back."

She went away, remaining in her room as long as she reasonably could, and Lester and Letty fell to discussing old times in earnest. He recounted as much of his experiences as he deemed wise, and Letty brought the history of her life up to date. "Now that you're safely married, Lester," she said daringly, "I'll confess to you that you were the one man I always wanted to have propose to me—and you never did."

"Maybe I never dared," he said, gazing into her superb black eyes, and thinking that perhaps she might know that he was not married. He felt that she had grown more beautiful in every way. She seemed to him now to be an ideal society figure—perfection itself—gracious, natural, witty, the type of woman who mixes and mingles well, meeting each newcomer upon the plane best suited to him or her.

"Yes, you thought! I know what you thought. Your real thought just left the table."

"Tut, tut, my dear. Not so fast. You don't know what I thought."

"Anyhow, I allow you some credit. She's charming."

"Jennie has her good points," he replied simply.

"And are you happy?"

"Oh, fairly so. Yes, I suppose I'm happy—as happy as any one can be who sees life as it is. You know I'm not troubled with many illusions."

"Not any, I think, kind sir, if I know you."

"Very likely, not any, Letty; but sometimes I wish I had a few. I think I would be happier."

"And I, too, Lester. Really, I look on my life as a kind of failure, you know, in spite of the fact that I'm almost as rich as Crœsus—not quite. I think he had some more than I have."

"What talk from you—you, with your beauty and talent, and money—good heavens!"

"And what can I do with it? Travel, talk, shoo away silly fortune-hunters. Oh, dear, sometimes I get so tired!"

Letty looked at Lester. In spite of Jennie, the old feeling came back. Why should she have been cheated of him? They were as comfortable together as old married people, or young lovers. Jennie had had no better claim. She looked at him, and her eyes fairly spoke. He smiled a little sadly.

"Here comes my wife," he said. "We'll have to brace up and talk of other things. You'll find her interesting—really."

"Yes, I know," she replied, and turned on Jennie a radiant smile.

Jennie felt a faint sense of misgiving. She thought vaguely that this might be one of Lester's old flames. This was the kind of woman he should have chosen—not her. She was suited to his station in life, and he would have been as happy —perhaps happier. Was he beginning to realize it? Then she put away the uncomfortable thought; pretty soon she would be getting jealous, and that would be contemptible.

Mrs. Gerald continued to be most agreeable in her attitude toward the Kanes. She invited them the next day to join her on a drive through Rotten Row. There was a dinner later at

Claridge's, and then she was compelled to keep some engagement which was taking her to Paris. She bade them both an affectionate farewell, and hoped that they would soon meet again. She was envious, in a sad way, of Jennie's good fortune. Lester had lost none of his charm for her. If anything, he seemed nicer, more considerate, more wholesome. She wished sincerely that he were free. And Lester—subconsciously perhaps—was thinking the same thing.

No doubt because of the fact that she was thinking of it, he had been led over mentally all of the things which might have happened if he had married her. They were so congenial now, philosophically, artistically, practically. There was a natural flow of conversation between them all the time, like two old comrades among men. She knew everybody in his social sphere, which was equally hers, but Jennie did not. They could talk of certain subtle characteristics of life in a way which was not possible between him and Jennie, for the latter did not have the vocabulary. Her ideas did not flow as fast as those of Mrs. Gerald. Jennie had actually the deeper, more comprehensive, sympathetic, and emotional note in her nature, but she could not show it in light conversation. Actually she was living the thing she was, and that was perhaps the thing which drew Lester to her. Just now, and often in situations of this kind, she seemed at a disadvantage, and she was. It seemed to Lester for the time being as if Mrs. Gerald would perhaps have been a better choice after all—certainly as good, and he would not now have this distressing thought as to his future.

They did not see Mrs. Gerald again until they reached Cairo. In the gardens about the hotel they suddenly encountered her, or rather Lester did, for he was alone at the time, strolling and smoking.

"Well, this is good luck," he exclaimed. "Where do you come from?"

"Madrid, if you please. I didn't know I was coming until last Thursday. The Ellicotts are here. I came over with them. You know I wondered where you might be. Then I remembered that you said you were going to Egypt. Where is your wife?"

"In her bath, I fancy, at this moment. This warm weather

makes Jennie take to water. I was thinking of a plunge myself."

They strolled about for a time. Letty was in light blue silk, with a blue and white parasol held daintily over her shoulder, and looked very pretty. "Oh, dear!" she suddenly ejaculated, "I wonder sometimes what I am to do with myself. I can't loaf always this way. I think I'll go back to the States to live."

"Why don't you?"

"What good would it do me? I don't want to get married. I haven't any one to marry now—that I want." She glanced at Lester significantly, then looked away.

"Oh, you'll find some one eventually," he said, somewhat awkwardly. "You can't escape for long—not with your looks and money."

"Oh, Lester, hush!"

"All right! Have it otherwise, if you want. I'm telling you."

"Do you still dance?" she inquired lightly, thinking of a ball which was to be given at the hotel that evening. He had danced so well a few years before.

"Do I look it?"

"Now, Lester, you don't mean to say that you have gone and abandoned that last charming art. I still love to dance. Doesn't Mrs. Kane?"

"No, she doesn't care to. At least she hasn't taken it up. Come to think of it, I suppose that is my fault. I haven't thought of dancing in some time."

It occurred to him that he hadn't been going to functions of any kind much for some time. The opposition his entanglement had generated had put a stop to that.

"Come and dance with me to-night. Your wife won't object. It's a splendid floor. I saw it this morning."

"I'll have to think about that," replied Lester. "I'm not much in practice. Dancing will probably go hard with me at my time of life."

"Oh, hush, Lester," replied Mrs. Gerald. "You make me feel old. Don't talk so sedately. Mercy alive, you'd think you were an old man!"

"I am in experience, my dear."

"Pshaw, that simply makes us more attractive," replied his old flame.

Chapter XLVI

THAT NIGHT after dinner the music was already sounding in the ball-room of the great hotel adjacent to the palm-gardens when Mrs. Gerald found Lester smoking on one of the verandas with Jennie by his side. The latter was in white satin and white slippers, her hair lying a heavy, enticing mass about her forehead and ears. Lester was brooding over the history of Egypt, its successive tides or waves of rather weak-bodied people; the thin, narrow strip of soil along either side of the Nile that had given these successive waves of population sustenance; the wonder of heat and tropic life, and this hotel with its modern conveniences and fashionable crowd set down among ancient, soul-weary, almost despairing conditions. He and Jennie had looked this morning on the pyramids. They had taken a trolley to the Sphinx! They had watched swarms of ragged, half-clad, curiously costumed men and boys moving through narrow, smelly, albeit brightly colored, lanes and alleys.

"It all seems such a mess to me," Jennie had said at one place. "They are so dirty and oily. I like it, but somehow they seem tangled up, like a lot of worms."

Lester chuckled. "You're almost right. But climate does it. Heat. The tropics. Life is always mushy and sensual under these conditions. They can't help it."

"Oh, I know that. I don't blame them. They're just queer."

To-night he was brooding over this, the moon shining down into the grounds with an exuberant, sensuous luster.

"Well, at last I've found you!" Mrs. Gerald exclaimed. "I couldn't get down to dinner, after all. Our party was so late getting back. I've made your husband agree to dance with me, Mrs. Kane," she went on smilingly. She, like Lester and Jennie, was under the sensuous influence of the warmth, the spring, the moonlight. There were rich odors abroad, floating subtly from groves and gardens; from the remote distance camel-bells were sounding and exotic cries, *"Ayah!"* and *"oosh! oosh!"* as though a drove of strange animals were being rounded up and driven through the crowded streets.

"You're welcome to him," replied Jennie pleasantly. "He ought to dance. I sometimes wish I did."

"You ought to take lessons right away then," replied Lester genially. "I'll do my best to keep you company. I'm not as light on my feet as I was once, but I guess I can get around."

"Oh, I don't want to dance that badly," smiled Jennie. "But you two go on, I'm going up-stairs in a little while, anyway."

"Why don't you come sit in the ball-room? I can't do more than a few rounds. Then we can watch the others," said Lester rising.

"No. I think I'll stay here. It's so pleasant. You go. Take him, Mrs. Gerald."

Lester and Letty strolled away. They made a striking pair— Mrs. Gerald in dark wine-colored silk, covered with glistening black beads, her shapely arms and neck bare, and a flashing diamond of great size set just above her forehead in her dark hair. Her lips were red, and she had an engaging smile, showing an even row of white teeth between wide, full, friendly lips. Lester's strong, vigorous figure was well set off by his evening clothes; he looked distinguished.

"That is the woman he should have married," said Jennie to herself as he disappeared. She fell into a reverie, going over the steps of her past life. Sometimes it seemed to her now as if she had been living in a dream. At other times she felt as though she were in that dream yet. Life sounded in her ears much as this night did. She heard its cries. She knew its large-mass features. But back of it were subtleties that shaded and changed one into the other like the shifting of dreams. Why had she been so attractive to men? Why had Lester been so eager to follow her? Could she have prevented him? She thought of her life in Columbus, when she carried coal; to-night she was in Egypt, at this great hotel, the chatelaine of a suite of rooms, surrounded by every luxury, Lester still devoted to her. He had endured so many things for her! Why? Was she so wonderful? Brander had said so. Lester had told her so. Still she felt humble, out of place, holding handfuls of jewels that did not belong to her. Again she experienced that peculiar feeling which had come over her the first time she went to New York with Lester—namely, that this fairy existence could not endure. Her life was fated. Something would happen. She would go back to simple things, to a side street, a poor cottage, to old clothes.

And then as she thought of her home in Chicago, and the attitude of his friends, she knew it must be so. She would never be received, even if he married her. And she could understand why. She could look into the charming, smiling face of this woman who was now with Lester, and see that she considered her very nice, perhaps, but not of Lester's class. She was saying to herself now no doubt as she danced with Lester that he needed some one like her. He needed some one who had been raised in the atmosphere of the things to which he had been accustomed. He couldn't very well expect to find in her, Jennie, the familiarity with, the appreciation of the niceties to, which he had always been accustomed. She understood what they were. Her mind had awakened rapidly to details of furniture, clothing, arrangement, decorations, manner, forms, customs, but—she was not to the manner born.

If she went away Lester would return to his old world, the world of the attractive, well-bred, clever woman who now hung upon his arm. The tears came into Jennie's eyes; she wished, for the moment, that she might die. It would be better so. Meanwhile Lester was dancing with Mrs. Gerald, or sitting out between the waltzes talking over old times, old places, and old friends. As he looked at Letty he marveled at her youth and beauty. She was more developed than formerly, but still as slender and shapely as Diana. She had strength, too, in this smooth body of hers, and her black eyes were liquid and lusterful.

"I swear, Letty," he said impulsively, "you're really more beautiful than ever. You're exquisite. You've grown younger instead of older."

"You think so?" she smiled, looking up into his face.

"You know I do, or I wouldn't say so. I'm not much on philandering."

"Oh, Lester, you bear, can't you allow a woman just a little coyness? Don't you know we all love to sip our praise, and not be compelled to swallow it in one great mouthful?"

"What's the point?" he asked. "What did I say?"

"Oh, nothing. You're such a bear. You're such a big, determined, straightforward boy. But never mind. I like you. That's enough, isn't it?"

"It surely is," he said.

They strolled into the garden as the music ceased, and he squeezed her arm softly. He couldn't help it; she made him feel as if he owned her. She wanted him to feel that way. She said to herself, as they sat looking at the lanterns in the gardens, that if ever he were free, and would come to her, she would take him. She was almost ready to take him anyhow— only he probably wouldn't. He was so straight-laced, so considerate. He wouldn't, like so many other men she knew, do a mean thing. He couldn't. Finally Lester rose and excused himself. He and Jennie were going farther up the Nile in the morning—toward Karnak and Thebes and the water-washed temples at Phylæ. They would have to start at an unearthly early hour, and he must get to bed.

"When are you going home?" asked Mrs. Gerald, ruefully.

"In September."

"Have you engaged your passage?"

"Yes; we sail from Hamburg on the ninth—the *Fulda*."

"I may be going back in the fall," laughed Letty. "Don't be surprised if I crowd in on the same boat with you. I'm very unsettled in my mind."

"Come along, for goodness sake," replied Lester. "I hope you do. . . . I'll see you to-morrow before we leave." He paused, and she looked at him wistfully.

"Cheer up," he said, taking her hand. "You never can tell what life will do. We sometimes find ourselves right when we thought we were all wrong."

He was thinking that she was sorry to lose him, and he was sorry that she was not in a position to have what she wanted. As for himself, he was saying that here was one solution that probably he would never accept; yet it was a solution. Why had he not seen this years before?

"And yet she wasn't as beautiful then as she is now, nor as wise, nor as wealthy." Maybe! Maybe! But he couldn't be unfaithful to Jennie nor wish her any bad luck. She had had enough without his willing, and had borne it bravely.

Chapter XLVII

THE TRIP HOME did bring another week with Mrs. Gerald, for after mature consideration she had decided to venture to America for a while. Chicago and Cincinnati were her destinations, and she hoped to see more of Lester. Her presence was a good deal of a surprise to Jennie, and it started her thinking again. She could see what the point was. If she were out of the way Mrs. Gerald would marry Lester; that was certain. As it was—well, the question was a complicated one. Letty was Lester's natural mate, so far as birth, breeding, and position went. And yet Jennie felt instinctively that, on the large human side, Lester preferred her. Perhaps time would solve the problem; in the mean time the little party of three continued to remain excellent friends. When they reached Chicago Mrs. Gerald went her way, and Jennie and Lester took up the customary thread of their existence.

On his return from Europe Lester set to work in earnest to find a business opening. None of the big companies made him any overtures, principally because he was considered a strong man who was looking for a control in anything he touched. The nature of his altered fortunes had not been made public. All the little companies that he investigated were having a hand-to-mouth existence, or manufacturing a product which was not satisfactory to him. He did find one company in a small town in northern Indiana which looked as though it might have a future. It was controlled by a practical builder of wagons and carriages—such as Lester's father had been in his day—who, however, was not a good business man. He was making some small money on an investment of fifteen thousand dollars and a plant worth, say, twenty-five thousand. Lester felt that something could be done here if proper methods were pursued and business acumen exercised. It would be slow work. There would never be a great fortune in it. Not in his lifetime. He was thinking of making an offer to the small manufacturer when the first rumors of a carriage trust reached him.

Robert had gone ahead rapidly with his scheme for reorganizing the carriage trade. He showed his competitors how much greater profits could be made through consolidation than through a mutually destructive rivalry. So convincing were his arguments that one by one the big carriage manufacturing companies fell into line. Within a few months the deal had been pushed through, and Robert found himself president of the United Carriage and Wagon Manufacturers' Association, with a capital stock of ten million dollars, and with assets aggregating nearly three-fourths of that sum at a forced sale. He was a happy man.

While all this was going forward Lester was completely in the dark. His trip to Europe prevented him from seeing three or four minor notices in the newspapers of some of the efforts that were being made to unite the various carriage and wagon manufactories. He returned to Chicago to learn that Jefferson Midgely, Imogene's husband, was still in full charge of the branch and living in Evanston, but because of his quarrel with his family he was in no position to get the news direct. Accident brought it fast enough, however, and that rather irritatingly.

The individual who conveyed this information was none other than Mr. Henry Bracebridge, of Cleveland, into whom he ran at the Union Club one evening after he had been in the city a month.

"I hear you're out of the old company," Bracebridge remarked, smiling blandly.

"Yes," said Lester, "I'm out."

"What are you up to now?"

"Oh, I have a deal of my own under consideration. I'm thinking something of handling an independent concern."

"Surely you won't run counter to your brother? He has a pretty good thing in that combination of his."

"Combination! I hadn't heard of it," said Lester. "I've just got back from Europe."

"Well, you want to wake up, Lester," replied Bracebridge. "He's got the biggest thing in your line. I thought you knew all about it. The Lyman-Winthrop Company, the Myer-Brooks Company, the Woods Company—in fact, five or six of the big companies are all in. Your brother was elected president of the new concern. I dare say he cleaned up a couple of millions out of the deal."

Lester stared. His glance hardened a little.

"Well, that's fine for Robert. I'm glad of it."

Bracebridge could see that he had given him a vital stab.

"Well, so long, old man," he exclaimed. "When you're in Cleveland look us up. You know how fond my wife is of you."

"I know," replied Lester. "By-by."

He strolled away to the smoking-room, but the news took all the zest out of his private venture. Where would he be with a shabby little wagon company and his brother president of a carriage trust? Good heavens! Robert could put him out of business in a year. Why, he himself had dreamed of such a combination as this. Now his brother had done it.

It is one thing to have youth, courage, and a fighting spirit to meet the blows with which fortune often afflicts the talented. It is quite another to see middle age coming on, your principal fortune possibly gone, and avenue after avenue of opportunity being sealed to you on various sides. Jennie's obvious social insufficiency, the quality of newspaper reputation which had now become attached to her, his father's opposition and death, the loss of his fortune, the loss of his connection with the company, his brother's attitude, this trust, all combined in a way to dishearten and discourage him. He tried to keep a brave face—and he had succeeded thus far, he thought, admirably, but this last blow appeared for the time being a little too much. He went home, the same evening that he heard the news, sorely disheartened. Jennie saw it. She realized it, as a matter of fact, all during the evening that he was away. She felt blue and despondent herself. When he came home she saw what it was—something had happened to him. Her first impulse was to say, "What is the matter, Lester?" but her next and sounder one was to ignore it until he was ready to speak, if ever. She tried not to let him see that she saw, coming as near as she might affectionately without disturbing him.

"Vesta is so delighted with herself to-day," she volunteered by way of diversion. "She got such nice marks in school."

"That's good," he replied solemnly.

"And she dances beautifully these days. She showed me some of her new dances to-night. You haven't any idea how sweet she looks."

"I'm glad of it," he grumbled. "I always wanted her to be perfect in that. It's time she was going into some good girls' school, I think."

"And papa gets in such a rage. I have to laugh. She teases him about it—the little imp. She offered to teach him to dance to-night. If he didn't love her so he'd box her ears."

"I can see that," said Lester, smiling. "Him dancing! That's pretty good!"

"She's not the least bit disturbed by his storming, either."

"Good for her," said Lester. He was very fond of Vesta, who was now quite a girl.

So Jennie tripped on until his mood was modified a little, and then some inkling of what had happened came out. It was when they were retiring for the night. "Robert's formulated a pretty big thing in a financial way since we've been away," he volunteered.

"What is it?" asked Jennie, all ears.

"Oh, he's gotten up a carriage trust. It's something which will take in every manufactory of any importance in the country. Bracebridge was telling me that Robert was made president, and that they have nearly eight millions in capital."

"You don't say!" replied Jennie. "Well, then you won't want to do much with your new company, will you?"

"No; there's nothing in that, just now," he said. "Later on I fancy it may be all right. I'll wait and see how this thing comes out. You never can tell what a trust like that will do."

Jennie was intensely sorry. She had never heard Lester complain before. It was a new note. She wished sincerely that she might do something to comfort him, but she knew that her efforts were useless. "Oh, well," she said, "there are so many interesting things in this world. If I were you I wouldn't be in a hurry to do anything, Lester. You have so much time."

She didn't trust herself to say anything more, and he felt that it was useless to worry. Why should he? After all, he had an ample income that was absolutely secure for two years yet. He could have more if he wanted it. Only his brother was moving so dazzlingly onward, while he was standing still—perhaps "drifting" would be the better word. It did seem a pity; worst of all, he was beginning to feel a little uncertain of himself.

Chapter XLVIII

L ESTER HAD been doing some pretty hard thinking, but so
far he had been unable to formulate any feasible plan
for his re-entrance into active life. The successful organization
of Robert's carriage trade trust had knocked in the head any
further thought on his part of taking an interest in the small
Indiana wagon manufactory. He could not be expected to
sink his sense of pride and place, and enter a petty campaign
for business success with a man who was so obviously his
financial superior. He had looked up the details of the combination, and he found that Bracebridge had barely indicated
how wonderfully complete it was. There were millions in the
combine. It would have every little manufacturer by the
throat. Should he begin now in a small way and "pike along"
in the shadow of his giant brother? He couldn't see it. It was
too ignominious. He would be running around the country
trying to fight a new trust, with his own brother as his tolerant rival and his own rightful capital arrayed against him. It
couldn't be done. Better sit still for the time being. Something else might show up. If not—well, he had his independent income and the right to come back into the Kane
Company if he wished. Did he wish? The question was always with him.

It was while Lester was in this mood, drifting, that he received a visit from Samuel E. Ross, a real estate dealer, whose
great, wooden signs might be seen everywhere on the windy
stretches of prairie about the city. Lester had seen Ross once
or twice at the Union Club, where he had been pointed out
as a daring and successful real estate speculator, and he had
noticed his rather conspicuous offices at La Salle and Washington streets. Ross was a magnetic-looking person of about
fifty years of age, tall, black-bearded, black-eyed, an arched,
wide-nostriled nose, and hair that curled naturally, almost
electrically. Lester was impressed with his lithe, cat-like figure,
and his long, thin, impressive white hands.

Mr. Ross had a real estate proposition to lay before Mr.
Kane. Of course Mr. Kane knew who he was. And Mr. Ross
admitted fully that he knew all about Mr. Kane. Recently, in

conjunction with Mr. Norman Yale, of the wholesale grocery firm of Yale, Simpson & Rice, he had developed "Yalewood." Mr. Kane knew of that?

Yes, Mr. Kane knew of that.

Only within six weeks the last lots in the Ridgewood section of "Yalewood" had been closed out at a total profit of forty-two per cent. He went over a list of other deals in real estate which he had put through, all well-known properties. He admitted frankly that there were failures in the business; he had had one or two himself. But the successes far outnumbered the bad speculations, as every one knew. Now Lester was no longer connected with the Kane Company. He was probably looking for a good investment, and Mr. Ross had a proposition to lay before him. Lester consented to listen, and Mr. Ross blinked his cat-like eyes and started in.

The idea was that he and Lester should enter into a one-deal partnership, covering the purchase and development of a forty-acre tract of land lying between Fifty-fifth, Seventy-first, Halstead streets, and Ashland Avenue, on the southwest side. There were indications of a genuine real estate boom there—healthy, natural, and permanent. The city was about to pave Fifty-fifth Street. There was a plan to extend the Halstead Street car line far below its present terminus. The Chicago, Burlington & Quincy, which ran near there, would be glad to put a passenger station on the property. The initial cost of the land would be forty thousand dollars which they would share equally. Grading, paving, lighting, tree planting, surveying would cost, roughly, an additional twenty-five thousand. There would be expenses for advertising—say ten per cent. of the total investment for two years, or perhaps three—a total of nineteen thousand five hundred or twenty thousand dollars. All told, they would stand to invest jointly the sum of ninety-five thousand, or possibly one hundred thousand dollars, of which Lester's share would be fifty thousand. Then Mr. Ross began to figure on the profits.

The character of the land, its salability, and the likelihood of a rise in value could be judged by the property adjacent, the sales that had been made north of Fifty-fifth Street and east of Halstead. Take, for instance, the Mortimer plot, at Halstead and Fifty-fifth streets, on the southeast corner. Here was a piece of land that in 1882 was held at forty-five dollars an acre. In 1886 it had risen to five hundred dollars an acre, as attested by its sale to a Mr. John L. Slosson at that time. In 1889, three years later, it had been sold to Mr. Mortimer for one thousand per acre, precisely the figure at which this tract was now offered. It could be parceled out into lots fifty by one hundred feet at five hundred dollars per lot. Was there any profit in that?

Lester admitted that there was.

Ross went on, somewhat boastfully, to explain just how real estate profits were made. It was useless for any outsider to rush into the game, and imagine that he could do in a few weeks or years what trained real estate speculators like himself had been working on for a quarter of a century. There was something in prestige, something in taste, something in psychic apprehension. Supposing that they went into the deal, he, Ross, would be the presiding genius. He had a trained staff, he controlled giant contractors, he had friends in the tax office, in the water office, and in the various other city departments which made or marred city improvements. If Lester would come in with him he would make him some money—how much he would not say exactly—fifty thousand dollars at the lowest—one hundred and fifty to two hundred thousand in all likelihood. Would Lester let him go into details, and explain just how the scheme could be worked out? After a few days of quiet cogitation, Lester decided to accede to Mr. Ross's request; he would look into this thing.

Chapter XLIX

THE PECULIARITY of this particular proposition was that
it had the basic elements of success. Mr. Ross had the
experience and the judgment which were quite capable of
making a success of almost anything he undertook. He was
in a field which was entirely familiar. He could convince almost any able man if he could get his ear sufficiently long to
lay his facts before him.

Lester was not convinced at first, although, generally speaking, he was interested in real estate propositions. He liked
land. He considered it a sound investment providing you did
not get too much of it. He had never invested in any, or
scarcely any, solely because he had not been in a realm where
real estate propositions were talked of. As it was he was land-
less and, in a way, jobless.

He rather liked Mr. Ross and his way of doing business. It
was easy to verify his statements, and he did verify them in
several particulars. There were his signs out on the prairie
stretches, and here were his ads in the daily papers. It seemed
not a bad way at all in his idleness to start and make some
money.

The trouble with Lester was that he had reached the time
where he was not as keen for details as he had formerly been.
All his work in recent years—in fact, from the very beginning—had been with large propositions, the purchasing of
great quantities of supplies, the placing of large orders, the
discussion of things which were wholesale and which had
very little to do with the minor details which make up the
special interests of the smaller traders of the world. In the
factory his brother Robert had figured the pennies and nickels
of labor-cost, had seen to it that all the little leaks were shut
off. Lester had been left to deal with larger things, and he
had consistently done so. When it came to this particular
proposition his interest was in the wholesale phases of it, not
the petty details of selling. He could not help seeing that Chicago was a growing city, and that land values must rise. What
was now far-out prairie property would soon, in the course
of a few years, be well built-up suburban residence territory.

Scarcely any land that could be purchased now would fall in value. It might drag in sales or increase, but it couldn't fall. Ross convinced him of this. He knew it of his own judgment to be true.

The several things on which he did not speculate sufficiently were the life or health of Mr. Ross; the chance that some obnoxious neighborhood growth would affect the territory he had selected as residence territory; the fact that difficult money situations might reduce real estate values—in fact, bring about a flurry of real estate liquidation which would send prices crashing down and cause the failure of strong promoters, even such promoters for instance, as Mr. Samuel E. Ross.

For several months he studied the situation as presented by his new guide and mentor, and then, having satisfied himself that he was reasonably safe, decided to sell some of the holdings which were netting him a beggarly six per cent. and invest in this new proposition. The first cash outlay was twenty thousand dollars for the land, which was taken over under an operative agreement between himself and Ross; this was run indefinitely—so long as there was any of this land left to sell. The next thing was to raise twelve thousand five hundred dollars for improvements, which he did, and then to furnish some twenty-five hundred dollars more for taxes and unconsidered expenses, items which had come up in carrying out the improvement work which had been planned. It seemed that hard and soft earth made a difference in grading costs, that trees would not always flourish as expected, that certain members of the city water and gas departments had to be "seen" and "fixed" before certain other improvements could be effected. Mr. Ross attended to all this, but the cost of the proceedings was something which had to be discussed, and Lester heard it all.

After the land was put in shape, about a year after the original conversation, it was necessary to wait until spring for the proper advertising and booming of the new section; and this advertising began to call at once for the third payment. Lester disposed of an additional fifteen thousand dollars worth of securities in order to follow this venture to its logical and profitable conclusion.

Up to this time he was rather pleased with his venture. Ross had certainly been thorough and business-like in his handling of the various details. The land was put in excellent shape. It was given a rather attractive title—"Inwood," although, as Lester noted, there was precious little wood anywhere around there. But Ross assured him that people looking for a suburban residence would be attracted by the name; seeing the vigorous efforts in tree-planting that had been made to provide for shade in the future, they would take the will for the deed. Lester smiled.

The first chill wind that blew upon the infant project came in the form of a rumor that the International Packing Company, one of the big constituent members of the packing house combination at Halstead and Thirty-ninth streets, had determined to desert the old group and lay out a new packing area for itself. The papers explained that the company intended to go farther south, probably below Fifty-fifth Street and west of Ashland Avenue. This was the territory that was located due west of Lester's property, and the mere suspicion that the packing company might invade the territory was sufficient to blight the prospects of any budding real estate deal.

Ross was beside himself with rage. He decided, after quick deliberation, that the best thing to do would be to boom the property heavily, by means of newspaper advertising, and see if it could not be disposed of before any additional damage was likely to be done to it. He laid the matter before Lester, who agreed that this would be advisable. They had already expended six thousand dollars in advertising, and now the additional sum of three thousand dollars was spent in ten days, to make it appear that Inwood was an ideal residence section, equipped with every modern convenience for the home-lover, and destined to be one of the most exclusive and beautiful suburbs of the city. It was "no go." A few lots were sold, but the rumor that the International Packing Company might come was persistent and deadly; from any point of view, save that of a foreign population neighborhood, the enterprise was a failure.

To say that Lester was greatly disheartened by this blow is to put it mildly. Practically fifty thousand dollars, two-thirds of all his earthly possessions, outside of his stipulated annual income, was tied up here; and there were taxes to pay, repairs to maintain, actual depreciation in value to face. He suggested to Ross that the area might be sold at its cost value, or a loan raised on it, and the whole enterprise abandoned; but that experienced real estate dealer was not so sanguine. He had had one or two failures of this kind before. He was superstitious about anything which did not go smoothly from the beginning. If it didn't go it was a hoodoo—a black shadow—and he wanted no more to do with it. Other real estate men, as he knew to his cost, were of the same opinion.

Some three years later the property was sold under the sheriff's hammer. Lester, having put in fifty thousand dollars all told, recovered a trifle more than eighteen thousand; and some of his wise friends assured him that he was lucky in getting off so easily.

Chapter L

WHILE THE real estate deal was in progress Mrs. Gerald decided to move to Chicago. She had been staying in Cincinnati for a few months, and had learned a great deal as to the real facts of Lester's irregular mode of life. The question whether or not he was really married to Jennie remained an open one. The garbled details of Jennie's early years, the fact that a Chicago paper had written him up as a young millionaire who was sacrificing his fortune for love of her, the certainty that Robert had practically eliminated him from any voice in the Kane Company, all came to her ears. She hated to think that Lester was making such a sacrifice of himself. He had let nearly a year slip by without doing anything. In two more years his chance would be gone. He had said to her in London that he was without many illusions. Was Jennie one? Did he really love her, or was he just sorry for her? Letty wanted very much to find out for sure.

The house that Mrs. Gerald leased in Chicago was a most imposing one on Drexel Boulevard. "I'm going to take a house in your town this winter, and I hope to see a lot of you," she wrote to Lester. "I'm awfully bored with life here in Cincinnati. After Europe it's so—well, you know. I saw Mrs. Knowles on Saturday. She asked after you. You ought to know that you have a loving friend in her. Her daughter is going to marry Jimmy Severance in the spring."

Lester thought of her coming with mingled feelings of pleasure and uncertainty. She would be entertaining largely, of course. Would she foolishly begin by attempting to invite him and Jennie? Surely not. She must know the truth by this time. Her letter indicated as much. She spoke of seeing a lot of him. That meant that Jennie would have to be eliminated. He would have to make a clean breast of the whole affair to Letty. Then she could do as she pleased about their future intimacy. Seated in Letty's comfortable boudoir one afternoon, facing a vision of loveliness in pale yellow, he decided that he might as well have it out with her. She would understand. Just at this time he was beginning to doubt the outcome of the real estate deal, and consequently he was feeling a little blue, and, as a concomitant, a little confidential. He could not as yet talk to Jennie about his troubles.

"You know, Lester," said Letty, by way of helping him to his confession—the maid had brought tea for her and some brandy and soda for him, and departed—"that I have been hearing a lot of things about you since I've been back in this country. Aren't you going to tell me all about yourself? You know I have your real interests at heart."

"What have you been hearing, Letty?" he asked, quietly.

"Oh, about your father's will for one thing, and the fact that you're out of the company, and some gossip about Mrs. Kane which doesn't interest me very much. You know what I mean. Aren't you going to straighten things out, so that you can have what rightfully belongs to you? It seems to me such a great sacrifice, Lester, unless, of course, you are very much in love. Are you?" she asked archly.

Lester paused and deliberated before replying. "I really don't know how to answer that last question, Letty," he said. "Sometimes I think that I love her; sometimes I wonder whether I do or not. I'm going to be perfectly frank with you. I was never in such a curious position in my life before. You like me so much, and I—well, I don't say what I think of you," he smiled. "But anyhow, I can talk to you frankly. I'm not married."

"I thought as much," she said, as he paused.

"And I'm not married because I have never been able to make up my mind just what to do about it. When I first met Jennie I thought her the most entrancing girl I had ever laid eyes on."

"That speaks volumes for my charms at that time," interrupted his *vis-a-vis*.

"Don't interrupt me if you want to hear this," he smiled.

"Tell me one thing," she questioned, "and then I won't. Was that in Cleveland?"

"Yes."

"So I heard," she assented.

"There was something about her so—"

"Love at first sight," again interpolated Letty foolishly. Her heart was hurting her. "I know."

"Are you going to let me tell this?"

"Pardon me, Lester. I can't help a twinge or two."

"Well, anyhow, I lost my head. I thought she was the most perfect thing under the sun, even if she was a little out of my world. This is a democratic country. I thought that I could just take her, and then—well, you know. That is where I made my mistake. I didn't think that would prove as serious as it did. I never cared for any other woman but you before and—I'll be frank—I didn't know whether I wanted to marry you. I thought I didn't want to marry any woman. I said to myself that I could just take Jennie, and then, after a while, when things had quieted down some, we could separate. She would be well provided for. I wouldn't care very much. She wouldn't care. You understand."

"Yes, I understand," replied his confessor.

"Well, you see, Letty, it hasn't worked out that way. She's a woman of a curious temperament. She possesses a world of feeling and emotion. She's not educated in the sense in which we understand that word, but she has natural refinement and tact. She's a good housekeeper. She's an ideal mother. She's the most affectionate creature under the sun. Her devotion to her mother and father was beyond words. Her love for her daughter—she's hers, not mine—is perfect. She hasn't any of the graces of the smart society woman. She isn't quick at repartee. She can't join in any rapid-fire conversation. She thinks rather slowly, I imagine. Some of her big thoughts never come to the surface at all, but you can feel that she is thinking and that she is feeling."

"You pay her a lovely tribute, Lester," said Letty.

"I ought to," he replied. "She's a good woman, Letty; but, for all that I have said, I sometimes think that it's only sympathy that's holding me."

"Don't be too sure," she said warningly.

"Yes, but I've gone through with a great deal. The thing for me to have done was to have married her in the first place. There have been so many entanglements since, so much rowing and discussion, that I've rather lost my bearings. This will of father's complicates matters. I stand to lose eight hundred thousand if I marry her—really, a great deal more, now that the company has been organized into a trust. I might better say two millions. If I don't marry her, I lose everything outright in about two more years. Of course, I might pretend that I have separated from her, but I don't care to lie. I can't work it out that way without hurting her feelings, and she's been the soul of devotion. Right down in my heart, at this minute, I don't know whether I want to give her up. Honestly, I don't know what the devil to do."

Lester looked, lit a cigar in a far-off, speculative fashion, and looked out of the window.

"Was there ever such a problem?" questioned Letty, staring at the floor. She rose, after a few moments of silence, and put her hands on his round, solid head. Her yellow, silken house-gown, faintly scented, touched his shoulders. "Poor Lester," she said. "You certainly have tied yourself up in a knot. But it's a Gordian knot, my dear, and it will have to be cut. Why don't you discuss this whole thing with her, just as you have with me, and see how she feels about it?"

"It seems such an unkind thing to do," he replied.

"You must take some action, Lester dear," she insisted. "You can't just drift. You are doing yourself such a great injustice. Frankly, I can't advise you to marry her; and I'm not speaking for myself in that, though I'll take you gladly, even if you did forsake me in the first place. I'll be perfectly honest—whether you ever come to me or not—I love you, and always shall love you."

"I know it," said Lester, getting up. He took her hands in his, and studied her face curiously. Then he turned away. Letty paused to get her breath. His action discomposed her.

"But you're too big a man, Lester, to settle down on ten thousand a year," she continued. "You're too much of a social figure to drift. You ought to get back into the social and financial world where you belong. All that's happened won't injure you, if you reclaim your interest in the company. You can dictate your own terms. And if you tell her the truth she won't object, I'm sure. If she cares for you, as you think she does, she will be glad to make this sacrifice. I'm positive of that. You can provide for her handsomely, of course."

"It isn't the money that Jennie wants," said Lester, gloomily.

"Well, even if it isn't, she can live without you; and she can live better for having an ample income."

"She will never want if I can help it," he said solemnly.

"You must leave her," she urged, with a new touch of decisiveness. "You must. Every day is precious with you, Lester! Why don't you make up your mind to act at once—to-day, for that matter? Why not?"

"Not so fast," he protested. "This is a ticklish business. To tell you the truth, I hate to do it. It seems so brutal—so unfair. I'm not one to run around and discuss my affairs with other people. I've refused to talk about this to any one heretofore—my father, my mother, any one. But somehow you have always seemed closer to me than any one else, and, since I met you this time, I have felt as though I ought to explain—I have really wanted to. I care for you. I don't know whether you understand how that can be under the circumstances. But I do. You're nearer to me intellectually and emotionally than I thought you were. Don't frown. You want the truth, don't you? Well, there you have it. Now explain me to myself, if you can."

"I don't want to argue with you, Lester," she said softly, laying her hand on his arm. "I merely want to love you. I understand quite well how it has all come about. I'm sorry for myself. I'm sorry for you. I'm sorry—" she hesitated—"for Mrs. Kane. She's a charming woman. I like her. I really do. But she isn't the woman for you, Lester; she really isn't. You need another type. It seems so unfair for us two to discuss her in this way, but really it isn't. We all have to stand on our merits. And I'm satisfied, if the facts in this case were put before her, as you have put them before me, she would see just how it all is, and agree. She can't want to harm you. Why, Lester, if I were in her position I would let you go. I would, truly. I think you know that I would. Any good woman would. It would hurt me, but I'd do it. It will hurt her, but she'll do it. Now, mark you my words, she will. I think I understand her as well as you do—better—for I am a woman. Oh," she said, pausing, "I wish I were in a position to talk to her. I could make her understand."

Lester looked at Letty, wondering at her eagerness. She was beautiful, magnetic, immensely worth while.

"Not so fast," he repeated. "I want to think about this. I have some time yet."

She paused, a little crestfallen but determined.

"This is the time to act," she repeated, her whole soul in her eyes. She wanted this man, and she was not ashamed to let him see that she wanted him.

"Well, I'll think of it," he said uneasily, then, rather hastily, he bade her good-by and went away.

Chapter LI

LESTER HAD thought of his predicament earnestly enough, and he would have been satisfied to act soon if it had not been that one of those disrupting influences which sometimes complicate our affairs entered into his Hyde Park domicile. Gerhardt's health began rapidly to fail.

Little by little he had been obliged to give up his various duties about the place; finally he was obliged to take to his bed. He lay in his room, devotedly attended by Jennie and visited constantly by Vesta, and occasionally by Lester. There was a window not far from his bed, which commanded a charming view of the lawn and one of the surrounding streets, and through this he would gaze by the hour, wondering how the world was getting on without him. He suspected that Woods, the coachman, was not looking after the horses and harnesses as well as he should, that the newspaper carrier was getting negligent in his delivery of the papers, that the furnace man was wasting coal, or was not giving them enough heat. A score of little petty worries, which were nevertheless real enough to him. He knew how a house should be kept. He was always rigid in his performance of his self-appointed duties, and he was so afraid that things would not go right. Jennie made for him a most imposing and sumptuous dressing-gown of basted wool, covered with dark-blue silk, and bought him a pair of soft, thick, wool slippers to match, but he did not wear them often. He preferred to lie in bed, read his Bible and the Lutheran papers, and ask Jennie how things were getting along.

"I want you should go down in the basement and see what that feller is doing. He's not giving us any heat," he would complain. "I bet I know what he does. He sits down there and reads, and then he forgets what the fire is doing until it is almost out. The beer is right there where he can take it. You should lock it up. You don't know what kind of a man he is. He may be no good."

Jennie would protest that the house was fairly comfortable, that the man was a nice, quiet, respectable-looking

American—that if he did drink a little beer it would not matter. Gerhardt would immediately become incensed.

"That is always the way," he declared vigorously. "You have no sense of economy. You are always so ready to let things go if I am not there. He is a nice man! How do you know he is a nice man? Does he keep the fire up? No! Does he keep the walks clean? If you don't watch him he will be just like the others, no good. You should go around and see how things are for yourself."

"All right, papa," she would reply in a genial effort to soothe him, "I will. Please don't worry. I'll lock up the beer. Don't you want a cup of coffee now and some toast?"

"No," Gerhardt would sigh immediately, "my stomach it don't do right. I don't know how I am going to come out of this."

Dr. Makin, the leading physician of the vicinity, and a man of considerable experience and ability, called at Jennie's request and suggested a few simple things—hot milk, a wine tonic, rest, but he told Jennie that she must not expect too much. "You know he is quite well along in years now. He is quite feeble. If he were twenty years younger we might do a great deal for him. As it is he is quite well off where he is. He may live for some time. He may get up and be around again, and then he may not. We must all expect these things. I have never any care as to what may happen to me. I am too old myself."

Jennie felt sorry to think that her father might die, but she was pleased to think that if he must it was going to be under such comfortable circumstances. Here at least he could have every care.

It soon became evident that this was Gerhardt's last illness, and Jennie thought it her duty to communicate with her brothers and sisters. She wrote Bass that his father was not well, and had a letter from him saying that he was very busy and couldn't come on unless the danger was an immediate one. He went on to say that George was in Rochester, working for a wholesale wall-paper house—the Sheff-Jefferson Company, he thought. Martha and her husband had gone to Boston. Her address was a little suburb named Belmont, just outside the city. William was in Omaha, working for a local electric company. Veronica was married to a man named Albert Sheridan, who was connected with a wholesale drug company in Cleveland. "She never comes to see me," complained Bass, "but I'll let her know." Jennie wrote each one personally. From Veronica and Martha she received brief replies. They were very sorry, and would she let them know if anything happened. George wrote that he could not think of coming to Chicago unless his father was very ill indeed, but that he would like to be informed from time to time how he was getting along. William, as he told Jennie some time afterward, did not get her letter.

The progress of the old German's malady toward final dissolution preyed greatly on Jennie's mind; for, in spite of the fact that they had been so far apart in times past, they had now grown very close together. Gerhardt had come to realize clearly that his outcast daughter was goodness itself—at least, so far as he was concerned. She never quarreled with him, never crossed him in any way. Now that he was sick, she was in and out of his room a dozen times in an evening or an afternoon, seeing whether he was "all right," asking how he liked his breakfast, or his lunch, or his dinner. As he grew weaker she would sit by him and read, or do her sewing in his room. One day when she was straightening his pillow he took her hand and kissed it. He was feeling very weak and despondent. She looked up in astonishment, a lump in her throat. There were tears in his eyes.

"You're a good girl, Jennie," he said brokenly. "You've been good to me. I've been hard and cross, but I'm an old man. You forgive me, don't you?"

"Oh, papa, please don't," she pleaded, tears welling from her eyes. "You know I have nothing to forgive. I'm the one who has been all wrong."

"No, no," he said; and she sank down on her knees beside him and cried. He put his thin, yellow hand on her hair. "There, there," he said brokenly, "I understand a lot of things I didn't. We get wiser as we get older."

She left the room, ostensibly to wash her face and hands, and cried her eyes out. Was he really forgiving her at last? And she had lied to him so! She tried to be more attentive, but that was impossible. But after this reconciliation he

seemed happier and more contented, and they spent a number of happy hours together, just talking. Once he said to her,
"You know I feel just like I did when I was a boy. If it wasn't
for my bones I could get up and dance on the grass."

Jennie fairly smiled and sobbed in one breath. "You'll get
stronger, papa," she said. "You're going to get well. Then I'll
take you out driving." She was so glad she had been able to
make him comfortable these last few years.

As for Lester, he was affectionate and considerate.

"Well, how is it to-night?" he would ask the moment he
entered the house, and he would always drop in for a few
minutes before dinner to see how the old man was getting
along. "He looks pretty well," he would tell Jennie. "He's apt
to live some time yet. I wouldn't worry."

Vesta also spent much time with her grandfather, for she
had come to love him dearly. She would bring her books, if
it didn't disturb him too much, and recite some of her lessons, or she would leave his door open, and play for him on
the piano. Lester had bought her a handsome music-box also,
which she would sometimes carry to his room and play for
him. At times he wearied of everything and everybody save
Jennie; he wanted to be alone with her. She would sit beside
him quite still and sew. She could see plainly that the end was
only a little way off.

Gerhardt, true to his nature, took into consideration all the
various arrangements contingent upon his death. He wished
to be buried in the little Lutheran cemetery, which was several miles farther out on the South Side, and he wanted the
beloved minister of his church to officiate.

"I want everything plain," he said. "Just my black suit and
those Sunday shoes of mine, and that black string tie. I don't
want anything else. I will be all right."

Jennie begged him not to talk of it, but he would. One day
at four o'clock he had a sudden sinking spell, and at five he was
dead. Jennie held his hands, watching his labored breathing;
once or twice he opened his eyes to smile at her. "I don't mind
going," he said, in this final hour. "I've done what I could."

"Don't talk of dying, papa," she pleaded.

"It's the end," he said. "You've been good to me. You're a
good woman."

She heard no other words from his lips.

The finish which time thus put to this troubled life affected Jennie deeply. Strong in her kindly, emotional relationships, Gerhardt had appealed to her not only as her father, but as a friend and counselor. She saw him now in his true perspective, a hard-working, honest, sincere old German, who had done his best to raise a troublesome family and lead an honest life. Truly she had been his one great burden, and she had never really dealt truthfully with him to the end. She wondered now if where he was he could see that she had lied. And would he forgive her? He had called her a good woman.

Telegrams were sent to all the children. Bass wired that he was coming, and arrived the next day. The others wired that they could not come, but asked for details, which Jennie wrote. The Lutheran minister was called in to say prayers and fix the time of the burial service. A fat, smug undertaker was commissioned to arrange all the details. Some few neighborhood friends called—those who had remained most faithful—and on the second morning following his death the services were held. Lester accompanied Jennie and Vesta and Bass to the little red brick Lutheran church, and sat stolidly through the rather dry services. He listened wearily to the long discourse on the beauties and rewards of a future life and stirred irritably when reference was made to a hell. Bass was rather bored, but considerate. He looked upon his father now much as he would on any other man. Only Jennie wept sympathetically. She saw her father in perspective, the long years of trouble he had had, the days in which he had had to saw wood for a living, the days in which he had lived in a factory loft, the little shabby house they had been compelled to live in in Thirteenth Street, the terrible days of suffering they had spent in Lorrie Street, in Cleveland, his grief over her, his grief over Mrs. Gerhardt, his love and care of Vesta, and finally these last days.

"Oh, he was a good man," she thought. "He meant so well." They sang a hymn, "A Mighty Fortress Is Our God," and then she sobbed.

Lester pulled at her arm. He was moved to the danger-line himself by her grief. "You'll have to do better than this," he whispered. "My God, I can't stand it. I'll have to get up and get out." Jennie quieted a little, but the fact that the last visible ties were being broken between her and her father was almost too much.

At the grave in the Cemetery of the Redeemer, where Lester had immediately arranged to purchase a lot, they saw the plain coffin lowered and the earth shoveled in. Lester looked curiously at the bare trees, the brown dead grass, and the brown soil of the prairie turned up at this simple graveside. There was no distinction to this burial plot. It was commonplace and shabby, a workingman's resting-place, but so long as he wanted it, it was all right. He studied Bass's keen, lean face, wondering what sort of a career he was cutting out for himself. Bass looked to him like some one who would run a cigar store successfully. He watched Jennie wiping her red eyes, and then he said to himself again, "Well, there is something to her." The woman's emotion was so deep, so real. "There's no explaining a good woman," he said to himself.

On the way home, through the wind-swept, dusty streets, he talked of life in general, Bass and Vesta being present. "Jennie takes things too seriously," he said. "She's inclined to be morbid. Life isn't as bad as she makes out with her sensitive feelings. We all have our troubles, and we all have to stand them, some more, some less. We can't assume that any one is so much better or worse off than any one else. We all have our share of troubles."

"I can't help it," said Jennie. "I feel so sorry for some people."

"Jennie always was a little gloomy," put in Bass. He was thinking what a fine figure of a man Lester was, how beautifully they lived, how Jennie had come up in the world. He was thinking that there must be a lot more to her than he had originally thought. Life surely did turn out queer. At one time he thought Jennie was a hopeless failure and no good.

"You ought to try to steel yourself to take things as they come without going to pieces this way," said Lester finally.

Bass thought so too.

Jennie stared thoughtfully out of the carriage window. There was the old house now, large and silent without Gerhardt. Just think, she would never see him any more. They finally turned into the drive and entered the library. Jeannette, nervous and sympathetic, served tea. Jennie went to look after various details. She wondered curiously where she would be when she died.

Chapter LII

THE FACT that Gerhardt was dead made no particular difference to Lester, except as it affected Jennie. He had liked the old German for his many sterling qualities, but beyond that he thought nothing of him one way or the other. He took Jennie to a watering-place for ten days to help her recover her spirits, and it was soon after this that he decided to tell her just how things stood with him; he would put the problem plainly before her. It would be easier now, for Jennie had been informed of the disastrous prospects of the real-estate deal. She was also aware of his continued interest in Mrs. Gerald. Lester did not hesitate to let Jennie know that he was on very friendly terms with her. Mrs. Gerald had, at first, formally requested him to bring Jennie to see her, but she never had called herself, and Jennie understood quite clearly that it was not to be. Now that her father was dead, she was beginning to wonder what was going to become of her; she was afraid that Lester might not marry her. Certainly he showed no signs of intending to do so.

By one of those curious coincidences of thought, Robert also had reached the conclusion that something should be done. He did not, for one moment, imagine that he could directly work upon Lester—he did not care to try—but he did think that some influence might be brought to bear on Jennie. She was probably amenable to reason. If Lester had not married her already, she must realize full well that he did not intend to do so. Suppose that some responsible third person were to approach her, and explain how things were, including, of course, the offer of an independent income? Might she not be willing to leave Lester, and end all this trouble? After all, Lester was his brother, and he ought not to lose his fortune. Robert had things very much in his own hands now, and could afford to be generous. He finally decided that Mr. O'Brien, of Knight, Keatley & O'Brien, would be the proper intermediary, for O'Brien was suave, good-natured, and well-meaning, even if he was a lawyer. He might explain to Jennie very delicately just how the family felt, and how much Lester stood to lose if he continued to maintain his connection with her. If Lester had married Jennie, O'Brien would find it out. A liberal provision would be made for her—say fifty or one hundred thousand, or even one hundred and fifty thousand dollars. He sent for Mr. O'Brien and gave him his instructions. As one of the executors of Archibald Kane's estate, it was really the lawyer's duty to look into the matter of Lester's ultimate decision.

Mr. O'Brien journeyed to Chicago. On reaching the city, he called up Lester, and found out to his satisfaction that he was out of town for the day. He went out to the house in Hyde Park, and sent in his card to Jennie. She came downstairs in a few minutes quite unconscious of the import of his message; he greeted her most blandly.

"This is Mrs. Kane?" he asked, with an interlocutory jerk of his head.

"Yes," replied Jennie.

"I am, as you see by my card, Mr. O'Brien, of Knight, Keatley & O'Brien," he began. "We are the attorneys and executors of the late Mr. Kane, your—ah—Mr. Kane's father. You'll think it's rather curious, my coming to you, but under your husband's father's will there were certain conditions stipulated which affect you and Mr. Kane very materially. These provisions are so important that I think you ought to know about them—that is if Mr. Kane hasn't already told you. I—pardon me—but the peculiar nature of them makes me conclude that—possibly—he hasn't." He paused, a very question-mark of a man—every feature of his face an interrogation.

"I don't quite understand," said Jennie. "I don't know anything about the will. If there's anything that I ought to know, I suppose Mr. Kane will tell me. He hasn't told me anything as yet."

"Ah!" breathed Mr. O'Brien, highly gratified. "Just as I thought. Now, if you will allow me I'll go into the matter briefly. Then you can judge for yourself whether you wish to hear the full particulars. Won't you sit down?" They had both been standing. Jennie seated herself, and Mr. O'Brien pulled up a chair near to hers.

"Now to begin," he said. "I need not say to you, of course, that there was considerable opposition on the part of

Mr. Kane's father, to this—ah—union between yourself and his son."

"I know—" Jennie started to say, but checked herself. She was puzzled, disturbed, and a little apprehensive.

"Before Mr. Kane senior died," he went on, "he indicated to your—ah—to Mr. Lester Kane, that he felt this way. In his will he made certain conditions governing the distribution of his property which made it rather hard for his son, your—ah—husband, to come into his rightful share. Ordinarily, he would have inherited one-fourth of the Kane Manufacturing Company, worth to-day in the neighborhood of a million dollars, perhaps more; also one-fourth of the other properties, which now aggregate something like five hundred thousand dollars. I believe Mr. Kane senior was really very anxious that his son should inherit this property. But owing to the conditions which your—ah—which Mr. Kane's father made, Mr. Lester Kane cannot possibly obtain his share, except by complying with a—with a—certain wish which his father had expressed."

Mr. O'Brien paused, his eyes moving back and forth sidewise in their sockets. In spite of the natural prejudice of the situation, he was considerably impressed with Jennie's pleasing appearance. He could see quite plainly why Lester might cling to her in the face of all opposition. He continued to study her furtively as he sat there waiting for her to speak.

"And what was that wish?" she finally asked, her nerves becoming just a little tense under the strain of the silence.

"I am glad you were kind enough to ask me that," he went on. "The subject is a very difficult one for me to introduce—very difficult. I come as an emissary of the estate, I might say as one of the executors under the will of Mr. Kane's father. I know how keenly your—ah—how keenly Mr. Kane feels about it. I know how keenly you will probably feel about it. But it is one of those very difficult things which cannot be helped—which must be got over somehow. And while I hesitate very much to say so, I must tell you that Mr. Kane senior stipulated in his will that unless, unless"—again his eyes were moving sidewise to and fro—"he saw fit to separate from—ah—you"—he paused to get breath—"he could not inherit this or any other sum—or, at least, only a very minor income of ten thousand a year; and that only on condition that he should marry you." He paused again. "I should add," he went on, "that under the will he was given three years in which to indicate his intentions. That time is now drawing to a close."

He paused, half expecting some outburst of feeling from Jennie, but she only looked at him fixedly, her eyes clouded with surprise, distress, unhappiness. Now she understood. Lester was sacrificing his fortune for her. His recent commercial venture was an effort to rehabilitate himself, to put himself in an independent position. The recent periods of preoccupation, of subtle unrest, and of dissatisfaction over which she had grieved were now explained. He was unhappy, he was brooding over this prospective loss, and he had never told her. So his father had really disinherited him!

Mr. O'Brien sat before her, troubled himself. He was very sorry for her, now that he saw the expression of her face. Still the truth had to come out. She ought to know.

"I'm sorry," he said, when he saw that she was not going to make any immediate reply, "that I have been the bearer of such unfortunate news. It is a very painful situation that I find myself in at this moment, I assure you. I bear you no ill will personally—of course you understand that. The family really bears you no ill will now—I hope you believe that. As I told your—ah—as I told Mr. Kane, at the time the will was read, I considered it most unfair, but, of course, as a mere executive under it and counsel for his father, I could do nothing. I really think it best that you should know how things stand, in order that you may help your—your husband"—he paused, significantly—"if possible, to some solution. It seems a pity to me, as it does to the various other members of his family, that he should lose all this money."

Jennie had turned her head away and was staring at the floor. She faced him now steadily. "He mustn't lose it," she said; "it isn't fair that he should."

"I am most delighted to hear you say that, Mrs.—Mrs. Kane," he went on, using for the first time her improbable title as Lester's wife, without hesitation. "I may as well be very frank with you, and say that I feared you might take this information in quite another spirit. Of course you know to begin with that the Kane family is very clannish. Mrs. Kane, your—ah—your husband's mother, was a very proud and rather distant woman, and his sisters and brothers are rather set in their notions as to what constitute proper family connections. They look upon his relationship to you as irregular, and—pardon me if I appear to be a little cruel—as not generally satisfactory. As you know, there had been so much talk in the last few years that Mr. Kane senior did not believe that the situation could ever be nicely adjusted, so far as the family was concerned. He felt that his son had not gone about it right in the first place. One of the conditions of his will was that if your husband—pardon me—if his son did not accept the proposition in regard to separating from you and taking up his rightful share of the estate, then to inherit anything at all—the mere ten thousand a year I mentioned before—he must—ah—he must—pardon me, I seem a little brutal, but not intentionally so—marry you."

Jennie winced. It was such a cruel thing to say this to her face. This whole attempt to live together illegally had proved disastrous at every step. There was only one solution to the unfortunate business—she could see that plainly. She must leave him, or he must leave her. There was no other alternative. Lester living on ten thousand dollars a year! It seemed silly.

Mr. O'Brien was watching her curiously. He was thinking that Lester both had and had not made a mistake. Why had he not married her in the first place? She was charming.

"There is just one other point which I wish to make in this connection, Mrs. Kane," he went on softly and easily. "I see now that it will not make any difference to you, but I am commissioned and in a way constrained to make it. I hope you will take it in the manner in which it is given. I don't know whether you are familiar with your husband's commercial interests or not?"

"No," said Jennie simply.

"Well, in order to simplify matters, and to make it easier for you, should you decide to assist your husband to a solution of this very difficult situation—frankly, in case you might possibly decide to leave on your own account, and maintain a separate establishment of your own—I am delighted to say that—ah—any sum, say—ah—"

Jennie rose and walked dazedly to one of the windows, clasping her hands as she went. Mr. O'Brien rose also.

"Well, be that as it may. In the event of your deciding to end the connection it has been suggested that any reasonable sum you might name, fifty, seventy-five, a hundred thousand dollars"—Mr. O'Brien was feeling very generous toward her—"would be gladly set aside for your benefit—put in trust, as it were, so that you would have it whenever you needed it. You would never want for anything."

"Please don't," said Jennie, hurt beyond the power to express herself, unable mentally and physically to listen to another word. "Please don't say any more. Please go away. Let me alone now, please. I can go away. I will. It will be arranged. But please don't talk to me any more, will you?"

"I understand how you feel, Mrs. Kane," went on Mr. O'Brien, coming to a keen realization of her sufferings. "I know exactly, believe me. I have said all I intend to say. It has been very hard for me to do this—very hard. I regret the necessity. You have my card. Please note the name. I will come any time you suggest, or you can write me. I will not detain you any longer. I am sorry. I hope you will see fit to say nothing to your husband of my visit—it will be advisable that you should keep your own counsel in the matter. I value his friendship very highly, and I am sincerely sorry."

Jennie only stared at the floor.

Mr. O'Brien went out into the hall to get his coat. Jennie touched the electric button to summon the maid, and Jeannette came. Jennie went back into the library, and Mr. O'Brien paced briskly down the front walk. When she was really alone she put her doubled hands to her chin, and stared at the floor, the queer design of the silken Turkish rug resolving itself into some curious picture. She saw herself in a small cottage somewhere, alone with Vesta; she saw Lester living in another world, and beside him Mrs. Gerald. She saw this house vacant, and then a long stretch of time, and then—

"Oh," she sighed, choking back a desire to cry. With her hands she brushed away a hot tear from each eye. Then she got up.

"It must be," she said to herself in thought. "It must be. It should have been so long ago." And then—"Oh, thank God that papa is dead! Anyhow, he did not live to see this."

Chapter LIII

THE EXPLANATION which Lester had concluded to be inevitable, whether it led to separation or legalization of
their hitherto banal condition, followed quickly upon the appearance of Mr. O'Brien. On the day Mr. O'Brien called he
had gone on a journey to Hegewisch, a small manufacturing
town in Wisconsin, where he had been invited to witness the
trial of a new motor intended to operate elevators—with a
view to possible investment. When he came out to the house,
interested to tell Jennie something about it even in spite of
the fact that he was thinking of leaving her, he felt a sense of
depression everywhere, for Jennie, in spite of the serious and
sensible conclusion she had reached, was not one who could
conceal her feelings easily. She was brooding sadly over her
proposed action, realizing that it was best to leave but finding
it hard to summon the courage which would let her talk to
him about it. She could not go without telling him what she
thought. He ought to want to leave her. She was absolutely
convinced that this one course of action—separation—was
necessary and advisable. She could not think of him as daring
to make a sacrifice of such proportions for her sake even if he
wanted to. It was impossible. It was astonishing to her that
he had let things go along as dangerously and silently as
he had.

When he came in Jennie did her best to greet him with her
accustomed smile, but it was a pretty poor imitation.

"Everything all right?" she asked, using her customary
phrase of inquiry.

"Quite," he answered. "How are things with you?"

"Oh, just the same." She walked with him to the library,
and he poked at the open fire with a long-handled poker
before turning around to survey the room generally. It was
five o'clock of a January afternoon. Jennie had gone to one
of the windows to lower the shade. As she came back he
looked at her critically. "You're not quite your usual self, are
you?" he asked, sensing something out of the common in her
attitude.

"Why, yes, I feel all right," she replied, but there was a

peculiar uneven motion to the movement of her lips—a rippling tremor which was unmistakable to him.

"I think I know better than that," he said, still gazing at her steadily. "What's the trouble? Anything happened?"

She turned away from him a moment to get her breath and collect her senses. Then she faced him again. "There is something," she managed to say. "I have to tell you something."

"I know you have," he agreed, half smiling, but with a feeling that there was much of grave import back of this.

"What is it?"

She was silent for a moment, biting her lips. She did not quite know how to begin. Finally she broke the spell with: "There was a man here yesterday—a Mr. O'Brien, of Cincinnati. Do you know him?"

"Yes, I know him. What did he want?"

"He came to talk to me about you and your father's will."

She paused, for his face clouded immediately. "Why the devil should he be talking to you about my father's will!" he exclaimed. "What did he have to say?"

"Please don't get angry, Lester," said Jennie calmly, for she realized that she must remain absolute mistress of herself if anything were to be accomplished toward the resolution of her problem. "He wanted to tell me what a sacrifice you are making," she went on. "He wished to show me that there was only a little time left before you would lose your inheritance. Don't you want to act pretty soon? Don't you want to leave me?"

"Damn him!" said Lester fiercely. "What the devil does he mean by putting his nose in my private affairs? Can't they let me alone?" He shook himself angrily. "Damn them!" he exclaimed again. "This is some of Robert's work. Why should Knight, Keatley & O'Brien be meddling in my affairs? This whole business is getting to be a nuisance!" He was in a boiling rage in a moment, as was shown by his darkening skin and sulphurous eyes.

Jennie trembled before his anger. She did not know what to say.

He came to himself sufficiently after a time to add:

"Well. Just what did he tell you?"

"He said that if you married me you would only get ten

thousand a year. That if you didn't and still lived with me you would get nothing at all. If you would leave me, or I would leave you, you would get all of a million and a half. Don't you think you had better leave me now?"

She had not intended to propound this leading question so quickly, but it came out as a natural climax to the situation. She realized instantly that if he were really in love with her he would answer with an emphatic "no." If he didn't care, he would hesitate, he would delay, he would seek to put off the evil day of reckoning.

"I don't see that," he retorted irritably. "I don't see that there's any need for either interference or hasty action. What I object to is their coming here and mixing in my private affairs."

Jennie was cut to the quick by his indifference, his wrath instead of affection. To her the main point at issue was her leaving him or his leaving her. To him this recent interference was obviously the chief matter for discussion and consideration. The meddling of others before he was ready to act was the terrible thing. She had hoped, in spite of what she had seen, that possibly, because of the long time they had lived together and the things which (in a way) they had endured together, he might have come to care for her deeply—that she had stirred some emotion in him which would never brook real separation, though some seeming separation might be necessary. He had not married her, of course, but then there had been so many things against them. Now, in this final hour, anyhow, he might have shown that he cared deeply, even if he had deemed it necessary to let her go. She felt for the time being as if, for all that she had lived with him so long, she did not understand him, and yet, in spite of this feeling, she knew also that she did. He cared, in his way. He could not care for any one enthusiastically and demonstratively. He could care enough to seize her and take her to himself as he had, but he could not care enough to keep her if something more important appeared. He was debating her fate now. She was in a quandary, hurt, bleeding, but for once in her life, determined. Whether he wanted to or not, she must not let him make this sacrifice. She must leave him—if he would not leave her. It was not important enough that she should stay. There might be but one answer. But might he not show affection?

"Don't you think you had better act soon?" she continued, hoping that some word of feeling would come from him. "There is only a little time left, isn't there?"

Jennie nervously pushed a book to and fro on the table, her fear that she would not be able to keep up appearances troubling her greatly. It was hard for her to know what to do or say. Lester was so terrible when he became angry. Still it ought not to be so hard for him to go, now that he had Mrs. Gerald, if he only wished to do so—and he ought to. His fortune was so much more important to him than anything she could be.

"Don't worry about that," he replied stubbornly, his wrath at his brother, and his family, and O'Brien still holding him. "There's time enough. I don't know what I want to do yet. I like the effrontery of these people! But I won't talk any more about it; isn't dinner nearly ready?" He was so injured in his pride that he scarcely took the trouble to be civil. He was forgetting all about her and what she was feeling. He hated his brother Robert for this affront. He would have enjoyed wringing the necks of Messrs. Knight, Keatley & O'Brien, singly and collectively.

The question could not be dropped for good and all, and it came up again at dinner, after Jennie had done her best to collect her thoughts and quiet her nerves. They could not talk very freely because of Vesta and Jeannette, but she managed to get in a word or two.

"I could take a little cottage somewhere," she suggested softly, hoping to find him in a modified mood. "I would not want to stay here. I would not know what to do with a big house like this alone."

"I wish you wouldn't discuss this business any longer, Jennie," he persisted. "I'm in no mood for it. I don't know that I'm going to do anything of the sort. I don't know what I'm going to do." He was so sour and obstinate, because of O'Brien, that she finally gave it up. Vesta was astonished to see her stepfather, usually so courteous, in so grim a mood.

Jennie felt a curious sense that she might hold him if she

would, for he was doubting; but she knew also that she should not wish. It was not fair to him. It was not fair to herself, or kind, or decent.

"Oh yes, Lester, you must," she pleaded, at a later time. "I won't talk about it any more, but you must. I won't let you do anything else."

There were hours when it came up afterward—every day, in fact—in their boudoir, in the library, in the dining-room, at breakfast, but not always in words. Jennie was worried. She was looking the worry she felt. She was sure that he should be made to act. Since he was showing more kindly consideration for her, she was all the more certain that he should act soon. Just how to go about it she did not know, but she looked at him longingly, trying to help him make up his mind. She would be happy, she assured herself—she would be happy thinking that he was happy once she was away from him. He was a good man, most delightful in everything, perhaps, save his gift of love. He really did not love her—could not perhaps, after all that had happened, even though she loved him most earnestly. But his family had been most brutal in their opposition, and this had affected his attitude. She could understand that, too. She could see now how his big, strong brain might be working in a circle. He was too decent to be absolutely brutal about this thing and leave her, too really considerate to look sharply after his own interests as he should, or hers—but he ought to.

"You must decide, Lester," she kept saying to him, from time to time. "You must let me go. What difference does it make? I will be all right. Maybe, when this thing is all over you might want to come back to me. If you do, I will be there."

"I'm not ready to come to a decision," was his invariable reply. "I don't know that I want to leave you. This money is important, of course, but money isn't everything. I can live on ten thousand a year if necessary. I've done it in the past."

"Oh, but you're so much more placed in the world now, Lester," she argued. "You can't do it. Look how much it costs to run this house alone. And a million and a half of dollars—why, I wouldn't let you think of losing that. I'll go myself first."

"Where would you think of going if it came to that?" he asked curiously.

"Oh, I'd find some place. Do you remember that little town of Sandwood, this side of Kenosha? I have often thought it would be a pleasant place to live."

"I don't like to think of this," he said finally in an outburst of frankness. "It doesn't seem fair. The conditions have all been against this union of ours. I suppose I should have married you in the first place. I'm sorry now that I didn't."

Jennie choked in her throat, but said nothing.

"Anyhow, this won't be the last of it, if I can help it," he concluded. He was thinking that the storm might blow over; once he had the money, and then—but he hated compromises and subterfuges.

It came by degrees to be understood that, toward the end of February, she should look around at Sandwood and see what she could find. She was to have ample means, he told her, everything that she wanted. After a time he might come out and visit her occasionally. And he was determined in his heart that he would make some people pay for the trouble they had caused him. He decided to send for Mr. O'Brien shortly and talk things over. He wanted for his personal satisfaction to tell him what he thought of him.

At the same time, in the background of his mind, moved the shadowy figure of Mrs. Gerald—charming, sophisticated, well placed in every sense of the word. He did not want to give her the broad reality of full thought, but she was always there. He thought and thought. "Perhaps I'd better," he half concluded. When February came he was ready to act.

Chapter LIV

THE LITTLE TOWN of Sandwood, "this side of Kenosha," as Jennie had expressed it, was only a short distance from Chicago, an hour and fifteen minutes by the local train. It had a population of some three hundred families, dwelling in small cottages, which were scattered over a pleasant area of lake-shore property. They were not rich people. The houses were not worth more than from three to five thousand dollars each, but, in most cases, they were harmoniously constructed, and the surrounding trees, green for the entire year, gave them a pleasing summery appearance. Jennie, at the time they had passed by there—it was an outing taken behind a pair of fast horses—had admired the look of a little white church steeple, set down among green trees, and the gentle rocking of the boats upon the summer water.

"I should like to live in a place like this some time," she had said to Lester, and he had made the comment that it was a little too peaceful for him. "I can imagine getting to the place where I might like this, but not now. It's too withdrawn."

Jennie thought of that expression afterward. It came to her when she thought that the world was trying. If she had to be alone ever and could afford it she would like to live in a place like Sandwood. There she would have a little garden, some chickens, perhaps, a tall pole with a pretty bird-house on it, and flowers and trees and green grass everywhere about. If she could have a little cottage in a place like this which commanded a view of the lake she could sit of a summer evening and sew. Vesta could play about or come home from school. She might have a few friends, or not any. She was beginning to think that she could do very well living alone if it were not for Vesta's social needs. Books were pleasant things—she was finding that out—books like Irving's *Sketch Book*, Lamb's *Elia*, and Hawthorne's *Twice Told Tales*. Vesta was coming to be quite a musician in her way, having a keen sense of the delicate and refined in musical composition. She had a natural sense of harmony and a love for those songs and instrumental compositions which reflect sentimental and passionate moods,

and she could sing and play quite well. Her voice was, of
course, quite untrained—she was only fourteen—but it was
pleasant to listen to. She was beginning to show the combined traits of her mother and father—Jennie's gentle, speculative turn of mind, combined with Brander's vivacity of
spirit and innate executive capacity. She could talk to her
mother in a sensible way about things, nature, books, dress,
love, and from her developing tendencies Jennie caught keen
glimpses of the new worlds which Vesta was to explore. The
nature of modern school life, its consideration of various
divisions of knowledge, music, science, all came to Jennie
watching her daughter take up new themes. Vesta was evidently going to be a woman of considerable ability—not irritably aggressive, but self-constructive. She would be able to
take care of herself. All this pleased Jennie and gave her great
hopes for Vesta's future.

The cottage which was finally secured at Sandwood was
only a story and a half in height, but it was raised upon red
brick piers between which were set green lattices and about
which ran a veranda. The house was long and narrow, its full
length—some five rooms in a row—facing the lake. There
was a dining-room with windows opening even with the
floor, a large library with built-in shelves for books, and a
parlor whose three large windows afforded air and sunshine
at all times. The plot of ground in which this cottage stood
was one hundred feet square and ornamented with a few
trees. The former owner had laid out flower-beds, and arranged green hardwood tubs for the reception of various
hardy plants and vines. The house was painted white, with
green shutters and green shingles.

It had been Lester's idea, since this thing must be, that
Jennie might keep the house in Hyde Park just as it was, but
she did not want to do that. She could not think of living
there alone. The place was too full of memories. At first, she
did not think she would take anything much with her, but
she finally saw that it was advisable to do as Lester suggested—to fit out the new place with a selection of silverware, hangings, and furniture from the Hyde Park house.

"You have no idea what you will or may want," he said.
"Take everything. I certainly don't want any of it."

A lease of the cottage was taken for two years, together with an option for an additional five years, including the privilege of purchase. So long as he was letting her go, Lester wanted to be generous. He could not think of her as wanting for anything, and he did not propose that she should. His one troublesome thought was, what explanation was to be made to Vesta. He liked her very much and wanted her life kept free of complications.

"Why not send her off to a boarding-school until spring?" he suggested once; but owing to the lateness of the season this was abandoned as inadvisable. Later they agreed that business affairs made it necessary for him to travel and for Jennie to move. Later Vesta could be told that Jennie had left him for any reason she chose to give. It was a trying situation, all the more bitter to Jennie because she realized that in spite of the wisdom of it indifference to her was involved. He really did not care *enough*, as much as he cared.

The relationship of man and woman which we study so passionately in the hope of finding heaven knows what key to the mystery of existence holds no more difficult or trying situation than this of mutual compatibility broken or disrupted by untoward conditions which in themselves have so little to do with the real force and beauty of the relationship itself. These days of final dissolution in which this household, so charmingly arranged, the scene of so many pleasant activities, was literally going to pieces was a period of great trial to both Jennie and Lester. On her part it was one of intense suffering, for she was of that stable nature that rejoices to fix itself in a serviceable and harmonious relationship, and then stay so. For her life was made up of those mystic chords of sympathy and memory which bind up the transient elements of nature into a harmonious and enduring scene. One of those chords—this home was her home, united and made beautiful by her affection and consideration for each person and every object. Now the time had come when it must cease.

If she had ever had anything before in her life which had been like this it might have been easier to part with it now, though, as she had proved, Jennie's affections were not based in any way upon material considerations. Her love of life and of personality were free from the taint of selfishness. She went

about among these various rooms selecting this rug, that set
of furniture, this and that ornament, wishing all the time with
all her heart and soul that it need not be. Just to think, in a
little while Lester would not come any more of an evening!
She would not need to get up first of a morning and see that
coffee was made for her lord, that the table in the dining-
room looked just so. It had been a habit of hers to arrange a
bouquet for the table out of the richest blooming flowers of
the conservatory, and she had always felt in doing it that it
was particularly for him. Now it would not be necessary any
more—not for him. When one is accustomed to wait for the
sound of a certain carriage-wheel of an evening grating upon
your carriage drive, when one is used to listen at eleven,
twelve, and one, waking naturally and joyfully to the echo of
a certain step on the stair, the separation, the ending of these
things, is keen with pain. These were the thoughts that were
running through Jennie's brain hour after hour and day after
day.

Lester on his part was suffering in another fashion. His was
not the sorrow of lacerated affection, of discarded and despised love, but of that painful sense of unfairness which
comes to one who knows that he is making a sacrifice of the
virtues—kindness, loyalty, affection—to policy. Policy was
dictating a very splendid course of action from one point of
view. Free of Jennie, providing for her admirably, he was free
to go his way, taking to himself the mass of affairs which
come naturally with great wealth. He could not help thinking
of the thousand and one little things which Jennie had been
accustomed to do for him, the hundred and one comfortable
and pleasant and delightful things she meant to him. The virtues which she possessed were quite dear to his mind. He had
gone over them time and again. Now he was compelled to go
over them finally, to see that she was suffering without making a sign. Her manner and attitude toward him in these last
days were quite the same as they had always been—no more,
no less. She was not indulging in private hysterics, as another
woman might have done; she was not pretending a fortitude
in suffering she did not feel, showing him one face while
wishing him to see another behind it. She was calm, gentle,
considerate—thoughtful of him—where he would go and

what he would do, without irritating him by her inquiries. He was struck quite favorably by her ability to take a large situation largely, and he admired her. There was something to this woman, let the world think what it might. It was a shame that her life was passed under such a troubled star. Still a great world was calling him. The sound of its voice was in his ears. It had on occasion shown him its bared teeth. Did he really dare to hesitate?

The last hour came, when having made excuses to this and that neighbor, when having spread the information that they were going abroad, when Lester had engaged rooms at the Auditorium, and the mass of furniture which could not be used had gone to storage, that it was necessary to say farewell to this Hyde Park domicile. Jennie had visited Sandwood in company with Lester several times. He had carefully examined the character of the place. He was satisfied that it was nice but lonely. Spring was at hand, the flowers would be something. She was going to keep a gardener and man of all work. Vesta would be with her.

"Very well," he said, "only I want you to be comfortable."

In the mean time Lester had been arranging his personal affairs. He had notified Messrs. Knight, Keatley & O'Brien through his own attorney, Mr. Watson, that he would expect them to deliver his share of his father's securities on a given date. He had made up his mind that as long as he was compelled by circumstances to do this thing he would do a number of other things equally ruthless. He would probably marry Mrs. Gerald. He would sit as a director in the United Carriage Company—with his share of the stock it would be impossible to keep him out. If he had Mrs. Gerald's money he would become a controlling factor in the United Traction of Cincinnati, in which his brother was heavily interested, and in the Western Steel Works, of which his brother was now the leading adviser. What a different figure he would be now from that which he had been during the past few years!

Jennie was depressed to the point of despair. She was tremendously lonely. This home had meant so much to her. When she first came here and neighbors had begun to drop in she had imagined herself on the threshold of a great career, that some day, possibly, Lester would marry her. Now, blow after blow had been delivered, and the home and dream were a ruin. Gerhardt was gone. Jeannette, Harry Ward, and Mrs. Frissell had been discharged, the furniture for a good part was in storage, and for her, practically, Lester was no more. She realized clearly that he would not come back. If he could do this thing now, even considerately, he could do much more when he was free and away later. Immersed in his great affairs, he would forget, of course. And why not? She did not fit in. Had not everything—everything illustrated that to her? Love was not enough in this world—that was so plain. One needed education, wealth, training, the ability to fight and scheme. She did not want to do that. She could not.

The day came when the house was finally closed and the old life was at an end. Lester traveled with Jennie to Sandwood. He spent some little while in the house trying to get her used to the idea of change—it was not so bad. He intimated that he would come again soon, but he went away, and all his words were as nothing against the fact of the actual and spiritual separation. When Jennie saw him going down the brick walk that afternoon, his solid, conservative figure clad in a new tweed suit, his overcoat on his arm, self-reliance and prosperity written all over him, she thought that she would die. She had kissed Lester good-by and had wished him joy, prosperity, peace; then she made an excuse to go to her bedroom. Vesta came after a time, to seek her, but now her eyes were quite dry; everything had subsided to a dull ache. The new life was actually begun for her—a life without Lester, without Gerhardt, without any one save Vesta.

"What curious things have happened to me!" she thought, as she went into the kitchen, for she had determined to do at least some of her own work. She needed the distraction. She did not want to think. If it were not for Vesta she would have sought some regular outside employment. Anything to keep from brooding, for in that direction lay madness.

Chapter LV

THE SOCIAL and business worlds of Chicago, Cincinnati, Cleveland, and other cities saw, during the year or two which followed the breaking of his relationship with Jennie, a curious rejuvenation in the social and business spirit of Lester Kane. He had become rather distant and indifferent to certain personages and affairs while he was living with her, but now he suddenly appeared again, armed with authority from a number of sources, looking into this and that matter with the air of one who has the privilege of power, and showing himself to be quite a personage from the point of view of finance and commerce. He was older of course. It must be admitted that he was in some respects a mentally altered Lester. Up to the time he had met Jennie he was full of the assurance of the man who has never known defeat. To have been reared in luxury as he had been, to have seen only the pleasant side of society, which is so persistent and so deluding where money is concerned, to have been in the run of big affairs not because one has created them, but because one is a part of them and because they are one's birthright, like the air one breathes, could not help but create one of those illusions of solidarity which is apt to befog the clearest brain. It is so hard for us to know what we have not seen. It is so difficult for us to feel what we have not experienced. Like this world of ours, which seems so solid and persistent solely because we have no knowledge of the power which creates it, Lester's world seemed solid and persistent and real enough to him. It was only when the storms set in and the winds of adversity blew and he found himself facing the armed forces of convention that he realized he might be mistaken as to the value of his personality, that his private desires and opinions were as nothing in the face of a public conviction; that he was wrong. The race spirit, or social avatar, the "Zeitgeist" as the Germans term it, manifested itself as something having a system in charge, and the organization of society began to show itself to him as something based on possibly a spiritual, or, at least, superhuman counterpart. He could not fly in the face of it. He could not deliberately ignore its mandates. The people of his time believed that some particular form of social arrangement was necessary, and unless he complied with that he could, as he saw, readily become a social outcast. His own father and mother had turned on him—his brother and sisters, society, his friends. Dear heaven, what a to-do this action of his had created! Why, even the fates seemed adverse. His real estate venture was one of the most fortuitously unlucky things he had ever heard of. Why? Were the gods battling on the side of a to him unimportant social arrangement? Apparently. Anyhow, he had been compelled to quit, and here he was, vigorous, determined, somewhat battered by the experience, but still forceful and worth while.

And it was a part of the penalty that he had become measurably soured by what had occurred. He was feeling that he had been compelled to do the first ugly, brutal thing of his life. Jennie deserved better of him. It was a shame to forsake her after all the devotion she had manifested. Truly she had played a finer part than he. Worst of all, his deed could not be excused on the grounds of necessity. He could have lived on ten thousand a year; he could have done without the million and more which was now his. He could have done without the society, the pleasures of which had always been a lure. He could have, but he had not, and he had complicated it all with the thought of another woman.

Was she as good as Jennie? That was a question which always rose before him. Was she as kindly? Wasn't she deliberately scheming under his very eyes to win him away from the woman who was as good as his wife? Was that admirable? Was it the thing a truly big woman would do? Was she good enough for him after all? Ought he to marry her? Ought he to marry any one seeing that he really owed a spiritual if not a legal allegiance to Jennie? Was it worth while for any woman to marry him? These things turned in his brain. They haunted him. He could not shut out the fact that he was doing a cruel and unlovely thing.

Material error in the first place was now being complicated with spiritual error. He was attempting to right the first by committing the second. Could it be done *to his own satisfaction*? Would it pay mentally and spiritually? Would it bring him peace of mind? He was thinking, thinking, all the while he was readjusting his life to the old (or perhaps better yet, new) conditions, and he was not feeling any happier. As a matter of fact he was feeling worse—grim, revengeful. If he married Letty he thought at times it would be to use her fortune as a club to knock other enemies over the head, and he hated to think he was marrying her for that. He took up his abode at the Auditorium, visited Cincinnati in a distant and aggressive spirit, sat in council with the board of directors, wishing that he was more at peace with himself, more interested in life. But he did not change his policy in regard to Jennie.

Of course Mrs. Gerald had been vitally interested in Lester's rehabilitation. She waited tactfully some little time before sending him any word; finally she ventured to write to him at the Hyde Park address (as if she did not know where he was), asking, "Where are you?" By this time Lester had become slightly accustomed to the change in his life. He was saying to himself that he needed sympathetic companionship, the companionship of a woman, of course. Social invitations had begun to come to him now that he was alone and that his financial connections were so obviously restored. He had made his appearance, accompanied only by a Japanese valet, at several country houses, the best sign that he was once more a single man. No reference was made by any one to the past.

On receiving Mrs. Gerald's note he decided that he ought to go and see her. He had treated her rather shabbily. For months preceding his separation from Jennie he had not gone near her. Even now he waited until time brought a 'phoned invitation to dinner. This he accepted.

Mrs. Gerald was at her best as a hostess at her perfectly appointed dinner-table. Alboni, the pianist, was there on this occasion, together with Adam Rascavage, the sculptor, a visiting scientist from England, Sir Nelson Keyes, and, curiously enough, Mr. and Mrs. Berry Dodge, whom Lester had not met socially in several years. Mrs. Gerald and Lester exchanged the joyful greetings of those who understand each other thoroughly and are happy in each other's company. "Aren't you ashamed of yourself, sir," she said to him when he made his appearance, "to treat me so indifferently? You are going to be punished for this."

"What's the damage?" he smiled. "I've been extremely rushed. I suppose something like ninety stripes will serve me about right."

"Ninety stripes, indeed!" she retorted. "You're letting yourself off easy. What is it they do to evil-doers in Siam?"

"Boil them in oil, I suppose."

"Well, anyhow, that's more like. I'm thinking of something terrible."

"Be sure and tell me when you decide," he laughed, and passed on to be presented to distinguished strangers by Mrs. De Lincum who aided Mrs. Gerald in receiving. The talk was stimulating. Lester was always at his ease intellectually, and this mental atmosphere revived him. Presently he turned to greet Berry Dodge, who was standing at his elbow.

Dodge was all cordiality. "Where are you now?" he asked. "We haven't seen you in—oh, when? Mrs. Dodge is waiting to have a word with you." Lester noticed the change in Dodge's attitude.

"Some time, that's sure," he replied easily. "I'm living at the Auditorium."

"I was asking after you the other day. You know Jackson Du Bois? Of course you do. We were thinking of running up into Canada for some hunting. Why don't you join us?"

"I can't," replied Lester. "Too many things on hand just now. Later, surely."

Dodge was anxious to continue. He had seen Lester's election as a director of the C. H. & D. Obviously he was coming back into the world. But dinner was announced and Lester sat at Mrs. Gerald's right hand.

"Aren't you coming to pay me a dinner call some afternoon after this?" asked Mrs. Gerald confidentially when the conversation was brisk at the other end of the table.

"I am, indeed," he replied, "and shortly. Seriously, I've been wanting to look you up. You understand though how things are now?"

"I do. I've heard a great deal. That's why I want you to come. We need to talk together."

Ten days later he did call. He felt as if he must talk with her; he was feeling bored and lonely; his long home life with Jennie had made hotel life objectionable. He felt as though he must find a sympathetic, intelligent ear, and where better than here? Letty was all ears for his troubles. She would have pillowed his solid head upon her breast in a moment if that had been possible.

"Well," he said, when the usual fencing preliminaries were over, " what will you have me say in explanation?"

"Have you burned your bridges behind you?" she asked.

"I'm not so sure," he replied gravely. "And I can't say that I'm feeling any too joyous about the matter as a whole."

"I thought as much," she replied. "I knew how it would be with you. I can see you wading through this mentally, Lester. I have been watching you, every step of the way, wishing you peace of mind. These things are always so difficult, but don't you know I am still sure it's for the best. It never was right the other way. It never could be. You couldn't afford to sink back into a mere shell-fish life. You are not organized temperamentally for that any more than I am. You may regret what you are doing now, but you would have regretted the other thing quite as much and more. You couldn't work your life out that way—now, could you?"

"I don't know about that, Letty. Really, I don't. I've wanted to come and see you for a long time, but I didn't think that I ought to. The fight was outside—you know what I mean."

"Yes, indeed, I do," she said soothingly.

"It's still inside. I haven't gotten over it. I don't know whether this financial business binds me sufficiently or not. I'll be frank and tell you that I can't say I love her entirely; but I'm sorry, and that's something."

"She's comfortably provided for, of course," she commented rather than inquired.

"Everything she wants. Jennie is of a peculiar disposition. She doesn't want much. She's retiring by nature and doesn't care for show. I've taken a cottage for her at Sandwood, a little place north of here on the lake; and there's plenty of money in trust, but, of course, she knows she can live anywhere she pleases."

"I understand exactly how she feels, Lester. I know how you feel. She is going to suffer very keenly for a while—we all do when we have to give up the thing we love. But we can get over it, and we do. At least, we can live. She will. It will go hard at first, but after a while she will see how it is, and she won't feel any the worse toward you."

"Jennie will never reproach me, I know that," he replied. "I'm the one who will do the reproaching. I'll be abusing myself for some time. The trouble is with my particular turn of mind. I can't tell, for the life of me, how much of this disturbing feeling of mine is habit—the condition that I'm accustomed to—and how much is sympathy. I sometimes think I'm the most pointless individual in the world. I think too much."

"Poor Lester!" she said tenderly. "Well, I understand for one. You're lonely living where you are, aren't you?"

"I am that," he replied.

"Why not come and spend a few days down at West Baden? I'm going there."

"When?" he inquired.

"Next Tuesday."

"Let me see," he replied. "I'm not sure that I can." He consulted his notebook. "I could come Thursday, for a few days."

"Why not do that? You need company. We can walk and talk things out down there. Will you?"

"Yes, I will," he replied.

She came toward him, trailing a lavender lounging robe. "You're such a solemn philosopher, sir," she observed comfortably, "working through all the ramifications of things. Why do you? You were always like that."

"I can't help it," he replied. "It's my nature to think."

"Well, one thing I know—" and she tweaked his ear gently. "You're not going to make another mistake through sympathy if I can help it," she said daringly. "You're going to stay disentangled long enough to give yourself a chance to think out what you want to do. You must. And I wish for one thing you'd take over the management of my affairs. You could advise me so much better than my lawyer."

He arose and walked to the window, turning to look back at her solemnly. "I know what you want," he said doggedly.

"And why shouldn't I?" she demanded, again approaching

him. She looked at him pleadingly, defiantly. "Yes, why shouldn't I?"

"You don't know what you're doing," he grumbled; but he kept on looking at her; she stood there, attractive as a woman of her age could be, wise, considerate, full of friendship and affection.

"Letty," he said. "You ought not to want to marry me. I'm not worth it. Really I'm not. I'm too cynical. Too indifferent. It won't be worth anything in the long run."

"It will be worth something to me," she insisted. "I know what you are. Anyhow, I don't care. I want you!"

He took her hands, then her arms. Finally he drew her to him, and put his arms about her waist. "Poor Letty!" he said; "I'm not worth it. You'll be sorry."

"No, I'll not," she replied. "I know what I'm doing. I don't care what you think you are worth." She laid her cheek on his shoulder. "I want you."

"If you keep on I venture to say you'll have me," he returned. He bent and kissed her.

"Oh," she exclaimed, and hid her hot face against his breast.

"This is bad business," he thought, even as he held her within the circle of his arms. "It isn't what I ought to be doing."

Still he held her, and now when she offered her lips coaxingly he kissed her again and again.

Chapter LVI

IT IS DIFFICULT to say whether Lester might not have returned to Jennie after all but for certain influential factors. After a time, with his control of his portion of the estate firmly settled in his hands and the storm of original feeling forgotten, he was well aware that diplomacy—if he ignored his natural tendency to fulfil even implied obligations—could readily bring about an arrangement whereby he and Jennie could be together. But he was haunted by the sense of what might be called an important social opportunity in the form of Mrs. Gerald. He was compelled to set over against his natural tendency toward Jennie a consciousness of what he was ignoring in the personality and fortunes of her rival, who was one of the most significant and interesting figures on the social horizon. For think as he would, these two women were now persistently opposed in his consciousness. The one polished, sympathetic, philosophic—schooled in all the niceties of polite society, and with the means to gratify her every wish; the other natural, sympathetic, emotional, with no schooling in the ways of polite society, but with a feeling for the beauty of life and the lovely things in human relationship which made her beyond any question an exceptional woman. Mrs. Gerald saw it and admitted it. Her criticism of Lester's relationship with Jennie was not that she was not worth while, but that conditions made it impolitic. On the other hand, union with her was an ideal climax for his social aspirations. This would bring everything out right. He would be as happy with her as he would be with Jennie—almost—and he would have the satisfaction of knowing that this Western social and financial world held no more significant figure than himself. It was not wise to delay either this latter excellent solution of his material problems, and after thinking it over long and seriously he finally concluded that he would not. He had already done Jennie the irreparable wrong of leaving her. What difference did it make if he did this also? She was possessed of everything she could possibly want outside of himself. She had herself deemed it advisable for him to leave. By such figments of the brain, in the face of unsettled and disturbing conditions, he was becoming used to the idea of a new alliance.

The thing which prevented an eventual resumption of relationship in some form with Jennie was the constant presence of Mrs. Gerald. Circumstances conspired to make her the logical solution of his mental quandary at this time. Alone he could do nothing save to make visits here and there, and he did not care to do that. He was too indifferent mentally to gather about him as a bachelor that atmosphere which he enjoyed and which a woman like Mrs. Gerald could so readily provide. United with her it was simple enough. Their home then, wherever it was, would be full of clever people. He would need to do little save to appear and enjoy it. She understood quite as well as any one how he liked to live. She enjoyed to meet the people he enjoyed meeting. There were so many things they could do together nicely. He visited West Baden at the same time she did, as she suggested. He gave himself over to her in Chicago for dinners, parties, drives. Her house was quite as much his own as hers—she made him feel so. She talked to him about her affairs, showing him exactly how they stood and why she wished him to intervene in this and that matter. She did not wish him to be much alone. She did not want him to think or regret. She came to represent to him comfort, forgetfulness, rest from care. With the others he visited at her house occasionally, and it gradually became rumored about that he would marry her. Because of the fact that there had been so much discussion of his previous relationship, Letty decided that if ever this occurred it should be a quiet affair. She wanted a simple explanation in the papers of how it had come about, and then afterward, when things were normal again and gossip had subsided, she would enter on a dazzling social display for his sake.

"Why not let us get married in April and go abroad for the summer?" she asked once, after they had reached a silent understanding that marriage would eventually follow. "Let's go to Japan. Then we can come back in the fall, and take a house on the drive."

Lester had been away from Jennie so long now that the first severe wave of self-reproach had passed. He was still doubtful, but he preferred to stifle his misgivings. "Very well," he replied, almost jokingly. "Only don't let there be any fuss about it."

"Do you really mean that, sweet?" she exclaimed, looking over at him; they had been spending the evening together quietly reading and chatting.

"I've thought about it a long while," he replied. "I don't see why not."

She came over to him and sat on his knee, putting her arms upon his shoulders.

"I can scarcely believe you said that," she said, looking at him curiously.

"Shall I take it back?" he asked.

"No, no. It's agreed for April now. And we'll go to Japan. You can't change your mind. There won't be any fuss. But my, what a trousseau I will prepare!"

He smiled a little constrainedly as she tousled his head; there was a missing note somewhere in this gamut of happiness; perhaps it was because he was getting old.

Chapter LVII

IN THE MEANTIME Jennie was going her way, settling herself in the markedly different world in which henceforth she was to move. It seemed a terrible thing at first—this life without Lester. Despite her own strong individuality, her ways had become so involved with his that there seemed to be no possibility of disentangling them. Constantly she was with him in thought and action, just as though they had never separated. Where was he now? What was he doing? What was he saying? How was he looking? In the mornings when she woke it was with the sense that he must be beside her. At night as if she could not go to bed alone. He would come after a while surely—ah, no, of course he would not come. Dear heaven, think of that! Never any more. And she wanted him so.

Again there were so many little trying things to adjust, for a change of this nature is too radical to be passed over lightly. The explanation she had to make to Vesta was of all the most important. This little girl, who was old enough now to see and think for herself, was not without her surmises and misgivings. Vesta recalled that her mother had been accused of not being married to her father when she was born. She had seen the article about Jennie and Lester in the Sunday paper at the time it had appeared—it had been shown to her at school—but she had had sense enough to say nothing about it, feeling somehow that Jennie would not like it. Lester's disappearance was a complete surprise; but she had learned in the last two or three years that her mother was very sensitive, and that she could hurt her in unexpected ways. Jennie was finally compelled to tell Vesta that Lester's fortune had been dependent on his leaving her, solely because she was not of his station. Vesta listened soberly and half suspected the truth. She felt terribly sorry for her mother, and, because of Jennie's obvious distress, she was trebly gay and courageous. She refused outright the suggestion of going to a boarding-school and kept as close to her mother as she could. She found interesting books to read with her, insisted that they go to see plays together, played to her on the piano, and asked for her mother's criticisms on her drawing and modeling. She found a few friends in the excellent Sandwood school, and brought them home of an evening to add lightness and gaiety to the cottage life. Jennie, through her growing appreciation of Vesta's fine character, became more and more drawn toward her. Lester was gone, but at least she had Vesta. That prop would probably sustain her in the face of a waning existence.

There was also her history to account for to the residents of Sandwood. In many cases where one is content to lead a secluded life it is not necessary to say much of one's past, but as a rule something must be said. People have the habit of inquiring—if they are no more than butchers and bakers. By degrees one must account for this and that fact, and it was so here. She could not say that her husband was dead. Lester might come back. She had to say that she had left him—to give the impression that it would be she, if any one, who would permit him to return. This put her in an interesting and sympathetic light in the neighborhood. It was the most sensible thing to do. She then settled down to a quiet routine of existence, waiting what dénouement to her life she could not guess.

Sandwood life was not without its charms for a lover of nature, and this, with the devotion of Vesta, offered some slight solace. There was the beauty of the lake, which, with its passing boats, was a never-ending source of joy, and there were many charming drives in the surrounding country. Jennie had her own horse and carryall—one of the horses of the pair they had used in Hyde Park. Other household pets appeared in due course of time, including a collie, that Vesta named Rats; she had brought him from Chicago as a puppy, and he had grown to be a sterling watch-dog, sensible and affectionate. There was also a cat, Jimmy Woods, so called after a boy Vesta knew, and to whom she insisted the cat bore a marked resemblance. There was a singing thrush, guarded carefully against a roving desire for bird-food on the part of Jimmy Woods, and a jar of goldfish. So this little household drifted along quietly and dreamily indeed, but always with the undercurrent of feeling which ran so still because it was so deep.

There was no word from Lester for the first few weeks following his departure; he was too busy following up the threads of his new commercial connections and too considerate to wish to keep Jennie in a state of mental turmoil over communications which, under the present circumstances, could mean nothing. He preferred to let matters rest for the time being; then a little later he would write her sanely and calmly of how things were going. He did this after the silence of a month, saying that he had been pretty well pressed by commercial affairs, that he had been in and out of the city frequently (which was the truth), and that he would probably be away from Chicago a large part of the time in the future. He inquired after Vesta and the condition of affairs generally at Sandwood. "I may get up there one of these days," he suggested, but he really did not mean to come, and Jennie knew that he did not.

Another month passed, and then there was a second letter from him, not so long as the first one. Jennie had written him frankly and fully, telling him just how things stood with her. She concealed entirely her own feelings in the matter, saying that she liked the life very much, and that she was glad to be at Sandwood. She expressed the hope that now everything was coming out for the best for him, and tried to show him that she was really glad matters had been settled. "You mustn't think of me as being unhappy," she said in one place, "for I'm not. I am sure it ought to be just as it is, and I wouldn't be happy if it were any other way. Lay out your life so as to give yourself the greatest happiness, Lester," she added. "You deserve it. Whatever you do will be just right for me. I won't mind." She had Mrs. Gerald in mind, and he suspected as much, but he felt that her generosity must be tinged greatly with self-sacrifice and secret unhappiness. It was the one thing which made him hesitate about taking that final step.

The written word and the hidden thought—how they conflict! After six months the correspondence was more or less perfunctory on his part, and at eight it had ceased temporarily.

One morning, as she was glancing over the daily paper, she saw among the society notes the following item:

The engagement of Mrs. Malcolm Gerald, of 4044 Drexel Boulevard, to Lester Kane, second son of the late Archibald Kane, of Cincinnati, was formally announced at a party given by the prospective bride on Tuesday to a circle of her immediate friends. The wedding will take place in April.

The paper fell from her hands. For a few minutes she sat perfectly still, looking straight ahead of her. Could this thing be so? she asked herself. Had it really come at last? She had known that it must come, and yet—and yet she had always hoped that it would not. Why had she hoped? Had not she herself sent him away? Had not she herself suggested this very thing in a roundabout way? It had come now. What must she do? Stay here as a pensioner? The idea was objectionable to her. And yet he had set aside a goodly sum to be hers absolutely. In the hands of a trust company in La Salle Street were railway certificates aggregating seventy-five thousand dollars, which yielded four thousand five hundred annually, the income being paid to her direct. Could she refuse to receive this money? There was Vesta to be considered.

Jennie felt hurt through and through by this dénouement, and yet as she sat there she realized that it was foolish to be angry. Life was always doing this sort of a thing to her. It would go on doing so. She was sure of it. If she went out in the world and earned her own living what difference would it make to him? What difference would it make to Mrs. Gerald? Here she was walled in this little place, leading an obscure existence, and there was he out in the great world enjoying life in its fullest and freest sense. It was too bad. But why cry? Why?

Her eyes indeed were dry, but her very soul seemed to be torn in pieces within her. She rose carefully, hid the newspaper at the bottom of a trunk, and turned the key upon it.

Chapter LVIII

Now that his engagement to Mrs. Gerald was an accomplished fact, Lester found no particular difficulty in reconciling himself to the new order of things; undoubtedly it was all for the best. He was sorry for Jennie—very sorry. So was Mrs. Gerald; but there was a practical unguent to her grief in the thought that it was best for both Lester and the girl. He would be happier—was so now. And Jennie would eventually realize that she had done a wise and kindly thing; she would be glad in the consciousness that she had acted so unselfishly. As for Mrs. Gerald, because of her indifference to the late Malcolm Gerald, and because she was realizing the dreams of her youth in getting Lester at last—even though a little late—she was intensely happy. She could think of nothing finer than this daily life with him—the places they would go, the things they would see. Her first season in Chicago as Mrs. Lester Kane the following winter was going to be something worth remembering. And as for Japan—that was almost too good to be true.

Lester wrote to Jennie of his coming marriage to Mrs. Gerald. He said that he had no explanation to make. It wouldn't be worth anything if he did make it. He thought he ought to marry Mrs. Gerald. He thought he ought to let her (Jennie) know. He hoped she was well. He wanted her always to feel that he had her real interests at heart. He would do anything in his power to make life as pleasant and agreeable for her as possible. He hoped she would forgive him. And would she remember him affectionately to Vesta? She ought to be sent to a finishing school.

Jennie understood the situation perfectly. She knew that Lester had been drawn to Mrs. Gerald from the time he met her at the Carlton in London. She had been angling for him. Now she had him. It was all right. She hoped he would be happy. She was glad to write and tell him so, explaining that she had seen the announcement in the papers. Lester read her letter thoughtfully; there was more between the lines than the written words conveyed. Her fortitude was a charm to him even in this hour. In spite of all he had done and what he was now going to do, he realized that he still cared for Jennie in a way. She was a noble and a charming woman. If everything else had been all right he would not be going to marry Mrs. Gerald at all. And yet he did marry her.

The ceremony was performed on April fifteenth, at the residence of Mrs. Gerald, a Roman Catholic priest officiating. Lester was a poor example of the faith he occasionally professed. He was an agnostic, but because he had been reared in the church he felt that he might as well be married in it. Some fifty guests, intimate friends, had been invited. The ceremony went off with perfect smoothness. There were jubilant congratulations and showers of rice and confetti. While the guests were still eating and drinking Lester and Letty managed to escape by a side entrance into a closed carriage, and were off. Fifteen minutes later there was pursuit pell-mell on the part of the guests to the Chicago, Rock Island and Pacific depot; but by that time the happy couple were in their private car, and the arrival of the rice throwers made no difference. More champagne was opened; then the starting of the train ended all excitement, and the newly wedded pair were at last safely off.

"Well, now you have me," said Lester, cheerfully pulling Letty down beside him into a seat, " what of it?"

"This of it," she exclaimed, and hugged him close, kissing him fervently. In four days they were in San Francisco, and two days later on board a fast steamship bound for the land of the Mikado.

In the meanwhile Jennie was left to brood. The original announcement in the newspapers had said that he was to be married in April, and she had kept close watch for additional information. Finally she learned that the wedding would take place on April fifteenth at the residence of the prospective bride, the hour being high noon. In spite of her feeling of resignation, Jennie followed it all hopelessly, like a child, hungry and forlorn, looking into a lighted window at Christmas time.

On the day of the wedding she waited miserably for twelve o'clock to strike; it seemed as though she were really present and looking on. She could see in her mind's eye the handsome residence, the carriages, the guests, the feast, the merriment, the ceremony—all. Telepathically and psychologically she received impressions of the private car and of the joyous journey they were going to take. The papers had stated that they would spend their honeymoon in Japan. Their honeymoon! Her Lester! And Mrs. Gerald was so attractive. She could see her now—the new Mrs. Kane—the only *Mrs.* Kane that ever was, lying in his arms. He had held her so once. He had loved her. Yes, he had! There was a solid lump in her throat as she thought of this. Oh, dear! She sighed to herself, and clasped her hands forcefully; but it did no good. She was just as miserable as before.

When the day was over she was actually relieved; anyway, the deed was done and nothing could change it. Vesta was sympathetically aware of what was happening, but kept silent. She too had seen the report in the newspaper. When the first and second day after had passed Jennie was much calmer mentally, for now she was face to face with the inevitable. But it was weeks before the sharp pain dulled to the old familiar ache. Then there were months before they would be back again, though, of course, that made no difference now. Only Japan seemed so far off, and somehow she had liked the thought that Lester was near her—somewhere in the city.

The spring and summer passed, and now it was early in October. One chilly day Vesta came home from school complaining of a headache. When Jennie had given her hot milk—a favorite remedy of her mother's—and had advised a cold towel for the back of her head, Vesta went to her room and lay down. The following morning she had a slight fever. This lingered while the local physician, Dr. Emory, treated her tentatively, suspecting that it might be typhoid, of which there were several cases in the village. This doctor told Jennie that Vesta was probably strong enough constitutionally to shake it off, but it might be that she would have a severe siege. Mistrusting her own skill in so delicate a situation, Jennie sent to Chicago for a trained nurse, and then began a period of watchfulness which was a combination of fear, longing, hope, and courage.

Now there could be no doubt; the disease was typhoid. Jennie hesitated about communicating with Lester, who was supposed to be in New York; the papers had said that he intended to spend the winter there. But when the doctor, after watching the case for a week, pronounced it severe, she thought she ought to write anyhow, for no one could tell what would happen. Lester had been so fond of Vesta. He would probably want to know.

The letter sent to him did not reach him, for at the time it arrived he was on his way to the West Indies. Jennie was compelled to watch alone by Vesta's sick-bed, for although sympathetic neighbors, realizing the pathos of the situation were attentive, they could not supply the spiritual consolation which only those who truly love us can give. There was a period when Vesta appeared to be rallying, and both the physician and the nurse were hopeful; but afterward she became weaker. It was said by Dr. Emory that her heart and kidneys had become affected.

There came a time when the fact had to be faced that death was imminent. The doctor's face was grave, the nurse was non-committal in her opinion. Jennie hovered about, praying the only prayer that is prayer—the fervent desire of her heart concentrated on the one issue—that Vesta should get well. The child had come so close to her during the last few years! She understood her mother. She was beginning to realize clearly what her life had been. And Jennie, through her, had grown to a broad understanding of responsibility. She knew now what it meant to be a good mother and to have children. If Lester had not objected to it, and she had been truly married, she would have been glad to have others. Again, she had always felt that she owed Vesta so much—at least a long and happy life to make up to her for the ignominy of her birth and rearing. Jennie had been so happy during the past few years to see Vesta growing into beautiful, graceful, intelligent womanhood. And now she was dying. Dr. Emory finally sent to Chicago for a physician friend of his, who came to consider the case with him. He was an old man, grave, sympathetic, understanding. He shook his head. "The treatment has been correct," he said. "Her system does not appear to be strong enough to endure the strain. Some physiques are more susceptible to this malady than others." It was agreed that if within three days a change for the better did not come the end was close at hand.

No one can conceive the strain to which Jennie's spirit was subjected by this intelligence, for it was deemed best that she should know. She hovered about white-faced—feeling intensely, but scarcely thinking. She seemed to vibrate consciously with Vesta's altering states. If there was the least improvement she felt it physically. If there was a decline her barometric temperament registered the fact.

There was a Mrs. Davis, a fine, motherly soul of fifty, stout and sympathetic, who lived four doors from Jennie, and who understood quite well how she was feeling. She had co-operated with the nurse and doctor from the start to keep Jennie's mental state as nearly normal as possible.

"Now, you just go to your room and lie down, Mrs. Kane," she would say to Jennie when she found her watching helplessly at the bedside or wandering to and fro, wondering what to do. "I'll take charge of everything. I'll do just what you would do. Lord bless you, don't you think I know? I've been the mother of seven and lost three. Don't you think I understand?" Jennie put her head on her big, warm shoulder one day and cried. Mrs. Davis cried with her. "I understand," she said. "There, there, you poor dear. Now you come with me." And she led her to her sleeping-room.

Jennie could not be away long. She came back after a few minutes unrested and unrefreshed. Finally one midnight, when the nurse had persuaded her that all would be well until morning anyhow, there came a hurried stirring in the sick-room. Jennie was lying down for a few minutes on her bed in the adjoining room. She heard it and arose. Mrs. Davis had come in, and she and the nurse were conferring as to Vesta's condition—standing close beside her.

Jennie understood. She came up and looked at her daughter keenly. Vesta's pale, waxen face told the story. She was breathing faintly, her eyes closed. "She's very weak," whispered the nurse. Mrs. Davis took Jennie's hand.

The moments passed, and after a time the clock in the hall struck one. Miss Murfree, the nurse, moved to the medicine-table several times, wetting a soft piece of cotton cloth with alcohol and bathing Vesta's lips. At the striking of the half-hour there was a stir of the weak body—a profound sigh. Jennie bent forward eagerly, but Mrs. Davis drew her back.

The nurse came and motioned them away. Respiration had ceased.

Mrs. Davis seized Jennie firmly. "There, there, you poor dear," she whispered when she began to shake. "It can't be helped. Don't cry."

Jennie sank on her knees beside the bed and caressed Vesta's still warm hand. "Oh no, Vesta," she pleaded. "Not you! Not you!"

"There, dear, come now," soothed the voice of Mrs. Davis. "Can't you leave it all in God's hands? Can't you believe that everything is for the best?"

Jennie felt as if the earth had fallen. All ties were broken. There was no light anywhere in the immense darkness of her existence.

Chapter LIX

THIS ADDED BLOW from inconsiderate fortune was quite enough to throw Jennie back into that state of hyper-melancholia from which she had been drawn with difficulty during the few years of comfort and affection which she had enjoyed with Lester in Hyde Park. It was really weeks before she could realize that Vesta was gone. The emaciated figure which she saw for a day or two after the end did not seem like Vesta. Where was the joy and lightness, the quickness of motion, the subtle radiance of health? All gone. Only this pale, lily-hued shell—and silence. Jennie had no tears to shed; only a deep, insistent pain to feel. If only some counselor of eternal wisdom could have whispered to her that obvious and convincing truth—there are no dead.

Miss Murfree, Dr. Emory, Mrs. Davis, and some others among the neighbors were most sympathetic and considerate. Mrs. Davis sent a telegram to Lester saying that Vesta was dead, but, being absent, there was no response. The house was looked after with scrupulous care by others, for Jennie was incapable of attending to it herself. She walked about looking at things which Vesta had owned or liked—things which Lester or she had given her—sighing over the fact that Vesta would not need or use them any more. She gave instructions that the body should be taken to Chicago and buried in the Cemetery of the Redeemer, for Lester, at the time of Gerhardt's death, had purchased a small plot of ground there. She also expressed her wish that the minister of the little Lutheran church in Cottage Grove Avenue, where Gerhardt had attended, should be requested to say a few words at the grave. There were the usual preliminary services at the house. The local Methodist minister read a portion of the first epistle of Paul to the Thessalonians, and a body of Vesta's classmates sang "Nearer My God to Thee." There were flowers, a white coffin, a world of sympathetic expressions, and then Vesta was taken away. The coffin was properly incased for transportation, put on the train, and finally delivered at the Lutheran cemetery in Chicago.

Jennie moved as one in a dream. She was dazed, almost to

the point of insensibility. Five of her neighborhood friends, at the solicitation of Mrs. Davis, were kind enough to accompany her. At the grave-side when the body was finally lowered she looked at it, one might have thought indifferently, for she was numb from suffering. She returned to Sandwood after it was all over, saying that she would not stay long. She wanted to come back to Chicago, where she could be near Vesta and Gerhardt.

After the funeral Jennie tried to think of her future. She fixed her mind on the need of doing something, even though she did not need to. She thought that she might like to try nursing, and could start at once to obtain the training which was required. She also thought of William. He was unmarried, and perhaps he might be willing to come and live with her. Only she did not know where he was, and Bass was also in ignorance of his whereabouts. She finally concluded that she would try to get work in a store. Her disposition was against idleness. She could not live alone here, and she could not have her neighbors sympathetically worrying over what was to become of her. Miserable as she was, she would be less miserable stopping in a hotel in Chicago, and looking for something to do, or living in a cottage somewhere near the Cemetery of the Redeemer. It also occurred to her that she might adopt a homeless child. There were a number of orphan asylums in the city.

Some three weeks after Vesta's death Lester returned to Chicago with his wife, and discovered the first letter, the telegram, and an additional note telling him that Vesta was dead. He was truly grieved, for his affection for the girl had been real. He was very sorry for Jennie, and he told his wife that he would have to go out and see her. He was wondering what she would do. She could not live alone. Perhaps he could suggest something which would help her. He took the train to Sandwood, but Jennie had gone to the Hotel Tremont in Chicago. He went there, but Jennie had gone to her daughter's grave; later he called again and found her in. When the boy presented his card she suffered an upwelling of feeling—a wave that was more intense than that with which she had received him in the olden days, for now her need of him was greater.

Lester, in spite of the glamor of his new affection and the restoration of his wealth, power, and dignities, had had time to think deeply of what he had done. His original feeling of doubt and dissatisfaction with himself had never wholly quieted. It did not ease him any to know that he had left Jennie comfortably fixed, for it was always so plain to him that money was not the point at issue with her. Affection was what she craved. Without it she was like a rudderless boat on an endless sea, and he knew it. She needed him, and he was ashamed to think that his charity had not outweighed his sense of self-preservation and his desire for material advantage. To-day as the elevator carried him up to her room he was really sorry, though he knew now that no act of his could make things right. He had been to blame from the very beginning, first for taking her, then for failing to stick by a bad bargain. Well, it could not be helped now. The best thing he could do was to be fair, to counsel with her, to give her the best of his sympathy and advice.

"Hello, Jennie," he said familiarly as she opened the door to him in her hotel room, his glance taking in the ravages which death and suffering had wrought. She was thinner, her face quite drawn and colorless, her eyes larger by contrast. "I'm awfully sorry about Vesta," he said a little awkwardly. "I never dreamed anything like that could happen."

It was the first word of comfort which had meant anything to her since Vesta died—since Lester had left her, in fact. It touched her that he had come to sympathize; for the moment she could not speak. Tears welled over her eyelids and down upon her cheeks.

"Don't cry, Jennie," he said, putting his arm around her and holding her head to his shoulder. "I'm sorry. I've been sorry for a good many things that can't be helped now. I'm intensely sorry for this. Where did you bury her?"

"Beside papa," she said, sobbing.

"Too bad," he murmured, and held her in silence. She finally gained control of herself sufficiently to step away from him; then wiping her eyes with her handkerchief, she asked him to sit down.

"I'm so sorry," he went on, "that this should have happened while I was away. I would have been with you if I had been here. I suppose you won't want to live out at Sandwood now?"

"I can't, Lester," she replied. "I couldn't stand it."

"Where are you thinking of going?"

"Oh, I don't know yet. I didn't want to be a bother to those people out there. I thought I'd get a little house somewhere and adopt a baby maybe, or get something to do. I don't like to be alone."

"That isn't a bad idea," he said, "that of adopting a baby. It would be a lot of company for you. You know how to go about getting one?"

"You just ask at one of these asylums, don't you?"

"I think there's something more than that," he replied thoughtfully. "There are some formalities—I don't know what they are. They try to keep control of the child in some way. You had better consult with Watson and get him to help you. Pick out your baby, and then let him do the rest. I'll speak to him about it."

Lester saw that she needed companionship badly. "Where is your brother George?" he asked.

"He's in Rochester, but he couldn't come. Bass said he was married," she added.

"There isn't any other member of the family you could persuade to come and live with you?"

"I might get William, but I don't know where he is."

"Why not try that new section west of Jackson Park," he suggested, "if you want a house here in Chicago? I see some nice cottages out that way. You needn't buy. Just rent until you see how well you're satisfied."

Jennie thought this good advice because it came from Lester. It was good of him to take this much interest in her affairs. She wasn't entirely separated from him after all. He cared a little. She asked him how his wife was, whether he had had a pleasant trip, whether he was going to stay in Chicago. All the while he was thinking that he had treated her badly. He went to the window and looked down into Dearborn Street, the world of traffic below holding his attention. The great mass of trucks and vehicles, the counter streams of hurrying pedestrians, seemed like a puzzle. So shadows march in a dream. It was growing dusk, and lights were springing up here and there.

"I want to tell you something, Jennie," said Lester, finally rousing himself from his fit of abstraction. "I may seem peculiar to you, after all that has happened, but I still care for you—in my way. I've thought of you right along since I left. I thought it good business to leave you—the way things were. I thought I liked Letty well enough to marry her. From one point of view it still seems best, but I'm not so much happier. I was just as happy with you as I ever will be. It isn't myself that's important in this transaction apparently; the individual doesn't count much in the situation. I don't know whether you see what I'm driving at, but all of us are more or less pawns. We're moved about like chessmen by circumstances over which we have no control."

"I understand, Lester," she answered. "I'm not complaining. I know it's for the best."

"After all, life is more or less of a farce," he went on a little bitterly. "It's a silly show. The best we can do is to hold our personality intact. It doesn't appear that integrity has much to do with it."

Jennie did not quite grasp what he was talking about, but she knew it meant that he was not entirely satisfied with himself and was sorry for her.

"Don't worry over me, Lester," she consoled. "I'm all right; I'll get along. It did seem terrible to me for a while— getting used to being alone. I'll be all right now. I'll get along."

"I want you to feel that my attitude hasn't changed," he continued eagerly. "I'm interested in what concerns you. Mrs.—Letty understands that. She knows just how I feel. When you get settled I'll come in and see how you're fixed. I'll come around here again in a few days. You understand how I feel, don't you?"

"Yes, I do," she said.

He took her hand, turning it sympathetically in his own. "Don't worry," he said. "I don't want you to do that. I'll do the best I can. You're still Jennie to me, if you don't mind. I'm pretty bad, but I'm not all bad."

"It's all right, Lester. I wanted you to do as you did. It's for the best. You probably are happy since—"

"Now, Jennie," he interrupted; then he pressed affectionately her hand, her arm, her shoulder. "Want to kiss me for old times' sake?" he smiled.

She put her hands over his shoulders, looked long into his eyes, then kissed him. When their lips met she trembled. Lester also felt unsteady. Jennie saw his agitation, and tried hard to speak.

"You'd better go now," she said firmly. "It's getting dark."

He went away, and yet he knew that he wanted above all things to remain; she was still the one woman in the world for him. And Jennie felt comforted even though the separation still existed in all its finality. She did not endeavor to explain or adjust the moral and ethical entanglements of the situation. She was not, like so many, endeavoring to put the ocean into a tea-cup, or to tie up the shifting universe in a mess of strings called law. Lester still cared for her a little. He cared for Letty too. That was all right. She had hoped once that he might want her only. Since he did not, was his affection worth nothing? She could not think, she could not feel that. And neither could he.

Chapter LX

THE DRIFT of events for a period of five years carried Lester and Jennie still farther apart; they settled naturally into their respective spheres, without the renewal of the old time relationship which their several meetings at the Tremont at first seemed to foreshadow. Lester was in the thick of social and commercial affairs; he walked in paths to which Jennie's retiring soul had never aspired. Jennie's own existence was quiet and uneventful. There was a simple cottage in a very respectable but not showy neighborhood near Jackson Park, on the South Side, where she lived in retirement with a little foster-child—a chestnut-haired girl taken from the Western Home for the Friendless—as her sole companion. Here she was known as Mrs. J. G. Stover, for she had deemed it best to abandon the name of Kane. Mr. and Mrs. Lester Kane when resident in Chicago were the occupants of a handsome mansion on the Lake Shore Drive, where parties, balls, receptions, dinners were given in rapid and at times almost pyrotechnic succession.

Lester, however, had become in his way a lover of a peaceful and well-entertained existence. He had cut from his list of acquaintances and associates a number of people who had been a little doubtful or overfamiliar or indifferent or talkative during a certain period which to him was a memory merely. He was a director, and in several cases the chairman of a board of directors, in nine of the most important financial and commercial organizations of the West—The United Traction Company of Cincinnati, The Western Crucible Company, The United Carriage Company, The Second National Bank of Chicago, the First National Bank of Cincinnati, and several others of equal importance. He was never a personal factor in the affairs of The United Carriage Company, preferring to be represented by counsel—Mr. Dwight L. Watson, but he took a keen interest in its affairs. He had not seen his brother Robert to speak to him in seven years. He had not seen Imogene, who lived in Chicago, in three. Louise, Amy, their husbands, and some of their closest acquaintances were practically strangers. The firm of Knight, Keatley & O'Brien had nothing whatever to do with his affairs.

The truth was that Lester, in addition to becoming a little phlegmatic, was becoming decidedly critical in his outlook on life. He could not make out what it was all about. In distant ages a queer thing had come to pass. There had started on its way in the form of evolution a minute cellular organism which had apparently reproduced itself by division, had early learned to combine itself with others, to organize itself into bodies, strange forms of fish, animals, and birds, and had finally learned to organize itself into man. Man, on his part, composed as he was of self-organizing cells, was pushing himself forward into comfort and different aspects of existence by means of union and organization with other men. Why? Heaven only knew. Here he was endowed with a peculiar brain and a certain amount of talent, and he had inherited a certain amount of wealth which he now scarcely believed he deserved, only luck had favored him. But he could not see that any one else might be said to deserve this wealth any more than himself, seeing that his use of it was as conservative and constructive and practical as the next one's. He might have been born poor, in which case he would have been as well satisfied as the next one—not more so. Why should he complain, why worry, why speculate?—the world was going steadily forward of its own volition, whether he would or no. Truly it was. And was there any need for him to disturb himself about it? There was not. He fancied at times that it might as well never have been started at all. "The one divine, far-off event" of the poet did not appeal to him as having any basis in fact. Mrs. Lester Kane was of very much the same opinion.

Jennie, living on the South Side with her adopted child, Rose Perpetua, was of no fixed conclusion as to the meaning of life. She had not the incisive reasoning capacity of either Mr. or Mrs. Lester Kane. She had seen a great deal, suffered a great deal, and had read some in a desultory way. Her mind had never grasped the nature and character of specialized knowledge. History, physics, chemistry, botany, geology, and sociology were not fixed departments in her brain as they were in Lester's and Letty's. Instead there was the feeling that the world moved in some strange, unstable way. Apparently no one knew clearly what it was all about. People were born and died. Some believed that the world had been made six thousand years before; some that it was millions of years old. Was it all blind chance, or was there some guiding intelligence—a God? Almost in spite of herself she felt there must be something—a higher power which produced all the beautiful things—the flowers, the stars, the trees, the grass. Nature was so beautiful! If at times life seemed cruel, yet this beauty still persisted. The thought comforted her; she fed upon it in her hours of secret loneliness.

It has been said that Jennie was naturally of an industrious turn. She liked to be employed, though she thought constantly as she worked. She was of matronly proportions in these days—not disagreeably large, but full bodied, shapely, and smooth-faced in spite of her cares. Her eyes were gray and appealing. Her hair was still of a rich brown, but there were traces of gray in it. Her neighbors spoke of her as sweet-tempered, kindly, and hospitable. They knew nothing of her history, except that she had formerly resided in Sandwood, and before that in Cleveland. She was very reticent as to her past.

Jennie had fancied, because of her natural aptitude for taking care of sick people, that she might get to be a trained nurse. But she was obliged to abandon that idea, for she found that only young people were wanted. She also thought that some charitable organization might employ her, but she did not understand the new theory of charity which was then coming into general acceptance and practice—namely, only to help others to help themselves. She believed in giving, and was not inclined to look too closely into the credentials of those who asked for help; consequently her timid inquiry at one relief agency after another met with indifference, if not unqualified rebuke. She finally decided to adopt another child for Rose Perpetua's sake; she succeeded in securing a boy, four years old, who was known as Henry—Henry Stover. Her support was assured, for her income was paid to her through a trust company. She had no desire for speculation or for the devious ways of trade. The care of flowers, the nature of children, the ordering of a home were more in her province.

One of the interesting things in connection with this

separation once it had been firmly established related to Robert and Lester, for these two since the reading of the will a number of years before had never met. Robert had thought of his brother often. He had followed his success since he had left Jennie with interest. He read of his marriage to Mrs. Gerald with pleasure; he had always considered her an ideal companion for his brother. He knew by many signs and tokens that his brother, since the unfortunate termination of their father's attitude and his own peculiar movements to gain control of the Kane Company, did not like him. Still they had never been so far apart mentally—certainly not in commercial judgment. Lester was prosperous now. He could afford to be generous. He could afford to make up. And after all, he had done his best to aid his brother to come to his senses—and with the best intentions. There were mutual interests they could share financially if they were friends. He wondered from time to time if Lester would not be friendly with him.

Time passed, and then once, when he was in Chicago, he made the friends with whom he was driving purposely turn into the North Shore in order to see the splendid mansion which the Kanes occupied. He knew its location from hearsay and description.

When he saw it a touch of the old Kane home atmosphere came back to him. Lester in revising the property after purchase had had a conservatory built on one side not unlike the one at home in Cincinnati. That same night he sat down and wrote Lester asking if he would not like to dine with him at the Union Club. He was only in town for a day or two, and he would like to see him again. There was some feeling he knew, but there was a proposition he would like to talk to him about. Would he come, say, on Thursday?

On the receipt of this letter Lester frowned and fell into a brown study. He had never really been healed of the wound that his father had given him. He had never been comfortable in his mind since Robert had deserted him so summarily. He realized now that the stakes his brother had been playing for were big. But, after all, he had been his brother, and if he had been in Robert's place at the time, he would not have done as he had done; at least he hoped not. Now Robert wanted to see him.

He thought once of not answering at all. Then he thought he would write and say no. But a curious desire to see Robert again, to hear what he had to say, to listen to the proposition he had to offer, came over him; he decided to write yes. It could do no harm. He knew it could do no good. They might agree to let by-gones be by-gones, but the damage had been done. Could a broken bowl be mended and called whole? It might be *called* whole, but what of it? Was it not broken and mended? He wrote and intimated that he would come.

On the Thursday in question Robert called up from the Auditorium to remind him of the engagement. Lester listened curiously to the sound of his voice. "All right," he said, "I'll be with you." At noon he went down-town, and there, within the exclusive precincts of the Union Club, the two brothers met and looked at each other again. Robert was thinner than when Lester had seen him last, and a little grayer. His eyes were bright and steely, but there were crow's-feet on either side. His manner was quick, keen, dynamic. Lester was noticeably of another type—solid, brusque, and indifferent. Men spoke of Lester these days as a little hard. Robert's keen blue eyes did not disturb him in the least—did not affect him in any way. He saw his brother just as he was, for he had the larger philosophic and interpretative insight; but Robert could not place Lester exactly. He could not fathom just what had happened to him in these years. Lester was stouter, not gray, for some reason, but sandy and ruddy, looking like a man who was fairly well satisfied to take life as he found it. Lester looked at his brother with a keen, steady eye. The latter shifted a little, for he was restless. He could see that there was no loss of that mental force and courage which had always been predominant characteristics in Lester's make-up.

"I thought I'd like to see you again, Lester," Robert remarked, after they had clasped hands in the customary grip. "It's been a long time now—nearly eight years, hasn't it?"

"About that," replied Lester. "How are things with you?"

"Oh, about the same. You've been fairly well, I see."

"Never sick," said Lester. "A little cold now and then. I don't often go to bed with anything. How's your wife?"

"Oh, Margaret's fine."

"And the children?"

"We don't see much of Ralph and Berenice since they married, but the others are around more or less. I suppose your wife is all right," he said hesitatingly. It was difficult ground for Robert.

Lester eyed him without a change of expression.

"Yes," he replied. "She enjoys pretty fair health. She's quite well at present."

They drifted mentally for a few moments, while Lester inquired after the business, and Amy, Louise, and Imogene. He admitted frankly that he neither saw nor heard from them nowadays. Robert told him what he could.

"The thing that I was thinking of in connection with you, Lester," said Robert finally, "is this matter of the Western Crucible Steel Company. You haven't been sitting there as a director in person I notice, but your attorney, Watson, has been acting for you. Clever man, that. The management isn't right—we all know that. We need a practical steel man at the head of it, if the thing is ever going to pay properly. I have voted my stock with yours right along because the propositions made by Watson have been right. He agrees with me that things ought to be changed. Now I have a chance to buy seventy shares held by Rossiter's widow. That with yours and mine would give us control of the company. I would like to have you take them, though it doesn't make a bit of difference so long as it's in the family. You can put any one you please in for president, and we'll make the thing come out right."

Lester smiled. It was a pleasant proposition. Watson had told him that Robert's interests were co-operating with him. Lester had long suspected that Robert would like to make up. This was the olive branch—the control of a property worth in the neighborhood of a million and a half.

"That's very nice of you," said Lester solemnly. "It's a rather liberal thing to do. What makes you want to do it now?"

"Well, to tell you the honest truth, Lester," replied Robert, "I never did feel right about that will business. I never did feel right about that secretary-treasurership and some other things that have happened. I don't want to rake up the past— you smile at that—but I can't help telling you how I feel. I've been pretty ambitious in the past. I was pretty ambitious just about the time that father died to get this United Carriage scheme under way, and I was afraid you might not like it. I have thought since that I ought not to have done it, but I did. I suppose you're not anxious to hear any more about that old affair. This other thing though—"

"Might be handed out as a sort of compensation," put in Lester quietly.

"Not exactly that, Lester—though it may have something of that in it. I know these things don't matter very much to you now. I know that the time to do things was years ago—not now. Still I thought sincerely that you might be interested in this proposition. It might lead to other things. Frankly, I thought it might patch up matters between us. We're brothers after all."

"Yes," said Lester, " we're brothers."

He was thinking as he said this of the irony of the situation. How much had this sense of brotherhood been worth in the past? Robert had practically forced him into his present relationship, and while Jennie had been really the only one to suffer, he could not help feeling angry. It was true that Robert had not cut him out of his one-fourth of his father's estate, but certainly he had not helped him to get it, and now Robert was thinking that this offer of his might mend things. It hurt him—Lester—a little. It irritated him. Life was strange.

"I can't see it, Robert," he said finally and determinedly. "I can appreciate the motive that prompts you to make this offer. But I can't see the wisdom of my taking it. Your opportunity is your opportunity. I don't want it. We can make all the changes you suggest if you take the stock. I'm rich enough anyhow. Bygones are bygones. I'm perfectly willing to talk with you from time to time. That's all you want. This other thing is simply a sop with which to plaster an old wound. You want my friendship and so far as I'm concerned you have that. I don't hold any grudge against you. I won't."

Robert looked at him fixedly. He half smiled. He admired Lester in spite of all that he had done to him—in spite of all that Lester was doing to him now.

"I don't know but what you're right, Lester," he admitted finally. "I didn't make this offer in any petty spirit though. I wanted to patch up this matter of feeling between us. I won't say anything more about it. You're not coming down to Cincinnati soon, are you?"

"I don't expect to," replied Lester.

"If you do I'd like to have you come and stay with us. Bring your wife. We could talk over old times."

Lester smiled an enigmatic smile.

"I'll be glad to," he said, without emotion. But he remembered that in the days of Jennie it was different. They would never have receded from their position regarding her. "Well," he thought, "perhaps I can't blame them. Let it go."

They talked on about other things. Finally Lester remembered an appointment. "I'll have to leave you soon," he said, looking at his watch.

"I ought to go, too," said Robert. They rose. "Well, anyhow," he added, as they walked toward the cloak-room, " we won't be absolute strangers in the future, will we?"

"Certainly not," said Lester. "I'll see you from time to time." They shook hands and separated amicably. There was a sense of unsatisfied obligation and some remorse in Robert's mind as he saw his brother walking briskly away. Lester was an able man. Why was it that there was so much feeling between them—had been even before Jennie had appeared? Then he remembered his old thoughts about "snaky deeds." That was what his brother lacked, and that only. He was not crafty; not darkly cruel, hence. "What a world!" he thought.

On his part Lester went away feeling a slight sense of opposition to, but also of sympathy for, his brother. He was not so terribly bad—not different from other men. Why criticize? What would he have done if he had been in Robert's place? Robert was getting along. So was he. He could see now how it all came about—why he had been made the victim, why his brother had been made the keeper of the great fortune. "It's the way the world runs," he thought. "What difference does it make? I have enough to live on. Why not let it go at that?"

Chapter LXI

THE DAYS of man under the old dispensation, or, rather, according to that supposedly biblical formula, which persists, are threescore years and ten. It is so ingrained in the race-consciousness by mouth-to-mouth utterance that it seems the profoundest of truths. As a matter of fact, man, even under his mortal illusion, is organically built to live five times the period of his maturity, and would do so if he but knew that it is spirit which endures, that age is an illusion, and that there is no death. Yet the race-thought, gained from what dream of materialism we know not, persists, and the death of man under the mathematical formula so fearfully accepted is daily registered.

Lester was one of those who believed in this formula. He was nearing sixty. He thought he had, say, twenty years more at the utmost to live—perhaps not so long. Well, he had lived comfortably. He felt that he could not complain. If death was coming, let it come. He was ready at any time. No complaint or resistance would issue from him. Life, in most of its aspects, was a silly show anyhow.

He admitted that it was mostly illusion—easily proved to be so. That it might all be one he sometimes suspected. It was very much like a dream in its composition truly—sometimes like a very bad dream. All he had to sustain him in his acceptance of its reality from hour to hour and day to day was apparent contact with this material proposition and that—people, meetings of boards of directors, individuals and organizations planning to do this and that, his wife's social functions. Letty loved him as a fine, grizzled example of a philosopher. She admired, as Jennie had, his solid, determined, phlegmatic attitude in the face of troubled circumstance. All the winds of fortune or misfortune could not apparently excite or disturb Lester. He refused to be frightened. He refused to budge from his beliefs and feelings, and usually had to be pushed away from them, still believing, if he were gotten away at all. He refused to do anything save as he always said, "Look the facts in the face" and fight. He could be made to fight easily enough if imposed upon, but only in a stubborn, resisting way. His plan was to resist every effort to coerce him to the last ditch. If he had to let go in the end he would when compelled, but his views as to the value of not letting go were quite the same even when he had let go under compulsion.

His views of living were still decidedly material, grounded in creature comforts, and he had always insisted upon having the best of everything. If the furnishings of his home became the least dingy he was for having them torn out and sold and the house done over. If he traveled, money must go ahead of him and smooth the way. He did not want argument, useless talk, or silly palaver as he called it. Every one must discuss interesting topics with him or not talk at all. Letty understood him thoroughly. She would chuck him under the chin mornings, or shake his solid head between her hands, telling him he was a brute, but a nice kind of a brute. "Yes, yes," he would growl. "I know. I'm an animal, I suppose. You're a seraphic suggestion of attenuated thought."

"No; you hush," she would reply, for at times he could cut like a knife without really meaning to be unkind. Then he would pet her a little, for, in spite of her vigorous conception of life, he realized that she was more or less dependent upon him. It was always so plain to her that he could get along without her. For reasons of kindliness he was trying to conceal this, to pretend the necessity of her presence, but it was so obvious that he really could dispense with her easily enough. Now Letty did depend upon Lester. It was something, in so shifty and uncertain a world, to be near so fixed and determined a quantity as this bear-man. It was like being close to a warmly glowing lamp in the dark or a bright burning fire in the cold. Lester was not afraid of anything. He felt that he knew how to live and to die.

It was natural that a temperament of this kind should have its solid, material manifestation at every point. Having his financial affairs well in hand, most of his holding being shares of big companies, where boards of solemn directors merely approved the strenuous efforts of ambitious executives to "make good," he had leisure for living. He and Letty were fond of visiting the various American and European watering-places. He gambled a little, for he found that there was considerable diversion in risking interesting sums on the spin of a wheel or the fortuitous roll of a ball; and he took more and more to drinking, not in the sense that a drunkard takes to it, but as a high liver, socially, and with all his friends. He was inclined to drink the rich drinks when he did not take straight whiskey—champagne, sparkling Burgundy, the expensive and effervescent white wines. When he drank he could drink a great deal, and he ate in proportion. Nothing must be served but the best—soup, fish, entrée, roast, game, dessert—everything that made up a showy dinner—and he had long since determined that only a high-priced chef was worth while. They had found an old *cordon bleu*, Louis Berdot, who had served in the house of one of the great dry goods princes, and this man he engaged. He cost Lester a hundred dollars a week, but his reply to any question was that he only had one life to live.

The trouble with this attitude was that it adjusted nothing, improved nothing, left everything to drift on toward an indefinite end. If Lester had married Jennie and accepted the comparatively meager income of ten thousand a year he would have maintained the same attitude to the end. It would have led him to a stolid indifference to the social world of which now necessarily he was a part. He would have drifted on with a few mentally compatible cronies who would have accepted him for what he was—a good fellow—and Jennie in the end would not have been so much better off than she was now.

One of the changes which was interesting was that the Kanes transferred their residence to New York. Mrs. Kane had become very intimate with a group of clever women in the Eastern four hundred, or nine hundred, and had been advised and urged to transfer the scene of her activities to New York. She finally did so, leasing a house in Seventy-eighth Street, near Madison Avenue. She installed a novelty for her, a complete staff of liveried servants, after the English fashion, and had the rooms of her house done in correlative periods. Lester smiled at her vanity and love of show.

"You talk about your democracy," he grunted one day. "You have as much democracy as I have religion, and that's none at all."

"Why, how you talk!" she denied. "I am democratic. We all run in classes. You do. I'm merely accepting the logic of the situation."

"The logic of your grandmother! Do you call a butler and doorman in red velvet a part of the necessity of the occasion?"

"I certainly do," she replied. "Maybe not the necessity exactly, but the spirit surely. Why should you quarrel? You're the first one to insist on perfection—to quarrel if there is any flaw in the order of things."

"You never heard me quarrel."

"Oh, I don't mean that literally. But you demand perfection—the exact spirit of the occasion, and you know it."

"Maybe I do, but what has that to do with your democracy?"

"I am democratic. I insist on it. I'm as democratic in spirit as any woman. Only I see things as they are, and conform as much as possible for comfort's sake, and so do you. Don't you throw rocks at my glass house, Mister Master. Yours is so transparent I can see every move you make inside."

"I'm democratic and you're not," he teased; but he approved thoroughly of everything she did. She was, he sometimes fancied, a better executive in her world than he was in his.

Drifting in this fashion, wining, dining, drinking the waters of this curative spring and that, traveling in luxurious ease and taking no physical exercise, finally altered his body from a vigorous, quick-moving, well-balanced organism into one where plethora of substance was clogging every essential function. His liver, kidneys, spleen, pancreas—every organ, in fact—had been overtaxed for some time to keep up the process of digestion and elimination. In the past seven years he had become uncomfortably heavy. His kidneys were weak, and so were the arteries of his brain. By dieting, proper exercise, the right mental attitude, he might have lived to be eighty or ninety. As a matter of fact, he was allowing himself to drift into a physical state in which even a slight malady might prove dangerous. The result was inevitable, and it came.

It so happened that he and Letty had gone to the North Cape on a cruise with a party of friends. Lester, in order to attend to some important business, decided to return to Chicago late in November; he arranged to have his wife meet him in New York just before the Christmas holidays. He wrote Watson to expect him, and engaged rooms at the Auditorium, for he had sold the Chicago residence some two years before and was now living permanently in New York.

One late November day, after having attended to a number of details and cleared up his affairs very materially, Lester was seized with what the doctor who was called to attend him described as a cold in the intestines—a disturbance usually symptomatic of some other weakness, either of the blood or of some organ. He suffered great pain, and the usual remedies in that case were applied. There were bandages of red flannel with a mustard dressing, and specifics were also administered. He experienced some relief, but he was troubled with a sense of impending disaster. He had Watson cable his wife—there was nothing serious about it, but he was ill. A trained nurse was in attendance and his valet stood guard at the door to prevent annoyance of any kind. It was plain that Letty could not reach Chicago under three weeks. He had the feeling that he would not see her again.

Curiously enough, not only because he was in Chicago, but because he had never been spiritually separated from Jennie, he was thinking about her constantly at this time. He had intended to go out and see her just as soon as he was through with his business engagements and before he left the city. He had asked Watson how she was getting along, and had been informed that everything was well with her. She was living quietly and looking in good health, so Watson said. Lester wished he could see her.

This thought grew as the days passed and he grew no better. He was suffering from time to time with severe attacks of griping pains that seemed to tie his viscera into knots, and left him very weak. Several times the physician administered cocaine with a needle in order to relieve him of useless pain.

After one of the severe attacks he called Watson to his side, told him to send the nurse away, and then said: "Watson, I'd like to have you do me a favor. Ask Mrs. Stover if she won't come here to see me. You'd better go and get her. Just send the nurse and Kozo (the valet) away for the afternoon, or while she's here. If she comes at any other time I'd like to have her admitted."

Watson understood. He liked this expression of sentiment. He was sorry for Jennie. He was sorry for Lester. He wondered what the world would think if it could know of this bit of romance in connection with so prominent a man. Lester was decent. He had made Watson prosperous. The latter was only too glad to serve him in any way.

He called a carriage and rode out to Jennie's residence. He found her watering some plants; her face expressed her surprise at his unusual presence.

"I come on a rather troublesome errand, Mrs. Stover," he said, using her assumed name. "Your—that is, Mr. Kane is quite sick at the Auditorium. His wife is in Europe, and he wanted to know if I wouldn't come out here and ask you to come and see him. He wanted me to bring you, if possible. Could you come with me now?"

"Why yes," said Jennie, her face a study. The children were in school. An old Swedish housekeeper was in the kitchen. She could go as well as not. But there was coming back to her in detail a dream she had had several nights before. It had seemed to her that she was out on a dark, mystic body of water over which was hanging something like a fog, or a pall of smoke. She heard the water ripple, or stir faintly, and then out of the surrounding darkness a boat appeared. It was a little boat, oarless, or not visibly propelled, and in it were her mother, and Vesta, and some one whom she could not make out. Her mother's face was pale and sad, very much as she had often seen it in life. She looked at Jennie solemnly, sympathetically, and then suddenly Jennie realized that the third occupant of the boat was Lester. He looked at her gloomily—an expression she had never seen on his face before—and then her mother remarked, "Well, we must go now." The boat began to move, a great sense of loss came over her, and she cried, "Oh, don't leave me, mamma!"

But her mother only looked at her out of deep, sad, still eyes, and the boat was gone.

She woke with a start, half fancying that Lester was beside her. She stretched out her hand to touch his arm; then she drew herself up in the dark and rubbed her eyes, realizing that she was alone. A great sense of depression remained with her, and for two days it haunted her. Then, when it seemed as if it were nothing, Mr. Watson appeared with his ominous message.

She went to dress, and reappeared, looking as troubled as were her thoughts. She was very pleasing in her appearance yet, a sweet, kindly woman, well dressed and shapely. She had never been separated mentally from Lester, just as he had never grown entirely away from her. She was always with him in thought, just as in the years when they were together. Her fondest memories were of the days when he first courted her in Cleveland—the days when he had carried her off, much as the cave-man seized his mate—by force. Now she longed to do what she could for him. For this call was as much a testimony as a shock. He loved her—he loved her, after all.

The carriage rolled briskly through the long streets into the smoky down-town district. It arrived at the Auditorium, and Jennie was escorted to Lester's room. Watson had been considerate. He had talked little, leaving her to her thoughts. In this great hotel she felt diffident after so long a period of complete retirement. As she entered the room she looked at Lester with large, gray, sympathetic eyes. He was lying propped up on two pillows, his solid head with its growth of once dark brown hair slightly grayed. He looked at her curiously out of his wise old eyes, a light of sympathy and affection shining in them—weary as they were. Jennie was greatly distressed. His pale face, slightly drawn from suffering, cut her like a knife. She took his hand, which was outside the coverlet, and pressed it. She leaned over and kissed his lips.

"I'm so sorry, Lester," she murmured. "I'm so sorry. You're not very sick though, are you? You must get well, Lester—and soon!" She patted his hand gently.

"Yes, Jennie, but I'm pretty bad," he said. "I don't feel right about this business. I don't seem able to shake it off. But tell me, how have you been?"

"Oh, just the same, dear," she replied. "I'm all right. You mustn't talk like that, though. You're going to be all right very soon now."

He smiled grimly. "Do you think so?" He shook his head, for he thought differently. "Sit down, dear," he went on, "I'm not worrying about that. I want to talk to you again. I want you near me." He sighed and shut his eyes for a minute.

She drew up a chair close beside the bed, her face toward his, and took his hand. It seemed such a beautiful thing that he should send for her. Her eyes showed the mingled sympathy, affection, and gratitude of her heart. At the same time fear gripped her; how ill he looked!

"I can't tell what may happen," he went on. "Letty is in Europe. I've wanted to see you again for some time. I was coming out this trip. We are living in New York, you know. You're a little stouter, Jennie."

"Yes, I'm getting old, Lester," she smiled.

"Oh, that doesn't make any difference," he replied, looking at her fixedly. "Age doesn't count. We are all in that boat. It's how we feel about life."

He stopped and stared at the ceiling. A slight twinge of pain reminded him of the vigorous seizures he had been through. He couldn't stand many more paroxysms like the last one.

"I couldn't go, Jennie, without seeing you again," he observed, when the slight twinge ceased and he was free to think again. "I've always wanted to say to you, Jennie," he went on, "that I haven't been satisfied with the way we parted. It wasn't the right thing, after all. I haven't been any happier. I'm sorry. I wish now, for my own peace of mind, that I hadn't done it."

"Don't say that, Lester," she demurred, going over in her mind all that had been between them. This was such a testimony to their real union—their real spiritual compatibility. "It's all right. It doesn't make any difference. You've been very good to me. I wouldn't have been satisfied to have you lose your fortune. It couldn't be that way. I've been a lot better satisfied as it is. It's been hard, but, dear, everything is hard at times." She paused.

"No," he said. "It wasn't right. The thing wasn't worked out right from the start; but that wasn't your fault. I'm sorry. I wanted to tell you that. I'm glad I'm here to do it."

"Don't talk that way, Lester—please don't," she pleaded. "It's all right. You needn't be sorry. There's nothing to be sorry for. You have always been so good to me. Why, when

I think—" she stopped, for it was hard for her to speak. She was choking with affection and sympathy. She pressed his hands. She was recalling the house he took for her family in Cleveland, his generous treatment of Gerhardt, all the long ago tokens of love and kindness.

"Well, I've told you now, and I feel better. You're a good woman, Jennie, and you're kind to come to me this way. I loved you. I love you now. I want to tell you that. It seems strange, but you're the only woman I ever did love truly. We should never have parted."

Jennie caught her breath. It was the one thing she had waited for all these years—this testimony. It was the one thing that could make everything right—this confession of spiritual if not material union. Now she could live happily. Now die so. "Oh, Lester," she exclaimed with a sob, and pressed his hand. He returned the pressure. There was a little silence. Then he spoke again.

"How are the two orphans?" he asked.

"Oh, they're lovely," she answered, entering upon a detailed description of their diminutive personalities. He listened comfortably, for her voice was soothing to him. Her whole personality was grateful to him. When it came time for her to go he seemed desirous of keeping her.

"Going, Jennie?"

"I can stay just as well as not, Lester," she volunteered. "I'll take a room. I can send a note out to Mrs. Swenson. It will be all right."

"You needn't do that," he said, but she could see that he wanted her, that he did not want to be alone.

From that time on until the hour of his death she was not out of the hotel.

Chapter LXII

THE END CAME after four days during which Jennie was by his bedside almost constantly. The nurse in charge welcomed her at first as a relief and company, but the physician was inclined to object. Lester, however, was stubborn. "This is my death," he said, with a touch of grim humor. "If I'm dying I ought to be allowed to die in my own way."

Watson smiled at the man's unfaltering courage. He had never seen anything like it before.

There were cards of sympathy, calls of inquiry, notices in the newspaper. Robert saw an item in the *Inquirer*, and decided to go to Chicago. Imogene called with her husband, and they were admitted to Lester's room for a few minutes after Jennie had gone to hers. Lester had little to say. The nurse cautioned them that he was not to be talked to much. When they were gone Lester said to Jennie, "Imogene has changed a good deal." He made no other comment.

Mrs. Kane was on the Atlantic three days out from New York the afternoon Lester died. He had been meditating whether anything more could be done for Jennie, but he could not make up his mind about it. Certainly it was useless to leave her more money. She did not want it. He had been wondering where Letty was and how near her actual arrival might be when he was seized with a tremendous paroxysm of pain. Before relief could be administered in the shape of an anesthetic he was dead. It developed afterward that it was not the intestinal trouble which killed him, but a lesion of a major blood-vessel in the brain.

Jennie, who had been strongly wrought up by watching and worrying, was beside herself with grief. He had been a part of her thought and feeling so long that it seemed now as though a part of herself had died. She had loved him as she had fancied she could never love any one, and he had always shown that he cared for her—at least in some degree. She could not feel the emotion that expresses itself in tears—only a dull ache, a numbness which seemed to make her insensible to pain. He looked so strong—her Lester—lying there still in death. His expression was unchanged—defiant, determined, albeit peaceful. Word had come from Mrs. Kane that she would arrive on the Wednesday following. It was decided to hold the body. Jennie learned from Mr. Watson that it was to be transferred to Cincinnati, where the Paces had a vault. Because of the arrival of various members of the family, Jennie withdrew to her own home; she could do nothing more.

The final ceremonies presented a peculiar commentary on the anomalies of existence. It was arranged with Mrs. Kane by wire that the body should be transferred to Imogene's residence, and the funeral held from there. Robert, who arrived the night Lester died; Berry Dodge; Imogene's husband, Mr. Midgely; and three other citizens of prominence were selected as pall-bearers. Louise and her husband came from Buffalo; Amy and her husband from Cincinnati. The house was full to overflowing with citizens who either sincerely wished or felt it expedient to call. Because of the fact that Lester and his family were tentatively Catholic, a Catholic priest was called in and the ritual of that Church was carried out. It was curious to see him lying in the parlor of this alien residence, candles at his head and feet, burning sepulchrally, a silver cross upon his breast, caressed by his waxen fingers. He would have smiled if he could have seen himself, but the Kane family was too conventional, too set in its convictions, to find anything strange in this. The Church made no objection, of course. The family was distinguished. What more could be desired?

On Wednesday Mrs. Kane arrived. She was greatly distraught, for her love, like Jennie's, was sincere. She left her room that night when all was silent and leaned over the coffin, studying by the light of the burning candles Lester's beloved features. Tears trickled down her cheeks, for she had been happy with him. She caressed his cold cheeks and hands. "Poor, dear Lester!" she whispered. "Poor, brave soul!" No one told her that he had sent for Jennie. The Kane family did not know.

Meanwhile in the house on South Park Avenue sat a woman who was enduring alone the pain, the anguish of an irreparable loss. Through all these years the subtle hope had persisted, in spite of every circumstance, that somehow life might bring him back to her. He had come, it is true—he really had in death—but he had gone again. Where? Whither

her mother, whither Gerhardt, whither Vesta had gone? She could not hope to see him again, for the papers had informed her of his removal to Mrs. Midgely's residence, and of the fact that he was to be taken from Chicago to Cincinnati for burial. The last ceremonies in Chicago were to be held in one of the wealthy Roman Catholic churches of the South Side, St. Michael's, of which the Midgelys were members.

Jennie felt deeply about this. She would have liked so much to have had him buried in Chicago, where she could go to the grave occasionally, but this was not to be. She was never a master of her fate. Others invariably controlled. She thought of him as being taken from her finally by the removal of the body to Cincinnati, as though distance made any difference. She decided at last to veil herself heavily and attend the funeral at the church. The paper had explained that the services would be at two in the afternoon. Then at four the body would be taken to the depot, and transferred to the train; the members of the family would accompany it to Cincinnati. She thought of this as another opportunity. She might go to the depot.

A little before the time for the funeral cortège to arrive at the church there appeared at one of its subsidiary entrances a woman in black, heavily veiled, who took a seat in an inconspicuous corner. She was a little nervous at first, for, seeing that the church was dark and empty, she feared lest she had mistaken the time and place; but after ten minutes of painful suspense a bell in the church tower began to toll solemnly. Shortly thereafter an acolyte in black gown and white surplice appeared and lighted groups of candles on either side of the altar. A hushed stirring of feet in the choir-loft indicated that the service was to be accompanied by music. Some loiterers, attracted by the bell, some idle strangers, a few acquaintances and citizens not directly invited appeared and took seats.

Jennie watched all this with wondering eyes. Never in her life had she been inside a Catholic church. The gloom, the beauty of the windows, the whiteness of the altar, the golden flames of the candles impressed her. She was suffused with a sense of sorrow, loss, beauty, and mystery. Life in all its vagueness and uncertainty seemed typified by this scene.

As the bell tolled there came from the sacristy a procession of altar-boys. The smallest, an angelic youth of eleven, came first, bearing aloft a magnificent silver cross. In the hands of each subsequent pair of servitors was held a tall, lighted candle. The priest, in black cloth and lace, attended by an acolyte on either hand, followed. The procession passed out the entrance into the vestibule of the church, and was not seen again until the choir began a mournful, responsive chant, the Latin supplication for mercy and peace.

Then, at this sound the solemn procession made its reappearance. There came the silver cross, the candles, the dark-faced priest, reading dramatically to himself as he walked, and the body of Lester in a great black coffin, with silver handles, carried by the pall-bearers, who kept an even pace. Jennie stiffened perceptibly, her nerves responding as though to a shock from an electric current. She did not know any of these men. She did not know Robert. She had never seen Mr. Midgely. Of the long company of notables who followed two by two she recognized only three, whom Lester had pointed out to her in times past. Mrs. Kane she saw, of course, for she was directly behind the coffin, leaning on the arm of a stranger; behind her walked Mr. Watson, solemn, gracious. He gave a quick glance to either side, evidently expecting to see her somewhere; but not finding her, he turned his eyes gravely forward and walked on. Jennie looked with all her eyes, her heart gripped by pain. She seemed so much a part of this solemn ritual, and yet infinitely removed from it all.

The procession reached the altar rail, and the coffin was put down. A white shroud bearing the insignia of suffering, a black cross, was put over it, and the great candles were set beside it. There were the chanted invocations and responses, the sprinkling of the coffin with holy water, the lighting and swinging of the censer and then the mumbled responses of the auditors to the Lord's Prayer and to its Catholic addition, the invocation to the Blessed Virgin. Jennie was overawed and amazed, but no show of form colorful, impression imperial, could take away the sting of death, the sense of infinite loss. To Jennie the candles, the incense, the holy song were beautiful. They touched the deep chord of melancholy in her, and made it vibrate through the depths of her being. She was as a house filled with mournful melody and the presence of death. She cried and cried. She could see, curiously, that Mrs. Kane was sobbing convulsively also.

When it was all over the carriages were entered and the body was borne to the station. All the guests and strangers departed, and finally, when all was silent, she arose. Now she would go to the depot also, for she was hopeful of seeing his body put on the train. They would have to bring it out on the platform, just as they did in Vesta's case. She took a car, and a little later she entered the waiting-room of the depot. She lingered about, first in the concourse, where the great iron fence separated the passengers from the tracks, and then in the waiting-room, hoping to discover the order of proceedings. She finally observed the group of immediate relatives waiting—Mrs. Kane, Robert, Mr. Midgely, Louise, Amy, Imogene, and the others. She actually succeeded in identifying most of them, though it was not knowledge in this case, but pure instinct and intuition.

No one had noticed it in the stress of excitement, but it was Thanksgiving Eve. Throughout the great railroad station there was a hum of anticipation, that curious ebullition of fancy which springs from the thought of pleasures to come. People were going away for the holiday. Carriages were at the station entries. Announcers were calling in stentorian voices the destination of each new train as the time of its departure drew near. Jennie heard with a desperate ache the description of a route which she and Lester had taken more than once, slowly and melodiously emphasized. "Detroit, Toledo, Cleveland, Buffalo, and New York." There were cries of trains for "Fort Wayne, Columbus, Pittsburg, Philadelphia, and points East," and then finally for "Indianapolis, Louisville, Columbus, Cincinnati, and points South." The hour had struck.

Several times Jennie had gone to the concourse between the waiting-room and the tracks to see if through the iron grating which separated her from her beloved she could get one last look at the coffin, or the great wooden box which held it, before it was put on the train. Now she saw it coming. There was a baggage porter pushing a truck into position near the place where the baggage car would stop. On it was Lester, that last shadow of his substance, incased in the honors of wood, and cloth, and silver. There was no thought on the part of the porter of the agony of loss which was represented here. He could not see how wealth and position in this hour were typified to her mind as a great fence, a wall, which divided her eternally from her beloved. Had it not always been so? Was not her life a patchwork of conditions made and affected by these things which she saw—wealth and force—which had found her unfit? She had evidently been born to yield, not seek. This panoply of power had been paraded before her since childhood. What could she do now but stare vaguely after it as it marched triumphantly by? Lester had been of it. Him it respected. Of her it knew nothing. She looked through the grating, and once more there came the cry of "Indianapolis, Louisville, Columbus, Cincinnati, and points South." A long red train, brilliantly lighted, composed of baggage cars, day coaches, a dining-car, set with white linen and silver, and a half dozen comfortable Pullmans, rolled in and stopped. A great black engine, puffing and glowing, had it all safely in tow.

As the baggage car drew near the waiting truck a trainhand in blue, looking out of the car, called to some one within.

"Hey, Jack! Give us a hand here. There's a stiff outside!"

Jennie could not hear.

All she could see was the great box that was so soon to disappear. All she could feel was that this train would start presently, and then it would all be over. The gates opened, the passengers poured out. There were Robert, and Amy, and Louise, and Midgely—all making for the Pullman cars in the rear. They had said their farewells to their friends. No need to repeat them. A trio of assistants "gave a hand" at getting the great wooden case into the car. Jennie saw it disappear with an acute physical wrench at her heart.

There were many trunks to be put aboard, and then the door of the baggage car half closed, but not before the warning bell of the engine sounded. There was the insistent calling of "all aboard" from this quarter and that; then slowly the great locomotive began to move. Its bell was ringing, its steam hissing, its smoke-stack throwing aloft a great black plume of smoke that fell back over the cars like a pall. The fireman, conscious of the heavy load behind, flung open a flaming furnace door to throw in coal. Its light glowed like a golden eye.

Jennie stood rigid, staring into the wonder of this picture, her face white, her eyes wide, her hands unconsciously clasped, but one thought in her mind—they were taking his body away. A leaden November sky was ahead, almost dark. She looked, and looked until the last glimmer of the red lamp on the receding sleeper disappeared in the maze of smoke and haze overhanging the tracks of the far-stretching yard.

"Yes," said the voice of a passing stranger, gay with the anticipation of coming pleasures. "We're going to have a great time down there. Remember Annie? Uncle Jim is coming and Aunt Ella."

Jennie did not hear that or anything else of the chatter and bustle around her. Before her was stretching a vista of lonely years down which she was steadily gazing. Now what? She was not so old yet. There were those two orphan children to raise. They would marry and leave after a while, and then what? Days and days in endless reiteration, and then—?

In Passing

IT IS USELESS to apostrophize a soul such as Jennie's which has reached the full measure of its being. Shall you say to the blown rose, " well done"? Or to the battered, wind-riven, lightning-scarred pine, "thou failure"? In the chemic drift and flow of things, how little we know of that which is either failure or success! Is there either? This daughter of the poor, born into the rush and hurry of a clamant world—a civilization, so called—eager to possess itself of shows and chattels—what a sorry figure! Not to be possessed of the power to strike and destroy; not to choose, because of an absence of lust and hunger, to run as a troubled current; not to be able to fall upon a fellow-being, tearing that which is momentarily desirable from his grasp, only to drop it and run wildly toward that which for another brief moment seems more worthy of pursuit. Not to be bitter, angry, brutal, feverish—what a loss!

And then how strange that there should be born into a soul a sense of its own fitness and place—that one should be able to say to himself, in a spirit of deep understanding, "My kingdom is not of this world"! Behold! there are hierarchies and powers above and below the measure of our perception. It is given to us to see in part and to believe in part. But of that which is perfect who shall prophesy? Only this daughter of the poor felt something—the beauty of the trees, the wonder of the rains, the color of existence. Marveling at these, feeling their call of community in spirit, how could it be that she should hurry—that she should seek? Was it not all with her from the beginning?

Those days of her earliest youth, when she felt that life was perfect; those hours of stress, when it seemed that life could not be wholly bad; those moments of prosperity, when she realized in her own soul that she held them lightly and that they would pass, leaving in their place the simplicities and the necessities only—were not these the hours of truest insight? Jennie loved, and loving, gave. Is there a superior wisdom? Are its signs and monuments in evidence? Of whom, then, have we life and all good things—and why?

TWELVE MEN

Contents

Peter

In any group of men I have ever known, speaking from the point of view of character and not that of physical appearance, Peter would stand out as deliciously and irrefutably different. In the great waste of American intellectual dreariness he was an oasis, a veritable spring in the desert. He understood life. He knew men. He was free—spiritually, morally, in a thousand ways, it seemed to me.

As one drags along through this inexplicable existence one realizes how such qualities stand out; not the pseudo freedom of strong men, financially or physically, but the real, internal, spiritual freedom, where the mind, as it were, stands up and looks at itself, faces Nature unafraid, is aware of its own weaknesses, its strengths; examines its own and the creative impulses of the universe and of men with a kindly and non-dogmatic eye, in fact kicks dogma out of doors, and yet deliberately and of choice holds fast to many, many simple and human things, and rounds out life, or would, in a natural, normal, courageous, healthy way.

The first time I ever saw Peter was in St. Louis in 1892; I had come down from Chicago to work on the St. Louis *Globe-Democrat*, and he was a part of the art department force of that paper. At that time—and he never seemed to change later even so much as a hair's worth until he died in 1908—he was short, stocky and yet quick and even jerky in his manner, with a bushy, tramp-like "get-up" of hair and beard, most swiftly and astonishingly disposed of at times only to be regrown at others, and always, and intentionally, I am sure, most amusing to contemplate. In addition to all this he had an air of well-being, force and alertness which belied the other surface characteristics as anything more than a genial pose or bit of idle gayety.

Plainly he took himself seriously and yet lightly, usually with an air of suppressed gayety, as though saying, "This whole business of living is a great joke." He always wore good and yet exceedingly mussy clothes, at times bespattered with ink or, worse yet, even soup—an amazing grotesquery that was the dismay of all who knew him, friends and relatives especially. In addition he was nearly always liberally besprinkled with tobacco dust, the source of which he used in all forms: in pipe, cigar and plug, even cigarettes when he could obtain nothing more substantial. One of the things about him which most impressed me at that time and later was this love of the ridiculous or the grotesque, in himself or others, which would not let him take anything in a dull or conventional mood, would not even permit him to appear normal at times but urged him on to all sorts of nonsense, in an effort, I suppose, to entertain himself and make life seem less commonplace.

And yet he loved life, in all its multiform and multiplex aspects and with no desire or tendency to sniff, reform or improve anything. It was good just as he found it, excellent. Life to Peter was indeed so splendid that he was always very much wrought up about it, eager to live, to study, to do a thousand things. For him it was a workshop for the artist, the thinker, as well as the mere grubber, and without really criticizing any one he was "for" the individual who is able to understand, to portray or to create life, either feelingly and artistically or with accuracy and discrimination. To him, as I saw then and see even more clearly now, there was no high and no low. All things were only relatively so. A thief was a thief, but he had his place. Ditto the murderer. Ditto the saint. Not man but Nature was planning, or at least doing, something which man could not understand, of which very likely he was a mere tool. Peter was as much thrilled and entendered by the brawling strumpet in the street or the bagnio as by the virgin with her starry crown. The rich were rich and the poor poor, but all were in the grip of imperial forces whose ruthless purposes or lack of them made all men ridiculous, pathetic or magnificent, as you choose. He pitied ignorance and necessity, and despised vanity and cruelty for cruelty's sake, and the miserly hoarding of anything. He was liberal, material, sensual and yet spiritual; and although he never had more than a little money, out of the richness and fullness of his own temperament he seemed able to generate a kind of atmosphere and texture in his daily life which was rich and warm, splendid really in thought (the true reality) if not in fact, and most grateful to all. Yet also, as I have said, always he wished to *seem* the clown, the scapegrace, the wanton and the loon even, mouthing idle impossibilities at times and declaring his profoundest faith in the most fantastic things.

Do I seem to rave? I am dealing with a most significant person.

In so far as I knew he was born into a mid-Western family of Irish extraction whose habitat was southwest Missouri. In the town in which he was reared there was not even a railroad until he was fairly well grown—a fact which amused but never impressed him very much. Apropos of this he once told me of a yokel who, never having seen a railroad, entered the station with his wife and children long before train time, bought his ticket and waited a while, looking out of the various windows, then finally returned to the ticket-seller and asked, "When does this thing start?" He meant the station building itself. At the time Peter had entered upon art work he had scarcely prosecuted his studies beyond, if so far as, the conventional high or grammar school, and yet he was most amazingly informed and but little interested in what any school or college had to offer. His father, curiously enough, was an educated Irish-American, a lawyer by profession, and a Catholic. His mother was an American Catholic, rather strict and narrow. His brothers and sisters, of whom there were four, were, as I learned later, astonishingly virile and interesting Americans of a rather wild, unsettled type. They were all, in so far as I could judge from chance meetings, agnostic, tense, quick-moving—so vital that they weighed on one a little, as very intense temperaments are apt to do. One of the brothers, K——, who seemed to seek me out ever so often for Peter's sake, was so intense, nervous, rapid-talking, rapid-living, that he frightened me a little. He loved noisy, garish places. He liked to play the piano, stay up very late; he was a high liver, a "good dresser," as the denizens of the Tenderloin would say, an excellent example of the flashy, clever promoter. He was always representing a new company, introducing something—a table or laxative water, a shaving soap, a chewing gum, a safety razor, a bicycle, an automobile tire or the machine itself. He was here, there, everywhere—in Waukesha, Wisconsin; San Francisco; New York; New Orleans.

"My, my! This is certainly interesting!" he would exclaim, with an air which would have done credit to a comedian and extending both hands. "Peter's pet friend, Dreiser! Well, well, well! Let's have a drink. Let's have something to eat. I'm only in town for a day. Maybe you'd like to go to a show—or hit the high places? Would you? Well, well, well! Let's make a night of it! What do you say?" and he would fix me with a glistening, nervous and what was intended no doubt to be a reassuring eye, but which unsettled me as thoroughly as the imminence of an earthquake. But I was talking of Peter.

The day I first saw him he was bent over a drawing-board illustrating a snake story for one of the Sunday issues of the *Globe-Democrat*, which apparently delighted in regaling its readers with most astounding concoctions of this kind, and the snake he was drawing was most disturbingly vital and reptilian, beady-eyed, with distended jaws, extended tongue, most fatefully coiled.

"My," I commented in passing, for I was in to see him about another matter, " what a glorious snake!"

"Yes, you can't make 'em too snaky for the snake-editor up front," he returned, rising and dusting tobacco from his lap and shirtfront, for he was in his shirt-sleeves. Then he expectorated not in but to one side of a handsome polished brass cuspidor which contained not the least evidence of use, the rubber mat upon which it stood being instead most disturbingly "decorated." I was most impressed by this latter fact although at the time I said nothing, being too new. Later, I may as well say here, I discovered why. This was a bit of his clowning humor, a purely manufactured and as it were mechanical joke or ebullience of soul. If any one inadvertently or through unfamiliarity attempted to expectorate in his "golden cuspidor," as he described it, he was always quick to rise and interpose in the most solemn, almost sepulchral manner, at the same time raising a hand. "Hold! Out—not in—to one side, on the mat! That cost me seven dollars!" Then he would solemnly seat himself and begin to draw again. I saw him do this to all but the chiefest of the authorities of the paper. And all, even the dullest, seemed to be amused, quite fascinated by the utter trumpery folly of it.

But I am getting ahead of my tale. In so far as the snake

was concerned, he was referring to the assistant who had these snake stories in charge. "The fatter and more venomous and more scaly they are," he went on, "the better. I'd like it if we could use a little color in this paper—red for eyes and tongue, and blue and green for scales. The farmers upstate would love that. They like good but poisonous snakes." Then he grinned, stood back and, cocking his head to one side in a most examining and yet approving manner, ran his hand through his hair and beard and added, "A snake can't be too vital, you know, for this paper. We have to draw 'em strong, plenty of vitality, plenty of go." He grinned most engagingly.

I could not help laughing, of course. The impertinent air! The grand, almost condescending manner!

We soon became fast friends.

In the same office in close contact with him was another person, one D—— W——, also a newspaper artist, who, while being exceedingly interesting and special in himself, still as a character never seems to have served any greater purpose in my own mind than to have illustrated how emphatic and important Peter was. He had a thin, pale, Dantesque face, coal black, almost Indian-like hair most carefully parted in the middle and oiled and slicked down at the sides and back until it looked as though it had been glued. His eyes were small and black and querulous but not mean—petted eyes they were—and the mouth had little lines at each corner which seemed to say he had endured much, much pain, which of course he had not, but which nevertheless seemed to ask for, and I suppose earned him some, sympathy. Dick in his way was an actor, a tragedian of sorts, but with an element of humor, cynicism and insight which saved him from being utterly ridiculous. Like most actors, he was a great poseur. He invariably affected the long, loose flowing tie with a soft white or blue or green or brown linen shirt (would any American imitation of the "Quartier Latin" denizen have been without one at that date?), yellow or black gloves, a round, soft crush hat, very soft and limp and very *different*, patent leather pumps, betimes a capecoat, a slender cane, a bouton-nière—all this in hard, smoky, noisy, commercial St. Louis, full of middle-West business men and farmers!

I would not mention this particular person save that for a

time he, Peter and myself were most intimately associated. We
temporarily constituted in our way a "soldiers three" of the
newspaper world. For some years after we were more or less
definitely in touch as a group, although later Peter and myself
having drifted Eastward and hob-nobbing as a pair had been
finding more and more in common and had more and more
come to view Dick for what he was: a character of Dicken-
sian, or perhaps still better, Cruikshankian, proportions and
qualities. But in those days the three of us were all but inseparable; eating, working, playing, all but sleeping together.
I had a studio of sorts in a more or less dilapidated factory
section of St. Louis (Tenth near Market; now I suppose
briskly commercial), Dick had one at Broadway and Locust,
directly opposite the then famous Southern Hotel. Peter lived
with his family on the South Side, a most respectable and
homey-home neighborhood.

It has been one of my commonest experiences, and one of
the most interesting to me, to note that nearly all of my keenest experiences intellectually, my most gorgeous *rapproche-
ments* and swiftest developments mentally, have been by, to,
and through men, not women, although there have been several exceptions to this. Nearly every turning point in my
career has been signalized by my meeting some man of great
force, to whom I owe some of the most ecstatic intellectual
hours of my life, hours in which life seemed to bloom forth
into new aspects, glowed as with the radiance of a gorgeous
tropic day.

Peter was one such. About my own age at this time, he was
blessed with a natural understanding which was simply God-
like. Although, like myself, he was raised a Catholic and still
pretending in a boisterous, Rabelaisian way to have some reverence for that faith, he was amusingly sympathetic to everything good, bad, indifferent—"in case there might be
something in it; you never can tell." Still he hadn't the least
interest in conforming to the tenets of the church and
laughed at its pretensions, preferring his own theories to any
other. Apparently nothing amused him so much as the
thought of confession and communion, of being shrived by
some stout, healthy priest as worldly as himself, and pref-
erably Irish, like himself. At the same time he had a hearty

admiration for the Germans, all their ways, conservatisms, their breweries, food and such things, and finally wound up by marrying a German girl.

As far as I could make out, Peter had no faith in anything except Nature itself, and very little in that except in those aspects of beauty and accident and reward and terrors with which it is filled and for which he had an awe if not a reverence and in every manifestation of which he took the greatest delight. Life was a delicious, brilliant mystery to him, horrible in some respects, beautiful in others; a great adventure. Unlike myself at the time, he had not the slightest trace of any lingering Puritanism, and wished to live in a lush, vigorous, healthy, free, at times almost barbaric, way. The negroes, the ancient Romans, the Egyptians, tales of the Orient and the grotesque Dark Ages, our own vile slums and evil quarters— how he reveled in these! He was for nights of wandering, endless investigation, reading, singing, dancing, playing!

Apropos of this I should like to relate here that one of his seemingly gross but really innocent diversions was occasionally visiting a certain black house of prostitution, of which there were many in St. Louis. Here while he played a flute and some one else a tambourine or small drum, he would have two or three of the inmates dance in some weird savage way that took one instanter to the wilds of Central Africa. There was, so far as I know, no payment of any kind made in connection with this. He was a friend, in some crude, artistic or barbaric way. He satisfied, I am positive, some love of color, sound and the dance in these queer revels.

Nor do I know how he achieved these friendships, such as they were. I was never with him when he did. But aside from the satiation they afforded his taste for the strange and picturesque, I am sure they reflected no gross or sensual appetite. But I wish to attest in passing that the mere witnessing of these free scenes had a tonic as well as toxic effect on me. As I view myself now, I was a poor, spindling, prying fish, anxious to know life, and yet because of my very narrow training very fearsome of it, of what it might do to me, what dreadful contagion of thought or deed it might open me to! Peter was not so. To him all, positively *all*, life was good. It was a fascinating spectacle, to be studied or observed and rejoiced in as a spectacle. When I look back now on the shabby, poorly-lighted, low-ceiled room to which he led me "for fun," the absolutely black or brown girls with their white teeth and shiny eyes, the unexplainable, unintelligible love of rhythm and the dance displayed, the beating of a drum, the sinuous, winding motions of the body, I am grateful to him. He released my mind, broadened my view, lengthened my perspective. For as I sat with him, watching him beat his drum or play his flute, noted the gayety, his love of color and effect, and feeling myself *low*, a criminal, disgraced, the while I was staring with all my sight and enjoying it intensely, I realized that I was dealing with a man who was "bigger" than I was in many respects, saner, really more wholesome. I was a moral coward, and he was not losing his life and desires through fear—which the majority of us do. He was strong, vital, unafraid, and he made me so.

But, lest I seem to make him low or impossible to those who instinctively cannot accept life beyond the range of their own little routine world, let me hasten to his other aspects. He was not low but simple, brilliant and varied in his tastes. America and its point of view, religious and otherwise, was simply amusing to him, not to be taken seriously. He loved to contemplate man at his mysteries, rituals, secret schools. He loved better yet ancient history, medieval inanities and atrocities—a most singular, curious and wonderful mind. Already at this age he knew many historians and scientists (their work), a most astonishing and illuminating list to me—Maspero, Froude, Huxley, Darwin, Wallace, Rawlinson, Froissart, Hallam, Taine, Avebury! The list of painters, sculptors and architects with whose work he was familiar and books about whom or illustrated by whom he knew, is too long to be given here. His chief interest, in so far as I could make out, in these opening days, was Egyptology and the study of things natural and primeval—all the wonders of a natural, groping, savage world.

"Dreiser," he exclaimed once with gusto, his bright beady eyes gleaming with an immense human warmth, "you haven't the slightest idea of the fascination of some of the old beliefs.

Do you know the significance of a scarab in Egyptian religious worship, for instance?"

"A scarab? What's a scarab? I never heard of one," I answered.

"A beetle, of course. An Egyptian beetle. You know what a beetle is, don't you? Well, those things burrowed in the earth, the mud of the Nile, at a certain period of their season to lay their eggs, and the next spring, or whenever it was, the eggs would hatch and the beetles would come up. Then the Egyptians imagined that the beetle hadn't died at all, or if it had that it also had the power of restoring itself to life, possessed immortality. So they thought it must be a god and began to worship it," and he would pause and survey me with those amazing eyes, bright as glass beads, to see if I were properly impressed.

"You don't say!"

"Sure. That's where the worship came from," and then he might go on and add a bit about monkey-worship, the Zoroastrians and the Parsees, the sacred bull of Egypt, its sex power as a reason for its religious elevation, and of sex worship in general; the fantastic orgies at Sidon and Tyre, where enormous images of the male and female sex organs were carried aloft before the multitude.

Being totally ignorant of these matters at the time, not a rumor of them having reached me as yet in my meagre reading, I knew that it must be so. It fired me with a keen desire to read—not the old orthodox emasculated histories of the schools but those other books and pamphlets to which I fancied he must have access. Eagerly I inquired of him where, how. He told me that in some cases they were outlawed, banned or not translated wholly or fully, owing to the puritanism and religiosity of the day, but he gave me titles and authors to whom I might have access, and the address of an old book-dealer or two who could get them for me.

In addition he was interested in ethnology and geology, as well as astronomy (the outstanding phases at least), and many, many phases of applied art: pottery, rugs, pictures, engraving, wood-carving, jewel-cutting and designing, and I know not what else, yet there was always room even in his most serious studies for humor of the bizarre and eccentric type, amounting to all but an obsession. He wanted to laugh, and he found occasion for doing so under the most serious, or at least semi-serious, circumstances. Thus I recall that one of the butts of his extreme humor was this same Dick, whom he studied with the greatest care for points worthy his humorous appreciation. Dick, in addition to his genuinely lively mental interests, was a most romantic person on one side, a most puling and complaining soul on the other. As a newspaper artist I believe he was only a fairly respectable craftsman, if so much, whereas Peter was much better, although he deferred to Dick in the most persuasive manner and seemed to believe at times, though I knew he did not, that Dick represented all there was to know in matters artistic.

Among other things at this time, the latter was, or pretended to be, immensely interested in all things pertaining to the Chinese and to know not only something of their language, which he had studied a little somewhere, but also their history—a vague matter, as we all know—and the spirit and significance of their art and customs. He sometimes condescended to take us about with him to one or two Chinese restaurants of the most beggarly description, and—as he wished to believe, because of the romantic titillation involved—the hang-outs of crooks and thieves and disreputable Tenderloin characters generally. (Of such was the beginning of the Chinese restaurant in America.) He would introduce us to a few of his Celestial friends, whose acquaintance apparently he had been most assiduously cultivating for some time past and with whom he was now on the best of terms. He had, as Peter pointed out to me, the happy knack of persuading himself that there was something vastly mysterious and superior about the whole Chinese race, that there was some Chinese organization known as the Six Companions, which, so far as I could make out from him, was ruling very nearly (and secretly, of course) the entire habitable globe. For one thing it had some governing connection with great constructive ventures of one kind and another in all parts of the world, supplying, as he said, thousands of Chinese laborers to any one who desired them, anywhere, and although they were employed by others, ruling them with a rod of iron,

cutting their throats when they failed to perform their bound-
en duties and burying them head down in a basket of rice,
then transferring their remains quietly to China in coffins
made in China and brought for that purpose to the country
in which they were. The Chinese who had worked for the
builders of the Union Pacific had been supplied by this company, as I understood from Dick. In regard to all this Peter
used to analyze and dispose of Dick's self-generated romance
with the greatest gusto, laughing the while and yet pretending to accept it all.

But there was one phase of all this which interested Peter
immensely. Were there on sale in St. Louis any bits of jade,
silks, needlework, porcelains, basketry or figurines of true
Chinese origin? He was far more interested in this than in the
social and economic sides of the lives of the Chinese, and was
constantly urging Dick to take him here, there and everywhere in order that he might see for himself what of these
amazing wonders were locally extant, leading Dick in the process a merry chase and a dog's life. Dick was compelled to
persuade nearly all of his boasted friends to produce all they
had to show. Once, I recall, a collection of rare Chinese porcelains being shown at the local museum of art, there was
nothing for it but that Dick must get one or more of his
Oriental friends to interpret this, that and the other symbol
in connection with this, that and the other vase—things
which put him to no end of trouble and which led to nothing, for among all the local Chinese there was not one who
knew anything about it, although they, Dick included, were
not honest enough to admit it.

"You know, Dreiser," Peter said to me one day with the
most delicious gleam of semi-malicious, semi-tender humor,
"I am really doing all this just to torture Dick. He doesn't
know a damned thing about it and neither do these Chinese,
but it's fun to haul 'em out there and make 'em sweat. The
museum sells an illustrated monograph covering all this, you
know, with pictures of the genuinely historic pieces and explanations of the various symbols in so far as they are known,
but Dick doesn't know that, and he's lying awake nights
trying to find out what they're all about. I like to see his
expression and that of those chinks when they examine those

things." He subsided with a low chuckle all the more disturbing because it was so obviously the product of well-grounded knowledge.

Another phase of this same humor related to the grand artistic, social and other forms of life to which Dick was hoping to ascend via marriage and which led him, because of a kind of anticipatory eagerness, into all sorts of exaggerations of dress, manners, speech, style in writing or drawing, and I know not what else. He had, as I have said, a "studio" in Broadway, an ordinary large, square upper chamber of an old residence turned commercial but which Dick had decorated in the most, to him, recherché or *different* manner possible. In Dick's gilding imagination it was packed with the rarest and most carefully selected things, odd bits of furniture, objects of art, pictures, books—things which the ordinary antique shop provides in plenty but which to Dick, having been reared in Bloomington, Illinois, were of the utmost artistic import. He had vaulting ambitions and pretensions, literary and otherwise, having by now composed various rondeaus, triolets, quatrains, sonnets, in addition to a number of short stories over which he had literally slaved and which, being rejected by many editors, were kept lying idly and inconsequentially and seemingly inconspicuously about his place— the more to astonish the poor unsophisticated "outsider." Besides it gave him the opportunity of posing as misunderstood, neglected, depressed, as becomes all great artists, poets, and thinkers.

His great scheme or dream, however, was that of marriage to an heiress, one of those very material and bovine daughters of the new rich in the West end, and to this end he was bending all his artistic thought, writing, dressing, dreaming the thing he wished. I myself had a marked tendency in this direction, although from another point of view, and speaking from mine purely, there was this difference between us: Dick being an artist, rather remote and disdainful in manner and decidedly handsome as well as poetic and better positioned than I, as I fancied, was certain to achieve this gilded and crystal state, whereas I, not being handsome nor an artist nor sufficiently poetic perhaps, could scarcely aspire to so gorgeous a goal. Often, as around dinnertime he ambled from the office arrayed in the latest mode—dark blue suit, patent leather boots, a dark, round soft felt hat, loose tie blowing idly about his neck, a thin cane in his hand—I was already almost convinced that the anticipated end was at hand, this very evening perhaps, and that I should never see him more except as the husband of a very rich girl, never be permitted even to speak to him save as an almost forgotten friend, and in passing! Even now perhaps he was on his way to her, whereas I, poor oaf that I was, was moiling here over some trucky work. Would my ship never come in? my great day never arrive? my turn? Unkind heaven!

As for Peter he was the sort of person who could swiftly detect, understand and even sympathize with a point of view of this kind the while he must laugh at it and his mind be busy with some plan of making a fol-de-rol use of it. One day he came into the city-room where I was working and bending over my desk fairly bursting with suppressed humor announced, "Gee, Dreiser, I've just thought of a delicious trick to play on Dick! Oh, Lord!" and he stopped and surveyed me with beady eyes the while his round little body seemed to fairly swell with pent-up laughter. "It's too rich! Oh, if it just works out Dick'll be sore! Wait'll I tell you," he went on. "You know how crazy he is about rich young heiresses? You know how he's always 'dressing up' and talking and writing about marrying one of those girls in the West end?" (Dick was forever composing a short story in which some lorn but perfect and great artist was thus being received via love, the story being read to us nights in his studio.) "That's all bluff, that talk of his of visiting in those big houses out there. All he does is to dress up every night as though he were going to a ball, and walk out that way and moon around. Well, listen. Here's the idea. We'll go over to Mermod & Jaccards to-morrow and get a few sheets of their best monogrammed paper, sample sheets. Then we'll get up a letter and sign it with the most romantic name we can think of—Juanita or Cyrene or Doris—and explain who she is, the daughter of a millionaire living out there, and that she's been strictly brought up but that in spite of all that she's seen his name in the paper at the bottom of his pictures and wants to meet him, see? Then we'll have her suggest that he come out to the

west gate of, say, Portland Place at seven o'clock and meet
her. We'll have her describe herself, see, young and beautiful,
and some attractive costume she's to wear, and we'll kill him.
He'll fall hard. Then we'll happen by there at the exact time
when he's waiting, and detain him, urge him to come into
the park with us or to dinner. We'll look our worst so he'll be
ashamed of us. He'll squirm and get wild, but we'll hang on
and spoil the date for him, see? We'll insist in the letter that
he must be alone, see, because she's timid and afraid of being
recognized. My God, he'll be crazy! He'll think we've ruined
his life—oh, ho, ho!" and he fairly writhed with inward joy.

The thing worked. It was cruel in its way, but when has
man ever grieved over the humorous ills of others? The paper was secured, the letter written by a friend of Peter's in a
nearby real estate office, after the most careful deliberation as
to wording on our part. Extreme youth, beauty and a great
mansion were all hinted at. The fascination of Dick as a romantic figure was touched upon. He would know her by a
green silk scarf about her waist, for it was spring, the ideal
season. Seven o'clock was the hour. She could give him only
a moment or two then—but later—and she gave no address!

The letter was mailed in the West end, as was meet and
proper, and in due season arrived at the office. Peter, working
at the next easel, observed him, as he told me, out of the
corner of his eye.

"You should have seen him, Dreiser," he exclaimed, hunting me up about an hour after the letter arrived. "Oh, ho!
Say, you know I believe he thinks it's the real thing. It
seemed to make him a little sick. He tried to appear nonchalant, but a little later he got his hat and went out, over to
Deck's," a nearby saloon, "for a drink, for I followed him.
He's all fussed up. Wait'll we heave into view that night! I'm
going to get myself up like a joke, a hobo. I'll disgrace him.
Oh, Lord, he'll be crazy! He'll think we've ruined his life,
scared her off. There's no address. He can't do a thing. Oh,
ho, ho, ho!"

On the appointed day—and it was a delicious afternoon
and evening, aflame with sun and in May—Dick left off his
work at three p. m., as Peter came and told me, and departed,

and then we went to make our toilets. At six we met, took a car and stepped down not more than a short block from the point of meeting. I shall never forget the sweetness of the air, the something of sadness in the thought of love, even in this form. The sun was singing its evensong, as were the birds. But Peter—blessings or curses upon him!—was arrayed as only he could array himself when he wished to look absolutely disconcerting—more like an unwashed, uncombed tramp who had been sleeping out for weeks, than anything else. His hair was over his eyes and ears, his face and hands dirty, his shoes ditto. He had even blackened one tooth slightly. He had on a collarless shirt, and yet he was jaunty withal and carried a cane, if you please, assuming, as he always could and in the most aggravating way, to be totally unconscious of the figure he cut. At one angle of his multiplex character the man must have been a born actor.

We waited a block away, concealed by a few trees, and at the exact hour Dick appeared, hopeful and eager no doubt, and walking and looking almost all that he hoped—delicate, pale, artistic. The new straw hat! The pale green "artists'" shirt! His black, wide-buckled belt! The cane! The dark-brown low shoes! The boutonnière! He was plainly ready for any fate, his great moment.

And then, before he could get the feeling that his admirer might not be coming, we descended upon him in all our wretched nonchalance and unworthiness—out of hell, as it were. We were most brisk, familiar, affectionate. It was so fortunate to meet him so, so accidentally and peradventure. The night was so fine. We were out for a stroll in the park, to eat afterward. He must come along.

I saw him look at Peter in that hat and no collar, and wilt. It was too much. Such a friend—such friends (for on Peter's advice I was looking as ill as I might, an easy matter)! No, he couldn't come. He was waiting for some friends. We must excuse him.

But Peter was not to be so easily shaken off. He launched into the most brisk and serious conversation. He began his badger game by asking about some work upon which Dick had been engaged before he left the office, some order, how he was getting along with it, when it would be done; and, when Dick evaded and then attempted to dismiss the subject, took up another and began to expatiate on it, some work he himself was doing, something that had developed in connection with it. He asked inane questions, complimented Dick on his looks, began to tease him about some girl. And poor Dick—his nervousness, his despair almost, the sense of the waning of his opportunity! It was cruel. He was becoming more and more restless, looking about more and more wearily and anxiously and wishing to go or for us to go. He was horribly unhappy. Finally, after ten or fifteen minutes had gone and various girls had crossed the plaza in various directions, as well as carriages and saddle-horses—each one carrying his heiress, no doubt!—he seemed to summon all his courage and did his best to dispose of us. "You two'll have to excuse me," he exclaimed almost wildly. "I can't wait." Those golden moments! She could not approach! "My people aren't coming, I guess. I'll have to be going on."

He smiled weakly and made off, Peter half following and urging him to come back. Then, since he would not, we stood there on the exact spot of the rendezvous gazing smirkily after him. Then we went into the park a few paces and sat on a bench in full view, talking—or Peter was—most volubly. He was really choking with laughter. A little later, at seven-thirty, we went cackling into the park, only to return in five minutes as though we had changed our minds and were coming out—and saw Dick bustling off at our approach. It was sad really. There was an element of the tragic in it. But not to Peter. He was all laughter, all but apoplectic gayety. "Oh, by George!" he choked. "This is too much! Oh, ho! This is great! his poor heiress! And he came back! Har! Har! Har!"

"Peter, you dog," I said, "aren't you ashamed of yourself, to rub it in this way?"

"Not a bit, not a bit!" he insisted most enthusiastically. "Do him good. Why shouldn't he suffer? He'll get over it. He's always bluffing about his heiresses. Now he's lost a real one. Har! Har! Har!" and he fairly choked, and for days and weeks and months he laughed, but he never told. He merely chortled at his desk, and if any one asked him what he was laughing about, even Dick, he would reply, "Oh, something—a joke I played on a fellow once."

If Dick ever guessed he never indicated as much. But that lost romance! That faded dream!

Not so long after this, the following winter, I left St. Louis and did not see Peter for several years, during which time I drifted through various cities to New York. We kept up a more or less desultory correspondence which resulted eventually in his contributing to a paper of which I had charge in New York, and later, in part at least I am sure, in his coming there. I noticed one thing, that although Peter had no fixed idea as to what he wished to be—being able to draw, write, engrave, carve and what not—he was in no way troubled about it. "I don't see just what it is that I am to do best," he said to me once. "It may be that I will wind up as a painter or writer or collector—I can't tell yet. I want to study, and meantime I'm making a living—that's all I want now. I want to live, and I am living, in my way."

Some men are masters of cities, or perhaps better, of all the elements which enter into the making of them, and Peter was one. I think sometimes that he was born a writer of great force and charm, only as yet he had not found himself. I have known many writers, many geniuses even, but not one his superior in intellect and romantic response to life. He was a poet, thinker, artist, philosopher and master of prose, as a posthumous volume ("Wolf, the Autobiography of a Cave Dweller") amply proves, but he was not ready then to fully express himself, and it troubled him not at all. He loved life's every facet, was gay and helpful to himself and others, and yet always with an eye for the undercurrent of human misery, error and tragedy as well as comedy. Immediately upon coming to New York he began to examine and grasp it in a large way, its museums, public buildings, geography, politics, but after a very little while decided suddenly that he did not belong there and without a by-your-leave, although once more we had fallen into each other's ways, he departed without a word, and I did not hear from him for months. Temporarily at least he felt that he had to obtain more experience in a lesser field, and lost no time in so doing. The next I knew he

was connected, at a comfortable salary, with the then dominant paper of Philadelphia.

It was after he had established himself very firmly in Philadelphia that we two finally began to understand each other
fully, to sympathize really with each other's point of view as
opposed to the more or less gay and casual nature of our
earlier friendship. Also here perhaps, more than before, we
felt the binding influence of having worked together in the
West. It was here that I first noticed the ease with which he
took hold of a city, the many-sidedness of his peculiar character which led him to reflect so many angles of it, which a
less varied temperament would never have touched upon.
For, first of all, wherever he happened to be, he was intensely
interested in the age and history of his city, its buildings and
graveyards and tombstones which pointed to its past life, then
its present physical appearance, the chief characteristics of the
region in which it lay, its rivers, lakes, parks and adjacent
places and spots of interest (what rambles we took!), as well
as its newest and finest things architecturally. Nor did any one
ever take a keener interest in the current intellectual resources
of a city—any city in which he happened to be—its museums, libraries, old bookstores, newspapers, magazines, and
I know not what else. It was he who first took me into
Leary's bookstore in Philadelphia, descanting with his usual
gusto on its merits. Then and lastly he was keenly and wisely
interested in various currents of local politics, society and finance, although he always considered the first a low mess, an
arrangement or adjustment of many necessary things among
the lower orders. He seemed to know or sense in some occult
way everything that was going on in those various realms.
His mind was so full and rich that merely to be with him was
a delight. He gushed like a fountain, and yet not polemically,
of all he knew, heard, felt, suspected. His thoughts were so
rich at times that to me they were more like a mosaic of var-
iegated and richly colored stones and jewels. I felt always as
though I were in the presence of a great personage, not one
who was reserved or pompous but a loose bubbling temperament, wise beyond his years or day, and so truly great that
perhaps because of the intensity and immense variety of his
interests he would never shine in a world in which the most

intensive specialization, and that of a purely commercial character, was the grand rôle.

And yet I always felt that perhaps he might. He attracted people of all grades so easily and warmly. His mind leaped from one interest to another almost too swiftly, and yet the average man understood and liked him. While in a way he contemned their mental states as limited or bigoted, he enjoyed the conditions under which they lived, seemed to wish to immerse himself in them. And yet nearly all his thoughts were, from their point of view perhaps, dangerous. Among his friends he was always talking freely, honestly, of things which the average man could not or would not discuss, dismissing as trash illusion, lies or the cunning work of self-seeking propagandists, most of the things currently accepted as true.

He was constantly commenting on the amazing dullness of man, his prejudices, the astonishing manner in which he seized upon and clung savagely or pathetically to the most ridiculous interpretations of life. He was also forever noting that crass chance which wrecks so many of our dreams and lives,—its fierce brutalities, its seemingly inane indifference to wondrous things,—but never in a depressed or morbid spirit; merely as a matter of the curious, as it were. But if any one chanced to contradict him he was likely to prove liquid fire. At the same time he was forever reading, reading, reading— history, archæology, ethnology, geology, travel, medicine, biography, and descanting on the wonders and idiosyncrasies of man and nature which they revealed. He was never tired of talking of the intellectual and social conditions that ruled in Greece and Rome from 600 B. C. on, the philosophies, the travels, the art, the simple, natural pagan view of things, and regretting that they were no more. He grieved at times, I think, that he had not been of that world, might not have seen it, or, failing that, might not see all the shards of those extinct civilizations. There was something loving and sad in the manner in which at times, in one museum and another, he would examine ancient art designs, those of the Egyptians, Greeks and Romans, their public and private house plans, their statues, book rolls, inscriptions, flambeaux, boats, swords, chariots. Carthage, Rome, Greece, Phœnicia—their

colonies, art and trade stuffs, their foods, pleasures and wor-
ships—how he raved! A book like Thaïs, Salammbo, Sonica,
Quo Vadis, touched him to the quick.

At the same time, and odd as it may seem, he was seemingly in intimate contact with a circle of friends that rather
astonished me by its catholicity. It included, for instance, and
quite naïvely, real estate dealers, clerks, a bank cashier or two,
some man who had a leather shop or cigar factory in the
downtown section, a drummer, a printer, two or three newspaper artists and reporters—a list too long to catalogue here
and seemingly not interesting, at least not inspiring to look at
or live in contact with. Yet his relations with all of these were
of a warm, genial, helpful, homely character, quite intimate.
He used them as one might a mulch in which to grow things,
or in other words he took them on their own ground; a thing
which I could never quite understand, being more or less
aloof myself and yet wishing always to be able so to do, to
take life, as he did.

For he desired, and secured, their good will and drew them
to him. He took a simple, natural pleasure in the kinds of
things they were able to do, as well as the kinds of things he
could do. With these, then, and a type of girl who might not
be classed above the clerk or manicure class, he and they managed to eke out a social life, the outstanding phases of which
were dances, "parties," dinners at one simple home and another, flirting, boating, and fishing expeditions in season, evenings out at restaurants or the theater, and I know not what
else. He could sing (a very fair baritone), play the piano, cor-
net, flute, banjo, mandolin and guitar, but always insisted that
his favorite instruments were the jews'-harp, the French harp
(mouth organ) and a comb with a piece of paper over it,
against which he would blow with fierce energy, making the
most outrageous sounds, until stopped. At any "party" he
was always talking, jumping about, dancing, cooking something—fudge, taffy, a rarebit, and insisting in the most mock-
serious manner that all the details be left strictly to him.
"Now just cut out of this, all of you, and leave this to your
Uncle Dudley. Who's doing this? All I want is sugar, chocolate, a pot, a big spoon, and I'll show you the best fudge you
ever ate." Then he would don an apron or towel and go to

work in a manner which would rob any gathering of a sense
of stiffness and induce a naturalness most intriguing, calculated to enhance the general pleasure an hundredfold.

Yes, Peter woke people up. He could convey or spread a
sense of ease and good nature and give and take among all.
Wise as he was and not so good-looking, he was still attractive to girls, very much so, and by no means unconscious of
their beauty. He could always, and easily, break down their
reserve, and was soon apparently on terms of absolute friendship, exchanging all sorts of small gossip and news with them
about this, that and the other person about whom they knew.
Indeed he was such a general favorite and so seemingly im-
partial that it was hard to say how he came close to any, and
yet he did. At odd tête-à-tête moments he was always making
confessions as to "nights" or "afternoons." "My God, Dreiser,
I've found a peach! I can't tell you—but oh, wonderful! Just
what I need. This world's a healthy old place, eh? Let's have
another drink, what?" and he would order a stein or a half-
schoppen of light German beer and pour it down, grinning
like a gargoyle.

It was while he was in Philadelphia that he told me the
beginnings of the love affair which eventually ended in his
marrying and settling down into the homiest of home men I
have ever seen and which for sheer naïveté and charm is one
of the best love stories I know anything about. It appears that
he was walking in some out-of-the-way factory realm of
North Philadelphia one Saturday afternoon about the first or
second year of his stay there, when, playing in the street with
some other children, he saw a girl of not more than thirteen
or fourteen who, as he expressed it to me, "came damned near
being the prettiest thing I ever saw. She had yellow hair and
a short blue dress and pink bows in her hair—and say,
Dreiser, when I saw her I stopped flat and said 'me for that'
if I have to wait fifteen years! Dutchy—you never saw the
beat! And poor! Her shoes were clogs. She couldn't even talk
English yet. Neither could the other kids. They were all sausage—a regular German neighborhood.

"But, say, I watched her a while and then I went over and
said, 'Come here, kid. Where do you live?' She didn't understand, and one of the other kids translated for her, and then

she said, 'Ich sprech nicht English,'" and he mocked her. "That fixed her for me. One of the others finally told me who she was and where she lived—and, say, I went right home and began studying German. In three months I could make myself understood, but before that, in two weeks, I hunted up her old man and made him understand that I wanted to be friends with the family, to learn German. I went out Sundays when they were all at home. There are six children and I made friends with 'em all. For a long time I couldn't make Madchen (that's what they call her) understand what it was all about, but finally I did, and she knows now all right. And I'm crazy about her and I'm going to marry her as soon as she's old enough."

"How do you know that she'll have you?" I inquired.

"Oh, she'll have me. I always tell her I'm going to marry her when she's eighteen, and she says all right. And I really believe she does like me. I'm crazy about her."

Five years later, if I may anticipate a bit, after he had moved to Newark and placed himself rather well in the journalistic field and was able to carry out his plans in regard to himself, he suddenly returned to Philadelphia and married, preparing beforehand an apartment which he fancied would please her. It was a fortunate marriage in so far as love and home pleasures were concerned. I never encountered a more delightful atmosphere.

All along in writing this I feel as though I were giving but the thinnest portrait of Peter; he was so full and varied in his moods and interests. To me he illustrated the joy that exists, on the one hand, in the common, the so-called homely and what some might think ugly side of life, certainly the very simple and ordinarily human aspect of things; on the other, in the sheer comfort and satisfaction that might be taken in things truly intellectual and artistic, but to which no great expense attached—old books, prints, things connected with history and science in their various forms, skill in matters relating to the applied arts and what not, such as the coloring and firing of pottery and glass, the making of baskets, hammocks and rugs, the carving of wood, the collection and imitation of Japanese and Chinese prints, the art of embalming as applied by the Egyptians (which, in connection with an undertaker to whom he had attached himself, he attempted to revive or at least play with, testing his skill for instance by embalming a dead cat or two after the Egyptian manner). In all of these lines he trained himself after a fashion and worked with skill, although invariably he insisted that he was little more than a bungler, a poor follower after the art of some one else. But most of all, at this time and later, he was interested in collecting things Japanese and Chinese: netsukes, inros, censors, images of jade and porcelain, teajars, vases, prints; and it was while he was in Philadelphia and seemingly trifling about with the group I have mentioned and making love to his little German girl that he was running here and there to this museum and that and laying the foundations of some of those interesting collections which later he was fond of showing his friends or interested collectors. By the time he had reached Newark, as chief cartoonist of the leading paper there, he was in possession of a complete Tokaido (the forty views on the road between Tokio and Kyoto), various prints by Hokusai, Sesshiu, Sojo; a collection of one hundred inros, all of fifty netsukes, all of thirty censers, lacquered boxes and teajars, and various other exceedingly beautiful and valuable things—Mandarin skirts and coats, among other things— which subsequently he sold or traded around among one collector friend and another for things which they had. I recall his selling his completed Tokaido, a labor which had extended over four years, for over a thousand dollars. Just before he died he was trading netsukes for inros and getting ready to sell all these latter to a man, who in turn was going to sell his collection to a museum.

But in between was this other, this ultra-human side, which ran to such commonplaces as bowling, tennis-playing, golf, billiards, cards and gambling with the dice—a thing which always struck me as having an odd turn to it in connection with Peter, since he could be interested in so many other things, and yet he pursued these commonplaces with as much gusto at times as one possessed of a mania. At others he seemed not to miss or think of them. Indeed, you could be sure of him and all his interests, whatever they were, feeling that he had himself well in hand, knew exactly how far he was

going, and that when the time came he could and would stop.
Yet during the process of his momentary relaxation or satiation, in whatever field it might be, he would give you a sense
of abandon, even ungovernable appetite, which to one who
had not known him long might have indicated a mania.

Thus I remember once running over to Philadelphia to
spend a Saturday and Sunday with him, visits of this kind, in
either direction, being of the commonest occurrence. At that
time he was living in some quiet-looking boarding-house in
South Fourth Street, but in which dwelt or visited the group
above-mentioned, and whenever I came there, at least, there
was always an atmosphere of intense gaming or playing in
some form, which conveyed to me nothing so much as a glorious sense of life and pleasure. A dozen or more men might
be seated at or standing about a poker or dice table, in summer (often in winter) with their coats off, their sleeves rolled
up, Peter always conspicuous among them. On the table or
to one side would be money, a pitcher or a tin pail of beer,
boxes of cigarettes or cigars, and there would be Peter among
the players, flushed with excitement, his collar off, his hair
awry, his little figure stirring about here and there or gesticulating or lighting a cigar or pouring down a glass of beer,
shouting at the top of his voice, his eyes aglow, "That's
mine!" "I say it's not!" "Two on the sixes!" "Three!" "Four!"
"Ah, roll the bones! Roll the bones!" "Get off! Get off!
Come on now, Spikes—cough up! You've got the money
now. Pay back. No more loans if you don't." "Once on the
fours—the fives—the aces!" "Roll the bones! Roll the bones!
Come on!" Or, if he saw me, softening and saying, "Gee,
Dreiser, I'm ahead twenty-eight so far!" or "I've lost thirty all
told. I'll stick this out, though, to win or lose five more, and
then I'll quit. I give notice, you fellows, five more, one way
or the other, and then I'm through. See? Say, these damned
sharks are always trying to turn a trick. And when they lose
they don't want to pay. I'm offa this for life unless I get a
better deal."

In the room there might be three or four girls—sisters,
sweethearts, pals of one or other of the players—some dancing, some playing the piano or singing, and in addition the
landlord and his wife, a slattern pair usually, about whose

past and present lives Peter seemed always to know much. He had seduced them all apparently into a kind of rakish camaraderie which was literally amazing to behold. It thrilled, fascinated, at times frightened me, so thin and inadequate and inefficient seemed my own point of view and appetite for life. He was vigorous, charitable, pagan, gay, full of health and strength. He would play at something, anything, indoors or out as occasion offered, until he was fairly perspiring, when, throwing down whatever implement he had in hand—be it cards, a tennis-racket, a golf club—would declare, "That's enough! That's enough! I'm done now. I've licked-cha," or "I'm licked. No more. Not another round. Come on, Dreiser, I know just the place for us——" and then descanting on a steak or fish planked, or some new method of serving corn or sweet potatoes or tomatoes, he would lead the way somewhere to a favorite "rat's killer," as he used to say, or grill or Chinese den, and order enough for four or five, unless stopped. As he walked, and he always preferred to walk, the latest political row or scandal, the latest discovery, tragedy or art topic would get his keen attention. In his presence the whole world used to look different to me, more colorful, more hopeful, more gay. Doors seemed to open; in imagination I saw the interiors of a thousand realms—homes, factories, laboratories, dens, resorts of pleasure. During his day such figures as McKinley, Roosevelt, Hanna, Rockefeller, Rogers, Morgan, Peary, Harriman were abroad and active, and their mental states and points of view and interests—and sincerities and insincerities—were the subject of his wholly brilliant analysis. He rather admired the clever opportunist, I think, so long as he was not mean in view or petty, yet he scorned and even despised the commercial viewpoint or trade reactions of a man like McKinley. Rulers ought to be above mere commercialism. Once when I asked him why he disliked McKinley so much he replied laconically, "The voice is the voice of McKinley, but the hands—are the hands of Hanna." Roosevelt seemed to amuse him always, to be a delightful if ridiculous and self-interested "grandstander," as he always said, "always looking out for Teddy, you bet," but good for the country, inspiring it with visions. Rockefeller was wholly admirable as a force driving the country on to autocracy, oligarchy, possibly revolution. Ditto Hanna, ditto Morgan, ditto Harriman, ditto Rogers, unless checked. Peary might have, and again might not have, discovered the North Pole. He refused to judge. Old "Doc" Cook, the pseudo discoverer, who appeared very shortly before he died, only drew forth chuckles of delight. "My God, the gall, the nerve! And that wreath of roses the Danes put around his neck! It's colossal, Dreiser. It's grand. Munchausen, Cook, Gulliver, Marco Polo—they'll live forever, or ought to!"

Some Saturday afternoons or Sundays, if he came to me or I to him in time, we indulged in long idle rambles, anywhere, either going first by streetcar, boat or train somewhere and then walking, or, if the mood was not so, just walking on and on somewhere and talking. On such occasions Peter was at his best and I could have listened forever, quite as the disciples of Plato and Aristotle must have to them, to his discourses on life, his broad and broadening conceptions of Nature—her cruelty, beauty, mystery. Once, far out somewhere beyond Camden, we were idling about an inlet where were boats and some fishermen and a trestle which crossed it. Just as we were crossing it some men in a boat below discovered the body of a possible suicide, in the water, days old and discolored, but still intact and with the clothes of a man of at least middle-class means. I was for leaving, being made a little sick by the mere sight. Not so Peter. He was for joining in the effort which brought the body to shore, and in a moment was back with the small group of watermen, speculating and arguing as to the condition and character of the dead man, making himself really one of the group. Finally he was urging the men to search the pockets while some one went for the police. But more than anything, with a hard and yet in its way humane realism which put any courage of mine in that direction to the blush, he was all for meditating on the state and nature of man, his chemical components—chlorine, sulphuric acid, phosphoric acid, potassium, sodium, calcium, magnesium, oxygen—and speculating as to which particular chemicals in combination gave the strange metallic blues, greens, yellows and browns to the decaying flesh! He had a great stomach for life. The fact that insects were at work shocked him not at all. He speculated as to *these*, their duties and functions! He asserted boldly that man was merely a chemical formula at best, that something much wiser than he had prepared him, for some not very brilliant purpose of his or its own perhaps, and that he or it, whoever or whatever he or it was, was neither good nor bad, as we imagined such things, but both. He at once went off into the mysteries—where, when with me at least, he seemed to prefer to dwell—talked of the divinations of the Chaldeans, how they studied the positions of the stars and the entrails of dead animals before going to war, talked of the horrible fetiches of the Africans, the tricks and speculations of the priests of Greek and Roman temples, finally telling me the story of the ambitious eel-seller who anchored the dead horse in the stream in order to have plenty of eels every morning for market. I revolted. I declared he was sickening.

"My boy," he assured me, "you are too thin-skinned. You can't take life that way. It's all good to me, whatever happens. We're here. We're not running it. Why be afraid to look at it? The chemistry of a man's body isn't any worse than the chemistry of anything else, and we're eating the dead things we've killed all the time. A little more or a little less in any direction—what difference?"

Apropos of this same a little later—to shock me, of course, as he well knew he could—he assured me that in eating a dish of chop suey in a Chinese restaurant, a very low one, he had found and eaten a part of the little finger of a child, and that "it was very good—very good, indeed."

"Dog!" I protested. "Swine! Thou ghoula!" but he merely chuckled heartily and stuck to his tale!

But if I paint this side of him it is to round out his wonderful, to me almost incredible, figure. Insisting on such things, he was still and always warm and human, sympathetic, diplomatic and cautious, according to his company, so that he was really acceptable anywhere. Peter would never shock those who did not want to be shocked. A minute or two or five after such a discourse as the above he might be describing some marvelously beautiful process of pollination among the flowers, the history of some medieval trade guild or gazing at a beautiful scene and conveying to one by his very attitude his unspoken emotion.

After spending about two or three years in Philadelphia—which city came to reflect for me the color of Peter's interests and mood—he suddenly removed to Newark, having been nursing an arrangement with its principal paper for some time. Some quarrel or dissatisfaction with the director of his department caused him, without other notice, to paste some crisp quotation from one of the poets on his desk and depart! In Newark, a city to which before this I had paid not the slightest attention, he found himself most happy; and I, living in New York close at hand, felt that I possessed in it and him an earthly paradise. Although it contained no more than 300,000 people and seemed, or had, a drear factory realm only, he soon revealed it to me in quite another light, because he was there. Very swiftly he found a wondrous canal running right through it, under its market even, and we went walking along its banks, out into the woods and fields. He found or created out of an existing boardinghouse in a back street so colorful and gay a thing that after a time it seemed to me to outdo that one of Philadelphia. He joined a country club near Passaic, on the river of that name, on the veranda of which we often dined. He found a Chinese quarter with a restaurant or two; an amazing Italian section with a restaurant; a man who had a $40,000 collection of rare Japanese and Chinese curios, all in his rooms at the Essex County Insane Asylum, for he was the chemist there; a man who was a playwright and manager in New York; another who owned a newspaper syndicate; another who directed a singing society; another who was president of a gun club; another who owned and made or rather fired pottery for others. Peter was so restless and vital that he was always branching out in a new direction. To my astonishment he now took up the making and firing of pottery for himself, being interested in reproducing various Chinese dishes and vases of great beauty, the originals of which were in the Metropolitan Museum of Art. His plan was first to copy the design, then buy, shape or bake the clay at some pottery, then paint or decorate with liquid porcelain at his own home, and fire. In the course of six or eight months, working in his rooms Saturdays and Sundays and some mornings before going to the office, he managed to produce three or four which satisfied him and which he kept, plates of real beauty. The others he gave away.

A little later, if you please, it was Turkish rug-making on a small scale, the frame and materials for which he slowly accumulated, and then providing himself with a pillow, Turkish-fashion, he crossed his legs before it and began slowly but surely to produce a rug, the colors and design of which were entirely satisfactory to me. As may be imagined, it was slow and tedious work, undertaken at odd moments and when there was nothing else for him to do, always when the light was good and never at night, for he maintained that the coloring required the best of light. Before this odd, homely, wooden machine, a combination of unpainted rods and cords, he would sit, cross-legged or on a bench at times, and pound and pick and tie and unravel—a most wearisome-looking task to me.

"For heaven's sake," I once observed, "couldn't you think of anything more interestingly insane to do than this? It's the slowest, most painstaking work I ever saw."

"That's just it, and that's just why I like it," he replied, never looking at me but proceeding with his weaving in the most industrious fashion. "You have just one outstanding fault, Dreiser. You don't know how to make anything out of the little things of life. You want to remember that this is an art, not a job. I'm discovering whether I can make a Turkish carpet or not, and it gives me pleasure. If I can get so much as one good spot of color worked out, one small portion of the design, I'll be satisfied. I'll know then that I can do it, the whole thing, don't you see? Some of these things have been the work of a lifetime of one man. You call that a small thing? I don't. The pleasure is in doing it, proving that you can, not in the rug itself." He clacked and tied, congratulating himself vastly. In due course of time three or four inches were finished, a soft and yet firm silky fabric, and he was in great glee over it, showing it to all and insisting that in time (how long? I often wondered) he would complete it and would then own a splendid carpet.

It was at this time that he built about him in Newark a structure of friendships and interests which, it seemed to me, promised to be for life. He interested himself intensely in the paper with which he was connected and although he was only the cartoonist, still it was not long before various departments and elements in connection with it seemed to reflect his presence and to be alive with his own good will and enthusiasm. Publisher, editor, art director, managing editor and business manager, were all in friendly contact with him. He took out life insurance for the benefit of the wife and children he was later to have! With the manager of the engraving department he was working out problems in connection with copperplate engraving and printing; with the official photographer, art photography; with the art director, some scheme for enlarging the local museum in some way. With his enduring love of the fantastic and ridiculous it was not long before he had successfully planned and executed a hoax of the most ridiculous character, a piece of idle drollery almost too foolish to think of, and yet which eventually succeeded in exciting the natives of at least four States and was telegraphed to and talked about in a Sunday feature way, by newspapers all over the country, and finally involved Peter as an actor and stage manager of the most vivid type imaginable. And yet it was all done really to amuse himself, to see if he could do it, as he often told me.

This particular hoax related to that silly old bugaboo of our boyhood days, the escaped and wandering wild man, ferocious, blood-loving, terrible. I knew nothing of it until Peter, one Sunday afternoon when we were off for a walk a year or two after he had arrived in Newark, suddenly announced apropos of nothing at all, "Dreiser, I've just hit upon a great idea which I am working out with some of the boys down on our paper. It's a dusty old fake, but it will do as well as any other, better than if it were a really decent idea. I'm inventing a wild man. You know how crazy the average dub is over anything strange, different, 'terrible.' Barnum was right, you know. There's one born every minute. Well, I'm just getting this thing up now. It's as good as the sacred white elephant or the blood-sweating hippopotamus. And what's more, I'm going to stage it right here in little old Newark—and they'll all fall for it, and don't you think they won't," and he chuckled most ecstatically.

"For heaven's sake, what's coming now?" I sighed.

"Oh, very well. But I have it all worked out just the same. We're beginning to run the preliminary telegrams every three or four days—one from Ramblersville, South Jersey, let us say, another from Hohokus, twenty-five miles farther on, four or five days later. By degrees as spring comes on I'll bring him north—right up here into Essex County—a genuine wild man, see, something fierce and terrible. We're giving him long hair like a bison, red eyes, fangs, big hands and feet. He's entirely naked—or will be when he gets here. He's eight feet tall. He kills and eats horses, dogs, cattle, pigs, chickens. He frightens men and women and children. I'm having him bound across lonely roads, look in windows at night, stampede cattle and drive tramps and peddlers out of the country. But say, wait and see. As summer comes on we'll make a regular headliner of it. We'll give it pages on Sunday. We'll get the rubes to looking for him in posses, offer rewards. Maybe some one will actually capture and bring in some poor lunatic, a real wild man. You can do anything if you just stir up the natives enough."

I laughed. "You're crazy," I said. "What a low comedian you really are, Peter!"

Well, the weeks passed, and to mark progress he occasionally sent me clippings of telegrams, cut not from his pages, if you please, but from such austere journals as the *Sun* and *World* of New York, the *North American* of Philadelphia, the *Courant* of Hartford, recording the antics of his imaginary thing of the woods. Longish articles actually began to appear here and there, in Eastern papers especially, describing the exploits of this very elusive and moving demon. He had been seen in a dozen fairly widely distributed places within the month, but always coming northward. In one place he had killed three cows at once, in another two, and eaten portions of them raw! Old Mrs. Gorswitch of Dutchers Run, Pennsylvania, returning from a visit to her daughter-in-law, Annie A. Gorswitch, and ambling along a lonely road in Osgoroola County, was suddenly descended upon by a most horrific figure, half man, half beast, very tall and with long hair and red, all but bloody eyes who, looking at her with avid glance, made as if to seize her, but a wagon approaching along the road from another direction, he had desisted and fled, leaving old Mrs. Gorswitch in a faint upon the ground. Barns and haystacks had been fired here and there, lonely widows in distant cotes been made to abandon their homes through fear . . . . I marveled at the assiduity and patience of the man.

One day in June or July following, being in Newark and asking Peter quite idly about his wild man, he replied, "Oh, it's great, great! Couldn't be better! He'll soon be here now. We've got the whole thing arranged now for next Sunday or Saturday—depends on which day I can get off. We're going to photograph him. Wanto come over?"

"What rot!" I said. "Who's going to pose? Where?"

"Well," he chuckled, "come along and see. You'll find out fast enough. We've got an actual wild man. I got him. I'll have him out here in the woods. If you don't believe it, come over. You wouldn't believe me when I said I could get the natives worked up. Well, they are. Look at these," and he produced clippings from rival papers. The wild man was actually being seen in Essex County, not twenty-five miles from Newark. He had ravaged the property of people in five different States. It was assumed that he was a lunatic turned savage, or that he had escaped from a circus or trading-ship wrecked on the Jersey coast (suggestions made by Peter himself). His depredations, all told, had by now run into thousands, speaking financially. Staid residents were excited. Rewards for his capture were being offered in different places. Posses of irate citizens were, and would continue to be, after him, armed to the teeth, until he was captured. Quite remarkable developments might be expected at any time. . . . I stared. It seemed too ridiculous, and it was, and back of it all was smirking, chuckling Peter, the center and fountain of it!

"You dog!" I protested. "You clown!" He merely grinned.

Not to miss so interesting a dénouement as the actual capture of this prodigy of the wilds, I was up early and off the following Sunday to Newark, where in Peter's apartment in due time I found him, his rooms in a turmoil, he himself busy stuffing things into a bag, outside an automobile waiting and within it the staff photographer as well as several others, all grinning, and all of whom, as he informed me, were to assist in the great work of tracking, ambushing and, if possible, photographing the dread peril.

"Yes, well, who's going to be him?" I insisted.

"Never mind! Never mind! Don't be so inquisitive," chortled Peter. "A wild man has his rights and privileges, as well as any other. Remember, I caution all of you to be respectful in his presence. He's very sensitive, and he doesn't like newspapermen anyhow. He'll be photographed, and he'll be wild. That's all you need to know."

In due time we arrived at as comfortable an abode for a wild man as well might be. It was near the old Essex and Morris Canal, not far from Boonton. A charming clump of brush and rock was selected, and here a snapshot of a posse hunting, men peering cautiously from behind trees in groups and looking as though they were most eager to discover something, was made. Then Peter, slipping away—I suddenly saw him ambling toward us, hair upstanding, body smeared with black muck, daubs of white about the eyes, little tufts of wool about wrists and ankles and loins—as good a figure of a wild man as one might wish, only not eight feet tall.

"Peter!" I said. "How ridiculous! You loon!"

"Have a care how you address me," he replied with solemn dignity. "A wild man is a wild man. Our punctilio is not to be trifled with. I am of the oldest, the most famous line of wild men extant. Touch me not." He strode the grass with the air of a popular movie star, while he discussed with the art director and photographer the most terrifying and convincing attitudes of a wild man seen by accident and unconscious of his pursuers.

"But you're not eight feet tall!" I interjected at one point.

"A small matter. A small matter," he replied airily. "I will be in the picture. Nothing easier. We wild men, you know——"

Some of the views were excellent, most striking. He leered most terribly from arras of leaves or indicated fright or cunning. The man was a good actor. For years I retained and may still have somewhere a full set of the pictures as well as the double-page spread which followed the next week.

Well, the thing was appropriately discussed, as it should

have been, but the wild man got away, as was feared. He went into the nearby canal and washed away all his terror, or rather he vanished into the dim recesses of Peter's memory. He was only heard of a few times more in the papers, his supposed body being found in some town in northeast Pennsylvania—or in the small item that was "telegraphed" from there. As for Peter, he emerged from the canal, or from its banks, a cleaner if not a better man. He was grinning, combing his hair, adjusting his tie.

"What a scamp!" I insisted lovingly. "What an incorrigible trickster!"

"Dreiser, Dreiser," he chortled, "there's nothing like it. You should not scoff. I am a public benefactor. I am really a creator. I have created a being as distinct as any that ever lived. He is in many minds—mine, yours. You know that you believe in him really. There he was peeking out from between those bushes only fifteen minutes ago. And he has made, and will make, thousands of people happy, thrill them, give them a new interest. If Stevenson can create a Jekyll and Hyde, why can't I create a wild man? I have. We have his picture to prove it. What more do you wish?"

I acquiesced. All told, it was a delightful bit of foolery and art, and Peter was what he was first and foremost, an artist in the grotesque and the ridiculous.

For some time thereafter peace seemed to reign in his mind, only now it was that the marriage and home and children idea began to grow. From much of the foregoing it may have been assumed that Peter was out of sympathy with the ordinary routine of life, despised the commonplace, the purely practical. As a matter of fact it was just the other way about. I never knew a man so radical in some of his viewpoints, so versatile and yet so wholly, intentionally and cravingly, immersed in the usual as Peter. He was all for creating, developing, brightening life along simple rather than outré lines, in so far as he himself was concerned. Nearly all of his arts and pleasures were decorative and homey. A good grocer, a good barber, a good saloon-keeper, a good tailor, a shoe maker, was just as interesting in his way to Peter as any one or anything else, if not a little more so. He respected their lines, their arts, their professions, and above all, where they had it, their industry, sobriety and desire for fair dealing. He believed that millions of men, especially those about him, were doing the best they could under the very severe conditions which life offered. He objected to the idle, the too dull, the swindlers and thieves as well as the officiously puritanic or dogmatic. He resented, for himself at least, solemn pomp and show. Little houses, little gardens, little porches, simple cleanly neighborhoods with their air of routine, industry, convention and order, fascinated him as apparently nothing else could. He insisted that they were enough. A man did not need a great house unless he was a public character with official duties.

"Dreiser," he would say in Philadelphia and Newark, if not before, "it's in just such a neighborhood as this that some day I'm going to live. I'm going to have my little *frau*, my seven children, my chickens, dog, cat, canary, best German style, my garden, my birdbox, my pipe; and Sundays, by God, I'll march 'em all off to church, wife and seven kids, as regular as clockwork, shined shoes, pigtails and all, and I'll lead the procession."

"Yes, yes," I said. "You talk."

"Well, wait and see. Nothing in this world means so much to me as the good old orderly home stuff. One ought to live and die in a family. It's the right way. I'm cutting up now, sowing my wild oats, but that's nothing. I'm just getting ready to eventually settle down and live, just as I tell you, and be an ideal orderly citizen. It's the only way. It's the way nature intends us to do. All this early kid stuff is passing, a sorting-out process. We get over it. Every fellow does, or ought to be able to, if he's worth anything, find some one woman that he can live with and stick by her. That makes the world that you and I like to live in, and you know it. There's a psychic call in all of us to it, I think. It's the genius of our civilization, to marry one woman and settle down. And when I do, no more of this all-night stuff with this, that and the other lady. I'll be a model husband and father, sure as you're standing there. Don't you think I won't. Smile if you want to—it's so. I'll have my garden. I'll be friendly with my neighbors. You can come over then and help us put the kids to bed."

"Oh, Lord! This is a new bug now! We'll have the vine-covered cot idea for a while, anyhow."

"Oh, all right. Scoff if you want to. You'll see."

Time went by. He was doing all the things I have indicated, living in a kind of whirl of life. At the same time, from time to time, he would come back to this thought. Once, it is true, I thought it was all over with the little yellow-haired girl in Philadelphia. He talked of her occasionally, but less and less. Out on the golf links near Passaic he met another girl, one of a group that flourished there. I met her. She was not unpleasing, a bit sensuous, rather attractive in dress and manners, not very well informed, but gay, clever, up-to-date; such a girl as would pass among other women as fairly satisfactory.

For a time Peter seemed greatly attracted to her. She danced, played a little, was fair at golf and tennis, and she was, or pretended to be, intensely interested in him. He confessed at last that he believed he was in love with her.

"So it's all day with Philadelphia, is it?" I asked.

"It's a shame," he replied, "but I'm afraid so. I'm having a hell of a time with myself, my alleged conscience, I tell you."

I heard little more about it. He had a fad for collecting rings at this time, a whole casket full, like a Hindu prince, and he told me once he was giving her her choice of them.

Suddenly he announced that it was "all off" and that he was going to marry the maid of Philadelphia. He had thrown the solitaire engagement ring he had given her down a sewer! At first he would confess nothing as to the reason or the details, but being so close to me it eventually came out. Apparently, to the others as to myself, he had talked much of his simple home plans, his future children—the good citizen idea. He had talked it to his new love also, and she had sympathized and agreed. Yet one day, after he had endowed her with the engagement ring, some one, a member of the golf club, came and revealed a tale. The girl was not "straight." She had been, mayhap was even then, "intimate" with other men—one anyhow. She was in love with Peter well enough, as she insisted afterward, and willing to undertake the life he suggested, but she had not broken with the old atmosphere completely, or if she had it was still not believed that she had.

There were those who could not only charge, but prove. A compromising note of some kind sent to some one was involved, turned over to Peter.

"Dreiser," he growled as he related the case to me, "it serves me right. I ought to know better. I know the kind of woman I need. This one has handed me a damned good wallop, and I deserve it. I might have guessed that she wasn't suited to me. She was really too free—a life-lover more than a wife. That home stuff! She was just stringing me because she liked me. She isn't really my sort, not simple enough."

"But you loved her, I thought?"

"I did, or thought I did. Still, I used to wonder too. There were many ways about her that troubled me. You think I'm kidding about this home and family idea, but I'm not. It suits me, however flat it looks to you. I want to do that, live that way, go through the normal routine experience, and I'm going to do it."

"But how did you break it off with her so swiftly?" I asked curiously.

"Well, when I heard this I went direct to her and put it up to her. If you'll believe me she never even denied it. Said it was all true, but that she was in love with me all right, and would change and be all that I wanted her to be."

"Well, that's fair enough," I said, "if she loves you. You're no saint yourself, you know. If you'd encourage her, maybe she'd make good."

"Well, maybe, but I don't think so really," he returned, shaking his head. "She likes me, but not enough, I'm afraid. She wouldn't run straight, now that she's had this other. She'd mean to maybe, but she wouldn't. I feel it about her. And anyhow I don't want to take any chances. I like her— I'm crazy about her really, but I'm through. I'm going to marry little Dutchy if she'll have me, and cut out this old-line stuff. You'll have to stand up with me when I do."

In three months more the new arrangement was consummated and little Dutchy—or Zuleika, as he subsequently named her—was duly brought to Newark and installed, at first in a charming apartment in a conventionally respectable and cleanly neighborhood, later in a small house with a "yard," lawn front and back, in one of the homiest of home neighborhoods in Newark. It was positively entertaining to observe Peter not only attempting to assume but assuming the rôle of the conventional husband, and exactly nine months after he had been married, to the hour, a father in this humble and yet, in so far as his particular home was concerned, comfortable world. I have no space here for more than the barest outline. I have already indicated his views, most emphatically expressed and forecasted. He fulfilled them all to the letter, up to the day of his death. In so far as I could make out, he made about as satisfactory a husband and father and citizen as I have ever seen. He did it deliberately, in cold reason, and yet with a warmth and flare which puzzled me all the more since it *was* based on reason and forethought. I misdoubted. I was not quite willing to believe that it would work out, and yet if ever a home was delightful, with a charming and genuinely "happy" atmosphere, it was Peter's.

"Here she is," he observed the day he married her, "me *frau*—Zuleika. Isn't she a peach? Ever see any nicer hair than that? And these here, now, pink cheeks? What? Look at 'em! And her little Dutchy nose! Isn't it cute? Oh, Dutchy! And right here in me vest pocket is the golden band wherewith I am to be chained to the floor, the domestic hearth. And right there on her finger is my badge of prospective serfdom." Then, in a loud aside to me, "In six months I'll be beating her. Come now, Zuleika. We have to go through with this. You have to swear to be my slave."

And so they were married.

And in the home afterward he was as busy and helpful and noisy as any man about the house could ever hope to be. He was always fussing about after hours "putting up" something or arranging his collections or helping Zuleika wash and dry the dishes, or showing her how to cook something if she didn't know how. He was running to the store or bringing home things from the downtown market. Months before the first child was born he was declaring most shamelessly, "In a few months now, Dreiser, Zuleika and I are going to have our first calf. The bones roll for a boy, but you never can tell. I'm offering up prayers and oblations—both of us are. I make Zuleika pray every night. And say, when it comes, no spoiling-the-kid stuff. No bawling or rocking it to sleep nights permitted. Here's one kid that's going to be raised right. I've worked out all the rules. No trashy baby-foods. Good old specially brewed Culmbacher for the mother, and the kid afterwards if it wants it. This is one family in which law and order are going to prevail—good old 'dichtig, wichtig' law and order."

I used to chuckle the while I verbally denounced him for his coarse, plebeian point of view and tastes.

In a little while the child came, and to his immense satisfaction it was a boy. I never saw a man "carry on" so, make over it, take such a whole-souled interest in all those little things which supposedly made for its health and well-being. For the first few weeks he still talked of not having it petted or spoiled, but at the same time he was surely and swiftly changing, and by the end of that time had become the most doting, almost ridiculously fond papa that I ever saw. Always the child must be in his lap at the most unseemly hours, when his wife would permit it. When he went anywhere, or they, although they kept a maid the child must be carried along by him on his shoulder. He liked nothing better than to sit and hold it close, rocking in a rocking-chair American style and singing, or come tramping into my home in New York, the child looking like a woolen ball. At night if it stirred or whimpered he was up and looking. And the baby-clothes!—and the cradle!—and the toys!—colored rubber balls and soldiers the first or second or third week!

"What about that stern discipline that was to be put in force here—no rocking, no getting up at night to coddle a weeping infant?"

"Yes, I know. That's all good stuff before you get one. I've got one of my own now, and I've got a new light on this. Say, Dreiser, take my advice. Go through the routine. Don't try to escape. Have a kid or two or three. There's a psychic punch to it you can't get any other way. It's nature's way. It's a great scheme. You and your girl and your kid."

As he talked he rocked, holding the baby boy to his breast. It was wonderful.

And Mrs. Peter—how happy she seemed. There was light in that house, flowers, laughter, good fellowship. As in his old rooms so in this new home he gathered a few of his old friends around him and some new ones, friends of this region. In the course of a year or two he was on the very best terms of friendship with his barber around the corner, his grocer, some man who had a saloon and bowling alley in the neighborhood, his tailor, and then just neighbors. The milkman, the coal man, the druggist and cigar man at the next corner—all could tell you where Peter lived. His little front "yard" had two beds of flowers all summer long, his lot in the back was a garden—lettuce, onions, peas, beans. Peter was always happiest when he could be home working, playing with the baby, pushing him about in a go-cart, working in his garden, or lying on the floor making something—an engraving or print or a box which he was carving, the infant in some simple gingham romper crawling about. He was always busy, but never too much so for a glance or a mock-threatening, "Now say, not so much industry there. You leave my things alone," to the child. Of a Sunday he sat out on the front porch smoking, reading the Sunday paper, congratulating himself on his happy married life, and most of the time holding the infant. Afternoons he would carry it somewhere, anywhere, in his arms to his friends, the Park, New York, to see me. At breakfast, dinner, supper the heir presumptive was in a high-chair beside him.

"Ah, now, here's a rubber spoon. Beat with that. It's less destructive and less painful physically."

"How about a nice prust" (crust) "dipped in bravery" (gravy) "—heh? Do you suppose that would cut any of your teeth?"

"Zuleika, this son of yours seems to think a spoonful of beer or two might not hurt him. What do you say?"

Occasionally, especially of a Saturday evening, he wanted to go bowling and yet he wanted his heir. The problem was solved by fitting the latter into a tight little sweater and cap and carrying him along on his shoulder, into the bar for a beer, thence to the bowling alley, where young hopeful was fastened into a chair on the side lines while Peter and myself or some of his friends bowled. At ten or ten-thirty or eleven, as the case might be, he was ready to leave, but before that hour les ongfong might be sound asleep, hanging against

Peter's scarf, his interest in his toes or thumbs having given out.

"Peter, look at that," I observed once. "Don't you think we'd better take him home?"

"Home nothing! Let him sleep. He can sleep here as well as anywhere, and besides I like to look at him." And in the room would be a great crowd, cigars, beers, laughter, and Peter's various friends as used to the child's presence and as charmed by it as he was. He was just the man who could do such things. His manner and point of view carried conviction. He believed in doing all that he wanted to do simply and naturally, and more and more as he went along people not only respected, I think they adored him, especially the simple homely souls among whom he chose to move and have his being.

About this time there developed among those in his immediate neighborhood a desire to elect him to some political position, that of councilman, or State assemblyman, in the hope or thought that he would rise to something higher. But he would none of it—not then anyhow. Instead, about this time or a very little later, after the birth of his second child (a girl), he devoted himself to the composition of a brilliant piece of prose poetry ("Wolf"), which, coming from him, did not surprise me in the least. If he had designed or constructed a great building, painted a great picture, entered politics and been elected governor or senator, I would have taken it all as a matter of course. He could have. The material from which anything may rise was there. I asked him to let me offer it to the publishing house with which I was connected, and I recall with interest the comment of the oldest and most experienced of the bookmen and salesmen among us. "You'll never make much, if anything, on this book. It's too good, too poetic. But whether it pays or not, I vote yes. I'd rather lose money on something like this than make it on some of the trash we do make it on."

Amen. I agreed then, and I agree now.

The last phase of Peter was as interesting and dramatic as any of the others. His married life was going forward about as he had planned. His devotion to his home and children, his loving wife, his multiplex interests, his various friends, was always a curiosity to me, especially in view of his olden days. One day he was over in New York visiting one of his favorite Chinese importing companies, through which he had secured and was still securing occasional objects of art. He had come down to me in my office at the Butterick Building to see if I would not come over the following Saturday as usual and stay until Monday. He had secured something, was planning something. I should see. At the elevator he waved me a gay "so long—see you Saturday!"

But on Friday, as I was talking with some one at my desk, a telegram was handed me. It was from Mrs. Peter and read: "Peter died today at two of pneumonia. Please come."

I could scarcely believe it. I did not know that he had even been sick. His little yellow-haired wife! The two children! His future! His interests! I dropped everything and hurried to the nearest station. En route I speculated on the mysteries on which he had so often speculated—death, dissolution, uncertainty, the crude indifference or cruelty of Nature. What would become of Mrs. Peter? His children?

I arrived only to find a home atmosphere destroyed as by a wind that puts out a light. There was Peter, stiff and cold, and in the other rooms his babies, quite unconscious of what had happened, prattling as usual, and Mrs. Peter practically numb and speechless. It had come so suddenly, so out of a clear sky, that she could not realize, could not even tell me at first. The doctor was there—also a friend of his, the nearest barber! Also two or three representatives from his paper, the owner of the bowling alley, the man who had the $40,000 collection of curios. All were stunned, as I was. As his closest friend, I took charge: wired his relatives, went to an undertaker who knew him to arrange for his burial, in Newark or Philadelphia, as his wife should wish, she having no connection with Newark other than Peter.

It was most distressing, the sense of dull despair and unwarranted disaster which hung over the place. It was as though impish and pagan forces, or malign ones outside life, had committed a crime of the ugliest character. On Monday, the day he saw me, he was well. On Tuesday morning he had a slight cold but insisted on running out somewhere without his overcoat, against which his wife protested. Tuesday night he had a fever and took quinine and aspirin and a hot whiskey. Wednesday morning he was worse and a doctor was called, but it was not deemed serious. Wednesday night he was still worse and pneumonia had set in. Thursday he was lower still, and by noon a metal syphon of oxygen was sent for, to relieve the sense of suffocation setting in. Thursday night he was weak and sinking, but expected to come round—and still, so unexpected was the attack, so uncertain the probability of anything fatal, that no word was sent, even to me. Friday morning he was no worse and no better. "If he was no worse by night he might pull through." At noon he was seized with a sudden sinking spell. Oxygen was applied by his wife and a nurse, and the doctor sent for. By one-thirty he was lower still, very low. "His face was blue, his lips ashen," his wife told me. "We put the oxygen tube to his mouth and I said 'Can you speak, Peter?' I was so nervous and frightened. He moved his head a little to indicate 'no.' 'Peter,' I said, 'you mustn't let go! You must fight! Think of me! Think of the babies!' I was a little crazy, I think, with fear. He looked at me very fixedly. He stiffened and gritted his teeth in a great effort. Then suddenly he collapsed and lay still. He was dead."

I could not help thinking of the force and energy—able at the last minute, when he could not speak—to "grit his teeth" and "fight," a minute before his death. What is the human spirit, or mind, that it can fight so, to the very last? I felt as though some one, something, had ruthlessly killed him, committed plain, unpunished murder—nothing more and nothing less.

And there were his cases of curios, his rug, his prints, his dishes, his many, many schemes, his book to come out soon. I gazed and marveled. I looked at his wife and babies, but could say nothing. It spelled, what such things always spell, in the face of all our dreams, crass chance or the willful, brutal indifference of Nature to all that relates to man. If he is to prosper he must do so without her aid.

That same night, sleeping in the room adjoining that in which was the body, a pale candle burning near it, I felt as though Peter were walking to and fro, to and fro, past me and into the room of his wife beyond, thinking and grieving.

His imagined wraith seemed horribly depressed and distressed. Once he came over and moved his hand (something) over my face. I felt him walking into the room where were his wife and kiddies, but he could make no one see, hear, understand. I got up and looked at his *cadaver* a long time, then went to bed again.

The next day and the next and the next were filled with many things. His mother and sister came on from the West as well as the mother and brother of his wife. I had to look after his affairs, adjusting the matter of insurance which he left, his art objects, the burial of his body "in consecrated ground" in Philadelphia, with the consent and aid of the local Catholic parish rector, else no burial. His mother desired it, but he had never been a good Catholic and there was trouble. The local parish assistant refused me, even the rector. Finally I threatened the good father with an appeal to the diocesan bishop on the ground of plain common sense and courtesy to a Catholic family, if not charity to a tortured mother and wife—and obtained consent. All along I felt as if a great crime had been committed by some one, foul murder. I could not get it out of my mind, and it made me angry, not sad.

Two, three, five, seven years later, I visited the little family in Philadelphia. The wife was with her mother and father in a simple little home street in a factory district, secretary and stenographer to an architect. She was little changed—a little stouter, not so carefree, industrious, patient. His boy, the petted F——, could not even recall his father, the girl not at all of course. And in the place were a few of his prints, two or three Chinese dishes, pottered by himself, his loom with the unfinished rug. I remained for dinner and dreamed old dreams, but I was uncomfortable and left early. And Mrs. Peter, accompanying me to the steps, looked after me as though I, alone, was all that was left of the old life.

A Doer of the Word

NOANK IS a little played-out fishing town on the south-eastern coast of Connecticut, lying half-way between New London and Stonington. Once it was a profitable port for mackerel and cod fishing. Today its wharves are deserted of all save a few lobster smacks. There is a shipyard, employing three hundred and fifty men, a yacht-building establishment, with two or three hired hands; a sail-loft, and some dozen or so shops or sheds, where the odds and ends of fishing life are made and sold. Everything is peaceful. The sound of the shipyard axes and hammers can be heard for miles over the quiet waters of the bay. In the sunny lane which follows the line of the shore, and along which a few shops struggle in happy-go-lucky disorder, may be heard the voices and noises of the workers at their work. Water gurgling about the stanchions of the docks, the whistle of some fisherman as he dawdles over his nets, or puts his fish ashore, the whirr of the single high-power sewing machine in the sail-loft, often mingle in a pleasant harmony, and invite the mind to repose and speculation.

I was in a most examining and critical mood that summer, looking into the nature and significance of many things, and was sitting one day in the shed of the maker of sailboats, where a half-dozen characters of the village were gathered, when some turn in the conversation brought up the nature of man. He is queer, he is restless; life is not so very much when you come to look upon many phases of it.

"Did any of you ever know a contented man?" I inquired idly, merely for the sake of something to say.

There was silence for a moment, and one after another met my roving glance with a thoughtful, self-involved and retrospective eye.

Old Mr. Main was the first to answer.

"Yes, I did. One."

"So did I," put in the sailboat maker, as he stopped in his work to think about it.

"Yes, and I did," said a dark, squat, sunny, little old fisherman, who sold cunners for bait in a little hut next door.

"Maybe you and me are thinking of the same one, Jacob," said old Mr. Main, looking inquisitively at the boat-builder.

"I think we've all got the same man in mind, likely," returned the builder.

"Who is he?" I asked.

"Charlie Potter," said the builder.

"That's the man!" exclaimed Mr. Main.

"Yes, I reckon Charlie Potter is contented, if anybody be," said an old fisherman who had hitherto been silent.

Such unanimity of opinion struck me forcibly. Charlie Potter—what a humble name; not very remarkable, to say the least. And to hear him so spoken of in this restless, religious, quibbling community made it all the more interesting.

"So you really think he is contented, do you?" I asked.

"Yes, sir! Charlie Potter is a contented man," replied Mr. Main, with convincing emphasis.

"Well," I returned, "that's rather interesting. What sort of a man is he?"

"Oh, he's just an ordinary man, not much of anybody. Fishes and builds boats occasionally," put in the boat-builder.

"Is that all? Nothing else?"

"He preaches now and then—not regularly," said Mr. Main.

A-ha! I thought. A religionist!

"A preacher is expected to set a good example," I said.

"He ain't a regular preacher," said Mr. Main, rather quickly. "He's just kind of around in religious work."

"What do you mean?" I asked curiously, not quite catching the import of this "around."

"Well," answered the boat builder, "he don't take any money for what he does. He ain't got anything."

"What does he live on then?" I persisted, still wondering at the significance of "around in religious work."

"I don't know. He used to fish for a living. Fishes yet once in a while, I believe."

"He makes models of yachts," put in one of the bystanders. "He sold the New Haven Road one for two hundred dollars here not long ago."

A vision of a happy-go-lucky Jack-of-all-trades arose before me. A visionary—a theorist.

"What else?" I asked, hoping to draw them out. "What makes you all think he is contented? What does he do that makes him so contented?"

"Well," said Mr. Main, after a considerable pause and with much of sympathetic emphasis in his voice, "Charlie Potter is just a good man, that's all. That's why he's contented. He does as near as he can what he thinks he ought to by other people—poor people."

"You won't find anybody with a kinder heart than Charlie Potter," put in the boat-builder. "That's the trouble with him, really. He's too good. He don't look after himself right, I say. A fellow has to look out for himself some in this world. If he don't, no one else will."

"Right you are, Henry," echoed a truculent sea voice from somewhere.

I was becoming both amused and interested, intensely so.

"If he wasn't that way, he'd be a darned sight better off than he is," said a thirty-year-old helper, from a far corner of the room.

"What makes you say that?" I queried. "Isn't it better to be kind-hearted and generous than not?"

"It's all right to be kind-hearted and generous, but that ain't sayin' that you've got to give your last cent away and let your family go hungry."

"Is that what Charlie Potter does?"

"Well, no, maybe he don't, but he comes mighty near to it at times. He and his wife and his adopted children have been pretty close to it at times."

You see, this was the center, nearly, for all village gossip and philosophic speculation, and many of the most important local problems, morally and intellectually speaking, were here thrashed out.

"There's no doubt but that's where Charlie is wrong," put in old Mr. Main a little later. "He don't always stop to think of his family."

"What did he ever do that struck you as being over-generous?" I asked of the young man who had spoken from the corner.

"That's all right," he replied in a rather irritated and peevish tone; "I ain't going to go into details now, but there's people around here that hang on him, and that he's give to, that he hadn't orter."

"I believe in lookin' out for Number One, that's what I believe in," interrupted the boat-maker, laying down his rule and line. "This givin' up everything and goin' without yourself may be all right, but I don't believe it. A man's first duty is to his wife and children, that's what I say."

"That's the way it looks to me," put in Mr. Main.

"Well, does Potter give up everything and go without things?" I asked the boat-maker.

"Purty blamed near it at times," he returned definitely, then addressing the company in general he added, "Look at the time he worked over there on Fisher's Island, at the Ellersbie farm—the time they were packing the ice there. You remember that, Henry, don't you?"

Mr. Main nodded.

"What about it?"

"What about it! Why, he give his rubber boots away, like a darned fool, to old drunken Jimmy Harper, and him loafin' around half the year drunk, and worked around on the ice without any shoes himself. He might 'a' took cold and died."

"Why did he do it?" I queried, very much interested by now.

"Oh, Charlie's naturally big-hearted," put in the little old man who sold cunners. "He believes in the Lord and the Bible. Stands right square on it, only he don't belong to no church like. He's got the biggest heart I ever saw in a livin' being."

"Course the other fellow didn't have any shoes for to wear," put in the boat-maker explanatorily, "but he never would work, anyhow."

They lapsed into silence while the latter returned to his measuring, and then out of the drift of thought came this from the helper in the corner:

"Yes, and look at the way Bailey used to sponge on him. Get his money Saturday night and drink it all up, and then Sunday morning, when his wife and children were hungry, go cryin' around Potter. Dinged if I'd 'a' helped him. But Potter'd take the food right off his breakfast table and give it to him. I saw him do it! I don't think that's right. Not when he's got four or five orphans of his own to care for."

"His own children?" I interrupted, trying to get the thing straight.

"No, sir; just children he picked up around, here and there."

Here is a curious character, sure enough, I thought—one well worth looking into.

Another lull, and then as I was leaving the room to give the matter a little quiet attention, I remarked to the boat-maker:

"Outside of his foolish giving, you haven't anything against Charlie Potter, have you?"

"Not a thing," he replied, in apparent astonishment. "Charlie Potter's one of the best men that ever lived. He's a good man."

I smiled at the inconsistency and went my way.

A day or two later the loft of the sail-maker, instead of the shed of the boat-builder, happened to be my lounging place, and thinking of this theme, now uppermost in my mind, I said to him:

"Do you know a man around here by the name of Charlie Potter?"

"Well, I might say that I do. He lived here for over fifteen years."

"What sort of a man is he?"

He stopped in his stitching a moment to look at me, and then said:

"How d'ye mean? By trade, so to speak, or religious-like?"

"What is it he has done," I said, "that makes him so popular with all you people? Everybody says he's a good man. Just what do you mean by that?"

"Well," he said, ceasing his work as though the subject were one of extreme importance to him, "he's a peculiar man, Charlie is. He believes in giving nearly everything he has away, if any one else needs it. He'd give the coat off his back if you asked him for it. Some folks condemn him for this, and for not giving everything to his wife and them orphans he has, but I always thought the man was nearer right than most of us. I've got a family myself—but, then, so's he, now, for that matter. It's pretty hard to live up to your light always."

He looked away as if he expected some objection to be made to this, but hearing none, he went on. "I always liked him personally very much. He ain't around here now any more—lives up in Norwich, I think. He's a man of his word, though, as truthful as kin be. He ain't never done nothin' for me, I not bein' a takin' kind, but that's neither here nor there."

He paused, in doubt apparently, as to what else to say.

"You say he's so good," I said. "Tell me one thing that he ever did that struck you as being preëminently good."

"Well, now, I can't say as I kin, exactly, offhand," he replied, "there bein' so many of them from time to time. He was always doin' things one way and another. He give to everybody around here that asked him, and to a good many that didn't. I remember once"—and a smile gave evidence of a genial memory—"he give away a lot of pork that he'd put up for the winter to some colored people back here—two or three barrels, maybe. His wife didn't object, exactly, but my, how his mother-in-law did go on about it. She was livin' with him then. She went and railed against him all around."

"She didn't like to give it to them, eh?"

"Well, I should say not. She didn't set with his views, exactly—never did. He took the pork, though—it was right in the coldest weather we had that winter—and hauled it back about seven miles here to where they lived, and handed it all out himself. Course they were awful hard up, but then they might 'a' got along without it. They do now, sometimes. Charlie's too good that way. It's his one fault, if you might so speak of it."

I smiled as the evidence accumulated. Houseless wayfarers, stopping to find food and shelter under his roof, an orphan child carried seven miles on foot from the bedside of a dead mother and cared for all winter, three children, besides two of his own, being raised out of a sense of affection and care for the fatherless.

One day in the local postoffice I was idling a half hour with the postmaster, when I again inquired:

"Do you know Charlie Potter?"

"I should think I did. Charlie Potter and I sailed together for something over eleven years."

"How do you mean sailed together?"

"We were on the same schooner. This used to be a great port for mackerel and cod. We were wrecked once together."

"How was that?"

"Oh, we went on rocks."

"Any lives lost?"

"No, but there came mighty near being. We helped each other in the boat. I remember Charlie was the last one in that time. Wouldn't get in until all the rest were safe."

A sudden resolution came to me.

"Do you know where he is now?"

"Yes, he's up in Norwich, preaching or doing missionary work. He's kind of busy all the time among the poor people, and so on. Never makes much of anything out of it for himself, but just likes to do it, I guess."

"Do you know how he manages to live?"

"No, I don't, exactly. He believes in trusting to Providence for what he needs. He works though, too, at one job and another. He's a carpenter for one thing. Got an idea the Lord will send 'im whatever he needs."

"Well, and does He?"

"Well, he lives." A little later he added:

"Oh, yes. There's nothing lazy about Charlie. He's a good worker. When he was in the fishing line here there wasn't a man worked harder than he did. They can't anybody lay anything like that against him."

"Is he very difficult to talk to?" I asked, meditating on seeking him out. I had so little to do at the time, the very idlest of summers, and the reports of this man's deeds were haunting me. I wanted to discover for myself whether he was real or not—whether the reports were true. The Samaritan in people is so easily exaggerated at times.

"Oh, no. He's one of the finest men that way I ever knew. You could see him, well enough, if you went up to Norwich, providing he's up there. He usually is, though, I think. He lives there with his wife and mother, you know."

I caught an afternoon boat for New London and Norwich at one-thirty, and arrived in Norwich at five. The narrow streets of the thriving little mill city were alive with people. I had no address, could not obtain one, but through the open door of a news-stall near the boat landing I called to the proprietor:

"Do you know any one in Norwich by the name of Charlie Potter?"

"The man who works around among the poor people here?"

"That's the man."

"Yes, I know him. He lives out on Summer Street, Number Twelve, I think. You'll find it in the city directory."

The ready reply was rather astonishing. Norwich has something like thirty thousand people.

I walked out in search of Summer Street and finally found a beautiful lane of that name climbing upward over gentle slopes, arched completely with elms. Some of the pretty porches of the cottages extended nearly to the sidewalk. Hammocks, rocking-chairs on verandas, benches under the trees— all attested the love of idleness and shade in summer. Only the glimpse of mills and factories in the valley below evidenced the grimmer life which gave rise mayhap to the need of a man to work among the poor.

"Is this Summer Street?" I inquired of an old darky who was strolling cityward in the cool of the evening. An umbrella was under his arm and an evening paper under his spectacled nose.

"Bress de Lord!" he said, looking vaguely around. "Ah couldn't say. Ah knows dat street—been on it fifty times— but Ah never did know de name. Ha, ha, ha!"

The hills about echoed his hearty laugh.

"You don't happen to know Charlie Potter?"

"Oh, yas, sah. Ah knows Charlie Potter. Dat's his house right ovah dar."

The house in which Charlie Potter lived was a two-story frame, overhanging a sharp slope, which descended directly to the waters of the pretty river below. For a mile or more, the valley of the river could be seen, its slopes dotted with houses, the valley itself lined with mills. Two little girls were upon the sloping lawn to the right of the house. A stout, comfortable-looking man was sitting by a window on the left side of the house, gazing out over the valley.

"Is this where Charlie Potter lives?" I inquired of one of the children.

"Yes, sir."

"Did he live in Noank?"

"Yes, sir."

Just then a pleasant-faced woman of forty-five or fifty issued from a vine-covered door.

"Mr. Potter?" she replied to my inquiry. "He'll be right out."

She went about some little work at the side of the house, and in a moment Charlie Potter appeared. He was short, thick-set, and weighed no less than two hundred pounds. His face and hands were sunburned and brown like those of every fisherman of Noank. An old wrinkled coat and a baggy pair of gray trousers clothed his form loosely. Two inches of a spotted, soft-brimmed hat were pulled carelessly over his eyes. His face was round and full, but slightly seamed. His hands were large, his walk uneven, and rather inclined to a side swing, or the sailor's roll. He seemed an odd, pudgy person for so large a fame.

"Is this Mr. Potter?"

"I'm the man."

"I live on a little hummock at the east of Mystic Island, off Noank."

"You do?"

"I came up to have a talk with you."

"Will you come inside, or shall we sit out here?"

"Let's sit on the step."

"All right, let's sit on the step."

He waddled out of the gate and sank comfortably on the little low doorstep, with his feet on the cool bricks below. I dropped into the space beside him, and was greeted by as sweet and kind a look as I have ever seen in a man's eyes. It was one of perfect courtesy and good nature—void of all suspicion.

"We were sitting down in the sailboat maker's place at Noank the other day, and I asked a half dozen of the old fellows whether they had ever known a contented man. They all thought a while, and then they said they had. Old Mr. Main and the rest of them agreed that Charlie Potter was a contented man. What I want to know is, are you?"

I looked quizzically into his eyes to see what effect this

would have, and if there was no evidence of a mist of pleasure and affection being vigorously restrained I was very much mistaken. Something seemed to hold the man in helpless silence as he gazed vacantly at nothing. He breathed heavily, then drew himself together and lifted one of his big hands, as if to touch me, but refrained.

"Yes, brother," he said after a time, "I *am*."

"Well, that's good," I replied, taking a slight mental exception to the use of the word brother. "What makes you contented?"

"I don't know, unless it is that I've found out what I ought to do. You see, I need so very little for myself that I couldn't be very unhappy."

"What ought you to do?"

"I ought to love my fellowmen."

"And do you?"

"Say, brother, but I do," he insisted quite simply and with no evidence of chicane or make-believe—a simple, natural enthusiasm. "I love everybody. There isn't anybody so low or so mean but I love him. I love you, yes, I do. I love you."

He reached out and touched me with his hand, and while I was inclined to take exception to this very moral enthusiasm, I thrilled just the same as I have not over the touch of any man in years. There was something effective and electric about him, so very warm and foolishly human. The glance which accompanied it spoke, it seemed, as truthfully as his words. He probably did love me—or thought he did. What difference?

We lapsed into silence. The scene below was so charming that I could easily gaze at it in silence. This little house was very simple, not poor, by no means prosperous, but well-ordered—such a home as such a man might have. After a while I said:

"It is very evident that you think the condition of some of your fellowmen isn't what it ought to be. Tell me what you are trying to do. What method have you for improving their condition?"

"The way I reason is this-a-way," he began. "All that some people have is their feelings, nothing else. Take a tramp, for instance, as I often have. When you begin to sum up to see where to begin, you find that all he has in the world, besides his pipe and a little tobacco, is his feelings. It's all most people have, rich or poor, though a good many think they have more than that. I try not to injure anybody's feelings."

He looked at me as though he had expressed the solution of the difficulties of the world, and the wonderful, kindly eyes beamed in rich romance upon the scene.

"Very good," I said, "but what do you do? How do you go about it to aid your fellowmen?"

"Well," he answered, unconsciously overlooking his own personal actions in the matter, "I try to bring them the salvation which the Bible teaches. You know I stand on the Bible, from cover to cover."

"Yes, I know you stand on the Bible, but what do you do? You don't merely preach the Bible to them. What do you do?"

"No, sir, I don't preach the Bible at all. I stand on it myself. I try as near as I can to do what it says. I go wherever I can be useful. If anybody is sick or in trouble, I'm ready to go. I'll be a nurse. I'll work and earn them food. I'll give them anything I can—that's what I do."

"How can you give when you haven't anything? They told me in Noank that you never worked for money."

"Not for myself alone. I never take any money for myself alone. That would be self-seeking. Anything I earn or take is for the Lord, not me. I never keep it. The Lord doesn't allow a man to be self-seeking."

"Well, then, when you get money what do you do with it? You can't do and live without money."

He had been looking away across the river and the bridge to the city below, but now he brought his eyes back and fixed them on me.

"I've been working now for twenty years or more, and, although I've never had more money than would last me a few days at a time, I've never wanted for anything and I've been able to help others. I've run pretty close sometimes. Time and time again I've been compelled to say, 'Lord, I'm all out of coal,' or 'Lord, I'm going to have to ask you to get me my fare to New Haven tomorrow,' but in the moment of my need He has never forgotten me. Why, I've gone down to the depot time and time again, when it was necessary for me to go, without five cents in my pocket, and He's been there to meet me. Why, He wouldn't keep you waiting when you're about His work. He wouldn't forget you—not for a minute."

I looked at the man in open-eyed amazement.

"Do you mean to say that you would go down to a depot without money and wait for money to come to you?"

"Oh, brother," he said, with the softest light in his eyes, "if you only knew what it is to have faith!"

He laid his hand softly on mine.

"What is car-fare to New Haven or to anywhere, to Him?"

"But," I replied materially, "you haven't any car-fare when you go there—how do you actually get it? Who gives it to you? Give me one instance."

"Why, it was only last week, brother, that a woman wrote me from Malden, Massachusetts, wanting me to come and see her. She's very sick with consumption, and she thought she was going to die. I used to know her in Noank, and she thought if she could get to see me she would feel better.

"I didn't have any money at the time, but that didn't make any difference.

" 'Lord,' I said, 'here's a woman sick in Malden, and she wants me to come to her. I haven't got any money, but I'll go right down to the depot, in time to catch a certain train,' and I went. And while I was standing there a man came up to me and said, 'Brother, I'm told to give you this,' and he handed me ten dollars."

"Did you know the man?" I exclaimed.

"Never saw him before in my life," he replied, smiling genially.

"And didn't he say anything more than that?"

"No."

I stared at him, and he added, as if to take the edge off my astonishment:

"Why, bless your heart, I knew he was from the Lord, just the moment I saw him coming."

"You mean to say you were standing there without a cent, expecting the Lord to help you, and He did?"

" 'He shall call upon me, and I shall answer him,' " he answered simply, quoting the Ninety-first Psalm.

This incident was still the subject of my inquiry when a little colored girl came out of the yard and paused a moment before us.

"May I go down across the bridge, papa?" she asked.

"Yes," he answered, and then as she tripped away, said:

"She's one of my adopted children." He gazed between his knees at the sidewalk.

"Have you many others?"

"Three."

"Raising them, are you?"

"Yes."

"They seem to think, down in Noank, that living as you do and giving everything away is satisfactory to you but rather hard on your wife and children."

"Well, it is true that she did feel a little uncertain in the beginning, but she's never wanted for anything. She'll tell you herself that she's never been without a thing that she really needed, and she's been happy."

He paused to meditate, I presume, over the opinion of his former fellow townsmen, and then added:

"It's true, there have been times when we have been right where we had to have certain things pretty badly, before they came, but they never failed to come."

While he was still talking, Mrs. Potter came around the corner of the house and out upon the sidewalk. She was going to the Saturday evening market in the city below.

"Here she is," he said. "Now you can ask her."

"What is it?" she inquired, turning a serene and smiling face to me.

"They still think, down in Noank, that you're not very happy with me," he said. "They're afraid you want for something once in a while."

She took this piece of neighborly interference in better fashion than most would, I fancy.

"I have never wanted for anything since I have been married to my husband," she said. "I am thoroughly contented."

She looked at him and he at her, and there passed between them an affectionate glance.

"Yes," he said, when she had passed after a pleasing little

conversation, "my wife has been a great help to me. She has never complained."

"People are inclined to talk a little," I said.

"Well, you see, she never complained, but she did feel a little bit worried in the beginning."

"Have you a mission or a church here in Norwich?"

"No, I don't believe in churches."

"Not in churches?"

"No. The sight of a minister preaching the word of God for so much a year is all a mockery to me."

"What do you believe in?"

"Personal service. Churches and charitable institutions and societies are all valueless. You can't reach your fellowman that way. They build up buildings and pay salaries—but there's a better way." (I was thinking of St. Francis and his original dream, before they threw him out and established monasteries and a costume or uniform—the thing he so much objected to.) "This giving of a few old clothes that the moths will get anyhow, that won't do. You've got to give something of yourself, and that's affection. Love is the only thing you can really give in all this world. When you give love, you give everything. Everything comes with it in some way or other."

"How do you say?" I queried. "Money certainly comes handy sometimes."

"Yes, when you give it with your own hand and heart—in no other way. It comes to nothing just contributed to some thing. Ah!" he added, with sudden animation, "the tangles men can get themselves into, the snarls, the wretchedness! Troubles with women, with men whom they owe, with evil things they say and think, until they can't walk down the street any more without peeping about to see if they are followed. They can't look you in the face; can't walk a straight course, but have got to sneak around corners. Poor, miserable, unhappy—they're worrying and crying and dodging one another!"

He paused, lost in contemplation of the picture he had conjured up.

"Yes," I went on catechistically, determined, if I could, to rout out this matter of giving, this actual example of the modus operandi of Christian charity. "What do you do? How do you get along without giving them money?"

"I don't get along without giving them some money. There are cases, lots of them, where a little money is necessary. But, brother, it is so little necessary at times. It isn't always money they want. You can't reach them with old clothes and charity societies," he insisted. "You've got to love them, brother. You've got to go to them and love them, just as they are, scarred and miserable and bad-hearted."

"Yes," I replied doubtfully, deciding to follow this up later. "But just what is it you do in a needy case? One instance?"

"Why, one night I was passing a little house in this town," he went on, "and I heard a woman crying. I went right to the door and opened it, and when I got inside she just stopped and looked at me.

" 'Madam,' I said, 'I have come to help you, if I can. Now you tell me what you're crying for.'

"Well, sir, you know she sat there and told me how her husband drank and how she didn't have anything in the house to eat, and so I just gave her all I had and told her I would see her husband for her, and the next day I went and hunted him up and said to him, 'Oh, brother, I wish you would open your eyes and see what you are doing. I wish you wouldn't do that any more. It's only misery you are creating.' And, you know, I got to telling about how badly his wife felt about it, and how I intended to work and try and help her, and bless me if he didn't up and promise me before I got through that he wouldn't do that any more. And he didn't. He's working today, and it's been two years since I went to him, nearly."

His eyes were alight with his appreciation of personal service.

"Yes, that's one instance," I said.

"Oh, there are plenty of them," he replied. "It's the only way. Down here in New London a couple of winters ago we had a terrible time of it. That was the winter of the panic, you know. Cold—my, but that was a cold winter, and thousands of people out of work—just thousands. It was awful. I tried to do what I could here and there all along, but finally things got so bad there that I went to the mayor. I saw they

were raising some kind of a fund to help the poor, so I told
him that if he'd give me a little of the money they were talking of spending that I'd feed the hungry for a cent-and-a-half
a meal."

"A cent-and-a-half a meal!"

"Yes, sir. They all thought it was rather curious, not possible at first, but they gave me the money and I fed 'em."

"Good meals?"

"Yes, as good as I ever eat myself," he replied.

"How did you do it?" I asked.

"Oh, I can cook. I just went around to the markets, and
told the market-men what I wanted—heads of mackerel, and
the part of the halibut that's left after the rich man cuts off
his steak—it's the poorest part that he pays for, you know.
And I went fishing myself two or three times—borrowed a
big boat and got men to help me—oh, I'm a good fisherman,
you know. And then I got the loan of an old covered brick-
yard that no one was using any more, a great big thing that
I could close up and build fires in, and I put my kettle in
there and rigged up tables out of borrowed boards, and got
people to loan me plates and spoons and knives and forks and
cups. I made fish chowder, and fish dinners, and really I set a
very fine table, I did, that winter."

"For a cent-and-a-half a meal!"

"Yes, sir, a cent-and-a-half a meal. Ask any one in New
London. That's all it cost me. The mayor said he was surprised at the way I did it."

"Well, but there wasn't any particular personal service in
the money they gave you?" I asked, catching him up on that
point. "They didn't personally serve—those who gave you
the money?"

"No, sir, they didn't," he replied dreamily, with unconscious simplicity. "But they gave through me, you see. That's
the way it was. I gave the personal service. Don't you see?
That's the way."

"Yes, that's the way," I smiled, avoiding as far as possible a
further discussion of this contradiction, so unconscious on his
part, and in the drag of his thought he took up another idea.

"I clothed 'em that winter, too—went around and got
barrels and boxes of old clothing. Some of them felt a little

ashamed to put on the things, but I got over that, all right. I was wearing them myself, and I just told them, 'Don't feel badly, brother. I'm wearing them out of the same barrel with you—I'm wearing them out of the same barrel.' Got my clothes entirely free for that winter."

"Can you always get all the aid you need for such enterprises?"

"Usually, and then I can earn a good deal of money when I work steadily. I can get a hundred and fifty dollars for a little yacht, you know, every time I find time to make one; and I can make a good deal of money out of fishing. I went out fishing here on the Fourth of July and caught two hundred blackfish—four and five pounds, almost, every one of them."

"That ought to be profitable," I said.

"Well, it was," he replied.

"How much did you get for them?"

"Oh, I didn't sell them," he said. "I never take money for my work that way. I gave them all away."

"What did you do?" I asked, laughing—"advertise for people to come for them?"

"No. My wife took some, and my daughters, and I took the rest and we carried them around to people that we thought would like to have them."

"Well, that wasn't so profitable, was it?" I commented amusedly.

"Yes, they were fine fish," he replied, not seeming to have heard me.

We dropped the subject of personal service at this point, and I expressed the opinion that his service was only a temporary expedient. Times changed, and with them, people. They forgot. Perhaps those he aided were none the better for accepting his charity.

"I know what you mean," he said. "But that don't make any difference. You just have to keep on giving, that's all, see? Not all of 'em turn back. It helps a lot. Money is the only dangerous thing to give—but I never give money—not very often. I give myself, rather, as much as possible. I give food and clothing, too, but I try to show 'em a new way—that's not money, you know. So many people need a new way.

They're looking for it often, only they don't seem to know how. But God, dear brother, however poor or mean they are—He knows. You've got to reach the heart, you know, and I let Him help me. You've got to make a man over in his soul, if you want to help him, and money won't help you to do that, you know. No, it won't."

He looked up at me in clear-eyed faith. It was remarkable.

"Make them over?" I queried, still curious, for it was all like a romance, and rather fantastic to me. "What do you mean? How do you make them over?"

"Oh, in their attitude, that's how. You've got to change a man and bring him out of self-seeking if you really want to make him good. Most men are so tangled up in their own errors and bad ways, and so worried over their seekings, that unless you can set them to giving it's no use. They're always seeking, and they don't know what they want half the time. Money isn't the thing. Why, half of them wouldn't understand how to use it if they had it. Their minds are not bright enough. Their perceptions are not clear enough. All you can do is to make them content with themselves. And that, giving to others will do. I never saw the man or the woman yet who couldn't be happy if you could make them feel the need of living for others, of doing something for somebody besides themselves. It's a fact. Selfish people are never happy."

He rubbed his hands as if he saw the solution of the world's difficulties very clearly, and I said to him:

"Well, now, you've got a man out of the mire, and 'saved,' as you call it, and then what? What comes next?"

"Well, then he's saved," he replied. "Happiness comes next—content."

"I know. But must he go to church, or conform to certain rules?"

"No, no, no!" he replied sweetly. "Nothing to do except to be good to others. 'True religion and undefiled before our God and Father is this,' " he quoted, " 'to visit the widow and the orphan in their affliction and to keep unspotted from the world. Charity is kind,' you know. 'Charity vaunteth not itself, is not puffed up, seeketh not its own.' "

"Well," I said, rather aimlessly, I will admit, for this high faith staggered me. (How high! How high!) "And then what?"

"Well, then the world would come about. It would be so much better. All the misery is in the lack of sympathy one with another. When we get that straightened out we can work in peace. There are lots of things to do, you know."

Yes, I thought, looking down on the mills and the driving force of self-interest—on greed, lust, love of pleasure, all their fantastic and yet moving dreams.

"I'm an ignorant man myself, and I don't know all," he went on, "and I'd like to study. My, but I'd like to look into all things, but I can't do it now. We can't stop until this thing is straightened out. Some time, maybe," and he looked peacefully away.

"By the way," I said, "whatever became of the man to whom you gave your rubber boots over on Fisher's Island?"

His face lit up as if it were the most natural thing that I should know about it.

"Say," he exclaimed, in the most pleased and confidential way, as if we were talking about a mutual friend, "I saw him not long ago. And, do you know, he's a good man now—really, he is. Sober and hard-working. And, say, would you believe it, he told me that I was the cause of it—just that miserable old pair of rubber boots—what do you think of that?"

I shook his hand at parting, and as we stood looking at each other in the shadow of the evening I asked him:

"Are you afraid to die?"

"Say, brother, but I'm not," he returned. "It hasn't any terror for me at all. I'm just as willing. My, but I'm willing."

He smiled and gripped me heartily again, and, as I was starting to go, said:

"If I die tonight, it'll be all right. He'll use me just as long as He needs me. That I know. Good-by."

"Good-by," I called back.

He hung by his fence, looking down upon the city. As I turned the next corner I saw him awakening from his reflection and waddling stolidly back into the house.

My Brother Paul

I LIKE BEST to think of him as he was at the height of his all-too-brief reputation and success, when, as the author and composer of various American popular successes ("On the Banks of the Wabash," "Just Tell Them That You Saw Me," and various others), as a third owner of one of the most successful popular music publishing houses in the city and as an actor and playwright of some small repute, he was wont to spin like a moth in the white light of Broadway. By reason of a little luck and some talent he had come so far, done so much for himself. In his day he had been by turn a novitiate in a Western seminary which trained aspirants for the Catholic priesthood; a singer and entertainer with a perambulating cure-all oil troupe or wagon ("Hamlin's Wizard Oil") traveling throughout Ohio, Indiana and Illinois; both end- and middle-man with one, two or three different minstrel companies of repute; the editor or originator and author of a "funny column" in a Western small city paper; the author of the songs mentioned and a hundred others; a black-face monologue artist; a white-face ditto, at Tony Pastor's, Miner's and Niblo's of the old days; a comic lead; co-star and star in such melodramas and farces as "The Danger Signal," "The Two Johns," "A Tin Soldier," "The Midnight Bell," "A Green Goods Man" (a farce which he himself wrote, by the way), and others. The man had a genius for the kind of gayety, poetry and romance which may, and no doubt must be, looked upon as exceedingly middle-class but which nonetheless had as much charm as anything in this world can well have. He had at this time absolutely no cares or financial worries of any kind, and this plus his health, self-amusing disposition and talent for entertaining, made him a most fascinating figure to contemplate.

My first recollection of him is of myself as a boy of ten and he a man of twenty-five (my oldest brother). He had come back to the town in which we were then living solely to find his mother and help her. Six or seven years before he had left without any explanation as to where he was going, tired of or irritated by the routine of a home which for any genuine opportunity it offered him might as well never have existed. It was run dominantly by my father in the interest of religious and moral theories, with which this boy had little sympathy. He was probably not understood by any one save my mother, who understood or at least sympathized with us all. Placed in a school which was to turn him out a priest, he had decamped, and now seven years later was here in this small town, with fur coat and silk hat, a smart cane—a gentleman of the theatrical profession. He had joined a minstrel show somewhere and had become an "end-man." He had suspected that we were not as fortunate in this world's goods as might be and so had returned. His really great heart had called him.

But the thing which haunts me, and which was typical of him then as throughout life, was the spirit which he then possessed and conveyed. It was one of an agile geniality, unmarred by thought of a serious character but warm and genuinely tender and with a taste for simple beauty which was most impressive. He was already the author of a cheap songbook, *"The Paul Dresser Songster"* ("All the Songs Sung in the Show"), and some copies of this he had with him, one of which he gave me. But we having no musical instrument of any kind, he taught me some of the melodies "by ear." The home in which by force of poverty we were compelled to live was most unprepossessing and inconvenient, and the result of his coming could but be our request for, or at least the obvious need of, assistance. Still he was as much an enthusiastic part of it as though he belonged to it. He was happy in it, and the cause of his happiness was my mother, of whom he was intensely fond. I recall how he hung about her in the kitchen or wherever she happened to be, how enthusiastically he related all his plans for the future, his amusing difficulties in the past. He was very grand and youthfully self-important, or so we all thought, and still he patted her on the shoulder or put his arm about her and kissed her. Until she died years later she was truly his uppermost thought, crying with her at times over her troubles and his. He contributed regularly to her support and sent home all his cast-off clothing to be made over for the younger ones. (Bless her tired hands!)

As I look back now on my life, I realize quite clearly that of all the members of my family, subsequent to my mother's death, the only one who truly understood me, or, better yet, sympathized with my intellectual and artistic point of view, was, strange as it may seem, this same Paul, my dearest brother. Not that he was in any way fitted intellectually or otherwise to enjoy high forms of art and learning and so guide me, or that he understood, even in later years (long after I had written "Sister Carrie," for instance), what it was that I was attempting to do; he never did. His world was that of the popular song, the middle-class actor or comedian, the middle-class comedy, and such humorous æsthetes of the writing world as Bill Nye, Petroleum V. Nasby, the authors of the Spoopendyke Papers, and "Samantha at Saratoga." As far as I could make out—and I say this in no lofty, condescending spirit, by any means—he was entirely full of simple, middle-class romance, middle-class humor, middle-class tenderness and middle-class grossness, all of which I am very free to say early disarmed and won me completely and kept me so much his debtor that I should hesitate to try to acknowledge or explain all that he did for or meant to me.

Imagine, if you can, a man weighing all of three hundred pounds, not more than five feet ten-and-one-half inches in height and yet of so lithesome a build that he gave not the least sense of either undue weight or lethargy. His temperament, always ebullient and radiant, presented him as a clever, eager, cheerful, emotional and always highly illusioned person with so collie-like a warmth that one found him compelling interest and even admiration. Easily cast down at times by the most trivial matters, at others, and for the most part, he was so spirited and bubbly and emotional and sentimental that your fiercest or most gloomy intellectual rages or moods could scarcely withstand his smile. This tenderness or sympathy of his, a very human appreciation of the weaknesses and errors as well as the toils and tribulations of most of us, was by far his outstanding and most engaging quality, and gave him a very definite force and charm. Admitting, as I freely do, that he was very sensuous (gross, some people might have called him), that he had an intense, possibly an undue fondness for women, a frivolous, childish, horse-playish sense of humor at times, still he had other qualities which were absolutely adorable. Life seemed positively to spring up fountain-like in him. One felt in him a capacity to do (in his possibly limited field); an ability to achieve, whether he was doing so at the moment or not, and a supreme willingness to share and radiate his success—qualities exceedingly rare, I believe. Some people are so successful, and yet you know their success is purely selfish—exclusive, not inclusive; they never permit you to share in their lives. Not so my good brother. He was generous to the point of self-destruction, and that is literally true. He was the mark if not the prey of all those who desired much or little for nothing, those who previously might not have rendered him a service of any kind. He was all life and color, and thousands (I use the word with care) noted and commented on it.

When I first came to New York he was easily the foremost popular song-writer of the day and was the cause of my coming, so soon at least, having established himself in the publishing field and being so comfortably settled as to offer me a kind of anchorage in so troubled a commercial sea. I was very much afraid of New York, but with him here it seemed not so bad. The firm of which he was a part had a floor or two in an old residence turned office building, as so many are in New York, in Twentieth Street very close to Broadway, and here, during the summer months (1894–7) when the various theatrical road-companies, one of which he was always a part, had returned for the closed season, he was to be found aiding his concern in the reception and care of possible applicants for songs and attracting by his personality such virtuosi of the vaudeville and comedy stage as were likely to make the instrumental publications of his firm a success.

I may as well say here that he had no more business skill than a fly. At the same time, he was in no wise sycophantic where either wealth, power or fame was concerned. He considered himself a personage of sorts, and was. The minister, the moralist, the religionist, the narrow, dogmatic and self-centered in any field were likely to be the butt of his humor, and he could imitate so many phases of character so cleverly that he was the life of any idle pleasure-seeking party anywhere. To this day I recall his characterization of an old Irish washerwoman arguing; a stout, truculent German laying down the law; lean, gloomy, out-at-elbows actors of the

Hamlet or classic school complaining of their fate; the stingy skinflint haggling over a dollar, and always with a skill for titillating the risibilities which is vivid to me even to this day. Other butts of his humor were the actor, the Irish day-laborer, the negro and the Hebrew. And how he could imitate them! It is useless to try to indicate such things in writing, the facial expression, the intonation, the gestures; these are not things of words. Perhaps I can best indicate the direction of his mind, if not his manner, by the following:

One night as we were on our way to a theater there stood on a nearby corner in the cold a blind man singing and at the same time holding out a little tin cup into which the coins of the charitably inclined were supposed to be dropped. At once my brother noticed him, for he had an eye for this sort of thing, the pathos of poverty as opposed to so gay a scene, the street with its hurrying theater crowds. At the same time, so inherently mischievous was his nature that although his sympathy for the suffering or the ill-used of fate was overwhelming, he could not resist combining his intended charity with a touch of the ridiculous.

"Got any pennies?" he demanded.

"Three or four."

Going over to an outdoor candystand he exchanged a quarter for pennies, then came back and waited until the singer, who had ceased singing, should begin a new melody. A custom of the singer's, since the song was of no import save as a means of attracting attention to him, was to interpolate a "Thank you" after each coin dropped in his cup and between the words of the song, regardless. It was this little idiosyncrasy which evidently had attracted my brother's attention, although it had not mine. Standing quite close, his pennies in his hand, he waited until the singer had resumed, then began dropping pennies, waiting each time for the "Thank you," which caused the song to go about as follows:

"Da-a-'ling" (Clink!—"Thank you!") "I am—" (Clink!— "Thank you!") "growing o-o-o-ld" (Clink!—"Thank you!"), "Silve-e-r—" (Clink!—"Thank you!") "threads among the—" (Clink!—"Thank you!") "go-o-o-ld—" (Clink! "Thank you!"). "Shine upon my-y" (Clink!—"Thank you!") "bro-o-ow toda-a-y" (Clink!—"Thank you!"), "Life is—" (Clink!—

"Thank you!") "fading fast a-a-wa-a-ay" (Clink!—"Thank you!")—and so on ad infinitum, until finally the beggar himself seemed to hesitate a little and waver, only so solemn was his rôle of want and despair that of course he dared not but had to go on until the last penny was in, and until he was saying more "Thank yous" than words of the song. A passerby noticing it had begun to "Haw-haw!", at which others joined in, myself included. The beggar himself, a rather sniveling specimen, finally realizing what a figure he was cutting with his song and thanks, emptied the coins into his hand and with an indescribably wry expression, half-uncertainty and half-smile, exclaimed, "I'll have to thank you as long as you keep putting pennies in, I suppose. God bless you!"

My brother came away smiling and content.

However, it is not as a humorist or song-writer or publisher that I wish to portray him, but as an odd, lovable personality, possessed of so many interesting and peculiar and almost indescribable traits. Of all characters in fiction he perhaps most suggests Jack Falstaff, with his love of women, his bravado and bluster and his innate good nature and sympathy. Sympathy was really his outstanding characteristic, even more than humor, although the latter was always present. One might recite a thousand incidents of his generosity and out-of-hand charity, which contained no least thought of return or reward. I recall that once there was a boy who had been reared in one of the towns in which we had once lived who had never had a chance in his youth, educationally or in any other way, and, having turned out "bad" and sunk to the level of a bank robber, had been detected in connection with three other men in the act of robbing a bank, the watchman of which was subsequently killed in the mêlée and escape. Of all four criminals only this one had been caught. Somewhere in prison he had heard sung one of my brother's sentimental ballads, "The Convict and the Bird," and recollecting that he had known Paul wrote him, setting forth his life history and that now he had no money or friends.

At once my good brother was alive to the pathos of it. He showed the letter to me and wanted to know what could be done. I suggested a lawyer, of course, one of those brilliant legal friends of his—always he had enthusiastic admirers in

all walks—who might take the case for little or nothing.
There was the leader of Tammany Hall, Richard Croker, who
could be reached, he being a friend of Paul's. There was the
Governor himself to whom a plain recitation of the boy's unfortunate life might be addressed, and with some hope of
profit.

All of these things he did, and more. He went to the prison
(Sing Sing), saw the warden and told him the story of the
boy's life, then went to the boy, or man, himself and gave
him some money. He was introduced to the Governor
through influential friends and permitted to tell the tale.
There was much delay, a reprieve, a commutation of the
death penalty to life imprisonment—the best that could be
done. But he was so grateful for that, so pleased. You would
have thought at the time that it was his own life that had
been spared.

"Good heavens!" I jested. "You'd think you'd done the man
an inestimable service, getting him in the penitentiary for
life!"

"That's right," he grinned—an unbelievably provoking
smile. "He'd better be dead, wouldn't he? Well, I'll write and
ask him which he'd rather have."

I recall again taking him to task for going to the rescue of
a "down and out" actor who had been highly successful and
apparently not very sympathetic in his day, one of that more
or less gaudy clan that wastes its substance, or so it seemed
to me then, in riotous living. But now being old and entirely
discarded and forgotten, he was in need of sympathy and aid.
By some chance he knew Paul, or Paul had known him, and
now because of the former's obvious prosperity—he was
much in the papers at the time—he had appealed to him. The
man lived with a sister in a wretched little town far out on
Long Island. On receiving his appeal Paul seemed to wish to
investigate for himself, possibly to indulge in a little lofty romance or sentiment. At any rate he wanted me to go along
for the sake of companionship, so one dreary November afternoon we went, saw the pantaloon, who did not impress
me very much even in his age and misery for he still had a
few of his theatrical manners and insincerities, and as we were
coming away I said, "Paul, why should you be the goat in

every case?" for I had noted ever since I had been in New York, which was several years then, that he was a victim of many such importunities. If it was not the widow of a deceased friend who needed a ton of coal or a sack of flour, or the reckless, headstrong boy of parents too poor to save him from a term in jail or the reformatory and who asked for fine-money or an appeal to higher powers for clemency, or a wastrel actor or actress "down and out" and unable to "get back to New York" and requiring his or her railroad fare wired prepaid, it was the dead wastrel actor or actress who needed a coffin and a decent form of burial.

"Well, you know how it is, Thee" (he nearly always addressed me thus), "when you're old and sick. As long as you're up and around and have money, everybody's your friend. But once you're down and out no one wants to see you any more—see?" Almost amusingly he was always sad over those who had once been prosperous but who were now old and forgotten. Some of his silliest tender songs conveyed as much.

"Quite so," I complained, rather brashly, I suppose, "but why didn't he save a little money when he had it? He made as much as you'll ever make." The man had been a star. "He had plenty of it, didn't he? Why should he come to you?"

"Well, you know how it is, Thee," he explained in the kindliest and most apologetic way. "When you're young and healthy like that you don't think. I know how it is; I'm that way myself. We all have a little of it in us. I have; you have. And anyhow youth's the time to spend money if you're to get any good of it, isn't it? Of course when you're old you can't expect much, but still I always feel as though I'd like to help some of these old people." His eyes at such times always seemed more like those of a mother contemplating a sick or injured child than those of a man contemplating life.

"But, Paul," I insisted on another occasion when he had just wired twenty-five dollars somewhere to help bury some one. (My spirit was not so niggardly as fearsome. I was constantly terrified in those days by the thought of a poverty-stricken old age for myself and him—why, I don't know. I was by no means incompetent.) "Why don't you save your money? Why should you give it to every Tom, Dick and

Harry that asks you? You're not a charity organization, and
you're not called upon to feed and clothe and bury all the
wasters who happen to cross your path. If you were down
and out how many do you suppose would help you?"

"Well, you know," and his voice and manner were largely
those of mother, the same wonder, the same wistfulness and
sweetness, the same bubbling charity and tenderness of heart,
"I can't say I haven't got it, can I?" He was at the height of
his success at the time. "And anyhow, what's the use being
so hard on people? We're all likely to get that way. You don't
know what pulls people down sometimes—not wasting always. It's thoughtlessness, or trying to be happy. Remember
how poor we were and how mamma and papa used to
worry." Often these references to mother or father or their
difficulties would bring tears to his eyes. "I can't stand to see
people suffer, that's all, not if I have anything," and his eyes
glowed sweetly. "And, after all," he added apologetically, "the
little I give isn't much. They don't get so much out of me.
They don't come to me every day."

Another time—one Christmas Eve it was, when I was
comparatively new to New York (my second or third year), I
was a little uncertain what to do, having no connections outside of Paul and two sisters, one of whom was then out of
the city. The other, owing to various difficulties of her own
and a temporary estrangement from us—more our fault than
hers—was therefore not available. The rather drab state into
which she had allowed her marital affections to lead her was
the main reason that kept us apart. At any rate I felt that I
could not, or rather would not, go there. At the same time,
owing to some difficulty or irritation with the publishing
house of which my brother was then part owner (it was publishing the magazine which I was editing), we twain were also
estranged, nothing very deep really—a temporary feeling of
distance and indifference.

So I had no place to go except to my room, which was in
a poor part of the town, or out to dine where best I might—
some moderate-priced hotel, was my thought. I had not seen
my brother in three or four days, but after I had strolled a
block or two up Broadway I encountered him. I have always
thought that he had kept an eye on me and had really

followed me; was looking, in short, to see what I would do. As usual he was most smartly and comfortably dressed.

"Where you going, Thee?" he called cheerfully.

"Oh, no place in particular," I replied rather suavely, I presume. "Just going up the street."

"Now, see here, sport," he began—a favorite expression of his, "sport"—with his face abeam, "what's the use you and me quarreling? It's Christmas Eve, ain't it? It's a shame! Come on, let's have a drink and then go out to dinner."

"Well," I said, rather uncompromisingly, for at times his seemingly extreme success and well-being irritated me, "I'll have a drink, but as for dinner I have another engagement."

"Aw, don't say that. What's the use being sore? You know I always feel the same even if we do quarrel at times. Cut it out. Come on. You know I'm your brother, and you're mine. It's all right with me, Thee. Let's make it up, will you? Put 'er there! Come on, now. We'll go and have a drink, see, something hot—it's Christmas Eve, sport. The old home stuff."

He smiled winsomely, coaxingly, really tenderly, as only he could smile. I "gave in." But now as we entered the nearest shining bar, a Christmas crowd buzzing within and without (it was the old Fifth Avenue Hotel), a new thought seemed to strike him.

"Seen E—— lately?" he inquired, mentioning the name of the troubled sister who was having a very hard time indeed. Her husband had left her and she was struggling over the care of two children.

"No," I replied, rather shamefacedly, "not in a week or two—maybe more."

He clicked his tongue. He himself had not been near her in a month or more. His face fell, and he looked very depressed.

"It's too bad—a shame really. We oughtn't to do this way, you know, sport. It ain't right. What do you say to our going around there," it was in the upper thirties, "and see how she's making out?—take her a few things, eh? Whaddya say?"

I hadn't a spare dollar myself, but I knew well enough what he meant by "take a few things" and who would pay for them.

"Well, we'll have to hurry if we want to get anything now,"

I urged, falling in with the idea since it promised peace, plenty and good will all around, and we rushed the drink and departed. Near at hand was a branch of one of the greatest grocery companies of the city, and near it, too, his then favorite hotel, the Continental. En route we meditated on the impossibility of delivery, the fact that we would have to carry the things ourselves, but he at last solved that by declaring that he could commandeer negro porters or bootblacks from the Continental. We entered, and by sheer smiles on his part and some blarney heaped upon a floor-manager, secured a turkey, sweet potatoes, peas, beans, a salad, a strip of bacon, a ham, plum pudding, a basket of luscious fruit and I know not what else—provender, I am sure, for a dozen meals. While it was being wrapped and packed in borrowed baskets, soon to be returned, he went across the way to the hotel and came back with three grinning darkies who for the tip they knew they would receive preceded us up Broadway, the nearest path to our destination. On the way a few additional things were picked up: holly wreaths, toys, candy, nuts—and then, really not knowing whether our plan might not miscarry, we made our way through the side street and to the particular apartment, or, rather, flat-house, door, a most amusing Christmas procession, I fancy, wondering and worrying now whether she would be there.

But the door clicked in answer to our ring, and up we marched, the three darkies first, instructed to inquire for her and then insist on leaving the goods, while we lagged behind to see how she would take it.

The stage arrangement worked as planned. My sister opened the door and from the steps below we could hear her protesting that she had ordered nothing, but the door being open the negroes walked in and a moment or two afterwards ourselves. The packages were being piled on table and floor, while my sister, unable quite to grasp this sudden visitation and change of heart, stared.

"Just thought we'd come around and have supper with you, E——, and maybe dinner tomorrow if you'll let us," my brother chortled. "Merry Christmas, you know. Christmas Eve. The good old home stuff—see? Old sport here and I thought we couldn't stay away—tonight, anyhow."

He beamed on her in his most affectionate way, but she, suffering regret over the recent estrangement as well as the difficulties of life itself and the joy of this reunion, burst into tears, while the two little ones danced about, and he and I put our arms about her.

"There, there! It's all over now," he declared, tears welling in his eyes. "It's all off. We'll can this scrapping stuff. Thee and I are a couple of bums and we know it, but you can forgive us, can't you? We ought to be ashamed of ourselves, all of us, and that's the truth. We've been quarreling, too, haven't spoken for a week. Ain't that so, sport? But it's all right now, eh?"

There were tears in my eyes, too. One couldn't resist him. He had the power of achieving the tenderest results in the simplest ways. We then had supper, and breakfast the next morning, all staying and helping, even to the washing and drying of the dishes, and thereafter for I don't know how long we were all on the most affectionate terms, and he eventually died in this sister's home, ministered to with absolutely restless devotion by her for weeks before the end finally came.

But, as I have said, I always prefer to think of him at this, the very apex or tower window of his life. For most of this period he was gay and carefree. The music company of which he was a third owner was at the very top of its success. Its songs, as well as his, were everywhere. He had in turn at this time a suite at the Gilsey House, the Marlborough, the Normandie—always on Broadway, you see. The limelight district was his home. He rose in the morning to the clang of the cars and the honk of the automobiles outside; he retired at night as a gang of repair men under flaring torches might be repairing a track, or the milk trucks were rumbling to and from the ferries. He was in his way a public restaurant and hotel favorite, a shining light in the theater managers' offices, hotel bars and lobbies and wherever those flies of the Tenderloin, those passing lords and celebrities of the sporting, theatrical, newspaper and other worlds, are wont to gather. One of his intimates, as I now recall, was "Bat" Masterson, the Western and now retired (to Broadway!) bad man; Muldoon, the famous wrestler; Tod Sloan, the jockey; "Battling" Nelson;

James J. Corbett; Kid McCoy; Terry McGovern—prize-fighters all. Such Tammany district leaders as James Murphy, "The" McManus, Chrystie and Timothy Sullivan, Richard Carroll, and even Richard Croker, the then reigning Tammany boss, were all on his visiting list. He went to their meetings, rallies and district doings generally to sing and play, and they came to his "office" occasionally. Various high and mighties of the Roman Church, "fathers" with fine parishes and good wine cellars, and judges of various municipal courts, were also of his peculiar world. He was always running to one or the other "to get somebody out," or they to him to get him to contribute something to something, or to sing and play or act, and betimes they were meeting each other in hotel grills or elsewhere and having a drink and telling "funny stories."

Apropos of this sense of humor of his, this love of horse-play almost, I remember that once he had a new story to tell—a vulgar one of course—and with it he had been making me and a dozen others laugh until the tears coursed down our cheeks. It seemed new to everybody and, true to his rather fantastic moods, he was determined to be the first to tell it along Broadway. For some reason he was anxious to have me go along with him, possibly because he found me at that time an unvarying fountain of approval and laughter, possibly because he liked to show me off as his rising brother, as he insisted that I was. At between six and seven of a spring or summer evening, therefore, we issued from his suite at the Gilsey House, whither he had returned to dress, and invading the bar below were at once centered among a group who knew him. A whiskey, a cigar, the story told to one, two, three, five, ten to roars of laughter, and we were off, over the way to Weber & Fields (the Musical Burlesque House Supreme of those days) in the same block, where to the ticket seller and house manager, both of whom he knew, it was told. More laughter, a cigar perhaps. Then we were off again, this time to the ticket seller of Palmer's Theater at Thirtieth Street, thence to the bar of the Grand Hotel at Thirty-first, the Imperial at Thirty-second, the Martinique at Thirty-third, a famous drug-store at the southwest corner of Thirty-fourth and Broadway, now gone of course, the manager of which

was a friend of his. It was a warm, moony night, and he took
a glass of vichy "for looks' sake," as he said.

Then to the quondam Hotel Aulic at Thirty-fifth and
Broadway—the center and home of the then much-berated
"Hotel Aulic or Actors' School of Philosophy," and a most
impressive actors' rendezvous where might have been seen in
the course of an evening all the "second leads" and "light comedians" and "heavies" of this, that and the other road company, all blazing with startling clothes and all explaining how
they "knocked 'em" here and there: in Peoria, Pasadena,
Walla-Walla and where not. My brother shone like a star
when only one is in the sky.

Over the way then to the Herald Building, its owls' eyes
glowing in the night, its presses thundering, the elevated
thundering beside it. Here was a business manager whom he
knew. Then to the Herald Square Theater on the opposite
side of the street, ablaze with a small electric sign—among
the newest in the city. In this, as in the business office of the
Herald was another manager, and he knew them all. Thence
to the Marlborough bar and lobby at Thirty-sixth, the manager's office of the Knickerbocker Theater at Thirty-eighth,
stopping at the bar and lobby of the Normandie, where some
blazing professional beauty of the stage waylaid him and exchanged theatrical witticisms with him—and what else?
Thence to the manager's office of the Casino at Thirty-ninth,
some bar which was across the street, another in Thirty-ninth
west of Broadway, an Italian restaurant on the ground floor
of the Metropolitan at Fortieth and Broadway, and at last but
by no means least and by such slow stages to the very door
of the then Mecca of Meccas of all theater- and sportdom, the
sanctum sanctorum of all those sportively au fait, " wise," the
"real thing"—the Hotel Metropole at Broadway and Forty-
second Street, the then extreme northern limit of the white-
light district. And what a realm! Rounders and what not were
here ensconced at round tables, their backs against the
leather-cushioned wall seats, the adjoining windows open to
all Broadway and the then all but somber Forty-second
Street.

It was wonderful, the loud clothes, the bright straw hats,
the canes, the diamonds, the "hot" socks, the air of security

and well-being, so easily assumed by those who gain an all too brief hour in this pretty, petty world of make-believe and pleasure and pseudo-fame. Among them my dearest brother was at his best. It was "Paul" here and "Paul" there—"Why, hello, Dresser, you're just in time! Come on in. What'll you have? Let me tell you something, Paul, a good one——" More drinks, cigars, tales—magnificent tales of successes made, "great shows" given, fights, deaths, marvelous winnings at cards, trickeries in racing, prize-fighting; the "dogs" that some people were, the magnificent, magnanimous "God's own salt" that others were. The oaths, stories of women, what low, vice-besmeared, crime-soaked ghoulas certain reigning beauties of the town or stage were—and so on and so on ad infinitum.

But his story?—ah, yes. I had all but forgotten. It was told in every place, not once but seven, eight, nine, ten times. We did not eat until we reached the Metropole, and it was ten-thirty when we reached it! The handshakes, the road stories— "This is my brother Theodore. He writes; he's a newspaper man." The roars of laughter, the drinks! "Ah, my boy, that's good, but let me tell you one—one that I heard out in Louisville the other day." A seedy, shabby ne'er-do-well of a songwriter maybe stopping the successful author in the midst of a tale to borrow a dollar. Another actor, shabby and distrait, reciting the sad tale of a year's misfortunes. Everywhere my dear brother was called to, slapped on the back, chuckled with. He was successful. One of his best songs was the rage, he had an interest in a going musical concern, he could confer benefits, favors.

Ah, me! Ah, me! That one could be so great, and that it should not last for ever and for ever!

Another of his outstanding characteristics was his love of women, a really amusing and at times ridiculous quality. He was always sighing over the beauty, innocence, sweetness, this and that, of young maidenhood in his songs, but in real life he seemed to desire and attract quite a different type—the young and beautiful, it is true, but also the old, the homely and the somewhat savage—a catholicity of taste I could never quite stomach. It was "Paul dearest" here and "Paul dearest" there, especially in his work in connection with the music-house and the stage. In the former, popular ballad singers of both sexes, some of the women most attractive and willful, were most numerous, coming in daily from all parts of the world apparently to find songs which they could sing on the American or even the English stage. And it was a part of his duty, as a member of the firm and the one who principally "handled" the so-called professional inquirers, to meet them and see that they were shown what the catalogue contained. Occasionally there was an aspiring female song-writer, often mere women visitors.

Regardless, however, of whether they were young, old, attractive or repulsive, male or female, I never knew any one whose manner was more uniformly winsome or who seemed so easily to disarm or relax an indifferent or irritated mood. He was positive sunshine, the same in quality as that of a bright spring morning. His blue eyes focused mellowly, his lips were tendrilled with smiles. He had a brisk, quick manner, always somehow suggestive of my mother, who was never brisk.

And how he fascinated them, the women! Their quite shameless daring where he was concerned! Positively, in the face of it I used to wonder what had become of all the vaunted and so-called "stabilizing morality" of the world. None of it seemed to be in the possession of these women, especially the young and beautiful. They were distant and freezing enough to all who did not interest them, but let a personality such as his come into view and they were all wiles, bending and alluring graces. It was so obvious, this fascination he had for them and they for him, that at times it took on a comic look.

"Get onto the hit he's making," one would nudge another and remark.

"Say, some tenderness, that!" This in reference to a smile or a melting glance on the part of a female.

"Nothing like a way with the ladies. Some baby, eh, boys?"—this following the flick of a skirt and a backward-tossed glance perhaps, as some noticeable beauty passed out.

"No wonder he's cheerful," a sour and yet philosophic vaudevillian, who was mostly out of a job and hung about the place for what free meals he could obtain, once remarked to me in a heavy and morose undertone. "If I had that many women crazy about me I'd be too."

And the results of these encounters with beauty! Always he had something most important to attend to, morning, noon or night, and whenever I encountered him after some such statement "the important thing" was, of course, a woman. As time went on and he began to look upon me as something more than a thin, spindling, dyspeptic and disgruntled youth, he began to wish to introduce me to some of his marvelous followers, and then I could see how completely dependent upon beauty in the flesh he was, how it made his life and world.

One day as we were all sitting in the office, a large group of vaudevillians, song-writers, singers, a chance remark gave rise to a subsequent practical joke at Paul's expense. "I'll bet," observed some one, "that if a strange man were to rush in here with a revolver and say, 'Where's the man that seduced my wife?' Paul would be the first to duck. He wouldn't wait to find out whether he was the one meant or not."

Much laughter followed, and some thought. The subject of this banter was, of course, not present at the time. There was one actor who hung about there who was decidedly skillful in make-up. On more than one occasion he had disguised himself there in the office for our benefit. Coöperating with us, he disguised himself now as a very severe and even savage-looking person of about thirty-five—side-burns, mustachios and goatee. Then, with our aid, timing his arrival to an hour when Paul was certain to be at his desk, he entered briskly and vigorously and, looking about with a savage air, demanded, "Where is Paul Dresser?"

The latter turned almost apprehensively, I thought, and at once seemed by no means captivated by the man's looks.

"That's Mr. Dresser there," explained one of the confederates most willingly.

The stranger turned and glared at him. "So you're the scoundrel that's been running around with my wife, are you?" he demanded, approaching him and placing one hand on his right hip.

Paul made no effort to explain. It did not occur to him to deny the allegation, although he had never seen the man before. With a rising and backward movement he fell against the rail behind him, lifting both hands in fright and exclaiming, "Why—why—Don't shoot!" His expression was one of guilt, astonishment, perplexity. As some one afterwards said, "As puzzled as if he was trying to discover which injured husband it might be." The shout that went up—for it was agreed beforehand that the joke must not be carried far—convinced him that a hoax had been perpetrated, and the removal by the actor of his hat, sideburns and mustache revealed the true character of the injured husband. At first inclined to be angry and sulky, later on he saw the humor of his own indefinite position in the matter and laughed as heartily as any. But I fancy it developed a strain of uncertainty in him also in regard to injured husbands, for he was never afterwards inclined to interest himself in the much-married, and gave such wives a wide berth.

But his great forte was of course his song-writing, and of this, before I speak of anything else, I wish to have my say. It was a gift, quite a compelling one, out of which, before he died, he had made thousands, all spent in the manner described. Never having the least power to interpret anything in a fine musical way, still he was always full of music of a tender, sometimes sad, sometimes gay, kind—that of the ballad-maker of a nation. He was constantly attempting to work them out of himself, not quickly but slowly, brooding as it were over the piano wherever he might find one and could have a little solitude, at times on the organ (his favorite instrument), improvising various sad or wistful strains, some of which he jotted down, others of which, having mastered, he strove to fit words to. At such times he preferred to be alone or with some one whose temperament in no way clashed but rather harmonized with his own. Living with one of my sisters for a period of years, he had a room specially fitted up for his composing work, a very small room for so very large a man, within which he would shut himself and thrum a melody by the hour, especially toward evening or at night. He seemed to have a peculiar fondness for the twilight hour, and at this time might thrum over one strain and another until over some particular one, a new song usually, he would be in tears!

And what pale little things they were really, mere bits and scraps of sentiment and melodrama in story form, most asinine sighings over home and mother and lost sweethearts and dead heroes such as never were in real life, and yet with something about them, in the music at least, which always appealed to me intensely and must have appealed to others, since they attained so wide a circulation. They bespoke, as I always felt, a wistful, seeking, uncertain temperament, tender and illusioned, with no practical knowledge of any side of life, but full of a true poetic feeling for the mystery and pathos of life and death, the wonder of the waters, the stars, the flowers, accidents of life, success, failure. Beginning with a song called "Wide Wings" (published by a small retail music-house in Evansville, Indiana), and followed by such national successes as "The Letter That Never Came," "I Believe It, For My Mother Told Me So" (!), "The Convict and the Bird," "The Pardon Came Too Late," "Just Tell Them That You Saw Me," "The Blue and the Grey," "On the Bowery," "On the Banks of the Wabash," and a number of others, he was never content to rest and never really happy, I think, save when composing. During this time, however, he was at different periods all the things I have described—a black-face monologue artist, an end- and at times a middle-man, a publisher, and so on.

I recall being with him at the time he composed two of his most famous successes: "Just Tell Them That You Saw Me," and "On the Banks of the Wabash," and noting his peculiar mood, almost amounting to a deep depression which ended a little later in marked elation or satisfaction, once he had succeeded in evoking something which really pleased him.

The first of these songs must have followed an actual encounter with some woman or girl whose life had seemingly if not actually gone to wreck on the shore of love or passion. At any rate he came into the office of his publishing house one gray November Sunday afternoon—it was our custom to go there occasionally, a dozen or more congenial souls, about as one might go to a club—and going into a small room which was fitted up with a piano as a "try-out" room (professionals desiring a song were frequently taught it in the office), he began improvising, or rather repeating over and over, a certain strain which was evidently in his mind. A little while later he came out and said, "Listen to this, will you, Thee?"

He played and sang the first verse and chorus. In the middle of the latter, so moved was he by the sentiment of it, his voice broke and he had to stop. Tears stood in his eyes and he wiped them away. A moment or two later he was able to go through it without wavering and I thought it charming for the type of thing it was intended to be. Later on (the following spring) I was literally astonished to see how, after those various efforts usually made by popular music publishers to make a song "go"—advertising it in the *Clipper* and *Mirror*, getting various vaudeville singers to sing it, and so forth—it suddenly began to sell, thousands upon thousands of copies being wrapped in great bundles under my very eyes and shipped express or freight to various parts of the country. Letters and telegrams, even, from all parts of the nation began to pour in—"Forward express today——copies of Dresser's 'Tell Them That You Saw Me.' " The firm was at once as busy as a bee-hive, on "easy street" again, as the expression went, "in clover." Just before this there had been a slight slump in its business and in my brother's finances, but now once more he was his most engaging self. Every one in that layer of life which understands or takes an interest in popular songs and their creators knew of him and his song, his latest success. He was, as it were, a revivified figure on Broadway. His barbers, barkeepers, hotel clerks, theatrical box-office clerks, hotel managers and the stars and singers of the street knew of it and him. Some enterprising button firm got out a button on which the phrase was printed. Comedians on the stage, newspaper paragraphers, his bank teller or his tailor, even staid business men wishing to appear "up-to-date," used it as a parting salute. The hand-organs, the bands and the theater orchestras everywhere were using it. One could scarcely turn a corner or go into a cheap music hall or variety house without hearing a parody of it. It was wonderful, the enormous furore that it seemed to create, and of course my dear brother was privileged to walk about smiling and secure, his bank account large, his friends numerous, in the pink of health, and gloating over the fact that he was a success, well known, a genuine creator of popular songs.

It was the same with "On the Banks of the Wabash," possibly an even greater success, for it came eventually to be adopted by his native State as its State song, and in that region streets and a town were named after him. In an almost unintentional and unthinking way I had a hand in that, and it has always cheered me to think that I had, although I have never had the least talent for musical composition or song versification. It was one of those delightful summer Sunday mornings (1896, I believe), when I was still connected with his firm as editor of the little monthly they were issuing, and he and myself, living with my sister E——, that we had gone over to this office to do a little work. I had a number of current magazines I wished to examine; he was always wishing to compose something, to express that ebullient and emotional soul of his in some way.

"What do you suppose would make a good song these days?" he asked in an idle, meditative mood, sitting at the piano and thrumming while I at a nearby table was looking over my papers. "Why don't you give me an idea for one once in a while, sport? You ought to be able to suggest something."

"Me?" I queried, almost contemptuously, I suppose. I could be very lofty at times in regard to his work, much as I admired him—vain and yet more or less dependent snip that I was. "I can't write those things. Why don't you write something about a State or a river? Look at 'My Old Kentucky Home,' 'Dixie,' 'Old Black Joe'—why don't you do something like that, something that suggests a part of America? People like that. Take Indiana—what's the matter with it—the Wabash River? It's as good as any other river, and you were 'raised' beside it."

I have to smile even now as I recall the apparent zest or feeling with which all at once he seized on this. It seemed to appeal to him immensely. "That's not a bad idea," he agreed, "but how would you go about it? Why don't you write the words and let me put the music to them? We'll do it together!"

"But I can't," I replied. "I don't know how to do those things. You write it. I'll help—maybe."

After a little urging—I think the fineness of the morning

had as much to do with it as anything—I took a piece of paper and after meditating a while scribbled in the most tentative manner imaginable the first verse and chorus of that song almost as it was published. I think one or two lines were too long or didn't rhyme, but eventually either he or I hammered them into shape, but before that I rather shamefacedly turned them over to him, for somehow I was convinced that this work was not for me and that I was rather loftily and cynically attempting what my good brother would do in all faith and feeling.

He read it, insisted that it was fine and that I should do a second verse, something with a story in it, a girl perhaps—a task which I solemnly rejected.

"No, you put it in. It's yours. I'm through."

Some time later, disagreeing with the firm as to the conduct of the magazine, I left—really was forced out—which raised a little feeling on my part; not on his, I am sure, for I was very difficult to deal with.

Time passed and I heard nothing. I had been able to succeed in a somewhat different realm, that of the magazine contributor, and although I thought a great deal of my brother I paid very little attention to him or his affairs, being much more concerned with my own. One spring night, however, the following year, as I was lying in my bed trying to sleep, I heard a quartette of boys in the distance approaching along the street in which I had my room. I could not make out the words at first but the melody at once attracted my attention. It was plaintive and compelling. I listened, attracted, satisfied that it was some new popular success that had "caught on." As they drew near my window I heard the words "On the Banks of the Wabash" most mellifluously harmonized.

I jumped up. They were my words! It was Paul's song! He had another "hit" then—"On the Banks of the Wabash," and they were singing it in the streets already! I leaned out of the window and listened as they approached and passed on, their arms about each other's shoulders, the whole song being sung in the still street, as it were, for my benefit. The night was so warm, delicious. A full moon was overhead. I was young, lonely, wistful. It brought back so much of my already spent youth that I was ready to cry—for joy principally. In

three more months it was everywhere, in the papers, on the
stage, on the street-organs, played by orchestras, bands, whistled and sung in the streets. One day on Broadway near the
Marlborough I met my brother, gold-headed cane, silk shirt,
a smart summer suit, a gay straw hat.

"Ah," I said, rather sarcastically, for I still felt peeved that
he had shown so little interest in my affairs at the time I was
leaving. "On the banks, I see."

"On the banks," he replied cordially. "You turned the trick
for me, Thee, that time. What are you doing now? Why don't
you ever come and see me? I'm still your brother, you know.
A part of that is really yours."

"Cut that!" I replied most savagely. "I couldn't write a song
like that in a million years. You know I couldn't. The words
are nothing."

"Oh, all right. It's true, though, you know. Where do you
keep yourself? Why don't you come and see me? Why be
down on me? I live here, you know." He looked up at the
then brisk and successful hotel.

"Well, maybe I will some time," I said distantly, but with
no particular desire to mend matters, and we parted.

There was, however, several years later, a sequel to all this
and one so characteristic of him that it has always remained
in my mind as one of the really beautiful things of life, and I
might as well tell it here and now. About five years later I had
become so disappointed in connection with my work and the
unfriendly pressure of life that I had suffered what subsequently appeared to have been a purely psychic breakdown or
relapse, not physical, but one which left me in no mood or
condition to go on with my work, or any work indeed in any
form. Hope had disappeared in a sad haze. I could apparently
succeed in nothing, do nothing mentally that was worth
while. At the same time I had all but retired from the world,
living on less and less until finally I had descended into those
depths where I was in the grip of actual want, with no place
to which my pride would let me turn. I had always been too
vain and self-centered. Apparently there was but one door,
and I was very close to it. To match my purse I had retired to
a still sorrier neighborhood in B——, one of the poorest. I
desired most of all to be let alone, to be to myself. Still I

could not be, for occasionally I met people, and certain prospects and necessities drove me to various publishing houses.
One day as I was walking in some street near Broadway (not
on it) in New York, I ran into my brother quite by accident,
he as prosperous and comfortable as ever. I think I resented
him more than ever. He was of course astonished, shocked,
as I could plainly see, by my appearance and desire not to be
seen. He demanded to know where I was living, wanted me
to come then and there and stay with him, wanted me to tell
him what the trouble was—all of which I rather stubbornly
refused to do and finally got away—not however without
giving him my address, though with the caution that I
wanted nothing.

The next morning he was there bright and early in a cab.
He was the most vehement, the most tender, the most disturbed creature I have ever seen. He was like a distrait mother
with a sick child more than anything else.

"For God's sake," he commented when he saw me, "living
in a place like this—and at this number, too!" (130 it was,
and he was superstitious as to the thirteen.) "I knew there'd
be a damned thirteen in it!" he ejaculated. "And me over in
New York! Jesus Christ! And you sick and run down this
way! I might have known. It's just like you. I haven't heard a
thing about you in I don't know when. Well, I'm not going
back without you, that's all. You've got to come with me
now, see? Get your clothes, that's all. The cabby'll take your
trunk. I know just the place for you, and you're going there
tomorrow or next day or next week, but you're coming with
me now. My God, I should think you'd be ashamed of yourself, and me feeling the way I do about you!" His eyes all but
brimmed.

I was so morose and despondent that, grateful as I felt, I
could scarcely take his mood at its value. I resented it, resented myself, my state, life.

"I can't," I said finally, or so I thought. "I won't. I don't
need your help. You don't owe me anything. You've done
enough already."

"Owe, hell!" he retorted. "Who's talking about 'owe'? And
you my brother—my own flesh and blood! Why, Thee, for
that matter, I owe you half of 'On the Banks,' and you know

it. You can't go on living like this. You're sick and discouraged. You can't fool me. Why, Thee, you're a big man. You've just got to come out of this! Damn it—don't you see—don't make me"—and he took out his handkerchief and wiped his eyes. "You can't help yourself now, but you can later, don't you see? Come on. Get your things. I'd never forgive myself if I didn't. You've got to come, that's all. I won't go without you," and he began looking about for my bag and trunk.

I still protested weakly, but in vain. His affection was so overwhelming and tender that it made me weak. I allowed him to help me get my things together. Then he paid the bill, a small one, and on the way to the hotel insisted on forcing a roll of bills on me, all that he had with him. I was compelled at once, that same day or the next, to indulge in a suit, hat, shoes, underwear, all that I needed. A bedroom adjoining his suite at the hotel was taken, and for two days I lived there, later accompanying him in his car to a famous sanitarium in Westchester, one in charge of an old friend of his, a well-known ex-wrestler whose fame for this sort of work was great. Here I was booked for six weeks, all expenses paid, until I should "be on my feet again," as he expressed it. Then he left, only to visit and revisit me until I returned to the city, fairly well restored in nerves if not in health.

But could one ever forget the mingled sadness and fervor of his original appeal, the actual distress written in his face, the unlimited generosity of his mood and deed as well as his unmerited self-denunciation? One pictures such tenderness and concern as existing between parents and children, but rarely between brothers. Here he was evincing the same thing, as soft as love itself, and he a man of years and some affairs and I an irritable, distrait and peevish soul.

Take note, ye men of satire and spleen. All men are not selfish or hard.

The final phase of course related to his untimely end. He was not quite fifty-five when he died, and with a slightly more rugged quality of mind he might have lasted to seventy. It was due really to the failure of his firm (internal dissensions and rivalries, in no way due to him, however, as I have been told) and what he foolishly deemed to be the end of his financial and social glory. His was one of those simple, confiding, non-hardy dispositions, warm and colorful but intensely sensitive, easily and even fatally chilled by the icy blasts of human difficulty, however slight. You have no doubt seen some animals, cats, dogs, birds, of an especially affectionate nature, which when translated to a strange or unfriendly climate soon droop and die. They have no spiritual resources wherewith to contemplate what they do not understand or know. Now his *friends* would leave him. Now that bright world of which he had been a part would know him no more. It was pathetic, really. He emanated a kind of fear. Depression and even despair seemed to hang about him like a cloak. He could not shake it off. And yet, literally, in his case there was nothing to fear, if he had only known.

And yet two years before he did die, I knew he would. Fantastic as it may seem, to be shut out from that bright world of which he deemed himself an essential figure was all but unendurable. He had no ready money now—not the same amount anyhow. He could not greet his old-time friends so gayly, entertain so freely. Meeting him on Broadway shortly after the failure and asking after his affairs, he talked of going into business for himself as a publisher, but I realized that he could not. He had neither the ability nor the talent for that, nor the heart. He was not a business man but a song-writer and actor, had never been anything but that. He tried in this new situation to write songs, but he could not. They were too morbid. What he needed was some one to buoy him up, a manager, a strong confidant of some kind, some one who would have taken his affairs in hand and shown him what to do. As it was he had no one. His friends, like winter-frightened birds, had already departed. Personally, I was in no position to do anything at the time, being more or less depressed myself and but slowly emerging from difficulties which had held me for a number of years.

About a year or so after he failed my sister E—— announced that Paul had been there and that he was coming to live with her. He could not pay so much then, being involved with all sorts of examinations of one kind and another, but neither did he have to. Her memory was not short; she gave him the fullness of her home. A few months later he was ostensibly connected with another publishing house, but by

then he was feeling so poorly physically and was finding consolation probably in some drinking and the caresses of those
feminine friends who have, alas, only caresses to offer. A little
later I met a doctor who said, "Paul cannot live. He has per-
nicious anæmia. He is breaking down inside and doesn't
know it. He can't last long. He's too depressed." I knew it
was so and what the remedy was—money and success once
more, the petty pettings and flattery of that little world of
which he had been a part but which now was no more for
him. Of all those who had been so lavish in their greetings
and companionship earlier in his life, scarcely one, so far as I
could make out, found him in that retired world to which he
was forced. One or two pegged-out actors sought him and
borrowed a little of the little that he had; a few others came
when he had nothing at all. His partners, quarreling among
themselves and feeling that they had done him an injustice,
remained religiously away. He found, as he often told my
sister, broken horse-shoes (a "bad sign"), met cross-eyed
women, another "bad sign," was pursued apparently by the
inimical number thirteen—and all these little straws depressed him horribly. Finally, being no longer strong enough
to be about, he took to his bed and remained there days at a
time, feeling well while in bed but weak when up. For a little
while he would go "downtown" to see this, that and the
other person, but would soon return. One day on coming
back home he found one of his hats lying on his bed, accidentally put there by one of the children, and according to my
sister, who was present at the time, he was all but petrified by
the sight of it. To him it was the death-sign. Some one had
told him so not long before!!!

Then, not incuriously, seeing the affectional tie that had
always held us, he wanted to see me every day. He had a
desire to talk to me about his early life, the romance of it—
maybe I could write a story some time, tell something about
him! (Best of brothers, here it is, a thin little flower to lay at
your feet!) To please him I made notes, although I knew most
of it. On these occasions he was always his old self, full of
ridiculous stories, quips and slight *mots*, all in his old and best
vein. He would soon be himself, he now insisted.

Then one evening in late November, before I had time to

call upon him (I lived about a mile away), a hurry-call came from E——. He had suddenly died at five in the afternoon; a blood-vessel had burst in the head. When I arrived he was already cold in death, his soft hands folded over his chest, his face turned to one side on the pillow, that indescribable sweetness of expression about the eyes and mouth—the empty shell of the beetle. There were tears, a band of reporters from the papers, the next day obituary news articles, and after that a host of friends and flowers, flowers, flowers. It is amazing what satisfaction the average mind takes in standardized floral forms—broken columns and gates ajar!

Being ostensibly a Catholic, a Catholic sister-in-law and other relatives insistently arranged for a solemn high requiem mass at the church of one of his favorite rectors. All Broadway was there, more flowers, his latest song read from the altar. Then there was a carriage procession to a distant Catholic graveyard somewhere, his friend, the rector of the church, officiating at the grave. It was so cold and dreary there, horrible. Later on he was removed to Chicago.

But still I think of him as not there or anywhere in the realm of space, but on Broadway between Twenty-ninth and Forty-second Streets, the spring and summer time at hand, the doors of the grills and bars of the hotels open, the rout of actors and actresses ambling to and fro, his own delicious presence dressed in his best, his "funny" stories, his songs being ground out by the hand organs, his friends extending their hands, clapping him on the shoulder, cackling over the latest idle yarn.

Ah, Broadway! Broadway! And you, my good brother! Here is the story that you wanted me to write, this little testimony to your memory, a pale, pale symbol of all I think and feel. Where are the thousand yarns I have laughed over, the music, the lights, the song?

Peace, peace. So shall it soon be with all of us. It was a dream. It is. I am. You are. And shall we grieve over or hark back to dreams?

The Country Doctor

HOW WELL I remember him—the tall, grave, slightly bent figure, the head like Plato's or that of Diogenes, the mild, kindly, brown-gray eyes peering, all too kindly, into the faces of dishonest men. In addition, he wore long, full, brown-gray whiskers, a long gray overcoat (soiled and patched toward the last) in winter, a soft black hat that hung darkeningly over his eyes. But what a doctor! And how simple and often non-drug-storey were so many of his remedies!

"My son, your father is very sick. Now, I'll tell you what you can do for me. You go out here along the Cheevertown road about a mile or two and ask any farmer this side of the creek to let you have a good big handful of peach sprigs—about so many, see? Say that Doctor Gridley said he was to give them to you for him. Then, Mrs. ——, when he brings them, you take a few, not more than seven or eight, and break them up and steep them in hot water until you have an amber-colored tea. Give Mr. —— about three or four tea-spoonfuls of that every three or four hours, and I hope we'll find he'll do better. This kidney case is severe, I know, but he'll come around all right."

And he did. My father had been very ill with gall stones, so weak at last that we thought he was sure to die. The house was so somber at the time. Over it hung an atmosphere of depression and fear, with pity for the sufferer, and groans of distress on his part. And then there were the solemn visits of the doctor, made pleasant by his wise, kindly humor and his hopeful predictions and ending in this seemingly mild prescription, which resulted, in this case, in a cure. He was seemingly so remote at times, in reality so near, and wholly thoughtful.

On this occasion I went out along the long, cold, country road of a March evening. I was full of thoughts of his importance as a doctor. He seemed so necessary to us, as he did to everybody. I knew nothing about medicine, or how lives were saved, but I felt sure that he did and that he would save my father in spite of his always conservative, speculative, doubtful manner. What a wonderful man he must be to know all these things—that peach sprouts, for instance, were an antidote to the agony of gall stones!

As I walked along, the simplicity of country life and its needs and deprivations were impressed upon me, even though I was so young. So few here could afford to pay for expensive prescriptions—ourselves especially—and Dr. Gridley knew that and took it into consideration, so rarely did he order anything from a drug-store. Most often, what he prescribed he took out of a case, compounded, as it were, in our presence.

A brisk wind had fluttered snow in the morning, and now the ground was white, with a sinking red sun shining across it, a sense of spring in the air. Being unknown to these farmers, I wondered if any one of them would really cut me a double handful of fresh young peach sprigs or suckers from their young trees, as the doctor had said. Did they really know him? Some one along the road—a home-driving farmer—told me of an old Mr. Mills who had a five-acre orchard farther on. In a little while I came to his door and was confronted by a thin, gaunt, bespectacled woman, who called back to a man inside:

"Henry, here's a little boy says Dr. Gridley said you were to cut him a double handful of peach sprigs."

Henry now came forward—a tall, bony farmer in high boots and an old wool-lined leather coat, and a cap of wool.

"Dr. Gridley sent cha, did he?" he observed, eyeing me most critically.

"Yes, sir."

"What's the matter? What does he want with 'em? Do ya know?"

"Yes, sir. My father's sick with kidney trouble, and Dr. Gridley said I was to come out here."

"Oh, all right. Wait'll I git my big knife," and back he went, returning later with a large horn-handled knife, which he opened. He preceded me out through the barn lot and into the orchard beyond.

"Dr. Gridley sent cha, did he, huh?" he asked as he went. "Well, I guess we all have ter comply with whatever the doctor orders. We're all apt ter git sick now an' ag'in," and talking trivialities of a like character, he cut me an armful, saying:

"I might as well give ya too many as too few. Peach sprigs! Now, I never heered o' them bein' good fer anythin', but I reckon the doctor knows what he's talkin' about. He usually does—or that's what we think around here, anyhow."

In the dusk I trudged home with my armful, my fingers cold. The next morning, the tea having been brewed and taken, my father was better. In a week or two he was up and around, as well as ever, and during this time he commented on the efficacy of this tea, which was something new to him, a strange remedy, and which caused the whole incident to be impressed upon my mind. The doctor had told him that at any time in the future if he was so troubled and could get fresh young peach sprigs for a tea, he would find that it would help him. And the drug expense was exactly nothing.

In later years I came to know him better—this thoughtful, crusty, kindly soul, always so ready to come at all hours when his cases permitted, so anxious to see that his patients were not taxed beyond their financial resources.

I remember once, one of my sisters being very ill, so ill that we were beginning to fear death, one and another of us had to take turn sitting up with her at night to help and to give her her medicine regularly. During one of the nights when I was sitting up, dozing, reading and listening to the wind in the pines outside, she seemed persistently to get worse. Her fever rose, and she complained of such aches and pains that finally I had to go and call my mother. A consultation with her finally resulted in my being sent for Dr. Gridley—no telephones in those days—to tell him, although she hesitated so to do, how sister was and ask him if he would not come.

I was only fourteen. The street along which I had to go was quite dark, the town lights being put out at two a.m., for reasons of thrift perhaps. There was a high wind that cried in the trees. My shoes on the board walks, here and there, sounded like the thuds of a giant. I recall progressing in a shivery ghost-like sort of way, expecting at any step to encounter goblins of the most approved form, until finally the well-known outlines of the house of the doctor on the main street—yellow, many-roomed, a wide porch in front—came, because of a very small lamp in a very large glass case to one side of the door, into view.

Here I knocked, and then knocked more. No reply. I then made a still more forceful effort. Finally, through one of the red glass panels which graced either side of the door I saw the lengthy figure of the doctor, arrayed in a long white nightshirt, and carrying a small glass hand-lamp, come into view at the head of the stairs. His feet were in gray flannel slippers, and his whiskers stuck out most grotesquely.

"Wait! Wait!" I heard him call. "I'll be there! I'm coming! Don't make such a fuss! It seems as though I never get a real good night's rest any more."

He came on, opened the door, and looked out.

"Well," he demanded, a little fussily for him, "what's the matter now?"

"Doctor," I began, and proceeded to explain all my sister's aches and pains, winding up by saying that my mother said "wouldn't he please come at once?"

"Your mother!" he grumbled. "What can I do if I do come down? Not a thing. Feel her pulse and tell her she's all right! That's every bit I can do. Your mother knows that as well as I do. That disease has to run its course." He looked at me as though I were to blame, then added, "Calling me up this way at three in the morning!"

"But she's in such pain, Doctor," I complained.

"All right—everybody has to have a little pain! You can't be sick without it."

"I know," I replied disconsolately, believing sincerely that my sister might die, "but she's in such awful pain, Doctor."

"Well, go on," he replied, turning up the light. "I know it's all foolishness, but I'll come. You go back and tell your mother that I'll be there in a little bit, but it's all nonsense, nonsense. She isn't a bit sicker than I am right this minute, not a bit——" and he closed the door and went upstairs.

To me this seemed just the least bit harsh for the doctor, although, as I reasoned afterwards, he was probably half-asleep and tired—dragged out of his bed, possibly, once or twice before in the same night. As I returned home I felt even more fearful, for once, as I was passing a woodshed which I could not see, a rooster suddenly flapped his wings and crowed—a sound which caused me to leap all of nineteen feet Fahrenheit, sidewise. Then, as I walked along a fence which later by day I saw had a comfortable resting board on top, two lambent golden eyes surveyed me out of inky darkness! Great Hamlet's father, how my heart sank! Once more I leaped to the cloddy roadway and seizing a cobblestone or hunk of mud hurled it with all my might, and quite involuntarily. Then I ran until I fell into a crossing ditch. It was an amazing—almost a tragic—experience, then.

In due time the doctor came—and I never quite forgave him for not making me wait and go back with him. He was too sleepy, though, I am sure. The seizure was apparently nothing which could not have waited until morning. However, he left some new cure, possibly clear water in a bottle, and left again. But the night trials of doctors and their patients, especially in the country, was fixed in my mind then.

One of the next interesting impressions I gained of the doctor was that of seeing him hobbling about our town on crutches, his medicine case held in one hand along with a crutch, visiting his patients, when he himself appeared to be so ill as to require medical attention. He was suffering from some severe form of rheumatism at the time, but this, apparently, was not sufficient to keep him from those who in his judgment probably needed his services more than he did his rest.

One of the truly interesting things about Dr. Gridley, as I early began to note, was his profound indifference to what might be called his material welfare. Why, I have often asked myself, should a man of so much genuine ability choose to ignore the gauds and plaudits and pleasures of the gayer, smarter world outside, in which he might readily have shone, to thus devote himself and all his talents to a simple rural community? That he was an extremely able physician there was not the slightest doubt. Other physicians from other towns about, and even so far away as Chicago, were repeatedly calling him into consultation. That he knew life—much of it—as only a priest or a doctor of true wisdom can know it, was evident from many incidents, of which I subsequently learned, and yet here he was, hidden away in this simple rural world, surrounded probably by his Rabelais, his Burton, his Frazer, and his Montaigne, and dreaming what dreams— thinking what thoughts?

"Say," an old patient, friend and neighbor of his once re-marked to me years later, when we had both moved to an-other city, "one of the sweetest recollections of my life is to picture old Dr. Gridley, Ed Boulder who used to run the ho-tel over at Sleichertown, Congressman Barr, and Judge Mor-gan, sitting out in front of Boulder's hotel over there of a summer's evening and haw-hawing over the funny stories which Boulder was always telling while they were waiting for the Pierceton bus. Dr. Gridley's laugh, so soft to begin with, but growing in force and volume until it was a jolly shout. And the green fields all around. And Mrs. Calder's drove of geese over the way honking, too, as geese will whenever peo-ple begin to talk or laugh. It was delicious."

One of the most significant traits of his character, as may be inferred, was his absolute indifference to actual money, the very cash, one would think, with which he needed to buy his own supplies. During his life, his wife, who was a thrifty, hard-working woman, used frequently, as I learned after, to comment on this, but to no result. He could not be made to charge where he did not need to, nor collect where he knew that the people were poor.

"Once he became angry at my uncle," his daughter once told me, "because he offered to collect for him for three per cent, dunning his patients for their debts, and another time he dissolved a partnership with a local physician who insisted that he ought to be more careful to charge and collect."

This generosity on his part frequently led to some very in-teresting results. On one occasion, for instance, when he was sitting out on his front lawn in Warsaw, smoking, his chair tilted back against a tree and his legs crossed in the fashion known as "jack-knife," a poorly dressed farmer without a coat came up and after saluting the doctor began to explain that his wife was sick and that he had come to get the doctor's advice. He seemed quite disturbed, and every now and then wiped his brow, while the doctor listened with an occasional question or gently accented "uh-huh, uh-huh," until the story was all told and the advice ready to be received. When this was given in a low, reassuring tone, he took from his pocket his little book of blanks and wrote out a prescription, which he gave to the man and began talking again. The latter took out a silver dollar and handed it to the doctor, who turned it idly between his fingers for a few seconds, then searched in his pocket for a mate to it, and playing with them a while as he talked, finally handed back the dollar to the farmer.

"You take that," he said pleasantly, "and go down to the drug-store and have the prescription filled. I think your wife will be all right."

When he had gone the doctor sat there a long time, meditatively puffing the smoke from his cob pipe, and turning his own dollar in his hand. After a time he looked up at his daughter, who was present, and said:

"I was just thinking what a short time it took me to write that prescription, and what a long time it took him to earn that dollar. I guess he needs the dollar more than I do."

In the same spirit of this generosity he was once sitting in his yard of a summer day, sunning himself and smoking, a favorite pleasure of his, when two men rode up to his gate from opposite directions and simultaneously hailed him. He arose and went out to meet them. His wife, who was sewing just inside the hall as she usually was when her husband was outside, leaned forward in her chair to see through the door, and took note of who they were. Both were men in whose families the doctor had practiced for years. One was a prosperous farmer who always paid his "doctor's bills," and the other was a miller, a "ne'er-do-well," with a delicate wife and a family of sickly children, who never asked for a statement and never had one sent him, and who only occasionally and at great intervals handed the doctor a dollar in payment for his many services. Both men talked to him a little while and then rode away, after which he returned to the house, calling to Enoch, his old negro servant, to bring his horse, and then went into his study to prepare his medicine case. Mrs. Gridley, who was naturally interested in his financial welfare, and who at times had to plead with him not to let his generosity stand wholly in the way of his judgment, inquired of him as he came out:

"Now, Doctor, which of those two men are you going with?"

"Why, Miss Susan," he replied—a favorite manner of addressing his wife, of whom he was very fond—the note of apology in his voice showing that he knew very well what she was thinking about, "I'm going with W——."

"I don't think that is right," she replied with mild emphasis. "Mr. N—— is as good a friend of yours as W——, and he always pays you."

"Now, Miss Susan," he returned coaxingly, "N—— can go to Pierceton and get Doctor Bodine, and W—— can't get any one but me. You surely wouldn't have him left without any one?"

What the effect of such an attitude was may be judged when it is related that there was scarcely a man, woman or child in the entire county who had not at some time or other been directly or indirectly benefited by the kindly wisdom of this Samaritan. He was nearly everybody's doctor, in the last extremity, either as consultant or otherwise. Everywhere he went, by every lane and hollow that he fared, he was constantly being called into service by some one—the well-to-do as well as by those who had nothing; and in both cases he was equally keen to give the same degree of painstaking skill, finding something in the very poor—a humanness possibly—which detained and fascinated him and made him a little more prone to linger at their bedsides than anywhere else.

"He was always doing it," said his daughter, "and my mother used to worry over it. She declared that of all things earthly, papa loved an unfortunate person; the greater the misfortune, the greater his care."

In illustration of his easy and practically controlling attitude toward the very well-to-do, who were his patients also, let me narrate this:

In our town was an old and very distinguished colonel, comparatively rich and very crotchety, who had won considerable honors for himself during the Civil War. He was a figure, and very much looked up to by all. People were, in the main, overawed by and highly respectful of him. A remote, stern soul, yet to Dr. Gridley he was little more than a child or schoolboy—one to be bossed on occasion and made to behave. Plainly, the doctor had the conviction that all of us, great and small, were very much in need of sympathy and care, and that he, the doctor, was the one to provide it. At any rate, he had known the colonel long and well, and in a public place—at the principal street corner, for instance, or in the postoffice where we school children were wont to congregate—it was not at all surprising to hear him take the old colonel, who was quite frail now, to task for not taking better care of himself—coming out, for instance, without his rubbers, or his overcoat, in wet or chilly weather, and in other ways misbehaving himself.

"There you go again!" I once heard him call to the colonel, as the latter was leaving the postoffice and he was entering (there was no rural free delivery in those days) "—walking around without your rubbers, and no overcoat! You want to get me up in the night again, do you?"

"It didn't seem so damp when I started out, Doctor."

"And of course it was too much trouble to go back! You wouldn't feel that way if you couldn't come out at all, perhaps!"

"I'll put 'em on! I'll put 'em on! Only, please don't fuss, Doctor. I'll go back to the house and put 'em on."

The doctor merely stared after him quizzically, like an old schoolmaster, as the rather stately colonel marched off to his home.

Another of his patients was an old Mr. Pegram, a large, kind, big-hearted man, who was very fond of the doctor, but who had an exceedingly irascible temper. He was the victim of some obscure malady which medicine apparently failed at times to relieve. This seemed to increase his irritability a great deal, so much so that the doctor had at last discovered that if he could get Mr. Pegram angry enough the malady would occasionally disappear. This seemed at times as good a remedy as any, and in consequence he was occasionally inclined to try it.

Among other things, this old gentleman was the possessor of a handsome buffalo robe, which, according to a story that long went the rounds locally, he once promised to leave to the doctor when he died. At the same time all reference to death both pained and irritated him greatly—a fact which the doctor knew. Finding the old gentleman in a most complaining and hopeless mood one night, not to be dealt with, indeed, in any reasoning way, the doctor returned to his home, and early the next day, without any other word, sent old

Enoch, his negro servant, around to get, as he said, the buffalo robe—a request which would indicate, of course, that
the doctor had concluded that old Mr. Pegram had died, or
was about to—a hopeless case. When ushered into the latter's
presence, Enoch began innocently enough:

"De doctah say dat now dat Mr. Peg'am hab subspired, he
was to hab dat ba—ba—buffalo robe."

"What!" shouted the old irascible, rising and clambering
out of his bed. "What's that? Buffalo robe! By God! You go
back and tell old Doc Gridley that I ain't dead yet by a
damned sight! No, sir!" and forthwith he dressed himself and
was out and around the same day.

Persons who met the doctor, as I heard years later from his
daughter and from others who had known him, were frequently asking him, just in a social way, what to do for certain ailments, and he would as often reply in a humorous and
half-vagrom manner that if he were in their place he would
do or take so-and-so, not meaning really that they should do
so but merely to get rid of them, and indicating of course any
one of a hundred harmless things—never one that could
really have proved injurious to any one. Once, according to
his daughter, as he was driving into town from somewhere,
he met a man on a lumber wagon whom he scarcely knew
but who knew him well enough, who stopped and showed
him a sore on the upper tip of his ear, asking him what he
would do for it.

"Oh," said the doctor, idly and jestingly, "I think I'd cut it
off."

"Yes," said the man, very much pleased with this free advice, " with what, Doctor?"

"Oh, I think I'd use a pair of scissors," he replied amusedly,
scarcely assuming that his jesting would be taken seriously.

The driver jogged on and the doctor did not see or hear of
him again until some two months later when, meeting him in
the street, the driver smilingly approached him and enthusiastically exclaimed:

"Well, Doc, you see I cut 'er off, and she got well!"

"Yes," replied the doctor solemnly, not remembering
anything about the case but willing to appear interested,
"—what was it you cut off?"

"Why, that sore on my ear up here, you know. You told me to cut it off, and I did."

"Yes," said the doctor, becoming curious and a little amazed, " with what?"

"Why, with a pair of scissors, Doc, just like you said."

The doctor stared at him, the whole thing coming gradually back to him.

"But didn't you have some trouble in cutting it off?" he inquired, in disturbed astonishment.

"No, no," said the driver, "I made 'em sharp, all right. I spent two days whettin' 'em up, and Bob Hart cut 'er off fer me. They cut, all right, but I tell you she hurt when she went through the gristle."

He smiled in pleased remembrance of his surgical operation, and the doctor smiled also, but, according to his daughter, he decided to give no more idle advice of that kind.

In the school which I attended for a period were two of his sons, Fred and Walter. Both were very fond of birds, and kept a number of one kind or another about their home—not in cages, as some might, but inveigled and trained as pets, and living in the various open bird-houses fixed about the yard on poles. The doctor himself was intensely fond of these and all other birds, and, according to his daughter and his sons, always anticipated the spring return of many of them—blackbirds, blue jays, wrens and robins—with a hopeful, "Well, now, they'll soon be here again." During the summer, according to her, he was always an interested spectator of their gyrations in the air, and when evening would come was never so happy as when standing and staring at them gathering from all directions to their roosts in the trees or the birdhouses. Similarly, when the fall approached and they would begin their long flight Southward, he would sometimes stand and scan the sky and trees in vain for a final glimpse of his feathered friends, and when in the gathering darkness they were no longer to be seen would turn away toward the house, saying sadly to his daughter:

"Well, Dollie, the blackbirds are all gone. I am sorry. I like to see them, and I am always sorry to lose them, and sorry to know that winter is coming."

"Usually about the 25th or 26th of December," his daughter

once quaintly added to me, "he would note that the days were beginning to get longer, and cheer up, as spring was certain to follow soon and bring them all back again."

One of the most interesting of his bird friendships was that which existed between him and a pair of crows he and his sons had raised, "Jim" and "Zip" by name. These crows came to know him well, and were finally so humanly attached to him that, according to his family, they would often fly two or three miles out of town to meet him and would then accompany him, lighting on fences and trees by the way, and cawing to him as he drove along! Both of them were great thieves, and would steal anything from a bit of thread up to a sewing machine, if they could have carried it. They were always walking about the house, cheerfully looking for what they might devour, and on one occasion carried off a set of spoons, which they hid about the eaves of the house. On another occasion they stole a half dozen tin-handled pocket knives, which the doctor had bought for the children and which the crows seemed to like for the brightness of the metal. They were recovered once by the children, stolen again by the crows, recovered once more, and so on, until at last it was a question as to which were the rightful owners.

The doctor was sitting in front of a store one day in the business-heart of town, where also he liked to linger in fair weather, when suddenly he saw one of his crows flying high overhead and bearing something in its beak, which it dropped into the road scarcely a hundred feet away. Interested to see what it was the bird had been carrying, he went to the spot where he saw it fall and found one of the tin-handled knives, which the crow had been carrying to a safe hiding-place. He picked it up and when he returned home that night asked one of his boys if he could lend him a knife.

"No," said his son. "Our knives are all lost. The crows took them."

"I knew that," said the doctor sweetly, "and so, when I met Zip uptown just now, I asked her to lend me one, and she did. Here it is."

He pulled out the knife and handed it to the boy and, when the latter expressed doubt and wonder, insisted that the crow had loaned it to him; a joke which ended in his always

asking one of the children to run and ask Zip if she would
lend him a knife, whenever he chanced to need one.

Although a sad man at times, as I understood, the doctor
was not a pessimist, and in many ways, both by practical jokes
and the humoring of odd characters, sought relief from the
intense emotional strain which the large practice of his profession put upon him. One of his greatest reliefs was the carrying out of these little practical jokes, and he had been known
to go to much trouble at times to work up a good laugh.

One of the, to him, richest jokes, and one which he always
enjoyed telling, related to a country singing school which was
located in the neighborhood of Pierceton, in which reading
(the alphabet, at least), spelling, geography, arithmetic, rules
of grammar, and so forth, were still taught by a process of
singing. The method adopted in this form of education was
to have the scholar memorize all knowledge by singing it.
Thus in the case of geography the students would sing the
name of the country, then its mountains, then the highest
peaks, cities, rivers, principal points of interest, and so on,
until all information about that particular country had been
duly memorized in song or rhyme. Occasionally they would
have a school-day on which the local dignitaries would be
invited, and on a number of these occasions the doctor was,
for amusement's sake merely, a grave and reverent listener.
On one occasion, however, he was merely passing the school,
when hearing "Africa-a, Africa-a, mountains of the moo-oo-
oon" drawled out of the windows, he decided to stop in and
listen a while. Having tethered his horse outside he knocked
at the door and was received by the little English singing
teacher who, after showing him to a seat, immediately called
upon the class for an exhibition of their finest wisdom. When
they had finished this the teacher turned to him and inquired
if there was anything he would especially like them to sing.

"No," said the doctor gravely, and no doubt with an
amused twinkle in his eye, "I had thought of asking you to
sing the Rocky Mountains, but as the mountains are so high,
and the amount of time I have so limited, I have decided that
perhaps it will be asking too much."

"Oh, not at all, *not at all*," airily replied the teacher, and
turning to his class, he exclaimed with a very superior smile:

"Now, ladies and gentlemen, 'ere is a scientific gentleman who thinks it is 'arder to sing of 'igh mountings than it is to sing of *low* mountings," and forthwith the class began to demonstrate that in respect to vocalization there was no difference at all.

Only those, however, who knew Dr. Gridley in the sickroom, and knew him well, ever discovered the really finest trait of his character: a keen, unshielded sensibility to and sympathy for all human suffering, that could not bear to inflict the slightest additional pain. He was really, in the main, a man of soft tones and unctuous laughter, of gentle touch and gentle step, and a devotion to duty that carried him far beyond his interests or his personal well-being. One of his chiefest oppositions, according to his daughter, was to telling the friends or relatives of any stricken person that there was no hope. Instead, he would use every delicate shade of phrasing and tone in imparting the fateful words, in order if possible to give less pain. "I remember in the case of my father," said one of his friends, " when the last day came. Knowing the end was near, he was compelled to make some preliminary discouraging remark, and I bent over with my ear against my father's chest and said, 'Doctor Gridley, the disease is under control, I think. I can hear the respiration to the bottom of the lungs.'

" 'Yes, yes,' he answered me sadly, but now with an implication which could by no means be misunderstood, 'it is nearly always so. The failure is in the recuperative energy. Vitality runs too low.' It meant from the first, 'Your father will not live.' "

In the case of a little child with meningitis, the same person was sent to him to ask what of the child—better or worse. His answer was: "He is passing as free from pain as ever I knew a case of this kind."

In yet another case of a dying woman, one of her relatives inquired: "Doctor, is this case dangerous?" "Not in the nature of the malady, madam," was his sad and sympathetic reply, "but fatal in the condition it meets. Hope is broken. There is nothing to resist the damage."

One of his patients was a farmer who lived in an old-time log house a few miles out from Silver Lake, who while working about his barn met with a very serious accident which involved a possible injury to the gall bladder. The main accident was not in itself fatal, but the possible injury to the gall bladder was, and this, if it existed, would show as a yellow tint in the eyeball on the tenth day. Fearing the danger of this, he communicated the possibility to the relatives, saying that he could do little after that time but that he would come just the same and make the patient as comfortable as possible. For nine days he came, sitting by the bedside and whiling away many a weary hour for the sufferer, until the tenth morning. On this day, according to his daughter, who had it from the sick man's relatives, his face but ill concealed the anxiety he felt. Coming up to the door, he entered just far enough to pretend to reach for a water bucket. With this in his hand he turned and gave one long keen look in the eye of the sick man, then walked down the yard to a chair under a tree some distance from the house, where he sat, drooping and apparently grieved, the certainty of the death of the patient affecting him as much as if he were his own child.

"There was no need for words," said one of them. "Every curve and droop of his figure, as he walked slowly and with bent head, told all of us who saw him that hope was gone and that death had won the victory."

One of his perpetual charges, as I learned later, was a poor old unfortunate by the name of Id Logan, who had a little cabin and an acre of ground a half dozen miles west of Warsaw, and who existed from year to year heaven only knows how.

Id never had any money, friends or relatives, and was always troubled with illness or hunger in some form or other, and yet the doctor always spoke of him sympathetically as "Poor old Id Logan" and would often call out there on his rounds to see how he was getting along. One snowy winter's evening as he was traveling homeward after a long day's ride, he chanced to recollect the fact that he was in the neighborhood of his worthless old charge, and fancying that he might be in need of something turned his horse into the lane which led up to the door. When he reached the house he noticed that no smoke was coming from the chimney and that the windows were slightly rimmed with frost, as if there were no heat within. Rapping at the door and receiving no response, he opened it and went in. There he found his old charge, sick and wandering in his mind, lying upon a broken-down bed and moaning in pain. There was no fire in the fireplace. The coverings with which the bed was fitted were but two or three old worn and faded quilts, and the snow was sifting in badly through the cracks where the chinking had fallen out between the logs, and under the doors and windows.

Going up to the sufferer and finding that some one of his old, and to the doctor well-known, maladies had at last secured a fatal grip upon him, he first administered a tonic which he knew would give him as much strength as possible, and then went out into the yard, where, after putting up his horse, he gathered chips and wood from under the snow and built a roaring fire. Having done this, he put on the kettle, trimmed the lamp, and after preparing such stimulants as the patient could stand, took his place at the bedside, where he remained the whole night long, keeping the fire going and the patient as comfortable as possible. Toward morning the sufferer died and when the sun was well up he finally returned to his family, who anxiously solicited him as to his whereabouts.

"I was with Id Logan," he said.

"What's ailing him now?" his daughter inquired.

"Nothing now," he returned. "It was only last night," and for years afterward he commented on the death of "poor old Id," saying always at the conclusion of his remarks that it must be a dreadful thing to be sick and die without friends.

His love for his old friends and familiar objects was striking, and he could no more bear to see an old friend move away than he could to lose one of his patients. One of his oldest friends was a fine old Christian lady by the name of Weeks, who lived down in Louter Creek bottoms and in whose household he had practiced for nearly fifty years. During the latter part of his life, however, this family began to break up, and finally when there was no one left but the mother she decided to move over into Whitley County, where she could stay with her daughter. Just before going, however, she expressed a wish to see Doctor Gridley, and he called in upon her. A little dinner had been prepared in honor of his coming. After it was over and the old times were fully discussed he was about to take his leave when Mrs. Weeks disappeared from the room and then returned, bearing upon her arm a beautiful yarn spread which she held out before her and, in her nervous, feeble way getting the attention of the little audience, said:

"Doctor, I am going up to Whitley now to live with my daughter, and I don't suppose I will get to see you very often any more. Like myself, you are getting old, and it will be too far for you to come. But I want to give you this spread that I have woven with my own hands since I have been sixty years of age. It isn't very much, but it is meant for a token of the love and esteem I bear you, and in remembrance of all that you have done for me and mine."

Her eyes were wet and her voice quivering as she brought it forward. The doctor, who had been wholly taken by surprise by this kindly manifestation of regard, had arisen during her impromptu address and now stood before her, dignified and emotionally grave, his own eyes wet with tears of appreciation.

Balancing the homely gift upon his extended hands, he waited until the force of his own sentiment had slightly subsided, when he replied:

"Madam, I appreciate this gift with which you have chosen to remember me as much as I honor the sentiment which has produced it. There are, I know, threads of feeling woven into it stronger than any cords of wool, and more enduring than all the fabrics of this world. I have been your physician now for fifty years, and have been a witness of your joys and sorrows. But, as much as I esteem you, and as highly as I prize this token of your regard, I can accept it but upon one condition, and that is, Mrs. Weeks, that you promise me that no matter how dark the night, how stormy the sky, or how deep the waters that intervene, you will not fail to send for me in your hour of need. It is both my privilege and my pleasure, and I should not rest content unless I knew it were so."

When the old lady had promised, he took his spread and going out to his horse, rode away to his own home, where he related this incident, and ended with, "Now I want this put on my bed."

His daughter, who lovingly humored his every whim, immediately complied with his wish, and from that day to the hour of his death the spread was never out of his service.

One of the most pleasing incidents to me was one which related to his last illness and death. Always, during his later years, when he felt the least bit ill, he refused to prescribe for himself, saying that a doctor, if he knew anything at all, was never such a fool as to take any of his own medicine. Instead, and in sequence to this humorous attitude, he would always send for one of the younger men of the vicinity who were beginning to practice here, one, for instance, who having other merits needed some assurance and a bit of superior recognition occasionally to help him along. On this occasion he called in a very sober young doctor, one who was greatly admired but had very little practice as yet, and saying, "Doctor, I'm sick today," lay back on his bed and waited for further developments.

The latter, owing to Dr. Gridley's great repute and knowledge, was very much flustered, so much so that he scarcely knew what to do.

"Well, Doctor," he finally said, after looking at his tongue, taking his pulse and feeling his forehead, "you're really a better judge of your own condition than I am, I'm sure. What do you think I ought to give you?"

"Now, Doctor," replied Gridley sweetly, "I'm your patient, and you're my doctor. I wouldn't prescribe for myself for anything in the world, and I'm going to take whatever you give me. That's why I called you in. Now, you just give me what you think my condition requires, and I'll take it."

The young doctor, meditating on all that was new or faddistic, decided at last that just for variation's sake he would give the doctor something of which he had only recently heard, a sample of which he had with him and which had been acclaimed in the medical papers as very effective. Without asking the doctor whether he had ever heard of it, or what he thought, he merely prescribed it.

"Well, now, I like that," commented Gridley solemnly. "I never heard of that before in my life, but it sounds plausible. I'll take it, and we'll see. What's more, I like a young doctor like yourself who thinks up ways of his own——" and, according to his daughter, he did take it, and was helped, saying always that what young doctors needed to do was to keep abreast of the latest medical developments, that medicine was changing, and perhaps it was just as well that old doctors died! He was so old and feeble, however, that he did not long survive, and when the time came was really glad to go.

One of the sweetest and most interesting of all his mental phases was, as I have reason to know, his attitude toward the problem of suffering and death, an attitude so full of the human qualities of wonder, sympathy, tenderness, and trust, that he could scarcely view them without exhibiting the emotion he felt. He was a constant student of the phenomena of dissolution, and in one instance calmly declared it as his belief that when a man was dead he was dead and that was the end of him, consciously. At other times he modified his view to one of an almost prayerful hope, and in reading Emily Brontë's somewhat morbid story of "Wuthering Heights," his copy of which I long had in my possession, I noted that he had annotated numerous passages relative to death and a future life with interesting comments of his own. To one of these passages, which reads:

"I don't know if it be a peculiarity with me, but I am seldom otherwise than happy while watching in the chamber of death, provided no frenzied or despairing mourner shares the duty with me. I see a repose that neither earth nor hell can break, and I feel an assurance of the endless and shadowless hereafter—the eternity they have entered—where life is boundless in its duration, and love in its sympathy, and joy in its fullness,"

he had added on the margin:

"How often I have felt this very emotion. How natural I know it to be. And what a consolation in the thought!"

Writing a final prescription for a young clergyman who was dying, and for whom he had been most tenderly solicitous, he added to the list of drugs he had written in Latin, the lines:

"In life's closing hour, when the trembling soul flies
    And death stills the heart's last emotion,
Oh, then may the angel of mercy arise
    Like a star on eternity's ocean!"

When he himself was upon his death-bed he greeted his old friend Colonel Dyer—he of the absent overcoat and overshoes—with:

"Dyer, I'm almost gone. I am in the shadow of death. I am standing upon the very brink. I cannot see clearly, I cannot speak coherently, the film of death obstructs my sight. I know what this means. It is the end, but all is well with me. I have no fear. I have said and done things that would have been better left unsaid and undone, but I have never willfully wronged a man in my life. I have no concern for myself. I am concerned only for those I leave behind. I never saved money, and I die as poor as when I was born. We do not know what there is in the future now shut out from our view by a very thin veil. It seems to me there is a hand somewhere that will lead us safely across, but I cannot tell. No one can tell."

This interesting speech, made scarcely a day before he closed his eyes in death, was typical of his whole generous, trustful, philosophical point of view.

"If there be green fields and placid waters beyond the river that he so calmly crossed," so ran an editorial in the local county paper edited by one of his most ardent admirers, "reserved for those who believe in and practice upon the principle of 'Do unto others as you would have them do unto you,' then this Samaritan of the medical profession is safe from all harm. If there be no consciousness, but only a mingling of that which was gentleness and tenderness here with the earth and the waters, then the greenness of the one and the sparkling limpidity of the other are richer for that he lived, and wrought, and returned unto them so trustingly again."

Culhane, the Solid Man

I MET HIM in connection with a psychic depression which only partially reflected itself in my physical condition. I might almost say that I was sick spiritually. At the same time I was rather strongly imbued with a contempt for him and his cure. I had heard of him for years. To begin with, he was a wrestler of repute, or rather ex-wrestler, retired undefeated champion of the world. As a boy I had known that he had toured America with Modjeska as Charles, the wrestler, in "As You Like It." Before or after that he had trained John L. Sullivan, the world's champion prize fighter of his day, for one of his most successful fights, and that at a time when Sullivan was unfitted to fight any one. Before that, in succession, from youth up, he had been a peasant farmer's son in Ireland, a scullion in a ship's kitchen earning his way to America, a "beef slinger" for a packing company, a cooks' assistant and waiter in a Bowery restaurant, a bouncer in a saloon, a rubber down at prize fights, a policeman, a private in the army during the Civil War, a ticket-taker, exhibition wrestler, "short-change man" with a minstrel company, later a circus, until having attained his greatest fame as champion wrestler of the world, and as trainer of John L. Sullivan, he finally opened a sporting sanitarium in some county in upper New York State which later evolved into the great and now decidedly fashionable institution in Westchester, near New York.

It has always been interesting to me to see in what awe men of this type or profession are held by many in the more intellectual walks of life as well as by those whose respectful worship is less surprising,—those who revere strength, agility, physical courage, so-called, brute or otherwise. There is a kind of retiring worshipfulness, especially in men and children of the lower walks, for this type, which must be flattering in the extreme.

However, in so far as Culhane was concerned at this time, the case was different. Whatever he had been in his youth he was not that now, or at least his earlier rawness had long since been glazed over by other experiences. Self-education, an

940

acquired politeness among strangers and a knowledge of the manners and customs of the better-to-do, permitted him to associate with them and to accept if not copy their manners and to a certain extent their customs in his relations with them. Literally, he owned hundreds of the best acres of the land about him, in one of the most fashionable residence sections of the East. He had already given away to some Sisters of Mercy a great estate in northern New York. His stables contained every type of fashionable vehicle and stalled and fed sixty or seventy of the worst horses, purposely so chosen, for the use of his "guests." Men of all professions visited his place, paid him gladly the six hundred dollars in advance which he asked for the course of six weeks' training, and brought, or attempted to, their own cars and retinues, which they lodged in the vicinity but could not use. I myself was introduced or rather foisted upon him by my dear brother, whose friend if not crony—if such a thing could have been said to exist in his life—he was. I was taken to him in a very somber and depressed mood and left; he rarely if ever received guests in person or at once. On the way, and before I had been introduced, I was instructed by my good brother as to his moods, methods, airs and tricks, supposed or rumored to be so beneficial in so many cases. They were very rough— purposely so.

The day I arrived, and before I saw him, I was very much impressed with the simplicity yet distinction of the inn or sanitarium or "repair shop," as subsequently I learned he was accustomed to refer to it, perched upon a rise of ground and commanding a quite wonderful panorama. It was spring and quite warm and bright. The cropped enclosure which surrounded it, a great square of green fenced with high, well-trimmed privet, was good to look upon, level and smooth. The house, standing in the center of this, was large and oblong and gray, with very simple French windows reaching to the floor and great wide balustraded balconies reaching out from the second floor, shaded with awnings and set with rockers. The land on which this inn stood sloped very gradually to the Sound, miles away to the southeast, and the spires of churches and the gables of villages rising in between, as well as various toy-like sails upon the water, were no small portion of its charm. To the west for a score of miles the green-covered earth rose and fell in undulating beauty, and here again the roofs and spires of nearby villages might in fair weather be seen nestling peacefully among the trees. Due south there was a suggestion of water and some peculiar configuration, which by day seemed to have no significance other than that which attached to the vague outlines of a distant landscape. By night, however, the soft glow emanating from myriads of lights identified it as the body and length of the merry, night-reveling New York. Northward the green waves repeated themselves unendingly until they passed into a dim green-blue haze.

Interiorly, as I learned later, this place was most cleverly and sensibly arranged for the purpose for which it was intended. It was airy and well-appointed, with, on the ground floor, a great gymnasium containing, outside of an alcove at one end where hung four or five punching bags, only medicine balls. At the other end was an office or receiving-room, baggage or store-room, and locker and dining-room. To the east at the center extended a wing containing a number of shower-baths, a lounging room and sun parlor. On the second floor, on either side of a wide airy hall which ran from an immense library, billiard and smoking-room at one end to Culhane's private suite at the other, were two rows of bedrooms, perhaps a hundred all told, which gave in turn, each one, upon either side, on to the balconies previously mentioned. These rooms were arranged somewhat like the rooms of a passenger steamer, with its center aisle and its outer decks and doors opening upon it. In another wing on the ground floor were kitchens, servants' quarters, and what not else! Across the immense lawn or campus to the east, four-square to the sanitarium, stood a rather grandiose stable, almost as impressive as the main building. About the place, and always more or less in evidence, were servants, ostlers, waiting-maids and always a decidedly large company of men of practically all professions, ages, and one might almost say nationalities. That is as nationalities are represented in America, by first and second generations.

The day I arrived I did not see my prospective host or manager or trainer for an hour or two after I came, being allowed to wait about until the very peculiar temperament which he possessed would permit him to come and see me. When he did show up, a more savage and yet gentlemanly-looking animal in clothes *de rigueur* I have never seen. He was really very princely in build and manner, shapely and grand, like those portraits that have come down to us of Richelieu and the Duc de Guise—fawn-colored riding trousers, bright red waistcoat, black-and-white check riding coat, brown leather riding boots and leggings with the essential spurs, and a riding quirt. And yet really, at that moment he reminded me not so much of a man, in his supremely well-tailored riding costume, as of a tiger or a very ferocious and yet at times purring cat, beautifully dressed, as in our children's storybooks, a kind of tiger in collar and boots. He was so lithe, silent, cat-like in his tread. In his hard, clear, gray animal eyes was that swift, incisive, restless, searching glance which sometimes troubles us in the presence of animals. It was hard to believe that he was all of sixty, as I had been told. He looked the very well-preserved man of fifty or less. The short trimmed mustache and goatee which he wore were gray and added to his grand air. His hair, cut a close pompadour, the ends of his heavy eyebrow hairs turned upward, gave him a still more distinguished air. He looked very virile, very intelligent, very indifferent, intolerant and even threatening.

"Well," he exclaimed on sight, "you wish to see me?"

I gave him my name.

"Yes, that's so. Your brother spoke to me about you. Well, take a seat. You will be looked after."

He walked off, and after an hour or so I was still waiting, for what I scarcely knew—a room, something to eat possibly, some one to speak a friendly word to me, but no one did.

While I was waiting in this rather nondescript antechamber, hung with hats, caps, riding whips and gauntlets, I had an opportunity to study some of the men with whom presumably I was to live for a number of weeks. It was between two and three in the afternoon, and many of them were idling about in pairs or threes, talking, reading, all in rather commonplace athletic costumes—soft woolen shirts, knee trousers, stockings and running or walking shoes. They were in the main evidently of the so-called learned professions or the arts—doctors, lawyers, preachers, actors, writers, with a goodly sprinkling of merchants, manufacturers and young and middle-aged society men, as well as politicians and monied idlers, generally a little the worse for their pleasures or weaknesses. A distinguished judge of one of the superior courts of New York and an actor known everywhere in the English-speaking world were instantly recognized by me. Others, as I was subsequently informed, were related by birth or achievement to some one fact or another of public significance. The reason for the presence of so many people rather above than under the average in intellect lay, as I came to believe later, in their ability or that of some one connected with them to sincerely appreciate or to at least be amused and benefited by the somewhat different theory of physical repair which the lord of the manor had invented, or for which at least he had become famous.

I have remarked that I was not inclined to be impressed. Sanitariums with their isms and theories did not appeal to me. However, as I was waiting here an incident occurred which stuck in my mind. A smart conveyance drove up, occupied by a singularly lean and haughty-looking individual, who, after looking about him, expecting some one to come out to him no doubt, clambered cautiously out, and after seeing that his various grips and one trunk were properly deposited on the gravel square outside, paid and feed his driver, then walked in and remarked:

"Ah—where is Mr. Culhane?"

"I don't know, sir," I replied, being the only one present. "He was here, but he's gone. I presume some one will show up presently."

He walked up and down a little while, and then added: "Um—rather peculiar method of receiving one, isn't it? I wired him I'd be here." He walked restlessly and almost waspishly to and fro, looking out of the window at times, at others commenting on the rather casual character of it all. I agreed.

Thus, some fifteen minutes having gone by without any one approaching us, and occasional servants or "guests" passing through the room or being seen in the offing without even so much as vouchsafing a word or appearing to be interested in us, the new arrival grew excited.

"This is very unusual," he fumed, walking up and down. "I wired him only three hours ago. I've been here now fully three-quarters of an hour! A most unheard-of method of doing business, I should say!"

Presently our stern, steely-eyed host returned. He seemed to be going somewhere, to be nowise interested in us. Yet into our presence, probably into the consciousness of this new "guest," he carried that air of savage strength and indifference, eyeing the stranger quite sharply and making no effort to apologize for our long wait.

"You wish to see me?" he inquired brusquely once more.

Like a wasp, the stranger was vibrant with rage. Plainly he felt himself insulted or terribly underrated.

"Are you Mr. Culhane?" he asked crisply.

"Yes."

"I am Mr. Squiers," he exclaimed. "I wired you from Buffalo and ordered a room," this last with an irritated wave of the hand.

"Oh, no, you didn't order any room," replied the host sourly and with an obvious desire to show his indifference and contempt even. "You wired to know if you *could engage* a room."

He paused. The temperature seemed to drop perceptibly. The prospective guest seemed to realize that he had made a mistake somewhere, had been misinformed as to conditions here.

"Oh! Um—ah! Yes! Well, have you a room?"

"I don't know. I doubt it. We don't take every one." His eyes seemed to bore into the interior of his would-be guest.

"Well, but I was told—my friend, Mr. X——," the stranger began a rapid, semi-irritated, semi-apologetic explanation of how he came to be here.

"I don't know anything about your friend or what he told you. If he told you you could order a room by telegraph, he's mistaken. Anyhow, you're not dealing with him, but with me. Now that you're here, though, if you want to sit down and rest yourself a little I'll see what I can do for you. I can't decide now whether I can let you stay. You'll have to wait a while." He turned and walked off.

The other stared. "Well," he commented to me after a time,

walking and twisting, "if a man wants to come here I suppose he has to put up with such things, but it's certainly unusual, isn't it?" He sat down, wilted, and waited.

Later a clerk in charge of the registry book took us in hand, and then I heard him explaining that his lungs were not in good shape. He had come a long way—Denver, I believe. He had heard that all one needed to do was to wire, especially one in his circumstances.

"Some people think that way," solemnly commented the clerk, "but they don't know Mr. Culhane. He does about as he pleases in these matters. He doesn't do this any more to make money but rather to amuse himself, I think. He always has more applicants than he accepts."

I began to see a light. Perhaps there was something to this place after all. I did not even partially sense the drift of the situation, though, until bedtime when, after having been served a very frugal meal and shown to my very simple room, a kind of cell, promptly at nine o'clock lights were turned off. I lit a small candle and was looking over some things which I had placed in a grip, when I heard a voice in the hall outside: "Candles out, please! Candles out! All guests in bed!" Then it came to me that a very rigorous régime was being enforced here.

The next morning as I was still soundly sleeping at five-thirty a loud rap sounded at my door. The night before I had noticed above my bed a framed sign which read: "Guests must be dressed in running trunks, shoes and sweater, and appear in the gymnasium by six sharp." "Gymnasium at six! Gymnasium at six!" a voice echoed down the hall. I bounced out of bed. Something about the very air of the place made me feel that it was dangerous to attempt to trifle with the routine here. The tiger-like eyes of my host did not appeal to me as retaining any softer ray in them for me than for others. I had paid my six hundred . . . I had better earn it. I was down in the great room in my trunks, sweater, dressing-gown, running shoes in less than five minutes.

And that room! By that time as odd a company of people as I have ever seen in a gymnasium had already begun to assemble. The leanness! the osseosity! the grandiloquent whiskers parted in the middle! the mustachios! the goatees!

the fat, Hoti-like stomachs! the protuberant knees! the thin arms! the bald or semi-bald pates! the spectacles or horn glasses or pince-nezes!—laid aside a few moments later, as the exercises began. Youth and strength in the pink of condition, when clad only in trunks, a sweater and running shoes, are none too acceptable—but middle age! And out in the world, I reflected rather sadly, they all wore the best of clothes, had their cars, servants, city and country houses perhaps, their factories, employees, institutions. Ridiculous! Pitiful! As lymphatic and flabby as oysters without their shells, myself included. It was really painful.

Even as I meditated, however, I was advised, by many who saw that I was a stranger, to choose a partner, any partner, for medicine ball practice, for it might save me being taken or called by *him*. I hastened so to do. Even as we were assembling or beginning to practice, keeping two or three light medicine balls going between each pair, our host entered— that iron man, that mount of brawn. In his cowled dressing-gown he looked more like some great monk or fighting abbot of the medieval years than a trainer. He walked to the center, hung up his cowl and revealed himself lithe and lion-like and costumed like ourselves. But how much more attractive as he strode about, his legs lean and sturdy, his chest full, his arms powerful and graceful! At once he seized a large leather-covered medicine ball, as had all the others, and calling a name to which responded a lean whiskerando with a semi-bald pate, thin legs and arms, and very much caricatured, I presume, by the wearing of trunks and sweater. Taking his place opposite the host, he was immediately made the recipient of a volley of balls and brow-beating epithets.

"Hurry up now! Faster! Ah, come on! Put the ball back to me! Put the ball back! Do you want to keep it all day? Great God! What are you standing there for? What are you standing there for? What do you think you're doing—drinking tea? Come on! I haven't all morning for you alone. Move! Move, you ham! You call yourself an editor! Why, you couldn't edit a handbill! You can't even throw a ball straight! Throw it straight! Throw it straight! For Christ's sake where do you think I am—out in the office? Throw it straight! Hell!" and all the time one and another ball, grabbed from anywhere, for the floor was always littered with them, would be thrown in the victim's direction, and before he could well appreciate what was happening to him he was being struck, once in the neck and again on the chest by the rapidly delivered six ounce air-filled balls, two of which at least he and the host were supposed to keep in constant motion between them. Later, a ball striking him in the stomach, he emitted a weak "Ooph!" and laying his hands over the affected part ceased all effort. At this the master of the situation only smirked on him leoninely and holding up a ball as if to throw it continued, "What's the matter with you now? Come on! What do you want to stop for? What do you want to stand there for? You're not hurt. How do you expect to get anywhere if you can't keep two silly little balls like these going between us?" (There had probably been six or eight.) "Here I am sixty and you're forty, and you can't even keep up with me. And you pretend to give the general public advice on life! Well, go on; God pity the public, is all I say," and he dismissed him, calling out another name.

Now came a fat, bald soul, with dewlaps and a protruding stomach, who later I learned was a manufacturer of clothing—six hundred employees under him—down in health and nerves, really all "shot to pieces" physically. Plainly nervous at the sound of his name, he puffed quickly into position, grabbing wildly after the purposely eccentric throws which his host made and which kept him running to left and right in an all but panicky mood.

"Move! Move!" insisted our host as before, and, if anything, more irritably. "Say, you work like a crab! What a motion! If you had more head and less guts you could do this better. A fine specimen you are! This is what comes of riding about in taxis and eating midnight suppers instead of exercising. Wake up! Wake up! A belt would have kept your stomach in long ago. A little less food and less sleep, and you wouldn't have any fat cheeks. Even your hair might stay on! Wake up! Wake up! What do you want to do—die?" and as he talked he pitched the balls so quickly that his victim looked at times as though he were about to weep. His physical deficiencies were all too plain in every way. He was generally obese and looked as though he might drop, his face a flaming red, his hands trembling and missing, when a "Well, go on," sounded and a third victim was called. This time it was a well-known actor who responded, a star, rather spry and well set up, but still nervous, for he realized quite well what was before him. He had been here for weeks and was in pretty fair trim, but still he was plainly on edge. He ran and began receiving and tossing as swiftly as he could, but as with the others so it was his turn now to be given such a grilling and tongue-lashing as falls to few of us in this world, let alone among the successful in the realm of the footlights. "Say, you're not an actor—you're a woman! You're a stewed onion! Move! Move! Come on! Come on! Look at those motions now, will you? Look at that one arm up! Where do you suppose the ball is? On the ceiling? It's not a lamp! Come on! Come on! It's a wonder when you're killed as Hamlet that you don't stay dead. You are. You're really dead now, you know. Move! Move!" and so it would go until finally the poor thespian, no match for his master and beset by flying balls, landing upon his neck, ear, stomach, finally gave up and cried:

"Well, I can't go any faster than I can, can I? I can't do any more than I can!"

"Ah, go on! Go back into the chorus!" called his host, who now abandoned him. "Get somebody from the baby class to play marbles with you," and he called another.

By now, as may well be imagined, I was fairly stirred up as to the probabilities of the situation. He might call me! The man who was playing opposite me—a small, decayed person who chose me, I think, because he knew I was new, innocuous and probably awkward—seemed to realize my thoughts as well as his own. By lively exercise with me he was doing his utmost to create an impression of great and valuable effort here. "Come on, let's play fast so he won't notice us," he said most pathetically at one point. You would have thought I had known him all my life.

But he didn't call us—not this morning at any rate. Whether owing to our efforts or the fact that I at least was too insignificant, too obscure, we escaped. He did reach me, however, on the fourth or fifth day, and no spindling failure could have done worse. I was struck and tripped and pounded until I all but fell prone upon the floor, half con-

vinced that I was being killed, but I was not. I was merely
sent stumbling and drooping back to the sidelines to recover
while he tortured some one else. But the names he called me!
The comments on my none too smoothly articulated bones—
and my alleged mind! As in my schooldays when, a laggard
in the fierce and seemingly malevolent atmosphere in which I
was taught my A B C's, I crept shamefacedly and beaten from
the scene.

It was in the adjoining bathroom, where the host daily personally superintended the ablutions of his guests, that even
more of his remarkable method was revealed. Here a goodly
portion of the force of his method was his skill in removing
any sense of ability, agility, authority or worth from those
with whom he dealt. Apparently to him, in his strength and
energy, they were all children, weaklings, failures, numb-
skulls, no matter what they might be in the world outside.
They had no understanding of the most important of their
possessions, their bodies. And here again, even more than in
the gymnasium, they were at the disadvantage of feeling
themselves spectacles, for here they were naked. However
grand an osseous, leathery lawyer or judge or doctor or politician or society man may look out in the world addressing a
jury or a crowd or walking in some favorite place, glistening
in his raiment, here, whiskered, thin of legs, arms and neck,
with bulging brow and stripped not only of his gown but
everything else this side of his skin—well, draw your own
conclusion. For after performing certain additional exercises—one hundred times up on your toes, one hundred
times (if you could) squatting to your knees, one hundred
times throwing your arms out straight before you from your
chest or up from your shoulders or out at right angles, right
and left from your body and back to your hips until your
fingers touched and the sweat once more ran—you were then
ready to be told (for once in your life) how to swiftly and
agilely take a bath.

"Well, now, you're ready, are you?" this to a noble jurist
who, like myself perhaps, had arrived only the day before.
"Come on, now. Now you have just ten seconds in which to
jump under the water and get yourself wet all over, twenty
seconds in which to jump out and soap yourself thoroughly,

ten seconds in which to get back in again and rinse off all the soap, and twenty seconds in which to rub and dry your skin thoroughly—now start!"

The distinguished jurist began, but instead of following the advice given him for rapid action huddled himself in a shivering position under the water and stood all but inert despite the previous explanation of the host that the sole method of escaping the weakening influence of cold water was by counteracting it with activity, when it would prove beneficial.

He was such a noble, stalky, bony affair, his gold eyeglasses laid aside for the time being, his tweeds and carefully laundered linen all dispensed with during his stay here. As he came, meticulously and gingerly and quite undone by his efforts, from under the water, where he had been most roughly urged by Culhane, I hoped that he and not I would continue to be seized upon by this savage who seemed to take infinite delight in disturbing the social and intellectual poise of us all.

"Soap yourself!" exclaimed the latter most harshly now that the bather was out in the room once more. "Soap your chest! Soap your stomach! Soap your arms, damn it! Soap your arms! And don't rub them all day either! Now soap your legs, damn it! Soap your legs! Don't you know how to soap your legs! Don't stand there all day! Soap your legs! Now turn round and soap your back—soap your back! For Christ's sake, soap your back! Do it quick—quick! Now come back under the water again and see if you can get it off. Don't act as though you were cold molasses! Move! Move! Lord, you act as though you had all day—as though you had never taken a bath in your life! I never saw such an old poke. You come up here and expect me to do some things for you, and then you stand around as though you were made of bone! Quick now, move!"

The noble jurist did as demanded—that is, as quickly as he could—only the mental inadequacy and feebleness which he displayed before all the others, of course, was the worst of his cruel treatment here, and in this as in many instances it cut deep. So often it was the shock to one's dignity more than anything else which hurt so, to be called an old poke when one was perhaps a grave and reverent senior, or to be told that one was made of bone when one was a famous doctor or merchant. Once under the water this particular specimen had begun by nervously rubbing his hands and face in order to get the soap off, and when shouted at and abused for that had then turned his attention to one other spot—the back of his left forearm.

Mine host seemed enraged. "Well, well!" he exclaimed irascibly, watching him as might a hawk. "Are you going to spend all day rubbing that one spot? For God's sake, don't you know enough to rub your whole body and get out from under the water? Move! Move! Rub your chest! Rub your belly! Hell, rub your back! Rub your toes and get out!"

When routed from the ludicrous effort of vigorously rubbing one spot he was continually being driven on to some other, as though his body were some vast complex machine which he had never rightly understood before. He was very much flustered of course and seemed wholly unable to grasp how it was done, let alone please his exacting host.

"Come on!" insisted the latter finally and wearily. "Get out from under the water. A lot you know about washing yourself! For a man who has been on the bench for fifteen years you're the dullest person I ever met. If you bathe like that at home, how do you keep clean? Come on out and dry yourself!"

The distinguished victim, drying himself rather ruefully on an exceedingly rough towel, looked a little weary and disgusted. "Such language!" some one afterwards said he said to some one else. "He's not used to dealing with gentlemen, that's plain. The man talks like a blackguard. And to think we pay for such things! Well, well! I'll not stand it, I'm afraid. I've had about enough. It's positively revolting, positively revolting!" But he stayed on, just the same—second thoughts, a good breakfast, his own physical needs. At any rate weeks later he was still there and in much better shape physically if not mentally.

About the second or third day I witnessed another such spectacle, which made me laugh—only not in my host's presence—nay, verily! For into this same chamber had come another distinguished personage, a lawyer or society man, I couldn't tell which, who was washing himself rather leisurely, as was *not* the prescribed way, when suddenly he was spied by mine host, who was invariably instructing some one in this swift one-minute or less system. Now he eyed the operation narrowly for a few seconds, then came over and exclaimed:

"Wash your toes, can't you? Wash your toes! Can't you wash your toes?"

The skilled gentleman, realizing that he was now living under very different conditions from those to which presumably he was accustomed, reached down and began to rub the tops of his toes but without any desire apparently to widen the operation.

"Here!" called the host, this time much more sharply, "I said wash your toes, not the outside of them! Soap them! Don't you know how to wash your toes yet? You're old enough, God knows! Wash between 'em! Wash under 'em!"

"Certainly I know how to wash my toes," replied the other irritably and straightening up, "and what's more, I'd like you to know that I am a gentleman."

"Well, then, if you're a gentleman," retorted the other, "you ought to know how to wash your toes. Wash 'em—and don't talk back!"

"Pah!" exclaimed the bather now, looking twice as ridiculous as before. "I'm not used to having such language addressed to me."

"I can't help that," said Culhane. "If you knew how to wash your toes perhaps you wouldn't have to have such language addressed to you."

"Oh, hell!" fumed the other. "This is positively outrageous! I'll leave the place, by George!"

"Very well," rejoined the other, "only before you go you'll have to wash your toes!"

And he did, the host standing by and calmly watching the performance until it was finally completed.

It was just this atmosphere which made the place the most astonishing in which I have ever been. It seemed to be drawing the celebrated and the successful as a magnet might iron, and yet it offered conditions which one might presume they would be most opposed to. No one here was really any one, however much he might be outside. Our host was all. He had a great blazing personality which dominated everybody, and he did not hesitate to show before one and all that he did so do.

Breakfast here consisted of a cereal, a chop and coffee—plentiful but very plain, I thought. After breakfast, between eight-thirty and eleven, we were free to do as we chose: write letters, pack our bags if we were leaving, do up our laundry to be sent out, read, or merely sit about. At eleven, or ten-thirty, according to the nature of the exercise, one had to join a group, either one that was to do the long or short block, as they were known here, or one that was to ride horseback, all exercises being so timed that by proper execution one would arrive at the bathroom door in time to bathe, dress and take ten minutes' rest before luncheon. These exercises were simple enough in themselves, consisting, as they did in the case of the long and the short blocks (the long block seven, the short four miles in length), of our walking, or walking and running betimes, about or over courses laid up hill and down dale, over or through unpaved mudroads in many instances, along dry or wet beds of brooks or streams, and across stony or weedy fields, often still damp with dew or the spring rains. But in most cases, when people had not taken any regular exercise for a long time, this was by no means easy. The first day I thought I should never make it, and I was by no means a poor walker. Others, the new ones especially, often gave out and had to be sent for, or came in an hour late to be most severely and irritatingly ragged by the host. He seemed to all but despise weakness and had apparently a thousand disagreeable ways of showing it.

"If you want to see what poor bags of mush some people can become," he once said in regard to some poor specimen who had seemingly had great difficulty in doing the short block, "look at this. Here comes a man sent out to do four measly country miles in fifty minutes, and look at him. You'd think he was going to die. He probably thinks so himself. In New York he'd do seventeen miles in a night running from barroom to barroom or one lobster palace to another—that's a good name for them, by the way—and never say a word. But out here in the country, with plenty of fresh air and a night's rest and a good breakfast, he can't even do four miles in fifty minutes! Think of it! And he probably thinks of himself as a man—boasts before his friends, or his wife, anyhow. Lord!"

A day or two later there arrived here a certain major of the United States Army, a large, broad-chested, rather pompous person of about forty-eight or -nine, who from taking his ease in one sinecure and another had finally reached the place where he was unable to endure certain tests (or he thought so) which were about to be made with a view to retiring certain officers grown fat in the service. As he explained to Culhane, and the latter was always open and ribald afterward in his comments on those who offered explanations of any kind, his plan was to take the course here in order to be able to make the difficult tests later.

Culhane resented this, I think. He resented people using him or his methods to get anywhere, do anything more in life than he could do, and yet he received them. He felt, and I think in the main that he was right, that they looked down on him because of his lowly birth and purely material and mechanical career, and yet having attained some distinction by it he could not forego this work which raised him, in a way, to a position of dominance over these people. Now the sight of presumably so efficient a person in need of aid or exercise, to be built up, was all that was required to spur him on to the most waspish or wolfish attitude imaginable. In part at least he argued, I think (for in the last analysis he was really too wise and experienced to take any such petty view, although there is a subconscious "past-lack" motivating impulse in all our views), that here he was, an ex-policeman, ex-wrestler, ex-prize fighter, ex-private, ex-waiter, beef-carrier, bouncer, trainer; and here was this grand major, trained at West Point, who actually didn't know any more about life or how to take care of his body than to be compelled to come here, broken down at forty-eight, whereas he, because of his stamina and Spartan energy, had been able to survive in perfect condition until sixty and was now in a position to rebuild all these men and wastrels and to control this great institution. And to a certain extent he was right, although he seemed to forget or not to know that he was not the creator of his own great strength, by any means, impulses and tendencies over which he had no control having arranged for that.

However that may be, here was the major a suppliant for his services, and here was he, Culhane, and although the major was paying well for his minute room and his probably greatly decreased diet, still Culhane could not resist the temptation to make a show of him, to picture him as the more or less pathetic example that he was, in order perhaps that he, Culhane, might shine by contrast. Thus on the first day, having sent him around the short block with the others, it was found at twelve, when the "joggers" were expected to return, and again at twelve-thirty when they were supposed to take their places at the luncheon table, that the heavy major had not arrived. He had been seen and passed by all, of course. After the first mile or two probably he had given out and was making his way as best he might up hill and down dale, or along some more direct road, to the "shop," or maybe he had dropped out entirely, as some did, via a kindly truck or farmer's wagon, and was on his way to the nearest railway station.

At any rate, as Culhane sat down at his very small private table, which stood in the center of the dining-room and far apart from the others (a vantage point, as it were), he looked about and, not seeing the new guest, inquired, "Has any one seen that alleged army officer who arrived here this morning?"

No one could say anything more than that they had left him two or three miles back.

"I thought so," he said tersely. "There you have a fine example of the desk general and major—we had 'em in the army—men who sit in a swivel chair all day, wear a braided uniform and issue orders to other people. You'd think a man like that who had been trained at West Point and seen service in the Philippines would have sense enough to keep himself in condition. Not at all. As soon as they get a little way up in their profession they want to sit around hotel grills or society ballrooms and show off, tell how wonderful they are. Here's a man, an army officer, in such rotten shape that if I sent a good horse after him now it's ten to one he couldn't get on him. I'll have to send a truck or some such thing."

He subsided. About an hour later the major did appear, much the worse for wear. A groom with a horse had been sent out after him, and, as the latter confided to some one afterward, he "had to help the major on." From that time on, on the short block and the long, as well as on those horseback tours which every second or third morning we were supposed to take, the major was his especial target. He loved to pick on him, to tell him that he was "nearly all guts"—a phrase which literally sickened me at that time—to ask him how he expected to stay in the army if he couldn't do this or that, what good was he to the army, how could any soldier respect a thing like him, and so on *ad infinitum* until, while at first I pitied the major, later on I admired his pluck. Culhane foisted upon him his sorriest and boniest nag, the meanest animal he could find, yet he never complained; and although he forced on him all the foods he knew the major could not like, still there was no complaint; he insisted that he should be out and around of an afternoon when most of us lay about, allowed him no drinks whatever, although he was accustomed to them. The major, as I learned afterwards, stayed not six but twelve weeks and passed the tests which permitted him to remain in the army.

But to return to Culhane himself. The latter's method always contained this element of nag and pester which, along with his brazen reliance on and pride in his brute strength at sixty, made all these others look so puny and ineffectual. They might have brains and skill but here they were in his institution, more or less undone nervously and physically, and here he was, cold, contemptuous, not caring much whether they came, stayed or went, and laughing at them even as they raged. Now and then it was rumored that he found some single individual in whom he would take an interest, but not often. In the main I think he despised them one and all for the puny machines they were. He even despised life and the pleasures and dissipations or swinish indolence which, in his judgment, characterized most men. I recall once, for instance, his telling us how as a private in the United States Army when the division of which he was a unit was shut up in winter quarters, huddled about stoves, smoking (as he characterized them) "filthy pipes" or chewing tobacco and spitting, actually lousy, and never changing their clothes for weeks on end—how he, revolting at all this and the disease and fevers ensuing, had kept out of doors as much as possible, even in the coldest weather, and finding no other way of keeping clean the single shift of underwear and the one uniform he possessed he had, every other day or so, washed all, uniform and underwear, with or without soap as conditions might compel, in a nearby stream, often breaking the ice to get to the water, and dancing about naked in the cold, running and jumping, while they dried on bushes or the branch of a tree.

"Those poor rats," he added most contemptuously, "used to sit inside and wonder at me or laugh and jeer, hovering over their stoves, but a lot of them died that very winter, and here I am today."

And well we knew it. I used to study the faces of many of the puffy, gelatinous souls, so long confined to their comfortable offices, restaurants and homes that two hours on horseback all but wore them out, and wonder how this appealed to them. I think that in the main they took it as an illustration of either one of two things: insanity, or giant and therefore not-to-be-imitated strength.

But in regard to them Culhane was by no means so tolerant. One day, as I recall, there arrived at the sanitarium a stout and mushy-looking Hebrew, with a semi-bald pate, protruding paunch and fat arms and legs, who applied to Culhane for admission. And, as much to irritate his other guests, I think, as to torture this particular specimen into some semblance of vitality, he admitted him. And thereafter, from the hour he entered until he left about the time I did, Culhane seemed to follow him with a wolfish and savage idea. He gave him a most damnable and savage horse, one that kicked and bit, and at mounting time would place Mr. Itzky (I think his name was) up near the front of the procession where he could watch him. Always at mount-time, when we were permitted to ride, there was inside the great stable a kind of preliminary military inspection of all our accouterments, seeing that we had to saddle and bridle and bring forth our own steeds. This particular person could not saddle a horse very well nor put on his bit and bridle. The animal was inclined to rear and plunge when he came near, to fix him with an evil eye and bite at him.

And above all things Culhane seemed to value strain of this kind. If he could just make his guests feel the pressure of necessity in connection with their work he was happy. To this end he would employ the most contemptuous and grilling comment. Thus to Mr. Itzky he was most unkind. He would look over all most cynically, examining the saddles and bridles, and then say, "Oh, I see you haven't learned how to tighten a belly-band yet," or "I do believe you have your saddle hind-side to. You would if you could, that's one thing sure. How do you expect a horse to be sensible or quiet when he knows that he isn't saddled right? Any horse knows that much, and whether he has an ass for a rider. I'd kick and bite too if I were some of these horses, having a lot of damned fools and wasters to pack all over the country. Loosen that belt and fasten it right" (there might be nothing wrong with it) "and move your saddle up. Do you want to sit over the horse's rump?"

Then would come the fateful moment of mounting. There was of course the accepted and perfect way—his way: left foot in stirrup, an easy balanced spring and light descent into the seat. One should be able to slip the right foot into the right stirrup with the same motion of mounting. But imagine fifty, sixty, seventy men, all sizes, weights and differing conditions of health and mood. A number of these people had never ridden a horse before coming here and were as nervous and frightened as children. Such mounts! Such fumbling around, once they were in their saddles, for the right stirrup! And all the while Culhane would be sitting out front like an army captain on the only decent steed in the place, eyeing us with a look of infinite and weary contempt that served to increase our troubles a thousandfold.

"Well, you're all on, are you? You all do it so gracefully I like to sit here and admire you. Hulbert there throws his leg over his horse's back so artistically that he almost kicks his teeth out. And Effingham does his best to fall off on the other side. And where's Itzky? I don't even see him. Oh, yes, there he is. Well" (this to Itzky, frantically endeavoring to get one fat foot in a stirrup and pull himself up), "what about you? Can't you get your leg that high? Here's a man who for twenty-five years has been running a cloak-and-suit business and employing five hundred people, but he can't get on a horse! Imagine! Five hundred people dependent on that for their living!" (At this point, say, Itzky succeeds in mounting.) "Well, he's actually on! Now see if you can stick while we ride a block or two. You'll find the right stirrup, Itzky, just a little forward of your horse's belly on the right side—see? A fine bunch this is to lead out through a gentleman's country! Hell, no wonder I've got a bad reputation throughout this section! Well, forward, and see if you can keep from falling off."

Then we were out through the stable-door and the privet gate at a smart trot, only to burst into a headlong gallop a little farther on down the road. To the seasoned riders it was all well enough, but to beginners, those nervous about horses, fearful about themselves! The first day, not having ridden in years and being uncertain as to my skill, I could scarcely stay on. Several days later, I by then having become a reasonably seasoned rider, it was Mr. Itzky who appeared on the scene, and after him various others. On this particular trip I am thinking of, Mr. Itzky fell or rolled off and could not again mount. He was miles from the repair shop and Culhane, discovering his plight, was by no means sympathetic. We had a short ride back to where he sat lamely by the roadside viewing disconsolately the cavalcade and the country in general.

"Well, what's the matter with you now?" It was Culhane, eyeing him most severely.

"I hef hurt my foot. I kent stay on."

"You mean you'd rather walk, do you, and lead your horse?"

"Vell, I kent ride."

"All right, then, you lead your horse back to the stable if you want any lunch, and hereafter you run with the baby-class on the short block until you think you can ride without falling off. What's the good of my keeping a stable of first-class horses at the service of a lot of mush-heads who don't even know how to use 'em? All they do is ruin 'em. In a week or two, after a good horse is put in the stable, he's not fit for a gentleman to ride. They pull and haul and kick and beat, when as a matter of fact the horse has a damned sight more sense than they have."

We rode off, leaving Itzky alone. The men on either side of me—we were riding three abreast—scoffed under their breath at the statement that we were furnished decent horses. "The nerve! This nag!" "This bag of bones!" "To think a thing like this should be called a horse!" But there were no outward murmurs and no particular sympathy for Mr. Itzky. He was a fat stuff, a sweat-shop manufacturer, they would bet; let him walk and sweat.

So much for sympathy in this gay realm where all were seeking to restore their own little bodies, whatever happened.

So many of these men varied so greatly in their looks, capacities and troubles that they were always amusing. Thus I recall one lean iron manufacturer, the millionaire president of a great "frog and switch" company, who had come on from Kansas City, troubled with anæmia, neurasthenia, "nervous derangement of the heart" and various other things. He was over fifty, very much concerned about himself, his family, his business, his friends; anxious to obtain the benefits of this celebrated course of which he had heard so much. Walking or running near me on his first day, he took occasion to make inquiries in regard to Culhane, the life here, and later on confidences as to his own condition. It appeared that his chief trouble was his heart, a kind of phantom disturbance which made him fear that he was about to drop dead and which came and went, leaving him uncertain as to whether he had it or not. On entering he had confided to Culhane the mysteries of his case, and the latter had examined him, pronouncing him ("Rather roughly," as he explained to me), quite fit to do "all the silly work he would have to do here."

Nevertheless while we were out on the short block his heart was hurting him. At the same time it had been made rather clear to him that if he wished to stay here he would have to fulfill all the obligations imposed. After a mile or two or three of quick walking and jogging he was saying to me, "You know, I'm not really sure that I can do this. It's very severe, more so than I thought. My heart is not doing very well. It feels very fluttery."

"But," I said, "if he told you you could stand it, you can, I'm sure. It's not very likely he'd say you could if you couldn't. He examined you, didn't he? I don't believe he'd deliberately put a strain on any one who couldn't stand it."

"Yes," he admitted doubtfully, "that's true perhaps."

Still he continued to complain and complain and to grow more and more worried, until finally he slowed up and was lost in the background.

Reaching the gymnasium at the proper time I bathed and dressed myself quickly and waited on the balcony over the bathroom to see what would happen in this case. As a rule Culhane stood in or near the door at this time, having just returned from some route or "block" himself, to see how the others were faring. And he was there when the iron manufacturer came limping up, fifteen minutes late, one hand over his heart, the other to his mouth, and exclaiming as he drew near, "I do believe, Mr. Culhane, that I can't stand this. I'm afraid there is something the matter with my heart. It's fluttering so."

"To hell with your heart! Didn't I tell you there was nothing the matter with it? Get into the bath!"

The troubled manufacturer, overawed or reassured as the case might be, entered the bath and ten minutes later might have been seen entering the dining-room, as comfortable apparently as any one. Afterwards he confessed to me on one of our jogs that there was something about Culhane which *gave him confidence* and made him believe that there wasn't anything wrong with his heart—which there wasn't, I presume.

The intensely interesting thing about Culhane was this different, very original and forthright if at times brutal point of view. It was a blazing material world of which he was the center, the sun, and yet always I had the sense of very great life. With no knowledge of or interest in the superior mental sciences or arts or philosophies, still he seemed to suggest and even live them. He was in his way an exemplification of that ancient Greek regimen and stark thought which brought back the ten thousand from Cunaxa. He seemed even to suggest in his rough way historical perspective and balance. He knew men, and apparently he sensed how at best and at bottom life was to be lived, with not too much emotional or appetitive swaying in any one direction, and not too little either.

Yet in "trapseing" about this particular realm each day with ministers, lawyers, doctors, actors, manufacturers, papa's or mamma's young hopefuls and petted heirs, young scapegraces and so-called "society men" of the extreme "upper crust," stuffed and plethoric with money and as innocent of sound knowledge or necessary energy in some instances as any one might well be, one could not help speculating as to how it was that such a man, as indifferent and all but discourteous as this one, could attract them (and so many) to him. They came from all parts of America—the Pacific, the Gulf, the Atlantic and Canada—and yet, although they did not relish him or his treatment of them, once here they stayed. Walking or running or idling about with them one could always hear from one or another that Culhane was too harsh, a "bounder," an "upstart," a "cheap pugilist" or "wrestler" at best (I myself thought so at times when I was angry), yet here they were, and here I was, and staying. He was low, vulgar—yet here we were. And yet, meditating on him, I began to think that he was really one of the most remarkable men I had ever known, for these people he dealt with were of all the most difficult to deal with. In the main they were of that order or condition of mind which springs from (1), too much wealth too easily acquired or inherited; or (2), from a blazing material success, the cause of which was their own savage self-interested viewpoint. Hence a colder and in some respects a more critical group of men I have never known. Most of them had already seen so much of life in a libertine way that there was little left to enjoy. They sniffed at almost everything, Culhane included, and yet they were obviously drawn to him. I tried to explain this to myself on the ground that there is some iron power in some people which literally compels this, whether one will or no; or that they were in the main so tired of life and so truly selfish and egotistic that it required some such different iron or caviar mood plus such a threatening regimen to make them really take an interest. Sick as they were, he was about the only thing left on which they could sharpen their teeth with any result.

As I have said, a part of Culhane's general scheme was to arrange the starting time for the walks and jogs about the long and short blocks so that if one moved along briskly he reached the sanitarium at twelve-thirty and had a few minutes in which to bathe and cool off and change his clothes before entering the dining-room, where, if not at the bathroom door beforehand, Culhane would be waiting, seated at his little table, ready to keep watch on the time and condition of all those due. Thus one day, a group of us having done the long block in less time than we should have devoted to it, came in panting and rejoicing that we had cut the record by seven minutes. We did not know that he was around. But in the dining-room as we entered he scoffed at our achievement.

"You think you're smart, don't you?" he said sourly and without any preliminary statement as to how he knew we had done it in less time. "You come out here and pay me one hundred a week and then you want to be cute and play tricks with your own money and health. I want you to remember just one thing: my reputation is just as much involved with the results here as your money. I don't need anybody's money, and I do need my orders obeyed. Now you all have watches. You just time yourselves and do that block in the time required. If you can't do it, that's one thing; I can forgive a man too weak or sick to do it. But I haven't any use for a mere smart aleck, and I don't want any more of it, see?"

That luncheon was very sad.

Another thing in connection with these luncheons and dinners, which were sharply timed to the minute, were these crisp table speeches, often made *in re* some particular offender or his offense, at other times mere sarcastic comments on life in general and the innate cussedness of human nature, which amused at the same time that they were certain to irritate some. For who is it that is not interested in hearing the peccadilloes of his neighbor aired?

Thus while I was there, there was a New York society man by the name of Blake, who unfortunately was given to severe periods of alcoholism, the results of which were, after a time, nervous disorders which sent him here. In many ways he was as amiable and courteous and considerate a soul as one could meet anywhere. He had that smooth, gracious something about him—good nature, for one thing, a kind of understanding and sympathy for various forms of life—which left him highly noncensorious, if genially examining at times. But his love of drink, or rather his mild attempts here to arrange some method by which in this droughty world he could obtain a little, aroused in Culhane not so much opposition as an amused contempt, for at bottom I think he really liked the man. Blake was so orderly, so sincere in his attempts to fulfill conditions, only about once every week or so he would suggest that he be allowed to go to White Plains or Rye, or even New York, on some errand or other—most of which requests were promptly and nearly always publicly refused. For although Culhane had his private suite at one end of the great building, where one might suppose one might go to make a private plea, still one could never find him there. He refused to receive complaints or requests or visits of any kind there. If you wanted to speak to him you had to do it when he was with the group in its entirety—a commonsense enough policy. But just the same there were those who had reasonable requests or complaints, and these, by a fine intuition as to who was who in this institution and what might be expected of each one, he managed to hear very softly, withdrawing slowly as they talked or inviting them into the office. In the main however the requests were very much like those of Blake—men who wanted to get off somewhere for a day or two, feeling, as they did after a week or two or three, especially fit and beginning to think no doubt of the various comforts and pleasures which the city offered.

But to all these he was more or less adamant. By hook or by crook, by special arrangements with friends or agents in nearby towns and the principal showy resorts of New York, he managed to know, providing they did leave the grounds, either with or without his consent, about where they were and what they had done, and in case any of his rules or their agreements were broken their privileges were thereafter cut off or they were promptly ejected, their trunks being set out on the roadway in front of the estate and they being left to make their way to shelter elsewhere as best they might.

On one occasion, however, Blake had been allowed to go to New York over Saturday and Sunday to attend to some urgent business, as he said, he on his honor having promised to avoid the white lights. Nevertheless he did not manage so to do but instead, in some comfortable section of that region,

was seen drinking enough to last him until perhaps he should
have another opportunity to return to the city.

On his return to the "shop" on Monday morning or late
Sunday night, Culhane pretended not to see him until noon-
day lunch, when, his jog over the long block done with
and his bath taken, he came dapperly into the dining-room,
wishing to look as innocent and fit as possible. But Culhane
was there before him at his little table in the center of the
room, and patting the head of one of the two pure-blooded
collies that always followed him about on the grounds or in
the house, began as follows:

"A dog," he said very distinctly and in his most cynical tone
and apparently apropos of nothing, which usually augured
that the lightning of his criticism was about to strike somewhere, "is so much better than the average man that it's an
insult to the dog to compare them. The dog's really decent.
He has no sloppy vices. You set a plate of food before a reg-
ularly-fed, blooded dog, and he won't think of gorging himself sick or silly. He eats what he needs, and then stops.
So does a cat" (which is of course by no means true, but
still——). "A dog doesn't get a red nose from drinking too
much." By now all eyes were turning in the direction of
Blake, whose nose was faintly tinged. "He doesn't get gon-
orrhea or syphilis." The united glances veered in the direction
of three or four young scapegraces of wealth, all of whom
were suspected of these diseases. "He doesn't hang around
hotel bars and swill and get his tongue thick and talk about
how rich he is or how old his family is." (This augured that
Blake did such things, which I doubt, but once more all eyes
were shifted to him.) "He doesn't break his word. Within the
limits of his poor little brain he's faithful. He does what he
thinks he's called upon to do.

"But you take a man—more especially a gentleman—one
of these fellows who is always very pointed in emphasizing
that he is a gentleman" (which Blake never did). "Let him
inherit eight or ten millions, give him a college education, let
him be socially well connected, and what does he do? Not a
damned thing if he can help it except contract vices—run
from one saloon to another, one gambling house to another,
one girl to another, one meal to another. He doesn't need to

know anything necessarily. He may be the lowest dog physically and in every other way, and still he's a gentleman—because he has money, wears spats and a high hat. Why, I've seen fifty poor boob prize fighters in my time who could put it all over most of the so-called gentlemen I have ever seen. They kept their word. They tried to be physically fit. They tried to stand up in the world and earn their own living and be somebody." (He was probably thinking of himself.) "But a gentleman wants to boast of his past and his family, to tell you that he must go to the city on business—his lawyers or some directors want to see him. Then he swills around at hotel bars, stays with some of his lady whores, and then comes back here and expects me to pull him into shape again, to make his nose a little less red. He thinks he can use my place to fall back on when he can't go any longer, to fix him up to do some more swilling later on.

"Well, I want to serve notice on all so-called gentlemen here, and *one gentleman* in particular" (and he heavily and sardonically emphasized the words), "that it won't do. This isn't a hospital attached to a whorehouse or a saloon. And as for the trashy little six hundred paid here, I don't need it. I've turned away more men who have been here once or twice and have shown me that they were just using this place and me as something to help them go on with their lousy drinking and carousing, than would fill this building. Sensible men know it. They don't try to use me. It's only the wastrels, or their mothers or fathers who bring their boys and husbands and cry, who try to use me, and I take 'em once or twice, but not oftener. When a man goes out of here cured, I know he is cured. I never want to see him again. I want him to go out in the world and stand up. I don't want him to come back here in six months sniveling to be put in shape again. He disgusts me. He makes me sick. I feel like ordering him off the place, and I do, and that's the end of him. Let him go and bamboozle somebody else. I've shown him all I know. There's no mystery. He can do as much for himself, once he's been here, as I can. If he won't, well and good. And I'm saying one thing more: There's one man here to whom this particularly applies today. This is his last call. He's been here twice. When he goes out this time he can't come back. Now see if some of you can remember some of the things I've been telling you."

He subsided and opened his little pint of wine.

Another day while I was there he began as follows:

"If there's one class of men that needs to be improved in this country, it's lawyers. I don't know why it is, but there's something in the very nature of the work of a lawyer which appears to make him cynical and to want to wear a know-it-all look. Most lawyers are little more than sharper crooks than the crooks they have to deal with. They're always trying to get in on some case or other where they have to outwit the law, save some one from getting what he justly deserves, and then they are supposed to be honest and high-minded! Think of it! To judge by some of the specimens I get up here," and then some lawyer in the place would turn a shrewd inquiring glance in his direction or steadfastly gaze at his plate or out the window, while the others stared at him, "you would think they were the salt of the earth or that they were following a really noble profession or that they were above or better than other men in their abilities. Well, if being conniving and tricky are fine traits, I suppose they are, but personally I can't see it. Generally speaking, they're physically the poorest fish I get here. They're slow and meditative and sallow, mostly because they get too little exercise, I presume. And they're never direct and enthusiastic in an argument. A lawyer always wants to stick in an 'if' or a 'but,' to get around you in some way. He's never willing to answer you quickly or directly. I've watched 'em now for nearly fifteen years, and they're all more or less alike. They think they're very individual and different, but they're not. Most of them don't know nearly as much about life as a good, all-around business or society man," this in the absence of any desire to discuss these two breeds for the time being. "For the life of me I could never see why a really attractive woman would ever want to marry a law-yer"—and so he would talk on, revealing one little unsatisfactory trait after another in connection with the tribe, sandpapering their raw places as it were, until you would about conclude, supposing you had never heard him talk concerning any other profession, that lawyers were the most ignoble, the pettiest, the most inefficient physically and mentally, of all the men he had ever encountered; and in his noble savage state there would not be one to disagree with him, for he had such an animal, tiger-like mien that you had the feeling that instead of an argument you would get a physical rip which would leave you bleeding for days.

The next day, or a day or two or four or six later—according to his mood—it would be doctors or merchants or society men or politicians he would discourse about—and, kind heaven, what a drubbing they would get! He seemed always to be meditating on the vulnerable points of his victims, anxious (and yet presumably not) to show them what poor, fallible, shabby, petty and all but drooling creatures they were. Thus in regard to merchants:

"The average man who has a little business of some kind, a factory or a wholesale or brokerage house or a hotel or a restaurant, usually has a distinctly middle-class mind." At this all the merchants and manufacturers were likely to give a very sharp ear. "As a rule, you'll find that they know just the one little line with which they're connected, and nothing more. One man knows all about cloaks and suits" (this may have been a slap at poor Itzky) "or he knows a little something about leather goods or shoes or lamps or furniture, and that's all he knows. If he's an American he'll buckle down to that little business and work night and day, sweat blood and make every one else connected with him sweat it, underpay his employees, swindle his friends, half-starve himself and his family, in order to get a few thousand dollars and seem as good as some one else who has a few thousand. And yet he doesn't want to be different from—he wants to be just like—the other fellow. If some one in his line has a house up on the Hudson or on Riverside Drive, when he gets his money he wants to go there and live. If the fellow in his line, or some other that he knows something about, belongs to a certain club, he has to belong to it even if the club doesn't want him or he wouldn't look well in it. He wants to have the same tailor, the same grocer, smoke the same brand of cigars and go to the same summer resort as the other fellow. They even want to look alike. God! And then when they're just like every one else, they think they're somebody. They haven't a single idea outside their line, and

yet because they've made money they want to tell other people how to live and think. Imagine a rich butcher or cloak-
maker, or any one else, presuming to tell me how to think
or live!"

He stared about him as though he saw many exemplifica-
tions of his picture present. And it was always interesting to
see how those whom his description really did fit look as
though he could not possibly be referring to them.

Of all types or professions that came here, I think he disliked doctors most. The reason was of course that the work
they did or were about to do in the world bordered on that
which he was trying to accomplish, and the chances were that
they sniffed at or at least critically examined what he was
doing with an eye to finding its weak spots. In many cases no
doubt he fancied that they were there to study and copy his
methods and ideas, without having the decency later on to
attribute their knowledge to him. It was short shrift for any
one of them with ideas or "notions" unfriendly to him advanced in his presence. For a little while during my stay there
was a smooth-faced, rather solid physically and decidedly self-
opinionated mentally, doctor who ate at the same small table
as I and who was never tired of airing his views, medical and
otherwise. He confided to me rather loftily that there was, to
be sure, something to Culhane's views and methods but that
they were "over-emphasized here, over-emphasized." Still,
one could over-emphasize the value of drugs too. As for himself he had decided to achieve a happy medium if possible,
and for this reason (for one) he had come here to study
Culhane.

As for Culhane, in spite of the young doctor's condescension and understanding, or perhaps better yet because of it,
he thoroughly disliked, barely tolerated, him, and was never
tired of commenting on little dancing medics with their "pill
cases" and easily acquired book knowledge, boasting of their
supposed learning " which somebody else had paid for," as he
once said—their fathers, of course. And when they were sick,
some of them at least, they had to come out here to him, or
they came to steal his theory and start a shabby grafting sanitarium of their own. He knew them.

One noon we were at lunch. Occasionally before seating himself at his small central table he would walk or glance about and, having good eyes, would spy some little defect or delinquency somewhere and of course immediately act upon it. One of the rules of the repair shop was that you were to eat what was put before you, especially when it differed from what your table companion received. Thus a fat man at a table with a lean one might receive a small portion of lean meat, no potatoes and no bread or one little roll, whereas his lean acquaintance opposite would be receiving a large portion of fat meat, a baked or boiled potato, plenty of bread and butter, and possibly a side dish of some kind. Now it might well be, as indeed was often the case, that each would be dissatisfied with his apportionment and would attempt to change plates.

But this was the one thing that Culhane would not endure. So upon one occasion, passing near the table at which sat myself and the above-mentioned doctor, table-mates for the time being, he noticed that he was not eating his carrots, a dish which had been especially prepared for him, I imagine— for if one unconsciously ignored certain things the first day or two of his stay, those very things would be all but rammed down his throat during the remainder of his stay; a thing concerning which one guest and another occasionally cautioned newcomers. However this may have been in this particular case, he noticed the uneaten carrots and, pausing a moment, observed:

"What's the matter? Aren't you eating your carrots?" We had almost finished eating.

"Who, me?" replied the medic, looking up. "Oh, no, I never eat carrots, you know. I don't like them."

"Oh, don't you?" said Culhane sweetly. "You don't like them, and so you don't eat them! Well, suppose you eat them here. They may do you a little good just as a change."

"But I never eat carrots," retorted the medic tersely and with a slight show of resentment or opposition, scenting perhaps a new order.

"No, not outside perhaps, but here you do. You eat carrots here, see?"

"Yes, but why should I eat them if I don't like them? They don't agree with me. Must I eat something that doesn't agree with me just because it's a rule or to please you?"

"To please me, or the carrots, or any damned thing you please—but eat 'em."

The doctor subsided. For a day or two he went about commenting on what a farce the whole thing was, how ridiculous to make any one eat what was not suited to him, but just the same while he was there he ate them.

As for myself, I was very fond of large boiled potatoes and substantial orders of fat and lean meat, and in consequence, having been so foolish as to show this preference, I received but the weakest, most contemptible and puling little spuds and pale orders of meat—with, it is true, plenty of other "side dishes"; whereas a later table-mate of mine, a distressed and neurasthenic society man, was receiving—I soon learned he especially abhorred them—potatoes as big as my two fists.

"Now look at that! Now look at that!" he often said peevishly and with a kind of sickly whine in his voice when he saw one being put before him. "He knows I don't like potatoes, and see what I get! And look at the little bit of a thing he gives you! It's a shame, the way he nags people, especially over this food question. I don't think there's a thing to it. I don't think eating a big potato does me a bit of good, or you the little one, and yet I have to eat the blank-blank things or get out. And I need to get on my feet just now."

"Well, cheer up," I said sympathetically and with an eye on the large potato perhaps. "He isn't always looking, and we can fix it. You mash up your big potato and put butter and salt on it, and I'll do the same with my little one. Then when he's not looking we'll shift."

"Oh, that's all right," he commented, "but we'd better look out. If he sees us he'll be as sore as the devil."

This system worked well enough for a time, and for days I was getting all the potato I wanted and congratulating myself on my skill, when one day as I was slyly forking potatoes out of his dish, moved helpfully in my direction, I saw Culhane approaching and feared that our trick had been discovered. It had. Perhaps some snaky waitress has told on us, or he had seen us, even from his table.

"Now I know what's going on here at this table," he growled savagely, "and I want you two to cut it out. This big boob here" (he was referring to my esteemed self) "who hasn't strength of will or character enough to keep himself in good health and has to be brought up here by his brother, hasn't brains enough to see that when I plan a thing for his benefit it is for his beneift, and not mine. Like most of the other damned fools that come up here and waste their money and my time, he thinks I'm playing some cute game with him—tag or something that will let him show how much cuter he is than I am. And he's supposed to be a writer and have a little horse-sense! His brother claims it, anyhow. And as for this other simp here," and now he was addressing the assembled diners while nodding toward my friend, "it hasn't been three weeks since he was begging to know what I could do for him. And now look at him—entering into a petty little game of potato-cheating!

"I swear," he went on savagely, talking to the room in general, "sometimes I don't know what to do with such damned fools. The right thing would be to set these two, and about fifty others in this place, out on the main road with their trunks and let them go to hell. They don't deserve the attention of a conscientious man. I prohibit gambling—what happens? A lot of nincompoops and mental lightweights with more money than brains sneak off into a field of an afternoon on the excuse that they are going for a walk, and then sit down and lose or win a bucket of money just to show off what hells of fellows they are, what sports, what big 'I ams.' I prohibit cigarette-smoking, not because I think it's literally going to kill anybody but because I think it looks bad here, sets a bad example to a lot of young wasters who come here and who ought to be broken of the vice, and besides, because I don't like cigarette-smoking here—don't want it and won't have it. What happens? A lot of sissies and mamma's boys and pet heirs, whose fathers haven't got enough brains to cut 'em off and make 'em get out and work, come up here, sneak in cigarettes or get the servants to, and then hide out behind the barn or a tree down in the lot and sneak and smoke like a lot of cheap schoolboys. God, it makes me sick! What's the use of a man working out a fact during a lifetime and letting other people have the benefit of it—not because he needs their money, but that they need his help—if all the time he is going to have such cattle to deal with? Not one out of twenty or forty men that come here really wants me to help him or to help himself. What he wants is to have some one drive him in the way he ought to go, kick him into it, instead of his buckling down and helping himself. What's the good of bothering with such damned fools? A man ought to take the whole pack and run 'em off the place with a dog-whip." He waved his hand in the air. "It's sickening. It's impossible.

"As for you two," he added, turning to us, but suddenly stopped. "Hell, what's the use! Why should I bother with you? Do as you damned well please, and stay sick or die!"

He turned on his heel and walked out of the dining-room, leaving us to sit there. I was so dumbfounded by the harangue our pseudo-cleverness had released that I could scarcely speak. My appetite was gone and I felt wretched. To think of having been the cause of this unnecessary tongue-lashing to the others! And I felt that we were, and justly, the target for their rather censorious eyes.

"My God!" moaned my companion most dolefully. "That's always the way with me. Nothing that I ever do comes out right. All my life I've been unlucky. My mother died when I was seven, and my father's never had any use for me. I started in three or four businesses four or five years ago, but none of them ever came out right. My yacht burned last summer, and I've had neurasthenia for two years." He catalogued a list of ills that would have done honor to Job himself, and he was worth nine millions, so I heard!

Two or three additional and amusing incidents, and I am done.

One of the most outré things in connection with our rides about the countryside was Culhane's attitude toward life and the natives and passing strangers as representing life. Thus one day, as I recall very well, we were riding along a back-woods country road, very shadowy and branch-covered, a great company of us four abreast, when suddenly and after his very military fashion there came a "Halt! Right by fours! Right dress! Face!" and presently we were all lined up in a row facing a greensward which had suddenly been revealed to the left and on which, and before a small plumber's stove standing outside some gentleman's stable, was stretched a plumber and his helper. The former, a man of perhaps thirty-five, the latter a lad of, say, fourteen or fifteen, were both very grimy and dirty, but taking their ease in the morning sun, a little pot of lead on the stove being waited for, I presume, that it might boil.

Culhane, leaving his place at the head of the column, returned to the center nearest the plumber and his helper and pointing at them and addressing us in a very clear voice, said:

"There you have it. There's American labor for you, at its best—union labor, the poor, downtrodden workingman. Look at him." We all looked. "This poor hard-working plumber here," and at that the latter stirred and sat up, scarcely even now grasping what it was all about, so suddenly had we descended upon him, "earns or demands sixty cents an hour, and this poor sweating little helper here has to have forty. They're working now. They're waiting for that little bit of lead to boil, at a dollar an hour between them. They can't do a thing, either of 'em, until it does, and lead has to be well done, you know, before it can be used.

"Well, now, these two here," he continued, suddenly shifting his tone from one of light sarcasm to a kind of savage contempt, "imagine they are getting along, making life a lot better for themselves, when they lie about this way and swindle another man out of his honest due in connection with the work he is paying for. He can't help himself. He can't know everything. If he did he'd probably find what's wrong in there and fix it himself in three minutes. But if he did that and the union heard of it they'd boycott him. They'd come around and blackmail him, blow up his barn, or make him pay for the work he did himself. I know 'em. I have to deal with 'em. They fix my pipes in the same way that these two are fixing his—lying on the grass at a dollar an hour. And they want five dollars a pound for every bit of lead they use. If they forget anything and have to go back to town for it, you pay

for it, at a dollar an hour. They get on the job at nine and
quit at four, in the country. If you say anything, they quit
altogether—they're *union* laborers—and they won't let any
one else do it, either. Once they're on the job they have to
rest every few minutes, like these two. Something has to boil,
or they have to wait for something. Isn't it wonderful! Isn't
it beautiful! And all of us of course are made free and equal!
They're just as good as we are! If you work and make money
and have any plumbing to do you have to support 'em—
Right by fours! Guide right! Forward!" and off we trotted,
breaking into a headlong gallop a little farther on as if he
wished to outrun the mood which was holding him at the
moment.

The plumber and his assistant, fully awake now to the import of what had occurred, stared after us. The journeyman
plumber, who was short and fat, sat and blinked. At last he
recovered his wits sufficiently to cry, "Aw, go to hell, you
____ ____ ____!" but by that time we were well along the
road and I am not sure that Culhane even heard.

Another day as we were riding along a road which led into
a nearby city of, say, twenty thousand, we encountered a beer
truck of great size and on its seat so large and ruddy and
obese a German as one might go a long way and still not see.
It was very hot. The German was drowsy and taking his time
in the matter of driving. As we drew near, Culhane suddenly
called a halt and, lining us up as was his rule, called to the
horses of the brewery wagon, who also obeyed his lusty
"Whoa!" The driver, from his high perch above, stared down
on us with mingled curiosity and wonder.

"Now, here's an illustration of what I mean," Culhane began, apropos of nothing at all, " when I say that the word
man ought to be modified or changed in some way so that
when we use it we would mean something more definite than
we mean now. That thing you see sitting up on that wagon-
seat there—call that a man? And then call me one? Or a man
like Charles A. Dana? Or a man like General Grant? Hell!
Look at him! Look at his shape! Look at that stomach! You
think a thing like that—call it a man if you want to—has any
brains or that he's really any better than a pig in a sty? If you
turn a horse out to shift for himself he'll eat just enough to

keep in condition; same way with a dog, a cat or a bird. But let one of these things, that some people call a *man*, come along, give him a job and enough money or a chance to stuff himself, and see what happens. A thing like that connects himself with one end of a beer hose and then he thinks he's all right. He gets enough guts to start a sausage factory, and then he blows up, I suppose, or rots. Think of it! And we call him a man—or some do!"

During this amazing and wholly unexpected harangue (I never saw him stop any one before), the heavy driver, who did not understand English very well, first gazed and then strained with his eyebrows, not being able quite to make out what it was all about. From the chuckling and laughter that finally set up in one place and another he began dimly to comprehend that he was being made fun of, used as an unsatisfactory jest of some kind. Finally his face clouded for a storm and his eyes blazed, the while his fat red cheeks grew redder. *"Donnervetter!"* he began gutturally to roar. *"Schweine hunde! Hunds knoche! Nach der polizei soll man reufen!"*

I for one pulled my horse cautiously back, as he cracked a great whip, and, charging savagely through us, drove on. Culhane, having made his unkind comments, gave orders for our orderly formation once more and calmly led us away.

Perhaps the most amusing phase of him was his opposition to and contempt for inefficiency of any kind. If he asked you to do anything, no matter what, and you didn't at once leap to the task ready and willing and able so to do, he scarcely had words enough with which to express himself. On one occasion, as I recall all too well, he took us for a drive in his tally-ho—one or two or three that he possessed—a great lumbering, highly lacquered, yellow-wheeled vehicle, to which he attached seven or eight or nine horses, I forget which. This tally-ho ride was a regular Sunday morning or afternoon affair unless it was raining, a call suddenly sounding from about the grounds somewhere at eleven or at two in the afternoon, "Tally-ho at eleven-thirty" (or two-thirty, as the case might be). "All aboard!" Gathering all the reins in his hands and perching himself in the high seat above, with perhaps one of his guests beside him, all the rest crowded willy-nilly on the seats within and on top, he would carry us off, careening about the countryside most madly, several of his hostlers acting as liveried footmen or outriders and one of them perched up behind on the little seat, the technical name of which I have forgotten, waving and blowing the long silver trumpet, the regulation blasts on which had to be exactly as made and provided for such occasions. Often, having been given no warning as to just when it was to be, there would be a mad scramble to get into our *de rigueur* Sunday clothes, for Culhane would not endure any flaws in our appearance, and if we were not ready and waiting when one of his stablemen swung the vehicle up to the door at the appointed time he was absolutely furious.

On the particular occasion I have in mind we all clambered on in good time, all spick and span and in our very best, shaved, powdered, hands appropriately gloved, our whiskers curled and parted, our shoes shined, our hats brushed; and up in front was Culhane, gentleman de luxe for the occasion, his long-tailed whip looped exactly as it should be, no doubt, ready to be flicked out over the farthest horse's head, and up behind was the trumpeter—high hat, yellow-topped boots, a uniform of some grand color, I forget which.

But, as it turned out on this occasion, there had been a hitch at the last minute. The regular hostler or stableman who acted as footman extraordinary and trumpeter plenipotentiary, the one who could truly and ably blow this magnificent horn, was sick or his mother was dead. At any rate, there he wasn't. And in order not to irritate Culhane, a second hostler had been dressed and given his seat and horn—only he couldn't blow it. As we began to clamber in I heard him asking, "Can any of you gentleman blow the trumpet? Do any of you gentleman know the regular trumpet call?"

No one responded, although there was much discussion in a low key. Some could, or thought they could, but hesitated to assume so frightful a risk. At the same time Culhane, hearing the fuss and knowing perhaps that his substitute could not trumpet, turned grimly around and said, "Say, do you mean to say there isn't any one back there who knows how to blow that thing? What's the matter with you, Caswell?" he called to one, and getting only mumbled explanations from that quarter, called to another, "How about you, Drewberry? Or you, Crashaw?"

All three apologized briskly. They were terrified by the mere thought of trying. Indeed no one seemed eager to assume the responsibility, until finally he became so threatening and assured us so volubly that unless some immediate and cheerful response were made he would never again waste one blank minute on a lot of blank-blank this and thats, that one youth, a rash young society somebody from Rochester, volunteered more or less feebly that he "thought" that "maybe he could manage it." He took a seat directly under the pompously placed trumpeter, and we were off.

"Heigh-ho!" Out the gate and down the road and up a nearby slope at a smart clip, all of us gazing cheerfully and possibly vainly about, for it was a bright day and a gay country. Now the trumpeter, as is provided for on all such occasions, lifted the trumpet to his lips and began on the grandiose "ta-ra-ta-ta," but to our grief and pain, although he got through fairly successfully on his first attempt, there was one place where there was a slight hitch, a "false crack," as some one rowdyishly remarked. Culhane, although tucking up his lines and stiffening his back irritably at this flaw, said nothing. For after all a poor trumpeter was better than none at all. A little later, however, the trumpeter having hesitated to begin again, he called back, "Well, what about the horn? What about the horn? Can't you do something with it? Have you quit for the day?"

Up went the horn once more, and a most noble and encouraging "Ta-ra-ta-ta" was begun, but just at the critical point, and when we were all most prayerfully hoping against hope, as it were, that this time he would round the dangerous curves of it gracefully and come to a grand finish, there was a most disconcerting and disheartening squeak. It was pathetic, ghastly. As one man we wilted. What would Culhane say to that? We were not long in doubt. "Great Christ!" he shouted, looking back and showing a countenance so black that it was positively terrifying. "Who did that? Throw him off! What do you think—that I want the whole country to know I'm airing a lot of lunatics? Somebody who can blow that thing, take it and blow it, for God's sake! I'm not going to drive around here without a trumpeter!"

For a few moments there was more or less painful gabbling in all the rows, pathetic whisperings and "go ons" or eager urgings of one and another to sacrifice himself upon the altar of necessity, insistences by the ex-trumpeter that he had blown trumpets in his day as good as any one—what the deuce had got into him anyhow? It must be the horn!

"Well," shouted Culhane finally, as a stop-gap to all this, "isn't any one going to blow that thing? Do you mean to tell me that I'm hauling all of you around, with not a man among you able to blow a dinky little horn? What's the use of my keeping a lot of fancy vehicles in my barn when all I have to deal with is a lot of shoe salesmen and floorwalkers? Hell! Any child can blow it. It's as easy as a fish-horn. If I hadn't these horses to attend to I'd blow it myself. Come on—come on! Kerrigan, what's the matter with you blowing it?"

"The truth is, Mr. Culhane," explained Mr. Kerrigan, the very dapper and polite heir of a Philadelphia starch million-aire, "I haven't had any chance to practice with one of those for several years. I'll try it if you want me to, but I can't guarantee——"

"Try!" insisted Culhane violently. "You can't do any worse than that other mutt, if you blow for a million years. Blow it! Blow it!"

Mr. Kerrigan turned back and being very cheerfully ten-dered the horn by the last failure, wetted and adjusted his lips, lifted it upward and backward—and——

It was pathetic. It was positively dreadful, the wheezing, grinding sounds that were emitted.

"God!" shouted Culhane, pulling up the coach to a dead stop. "Stop that! Whoa! Whoa!!! Do you mean to say that that's the best you can do? Well, this finishes me! Whoa! What kind of a bunch of cattle have I got up here, anyhow? Whoa! And out in this country too where I'm known and where they know all about such things! God! Whoa! Here I spend thousands of dollars to get together an equipment that will make a pleasant afternoon for a crowd of gentlemen, and this is what I draw—hams! A lot of barflies who never saw a tally-ho! Well, I'm done! I'm through! I'll split the damned thing up for firewood before I ever take it out again! Get down! Get out, all of you! I'll not haul one of you back a step! Walk back or anywhere you please—to hell, for all I care! I'm through! Get out! I'm going to turn around and get back to the barn as quick as I can—up some alley if I can find one. To think of having such a bunch of hacks to deal with!"

Humbly and wearily we climbed down and, while he drove savagely on to some turning-place, stood about first in small groups, then by twos and threes began making our way—rather gingerly, I must confess, in our fine clothes—along the winding road back to the place on the hill. But such swearing! Such un-Sabbath-like comments! The number of times his sturdy Irish soul was wished into innermost and almost sacrosanct portions of Sheol! He was cursed from more angles and in more artistically and architecturally nobly constructed phrases and even paragraphs than any human being that I have ever heard of before or since, phrases so livid and glistening that they smoked.

Talk about the carved ivories of speech! The mosaics of verbal precious stones!

You should have heard us on our way back!

And still we stayed.

Some two years later I was passing this place in company with some friends, when I asked my host, who also knew of the place, to turn in. During my stay it had been the privilege and custom among those who knew much of this institution to drive through the grounds and past the very doors of the "repair shop," even to stop if Culhane chanced to be visible and talking to or at least greeting him, in some cases. A custom of Culhane's was, in the summer time, to have erected on the lawn a large green-and-white striped marquee tent, a very handsome thing indeed, in which was placed a field-officer's table and several camp chairs, and some books and papers. Here of a hot day, when he was not busy with us, he would sit and read. And when he was in here or somewhere about, a little pennant was run up, possibly as guide to visiting guests or friends. At any rate, it was the presence of this pennant which caused me to know that he was about and to wish that I might have a look at him once more, great lion that he was. As "guests," none of us were ever allowed to come within more than ten feet of it, let alone in it. As passing visitors, however, we might, and many did, stop, remind him that we had once been his humble slaves, and ask leave to congratulate him on his health and sturdy years. At such times, if the visitors looked interesting enough, or he remembered them well, he would deign to come to the tent-fly and, standing there à la Napoleon at Lodi or Grant in the Wilderness, be for the first time in his relations with them a bit civil.

Anyway, on this occasion, urged on by curiosity to see my liege once more and also to learn whether he would remember me at all, I had my present host roll his car up to the tent door, where Culhane was reading. Feeling that by this venturesome deed I had "let myself in for it" and had to "make a showing," I climbed briskly out and, approaching, recalled myself to him. With a semi-wry expression, half smile, half contemptuous curl of the corners of his mouth, he recalled me and took my extended hand; then seeing that possibly my friends if not myself looked interesting, he arose and came to the door. I introduced them—one a naval officer of distinction, the other the owner of a great estate some miles farther on. For the first time in my relations with him I had an opportunity to note how grandly gracious he could be. He accepted my friends' congratulations as to the view with a princely nod and suggested that on other days it was even better. He was soon to be busy now or he would have some one show my friends through the shop. Some Saturday afternoon, if they would telephone or stop in passing, he would oblige.

I noted at once that he had not aged in the least. He was sixty-two or -three now and as vigorous and trim as ever. And now he treated me as courteously and formally as though he had never browbeaten me in the least. "Good heavens," I said, "how much better to be a visitor than a guest!" After a moment or two we offered many thanks and sped on, but not without many a backward glance on my part, for the place fascinated me. That simply furnished institution! That severe regimen! This latter-day Stoic and Spartan in his tent! And, above all things, and the most astounding to me, so little could one know him, the book he had been reading and which he had laid upon his little table as I entered—I could not help noting the title for he laid it back up, open face down—was Lecky's "History of European Morals"!

Now!

Well!

IN RETROSPECT

Two years after this visit, in a serious attempt to set down what I really did think of him, I arranged the following thoughts with which I closed my sketch then and which I now append for what they may be worth. They represented my best thought concerning him then:

"Thomas Culhane belongs to that class of society which the preachers and the world's army of conventional merchants, lawyers, judges and reputable citizens generally are presumably, if one may judge by the moral and religious literature of the day, trying to reach and reform. Yet here at his sanitarium are gathered representatives of those same orders, the so-called better element. And here we see them suddenly dominated, mind and soul, by this being whom they, theoretically at least, look upon as a brand to be snatched from the burning.

"As the Church and society view Culhane, so they view all life outside their own immediate circles. Culhane is in fact a conspicuous figure among the semi-taboo. He has been referred to in many an argument and platform and pulpit and in the press as a type of man whose influence is supposed to be vitiating. Now a minister enters the sanitarium, broken down by his habits of life, and this same Culhane is able to penetrate him, to see that his dogmatic and dictatorial mental habits are the cause of his ailment, and he has the moral courage to shock him, to drag him by apparently brutal processes out of his rut. He reads the man accurately, he knows him better than he knows himself, and he effects a cure.

"This astonishing condition is certainly a new light for those seeking to labor among men. Those who are successful gamblers, pugilists, pickpockets, saloon-keepers, book-

makers, jockeys and the like are so by reason of their intelligence, their innate mental acumen and perception. It is a
fact that in the sporting world and among the unconven-
tional men-about-town you will often find as good if not
better judges of human nature than elsewhere. Contact with
a rough and ready and all-too-revealing world teaches them
much. The world's customary pretensions and delusions are
in the main ripped away. They are bruised by rough facts.
Often the men gathered in some such café and whom
preachers and moralists are most ready to condemn have a
clearer perception of preachers, church organizations and reformers and their relative importance in the multitudinous
life of the world than the preachers, church congregations
and reformers have of those in the café or the world outside
to which they belong.

"This is why, in my humble judgment, the Church and
those associated with its aims make no more progress than
they do. While they are consciously eager to better the world,
they are so wrapped up in themselves and their theories, so
hampered by their arbitrary and limited conceptions of good
and evil, that the great majority of men move about them
unseen, except in a far-away and superficial manner. Men are
not influenced at arm's length. It would be interesting to
know if some day a preacher or judge, who, offended by Mr.
Culhane's profanity and brutality, will be able to reach the
gladiator and convert him to his views as readily as the gladiator is able to rid him of his ailment."

In justice to the preachers, moralists, et cetera, I should
now like to add that it is probably not any of the virtues or
perfections represented by a man like Culhane with which
they are quarreling, but the vices of many who are in no wise
like him and do not stand for the things he stands for. At the
same time, the so-called "sports" might well reply that it is
not with any of the really admirable qualities of the "unco
guid" that they quarrel, but their too narrow interpretations
of virtue and duty and their groundless generalization as to
types and classes.

Be it so.

Here is meat for a thousand controversies.

A True Patriarch

IN THE STREETS of a certain moderate-sized county seat in Missouri not many years ago might have been seen a true patriarch. Tall, white-haired, stout in body and mind, he roamed among his neighbors, dispensing sympathy and a curiously genial human interest through the leisure of his day. One might have taken him to be Walt Whitman, of whom he was the living counterpart; or, in the clear eye, high forehead and thick, appealing white hair, have seen a marked similarity to Bryant as he appeared in his later years. Already at this time he had seen man's allotted term on earth, and yet he was still strong in the councils of his people and rich in the accumulated interests of a lifetime.

At the particular time in question he was most interesting for the eccentricities which years of stalwart independence had developed, but these were lovable peculiarities and only severed from remarkable actions by the compelling power of time and his increasing infirmities. The loud, though pleasant, voice, and strong, often fiery, declamatory manner, were remnants of the days when his fellow-citizens were wholly swayed by the magnificence of his orations. Charmingly simple in manner, he still represented with it that old courtesy which made every stranger his guest. When moved by righteous indignation, there cropped out the daring and domineering insistence of one who had always followed what he considered to be the right, and who knew its power.

Even then, old as he was, if there were any topic worthy of discussion, and his fellow-citizens were in danger of going wrong, he became an haranguing prophet, as it were, a local Isaiah or Jeremiah. Every gate heard him, for he stopped on his rounds in front of each, and calling out the inhabitant poured forth such a volume of fact and argument as tended to remove all doubt of what he, at least, considered right. All of this he invariably accompanied by a magnificence of gesture worthy of a great orator.

At such times his mind, apparently, was almost wholly engrossed with these matters, and I have it from one of his daughters, who, besides being his daughter, was a sincere admirer of his, that often he might have been seen coming down his private lawn, and even the public streets when there was no one near to hear him, shaking his head, gesticulating, sometimes sweeping upward with his arms, as if addressing his fellow-citizens in assemblage.

"He used to push his big hat well back upon his forehead," she said on one occasion, "and often in winter, forgetful of the bitter cold, would take off his overcoat and carry it on his arm. Occasionally he would stop quite still, as if he were addressing a companion, and with sweeping gestures illustrate some idea or other, although, of course, there was no one present. Then, planting his big cane forcibly with each step, as though still emphasizing his recently stated ideas, he would come forward and enter the house."

The same suggestion of mental concentration might have been seen in everything that he did, and I personally have seen him leading a pet Jersey cow home for milking with the same dignity of bearing and forcefulness of manner that characterized him when he stood before his fellow-citizens at a public meeting addressing them on some important topic. He never appeared to have a sense of difference from or superiority over his fellowmen, but only the keenest sympathy with all things human. Every man was his brother, every human being honest. A cow or a horse was as much to be treated with sympathy and charity as a man or a woman. If a purse was lost, forty-nine out of every fifty men would return it without thought of reward, if you were to believe him.

In the little town where he had lived so many years, and where he finally died, he knew every living creature from cattle upwards, and could call each by name. The sick, the poor, the widows, the orphans, the insane, and dependents of all kinds, were his especial care. Every Sunday afternoon for years, it was his custom to go the rounds of the indigent, frequently carrying a basket of his good wife's dinner. This he distributed, along with consolation and advice. Occasionally he would return home of a winter's day very much engrossed with the discovery of some condition of distress hitherto unseen.

"Mother," he would say to his wife in that same oratorical manner previously noted, as he entered the house, "I've found such a poor family. They have moved into the old saloon below Solmson's. You know how open that is." This was delivered in the most dramatic style after he had indicated something important by throwing his overcoat on the bed and standing his cane in the corner. "There's a man and several children there. The mother is dead. They were on their way to Kansas, but it got so cold they've had to stop here until the winter is broken. They're without food; almost no clothing. Can't we find something for them?"

"On these occasions," said his daughter to me once, "he would, as he nearly always did, talk to himself on the way, as if he were discussing politics. But you could never tell what he was coming for."

Then with his own labor he would help his wife seek out the odds and ends that could be spared, and so armed, would return, arguing by the way as if an errand of mercy were the last thing he contemplated. Nearly always the subject of these orations was some public wrong or error which should receive, although in all likelihood it did not, immediate attention.

Always of a reverent, although not exactly religious, turn of mind, he took considerable interest in religious ministration, though he steadily and persistently refused, in his later years, to go to church. He had St. James's formula to quote in self-defense, which insists that "Pure religion and undefiled before our God and Father is this, To visit the fatherless and widows in their affliction, and to keep himself unspotted from the world." Often, when pressed too close, he would deliver this with kindly violence. One of the most touching anecdotes representative of this was related to me by his daughter, who said:

"Mr. Kent, a poor man of our town, was sick for months previous to his death, and my father used to go often, sometimes daily, to visit him. He would spend perhaps a few minutes, perhaps an hour, with him, singing, praying, and ministering to his spiritual wants. The pastor of the church living so far away and coming only once a month, this duty devolved upon some one, and my father did his share, and always felt more than repaid for the time spent by the gratitude shown by the many poor people he aided in this way.

"Mr. Kent's favorite song, for instance, was 'On Jordan's Stormy Banks I Stand.' This he would have my father sing, and his clear voice could often be heard in the latter's small house, and seemed to impart strength to the sick man.

"Upon one occasion, I remember, Mr. Kent expressed a desire to hear a certain song. My father was not very familiar with it but, anxious to grant his request, came home and asked me if I would get a friend of mine and go and sing the song for him.

"We entered the sick-room, he leading us by the hand, for we were children at the time. Mr. Kent's face at once brightened, and father said to him:

" 'Mr. Kent, I told you this morning that I couldn't sing the song you asked for, but these girls know it, and have come to sing it for you.'

"Then, waving his hand gently toward us, he said:

" 'Sing, children.'

"We did so, and when we had finished he knelt and offered a prayer, not for the poor man's recovery but that he might put his trust in the Lord and meet death without fear. I have never been more deeply impressed nor felt more confident in the presence of death, for the man died soon after, soothed into perfect peace."

On another occasion he was sitting with some friends in front of the courthouse in his town, talking and sunning himself, when a neighbor came running up in great excitement, calling:

"Mr. White, Mr. White, come, right quick. Mrs. Sadler wants you."

He explained that the woman in question was dying, and, being afraid she would strangle in her last moments, had asked the bystanders to run for him, her old acquaintance, in the efficacy of whose prayers she had great faith. The old patriarch was without a coat at the time, but, unmindful of that, hastened after.

"Mr. White," exclaimed the sick woman excitedly upon seeing him, "I want you to pray that I won't strangle. I'm not afraid to die, but I don't want to die that way. I want you to offer a prayer for me that I may be saved from that. I'm so afraid."

Seeing by the woman's manner that she was very much overwrought, he used all his art to soothe her.

"Have no fear, Mrs. Sadler, now," he exclaimed solemnly. "You won't strangle. I will ask the Lord for you, and this evil will not come upon you. You need not have any fear."

"Kneel down, you," he commanded, turning upon the assembled neighbors and relatives who had followed or had been there before him, while he pushed back his white hair from his forehead. "Let us now pray that this good woman here be allowed to pass away in peace." And even with the rustle of kneeling that accompanied his words he lifted up his coatless arms and began to pray.

Through his magnificent phraseology, no doubt, as well as his profound faith, he succeeded in inducing a feeling of peace and quiet in all his hearers, the sick woman included, who, listening, sank into a restful stupor, from which all agony of mind had apparently disappeared. Then when the physical atmosphere of the room had been thus reorganized, he ceased and retired to the yard in front of the house, where on a bench under a shade tree he seated himself to wipe his moist brow and recover his composure. In a few moments a slight commotion in the sick-room denoted that the end had come. Several neighbors came out, and one said, "Well, it is all over, Mr. White. She is dead."

"Yes," he replied with great assurance. "She didn't strangle, did she?"

"No," said the other, "the Lord granted her request."

"I knew He would," he replied in his customary loud and confident tone. "Prayer is always answered."

Then, after viewing the dead woman and making additional comments, he was off, as placid as though nothing had occurred.

I happened to hear of this some time after, and one day, while sitting with him on his front porch, said, "Mr. White, do you really believe that the Lord directly answered your prayer in that instance?"

"Answered!" he almost shouted defiantly and yet with a kind of human tenderness that one could never mistake. "Of course He answered! Why wouldn't He—a faithful old servant like that? To be sure, He answered."

"Might it not have been merely the change of atmosphere which your voice and strength introduced? The quality of your own thoughts goes for something in such matters. Mind acts on mind."

"Certainly," he said, in a manner as agreeable as if it had always been a doctrine with him. "I know that. But, after all, what is *that*—my mind, your mind, the sound of voices? It's all the Lord anyhow, whatever you think."

How could one gainsay such a religionist as that?

The poor, the blind, the insane, and sufferers of all sorts, as I have said before, were always objects of his keenest sympathies. Evidence of it flashed out at the most unexpected moments—loud, rough exclamations, which, however, always contained a note so tender and suggestive as to defy translation. Thus, while we were sitting on his front porch one day and hotly discussing politics to while away a dull afternoon, there came down the street, past his home, a queer, ragged, half-demented individual, who gazed about in an aimless sort of way, peering queerly over fences, looking idly down the road, staring strangely overhead into the blue. It was apparent, in a moment, that the man was crazy, some demented creature, harmless enough, however, to be allowed abroad and so save the county the expense of caring for him. The old man broke a sentence short in order to point and shake his head emotionally.

"Look at that," he said to me, with a pathetic sweep of the arm, "now just look at that! There's a poor, demented soul, with no one to look after him. His brother is a hard-working saddler. His sister is dead. No money to speak of, any of them." He paused a moment, and then added, "I don't know what we're to do in such cases. The state and the county don't always do their duty. Most people here are too poor to help, there are so many to be taken care of. It seems almost at times as if you can't do anything but leave them to the mercy of God, and yet you can't do that either, quite," and he once more shook his head sadly.

I was for denouncing the county, but he explained very charitably that it was already very heavily taxed by such cases. He did not seem to know exactly what should be done at the time, but he was very sorry, very, and for the time being the

warm argument in which he had been indulging was completely forgotten. Now he lapsed into silence and all communication was suspended, while he rocked silently in his great
chair and thought.

One day in passing the local poor-farm (and this is of my
own knowledge), he came upon a man beating a poor idiot
with a whip. The latter was incapable of reasoning and therefore of understanding why it was that he was being beaten.
The two were beside a wood-pile and the demented one was
crying. In a moment the old patriarch had jumped out of his
conveyance, leaped over the fence, and confronted the amazed
attendant with an uplifted arm.

"Not another lick!" he fairly shouted. "What do you mean
by striking an idiot?"

"Why," explained the attendant, "I want him to carry in
the wood, and he won't do it."

"It is not his place to bring in the wood. He isn't put here
for that, and in the next place he can't understand what you
mean. He's put here to be taken care of. Don't you dare strike
him again. I'll see about this, and you."

Knowing his interrupter well, his position and power in
the community, the man endeavored to explain that some
work must be done by the inmates, and that this one was
refractory. The only way he had of making him understand
was by whipping him.

"Not another word," the old man blustered, overawing the
county hireling. "You've done a wrong, and you know it. I'll
see to this," and off he bustled to the county courthouse, leaving the transgressor so badly frightened that whips thereafter
were carefully concealed, in this institution at least. The court,
which was held in his home town, was not in session at the
time, and only the clerk was present when he came tramping
down the aisle and stood before the latter with his right hand
uplifted in the position of one about to make oath.

"Swear me," he called solemnly, and without further explanation, as the latter stared at him. "I want you to take this
testimony under oath."

The clerk knew well enough the remarkable characteristics
of his guest, whose actions were only too often inexplicable
from the ground point of policy and convention. Without

ado, after swearing him, he got out ink and paper, and the patriarch began.

"I saw," he said, "in the yard of the county farm of this county, not over an hour ago, a poor helpless idiot, too weak-minded to understand what was required of him, and put in that institution by the people of this county to be cared for, being beaten with a cowhide by Mark Sheffels, who is an attendant there, because the idiot did not understand enough to carry in wood, which the people have hired Mark Sheffels to carry in. Think of it," he added, quite forgetting the nature of his testimony and that he was now speaking for dictation and not for an audience to hear, and going off into a most scorching and brilliant arraignment of the entire system in which such brutality could occur, "a poor helpless idiot, unable to frame in his own disordered mind a single clear sentence, being beaten by a sensible, healthy brute too lazy and trifling to perform the duties for which he was hired and which he personally is supposed to perform."

There was more to the effect, for instance, that the American people and the people of this county should be ashamed to think that such crimes should be permitted and go unpunished, and that this was a fair sample. The clerk, realizing the importance of Mr. White in the community, and the likelihood of his following up his charges very vigorously, quietly followed his address in a very deferential way, jotting down such salient features as he had time to write. When he was through, however, he ventured to lift his voice in protest.

"You know, Mr. White," he said, "Sheffels is a member of our party, and was appointed by us. Of course, now, it's too bad that this thing should have happened, and he ought to be dropped, but if you are going to make a public matter of it in this way it may hurt us in the election next month."

The old patriarch threw back his head and gazed at him in the most blazing way, almost without comprehension, apparently, of so petty a view.

"What!" he exclaimed. "What's that got to do with it? Do you want the Democratic Party to starve the poor and beat the insane?"

The opposition was rather flattened by the reply, and left

the old gentleman to storm out. For once, at least, in this particular instance, anyhow, he had purified the political atmosphere, as if by lightning, and within the month following the offending attendant was dropped.

Politics, however, had long known his influence in a similar way. There was a time when he was the chief political figure in the county, and possessed the gift of oratory, apparently, beyond that of any of his fellow-citizens. Men came miles to hear him, and he took occasion to voice his views on every important issue. It was his custom in those days, for instance, when he had anything of special importance to say, to have printed at his own expense a few placards announcing his coming, which he would then carry to the town selected for his address and personally nail up. When the hour came, a crowd, as I am told, was never wanting. Citizens and farmers of both parties for miles about usually came to hear him.

Personally I never knew how towering his figure had been in the past, or how truly he had been admired, until one day I drifted in upon a lone bachelor who occupied a hut some fifteen miles from the patriarch's home and who was rather noted in the community at the time that I was there for his love of seclusion and indifference to current events. He had not visited the nearest neighboring village in something like five years, and had not been to the moderate-sized county seat in ten. Naturally he treasured memories of his younger days and more varied activity.

"I don't know," he said to me one day, in discussing modern statesmen and political fame in general, "but getting up in politics is a queer game. I can't understand it. Men that you'd think ought to get up don't seem to. It doesn't seem to be real greatness that helps 'em along."

"What makes you say that?" I asked.

"Well, there used to be a man over here at Danville that I always thought would get up, and yet he didn't. He was the finest orator I ever heard."

"Who was he?" I asked.

"Arch White," he said quietly. "He was really a great man. He was a good man. Why, many's the time I've driven fifteen miles to hear him. I used to like to go into Danville just for that reason. He used to be around there, and sometimes he'd talk a little. He could stir a fellow up."

"Oratory alone won't make a statesman," I ventured, more to draw him out than to object.

"Oh, I know," he answered, "but White was a good man. The plainest-spoken fellow I ever heard. He seemed to be able to tell us just what was the matter with us, or at least I thought so. He always seemed a wonderful speaker to me. I've seen as many as two thousand people up at High Hill hollerin' over what he was saying until you could hear them for miles."

"Why didn't he get up, then, do you suppose?" I now asked on my part.

"I dunno," he answered. "Guess he was too honest, maybe. It's sometimes that way in politics, you know. He was a mighty determined man, and one that would talk out in convention, whatever happened. Whenever they got to twisting things too much and doing what wasn't just honest, I suppose he'd kick out. Anyhow, he didn't get up, and I've always wondered at it."

In Danville one might hear other stories wholly bearing out this latter opinion, and always interesting—delightful, really. Thus, a long, enduring political quarrel was once generated by an incident of no great importance, save that it revealed an odd streak in the old patriarch's character and his interpretation of charity and duty.

A certain young man, well known to the people of this county and to the patriarch, came to Danville one day and either drank up or gambled away a certain sum of money intrusted to him by his aunt for disposition in an entirely different manner. When the day was all over, however, he was not too drunk to realize that he was in a rather serious predicament, and so, riding out of town, traveled a little way and then tearing his clothes and marking his skin, returned, complaining that he had been set upon by the wayside, beaten, and finally robbed. His clothes were in a fine state of dilapidation after his efforts, and even his body bore marks which amply seconded his protestation. In the slush and rain of the dark village street he was finally picked up by the county treasurer seemingly in a wretched state, and the latter, knowing the generosity of White and the fact that his door was always open to those in distress, took the young man by the arm and led him to the patriarch's door, where he personally applied for him. The old patriarch, holding a lamp over his head, finally appeared and peered outward into the darkness.

"Yes," he exclaimed, as he always did, eyeing the victim; " what is it you want of me?"

"Mr. White," said the treasurer, "it's me. I've got young Squiers here, who needs your sympathy and aid tonight. He's been beaten and robbed out here on the road while he was on his way to his mother's home."

"Who?" inquired the patriarch, stepping out on the porch and eyeing the newcomer, the while he held the lamp down so as to get a good look. "Billy Squiers!" he exclaimed when he saw who it was. "Mr. Morton, I'll not take this man into my house. I know him. He's a drunkard and a liar. No man has robbed him. This is all a pretense, and I want you to take him away from here. Put him in the hotel. I'll pay his expenses for the night, but he can't come into my home," and he retired, closing the door after him.

The treasurer fell back amazed at this onslaught, but recovered sufficiently to knock at the door once more and declare to his friend that he deemed him no Christian in taking such a stand and that true religion commanded otherwise, even though he suspected the worst. The man was injured and penniless. He even went so far as to quote the parable of the good Samaritan who passed down by way of Jericho and rescued him who had fallen among thieves. The argument had long continued into the night and rain before the old patriarch finally waved them both away.

"Don't you quote Scripture to me," he finally shouted defiantly, still holding the light and flourishing it in an oratorical sweep. "I know my Bible. There's nothing in it requiring me to shield liars and drunkards, not a bit of it," and once more he went in and closed the door.

Nevertheless the youth was housed and fed at his expense and no charge of any kind made against him, although many believed, as did Mr. White, that he was guilty of theft, whereas others of the opposing political camp believed not. However, considerable opposition, based on old Mr. White's lack of humanity in this instance, was generated by this argument, and for years he was taunted with it although he always maintained that he was justified and that the Lord did not require any such service of him.

The crowning quality of nearly all of his mercies, as one may easily see, was their humor. Even he was not unaware, in retrospect, of the figure he made at times, and would smilingly tell, under provocation, of his peculiar attitude on one occasion or another. Partially from himself, from those who saw it, and the judge presiding in the case, was the following characteristic anecdote gathered.

In the same community with him at one time lived a certain man by the name of Moore, who in his day had been an expert tobacco picker, but who later had come by an injury to his hand and so turned cobbler, and a rather helpless, although not hopeless, one at that. Mr. White had known this man from boyhood up, and had been a witness at various times to the many changes in his fortunes, from the time, for instance, when he had earned as much as several dollars a day—good pay in that region—to the hour when he took a cobbler's kit upon his back and began to eke out a bare livelihood for his old age by traveling about the countryside mending shoes. At the time under consideration, this ex-tobacco picker had degenerated into so humble a thing as Uncle Bobby Moore, a poor, half-remembered cobbler, whose earlier state but few knew, and who at this time had only a few charitably inclined friends, with some of whom he spent the more pleasant portion of the year from spring to fall. Thus, it was his custom to begin his annual pilgrimage with a visit of ten days to Mr. White, where he would sit and cobble shoes for all the members of the household. From here he would go to another acquaintance some ten miles farther on, where he could enjoy the early fruit which was then ripening in delicious quantity. Then he would visit a friendly farmer whose home was upon the Missouri River still farther away, where he did his annual fishing, and so on by slow degrees, until at last he would reach a neighborhood rich in cider presses, where he would wind up the fall, and so end his travel for the winter, beginning his peculiar round once more the following spring at the home of Mr. White. Naturally the old patriarch knew him and liked him passing well.

As he grew older, however, Uncle Bobby reached the place where even by this method and his best efforts he could scarcely make enough to sustain him in comfort during the winter season, which was one of nearly six months, free as his food and lodging occasionally were. He was too feeble. Not desiring to put himself upon any friend for more than a short visit, he finally applied to the patriarch.

"I come to you, Mr. White," he said, "because I don't think I can do for myself any longer in the winter season. My hand hurts a good deal and I get tired so easily. I want to know if you'd won't help me to get into the county farm during the winter months, anyhow. In summer I can still look out for myself, I think."

In short, he made it clear that in summer he preferred to be out so that he might visit his friends and still enjoy his declining years.

The old patriarch was visibly moved by this appeal, and seizing him by the arm and leading off toward the courthouse where the judge governing such cases was then sitting he exclaimed, "Come right down here, Uncle Bobby. I'll see what can be done about this. Your old age shouldn't be troubled in this fashion—not after all the efforts you have made to maintain yourself," and bursting in on the court a few moments later, where a trial was holding at the time, he deliberately led his charge down the aisle, disturbing the court proceedings by so doing, and calling as he came:

"Your Honor, I want you to hear this case especially. It's a very important and a very sad case, indeed."

Agape, the spectators paused to listen. The judge, an old and appreciative friend of his, turned a solemn eye upon this latest evidence of eccentricity.

"What is it, Mr. White?" he inquired.

"Your Honor," returned the latter in his most earnest and oratorical manner, "this man here, as you may or may not know, is an old and honorable citizen of this county. He has been here nearly all the days of his life, and every day of that time he has earned an honest living. These people here," he said, gazing about upon the interested spectators, "can witness whether or not he was one of the best tobacco pickers this county ever saw. Mayhew," he interrupted himself to call to a spectator on one of the benches, "you know whether Uncle Bobby always earned an honest living. Speak up. Tell the Court, did he?"

"Yes, Mr. White," said Mayhew quickly, "he did."

"Morrison," he called, turning in another direction, where an aged farmer sat, " what do you know of this man?"

Mr. Morrison was about to reply, when the Court interfered.

"The Court knows, Mr. White, that he is an honest man. Now what would you have it do?"

"Well, your Honor," resumed the speaker, indifferently following his own oratorical bent, the while the company surveyed him, amused and smiling, "this man has always earned an honest living until he injured his hand here in some way a number of years ago, and since then it has been difficult for him to make his way and he has been cobbling for a living. However, he is getting so old now that he can't even earn much at that, except in the spring and summer, and so I brought him here to have him assigned a place in the county infirmary. I want you to make out an order admitting him to that institution, so that I can take it and go with him and see that he is comfortably placed."

"All right, Mr. White," replied the judge, surveying the two figures in mid-aisle, "I so order."

"But, your Honor," he went on, "there's an exception I want made in this case. Mr. Moore has a few friends that he likes to visit in the summer, and who like to have him visit them. I want him to have the privilege of coming out in the summer to see these people and to see me."

"All right, Mr. White," said the judge, "he shall have that privilege. Now, what else?"

Satisfied in these particulars, the aged citizen led his charge away, and then went with him to the infirmary, where he presented the order of the Court and then left him.

Things went very well with his humble client for a certain time, and Uncle Bobby was thought to be well disposed of, when one day he came to his friend again. It appeared that only recently he had been changed about in his quarters at the infirmary and put into a room with a slightly demented individual, whose nocturnal wanderings greatly disturbed his very necessary sleep.

"I want to know if you won't have them put me by myself, Mr. White," he concluded. "I need my sleep. But they say they can't do it without an order."

Once more the old patriarch led his charge before the Court, then sitting, as it happened, and breaking in upon the general proceedings as before, began:

"Your Honor, this man here, Mr. Moore, whom I brought before you some time ago, has been comfortably housed by your order, and he's deeply grateful for it, as he will tell you, and as I can, but he's an old man, your Honor, and, above all things, needs his rest. Now, of late they've been quartering him with a poor, demented sufferer down there who walks a good deal in his sleep, and it wears upon him. I've come here with him to ask you to allow him to have a room by himself, where he will be alone and rest undisturbed."

"Very well, Mr. White," said the Court, "it shall be as you request."

Without replying, the old gentleman turned and led the supplicant away.

Everything went peacefully now for a number of years, until finally Uncle Bobby, having grown so feeble with age that he feared he was soon to die, came to his friend and asked him to promise him one thing.

"What is it?" asked the latter.

By way of replying, the supplicant described an old oak tree which grew in the yard of the Baptist Church some miles from Danville, and said:

"I want you to promise that when I am dead, wherever I happen to be at the time, that you will see that I am buried under that tree." He gave no particular reason save that he had always liked the tree and the view it commanded, but made his request a very secret matter and begged to be assured that Mr. White would come and get his body and carry it to the old oak.

The latter, always a respecter of the peculiarities and crotchets of his friends, promised. After a few years went by, suddenly one day he learned that Uncle Bobby was not only dead but buried, a thing which astonished him greatly. No one locally being supposed to know that he was to have had any special form of burial, the old patriarch at once recalled his promise.

"Where is his body?" he asked.

"Why, they buried it under the old white oak over at Mt. Horeb Church," was the answer.

"What!" he exclaimed, too astonished to think of anything save his lost privilege of mercy, " who told them to bury him there?"

"Why, *he* did," said the friend. "It was his last wish, I believe."

"The confounded villain," he shouted, amusingly enough. "He led me to believe that I was the only one he told. I alone was to have looked after his burial, and now look at him— going and having himself buried without a word. The scoundrel! Would you believe that an old friend like Uncle Bobby would do anything like that? However," he added after a time, "I think I know how it was. He got so old and feeble here of late that he must have lost his mind—otherwise he would never have done anything like that to me."

And with this he was satisfied to rest and let bygones be bygones.

De Maupassant, Junior

H<small>E DAWNED</small> on me in the spring of 1906, a stocky, sturdy, penetrative temperament of not more than twenty-four or -five years of age, steady of eye, rather aloof and yet pervasive and bristling; a devouring type. Without saying much, and seeming to take anything I had to say with a grain of salt, he managed to impress himself on me at once. Frankly, I liked him very much, although I could see at a glance that he was not so very much impressed with me. I was an older man than he by, say, ten years, an editor of an unimportant magazine, newly brought in (which he did not know) to turn it into something better. In order to earn a few dollars he had undertaken to prepare for the previous editor a most ridiculous article, some silly thing about newspaper writing as a career for women. It had been ordered or encouraged, and I felt that it was but just that it should be paid for.

"Why do you waste your time on a thing like that?" I inquired, smiling and trying to criticize and yet encourage him at one and the same time, for I had been annoyed by many similar assignments given out by the old management which could not now be used. "You look to me to have too much force and sense for that. Why not undertake something worth your time?"

"My time, hell!" he bristled, like a fighting sledge-dog, of which by the way he reminded me. "You show me a magazine in this town that would buy anything that I thought worthy of my time! You're like all the rest of them: you talk big, but you really don't want anything very important. You want little things probably, written to a theory or down to 'our policy.' I know. Give me the stuff. You don't have to take it. It was ordered, but I'll throw it in the waste basket."

"Not so fast! Not so fast!" I replied, admiring his courage and moved by his contempt of the editorial and book publishing conditions in America. He was so young and raw and savage in his way, quite animal, and yet how interesting! There was something as fresh and clean about him as a newly plowed field or the virgin prairies. He typified for me all the young unsophisticated strength of my country, but with more "punch" than it usually manifests, in matters intellectual at least. "Now, don't get excited, and don't snarl," I cooed. "I know what you say is true. They don't really want much of what you have to offer. I don't. Working for some one else, as most of us do, for the dear circulation department, it's not possible for us to get very far above crowd needs and tastes. I've been in your position exactly. I am now. Where do you come from?"

He told me—Missouri—and some very few years before from its state university.

"And what is it you want to do?"

"What's that to you?" he replied irritatingly, with an ingrowing and obvious self-conviction of superiority and withdrawing as though he highly resented my question as condescending and intrusive. "You probably wouldn't understand if I told you. Just now I want to write enough magazine stuff to make a living, that's all."

"Dear, dear!" I said, laughing at the slap. "What a bravo we are! Really, you're interesting. But suppose now you and I get down to brass tacks. You want to do something interesting, if you can, and get paid for it. I rather like you, and anyhow you look to me as though you might do the things I want, or some of them. Now, you want to do the least silly thing you can—something better than this. I want the least silly stuff I can get away with in this magazine—genuine color out of the life of New York, if such a thing can be published in an ordinary magazine. Roughly, here's the kind of thing I want," and I outlined to him the probable policy of the magazine under my direction. I had taken an anæmic "white-light" monthly known as *The Broadway* (!) and was attempting to recast it into a national or international metropolitan picture. He thawed slightly.

"Well, maybe with that sort of idea behind it, it might come to something. I don't know. It's *possible* that you may be the one to do it." He emphasized the "possible." "At any rate, it's worth trying. Judging by the snide editors and publications in this town, no one in America wants anything decent." His lip curled. "I have ambitions of my own, but I don't expect to work them out through the magazines of this town; maybe not of this country. I didn't know that any change was under way here."

"Well, it is," I said. "Still, you can't expect much from this either, remember. After all, it seeks to be a popular magazine. We'll see how far we can go with really interesting material. And now if you know of any others like yourself, bring them in here. I need them. I'll pay you for that article, only I'll include it in a better price I'll give you for something else later, see?"

I smiled and he smiled. His was a warmth which was infectious when he chose to yield, but it was always a repressed warmth, cynical, a bit hard; heat chained to a purpose, I thought. He went away and I saw him no more until about a week later when he brought me his first attempt to give me what I wanted.

In the meantime I was busy organizing a staff which should if possible, I decided after seeing him, include him. I could probably use him as a salaried "special" writer, provided he could be trained to write "specials." He looked so intelligent and ambitious that he promised much. Besides, the little article which he had left when he came again, while not well organized or arranged as to its ideas or best points, was exceedingly well written from the point of mere expression.

And the next thing I had given him to attempt was even better. It was, if I recall correctly, a stirring picture of the East Side, intended to appeal to readers elsewhere than in the city, but while in the matter of color and definiteness of expression as well as choice of words it was exceptional, it was lacking in, quite as the first one had been, the arrangement of its best points. This I explained to him, and also made it clear to him that I could show him how if he would let me. He seemed willing enough, quite anxious, although always with an air of reserve, as if he were accommodating himself to me in this much but no more. He grasped the idea of order swiftly, and in a little while, having worked at a table in an outer room, brought me the rearranged material, almost if not quite satisfactory. During a number of weeks and months thereafter, working on one "special" and another in this way with me, he seemed finally to grasp the theory I had, or at least to develop a method of his own which was quite as satisfactory to me, and I was very much pleased. A little later I employed him at a regular salary.

It was pathetic, as I look at it now, the things we were trying to do and the conditions under which we were trying to do them—the raw commercial force and theory which underlay the whole thing, the necessity of explaining and fighting for so much that one should not, as I saw it then, have to argue over at all. We were in new rooms, in a new building, filled with lumber not yet placed and awaiting the completion of partitions which, as some one remarked, "would divide us up." Our publisher and owner was a small, energetic, vibrant and colorful soul, all egotism and middle-class conviction as to the need of "push," ambition, "closeness to life," "punch," and what not else, American to the core, and descending on us, or me rather, hourly as it were, demanding the "hows" and the "whyfors" of the dream which the little group I was swiftly gathering about me was seeking to make real.

It was essential to me, therefore, that something different should be done, some new fresh note concerning metropolitan life and action be struck; the old, slow and somewhat grandiose methods of reporting and describing things dispensed with, at least in this instance, and here was a youth who seemed able to help me do it. He was so vigorous, so avid of life, so anxious to picture the very atmosphere which this magazine was now seeking to portray. I felt stronger, better for having him around. The growth of the city, the character and atmosphere of a given neighborhood, the facts concerning some great social fortune, event, condition, crime interested him intensely; on the other hand he was so very easy to teach, quick to sense what was wanted and the order in which it must be presented. A few brief technical explanations from me, and he had the art of writing a "special" at his fingertips, and thereafter gave me no real difficulty.

But what was more interesting to me than his success in grasping my theory of "special" writing was his own character as it was revealed to me from day to day in intimate working contact with him under these conditions. Here, as I soon learned, and was glad to learn, was no namby-pamby scribbler of the old happy-ending, pretty-nothing school of literary composition. On the contrary he sounded, for the first time in my dealings with literary aspirants of every kind, that sure, sane, penetrating, non-sentimental note so common to the best writers of the Continent, a note entirely free from mush, bravado and cant. He had a style as clear as water, as simple as rain; color, romance, humor; and if a little too much of vanity and self-importance, still one could forgive him for they were rather well-based. Already used to dealing with literary and artistic aspirants of different kinds in connection with the publications of which I had been a part, this one appealed to me as being the best of them all and a very refreshing change.

One day, only a few weeks after I had met him, seeing that I was alert for fiction, poetry and short essays or prose phantasies, all illustrative of the spirit of New York, he brought me a little poem entitled "Neuvain," which interested me greatly. It was so brief and forceful and yet so delicate, a double triolet of the old French order, but with the modernity and flavor of the streets outside, the conduit cars, hand-organs and dancing children of the pavements. The title seemed affected, seeing that the English word "Spring" would have done as well, but it was typical of his mood at the time, his literary adorations. He was in leash to the French school of which de Maupassant was the outstanding luminary, only I did not know it at the time.

"Charming," I exclaimed quite enthusiastically. "I like this. Let me see anything else you have. Do you write short stories?"

For answer he merely stared at me for a little while in the most examining and arrogant and contemptuous way, as much as to say, "Let me see if you are really worth my time and trouble in this matter," or "This sad specimen of alleged mentality is just beginning to suspect that I might write a short story." Seeing that I merely smiled most genially in return, he finally deigned to say, "Sure, I write short stories. What do you think I'm in the writing game for?"

"But you might be interested in novels only or plays, or poetry."

"No," he returned after a pause and with that same air of unrelieved condescension, "the short story is what I want to specialize in."

"Well," I said to myself, "here is a young cub who certainly has talent, is crowded with it, and yet owing to the kind of thing he is starting out to do and the fact that life will give him slaps and to spare before he is many years older, he needs to be encouraged. I was like that myself not so long ago. And besides, if I do not encourage this type of work financially (which is the best way of all), who will?"

About a week later I was given another and still more gratifying surprise, for one day, in his usual condescending manner, he brought to me two short pieces of fiction and laid them most gingerly on my desk with scarcely a word—"Here was something I might read if I chose," I believe. The reading of these two stories gave me as much of a start as though I had discovered a fully developed genius. They were so truly new or different in their point of view, so very clear, incisive, brief, with so much point in them (*The Second Motive*; *The Right Man*). For by then having been struggling with the short-story problem in other magazine offices before this, I had become not a little pessimistic as to the trend of American short fiction, as well as long—the impossibility of finding any, even supposing it publishable once we had it. My own experience with "Sister Carrie" as well as the fierce opposition or chilling indifference which, as I saw, overtook all those who attempted anything even partially serious in America, was enough to make me believe that the world took anything even slightly approximating the truth as one of the rankest and most criminal offenses possible. One dared not "talk out loud," one dared not report life as it was, as one lived it. And one of the primary warnings I had received from the president of this very organization—a most eager and ambitious and distressing example of that American pseudo-morality which combines a pirate-like acquisitiveness with an inward and absolute conviction of righteousness—was that while he wanted something new in fiction, something more virile and life-like than that "mush," as he characterized it, to be found in the current magazines, still (1), it must have a strong appeal for the general reader (!); and (2), be very compelling in fact

and *clean*, as the dear general reader would of course understand that word—a solid little pair of millstones which would
unquestionably end in macerating everything vital out of any
good story.

Still I did not despair; something might be done. And
though I sighed, I hoped to be able to make my superior
stretch a point in favor of the exceptional thing, or, as the
slang phrase went, "slip a few over on him," but that of
course meant nothing or something, as you choose. My
dream was really to find one or many like this youth, or a
pungent kind of realism that would be true and yet within
such limits as would make it usable. Imagine, then, my satisfaction in finding these two things, tales that I could not only
admire genuinely but that I could publish, things that ought
to have an interest for all who knew even a little about life.
True, they were ironic, cruel, but still with humor and color,
so deftly and cleanly told that they were smile-provoking. I
called him and said as much, or nearly so—a mistake, as I
sometimes think now, for art should be long—and bought
them forthwith, hoping, almost against hope, to find many
more such like them.

By this time, by the way, and as I should have said before,
I had still further enlarged my staff by one art director of the
most flamboyant and erratic character, a genius of sorts, volatile, restless, emotional, colorful, a veritable Verlaine-Baude-
laire-Rops soul, who, not content to arrange and decorate the
magazine each month, must needs wish to write, paint, compose verse and music and stage plays, as well as move in an
upper social world, *entrée* to which was his by birth. Again,
there was by now an Irish-Catholic makeup editor, a graduate
of some distinguished sectarian school, who was more interested in St. Jerome and his *Vulgate*, as an embodiment of
classic Latin, than he was in getting out the magazine. Still
he had the advantage of being interesting—"and I learned
about Horace from him." Again, there was a most interesting
and youthful and pretty, if severe, example of the Wellesley-
Mt. Holyoke-Bryn Mawr school of literary art and criticism,
a most engagingly interesting intellectual maiden, who func-
tioned as assistant editor and reader in an adjoining room,
along with the art-director, the makeup editor and an office

boy. This very valuable and in some respects remarkable young woman, who while holding me in proper contempt, I fear, for my rather loose and unliterary ways, was still, as I had suspected before employing her, as keen for something new and vital in fiction and every other phase of the scriptic art as any one well could be. She was ever for culling, sorting, eliminating—repression carried to the N-th power. At first L—— cordially hated her, calling her a "simp," a "bluff," a "la-de-da," and what not. In addition to these there was a constantly swelling band of writers, artists, poets, critics, dreamers of reforms social, and I know not what else, who, holding the hope of achieving their ends or aims through some really forceful magazine, were by now beginning to make our place a center. It fairly swarmed for a time with aspirants; an amusing, vivid, strident world.

As for L——, all this being new to him, he was as interested, fascinated even, as any one well might be. He responded to it almost gayly at times, wondering whether something wonderful, international, enduring might not be made to come of it. He rapidly developed into one of the most pertinacious and even disconcerting youths I have ever met. At times he seemed to have a positive genius for saying and doing irritable and disagreeable things, not only to me but to others. Never having heard of me before he met me here, he was convinced, I think, that I was a mere nothing, with some slight possibilities as an editor maybe, certainly with none as a writer or as one who could even suggest anything to writers. I had helped him, but that was as it should be. As for my art-director, he was at first a fool, later a genius; ditto my makeup man.

As for Miss E——, the Wellesley-Bryn Mawr-Mt. Holyoke assistant, who from the first had agreed with me that here indeed was a writer of promise, a genius really, he, as I have said, at first despised her. Later, by dint of exulting in his force, sincerity of purpose, his keen insight and all but braggart strength, she managed, probably on account of her looks and physical graces, to install herself in his confidence and to convince him that she was not only an honest admirer of his skill but one who had taste and judgment of no mean caliber.

Thereafter he was about as agreeable as a semi-caged wild animal would be about any office.

But above all he was affronted by M——, the publisher of the paper, concerning whom he could find no words equal to his contemptuous thoughts of him. The publisher, as L—— made quite bold to say to me, was little more than a "dodging, rat-like financial ferret," a "financial stool-pigeon for some trust or other," a "shrewd, material little shopkeeper." This because M—— was accustomed to enter and force a conversation here and there, anxious of course to gather the full import of all these various energies and enthusiasms. One of the things which L—— most resented in him at the time was his air of supreme material well-being, his obvious attempt and wish not to convey it, his carefully-cut clothes, his car, his numerous assistants and secretaries following him here and there from various other organizations with which he was connected.

M——'s idea, as he always said, was to spend and to live, only it wasn't. He merely induced others so to do. One of his customs (and it must have impressed L—— very much, innocent newcomer that he was) was to have one or another of his hirelings announce his passing from one "important" meeting to another, within or without his own building, telephone messages being "thrown in" on his line or barred out, wherever he happened to be at the moment and when, presumably, he was deep in one of those literary conferences or confidences with one employee or another or with a group, for which he rapidly developed a passion. Another of his vanities was to have his automobile announced and he be almost forced into it by impetuous secretaries, who, because of orders previously given, insisted that he must be made to keep certain important engagements. Or he would send for one of his hirelings, wherever he chanced to be—club, restaurant, his home—midnight if necessary, to confer with him on some subject of great moment, and the hireling was supposed to call a taxi and come post haste in order that he might not be kept waiting.

"God!" L—— once remarked in my presence. "To think that a thinking being has to be beholden to a thing like that for his weekly income! Somebody ought to tap him with a feather-duster and kill him!"

But the manner in which L—— developed in this atmosphere! It was interesting. At first, before the magazine became so significant or well-organized, it was a great pleasure for me to associate with him outside office hours, and a curious and vivid companion he made. He was so intensely avid of life, so intolerant of the old, of anything different to that which he personally desired or saw, that at times it was most difficult to say anything at all for fear of meeting a rebuff or at least a caustic objection. As I was very pleased to note, he had a passion for seeing, as all youth should have when it first comes to the great city—the great bridges, the new tunnels just then being completed or dug, the harbor and bay, Coney Island, the two new and great railway terminals, then under construction. Most, though, he reveled in different and even depressing neighborhoods—Eighth Avenue, for instance, about which he later wrote a story, and a very good one ("A Quiet Duet"); Hell's Kitchen, that neighborhood that lies (or did), on the West Side of Manhattan, between Eighth and Tenth Avenues, Thirty-sixth and Forty-first Streets; Little Italy, the region below Delancey and north of Worth Street on the East Side; Chinatown; Washington Street (Syria in America); the Greeks in Twenty-seventh and -eighth Streets, West Side. All these and many more phases of New York's multiplex life took his full and restless attention. Once he said to me quite excitedly, walking up Eighth Avenue at two in the morning—I was showing him some rear tenement slums in the summertime—"God, how I hate to go to bed in this town! I'm afraid something will happen while I'm asleep and I won't see it!" That was exactly how he felt all the time, I am sure.

And in those days he was most simple, a very Spartan of a boy. He hadn't the least taste for drink, lived in a small hall-bedroom somewhere—Eighth Avenue, I believe—and took his meals in those shabby little quick-lunch rooms where the characters were more important to him than the food. (My hat—my hat is in my hand!) Intellectually he was so stern and ambitious that I all but stood in awe of and reverence before him. Here, I said to myself, is one who will really do;

let him be as savage as he pleases. In America he probably needs to be.

And during this short time, what scraps of his early life he revealed! By degrees I picked up bits of his early deprivations and difficulties, if such they might be called. He had been a newspaper reporter, or had tried to be, in Kansas City, had worked in the college restaurant and laundry of the middle-West State university from which he had graduated, to help pay his way. Afterward he had assisted the janitor of some great skyscraper somewhere—Kansas City, I believe—and, what was most pleasing to me, he in nowise emphasized these as youthful difficulties or made any comment as to their being "hard." Neither did he try to boastingly minimize them as nothing at all—another wretched pose. From him I learned that throughout his youth he had been carried here and there by the iron woman who was his mother and whom he seemed to adore in some grim contentious way, smothering his comments as though he disliked to say anything at all, and yet describing her at times as coarse and vulgar, but a mother to him "all right," someone who had made marked sacrifices for him.

She had once "run" a restaurant in a Western mining camp, had then or later carried him as a puling baby under her shawl or cloak across the Mojave Desert, on foot a part of the way. Apparently he did not know who his father was, and he was not very much concerned to know whether she did or not. His father had died, he said, when he was a baby. Later his mother, then a cook in some railroad hotel in Texas, had sent him to school there. Later still she had been a "bawler out," if you know what that means, an employee of a loan shark and used by him to compel delinquent, albeit petty and pathetic, creditors to pay their dues or then and there, before all their fellow-workers, be screamed at for their delinquency about the shop in which they worked! Later she became a private detective! an insurance agent—God knows what—a kind of rough man-woman, as she turned out to be, but all the while clinging to this boy, her pet, no doubt her dream of perfection. She had by turns sent him to common and high school and to college, remitting him such sums of money as she might to pay his way. Later still (at that very time in fact) she was seeking to come to New York to keep house for him, only he would not have that, perhaps sensing the need of greater freedom. But he wrote her regularly, as he confessed to me, and in later years I believe sent her a part of his earnings, which were to be saved by her for him against a rainy day. Among his posthumous writings later I found a very lovely story ("His Mother"), describing her and himself in unsparing and yet loving terms, a compound of the tender and the brutal in his own soul.

The thing that always made me hope for the best was that at that time he was not at all concerned with the petty little *moralic* and economic definitions and distinctions which were floating about his American world in one form and another. Indeed he seemed to be entirely free of and even alien to them. What he had heard about the indwelling and abiding perfections of the human soul had gone, and rightly so, in one ear and out the other. He respected the virtues, but he knew of and reckoned with the antipathetic vices which gave them their reason for being. To him the thief was almost as important as the saint, the reason for the saint's being. And, better still, he had not the least interest in American politics or society—a wonderful sign. The American dream of "getting ahead" financially and socially was not part of him—another mark royal. All life was fascinating, acceptable, to be interpreted if one had the skill; it was a great distinction to have the skill—worth endless pains to acquire it.

But how unwilling would the average American of his day have been, stuffed as he was and still is with book and picture drivel about artists and art, to accept L—— as anything more than a raw, callow yokel, presuming to assail the outer portals of the temple with his muddy feet! A romping, stamping, irritable soul, with more the air of a young railroad brakeman or "hand," than an artist, and with so much coarse language at times and such brutality of thought as to bar him completely, one might say, from having anything to do with great fiction, great artistic conceptions, or the temple of art. What, sit with the mighty!—that coarse youth, with darkish-brown hair parted at one side and combed over one ear, in the manner of a grandiose barber; with those thick-soled and none too shapely brown shoes, that none too well-made store suit of clothes, that little round brown hat, more often a cap, pulled rather savagely and vulgarly, even insultingly, over one eye; that coarse frieze overcoat, still worn on cold spring days, its "corners" back and front turned up by the damp and from being indifferently sat on; that brash corn-cob pipe and bag of cheap tobacco, extracted and lit at odd moments; what, that youth with the aggressive, irritating vibrant manner— almost the young tough with a chip on his shoulder looking for one to even so much as indicate that he is not all he should be! Positively, there was something brutal and yet cosmic (not comic) about him, his intellectual and art preten- sions considered. At times his waspishness and bravado palled even on me. He was too aggressive, too forceful, too intoler- ant, I said. He should be softer. At other times I felt that he needed to be all that and more to "get by," as he would have said. I wanted to modify him a little—and yet I didn't—and I remained drawn to him in spite of many irritating little cir- cumstances, all but infuriating at times, and actually calcu- lated, it seemed, with a kind of savage skill to reduce what he conceived to be my lofty superiority. At times I thought he ought to be killed—like a father meditating on an unruly son—but the mood soon passed and his literary ability made amends for everything.

In so far as the magazine was concerned, once it began to grow and attract attention he was for me its most important asset; not that he did so much directly as that he provided a definite standard toward which we all had to work. Not in- curiously, he was swiftly recognized for what he was by all who came in touch with the magazine. In the first place, in- terested in his progress, I had seen to it that he was properly introduced wherever that was possible and of benefit to him, and later on, by sheer force of his mental capacity and integ- rity, his dreams and his critical skill, he managed to center about him an entire band of seeking young writers, artists, poets, playwrights, aspiring musicians; an amusing and as in- teresting a group as I have ever seen. Their points of rendez- vous appeared to be those same shabby quick-lunches in back streets or even on the principal thoroughfares about Times Square, or they met in each other's rooms or my office at night after I had gone, giving me as an excuse that they had work to do. And during all this time the air fairly hummed with rumors of new singers, dancers, plays, stories being begun or under way, articles and essays contemplated; avid, if none too well financed frolics or bohemian midnight suppers here and there. Money was by no means plentiful, and in consequence there was endless borrowing and "paying up" among them. Among the most enthusiastic members of this circle, as I had begun to note, and finally rather nervously, were my art-director, a valiant knight in Bohemia if ever there was one, and she of Bryn Mawr-Wellesley standards. My makeup editor, as well as various contributors who had since become more or less closely identified with the magazine, were also following him up all the time.

If not directly profitable it was enlivening, and I was fairly well convinced by now that from the point of view of being "aware," "in touch with," "in sympathy with" many of the principal tendencies and undercurrents which make for a magazine's success and precedence, this group was as valuable to me as any might well be. It constituted a "kitchen cabinet" of sorts and brought hundreds of interesting ideas to the surface, and from all directions. Now it would be a new and hitherto unheard-of tenor who was to be brought from abroad and introduced with great noise to repute-loving Americans; a new sculptor or painter who had never been heard of in America; a great actor, perhaps, or poet or writer. I listened to any quantity of gossip in regard to new movements that were ready to burst upon the world, in sculpture, painting, the scriptic art. About the whole group there was much that was exceedingly warm, youthful, full of dreams. They were intensely informative and full of hope, and I used to look at them and wonder which one, if any, was destined to have his dreams realized.

Of L—— however I never had the least doubt. He began, it is true, to adopt rather more liberal tendencies, to wish always to be part and parcel of this gayety, this rushing here and there; and he drank at times—due principally, as I thought, to my wildling art-director, who had no sense or reserve in matters material or artistic and who was all for a bacchanalian career, cost what it might. On more than one occasion I heard L—— declaring roundly, apropos of some group scheme of pilgrimage, "No, no! I will not. I am going *home* now!" He had a story he wanted to work on, an article to finish. At the same time he would often agree that if by a certain time, when he was through, they were still at a certain place, or a second or third, he would look them up. Never, apparently, did his work suffer in the least.

And it was about this time that I began to gather the true source and import of his literary predisposition. He was literally obsessed, as I now discovered, with Continental and more especially the French conception of art in writing. He had studied the works as well as the temperaments and experiences (more especially the latter, I fear) of such writers as de Maupassant, Flaubert, Baudelaire, Balzac, de Musset, Sand, Daudet, Dumas junior, and Zola, as well as a number of the more recent writers: Hervieu, Bourget, Louys and their contemporaries. Most of all, though, he was impressed, and deeply, by the life and art of de Maupassant, his method of approach, his unbiased outlook on life, his freedom from moral and religious and even sentimental predisposition. In the beginning of his literary career I really believe he slaved to imitate him exactly, although he could not very well escape the American temperament and rearing by which he was hopelessly conditioned. A certain Western critic and editor, to whom he had first addressed his hopes and scribblings before coming to me, writing me after L——'s death in reference to a period antedating that in which I had known him, observed, "He was crazy about the *fin de siècle* stuff that then held the boards and from which (I hope the recording angel will put it to my credit) I steered him clear." I think so; but he was still very much interested in it. He admired Aubrey Beardsley, the poster artists of France, Verlaine, Baudelaire, Rops, the Yellow Book, even Oscar Wilde, although his was a far more substantial and plebeian and even radical point of view.

Unfortunately for L——, I have always thought, there now thrust himself forward the publisher and owner of the magazine, who from previously having been content to see that the mercantile affairs of the magazine were in good order, had decided that since it was attracting attention he should be allowed to share in its literary and artistic prestige, should indeed be closely identified with it and recognized as its true source and inspiration—a thing which in no fashion had been contemplated by me when I went there. From having agreed very distinctly with me that no such interference would at any time be indulged in, he now came forward with a plan for an advisory council which was to consist of himself and the very members of the staff which I had created.

I could not object and it did not disturb me so much personally. For some time I had been sensing that the thing was for me no end in itself, but an incident. This same I felt to be true for L——, who had been taking more and more interest in the magazine's technical composition. At the same time I saw no immediate way of arranging my affairs and departing, which left me, for a very little while, more or less of a spectator. During this time I had the dissatisfaction of noting the growth of an influence with L—— which could, as I saw, prove only harmful. M—— was no suitable guide for him. He was a brilliant but superficial and very material type who was convinced that in the having and holding of many things material—houses, lands, corporation stocks, a place in the clubs and circles of those who were materially prosperous—was really to achieve all that was significant in the now or the hereafter. Knowing comparatively nothing of either art or letters, or that subtle thing which makes for personality and atmosphere in a magazine or in writing (and especially the latter), that grateful something which attracts and detains one, he was nevertheless convinced that he did. And what was more, he was determined not only to make friends with and hold all those whom I might have attracted, providing they could prove useful to him, but also a number of a much more successful group in these fields, those who had already achieved repute in a more commonplace and popular way and were therefore presumably possessed of a following and with the power to exact a high return for their product, and for the magazine, regardless of intrinsic merit. His constant talk was of money, its power to attract and buy, the significance of all things material. He now wanted the magazine to be representative of this glowing element, and at the same time, paradoxical as it might seem, the best that might be in literary and artistic thought.

Naturally the thing was impossible, but he had a facile and specious method of arguing, a most gay and in some respects magnetic personality, far from stodgy or gross, which for a time attracted many to him. Very briskly then indeed he proceeded to make friends with all those with whom I had surrounded myself, to enter into long and even private discussions with them as to the proper conduct of the magazine, to hint quite broadly at a glorious future in which all, each one particularly to whom he talked, was to share. Curiously, this new and (as I would have thought) inimical personality of M—— seemed to appeal to L—— very much.

I do not claim that the result was fatal. It may even, or at least might, have had value, combined with an older or slightly more balanced temperament. But it seemed to me that it offered too quickly what should have come, if at all, as the result of much effort. For in regard to the very things L—— should have most guarded against—show and the shallow pleasures of social and night and material life in New York—M—— was most specious. I never knew a more intriguing and fascinating man in this respect nor one who cared less for those he used to obtain his unimportant ends. He had positive genius for making the gaudy and the unworthy seem worthy and even perfect. During his earlier days there, L—— had more than once "cursed him out" (in his absence, of course), to use his own expressive phrase, for his middle-West trade views, as he described them, his shabby social and material ideals, and yet, as I could plainly see, even at that time the virus of his theories was working. For it must be remembered that L—— was very new to New York, very young, and never having had much of anything he was no doubt slightly envious of the man's material facility, the sense of all-sufficiency, exclusiveness and even a kind of petty trade grandeur with which he tried to surround himself.

Well, that might not have proved fatal either, only L—— needed some one to keep him true to himself, his individual capabilities, to constantly caution and if possible sober him to his very severe taste, and as it was he was all but surrounded by acolytes and servitors.

A little later, having left M——'s and assumed another editorial position, and being compelled to follow the various current magazines more or less professionally, I was disturbed to note that there began to appear in various publications— especially M——'s, which was flourishing greatly for the moment—stories which while exhibiting much of the deftness and repression as well as an avidity for the true color of things, still showed what I had at first feared they might: a decided compromise. That curse of all American fiction, the necessarily happy ending, had been impressed on him—by whom? To my sincere dissatisfaction, he began writing stories, some at least, which concerned (1), a young woman who successfully abandoned art dreams for advertising; (2), a middle-aged charmer, female, who attempted *libertinage* and was defeated, American style; (3), a Christmas picture with sweetness and light reigning on every hand (Dickens at his sentimentalest could have done no worse); (4), a Broadway press agent who, attempting to bring patronage to a great hotel via chic vice, accidentally and unintentionally mates an all-too-good young society man turned hotel manager to a grand heiress. And so on and so on, not ad infinitum but for a period at least—the ten years in which he managed to live and work.

And, what was more, during this new period I heard and occasionally saw discouraging things in connection with him from time to time. True to his great promise, for I sincerely think M—— had a genuine fondness for his young protégé, as much of a fondness as he could well have for anything, he guaranteed him perhaps as much as three thousand a year; sent him to Stockholm at the age of twenty-four or -five to meet and greet the famous false pole discoverer, Doctor Cook; allowed him to go to Paris in connection with various articles; to Rome; sent him into the middle and far West; to Broadway for dramatic and social studies. Well and good, only he wanted always in what was done for him the "uplift" note, the happy ending—or at least one not vulgar or low— whereas my idea in connection with L——, gifted as he was, was that he should confine himself to fiction as an art and without any regard to theories or types of ending, believing, as I did, that he would definitely establish himself in that way in the long run. I had no objection of course to experiences of various kinds, his taking up with any line of work which might seem at the moment far removed from realistic writing, providing always that the star of his ideal was in sight. Whenever he wrote, be it early or late, it must be in the clear, incisive, uncompromising vein of these first stories and with that passion for revelation which characterized him at first, that same unbiased and unfettered non-moral viewpoint.

But after meeting with and working for M—— under this new arrangement and being apparently fascinated for the moment by his personality, he seemed to me to gradually lose sight of his ideal, to be actually taken in by the plausible arguments which the latter could spin with the ease that a spider spins gossamer. In that respect I insist that M—— was a bad influence. Under his tutelage L—— gradually became, for instance, an habitué of a well-known and pseudo-bohemian chop-house, a most mawkish and naïvely imitative affair, intended frankly to be a copy or even the original, forsooth, of an old English inn, done, in so far as its woodwork was concerned, in smoked or dark-stained oak to represent an old English interior, its walls covered with long-stemmed pipes and pictures of English hunting and drinking scenes, its black-stained but unvarnished tables littered with riding, driving and country-life society papers, to give it that air of *sans ceremonie* with an upper world of which its habitués probably possessed no least inkling but most eagerly craved. Here, along with a goodly group of his latter-day friends, far different from those by whom he had first been surrounded—a pretentious society poet of no great merit but considerable self-emphasis, a Wall Street broker, posing as a club man, *raconteur*, "first-nighter" and what not, and several young and ambitious playwrights, all seeking the heaven of a Broadway success—he began to pose as one of the intimates of the great city, its bosom child as it were, the cynosure and favorite of its most glittering precincts—a most M——like proceeding. His clothes by now, for I saw him on occasion, had taken on a more lustrous if less convincing aspect than those he had worn when I first knew him. The small round hat or rakish cap, typical of his Western dreams, had now given way to a most pretentious square-topped derby, beloved, I believe, of undertakers and a certain severe type of banker as well as some clergymen, only it was a light brown.

His suit and waistcoat were of a bright English tweed, reddish-brown or herring-bone gray by turns, his shoes box-toed perfections of the button type. He carried a heavy cane, often a bright leather manuscript case, and seemed intensely absorbed in the great and dramatic business of living and writing. "One must," so I read him at this time, "take the pleasures as well as the labors of this world with the utmost severity." Here, with a grand manner, he patronized the manager and the waiters, sent word to his friend the cook, who probably did not know him at all, that his chop or steak was to be done just so. These friends of his, or at least one of them (the poet) he met every day at five for an all-essential game of chess, after which an evening paper was read and the chop ordered. Ale—not beer—in a pewter mug was *comme il faut*, the only thing for a gentleman of letters, worthy of the name, to drink.

I am sorry to write so, for after all youth must have its fling. Still, I had expected better of L——, and I was a little disappointed to see that earlier dream of simplicity and privation giving way to an absolutely worthless show. Besides, twenty or thirty such stories as "The Right Man," "Sweet Dreams," "The Man With the Broken Fingers," "The Second Motive," would outweigh a thousand of the things he was getting published and the profits of which permitted him these airs.

Again, during the early days of his success with M——, he had married—a young nurse who had previously been a clerk in a store, a serious, earnest and from one point of view helpful person, seeing that she could keep his domestic affairs in order and bear him children, which she did, but she had no understanding of, or flair for, the type of thing he was called upon to do. She had no instinct for literature or the arts, and aside from her domestic capacities little skill or taste for "socializing." And, naturally, he was neglecting her. His head was probably surging with great ideas of art and hence a social supremacy which might well carry him anywhere. He had bought a farm some distance from New York, where in a community supposedly inhabited by successful and superior men of letters he posed as a farmer at times, mowing and cocking hay as became a Western plow-boy; and also, as the mood moved him, and as became a great and secluded writer, working in a den entirely surrounded by books in fine leather bindings (!) and being visited by those odd satellites of the scriptic art who see in genius of this type the *summum bonum* of life. It was the thing to do at that time, for a writer to own a farm and work it. Horace had. One individual in particular, a man of genuine literary and critical ability and great taste in the matter of all the arts but with no least interest in or tolerance for the simplicities of effort, came here occasionally, as I heard, to help him pile hay, and this in a silk shirt and a monocle; a second—and a most fascinating intellectual *flaneur*, who, however, had no vision or the gift of dreams—came to eat, drink, talk of many things to be done, to steal a few ideas, borrow a little money perhaps or consume a little morphine, and depart; a third came to spout of his success in connection with plays, or his proposed successes; a fourth to paint a picture, urged on by L——; a fifth to compose rural verse; a sixth, a broker or race-track tout or city bar-tender (for color, this last), to marvel that one of L——'s sense, or any one indeed, should live in the country at all. There were drinking bouts, absolute drunkenness, in which, according to the Johnsonian tradition and that of Messieurs Rabelais and Molière, the weary intellect and one's guiding genius were immersed in a comforting Lethe of rye.

Such things cost money, however. In addition, my young friend, due to a desire no doubt to share in the material splendors of his age (a doctrine M—— was ever fond of spouting—and as a duty, if you please), had saddled himself, for a time at least, with an apartment in an exclusive square on the East Side, the rent of which was a severe drain. Before this there had been, and after it were still, others, obligations too much for him to bear financially, all in the main taken for show, that he might be considered a literary success. Now and again (so I was told by several of his intimates), confronted by a sudden exhaustion of his bank balance, he would leave some excellent apartment house or neighborhood, where for a few months he had been living in grand style, extracting his furniture as best he might, or leaving it and various debts beside, and would take refuge in some shabby tenement, or rear rooms even, and where, touched by remorse or encouraged by the great literary and art traditions (Balzac, Baudelaire, Johnson, Goldsmith, Verlaine) he would toil unendingly at definite money-yielding manuscripts, the results of which carried to some well-paying *successful magazine* would yield him sufficient to return to the white lights— often even to take a better apartment than that which last had been his. By now, however, one of the two children he eventually left behind him had been born. His domestic cares were multiplying, the marriage idea dull. Still he did not hesitate to continue those dinners given to his friends, the above-mentioned group or its spiritual kin, either in his apartment or in a bohemian restaurant of great show in New York. In short, he was a fairly successful short-story writer and critic in whom still persisted a feeling that he would yet triumph in the adjacent if somewhat more difficult field of popular fiction.

It was during this period, if I may interpolate an incident, that I was waiting one night in a Broadway theater lobby for a friend to appear, when who should arrive on the scene but L——, most outlandishly dressed in what I took to be a *reductio ad absurdum* of his first pose, as I now half-feared it to be: that of the uncouth and rugged young American, disclaiming style in dress at least, and content to be a clod in looks so long as he was a Shelley in brains. His suit was of that coarse ill-fitting character described as Store, and shelf-worn; his shoes all but dusty brogans, his headgear a long-visored yellowish-and-brown cross-barred cap. He had on a short, badly-cut frieze overcoat, his hands stuck defiantly in his trousers pockets, forcing its lapels wide open. And he appeared to be partially if not entirely drunk, and very insolent. I had the idea that the drunkenness and the dress were a pose, or else that he had been in some neighborhood in search of copy which required such an outfit. Charitably let us accept the last. He was accompanied by two satellic souls who were doing their best to restrain him.

"Come, now! Don't make a scene. We'll see the show all right!"

"Sure we'll see the show!" he returned contentiously. "Where's the manager?"

A smug mannikin whose uniform was a dress suit, the

business manager himself, eyed him in no friendly spirit from a nearby corner.

"This is Mr. L——," one of the satellites now approached and explained to the manager. "He's connected with M——'s Magazine. He does short stories and dramatics occasionally."

The manager bowed. After all, M——'s Magazine had come to have some significance on Broadway. It was as well to be civil. Courtesy was extended for three, and they went in.

As for myself, I resented the mood and the change. It was in no way my affair—his life was his own—and still I resented it. I did not believe that he was as bad as he seemed. He had too much genuine sense. It was just boyish swagger and show, and still it was time that he was getting over that and settling down. I really hoped that time would modify all this.

One thing that made me hope for the best was that very shortly after this M——'s Magazine blew completely up, leaving him without that semi-financial protection which I felt was doing him so much harm. The next favorable sign that I observed was that a small volume of short stories, some sixteen in number, and containing the cream of his work up to that time, was brought to a publishing house with which I was financially identified at the time, and although no word was said to me (I really think he took great care not to see me), still it was left and on my advice eventually published (it sold, I believe, a little under five hundred copies). But the thing that cheered me was that it contained not one story which could be looked upon as a compromise with his first views. And better, it had been brought to the concern with which I was connected—intentionally, I am sure. I was glad to have had a hand in its publication. "At least," I said, "he has not lost sight of his first ideal. He may go on now."

And thereafter, in one magazine and another, excellent enough to have but a small circulation, I saw something of his which had genuine merit. A Western critical journal began to publish a series of essays by him, for which I am sure he received nothing at all. Again, three or four years later, a second volume of stories, almost if not quite as good as his first, was issued by this same Western paper. He was trying to do serious work; but he still sought and apparently craved those grand scenes on the farm or in some New York restaurant or an expensive apartment, and when he could no longer afford it. He still wrote happy-ending, or compromise, stories for any such magazine as would receive him, and was apparently building up a reasonably secure market for them. In the meantime the moving-picture scenario market had developed, and he wrote for it. His eyes were also turning toward the stage, as one completed manuscript and several "starts" turned over to me after his death proved. One day some one who knew him and me quite well assured me that L——, having sent out many excellent stories only to have them re-turned, had one day cried and then raged, cursing America for its attitude toward serious letters—an excellent sign, I thought, good medicine for one who must eventually forsake his hope of material grandeur and find himself. "In time, in time," I said, "he will eat through the husks of these other things, the 'M—— complex,' and do something splendid. He can't help it. But this fantastic dream of grandeur, of being a popular success, will have to be lived down."

For a time now I heard but little more save once that he was connected with a moving-picture concern, suggesting plots and making some money. Then I saw a second series of essays in the same Western critical paper—that of the editor who had published his book—and some of them were excel-lent, very searching and sincere. I felt that he was moving along the right line, although they earned him nothing. Then one week, very much to my surprise, there was a very glow-ing and extended commentary on myself, concerning which for the time being I decided to make no comment; and a little later, perhaps three weeks, a telephone call. Did I recall him? (!) Could he come and see me? (!) I invited him to dinner, and he came, carrying, of all things—and for him, the ex-railroad boy—a great armful of red roses. This touched me.

"What's the idea?" I inquired jovially, laughing at him.

He blushed like a girl, a little irritably too, I thought, for he found me (as perhaps he had hoped not to) examining and critical, and he may have felt that I was laughing at him, which I wasn't. "I wished to give them to you, and I brought 'em. Why shouldn't I?"

"You know you should bring them if you want me to have them, and I'm only too glad to get them, anyway. Don't think I'm criticizing."

He smiled and began at once on the "old days," as he now called them, a sad commentary on our drifting days. Indeed he seemed able to talk of little else or fast enough or with too much enthusiasm. He went over many things and people— M——; K——, the wonderful art-director, now insane and a wreck; the group of which he and I had once been a part; his youthful and unsophisticated viewpoint at the time. "You know," he confessed quite frankly finally, "my mother always told me then and afterwards that I made a mistake in leaving you. You were the better influence for me. She was right. I know it now. Still, a life's a life, and we have to work through it and ourselves somehow."

I agreed heartily.

He told me of his wife, children, farm, his health and his difficulties. It appeared that he was making a bare living at times, at others doing very well. His great bane was the popular magazine, the difficulty of selling a good thing. It was true, I said, and at midnight he left, promising to come again, inviting me to come to his place in the country at my convenience. I promised.

But one thing and another interfered. I went South. One day six months later, after I had returned, he called up once more, saying he wished to see me. Of course I asked him down and he came and spoke of his health. Some doctor, an old college pal of his, was assuring him that he had Bright's disease and that he might die at any time. He wanted to know, in case anything happened to him, would I look after his many mss., most of which, the most serious efforts at least, had never been published. I agreed. Then he went away and I never saw him again. A year later I was one day informed that he had died three days before of kidney trouble. He had been West to see a moving-picture director; on his way East he had been taken ill and had stopped off with friends somewhere to be treated, or operated upon. A few weeks later he had returned to New York, but refusing to rest and believing that he could not die, so soon, had kept out of doors and in the city, until suddenly he did collapse. Or, rather, he met his favorite doctor, an intellectual savage like himself, who with some weird desire to appear forceful, definite, unsentimental perhaps—a mental condition L——— most fancied—had told him to go home and to bed, for he would be dead in forty-eight hours!—a fine bit of assurance which perhaps as much as anything else assisted L——— to die. At any rate and in spite of the ministrations of his wife, who wished to defy the doctor and who in her hope for herself and her children as well as him strove to contend against this gloom, he did so go to bed and did die. On the last day, realizing no doubt how utterly indifferent his life had been, how his main aspirations or great dreams had been in the main nullified by passions, necessities, crass chance (how well he was fitted to understand that!) he broke down and cried for hours. Then he died.

A friend who had known much of this last period, said to me rather satirically, "He was dealing with death in the shape of a medic. Have you ever seen him?" The doctor, he meant. "He looks like an advertisement for an undertaker. I do believe he was trying to discover whether he could kill somebody by the power of suggestion, and he met L——— in the nick of time. You know how really sensitive he was. Well, that medic killed him, the same as you would kill a bird with a bullet. He said 'You're already dead,' and he was."

And—oh yes—M———, his former patron. At the time of L———'s sickness and death he was still owing him $1100 for services rendered during the last days of that unfortunate magazine. He had never been called upon to pay his debts, for he had sunk through one easy trapdoor of bankruptcy only to rise out of another, smiling and with the means to continue. Yes, he was rich again, rated A No. 1, the president of a great corporation, and with L———'s $1100 still unpaid and now not legally "collectible." His bank balance, established by a friend at the time, was exactly one hundred thousand.

But Mrs. L———, anxious to find some way out of her difficulty since her husband was lying cold, and knowing of no one else to whom to turn, had written to him. There was no food in the house, no medicine, no way to feed the children at the moment. That matter of $1100 now—could he spare a little? L——— had thought———

A letter in answer was not long in arriving, and a most moving M——y document it was. M—— had been stunned by the dreadful news, stunned. Could it really be? Could it? His young brilliant friend? Impossible! At the dread, pathetic news he had cried—yes he had—cried—and cried—and cried—and then he had even cried some more. Life was so sad, so grim. As for him, his own affairs were never in so wretched a condition. It was unfortunate. Debts there were on every hand. They haunted him, robbed him of his sleep. He himself scarcely knew which way to turn. They stood in serried ranks, his debts. A slight push on the part of any one, and he would be crushed—crushed—go down in ruin. And so, as much as he was torn, and as much as he cried, even now, he could do nothing, nothing, nothing. He was agonized, beaten to earth, but still—— Then, having signed it, there was a P. S. or an N. B. This stated that in looking over his affairs he had just discovered that by stinting himself in another direction he *could* manage to scrape together twenty-five dollars, and this he was enclosing. Would that God had designed that he should be better placed at this sad hour!

* * *

However that may be, I at once sent for the mss. and they came, a jumbled mass in two suitcases and a portfolio; and a third suitcase, so I was informed, containing all of a hundred mss., mostly stories, had been lost somewhere! There had been much financial trouble of late and more than one enforced move. Mrs. L—— had been compelled—but I will not tell all. Suffice it to say that he had such an end as his own realistic pen might have satirically craved.

The mss., finally sorted, tabulated and read, yielded two small volumes of excellent tales, all unpublished, the published material being all but uniformly worthless. There was also the attempt at a popular comedy, previously mentioned, a sad affair, and a volume of essays, as well as a very, very slender but charming volume of verse, in case a publisher could ever be found for them—a most agreeable little group, showing a pleasing sense of form and color and emotion. I arranged them as best I could and finally——

But they are still unpublished.

* * *

P. S. As for the sum total of the work left by L——, its very best, it might be said that although he was not a great psychologist, still, owing to a certain pretentiousness of assertion at times, one might unthinkingly suppose he was. Neither had he, as yet, any fixed theories of art or definite style of his own, imitating as he was now de Maupassant, now O. Henry, now Poe; but also it must be said that slowly and surely he was approximating one, original and forceful and water-clear in expression and naturalness. At times he veered to a rather showy technique, at others to a cold and even harsh simplicity. Yet always in the main he had color, beauty, emotion, poignance when necessary. Like his idol, de Maupassant, he had no moral or strong social prejudices, no really great or disturbing imagination, no wealth of perplexing ideas. He saw America and life as something to be painted as all masters see life and paint it. Gifted with a true vein of satire, he had not, at the time of his death, quite mastered its possibilities. He still retained prejudice of one type or another, which he permitted to interfere with the very smooth arrangement of his colors. At the same time, had he not been disturbed by so many of the things which in America, as elsewhere, ordinarily assail an ambitious and earnest writer—the prejudice against naturalness and sincerity in matters of the intellect and the facts of life, and the consequent difficulty of any one so gifted in obtaining funds at any time—he might have done much better sooner. He was certain to come into his own eventually had he lived. His very accurate and sensitive powers of observation, his literary taste, his energy and pride in his work, were destined to carry him there. It could not have been otherwise. Ten years more, judging by the rate at which he worked, his annual product and that which he did leave, one might say that in the pantheon of American letters it is certain that he would have proved a durable if not one of its great figures, and he might well have been that. As it stands, it is not impossible that he will be so recognized, if for no more than the sure promise of his genius.

The Village Feudists

IN A CERTAIN Connecticut fishing-town sometime since, where, besides lobstering, a shipyard and some sail-boat-building there existed the several shops and stores which catered to the wants of those who labored in those lines, there dwelt a groceryman by the name of Elihu Burridge, whose life and methods strongly point the moral and social successes and failures of the rural man.

Sixty years of age, with the vanities and desires of the average man's life behind rather than before him, he was at the time not unlike the conventional drawings of Parson Thirdly, which graced the humorous papers of that day. Two moon-shaped eyes, a long upper lip, a mouth like the sickle moon turned downward, prominent ears, a rather long face and a mutton-chop-shaped whisker on either cheek, served to give him that clerical appearance which the humorous artists so religiously seek to depict. Add to this that he was middle-sized, clerically spare in form, reserved and quiet in demeanor, and one can see how he might very readily give the impression of being a minister. His clothes, however, were old, his trousers torn but neatly mended, his little blue gingham jumper which he wore about the store greasy and aged. Everything about him and his store was so still and dark that one might have been inclined on first sight to consider him crusty and morose.

Even more remarkable than himself, however, was his store. I have seen many in my time that were striking because of their neatness; I never saw one before that struck me as more remarkable for its disorder. In the first place it was filled neck-deep with barrels and boxes in the utmost confusion. Dark, greasy, provision-lined alleys led off into dingy sections which the eye could not penetrate. Old signs hung about, advertising things which had long since ceased to sell and were forgotten by the public. There were pictures in once gilt but now time-blackened frames, wherein queerly depicted children and pompous-looking grocers offered one commodity and another, all now almost obliterated by fly-specks. Shelves were marked on the walls by

signs now nearly illegible. Cobwebs hung thickly from corners and pillars. There were oil, lard, and a dust-laden scum
of some sort on three of the numerous scales with which he
occasionally weighed things and on many exteriors of once
salable articles. Pork, lard, molasses, and nails were packed
in different corners of the place in barrels. Lying about
were household utensils, ship-rigging, furniture and a hundred other things which had nothing to do with the grocery
business.

As I entered the store the first afternoon I noticed a Bible
open at Judges and a number of slips of paper on which questions had been written. On my second visit for oil and vine-
gar, two strangers from off a vagrant yacht which had entered
the little harbor nudged one another and demanded to know
whether either had ever seen anything like it. On the third,
my companion protested that it was not clean, and seeing that
there were other stores we decided to buy our things elsewhere. This was not so easily accomplished.

"Where can I get a flatiron?" I inquired at the Postoffice
when I first entered the village.

"Most likely at Burridge's," was the reply.

"Do you know where I can get a pair of row-locks?" I
asked of a boy who was lounging about the town dock.

"At Burridge's," he replied.

When we wanted oars, pickles of a certain variety, golden
syrup, and a dozen other things which were essential at times,
we were compelled to go to Burridge's, so that at last he obtained a very fair portion of our trade despite the condition
of his store.

During all these earlier dealings there cropped up something curt and dry in his conversation. One day we lost a fruit
jar which he had loaned, and I took one very much like it
back in its place. When I began to apologize he interrupted
me with, "A jar's a jar, isn't it?"

Another time, when I remarked in a conciliatory tone that
he owed me eight cents for a can of potted ham which had
proved stale, he exclaimed, "Well, I won't owe you long," and
forthwith pulled the money out of the loose jacket of his
jumper and paid me.

I inquired one day if a certain thing were good. "If it isn't," he replied, with a peculiar elevation of the eyebrows, "your money is. You can have that back."

"That's the way you do business, is it?"

"Yes, sir," he replied, and his long upper lip thinned out along the line of the lower one like a vise.

I was in search of a rocking-chair one day and was directed to Burridge's as the only place likely to have any!

"Do you keep furniture?" I inquired.

"Some," he said.

"Have you a rocking-chair?"

"No, sir."

A day or two later I was in search of a table and on going to Burridge's found that he had gone to a neighboring city.

"Have you got a table?" I inquired of the clerk.

"I don't know," he replied. "There's some furniture in the back room, but I don't know as I dare to sell any of it while he's away."

"Why?"

"Well, he don't like me to sell any of it. He's kind of queer that way. I dunno what he intends to do with it. Gar!" he added in a strangely electric way, "he's a queer man! He's got a lot of things back there—chairs and tables and everything. He's got a lot more in a loft up the street here. He never seems to want to sell any of 'em. Heard him tell people he didn't have any."

I shook my head in puzzled desperation.

"Come on, let's go back and look anyway. There's no harm in seeing if he has one."

We went back and there amid pork and molasses barrels, old papers, boxes and signs, was furniture in considerable quantity—tables, rocking-chairs, washstands, bureaus—all cornered and tumbled about.

"Why, here are rocking-chairs, lots of them," I exclaimed. "Just the kind I want! He said he didn't have any."

"Gar! I dunno," replied the clerk. "Here's a table, but I wouldn't dare sell it to you."

"Why should he say he didn't have a rocking-chair?"

"Gar! I dunno. He's goin' out of the furniture business. He don't want to sell any. I don't know what he intends to do with it."

"Well," I said in despair, "what about the table? You can sell that, can't you?"

"I couldn't—not till he comes back. I don't know what he'd want to do about it."

"What's the price of it?"

"I dunno. He could tell you."

I went out of the thick-aired stuffy backroom with its unwashed windows, and when I got opposite the Bible near the door I said:

"What's the matter with him anyhow? Why doesn't he straighten things out here?"

Again the clerk awoke. "Huh!" he exclaimed. "Straighten it out! Gar! I'd like to see anybody try it."

"It could be," I said encouragingly.

"Gar!" he chuckled. "One man did try to straighten it out once when Mr. Burridge was away. Got about a third of it cleaned up when he come back. Gar! You oughta seen him! Gar!"

"What did he do?"

"What did he do! What didn't he do! Gar! Just took things an' threw them about again. Said he couldn't find anything."

"You don't say!"

"Gar! I should say so! Man come in an' asked for a hammer. Said he couldn't find any hammer, things was so mixed up. Did it with screws, water-buckets an' everything just the same. Took 'em right off the shelves, where they was all in groups, an' scattered 'em all over the room. Gar! 'Now I guess I can find something when I want it,' he said." The clerk paused to squint and add, "There ain't anybody tried any straightenin' out around here since then, you bet. Gar!"

"How long ago has that been?"

"About fourteen years now."

Surprised by this sharp variation from the ordinary standards of trade, I began thinking of possible conditions which had produced it, when one evening I happened in on the local barber. He was a lean, inquisitive individual with a shock of sandy hair and a conspicuous desire to appear a well-rounded social factor.

"What sort of person is this Burridge over here? He keeps such a peculiar store."

"Elihu is a bit peculiar," he replied, his smile betraying a desire to appear conservative. "The fault with Elihu, if he has one, is that he's terribly strong on religion. Can't seem to agree with anybody around here."

"What's the trouble?" I asked.

"It's more'n I could ever make out, what is the matter with him. They're all a little bit cracked on the subject around here. Nothing but revivals and meetin's, year in and year out. They're stronger on it winters than they are in summer."

"How do you mean?"

"Well, they'll be more against yachtin' and Sunday pleasures when they can't go than when they can."

"What about Elihu?" I asked.

"Well, he can't seem to get along, somehow. He used to belong to the Baptist Church, but he got out o' that. Then he went to a church up in Graylock, but he had a fallin' out up there. Then he went to Northfield and Eustis. He's been all around, even over on Long Island. He goes to church up at Amherst now, I believe."

"What seems to be the trouble?"

"Oh, he's just strong-headed, I guess." He paused, and ideas lagged until finally I observed:

"It's a very interesting store he keeps."

"It's just as Billy Drumgold told him once: 'Burridge,' he says, 'you've got everything in this store that belongs to a full-rigged ship 'cept one thing.' 'What's that?' Burridge asks. 'A second-hand pulpit.' 'Got that too,' he answered, and takes him upstairs, and there he had one sure enough."

"Well," I said, " what was he doing with it?"

"Danged if I know. He had it all right. Has it yet, so they say."

Days passed and as the summer waned the evidences of a peculiar life accumulated. Noank, apparently, was at outs with Burridge on the subject of religion, and he with it. There were instances of genuine hard feeling against him.

Writing a letter in the Postoffice one day I ventured to take up this matter with the postmaster.

"You know Mr. Burridge, don't you—the grocer?"

"Well, I should guess I did," he replied with a flare.

"Anything wrong with him?"

"Oh, about everything that's just plain cussed—the most wrangling man alive. I never saw such a man. He don't get his mail here no more because he's mad at me, I guess. Took it away because I had Mr. Palmer's help in my fight, I suppose. Wrote me that I should send all his mail up to Mystic, and he goes there three or four miles out of his way every day, just to spite me. It's against the law. I hadn't ought to be doing it, re-addressing his envelopes three or four times a day, but I do do it. He's a strong-headed man, that's the trouble with Elihu."

I had no time to follow this up then, but a little later, sitting in the shop of the principal sailboat maker, which was situated in the quiet little lane which follows the line of the village, I was one day surprised by the sudden warm feeling which the name of Elihu generated. Something had brought up the subject of religion, and I said that Burridge seemed rather religious.

"Yes," said the sailboat maker quickly, "he's religious, all right, only he reads the Bible for others, not for himself."

"What do you mean by that?"

"Why, he wants to run things, that's what. As long as you agree with Elihu, why, everything's all right. When you don't, the Bible's against you. That's the way he is."

"Did he ever disagree with you?" I asked, suspecting some personal animus in the matter.

"Me and Elihu was always good friends as long as I agreed with him," he went on bitterly. "We've been raised together, man and boy, for pretty near sixty years. We never had a word of any kind but what was friendly, as long as I agreed with him, but just as soon as I didn't he took a set against me, and we ain't never spoke a word since."

"What was the trouble?" I inquired sweetly, anxious to come at the kernel of this queer situation.

"Well," he said, dropping his work and looking up to impress me, "I'm a man that'll sometimes say what I don't believe; that is, I'll agree with what I hadn't ought to, just to be friendly like. I did that way a lot o' times with Elihu till one day he came to me with something about particular salvation. I'm a little more liberal myself. I believe in universal redemption by faith alone. Well, Elihu came to me and began telling me what he believed. Finally he asked me something about particular salvation and wanted to know whether I didn't agree with him. I didn't, and told him so. From that day on he took a set against me, and he ain't never spoke a word to me since."

I was unaware that there was anything besides a religious disagreement in this local situation until one day I happened to come into a second friendly contact with the postmaster. We were speaking of the characteristics of certain individuals, and I mentioned Burridge.

"He's all right when you take him the way he wants to be taken. When you don't you'll find him quite a different man."

"He seems to be straightforward and honest," I said.

"There ain't anything you can tell me about Elihu Burridge that I don't know," he replied feelingly. "Not a thing. I've lived with him, as you might say, all my life. Been raised right here in town with him, and we went to school together. Man and boy, there ain't ever been a thing that Elihu has agreed with, without he could have the running of it. You can't tell me anything about him that I don't know."

I could not help smiling at the warmth of feeling, although something about the man's manner bespoke a touch of heart-ache, as if he were privately grieving.

"What was the trouble between you two?" I asked.

"It's more'n I could ever find out," he replied in a voice that was really mournful, so difficult and non-understandable was the subject to him. "Before I started to work for this office there wasn't a day that I didn't meet and speak friendly with Elihu. He used to have a good many deeds and papers to sign, and he never failed to call me in when I was passing. When I started to work for this office I noticed he took on a cold manner toward me, and I tried to think of something I might have done, but I couldn't. Finally I wrote and asked him if there was anything between us if he wouldn't set a time and place so's we might talk it over and come to an under-standing." He paused and then added, "I wish you could see the letter he wrote me. Comin' from a Christian man—from him to me—I wish you could see it."

"Why don't you show it to me?" I asked inquisitively.

He went back into the office and returned with an ancient-looking document, four years old it proved to be, which he had been treasuring. He handed me the thumbed and already yellowed page, and I read:

"MATTHEW HOLCOMB, ESQUIRE,

"DEAR SIR:—In reply to your letter asking me to set a time and place in which we might talk over the trouble between us, would say that the time be Eternity and the place where God shall call us to judgment.

"Very truly,

"ELIHU BURRIDGE."

His eyes rested on me while I read, and the moment I finished he began with:

"I never said one word against that man, not one word. I never did a thing he could take offense at, not one thing. I don't know how a man can justify himself writing like that."

"Perhaps it's political," I said. "You don't belong to the same party, do you?"

"Yes, we do," he said. "Sometimes I've thought that maybe it was because I had the support of the shipyard when I first tried to get this office, but then that wasn't anything between him and me," and he looked away as if the mystery were inexplicable.

This shipyard was conducted by a most forceful man but one as narrow and religionistic as this region in which it had had its rise. Old Mr. Palmer, the aged founder of it, had long been a notable figure in the streets and private chambers of the village. The principal grocery store, coal-yard, sail-loft, hotel and other institutions were conducted in its interests. His opinion was always foremost in the decision of the local authorities. He was still, reticent, unobtrusive. Once I saw him most considerately helping a cripple up the lane to the local Baptist Church.

"What's the trouble between Burridge and Palmer?" I asked of the sail-maker finally, coming to think that here, if anywhere, lay the solution of the difficulty.

"Two big fish in too small a basket," he responded laconically.

"Can't agree, eh?"

"They both want to lead, or did," he said. "Elihu's a beaten man, though, now." He paused and then added, "I'm sorry for Elihu. He's a good man at heart, one of the kindest men you ever saw, when you let him follow his natural way. He's good to the poor, and he's carried more slow-pay people than any man in this country, I do believe. He won't collect an old debt by law. Don't believe in it. No, sir. Just a kind-hearted man, but he loves to rule."

"How about Palmer?" I inquired.

"Just the same way exactly. He loves to rule, too. Got a good heart, too, but he's got a lot more money than Elihu and so people pay more attention to him, that's all. When Elihu was getting the attention he was just the finest man you ever saw, kind, generous, good-natured. People love to be petted, at least some people do—you know they do. When you don't pet 'em they get kind o' sour and crabbed like. Now that's all that's the matter with Elihu, every bit of it. He's sour, now, and a little lonely, I expect. He's drove away every one from him, or nearly all, 'cept his wife and some of his kin. Anybody can do a good grocery business here, with the strangers off the boats"—the harbor was a lively one— "all you have to do is carry a good stock. That's why he gets along so well. But he's drove nearly all the local folks away from him."

I listened to this comfortable sail-loft sage, and going back to the grocery store one afternoon took another look at the long, grim-faced silent figure. He was sitting in the shadow of one of his moldy corners, and if there had ever been any light of merriment in his face it was not there now. He looked as fixed and solemn as an ancient puritan, and yet there was something so melancholy in the man's eye, so sad and disappointed, that it seemed anything but hard. Two or three little children were playing about the door and when he came forward to wait on me one of them sidled forward and put her chubby hand in his.

"Your children?" I asked, by way of reaching some friendly understanding.

"No," he replied, looking fondly down, "she belongs to a French lady up the street here. She often comes down to see me, don't you?" and he reached over and took the fat little cheek between his thumb and forefinger.

The little one rubbed her face against his worn baggy trousers' leg and put her arm about his knee. Quietly he stood there in a simple way until she loosened her hold upon him, when he went about his labor.

I was sitting one day in the loft of the comfortable sailmaker, who, by the way, was brother-in-law to Burridge, when I said to him:

"I wish you'd tell me the details about Elihu. How did he come to be what he is? You ought to know; you've lived here all your life."

"So I do know," he replied genially. "What do you want me to tell you?"

"The whole story of the trouble between him and Palmer; how he comes to be at outs with all these people."

"Well," he began, and here followed with many interruptions and side elucidations, which for want of space have been eliminated, the following details:

Twenty-five years before Elihu had been the leading citizen of Noank. From operating a small grocery at the close of the Civil War he branched out until he sold everything from ship-rigging to hardware. Noank was then in the height of its career as a fishing town and as a port from which expeditions of all sorts were wont to sail. Whaling was still in force, and vessels for whaling expeditions were equipped here. Wealthy sea-captains frequently loaded fine three-masted schooners here for various trading expeditions to all parts of the world; the fishers for mackerel, cod and herring were making three hundred and fifty dollars a day in season, and thousands of dollars' worth of supplies were annually purchased here.

Burridge was then the only tradesman of any importance and, being of a liberal, strong-minded and yet religious turn, attracted the majority of this business to him. He had houses and lands, was a deacon in the local Baptist Church and a counselor in matters political, social and religious, whose advice was seldom rejected. Every Fourth of July during these years it was his custom to collect all the children of the town in front of his store and treat them to ice-cream. Every Christmas Eve he traveled about the streets in a wagon, which carried half a dozen barrels of candy and nuts, which he would ladle out to the merry shouting throng of pursuing youngsters, until all were satisfied. For the skating season he prepared a pond, spending several thousand dollars damming up a small stream, in order that the children might have a place to skate. He created a library where all might obtain suitable reading, particularly the young.

On New Year's morning it was his custom to visit all the poor and bereaved and lonely in Noank, taking a great dray full of presents and leaving a little something with his greetings and a pleasant handshake at every door. The lonely rich as well as the lonely poor were included, for he was certain, as he frequently declared, that the rich could be lonely too.

He once told his brother-in-law that one New Year's Day a voice called to him in church: "Elihu Burridge, how about the lonely rich and poor of Noank?" "Up I got," he concluded, "and from that day to this I have never neglected them."

When any one died who had a little estate to be looked after for the benefit of widows or orphans, Burridge was the one to take charge of it. People on their deathbeds sent for him, and he always responded, taking energetic charge of everything and refusing to take a penny for his services. After a number of years the old judge to whom he always repaired with these matters of probate, knowing his generosity in this respect, also refused to accept any fee. When he saw him coming he would exclaim:

"Well, Elihu, what is it this time? Another widow or orphan that we've got to look after?"

After Elihu had explained what it was, he would add:

"Well, Elihu, I do hope that some day some rich man will call you to straighten out his affairs. I'd like to see *you* get a little something, so that *I* might get a little something. Eh, Elihu?" Then he would jocularly poke his companion in charity in the ribs.

These general benefactions were continuous and coeval with his local prosperity and dominance, and their modification as well as the man's general decline the result of the rise of this other individual—Robert Palmer,—"operating" to take the color of power and preëminence from him.

Palmer was the owner of a small shipyard here at the time, a thing which was not much at first but which grew swiftly.

He was born in Noank also, a few years before Burridge, and as a builder of vessels had been slowly forging his way to a moderate competence when Elihu was already successful. He was a keen, fine-featured, energetic individual, with excellent commercial and strong religious instincts, and by dint of hard labor and a saving disposition he obtained, soon after the Civil War, a powerful foothold. Many vessels were ordered here from other cities. Eventually he began to build barges in large numbers for a great railroad company.

Early becoming a larger employer of labor than any one else in the vicinity he soon began to branch out, possessed himself of the allied industries of ship-rigging, chandlering, and finally established a grocery store for his employees, and opened a hotel. Now the local citizens began to look upon him as their leading citizen. They were always talking of his rise, frequently in the presence of Burridge. He said nothing at first, pretending to believe that his quondam leadership was unimpaired. Again, there were those who, having followed the various branches of labor which Palmer eventually consolidated, viewed this growth with sullen and angry eyes. They still sided with Burridge, or pretended still to believe that he was the more important citizen of the two. In the course of time, however—a period of thirty years or more—some of them failed; others died; still others were driven away for want of a livelihood. Only Burridge's position and business remained, but in a sadly weakened state. He was no longer a man of any great importance.

Not unnaturally, this question of local supremacy was first tested in the one place in which local supremacy is usually tested—the church where they both worshiped. Although only one of five trustees, Burridge had been the will of the body. Always, whatever he thought, the others had almost immediately agreed to it. But now that Palmer had become a power, many of those ardent in the church and beholden to him for profit became his humble followers. They elected him trustee and did what he wished, or what they thought he wished. To Burridge this made them sycophants, slaves.

Now followed the kind of trivialities by which most human feuds are furthered. The first test of strength came when a vagrant evangelist from Alabama arrived and desired to use the church for a series of evening lectures. The question had to be decided at once. Palmer was absent at the time.

"Here is a request for the use of the church," said one of the trustees, explaining its nature.

"Well," said Burridge, "you'd better let him have it."

"Do you think we ought to do anything about it," the trustee replied, "until Mr. Palmer returns?"

Although Burridge saw no reason for waiting, the other trustees did, and upon that the board rested. Burridge was furious. By one fell stroke he was put in second place, a man who had to await the return of Palmer—and that in his own church, so to speak.

"Why," he told some one, "the rest of us are nothing. This man is a king."

From that time on differences of opinion within the church and elsewhere were common. Although no personal animosity was ever admitted, local issues almost invariably found these two men opposed to each other. There was the question of whether the village should be made into a borough—a most trivial matter; another, that of creating public works for the manufacture of gas and distribution of water; a third, that of naming a State representative. Naturally, while these things might be to the advantage of Palmer or not, they were of no great import to Burridge, but yet he managed to see in them an attempt or attempts to saddle a large public debt upon widows and orphans, those who could not afford or did not need these things, and he proceeded to so express himself at various public meetings. Slowly the breach widened. Burridge became little more than a malcontent in many people's eyes. He was a "knocker," a man who wanted to hold the community back.

Although defeated in many instances he won in others, and this did not help matters any. At this point, among other things the decay of the fishing industry helped to fix definitely the position of the two men as that of victor and vanquished. Whaling died out, then mackerel and cod were caught only at farther and farther distances from the town, and finally three- and even two-masted schooners ceased entirely to buy their outfits here, and Burridge was left dependent upon local patronage or smaller harbor trade for his support. Coextensively, he had the dissatisfaction of seeing Palmer's industries grow until eventually three hundred and fifty men were upon his payrolls and even his foremen and superintendents were considered influential townspeople. Palmer's son and two daughters grew up and married, branched out and became owners of industries which had formerly belonged to men who had traded with Burridge. He saw his grocery trade dwindle and sink, while with age his religiosity grew, and he began to be little more than a petty disputant, one constantly arguing as to whether the interpretation of the Bible as handed down from the pulpit of what he now considered *his* recalcitrant church was sound or not. When those who years before had followed him obediently now pricked him with theological pins and ventured to disagree with him, he was quick and sometimes foolish in his replies. Thus, once a former friend and fellow-church-member who had gone over to the opposition came into his store one morning and said:

"Elihu, for a man that's as strong on religion as you are, I see you do one thing that can't quite be justified by the Book."

"What's that?" inquired Burridge, looking up.

"I see you sell tobacco."

"I see you chew it," returned the host grimly.

"I know I do," returned his visitor, "but I'll tell you what I'll do, Elihu. If you'll quit selling, I'll quit chewing it," and he looked as if he had set a fancy trap for his straw-balancing brother, as he held him to be.

"It's a bargain," said Burridge on the instant. "It's a bargain!"

And from that day on tobacco was not offered for sale in that store, although there was a large local demand for it.

Again, in the pride of his original leadership, he had accepted the conduct of the local cemetery, a thing which was more a burden than a source of profit. With his customary liberality in all things reflecting credit upon himself he had spent his own money in improving it, much more than ever the wardens of the church would have thought of returning to him. In one instance, when a new receiving vault was desired, he had added seven hundred dollars of his own to three hundred gathered by the church trustees for the purpose, and the vault was immediately constructed. Frequently also, in his pride of place, he had been given to asserting he was tired of conducting the cemetery and wished he could resign.

In these later evil days, therefore, the trustees, following the star of the newer power, saw fit to intimate that perhaps some one else would be glad to look after it if he was tired of it. Instantly the fact that he could no longer boast as formerly came home to him. He was not essential any longer in anything. The church did not want him to have a hand in any of its affairs! The thought of this so weighed on him that eventually he resigned from this particular task, but thereafter also every man who had concurred in accepting his resignation was his bitter enemy. He spoke acidly of the seven hundred he had spent, and jibed at the decisions of the trustees in other matters. Soon he became a disturbing element in the church, taking a solemn vow never to enter the graveyard again, and not long after resigned all his other official duties—passing the plate, et cetera—although he still attended services there.

Decoration Day rolled around, the G. A. R. Post of which he was an ardent member prepared for the annual memorial services over the graves of its dead comrades. Early on the morning of the thirtieth of May they gathered before their lodge hall, Burridge among them, and after arranging the details marched conspicuously to the cemetery where the placing of the wreaths and the firing of the salute were to take place. No one thought of Burridge until the gate was reached, when, gun over shoulder and uniform in perfect trim, he fell conspicuously out of line and marched away home alone. It was the cemetery he had vowed not to enter, his old pet and protégé.

Men now looked askance at him. He was becoming queer, no doubt of it, not really sensible—or was he? Up in Northfield, a nearby town, dwelt a colonel of the Civil War who had led the very regiment of which Burridge was a member but who during the war had come into serious difficulty through a tangle of orders, and had been dishonorably discharged. Although wounded in one of the engagements in which the regiment had distinguished itself, he had been allowed to languish almost forgotten for years and finally, failing to get a pension, had died in poverty. On his deathbed he had sent for Burridge, and reminding him of the battle in which he had led him asked that after he was gone, for the sake of his family, he would take up the matter of a pension and if possible have his record purged of the stigma and the pension awarded.

Burridge agreed most enthusiastically. Going to the local congressman, he at once began a campaign, but because of the feeling against him two years passed without anything being done. Later he took up the matter in his own G. A. R. Post, but there also failing to find the measure of his own enthusiasm, he went finally direct to one of the senators of the State and laying the matter before him had the records examined by Congress and the dead colonel honorably discharged.

One day thereafter in the local G. A. R. he commented unfavorably upon the indifference which he deemed had been shown.

"There wouldn't have been half so much delay if the man hadn't been a deserter," said one of his enemies—one who was a foreman in Palmer's shipyard.

Instantly Burridge was upon his feet, his eyes aflame with feeling. Always an orator, with a strangely declamatory style he launched into a detailed account of the late colonel's life and services, his wounds, his long sufferings and final death in poverty, winding up with a vivid word picture of a battle (Antietam), in which the colonel had gallantly captured a rebel flag and come by his injury.

When he was through there was great excitement in the Post and much feeling in his favor, but he rather weakened the effect by at once demanding that the traitorous words be withdrawn, and failing to compel this, preferred charges against the man who had uttered them and attempted to have him court-martialed.

So great was the bitterness engendered by this that the Post was now practically divided, and being unable to compel what he considered justice he finally resigned. Subsequently he took issue with his former fellow-soldiers in various ways, commenting satirically on their church regularity and professed Christianity, as opposed to their indifference to the late colonel, and denouncing in various public conversations the double-mindedness and sharp dealings of the "little gods," as he termed those who ran the G. A. R. Post, the church, and the shipyards.

Not long after his religious affairs reached a climax when the minister, once a good friend of his, following the lead of the dominant star, Mr. Palmer, publicly denounced him from the pulpit one Sunday as an enemy of the church and of true Christianity!

"There is a man in this congregation," he exclaimed in a burst of impassioned oratory, "who poses as a Christian and a Baptist, who is in his heart's depth the church's worst enemy. Hell and all its devils could have no worse feelings of evil against the faith than he, and he doesn't sell tobacco, either!"

The last reference at once fixed the identity of the person, and caused Burridge to get up and leave the church. He pondered over this for a time, severed his connections with the body, and having visited Graylock one Sunday drove there every Sabbath thereafter, each time going to a different church. After enduring this for six months he generated a longing for a more convenient meeting-place, and finally allied himself with the Baptist Church of Eustis. Here his anchor might possibly have remained fast had it not been that subtle broodings over his wrongs, a calm faith in the righteousness of his own attitude, and disgust with those whom he saw calmly expatiating upon the doctrines and dogmas of religion in his own town finally caused him to suspect a universal misreading of the Bible. This doubt, together with his own desire for justification according to the Word, finally put the idea in his mind to make a study of the Bible himself. He would read it, he said. He would study Hebrew and Greek, and refer all questionable readings of words and passages back to the original tongue in which it had been written.

With this end in view he began a study of these languages, the importance of the subject so growing upon him that he neglected his business. Day after day he labored, putting a Bible and a Concordance upon a pile of soap-boxes near the door of his store and poring over them between customers, the store meantime taking care of itself. He finally mastered

Greek and Hebrew after a fashion, and finding the word "re-pent" frequently used, and that God had made man in the image of Himself, with a full knowledge of right and wrong, he gravitated toward the belief that therefore his traducers in Noank knew what they were doing, and that before he needed to forgive them—though his love might cover all—they must repent.

He read the Bible from beginning to end with this one feeling subconsciously dominant, and all its loving commands about loving one another, forgiving your brother seventy times seven, loving those that hate you, returning good for evil, selling all that you have and giving it to the poor, were made to wait upon the duty of others to repent. He began to give this interpretation at Eustis, where he was allowed to have a Sunday-school, until the minister came and told him once, "to his face," as the local report ran: "We don't want you here."

Meekly he went forth and, joining a church across the Sound on Long Island, sailed over every Sunday and there advanced the same views until he was personally snubbed by the minister and attacked by the local papers. Leaving there he went to Amherst, always announcing now that he held distinctive views about some things in the Bible and asking the privilege of explaining. In this congregation he was still comfortably at rest when I knew him.

"All sensitiveness," the sail-maker had concluded after his long account. "There ain't anything the matter with Elihu, except that he's piqued and grieved. He wanted to be the big man, and he wasn't."

I was thinking of this and of his tender relationship with children as I had noticed it, and of his service to the late colonel when one day being in the store, I said:

"Do you stand on the Bible completely, Mr. Burridge?"

"Yes, sir," he replied, "I do."

"Believe every word of it to be true?"

"Yes, sir."

"If your brother has offended you, how many times must you forgive him?"

"Seventy times seven."

"Do you forgive your brothers?"

"Yes, sir—if they repent."

"If they repent?"

"Yes, sir, if they repent. That's the interpretation. In Matthew you will find, 'If he repent, forgive him.'"

"But if you don't forgive them, even before they repent," I said, "aren't you harboring enmity?"

"No, sir, I'm not treasuring up enmity. I only refuse to forgive them."

I looked at the man, a little astonished, but he looked so sincere and earnest that I could not help smiling.

"How do you reconcile that with the command, 'Love one another?' You surely can't love and refuse to forgive them at the same time?"

"I don't refuse to forgive them," he repeated. "If John there," indicating an old man in a sun-tanned coat who happened to be passing through the store at the time, "should do me a wrong—I don't care what it was, how great or how vile—if he should come to me and say, 'Burridge, I'm sorry,'" he executed a flashing oratorical move in emphasis, and throwing back his head, exclaimed: "It's gone! It's gone! There ain't any more of it! All gone!"

I stood there quite dumbfounded by his virility, as the air vibrated with his force and feeling. So manifestly was his reading of the Bible colored by the grief of his own heart that it was almost painful to tangle him with it. Goodness and mercy colored all his ideas, except in relation to his one-time followers, those who had formerly been his friends and now left him to himself.

"Do you still visit the poor and the afflicted, as you once did?" I asked him once.

"I'd rather not say anything about that," he replied sternly.

"But do you?"

"Yes, sir."

"Still make your annual New Year round?"

"Yes, sir."

"Well, you'll get your reward for that, whatever you believe."

"I've had my reward," he said slowly.

"Had it?"

"Yes, sir, had it. Every hand that's been lifted to receive the little I had to offer has been my reward."

He smiled, and then said in seemingly the most untimely way:

"I remember once going to a lonely woman here on New Year's Day and taking her a little something—basket of grapes or fruit of some kind it was. I was stopping a minute—never stay long, you know; just run in and say 'Happy New Year!' leave what I have and get out—and so said, 'Good morning, Aunt Mary!'

" 'Good morning, Elihu,' says she.

" 'Can't stay long, Aunt Mary,' I said. 'Just want to leave you these. Happy New Year!'

"Well, sir, you know I was just turning around and starting when she caught hold of my sleeve and says:

" 'Elihu Burridge,' she says, 'give me that hand!' and do you know, before I knew what she was about she took it up to her lips and kissed it! Yes, she did—kissed my hand!

"Now," he said, drawing himself up, with eyes bright with intense feeling, "you know whether I've had my reward or not, don't you?"

"Vanity, Vanity,"
Saith the Preacher

SOMETIMES a single life will clearly and effectively illustrate a period. Hence, to me, the importance of this one.

I first met X—— at a time when American financial methods and American finances were at their apex of daring and splendor, and when the world was in a more or less tolerant mood toward their grandiose manners and achievements. It was the golden day of Mr. Morgan, Senior, Mr. Belmont, Mr. Harriman, Mr. Sage, Mr. Gates, Mr. Brady, and many, many others who were still extant and ruling distinctly and drastically, as was proved by the panic of 1907. In opposition to them and yet imitating their methods, now an old story to those who have read "Frenzied Finance," "Lawless Wealth," and other such exposures of the methods which produced our enormous American fortunes, were such younger men as Charles W. Morse (the victim of the 1907 panic), F. Augustus Heinze (another if less conspicuous victim of the same "panic"), E. R. Thomas, an ambitious young millionaire, himself born to money, David A. Sullivan, and X——. I refuse to mention his name because he is still alive although no longer conspicuous, and anxious perhaps to avoid the uncomfortable glare of publicity when all the honors and comforts which made it endurable in the first place are absent.

The person who made X—— essentially interesting to me long before I met him was one Lucien de Shay, a ne'er-do-well pianist and voice culturist, who was also a connoisseur in the matters of rugs, hangings, paintings and furniture, things in which X—— was just then most intensely interested, erecting, as he was, a great house on Long Island and but newly blossoming into the world of art or fashion or culture or show—those various things which the American multi-millionaire always wants to blossom or bloom into and which he does not always succeed in doing. De Shay was one of those odd natures so common to the metropolis—half artist and half man of fashion who attach themselves so readily to men of strength and wealth, often as advisors and

counselors in all matters of taste, social form and social progress. How this particular person was rewarded I never quite
knew, whether in cash or something else. He was also a semi-
confidant of mine, furnishing me "tips" and material of one
sort and another in connection with the various publications
I was then managing. As it turned out later, X—— was not
exactly a multi-millionaire as yet, merely a fledgling, although
the possibilities were there and his aims and ambitions were
fast nearing a practical triumph the end of which of course
was to be, as in the case of nearly all American multi-million-
aires of the newer and quicker order, bohemian or exotic and
fleshly rather than cultural or æsthetic pleasure, although the
latter were never really exactly ignored.

But even so. He was a typical multi-millionaire in the
showy and even gaudy sense of the time. For if the staid and
conservative and socially well-placed rich have the great
houses and the ease and the luxury of paraphernalia, the bohemian rich of the X—— type have the flare, recklessness and
imagination which lend to their spendings and flutterings a
sparkle and a shine which the others can never hope to match.

Said this friend of mine to me one day: "Listen, I want you
to meet this man X——. You will like him. He is fine. You
haven't any idea what a fascinating person he really is. He
looks like a Russian Grand Duke. He has the manners and
the tastes of a Medici or a Borgia. He is building a great
house down on Long Island that once it is done will have
cost him five or six hundred thousand. It's worth seeing already. His studio here in the C—— studio building is a
dream. It's thick with the loveliest kinds of things. I've helped
buy them myself. And he isn't dull. He wrote a book at
twenty, 'Icarus,' which is not bad either and which he says is
something like himself. He has read your book ("Sister Carrie") and he sympathizes with that man Hurstwood. Says
parts of it remind him of his own struggles. That's why he
wants to meet you. He once worked on the newspapers too.
God knows how he is making his money, but I know how he
is spending it. He's decided to live, and he's doing it splen-
didly. It's wonderful."

I took notice, although I had never even heard of the man.
There were so very, very many rich men in America. Later I

heard much more concerning him from this same de Shay. Once he had been so far down in the scale that he had to shine shoes for a living. Once he had walked the streets of New York in the snow, his shoes cracked and broken, no overcoat, not even a warm suit. He had come here a penniless emigrant from Russia. Now he controlled four banks, one trust company, an insurance company, a fire insurance company, a great real estate venture somewhere, and what not. Naturally all of this interested me greatly. When are we indifferent to a rise from nothing to something?

At de Shay's invitation I journeyed up to X——'s studio one Wednesday afternoon at four, my friend having telephoned me that if I could I must come at once, that there was an especially interesting crowd already assembled in the rooms, that I would meet a long list of celebrities. Two or three opera singers of repute were already there, among them an Italian singer and sorceress of great beauty, a veritable queen of the genus adventuress, who was setting the town by the ears not only by her loveliness but her voice. Her beauty was so remarkable that the Sunday papers were giving full pages to her face and torso alone. There were to be several light opera and stage beauties there also, a basso profundo to sing, writers, artists, poets.

I went. The place and the crowd literally enthralled me. It was so gay, colorful, thrilling. The host and the guests were really interesting—to me. Not that it was so marvelous as a studio or that it was so gorgeously decorated and furnished—it was impressive enough in that way—but that it was so gracefully and interestingly representative of a kind of comfort disguised as elegance. The man had everything, or nearly so—friends, advisors, servants, followers. A somewhat savage and sybaritic nature, as I saw at once, was here disporting itself in velvets and silks. The iron hand of power, if it was power, was being most gracefully and agreeably disguised as the more or less flaccid one of pleasure and friendship.

My host was not visible at first, but I met a score of people whom I knew by reputation, and listened to clatter and chatter of the most approved metropolitan bohemian character. The Italian sorceress was there, her gorgeous chain earrings tinkling mellifluously as she nodded and gesticulated. De Shay at once whispered in my ear that she was X——'s very latest flame and an expensive one too. "You should see what he buys her!" he exclaimed in a whisper. "God!" Actresses and society women floated here and there in dreams of afternoon dresses. The automobiles outside were making a perfect uproar. The poets and writers fascinated me with their praises of the host's munificence and taste. At a glance it was plain to me that he had managed to gather about him the very element it would be most interesting to gather, supposing one desired to be idle, carefree and socially and intellectually gay. If America ever presented a smarter drawing-room I never saw it.

My friend de Shay, being the fidus Achates of the host, had the power to reveal the inner mysteries of this place to me, and on one or two occasions when there were not so many present and while the others were chattering in the various rooms—music-, dining-, ball-, library and so forth—I was being shown the kitchen, pantry, wine cellar, and also various secret doors and passages whereby mine host by pressing a flower on a wall or a spring behind a picture could cause a door to fly open or close which gave entrance to or from a room or passage in no way connected with the others save by another secret door and leading always to a private exit. I wondered at once at the character of the person who could need, desire or value this. A secret bedroom, for instance; a lounging-room! In one of these was a rather severe if handsome desk and a steel safe and two chairs—no more; a very bare room. I wondered at this silent and rather commercial sanctum in the center of this frou-frou of gayety, no trace of the sound of which seemed to penetrate here. What I also gained was a sense of an exotic, sybaritic and purely pagan mind, one which knew little of the conventions of the world and cared less.

On my first visit, as I was leaving, I was introduced to the host just within his picture gallery, hung with many fine examples of the Dutch and Spanish schools. I found him to be as described: picturesque and handsome, even though somewhat plump, phlegmatic and lethargic—yet active enough. He was above the average in height, well built, florid, with a huge, round handsome head, curly black hair, keen black eyes, heavy overhanging eyebrows, full red lips, a marked chin ornamented by a goatee. In any costume ball he would have made an excellent Bacchus or Pan. He appeared to have the free, easy and gracious manner of those who have known much of life and have achieved, in part at least, their desires. He smiled, wished to know if I had met all the guests, hoped that the sideboard had not escaped me, that I had enjoyed the singing. Would I come some evening when there was no crowd—or, better yet, dine with him and my friend de Shay, whose personality appeared to be about as agreeable to him as his own. He was sorry he could not give me more attention now.

Interestingly enough, and from the first, I was impressed with this man; not because of his wealth (I knew richer men) but because of a something about him which suggested dreams, romance, a kind of sense or love of splendor and grandeur which one does not often encounter among the really wealthy. Those cracked shoes were in my mind, I suppose. He seemed to live among great things, but in no niggardly, parsimonious or care-taking way. Here was ease, largess, a kind of lavishness which was not ostentation but which seemed rather to say, "What are the minute expenses of living and pleasuring as contrasted with the profits of skill in the world outside?" He suggested the huge and Aladdin-like adventures with which so many of the great financiers of the day, the true tigers of Wall Street, were connected.

It was not long thereafter that I was once more invited, this time to a much more lavish affair and something much more sybaritic in its tone, although I was really not conscious of what it was to be like when I went there. It began at twelve midnight, and to this day it glitters in my mind as among the few really barbaric and exotic things that I have ever witnessed. Not that the trappings or hangings or setting were so outré or amazing as that the atmosphere of the thing itself was relaxed, bubbling, pagan. There were so many daring and seeking people there. The thing sang and was talked of for months after—in whispers! The gayety! The abandon! The sheer intoxication, mental and physical! I never saw more daring costumes, so many really beautiful women (glitteringly so) in one place at one time, wonderful specimens of exotic and in the main fleshy or sensuous femininity. There was, among other things, as I recall, a large nickeled ice-tray on wheels packed with unopened bottles of champagne, and you had but to lift a hand or wink an eye to have another opened for you alone, ever over and over. And the tray was always full. One wall of the dining-room farther on was laden with delicate novelties in the way of food. A string quartette played for the dancers in the music-room. There were a dozen corners in different rooms screened with banks of flowers and concealing divans. The dancing and singing were superb, individual, often abandoned in character, as was the conversation. As the morning wore on (for it did not begin until after midnight) the moods of all were either so mellowed or inflamed as to make intentions, hopes, dreams, the most secret and sybaritic, the order of expression. One was permitted to see human nature stripped of much of its repression and daylight reserve or cant. At about four in the morning came the engaged dancers, quite the pièce de résistance—with wreaths about heads, waists and arms for clothing and well, really nothing more beyond their beautiful figures—scattering rose leaves or favors. These dancers the company itself finally joined, single file at first, pellmell afterwards—artists, writers, poets—dancing from room to room in crude Bacchic imitation of their leaders—the women too—until all were singing, parading, swaying and dancing in and out of the dozen rooms. And finally, liquor and food affecting them, I suppose, many fell flat, unable to do anything thereafter but lie upon divans or in corners until friends assisted them elsewhere—to taxis finally. But mine host, as I recall him, was always present, serene, sober, smiling, unaffected, bland and gracious and untiring in his attention. He was there to keep order where otherwise there would have been none.

I mention this merely to indicate the character of a long series of such events which covered the years 19— to 19—. During that time, for the reason that I have first given (his curious pleasure in my company), I was part and parcel of a dozen such more or less vivid affairs and pleasurings, which stamped on my mind not only X—— but life itself, the possibilities and resources of luxury where taste and appetite are involved, the dreams of grandeur and happiness which float

in some men's minds and which work out to a wild fruition—dreams so outré and so splendid that only the tyrant
of an obedient empire, with all the resources of an enslaved
and obedient people, could indulge with safety. Thus once, I
remember, that a dozen of us—writers and artists—being assembled in his studio in New York one Friday afternoon for
the mere purpose of idling and drinking, he seeming to have
nothing better to do for the time being, he suddenly suggested, and as though it had but now occurred to him, that
we all adjourn to his country house on Long Island, which
was not yet quite finished (or, rather, furnished), but which
was in a sufficient state of completion to permit of appropriate entertainment providing the necessaries were carried out
there with us.

As I came to think of this afterward, I decided that after all
it was not perhaps so unpremeditated as it seemed and that
unconsciously we served a very useful purpose. There was
work to do, suggestions to be obtained, an overseer, decora-
tor and landscape gardener with whom consultations were absolutely necessary; and nothing that X—— ever did was
without its element of calculation. Why not make a gala affair
of a rather dreary November task—

Hence—

At any rate the majority of us forthwith agreed, since
plainly it meant an outing of the most lavish and pleasing
nature. At once four automobiles were pressed into service,
three from his own garage and one specially engaged elsewhere. There was some telephoning *in re* culinary supplies to
a chef in charge of the famous restaurant below who was *en
rapport* with our host, and soon some baskets of food were
produced and subsequently the four cars made their appearance at the entryway below. At dusk of a gray, cold, smoky
day we were all bundled into these—poets, playwrights, nov-
elists, editors (he professed a great contempt for actors), and
forthwith we were off, to do forty-five miles between five-
thirty and seven p. m.

I often think of that ride, the atmosphere of it, and what it
told of our host's point of view. He was always so grave,
serene, watchful yet pleasant and decidedly agreeable, gay
even, without seeming so to be. There was something so

amazingly warm and exotic about him and his, and yet at the same time something so cold and calculated, as if after all he were saying to himself, "I am the master of all this, am stage-managing it for my own pleasure." I felt that he looked upon us all not so much as intimates or friends as rather fine birds or specimens of one kind and another, well qualified to help him with art and social ideas if nothing more—hence his interest in us. Also, in his estimation no doubt, we reflected some slight color or light into his life, which he craved. We had done things too. Nevertheless, in his own estimation, he was the master, the Can Grande. He could at will "take us up or leave us out," or so he thought. We were mere toys, fine feathers, cap-and-bell artists. It was nice to "take us around," have us with him. Smothered in a great richly braided fur coat and fur cap, he looked as much the Grand Duke as one might wish.

But I liked him, truly. And what a delicious evening and holiday all told he made of it for us. By leaving a trail of frightened horses, men and women, and tearing through the gloom as though streets were his private race-track—I myself as much frightened as any at the roaring speed of the cars and the possibilities of the road—we arrived at seven, and by eight were seated to a course dinner of the most gratifying character. There was no heat in the house as yet, but from somewhere great logs had been obtained and now blazed in the large fireplaces. There was no electricity as yet—a private plant was being installed—but candles and lamps blazed in lovely groups, casting a soft glow over the great rooms. One room lacked a door, but an immense rug took its place. There were rugs, hangings and paintings in profusion, many of them as yet unhung. Some of the most interesting importations of furniture and statuary were still in the cases in which they had arrived, with marks of ships and the names of foreign cities upon the cases. Scattered about the great living-room, dining-room, music-room and library were enough rugs, divans and chairs as well as musical instruments—a piano among others—to give the place an air of completeness and luxury. The walls and ceilings had already been decorated—in a most florid manner, I must say. Outside were great balconies and verandahs commanding, as the following

morning proved, a very splendid view of a very bleak sea. The
sand dunes! The distant floor of the sea! The ships! Upstairs
were nine suites of one- and two-rooms and bath. The basement was an intricate world of kitchen, pantry, engine-room,
furnace, wine cellars and what not. Outside was a tawny
waste of sand held together in places in the form of hummocks and even concealing hills by sand-binding grasses.

That night, because it was windy and dull and bleak, we
stayed inside, I for one going outside only long enough to
discover that there were great wide verandahs of concrete
about the house, fit for great entertainments in themselves,
and near at hand hummocks of sand. Inside all was warm and
flaring enough. The wine cellar seemed to contain all that one
might reasonably desire. Our host once out here was most
gay in his mood. He was most pleasantly interested in the
progress of his new home, although not intensely so. He
seemed to have lived a great deal and to be making the best
of everything as though it were something to go through
with. With much talking on the part of us all, the evening
passed swiftly enough. Some of the men could play and sing.
One poet recited enchanting bits of verse. For our inspection
certain pieces of furniture and statuary were unpacked and
displayed—a bronze faun some three feet in height, for one
thing. All the time I was sensible of being in contact with
some one who was really in touch with life in a very large
way, financially and otherwise. His mind seemed to be busy
with all sorts of things. There were two Syrians in Paris, he
said, who owned a large collection of rugs suitable for an
exhibition. He had an agent who was trying to secure the best
of them for his new home. De Shay had recently introduced
him to a certain Italian count who had a great house in Italy
but could not afford its upkeep. He was going to take over a
portion of its furnishings, after due verification, of course.
Did I know the paintings of Monticelli and Mancini? He had
just secured excellent examples of both. Some time when his
new home was further along I must come out. Then the pictures would be hung, the statuary and furniture in place. He
would get up a week-end party for a select group.

The talk drifted to music and the stage. At once I saw that
because of his taste, wealth and skill, women formed a large

and yet rather toy-like portion of his life, holding about as much relation to his inner life as do the concubines of an Asiatic sultan. Madame of the earrings, as I learned from de Shay, was a source of great expense to him, but at that she was elusive, not easily to be come at. The stage and Broadway were full of many beauties in various walks of life, many of whom he knew or to whom he could obtain access. Did I know thus and so—such-and-such an one?

"I'll tell you," he said after a time and when the wine glasses had been refilled a number of times, " we must give a party out here some time, something extraordinary, a real one. De Shay and Bielow" (naming another artist) "and my-self must think it out. I know three different dancers"—and he began to enumerate their qualities. I saw plainly that even though women played a minor part in his life, they were the fringe and embroidery to his success and power. At one a. m. we went to our rooms, having touched upon most of the themes dear to metropolitan lovers of life and art.

The next morning was wonderful—glittering, if windy. The sea sparkled beyond the waste of sand. I noted anew the richness of the furnishings, the greatness of the house. Set down in so much sand and facing the great sea, it was won-derful. There was no order for breakfast; we came down as we chose. A samovar and a coffee urn were alight on the table. Rolls, chops, anything, were brought on order. Possibly because I was one of the first about, my host singled me out—he was up and dressed when I came down—and we strolled over the estate to see what we should see.

Curiously, although I had seen many country homes of pretension and even luxury, I never saw one that appealed to me more on the ground of promise and, after a fashion, of partial fulfillment. It was so unpretentiously pretentious, so really grand in a limited and yet poetic way. Exteriorly its placement, on a rise of ground commanding that vast sweep of sea and sand, its verandahs, so very wide—great smooth floors of red concrete—bordered with stone boxes for flowers and handsomely designed stone benches, its long walks and drives but newly begun, its stretch of beach, say a half mile away and possibly a mile and a half long, to be left, as he remarked, "au naturel," driftwood, stones and all, struck me most favorably. Only one long pier for visiting yachts was to be built, and a certain stretch of beach, not over three hundred feet, cleared for bath houses and a smooth beach. On one spot of land, a high hummock reaching out into the sea, had already been erected a small vantage tower, open at the bottom for shade and rest, benches turning in a circle upon a concrete floor, above it a top looking more like a small bleak lighthouse than anything else. In this upper portion was a room reached by small spiral concrete stairs!

I could not help noting the reserve and *savoir faire* with which my host took all this. He was so healthy, assured, interested and, I am glad to say, not exactly self-satisfied; at least he did not impress me in that way—a most irritating condition. Plainly he was building a very splendid thing. His life was nearing its apex. He must not only have had millions but great taste to have undertaken, let alone accomplished, as much as was already visible here. Pointing to a bleak waste of sand between the house and the sea—and it looked like a huge red and yellow bird perched upon a waste of sand—he observed, "When you come again in the spring that will contain a garden of 40,000 roses. The wind is nearly always off the sea here. I want the perfume to blow over the verandahs. I can rotate the roses so that a big percentage of them will always be in bloom."

We visited the stables, the garage, an artesian well newly driven, a drive that was to skirt the sea, a sunken garden some distance from the house and away from the sea.

Next spring I came once more—several times, in fact. The rose garden was then in bloom, the drives finished, the pictures hung. Although this was not a world in which society as yet deigned to move it was entirely conceivable that at a later period it might, and betimes it was crowded with people smart enough and more agreeable in the main than the hardy, strident members of the so-called really inner circles. There were artists, writers, playwrights, singers, actresses, and some nondescript figures of the ultra-social world—young men principally who seemed to come here in connection with beautiful young women, models and other girls whose beauty was their only recommendation to consideration.

The scene was not without brilliance. A butler and nu-

merous flunkeys fluttered to and fro. Guests were received at
the door by a footman. A housekeeper and various severe-
looking maids governed in the matter of cleaning. One could
play golf, tennis, bridge, motor, fish, swim, drink in a free
and even disconcerting manner or read quietly in one angle
or another of the grounds. There were affairs, much flirting
and giggling, suspicious wanderings to and fro at night—no
questions asked as to who came or whether one was married,
so long as a reasonable amount of decorum was maintained.
It was the same on other occasions, only the house and
grounds were full to overflowing with guests and passing
friends, whose machines barked in the drives. I saw as many
gay and fascinating costumes and heard as much clever and at
times informative talk here as anywhere I have been.

During this fall and winter I was engaged in work which
kept me very much to myself. During the period I read much
of X——, banks he was combining, new ventures he was undertaking. Yet all at once one winter's day, and out of a clear
sky, the papers were full of an enormous financial crash of
which he was the center. According to the newspapers, the
first and foremost of a chain of banks of which he was the
head, to say nothing of a bonding and realty company and
some street railway project on Long Island, were all involved
in the crash. Curiously, although no derogatory mention had
previously been made of him, the articles and editorials were
now most vituperative. Their venom was especially noticeable. He was a get-rich-quick villain of the vilest stripe; he
had been juggling a bank, a trust company, an insurance company and a land and street railway speculative scheme as one
would glass balls. The money wherewith he gambled was not
his. He had robbed the poor, deceived them. Yet among all
this and in the huge articles which appeared the very first day,
I noted one paragraph which stuck in my mind, for I was
naturally interested in all this and in him. It read:

"Wall Street heard yesterday that Superintendent H——
got his first information concerning the state in which
X——'s affairs were from quarters where resentment may
have been cherished because of his activity in the Long Island
Traction field. This is one of the Street's 'clover patches' and

the success which the newcomer seemed to be meeting did not provoke great pleasure."

Another item read:

"A hitch in a deal that was to have transferred the South Shore to the New York and Queens County System, owned by the Long Island Railroad, at a profit of almost $2,000,000 to X——, was the cause of all the trouble. Very active displeasure on the part of certain powers in Wall Street blocked, it is said, the closing of the deal for the railroad. They did not want him in this field, and were powerful enough to prevent it. At the same time pressure from other directions was brought to bear on him. The clearing-house refused to clear for his banks. X—— was in need of cash, but still insisting on a high rate of remuneration for the road which he had developed to an important point. Their sinister influences entered and blocked the transfer until it was no longer possible for him to hold out."

Along with these two items was a vast mass of data, really pages, showing how, when, where he had done thus and so, "juggled accounts" between one bank and another, all of which he controlled however and most of which he owned, drew out large sums and put in their place mortgages on, or securities in, new companies which he was organizing—tricks which were the ordinary routine of Wall Street and hence rather ridiculous as the sub-stone of so vast a hue and cry.

I was puzzled and, more than that, moved by the drama of the man's sudden end, for I understood a little of finance and its ways, also of what place and power had plainly come to mean to him. It must be dreadful. Yet how could it be, I asked myself, if he really owned fifty-one per cent or more in so many companies that he could be such a dark villain? After all, ownership is ownership, and control, control. On the face of the reports themselves his schemes did not look so black. I read everything in connection with him with care.

As the days passed various other things happened. For one thing, he tried to commit suicide by jumping out of a window of his studio in New York; for another, he tried to take poison. Now of a sudden a bachelor sister, of whom I had never heard in all the time I had known him, put in an appearance as his nearest of kin—a woman whose name was not his own but a variation of it, an "-ovitch" having suddenly been tacked onto it. She took him to a sanitarium, from which he was eventually turned out as a criminal, then to a hospital, until finally he surrendered himself to the police. The names of great lawyers and other bankers began to enter the case. Alienists of repute, those fine chameleons of the legal world, were employed who swore first that he was insane, then that he was not. His sister, who was a physician and scientist of repute, asked the transfer of all his property to her on the ground that he was incompetent and that she was his next of kin. To this she swore, giving as her reasons for believing him insane that he had "illusions of grandeur" and that he believed himself "persecuted by eminent financiers," things which smacked more of sanity than anything else to me. At the same time he and she, as time rather indicated, had arranged this in part in the hope of saving something out of the great wreck. There were other curious features: Certain eminent men in politics and finance who from revelations made by the books of the various banks were in close financial if not personal relations with X—— denied this completely. Curiously, the great cry on the part of these was that he was insane, must be, and that he was all alone in his schemes. His life on Broadway, on Long Island, in his studio in New York, were ransacked for details. Enough could not be made of his gay, shameful, spendthrift life. No one else, of course, had ever been either gay or shameful before—especially not the eminent and hounding financiers.

Then from somewhere appeared a new element. In a staggeringly low tenement region in Brooklyn was discovered somehow or other a very old man and woman, most unsatisfactory as relatives of such imposing people, who insisted that they were his parents, that years before because he and his sister were exceedingly restless and ambitious, they had left them and had only returned occasionally to borrow money, finally ceasing to come at all. In proof of this, letters, witnesses, old photos, were produced. It really did appear as if he and his sister, although they had long vigorously denied it, really were the son and daughter of the two who had been petty bakers in Brooklyn, laying up a little competence of their own. I never knew who "dug" them up, but the reason why was plain enough. The sister was laying claim to the property as the next of kin. If this could be offset, even though X—— were insane, the property would at once be thrown into the hands of the various creditors and sold under a forced sale, of course—in other words, for a song—for their benefit. Naturally it was of interest to those who wished to have his affairs wound up to have the old people produced. But the great financier had been spreading the report all along that he was from Russia, that his parents, or pseudo-parents, were still there, but that really he was the illegitimate son of the Czar of Russia, boarded out originally with a poor family. Now, however, the old people were brought from Brooklyn and compelled to confront him. It was never really proved that he and his sister had neglected them utterly or had done anything to seriously injure them, but rather that as they had grown in place and station they had become more or less estranged and so ignored them, having changed their names and soared in a world little dreamed of by their parents. Also a perjury charge was made against the sister which effectually prevented her from controlling his estate, a lease long enough to give the financiers time for their work. Naturally there was a great hue and cry over her, the scandal, the shame, that they should thus publicly refuse to recognize their parents as they did or had when confronted by them. Horrible! There were most heavily illustrated and tearful Sunday articles, all blazoned forth with pictures of his house and studio, his banks, cars, yacht, groups of guests, while the motives of those who produced the parents were overlooked. The pictures of the parents confronting X—— and his sister portrayed very old and feeble people, and were rather moving. They insisted that they were his parents and wept brokenly in their hands. But why? And he denying it! His sister, who resented all this bitterly and who stood by him valiantly, repudiated, for his sake of course, his and her so-called parents and friends.

I never saw such a running to cover of "friends" in all my life. Of all those I had seen about his place and in his company, scores on scores of people reasonably well known in the arts, the stage, the worlds of finance and music, all eating his dinners, riding in his cars, drinking his wines, there was scarcely any one now who knew him anything more than "casually" or "slightly"—oh, so slightly! When rumors as to the midnight suppers, the Bacchic dancing, the automobile parties to his great country place and the spirited frolics which occurred there began to get abroad, there was no one whom I knew who had ever been there or knew anything about him or them. For instance, of all the people who had been close or closest and might therefore have been expected to be friendly and deeply concerned was de Shay, his fidus Achates and literally his pensioner—yet de Shay was almost the loudest in his denunciation or at least deprecation of X——, his habits and methods! Although it was he who had told me of Mme. —— and her relation to X——, who urged me to come here, there and the other place, especially where X—— was the host, always assuring me that it would be so wonderful and that X—— was really such a great man, so generous, so worth-while, he was now really the loudest or at least the most stand-offish in his comments, pretending never to have been very close to X——, and lifting his eyebrows in astonishment as though he had not even guessed what he had actually engineered. His "Did-you-hears," "Did-you-knows" and "Wouldn't-have-dreamed" would have done credit to a tea-party. He was so shocked, especially at X——'s robbing poor children and orphans, although in so far as my reading of the papers went I could find nothing that went to prove that he had any intention of robbing anybody—that is, directly. In the usual Wall Street high finance style he was robbing Peter to pay Paul, that is, he was using the monies of one corporation which he controlled to bolster up any of the others which he controlled, and was " washing one hand with the other," a proceeding so common in finance that to really radically and truly oppose it, or do away with it, would mean to bring down the whole fabric of finance in one grand crash.

Be that as it may. In swift succession there now followed the so-called "legal" seizure and confiscation of all his properties. In the first place, by alienists representing the District Attorney and the State banking department, he was declared sane and placed on trial for embezzlement. Secondly, his sister's plea that his property be put into her hands as trustee or administrator was thrown out of court and she herself arrested and confined for perjury on the ground that she had perjured herself in swearing that she was his next of kin when in reality his real parents, or so they swore, were alive and in America. Next, his banks, trust companies and various concerns, including his great country estate, were swiftly thrown into the hands of receivers (what an appropriate name!) and wound up "for the benefit of creditors." All the while X——— was in prison, protesting that he was really not guilty, that he was solvent, or had been until he was attacked by the State bank examiner or the department back of him, and that he was the victim of a cold-blooded conspiracy which was using the State banking department and other means to drive him out of financial life, and that solely because of his desire to grow and because by chance he had been impinging upon one of the choicest and most closely guarded fields of the ultra-rich of Wall Street—the street railway area in New York and Brooklyn.

One day, so he publicly swore to the grand jury, by which he was being examined, as he was sitting in his great offices, in one of the great sky-scrapers of New York, which occupied an entire floor and commanded vast panoramas in every direction (another evidence of the man's insane "delusion of grandeur," I presume), he was called to answer the telephone. One Mr. Y———, so his assistant said, one of the eminent financiers of Wall Street and America, was on the wire. Without any preliminary and merely asking was this Mr. X——— on the wire, the latter proceeded, "This is Mr. Y———. Listen closely to what I am going to say. I want you to get out of the street railway business in New York or something is going to happen to you. I am giving you a reasonable warning. Take it." Then the phone clicked most savagely and ominously and superiorly at the other end.

"I knew at the time," went on X———, addressing the grand jury, "that I was really listening to the man who was most powerful in such affairs in New York and elsewhere and that he meant what he said. At the same time I was in no position to get out without closing up the one deal which stood to net me two million dollars clear if I closed it. At the same time I wanted to enter this field and didn't see why I shouldn't. If I didn't it spelled not ruin by any means but a considerable loss, a very great loss, to me, in more ways than one. Oddly enough, just at this time I was being pressed by those with whom I was associated to wind up this particular venture and turn my attention to other things. I have often wondered, in the light of their subsequent actions, why they should have become so pressing just at this time. At the same time, perhaps I was a little vain and self-sufficient. I had once got the better of some agents of another great financier in a Western Power deal, and I felt that I could put this thing through too. Hence I refused to heed the warning. However, I found that all those who were previously interested to buy or at least develop the property were now suddenly grown cold, and a little later when, having entered on several other matters, I needed considerable cash, the State banking department descended on me and, crying fraud and insolvency, closed all my banks.

"You know how it is when they do this to you. Cry 'Fire!' and you can nearly wreck a perfectly good theater building. Depositors withdraw, securities tumble, investigation and legal expenses begin, your financial associates get frightened or ashamed and desert you. Nothing is so squeamish or so retiring and nervous as money. Time will show that I was not insolvent at the time. The books will show a few technically illegal things, but so would the books or the affairs of any great bank, especially at this time, if quickly examined. I was doing no more than all were doing, but they wanted to get me out—and they did."

Regardless of proceedings of various kinds—legal, technical and the like—X—— was finally sent to the penitentiary, and spent some time there. At the same time his confession finally wrecked about nine other eminent men, financiers all. A dispassionate examination of all the evidence eight years later caused me to conclude without hesitation that the man had been a victim of a cold-blooded conspiracy, the object of which was to oust him from opportunities and to forestall him in methods which would certainly have led to enormous wealth. He was apparently in a position and with the brains to do many of the things which the ablest and coldest financiers of his day had been and were doing, and they did not want to be bothered with, would not brook, in short, his approaching rivalry. Like the various usurpers of regal powers in ancient days, they thought it best to kill a possible claimant to the throne in his infancy.

But that youth of his! The long and devious path by which he had come! Among the papers relating to the case and to a time when he could not have been more than eighteen, and when he was beginning his career as a book agent, was a letter written to his mother (August, 1892), which read:

"MY DEAR PARENTS: Please answer me at once if I can have anything of you, or something of you or nothing. Remember this is the first and the last time in my life that I beg of you anything. You have given to the other child not $15 but hundreds, and now when I, the very youngest, ask of you, my parents, $15, are you going to be so hard-hearted as to refuse me? Without these $15 it is left to me to be without income for two or three weeks.

"For God's sake, remember what I ask of you, and send me at once so that I should cease thinking of it. Leon, as I have told you, will give me $10, $15 he has already paid for the contract, and your $15 will make $25. Out of this I need $10 for a ticket and $15 for two or three weeks' board and lodging.

"Please answer at once. Don't wait for a minute, and send me the money or write me one word 'not.' Remember this only that if you refuse me I will have nothing in common with you.

"Your son,

"_____"

There was another bit of testimony on the part of one Henry Dom, a baker, who for some strange reason came forward to identify him as some one he had known years before in Williamsburgh, which read:

"I easily recognize them" (X—— and his sister) "from their pictures in the newspapers. I worked for X——'s father, who was a baker in Williamsburgh, and frequently addressed letters that were written by X—— Senior and his wife to Dr. Louise X—— who was then studying medicine in Philadelphia. X—— was then a boy going to school, but working in his father's bakery mornings and evenings. He did not want to do that, moaned a great deal, and his parents humored him in his attitude. He was very vain, liked to appear intellectual. They kept saying to their friends that he should have a fine future. Five years later, after I had left them once, I met the mother and she told me that X—— was studying banking and getting along fine."

Some seven years after the failure and trial by which he had so summarily been disposed of and after he had been released from prison, I was standing at a certain unimportant street corner in New York waiting for a car when I saw him. He was passing in the opposite direction, not very briskly, and, as I saw, plainly meditatively. He was not so well dressed. The clothes he wore while good were somehow different, lacking in that exquisite something which had characterized him years before. His hat—well, it was a hat, not a Romanoff shako nor a handsome panama such as he had affected in the old days. He looked tired, a little worn and dusty, I thought.

My first impulse was of course to hail him, my second not, since he had not seen me. It might have been embarrassing, and at any rate he might not have even remembered me. But as he walked I thought of the great house by the sea, the studio, the cars, the 40,000 roses, the crowds at his summer place, the receptions in town and out, Madame of the earrings (afterward married to a French nobleman), and then of the letter to his mother as a boy, the broken shoes in the winter time, his denial of his parents, the telephone message from the financial tiger. "Vanity, vanity," saith the preacher. The shores of our social seas are strewn with pathetic wrecks, the whitening bone of half-sand-buried ships.

At the next corner he paused, a little uncertain apparently as to which way to go, then turned to the left and was lost. I have never seen nor heard of him since.

The Mighty Rourke

WHEN I FIRST met him he was laying the foundation for a small dynamo in the engine-room of the repair shop at Spike, and he was most unusually loud in his protestations and demands. He had with him a dozen Italians, all short, swarthy fellows of from twenty-five to fifty years of age, who were busy bringing material from a car that had been pushed in on the side-track next to the building. This was loaded with crushed stone, cement, old boards, wheelbarrows, tools, and the like, all of which were to be used in the labor that he was about to undertake. He himself was standing in the doorway of the shop where the work was to be conducted, coat off, sleeves rolled up, and shouting with true Irish insistence, "Come, Matt! Come, Jimmie! Get the shovels, now! Get the picks! Bring some sand here! Bring some stone! Where's the cement, now? Where's the cement? Jasus Christ! I must have some cement! What arre ye all doin'? What do ye think ye're up here fer? Hurry, now, hurry! Bring the cement!" and then, having concluded this amazing fanfare, calmly turning to gaze about as if he were the only one in the world who had the right to stand still.

More or less oppressed with life myself at the time, I was against all bosses, and particularly against so seemingly a vicious one as this. "What a slave driver!" I thought. "What a brute!" And yet I remember thinking that he was not exactly unpleasant to look at, either—quite the contrary. He was medium in height, thick of body and neck, with short gray hair and mustache, and bright, clear, twinkling Irish gray eyes, and he carried himself with an air of unquestionable authority. It was much as if he had said, "I am the boss here"; and, indeed, he was. Is it this that sends the Irish to rule as captains of hundreds the world over?

The job he was bossing was not very intricate or important, but it was interesting. It consisted of digging a trench ten by twelve feet, and shaping it up with boards into a "form," after which concrete was to be mixed and poured in, and some iron rods set to fasten the engine to—an engine bed, no less. It was not so urgent but that it might have been conducted with far less excitement, but what are you to do when you are naturally excitable, love to make a great noise, and feel that things are going forward whether they are or not? Plainly this particular individual loved noise and a great stir. So eager was he to have done with it, no matter what it was or where, that he was constantly trotting to and fro, shouting, "Come, Matt! Come, Jimmie! Hurry, now, bring the shovels! Bring the picks!" and occasionally bursting forth with a perfect avalanche of orders. "Up with it! Down with it! Front with it! Back with it! In with it! Out with it!" all coupled with his favorite expletive, "Jasus Christ," which was as innocent of evil, I subsequently came to know, as a prayer. In short, he was simply wild Irish, and that was all there was to him—a delightful specimen, like Namgay Doola.

But, as I say, at the time he seemed positively appalling to me, a virulent specimen, and I thought, "The Irish brute! To think of human beings having to work for a brute like that! To think of his driving men like that!" However, I soon began to discover that he was not so bad as he seemed, and then I began to like him.

The thing that brought about this swift change of feeling in me was the attitude of his men toward him. Although he was so insistent with his commands, they did not seem to mind nor to strain themselves working. They were not killing themselves, by any means. He would stand over them, crying, "Up with it! Up with it! Up with it! Up with it!" or "Down with it! Down with it! Down with it!" until you would have imagined their nerves would be worn to a frazzle. As it was, however, they did not seem to care any more than you would for the ticking of a clock; rather, they appeared to take it as a matter of course, something that had to be, and that one was prepared for. Their steps were in the main as leisurely as those of idlers on Fifth Avenue or Broadway. They carried boards or stone as one would objects of great value. One could not help smiling at the incongruity of it; it was farcical. Finally gathering the full import of it all, I ventured to laugh, and he turned on me with a sharp and yet not unkindly retort.

"Ha! ha! ha!" he mocked. "If ye had to work as hard as these min, ye wouldn't laugh."

I wanted to say, "Hard work, indeed!" but instead I

replied, "Is that so? Well, I don't see that they're killing themselves, or you either. You're not as fierce as you sound."

Then I explained that I was not laughing at them but at him, and he took it all in good part. Since I was only a nominal laborer here, not a real one—permitted to work for my health, for twelve cents an hour—we fell to conversing upon railroad matters, and in this way our period of friendship began.

As I learned that morning, Rourke was the foreman-mason for minor tasks for all that part of the railroad that lay between New York and fifty miles out, on three divisions. He had a dozen or so men under him and was in possession of one car, which was shunted back and forth between the places in which he happened to be working. He was a builder of concrete platforms, culverts, coal-bins, sidewalks, bridge and building piers, and, in fact, anything that could be made out of crushed stone and cement, or bricks and stone, and he was sent here and there, as necessity required. As he explained to me at the time, he sometimes rose as early as four a. m. in order to get to his place of labor by seven. The great railroad company for which he toiled was no gentle master, and did not look upon his ease, or that of his men, as important. At the same time, as he himself confessed, he did not mind hard work—liked it, in short. He had been working now for the company for all of twenty-two years, "rain or shine." Darkness or storm made no difference to him. "Shewer, I have to be there," he observed once with his quizzical, elusive Irish grin. "They're not payin' me wages fer lyin' in bed. If ye was to get up that way yerself every day fer a year, me b'y," he added, eyeing my spare and none too well articulated frame, "it'd make a man av ye."

"Yes?" I said tolerantly. "And how much do you get, Rourke?"

"Two an' a half a day."

"You don't say!" I replied, pretending admiration.

The munificence of the corporation that paid him two and a half dollars a day for ten hours' work, as well as for superintending and constructing things of such importance, struck me forcibly. Perhaps, as we say in America, he "had a right" to be happy, only I could not see it. At the same time, I could not help thinking that he was better situated than myself at the time. I had been ill, and was now earning only twelve cents an hour for ten hours' work, and the sight of the foreman for whom I was working was a torture to my soul. He was such a loud-mouthed, blustering, red-headed ignoramus, and I wanted to get out from under him. At the same time, I was not without sufficient influence so to do, providing I could find a foreman who could make use of me. The great thing was to do this, and the more I eyed this particular specimen of foreman the better I liked him. He was genial, really kindly, amazingly simple and sincere. I decided to appeal to him to take me on his staff.

"How would you like to take me, Mr. Rourke, and let me work for you?" I asked hopefully, after explaining to him why I was here.

"Shewer," he replied. "Ye'd do fine."

"Would I have to work with the Italians?" I asked, wondering how I would make out with a pick and shovel. My frame was so spare at the time that the question must have amused him, considering the type of physique required for day labor.

"There'll be plenty av work fer ye to do without ever yer layin' a hand to a pick er shovel," he replied comfortingly. "Shewer, that's no work fer white min. Let the nagurs do it. Look at their backs an' arrms, an' then look at yers."

I was ready to blush for shame. These poor Italians whom I was so ready to contemn were immeasurably my physical superiors.

"But why do you call them negroes, Rourke?" I asked after a time. "They're not black."

"Well, bedad, they're not white, that's waan thing shewer," he added. "Aany man can tell that be lookin' at thim."

I had to smile. It was so dogmatic and unreasoning.

"Very well, then, they're black," I said, and we left the matter.

Not long after I put in a plea to be transferred to him, at his request, and it was granted. The day that I joined his flock, or gang, as he called it, he was at Williamsbridge, a little station north on the Harlem, building a concrete coal-bin. It was a pretty place, surrounded by trees and a grass-plot, a vast improvement upon a dark indoor shop, and seemed to me a veritable haven of rest. Ah, the smiling morning sun, the green leaves, the gentle fresh winds of heaven!

Rourke was down in an earthen excavation under the depot platform when I arrived, measuring and calculating with his plumb-bob and level, and when I looked in on him hopefully he looked up and smiled.

"So here ye arre at last," he said with a grin.

"Yes," I laughed.

"Well, ye're jist in time; I waant ye to go down to the ahffice."

"Certainly," I replied, but before I could say more he climbed out of his hole, his white jeans odorous of the new-turned earth, and fished in the pocket of an old gray coat which lay beside him for a soiled and crumpled letter, which he finally unfolded with his thick, clumsy fingers. Then he held it up and looked at it defiantly.

"I waant ye to go to Woodlawn," he continued, "an' look after some bolts that arre up there—there's a keg av thim—an' sign the bill fer thim, an' ship thim down to me. An' thin I waant ye to go down to the ahffice an' take thim this o. k." Here again he fished around and produced another crumpled slip, this time of a yellow color (how well I came to know them!), which I soon learned was an o. k. blank, a form which had to be filled in and signed for everything received, if no more than a stick of wood or a nail or a bolt. The company demanded these of all foremen, in order to keep its records straight. Its accounting department was useless without them. At the same time, Rourke kept talking of the "nonsinse av it," and the "onraisonableness" of demanding o. k.s for everything. "Ye'd think some one was goin' to sthale thim from thim," he declared irritably and defiantly.

I saw at once that some infraction of the railroad rules had occurred and that he had been "called down," or "jacked up" about it, as the railroad men expressed it. He was in a high state of dudgeon, and as defiant and pugnacious as his royal Irish temper would allow. At the same time he was pleased to think that I or some one had arrived who would relieve him of this damnable "nonsinse," or so he hoped. He was not so inexperienced as not to imagine that I could help him with all this. In fact, as time proved, this was my sole reason for being here.

He flung a parting shot at his superior as I departed.

"Tell him that I'll sign fer thim when I get thim, an' not before," he declared.

I went on my way, knowing full well that no such message was for delivery, and that he did not intend that it should be. It was just the Irish of it. I went off to Woodlawn and secured the bolts, after which I went down to the "ahffice" and reported. There I found the chief clerk, a mere slip of a dancing master in a high collar and attractive office suit, who was also in a high state of dudgeon because Rourke, as he now explained, had failed to render an o. k. for this and other things, and did not seem to understand that he, the chief clerk, must have them to make up his reports. Sometimes o. k.s did not come in for a month or more, the goods lying around somewhere until Rourke could use them. He wanted to know what explanation Rourke had to offer, and when I suggested that the latter thought, apparently, that he could leave all consignments of goods in one station or another until such time as he needed them before he o. k.ed for them, he fairly foamed.

"Say," he almost shouted, at the same time shoving his hands distractedly through his hair, "what does he think I am? How does he think I'm going to make up my books? He'll leave them there until he needs them, will he? Well, he's a damned fool, and you go back and tell him I said so. He's been long enough on the road to know better. You go back and tell him I said that I want a signed form for everything consigned to him the moment he learns that it's waiting for him, and I want it right away, without fail, whether it's a single nut or a car of sand. I want it. He's got to come to time about this now, or something's going to drop. I'm not going to stand it any longer. How does he think I'm going to make up my books? I wish he'd let you attend to these matters while you're up there. It will save an awful lot of trouble in this office and it may save him his job. There's one thing sure: he's got to come to time from now on, or either he quits or I do."

These same o. k.s plus about twenty-five long-drawn-out

reports or calculations, retroactive and prospective, covering every possible detail of his work from the acknowledgment of all material received up to and including the expenditure of even so much as one mill's worth of paper, were the bane of my good foreman's life. As I learned afterward, he had nearly his whole family, at least a boy and two girls, assisting him nights on this part of the work. In addition, while they were absolutely of no import in so far as the actual work of construction was concerned—and that was really all that interested Rourke—they were an essential part of the system which made it possible for him to do the work at all—a point which he did not seem to be able to get clear. At the same time, there was an unsatisfactory side to this office technicalia, and it was this: If a man could only sit down and reel off a graphic account of all that he was doing, accompanied by facts and figures, he was in excellent standing with his superiors, no matter what his mechanical defects might be; whereas, if his reports were not clear, or were insufficient, the efficiency of his work might well be overlooked. In a vague way, Rourke sensed this and resented it. He knew that his work was as good as could be done, and yet here were these constant reports and o. k.s to irritate and delay him. Apparently they aided actual construction no whit—but, of course, they did. Although he was a better foreman than most, still, because of his lack of skill in this matter of accounting, he was looked upon as more or less a failure, especially by the chief clerk. Naturally, I explained that I would do my best, and came away.

When I returned, however, I decided to be politic. I could not very well work with a pick and shovel, and this was about all that was left outside of that. I therefore explained as best I could the sad plight of the chief clerk, who stood in danger of losing his job unless these things came in promptly.

"You see how it is, Rourke, don't you?" I pleaded.

He seemed to see, but he was still angry.

"An o. k. blank! An o. k. blank!" he echoed contentiously, but in a somewhat more conciliatory spirit. "He wants an o. k. blank, does he? Well, I expect ye might as well give thim to him, thin. I think the man lives on thim things, the way he's aalways caallin' fer thim. Ye'd think I

was a bookkeeper an' foreman at the same time; it's some-
thin' aaful. An o. k. blank! An o. k. blank!" and he sput-
tered to silence.

A little while later he humorously explained that he had
"clane forgot thim, anyhow."

The ensuing month was a busy one for us. We had a platform to lay at Morrisania, a chimney to build at Tarrytown, a
sidewalk to lay at White Plains, and a large cistern to dig and
wall in at Tuckahoe. Besides these, there were platforms to
build at Van Cortlandt and Mount Kisco, water-towers at
Highbridge and Ardsley, a sidewalk and drain at Caryl, a cul-
vert and an ash-pit at Bronx Park, and some forty concrete
piers for a building at Melrose—all of which required any
amount of running and figuring, to say nothing of the actual
work of superintending and constructing, which Rourke
alone could look after. It seemed ridiculous to me at the time
that any one doing all this hard practical labor should not be
provided with a clerk or an accountant to take at least some
of this endless figuring off his hands. At the same time, if he
had been the least bit clever, he could have provided himself
with one permanently by turning one of his so-called laborers
into a clerk—carrying a clerk as a laborer—but plainly it had
never occurred to him. He depended on his family. The preliminary labor alone of ordering and seeing that the material
was duly shipped and unloaded was one man's work; and yet
Rourke was expected to do it all.

In spite of all this, however, he displayed himself a masterful worker. I have never seen a better. He preferred to super-
intend, of course, to get down into the pit or up on the wall,
and measure and direct. At the same time, when necessary to
expedite a difficult task, he would toil for hours at a stretch
with his trowel and his line and his level and his plumb-bob,
getting the work into shape, and you would never hear a personal complaint from him concerning the weariness of labor.
On the contrary, he would whistle and sing until something
went wrong, when suddenly you would hear the most terrific
uproar of words: "Come out av that! Come out, now! Jasus
Christ, man, have ye no sinse at aall? Put it down! Put it
down! What arre ye doin'? What did I tell ye? Have ye no
raison in ye, no sinse, ye h'athen nagur?"

"Great heavens!" I used to think, "what has happened now?"

You would have imagined the most terrible calamity; and yet, all told, it might be nothing of any great import—a little error of some kind, more threatening than real, and soon adjusted. It might last for a few moments, during which time the Italians would be seen hurrying excitedly to and fro; and then there would come a lull, and Rourke would be heard to raise his voice in tuneful melody, singing or humming or whistling some old-fashioned Irish "Come-all-ye."

But the thing in Rourke that would have pleased any one was his ready grasp for the actualities of life—his full-fledged knowledge that work is the thing, not argument, or reports, or plans, but the direct accomplishment of something tangible, the thing itself. Thus, while I was working with him, at least nothing that might concern the clerical end of the labor could disturb him, but, if the sky fell, and eight thousand chief clerks threatened to march upon him in a body demanding reports and o. k.s, he would imperturbably make you wait until the work was done. Once, when I interrupted him to question him concerning some of these same wretched, pestering aftermaths of labor, concerning which he alone could answer, he shut me off with: "The reports! The reports! What good arre the reports! Ye make me sick. What have the reports to do with the work? If it wasn't fer the work, where would the reports be?" And I heartily echoed "Where?"

Another thing was his charming attitude toward his men, kindly and sweet for all his storming, that innate sense of something intimate and fatherly. He had a way of saying kindly things in a joking manner which touched them. When he arrived in the morning, for instance, it was always in the cheeriest way that he began. "Come, now, b'ys, ye have a good day's work before ye today. Get the shovels, Jimmie. Bring the line, Matt!" and then he would go below himself, if below it was, and there would be joy and peace until some obstacle to progress interfered. I might say in passing that Matt and Jimmie, his faithful henchmen, were each between forty and fifty, if they were a day—poor, gnarled, dusty, storm-tossed Italians who had come from heaven knows where, had endured God knows what, and were now rounding

out a work-a-day existence under the sheltering wing of this
same Rourke, a great and protecting power to them.

This same Matt was a funny little Italian, soft of voice and
gentle of manner, whom Rourke liked very much, but with
whom he loved to quarrel. He would go down in any hole
where the latter was working, and almost invariably shortly
after you would hear the most amazing uproar issuing therefrom, shouts of: "Put it here, I say! Put it here! Down with
it! Here! Here! Jasus Christ, have ye no sinse at aall?"—coupled, of course, with occasional guttural growls from Matt,
who was by no means in awe of his master and who feared
no personal blows. The latter had been with Rourke for so
long that he was not in the least overawed by his yelling and
could afford to take such liberties. Occasionally, not always,
Rourke would come climbing out of the hole, his face and
neck fairly scarlet with heat, raging and shouting, "I'll get
shut av ye! I'll have no more thruck with ye, ye blitherin',
crazy loon! What good arre ye? What work can ye do? Naathin'! Naathin'! I'll be shut av ye now, an' thin maybe I'll have
a little p'ace." Then he would dance around and threaten and
growl until something else would take his attention, when he
would quiet down and be as peaceful as ever. Somehow, I
always felt that in spite of all the difficulties involved, he enjoyed these rows—must fight, in short, to be happy. Sometimes he would go home without saying a word to Matt, a
conclusion which at first I imagined portended the end of the
latter, but soon I came to know better. For the next morning
Matt would reappear as unconcernedly as though nothing
had happened, and Rourke would appear not to notice or
remember.

Once, anent all this, I said to him, "Rourke, how many
times have you threatened to discharge Matt in the last three
years?"

"Shewer," he replied, with his ingratiating grin, "a man
don't mane aall he says aall the time."

The most humorous of all his collection of workingmen,
however, was the aforementioned Jimmie, a dark, mild-eyed,
soft-spoken Calabrian, who had the shrewdness of a Machia-
velli and the pertness of a crow. He lived in the same neighborhood as Rourke, far out in one of those small towns on

the Harlem, sheltering so many Italians, for, like a hen with a brood of chicks, Rourke kept all his Italians gathered close about him. Jimmie, curiously, was the one who was always selected to run his family errands for him, a kind of valet to Rourke, as it were—selected for some merit I could never discover, certainly not one of speed. He was nevertheless constantly running here and there like an errand boy, his worn, dusty, baggy clothes making him look like a dilapidated bandit fresh from a sewer. On the job, however, no matter what it might be, Jimmie could never be induced to do real, hard work. He was always above it, or busy with something else. But as he was an expert cement-mixer and knew just how to load and unload the tool-car, two sinecures of sorts, nothing was ever said to him. If any one dared to reprove him, myself for instance (a mere interloper to Jimmie), he would reply: "Yeh! Yeh! I know-a my biz. I been now with Misha Rook fifteen year. I know-a my biz." If you made any complaint to Rourke, he would merely grin and say, "Ha! Jimmie's the sharp one," or perhaps, "I'll get ye yet, ye fox," but more than that nothing was ever done.

One day, however, Jimmie failed to comply with an extraordinary order of Rourke's, which, while it resulted in no real damage, produced a most laughable and yet characteristic scene. A strict rule of the company was that no opening of any kind into which a person might possibly step or fall should be left uncovered at any station during the approach, stay, or departure of any train scheduled to stop at that station. Rourke was well aware of this rule. He had a copy of it on file in his collection of circulars. In addition, he had especially delegated Jimmie to attend to this matter, a task which just suited the Italian as it gave him ample time to idle about and pretend to be watching. This it was which made the crime all the greater.

On this particular occasion Jimmie had failed to attend to this matter. We had been working on the platform at Williamsbridge, digging a pit for a coal-bin, when a train bearing the general foreman came along. The latter got off at the station especially to examine the work that had been done so far. When the train arrived there was the hole wide open with Rourke below shouting and gesticulating about something, and totally unconscious, of course, that his order had been neglected. The general foreman, who was, by the way, I believe, an admirer of Rourke, came forward, looked down, and said quietly: "This won't do, Rourke. You'll have to keep the work covered when a train is approaching. I've told you that before, you know."

Rourke looked up, so astonished and ashamed that he should have been put in such a position before his superior that he hardly knew what to say. I doubt if any one ever had a greater capacity for respecting his superiors, anyhow. Instead of trying to answer, he merely choked and began to shout for Jimmie, who came running, crying, as he always did, "What's da mat'? What's da mat'?"

"What's da mat'? What's da mat'?" mocked Rourke, fairly seething with a marvelous Irish fury. "What the devil do ye suppose is the mat'? What do ye mane be waalkin' away an' l'avin' the hole uncovered? Didn't I tell ye niver to l'ave a hole when a train's comin'? Didn't I tell ye to attind to that an' naathin' else? An' now what have ye been doin'? Be all the powers, what d'ye mane be l'avin' it? What else arre ye good fer? What d'ye mane be lettin' a thing like that happen, an' Mr. Wilson comin' along here, an' the hole open?"

He was as red as a beet, purple almost, perspiring, apoplectic. During all this tirade Mr. Wilson, a sad, dark, anæmic-looking person, troubled with acute indigestion, I fancy, stood by with an amused, kindly, and yet mock severe expression on his face. I am sure he did not wish to be severe.

Jimmie, dumbfounded, scarcely knew what to say. In the face of Rourke's rage and the foreman's presence, he did his best to remedy his error by covering the hole, at the same time stuttering something about going for a trowel.

"A trowel!" cried Rourke, glaring at him. "A trowel, ye h'athen ginny! What'd ye be doin' lookin' fer a trowel, an' a train comin' that close on ye it could 'a' knocked ye off the thrack? An' the hole open, an' Mr. Wilson right here! Is that what I told ye? Is that what I pay ye fer? Be all the saints! A trowel, is it? I'll trowel ye! I'll break yer h'athen Eyetalian skull, I will. Get thim boards on, an' don't let me ketch ye l'avin' such a place as that open again. I'll get shut av ye, ye blitherin' lunatic."

When it was all over and the train bearing the general fore-man had gone, Rourke quieted down, but not without many fulgurous flashes that kept the poor Italian on tenterhooks.

About an hour later, however, another train arrived, and, by reason of some intervening necessity and the idle, wander-ing mood of the Italian, the hole was open again. Jimmie was away behind the depot somewhere, smoking perhaps, and Rourke was, as usual, down in the hole. This time misfortune trebled itself, however, by bringing, not the general foreman, but the supervisor himself, a grave, quiet man, of whom Rourke stood in the greatest awe. He was so solid, so pro-found, so severe. I don't believe I ever saw him smile. He walked up to the hole, and looking reproachfully down, said: "Is this the way you leave your excavations, Rourke, when a train is coming? Don't you know better than to do a thing like that?"

"Jimmie!" shouted Rourke, leaping to the surface of the earth with a bound, "Jimmie! Now, be Jasus, where is that bla'guard Eyetalian? Didn't I tell him not to l'ave this place open!" and he began shoving the planks into place himself.

Jimmie, suddenly made aware of this new catastrophe, came running as fast as his short legs would carry him, scared almost out of his wits. He was as pale as a very dark and dirty Italian could be, and so wrought up that his facial expression changed involuntarily from moment to moment. Rourke was in a fairly murderous mood, only he was so excited and ashamed that he could not speak. Here was the supervisor, and here was himself, and conditions—necessity for order, etc.—would not permit him to kill the Italian in the former's presence. He could only choke and wait. To think that he should be made a mark of like this, and that in the face of his great supervisor! His face and neck were a beet-red, and his eyes flashed with anger. He merely glared at his recalcitrant henchman, as much as to say, "Wait!" When this train had departed and the dignified supervisor had been carried safely out of hearing he turned on Jimmie with all the fury of a masterful and excitable temper.

"So ye'll naht cover the hole, after me tellin' ye naht fifteen minutes ago, will ye?" he shouted. "Ye'll naht cover the hole! An' what'll ye be tellin' me ye was doin' now?"

"I carry da waut (water) for da concrete," pleaded Jimmie weakly.

"Waut fer the concrete," almost moaned Rourke, so great was his fury, his angry face shoved close to the Italian's own. "Waut fer the concrete, is it? It's a pity ye didn't fall into yer waut fer the concrete, ye damned nagur, an' drown! Waut fer the concrete, is it, an' me here, an' Mr. Mills steppin' off an' lookin' in on me, ye black-hearted son of a Eyetalian, ye! I'll waut fer the concrete ye! I'll crack yer blitherin' Eyetalian skull with a pick, I will! I'll chuck ye in yer waut fer the concrete till ye choke, ye flat-footed, leather-headed lunatic! I'll tache ye to waalk aaf an' l'ave the hole open, an' me in it. Now, be Jasus, get yer coat an' get out av this. Get—I'm tellin' ye! I'll have no more thruck with ye! I'll throuble no more with ye. Ye're no damned good. Out with ye! An' niver show me yer face again!" And he made a motion as if he would grab him and rend him limb from limb.

Jimmie, well aware of his dire position, was too clever, however, to let Rourke seize him. During all this conversation he had been slowly backing away, always safely beyond Rourke's reach, and now ran—an amazing feat for him. He had evidently been through many such scenes before. He retreated first behind the depot, and then when Rourke had gone to work once more down in his hole, came back and took a safe position on guard over the hitherto sadly neglected opening. When the next train came he was there to shove the boards over before it neared the station, and nothing more was said about the matter. Rourke did not appear to notice him. He did not even seem to see that he was there. The next morning, however, when the latter came to work as usual, it was, "Come, Matt! Come, Jimmie!" just as if nothing had happened. I was never more astonished in my life.

An incident, even more ridiculous, but illustrative of the atmosphere in which Rourke dwelt, occurred at Highbridge one frosty October Sunday morning, where because of seepage from a hill which threatened to undermine some tracks, Rourke was ordered to hurry and build a drain—a thing which, because the order came on Saturday afternoon, required Sunday labor, a most unusual thing in his case. But in spite of the order, Rourke, who was a good Catholic, felt impelled before coming to go to at least early mass, and in addition—a regular Sunday practice with him, I presume—to put on a long-skirted Prince Albert coat, which I had never seen before and which lent to his stocky figure some amusing lines. It was really too tight, having been worn, I presume, every Sunday regularly since his wedding day. In addition, he had donned a brown derby hat which, to me at least, gave him a most unfamiliar look..

I, being curious more than anything else and wishing to be out of doors as much as possible, also went up, arriving on the scene about nine. Rourke did not arrive until ten. In the meantime, I proceeded to build myself a fire on the dock, for we were alongside the Harlem River and a brisk wind was blowing. Then Rourke came, fresh from church, smiling and genial, in the most cheerful Sunday-go-to-meeting frame of mind, but plainly a little conscious of his grand garb.

"My," I said, surveying him, "you look fine. I never saw you dressed up before."

"L'ave aaf with yer taalk," he replied. "I know well enough how I look—good enough."

Then he bestirred himself about the task of examining what had been done so far. But I could see, in spite of all the busy assurance with which he worked, that he was still highly conscious of his clothes and a little disturbed by what I or others might think. His every-day garb plainly suited his mood much better.

Everything went smoothly until noon, not a cloud in the sky, when, looking across the tracks at that hour, I beheld coming toward us with more or less uncertain step another individual, stocky of figure and evidently bent on seeing Rourke—an Irishman as large as Rourke, younger, and, if anything, considerably coarser in fiber. He was very red-faced, smooth shaven, with a black derby hat pulled down over his eyes and wearing a somewhat faded tight-fitting brown suit. He was drunk, or nearly so, that was plain from the first. From the moment Rourke beheld him he seemed beside himself with anger or irritation. His expression changed completely and he began to swell, as was customary with him when he was angry, as though suffering from an internal eruption of some kind.

"The bla'guard!" I heard him mutter. "Now, be gob, what'll that felly be waantin'?" and then as the stranger drew nearer, "Who was it tould him I was here? Maybe some waan at the ahffice."

Regardless of his speculations on this score, the stranger picked his way across the tracks and came directly to him, his face and manner indicating no particularly friendly frame of mind.

"Maybe ye'll be lettin' me have that money now," he began instanter, and when Rourke made no reply, merely staring at him, he added, "I'll be waantin' to know now, when it is ye're goin' to give me the rest av me time fer that Scarborough job. I've been waitin' long enough."

Rourke stirred irritably and aggressively before he spoke. He seemed greatly put out, shamed, to think that the man should come here so, especially on this peaceful Sabbath morning.

"I've tould ye before," he replied defiantly after a time, "that ye've had aall ye earned, an' more. Ye left me without finishin' yer work, an' ye'll get no more time from me. If ye waant more, go down to the ahffice an' see if they'll give it to ye. I have no money fer ye here," and he resumed a comfortable position before the fire, his hands behind his back.

"It's siven dollars ye still owe me," returned the other, ignoring Rourke's reply, "an' I waant it now."

"Well, ye'll naht get it," replied my boss. "I've naathin' fer ye, I'm tellin' ye. I owe ye naathin'."

"Is that so?" returned the other. "Well, we'll see about that. Ye'll be after givin' it to me, er I'll get it out of ye somehow. It's naht goin' to be ch'ated out av me money I am."

"I'm owin' ye naathin'," insisted Rourke. "Ye may as well go away from here. Ye'll get naathin'. If ye waant anything more, go an' see the ahffice," and now he strode away to where the Italians were, ignoring the stranger completely and muttering something about his being drunk. The latter followed him, however, over to where he stood, and continued the dispute. Rourke ignored him as much as possible, only exclaiming once, "L'ave me be, man. Ye're drunk."

"I'm naht drunk," returned the other. "Once an' fer all now, I'm askin' ye, arre ye goin' to give me that money?"

"No," replied Rourke, "I'm naht."

"Belave me," said the stranger, "I'll get it out av ye some-how," but for the moment he made no move, merely hanging about in an uncertain way. He seemed to have no definite plan for collecting the money, or if he had he had by now abandoned it.

Without paying any more attention to him, Rourke, still very irritated and defiant, returned to the fire. He tried to appear calm and indifferent, but the ex-workman, a non-union mason, I judged, followed after, standing before him and staring in the defiant, irritating way a drunken man will, not quite able to make up his mind what else to do. Presently Rourke, more to relieve the tedium of an embarrassing situation than anything else (a number of accusatory remarks having been passed), turned and began poking at the blaze, finally bending over to lay on a stick of wood. On the instant, and as if seized by sudden inspiration, whether because the tails of Rourke's long coat hung out in a most provoking fashion and suggested the thing that followed or not, I don't know, but now the red-faced intruder jumped forward, and seizing them in a most nimble and yet vigorous clutch, gave an amazing yank, which severed them straight up the back, from seat to nape, at the same time exclaiming:

"Ye'll naht pay me, will ye? Ye'll naht, will ye?"

On the instant a tremendous change came over the scene. It was as swift as stage play. Instantly Rourke was upright and faced about, shouting, "Now, be gob, ye've torn me coat, have ye! Now I'll tache ye! Now I'll show ye! Wait! Get ready, now. Now I'll fix ye, ye drunken, thavin' loafer," and at the same time he began to move upon the enemy in a kind of rhythmic, cryptic circle (some law governing anger and emotion, I presume), the while his hands opened and shut and his eyes looked as though they would be veiled completely by his narrowing lids. At the same time the stranger, apparently seeing his danger, began backing and circling in the same way around Rourke, as well as around the fire, until it looked as though they were performing a war dance. Round and round they went like two Hopi bucks or Zulu warriors, their faces displaying the most murderous cunning and intention to slay—only, instead of feathers and beads, they had on their negligible best. All the while Rourke was calling, "Come on, now! Get ready, now! I'll show ye, now! I'll fix ye, now! It's me coat ye'll rip, is it? Come on, now! Get ready! Make yerself ready! I'm goin' to give ye the lickin' av yer life! Come on, now! Come on, now! Come on, now!"

It was as though each had been secreted from the other and had to be sought out in some mysterious manner and in a circle. In spite of the feeling of distress that an impending struggle of this kind gives one, I could not help noting the comic condition of Rourke's back—the long coat beautifully ripped straight up the back, its ends fluttering in the wind like fans, and exposing his waistcoat and Sunday boiled white shirt—and laying up a laugh for the future. It was too ridiculous. The stranger had a most impressive and yet absurd air of drunken sternness written in his face, a do-or-die look.

Whether anything serious would really have happened I was never permitted to learn, for now, in addition to myself and the Italians, all of them excited and ready to defend their lord and master, some passengers from the nearby station and the street above as well as a foreman of a section gang helping at this same task, a great hulking brute of a man who looked quite able to handle both Rourke and his opponent at one and the same time, came forward and joined in this excited circle. Considerable effort was made on the part of the latter to learn just what the trouble was, after which the big foreman interposed with:

"What's the trouble here? Come, now! What's all this row, Rourke? Ye wouldn't fight here, would ye? Have him arristed, er go to his home—ye say ye know him—but don't be fightin' here. Supposin' waan av the bosses should be comin' along now?" and at the same time he interposed his great bulk between the two.

Rourke, quieted some by this interruption but still sputtering with rage and disgrace, shouted, "Lookit me coat! Lookit what he done to me coat! See what he done to me coat! Man alive, d'ye think I'm goin' to stand fer the likes av that? It's naht me that can be waalked on by a loafer like that—an' me payin' him more than ever he was worth, an' him waalkin' aaf an' l'avin' the job half done. I'll fix him this time. I'll show him. I'll tache him to be comin' around an' disturbin' a man when he's at his work. I'll fix him now," and once more he began to move. But the great foreman was not so easily to be disposed of.

"Well then, let's caall the police," he argued in a highly conciliatory mood. "Ye can't be fightin' him here. Sure, ye don't waant to do that. What'll the chafe think? What is it ye'll think av yerself?"

At the same time he turned to find the intruder and demand to know what he meant by it, but the latter had already decamped. Seeing the crowd that had and was gathering, and that he was likely to encounter more forms of trouble than he had anticipated, he had started down the track toward Mott Haven.

"I'll fix ye!" Rourke shouted when he saw him going. "Ye'll pay fer this. I'll have ye arristed. Wait! Ye'll naht get aaf so aisy this time."

But just the same the storm was over for the present, anyhow, the man gone, and in a little while Rourke left for his home at Mount Vernon to repair his tattered condition. I never saw a man so crestfallen, nor one more determined to "have the laa on him" in my life. Afterwards, when I inquired very cautiously what he had done about it—this was a week or two later—he replied, "Shewer, what can ye do with a loafer like that? He has no money, an' lockin' him up won't help his wife an' children any."

Thus ended a perfect scene out of Kilkenny.

It was not so very long after I arrived that Rourke began to tell me of a building which the company was going to erect in Mott Haven Yard, one of its great switching centers. It was to be an important affair, according to him, sixty by two hundred feet in breadth and length, of brick and stone, and was to be built under a time limit of three months, an arrangement by which the company hoped to find out how satisfactorily it could do work for itself rather than by outside contract, which it was always hoping to avoid. From his manner and conversation, I judged that Rourke was eager to get this job, for he had been a contractor of some ability in his day before he ever went to work for the company, and felt, I am sure, that fate had done him an injustice in not allowing him to remain one. In addition, he felt a little above the odds and ends of masonry that he was now called on to do, where formerly he had done so much more important work. He was eager to be a real foreman once more, a big one, and to show the company that he could erect this building and thus make a little place for himself in the latter's good graces, although to what end I could not quite make out. He would never have made a suitable general foreman. At the same time, he was a little afraid of the clerical details, those terrible nightmares of reports, o. k.s and the like.

"How arre ye feelin', Teddy, b'y?" he often inquired of me during this period, with a greater show of interest in my troublesome health than ever before. I talked of leaving, I suppose, from time to time because sheer financial necessity was about to compel it.

"Fine, Rourke," I would say, "never better. I'm feeling better every day."

"That's good. Ye're the right man in the right place now. If ye was to sthay a year er two at this work it would be the makin' av ye. Ye're too thin. Ye need more chist," and he would tap my bony chest in a kindly manner. "I niver have a sick day, meself."

"That's right, Rourke," I replied pleasantly, feeling keenly the need of staying by so wonderful a lamp of health. "I intend to stick at it as long as I can."

"Ye ought to; it'll do ye good. If we get the new buildin' to build, it'll be better yet for ye. Ye'll have plenty to do there to relave yer mind."

"Relieve, indeed!" I thought, but I did not say so. On the contrary I felt so much sympathy for this lusty Irishman and his reasonable ambitions that I desired to help him, and urged him to get it. I suggested indirectly that I would see him through, which touched him greatly. He was a grateful creature in his way, but so excitable and so helplessly self-reliant that there was no way of aiding him without doing it in a secret or rather self-effacing manner. He would have much preferred to struggle along alone and fail, though I doubt whether real failure could have come to Rourke so essentially capable was he.

In another three weeks the work was really given him to do, and then began one of the finest exhibitions of Irish domination and self-sufficiency that I have ever witnessed. We moved to Mott Haven Yard, a great network of tracks and buildings, in the center of which this new building was to be erected. Rourke was given a large force of men, whom he fairly gloried in bossing. He had as many as forty Italians, to say nothing of a number of pseudo-carpenters and masons (not those shrewd hawks clever enough to belong to the union, but wasters and failures of another type) who did the preliminary work of digging for the foundation, etc. Handling these, Rourke was in his element. He loved to see so much brisk work going on. He would trot to and fro about the place, beaming in the most angelic fashion, and shouting orders that could be heard all over the neighborhood. It was delicious to watch him. At times he would stand by the long trenches where the men were digging for the foundation, a great line of them, their backs bent over their work, and rub his hands in pleasingly human satisfaction, saying, "We're goin' along fine, Teddy. I can jist see me way to the top av the buildin'," and then he would proceed to harass and annoy his men out of pure exuberance of spirits.

"Ye waant to dig it so, man," or, "Ye don't handle yer pick right; can't ye see that? Hold it this way." Sometimes he would get down in the trench and demonstrate just how it was to be done, a thing which greatly amused some of the workmen. Frequently he would exhibit to me little tricks or knacks of his trade, such as throwing a trowel ten feet so that it would stick in a piece of wood; turning a shovel over with a lump of dirt on it and not dropping the lump, and similar simple acts, always adding, "Ye'll niver be a mason till ye can do that."

When he was tired of fussing with the men outside he would come around to the little wooden shed, where I was keeping the mass of orders and reports in shape and getting his material ready for him, and look over the papers in the most knowing manner. When he had satisfied himself that everything was going right, he would exclaim, "Ye're jist the b'y fer the place, Teddy. Ye'd made a good bookkeeper. If ever I get to be President, I'll make ye me Sicretary av State."

But the thing which really interested and enthralled Rourke was the coming of the masons—those hardy buccaneers of the laboring world who come and go as they please, asking no favors and brooking no interference. Plainly he envied them their reckless independence at the same time that he desired to control their labor in his favor—a task worthy of the shrewdest diplomat. Never in my life have I seen such a gay, ruthless, inconsiderate point of view as these same union masons represented, a most astounding lot. They were—are, I suppose I should say—our modern buccaneers and Captain Kidds of the laboring world, demanding, if you please, their six a day, starting and stopping almost when they please, doing just as little as they dare and yet face their own decaying conscience, dropping any task at the most critical and dangerous point, and in other ways rejoicing in and disporting themselves in such a way as to annoy the representatives of any corporation great or small that suffered the sad compulsion of employing them. Seriously, I am not against union laborers. I like them. They spell rude, blazing life. But when you have to deal with them!

Plainly, Rourke anticipated endless rows. Their coming promised him the opportunity he inmostly desired, I suppose, of once more fussing and fuming with real, strong, determined and pugnacious men like himself, who would not take his onslaughts tamely but would fight him back, as he wished strong men to do. He was never weary of talking of them.

"Wait till we have thirty er forty av thim on the line," he once observed to me in connection with them, "every man layin' his six hundred bricks a day, er takin' aaf his apron! Thim's the times ye'll see what excitement manes, me b'y. Thim's the times."

"What'll I see, Rourke?" I asked interestedly.

"Throuble enough. Shewer, they're no crapin' Eyetalians, that'll let ye taalk to thim as ye pl'ase. Indade not. Ye'll have to fight with them fellies."

"Well, that's a queer state of affairs," I remarked, and then added, "Do you think you can handle them, Rourke?"

"Handle thim!" he exclaimed, his glorious wrath kindling in anticipation of a possible conflict. "Handle thim, an' the likes av a thousand av thim! I know them aall, every waan av thim, an' their thricks. It's naht foolin' me they'll be. But, me b'y," he added instructively, "it's a fine job ye'll have runnin' down to the ahffice gettin' their time." (This is the railroad man's expression for money due, or wages.) "Ye'll have plenty av that to do, I'm tellin' ye."

"You don't mean to say that you're going to discharge them, Rourke, do you?" I asked.

"Shewer!" he exclaimed authoritatively. "Why shouldn't I? They're jist the same as other min. Why shouldn't I?" Then he added, after a pause, "But it's thim that'll be comin' to me askin' fer their time instid av me givin' it to thim, niver fear. They're not the kind that'll let ye taalk back to thim. If their work don't suit ye, it's 'give me me time.' Wait till they'll be comin' round half drunk in the mornin', an' not feelin' just right. Thim's the times ye'll find out what masons arre made av, me b'y."

I confess this probability did not seem as brilliant to me as it did to him, but it had its humor. I expressed wonder that he would hire them if they were such a bad lot.

"Where else will ye get min?" he demanded to know. "The unions have the best, an' the most av thim. Thim outside fellies don't amount to much. They're aall pore, crapin' creatures. If it wasn't fer the railroad bein' against the union I wouldn't have thim at aall, and besides," he added thoughtfully, and with a keen show of feeling for their point of view, "they have a right to do as they pl'ase. Shewer, it's no common workmen they arre. They can lay their eight hundred bricks a day, if they will, an' no advice from any waan. If ye was in their place ye'd do the same. There's no sinse in allowin' another man to waalk on ye whin ye can get another job. I don't blame thim. I was a mason wanst meself."

"You don't mean to say that you acted as you say these men are going to act?"

"Shewer!"

"Well, I shouldn't think you'd be very proud of it."

"I have me rights," he declared, flaring up. "What kind av a man is it that'll let himself be waalked on? There's no sinse in it. It's naht natchral. It's naht intinded that it should be so."

"Very well," I said, smoothing the whole thing over, and so that ended.

Well, the masons came, and a fine lot of pirates they surely

were. Such independence! Such defiance! Such feverish punctilio in regard to their rights and what forms and procedures
they were entitled to! I stared in amazement. For the most
part they were hale, healthy, industrious looking creatures,
but so obstreperously conscious of their own rights, and so
proud of their skill as masons, that there was no living with
them. Really, they would have tried the patience of a saint,
let alone a healthy, contentious Irish foreman-mason. "First
off," as the railroad men used to say, they wanted to know
whether there were any non-union men on the job, and if so,
would they be discharged instanter?—if not, no work—a situation which gave Rourke several splendid opportunities for
altercations, which he hastened to improve, although the
non-union men *went*, of course. Then they wanted to know
when, where, and how they were to get their money, whether
on demand at any time they chose, and this led to more trouble, since the railroad paid only once a month. However, this
was adjusted by a special arrangement being made whereby
the building department stood ready to pay them instantly on
demand, only I had to run down to the division office each
time and get their pay for them at any time that they came to
ask for it! Then came an argument (or many of them) as to
the number of bricks they were to lay an hour; the number
of men they were to carry on one line, or wall; the length of
time they were supposed to work, or had worked, or would
work—all of which was pure food and drink to Rourke. He
was in his element at last, shouting, gesticulating, demanding
that they leave or go to ——. After all these things had been
adjusted, however, they finally consented to go to work, and
then of course the work flew. It was a grand scene, really
inspiring—forty or fifty masons on the line, perhaps half as
many helpers or mixers, the Italians carrying bricks, and a
score of carpenters now arriving under another foreman to
set the beams and lay the joists as the walls rose upward.

Rourke was about all the time now, arguing and gesticulating with this man or that, fighting with this one or the
other, and calling always to some mason or other to "come
down" and get his "time." "Come down! Come down!" I
would hear, and then would see him rushing for the office, a
defiant and even threatening mason at his heels; Rourke

demanding that I make out a time-check at once for the latter and go down to the "ahffice" and get the money, the
while the mason hung about attempting to seduce other
men to a similar point of view. Once in a while, but only on
rare occasions, Rourke would patch up a truce with a man.
As a rule, the mason was only too eager to leave and spend
the money thus far earned, while Rourke was curiously indifferent as to whether he went or stayed. " 'Tis to drink he
waants," he would declare amusedly. To me it was all like a
scene out of comic opera.

Toward the last, however, a natural calm set in, the result
no doubt of weariness and a sense of surfeit, which sent the
building forward apace. During this time Rourke was to be
seen walking defiantly up and down the upper scaffolding of
the steadily rising walls, or down below on the ground in
front of his men, his hands behind his back, his face screwed
into a quizzical expression, his whole body bearing a look of
bristling content and pugnacity which was too delicious for
words. Since things were going especially well he could not
say much, but still he could look his contentiousness, and did.
Even now he would occasionally manage to pick a quarrel
with some lusty mason or other, which resulted in the customary descent to the office, but not often.

But one cold December day, about three weeks later, when
I was just about to announce that I could no longer delay my
departure, seeing that my health was now as good, or nearly
so, as my purse was lean, and that, whether I would or no, I
must arrange to make more money, that a most dreadful accident occurred. It appeared that Rourke and a number of
Italians, including Matt and Jimmie, were down in the main
room of the building, now fast nearing completion, when the
boiler of the hoisting engine, which had been placed inside
the building and just at the juncture of three walls, blew up
and knocked out this wall and the joists of the second and
third floors loose, thus precipitating all of fifteen thousand
bricks, which had been placed on the third floor, into this
room below. For a few moments there had been a veritable
hurricane of bricks and falling timber; and then, when it was
over, it was found that the mighty Rourke and five Italians
were embedded in or under them, and all but Jimmie more

or less seriously injured or killed. Two Italians were killed outright. A third died later. Rourke, in particular, was unfortunately placed and terribly injured. His body from the waist down was completely buried by a pile of bricks, and across his shoulder lay a great joist pressing where it had struck him, and cutting his neck and ear. He was a pathetic sight when we entered, bleeding and pain-wrenched yet grim and undaunted, as one might have expected.

"I'm tight fast, me lad," he said when he could speak. "It's me legs that's caught, not me body. But give a hand to the min, there. The Eyetalians are underneath."

Disregarding his suggestion, however, we began working about him, every man throwing away bricks like a machine; but he would not have it.

" 'Tind to the min!" he insisted with all of his old firmness. "The Eyetalians are under there—Matt an' Jimmie. Can't ye see that I'll be all right till ye get thim out? Come, look after the min!"

We fell to this end of the work, although by now others had arrived, and soon there was a great crowd assisting— men coming from the yard and the machine shop. Although embedded in this mass of material and most severely injured, there was no gainsaying him, and he still insisted on directing us as best he could. But now he was so picturesque, so much nobler, really, than he had been in his healthier, uninjured days. A fabled giant, he seemed to me, half-god, half-man, composed in part of flesh, in part of brick and stone, gazing down on our earthly efforts with the eye of a demi-god.

"Come, now—get the j'ists from aaf the end, there. Take the bricks away from that man. Can't ye see? There's where his head is—there. There! Jasus Christ—theyer!"

You would have thought we were Italians ourselves, poor wisps of nothing, not his rescuers, but slaves, compelled to do his lordly bidding.

After a time, however, we managed to release him and all his five helpers—two dead, as I say, and Matt badly cut about the head and seriously injured, while Jimmie, the imperturbable, was but little the worse for a brick mark on one shoulder. He was more or less frightened, of course, and comic to look at, even in this dread situation. "Big-a smash," he exclaimed when he recovered himself. "Like-a da worl' fall. Misha Rook! Misha Rook! Where Misha Rook?"

"Here I am, ye Eyetalian scalawag," exclaimed the unyielding Rourke genially, who was still partially embedded when Jimmie was released. There was, however, a touch of sorrow in his voice as he added weakly, "Arre ye hurted much?"

"No, Misha Rook. Help Misha Rook," replied Jimmie, grabbing at bricks himself, and so the rescue work of "Rook" went on.

Finally he was released, although not without deprecating our efforts the while (this wonderful and exceptional fuss over him), and exclaiming at one point as we tugged at joists and beams rather frantically, "Take yer time. Take yer time. I'm naht so bad fixed as aall that. Take yer time. Get that board out o' the way there, Jimmie."

But he was badly "fixed," and "hurted" unto death also, as we now found, and as he insisted he was not. His hip was severely crushed by the timbers and his legs broken, as well as his internal organs disarranged, although we did not know how badly at the time. Only after we had removed all the weight did he collapse and perhaps personally realize how serious was his plight. He was laid on a canvas tarpaulin brought by the yard-master and spread on the chip-strewn ground, while the doctors from two ambulances worked over him. While they were examining his wounds he took a critical and quizzical interest in what they were doing, and offered one or two humorous suggestions. Finally, when they were ready to move him he asked how he was, and on being told that he was all right, looked curiously about until he caught my eye. I could see that he realized how critical it was with him.

"I'd like to see a priest, Teddy," he whispered, "and, if ye don't mind, I'd like ye to go up to Mount Vernon an' tell me wife. They'll be after telegraphin' her if ye don't. Break it aisy, if ye will. Don't let 'er think there's anything serious. There's no need av it. I'm naht hurted so bad as aall that."

I promised, and the next moment one of the doctors shot a spray of cocaine into his hip to relieve what he knew must be his dreadful pain. A few moments later he lost consciousness, after which I left him to the care of the hospital authorities and hurried away to send the priest and to tell his wife.

For a week thereafter he lingered in a very serious condition and finally died, blood-poisoning having set in. I saw him at the hospital a day or two before, and, trying to sympathize with his condition, I frequently spoke of what I deemed the dreadful uncertainty of life and the seeming carelessness of the engineer in charge of the hoisting engine. He, however, had no complaint to make.

"Ye must expect thim things," was his only comment. "Ye can't aalways expect to go unhurted. I niver lost a man before, nor had one come to haarm. 'Tis the way av things, ye see."

Mighty Rourke! You would have thought the whole Italian population of Mount Vernon knew and loved him, the way they turned out at his funeral. It was a state affair for most of them, and they came in scores, packing the little brick church at which he was accustomed to worship full to overflowing. Matt was there, bandaged and sore, but sorrowful; and Jimmie, artful and scheming in the past, but now thoroughly subdued. He was all sorrow, and sniveled and blubbered and wept hot, blinding tears through the dark, leathery fingers of his hands.

"Misha Rook! Misha Rook!" I heard him say, as they bore the body in; and when they carried it out of the church, he followed, head down. As they lowered it to the grave he was inconsolable.

"Misha Rook! Misha Rook! I work-a for him fifteen year!"

A Mayor and His People

HERE IS the story of an individual whose political and social example, if such things are ever worth anything (the moralists to the contrary notwithstanding), should have been, at the time, of the greatest importance to every citizen of the United States. Only it was not. Or was it? Who really knows? Anyway, he and his career are entirely forgotten by now, and have been these many years.

He was the mayor of one of those dreary New England mill towns in northern Massachusetts—a bleak, pleasureless realm of about forty thousand, where, from the time he was born until he finally left at the age of thirty-six to seek his fortune elsewhere, he had resided without change. During that time he had worked in various of the local mills, which in one way and another involved nearly all of the population. He was a mill shoe-maker by trade, or, in other words, a factory shoe-hand, knowing only a part of all the processes necessary to make a shoe in that fashion. Still, he was a fair workman, and earned as much as fifteen or eighteen dollars a week at times—rather good pay for that region. By temperament a humanitarian, or possibly because of his own humble state one who was compelled to take cognizance of the difficulties of others, he finally expressed his mental unrest by organizing a club for the study and propagation of socialism, and later, when it became powerful enough to have a candidate and look for political expression of some kind, he was its first, and thereafter for a number of years, its regular candidate for mayor. For a long time, or until its membership became sufficient to attract some slight political attention, its members (following our regular American, unintellectual custom) were looked upon by the rest of the people as a body of harmless kickers, filled with fool notions about a man's duty to his fellowman, some silly dream about an honest and economical administration of public affairs—their city's affairs, to be exact. We are so wise in America, so interested in our fellowman, so regardful of his welfare. They were so small in number, however, that they were little more than an object of pleasant jest, useful for that purpose alone.

This club, however, continued to put up its candidate until about 1895, when suddenly it succeeded in polling the very modest number of fifty-four votes—double the number it had succeeded in polling any previous year. A year later one hundred and thirty-six were registered, and the next year six hundred. Then suddenly the mayor who won that year's battle died, and a special election was called. Here the club polled six hundred and one, a total and astonishing gain of one. In 1898 the perennial candidate was again nominated and received fifteen hundred, and in 1899, when he ran again, twenty-three hundred votes, which elected him.

If this fact be registered casually here, it was not so regarded in that typically New England mill town. Ever study New England—its Puritan, self-defensive, but unintellectual and selfish psychology? Although this poor little snip of a mayor was only elected for one year, men paused astounded, those who had not voted for him, and several of the older conventional political and religious order, wedded to their church and all the routine of the average puritanic mill town, actually cried. No one knew, of course, who the new mayor was, or what he stood for. There were open assertions that the club behind him was anarchistic—that ever-ready charge against anything new in America—and that the courts should be called upon to prevent his being seated. And this from people who were as poorly "off" commercially and socially as any might well be. It was stated, as proving the worst, that he was, or had been, a mill worker!—and, before that a grocery clerk—both at twelve a week, or less!! Immediate division of property, the forcing of all employers to pay as much as five a day to every laborer (an unheard-of sum in New England), and general constraint and subversion of individual rights (things then unknown in America, of course), loomed in the minds of these conventional Americans as the natural and immediate result of so modest a victory. The old-time politicians and corporations who understood much better what the point was, the significance of this straw, were more or less disgruntled, but satisfied that it could be undone later.

An actual conversation which occurred on one of the outlying street corners one evening about dusk will best illustrate the entire situation.

"Who is the man, anyway?" asked one citizen of a total stranger whom he had chanced to meet.

"Oh, no one in particular, I think. A grocery clerk, they say."

"Astonishing, isn't it? Why, I never thought those people would get anything. Why, they didn't even figure last year."

"Seems to be considerable doubt as to just what he'll do."

"That's what I've been wondering. I don't take much stock in all their talk about anarchy. A man hasn't so very much power as mayor."

"No," said the other.

"We ought to give him a trial, anyway. He's won a big fight. I should like to see him, see what he looks like."

"Oh, nothing startling. I know him."

"Rather young, ain't he?"

"Yes."

"Where did he come from?"

"Oh, right around here."

"Was he a mill-hand?"

"Yes."

The stranger made inquiry as to other facts and then turned off at a corner.

"Well," he observed at parting, "I don't know. I'm inclined to believe in the man. I should like to see him myself. Good-night."

"Good-night," said the other, waving his hand. "When you see me again you will know that you are looking at the mayor."

The inquirer stared after him and saw a six-foot citizen, of otherwise medium proportions, whose long, youthful face and mild gray eyes, with just a suggestion of washed-out blue in them, were hardly what was to be expected of a notorious and otherwise astounding political figure.

"He is too young," was the earliest comments, when the public once became aware of his personality.

"Why, he is nothing but a grocery clerk," was another, the skeptical and condemnatory possibilities of which need not be dilated upon here.

And he was, in his way—nothing much of a genius, as such things go in politics, but an interesting figure. Without much taste (or its cultivated shadow) or great vision of any kind, he was still a man who sensed the evils of great and often unnecessary social inequalities and the need of reorganizing influences, which would tend to narrow the vast gulf between the unorganized and ignorant poor, and the huge beneficiaries of unearned (yes, and not even understood) increment. For what does the economic wisdom of the average capitalist amount to, after all: the narrow, gourmandizing hunger of the average multi-millionaire?

At any rate, people watched him as he went to and fro between his office and his home, and reached the general conclusion after the first excitement had died down that he did not amount to much.

When introduced into his office in the small but pleasant city hall, he came into contact with a "ring," and a fixed condition, which nobody imagined a lone young mayor could change. Old-time politicians sat there giving out contracts for street-cleaning, lighting, improvements and supplies of all kinds, and a bond of mutual profit bound them closely together.

"I don't think he can do much to hurt us," these individuals said one to another. "He don't amount to much."

The mayor was not of a talkative or confiding turn. Neither was he cold or wanting in good and natural manners. He was, however, of a preoccupied turn of mind, "up in the air," some called it, and smoked a good many cigars.

"I think we ought to get together and have some sort of a conference about the letting of contracts," said the president of the city council to him one morning shortly after he had been installed. "You will find these gentlemen ready to meet you half-way in these matters."

"I'm very glad to hear that," he replied. "I've something to say in my message to the council, which I'll send over in the morning."

The old-time politician eyed him curiously, and he eyed the old-time politician in turn, not aggressively, but as if they might come to a very pleasant understanding if they wanted to, and then went back to his office.

The next day his message was made public, and this was its key-note:

"All contract work for the city should be let with a proviso, that the workmen employed receive not less than two dollars a day."

The dissatisfied roar that followed was not long in making itself heard all over the city.

"Stuff and nonsense," yelled the office jobbers in a chorus. "Socialism!" "Anarchy!" "This thing must be put down!" "The city would be bankrupt in a year." "No contractor could afford to pay his ordinary day laborers two a day. The city could not afford to pay any contractor enough to do it."

"The prosperity of the city is not greater than the prosperity of the largest number of its component individuals," replied the mayor, in a somewhat altruistic and economically abstruse argument on the floor of the council hall. "We must find contractors."

"We'll see about that," said the members of the opposition. "Why, the man's crazy. If he thinks he can run this town on a goody-good basis and make everybody rich and happy, he's going to get badly fooled, that's all there is to that."

Fortunately for him three of the eight council members were fellows of the mayor's own economic beliefs, individuals elected on the same ticket with him. These men could not carry a resolution, but they could stop one from being carried over the mayor's veto. Hence it was found that if the contracts could not be given to men satisfactory to the mayor they could not be given at all, and he stood in a fair way to win.

"What the hell's the use of us sitting here day after day!" were the actual words of the leading members of the opposition in the council some weeks later, when the fight became wearisome. "We can't pass the contracts over his veto. I say let 'em go."

So the proviso was tacked on, that two a day was the minimum wage to be allowed, and the contracts passed.

The mayor's followers were exceedingly jubilant at this, more so than he, who was of a more cautious and less hopeful temperament.

"Not out of the woods yet, gentlemen," he remarked to a group of his adherents at the reform club. "We have to do a great many things sensibly if we expect to keep the people's confidence and ' win again.' "

Under the old system of letting contracts, whenever there was a wage rate stipulated, men were paid little or nothing, and the work was not done. There was no pretense of doing it. Garbage and ashes accumulated, and papers littered the streets. The old contractor who had pocketed the appropriated sum thought to do so again.

"I hear the citizens are complaining as much as ever," said the mayor to this individual one morning. "You will have to keep the streets clean."

The contractor, a robust, thick-necked, heavy-jawed Irishman, of just so much refinement as the sudden acquisition of a comfortable fortune would allow, looked him quizzically over, wondering whether he was "out" for a portion of the appropriation or whether he was really serious.

"We can fix that between us," he said.

"There's nothing to fix," replied the mayor. "All I want you to do is to clean the streets."

The contractor went away and for a few days after the streets were really clean, but it was only for a few days.

In his walks about the city the mayor himself found garbage and paper uncollected, and then called upon his new acquaintance again.

"I'm mentioning this for the last time, Mr. M——," he said. "You will have to fulfill your contract, or resign in favor of some one who will."

"Oh, I'll clean them, well enough," said this individual, after five minutes of rapid fire explanation. "Two dollars a day for men is high, but I'll see that they're clean."

Again he went away, and again the mayor sauntered about, and then one morning sought out the contractor in his own office.

"This is the end," he said, removing a cigar from his mouth and holding it before him with his elbow at right angles. "You are discharged from this work. I'll notify you officially to-morrow."

"It can't be done the way you want it," the contractor exclaimed with an oath. "There's no money in it at two dollars. Hell, anybody can see that."

"Very well," said the mayor in a kindly well-modulated tone. "Let another man try, then."

The next day he appointed a new contractor, and with a schedule before him showing how many men should be employed and how much profit he might expect, the latter succeeded. The garbage was daily removed, and the streets carefully cleaned.

Then there was a new manual training school about to be added to the public school system at this time, and the contract for building was to be let, when the mayor threw a bomb into the midst of the old-time jobbers at the city council. A contractor had already been chosen by them and the members were figuring out their profits, when at one of the public discussions of the subject the mayor said:

"Why shouldn't the city build it, gentlemen?"

"How can it?" exclaimed the councilmen. "The city isn't an individual; it can't watch carefully."

"It can hire its own architect, as well as any contractor. Let's try it."

There were sullen tempers in the council chamber after this, but the mayor was insistent. He called an architect who made a ridiculously low estimate. Never had a public building been estimated so cheaply before.

"See here," said one of the councilmen when the plans were presented to the chamber—"This isn't doing this city right, and the gentlemen of the council ought to put their feet down on any such venture as this. You're going to waste the city's money on some cheap thing in order to catch votes."

"I'll publish the cost of the goods as delivered," said the mayor. "Then the people can look at the building when it's built. We'll see how cheap it looks then."

To head off political trickery on the part of the enemy he secured bills for material as delivered, and publicly compared them with prices paid for similar amounts of the same material used in other buildings. So the public was kept aware of what was going on and the cry of cheapness for political purposes set at naught. It was the first public structure erected by the city, and by all means the cheapest and best of all the city's buildings.

Excellent as these services were in their way, the mayor realized later that a powerful opposition was being generated and that if he were to retain the interest of his constituents

he would have to set about something which would endear
him and his cause to the public.

"I may be honest," he told one of his friends, "but honesty
will play a lone hand with these people. The public isn't interested in its own welfare very much. It can't be bothered or
hasn't the time. What I need is something that will impress it
and still be worth while. I can't be reëlected on promises, or
on my looks, either."

When he looked about him, however, he found the possibility of independent municipal action pretty well hampered
by mandatory legislation. He had promised, for instance, to
do all he could to lower the exorbitant gas rate and to abolish
grade crossings, but the law said that no municipality could
do either of these things without first voting to do so three
years in succession—a little precaution taken by the corporation representing such things long before he came into
power. Each vote must be for such contemplated action, or it
could not become a law.

"I know well enough that promises are all right," he said
to one of his friends, "and that these laws are good enough
excuses, but the public won't take excuses from me for three
years. If I want to be mayor again I want to be doing something, and doing it quick."

In the city was a gas corporation, originally capitalized at
$45,000, and subsequently increased to $75,000, which was
earning that year the actual sum of $58,000 over and above
all expenses. It was getting ready to inflate the capitalization,
as usual, and water its stock to the extent of $500,000, when
it occurred to the mayor that if the corporation was making
such enormous profits out of a $75,000 investment as to be
able to offer to pay six per cent on $500,000 to investors, and
put the money it would get for such stocks into its pocket,
perhaps it could reduce the price of gas from one dollar and
nineteen cents to a more reasonable figure. There was the
three years' voting law, however, behind which, as behind an
entrenchment, the very luxurious corporation lay comfortable
and indifferent.

The mayor sent for his corporation counsel, and studied
gas law for awhile. He found that at the State capital there
was a State board, or commission, which had been created to

look after gas companies in general, and to hear the complaints of municipalities which considered themselves unjustly treated.

"This is the thing for me," he said.

Lacking the municipal authority himself, he decided to present the facts in the case and appeal to this commission for a reduction of the gas rate.

When he came to talk about it he found that the opposition he would generate would be something much more than local. Back of the local reduction idea was the whole system of extortionate gas rates of the State and of the nation; hundreds of fat, luxurious gas corporations whose dividends would be threatened by any agitation on this question.

"You mean to proceed with this scheme of yours?" asked a prominent member of the local bar who called one morning to interview him. "I represent the gentlemen who are interested in our local gas company."

"I certainly do," replied the mayor.

"Well," replied the uncredentialed representative of private interests, after expostulating a long time and offering various "reasons" why it would be more profitable and politically advantageous for the new mayor not to proceed, "I've said all I can say. Now I want to tell you that you are going up against a combination that will be your ruin. You're not dealing with this town now; you're dealing with the State, the whole nation. These corporations can't afford to let you win, and they won't. You're not the one to do it; you're not big enough."

The mayor smiled and replied that of course he could not say as to that.

The lawyer went away, and that next day the mayor had his legal counsel look up the annual reports of the company for the consecutive years of its existence, as well as a bulletin issued by a firm of brokers, into whose hands the matter of selling a vast amount of watered stock it proposed to issue had been placed. He also sent for a gas expert and set him to figuring out a case for the people.

It was found by this gentleman that since the company was first organized it had paid dividends on its capital stock at the rate of ten per cent per annum, for the first thirty years; had made vast improvements in the last ten, and notwithstanding this fact, had paid twenty per cent, and even twenty-five per cent per annum in dividends. All the details of cost and expenditure were figured out, and then the mayor with his counsel took the train for the State capitol.

Never was there more excitement in political circles than when this young representative of no important political organization whatsoever arrived at the State capitol and walked, at the appointed time, into the private audience room of the commission. Every gas company, as well as every newspaper and every other representative of the people, had curiously enough become interested in the fight he was making, and there was a band of reporters at the hotel where he was stopping, as well as in the commission chambers in the State capitol where the hearing was to be. They wanted to know about him—why he was doing this, whether it wasn't a "strike" or the work of some rival corporation. The fact that he might foolishly be sincere was hard to believe.

"Gentlemen," said the mayor, as he took his stand in front of an august array of legal talent which was waiting to pick his argument to pieces in the commission chambers at the capitol, "I miscalculated but one thing in this case which I am about to lay before you, and that is the extent of public interest. I came here prepared to make a private argument, but now I want to ask the privilege of making it public. I see the public itself is interested, or should be. I will ask leave to postpone my argument until the day after tomorrow."

There was considerable hemming and hawing over this, since from the point of view of the corporation it was most undesirable, but the commission was practically powerless to do aught but grant his request. And meanwhile the interest created by the newspapers added power to his cause. Hunting up the several representatives and senators from his district, he compelled them to take cognizance of the cause for which he was battling, and when the morning of the public hearing arrived a large audience was assembled in the chamber of representatives.

When the final moment arrived the young mayor came forward, and after making a very simple statement of the cause which led him to request a public hearing and the local condition which he considered unfair begged leave to introduce an expert, a national examiner of gas plants and lighting facilities, for whom he had sent, and whose twenty years of experience in this line had enabled him to prepare a paper on the condition of the gas-payers in the mayor's city.

The commission was not a little surprised by this, but signified its willingness to hear the expert as counsel for the city, and as his statement was read a very clear light was thrown upon the situation.

Counsel for the various gas corporations interrupted freely. The mayor himself was constantly drawn into the argument, but his replies were so simple and convincing that there was not much satisfaction to be had in stirring him. Instead, the various counsel took refuge in long-winded discussions about the methods of conducting gas plants in other cities, the cost of machinery, labor and the like, which took days and days, and threatened to extend into weeks. The astounding facts concerning large profits and the present intentions of not only this but every other company in the State could not be dismissed. In fact the revelation of huge corporation profits everywhere became so disturbing that after the committee had considered and re-considered, it finally, when threatened with political extermination, voted to reduce the price of gas to eighty cents.

It is needless to suggest the local influence of this decision. When the mayor came home he received an ovation, and that at the hands of many of the people who had once been so fearful of him, but he knew that this enthusiasm would not last long. Many disgruntled elements were warring against him, and others were being more and more stirred up. His home life was looked into as well as his past, his least childish or private actions. It was a case of finding other opportunities for public usefulness, or falling into the innocuous peace which would result in his defeat.

In the platform on which he had been elected was a plank which declared that it was the intention of this party, if elected, to abolish local grade crossings, the maintenance of which had been the cause of numerous accidents and much public complaint. With this plank he now proposed to deal.

In this of course he was hampered by the law before mentioned, which declared that no city could abolish its grade crossings without having first submitted the matter to the people during three successive years and obtained their approval each time. Behind this law was not now, however, as in the case of the gas company, a small $500,000 corporation, but all the railroads which controlled New England, and to which brains and legislators, courts and juries, were mere adjuncts. Furthermore, the question would have to be voted on at the same time as his candidacy, and this would have deterred many another more ambitious politician. The mayor was not to be deterred, however. He began his agitation, and the enemy began theirs, but in the midst of what seemed to be a fair battle the great railway company endeavored to steal a march. There was suddenly and secretly introduced into the lower house of the State legislature a bill which in deceptive phraseology declared that the law which allowed all cities, by three successive votes, to abolish grade crossings in three years, was, in the case of a particular city mentioned, hereby abrogated for a term of four years. The question might not even be discussed politically.

When the news of this attempt reached the mayor, he took the first train for the State capitol and arrived there just in time to come upon the floor of the house when the bill was being taken up for discussion. He asked leave to make a statement. Great excitement was aroused by his timely arrival. Those who secretly favored the bill endeavored to have the matter referred to a committee, but this was not to be. One member moved to go on with the consideration of the bill, and after a close vote the motion carried.

The mayor was then introduced.

After a few moments, in which the silent self-communing with which he introduced himself impressed everyone with his sincerity, he said:

"I am accused of objecting to this measure because its enactment will remove, as a political issue, the one cause upon which I base my hope for reëlection. If there are no elevated crossings to vote for, there will be no excuse for voting for me. Gentlemen, you mistake the temper and the intellect of the people of our city. It is you who see political significance in this thing, but let me assure you that it is of a far different kind from that which you conceive. If the passing of this measure had any significance to me other than the apparent wrong of it, I would get down on my knees and urge its immediate acceptance. Nothing could elect me quicker. Nothing could bury the opposition further from view. If you wish above all things to accomplish my triumph you will only need to interfere with the rights of our city in this arbitrary manner, and you will have the thing done. I could absolutely ask nothing more."

The gentlemen who had this measure in charge weighed well these assertions and trifled for weeks with the matter, trying to make up their minds.

Meanwhile election time approached, and amid the growing interest of politics it was thought unwise to deal with it. A great fight was arranged for locally, in which every conceivable element of opposition was beautifully harmonized by forces and conceptions which it is almost impossible to explain. Democrats, republicans, prohibitionists, saloon men and religious circles, all were gathered into one harmonious body and inspired with a single idea, that of defeating the mayor. From some quarter, not exactly identified, was issued a call for a civic committee of fifty, which should take into its hands the duty of rescuing the city from what was termed a "throttling policy of commercial oppression and anarchy." Democrats, republicans, liquor and anti-liquorites, were invited to the same central meeting place, and came. Money was not lacking, nor able minds, to prepare campaign literature. It was openly charged that a blank check was handed in to the chairman of this body by the railway whose crossings were in danger, to be filled out for any amount necessary to the destruction of the official upstart who was seeking to revolutionize old methods and conditions.

As may be expected, this opposition did not lack daring in making assertions contrary to facts. Charges were now made that the mayor was in league with the railroad to foist upon the city a great burden of expense, because the law under which cities could compel railroads to elevate their tracks declared that one-fifth of the burden of expense must be borne by the city and the remaining four-fifths by the railroad. It would saddle a debt of $250,000 upon the taxpayers, they said, and give them little in return. All the advantage would be with the railroad. "Postpone this action until the railroad can be forced to bear the entire expense, as it justly should," declared handbill writers, whose services were readily rendered to those who could afford to pay for them.

The mayor and his committee, although poor, answered with handbills and street corner speeches, in which he showed that even with the extravagantly estimated debt of $250,000, the city's tax-rate would not be increased by quite six cents to the individual. The cry that each man would have to pay five dollars more each year for ten years was thus wholesomely disposed of, and the campaign proceeded.

Now came every conceivable sort of charge. If he were not defeated, all reputable merchants would surely leave the city. Capital was certainly being scared off. There would be idle factories and empty stomachs. Look out for hard times. No one but a fool would invest in a city thus hampered.

In reply the mayor preached a fair return by corporations for benefits received. He, or rather his organization, took a door-to-door census of his following, and discovered a very considerable increase in the number of those intending to vote for him. The closest calculations of the enemy were discovered, the actual number they had fixed upon as sufficient to defeat him. This proved to the mayor that he must have three hundred more votes if he wished to be absolutely sure. These he hunted out from among the enemy, and had them pledged before the eventual morning came.

The night preceding election ended the campaign, for the enemy at least, in a blaze of glory, so to speak. Dozens of speakers for both causes were about the street corners and in the city meeting room.

Oratory poured forth in streams, and gasoline-lighted band-wagons rattled from street to street, emitting song and invective. Even a great parade was arranged by the anti-mayoral forces, in which horses and men to the number of hundreds were brought in from nearby cities and palmed off as enthusiastic citizens.

"Horses don't vote," a watchword handed out by the mayor, took the edge off the extreme ardor of this invading throng, and set to laughing the hundreds of his partisans, who needed such encouragement.

Next day came the vote, and then for once, anyhow, he was justified. Not only was a much larger vote cast than ever, but he thrashed the enemy with a tail of two hundred votes to spare. It was an inspiring victory from one point of view, but rather doleful for the enemy. The latter had imported a carload of fireworks, which now stood sadly unused upon the very tracks which, apparently, must in the future be raised. The crowning insult was offered when the successful forces offered to take them off their hands at half price.

For a year thereafter (a mayor was elected yearly there), less was heard of the commercial destruction of the city. Gas stood, as decided, at eighty cents a thousand. A new manual training school, built at a very nominal cost, a monument to municipal honesty, was also in evidence. The public waterworks had also been enlarged and the rates reduced. The streets were clean.

Then the mayor made another innovation. During his first term of office there had been a weekly meeting of the reform club, at which he appeared and talked freely of his plans and difficulties. These meetings he now proposed to make public.

Every Wednesday evening for a year thereafter a spectacle of municipal self-consciousness was witnessed, which those who saw it felt sure would redound to the greater strength and popularity of the mayor. In a large hall, devoted to public gatherings, a municipal meeting was held. Every one was invited. The mayor was both host and guest, an individual who chose to explain his conduct and his difficulties and to ask advice. There his constituents gathered, not only to hear but to offer counsel.

"Gentlemen," so ran the gist of his remarks on various of these occasions, "the present week has proved a most trying one. I am confronted by a number of difficult problems, which I will now try to explain to you. In the first place, you know my limitations as to power in the council. But three members now vote for me, and it is only by mutual concessions that we move forward at all."

Then would follow a detailed statement of the difficulties, and a general discussion. The commonest laborer was free to offer his advice. Every question was answered in the broadest spirit of fellowship. An inquiry as to " what to do" frequently brought the most helpful advice. Weak and impossible solutions were met as such, and shown to be what they were. Radicals were assuaged, conservatives urged forward. The whole political situation was so detailed and explained that no intelligent person could leave, it was thought, with a false impression of the mayor's position or intent.

With five thousand or more such associated citizens abroad each day explaining, defending, approving the official conduct of the mayor, because they understood it, no misleading conceptions, it was thought, could arise. Men said that his purpose and current leaning in any matter was always clear. He was thought to be closer to his constituency than any other official within the whole range of the Americas and that there could be nothing but unreasoning partisan opposition to his rule.

After one year of such service a presidential campaign drew near, and the mayor's campaign for reëlection had to be contested at the same time. No gas monopoly evil was now a subject of contention. Streets were clean, contracts fairly executed; the general municipal interests as satisfactorily attended to as could be expected. Only the grade crossing war remained as an issue, and that would require still another vote after this. His record was the only available campaign argument.

On the other side, however, were the two organizations of the locally defeated great parties, and the railroad. The latter, insistent in its bitterness, now organized these two bodies into a powerful opposition. Newspapers were subsidized; the national significance of the campaign magnified; a large number of railroad-hands colonized. When the final weeks of the campaign arrived a bitter contest was waged, and money triumphed. Five thousand four hundred votes were cast for the mayor. Five thousand four hundred and fifty for the opposing candidate, who was of the same party as the successful presidential nominee.

It was a bitter blow, but still one easily borne by the mayor, who was considerable of a philosopher. With simple, undisturbed grace he retired, and three days later applied to one of the principal shoe factories for work at his trade.

"What? You're not looking for a job, are you?" exclaimed the astonished foreman.

"I am," said the mayor.

"You can go to work, all right, but I should think you could get into something better now."

"I suppose I can later," he replied, "when I complete my law studies. Just now I want to do this for a change, to see how things are with the rank and file." And donning the apron he had brought with him he went to work.

It was not long, however, before he was discharged, largely because of partisan influence anxious to drive him out of that region. It was said that this move of seeking a job in so simple a way was a bit of "grand standing"—insincere—that he didn't need to do it, and that he was trying to pile up political capital against the future. A little later a local grocery man of his social faith offered him a position as clerk, and for some odd reason—humanitarian and sectarian, possibly—he accepted this. At any rate, here he labored for a little while. Again many said he was attempting to make political capital out of this simple life in order to further his political interests later, and this possibly, even probably, was true. All men have methods of fighting for that which they believe. So here he worked for a time, while a large number of agencies pro and con continued to denounce or praise him, to ridicule or extol his so-called Jeffersonian simplicity. It was at this time that I encountered him—a tall, spare, capable and interesting individual, who willingly took me into his confidence and explained all that had hitherto befallen him. He was most interesting, really, a figure to commemorate in this fashion.

In one of the rooms of his very humble home—a kind of office or den, in a small house such as any clerk or workingman might occupy—was a collection of clippings, laudatory, inquiring, and abusive, which would have done credit to a candidate for the highest office in the land. One would have judged by the scrap-books and envelopes stuffed to overflowing with long newspaper articles and editorials that had been cut from papers all over the country from Florida to Oregon, that his every movement at this time and earlier was all-essential to the people. Plainly, he had been watched, spied upon, and ignored by one class, while being hailed, praised and invited by another. Magazine editors had called upon him for contributions, journalists from the large cities had sought him out to obtain his actual views, citizens' leagues in various parts of the nation had invited him to come and speak, and yet he was still a very young man in years, not over-intelligent politically or philosophically, the ex-mayor of a small city, and the representative of no great organization of any sort.

In his retirement he was now comforted, if one can be so comforted, by these memories, still fresh in his mind and by the hope possibly for his own future, as well as by a droll humor with which he was wont to select the sharpest and most willful slur upon his unimpeachable conduct as an offering to public curiosity.

"Do you really want to know what people think of me?" he said to me on one occasion. "Well, here's something. Read this." And then he would hand me a bunch of the bitterest attacks possible, attacks which pictured him as a sly and treacherous enemy of the people—or worse yet a bounding anarchistic ignoramus. Personally I could not help admiring his stoic mood. It was superior to that of his detractors. Apparent falsehoods did not anger him. Evident misunderstandings could not, seemingly, disturb him.

"What do you expect?" he once said to me, after I had made a very careful study of his career for a current magazine, which, curiously, was never published. I was trying to get him to admit that he believed that his example might be fruitful of results agreeable to him in the future. I could not conclude that he really agreed with me. "People do not remember; they forget. They remember so long as you are directly before them with something that interests them. That may be a lower gas-rate, or a band that plays good music. People like strong people, and only strong people, characters of that sort—good, bad or indifferent—I've found that out. If a man or a corporation is stronger than I am, comes along and denounces me, or spends more money than I do (or can), buys more beers, makes larger promises, it is 'all day' for me. What has happened in my case is that, for the present, anyhow, I have come up against a strong corporation, stronger than I am. What I now need to do is to go out somewhere and get some more strength in some way, it doesn't matter much how. People are not so much interested in me or you, or your or my ideals in their behalf, as they are in strength, an interesting spectacle. And they are easily deceived. These big fighting corporations with their attorneys and politicians and newspapers make me look weak—puny. So the people forget me. If I could get out, raise one million or five hundred thousand dollars and give the corporations a good drubbing, they would adore me—for awhile. Then I would have to go out and get another five hundred thousand somewhere, or do something else."

"Quite so," I replied. "Yet *Vox populi, vox dei.*"

Sitting upon his own doorstep one evening, in a very modest quarter of the city, I said:

"Were you very much depressed by your defeat the last time?"

"Not at all," he replied. "Action, reaction, that's the law. All these things right themselves in time, I suppose, or, anyhow, they ought to. Maybe they don't. Some man who can hand the people what they really need or ought to have will triumph, I suppose, some time. I don't know, I'm sure. I hope so. I think the world is moving on, all right."

In his serene and youthful face, the pale blue, philosophical eyes, was no evidence of dissatisfaction with the strange experiences through which he had passed.

"You're entirely philosophical, are you?"

"As much as any one can be, I suppose. They seem to think that all my work was an evidence of my worthlessness," he said. "Well, maybe it was. Self-interest may be the true law, and the best force. I haven't quite made up my mind yet. My sympathies of course are all the other way. 'He ought to be sewing shoes in the penitentiary,' one paper once said of me. Another advised me to try something that was not above my intelligence, such as breaking rock or shoveling dirt. Most of them agreed, however," he added with a humorous twitch of his large, expressive mouth, "that I'll do very well if I will only stay where I am, or, better yet, get out of here. They want me to leave. That's the best solution for them."

He seemed to repress a smile that was hovering on his lips.

"The voice of the enemy," I commented.

"Yes, sir, the voice of the enemy," he added. "But don't think that I think I'm done for. Not at all. I have just returned to my old ways in order to think this thing out. In a year or two I'll have solved my problem, I hope. I may have to leave here, and I may not. Anyhow, I'll turn up somewhere, with something."

He did have to leave, however, public opinion never being allowed to revert to him again, and five years later, in a fairly comfortable managerial position in New York, he died. He had made a fight, well enough, but the time, the place, the stars, perhaps, were not quite right. He had no guiding genius, possibly, to pull him through. Adherents did not flock to him and save him. Possibly he wasn't magnetic enough—that pagan, non-moral, non-propagandistic quality, anyhow. The fates did not fight for him as they do for some, those fates that ignore the billions and billions of others who fail. Yet are not all lives more or less failures, however successful they may appear to be at one time or another, contrasted, let us say, with what they hoped for? We compromise so much with everything—our dreams and all.

As for his reforms, they may be coming fast enough, or they may not. *In medias res.*

But as for him . . . ?

W. L. S.

LIFE'S LITTLE IRONIES are not always manifest. We hear distant rumbling sounds of its tragedies, but rarely are we
permitted to witness the reality. Therefore the real incidents
which I am about to relate may have some value.

I first called upon W. L. S——, Jr., in the winter of 1895. I
had known of him before only by reputation, or, what is
nearer the truth, by seeing his name in one of the great
Sunday papers attached to several drawings of the most lively
interest. These drawings depicted night scenes of the city
of New York, and appeared as colored supplements, eleven
by eighteen inches. They represented the spectacular scenes
which the citizen and the stranger most delight in—Madison
Square in a drizzle; the Bowery lighted by a thousand lamps
and crowded with "L" and surface cars; Sixth Avenue looking
north from Fourteenth Street.

I was a youthful editor at the time and on the lookout for
interesting illustrations of this sort, and when a little later I
was in need of a colored supplement for the Christmas number I decided to call upon S——. I knew absolutely nothing
about the world of art save what I had gathered from books
and current literary comment of all sorts, and was, therefore,
in a mood to behold something exceedingly bizarre in the
atmosphere with which I should find my illustrator surrounded.

I was not disappointed. It was at the time when artists—I
mean American artists principally—went in very strongly for
that sort of thing. Only a few years before they had all been
going to Paris, not so much to paint as to find out and imitate how artists *do* and live. I was greeted by a small, wiry,
lean-looking individual arrayed in a bicycle suit, whose countenance could be best described as wearing a perpetual look
of astonishment. He had one eye which fixed you with a
strange, unmoving solemnity, owing to the fact that it was
glass. His skin was anything but fair, and might be termed
sallow. He wore a close, sharp-pointed Vandyke beard, and
his gold-bridge glasses sat at almost right angles upon his
nose. His forehead was high, his good eye alert, his hair

sandy-colored and tousled, and his whole manner indicated thought, feeling, remarkable nervous energy, and, above all, a rasping and jovial sort of egotism which pleased me rather than otherwise.

I noticed no more than this on my first visit, owing to the fact that I was very much overawed and greatly concerned about the price which he would charge me, not knowing what rate he might wish to exact, and being desirous of coming away at least unabashed by his magnificence and independence.

"What's it for?" he asked, when I suggested a drawing.

I informed him.

"You say you want it for a double-page center?"

"Yes."

"Well, I'll do it for three hundred dollars."

I was taken considerably aback, as I had not contemplated paying more than one hundred.

"I get that from all the magazines," he added, seeing my hesitation, " wherever a supplement is intended."

"I don't think I could pay more than one hundred," I said, after a few moments' consideration.

"You couldn't?" he said, sharply, as if about to reprove me.

I shook my head.

"Well," he said, "let's see a copy of your publication."

The chief value of this conversation was that it taught me that the man's manner was no indication of his mood. I had thought he was impatient and indifferent, but I saw now that he was not so, rather brusque merely. He was simply excitable, somewhat like the French, and meant only to be businesslike. The upshot of it all was that he agreed to do it for one hundred and fifty, and asked me very solemnly to say nothing about it.

I may say here that I came upon S—— in the full blush of his fancies and ambitions, and just when he was verging upon their realization. He was not yet successful. A hundred and fifty dollars was a very fair price indeed. His powers, however, had reached that stage where they would soon command their full value.

I could see at once that he was very ambitious. He was bubbling over with the enthusiasm of youth and an intense desire for recognition. He knew he had talent. The knowledge of it gave him an air and an independence of manner which might have been irritating to some. Besides, he was slightly affected, argue to the contrary as he would, and was altogether full of his own hopes and ambitions.

The matter of painting this picture necessitated my presence on several occasions, and during this time I got better acquainted with him. Certain ideas and desires which we held in common drew us toward each other, and I soon began to see that he was much above the average in insight and skill. He talked with the greatest ease upon a score of subjects—literature, art, politics, music, the drama, and history. He seemed to have read the latest novels; to have seen many of the current plays; to have talked with important people. Theodore Roosevelt, previously Police Commissioner but then Governor, often came to his studio to talk and play chess with him. A very able architect was his friend. He had artist associates galore, many of whom had studios in the same building or the immediate vicinity. And there were literary and business men as well, all of whom seemed to enjoy his company, and who were very fond of calling and spending an hour in his studio.

I had only called the second time, and was going away, when he showed me a steamship he had constructed with his own hands—a fair-sized model, complete in every detail, even to the imitation stokers in the boiler-room, and which would run by the hour if supplied with oil and water. I soon learned that his skill in mechanical construction was great. He was a member of several engineering societies, and devoted some part of his carefully organized days to studying and keeping up with problems in mechanics.

"Oh, that's nothing," he observed, when I marveled at the size and perfection of the model. "I'll show you something else, if you have time some day, which may amuse you."

He then explained that he had constructed several model warships, and that it was his pleasure to take them out and fight them on a pond somewhere out on Long Island.

"We'll go out some day," he said when I showed appropriate interest, "and have them fight each other. You'll see how it's done!"

I waited some time for this outing, and finally mentioned it.

"We'll go tomorrow," he said. "Can you be around here by ten o'clock?"

Ten the next morning saw me promptly at the studio, and five minutes later we were off.

When we arrived at Long Island City we went to the first convenient arm of the sea and undid the precious fighters, in which he much delighted.

After studying the contour of the little inlet for a few moments he took some measurements with a tape-line, stuck up two twigs in two places for guide posts, and proceeded to fire and get up steam in his war-ships. Afterwards he set the rudders, and then took them to the water-side and floated them at the points where he had placed the twigs.

These few details accomplished, he again studied the situation carefully, headed the vessels to the fraction of an inch toward a certain point of the opposite shore, and began testing the steam.

"When I say ready, you push this lever here," he said, indicating a little brass handle fastened to the stern-post. "Don't let her move an inch until you do that. You'll see some tall firing."

He hastened to the other side where his own boat was anchored, and began an excited examination. He was like a school-boy with a fine toy.

At a word, I moved the lever as requested, and the two vessels began steaming out toward one another. Their weight and speed were such that the light wind blowing affected them not in the least, and their prows struck with an audible crack. This threw them side by side, steaming head on together. At the same time it operated to set in motion their guns, which fired broadsides in such rapid succession as to give a suggestion of rapid revolver practice. Quite a smoke rose, and when it rolled away one of the vessels was already nearly under water and the other was keeling with the inflow of water from the port side. S—— lost no time, but throwing off his coat, jumped in and swam to the rescue.

Throughout this entire incident his manner was that of an enthusiastic boy who had something exceedingly novel. He did not laugh. In all our acquaintance I never once heard him give a sound, hearty laugh. Instead he cackled. His delight apparently could only express itself in that way. In the main it showed itself in an excess of sharp movements, short verbal expressions, gleams of the eye.

I saw from this the man's delight in the science of engineering, and humored him in it. He was thereafter at the greatest pains to show all that he had under way in the mechanical line, and schemes he had for enjoying himself in this work in the future. It seemed rather a recreation for him than anything else. Like him, I could not help delighting in the perfect toys which he created, but the intricate details and slow process of manufacture were brain-racking. For not only would he draw the engine in all its parts, but he would buy the raw material and cast and drill and polish each separate part.

Upon my second visit I was deeply impressed by the sight of a fine passenger engine, a duplicate of the great 999 of the New York Central, of those days. It stood on brass rails laid along an old library shelf that had probably belonged to the previous occupant of the studio. This engine was a splendid object to look upon, strong, heavy, silent-running, with the fineness and grace of a perfect sewing-machine. It was duly trimmed with brass and nickel, after the manner of the great "flyers," and seemed so sturdy and powerful that one could not restrain the desire to see it run.

"How do you like that?" S—— exclaimed when he saw me looking at it.

"It's splendid," I said.

"See how she runs," he exclaimed, moving it up and down. "No noise about that."

He fairly caressed the mechanism with his hand, and went off into a most careful analysis of its qualities.

"I could build that engine," he exclaimed at last, enthusiastically, "if I were down in the Baldwin Company's place. I could make her break the record."

"I haven't the slightest doubt in the world," I answered.

This engine was a source of great expense to him, as well as the chief point in a fine scheme. He had made brass rails for it—sufficient to extend about the four sides of the studio—something like seventy feet. He had made most handsome passenger-cars with full equipment of brakes, vestibules, Pintsch gas, and so on, and had painted on their sides "The Great Pullman Line." One day, when we were quite friendly, he brought from his home all the rails, in a carpet-bag, and gave an exhibition of his engine's speed, attaching the cars and getting up sufficient steam to cause the engine to race about the room at a rate which was actually exciting. He had an arrangement by which it would pick up water and stop automatically. It was on this occasion that he confided what he called his great biograph scheme, the then forerunner of the latter day moving pictures. It was all so new then, almost a rumor, like that of the flying machine before it was invented.

"I propose to let the people see the photographic representation of an actual wreck—engine, cars, people, all tumbled down together after a collision, and no imitation, either—the actual thing."

"How do you propose to do it?" I asked.

"Well, that's the thing," he said, banteringly. "Now, how do you suppose I'd do it?"

"Hire a railroad to have a wreck and kill a few people," I suggested.

"Well, I've got a better thing than that. A railroad couldn't plan anything more real than mine will be."

I was intensely curious because of the novelty of the thing at that time. The "Biograph" was in its infancy.

"This is it," he exclaimed suddenly. "You see how realistic this engine is, don't you?"

I acknowledged that I did.

"Well," he confided, "I'm building another just like it. It's costing me three hundred dollars, and the passenger-cars will cost as much more. Now, I'm going to fix up some scenery on my roof—a gorge, a line of woods, a river, and a bridge. I'm going to make the water tumble over big rocks just above the bridge and run underneath it. Then I'm going to lay this track around these rocks, through the woods, across the bridge and off into the woods again.

"I'm going to put on the two trains and time them so they'll meet on the bridge. Just when they come into view where they can see each other, a post on the side of the track

will strike the cabs in such a way as to throw the firemen out
on the steps just as if they were going to jump. When the
engines take the bridge they'll explode caps that will set fire
to oil and powder under the cars and burn them up."

"Then what?" I asked.

"Well, I've got it planned automatically so that you will see
people jumping out of the cars and tumbling down on the
rocks, the flames springing up and taking to the cars, and all
that. Don't you believe it?" he added, as I smiled at the idea.
"Look here," and he produced a model of one of the occupants of the cars. He labored for an hour to show all the
intricate details, until I was compelled to admit the practica-
bility and novelty of the idea. Then he explained that instan-
taneous photography, as it was then called, was to be applied
at such close range that the picture would appear life size. The
actuality of the occurrence would do the rest.

Skepticism still lingered with me for a time, but when I saw
the second train growing, the figures and apparatus gradually
being modeled, and the correspondence and conferences
going on between the artist and several companies which
wished to gain control of the result, I was perfectly sure that
his idea would some day be realized.

As I have said, when I first met S—— he had not realized
any of his dreams. It was just at that moment that the tide
was about to turn. He surprised me by the assurance, born of
his wonderful virility, with which he went about all things.

"I've got an order from the *Ladies' Home Journal*," he said
to me one day. "They came to me."

"Good," I said. "What is it?"

"Somebody's writing up the terminal facilities of New
York."

He had before him an Academy board, on which was
sketched, in wash, a midnight express striking out across the
Jersey meadows with sparks blazing from the smoke stacks
and dim lights burning in the sleepers. It was a vivid thing,
strong with all the strength of an engine, and rich in the go
and enthusiasm which adhere to such mechanisms.

"I want to make a good thing of this," he said. "It may do
me some good."

A little later he received his first order from Harper's. He could not disguise that he was pleased, much as he tried to carry it off with an air. It was just before the Spanish war broke out, and the sketches he was to do related to the navy.

He labored at this order with the most tireless enthusiasm. Marine construction was his delight anyhow, and he spent hours and days making studies about the great vessels, getting not only the atmosphere but the mechanical detail. When he made the pictures they represented all that he felt.

"You know those drawings?" he said the day after he delivered them.

"Yes."

"I set a good stiff price on them and demanded my drawings back when they were through."

"Did you get them?"

"Yep. It will give them more respect for what I'm trying to do," he said.

Not long after he illustrated one of Kipling's stories.

He was in high feather at this, but grim and repressed withal. One could see by the nervous movements of his wiry body that he was delighted over it.

At this time Kipling came to his studio. It was by special arrangement, but S—— received him as if he were—well, as artists usually receive authors. They talked over the galley proofs, and the author went away.

"It's coming my way now," he said, when he could no longer conceal his feelings. "I want to do something good on this."

Through all this rise from obscurity to recognition he lived close to his friends—a crowd of them, apparently, always in his studio jesting, boxing, fencing—and interested himself in the mechanics I have described. His drawing, his engine-building, his literary studies and recreations were all mixed, jumbled, plunging him pell-mell, as it were, on to distinction. In the first six months of his studio life he had learned to fence, and often dropped his brush to put on the mask and assume the foils with one of his companions.

As our friendship increased I found how many were the man's accomplishments and how wide his range of sympathies. He was an expert bicyclist, as well as a trick rider, and

used a camera in a way to make an amateur envious. He could
sing, having a fine tenor voice, which I heard the very day I
learned that he could sing. It so happened that it was my turn
to buy the theater tickets, and I invited him to come with me
that especial evening.

"Can't do it," he replied.

"All right," I said.

"I'm part of an entertainment tonight, or I would," he
added apologetically.

"What do you do?" I inquired.

"Sing."

"Get out!" I said.

"So be it," he answered. "Come up this evening."

To this I finally agreed, and was surprised to observe the
ease with which he rendered his solo. He had an exquisitely
clear and powerful voice and received a long round of applause, which he refused to acknowledge by singing again.

The influence of success is easily observable in a man of so
volatile a nature. It seems to me that I could have told by his
manner, day by day, the inwash of the separate ripples of the
inrolling tide of success. He was all alive, full of plans, and
the tale of his coming conquests was told in his eye. Sometime in the second year of our acquaintance I called at his
studio in response to a card which he had stuck under my
office door. It was his habit to draw an outline head of himself, something almost bordering upon a caricature, writing
underneath it "I called," together with any word he might
have to say. This day he was in his usual good spirits, and
rallied me upon having an office which was only a blind. He
had a roundabout way of getting me to talk about his personal affairs with him, and I soon saw that he had something
very interesting, to himself, to communicate. At last he
said,—

"I'm going to Europe next summer."

"Is that so?" I replied. "For pleasure?"

"Well, partly."

"What's up outside of that?" I asked.

"I'm going to represent the American Architectural League
at the international convention."

"I didn't know you were an architect," I said.

"Well, I'm not," he answered, "professionally. I've studied it pretty thoroughly."

"Well, you seem to be coming up, Louis," I remarked.

"I'm doing all right," he answered.

He went on working at his easel as if his fate depended upon what he was doing. He had the fortunate quality of being able to work and converse most entertainingly at the same time. He seemed to enjoy company under such circumstances.

"You didn't know I was a baron, did you?" he finally observed.

"No," I answered, thinking he was exercising his fancy for the moment. "Where do you keep your baronial lands, my lord?"

"In Germany, kind sir," he replied, banteringly.

Then in his customary excitable mood he dropped his brushes and stood up.

"You don't believe me, do you?" he exclaimed, looking over his drooping glasses.

"Why, certainly I believe you, if you are serious. Are you truly a baron?"

"It was this way," he said. "My grandfather was a baron. My father was the younger of two brothers. His brother got the title and what was left of the estate. That he managed to go through with, and then he died. Now, no one has bothered about the title——"

"And you're going back to claim it?"

"Exactly."

I took it all lightly at first, but in time I began to perceive that it was a serious ambition. He truly wanted to be Baron S—— and add to himself the luster of his ancestors.

With all this, the man was really not so much an aristocrat in his mood as a seeker after life and new experiences. Being a baron was merely a new experience, or promised to be. He had the liveliest sympathies for republican theories and institutions—only he considered his life a thing apart. He had a fine mind, philosophically and logically poised. He could reason upon all things, from the latest mathematical theorem to Christian Science. Naturally, being so much of an individualist, he was not drifting toward any belief in the latter, but was never weary of discussing the power of mind—a universal mind even—its wondrous ramifications and influences. Also he was a student of the English school of philosophy, and loved to get up mathematical and mechanical demonstrations of certain philosophic truths. Thus he worked out by means of a polygon, whose sides were of unequal lengths, a theory of friendship which is too intricate to explain here.

From now on I watched his career with the liveliest interest. He was a charming and a warm friend, and never neglected for a moment the obligations which such a relationship demands.

I heard from him frequently in many and various ways, dined with him regularly every second or third week, and rejoiced with him in his triumphs, now more and more frequent. One spring he went to Europe and spent the summer in tracing down his baronial claims, looking up various artists and scientists and attending several scientific meetings here and there at the same time. He did the illustrations for one of Kipling's fast express stories which one of the magazines published, and came back flushed and ready to try hard for a membership in the American Water-Color Society.

I shall never forget his anxiety to get into that mildly interesting body. He worked hard and long on several pictures which should not only be hung on the line but enlist sufficient interest among the artists to gain him a vote of admission. He mentioned it frequently and fixed me with his eyes to see what I thought of him.

"Go ahead," I said; "you have more right to membership perhaps than many another I know. Try hard."

He painted not one, but four, pictures, and sent them all. They were very interesting after their kind. Two were scenes from the great railroad terminal yards; the others, landscapes in mist or rain. Three of these pictures were passed and two of them hung on the line. The third was *skyed*, but he was admitted to membership.

I was delighted for his sake, for I could see, when he gave me the intelligence, that it was a matter which had keyed up his whole nervous system.

Not long after this we were walking on Broadway, one drizzly autumn evening, on our way to the theater. Life, ambition, and our future were the *small* subjects under discussion. The street, as usual, was crowded. On every hand blazed the fire signs. The yellow lights were beautifully reflected in the wet sidewalks and gray wet cobblestones glistening with water.

When we reached Greeley Square (at that time a brilliant and almost sputtering spectacle of light and merriment), S—— took me by the arm.

"Come over here," he said. "I want you to look at it from here."

He took me to a point where, by the intersection of the lines of the converging streets, one could not only see Greeley Square but a large part of Herald Square, with its then huge theatrical sign of fire and its measure of store lights and lamps of vehicles. It was a kaleidoscopic and inspiring scene. The broad, converging walks were alive with people. A perfect jam of vehicles marked the spot where the horse and cable cars intersected. Overhead was the elevated station, its lights augmented every few minutes by long trains of brightly lighted cars filled with changing metropolitan crowds—crowds like shadows moving in a dream.

"Do you see the quality of that? Look at the blend of the lights and shadows in there under the L."

I looked and gazed in silent admiration.

"See, right here before us—that pool of water there—do you get that? Now, that isn't silver-colored, as it's usually represented. It's a prism. Don't you see the hundred points of light?"

I acknowledged the variety of color, which I had scarcely observed before.

"You may think one would skip that in viewing a great scene, but the artist mustn't. He must get all, whether you notice it or not. It gives feeling, even when you don't see it."

I acknowledged the value of this ideal.

"It's a great spectacle," he said. "It's got more flesh and blood in it than people usually think. It's easy to make it too mechanical and commonplace."

"Why don't you paint it?" I asked.

He turned on me as if he had been waiting for the suggestion.

"That's something I want to tell you," he said. "I am. I've sketched it a half-dozen times already. I haven't got it yet. But I'm going to."

I heard more of these dreams, intensifying all the while, until the Spanish-American war broke out. Then he was off in a great rush of war work. I scarcely saw him for six weeks, owing to some travels of my own, but I saw his name. One day in Broadway I stopped to see why a large crowd was gathered about a window in the Hoffman House. It was one of S——'s drawings of our harbor defenses, done as if the artist had been sitting at the bottom of the sea. The fishes, the green water, the hull of a massive war-ship—all were there—and about, the grim torpedoes. This put it into my head to go and see him. He was as tense and strenuous as ever. The glittering treasure at the end of the rainbow was more than ever in his eye. His body was almost sore from traveling.

"I am in now," he said, referring to the war movement. "I am going to Tampa."

"Be gone long?" I asked.

"Not this first time. I'll only be down there three weeks."

"I'll see you then."

"Supposing we make it certain," he said. "What do you say to dining together this coming Sunday three weeks?"

I went away, wishing him a fine trip and feeling that his dreams must now soon begin to come true. He was growing in reputation. Some war pictures, such as he could do, would set people talking. Then he would paint his prize pictures, finish his wreck scheme, become a baron, and be a great man.

Three weeks later I knocked at his studio door. It was a fine springlike day, though it was in February. I expected confidently to hear his quick aggressive step inside. Not a sound in reply. I knocked harder, but still received no answer. Then I went to the other doors about. He might be with his friends, but they were not in. I went away thinking that his war duties had interfered, that he had not returned.

Nevertheless there was something depressing about that portion of the building in which his studio was located. I felt as if it should not be, and decided to call again. Monday it was the same, and Tuesday.

That same evening I was sitting in the library of the Salmagundi Club, when a well-known artist addressed me.

"You knew S——, didn't you?" he said.

"Yes; what of it?"

"You knew he was dead, didn't you?"

"What!" I said.

"Yes, he died of fever, this morning."

I looked at him without speaking for a moment.

"Too bad," he said. "A clever boy, Louis. Awfully clever. I feel sorry for his father."

It did not take long to verify his statement. His name was in the perfunctory death lists of the papers the next morning. No other notice of any sort. Only a half-dozen seemed to know that he had ever lived.

And yet it seemed *to me* that a great tragedy had happened—he was so ambitious, so full of plans. His dreams were so near fulfillment.

I saw the little grave afterward and the empty studio. His desks revealed several inventions and many plans of useful things, but these came to nothing. There was no one to continue the work.

My feeling at the time was as if I had been looking at a beautiful lamp, lighted, warm and irradiating a charming scene, and then suddenly that it had been puffed out before my eyes, as if a hundred bubbles of iridescent hues had been shattered by a breath. We toil so much, we dream so richly, we hasten so fast, and, lo! the green door is opened. We are through it, and its grassy surface has sealed us forever from all which apparently we so much crave—even as, breathlessly, we are still running.

Chronology

Born August 27 in Terre Haute, Indiana, ninth living child of Johann Paul and Sarah Schänäb Dreiser. (His mother, Sarah Schänäb, daughter of German Mennonite farmers from near Dayton, Ohio, eloped in 1851 at age seventeen with 29-year-old Johann Paul Dreiser, a devout Roman Catholic who emigrated from Mayen in the German Rhineland in 1844 to avoid conscription and worked in eastern woolen mills before moving to Dayton. Parents lived in Fort Wayne, Terre Haute, and Sullivan, Indiana, where father supervised woolen factory until slump in industry and change in ownership caused him to lose his job.) Baptized Herman Theodore (called Theo, Thee, Dorsh, and Teddy) at Church of St. Benedict, September 10. Brothers and sisters are Johann Paul, Jr. (Paul), b. 1858; Markus Romanus (Rome), b. 1860; Maria Franziska (Mame), b. 1861; Emma Wilhelmina (Em), b. 1863; Mary Theresa (Tres), b. 1865; Cacilia (Sylvia), b. 1866; Alphons Joachim (Al), b. 1867; Clara Clothilde (Claire, Tillie), b. 1869. Shortly after Dreiser's birth, family moves to newly purchased home at 12th Street and Walnut in Terre Haute. Another brother, Eduard Minerod (Ed), born 1873. Father works sporadically. Paul arrested for stealing (Feb. 1876) and father pays $300 bond.

1877–78 Enters St. Benedict's Catholic School; classes are conducted in German. Attends German Mass daily and hears German at home. Does poorly in sports, develops stutter, and is bullied by other boys. Gathers coal from railroad tracks; sometimes has nothing to eat but potatoes and fried mush. May 1878, father sells home for $1,400 and moves family to smaller house at 2533 North 7th Street. Hears parents fight over "what should be done for the children." (Remembers Terre Haute years as "a dour and despondent period which seems to have colored my life forever.")

1879–81 Father, now employed as rug-maker, finds jobs for Mame, Emma, Sylvia, and Theresa as loom-workers in Terre Haute, and they help support family. Al works on relative's farm. Rome runs away and works as vendor on railroad. With mother, Ed, and Claire, moves in spring to Vincennes, Indiana; they occupy small, rent-free room in firehouse at invitation of young woman mother had once befriended. Enjoys the firehouse and winding streets of Vincennes and sees first telephone. After five weeks, mother discovers that friend runs bordello for the firemen and moves with children to Sullivan, Indiana. Older sisters quarrel with father and take jobs as housemaids in Terre Haute. Rome visits, penniless, but full of tales of adventure in the West. Dreiser often sent home from school because mother cannot pay parochial school fees. Picks coal with Ed and, with Claire, teaches mother to write English. Fall 1880, mother opens boarding house, but coal mines close in fall 1881, and some boarders leave without paying. Winter is severe and food scarce.

1882–84   Family fears eviction. February, Paul, absent for years, arrives, bringing gifts and money; has played in minstrel shows, changed his name to "Paul Dresser" and published *The Paul Dresser Songster*. In May, Dreiser, Ed, and Claire move with mother to Evansville, Indiana, and occupy a furnished brick cottage at 1415 East Franklin Street that Paul has rented for them. Groceries and secondhand clothes are sent regularly by Sallie Walker (real name Annie Brace), prosperous madam of Evansville brothel with whom Paul now lives. Reads books found in attic of house, including Ouida's *Wanda*, Bulwer's *Ernest Maltravers*, Horatio Alger's stories, as well as *The Family Story Paper*, *The Fireside Companion*, and *The New York Weekly*. Father visits from Terre Haute and enrolls children in *Heilige Dreifaltighet Kirchet* (Holy Trinity Parochial School). Brother Al comes from Chicago and sisters Emma and Sylvia rejoin family. Dreiser works in five-and-dime store on Saturday nights, earning pocket money and free ice cream. Rome visits, drinks heavily, is arrested and bailed out by Paul.

1884–85   Summer, Paul breaks up with Sallie Walker and is no longer able to provide sufficient support. Mother moves family to apartment found by Theresa in Chicago at West Madison and Throop Street. Dreiser sells newspapers with Ed. Father, unemployed, arrives. Sisters Mame, Emma, and Theresa date older men. By fall, Chicago proves too expensive and Dreiser, Ed, and Claire move with mother to Warsaw, Indiana. Father (now working again in Terre Haute), older sisters, and Paul send money for support. Enters seventh grade in West Ward, first public school; is delighted by coeducational classes and attractive 21-year-old teacher, May Calvert. Feels self-conscious because of cast in right eye and buck teeth. Does well in all subjects except mathematics and grammar and pleases father, who approves purchase of sets of works by Irving, Dickens, and Scott. Reads Kingsley's *Water Babies*, Hawthorne's *The House of the Seven Gables* and *The Scarlet Letter*, Lew Wallace's *Ben Hur*, Samuel Smiles's *Self-help*, and works by Cooper, Bryant, Whittier, Poe, and Longfellow. Late spring, Rome visits, drinks heavily, and causes trouble. Summer, Sylvia loses her job in Chicago and comes to stay; Emma, who has broken up with her architect lover, visits. Dreiser embarrassed by ostentatious dress and free behavior of sisters and violent quarrels between them and father. Emma returns to Chicago.

1885–86   Enters eighth grade of Central High School and is encouraged by teacher Mildred Fielding. Fall, family moves to fourteen-room "Thrall's House" on three acres with grove of pine trees ("of all the places we lived this was the most charming"). Theresa, deserted by Chicago manufacturer, comes to Warsaw to recuperate from severe illness. February 1886, family, learning that Emma has married L. A. Hopkins and moved to New York, is pleased with his apparent prosperity and Roman Catholic background. (Later they learn that Hopkins was already married and had stolen $3,500 from saloon where he worked.) Reads Thackeray, Bunyan, Dryden, Pope, Emerson, Thoreau, and Mark Twain, as well as *Tom Jones*, *Moll Flanders*, and pamphlets on sex circulating among his friends. Suffers dizzy spells and ringing in ears. April, has first sexual experience with 15-year-old baker's daughter. Takes course in German literature at urging of ninth-grade teacher, Alvira Skarr. ("At once my estimate of my father's native land [hitherto, because of his religious dogmatizing, exceedingly low] rose.") Sylvia reveals she is carrying the child of son of wealthy Warsaw family; after attempts to bring charges of abandonment against him are unsuccessful, she joins Emma and Hopkins in New York to have baby. Dreiser, Ed, and Claire feel socially ostracized. Spring, Sylvia brings baby boy, Carl, to mother in Warsaw and returns to New York. With advice from superintendent of schools, who praises his academic abilities, Dreiser reads Shakespeare and studies German history; also reads Carlyle, Macaulay's *History of England*, Guizot's *History of France*, and Taine's *History of English Literature*.

1887–88   Summer, after a brief attempt at farm work moves to Chicago and takes cheap room on West Madison Street. Gets job as dishwasher in Paradiso Restaurant for $5/week plus meals; tells sisters that he is haberdashery clerk for $7. Mother, Claire, Ed, and Sylvia's child, Carl, arrive in September, and family, joined by Theresa and Al, moves to apartment on Ogden Avenue. Quits restaurant and is out of work for a month. Family moves to cheaper apartment at 61 Flourney Street in October. Works as stock boy at wholesale hardware firm for $5/week; gives mother $3/week. Dislikes job but forms friendship with 45-year-old intellectual and alcoholic Danish immigrant, Christian Aaberg, who talks to him about Voltaire, Ibsen, Goethe, Wagner, and Schopenhauer, ancient Greece, Peter the Great, and Napoleon. Fired, but rehired after appeal to company director. Develops stomach problems, chronic cough, and fears consumption.

1889   Summer, former teacher Mildred Fielding, now principal of suburban Chicago high school, arranges for his admission as special student to Indiana University at Bloomington, and pays living expenses ($300) for year. Resents not being invited to join fraternity. Elected secretary of Philomathean, school literary society. Shyness with girls is excruciating; finds concentration difficult.

1890   Takes final exams and passes all classes. In June, returns to Chicago. Paul has written hit song "I Believe It for My Mother Told Me So," and is now the leading comedian in road show of *The Tin Soldier*. Dreiser's health is improved, stomach troubles and cough are gone. Finds job selling real estate at $3/week plus commission; though boss is unable to pay his wages, enjoys free use of buggy and takes ailing mother for rides. Mother dies November 14 in Dreiser's arms. (Later writes, "Our youth and home were over . . . now I was I. And alone. Her part—her strength and living sustaining love—had gone from me.") Owed $21 for seven weeks' back pay, uses employer's credit to buy clothes. Finds work as driver with laundry company at $8/week.

1891   After family quarrels, takes small apartment on Taylor Street with Claire and Ed. Gets better-paying job collecting installments on cheap household goods sold to the poor. Writes pieces about Chicago influenced by Eugene Field's *Daily News* column "Sharps and Flats"; sends them to Field, but receives no response. November, uses $25 of company's money to buy new overcoat, gloves, and cane, intending to pay it back a little each week, but is discovered and fired. Gets job with Chicago *Herald* Christmas promotion giving away toys; hopes to become a newspaper reporter.

1892   Stands 6 feet 1 1/2 inches tall, weighs 137 pounds. Gets job with another collection firm. Quarrels with Claire and moves with Ed to room of their own. June, becomes reporter for Chicago *Daily Globe* for $15/week. Learns how to write news stories from copy editor John Milo Maxwell. Covers Democratic National Convention and by luck scoops other reporters with news of Grover Cleveland's nomination. Takes room alone on Ogden Place. Publishes first fiction, "The Return of Genius," in the *Globe* under the name Carl Dreiser. Moves to St. Louis when city editor helps him get job with respected St. Louis *Globe-Democrat* in November at $20/week; covers night beat at North 7th Street police station. Depressed and lonely at first, meets Peter B. McCord (who will become a close friend) and Richard Wood, bohemian staff artists.

1893   Interviews celebrities passing through town, including former boxing champion John L. Sullivan (acting in touring theater company) and theosophist Annie Besant. January, eyewitness account of railroad disaster in Alton, Illinois, earns a bonus and a raise in pay. Becomes drama critic and plans play, *Jeremiah I*, with McCord to design costumes and sets. Favorable review of black singer Sissieretta Jones is criticized as "black Republicanism" by rival newspapers. April, unable to attend three plays because of crime assignment, writes reviews from advance clippings. Next day, discovers none of the touring companies had reached town because of floods. Humiliated, resigns from job. Becomes reporter for the St. Louis *Republic* at $18/week. Accompanies twenty Missouri schoolteachers (including 24-year-old Sara Osborne "Jug" White), winners of *Republic*-sponsored popularity contest, to Chicago World's Fair. Visits 72-year-old father, and brothers Al, now an electrician, and Ed, who drives a delivery wagon, in Chicago. Sara White comes to St. Louis in mid-September and they become engaged.

1894   January, covers story of lynching of black youth. Feeling restless, decides to leave St. Louis in spite of the *Republic*'s offer of an editorial post and more money. Considers buying small country weekly in Ohio, but is disappointed by its condition. Goes to Toledo, where Toledo *Blade* city editor Arthur Henry gives him temporary job covering streetcar strike and becomes very close friend. Then goes to Cleveland and Buffalo, and finally to Pittsburgh in April; impressed by the city, decides to stay. Receives wire from Henry offering job at $18/week at the *Blade*; changes figure to $25 and uses it to negotiate successfully with city editor of Pittsburgh *Dispatch*. Assigned to cover police and court news. Spends free time in nearby Carnegie Library; reads Balzac, beginning with *The Wild Ass's Skin* and *The Great Man from the Provinces* ("For a period of four or five months I ate, slept, dreamed, lived him and his characters and his views and his city"), George Eliot, John Tyndall, Thomas Huxley, and Herbert Spencer's *First Principles*. July, makes brief visit to Montgomery City, Missouri, to see Sara White and to meet her parents. Goes to New York to visit brother Paul, now successful and living with sister Emma and Hopkins and their two children. Feels overwhelmed by New York ("here were huge dreams and lusts and vanities being gratified hourly"). In November returns to New York to live. Works as space-rate reporter for the New York *World* at $7.50 for 21-inch-column, but rarely fills more than two inches.

1895   February, helps Emma leave Hopkins (now unemployed and alcoholic). Quits job on newspaper, tries to write articles and stories but is unsuccessful. Convinces Paul's business partners to let him put out magazine to sell their music. October, large format magazine *Ev'ry Month* appears, containing four songs per issue. Selects fiction, poetry, and pictures, gives household hints, writes captions, book reviews, occasional interviews, and editorial column "Reflections," signed "The Prophet." Salary is $10/week during summer and $15 when magazine appears. Becomes friend of William Louis Sonntag, Jr., painter of street scenes, who introduces him to other artists.

1896   April, visits Sara White, now teaching in Danville, Missouri. *Ev'ry Month* becomes modest success (circulation 65,000), publishing Bret Harte and Stephen Crane. Salary is raised. Goes to theater regularly and reads Darwin. Ed comes to New York determined to be an actor. Sylvia moves to New York to become a songwriter. Mame and husband, Austin Brennan, arrive for Christmas from Chicago with Claire, who is ill.

1897   At Paul's urging, writes words to first verse of "On the Banks of the Wabash." Increasingly resents publishing second-rate material. Quarrels with Paul and his partners over magazine's contents and leaves *Ev'ry Month* in August. Writes articles and occasional verse for *Munsey's*, *Ainslee's*, *Metropolitan*, and *Cosmopolitan*. Receives news that sister Theresa has been killed by train in Chicago.

1898   Hired by Orison Swett Marden, founder of new magazine *Success*, to write series of "inspirational" pieces about famous people for $100 each. Series impresses Richard Duffy of *Ainslee's*, who hires Dreiser as writer and part-time editor at $150/month. Continues to write articles for other magazines as well, and total earnings reach almost $100/week. Joins artists' Salmagundi Club and becomes friend of painters J. Francis Murphy and Bruce Crane. Lives at 232 West 15th Street. Pleased when "On the Banks of the Wabash" is a huge success, but still angry with Paul. In Chicago, interviews Philip D. Armour and Marshall Field for *Success*, as well as Abraham Lincoln's son, Robert Todd Lincoln, president of the Pullman Company, for *Ainslee's*. Writes articles on writers and artists, including Alfred Stieglitz. Arranges to meet Sara, accompanied by her sister Rose, in Washington, D.C., where they are married December 28.

1899   Dreisers move to 6 West 102nd Street. July, Dreiser and Sara join Arthur Henry and his wife, Maud, at their large house on the Maumee River outside Toledo. At Henry's urging, writes short stories: "McEwen of the Shining Slave Makers," "Old Rogaum and His Theresa," "Nigger Jeff," and "When the Old Century Was New." Dreisers return to New York in September with Arthur Henry, who lives with them. "Curious Shifts of the Poor," Bowery sketch inspired by Stephen Crane's "The Men in the Storm," appears as lead article in November *Demorest's Family Magazine*. Accepts invitation to call on William Dean Howells and writes "The Real Howells" (*Ainslee's*, March 1900). Begins writing *Sister Carrie* with encouragement and collaboration of Henry and Sara. ("I took a piece of yellow paper and . . . wrote down a title at random—*Sister Carrie*—and began!")

1900   Works on *Sister Carrie*. Writes magazine articles. Finishes *Sister Carrie*, which is rejected by Harper & Brothers but accepted by Doubleday, Page on recommendation of editor Frank Norris ("it pleased me as well as any novel I have read in *any* form, published or otherwise"). Vacations with in-laws in Missouri. When Frank Doubleday attempts to reject novel, insists Doubleday, Page honor its promise. Contract signed in August. *Sister Carrie*, published November 8, is distributed without publicity. Norris sends copies to reviewers. Reviews are mixed, but only 450 copies are sold; royalties total $68.40. Father dies on Christmas Day.

1901   January, begins work on *Jennie Gerhardt*. Depressed by reception of *Sister Carrie*. Has difficulty selling articles to magazines. Asks Henry to cut *Sister Carrie* when British publisher requests shorter version for Dollar Library of American Fiction. Summer, with Sara, joins Henry and his mistress, Anna Mallon, at her cabin on Dumpling Island off Noank, Connecticut. Quarrels with them, and returns earlier than planned to New York at end of July. Dreisers take cheaper apartment at 1599 East End Avenue. *Sister Carrie* receives good reviews in England. Tries without success to interest American publishers in reissuing it. Worries about money as income declines; often sits in rocking chair, folding and unfolding handkerchief (a habit continued throughout his life). Signs contract for *The Transgressor (Jennie Gerhardt)* with J. F. Taylor Company, which agrees to pay him $100/month to finish novel by following summer. November, unable to write, decides to go to Bedford City, east of Roanoke, Virginia, for winter with Sara to improve spirits. Makes slow progress on novel; still suffers from depression. Spends holidays with in-laws at their farm in Missouri.

1902   Dreisers travel through South. Goes alone to Lynchburg and Charlottesville, Virginia, in April. June and July, walks from Charlottesville to Philadelphia; joined by Sara in September. Consults dermatologist Dr. Louis Adolphus Duhring about skin disorders, chest pains, headaches, insomnia, weariness, and inordinate appetite. Doctor prescribes experimental treatment for neurasthenia (analgesics and bromides taken in sequence) and for lethargy (tonic of small amounts of arsenic, strychnine, and quinine). Health fails to improve. Unable to complete *Jennie Gerhardt*; payments from J. F. Taylor cease. Writes occasional pieces for local periodicals. Sketch "Christmas in the Tenements" appears in *Harper's Weekly* in December.

1903   Sends Sara to her family in Missouri when money is almost gone. February, moves to cheap lodgings in Brooklyn. Suffers from insomnia, pain in fingers and toes, and has hallucinations. Lives on bread and milk; weight drops to 130 pounds. Refuses to seek help from family, although Mame, Paul, Ed, and Emma all live in New York. On city street, encounters Paul, who persuades him to enter former wrestler William Muldoon's sanatorium in Westchester County. After six weeks of long walks, rigorous exercise, and regular meals, condition improves. Paul pays $256 bill. June, gets job on railroad at Spuyten Duyvil shop on Hudson River at 15¢/hour, later 17¢. Lives in Kingsbridge, New York, and is joined by Sara in August. Receives occasional financial help from Paul. Resigns from railroad Christmas Eve.

1904   January, gets job with Paul's help as feature editor on New York *Daily News*, and takes apartment with Sara at 399 Mott Avenue in the Bronx. Quarrels with Henry about portrayal of him in Henry's novel *An Island Cabin*. Fall, takes job with publisher Street & Smith updating, cutting, and editing dime novels for $15/week. With co-worker Charles Agnew MacLean, plans to start publishing company; MacLean buys plates of *Sister Carrie* from J. F.

Taylor (which had bought them from Doubleday, Page) for $500.

1905   Still unable to complete *Jennie Gerhardt*, owes J. F. Taylor $750 for advances. Writes poetry and articles for Richard Duffy, now editor at *Tom Watson's Magazine*. Becomes editor, with raise in pay, of new pulp journal *Smith's Magazine*, which appears in April. Begins lifelong friendship with Charles Fort, eccentric contributor. Sara is unhappy about infidelities and his unwillingness to have children. Paul, suffering from financial pressure and poor health, moves in with Emma; Dreiser visits nearly every day.

1906   Paul Dresser dies penniless January 30 of heart attack (family will later receive royalties from songs, including "My Gal Sal," which becomes a hit). After raising *Smith's* circulation to 125,000, takes new job as editor of the *Broadway Magazine* at $40/week. Uses generous budget to buy work from O. Henry, Kipling, and Channing Pollock. Buys plates and sheets of *Sister Carrie* from MacLean for $550 and moves with Sara to 439 West 123rd Street, overlooking Morningside Park.

1907   Circulation of *Broadway Magazine* goes to 100,000; now earns $100/week salary. With investment of $5,000 becomes secretary and editor of B. W. Dodge & Company. Lends plates of *Sister Carrie* to company. Reissued *Sister Carrie* receives good reviews and sells well. June, accepts offer to become chief editor, at $5,000/year, of the Butterick Company's "Trio" of women's magazines: *The Delineator*, *The Designer*, and the *New Idea Woman's Magazine*. June, has appendix removed at St. Luke's Hospital. Starts campaign to find homes for orphaned children. Repays debt to J. F. Taylor for *Jennie Gerhardt*.

1908   Spring, meets and begins close friendship with H. L. Mencken. Invests in two lots near Nyack, New York, and a 150-acre tract near Nanuet, New York; buys ten-acre orchard in North Yakima, Washington, with Arthur Henry and his brother Albert. Grosset & Dunlap publishes inexpensive edition of *Sister Carrie* (5,248 copies sold by end of year). Prepares twenty chapters of *Jennie Gerhardt* to show publishers. Travels to Washington, D.C., and persuades President Theodore Roosevelt to support the

Delineator campaign for orphans (forerunner of National Child Rescue League). Receives increase in salary when circulation of magazines goes up.

1909   July, with William Neil Smith, secures control of bankrupt magazine *The Bohemian* for $1,000. Keeps involvement secret from employers. Fall, begins romantic affair with Thelma Cudlipp, 17-year-old daughter of Butterick assistant editor. Drops *The Bohemian* as losing proposition in December.

1910   Attends social gatherings at home of Elias Rosenthal, wealthy attorney and admirer of *Sister Carrie*, and meets daughter Lillian (who will become lover and lifelong friend). Spring, hires William C. Lengel, 21-year-old lawyer, as private secretary at *The Delineator*, beginning long friendship. Wants to marry Thelma and asks for divorce, but Sara, ill with rheumatic fever, refuses. Fired by Butterick Company October 1, after firm is threatened by scandalous publicity from Thelma's mother. Leaves wife and moves to Park Avenue Hotel. Denied permission to see Thelma; angry, depressed, and suffering from insomnia, loses weight and writes her daily letters (which are intercepted by her mother). Dodge & Company taken over by creditors. Disconsolate when Thelma sails with mother to England for a year. Continues to see Sara, though they live separately. At Christmas attends Anarchists' Ball; sits with Sinclair Lewis and Emma Goldman. Finishes first draft of *Jennie Gerhardt*.

1911   Revises ending of *Jennie Gerhardt*, and Sara cuts and edits the manuscript. Shows new version to Mencken, Flora Mai Holly, James Huneker, and other friends, who admire the novel, but, except for Mencken, advise cutting it. Sara sails for England in January with copy to show Curtis Brown & Massie, London literary agency. July, moves to 3609 Broadway; joined by Sara on her return from Europe. Finishes first draft of *The "Genius"* by August, but puts it aside to work on *The Financier*, first volume of Frank Cowperwood trilogy based on life of Charles Tyson Yerkes. *Jennie Gerhardt* published by Harper & Brothers in New York and London on October 19. Novel is praised by Floyd Dell in *The Bookman* and Mencken in *The Smart Set*; Arnold Bennett, in New York, tells interviewer he knows little about American literature except, "I know there is one novel called *Sister Carrie*, by a man named Theodore Dreiser." Wants to travel to Europe to continue research on life of Yerkes, and is grateful when British publisher Grant Richards helps arrange luxurious European trip (in the style of Yerkes); Century Company offers $1,000 advance for three travel articles. Harpers advances $500 for *Jennie Gerhardt* and $2,000 for *The Financier*. Embarks November 22 on the *Mauretania* with Richards. Spends three weeks at Richards's country home at Cookham Dean, Berkshire. Visits Oxford, hikes along the Thames, stays at the Capitol Hotel in London. Buys expensive Bond Street clothes.

1912   Visits Manchester. Goes to Paris January 11. Joined by Richards, who shows him Paris night life. Goes to Monte Carlo and Cap Martin with Richards and Sir Hugh Lane, art collector and director of Dublin Municipal Art Gallery. February, stays two weeks in Rome at the Grand Continental Hotel. Worries about sales of *Jennie Gerhardt* and expense of trip. Sees Pope Pius X. March, tours Florence and Venice. Travels through Switzerland to Germany, where he visits father's birthplace in Mayen, then to Amsterdam. Sails April 13 from Dover on the *Kroonland*; arrives in New York April 23. Stays at St. Paul Hotel. Relieved to find that *Jennie Gerhardt* has sold 12,717 copies since February. Meets Anna Tatum and finds her Quaker background and literary abilities fascinating; she becomes his lover for a short time and later acts as literary agent. Moves temporarily to 605 West 111th Street. Late June, rejoins Sara at 3609 Broadway. Decides to remain with Harpers rather than sign with Richards. Completes *The Financier*, which is published in October by Harpers and receives good reviews. Works on travel articles. November, asks Mencken to be his literary executor. December, goes to Chicago for further research on Yerkes. Meets Edgar Lee Masters, lawyer and (then unknown) poet, to talk about Yerkes, beginning lifelong friendship.

1913   Introduced by Floyd Dell to Maurice Browne (founder of early Little Theater), actress Kirah Markham (with whom he is to have an affair), novelist John Cowper Powys, poet Arthur Davison Ficke, and Sherwood Anderson, who will all become close friends. Urges Browne to bring theater to New York. On return to New York, works on *A Traveler at Forty*, account of European trip, and *The Titan*, second volume of Cowperwood trilogy. Worries about declining sales of *The Financier*. Summer, writes one-act play "The Girl in the Coffin" (*The Smart Set*, Oct. 1913). Stays often with Kirah Markham, who has come to live in New York. *A Traveler at Forty* published by Century November 25. Through Dell, becomes member of Liberal Club in Greenwich Village. Goes to New Year's party at Emma Goldman's house with Markham.

1914   Financial worries continue. Markham learns that Dreiser still spends time with Sara and returns to Chicago. Goes to Chicago for more research and sees Markham and Edgar Lee Masters. Hears from Anna Tatum that Harpers, after printing 8,500 sets of sheets, has refused to publish *The Titan*, claiming its realism is too uncompromising. John Lane Company, under direction of J. Jefferson Jones, accepts the book, giving $1,000 advance plus 20 percent royalty. Dreiser agrees to repay Harpers' $3,000 advance. Returns to New York in March and stays with Mame and husband, Austin Brennan, in New Brighton, Staten Island. Pays Sara $100 a month; keeps separation secret from friends. *The Titan* published by John Lane, May 10. Reviews are mixed (8,016 copies sold by year-end). July, moves with Markham to 165 West 10th Street (his residence for five years). Revises *The "Genius"* and works on *The Bulwark* (story based on Anna Tatum's Quaker father). August, gives Mencken manuscript of *Sister Carrie* as gift. Tries to sell serial rights to *The "Genius"* (cut by Lengel); considers it his best novel. Writes five one-act plays: "The Blue Sphere," "In the Dark," "Laughing Gas," "The Spring Recital," and "The Light in the Window"; also writes a film scenario "The Born Thief," a philosophical essay "Saving the Universe," and first part of autobiography (put aside for later publication as *Dawn*).

1915   Unable to continue $100 monthly support to Sara, signs over land in Nyack, apple orchard, and furniture to her in lieu of eighteen months' payments. Receives $1,500 advance from John Lane for *The "Genius"* and smaller advance for *Plays of the Natural and the Supernatural*. Tries to find publishers for friends Masters, Sherwood Anderson, Harris Merton Lyon, Charles Fort, and Benjamin De

Casseres. Refuses request to write recommendation for Mencken's *The Smart Set* because he distrusts co-editor George Jean Nathan's influence ("too debonair, too Broadwayesque"). Sells story "The Lost Phoebe" for $200 (*Century*, April 1916). Gets a room in New York Public Library to study physics and chemistry, especially work of Jacques Loeb, biophysiologist working in comparative physiology and psychology (subjects that will interest Dreiser for the rest of his life). Agrees to do book on Indiana with old Indiana friend Franklin Booth, prosperous advertising illustrator, and in August drives with him to Warsaw, Terre Haute, Bloomington, Sullivan, Vincennes, Indianapolis, and Evansville, Indiana, in chauffered car. October, *The "Genius"* published by John Lane; receives negative reviews, including attacks on Dreiser's German ancestry.

1916   Suffers depression and prostate trouble. Takes ship to Savannah, Georgia, and works on *A Hoosier Holiday*. Markham joins him after her play, Hauptmann's *The Weavers*, closes. *Plays of the Natural and the Supernatural* published by John Lane. Returns to New York in early April. Unhappy when Markham leaves because of his infidelity (she joins the Provincetown Players). Sends manuscript of *A Hoosier Holiday* to Mencken for editing. July, learns that New York Society for the Suppression of Vice, headed by John S. Sumner, seeks to ban *The "Genius"* as blasphemous and obscene. Angry when Jones of John Lane agrees to withdraw the book (which has sold 8,887 copies) pending legal decision; begins campaign against Sumner aided by Mencken and Harold Hersey of the Author's League of America. August, meets with executive committee of Author's League, but its support is lukewarm. Ships plates of *The "Genius"* to New Jersey for safekeeping. Mencken and Hersey, with some help from Dreiser, collect 500 signatures in his support, including Robert Frost, George Ade, Mary Wilkins Freeman, Jack London, William Allen White, Sinclair Lewis, Willa Cather, John Reed, Max Eastman, Edwin Arlington Robinson, and Sherwood Anderson. Through Mencken meets Estelle Bloom Kubitz, who becomes secretary and lover. Begins lifelong friendship with Dorothy Dudley, a friend of Masters. *A Hoosier Holiday*, published by John Lane November 17, sells 1,665 copies by end of year. "Laughing

Gas" produced by Indianapolis Little Theatre Society December 7; runs for three performances. Completes play *The Hand of the Potter*, about sexually driven murderer, and sends it to Mencken. Mencken tells Dreiser that he is ruining all efforts on his behalf in the anti-censorship campaign by writing this play and warns, "Nothing is more abhorrent to the average man than sexual perversion." Feeling that Mencken has joined ranks of the conventional, Dreiser answers, "Tragedy is tragedy and I will go where I please for my subject."

1917   Writes pro-German article, "American Idealism and German Frightfulness," but fails to get it published. Meets Philadelphian Louise Campbell, who becomes his lover, editor, adviser, and typist. June, goes to farm near Westminster, Maryland, with Estelle Kubitz to work on *The Bulwark* and second volume of autobiography (*Newspaper Days*). Has low blood pressure, and takes medication for nervousness and fatigue. Gives Boni & Liveright permission to reissue *Sister Carrie* (its sixth printing) and discusses future publications with Horace Liveright. Revises stories for *Free and Other Stories*. November, buys Paul's piano from Mame and has it made into desk. Feels less pressure about money due to placement of stories in *Cosmopolitan* and *The Saturday Evening Post*. "The Girl in the Coffin" produced by Washington Square Players December 3 (staged earlier by groups in St. Louis and San Francisco).

1918   Obscenity case against *The "Genius"* dismissed on technicality by New York appellate court in May. Sells articles and stories to *Harper's Monthly*, *Metropolitan*, *Scribner's*, and *Munsey's*. Receives from Boni & Liveright $500 advance for *Free and Other Stories* (published Aug.). Sends essay "Hey Rub-a-Dub-Dub" and the play *Phantasmagoria* to *The Smart Set* in June but Mencken rejects them. Meets A. A. Brill, translator of Freud and founder of New York Psychoanalytic Society; reads works of Freud. Begins close friendship with San Francisco poet George Sterling. Plans book of personality sketches, *Twelve Men*, drawn from pieces written over the years.

1919   *Twelve Men*, published in April by Boni & Liveright, is praised by critics but sells poorly. Threatens to leave

Liveright unless they publish Charles Fort's *The Book of the Damned* (published 1920). May, hit by car while crossing New York City intersection and suffers cuts in scalp and broken ribs. Spends night in Roosevelt Hospital; refuses to press charges against driver. Recuperates at apartment of Estelle Kubitz. June, goes to Indiana to visit former teacher May Calvert Baker and old friend John Milo Maxwell, now on staff of Indianapolis *Star* and at work on book attempting to prove that Robert Cecil wrote Shakespeare's plays (Dreiser later tries to find publisher for it). *The Hand of the Potter* published by Boni & Liveright in September. Visited by and falls in love with Oregon-born Helen Patges Richardson, 25-year-old granddaughter of Dreiser's maternal aunt. October, secretly travels by ship with her to New Orleans and from there by train to Los Angeles; Dreiser hopes to write and sell scenarios for movies and Helen to act in movies. Boni & Liveright advances $333.33/month for one year on *The Bulwark*. Rents rooms at 338 Alvarado Street, keeping address secret and using post office box for mail. Moves to Highland Park in December. Takes trips to San Diego and Santa Barbara.

1920   *Hey Rub-a-Dub-Dub*, book of philosophical essays and plays published by Boni & Liveright in January, receives negative reviews. Signs protest over suppression of James Branch Cabell's *Jurgen*. April, moves to Hollywood to be closer to movie studios. (Helen has minor roles as extra at $7.50, then $20/day; later gets supporting roles in *The Flame of Youth* and Rudolph Valentino's first film, *The Four Horsemen of the Apocalypse*.) Learns from Boni & Liveright that Anna Tatum threatens to sue if they publish *The Bulwark* (story based on her family). Writes movie scenarios but is unable to sell them. Begins work on *An American Tragedy*. Reads Poe and critical biographical works about him. October, travels to San Francisco to see his friend George Sterling and begins another lifelong friendship with George Douglas, literary editor of San Francisco *Bulletin*. December, pays for Estelle Kubitz's appendectomy in New York.

1921   Tries unsuccessfully to find a publisher who will issue all his books as a set. April, with Helen visits San Francisco, Portland, Seattle, and Vancouver. Enjoys drives in used Overland car bought by Helen. August, after several moves, decides to purchase cottage at 652 North Columbus in Glendale for $4,500. Sells articles on Hollywood. *The Hand of the Potter*, produced by Provincetown Players in New York City December 5, receives negative reviews.

1922 Hopes for reissue of *The "Genius"*, and despite distaste for an expurgated version, discusses cuts with Mencken, who negotiates successfully with John Sumner. Drives with Helen in new Maxwell to San Francisco and Yosemite. Sells house in October and returns to New York with Helen, taking apartment at 16 St. Luke's Place in Greenwich Village. Conceals address from all but a few friends. Sells manuscript of *Jennie Gerhardt* for $1,000 to W. W. Lange, admirer prosecuted in 1921 for giving *Sister Carrie* and *Jennie Gerhardt* to a minor. Receives $1,000 advance for *Newspaper Days*. Works on *The Stoic* (final novel in Cowperwood trilogy), two new plays, film scenarios, short stories, and sketches of women. Angry when *Newspaper Days* is published under title *A Book About Myself* by Boni & Liveright in December; intended *A History of Myself* to be overall title of four projected autobiographical volumes.

1923 Finally meets Jacques Loeb, with whom he has been corresponding for several years, at Rockefeller Institute in January. Horace Liveright buys plates from other publishers and takes five-year leases on all books; in new contract, signed February 7, agrees to pay Dreiser $4,000 a year for four years, to reprint *The "Genius"* unexpurgated, to publish book of poems and uniform collected edition of Dreiser's works (starting Jan. 1927), and, after sale of 1,000 sets, to pay Dreiser $10,000. Dreiser agrees to deliver two novels in three years. Feels business affairs are in order for the first time. Receives $900 first installment from *Metropolitan* for short version of *The "Genius"*. Sells various shorter pieces to magazines. June, with Helen driving, tours upstate New York visiting scenes of *An American Tragedy* in Cortland, South Otselic, Herkimer, and Big Moose Lake in the Adirondacks. Suffers from chronic nausea and headaches. September, moves to apartment at 118 West 11th Street. *The Color of a Great City*, made up of earlier articles, published in December by Liveright. By end of year *The "Genius"* has sold 12,301 copies.

1924   Modern Library publishes edition of *Free and Other Stories* with foreword by Sherwood Anderson. March, Helen returns to Portland because of his continuing infidelities. Interviews Ty Cobb in Detroit ("The Most Successful Ball-Player of Them All" published in *Hearst's International*, Feb. 1925). Helen returns in late October. Finds work on *An American Tragedy* difficult, but continues, with Louise Campbell in Philadelphia typing and cutting.

1925   Moves with Helen to apartment at 1799 Bedford Avenue in Brooklyn. Takes office on Union Square; Helen types at home, and Louise Campbell and Sally Kusell, his secretary-editor, cut, edit, and retype. Delivers manuscript of *An American Tragedy* in July. Makes extensive revisions in proofs. December, exhausted from work on novel, goes on motor trip to Florida with Helen to rest and to avoid being in New York when *An American Tragedy* is published December 17; after visiting Louise Campbell, artist friend Wharton Esherick, and Mencken en route, arrives Christmas Day.

1926   Researches real estate boom in Florida, puts $200 down on lot, and takes notes for articles (later published by *Vanity Fair*). Hears that *An American Tragedy* has already sold 17,000 two-volume sets. Sails back to New York January 24 on *Kroonland*. Hurt by Mencken's negative review of *An American Tragedy*. March, moves temporarily to Hotel Pasadena; Liveright has commissioned Patrick Kearney to dramatize novel and Dreiser wants to be near production. March 23, sells film rights for *An American Tragedy* to director and producer Jesse L. Lasky for $90,000. Quarrels publicly over his share with Liveright, who calls Dreiser a liar; Dreiser throws coffee in his face. Pays $10,000 to Liveright as agreed in contract (Liveright had wanted more). Dreiser signs new contract with Liveright for 20 percent royalties on all subsequent works, $500/month on account, and invitation to sit on board of directors; Liveright is to begin publishing limited edition of collected works in 1927, followed by library edition in 1929. Resumes support to Sara Dreiser, sending $200/month. June 22, sails with Helen for Oslo to consult foreign publishers and collect further material for *The Stoic*. Tours Norway, Sweden, Denmark, Berlin, Prague, Vienna (fails to meet Freud, though Brill has written a letter of introduction),

Salzburg, Budapest, and Munich. Arrives in Paris early September. Visits Emma Goldman, now in exile. Goes to London in October and begins warm friendship with Otto Kyllmann, director of Constable, his British publisher. Visits George Bernard Shaw (later says Shaw is "witty, delightful, flashing with ideas. . . . He reminds me of H. L. Mencken"). Returns in October to Hotel Pasadena in New York. Dramatized version of *An American Tragedy* opens October 11 at Longacre Theater on Broadway, runs for 216 performances, and grosses over $30,000/week. Dreiser moved to tears by performance. Grieves over suicide of friend George Sterling. Sells rights for novels to eight European publishers. Late December, moves with Helen to duplex apartment in Rodin Studios, 200 West 57th Street; buys Russian wolfhound, Steinway grand piano, Oriental rugs, and hires maid. Invites friends to call Thursday evenings. *An American Tragedy* sells more than 50,000 two-volume sets (royalties total over $47,000). Sets up corporation, Author Royalties, with Helen as president and himself as vice-president.

1927   Hears from brother Rome, whom he had presumed dead, and sends money. Introduces Louise Campbell to Helen. March, takes three-week walking trip for health from Elizabeth, New Jersey, through Pennsylvania, Maryland, and West Virginia, to the Shenandoah Valley and Virginia. *The Financier*, revised and shortened, mostly by Campbell, published April 16. Buys thirty-seven acres with cottage near Mt. Kisco, New York. Agrees to visit Soviet Union on condition that all expenses will be paid and he be allowed to travel freely. Leaves October 19 aboard the *Mauretania*. Fellow passengers include publisher Ben Huebsch and painter Diego Rivera. Lands at Cherbourg, goes to Paris, where he briefly meets Ernest Hemingway. In Berlin sees Sinclair Lewis and Dorothy Thompson, also on her way to Soviet Union. November, leaves for Moscow, though ill with bronchitis and advised not to go. Stays in Grand Hotel near Red Square. Attempts unsuccessfully to interview Stalin and Trotsky. Meets German writer Lina Goldschmidt, Konstantin Stanislavski of the Art Theater, film director Sergei Eisenstein, poet Vladimir Mayakovski, Politburo member Nikolai Bukharin, and longtime correspondent Sergei Dinamov, state publishing house expert in American and English literature. Visits

Tolstoi's country estate, Yasnaya Polyana, and meets his daughter and niece. Goes to Leningrad, and in December is finally allowed to widen tour to other cities.

1928   Leaves Soviet Union from Odessa January 13; stops in Berlin to visit Lina Goldschmidt. Meets Helen in Paris and goes with her to Menton for rest. London, interviews Winston Churchill, sees Kyllmann and George Moore. Sails from Southampton and arrives in New York February 21. Writes articles on Soviet Union for New York *World*, *The Saturday Evening Post*, *Vanity Fair*, and others; declares that it offers hope to the world. Because of interest in science, goes with Helen to Woods Hole Marine Biological Laboratory at invitation of Boris Sokoloff, friend from Rockefeller Institute. Begins warm friendship with geneticist Calvin Bridges of Carnegie Institute at Washington, D.C. Oversees building of country house on property near Mt. Kisco, now called Iroki—Japanese for "beauty." Returns to New York, and with Helen dines with Thelma Cudlipp, who has married a wealthy attorney. Works on *A Gallery of Women* (collection of biographical sketches of women) with Louise Campbell and collects poems for volume *Moods*. With H. S. Kraft, arranges for John Howard Lawson to adapt *Sister Carrie* for stage, hoping to have Paul Muni play Hurstwood (project is never finished). *Dreiser Looks at Russia* published by Horace Liveright in November. Accused of plagiarism by Dorothy Thompson, whose book *The New Russia*, based on her newspaper articles, had appeared in September. Denies accusation (suit by Thompson eventually dropped). Writes to California governor C. C. Young on behalf of Thomas Mooney, imprisoned in San Quentin for 1916 San Francisco political bombings, arguing that he is innocent.

1929   *This Madness* (more sketches of women) serialized in *Hearst's International-Cosmopolitan* February–July. Considers leaving publisher Horace Liveright because promise of collected edition has not been kept, but stays when Liveright offers larger advance ($50,000 for ten-year contract). April, attends trial on 1927 suppression of *An American Tragedy* in Boston; Clarence Darrow and Arthur Garfield Hays appear unsuccessfully for the defense. Continues work on Iroki with help of artist friends Ralph

Fabri, Wharton Esherick, Jerome Blum, Henry Varnum Poor, and Hubert Davis. Hears from Lina Goldschmidt that she and others are trying to secure 1930 Nobel Prize for him. *A Gallery of Women* published by Horace Liveright November 30, in two volumes at $5. Loses only part of savings in Wall Street crash.

1930   March–May, makes tours by train of Grand Canyon, Tucson, Albuquerque, Santa Fe, El Paso, and Dallas. Meets Helen in Galveston and drives with her to San Francisco. Visits Mooney in San Quentin prison and receives help for his defense from William Randolph Hearst. Brings brother Rome, now physically weak and mentally confused, to sister Mame in New York. *The Hand of the Potter* produced in Hamburg, Germany. Hopes for Nobel Prize are disappointed when it is awarded to Sinclair Lewis. Meets Indian poet Rabindranath Tagore. Negotiates with Jesse Lasky, now at Paramount, over sound production of *An American Tragedy*. Visited by Sergei Eisenstein and Ivor Montague at Iroki and is impressed by their scenario version of *An American Tragedy*; Paramount, however, decides it is too long and costly (a million dollars) and assigns film to screenwriter Samuel Hoffenstein and director Josef von Sternberg.

1931   January 2, signs contract with Paramount for sound rights to *An American Tragedy* for $55,000, with stipulation that he will see script and be allowed to suggest revisions. When he reads Hoffenstein's script, writes, "To me, it is nothing less than an insult to the book—its scope, actions, emotions and psychology." Slaps Sinclair Lewis at Metropolitan Club dinner, angered by accusation of plagiarizing Dorothy Thompson's book on Russia. March 22, flies to Hollywood to revise Paramount script. April, chairs meeting in his apartment of the National Committee for the Defense of Political Prisoners ("The time has come for American intellectuals to render some service to the American worker"). Writes articles on arrests of Communists, and supports Scottsboro defendants. May 8, *Dawn*, second volume of autobiography covering childhood years, published by Liveright. Critics praise the book, but are amazed at frankness of revelations about himself and family; sisters are upset. June, investigates conditions of miners in Pittsburgh area at urging of

Communist leaders William Z. Foster and Joseph Pass. Accuses American Federation of Labor and United Mine Workers of close relations with corporations and defends Communist-organized National Mining Union. After viewing film *An American Tragedy* in June, files suit to prevent distribution. Loses case in trial July 22, but Paramount adds eight minutes of film, following some of Dreiser's suggestions. Income declines; September, moves from 200 West 57th Street to Ansonia Hotel. November, visits Harlan County, Kentucky, with committee including John Dos Passos, to investigate situation of striking and unemployed miners. Returns to New York moved by what he has seen. Committee is indicted in Kentucky on charges of "criminal syndicalism"; offense carries prison term of up to twenty-one years and/or $10,000 fine. Refuses to stop publicity in exchange for dropping of charges; collects relief funds for miners and publicizes conditions in newsreel and on radio. Attorney John W. Davis offers to defend him; New York governor Franklin D. Roosevelt promises open hearing if extradition is requested. Senator George Norris calls for Senate investigation of Harlan County situation. *Tragic America*, published by Liveright December 30, receives negative reviews.

1932   Redraws will, leaving Helen two-thirds of property. Saddened when Charles Fort dies May 3 ("the most fascinating literary figure since Poe"). Works on *The Stoic* with Louise Campbell's help. Liveright firm suffers financial setbacks and stops monthly payments. Dreiser reduces monthly support to sisters Emma and Sylvia ($100) and Mame and Rome ($80); continues payments to wife, Sara ($200). With George Jean Nathan, Eugene O'Neill, James Branch Cabell, and Ernest Boyd, becomes editor of new literary journal, *American Spectator*. August, refuses to endorse Soviet statement condemning Dostoyevski ("he is a great artist"). Becomes interested in possibilities of Technocracy, Inc., group formed by friend Howard Scott of Columbia University Department of Industrial Engineering that believes government should be ruled and goods distributed by social engineers. First issue of *American Spectator* is successful and 20,000 more are printed. November, flies to San Francisco to visit Tom Mooney in San Quentin and addresses rally of 15,000. (Mooney is pardoned January 1939.) In Hollywood, sells producer B. P. Schulberg film rights to *Jennie Gerhardt* for $25,000 and seven percent of Schulberg's one-third interest in profits.

1933   February, goes to Nashville, Tennessee, and Hopkinsville, Kentucky, for research and interviews for film about 1906–07 rebellion of tobacco farmers against Duke trust; writes scenarios with Hy Kraft and Milton Goldberg, but film is never made. Lectures at colleges on problems in America. Though uneasy about suppression of Trotskyists in Soviet Union, refuses to make public condemnation. Delighted by film version of *Jennie Gerhardt* starring Sylvia Sidney. Visits old friends: poet Arthur Davison Ficke and his wife, artist Gladys Brown, and John Cowper Powys in upstate New York and the Eshericks in Paoli, Pennsylvania. October, begins correspondence with Hutchins Hapgood on the subject of Dreiser's anti-Semitism (published as "Is Dreiser Anti-Semitic?", *The Nation*, April 17, 1935). Visited at Iroki by Diego Rivera, Floyd Dell, Sherwood Anderson, George Jean Nathan, Lillian Gish, George Douglas, and others. Attends funeral of Horace Liveright, dead of pneumonia at 49. When Liveright's firm goes bankrupt, offers $5,250 for books and plates; receiver asks $25,000, and dispute goes to arbitration.

1934   January, resigns from *American Spectator*, thinking its emphasis is frivolous. Sells stories to *Esquire* and *Scribner's*. Works on book of philosophy; parts appear as "The Myth of Individuality" (*American Mercury*, March 1934), "You, the Phantom" (*Esquire*, Nov. 1934), and "Kismet" (*Esquire*, Jan. 1935). Arbitration with Liveright firm settled in September; Dreiser buys plates for $6,500. Signs contract with Simon & Schuster, which pays $5,000 advance, promises uniform edition of his works, and gives large party at Iroki in October to celebrate. Almost 300 actors, filmmakers, dancers, artists, and writers attend. Article on Upton Sinclair, "The Epic Sinclair," appears in December *Esquire*. Renews friendship with Mencken in November after nine-year break.

1935   On Mencken's advice and because of his own lack of respect for most of the members, refuses Henry Seidel Canby's offer to join the National Institute of Arts and Letters. Suffers from grippe, bronchitis, and depression ("a sense of psychic earthquake as though something abysmal and final were first opening under or splitting once and for all the so-called conscious something which is me"). Works intensely on book of philosophy titled *The Formula Called Man*. Moves from Ansonia Hotel to Iroki for rest. Corresponds with scientists on problems of chemical and physical processes and asks about order and chaos in universal laws. In Los Angeles, stays with friend George Douglas, who works with him on philosophy book. Returns to New York in October. Hires Harriet Bissell as new secretary. Tries to sell Iroki; feels health will be better in Los Angeles. Urges Upton Sinclair to include Howard Scott's Technocracy in his EPIC (End Poverty in California) movement, but receives no encouragement from Scott or Sinclair.

1936   Continues study of science for philosophy book and writes Sherwood Anderson that he finds science "enormously rich, mysterious, varied, and in fact, entirely satisfactory in an emotional way." Saddened by news of death of George Douglas from heart attack, February 11. Rents out main house at Iroki for summer and lives in cabin until October 1. Late December, moves with Helen to Park Plaza Hotel.

1937   Loses suit brought by Liveright firm and is ordered in June to pay $16,394 for unearned advances and special editions of books purchased by him between 1929 and 1932. Summer, visits Calvin Bridges and researchers at Carnegie Biological Laboratory at Cold Spring Harbor, New York, and Woods Hole, Massachusetts. October, moves to 116 West 11th Street to save money. Exchanges visits with novelist Edward Dahlberg. Finds it impossible to pay Sara $200/month. Receives some royalties: $500 from Limited Editions Club for special issue of *Sister Carrie* and $200 from Czech publisher. Discusses Moscow trials with Dos Passos (disturbed when Nikolai Bukharin is shot as traitor, March 1938). Emma dies.

1938   January, learning that Eisenstein has resumed making films in Soviet Union, asks him to produce earlier script of *An American Tragedy* or to write one for *The Financier*. June, leases Iroki. Stays at friend Marguerite Tjader Harris's beach house in Noroton, Connecticut; works on philosophy book with her and Harriet Bissell. Agrees to edit *The Living Thoughts of Thoreau* for Longmans, Green. July, attends meeting in Paris of the International Association of Writers for the Defense of Culture. Writes to Harriet Bissell: "My morning depressions are stupendous. . . . I am wholly too miserable to think of anything except dying or finding some soothing drug. All this detail of living begins to pall on me. When I get enough whisky in me I'm all right for a little while, but then come the blues again . . ." Meets Louis Aragon ("one of those parlor radicals") and Paul Blech, secretary of International Association of Writers. Gives talk on Spanish Civil War. July 28, goes to Loyalist-held Barcelona and meets with President Manuel Azaña. Impressed by bravery in midst of destruction; agrees to ask President Roosevelt for food and supplies. Visits close friends Otto Kyllmann in London and John Cowper Powys in Corwin, Wales. Sails for New York August 13. Stays at George Washington Hotel. September 7, discusses Spanish relief at lunch with Franklin D. Roosevelt on presidential yacht *Potomac* in Hudson River. Agrees to form Spanish relief committee, but is not successful (it is later formed by Roosevelt). Writes articles on Spain for North American Newspaper Alliance. Works with Harriet Bissell on Thoreau book; finishes preface in November. Impressed by Quaker Rufus M. Jones when he visits him at Haverford College in Haverford, Pennsylvania, to discuss Spanish relief (later reads his book on Quakers). Attends farewell party at Sherwood Anderson's and has Thanksgiving dinner with Masters. Moves to California with Helen and rents apartment in Glendale.

1939   January, attends séance at house of Upton and May Craig Sinclair in Pasadena. Resumes work on *The Bulwark*. Lectures at various colleges. Dismayed by Loyalist losses in Spain; stops relief activities. Tries to sell *Sister Carrie* to movie studios; writes John Barrymore, "Live to present Hurstwood for me. I have, for so long, thought of *you* treading—in art—his sorrowful way. . . ." August, calls Britain worse than Hitler's Germany and approves of Nazi-Soviet pact. Fall, sees Sherwood Anderson for last time. Looks for new publisher because Simon & Schuster has not fulfilled agreement to bring out uniform edition of his works.

1940   Ill in January and February; feels neglected. RKO Studios buys option on *Sister Carrie* for $3,000. Dreiser actively opposes Hoover's Finnish Relief Fund (established after the U.S.S.R. invaded Finland in 1939), claiming Finland is being used by the British as a tool against Soviet Union. Accepts $5,000 from Oskar Piest of Veritas Press for book urging America to stay out of war and pays English novelist Cedric Belfrage $1,000 to assist him. Exhausted, works only three hours a day. Makes radio speech in support of Earl Browder, Communist Party candidate for president. Elected a vice-president of American Peace Mobilization. November 9, makes radio speech and addresses mass meeting in Washington, D.C. RKO buys *Sister Carrie* for $40,000. Pays alimony owed Sara and buys six-room Spanish-style white stucco house at 1015 N. Kings Road in Los Angeles for $20,000. Brother Rome dies.

1941   January, *America Is Worth Saving* published by Modern Age Books, which had difficulty finding printer because of anti-British, pro-Communist contents. Sells story titled "My Gal Sal," based on "My Brother Paul" in *Twelve Men*, to Twentieth Century-Fox for $50,000. March, in New York addresses American Council on Soviet Relations. Objects to Communist Party's use of his name without permission. Addresses American Peace Mobilization meeting in Philadelphia. Writes eulogy for Sherwood Anderson (appears in May *Clipper*). June 22, stunned by Nazi invasion of Soviet Union; now feels America must enter war. July, receives letter from closest English friend, Otto Kyllmann, expressing anger and pain over Dreiser's violently anti-British opinions in *America Is Worth Saving*; appeals to Kyllmann not to allow anything to interfere with their friendship ("surely you could continue to like me who truly loves and respects and admires you so much"). Fall, buys out contract with Simon & Schuster for $8,500. In New York signs agreement with G. P. Putnam's Sons to deliver *The Bulwark* by June 1, 1942.

1942   Work on *The Bulwark* hampered by arthritis in shoulder and intestinal flu. Decides to deposit his papers in University of Pennsylvania library. September 21, in Toronto, Ontario, for speech, denounces England in press interview for delaying opening of second front against Germany; says if Soviet Union should fall, he hopes that Hitler will invade England and oust the British ruling class. Speech is canceled by order of Ontario attorney general. Leaves secretly for Detroit, fearing arrest. Writes thanks to George Bernard Shaw for his defense in the press. Sara Dreiser dies October 1. Works on *The Bulwark* and on film scenarios.

1943   March, stops work on *The Bulwark* and returns to the philosophy book, now retitled *The Mechanism Called Man*, but finds writing difficult (work is never completed). Worries about money; still unable to sell Iroki. Suffers from colds, shingles, deterioration of one good eye, and weight loss. September, returns to work on *The Bulwark*. Conceives series for *Esquire* about "black sheep characters," in contrast to *Reader's Digest* series of "unforgettable characters." Invites Louise Campbell and other women to write pieces for pay that will be published under his name.

1944   January, informed by Walter Damrosch, president of Academy of Arts and Letters, that he has won Award of Merit Medal, given every five years; prize includes $1,000 and travel expenses to New York (other awards go to Willa Cather, S. S. McClure and Paul Robeson). Leaves on train May 10 for three-week stay. Sees family and old friends. Looks for new publisher to reissue works in uniform edition, but is told that paper shortage prevents it. Makes two recordings for Office of War Information to be broadcast to Germany and occupied countries urging the overthrow of Nazi leaders. May 19, accompanied by Edgar Lee Masters, receives award from Academy. Sells Iroki and half of land for $15,000, and makes last visit. Attends funeral of Mame June 4. Sees brother Ed for the last time. Exhausted, cancels planned trip to Philadelphia to see Mencken, Markham, Esherick, and Campbell. June 5, takes train to Stevenson, Washington, to meet Helen. Marries her there under name Herman Dreiser; only witnesses are Helen's sister Myrtle Patges and her fiancé. Invites Marguerite Tjader Harris to come to California to work on *The Bulwark*. August 20, celebrates birthday with fifty-seven guests. Repays advance to Putnam's, severing connection. Renews work on novel, dictating to Marguerite Tjader Harris. Suffers from rashes, kidney trouble, and various ailments; finds work difficult. Sees friends Paul

Robeson, John Howard Lawson, Charlie Chaplin, Clifford Odets, and others.

1945   May 6, finishes *The Bulwark* and sends it to Louise Campbell for opinion and to new publisher, Doubleday & Co. Disappointed by Campbell's response, tells her to indicate cuts and send manuscript to James T. Farrell, author of recent two-part essay on Dreiser in *The New York Times Book Review*. Reassured by Farrell's opinion (many cuts and changes made by Louise Campbell are restored by Farrell and Donald B. Elder, editor at Doubleday, when novel is published in March 1946). Works on *The Stoic*. Receives $34,600 payment of royalties from Soviet Union for works published there. July, goes to Portland with Helen for several weeks. August, becomes member of Communist Party. Occasionally attends church services of different denominations. September, begins to have periods of disorientation and loses appetite. December 3, finishes *The Stoic* and sends it to Farrell. Responds to Farrell's comments about last chapters, "I simply stopped writing at the end because I was tired. . . ." December 22, reads proofs of *The Bulwark* and returns them to Doubleday. Spends Christmas with Lillian Rosenthal Goodman and her husband, and visits Clare Kummer (widow of Arthur Henry), who plays brother Paul's songs. December 27, rewrites penultimate chapter of *The Stoic* (published Nov. 1947). Drives to beach with Helen to watch sunset. Suffers intense pain 3:00 A.M., December 28; dies of heart failure 6:50 P.M. Buried in Whispering Pines section at Forest Lawn, Glendale, January 3, 1946. John Howard Lawson delivers eulogy; Charlie Chaplin reads Dreiser's poem "The Road I Came."

Note on the Texts

This volume prints the texts of the first editions of *Sister Carrie*, *Jennie Gerhardt*, and *Twelve Men*.

Dreiser began work on his first novel, *Sister Carrie*, in the fall of 1899 and, with a few interruptions, worked on it steadily through March 1900. Revisions and cuts were made as he wrote, with the help of his wife, Sara White Dreiser, and his friend Arthur Henry, who then lived with the Dreisers. A typescript was prepared from the revised manuscript by Anna Mallon and a pool of typists. Dreiser, again aided by his wife and Henry, made further cuts and revisions in this typescript and rewrote the ending. He submitted the revised typescript to Harper & Brothers, who rejected it May 2, 1900. In the meantime, Dreiser had read and admired *McTeague*, by Frank Norris, and probably because Norris was an editor at the newly established company of Doubleday, Page, decided to submit the novel to that firm for publication. Norris was very enthusiastic about the novel, as apparently were others at the firm, and early in June it was accepted for fall publication without a formal contract. Soon after, Dreiser left New York to visit his wife's family in Missouri, confident that all was in order. Frank N. Doubleday, the senior member of the firm, returned to New York from Europe in July, read the novel, and decided that his firm should not publish it. However, Dreiser held Doubleday, Page to their promise to publish the book, and a formal contract was signed August 20, 1900. The publisher insisted on certain revisions, such as disguising the names of real places and people and eliminating all profanity. Although Dreiser agreed to some changes and wrote in September that "the names of Francis Wilson, Charles Frohman, Schlesinger and Meyer, the Waldorf, the Morton House, the Broadway and so on have been removed," in fact Charles Frohman, the Waldorf Hotel, the Morton House Hotel, and the Broadway Theatre are still present in the published novel. In the same letter, Dreiser disagreed with some of the judgments of "profanity" as queried in the typescript, writing, "Since when has the expression 'Lord Lord,' become profane.

Wherein is 'Damn,' 'By the Lord,' and 'By God.' " Existing correspondence shows that Dreiser saw galleys and page proofs, and some of the variants between the typescript and book version of the novel are stylistic revisions that only the author would make. There is also evidence of further censoring by the publishers: for example, "you bastards!" was cut from the strike episode (382.10), "dingy lavatory" was changed to "dingy hall" (417.32), and Carrie and Hurstwood get married in the afternoon of the day they arrive at the hotel rather than the morning after (263.39–264.2). The book was published November 8, 1900. Only 1,008 sets of sheets were printed, of which 450 were left unbound. Distribution was kept to the minimum necessary to satisfy the legal obligation and the book was not publicized except by Frank Norris, who sent out 127 copies for review. From its publication to February 1902, only 456 copies of *Sister Carrie* were sold, and Dreiser received $68.40 in royalties. In 1901, Heinemann in London brought out an abridged edition for its Dollar Library of American Fiction. Dreiser himself took no part in preparing this edition; the work of abridgment was done by his friend Arthur Henry. Though the British edition received good reviews, Dreiser's royalties from it were less than $100.

Dreiser bought the plates for *Sister Carrie* in 1906 and at that time eliminated the dedication to Arthur Henry; he also rewrote a passage that one reviewer had noted was taken from George Ade's "The Fable of the Two Mandolin Players and the Willing Performer" ("Let . . . regard.", 6.7–25). A new printing from these altered plates was brought out by B. W. Dodge in 1907. Though Dreiser owned the plates and the book was reprinted many times during his lifetime, he never made any further alterations, not even when the Limited Editions Club brought out a new edition in 1939. This volume prints the text of the first printing, which includes the dedication to Arthur Henry and the original Ade passage.

Dreiser began work on *Jennie Gerhardt* in January 1901 and wrote forty chapters in four months; then he discovered he had made an "error in character analysis" and would have to revise the work completely. He contracted with the J. F. Taylor Company in September 1901 to deliver the novel (then titled *The Transgressor*) within a year and received advances against royalties of $100 a month.

By mid-June 1902, suffering from depression and nervous collapse, he realized he would be unable to complete the novel in time for fall publication, and not long after, payments from Taylor stopped. When he recovered his health, Dreiser worked as an editor with the New York *Daily News*, Street & Smith, *Smith's Magazine*, *Broadway Magazine*, and the Butterick Company and by 1907 was able to repay J. F. Taylor the $750 advanced. There is evidence that he did some work on the novel between 1903 and 1905 and that he prepared twenty chapters to show publishers in 1908. After losing his job with the Butterick Company in 1910, he again took up the manuscript and by the end of December completed the first draft. This draft was read by Sara Dreiser, who advised cutting it, and Lillian Rosenthal and Fremont Rider, who both thought that the "happy ending" was wrong. The manuscript was cut and the ending was rewritten. The new version was sent to H. L. Mencken, James Huneker, and others. Every reader but Mencken advised cutting, and Huneker did not like the epilogue and thought it should be left out. The manuscript was rejected by Macmillan, but it was accepted by Ripley Hitchcock for Harper & Brothers in April 1911. Hitchcock insisted on further cuts and revisions, and Dreiser was charged $600 against royalties for editorial work. The novel was published October 19, 1911, and received good reviews. Some alterations were later made in the plates: for example, the second printing contains a correction of "is" to "it" (477.9), and at some time still later Harpers eliminated the epilogue, "In Passing."

Dreiser's role in dropping the epilogue, however, is unclear. Subsequent printings by Burt (1924), Boni & Liveright (1924), and others reprint the cut version. No other changes were made in the later printings or editions of the novel during Dreiser's lifetime. The text of the first printing of the first edition, which includes the epilogue, is printed in this volume.

Dreiser published versions of seven of the twelve "narratives" (the term is Dreiser's) that make up *Twelve Men* in various magazines over a period of seventeen years: "A Doer of the Word" in *Ainslee's* (June 1902); "The Country Doctor" in *Harper's Monthly* (July 1918); "Culhane, the Solid Man," based on "Scared Back to Nature," in *Harper's Weekly* (May 16, 1903); "A True Patriarch" in *McClure's* (Dec. 1901); "The Mighty Rourke," as "The Mighty Burke," in *McClure's* (May 1911); "A Mayor and His People" in *Era* (June 1903); and "W. L. S." as "The Color of To-Day" in *Harper's Weekly* (Dec. 14, 1901). The magazine publication dates are misleading: "The Country Doctor" was written before July 1902, and "The Mighty Rourke" was written before June 1904. Other narratives, though they appeared first in *Twelve Men*, were written much earlier. "Peter" and "My Brother Paul" were probably written between 1908 and 1909; "The Village Feudists" was written soon after the summer of 1901. Only two of the narratives seem to have been written close to the time of the book's appearance: "De Maupassant, Jr." and "Vanity, Vanity." In 1918, Dreiser gave these narratives to Dorothy Dudley for preliminary editing and then carefully went over them himself. Collation of the published articles with the book versions reveals that he made few cuts in the articles and added many passages of social commentary and criticism. Some of the additions, of course, may simply be to restore sections that had been removed for the magazine publication. *Twelve Men* was published by Boni & Liveright April 14, 1919. It was not revised in later printings or editions. The first printing of the first edition published by Boni & Liveright furnishes the text printed in this volume.

This volume presents the texts of the original editions chosen for inclusion here. It does not attempt to reproduce features of the typographic design, such as the display capitalization of chapter openings. The texts are reproduced without change, except for the correction of typographical errors. Spelling, punctuation, and capitalization are often expressive features, and they are not altered, even when inconsistent or irregular. The following is a list of typographical errors corrected, cited by page and line number: 63.19, distress;; 171.40, pears; 172.25, overcast.'; 178.21, departure.; 179.8, attion; 286.26, "A Gold Mine."; 390.19, struck; 400.33, meropolitan; 453.24, semed; 477.9, is; 481.26, coal?; 488.10,

answer"; 498.31, present,; 550.8, promptly.; 551.8, heerful;
559.8, gingery; 561.16, require; 586.7, "no"; 587.14, mential;
598.4, atranged; 601.25, Jennie; 605.10, pretty; 607.33,
chance."; 614.11, massages; 621.8, make?"; 629.22, shop.;
629.24—25, observation; 631.7, self possession; 680.6, tall;
684.6, Fields; 685.24, month's; 689.20, seasons'; 711.8, him;;
725.25, have'nt; 734.32, fifty-years; 762.27, me.; 817.11, Dodge,;
817.11, husband;; 817.12, Midgely,; 820.14, Mrs. Midgely;
848.36, he; 851.21, censors; 862.34, outre; 876.34, him; 890.35,
others."; 890.35, "True; 890.36, this,"; 890.36, "to; 890.38,
kind,"; 901.17—18, drink, but as for dinner I have another engagement."; 903.40, Sloane: 905.3, quondom; 912.11, E——;
917.1, disposition; 925.32, come; 940.7, undefeated; 943.4, *ri-
guer*; 972.7, or; 976.9, any plumber's stove standing outside
some gentleman's stable,; 977.19, *Nack*; 994.36—37, delapida-
tion; 1004.16, whyfores; 1007.3, mascerating; 1020.31, flare;
1042.11, considere; 1053.34, outre; 1054.1, feminity; 1054.15,
syhoritic; 1055.2, outre; 1058.24, a light; 1106.4, capital; 1110.10,
and thus; 1114.34, "all day".

Notes

In the notes below, the reference numbers denote page and line of the present volume (the line count includes chapter headings). No note is made for material included in a standard desk-reference book. For more detailed notes, references to other studies, and further biographical background for *Sister Carrie*, see the edition by Donald Pizer (New York: W. W. Norton & Company, 1970) and the Pennsylvania Edition, edited by John C. Berkey, Alice M. Winters, James L. W. West III, and Neda M. Westlake (Philadelphia: University of Pennsylvania Press, 1981). For further information on biography and sources, see *A Traveler at Forty* (New York: The Century Co., 1913); *A Hoosier Holiday* (New York: John Lane Company, 1916); *A Book About Myself* (New York: Boni & Liveright, Inc., 1922); *Dawn* (New York: Horace Liveright, Inc., 1931); *Letters of Theodore Dreiser: A Selection*, ed. Robert H. Elias, 3 volumes (Philadelphia: University of Pennsylvania Press, 1959); *Dreiser-Mencken Letters: The Correspondence of Theodore Dreiser & H. L. Mencken 1907–1945*, ed. Thomas P. Riggio, 2 volumes (Philadelphia: University of Pennsylvania Press, 1986); *American Diaries 1902–1926*, ed. Thomas P. Riggio (Philadelphia: University of Pennsylvania Press, 1982); *Theodore Dreiser: A Primary and Secondary Bibliography*, ed. Donald Pizer, Richard W. Dowell, and Frederic E. Rusch (Boston: G. K. Hall & Co., 1975); Walker Gilmer, *Horace Liveright: Publisher of the Twenties* (New York: David Lewis, 1970); Richard Lehan, *Theodore Dreiser: His World and His Novels* (Carbondale, Illinois: University of Southern Illinois Press, 1969); Richard Lingeman, *Theodore Dreiser: At the Gates of the City 1871–1907* (New York: G. P. Putnam's Sons, 1986); Ellen Moers, *Two Dreisers* (New York: The Viking Press, 1969); W. A. Swanberg, *Dreiser* (New York: Charles Scribner's Sons, 1965).

SISTER CARRIE

40.9   Fitzgerald and Moy's]   In Dreiser's typescript the place is named "Hannah and Hogg's," after a real establishment at 146 Madison Street. The publisher, Doubleday, Page, asked Dreiser to eliminate such references to real persons and concerns. (It was actually another Chicago "resort," Chapin & Gore, that had employed L. A. Hopkins, the model for Hurstwood.)

43.25   "Old Pepper,"]   "Old Hennessy" in Dreiser's typescript; evidently changed at the insistence of Doubleday, Page.

45.31   Jules Wallace]   Spiritualist healer, subject of three articles by Dreiser in the St. Louis *Republic*, September 9–11, 1898.

46.1   'The Hole in the Ground,'] Farce by Charles Hoyt (1860–1900), first performed in Chicago in 1889.

72.33   "The Mikado"] Comic opera by Gilbert and Sullivan, first performed in 1885.

80.34   Vega-cure] A patent medicine.

81.5   McVicker's] A leading Chicago theater, at 25 West Madison Street. Elsewhere (pp. 104, 226, 230) spelled "McVickar's," possibly to conform with the publisher's instructions to disguise the names of actual places.

100.24–25   Exposition] The Inter-State Industrial Exposition on Michigan Avenue featured paintings and sculpture, displays of manufactured goods, and a beer garden.

104.30   'Rip Van Winkle.'] Adaptation by Dion Boucicault (1820–90) of the story by Washington Irving, written for the actor Joseph Jefferson III (1829–1905), who played the title role for over forty years.

141.3   'Over the Hills'] "Over the Hill to the Poor House" (1873), popular sentimental poem by Will Carleton (1845–1912).

141.9   'Under the Gaslight,'] Melodrama by American dramatist Augustin Daly (1839–99), first performed in 1867. In the play, the virtuous heroine Laura (played by Carrie) is driven from polite society and forced to renounce her fiancé when it is mistakenly suspected that she is of low birth.

197.18   bunco-steerer] A confidence man who directs strangers to places where they are robbed or cheated.

225.26–27   Chicago Opera House] A vaudeville theater.

230.19   "The Old Homestead"] Play by Denman Thompson (1833–1911), first produced in 1886; an earlier version was titled *Joshua Whitcomb*.

259.33–34   Pinkerton . . . Boland] Private detectives.

265.19   Gilsey] Hotel at Broadway and 29th Street in New York.

265.36   Belford] Dreiser's typescript reads "the Continental," a hotel at Broadway and 20th Street.

282.34   "What . . . Broadway?"] Written in 1895, with words by Harry Dillon and music by Nat Mann.

284.2   FEAST OF BELSHAZZAR] In Daniel, chapter 5, Daniel interprets writing that appears on the wall during a feast, predicting the murder of Belshazzar, king of Babylon, and the fall of his kingdom.

286.26   'A Gold Mine.'] Comedy (1889) by James Brander Matthews (1852–1929) and George H. Jessop (d. 1915).

287.5   Lyceum] The New Lyceum Theater, at Fourth Avenue and 23rd Street, opened in 1885 and was managed by Daniel Frohman.

287.31 Lord & Taylor's] In the typescript, "Stewart's."

289.27 "Sothern . . . Chumley.' "] In the typescript, "Florence, . . . in 'Judge Dockitt.' "

294.18 Albert Ross] Pseudonym of American writer Linn Boyd Porter (1851–1916). In the typescript, the book named is *The Opening of a Chestnut Burr*, by E. P. Roe.

294.29 'Dora Thorne,'] Popular romance by Charlotte Monica Braeme or Brame (1836–1884), published in 1883 under her pseudonym "Bertha M. Clay" (see 96.10).

299.38–40 katastates . . . anastates.] Based on theories elaborated by Elmer Gates, physiological psychologist and inventor, whose laboratory Dreiser visited in 1900. Gates conducted research to prove that thoughts had specific chemical causes and consequences in the brain.

314.10–11 the Fifth Avenue] Theater at Broadway and 28th Street.

316.18–19 restaurant . . . Square.] In the typescript, "Dorlon's"— Dorlon's Oyster House at 6 East 23rd Street.

338.28 Madison Square Theatre] On 24th Street near Broadway, opened in 1879.

338.33 the 'Clipper,'] The *New York Clipper* (1853–1924) was a theatrical newspaper which later became *Billboard Magazine*.

343.4 the Casino,] The Casino Theater, on the southeast corner of Broadway and 39th Street, opened in 1883 and featured musical comedy.

343.27 Mr. Dorney.] Richard Dorney, business manager for Augustin Daly.

343.30 Empire Theatre] At Broadway and 41st Street, the theater opened in 1893 and presented sophisticated comedies.

343.33 the Lyceum] See note 287.5.

354.25 Manon,] A naïve country girl corrupted by the city. The term is derived from *Manon Lescaut* (1731), novel by Abbé Prévost that became the basis for operas by Auber, Massenet, and Puccini.

355.3–4 'The Queen's Mate'] Musical comedy by Henry Paulton, first performed in 1888. Lillian Russell frequently starred in it.

366.34–35 strike . . . Brooklyn.] The strike by Brooklyn streetcar workers began January 14, 1895, and lasted nearly a month. Dreiser's description is based on accounts in *The New York Times* and on his own observation of the Toledo trolley strike of March 1894, which he reported for the Toledo *Blade*.

400.38 Sarony.] Napoleon Sarony (1821–96) was a lithographer and theatrical photographer.

411.9   the Chelsea]   Hotel at 222 West 23rd Street.

416.2   CURIOUS . . . POOR]   Dreiser had published an article by this name in *Demorest's Family Magazine* in November 1899. Much of that article is used verbatim in this chapter, beginning at 423.5.

420.38   Bellevue]   Charity hospital at First Avenue and 26th Street.

423.10   Fire signs]   Outdoor electric signs.

444.6   Single Tax]   Plan proposed by Henry George (1839–97) in his *Progress and Poverty* (1879) to reform the economic system through a 100 percent tax on income from land.

455.5   Potter's Field.]   Charity cemetery located on Hart's Island, off the eastern shore of the Bronx in Long Island Sound.

JENNIE GERHARDT

521.40–522.21   The English . . . sad."]   Quoted almost exactly from Richard Jefferies (1848–87) in *The Open Air*, a collection of essays published in 1885. This extract is from "Beauty in the Country": Part I, "The Making of Beauty."

723.40   Rotten Row]   A road in Hyde Park extending from Apsley Gate to Kensington Gardens used for fashionable horse and carriage exercise. The origin of the name is uncertain.

TWELVE MEN

829.1   *Peter*]   Peter B. McCord.

833.16   D—— W——]   Richard Wood.

838.33   Chinese . . . Companions]   Usually called "Six Companies"; Chinese emigrant mutual aid societies that began in California about 1850, representing six districts in Kwantung Province, China.

845.26–27   "Wolf . . . Dweller"]   Published by B. W. Dodge in 1908 when Dreiser was connected with the firm. See 869.23.

848.2–3   Thaïs . . . Quo Vadis]   Respectively by Anatole France, Gustave Flaubert, Vicente Blasco-Ibáñez (title should be *Sónnica*), and Henryk Sienkiewicz.

867.4   Culmbacher]   Sweet Bavarian beer preferred by women.

874.6   Charlie Potter]   After this piece was published in *Ainslee's*, June 1902, Charlie Potter wrote the magazine asking for a copy to be made into a tract.

892.17–18   editor . . . paper;]   The Evansville (Indiana) *Argus*.

892.20–21   Tony . . . Niblo's]   Vaudeville houses in New York City.

894.12   Spoopendyke . . . Saratoga."]   The first by Stanley Huntley (d. 1883), the second by Marietta Holley (1836–1926).

920.1   *The Country Doctor*]   Dr. Woolley, the Dreiser family doctor in Warsaw, Indiana.

940.1   *Culhane*]   William Muldoon (1852–1933), born in Allegany County in western New York, bought the resort in 1900.

962.35–36   ancient . . . Cunaxa]   Battle fought in 401 B.C. north of Babylon between the Greeks, led by Cyrus the Younger, and the Persians, led by his brother Artaxerxes. Cyrus was killed and the "Retreat of the Ten Thousand" through hostile territory was led (and later written about) by Xenophon, a disciple of Socrates.

984.34–35   "unco guid"]   Those professedly strict in matters of morals and religion.

985.1   *A True Patriarch*]   Dreiser's father-in-law, Archibald Herndon White.

987.25–28   "Pure . . . world."]   James 1:27.

1001.1   *De Maupassant, Junior*]   Harris Merton Lyon (1883–1916), author of two books of short stories, *The Sardonics* (1908) and *Graphics* (1913).

1004.11   Our . . . owner]   Benjamin Bowles Hampton.

1007.38   intellectual maiden]   Ethel M. Kelley.

1049.1–2   "*Vanity . . . Preacher*]   Eccles. 1:2 and 12:8.

1049.5   X——]   James G. Robin. He later wrote a verse tragedy, *Caius Gracchus* (1920), using pseudonym Odin Gregory, for which Dreiser wrote an introduction.

1049.14   "Frenzied . . . Wealth,"]   Respectively by Thomas W. Lawson (1857–1925) and Charles Edward Russell (1860–1941).

1069.1   *The Mighty Rourke*]   His real name was Mike Burke.

1117.1   *W. L. S.*]   W. Louis Sonntag, Jr., died in 1898.

CATALOGING INFORMATION

Dreiser, Theodore, 1871–1945.
  Sister Carrie, Jennie Gerhardt, Twelve men.
  Edited by Richard Lehan.

  (The Library of America ; 36)
I. Title: Sister Carrie. II. Title: Jennie Gerhardt. III. Title: Twelve
men. IV. Series.
PS3507.R55A6   1987   813'.52   87–27583
ISBN 0–940450–41–0

This book is set in 10 point Linotron Galliard,
a face designed for photocomposition by Matthew Carter
and based on the sixteenth-century face Granjon. The paper
is acid-free Ecusta Nyalite and meets the requirements for perma-
nence of the American National Standards Institute. The binding
material is Brillianta, a 100% woven rayon cloth made by
Van Heek-Scholco Textielfabrieken, Holland. The com-
position is by Haddon Craftsmen, Inc., and The
Clarinda Company. Printing and binding
by R. R. Donnelley & Sons Company.
Designed by Bruce Campbell.